# SANDRA GULLAND

# *The Josephine B. Trilogy*

The Many Lives & Secret Sorrows
of Josephine B.

Tales of Passion, Tales of Woe

The Last Great Dance on Earth

HARPER  PERENNIAL

*The Josephine B. Trilogy*
© 2005 by Sandra Gulland.
*The Many Lives & Secret Sorrows of Josephine B.*
© 1995 by Sandra Gulland.
*Tales of Passion, Tales of Woe*
© 1998 by Sandra Gulland.
*The Last Great Dance on Earth*
© 2000 by Sandra Gulland.
P.S. section © 2006 by Sandra Gulland.

Published by Harper Perennial, an imprint of
HarperCollins Publishers Ltd

*The Many Lives & Secret Sorrows of Josephine B.*
Originally published in hardcover by HarperCollins
Publishers Ltd, 1995.
First trade paperback edition 1996.

*Tales of Passion, Tales of Woe*
Originally published in hardcover by HarperCollins
Publishers Ltd, 1998.
First published in trade paperback by Harper Perennial
Canada, 1999.

*The Last Great Dance on Earth*
Originally published in hardcover by HarperFlamingo
Canada, an imprint of HarperCollins Publishers Ltd,
2000.
First published in trade paperback by Harper Perennial
Canada 2001.

These three books were first published together in this
omnibus edition in 2006.

HarperCollins books may be purchased for educational,
business, or sales promotional use through our Special
Markets Department.

HarperCollins Publishers Ltd
2 Bloor Street East, 20th Floor
Toronto, Ontario, Canada
M4W 1A8

*www.harpercollins.ca*

Library and Archives Canada Cataloguing in Publication

Gulland, Sandra
The Josephine B. trilogy / Sandra Gulland.

Contents: The many lives and secret sorrows of
Josephine B.—Tales of passion, tales of woe—
The last great dance on Earth.

ISBN-13: 978-0-00-639557-7
ISBN-10: 0-00-639557-0

1. Joséphine, Empress, consort of Napoleon I,
Emperor of the French.

1763-1814—Fiction. I. Title.

PS8563.U643J67 2006          C813'.54
C2005-905570-7

H C  9  8  7  6

Printed and bound in the United States
Set in Garamond and Kuenstler Script

# Contents

BOOK ONE

*The Many Lives*
*& Secret Sorrows*
*of Josephine B.*

History is fiction. — *Robespierre*

The Many Lives & Secret Sorrows of Josephine B.
*is a work of fiction based on (and inspired by)
the extraordinary life of an extraordinary woman.*

*For Richard, who insisted*

. . . the ghosts of our future
are unpredictable
and out of control.
— *Wendy Rose*,
from "The Fifties"

*The Many Lives
& Secret Sorrows
of Josephine B.*

# I

*Mademoiselle*

# *In which I am told an extraordinary fortune*

*June 23, 1777—Trois-Ilets, Martinico.*

I am fourteen today and unmarried still. Without a dowry, what hope is there? Mother says the wind takes hope and dashes it into the sky, just as the big wind took our house, picked it up and dashed it, leaving nothing but debts in its place.

Oh, what a black mood has possessed me. Is not the celebration of one's birthday supposed to bring one joy? After dinner, after eating too many doughnut fritters with guava jelly, I took my leave and climbed up to my special place in the kapok tree. It was cool in the shade of the leaves. I could hear Grandmother Sannois and Mother arguing in the front parlor, the slaves chanting as they pushed the cane stalks through the rollers in the crushing hut, a chicken scratching in the honeysuckle bushes. I felt strange up there—peering out at my world, enveloped in gloom on my happy day.

It's the voodoo, surely, the bitter-tasting quimbois Mimi got me to drink this morning, a drink of secret spells. "Something manbo Euphémie made for you," she whispered. She'd knotted a red and yellow scarf tight around her head.

"Euphémie David—the teller of fortunes?" The obeah woman, the voodoo priestess who lived in the shack up the river.

Mimi pushed the coconut bowl into my hands. "It will bring you a *man.*"

I regarded the liquid cautiously, for it smelled vile.

"Quick!" She glanced over her shoulder. For Mother doesn't hold with voodoo. Mother says the Devil speaks through the mouths of the voodoo spirits. Mother says the Devil is hungry for girls like me. Mother says the Devil sent her too many girls and is hungry to get one back.

So this is confession number one in this, my new diary, sent to me all the way from Paris by my beautiful Aunt Désirée: I drank a magic potion and I'll not tell Mother. I drank a magic potion and I'm filled with woe.

A note Aunt Désirée enclosed with her gift read: "A little book in which to record your wishes and dreams, your secret confessions." I shook the book over the table. Ten livres fell out.

"Confessions?" my sister Catherine asked. She is twelve now, almost thirteen, but even so, always into mischief. At convent school the nuns make a fuss over Catherine. They don't know it is Catherine who lets the chicken into the rectory, that it is Catherine who steals the sugar cakes before they are cooled. Catherine has the soul of a trickster, Mimi says.

"Tell us your wish," my youngest sister, Manette, said, lisping through the gap in her teeth. I was saddened by the light in her eyes, for she is only ten, young enough to believe that wishes are granted.

I shrugged. "My wish is the same every year." I glanced at Father. He had started the day with rum and absinthe and followed it with ti-punches all through the afternoon. "To go to France." Send Rose to France, my beautiful Aunt Désirée would write every year—send her to me, to *Paris*.

Father looked away. His skin was yellow; it is the malaria again, surely. So then I felt bad, for is it Father's fault he'd inherited only debts? Is it his fault he has been cursed with three daughters and no son, that Mother's dowry turned to dust in his hands, that his dream of sending me to France had never materialized for want of the price of passage?

"France!" Grandmother Sannois pushed her two pug dogs off her lap. "I'd keep that girl well away from Madame Désirée." Grandmother Sannois doesn't approve of Aunt Désirée, or any of the Taschers for that matter (*especially* Father). "What's wrong with that boy over near Laniantin," she said, downing her laudanum: seven drops in a jigger of brandy. "What's wrong with that Beal boy?"

Algernon Beal! The fat boy we all call Algie.

"Monsieur Beal requires a dowry," Mother said.

"Monsieur *de* Beal, I believe it is now," Father said, "the manufacturer of shackles and branding irons, the owner of three gilded carriages, twenty-two fighting cocks, an English Thoroughbred stallion and one dim-witted son." Father coughed and emptied his glass. "Monsieur *de* Beal and I had occasion to converse at the slave auction in Fort-Royal last month. He told me at *length* and in great *detail* how large a girl's dowry would have to be, how noble her bloodline, how abundant her bosom and intact her maiden-hood even to dream of marrying his pimple-faced boy—"

Manette had her napkin stuffed in her mouth to keep from laughing.

"Well, there's always the convent," Grandmother Sannois said.

*The convent.* Always the *convent.* Is this to be my future? I yearn for so much more! But it's too late now, I know, for on this, my fourteenth birth-day, Aunt Désirée made no offer, and, for the first time since I can remem-ber, Father made no promise . . . and I liked it better before, to tell the truth, with glittering false hopes to brighten my day.


*June 24.*

This morning I gave my ten livres to the slave-master to divide among the field-hands. I am grown now and more aware of the sufferings of the world.

But Mother found out and got cross, accusing me of being like Father. "Generous" Father who would let his family starve to feed a friend. "Crazy" Father with his wild stories and dreams of glory. "Dreams from the rum god," she cursed. "Promises like clouds on a summer day."

Father who is never home. Already he's off to Fort-Royal—"to play games with the Devil," Grandmother Sannois said.

"To play games with the *she*-devils," Mother said quietly under her breath.


*Sunday, June 29.*

Dear Diary, I have been giving thought to my sins, making repentance.

I am guilty of wishful thinking, of extravagant imaginings.

I am guilty of gazing at myself in the pond.

I am guilty of sleeping with my hands under my bedsheets.

There, it is written. The ink is drying as I write. I must close this book now—I cannot bear to look at these words.

*Sunday, July 6.*

"Mademoiselle Tascher," Father Droppet called to me after church this morning. "Your grandmother asked me to talk to you."

I fingered the pages of my missal. Outside I heard a horse whinny and a man shouting.

"You are coming to an age of decision," he said. His big nose twitched.

"Yes, Father." I could see the outline of his vest under his white frock.

He paused. "I advise you to bend to God's will, to accept a life of service."

I felt my cheeks becoming heated.

Father Droppet handed me a handkerchief. "The life of a nun might satisfy that hungry heart of yours."

Through the high open window I could see the head of the statue of Christ in the cemetery, His eyes looking up at the clouds. The hunger I felt was for fêtes and silk slippers, for the love of a comely beau.

He bent toward me. "I was young once, too," he said. I could smell rum on his breath.

"I would die in a convent!"

*Forgive me, Father.* I backed away. At the door I turned and ran.


*July 24.*

This afternoon Mimi and I were playing in the ruins* when Mimi saw a spot on my chemise.

I twisted and pulled my skirt around. Blood?

"It's the flowers," Mimi said.

I didn't know what to do.

"Tell your mother," she said.

"I can't do that!" Mother is proper.

So Mimi got me a rag which she instructed me on how to use. She told me she washes hers out in the creek, early, when no one is around to see.

"Where we bathe?" How disgusting.

"Farther down the river."

---

* *The family home was destroyed by a hurricane in 1766. They moved into the sucrerie, the building used to boil down sugar syrup.*

I move around the house aware of this great cloth between my legs, thinking that surely everyone notices. This is supposed to be the big change in me, but all I feel is ill.

*Saturday.*
Mimi is teaching me how to tell the future from cards, how to lay them out, how to know the meaning. Today we practised on my sister Catherine. The card in the ninth place was Death.

Catherine protested.

"It's not *really* death," Mimi said, taking up the cards. She sniffed the air. Later, I questioned her. "Why did you stop?"

"Didn't you smell cigar smoke?" she whispered. "The spirit of Death is a trickster. Never believe *him*."

*Thursday, July 31.*
Dear Diary, something terrible has happened; it hangs over my heart like a curse.

It began with a lie. I told my little sister Manette that Mimi and I were going to the upper field to see if Father's ship was in the harbour yet. "You stay here," I told her.

Mimi and I headed up the trace behind the manioc hut, but at the top of the hill we took the path that led back down to the river, toward Morne Croc-Souris. We hadn't gone far when Manette caught up with us.

"I told you to stay," I told her.

"You lied. You said you were going up the hill."

Mimi glared at her. "Can you keep a secret?"

"I never tell!"

It was dark by the river; the moss hung thick from the trees. We heard a chicken squawking before we came upon the fortuneteller's shack.

"That's where the werewolf lives," Manette said, taking my hand.

I looked at Mimi. "Is this it?"

In front of the hut was a charcoal brazier. The air was thick with the smell of roasted goat. In the shadows of a verandah roofed over with banana tree leaves, I saw an old Negro woman sitting cross-legged. Euphémie David—the voodoo priestess.

As we approached she stood up. She was wearing a red satin ball gown fringed with gold, much tattered and stained and too big for her. Her hair was white and woolly, standing out around her head like a halo. A rusty machete was propped up against the wall behind her.

Mimi called out something I couldn't understand. The old woman said something in the African tongue.

"What did she say?" I asked.

"Come," the old woman said. A puppy came out of the shack and growled at us.

"I'll stay back here," Manette said.

Mimi pushed me forward.

"Aren't you coming too?" I asked.

The two of us approached. What was there to be afraid of?

Entering the shade of the verandah, I was surprised how small the old woman was, not much bigger than Manette. Her loose black skin hung from her neck. She held a shell bowl in one hand—pigs' knuckles and coconut, it looked like—and was eating it with her fingers. She threw a bone to the puppy to finish. The old woman and Mimi began talking in the African tongue. I looked back over my shoulder. Manette was standing by a calabash tree, watching. A crow called out warning sounds.

Mimi touched my arm. "She says your future is all around you."

"What does that mean?"

The old woman went into the shack. She returned with a basket which she pushed into my hands. In the basket was a gourd rattle, a wooden doll, a stick, two candles, a bone, bits of frayed ribbon and a crucifix.

The old woman said something to Mimi.

"She wants you to pick out three things," Mimi told me.

"Anything?" I took a candle, the doll and the crucifix out of the basket.

"She wants you to put them down," Mimi said.

"In the dirt?"

The old woman began chanting. I looked to see if Manette was still by the calabash tree. I shrugged at her. I remember thinking: *See, there is nothing to fear.*

The old woman began to moan, rolling her head from side to side, the whites of her eyes cloudy. Then she looked at me and screamed—a sound I will never forget, not unlike a pig being stuck.

"What is it!" I demanded. I was not without fear. "Mimi! Why is she crying?"

The old woman was shaking her head and mumbling. Finally she spoke, slowly, but strangely. "You will be unhappily married. You will be widowed."

I put my hand to my throat.

The old woman began to shake. She shook her hands, crying out words I could not understand.

"Mimi, what is she saying!"

The old woman began to dance, singing with the voice of a man. I backed away, stumbling over a gnarled tree root. I fell in the dirt and scrambled to my feet.

*You will be Queen*, she said.

# *In which I am punished*

Monday, August 4, 1777.

When I saw Father Droppet coming up the laneway on his grey mare, fear came into my heart. I ran up the trace to the manioc hut. Mimi was turning the big iron scraper.

"Father Droppet is here!" I said. "Why? It's not a feast-day."

Mimi stopped turning the wheel.

"I made confession yesterday morning," I told her.

"Did you tell?"

"About the voodoo witch?" I nodded.

"Did you tell I took you?" There was fear in her eyes.

"I *wouldn't.*" I turned, suddenly anxious. "I wonder what's happening."

I did not intend to eavesdrop. That was not my plan. But instead of going directly toward the sucrerie, I went down into the ravine. From my place in the kapok tree I could hear voices on the verandah—Mother, Grandmother Sannois. Then Father Droppet saying, "You understand, this is a matter of . . . I don't have to . . ."

"Goodness!" Mother exclaimed.

Father Droppet said something I couldn't understand. I heard the front door open and close. Then I heard Manette's voice.

*Manette!* I strained to hear, but all I could make out was Grandmother Sannois saying, "I told you. I told you this would happen."

I heard the door open and close again and, before long, the sound of

Manette weeping in an upstairs bedchamber. Then I heard Father Droppet say, "If the Devil is permitted . . . You must . . ."

"But Father Droppet!" I heard Mother exclaim. I strained to hear more but a black finch landed on the branch above me and began to scold so vigorously I couldn't make out a word. I shook the branch to chase the bird away. Then, Father Droppet's voice: "If you don't . . ."

It grew dark suddenly and began to rain, a light shower at first, followed by big, heavy drops.

"Rose!" I heard Mother calling.

I climbed down and approached the verandah.

"Why, it's Rose," my mother said. "You're soaking wet."

Grandmother Sannois was slouched in a cane chair. Father Droppet was standing by the door with an empty glass in his hand. He nodded.

"What can you be thinking of, standing out in such a downpour. Go put some dry clothes on and come back. There is something we must discuss," Mother said.

Gladly I escaped. Catherine met me at the top of the stairs, an embroidery hoop in her hand. "Manette says you will be Queen! She said the old witch told you. But she won't stop crying! What happened?"

I could hear Manette bawling even from the foyer. I went down the dark hallway to the door to her room. I knocked. "Manette? It's me."

The weeping stopped but she did not answer.

"I won't hurt you, I promise." I pushed the door open. She was huddled in the corner of the little four-poster bed. I stooped down under the canopy and sat down across from her. Her eyes were red and her nose was runny. I felt around in my bodice for a handkerchief and handed it to her. "I know you told," I said.

"You're not mad?" she asked, her breathing jagged. She glanced up at Catherine, who had come to the door.

I shook my head no. "I should never have taken you there. Did you say anything about Mimi?"

"No!"

"Do you understand what might happen if you did, Manette? She'd be sold—or put on a field gang." Or worse. . . .

"I didn't say anything!" she sobbed, so hard my heart was full of fear.

The rain had stopped when I emerged onto the verandah. I could hear Mother and Grandmother Sannois bidding farewell to Father Droppet on the laneway. I stood by the front door, my hands clasped in front of me, waiting. It sounded like Father Droppet's grey was being fractious. I heard the stable boy cursing in the African tongue. The horse quieted. Then I heard the steady clip-clop of the horse's hoofs on the stones.

Mother appeared on the path, Grandmother Sannois on her arm, the two pugs sniffing in the weeds behind them. They were wet and looked like big rats. Grandmother Sannois was saying something to Mother as they walked along. Then Mother looked up, saw me.

I held my breath.

"I'll tell her if you won't," Grandmother Sannois said, lowering herself into the chair with the sisal seat. One of her pugs jumped up onto her lap and she pushed him off.

Mother turned to face me.

I bowed my head. I considered throwing myself at her feet. Was that not how it was done?

"And to think that you *made* little Manette go along with you!" she whispered, so low I almost couldn't hear her.

"Let me tell her," Grandmother Sannois said.

Mother took a deep breath. "Mimi, of course, will have to be—"

"No!" A violent emotion filled me. "Mimi had nothing to do with it! I *begged* her to take me, but she refused. I was the one, it was only *me!*" My breath was coming in spurts; I could not still it.

Mother took the chain from around her neck, the chain with the big silver cross hanging from it. She took my two hands, put the cross between them. "Look at me, Rose," she said.

I looked into her eyes.

"Swear that you speak the truth."

"Mimi is innocent. It is all my doing, all my fault," I cried out, not untruly.

"She did not take you to see the unholy woman in the woods?"

I shook my head no, violently.

"Say it."

"Mimi did not go," I lied. The cross felt cold and heavy in my hands. I pushed it back into my mother's hands.

"Call the child down," Grandmother Sannois said.

Mother sat down on a wood stool. "Come here, Rose," she said. She pulled me down on the stones in front of her. She wiped several strands of damp hair from my forehead. Her touch was tender. "Sometimes it's not easy to be a mother," she said. Her voice was cold when she said, "You will be put in the storm room, in the cellar. You will stay there for eight days." She looked over at Grandmother Sannois and then back at me. She took a deep breath. "You will be fed nothing but dry bread and water."

I looked at her without comprehending. Eight days? Eight *nights?* In the cellar? "Alone?" My voice trembled. In the *dark?*

Mother slipped the chain with the cross over my head. "You will be needing this," she said.

I've been sent to my room to await my fate. I'm to eat supper with my family, and make my farewells. It will be my last meal.

Mimi and Manette are more upset than I am. Catherine, however, can only think of the fortune I was told. "That *you* will be a queen, Rose. Imagine!"

My nanny Da Gertrude appeared, her face wet with tears. She crushed me to her bosom. Then she washed me with a fragrant liquid, beginning at my feet.

"Why?" I asked, for her method was curious. A floating feeling came over me, as if my body were not my own.

"This will protect you," she said.

"I will be strong," I said. The thought came to me: *As befits one who will be Queen.*

It was true, then, I knew, I *had* been cursed.

At supper I could hardly eat. After, everyone embraced me as if I was going on an ocean voyage. Grandmother Sannois presented me with her Bible. Da Gertrude grasped me so hard I feared my bones would crack.

Mother held the lamp high as we descended into the basement. It was cool, the air damp—old air. I watched where I stepped, fearing cockroaches.

I followed Mother into the storm room—a large room with a narrow bed in it. There was a chair with a frayed wicker seat and a three-legged table propped up in one corner. On the table was a lantern, a candle, an earthenware jug and a cracked china cup. That was all but for one small opening high up on the wall, covered with a wooden shutter.

I set my basket down on the bed. I recognized the patchwork counterpane as one that Catherine and I had worked on together. Mother put the lantern down on the table and felt with her finger to see if it had been dusted. She turned to me. "Rose—I hope you understand why this is necessary."

"I do," I lied. I didn't know what to say.

She began to weep. It was more of a shuddering movement than a sound, for there were no tears. It seemed an unnatural thing. I put my arm around her shoulders. I was surprised how small she seemed. She wiped her face with the back of her hand. "May God be with you," she said.

And then she was gone and I was alone.

*Later.*

Dear Diary, it is night, my first. I pried open the shutters; the night sounds filled my room. Then I closed the shutters tight, for fear of the wandering night spirits, the hungry mystères.

I fear I am not alone. In the shadows I feel the presence of some spirit. I cannot sleep, will not sleep, for fear it will approach. My eyes open, ever alert, I watch the dark.

The oil in my lantern is low. I must blow it out, I know, forsake this island of light. Courage, I say.

*Faith*, I hear something whisper.

*August 5.*

I woke at the sound of the slave-master blowing his conch shell up in the slave village. I lay there for a time, staring at the ceiling, looking for faces in the cracks. I thought I heard a voice and a giggle. I pushed the chair to the wall and opened the shutters. There, peering at me through the long grass, were Catherine's dark eyes.

"We have to be quick!" she whispered through the grate.

I heard Manette behind her: "Let me see! Let me see!"

"Quiet!" Catherine hissed.

Manette's little face came into view. Her hand reached down. I took the handful of moist crumbs. "A mango tart. I stole it!"

Then some more quarrelling and Catherine came back into view. "How is it down there?"

"Boring."

"Run!" I heard Manette cry out.

And then there was only grass.


*August 6.*

Toward evening I heard a scratching at the window again. I stood on the chair and looked out. It was Catherine again. She was crying.

"What's the matter!"

"You have to promise not to tell."

"What *is* it!"

She started to speak but tears came. "Just a minute," she said, taking out her handkerchief and blowing her nose. She pressed her face closer to the grate. "I went to the fortuneteller."

"To Euphémie David?"

She nodded.

"But Catherine! How could you!"

"Just because she told *you* you would be Queen."

"Did Mimi take you?" I was angry now.

"I went alone."

"*Alone?*" I couldn't imagine anyone being *that* brave.

She was beginning to gasp now, sobs overcoming her. I stuck my finger through the grate to try to touch her. "What happened! Did she say something?"

And then she told me. At first the sorcerer had told her to go away, she would not say her future, she said she could not see it. But then the old woman said an awful thing—that Catherine would be in the ground before her next birthday.

"Mother's right—she is the Devil!" I hissed, but already Catherine was gone, scrambling through the grass.

*[Undated]*
Is it the Devil or a kind spirit that takes the form of a bat? Last night there were several. I have begun to feel dizzy and not at all hungry. Why am I here? I can't recall.

*[Undated]*
I went for a walk. I remember an old woman's face. I remember her eyes and dust on the back of her hand. I remember watching as she picked through a basket of dried leaves and put them one by one on the dirt in front of me. I remember her chant, her strange wail. I remember an earthenware bowl with two little hearts in it, swarming with flies. I remember seeing a maggot in the bowl.

Was this a dream?

I remember a crippled old woman standing, raising her arms. I remember her lifting a flask of devil-fire to her lips, drinking it like water. I remember her jumping up and down on the ground in front of me, swiping the air with her outstretched hands.

I remember the words: *You will be Queen.*

This must have been a dream.

*Tuesday, August 12, late.*
It was Mother who came for me, at the last. I was lying on the bed. She stood at the door with a lantern in her hand. "Rose?"

I did not answer. I tried, but could not—it seemed too hard a task.

She came to the bed. She was wearing a white gown and a white head scarf and by the light of the lantern she looked like an angel. "You look like an angel," I said, my voice strange, hoarse.

I felt her fingers fluttering over my face. I heard a snuffling sound. "Oh, sweet Jesus!" she whispered.

I looked at her with confusion. Why was she weeping? I saw a brilliant light all around her. She was the Virgin Mary come to bless me. "Maman!" I cried out, kissing her fingers, pressing her hand to my cheek, marvelling at her beauty.

*In which the mystères have their way*

Thursday, August 21, 1777.
I woke to the sound of a soft rap-rap-rap on my bedchamber door. "Who is it?" I hissed, fearful.

The door creaked open.

"Father!" He was wearing a riding jacket, blue with gold buttons.

"I've ordered your pony saddled," he whispered, so as not to waken Da Gertrude. Steam was rising from the earthenware mug in his hand. It smelled of coffee and rum. "I want you to meet my new lady," he said, tossing me a chocolate roll.

Father's new lady was a black mare with white socks—a bold well-built girl with big eyes, young still. "Lady Luck, I've named her," he said proudly, "won at the tables."

I reached out to touch her muzzle. She jerked her head away. "Sucre is small for me now," I said. My little pony was standing by the wall with flies on her eyes.

"This one's a little hot for you," Father said. I held the bridle as he mounted.

The horses snorted as we headed down the laneway, shaking their heads against the flies. The sun had just come up; the shadows were long yet, the grass damp. A blue heron flew up as we approached the canefields, still in chaos from the harvest. On the far horizon, at the edge of the sea, the field-slaves were working, preparing a field for burning.

"King Sugar," Father said with an ironic smile, slapping at a mosquito. He pulled a leather flask from his coat pocket, tipped back his head.

Other planters lived like kings. Why did we have no fortune? But I knew the answer. Your father courts Lady Luck, Mother said. But the Lady mistreats him.

"Tell me a story about when you were at Court, Father."

He groaned.

"The hunt story?"

"You know it by heart," he said.

It was true. I knew the story of the hunt so well I could tell it myself. How the King set out each morning with his lieutenants and under-lieutenants, the gentlemen of the chase, his squires and under-squires and pages. How the dogs howled, how the King knew each by name. How the fine-blooded horses pranced in the morning mist—so many of them sixty men were needed just to give them water!

I leaned my head on Sucre's neck, inhaled her warm, clean scent. Imagine such a world. "A story about the Queen, then," I said. "About the birth of the Dauphin." About fireworks lighting up the night.

Father let loose his reins, allowed his mare to graze. "Speaking of queens, I was told the most extraordinary thing." He turned to look at me. "I was told you went to see that old voodoo woman up river."

I sat up. "Who told you that?" I tried not to sound alarmed.

"A woman in Fort-Royal."

"Oh?" I didn't like my father talking about me with "a woman."

"It's said you will be Queen," he said.

I felt my cheeks burn. I looked away.

"So it's true," he said. He held out the flask. I shook my head. "You are looking a little pale, Rose, a little thin. Have you been ill?"

"No." I'd been warned not to tell.

"You know, I wanted you to be a boy." He took another swig from his flask. Then he laughed. "But a queen might not be so bad," he said, urging his mare into a walk. "A queen might help pay off my gambling debts."

"I was punished, Father!" The words leapt from me unbidden.

His saddle creaked as he turned to face me. "Punished?"

Tears came to my eyes.

"For being told you will be Queen?" he asked.

I took a shaky breath. "For talking to the Devil," I whispered.

"The strap?" His voice cold.

I nodded. I wanted to tell him the truth, but I did not dare. I wanted to tell him about the room in the basement, about the bats and the spirits and the faces in the night. I wanted to tell him about the voices. But it would only anger him, I knew, and there would be fights. There were fights enough.

"The Old Women did this?" That is what Father called Mother and Grandmother Sannois.

"Father Droppet made them!"

"The Devil be damned," he cursed, under his breath. His mare bucked as he spurred her, bucked again as she broke into a gallop.

I kicked my pony hard and held on, tears blinding me. Father cried out as I passed him at the hanging tree.


*August 25.*

Catherine and I are getting ready to return to the convent school in Fort-Royal. Little Manette watches us enviously, offering to help, getting in the way.

We leave day after tomorrow, in spite of the rains. The weather is hot and terribly humid. We have to push our embroidery needles through the heavy cotton cloth.


*A week later, 6:00 P.M.—Fort-Royal.*

Catherine and I are back at school again, back at dreary Dames de la Providence, back to Sister Gretch's scowls. Mass at seven, classes from eight until eleven, and again from one until five. Drawing and embroidery. Reading and penmanship. Lectures on virtue and modesty. My backside is sore from sitting all day on hard benches.

*September 7.*
This rainy season will never end. The streets are rivers of mud. Catherine and I are stuck here at the convent—we can't even go to Uncle Tascher's for Sunday supper. Instead we eat salt fish, the third evening in a row. A cockroach, the biggest I'd ever seen, was running under the tables. Catherine screamed, though I know for a fact she's braver than most boys. She stood up on the table and stepped into at least two dinner plates and sent her own crashing to the floor. If it weren't for Catherine, we'd die of boredom.

*Wednesday, September 10, 11:00 A.M .*
This morning at bath Catherine lifted her chemise when the sisters weren't looking. I gestured to her to lower it, but she only giggled and did it again. Soon we were all being bad.

*Sunday, September 14, 1:00 P.M.*
After mass this morning we were led on a promenade across the Savane. The smell of the slave ships in the harbour was strong. And then, a disturbing thing. As we turned back, Catherine whispered, "I don't want to die!"

"Your face is flushed," I said, alarmed by her curious statement. "Are you ill?" She looked inflamed.

Tonight Catherine was the first to fall asleep. This is the most worrisome sign. Usually she gets the paddle for staying up late.

*Tuesday, September 16.*
Catherine is so sick now, she has to return home. I have insisted I go with her. Sister Gretch told me I am using my sister's misfortune as an excuse not to go to school. It wouldn't be honest, dear Diary, not to say that there is some truth in what Sister Gretch said. I hate being at the convent school, but it is also true that I am worried about Catherine. I've been nursing her for two days. We leave in the morning.

*September 22—Trois-Ilets.*
We've been home five days and Catherine's sicker still, always in a drowsy stupor. Da Gertrude has been making smelly salves to spread on her chest, but they haven't helped. All day Mother sits and watches her, fanning her with a big palm leaf. Every so often she sponges her all over with rum, her prayers filling the rooms with a monotonous drone.


*September 23.*
I found chicken feathers and bits of bone under Catherine's bed. Voodoo magic, I hope.


*4:00 P.M.*
Grandmother Sannois says Catherine has yellow fever.

Yellow fever! I try not to think of Madame Laveaux's little boy who died in the summer, try not to think what the slaves say, how Madame Laveaux pierced her dead boy's heart with a butcher knife to keep the bokor from his grave.


*Friday afternoon, September 26.*
The doctor finally came and looked at Catherine. He prescribed Hoffman's Drops with sugar. He said she's been seized by an ague that has been succeeded by a fever, but that it's not *yellow* fever, that there's nothing to worry about—but why is she getting worse?

I told Mother she should call the doctor back, but she said, "What's the point? He'll just say the same thing and charge another livre."


*September 27, 10:00 P.M.*
Tonight Catherine was talking in a dream, crying out and screaming. Then she jumped out of bed and ran around the room. She thought little Manette was a giant crab trying to pinch her. Mother, Da Gertrude and I tried to hold on to her but she was strong. I couldn't believe it, she's so

thin. Finally she weakened and Da Gertrude put some herbs in a pair of socks and tied the socks onto her feet. It helped, she went to sleep.


*October 6.*
Catherine gets worse. Manette and I are not allowed to go in her bed-chamber. We stand at the door, but it's hard to see her through the nets.


*Thursday, October 8.*
Tonight I sneaked into Catherine's room after Mother fell asleep. I sat on her bed under the nets and we talked, whispering in the dark. Before I left I took her hand.

"You mustn't touch me," she said, pulling away.

"Imagine this. Imagine that I'm holding you," I said.

She began to cry, so I put my arms around her and held her close. How could I not?


*October 10.*
Father came home late tonight. I heard him stumbling in and then I heard Mother: "Catherine is dying and where are you? Getting drunk, you damn fool!"

Sheet lightning lit up my room and in the dark silence I heard the shrill whistle of the fruit bats. Catherine is *dying?*


*Monday.*
After morning chores I went down to the river, looking for Mimi. I needed her help. Mimi knew the ways of the spirits, the mystères.

She was up to her knees in the bathing-pool washing linens, her flour-sack chemise soaked. Under a lilac bush the two pugs sat watching. A chicken was scratching in the mud nearby.

It began to rain. We took shelter under a tree laden with green oranges. The pugs scuffed around at Mimi's feet.

"Remember when we went to the obeah woman's hut?" I said.

"You think I'd forget?" She threw a pebble at the chicken, to shoo it away.

"I never told you something." I paused. The rain was coming down heavily now, dripping through the leaves. I began to feel a little ill, the way I do when a wind starts up. "The old woman told Catherine she'd be in the ground before her birthday this December. And now Mother says Catherine's—"

"*Catherine* went?"

"When I was in the basement room."

"You never told me!"

"I *promised* not to tell."

"That girl—!"

"And now Mother says Catherine is . . ." I stopped, tears choking. "What if what the obeah woman said comes true?" I blurted out. "Can't you change it?"

"Undo it?"

"Yes!"

Mimi rested her chin on her knees, thinking. "A paquets Congo," she said finally.

"Yes," I said, taking a breath. A paquets Congo, properly made . . .

I spent the afternoon helping Mimi gather the ingredients: a toad (which Mimi killed, not me), a tcha-tcha root, a bag of mombin leaves and some hairs I took from Catherine's comb.

"It must be buried under a mapou tree," Mimi said, securing the bundle with a bit of red string, the type barren women wear at voodoo ceremonies. "By moonlight."

"I can't," I said. "Not at night."

"It's safe if you keep your eyes down."

"It's Mother." Mother doesn't believe in voodoo, but she fears the mystères, the voodoo spirits.

"I'll do it then," Mimi said.

"Alone?" I asked, in awe of her courage.

I don't know how late it was when Mimi climbed in my window. "I did it," she hissed, shaking me awake. I could hardly see her in the dark. "I buried the paquets." Faintly, through the steady drone of the rain, I heard drums.

"You're wet," I said, touching her hand.

"I can't stay." She tightened her kerchief around her head. "There's a séance."

I watched her climb down the mango tree, watched until I could see her no longer. I felt a chill pass through me, smelled the faint scent of a cigar. Trembling, I shut the window, pulled the drapes tight against the dark night.


*October 15.*

Father Droppet came today. I must have looked suddenly pale, for he guided me to the sofa in the parlour and suggested I rest for a moment. Mother came in then. She took his soaking wet cloak and hat. "I was afraid you would not be able to make it," she said. "The roads are so bad."

"The roads are bad," he said.

He was in with Catherine for a very short time. When he came out, Mother offered him tea, but he said he must be on his way, because of the roads.

After he left I went to my bedchamber. I took the heavy wood cross down from the wall and kissed it, pressed it to my heart. Don't take Catherine, I prayed. Don't. *Don't!*


*October 16.*

When I woke it was quiet in the house except for the sound of Mother crying and Father talking in a tired, sad voice.

I tiptoed into Catherine's room and I saw her lying there, still and all alone with no one fanning her, no one praying. I watched to see her chest rise and fall, her eyelids flicker, but there was no movement, only silence.

I willed myself to touch her, to wake her, but I could not. I stumbled back down the hall to my room. *Catherine is dead.* I began to shake.

I climbed out my window and down the mango tree. I ran up the trace to the slave shacks. Mimi was asleep on her straw pallet. She opened her eyes, seeing me slowly.

"You said it would work!" I cried. I hit her with my fist.

"Oh . . ." She grabbed my wrists, hard.

"Do something!" I was blubbering. "Make her come back!"

Mimi began to cry then too. "Oh, that little brat," she moaned. She held me in her arms and rocked me, whispering, "It's done, it's done, rest now."

*7:00 P.M.*

The rains stopped. "We are blessed," Mother said, her eyes shining. She washed Catherine all over with rum and laid her out in her festival gown on a patchwork counterpane. Father told me and Manette to go gather flowers. We were bringing in baskets of roses, red jasmine, orchids and honeysuckle all morning. Mother laced the orchids through Catherine's hair and arranged the other blossoms nicely all around her.

"She looks beautiful," Manette said, awed.

But so still.

Mother tried to get her best crucifix, the iron one with the tiny ruby in the centre, to stay in Catherine's hands, but it kept slipping to the floor.

"That will do," Father said. I don't think he liked Mother fussing so.

Mother laid the cross on Catherine's chest and it stayed.

In the afternoon, neighbours began to arrive, gaping at our worn rugs. Later we began the journey to Trois-Ilets, two carriages and a wagon through the mud to the graveyard behind the church. The roads were perilous but it was so hot we dared not wait a day. One of the horses foundered in the deep footing and several times we had to stop to pull a carriage out of the ruts.

The sun was going down as the box was lowered into the tomb. My knees gave way as the top was fastened on. Da Gertrude helped me to my feet. All the way home, fireflies circled us. Circled us and circled us.

It is late now. The air is heavy with the threat of rain. I listen to the land breezes stirring the mango tree outside my window, the noisy cabri-bois.

Father Droppet says Catherine's in Heaven, that she's with God. Yet I feel her in the wind, in the dark shadows. I feel her tears and I think, Why *Catherine?* Why not *me?* The beating of my heart such a terrible sin.


*Sunday, October 19.*
Mother and I took a potted ginger lily to town today to put on Catherine's tomb. Then Mother told me to go sit in the wagon. When I looked back I saw her kneeling in the dirt. I ran to see if she was hurt. She had her fist in her mouth and her face was wet. It frightened me, seeing her thus. I didn't know what to say or do.

"Is there a God?" she cried out. I could see rage in her eyes.

I was afraid to answer, afraid that something I said might condemn Catherine to eternal Hell. "We'd better go," I said quickly, reaching out for her, fearful of what she might do in that holy place.

Once home I persuaded Mother to have a rum and syrup and got her to lie down. Her cry fills me still: *Is there a God?*

My quill trembles and tiny blots of ink like a flurry of tears cover the page.

## In which I suffer a bitter disappointment
## & hope is offered anew

*January 3, 1778.*

Uncle Tascher came from Fort-Royal today with a buggy-load of provisions: coarse cotton fabric for the slaves' clothing, black crêpe for mourning clothes for us. Then he pulled a letter out of his vest pocket—a letter from Paris! From Aunt Désirée.

Father read the letter. He looked up at his brother. "It's about Désirée's godson—the Marquis's boy." He snorted. "*My.*"

"Are you not going to read it aloud, Father?" I sat down beside Mother on the sofa. Outside a gentle breeze stirred the palms. Our lovesick bull was bellowing in his pen.

Father began to read. In the letter Aunt Désirée informed Father that the Marquis's son, Alexandre—"handsome and well educated"—was now seventeen. If he married, he would come into his mother's inheritance, so Aunt Désirée has suggested he marry one of her nieces—one of *us*.

At last! I thought. My prayers had been answered.

But then Father read out a part about Alexandre preferring Catherine. *Catherine?*

"But . . ." I stuttered. It was only two months ago we buried Catherine.

Mother put down her mending. "Let him have her then," she said. She is like that still—strange somehow.

Father paced the room. "The young chevalier will command an annual income of at least forty thousand livres."

"Forty thousand?" Grandmother Sannois said, coming into the room. "Did he say forty thousand? Or four?"

Father stood by the window. "Maybe they would take Manette instead," he said.

"My thinking exactly, Joseph," Uncle Tascher said, rubbing his chin.

I didn't understand. Why not *me?*

"Manette's too young," Mother said.

"Four thousand would be an acceptable income," Grandmother Sannois said.

"Manette's *eleven*," Father said. "By the time—"

"Only just," Mother said.

"Eleven and a half. You're not being reasonable!" Father raised his voice.

Uncle Tascher coughed and poured himself a rum. "Opportunities like this don't come along every day," he said.

"Why not *me?*" I said, standing.

Father looked uneasy. He sighed. "Rose—" He glanced at the letter again. Then he cleared his throat. "The chevalier has expressed a preference for a younger bride. You are too close to him in age—you wouldn't look up to him the way a wife should."

Mother snorted.

"That's it exactly," Father said. He stomped to the door. "God help me!" He slammed the door behind him.

"I won't let you take my baby!" Mother cried.

I ran to my room. I started to throw things into an old haversack. I was going to run, I didn't care where. Anywhere. Even the empty slave shack down by the shore would be better than this. Even a cave in the mountains, with the runaways.

That's when I saw Manette, standing in the door sucking on a stick of sugarcane, her battered wood doll under one arm.

"I thought you were playing outside," I said. I didn't care about Manette, to tell the truth.

I heard sniffles. "I don't want to go!"

"Oh . . . ," I said. "You heard all that." I took her in my arms. "Poor little scarecrow," calling her the name the slaves had given her.

*Sunday night, January 4.*

I woke to the sound of billiard balls knocking against each other, the sound of men laughing. Uncle Tascher and Father were in the game room, I thought. How late was it?

"Why one of *your* girls, Joseph?" I heard Uncle demand.

I went to the door, pressed my ear to the crack.

"Not that they aren't lovely," he went on, "and of baptismal innocence, both of them—but face it, a girl without a dowry? The lad must be desperate. And if he's such a fine specimen, why must he go halfway around the world for a girl he's never even seen? And a penniless one at that. If he's all our sister says he is, it seems to me he would have his pick of any of the pedigreed strumpets in France."

"Désirée's no fool," I heard my father answer. "How old is the Marquis now anyway? Sixty? Seventy? When he hangs up his fiddle, Désirée will be—" Father made a rude noise.

Then Uncle Robert said something, but I couldn't make it out.

"If she can make this"—Father's words became unclear for a moment—"she'll be legally related. And it wouldn't do, would it, for a *relative* to end her days in a charity hospital."

I heard a chair scrape on the wood floor. "I can see the advantage to Désirée—but why would the *son* go along with it?" Uncle Tascher asked.

"Does the boy have a choice? Until he's twenty-one, if his father tells him to jump in the Seine, he's got to jump in the Seine. And if our sister tells the Marquis to make his son go jump in the Seine, I believe the old bastard would do it. The Devil knows what she does for him in return." He laughed.

"So you think young Alexandre is being forced into this arrangement?"

"Not so much forced as bribed. Happiness is an unlimited income, if you ask me. The only way the young chevalier can get his hands on his fortune is to marry. And my guess is that his piss-proud father told him (at our beloved sister's *suggestion*, God bless her): Look, if you want my permission to marry, it must be a Tascher girl."

There was another burst of laughter and the talk turned to slave prices. I climbed back into bed. I felt a strange tingling in my belly. What did Father mean, that Aunt Désirée had *done* something to the Marquis—something that made him do her bidding?

*January 5.*

I told Mimi that Manette might be going to France to be married. "She's scared," I said.

"What's to be scared of?" Mimi asked, mashing the plaintain with violent strokes.

I wasn't really sure what it was Manette had to be afraid of, but I knew it was something—something to do with dogs climbing over each other, trembling in that pathetic way. "You know, marriage duty."

"Is she in flowers yet?"

I shook my head. "What does that have to do with it?" All I know is that the cook isn't allowed to cure pork when she's in flowers.*

"Child, don't they tell you *anything!*" But Mimi didn't tell me anything either.


*March 17.*

Now Manette is ill—she has a fever, just as Catherine had. Mother says it's her fear of getting married that brought it on.

I crawl in under the covers beside her and try to cheer her. I tell her how grand it will be in France. I tell her about the wonderful dolls they have there, and how our beautiful Aunt Désirée will look after her. I tell her how handsome the chevalier is, how smart and how educated, how noble and how rich. I tell her how envious I am. (Oh, but I am!)

But in her fever she only cries. There are nights when I'm so afraid she will die, as Catherine did, in one big moment gone, just a limp body on a rumpled bed, no more or less than a rag doll.


*June 23, 9:00 P.M.*

Father came back from Sainte-Lucie yesterday. Right away he and Mother got into a quarrel.

---

* The belief that a menstruating woman could spoil a ham was maintained into the nineteenth century. Doctors published papers in medical journals theorizing that when a woman was menstruating her skin became moist, preventing the pork from taking in salt.

"But Manette never did want to go!" I heard Mother say. "It was *you* put those words in her mouth."

She started crying that he *couldn't* take Manette from her, not so soon after losing Catherine. Father yelled, "You crazy créole women and your children!" I felt the walls shake as the door slammed shut.

*June 24.*
Father has relented. He wrote to Aunt Désirée, telling her he wouldn't be able to bring Manette, she was too sick to go, but how about me? He explained that I wasn't all *that* old, and already well developed.

"You know they may not like the idea, Rose," he told me, sealing the letter with wax. "After all, you're already fifteen."

"When will you find out?"

"It will take a few months for my letter to get there and what with the war on—" He stopped to calculate. "Five months?"

I moaned. Five months! I want to know *now!*

*In which I fall in love*

*Sunday, July 19, 1778.*
There is talk of a new family in town, a woman and her son. At church I
saw them after mass. The boy—about sixteen, I guessed, and comely—
was watching three village boys chase a scorpion that had slipped under a
pew. He fiddled with the handle of his cutlass, his long dark bangs hiding
his eyes. His linen frock and leather breeches were patched.

"Béké-goyave," Mother said under her breath, pushing me outside,
"vagabonds!"


*July 25.*
Mother allowed me to go with Mimi and Sylvester to market today. "So
long as your chores are done," she said. We set off for town in the back of
the ox-cart.

It was busy in the village; I confess I was hoping to see the new boy,
but there were only sailors who'd come over from Fort-Royal for the
cock-fights. I kept my eyes to the ground, the way the nuns had taught.

At the dock we bought a bonito and three coral fish from a fisherman
with light frizzy hair. He stared at me while we went through his catch. Then
he said something to Sylvester and laughed in a way that made me blush.

We walked back up to the village square to buy pawpaws, guavas, avo-
cado pears and tapioca. At a table displaying pictures of the saints, little
mirrors and beads, a woman told us about the runaway slave who had
turned into a dog and eaten a baby on the Desfieux plantation. Just at

the frightful part the new boy's mother arrived, followed at some distance by the boy, laden with parcels.

His mother nodded at me, her eyes deep set. "I saw you at church," she said. She talked like a nun, proper. Between sentences she pressed her lips together.

I nodded. She introduced herself as Madame Browder, a British name. The boy's name is William.

"We're at the foot of Morne Croc-Souris," I told them.

Mimi spat onto the dirt.

"On the river?" Madame Browder asked, tucking a wisp of red hair under her plain white téte.

"Farther on, La Pagerie." From across the bay, I could see a gommier making its way slowly to the shore. A swarm of gulls hovered above it like mosquitoes in rainy season.

"We're closer in toward town," Madame Browder said.

"The old Laignelot homestead," Mimi said. She was scratching the ears of a mangy dog. "Neighbours, if you go by the river."

I felt I should invite them for tea and cakes, but I dared not, remembering my mother's harsh words: béké-goyave. I was saved by Sylvester pulling up in the wagon. Hurriedly I took my leave.

"Sweet eyes," Mimi teased on the way home, jabbing me with her elbow. "I saw you making sweet eyes."


*Sunday, August 9.*
William and his mother sat near the front of church this morning. Mother, Manette (who is better now) and I sat on a bench several rows behind. All through mass I watched him, my heart fluttering like a trapped baby bird.


*August 10.*
I sneaked down to the lower pond this afternoon for a swim. But when I got there I saw the new boy William Browder. He was fishing, his pantaloons rolled up to his knees. He startled when he saw me, as if he

shouldn't be there. He pulled his line out of the water, a long length of white horsehair attached to a bamboo pole.

"Caught anything?" It was hot and I longed to go in, but I didn't know if I should, now that he was there. Instead I sat down on the bank. I picked a long blade of razor grass and split it so I could whistle through it.

"How do you do that?" William Browder asked, rolling down his pantaloons.

I showed him and we sat whistling.

"Why did you move to Trois-Ilets?" I asked finally. Cul-de-sac à vaches—cow-field—that's what we call it. "Not that it's my business," I added, in an attempt to show manners.

"It was hard for my mother in Saint-Pierre," he said. He looked up at the sky. A hawk was circling. "It's hard for her here, too." He shrugged.

I'd heard that his mother used to be an actress, that she'd fallen in love with a sailor in the British navy during the Seven Years' War. Imagine having a mother like that, I thought. An actress! The shame and the glory of it. An actress couldn't be buried in a church graveyard, or even marry—the Church forbade it.

"You're English? But you don't have an accent." I swatted at a red ant crawling up my arm.

"My father was from Scotland actually."

I didn't know where Scotland was, but I was relieved he wasn't British. The British are not Christian—they eat children.

"I never knew him," he went on. He stretched out on the grass, twirling a blade of grass between his fingers.

"Never?"

William looked at me. His eyes were the lightest blue I'd ever seen. "I remember his face, remember him smiling. But that's all."

"My father is rarely home, so I don't suppose it's that much different," I told him.

"When I was young," William said, "I liked to think that my mother and father had loved each other very much, and had parted tragically. I thought that better than some long drawn-out marriage where the husband and wife only grow bitter and cold."

A fish jumped from the water, making rings over the glassy surface of the pond. I thought of my own mother and father, of the bitterness between them. Had there ever been love?

William pushed his hair away from his eyes. "I'm a romantic, I guess." He smiled. "Like my hero, Jean-Jacques Rousseau."

I got to my feet, uneasy. No one, most especially a boy, had ever talked to me about such things. I feared it was improper and didn't know how to respond. "I must go," I said.

"Yes," William said, also rising. He stood before me, awkward and hesitant, no longer a mysterious young man, the son of an actress who had been tragically loved, but instead only William, a béké-goyave in patched clothes.

I hurried up the trace. At the stone bridge I glanced back. William was watching me.

"Tomorrow?" he called out.

I ran up the hill, my face burning.


*Wednesday, August 12.*
All morning I told myself: I'm not going to go, I'm not going to go. And then, after chores, there I was, heading for the swimming pond. . . .

William grinned when he saw me coming down the trace. I pretended to be surprised to see him there. I didn't know what to say so I sat on the bank and threw pebbles in the water. Then I ran home singing.

If anyone ever found out, I hate to think what might become of me.

I will never go again.


*September 2.*
Whenever I can I go to the fishing pond. William is often there. Mostly we sit and talk. I tell him how I long to go to France, to *Paris*, how I feel there is so much to experience and see, how exciting it is to be young and looking forward to it all, how hard to be told your dreams are impossible.

William is the same. He longs to see the world. He reads the journals that come over on the boats. He tells me all about the things that are going on in the American colonies. He talks of "freedom" and "equality."

He asks me what I think about it all, but I tell him I don't read, so how do I know?

"You don't have to read to know how you feel about something like freedom. It's in your heart," he says, "not in words on a page."

This afternoon he read a passage from a book: *Man is born free, but is everywhere in chains*.* "*Born* free," he said. "Imagine that."

"Everyone?"

"Free *and* equal."

"Slaves, too?"

"A master and his slaves." He paused. "A king and his subjects."

"Is *that* what's written in that book?" I regarded it with apprehension, as if it might burst into flames before my eyes. "But William," I said, "if that were true, the world would—" I stopped. I couldn't think of a word big enough.

"Yes!" he said.


*Friday, September 18.*
William and I have quarrelled. It started when I told him Mimi casts my cards, that she's teaching me how.

"How can your life be in those little pieces of paper?" he demanded.

"I just know the cards are right. I have seen that it is so."

"You can't believe in freedom then," he said.

"Show me freedom!" I cried, and he had no answer. For there is no such thing.


*September 20, 8:30 P.M.*
William has apologized and I have accepted. He confessed that it distressed him to think that there might be no such thing as freedom, that everything was written. "Then what would it matter what a person did?" he asked.

I told him about Catherine, and the fortune the old woman had given

* *From* The Social Contract *by Jean-Jacques Rousseau.*

her, and how it had so tragically come to pass. Then I told him about the fortune the old woman had given me.

"Do you believe this is your destiny—to be *Queen* of France?" he asked.

"How frightful that would be," I said. A flock of crows were making a racket in some bushes down in a ravine.

William picked a bough of scarlet bougainvillea and crowned my head. He stood back to look at me. "You would make a lovely queen," he said.

I turned away, for I felt so shamelessly beautiful in his eyes.

He made a mock bow. "But who will be your king?"

The bougainvillea fell from my head. I stooped to pick it up. I stood and faced him, suddenly dizzy. "You?"

Then he kissed me, and I allowed him to do so.

*October 16.*
This afternoon William and I hiked up the mountain in hopes of seeing the green flash.\* We waited until just after dusk, but even so, we did not see it, for too much kissing.

*Sunday, November 1, All Saints' Day.*
Oh . . . holidays, holidays, holidays, I'm so anxious for them to be over.

This morning, after lighting candles at Catherine's tomb, Mother, Manette and I returned to a holiday "feast" at home: boiled green bananas and féroce. The féroce tasted terrible without salt, which we have had to do without ever since the British have blockaded the port.\*\* We said a prayer for Father, who is engaged in conflict in Sainte-Lucie.

I've not seen William for five days.

---

\* *A narrow line of green that can occasionally be seen as the sun sets or rises. It is believed to bring luck to those who see it.*

\*\* *France was unofficially supporting the American War of Independence against England by providing supplies to the American troops from Fort-Royal, so British ships blockaded the port.*

*December 15.*
The British have captured Sainte-Lucie. Father is safe—he's on his way home.


*New Year's Day, 1779 .*
Today I brought William a gift of ginger sweets. "You have found the way to my heart," he said. Sometimes he talks like that—like an old-fashioned knight.

It was hot so we stayed in the water a long time. When we got out we stretched out on the bank to dry. He untied my hair. Then he kissed me and held me close. There were no sounds, no birds singing, only the beating of my heart. I pulled away then, for it frightened me, this.

"Where have you been?" Mother said when I got home. The shadows had grown long.

"At the river with Mimi," I lied.

"Your cheeks are burned," she said. "You're neglecting to wear your bonnet."

It is night now, late. The hills are silent. I couldn't sleep so I got up and lit a candle and opened this dear little book, that I might write down the thoughts that burn in my heart.

I love William. I love William. I love William.

## *In which I am betrothed*

*Friday, January 29, 1779* .

The letter from Paris came today. Aunt Désirée wrote Father: Whatever, just bring a girl, me or Manette, it didn't matter. "We must have one of your daughters." She urged Father to act with haste; the young chevalier might change his mind if forced to wait too long.

There was a note to Father from the Marquis as well: "The one whom you judge most suitable for my son will be the one whom we desire." He enclosed permission to have the banns read and left a space where a name should go.

Father looked at me. "Well, Rose—your prayers have been answered," he said, writing out my name on the form.

I looked away.

"What a funny girl you are. Always crying when you're happy."

I wiped my cheeks with the back of my hand. "Yes, Father," I said.


*January 31* .

At church this morning I saw William. I made our signal and he acknowledged it.

Back home, I hurried with my chores. I asked leave to go down to the river—with Mimi, I said, praying for forgiveness for lying, especially on a Sunday.

Mother consented and I was gone before she could think otherwise, down the trace and into the forest. At the bridge I stopped, my breath coming in short jabs. Why was I running? I proceeded at a walk, my troubled thoughts catching up with me. What was I going to tell him?

William was fishing at the pond. He turned when he heard me on the path.

"I'm glad you could come," I said, standing nervously beside him, as a stranger. "I have something to tell you." I heard the cry of a raven.

William pulled in his line. There was a live frog on the hook.

"Father received a letter from his sister in Paris," I said. "His offer has been accepted."

"What offer?"

"I'm to be betrothed—to a man in France."

William fiddled with the hook, trying to slide the frog off. He cursed under his breath and did not beg my forgiveness for doing so.

"I'm to go live in Paris. I will be a vicomtesse." In spite of myself, there was pride in my voice.

William looked at me. His eyes seemed unnaturally blue.

"Are you not going to say anything?" I felt uneasy.

William threw his fishing gear into his basket. "Thank you for telling me? Is that what I'm supposed to say?" He untied his dusty donkey from a gum-tree branch.

"William . . ." I put one hand on his shoulder.

He jerked away, pulling himself onto his donkey's back. Then he kicked her, taking off down the trace at a trot.

I sat by the river, trying hard not to cry.


*Sunday, April 11.*

This morning, after mass, Father Droppet read the banns of marriage between Alexandre-François, Chevalier de Beauharnais, and Marie-Joseph-Rose de Tascher de la Pagerie.

Manette made monkey eyes at me. Everyone turned to stare. I felt Father Droppet had been speaking of someone else, not me.

Now this is the big news in the village: at last I will be married, and to a rich man in Paris, to a *Beauharnais*, the son of the former governor of all the Windward Islands. I will be Madame la vicomtesse. I am regarded as an adult now and I feel older, I admit.

*May 8.*
Mother is having a dress made for me, in the Parisian style, an amaranth brocade with gauze around the sleeves and neck. I'm not to wear it until I reach France. That way at least I'll have one thing decent to wear, she said. I go for my first fitting today.

*Monday, June 7.*
Mother insists I learn a proper toilette. I'm to wear a corps de baleine, a corset with stays so stiff it pushes my bosom up and forces me to sit straight. It even hurts to breathe. "When can I take it off?" I asked after one long hour sitting at my vanity, applying pommades.

"You must never take it off," Mother said, showing Mimi how my hair is to be powdered. "You are a woman now."

*June 23.*
I'm sixteen today—how quickly youth passes. Mimi gave me tarot cards of my own as a gift. "Blessed by holy water," she whispered.

Carefully, I laid them out. In the tenth position was the hanged man, his hair hanging down.

"Life turned upside-down," she snorted. "That's you!"

*Saturday, July 10.*
Father is having difficulty getting enough money to pay for passage. I overheard him having an argument with Uncle Robert. "I've loaned you enough already, Joseph!" I heard Uncle Tascher say.

*July 16, 3:00 P.M.*
Father finally has enough money. Uncle Robert gave in. Now Father has to find a ship that can take us. With the war on, it won't be easy, he says.

I worry, for his health is poor.

"You won't survive this voyage, Joseph," I heard Mother tell him this morning. "And then where will we be?"

"It's my only hope. Those doctors in Paris know things," he said, coughing.

What if Mother is right? What if Father dies?


*July 28.*

We leave in two weeks. Mother has had the two big sea chests hauled up to the parlour and there are stacks of clothing everywhere. There is so much to be done, deciding what to take, what to leave behind.

Mother is intent on sending Da Gertrude with me, but Da Gertrude begs to stay. The journey would kill her, she says.

"It's Lasyrenn that scares her," Mimi whispered.

Lasyrenn, the voodoo spirit of the sea, the mermaid with the long black hair. Lasyrenn just below the surface of the water, calling.


*July 29.*

Mimi's coming with me!


*Sunday, August 8.*

We leave for Fort-Royal day after tomorrow, and the day after that we sail. At Saint-Domingue we will change over to the *Ile de France*, a naval store ship which Father warns might not be too comfortable. The frigate *La Pomone* will accompany us all the way to France, to defend us in case we're attacked by the English at sea.

"I don't like sailing when there's a war on," Father told me, "but if we wait for peace, we will never get there."

It's scary, but thrilling—what if we were in a battle!


*1:00 P.M.*

A wind rises, bending the palms. The hot air rushes at my skirts, pulling my plaits loose, my dangling silver earrings. It is midday, but dark as midnight. Inside, in my room, I fasten the wooden shutters with some effort and light a wax taper on my toilette table. I scribble over the pages, seeking a path to my heart, one word, one name: *William*.

From somewhere a breeze catches the flame and snuffs it out, plunging me into dark.


*August 9.*

Dawn was breaking when I got up. I slipped on my clothes and went out into the fields. Sucre was hard to catch. I had to use a custard apple to tempt her. Finally I got a bridle on her and headed off toward the river, my petticoats up around my thighs, my pony's warm body between my legs.

I waited by the stone bridge. Before long William came poking along the trace on his donkey, reading a book. He was surprised when he saw me.

"Come up the mountain with me," I said.

"You're betrothed."

"I'm leaving tomorrow!"

That seemed to startle him.

I took the lead going up the slope. At the top of the path, where it opens onto a clearing, I stopped. "This is a good place." I slid off Sucre.

"Good as any." William tied his donkey to a coconut tree.

"You're not the only one who—"

"Who *what?* What is it that you feel, Rose?" He turned away. "I'm sorry," he said. "I know it can't be helped."

I pressed my forehead into his back. "Do you think it possible we will always love one another?"

"Do not speak of love, I beg you," he said, his voice full of tears.

We stayed on the hill until the mosquitoes began to swarm. He kissed me on my cheek. I longed for more, much more, but I no longer had the right.

We rode down the mountain, through the long shadows. At the bottom he turned to me. "We never saw the green flash."

I'd forgotten.

"Some other day," he said, shading his eyes against the sun.

*August 11—Fort-Royal.*

We were eight of us in the covered wagon—myself, Father and Mimi, plus Mother, Manette, Grandmother Sannois, even Da Gertrude. And Sylvester driving. Plus the two big sea trunks. So it was a wonder the horses could pull us at all. More than once we were up to the hub in mud and had to walk.

It was dangerously after dusk by the time we pulled into Uncle Tascher's courtyard. His wife came running down to greet us, her hair let down and looking wild, Uncle Tascher behind her all red in the face.

We were all of us put in two rooms on the second floor. Uncle Tascher's waiting woman brought us cassava bread with sugar syrup and a saucepan of hot chocolate, to which Father added brandy from his case-bottle. We ate and made ready for bed. As we said our evening prayers together, I could hear sniffling. Da Gertrude had her face in her hands.

I woke before dawn. I lay there for a time, dreaming. What will Monsieur de Beauharnais be like, I wondered. I imagined that he would be handsome and gallant, but perhaps a little shy, so that I would have to coquette a little to put him at his ease. I practised rolling my eyes, which I am told are my best feature, and kissing the back of my hand, but this only made my hand wet, and reminded me of William. I hoped that Monsieur de Beauharnais would be very much like William, only titled and rich, and that he would come to love me very much. As for myself, I know I will come to love him, for Da Gertrude says I could love a flea.

Grandmother stirred, poked Mother to help her up, and the day began. I went to the window and pulled back the heavy brocade. Our sailing ship was still there, beside the little fishing boats. One of the sails had been unfurled. I was anxious to be on deck, for what if a wind came and we were left behind?

For once Mother didn't have to tell me to get ready. Da Gertrude laced me into my best gown, the yellow one with the fichu I'd embroidered myself.

Mimi, still in her petticoats, joined us from the other room. "I had a bad dream last night." She wiped her sleepy eyes.

Da Gertrude threw her hands to her ears. "Don't say that!"

"Hush!" Mother said, crossing herself.

Finally, we were ready, dressed in our church clothes. We'd eaten, had coffee and milk, said our morning prayers, which went on for so long my knees ached.

Uncle Tascher ordered two teams harnessed. His coachman (in new livery—very handsome) and Sylvester loaded the trunks onto an open wagon harnessed to two sleepy mules. Mimi, clutching her wicker basket, and a sniffling Da Gertrude climbed in behind. Sylvester swung himself up onto the driver's seat. Uncle's coachman—looking liquorish, in spite of the hour—helped us into Uncle's new carriage.

"My," Mother said, touching the blue silk upholstery. "Are you sure we are supposed to sit on it, Robert?"

Grandmother knocked on the glass to see if it was real and pulled down one of the shades to see if it worked. "Pity it's that colour," she said.

"Oh yes, oh yes, oh yes, do sit." Uncle Tascher's wife arranged her pleated skirt of brown taffeta (from *Milan*). "I never walk anywhere any more." She looked in the glass to make sure her frightful red hair was well hidden under her lace cap.

"I feel like a queen in such a carriage," I said. Then I slapped my hand over my mouth, for there was talk of my fortune still.

The coachman cracked his whip and the horses jumped forward, throwing us into a tumble.

As we approached the docks, Father took my hand. "Nervous?"

"Mon Dieu," Mother said. "That ship's not so very big, Joseph."

"We'll be changing to a bigger one at Saint-Domingue." Father jumped down onto the dock as if he were a young man. He let down the metal step.

"A ship *and* an escort." Uncle Tascher adjusted his hat, for he was Port Commander now. He took Mother's hand as she stepped down. "They should be safe from attack."

Sylvester pulled the wagon carrying Da Gertrude and Mimi up behind us. Our two sea trunks were loaded into a rowboat and suddenly we were all saying goodbye.

"Send me a doll!" Manette demanded, clasping me tightly around the waist.

I kissed her dear, tear-streaked face. "You'll write?"

She nodded, but I knew she wouldn't.

Mother took my hands. "You must remember to wash under your nails."

"Maman!"

She put her hand on my shoulder. "You'll be a good girl?"

I embraced her then. I feared she might cry.

Mimi and Father were already seated in the little passenger dingy. Father was yelling for me to get in.

Da Gertrude took me in her arms. "My baby!" I began to weep as well.

I kissed her wet cheeks and pulled away. A sailor with a beard helped me into the boat. Father handed me his kerchief. Mimi looked terrified. And then we were on the water, waving and throwing kisses.

I looked back. Da Gertrude had fallen to her knees and was praying. Mother stood silently, her hands pressed to her chest. It was only Manette and Sylvester, at the last, who stood waving.

# II

## *Vicomtesse*

## In which I come to the Old World

*Tuesday, October 12, 1779—Brest, France.*
My knees trembled climbing onto the dock. I held on to Mimi to steady myself. I hadn't realized how frightened I'd been that we would never make it.

France! So many people, horses, carriages! A porter balancing a load on his head barked out to us to move. A newsmonger yelled from the edge of the crowd. It seemed strange, all these white faces rushing about, crying out words I couldn't understand.

Captain and the flag-lieutenant helped with Father. He was so sick he could hardly walk. He has been taking a syrup of maidenhair and brandy concoction the ship's surgeon had made him, but it hadn't helped.

I asked a painted lady standing by some sea chests where we might hire a hackney coach but she only looked at me. "She can't understand your dialect," Captain explained, getting Father seated on a crate. He hailed a hackney cab and helped get us settled in a public house. He even sent word to Aunt Désirée that we have arrived. He said it would take about ten days for her to get here, maybe longer.

At first we tried to take a lodging in the Hôtel du Monarque, an airy and lightsome place with chandeliers, carpets and a buffet on which a few plates were set out. We were led into a parlour where a lady stood by the fire in a dress over a hoop so big I don't know how she got through the door.

We were all set to settle when Father, whom we had propped up in a chair, doubled over coughing and the innkeeper told us we couldn't stay.

Captain, who doesn't hold his temper at the best of times, started to speak. I quickly assured him we would *prefer* to stay somewhere else. So here we are now, at the Hôtel Graves, which is at least clean, although not nearly so grand.

Father and I each have a room on the second floor, facing the street. Mimi was given a room by the stables and privies. I told the innkeeper, Madame Mignon Lodi-Clarion, a cross sort, and thin as a stick, that I wanted Mimi with me, that I needed her help during the night, with Father, but Madame insisted. "We'll have the boy fetch her when you need her" is what she said, somewhat curtly.

The first thing I did after getting Father settled was ask to have a bath. Madame provided me with a hand-basin of hot water and some Joppa soap, immersion being unsafe, she said. I washed myself as best I could.

When poor Mimi came in she smelled like the barn. I let her use my water for a wash of her own, and then we put our small linens in. We draped them over chairs in front of the coal grate. It's so cold and damp I fear they will never dry.


*That evening.*
All the people staying at this inn eat together. I went down without Father. We had cod's head with shrimps and oysters, and then mutton, eggs and a dish of broiled eels which I did not care for but forced myself to eat, to be polite. After the meal a man across the table rubbed his teeth with a sponge and scraper. I thought perhaps that was the custom here, but he was the only one who did it. Then he asked for the chamber-pot. Hastily, I took my leave.


*Thursday, October 14.*
Father didn't sleep last night, suffering feverish dreams. He kept saying he *couldn't* die now.

I tried to get him to take some fish broth but he couldn't keep it down, coughing up blood. "I'll get Madame." I didn't want him to see me crying.

"No." He fell back against his pillows.

I'm back in my room now, but I cannot sleep, listening for sounds on the other side of the wall. Listening for life—but fearing death.

*That evening.*
At last, the doctor came, his tall assistant carrying his big bag. He prescribed a tincture which Father's to take three times a day. That and his visit cost five livres! At least Father's not to be bled.

*October 16.*
Yesterday evening, after Father was asleep, I joined several of the guests in the front parlour. I taught them how to play piquet, which I learned on the boat. I was naughty and wagered a bit of money on it and won two sous from Monsieur d'Aelders, a dear old man from Dijon. I tried to give him the money back after, but he insisted I keep it, somewhat proudly. He's vowed revenge tonight!

Even Madame played. She was sipping wine and humming.

Everyone wanted to know what it was like to live on a sugar plantation. Madame said it was a well-known fact that an owner of a sugar plantation earned more money than a king. Monsieur d'Aelders wanted to know if it was true that the slaves went about naked.

"Not all the time," I said, an answer that seemed to please him.

I told them that I've come to France to meet my fiancé. Madame told a story about how when she was introduced to her husband (who died six years ago), she was wearing false eyebrows, mouse skin ones. She didn't know it, but one eyebrow had fallen off! Her fiancé kept looking at her strangely.

I like Madame better now. She informed me that I may address her as Madame Mignonette. She told me how to get mildew out of linen: rub soap on it, scrape some chalk and rub that in and put it into the sun, wetting it a little. She says I might have to do it twice, but it should come out.

I told her I liked France, but that I had to confess that sometimes the smells quite overpowered me. She gave me a vial to hang around my neck. Inside there is flower water I can sniff. Also, I can dab little bits on my wrists and behind my ears and even on my bosom. She told me to dab it "everywhere," wiggling her eyebrows. When she has time, she said, she'll show me how to dress like a *proper* French lady.

*October 21.*
Still no word from Aunt Désirée.

*October 22, evening.*
Shortly before noon Madame came to inform Father that there was a woman wishing to see him. "Are you receiving, Monsieur?"

I glanced around his room, over his person. He had not been shaved yet and the room had not been freshened.

"Comtesse de la Touche de Longpré." Madame stuck her nose in the air and wiggled her fingers, pretending to put on airs. "The daughter of Madame de Girardin, she said to tell you."

I looked at Father, confused. Wasn't Girardin the name of Mother's sister-in-law? I had only met her a few times. I remembered her as a haughty woman who treated Mother poorly.

Father groaned. "Mon Dieu, Laure Longpré—Brigitte's daughter. . . ."

My *cousin* Laure? I hadn't seen her since I was a child. She was much older than I was, almost fifteen years as I recalled, married and with children. I remembered that the boys used to ogle and follow her about, which she didn't discourage.

"Why in God's name would *she* be here?" Father snorted.

Shortly after, Madame Longpré was admitted, filling the room with a heavy iris fragrance that made Father cough. Quickly I opened the windows.

"Rose, how you've grown," she said, accepting my offer of a chair. She was wearing a frothy pink dress looped in gauze with tassel decorations.

I curtsied, not knowing what to say. She was quite heavily made-up with jewels on every part of her, particularly over her bosom, which was displayed in such a way as to make one blush.

"How *charming* to have relatives in France," she said. Her eyebrows had been plucked into a thin line and blackened with charcoal and the lids of her eyes were painted silver. "I understand there may be a wedding soon."

Father began to choke.

"Would you care for a dish of tea?" I said. "Sweetmeats, perhaps?"

"No, thank you, child. I won't keep you. I can see that my uncle is not well, and as for myself, I must be returning home as I have only *recently* risen from childbed."

Before Father and I could offer our blessings, Madame Longpré turned to me. "In the last two years I have had the good fortune to make the acquaintance of your fiancé, Chevalier Alexandre de Beauharnais, whom I assure you is the most *charming* young man one could ever hope to find."

Father spit up into his kerchief.

I searched my mind for something to say. "A glass of wine perhaps?"

Madame Longpré smiled at me. She stood, taking up her pink parasol. "When the chevalier does arrive, would you please be so kind as to convey to him my warmest congratulations. Inform him that it would be my *greatest* pleasure to tell him so *personally*."

Immediately after Madame Longpré left, Father demanded a glass of brandy.

"Mother didn't mention that Laure Longpré lived here," I said.

"I doubt that she even knows. Your mother and I are none too fond of the Girardins—and they, I must say, are none too fond of us."

"Madame Longpré seemed *very* friendly."

"Like a rabid fox," Father cursed, downing the glass.


*October 23.*

Madame showed me fashion "tricks" this afternoon. Mimi and I giggled, which Madame didn't appreciate, but we couldn't help it, especially when she showed us the false bottoms and bosoms. She showed me how to put a small cork ball in my cheek to fill it out where I'd had a tooth pulled. Madame does this herself, on the right side. (Now I understand why she's a little hard to understand sometimes.) She also showed me how I could glue little patches on my face to cover up my pockmarks. She gave me two small ones made of thick blue wool: one in the shape of a diamond, the other an oval. Then she showed Mimi how to tighten my corset for me by bracing her feet against the bedstead and pulling. We got me all done up with a bottom and a bosom and a tiny, tiny waist. I looked beautiful, but I couldn't breathe and I very nearly fainted!

*October 26.*
Aunt Désirée and Monsieur de Beauharnais will be arriving tomorrow! I fear I'm going to be sick.

## *In which I am introduced to my fiancé*

*October 27, 1779.*

Mimi and I spent the morning in my room fussing over my make-up, my clothes and hair. Every few minutes we would go to the window. At around eleven, I heard Madame's man-of-all-work talking loudly in the street. I looked out and saw a large woman being helped from a conveyance, but no sign of a young man—so I knew it wasn't them.

Then suddenly there was a woman at my door. It was my Aunt Désirée! I last saw her when I was only three or four, so I had no recollection of her, although I'd *imagined* her: my "beautiful Aunt Désirée," the tall woman with golden hair who had bewitched a wealthy marquis. And now here she was—stout, cross and bossy.

"So." She looked me up and down with a bit of a frown—"you must be Rose." She was wearing a red- and white-striped taffeta gown and a hat quivering with red feathers. She thrust me into a hug. I choked on the powder in her wig.

She wanted to know where Father was. "That brother of mine—is he dead yet?" she barked.

I opened the sash doors to Father's room, hoping she wouldn't detect the scent of spirits.

"Joseph," Aunt Désirée commanded, from the door, "you're not to die!"

"I'm not *trying* to die, Désirée," my father said, sitting up in bed with some evidence of discomfort, made the more so by his sister's vigorous greeting. I helped adjust the pillows behind his back. "Where's the young chevalier?" he asked, a question that was foremost in my mind as well.

"I sent him on an errand." Aunt Désirée helped herself to a cordial from the case near the bed. She looked me over. "Are you going to hold your tongue, young lady? Your mother warned me you've got a bit of a tongue."

I had to hold my tongue just then.

"Désirée, don't you be . . . Grand Dieu! I'd forgotten what a—"

"If I were you, I'd keep quiet, Joseph. I've already been attacked by Madame downstairs for the eighty-six livres you owe. And there will be other bills, no doubt."

I sighed and went to the window. A barber covered in flour crossed the street, dodging a man on horseback. "When will Monsieur de Beauharnais be returning?" I asked.

Aunt Désirée took me by the shoulders and turned me toward the light. "None too soon, I hope. You're wearing far too much rouge. And what are these things you've got stuck to your face? Patches have been out of style since King Louis XV died!"

I glanced over at Mimi, who was standing by the door trying hard not to giggle. "Madame has been helping me with my toilette," I confessed.

"Madame downstairs? No wonder you look like a tart!"

I fought back tears. Aunt Désirée sighed and pursed her lips. I detected a flicker of affection beneath her crusty exterior. "My dear child, you will find that your fiancé—should he approve of you, that is, and consent to this union—values *simplicity*, not artifice. He's a strong advocate, as the young man will *no* doubt inform you, of the 'Cult of Sensibility,' God help us all."

She made this proclamation as if it were a badge of both honour and ridicule. I hadn't the faintest notion what she meant.

"What your Aunt Désirée is trying to suggest, Rose," my father said, sinking back under the quilt, "is that you change your toilette."

And so it was that I received still another lesson in how to dress like a proper French lady.

"There now, Joseph, what do you think?" Aunt Désirée pushed me to the foot of Father's bed. She had clothed me in a simple lawn dress and a straw hat covered with silk flowers.

"You've got her looking like a peasant, Désirée. Are you crazy? She will catch her death in that get-up."

The dress was not too different from the chemises we wore back home, around the house doing our chores. I felt disappointed changing out of the amaranth brocade gown Mother had had made for me, but Aunt Désirée insisted it was out of style and that Monsieur de Beauharnais would *never* consent to marry me if he saw me in a dress like *that*.

"You never did have taste, Joseph." Aunt Désirée pulled at my side-curls, trying to get them to fall in loose locks around my face—à la négligence, she called it. "Although I must confess I rather agree with you in this instance. But whatever the Queen wears, all the young people follow, and God knows she's leading them on a merry chase." She pulled a timepiece out of her bosom. "Come now, child, we mustn't linger."

I was more confused than nervous following Aunt Désirée down the stairs to the front parlour. The efforts of the last hours had bewildered me, and for some reason I wasn't expecting to meet Monsieur de Beauharnais at that moment—so when I saw a young man in uniform sitting on the sofa, absorbed in a book, I didn't think anything of it.

"Alexandre, if you please," Aunt Désirée called out with a theatrical flourish, "it is my pleasure to introduce you to my niece—and *your* fiancée."

Monsieur de Beauharnais looked up, startled, as if he'd been waiting for a coach and suddenly it had arrived. "Oh!" He put a bookmark in his little leather volume before carefully setting it down on the side-table. He stood up.

"Mademoiselle Tascher de la Pagerie," Aunt Désirée said grandly, "Monsieur le chevalier de Beauharnais."

I felt there had been a mistake. *This* young man was so *very* distinguished in his white uniform with silver facings. His hair (his own, not a wig—I like that) was brushed back from his forehead and nicely powdered. His nose was perhaps too long, but gracefully so. His arched eyebrows gave him an intelligent, questioning look. His eyes were dark, and quite deep set.

I dropped a curtsy all the way down to the ground (displaying my bosom to good effect, I confess) and on rising offered my hand as Father had taught me, delicately, with my little finger slightly raised. I smiled, remembering to keep my mouth closed,* which was not difficult, for I was terrified of speaking. Fortunately, Aunt Désirée was not. She stationed herself on the sofa and pulled me down beside her. Then she and Monsieur de Beauharnais talked about whether or not they should get accommodation elsewhere. Apparently Monsieur de Beauharnais was not content with the Hôtel Graves. Aunt Désirée observed that Father should not be moved; he needed to gather strength for the long journey back to Paris. Monsieur de Beauharnais said that in that case he would take a room at the Hôtel du Grand Monarque. I turned my head from one to the other.

At that point Madame Mignonette stumbled in, carrying a basket of soiled laundry. She quickly perceived the situation and, stuttering, asked if we wished refreshment.

"What's wrong with that woman?" Monsieur de Beauharnais asked after she had left, backing out of the room in the most comical way. He pulled a cigar out of a silver case.

"She's no doubt a bit ruffled by the purpose of this meeting," Aunt Désirée answered.

"She *knows?*"

"So far as I can ascertain, *everyone* knows." Aunt Désirée rolled her eyes.

"Surely that wasn't necessary."

Madame's maid came in with wine in a decanter, a little dish of chewing marzipan and a plate of buttered burnt toast. I declined the wine and the sweetmeats, but accepted a piece of toast, eating it in little bites and trying to be ladylike, in spite of the crumbs falling onto my lap. Whenever Monsieur de Beauharnais happened to glance at me, I smiled and made sweet eyes.

I searched my mind for something to say. "Madame Longpré came to call," I announced finally. "She said she would welcome the opportunity to see Monsieur de Beauharnais."

There was a moment's commotion, for a bit of toast had caught dangerously in Aunt Désirée's throat. "Madame *Laure* Longpré?" she asked, her eyes watering.

* *Like all the other members of her family, Rose had terrible teeth.*

I nodded. "Didn't Mother take care of her when she was a child?"

"Your mother and I together. Laure was a handful."

"Still is," Monsieur de Beauharnais said.

"What a pity that we won't be able to call on her," Aunt Désirée said.

Then Madame Mignonette announced that supper was served. As I feared, the main course was eels. I noticed that Monsieur de Beauharnais was not fond of them either—so at least we have that in common.

Later we sat around the fire in the front parlour. Some of the others in the inn were playing whist. They were being so boisterous I sometimes had difficulty following what Monsieur de Beauharnais was saying— "A groundswell of enlightened liberalism is sweeping the land," or something like that. Then Aunt Désirée would nod and smile, and I would nod and smile, and Monsieur de Beauharnais would speak another sentence.

And so, in this way, my fiancé and I spent our first evening together.

*October 28.*

"Well?" Father demanded when I brought him his morning bowl of fish bouillon. (I've succeeded in persuading him to refrain from spirits—at least until noon.) "The chevalier is to your liking?"

"He's a gentleman." I pushed back the bedcurtains. "And comely," I added. My cheeks felt flushed.

"Indeed. I gather the ladies quite like him."

"Philosophy is his passion," I told him proudly.

"Mon Dieu—a *philosophe?*" Father sank back onto the pillows. "Well," he sighed, "it could be worse, I guess."

*Later.*

This afternoon Aunt Désirée met with a notary. Now she has the authority to arrange the marriage herself, she said, "should anything happen."

Should Father die, she meant.

*That evening.*

Monsieur de Beauharnais has gone to the country to call on friends from his regiment. Aunt Désirée has taken advantage of his absence to instruct me on how to be a good wife. This afternoon, after the midday meal (I'm not to eat with my fingers), she presented me with a book which I'm to study. In it are a number of essays on continence and obedience as well as one on how to prepare viands and address servants. She informed me that I treat Mimi too much as a familiar, that in order to command the respect due my station I must observe correct forms.

Also, as a grown woman now, I must take responsibility for the instruction of my servant: Mimi is not to spit and she is to refrain from using a word such as *pisspot* in polite company. She is to drop a curtsy when she sees me and address me as Mademoiselle de la Pagerie. After I am married she's to call me Madame la vicomtesse. Then Aunt Désirée demonstrated a curtsy and made Mimi practise until she had it right. Mimi has never been noted for grace and it was all I could do not to burst.

*October 30.*

Monsieur de Beauharnais returned from his visit to the country all good cheer, taking my hand and promising to be a faithful companion "on the journey of life." I said, "Me, too," and Aunt Désirée looked happy and clucked around us like a mother hen.

We played trictrac after supper. (I let Monsieur de Beauharnais win.) He is so educated and so talented, I am in awe of him. He draws portraits, he has a good singing voice, and he plays the harpsichord. He reads Latin, speaks German, and even a little English. He told me I have lovely eyes and called me "mathia mou," Greek for "light of his eyes," he said. I wish I knew something Greek I could call him.

*October 31, All Saints' Day Eve.*

The doctor feels that Father has improved sufficiently to travel. We leave in the morning. Monsieur de Beauharnais has purchased a closed carriage for the journey. (For forty louis! So much!) It is dark green with black leather seats—*very* pretty. Aunt Désirée lectured him on the evils of going into debt but he said that the expenditure was necessary for Father's comfort. And, he added, "If Mademoiselle Tascher and I marry, debt will not be an issue."

*If* we marry?

# *In which I come to my city of dreams*

*Wednesday, November 10, 1779—Paris.*

*Paris!* As we crossed the Seine Father gave me a sou to throw in. "Make a wish."

"This *is* my wish."

Paris is bigger and more beautiful than I had imagined, but so muddy!

"*Boue de Paris,*" Monsieur de Beauharnais cursed, for a bit had splashed onto the sleeve of his lavender grosgrain riding jacket.

"*Lutetia,* city of mud—that's what we call it," Aunt Désirée said.

I had to confess that there was a strange smell. Aunt Désirée said one got used to it, but she cautioned me to be careful of getting any mud on my skirts—it can burn a hole if left on too long.

We made our way at a footpace through crowded streets. I was in a daze, taking it all in. It was cold; everyone in the market was wearing shoes. A man in a beribboned wig was selling vinegar from a wheelbarrow. A squat little soap dealer with a pockmarked face had twisted pretty scarves together to hold up his buckskin breeches. I saw a fish lady wearing a fluted cap.

And so many smells! So many sounds! Everywhere foot passengers were talking, arguing, singing, but I couldn't understand a word—it's French, but poissard, Aunt Désirée said, the language of the market.

It was late by the time we got to the district of Monsieur de Beauharnais's family home. The street lamps hanging out on great brackets were just being lit. The house is on a street so narrow the carriage couldn't turn around. Aunt Désirée expressed warnings regarding the neighbourhood.

"A short distance away thieves are known to gather," she said.*

The house is tall, with big shutters. There is a stone face of a woman above the front door. "Vesta," Monsieur de Beauharnais said, helping Father up the steps. "A Roman goddess."

"A guiablesse!" Mimi whispered, and refused to pass.

I grabbed her hand and pulled her in. "There are no voodoo spirits in Paris," I hissed.

Inside it was very grand—more grand than Uncle Tascher's home in Fort-Royal even—with a big fireplace and many fine furnishings. In the front parlour white and gold brocade curtains hung from gold rods.

"Ohhhhh," Mimi sighed. The slippery wood floors squeaked when she walked over them, reminding me of crick cracks.

Father took my arm. "This will do?" he asked, giving me a wink.

"It's like a palace," I whispered. I had a sad thought of Mother and Manette, of our worn grey rugs.

"This way!" Aunt Désirée called out, following Monsieur de Beauharnais up a sweeping staircase.

Monsieur de Beauharnais's father, Marquis de Beauharnais, received us in his bedchamber, standing with the help of two walking sticks. He was dressed in a flannel night-shirt and a quilted gold satin dressing gown. He was wearing an old-fashioned white powdered wig of thick curls which flowed over his shoulders and down his back. He was a lot older than I expected—in his sixties or seventies I think—but he had an air of distinction, in spite of his state of undress.

I made a half-curtsy and accepted his offer of a chair by the fireside, where a tea board had been set.

"Content, Alexandre?" the Marquis asked, after we'd been introduced. I was relieved that Monsieur de Beauharnais answered in the affirmative.

"I believe you will find her pleasing," Aunt Désirée said.

"I can see that for myself," the Marquis said. He winked at me.

* The once-prosperous neighbourhood was now quite poor, situated close to the entrance of the "cour des miracles"—a haven for beggars and thieves made famous in Victor Hugo's Hunchback of Notre-Dame, written in 1831.

After a light supper and a family prayer we retired, weary travellers all. Aunt Désirée showed me to my room, which is large and filled with the most elegant furnishings. Father is in the room next to mine so that I might easily tend him. Mimi is in a room on the third floor with the other household servants.

And so, dear Diary, I must blow out the candle. I hear church bells ringing. I am here, at last. *Paris!*

*November 13.*

Father is more comfortable now that he's taken to bed and doesn't have to move, although he's none too happy about all the concoctions Aunt Désirée makes him take. In the morning he's to eat a paste of powdered rhubarb and currants. In the evening she brings him pennyroyal mixed with sugar. He doesn't mind that so much, but the poultice Mimi must smear on his chest is disgusting: bread mashed with milk, egg yolks and raisins.

*November 14.*

The doctor spent only a moment examining Father. Nevertheless, he is confident of success. He prescribed a half a grain of tartar emetic followed by a purgative when nausea commences. Father was pleased; he's to ingest claret as a remedy.

*November 20.*

I've been ill, "homesick," Aunt Désirée says. It was true. I'd been dreaming of home. "Nothing an afternoon shopping won't cure," she said.

So after our morning chocolate she ordered the carriage. Aubin, the footman, escorted us, running in front of our coach in his yellow petticoat with a fringe around the bottom and no breeches.* Mimi told me that there's wine in the silver ball on top of his staff and nothing at all on under

---

* Breeches were difficult to run in so footmen wore skirts. They also wore bright colours so that they could be more easily seen in the dark.

his skirt! (Now every time I see him, that's all I can think of.)

Paris is a dirty, crowded city—but everywhere one goes there is gaiety. There are beggars *everywhere*. Some are quite aggressive. Others play tricks to catch your attention. A gang of street urchins crowded us outside a billiard parlour until Aubin chased after them. One hit Aubin with his flute, on the leg, causing him to curse mightily.

I was overwhelmed by the beauty of all the things on display, all the trimmings and accessories, the laces, ribbons and silks. Everything I saw, I longed for—until I learned the price, that is. I did purchase a sketching pad and some charcoal at a stall in the market. The vendor reminded me of William, which brought on a mournful reverie in me. Secretly, I've started a portrait of him, but already I can't remember his face.


*Saturday, November 27.*
It is late. We've just returned from the home of the Marquis's brother, Comte Charles, who gave a reception on our behalf. I wore a new dress Aunt Désirée had had made for me: an ivory white silk, cut low—quite low!—with a tiny waist. (As tiny as I can get, anyway—I've been trying to lose weight.) The sleeves have gold frogs on them, very pretty. The full skirt is tucked up by pretty little bunches of flowers, revealing a skirt of gauze and a quilted silk petticoat.

It took more than two hours for Aubin to get my hair piled up into what is called a hedgehog—in three waves over my forehead. First my hair was greased and combed over a wire mesh secured into place with pins. Then I went into the powder closet to be powdered (I almost choked). At the last he attached ribbons, feathers and silk flowers all over. In a wind, I fear I might topple! I'm to wear a cap over this heavy confection days and nights so that it will stay nice until after the wedding.

Before we left, I went to Father's room to show him my ensemble.

"It's too . . . !" He sighed, lay back on the pillows. "You look *lovely*." He smiled. "Your mother would never approve."

"This is Paris, Father," I said, preparing his evening elixir. "This isn't Trois-Ilets."

"I should say," he said, taking his glass. "Remember to leave your gloves on."

"And to sit up straight, and to keep my mouth closed when I chew, and to—"

"Have a wonderful time," he said.

Everyone cheered when Monsieur de Beauharnais and I made our entrance. There were a number of guests: uncles, aunts, several cousins as well as friends of the family. I was introduced to Monsieur de Beauharnais's older brother, François. He's not nearly as good-looking as Monsieur de Beauharnais, nor as clever, but he seemed a gentle man, and very courteous. He looked distinguished in a black satin waistcoat with blue glass ornaments. He is married to Marie (his cousin), who is big with child. She looked ill and did not speak. Her hair, which was not dressed, was hidden under a cap ornamented with vulture feathers. They left soon after the meal, for Marie's time of confinement is approaching. Aunt Désirée told me that her first baby died not too long ago and that Marie has not taken it well.

There were a number of distinguished men and women there. A Monsieur de la Chevalerie* and his daughter were charming. Monsieur had spent his youth in the military on Saint-Domingue, so we talked of the Islands. Mademoiselle de la Chevalerie invited me to the next meeting of her Masonic lodge. "We have feasts and perform good works." Her hair was back-combed all around her face, giving her a woolly look.

Supper was elegant and abundant, served on a table laid with eighteen covers. We had sole fried, rump of beef boiled, boiled rabbit and onion sauce, jigget of mutton roasted with sweet sauce, batter pudding and drippings, macaroni and tarts all together with wine in abundance and brandy. By way of dessert we had filberts, apple pudding and some cheesecakes. So much! I was thankful for the severity of my stays, for surely I would have split a seam. As we dined, a violinist played.

After dessert, in the game room playing billiards, Monsieur de

---

* Jean-Jacques Bacon de la Chevalerie (1731–1821) was a celebrated Freemason. In 1773 he'd been Grand Orateur of the Grand Orient of France.

Beauharnais and his brother played billiards while "discussing" politics (it was more of an argument).

"Oh politics, always politics," Mademoiselle de la Chevalerie whispered to me. "At the lodge we only talk of lofty things."

I was tempted to advise Monsieur de Beauharnais on a more likely angle for a shot he was setting up, but held my tongue. He shot and missed, leaving the way clear for his brother to sink four running.

Someone began to play the harpsichord in the front parlour. "Your fiancé may not be good at billiards," Mademoiselle de la Chevalerie whispered as we left the game room, "but he is so very charming. He is the favourite with all the ladies."

In the parlour Aunt Désirée was playing the harpsichord as a woman sang. I was introduced to several people who had newly arrived. Soon Monsieur de Beauharnais and his brother joined us and the gathering became gay. At Monsieur de Beauharnais's insistence there was dancing, first a polonaise, which is a bit of a walk, and then contredanses, which are more involved.

"Alexandre is the best dancer in all of Paris," one of the younger cousins said to me. A plain girl, she was strikingly attired in a lavender silk brocade dress with huge flounces and a bustle. Her braided shoes had little gold buckles on them that looked like flowers.

"Even the *Queen* has taken notice," Mademoiselle de la Chevalerie whispered.

"The Queen?" I accepted another glass of champagne which a servant brought around. The three of us were sitting close to the musicians and it was a little difficult to hear.

Mademoiselle de la Chevalerie giggled behind her gold-painted fan. "But then the Queen fancies any number of men."

I was feeling a little light-headed and refrained from responding. I turned to watch Monsieur de Beauharnais move through the intricate forms. He *did* move elegantly. I could understand why everyone so admired him.

After the piece, which went on for over twenty minutes, Monsieur de Beauharnais invited me to be his partner for a polonaise. I declined. I love dancing, but these forms were entirely new to me. I feared I would embarrass him.

Nevertheless, it was an enjoyable evening. Even the Marquis seemed spry—I saw him dancing hatless.*

On the return, in the carriage (I had to sit on a low stool between the seats because my headdress was so high), Aunt Désirée informed Monsieur de Beauharnais that she had decided that the wedding would take place at her country home in Noisy-le-Grand and that she intended to arrange a special dispensation from the archbishop of Paris so that the banns wouldn't have to be read three times. "This way, you and Rose will be able to get married before Christmas."

"Excellent," Monsieur de Beauharnais said. "I shall talk to my accountant tomorrow."

Before *Christmas?* So *soon* . . .

---

* *Men who intended to dance wore a hat to a soirée. However, it was considered inappropriate for an elderly man to dance, much less to declare his intention to do so. It was acceptable, however, for an elderly man to be spontaneously recruited—to dance hatless.*

## *In which I am married*
## *& learn the facts of life*

*December 14, 1779—Noisy-le-Grand.*

At nine the morning of my wedding I began my toilette. I allowed four hours in order to indulge in a number of rituals: a wash with water perfumed with jasmine (which made me homesick), a massage (which made me ache) and a facial mask of cucumber and vinegar (which made my skin blotchy). So right from the start my wedding day was not as I had planned.

After being bled (not too much—just enough to give me a pale complexion), my make-up applied, it took almost an *hour*—and my headdress freshly powered, Mimi and Aunt Désirée helped tie me into a stiff, boned corset to which the paniers were fastened. I kept bumping into the furniture. Over this came the dress: a white satin gown with a train, embroidered and trimmed with lace. This was fixed to the stomacher, an embroidered panel that goes down the front. It wasn't easy, for the gown was tight. I viewed myself in the looking glass. I looked beautiful, but not radiant. It was *torture* being inside this construction.

Last, I slipped on my new shoes laced with silver. I stood in front of the looking-glass.

"You look like a bride!" Mimi said. She gave a squeal.

"You sounded like Da Gertrude just then," I said, turning to see my profile. Tears came to my eyes. How I longed for Mother and Manette—and even Grandmother Sannois! If only they could see me now.

"Don't cry! You'll spoil your rouge," Aunt Désirée exclaimed.

Aunt Désirée and I went down to await the guests. I sat by the window. My veil was secured to my towering headdress by a pearl-studded cap which kept slipping.

First Abbé Tascher arrived, to stand in for Father, who was too ill to come to Noisy-le-Grand with us. Then, shortly after, Monsieur de Beauharnais's cousin Comte Claude, who brought word that François would not be able to attend as Marie was indisposed. Of course then we were all of us concerned that her time of confinement had begun, but we were assured that that was not the case. Three men in uniform arrived, colleagues from Monsieur de Beauharnais's regiment. They apologized that one of their number was unable to attend as he was suffering from an indisposition going around Versailles. Monsieur Patricol, who had been Monsieur de Beauharnais's tutor when he was a child, arrived a bit late and somewhat flustered, saying he'd had trouble with the wheel of his carriage. But he didn't put it that way. He said, "There has been an apparent altercation with the drive mechanism." I was struck by his eyes, which are protruding, and his ponderous forehead.

Finally Monsieur de Beauharnais came downstairs to join us. He looked elegant in a black silk coat, gold embroidered waistcoat and a lace cravat. I felt proud sitting beside him.

Aunt Désirée ordered refreshments. I sipped from a glass of champagne, now and again sighing from nerves, fearful that I might faint from the lack of air my corset was causing me.

We set out for the chapel. Some children cried out, "Long live the bride and bridegroom!" The church was small and quite cold. We were received and Monsieur de Beauharnais and I said our vows. (It took longer to dress than to marry.) As we were leaving the priest almost tripped on his robes thanking Aunt Désirée for the gift of two copper candelabras and six hundred livres, which he assured her would be used in its *entirety* to make up a dowry for some unfortunate girl of his parish.

Back at the cottage, the toasts began. Aunt Désirée touched her glass to mine. "To the vicomtesse."

I felt light-headed and had to lie down. I was still a little weak when I rejoined the guests. The men were teasing Monsieur de Beauharnais about the night that lay ahead.

It was almost midnight when the last guest departed. On Aunt Désirée's instruction Mimi accompanied me to Monsieur de Beauharnais's room. A fire had been laid, but even so it was chilly. In the dressing room, Mimi helped me out of my gown and into a new lace-trimmed chemise, which was lovely, although scratchy. "You look like an angel," she said. Mimi tucked my greased and powdered headdress under a boned calash. She began humming: *Calypso, you are a woman just like me. . . .*

"How does that song go?" It was familiar.

Mimi sang, "I caressed Sonson, fondled Sonson, I even went so far I nibbled Sonson!"

A dizzy feeling came over me. I grabbed hold of a wig stand.

"Are you all right?" Mimi asked.

"Yes." Although I wasn't sure. I heard footsteps in the bedchamber, heard the door close, the bed boards creak. The light in the bedchamber suddenly went out.

"Ooooh!" Mimi hurriedly dabbed jasmine fragrance on my neck, bosom and behind my ears. Then she pushed me through the dressing-room curtains.

I was comforted by the darkness. "I am here," I heard Monsieur de Beauharnais say. I heard someone coughing downstairs.

I felt my way to the side of the bed. His hand reached out for me. "You startled me!" I said.

"I'm sorry," he said, pulling back the covers. "I should have left a candle burning."

I slipped under the covers, felt the warming pan at the foot of the bed. I was trying to think what to say. Was I supposed to say something? I was suddenly aware of the dull, constant ache of my bad tooth. Would I have to have it pulled? Did I have worms in my teeth, like Mimi said? Should I let Monsieur de Beauharnais kiss me if I did?

"What are you thinking?" Monsieur de Beauharnais asked. He turned onto his side, facing me. My eyes were growing accustomed to the dark. I could make out the outline of his head, his shoulder. He wasn't wearing a nightcap.

"Nothing." I'd been thinking that in the morning I should rinse my mouth with urine to stop the ache. The thought made me ill, but if doing so would save the tooth— "What are *you* thinking?" I asked.

"I'm thinking what a strange situation this is. We hardly know one another." His words slurred a little.

I made a little laugh.

"Perhaps you would prefer to wait," he said.

"Yes." Was that what he wanted me to say? I wondered.

The room suddenly became brighter. The moon had come out from behind a cloud. I could see his eyes. His lips were thin, a little disdaining, his nose prominent, giving him an aristocratic profile. My husband, the man for whom God intended me. I had only met him six weeks before, and now I was his wife.

"Perhaps if I just kissed you," he said.

"Yes." A pin had come loose in my headdress and was poking into my scalp uncomfortably.

He moved over to my side of the big bed. His head blocked the light from the window. I could no longer see his features. He put his hand on my shoulder. His breath smelled of brandy and cigars. His lips touched mine, and then he pulled away. Was that it? I wondered. Did I do something wrong?

"I forgot something," he said.

He reached back and opened the cabinet beside the bed. "Aunt Désirée doesn't want the sheets stained," he said, handing me a cloth.

What was I supposed to do with it?

"Put it under your . . . you know."

Under my bottom?

He lay down beside me. I felt him fumbling with my bed jacket. "Do you mind?" he asked.

"Do you want me to take it off?" I didn't want to take it off.

He kissed my nose. I wondered, did he miss my mouth? His hand slipped into the bodice of my night-dress. His lips covered my mouth. Then he slipped his hand under my night-dress, found the place between my legs. I cried out, surprised. His fingers were cold. He kissed me hard. He pushed my night-dress up around my waist, got on top of me. His manhood felt warm against my skin. He poked it here and there. I lay still. I wasn't sure what I was supposed to do. Then I felt a sharp pain. I cried out and tried to pull away, but he held me. And then he was inside me.

He kissed my wet cheeks. He was moaning and moving around. I wondered how long it would go on. I tried not to cry, but it hurt! Then he clasped me to him hard, his feet kicking, and collapsed on top of me, groaning.

Had he had an attack? Was he dead? "Are you all right?" I whispered. What had happened? He rolled over beside me, grunting.

Soon he was snoring. The image of William's face came to me, his smile. *You would make a lovely queen*, he had told me.

Tears trickled down the side of my face onto the pillow. Was I a woman now?

*January 1, 1780, New Year's Day—Paris.*
I have resolved to go to mass every morning. I want to become a good wife. I have asked for divine help in this, for so often a pained expression covers Monsieur de Beauharnais's brow.

"What is it I do?" I asked Aunt Désirée. "What is the reason?"

"*Reason*," she said, correcting my pronunciation. "You continue to drop your *r*'s, Rose."

Aunt Désirée wrote out a list of words. I am to practise them, recite them to her every evening. I try to accept her correction without temper, for I know that it is in *this* that I must strive—to obey without question, to become Madame la vicomtesse, a most excellent wife.

*January 13.*
Monsieur de Beauharnais practises dance steps all the day long, watching himself in the big looking glass. He has been invited to the Queen's ball at Versailles . . . but I have not.

"Why?" I asked Father and Aunt Désirée. "Why might *I* not go?"

"You haven't been presented at Court, Rose," Father said.

"Neither has Alexandre."*

"But Alexandre is the best dancer in all of Paris," Aunt Désirée said. "This is quite an honour, Rose. You should rejoice on your husband's behalf."

* *To be presented at Court, one had to prove noble blood back to 1400. Alexandre's nobility was relatively new and made less impressive by the fact that the government was selling titles by the thousands in order to raise money.*

*Sunday, January 23.*

Monsieur de Beauharnais has returned from Versailles. He danced with the Queen!

Aunt Désirée looked like she might faint. "Alexandre, tell us the truth. You didn't dance with the *Queen.*"

It was true, he had, for one-quarter turn of a polonaise, he said.

"Did she touch your glove?" Aunt Désirée asked. "This one?"

"Behold, Madame, I give you my blessing." Monsieur de Beauharnais made an elegant sweep through the air and touched his hand to her shoulder.

We gathered in the front parlour to listen to his account. Even Father came downstairs to join us, interrupting Monsieur de Beauharnais to fill us in on details of proper royal deportment.

Monsieur de Beauharnais said the Queen is graceful—although she doesn't dance too much now, now that she is a mother, allowing herself only a few quadrilles or a colonne anglaise or two in an evening. When the King joins her he has to dance without turning his back to her, which gets him hopelessly mixed up and behind the music.

Monsieur de Beauharnais said the Queen is an accomplished hostess, keeping the young men from staying in the corners all night talking of horses and duelling.

Oh, there was so much that he told us, it is hard to remember it all: the Swiss Guards in starched ruffs, their spaniels on leashes; a door of glass so clear people almost walked through it; a room of maids to attend to dresses in need of repair; the firemen standing ready with buckets of water and large sponges. . . .

All this evening I have been in a reverie. I imagine myself strolling, cooling myself with a fan of mother-of-pearl. Men in black velvet dance around me, their long plumes bobbing. I imagine the music, the women in court hoops twirling, the swish of silk on silk. . . .

It is dawn. I have danced all night. Around the walls of the gilded room are the slumped bodies of the sleeping pages, the maids, the exhausted dancers. But still, I dance. . . .

*Tuesday, February 29.*

Oh, sorrow beyond measure. One week ago Alexandre's sister-in-law, Marie, gave birth to a girl. Aunt Désirée and I have been going to mass every morning, praying for the health of this infant, but in spite of our efforts, she died this morning, at seven days. This is the second infant Marie has lost.

*Friday, June 23, Saint John's Day.*

I am seventeen today. Monsieur de Beauharnais presented me with a ruby. Then he informed me that he must return to his regiment. "How long will you be gone?" I asked.

"Six months."

Six months!

*July 18, 3:00 P.M.*

Monsieur de Beauharnais is gone. He left a list of readings for me to complete: Agesilaus, Brutus, Aristides. I fall asleep reading.

*July 25, 1780—Brest*

*Dear Rose,*

*I am glad you have been attending to your studies but disheartened that your efforts are not better reflected in your written expression. Are you sitting at the writing desk properly, as I showed you? Are you holding your quill correctly, bending your arm at the right angle?*

*As for content, I suggest you ask Aunt Désirée if she has a book of letters you might copy. In this way you might learn correct expression.*

*My heart is filled with longing for the one whom I hold most dear. In rapture, I fall asleep each night, pressing your image to my lips. Oh, that it were you! How cruel Time, who keeps us apart.*

*Write, Rose. Do not neglect your studies.*

*Your husband, Alexandre de Beauharnais, vicomte*

*August 2.*
I stood in front of the looking glass this morning, examining my belly, turning to the right and the left, trying to see if there has been any change. I should have started the flowers two weeks ago. . . .

*Thursday, August 31.*
This morning when I woke, feeling sick in the way I do so often now, I decided it was time to talk to Aunt Désirée. After the midday meal I asked her if we could talk. She invited me into her apartment. I sat down on the settee with some sense of formality. I told her I'd come to ask her advice.

She looked at me with a cautious but satisfied look. "Yes?"

"How would I know if I were with child?"

I thought for a moment Aunt Désirée had stopped breathing, for the rise and fall of her chest is usually remarkable. She squared her shoulders and said, "Very well," and proceeded to ask me questions. When I told her I hadn't had flowers for over two months, she stood up and put me directly to bed, where she's been feeding me hot chicken broth and wine ever since.

The doctor comes every morning, to see Father. Hopefully he will release me from this prison.

*September 1.*
The doctor prescribed ten drops of tincture of iron in the morning, meat two times a day, and a pint of beer or a glass of port with supper. I can get out of bed, but for two months I'm not to ride in a carriage.

I endure with joy. I am more than myself.

*September 14, 7:00 P.M.*
Monsieur de Beauharnais writes words of love now that he has received my news. But, oh, woe, I fear it is too late. A week ago I began to bleed—not much, but I was cautious and took to bed. The baby was held, Mimi said, kept from growing. She made a dragon's blood mixture that I dutifully ingested two times a day with powdered dried almonds mixed with the

yolks of eggs. This went on for several days. Nevertheless yesterday I was seized with the most terrible pain. Mimi asked if she should fetch Aunt Désirée, but I insisted no.

So it was Mimi who was with me, for which I shall always be grateful. It was hard—it was *all* I could do not to scream—but Mimi knew how to help it pass. When it was over she prayed for me, not a Christian prayer, I confess, but a sweet crooning sort of chant about a woman's pain and the earth bringing life anew.

I wept the night through. I am no longer with child.

*In which I am too much alone*

*November 1, 1780, All Saints' Day.*
At table the Marquis and Aunt Désirée talked of Marie's mother "Aunt
Fanny," who has recently returned from Rome. She's a writer and keeps a
*salon.* She has published a booklet, *Hail to All Thinkers!* (which the Marquis *insists* "one of" her lovers must have written) and a romance novel
called *Triumph of Love* (which Aunt Désirée forbids me to read).

"Her salon stays open until five in the morning," the Marquis exclaimed.
"I'd like to know what people can be doing at that hour!" It was a small
entertainment to see him worked up so.

*Tuesday, November 7.*
My room is full of the heavy scent of attar of roses, Aunt Fanny's per-
fume. I confess to being captivated. Her face is tiny, giving the impression of a fairy. She wears a frightful amount of make-up, especially on her
eyes, which are quite lively, never resting. She's very *theatrical.* (It is hard
to imagine that she is Marie's mother. Marie is so timid.)

Her dress was simple, but she wore it without a corset—I was shocked!
There was a mannish quality to her hat, which was mellowed charmingly
by a wreath of flowers which she wore in abundance in defiance of her age.

"So," she said when we met, "this is the beauty all of Paris will be talking about."

I blushed. Were that it were true! I don't believe I'll ever see Paris, in
spite of living in the heart of it.

She stayed for only one hour, drinking brandy in her tea. The Marquis seemed only too willing to listen to her wild stories, in spite of his disapproval, which he made clear. She knows artists and politicians, philosophers and poets, all manner of people. She has just finished writing a romantic novel which will be published soon, and has already begun composing yet another. But mostly she was concerned about *me*.

"What events have you taken the girl to?" she demanded.

"Events?" Aunt Désirée asked.

"You know—*out*." Fanny has a clipped and energetic way of talking. "Lodge meetings, the fairs—"

"We're quite content to stay in," the Marquis said.

"You didn't take her to the Saint-Germain Fair?" Fanny was clearly horrified.

"That's gotten so dirty," Aunt Désirée protested. "And the last time we went, we practically got run down by a carriage coming in through the gates at a gallop." She turned to the Marquis to confirm this fact.

"Ermenonville is quiet—you could take her there."

"I am perhaps the only person in France who is not enraptured with Rapture," the Marquis said. "Forgive me, but your hero Jean-Jacques is not to my liking."

"Young Alexandre and his dear Patricol have not made a convert of you?"

"They have not."

"They've not lured you to one of their Masonic meetings?"

The Marquis made a sputtering sound.

"He could never remember the password," Aunt Désirée said, covering a disloyal smile with her fan.

"That wasn't the problem in the least," the Marquis objected. "It was all that nonsense about liberty and equality and brotherly love. And the red caps they wore were itchy as well as ugly."

"Perhaps the theatre? You have taken her to some spectacles, surely."

Aunt Désirée shook her head. "Alexandre would not approve, I am afraid," she said. "Something to do with theatre fostering a sense of detachment in the modern age."

Fanny hooted, a most unladylike snort. "I suppose he would have us all out on the street, singing and dancing around Maypoles with ribbons! I'm weary of all this longing for 'The Olden Days.' One can take the precepts of Rousseau too far. The question, quite simply, is how can you bring this girl to Paris and *not* take her to the theatre?"

"Perhaps we could take her to the Théâtre Français," Aunt Désirée suggested cautiously, glancing over at the Marquis.

"Mon Dieu!" Fanny said. "The only show there worth watching is the King . . . and the Queen, sometimes, when he manages to drag her along to those tedious productions. 'Ah, Virtue!'. . ." Fanny paraded across the room, demonstrating an actor reciting lines in the most superficial way. I turned to see Mimi giggling in the door.

"The Queen, on the other hand, who may not have sense, but who at least has *taste*," Fanny went on, "is more likely to be seen taking in the entertainment on the Boulevard du Temple."

"The Boulevard of *Crime* you mean?" the Marquis asked.

"Of course that's what we've come to expect of her," Aunt Désirée said.

"Have you ever seen her?" I blurted out, revealing myself to be what I truly was: a star-struck girl from the Islands.

"What's to see?" the Marquis bristled.

"How can one *not* see her?" Fanny moaned. "The woman is everywhere—at the theatre, the gaming tables, the concerts spirituels, the salons . . . not *mine*, of course—but I heard from Comte Clairon that she was at Comtesse d'Autricourt's, feigning disguise, which of course everyone sees right through. Poor woman. I feel sorry for her. Hope she's not allergic to cats.* Clearly she's not allergic to *men*. I understand she's moved into the little Trianon—for more *freedom* (Fanny indulged me with a wink)—where she can give full expression to her 'bucolic' affectations, playing shepherdess, tying pretty ribbons around the cows and sheep. It's all so fashionable, it makes me sick, frankly. Although I admit I couldn't stand being Queen for more than a minute. The palace is full of strangers watching the royal comings and goings as if they were on exhibit, relieving themselves in the

---

* *The Comtesse de Lingiville d'Autricourt ran what some considered the most brilliant salon in Paris, surrounding herself with Angora cats, each with a bright silk ribbon.*

corners. People even watch them eat—can you imagine?* Goodness knows *I'm* all in favour of giving up corsets—who can stand them?—but don't you think our Queen carries it a bit far?" Fanny did not wait for a response. "But, of course, who wouldn't go wild with a man like King Louis for a husband? The only thing he's passionate about is food."

"And carrying on like a child," the Marquis muttered in turn, "turning the fountains on strollers, for amusement. It's time His Majesty grew up, don't you think?"

"Did you know that in Strasbourg they've actually *minted* a coin showing our dear King with cuckold's horns?" Fanny said. "It's true—a friend of a friend of mine has one."

Fanny could have gone on and on, much to my delight, but Aunt Désirée changed the subject, informing Fanny that I was learning to play the harp, that I sang quite nicely and that I was interested in drawing as well. I was embarrassed to be paraded in this way, but eager, nevertheless, to be the object of Fanny's notice.

She insisted on seeing a drawing I've been working on, an island scene. Quite by accident she came upon one I'd done of the stone wall of the neighbour's house—the view out my window—and she laughed. She thought it showed originality and a sense of humour. "Or a serious case of vapours." She looked at me closely.

She noticed an open volume of Helvétius on a table. She asked if I was reading it. "I'm trying to," I confessed.

"Why?" she asked. "Not that it isn't an admirable pursuit."

"Monsieur de Beauharnais wishes me to," I explained. "He aims to educate me."

"How good of him," she said with a sarcastic tone.

"My spelling is terrible," I said, defending my husband's intent.

"Voltaire's letters were *full* of spelling errors," she said, noticing my guitar propped in a corner. "Do you play?"

I somewhat reluctantly confessed that I did, for Monsieur de Beauharnais

---

* At Versailles, the public was allowed to watch members of the royal family eat. Crowds would race from one part of the palace to another in order to observe various courses being consumed by the different members of the royal family.

had given me to believe that only members of the lower social orders played such a primitive instrument.

"A lovely instrument—so expressive. What pieces do you know?"

I told her I was trying to learn the cantatas of Clérambault, but finding them challenging. "I should think so," she said, which was heartening.

She turned to me at the door. "Tell me, my dear—what *do* you think of our fair city?"

I flushed.

"Don't be shy. Do you not think your misery is written on your face? As is every thought and emotion that comes to you? Really, you are the most transparent creature. But come now, admit it—one cannot be French and not love it."

I felt she could see into my most private thoughts, penetrate my spirit, my very dreams. For all my life, had I not dreamed of France? Had not the word meant romance and all good things to me? "I am, I confess, familiar only with these four walls," I said.

"*That* we will have to remedy, my dear. You will begin by coming to my salon—tomorrow evening." She raised a finger to still my objection. "I *insist*. I will send my footman for you, at nine."

And so, it is set. A *salon*? I don't even know what a salon is.

*Thursday, November 9.*

There were a number of men and women gathered in Fanny's parlour when I arrived—twelve, I counted. Fanny introduced me as a student of painting and music, which flattered my modest pursuits greatly. After supper, music was played and poetry read. There was lots of laughter and argument. All the while Fanny was stretched out on a silver and blue settee with a garland of flowers on her head, looking like a goddess. A poet named Michel de Cubières (short, with a booming voice and big lips) read some of Fanny's poems, which I didn't understand, but everyone seemed to appreciate. I felt nervous, but of course quite proud once the reading was over and everyone praised her.

I can't begin to describe the interesting people I met and the vitality of the conversation. I felt tongue-tied, but nevertheless was kindly received.

An older gentleman in a tight old-fashioned wig guessed immediately I was créole.

"How did you know?" I asked.

"Your accent gives you away. And the intoxicating way you move."

The intoxicating way I move, indeed!


*Monday, November 13.*

I have been to a meeting of a Masonic lodge—the lodge of the Triple Lumière. I went with Alexandre's brother François and Mademoiselle de la Chevalerie, whom I had met shortly before Alexandre and I were married. The banquet was elegant, the company delightful and but for the length of some of the speeches, it was a pleasant evening. A number of men and women from the Islands are members, so I felt very much at home. (There was even cassava bread served!) The songs were pretty, all about brotherhood and love.

Mademoiselle de la Chevalerie has promised to put my name forward. Already she showed me a secret hand-signal. "I tried this at the Saint-Germain Fair and *hundreds* signalled back," she said.

"That many?" It was hard to imagine.

"If you are ever in distress, all you need to do is make a sign, and help will come," she said with fervour.


*Saturday, November 18.*

Fanny took me to see a play tonight. She arrived early in order to help supervise my toilette. We were sipping brandy and being perhaps a bit silly, for Aunt Désirée stuck her head in and frowned at us. After the door closed Fanny made a funny face. Really, I've never met anyone quite like her.

Fanny gave her coachman orders to drive to the Boulevard du Temple. After what the Marquis had said—about it being called the Boulevard of Crime—I was looking out everywhere for ruffians, but it didn't take long for me to be overtaken by the gay spirit of the place. We were inundated all around with tightrope acrobats, puppeteers, mime artists, performing animals—it was as if a circus had been let loose in the streets! Every balladeer and vendor had a song to sing—about liberty in America, about the Queen's naughtiness, and lots of songs about love, of course. There were even actors performing a sentimental sort of romance, a woman on one side of the street, a man on the other, yelling words to each other. It was impossible not to be swept up into the excitement of it all.

It was with some reluctance, therefore, that I entered the theatre, only to be drawn into still another world. After Fanny and I had seated ourselves in her loge—I was trying very hard not to look this way and that like a child at a fair—I noticed a commotion in the audience. Everyone was looking toward a loge at the front. It was the Queen!

I had a very clear view of her face. She is younger than I expected, not much older than myself, and pretty, with a kindly expression, almost shy. Of course I took in all the details of what she was wearing, especially her headdress, which was a most fanciful construction of mauve feathers that fluttered with every move she made. With her was a blonde woman and a tall, handsome man.

"That's Yolande de Polignac and the Comte de Vaudreuil," Fanny whispered. "She's the Comte's mistress. They have what is called 'a secret marriage'—complicated, one would think, by *his* relationship with the Queen." She looked at me over her fan.

"The *Queen?*" I whispered.

"And furthermore," Fanny raised her eyebrows, "it is my understanding that the Queen and Yolande are—" Fanny held up two fingers entwined. "If you can believe what people say," she went on. "Which of course I don't."

Just then the lights went out and the audience fell into a hush. I could hear a woman giggling in the loge next to ours.

"Is there someone in there?" I asked. For the curtains were drawn tight.

"In one's loge at the theatre, one may receive *anyone*." Fanny rolled her eyes.

I heard another peal of laughter, followed by a man's low voice. "You mean—"

"I can see I am going to have to give you one of my novels to read, darling," Fanny whispered as the curtain went up. "Disguised as a text on aesthetics, of course."

The play we saw was *The Beaten* and I laughed so hard I feared my corset ties would break. In it, Janot, a servant, has a chamber-pot emptied on his head. He tries to take legal action, but ends up in jail. It was terribly silly, but well done. Between acts there were speeches, singing and announcements.

Oh, I'm in love with the theatre! Fanny has promised to take me to another performance soon.


*November 22.*
Monsieur de Beauharnais wrote to me: *Labour omnia vincit improbus.* I had to ask Father to translate it. "Persistent effort overcomes all difficulties," he told me. I should have known it would have to do with studies, and nothing whatsoever to do with *love.*


*Saturday, November 25.*
Fanny has had her newest novel published, titled *Abailard the Pretender.* We all went to a ballet tonight to celebrate—Fanny, my brother-in-law François (Marie is confined to bed), Aunt Désirée and even the Marquis. When the dancers leaped into the air one could see their garters and drawers. Fanny thought nothing of it, but I could see that the Marquis and Aunt Désirée were discomfited.


*November 27.*
Aunt Désirée is reading Fanny's new novel to determine if I should be permitted to read it. I doubt that I shall—she makes the sign of the cross before picking it up.


*December 7.*
Monsieur de Beauharnais sent word that he is coming home. I haven't seen him for five months.

*Wednesday, December 13, 11:30 A.M.*
Today is our first anniversary. But already Monsieur de Beauharnais is gone, on his way to join his regiment in Verdun. He was here for only four days.

*In which I become a mother*
*& discover a terrible truth*

*Sunday, January 28, 1781.*
Aunt Désirée and I were summoned in the night. Marie's labour had com-
menced. We hurried to her bedside, the horses slipping on the icy cobblestones. When we arrived, we were immediately taken to Marie's
bedchamber where Fanny informed us that Marie had fallen into uncon-
sciousness. Aunt Désirée was overcome with uneasiness and took leave of
the room, Fanny following. Soon after, the child was born. The accoucher
asked me to hold the infant while she tied the cord. The baby did not cry;
her eyes opened, her blue skin slowly turning pink, the miracle of life in
my hands. My tears fell on her cheeks.

   The priest was delayed and Fanny was anxious that the infant quickly
be baptized. I held the crying baby as Aunt Désirée poured water over
her head, uttering the words, "I baptize thee." Her name is Émilie. We
pray for her. I pray for her.


*February 19.*
I'm with child again. I move with great caution.

*February 28—Brest*
*Darling,*

*Joy filled my spirit on receipt of your wonderful news. Be sure to do all as the doctor instructs. I have asked Patricol to outline a program of reading for you, for it is currently understood that a mother's thoughts will produce a result on the infant she carries, both for good and for ill. I do not need to remind you that any reading of novels is forbidden—especially romantic novels. Refrain from situations that occasion strong emotions, and above all, do not go to the theatre!*

*I have asked Aunt Désirée to obtain etchings of inspiring moments in Roman and Greek history to position beside your bed. In this way, by casting your eyes upon these heroic images, you will guarantee a good result. I forbid you to hire a wet-nurse as the milk will influence the character of the baby. If mothers nursed their own babies, many of the ills of society would be eliminated.*

*I embrace you, ma tendre amie.*

*Your husband, Alexandre de Beauharnais, vicomte*
*Note—I suggest for this period of waiting you absent yourself from the company of Aunt Fanny.*


*March 7.*

Fanny came by around eleven for tea. As she was going she put a small parcel in my hand. "Don't tell Désirée," she whispered. "And certainly not your father."

I've just now opened it. It's Rousseau's *Confessions*, which have been banned. I started reading it and was immediately shocked. I've hidden it under my mattress.


*March 15.*

Fanny came by before dinner. I didn't think I'd get a chance to ask her about something in *Confessions*, but finally Aunt Désirée went out to see how the cook was managing with the rabbits Fanny had brought and I got up the courage. "You want me to explain?" she demanded.

I realized from the look on her face that I shouldn't have asked.

"You know how certain things can . . . *arouse* a man?" she asked.

Now it was my turn to blush.

"Well—for Rousseau, he fancied a bit of a spanking."

I was shocked. "You mean . . . ?"

"For a man like that, carry a birch rod and make him beg, I say." She sat back on the sofa with a maternal air. "Perhaps that's what your Alexandre needs," she mused.

When Aunt Désirée returned I was in such a state of giddiness she grew alarmed on my behalf. After Fanny left and I was alone again I got out the book, searching for the passages that had previously eluded my understanding. In this naughty way I am pleasantly passing the Lord's day.


*Sunday, March 25.*

Yesterday, the eve of Lady Day, I felt my child flutter in my belly like a butterfly. I grew still. It did it again, fluttering—oh, so faintly!

Mimi cast my cards. I will have a boy, she said.

A *boy!* I think of all the things a boy must do, all the things a mother must let him do, and I want to cry. Is this what being a mother means, this bewildering sentiment flooding one's heart?


*Sunday, April 15.*

In church we learned that the Queen is expecting another child. There was much rejoicing. I felt the festivities as if they were for me, for I know what she feels, I know her joy.


*April 18.*

Monsieur de Beauharnais complains I haven't written, yet when I do my letters are corrected and returned. Now he suggests I send *all* my letters to him—even those I write to Mother and Manette—so that I might be instructed on correct spelling and construction. I cannot write at all, now, I am so distressed.

*Later.*
Father has suggested that Aunt Désirée help me with my letters to Monsieur de Beauharnais—she will write them out for me, to ensure that no errors are made.


*April 30.*
Monsieur de Beauharnais has accused Aunt Désirée of writing my letters for me. He is furious!


*May 4—Noisy-le-Grand.*
I received a letter from Monsieur de Beauharnais this afternoon, posted from La Roche-Guyon, the country estate of his patron, the Duc de la Rochefoucauld.

"But Monsieur de Beauharnais is in Verdun," I told Aunt Désirée. Surely Monsieur de Beauharnais would not have travelled to La Roche-Guyon without coming to see us—to see *me*. It was but a short detour along the route.

"No doubt Alexandre was under orders," Aunt Désirée said, but I saw doubt in her eyes.

"Under orders to live as he pleases without any regard for his pregnant wife," I said angrily. Without any *love* for his wife.

"You must try harder, Rose," Aunt Désirée said. "It is a wife's duty to please."

"Monsieur de Beauharnais is impossible to please!" I went to the window. Even the country vista did not soothe me. "Laughing one minute, morose the next, serious and then frivolous, feverish and then cold—one never knows how it will be with him!"

Aunt Désirée sighed, putting down her lacework. "We need help," she said.


*Thursday, June 7.*
Aunt Désirée sent Patricol, Alexandre's childhood tutor, to La Roche-

Guyon to talk with him. Now Patricol has written Aunt Désirée suggesting a solution to "our" problem: that others get involved in my schooling. So now Aunt Désirée is hiring tutors for me. Everyone—even Father—is being recruited in this effort to educate me.

*June 23.*
I am eighteen today. It is terribly hot, and in my condition I suffer. Nevertheless, I've been trying to get through the first volume of Vertot's *Roman History*—but then the baby moves within me, inspiring a reverie.

My letters to Monsieur de Beauharnais report only my studies. I do not tell him of the changes in my heart.

*Monday, September 3—Paris.*
My baby was born this morning—a boy, on the very day of my dear sister Manette's birth. A good omen.

It was a hard labour, more painful than I could have imagined, but the love I feel for this little creature, this little sucking thing, overwhelms me, puts all at peace. I clasp my squalling baby to me and sing sweet songs, baptizing him with tears of wonder. I curl under the covers with him, bringing him to my breast. He grabs at my nipple greedily, pulling the watery liquid out of me, and we are silent then together but for his chirps and sucking sounds. We fall into a sweet-smelling sleep, then, my baby and I, and I think, as we drift into dreams, this is Heaven, isn't it? Is this not what Heaven is?

*Later.*
"Rose, there is someone here to see you," Aunt Désirée said. Something in her voice warned me.

Behind her I saw Monsieur de Beauharnais. I caught my breath. I hadn't seen him for—how many months? Eight? I'd lost count. He looked exceedingly well, dressed in an elegant black coat, a red-striped waistcoat and flesh-coloured breeches. The toes of his glistening black boots were pointed.

He smiled and tipped his top hat. "My apologies. I intended to be here for the event, but—"

"No need to apologize, Alexandre. I wasn't expecting you," I said.

"I recall that when you address me by my Christian name, it means that you are angry."

"I am too tired to be angry." I felt pressure in my breasts. Soon it would be time to nurse.

"I have a gift for you." He pulled a jeweller's case out of his vest pocket. Inside was a gold pin with a tiny image of himself painted on it.

Mimi came into the room, my baby bundled in her arms. She startled when she saw Monsieur de Beauharnais.

"Alexandre, you remember—"

"Rose, of course I . . ." He faltered.

"Mimi," I said, reminding him.

But his eyes were on the baby. "And this is—?"

Mimi gently put the baby into Monsieur de Beauharnais's outstretched arms. He lifted the corner of the coverlet, looked upon the face of his son. Then he looked over at me, his eyes filled with tears. "Have you named him?" he asked, his voice full of emotion.

"The honour is yours."

"I would like him to be Eugène," he said.

"I like that name," I said. The baby began to fuss. "He's hungry."

Monsieur de Beauharnais put our son into my arms.

"Welcome home, Alexandre." I touched his hand.


*Friday, September 7, 3:00 P.M.*

Monsieur de Beauharnais is attentive. He goes on in a rapture about new life. He has studied the newest theories and is intent on doing everything properly. He talks of Rousseau, of nursing, of a child's "development"— he talks of all the wrong a mother might do. He's in a fit of worry.

I want to take his head and place it on my heart. I want to say, do not be afraid. I want to stroke his fine, long hair and mother him—Monsieur de Beauharnais, my husband, the motherless one.

*Monday, October 22.*

The tocsins are ringing, there is celebrating in the streets. The Queen has had her baby—a *boy!* One hundred and one guns were fired. Everywhere people call out, "Long live the Dauphin!"

I clasp my baby to my heart and pray for the Queen. I do not envy her, for her baby is not her own. Her boy will be King. He belongs to God, to France—he belongs to us all.


*October 23.*

Last night I had a dream in which Monsieur de Beauharnais told me: "You are not my only wife."

I woke in a feverish sweat.

This morning I told Mimi about the dream. Her face is like water, it shows the slightest disturbance. So I watched her.

"What a crazy dream," she said. But she had that look of caution.

"If there were some truth in it, would you tell me?"

"Ask Charlotte." Charlotte is Aunt Désirée's cook. Charlotte is a gossip and wields considerable power, and not just with a knife.

"Mimi—don't make me suffer the humiliation of learning this from Charlotte."

Mimi's dark eyes filled with doubt.

"Please!" For the truth was more and more evident.

Mimi collected herself before continuing, in that proud and silent way she has. "Monsieur le vicomte keeps a mistress," she said.

A *mistress.* It did not surprise me. Monsieur de Beauharnais was rarely home. "Who?" I asked.

Mimi bowed her head. The light glittered off her black hair. "Madame Longpré."

"Madame Laure Longpré?" I stuttered. "My *cousin* Laure Longpré?" I recalled the buxom woman who had called on Father and me when we had just arrived in France. I remembered her bosom adorned with glittering gems, her frothy pink gown.

Mimi nodded.

"But she's so much older than Alexandre," I objected. I was more confused than upset. I remembered the rhyme the boys used to sing: *Laure, Laure, goes down to the lorry.* I never knew what happened down at the lorry, but something told me it had to do with taking up petticoats.

"There is more, there is a child. A boy."

"Monsieur de Beauharnais is the father? How do you know this? Who told you?"

"Charlotte."

"It's common knowledge? The Marquis? My father?"

"I don't know about your father."

I sat down on the edge of my bed. I held my face in my hands. Then I stood up.

"Where are you going?"

I went downstairs. I found Aunt Désirée in the pantry, checking the supplies. "May I talk to you?" I asked.

"Can it wait, Rose?"

I shook my head.

"Go to the front parlour. I will join you in a moment."

I went into the parlour.

Aunt Désirée entered the room and sat down, her hands planted purposefully in her lap. "Yes?" She had things to do.

"I just found out about Madame Longpré." I was relieved that I was tearless and that my voice was steady. "And about her child, Alexandre's son."

"Oh," Aunt Désirée said, with an appearance of calm.

"Does it not matter?" I asked, emotion giving way.

"Laure poses no threat to you, Rose. Alexandre cares for you, if that's what concerns you."

"How do *you* know?" A mean-spirited bitterness had come over me.

"Alexandre tells me everything." Aunt Désirée sat back with a proprietorial air.

I stood. I felt light-headed and needed to lie down. Aunt Désirée reached for my hand. "Rose, please—don't be so provincial."

I headed for the stairs.

Shortly after, Father came into my room. I refused to look at him, attending to a drawing I was reworking. He sat down beside my writing table, toying with a split quill. "Désirée suggested I talk to you," he said.

I held the drawing out at arm's length. It was a portrait of Eugène. I was not content with the features.

Father coughed. "I am told you are not happy."

"I am perfectly happy," I said. Nevertheless, I could not disguise the trembling of my lower lip.

"Rose, you were never one to be overly proud," Father said, sighing. "And more than once you were blessed with the strength of forgiveness. Look how many times you have forgiven *me*." He smiled, stilled another cough.

"You are my father."

"I am a man. You have to understand, it is not easy for the young chevalier—"

"Do not ask me to accept this, Father!" I stood up abruptly and went to the fire. I kneeled, picked up the bellows.

"It is natural for any man to have . . . interests," my father went on, breaking the quill in his hands. "But that doesn't mean Alexandre doesn't love you. A wife must learn to . . . to be accepting."

The ashes blew back in my face. "Do you think I do not notice when Alexandre puts his hand down the chambermaid's bodice? Do you think I do not know that he slips his hand under her skirts when she is doing his hair, that he visits her bedchamber? Do you think I do not know that he gave Vicomtesse de Rosin-Mallarmé his portrait? That he keeps a collection of silk stockings—victory trophies!—in his cupboard? Do you think I am blind? I see, I know—*and* I look the other way. But this, *this* is different. Laure Longpré is my *cousin!*"

I put the bellows to one side, stood up, brushing the ashes off my skirt. "You said yourself that no good would come of Laure. Remember when she visited when we first came to France? That child she had just given birth to was *Alexandre's*, Father. Remember how she asked *me* to invite Monsieur de Beauharnais to call on her? And I—so stupidly! so innocently! so *kindly!*—obliged her. Remember how he left the very next week? To visit friends from his regiment, he said!"

"If it makes you feel any better" —Father handed me a cap of whisky from the flask he carried—"I believe I am to blame."

I sat down on the footstool. The liquor burned going down. "What do you mean?" I handed him back the cap.

"Laure's family, as you know, has long hated ours—resented the favours the Marquis bestowed on me, such as they were, all because I was Désirée's brother. I think it is no accident that Laure has meddled in your marriage. That family has spite in their blood. She is a cat, playing a mouse."

"*Playing*, Father? This *game* will be the death of me!"

At five Monsieur de Beauharnais arrived home. I heard his voice in the entryway, heard Father's low warning tones, hushed whispers.

After a short time Monsieur de Beauharnais appeared at the door. "Aren't you coming down for supper?"

I refused to answer.

"Désirée tells me you talked to her about Laure." He came into the room. *Laure*. Not Laure Longpré. Not Madame Longpré. But *Laure*. I pressed my hand to my lips to check the feelings that were rising in me.

"Oh, Rose, please!" Monsieur de Beauharnais had that same impatient tone: *provincial*. It was *provincial* of me to be upset about such a thing.

"Don't take that tone with me, Alexandre." There were wet spots on my dress, splotches from my tears.

Monsieur de Beauharnais walked to the window. "It's stuffy in here." He opened the window with some effort, for it tended to stick.

"How can you be so nonchalant!"

"You'll wake the baby," he warned.

"*You*, who know so much about babies." I turned away. "When shall we tell Eugène that he is not your firstborn—on his fifth birthday? Or perhaps we should tell him sooner, on his third—"

"For God's sake, Eugène is my only legal son."

"And Madame Longpré?" I could not stop myself. "Who is *she?*"

"Do you want me to be honest?"

"I've had enough of deceit."

"You are my wife." He pulled aside a drape and looked out onto the street.

"And . . . ?"
"And Laure is the woman I love."
"Get out!"
"You wanted the truth!"
I flung a pillow, and another. I was trembling as I reached for a vase.

## *In which I come to the end of my endurance*

*December 13, 1781.*

"My daughter wears a long face," Father said as I brought him his evening glass of claret. Ever since Monsieur de Beauharnais left for Italy six weeks ago, Father has been kindly.

"Do I?" I knew it to be true. It was the day of my marriage to Monsieur de Beauharnais, two years before. Our anniversary.

Father grabbed my hand. "Come back with me, Rose."

"To Martinico?" Father's health had improved and he'd succeeded in getting a small increase in his pension. Soon he would be returning home.

"Your husband does not honour you sufficiently."

I was surprised by his words. Had he "honoured" my mother sufficiently?

"I couldn't," I said. Eugène was too young—the journey could kill him.

"Leave your baby with a wet-nurse. You may send for him in time, when he is old enough to travel."

Leave Eugène? It was the common practice, I knew. Yet I could not bear the thought. "Forgive me, Father, but I could not." My baby was my only joy.

Father looked at me for a long moment. "You créole mothers," he sighed.

*January 19, 1782.*

Father left this morning. He didn't look back as the carriage pulled away.

I'm on my own now. I feel a lifetime older.

*[Undated]*
A feeling of loneliness continues to haunt me. This Easter week I have
been examining my conscience. Monsieur de Beauharnais and I were
united by God. Is it my right to question this union? I have vowed to the
Virgin that I would write to my husband, and in my pitiful prose, which
he so detests, I will offer him my heart.

*July 25—Noisy-le-Grand.*
A courier came this morning with a message: Monsieur de Beauharnais
was in Paris. Immediately I called for a carriage. I asked Mimi to prepare
the baby. She dressed Eugène in his sailor suit—an ensemble intended
for a child one year older. I kissed his fat little nose. He rewarded me
with a smile, his feet kicking. I tried to nurse before I dressed, but I was
too anxious. Eugène fretted and began to cry. "I will try again on the
way," I told Mimi, handing Eugène back to her. Nervously I prepared
my own toilette, choosing a cream silk visiting suit and a big straw hat
with wide cream ribbons that tied under my chin. The jacket was a little
tight for me.

All the way in I thought of what I was going to say. At the edge of a
woods I instructed the driver to pull into a shady glen. This time Eugène
was hungry enough that he nursed no matter my emotional state. I held
a handkerchief to my other nipple to keep from staining my jacket. "I'm
nervous," I told Mimi.

At the Hôtel de la Rochefoucauld I presented my card. Mimi stood
behind me with Eugène, humming to him. I adjusted his funny little
sailor hat, which had fallen down over his eyes.

"Rose."

I turned. It was Monsieur de Beauharnais, standing in the open doorway. He looked stylish in a double-breasted waistcoat embroidered in
gold. I offered my hand. "It's good to see you, Alexandre." The baby let
out a squeal. Mimi lifted him into his father's arms. For a moment I
feared Eugène might take fright in the arms of this stranger, but he
didn't. He stared at the gold buttons on his father's waistcoat, reached out
to touch one.

"Is it all right to hold him this way?" Monsieur de Beauharnais asked nervously.

"He's a strong, healthy boy, you will not hurt him," I said, following him into the parlour.

Monsieur de Beauharnais touched the baby's chin with his finger. Eugène rewarded him with a grin. "He smiled at me! Do you think he knows who I am?" Eugène began to fuss. "I must have done something wrong." Monsieur de Beauharnais handed his son to Mimi. Eugène began to howl.

"Is there somewhere I could walk with him?" Mimi asked.

"The garden is through those doors," he said.

I removed my hat, touched my hair. Monsieur de Beauharnais filled a pipe with tobacco. I sat down, for my knees felt insecure. "How was Italy?" I asked.

"Rainy." He paused. "Lonely."

In spite of my prayers, I could feel anger rising within me. I willed such feelings away. They were the work of the Devil, not of God. For within me, too, was the longing that had become so much a part of me. For the sake of my son, for my own sake, I wanted my husband with me. For this, I was willing to forget, to give my heart anew.

Monsieur de Beauharnais lit his pipe, sucking in air through the stem. "I received your letter," he said, exhaling smoke.

There was a moment of silence. I heard my baby shriek from outside. Eugène, happy again.

"It was the reason for my return." He examined his fingertips.

I stood, went to the window, looked out. I feared I might say the wrong thing.

Monsieur de Beauharnais put his pipe down on the fireplace mantle. "I . . . I know it has not been easy for you, Rose, but on my travels I've had time to reflect, to examine the past . . . and to consider the future." He cleared his throat. "I have decided . . . that is, I have made the decision, to forsake a certain woman."

*A certain woman.* I turned to him. "Will that be difficult, Alexandre?"

He came to me and kissed me, lightly at first. "No," he said. I put my hand on the back of his neck. He embraced me with feeling. My heart weakened.

I heard my baby crying. I pulled away. Mimi was at the door, holding a crying Eugène in her arms. "I could come back later," she said, grinning.

Monsieur de Beauharnais ran his fingers over his hair. "No, come in. . . ." He kissed my hand.

We have returned to the country, Monsieur de Beauharnais and I, Mimi and our son. Now and again a voice of warning sounds in me; I do not pay it heed. I am intent on putting loneliness behind me.

*September 1.*
I woke with the most delicious feeling of warmth, curled next to my husband, a sense of peace filling me. I am with child again. . . .

*September 3, evening.*
Eugène's first birthday. I've had the most shattering news. Monsieur de Beauharnais has applied for the position of aide-de-camp to the governor of Martinico.

"But Alexandre, our son is too young. I couldn't leave him behind. And if I'm—"

"I don't think it would be safe for either of you."

"You would leave us?"

"I have much to gain in taking this opportunity—"

"And *everything* to lose," I cried, which set the baby howling.

*September 7.*
This morning I woke and Monsieur de Beauharnais was gone. He had left in the night.

*December 10.*
I've learned that Laure Longpré, now a widow, is on the same boat as Monsieur de Beauharnais, also headed for Martinico.

A feeling of bitterness overwhelms me. I've been betrayed.

I pray for strength. I must endure—for my boy's sake, for the sake of the child within me.

*April 10, 1783.*
In the morning I gave birth, earlier than expected. She is red, frail—she sleeps the sleep of the dead.

After the cord was cut, after the accoucher had bathed her in red wine and wrapped her in cotton wool, Mimi bathed me with a fragrant tea. I began to say something but she silenced me. A woman who has just given birth should never speak. "Else a wind come inside you," she said.

I closed my eyes, my lips. I closed my heart. A wind has already come inside me, a storm carrying tears.

*April 11.*
My baby was baptized this afternoon. Fanny, as godmother, has suggested the name Hortense. It is not a name I care for. I am too weary to object. I had to sell a medallion in order to pay the priest.

I don't remember feeling this way after Eugène was born . . . so sad, so sad.

*April 22—Noisy-le-Grand.*
Hortense is not growing. The doctor insists I put her in the care of a wet-nurse. He has recommended Madame Rousseau in the village here.

"A wet-nurse in Noisy-le-Grand would be better than one in Paris," Aunt Désirée said, in answer to my concerns. "In Paris the wet-nurses starve their charges. They take in laundry and overexert themselves, which spoils their milk."

I regarded the screaming baby in my arms. She'd sucked for hours and, even so, writhed with discontent. Was my own milk spoiled? Could grief spoil a mother's milk?

So today Aunt Désirée and I went to interview Madame Rousseau. Her abode is humble but clean. No animals are kept inside. She has a one-year-old boy (healthy, I noted), still nursing but ready to wean, she assured us. Her bosom seemed ample—she displayed it for inspection.

"I can come for your baby this evening," she said.

So soon? "I was thinking tomorrow," I said.

"This evening would be better," Aunt Désirée said. My baby's crying distressed the Marquis, I knew.

Hortense was wailing when we returned. Mimi was pacing the floor with her. I took my miserable baby from her, put her to suck, but in a short time she was screaming once again. I walked her in the garden for over an hour, until mercifully she fell into an exhausted sleep. If Madame Rousseau's milk will ease my baby's cries, I will rest content.

*April 24.*
I am ill, in terrible pain still, I have not slept. After my baby was taken from me Mimi bound my breasts, but even so, one became inflamed, my milk blocked. The doctor has been coming each morning to bleed me. After, I am able to sleep, but wake weeping.

Eugène brings me leaves torn from the lilac bush in the garden. His sweet kisses are my only consolation. That and the news that my baby has stopped crying. I have been advised not to visit her until my milk dries.

Who would have thought this would have been such a heart-wrenching process? I keep one of my baby's night-shirts under my pillow at night, press it to my lips as I sleep, inhale her sweet scent. My longing to hold her is so strong it makes me ill. I mourn for mothers everywhere.

*June 30.*
The Marquis has received several letters regarding Alexandre's dissolute behaviour in Martinico, where, he has learned, his son drinks, gambles and consorts publicly with a number of women (not only Laure), oblivious to the disgrace to his family name. Dangerously enraged, the Marquis composed a letter to the King demanding that his son be arrested under a lettre de cachet. With some effort Aunt Désirée apprehended it before it was sent.

*September 2.*

I was finishing the embroidery on a vest for Eugène when Mimi brought me an envelope. "It's from your husband," she said.

"A courier brought it?" It was unusual for a courier to come so early.

"A woman." Mimi stared at the floor. "Madame Longpré."

"Madame Laure Longpré?" Was she not in Martinico? "She came *here?*" I regarded the envelope in my hand. It smelled of iris powder. I broke the seal and slipped out the paper.

It was a letter—a letter from Monsieur de Beauharnais.

"What is it?" Mimi asked, perceiving my distress.

"Monsieur de Beauharnais has ordered me out of the house . . . into a convent. He claims—" I stopped. I could not say it. Alexandre claimed that Hortense was not his child.

"Allow me to fetch Madame!"

I did not protest. I felt myself weakening. Aunt Désirée came rushing into the room. She took the letter from me.

In it Monsieur de Beauharnais called me a vile creature. He accused me of having had numerous affairs as a girl. He claimed I'd lain with a man the night before I left to be betrothed to him, and with another in Saint-Pierre on the voyage to France. He claimed to have proof.

Aunt Désirée sank into the chair beside me. "Mon Dieu," I heard her whisper.

I felt the world become heavy around me.

# III

*Madame*

## In which I am banished to a convent

*October 29, 1783.*

"The fee is six hundred livres a year for a room, eight hundred livres for board," the Abbesse of the abbey de Penthémont informed us. She is a small woman of middle age, pretty in spite of a pocked face. She speaks with that particular cadence that identifies a member of the highest level of the noble class.

I nodded. I had expected it to be more. The convent of Penthémont was an elegant establishment for aristocratic ladies in distress. The Princess of Condé had been a boarder there.

The apartment that is available is parlour number three, on the second floor, overlooking a stone courtyard. The rooms, four in number, are not large, but sunny and simply furnished. Through two huge oak trees I could see the glittering dome of the Invalides.

Aunt Renaudin felt along the windowsill for dust.

"Satisfied, Madame?" the Abbesse inquired with a forgiving smile.

I move in at the end of November.

*November 1.*

"Why should *you* move out!" the Marquis stormed. He can't even look at me without sputtering. His son has disappointed him in the most grievous way. Since returning to Paris, Alexandre has refused to even speak to his family. As a result, the Marquis's gout has flared.

I am touched by his loyalty, yet what can I do? By law I must do as

Alexandre commands, in spite of the fact that he hasn't contributed an écu toward my support since he abandoned me over a year ago, in spite of his dissolute behaviour, his attack on my honour.

Eugène burst into tears when I told him. He wants to stay with "Papa," he wept, his beloved Marquis. How can I explain?


*November 27.*
We've moved, Mimi, Eugène and I. "I want to go home!" Eugene cried when I showed him his new bed.


*December 1.*
Yesterday morning I received an elegantly scribed invitation to dine with the Abbesse.

Her rooms are on the ground floor, directly below my own. We were joined by three other boarders—Vicomtesse de Douai (tall, elegant), Duchesse de Monge (witty, plump) and Madame de Crény (tiny, sweet). We enjoyed an elegant meal of fresh oysters, brochette de rognons, foie gras aux truffles and, last, a fondue, which was put on the table in a casserole with a chafing-dish and a spirit lamp. After we sat by the fire drinking les régals à gloire—a hot coffee and cognac drink that is popular now.

That evening there was a gathering in the apartment of Vicomtesse de Sotin. Monsieur Beaumarchais, the playwright, attended. After readings and song there were the usual discussions concerning the weather, theatre and politics. Then we got on to the more relaxing pursuits—gossip and games. (The Abbesse is unbeatable at trictrac, I discovered.) I feared the sound of our laughter would disturb our neighbours, but the Abbesse said I need not be concerned—that over the years they have had to become accustomed to it.

Life here is not at all what I expected.


*Tuesday, December 2, 11:00 P.M.*
This afternoon, taking in yet another one of my dresses (I've become thin), I informed Aunt Désirée that I intended to seek a legal separation.

Aunt Désirée looked concerned. "A separation, Rose? Have you any idea what that would entail—the social stigma that would attach to you and your children?"

"Yet you obtained a legal separation from your husband." In the first year of her marriage, Aunt Désirée's husband had tried to poison her.

"And I have paid the price. Many a time I have been excluded from gatherings. It matters not at all if a woman is innocent. She has been tarnished and is not considered fit for *proper* society." Aunt Désirée put down her needlework. "And what if Alexandre proved contentious, Rose? Are you willing to expose the details of your private life for all of Paris to see? A woman is rarely the victor in such a battle. Even if you were beaten black and blue, it would be viewed as your husband's right—and your *duty* to be submissive to his wish, *whatever* his wish might be."

"Am I to do nothing?" I demanded, jabbing the needle into my thumb by mistake. With some effort, I refrained from cursing. "Alexandre has attacked my honour in an entirely public way."

"But what of your son? Think how it will affect him. Eugène is old enough to understand the taunts of his playmates."

"Think how a stain on my honour will affect him. Imagine what it will be like for him, having a mother who is forced to live in a convent until the end of her days. And what of Hortense? Her prospects for a good marriage will be seriously diminished. A legal separation is my only alternative—both for my sake *and* for the sake of my children."

Aunt Désirée sighed. "I will pray for you, Rose."


*December 8, late afternoon.*
This afternoon I met with Monsieur Joron, King's Counsel and commissioner at Chastelet, to make official my record of complaint. He came with his father\* and his secretary. It was trying, laying bare the failure of my marriage, but they were tactful and put me at my ease.

---

\* *Monsieur Joron's father described Rose in the following way to his wife: "a fascinating young person, a lady of distinction and elegance, with perfect style, a multitude of graces and the most beautiful of speaking voices."*

Monsieur Joron told me that it will take a few months for an order for a separation of person and dwelling to be issued, and that I shouldn't expect settlement for more than a year after that. Until then, I must live according to my husband's wishes.

"One full year?"

The secretary transcribed my testimony in his careful hand. I was asked to read it over and sign each page. "How shall I sign?" I asked. "As Beauharnais, or Tascher de la Pagerie?"

"However you prefer."

I wrote: Tascher de la Pagerie.

And so it is—my marriage undone.


*December 13—Noisy-le-Grand.*

We are at Noisy-le-Grand for a few days. Four years ago Alexandre and I were married here, shared the bed I sleep in now. I remember so clearly the first time I saw him, a handsome young man reading Cicero's *Treatise on Laws* in the salon of the Hôtel Graves in Brest. It seems another world, another time—another Rose.

After Eugène woke from his nap we walked to Madame Rousseau's to see Hortense. She giggled in her brother's clumsy embrace. I held them both in my arms. How can I regret a union that has given me two such beautiful children?


*Monday, December 22.*

The women here make a fuss over me. Their warmth puzzles me. Well-bred, wealthy and titled, they are much above my station.

"They perceive a natural elegance in your demeanour," the Abbesse told me this morning. (I read to her; in return she helps me with my enunciation.) "And, too, there is nothing so rewarding as an avid student."

An avid student I confess I have become. I long to feel at ease in this world, among these women—but there is so much to learn: how to bow, how to enter a room, how to take a seat, how to speak. Quietly I observe the way Vicomtesse de Douai orders her coach, how Duchesse de Monge bows (and for whom, and how low, depending), watch for whom her footman opens both double doors and for whom only one is opened, listen to the way the Abbesse speaks, her aristocratic inflection.

In the privacy of my room, I practise before the long looking glass, bow deeply to my image in the glass. "Don't laugh!" I tell Mimi, who watches me with a mocking smile.

*February 4, 1784.*

Alexandre is suing for the return of my jewellry, including the medallion I had to sell in order to pay for Hortense's baptism. He claims that it was part of his inheritance, that I had no right to sell it.

I am so enraged I cannot sleep. Alexandre provides nothing for my support. I am increasingly desperate for funds. Every day, it seems, there is a creditor at my door. Yesterday I was presented with a bill for jewels I had never even seen. I gave the man Alexandre's address and directed him there, trying not to reveal my rage.

*February 23.*

Fanny called early this morning, her heavily powdered face streaked with tears. Her daughter Marie has suffered yet another infant death. The youngest, Amédée, died in the night, succumbing to a fever. She was not even two. It was three-year-old Émilie who'd discovered her "sleeping" sister.

"Can you come with me?" Fanny asked. "I can't face her alone. Not again." This is the third child Marie has lost.

It was Alexandre's brother François who came to the door to meet us, wearing a nightcap and a blue waistcoat over a bed gown. He looked distressed. I don't know why this surprised me, for he is a man of feeling, with a tender regard for children. He led us into Marie's bedchamber, where she was resting on a chaise longue, a dish of tea on the side-table. She was pale, without expression, like a dead person herself. Little Émilie was sitting quietly beside her mother, looking confused.

We were told that the child was in her bed in the next room. I stayed with Marie while Fanny went to help prepare the body, the sobbing nanny assisting.

After the priest came, and then the doctor (who prescribed laudanum drops for Fanny as well as for Marie and François), I left, taking little Émilie back with me to Penthémont. Mimi, Eugène and I fuss over her gently. Even so, she refuses to speak.

*March 2.*
Eugène has worked his magic on Émilie. She follows him everywhere. She is a bright little thing, a little pixie with fair pink cheeks and coal black hair and eyes—but oh, so serious! Only Eugène can coax a smile from her.

"I'm afraid we will have to take Émilie back home soon." I broke the news to him gently. "To her own mother." Marie was in need of her now, in need of her one surviving child.

*April 10—Noisy-le-Grand.*
Hortense is one today. She's walking!

*April 27, 1784, Noisy-le-Grand*
*Dear Madame Beauharnais,*

*I am returning the money you sent me. Your husband came for a visit last week and paid for two months. He brought some pretty baubles from the fun-fair for the baby. She didn't make strange at all. He sang her a ballad and danced about with her, which made her spit up but he didn't mind too much. You never mentioned your husband. I hope I did the right thing.*

*Respectfully, Madame Rousseau*

*Tuesday, January 11, 1785—Noisy-le-Grand.*
Aunt Désirée has received word that Alexandre would like to see Eugène. "And he would consent to see me as well," she said, examining the letter.

The Marquis snorted. "How good of him."

"I think you should go," I told her.

Aunt Désirée spent the morning getting ready. She settled on her blue silk robe with a black velvet cape. I loaned her my hat with the blue ribbons, which complemented the dress nicely. She was flustered, which brought some colour to her cheeks.

I dressed Eugène in his best clothes. "Am I going to church?" he asked. He is too young to grasp the situation. To him, "father" is the Marquis—why should it be otherwise?

Aunt Désirée returned at nightfall looking relieved. Eugène was quite excited about the bounty of presents this "stranger" had heaped upon him.

"Alexandre asked if I could bring Eugène once a week." Aunt Désirée took off her hat and tidied her hair.

"What do you think?" I asked.

"It might help." She paused. "Although there will be no changing his mind."

I stiffened. Even if Alexandre were to relent, could my heart open? "And you? How did you find him?"

"Oh, he was full of pretty words—"

I knew Alexandre's pretty words. "But his heart was not there?"

Aunt Désirée looked at me, her eyes filling with tears. "How can that be?"

*Friday, February 4.*

Today, as I returned from my clothier, Mimi rushed to me in the most terrible state, crying out in the African tongue.

"Speak!" I demanded. She had fallen to her knees. "Mimi, mon Dieu!"

"The boy! He's gone!"

I could not comprehend. Eugène? *Gone?* What did that mean?

In a rush her story came out. She'd allowed Eugène to play in the courtyard, as was our custom. Every few minutes she looked out. Eugène had been beating on a drum and the din served as a means of keeping track of him. She'd gone into her room to search for a particular colour thread. When she came back out she noticed that the courtyard had become silent. She looked out the window. The courtyard was empty.

She ran down to the courtyard and out the iron gates—which were closed, she assured me—and onto the street. Eugène was nowhere to be seen. She questioned the tenants, but could get no answers. She ran for the Abbesse, but she was out.

I went to the open window, looked out at the empty courtyard. "Eugène!" I called out. I hurried through our rooms, looking into every closet, under the beds. I could not believe that Eugène was not there. It was then that I noticed a piece of paper sticking out from under the carpet. Apparently it had been pushed under the door. I picked it up, knowing even before I read it what it would reveal.

It was from Alexandre. He had taken Eugène.

It did not take long to send for a fiacre and find our way to the Rochefoucauld town house on Rue de Seine. The big doors to the courtyard were still open, the horses had not yet been unhitched. A footman in livery opened the door.

Alexandre came to the foyer with a cautious look. We hadn't seen each other since he'd left my bed in the night, two years before. He looked the same, if pale and thin, no doubt from the lingering effects of the malignant fever he had contracted in Martinico. He was without a wig, his hair long, hanging about his shoulders.

"I've come for Eugène." I tried to calm myself.

"I won't have my son growing up in a house of women!" he said.

"Then permit me to live elsewhere with him!" I cried.

He turned his back, commanding the footman to shut the heavy door. Mimi pulled me away.

*February 5.*
I've notified the authorities. A hearing has been set one month from today, but until then I am powerless. Alexandre, as the father, may do as he pleases with Eugène.

Mimi has gone to stay at Alexandre's in order to look after Eugène. I am unbearably alone here.

*Saturday, February 7.*

As I was packing to go to Noisy-le-Grand, tiny Madame de Crény called. She was in need of diversion, she said. Her coach had been tied up in traffic at Saint-Sulpice for over an hour. "An enormous wedding." She removed her hat. She was wearing a travelling suit of grey silk with abundant lace trimming that overwhelmed her tiny figure. At her neck and elbows were huge pink-and-white-striped bows. "General Arthur Dillon and that woman with the bosom. Créole, I am told. Perhaps you know her. Apparently she met Dillon in Martinico. Her name is Longbeau, Longpreid . . . something like that. She chews candles, I've heard."

*Laure Longpré.*

"You should have seen the equipages. The Queen and King signed the wedding contract." Madame de Crény rolled her eyes. "Even Duchesse de Monge's sister couldn't get *that* honour, and she practically lives with the Queen."

I sat down, stunned. The Queen and King? Signed their wedding contract? Alexandre's bloodline wasn't even noble enough to permit him to sit in a royal equipage. "Madame Longpré is a cousin of mine." I paused. "My husband fancied her," I said.

"Was *she* the one?" Madame de Crény said sweetly. "Oh . . . !" She took my hand. "And now she has married General Dillon?"

I recalled the deranged expression in Alexandre's eyes. "Curious," I said, "is it not?" Curious and cruel.

*March 3.*

After mass this morning the Abbesse came to my door. "Your husband wishes to speak with you."

"Alexandre?" Tomorrow both Alexandre and I are to appear in court. Why would he come at this time? "Is Eugène with him?"

The Abbesse shook her head. "You must consider whether or not *you* wish to speak with him."

"What harm might there be?"

"If you do consent to receive him, Rose, I recommend that you do so in the presence of your lawyer."

"I'll agree to nothing, I promise you."

"You'll receive him?"

"If you will stay with me."

"That is wise."

She was gone for what seemed a long time. When Alexandre entered, I was puzzled by the look in his eyes. It has always been difficult to interpret Alexandre's emotions, and this time was no different.

The Abbesse settled herself into a chair by the door. Alexandre seemed uncomfortable about her presence, and for a moment I thought he was going to protest. Then, he spoke. "Rose, after a period of deliberation I have come to the conclusion—" He stopped to clear his throat. "I have come to the conclusion that I have been in error."

I was shocked by his confession, but remained, nevertheless, cautious. How many times has Alexandre fooled me with his golden words, jewels given but not paid for?

Alexandre turned to the Abbesse. "I have come to comprehend the . . . grievousness of my actions—while I was in Martinico, and again, most recently, in taking Eugène. I have no defence," he went on, addressing me now, "but that I was possessed by emotions I could not control. I have vowed to make amends. Eugène will be returned to you shortly. At the hearing tomorrow I will plead guilty, for it is guilty I stand before you."

It was silent but for the steady ticking of the clock. "Madame de Beauharnais—if I may address your husband," the Abbesse said.

I nodded.

"Vicomte de Beauharnais, I urge you to continue in this line of thinking. It will only bear fruit. The appearance of a fiat lux* in one's life helps not only oneself, but all those around one, and puts in motion any number of blessed events. But it is not to this purpose I wish to speak. I would advise your wife to accept your apology—but only were it to be expressed in a more tangible form, such as an equitable and prompt settling of accounts overdue. But at the same time I would caution her to be aware of the benefits that might accrue to *you* in light of your confession of guilt, for your sins might perhaps be judged less severely, and you might stand

---

* She is referring to Genesis, "Let there be light."

to gain in this way. Is this not so? Tell me truthfully," she went on, "how does your lawyer feel about this . . . this 'confession' of yours?"

"Abbesse, respectfully," I interrupted. "I thank you for your counsel. I will hold your words close to my heart. But at this moment I would like to have a word with my husband, in private."

The Abbesse looked at me with concern.

"I promise I will not do anything foolish," I whispered, accompanying her to the door.

She touched my shoulder as she departed.

I closed the door behind me and turned to Alexandre, pulling my shawl around my shoulders. "Alexandre, tell me what this means—I have lived with uncertainty too long."

"I am prepared to give you whatever you ask, Rose. I look back with regret on the things I did, the things I said. I can only conclude that I was not myself. Perhaps it was the delirium I suffered in Martinico, occasioned by the fever."

Relief filled my soul, followed by caution. I recalled the Abbesse's words. "What will you be demanding at the court hearing, in the way of a settlement?"

Alexandre turned his face to the embers in the fireplace. "I will agree to anything. A public apology, an admission of error, a monthly allowance, your freedom to live where you please . . . whatever you require."

I went to the window. A bricklayer was working on the courtyard wall. "And in exchange?"

"I only ask for custody of my son, when he turns five."

Eugène!

"You will have Hortense," he pleaded. "Can't you grant me Eugène? A boy needs his father. He will need what I can teach him. You know that, Rose. For the boy's sake."

For the boy's sake. . . .

## *In which ill-fortune plagues us*

March 12, 1785—Fontainebleau
Darling!

Congratulations! Who would have imagined that a woman could take her husband to court and win!* How unthinkable! All the ladies are in a fever of excitement over your victory. I've been told that even the Queen talks of it. You are a heroine now!

I've finally persuaded your aunt and the Marquis to join me here in Fontainebleau. The estate she has leased on Rue de Montmorin is well located, and big—stables for twelve horses! And all for the price of some Paris hovel, no doubt.

Is it true that you intend to join us soon? I pray that it is so. My salon here in Fontainebleau could use your lively heart.

Your loving Aunt Fanny

March 24, 1785—Fontainebleau
Dear Rose,

With the proceeds from the sale of Noisy-le-Grand, I've been able to secure a long-term lease on an estate here in Fontainebleau. You will love

* The separation agreement stipulated that Alexandre would pay Rose an annual allowance of five thousand livres plus an additional one thousand livres for Hortense's expenses up to the age of seven, fifteen hundred livres thereafter. (Unfortunately, this was rarely paid.) As for Eugène, the agreement stipulated that Alexandre would take custody when the boy turned five.

*it. There is a lovely suite of rooms for you and the children overlooking the garden.*

*You will be pleased to know that Alexandre paid us a call to inform us personally of the results of the settlement. He and his father have come to terms. What a great joy this is to me. Already I can see an improvement in the Marquis's health.*

*Do join us soon. The garden, quite large, is much in need of your special attention. The prices are reasonable and there isn't all that disagreeable mob one encounters in Paris now.*

*We miss Eugène. Alexandre told us a number of charming stories—it is clear that he is quite fond of the boy. As for Hortense, he made a point of mentioning that he would like "his daughter" (his exact words) weaned from her wet-nurse. I told him it would be best for her to be weaned after you move. I know it is hard to wait, but it is not an easy process. Best to be settled first.*

*Your loving Aunt Désirée*

*July 22, Saint Mary Magdalen's Day—Fontainebleau.*
How quiet Fontainebleau is—so unlike Paris, which never rests. This morning I took my morning cup of chocolate into the garden, breathing in the cleansing air. I could hear the soothing clip-clop of the chimney sweep's horse, the creaking of the rag collector's wagon. From somewhere close a rooster crowed. We will be happy here.

*July 24, evening.*
This afternoon Madame Rousseau, the wet-nurse, brought Hortense. The good woman bawled leaving "her" girl behind, she has formed such a strong attachment. When Hortense saw the carriage pull away she began screaming as if she were being tortured. This horrible state lasted for over two hours.

Now, at last, she has fallen into an exhausted sleep. I look upon the face of my daughter with apprehension. Will she ever love me?

*Friday, September 23.*

Father writes that there has been no income earned on La Pagerie, or even on the Marquis's properties in Saint-Domingue.*

"No income at *all?* But how is that possible?" Aunt Désirée exclaimed when I read out the letter. "How are we to manage?"

Indeed. Already my debts are mounting. Alexandre hasn't paid support for four months. He recently bought a country property in the Loire from his brother and claims to have no cash. And now, without income from the Islands . . .


*May 4, 1786.*

A Madame Croÿ came to call this afternoon. She'd sent a letter from Paris a week ago requesting an audience on a matter she said concerned us.

She is a humble woman of quiet composure. Although her clothes were tattered, she wore them with grace. She was nervous in our company, but when she perceived that we were kindly, she was able to speak her mind.

Her daughter, a married woman with three children, is about to have another. She explained that her daughter intended to put this baby into the charities, for she could not afford to provide for it. Madame Croÿ was concerned about this possibility, for she knew what the fate of that child would be. Indeed, more than half the babies given over each year die.**

"Why have you come to us?" I asked.

"Because the Vicomte de Beauharnais is the father—"

"Alexandre?" Aunt Désirée interrupted.

"I do not believe he would deny it." The spots of rouge on Madame Croÿ's cheeks were garishly bright in the afternoon sun.

I sat back. I had falsely assumed I would no longer be affected by Alexandre's reprehensible behaviour. I was mistaken.

"You're not going to suggest that *we* take the child," Aunt Désirée said.

"No—I thought perhaps you . . . I thought if you could help—"

---

* *Joseph acted as manager of all the Beauharnais properties in the Caribbean. Unfortunately, he was not a good one.*
** *Approximately forty thousand babies were abandoned a year.*

"Financially, you mean." Aunt Désirée sighed.

"It wouldn't take much, but it is more than I can offer. I had to sell my winter cloak to purchase a coach ticket to come see you today."

"How much would your daughter require in order to keep the child?" I asked.

"I do not believe she has the heart for it," Madame Croÿ said. "I am ashamed to say so, but the baby would be better in the care of a foster parent. I do laundry for a woman, a Madame d'Antigny, the wife of a goldsmith, but a paresseuse—she has no children of her own. She might be willing, were the financial needs looked after."

"You have discussed this with her?" Aunt Désirée asked.

"Aunt Désirée, I think we should talk to Alexandre," I said.


*May 6.*

Alexandre arrived in the rain. He'd set out from Paris the day before, but the roads were so muddy a linchpin had been lost from one of the fore wheels and they had had to stop at an inn along the way.

He'd been alarmed by my use of a mounted courier. "Bad news always comes fast. Is it Father? Do not keep me in suspense, I beg you." His yellow velvet frock coat was splattered with mud.

"A Madame Croÿ came to see us," I said.

Alexandre leaned his sword against the wall. "Do I know this Madame Croÿ?" Aubin cleaned the mud off his boots.

"She claims you enjoyed an amourette with her daughter." Aunt Désirée appeared in the doorway behind us, wearing a brocade dressing gown over her corset and petticoat. She'd interrupted her toilette to come to the door, her hair greased but unpowdered.

Alexandre groaned.

"You recall?" Aunt Désirée asked.

He sighed with exasperation and entered the parlour. "I believe you mean Madame Darigrand—a certain Geneva-Louise." He sat down by the fire, blowing into his hands and rubbing them together. "It's so cold out there! Who would believe it's May? What's come over this country? The weather has become so unpredictable!"

The parlourmaid came to the door. "Would Vicomte de Beauharnais wish for something?"

"I'll have a pint of claret—warm."

"Alexandre!" Aunt Désirée said. "It's not yet eleven."

"And *you* haven't been travelling all day in this miserable weather. When you think of the nonsense they concern themselves with, you'd think they'd figure out a way to heat a diligence."

I sat opposite him, ready to speak to the subject at hand, when Mimi came to the door holding Hortense's hand, Eugène following behind, carrying a toy crossbow he'd made the day before from sticks and bits of string.

"Take the children away," Aunt Désirée told Mimi.

"Please allow a moment." I knew how much his father's visits meant to Eugène. Hortense squirmed to escape Mimi's grasp.

Alexandre examined Eugène's crossbow. "Do you want to try it?" Eugène asked.

"I must talk with your mother and Aunt Désirée first."

Mimi picked Hortense up, setting off a howl. "You will see your father soon," I assured her.

After the children had gone, the three of us sat for a moment in uncomfortable silence. Aunt Désirée cleared her throat. "Madame Croÿ is concerned about the welfare of the child," she said finally.

"The child?" Alexandre stood in front of the fire. There were only a few small sticks on a deep bed of ashes—they gave off little heat. "What child?"

"You don't know?" I asked. Aunt Désirée and I exchanged a confused look.

Aunt Désirée explained: "Madame Croÿ claims that her daughter—Madame Darigrand—is soon to be having your child."

Alexandre sat down in a chair, crossing and uncrossing his legs in an agitated manner.

"Alexandre," I said, "you look upset. Please explain."

"I . . . knew Geneva-Louise—or Madame Darigrand, as you so honour her—for a period of six months. I wasn't the first and I won't be the last. We broke off, and a month later she came to me, claiming to be with child."

"Why does this news surprise you?" I asked.

"Because I gave Madame Darigrand a considerable sum of money to . . . to *resolve* her condition."

"I see." Aunt Désirée crossed herself. "And what do you propose to do now, Alexandre?"

"I told Madame Darigrand I wanted nothing more to do with her," Alexandre said, "and certainly nothing to do with a child."

"But, Alexandre," I said, "you are the father of that—"

"I did not journey all the way from Paris to be lectured," Alexandre said. He strode back into the foyer.

"Hortense and Eugène will be heartbroken if you leave!" I cried out, running after him.

He stayed. I promised not to mention Madame Darigrand again.[*]

*August 10.*

We are besieged by financial troubles, which I greatly resent for I consider money one of the least important things in life. Yet the want of it can certainly be distracting.

The Marquis's Saint-Domingue plantation is not earning, nor La Pagerie in Martinico. Aunt Désirée and I have written letter after letter to Father, but without solution. He claims it's the British, the weather, inflation . . . all adding up to the same result: no income. I've had to depend on Alexandre's contribution, which is rarely forthcoming. There are times when I am entirely without. . . .

*September 3, 1:15 P.M.*

It is said that autumn is beautiful in Fontainebleau, but the charm is dulled for me in this season. In three hours Alexandre will arrive and we will partake of the refreshments the cook has made in honour of Eugène's

---

[*] *In June, Marie-Adélaïde (Adèle) was born. Monsieur and Madame d'Antigny became her foster parents. Rose contributed to the child's upkeep. In 1804, Rose—as Empress—arranged Adèle's marriage to a Captain Lecomte, and provided her with a farm as a dowry and a trousseau.*

fifth birthday. I've just finished decorating the cake, fulfilling his request for liquorice comfits all around on top. Oh, how my heart went out with each comfit I placed, how the tears started as I positioned each candle.


*September 4.*

Eugène and Alexandre left this morning, Eugène holding on to his new book bag, looking very grown-up but for the baby-blanket he clasped in his other hand. I tried hard not to cry, for he might cry in turn, and that would have distressed him, I knew, trying so hard to be big. We are all of us trying.


*Wednesday, January 3, 1787.*

Creditors pester our door like flies in autumn. Years ago, the Marquis's annual pension was set at one hundred and fifty thousand livres. In the last decade, it was reduced to twelve thousand. And now, because of the impoverishment of the government treasury,* it has been further reduced to under three thousand livres a year.

Three thousand! How can the Marquis and my aunt be expected to live on such a sum? After all his years of distinguished service, is this his reward? I have written the Minister of War to try to persuade him to have the pension increased. We are renting a house that can stable twelve horses, but can't afford to keep a pair.

The Marquis maintains his humour: "I used to think someone impover-ished if he couldn't enjoy the privilege of raising three armed men. I'll soon be so poor I'll have to stay in bed while my breeches are mended." He's in bed all the time anyway; it's unlikely he'll ever wear out a pair of breeches again.


*May 1, 1788.*

The letters from home are distressing. Father is not well and now Manette is seriously ill. Mother begs me to come home—her words have an ominous tone. I must go, surely . . . but how could I leave Eugène?

---

* *France was bankrupt in part because of its support of the American Revolution.*

*Tuesday, May 27.*

We've received the most bewildering news: the Island properties have been earning a profit. According to information Uncle Tascher provided, last year La Pagerie earned seventy thousand livres.

"Seventy thousand! Why hasn't Joseph sent you your share?" Aunt Désirée demanded. "Has he sent you anything?"

"He's been ill. No doubt—"

"I wonder if the Marquis's properties earned a profit as well." She began pacing in an agitated state. I no longer feared that she might faint.

"If only I could talk to him," I said.

Aunt Désirée stopped. "You must go, Rose."

"To Martinico?" I stuttered.

"I would gladly go myself were it not for the Marquis's health."

"But—" What about Eugène? Alexandre would never permit me to take him. "But Eugène is coming in a few weeks to spend his summer holiday with me." I'd been looking forward to it, making plans.

"Yet it is precisely for his sake that you must go, Rose. It is his inheritance, his future, after all."

I was at a loss. I longed to see my family, my ailing father and sister, but the very thought of an ocean voyage made me ill. "It would cost a small fortune to go," I said. Last week Alexandre had informed me that he didn't have the two thousand livres required to pay for Eugène's schooling. As well, my own debts had mounted.

"It will cost you *not* to go."

"But it's almost June. I would have to leave immediately." It would be dangerous to be at sea in August, the month of hurricanes.

"Exactly." Aunt Désirée dipped a quill in the inkwell. "The Marquis may be feeble but as a former commander in the navy there are a few things he can arrange—I should think passage on the next ship to Fort-Royal would be one of them," she said, writing out a note. "There—" She sprinkled the letter with sand and shook it clean. "Take this up for his signature and I'll send it out on the next post."

*June 2.*

It has happened very quickly. Passage has been found. I've borrowed six thousand livres for the journey. As well, Aunt Désirée will loan me one thousand livres. Already she's found a buyer for my harp—that should help pay for Eugène's tuition.

And so it is set—Mimi, Hortense and I will be leaving in a few weeks for Paris. From there it will be a three-day journey by coach to Rouen, where we'll take a river barge to Le Havre to wait ship.

There is so much to do, so many things to remember to do, so many things to worry about.

I told Hortense last night, at bedtime. She likes the idea of a boat. She is five now, and a strong girl.

Mimi is ecstatic, of course.

I can't believe we are doing this.

*June 20—Paris.*

Hortense and I are in Paris, saying our farewells to Eugène and Alexandre. We leave for Le Havre in the morning.

It was difficult explaining to Eugène that we are going to be away for a very long time. "I must see my father and my sister," I explained. "They are ill." He is only six; it was the explanation he could most easily understand.

He said he would come visit us, and I had to explain that he couldn't. "Your sister and I will be on the boat for a very long time, just to get there."

I gave him a music box with a toy soldier that popped up. I turned the box over. I'd had an inscription engraved on the bottom.

"I can't read it," he confessed.

I pointed to each word as I pronounced it: "For Eugène, whom I will always love, Maman."

He turned the box over in his hands. "Is that all?" he asked.

"That's all," I said, too close to tears to say more.

## In which I return home

*Thursday, July 3, 1788.*

As we approached the open sea it grew dark. Soon there was a great wind and one of the sails began flapping, making a cracking sound. Quickly the men began taking down the sails.

"Get below," a flagman yelled. "Take the child!"

I grabbed Hortense for fear the wind might snatch her away.

The swells were growing. The rain began hitting us violently. Just before I climbed down into the passage, I looked out to sea. In the dark I could see a darker dark, a thickening of wind and rain. Then, a deafening roar; the rain had turned to stone. Mimi appeared, falling down the ladder behind us.

We stumbled into our cabin as best we could, for we were thrown from one side of the narrow passage to the other. Hortense cried out; I held her too tightly. I braced myself against the bunk. I could feel the sickness rising within me. We'd sunk into the pit of Hell, into an elemental fury. "Mimi!" I called out.

"I am here." A voice in the dark, barely discernible over the frightful howling. I felt her curled at the foot of the bunk.

The sickness filled me again. I fought it, weakly. Oh, please, God, I prayed, shameful for having neglected Him.

We emerged into the light, giddy with the memory of terror. The deck was covered with stones of ice, glittering like a wealth of diamonds. And, as far as I could see, the undulating surface of the sea, smooth and untroubled.

*[Undated]*

We've hit a calm, and are helpless, unmoving. For two days we've not moved, merely drifted. I never thought I'd pray for wind.

I feel cut loose from the world, detached. The most horrifying thing might happen and I would never know.

When I think about this, looking out on the vast watery surface, standing on the deck under the bright and crowded stars, when I think of the enormity of it all and the meaninglessness of my own small life, I am both sickened and comforted.

"Time is longer than rope," Mimi says, a Carib proverb. And now I understand.


*August 7.*

At last, we've caught a wind. It pulls us forward. With the rising and the falling of the waves, the sickness fills me again. I tolerate it gladly. I'm anxious to be done with this voyage.


*[Undated]*

We're approaching Martinico. I can smell it. I stand on the deck and pretend it is the wind that brings tears to my eyes.


*August 10.*

Sighting the mountains I held Hortense in my arms and wept. "Is that 'Tinico?'" she asked, perhaps four times before I gave up answering.

Mimi leans on the railing and stares, as if turning away would cause this vision to disappear.

Oh, my beautiful island—in the midst of such a great water.


*August 11—Fort-Royal.*

We pulled into port in a torrent of rain. Uncle Tascher braved the weather to meet us, drenched.

The roads were rivers of mud. We made it with difficulty to his new estate in the hills, where the house-slaves relieved us of our mud-splattered clothes. Hortense escaped and went running through the rooms in her petticoat (Mimi chasing after), much to the delight of her cousins.

I was astonished by the luxury of Uncle's home. He is Mayor now, as well as Port Commander. "And all he has to do is keep the young men from killing themselves off in duels," his wife said, giggling. Her time of confinement is approaching, it is clear.

Uncle seemed cheerful in spite of his gout, inflamed due to the rain.

*August 12.*
The bay was too rough to cross by gommier so we made the trip to Trois-Ilets overland in a carriage.

A "carriage" I say—it was more of a partially covered wagon, crudely fashioned from canvas, and leaking terribly whenever we were over-come by a squall. Hortense, bounding with eagerness, flung herself from one side to the other in spite of my efforts to still her. At last she fell into an exhausted sleep, her sweat-damp head on my lap, and I was left with my thoughts.

Now and again the sky cleared and the sun came out, illuminating the thick foliage with an intensity I'd forgotten. The smell was dank, fertile, salted by the sea. I was in a reverie of emotion for all I had missed and was missing still. The incessant noise of the cicadas, the bullfrogs croak-ing, even the buzzing of the mosquitoes was like a song I'd been longing to hear. I felt I'd been a lifetime away, and was assaulted by memories both of pleasure and pain.

Coming down the hill into Trois-Ilets I asked Morin, the driver, to stop in the square in front of the church. The market women were there, as before, selling fruit. The fishing boats were moored down the hill at the pier. Behind the church, the bright white of the tombs, littered with flowers and trinkets. Nothing had changed. Only I had changed—thin-ner, dressed in elegant silk and lace, wearing a bonnet that hid the sad-ness in my eyes.

Mimi cried out—she recognized one of the women in the market. She climbed down out of the wagon and sprinted across the square, her skirts pulled up to her knees, in one instant forgetting the ladylike saunter she'd acquired in Paris.

Hortense sat up, wiped her eyes. "I'm thirsty," she said.

"Maybe one of the market women would sell us a juice." I climbed down from the wagon, took Hortense in my arms. Her clothes were damp from the heat. "This is the church I was baptized in."

"It's little."

"Yes." It looked small to me, too. I pressed her to my heart, inhaling the sweet scent of her damp hair, kissed her nose before lowering her onto the dirt. "Do you want to come inside with me?" I took her hand, dirty now.

"And then a juice?"

I nodded. I had forgotten her thirst.

We climbed the three steps to the door. It creaked as I pulled it open. The dark interior was cool—and empty, for which I was grateful. We stood together, made the sign of the cross (Hortense so sweetly), walked down the aisle, the sound of our footsteps echoing on the black-and-white tiles. "I'm just going to say a prayer and we'll go," I whispered to her, edging into the second row of pews.

"A prayer for what?"

"For juice, for you," I teased.

"Mother!" She frowned, alarmed, for she perceived my jest, and no doubt believed jesting in church a sin.

"For thanks, for our safe journey," I whispered, adjusting my skirts and kneeling. And for the soul of my dead sister Catherine. And for my ailing sister Manette and my ever-ailing beloved Father. And for my Mother, who held them all in her arms, both the dead and the dying. And for my own small soul.

After a moment I rose. Hortense was sitting on the bench beside me, her eyes pinched shut, her brow furrowed, her hands clenched in a fist under her chin. I touched her shoulder. Her eyes flew open. "One moment." Her eyes shut tight again.

"And what was it *you* were praying for?" I asked as we emerged into the light. Mimi was already in the wagon, sharing a mango with Morin. Flirting, I thought, by the way she moved.

"For Father." Hortense jumped three steps in one leap.

"Alexandre?" I was taken aback. I took her hand and we headed over to the market.

"For his blessing." Hortense looked around the market. Trunks of felled banana trees, thick with green fruit, were stacked next to a basket of overly ripe mangoes, buzzing with flies.

I asked the eldest of the women if she had juice. She smiled a toothless grin and pointed to the pile of ripe oranges stacked before her. She hadn't understood and my memory of the African tongue had abandoned me. I took three oranges, gave the woman a coin.

"An orange will be wonderfully juicy," I told Hortense, who was about to object. "For his love, you mean?" I stripped an orange of peel and gave her a section, popping one in my mouth as well. The sweetness of the fruit brought on a distant recollection of standing in this very market, sucking on orange sections after mass on a Sunday morning. A girl with an aching heart, sucking on orange sections and watching the door of the church, searching the crowd for a boy named William. I took Hortense's hand and headed back to the wagon.

"Yes—for you." The juice from the orange dribbled down her chin.

I stopped under the shade of a manchineel tree.

"For him to love you," she said.

I heard Mimi laugh. I looked toward the wagon. The two horses were asleep on their feet. "You prayed for your father to love *me?*"

Hortense looked confused. "Was that bad?"

"Stay," I told Mimi, hoisting Hortense up onto the wagon seat, taking care (without success) not to soil my skirts on the muddy wagon wheels. "We're fine back here," I added, handing two oranges forward, one for Mimi and one for Morin.

The road leading out of Trois-Ilets was as rough as I remembered it, the wagon almost overturning. Before long, we came to my family's cane-fields, black with ash. In the distance, a field yet to be burned, still in chaos from the harvest, and beyond that, newly planted coffee trees.

"All of this belongs to my family," I told Hortense.

"It's burned." She stood on my lap to look.

"They do that after the harvest, to scare away bugs and snakes."

"Snakes!"

At the river we had to get down. The horses refused to put hoof to the old wooden bridge. They had to be coaxed and in the end whipped, but finally they made a bolt for it, cantering across in a lather of fear, the wagon clattering behind them.

We climbed back in. I noticed a gang of field-slaves in big straw hats labouring in a field—replanting likely. "Do you recognize anyone?" I asked Mimi.

"I can't see that far." Mimi threw an orange peel into the canebrake. "Turn left up ahead," she told Morin, adjusting her skirt. "By the cabbage-palms." She turned to me and grinned.

The horses slowed, beginning their ascent up the gentle slope. The road was more overgrown than I remembered it, the moss hanging heavy from the trees, reminding me of dreams. As we passed the kitchen gardens, several of the Negro women waved.

"They aren't wearing tops." Hortense pressed her hands over her eyes.

"It's hot working in the sun." My own clothes were already damp, the heat was so intense. As we neared the homestead it began to rain, a soft, cooling shower more like a mist. I fussed over Hortense, cleaning her face, attempting to push her unruly hair under her new hat.

"It that it?" she asked, pushing her hat back off her head. I turned as we pulled up in front of the old stone building—the sucrerie my family called home. I nodded wordlessly, climbing down, looking upon the graceless structure with a stranger's critical eyes. The massive stone chimney seemed to tower above us, ominous and dark from the rain. One corner of the verandah roof had given slightly.

Where were Mother and Father? I searched for some sign in the windows, but they had all been shuttered against the midday sun.

It was Da Gertrude who came first to greet us, running down the path from the crushing hut screaming, "They're here! They're here!" Her big arms circling like a windmill, her big lower lip quivering, catching first

Mimi and then me in a hug so hard it forced the air right out of me. She twirled me in her hands, admiring my Parisian finery. "Lord, girl, look at you now, a *lady!* But you're too thin!" She was weeping now, uttering cries in the African tongue, a musical clicking sound. She had aged in the nine years I had been away, her face etched with lines like crevasses in an ancient hillside. But her eyes were bright, her spirit as clear as my heart remembered. In her arms I felt myself a girl again.

And then, magically it seemed, we were surrounded by all the household slaves, by the familiar faces of my youth, crying out in the cooling mist. One after another they took us in their arms, did joyful little dances all about us. "Oh, look at you both, so elegant! Look! Even the little girl is in ribbons! So precious in her little hat!" Sylvester was there, elderly now, as comical as ever, his pipe extinguished by the rain. My heart was full to bursting with the love I felt around me. I had been starving for them all and hadn't known it.

Embarrassed by the choking emotion that had welled up in me, I searched in my velvet bag for a handkerchief. "And this is Hortense," I said, wiping my eyes.

"Oh, and when she smiles!" Da Gertrude pulled a section of cane stalk out of her pocket. "Have you ever sucked on a sugarcane?"

Hortense regarded the stalk suspiciously, looked at me for approval.

I kissed her dirty cheek. "Chew it. It's like a comfit."

With a rush of wind, the gentle mist turned to pelting drops of rain. I ran with Hortense for the shelter of the verandah, Da Gertrude chasing after.

"Mother? Father?" I lowered Hortense to the ground. I was puzzled by their absence.

"Your father's not well." Da Gertrude pushed open the heavy door to the refinery. She'd taken Hortense's hand, wooed my girl with her big-hearted magic. I followed, stepped inside.

The floor of the boiling room was littered with cane stalks. I was struck by the familiar scent of sugar syrup, the sound of buzzing flies. I saw the stairs that descended into the basement—to the room where I had been punished. Had that really happened?

I heard voices up above. I headed up the rickety wooden stairs.

It was dark in the foyer. "Mother?"

She appeared before me, as stern as I remembered her, but for her eyes, which were etched with something different, I knew not what. She was wearing a brown muslin gown of a simple design and a white fluted cap.

"Look at you." She took my hands in hers. She stood back and appraised me. "You're thin, Rose."

"And you." She was so much older than I remembered her, older than I'd ever imagined her being.

"Only *you* look like a lady of fashion."

Her hands felt rough, dry. "Have you seen Hortense?" I asked.

"The child?"

We both turned at the sound of Hortense's giggle. Da Gertrude came striding in, my girl on her shoulders. Hortense was grinning, one hand covering Da Gertrude's left eye, the other still clutching the sugarcane stalk. "I used to carry you this way, Rose," Da Gertrude said. "Remember?"

I smiled, reaching up to take Hortense. I cradled her in my arms, turned to Mother. "My girl," I said.

Mother reached out a finger, stroked the smooth skin on Hortense's arm. Hortense was suddenly still, sucking on the cane stalk. "She's lovely." Mother's eyes were glistening. "She takes after her father, doesn't she."

"Yes."

"I'm not a man!" Hortense said.

I let her down. "She's big for her age," I said, "healthy—quite bright. And *active*," I sighed, watching Hortense spinning circles on the slippery wooden floor.

"Having a child in the house will be good for us," Mother said. "We are all of us too old here."

I heard a voice boom from the parlour: "This must be Yeyette's girl!" It was Father, addressing Hortense no doubt, who had spun into the other room.

"No," I heard Hortense answer. "Who is Yeyette?"

"You don't know!"

I followed Mother into the parlour. There was Father, leaning on a tasselled cane, addressing Hortense. He was wearing a patched hunting jacket over a night-dress. At his feet snuffled one of the pugs, now white around the muzzle and quite thin. Grandmother Sannois had died almost three years ago, the other pug the year after.

"She's not Yeyette any more," Mother said. "She's a woman now."

"Father!" I kissed him on both cheeks, taking care not to bump his cane. He looked so weak—so fragile. "You look wonderful," I said.

Father looked down at Hortense. "Now you would never do such a thing, would you? Tell an ugly old man that he looked wonderful. The *wonder* is I'm still alive." He paused for a moment, studied my face. "My—but you have become so very, very lovely." He turned to my mother. "Claire—who would have thought that that scrappy, plump, dirty-faced little thing would ever have turned into this!" He swung one hand wide, too wide, for he began to lose his balance.

Quickly Mother was at his side, one arm around his back, her shoulder braced under his arm. Father started to cough. "You're too flamboyant, Joseph," she said, pounding his back with her fist.

Da Gertrude appeared with a tray. "Some juice—and sugar cakes," she announced. "But I bet you don't like sugar cakes," she said to Hortense.

"Yessss." Hortense swung her skirts. "Yes I do!"

Mother nodded toward the hall. "Manette's in her room, Rose."

"Go," Father said, waving me away. "She's been waiting."

"Rose, she is—" Mother didn't finish her sentence.

I traced my way through the dark rooms, thick with the scent of sugar syrup, the musky faint scent of mould, the sound of flies buzzing at every window. At the end of the narrow passage was the door to Manette's room. I stood for a moment before opening it. I remembered standing before this same door, listening to the sound of Manette weeping. Now, there was only silence.

It was dark in the room. One shutter had been closed. Manette was lying on top of the bedclothes in a stained white muslin shift, her long dark hair dishevelled, wet tendrils curling around her neck. A plump Negro girl I didn't recognize was sitting at the foot of her bed, fanning her lazily with a palm-tree leaf.

I approached the bed slowly. I tried to put on a brave face, but tears broke free as soon as I caught my sister's eyes. I pretended my tears were tears of joy—but they were not. Oh, my little Manette, how she has wizened and aged, an old crone in a young woman's body.

Manette spoke slowly, pushing the words from her with some effort. "Rose . . ." She stopped. She took my hand. "I'm sorry," she whispered.

I laid my head on her hollow belly. Already I knew there was no hope.

# *In which storms rage*

*August 17, 1788.*

As the Carib chief approached, the slaves went running. He stood in the laneway in his loose shirt made of old flour sacks, his long hair blowing in the wind. Mother stood to greet him.

It was a windy morning, without mosquitoes. The leaves of the gum tree fluttered onto the ground.

I could overhear little, understand nothing. He spoke to Mother in his language, an ancient tongue beyond my understanding, and my mother answered him in kind, slowly and with some effort. He turned and left, the back of his shirt stained with sweat.

I went down to the verandah.

"There's a storm coming." Mother stood looking out toward Morne Croc-Souris.

"Does he always come?"

"Once before he came." She turned toward the sucrerie. "Before the big storm."

The big storm. Seventeen-sixty-six. I was only three at the time, yet even now, when a wind rises, a sick feeling comes over me. All through my childhood, I'd heard stories of the wind that had blown our house away, the rain that drowned an entire town, the wave that swallowed a hundred ships whole, not even a shoe washed up on the shore.

"We must see to the shutters," Mother said.

The morning hours turned frantic. The field-gang was called in, the house-slaves alerted, the children in the garden crew located, the animals put back in their stalls.

After the midday meal, the air thickened. The wind howled. A wood bucket on the verandah clattered across the stones. Drops of rain splashed hard against the shutters. A chicken screeched, caught in the rising gale.

We descended into the stone basement, the air heavy with the odour of rotting potatoes. I was sickened for a moment entering that dark room—the room in which I had been kept as a girl, the room of my imprisonment. The bed was still there. The three-legged table was gone. I reached up to make sure the shutters were tightly fastened.

Sylvester carried Manette down the narrow steps, let her down gently on the bed. She looked around dreamily. Mother put the pug dog down and arranged the bedclothes over her. Mimi and I sat on a straw mat, our backs against the rough stone wall. Da Gertrude squeezed in beside me, trying to hold on to Hortense, who nevertheless wiggled free to chase a lizard. Father squatted by the door drinking pétépié from a bottle, his cane by his side.

Everyone was crowding in, the house-slaves and their children in with us, the slave-master and the field slaves in the other basement room.

A blast of wind rattled the window. The slaves in the other room began to chant.

"I want to go in there," Hortense said.

"What happened to the lizard?"

"He lost his tail and ran away. I want to find Max."

"See if Max can come in here." I wanted Hortense near me.

"You're letting Hortense go in there?" Mother had her Bible open on her lap. The chanting in the other room had grown louder. Someone had started beating on a drum. "I wish they'd stop," she sighed, closing her eyes.

"She's gone to find a friend. She'll be back."

Mother started to say something but then there was a terrible roaring sound. The roof beam above us cracked. Mother clutched her cross.

I looked over at Da Gertrude. Her upper lip was beaded with sweat. I thought of the dark nights I had trembled in her arms, suckled her milk, slept in her bed. When I was an infant she'd protected me from the ants that had infested our island, swarming the hills and valleys, consuming everything in their path. She'd held me during every storm, singing prayers to the howling winds. I took her hand.

"So now it is *you* who comforts me," she said.

We emerged at dawn, squinting against the sun, faint from terror and constant prayer. Four chickens were perched in an uprooted orange tree. Deep cracks had been etched in the earth, like a network of snakes. Everywhere a thick carpet of torn trees and bushes—even the giant kapok tree had fallen, crashing across a river now raging with debris. The devastation was everywhere, pink and pure in the early morning light.

Hortense began to cry. "My cricket cage!"

"Hush," I said. We had survived.

*Later.*
We spent all this day picking through splinters. The slave huts have been destroyed. There has been considerable damage to the stables and the crushing hut as well. The stone kitchen shack only suffered two broken windows and a deluge of water. Two horses, nine cows and a goat are missing. The sow was badly injured and had to be slaughtered, so weak she did not even squeal.

*August 19.*
We've received word from Fort-Royal. The roof of Uncle Tascher's house was blown off and the furniture ruined. But no one hurt, thank God.

*September 14.*
Mail—*at last.*

*July 16, 1788—Fontainebleau*
*Darling!*
*Two weeks after you set sail we had a dreadful hailstorm—in July, the hottest month of the year! Imagine. Really, we begin to think France is being*

visited by a destroying angel.* The ice stones were so big they killed birds and ripped the branches off the oak trees in the Luxembourg gardens. My servants are blaming the priests, for ineffective influence.

My darling pixie of a granddaughter Émilie, quite tall for seven, continues to thrive. I had Eugène over the other day as well—the two are a charm for the vapours.

*A million kisses, your loving Aunt Fanny*


*July 18, 1788—Fontainebleau*
*Dear Rose,*

We've been busy attending to finance and health. It is maddening how much time these two matters consume. Fortunately, with respect to health at least, I am beginning to make progress. A doctor suggested I take purgatives and clysters, followed by Peruvian bark. I am following his program with excellent results. I am enclosing three ounces of this bark at a cost of ten livres, which I will add to your father's account. I urge you to get Joseph (and your sister?) to take it. As well, restrain him from consuming milk foods and salt meat—not to mention spirits.

The situation here worsens. . . . there was a dreadful ice storm which destroyed the crops, just when everyone had been praying for grain. No doubt this is God's punishment for the riots in Paris. My chambermaid's brother vows he saw King Henry IV's statue bleeding.

Do not neglect to say your prayers—morning and night—as well as your hours. Have you talked to your father regarding the accounts? We anxiously await news.

*Your loving Aunt Désirée*


*July 5, 1788—Paris*
*Dear Rose,*

A quick note (I have a meeting to attend)—I have decided to enter the realm of politics. It is a labour I do willingly; my country needs me.

*Your husband, Alexandre Beauharnais*
Note—Eugène is well.

---

* Fanny is plagiarizing, something she was known to do with regularity. The statement about the destroying angel was in fact made by the great economist Mirabeau.

*Sunday*
*Chère Maman,*
   *Ice came out of the sky. Are you coming home yet?*
                                          *A thousand kisses, Eugène*


*January 29, 1789.*
A talk with Mother, regarding the accounts. She is reluctant to bring in anyone from outside.

"What can be the harm?" I insisted. Father wasn't able, Mother was unwilling and I had no experience, much less knowledge.

"Our only problem is your father's debts," she said. "His *vice*."

But at last she relented. She has agreed to allow me to consult with Monsieur de Couvray, an accountant of merit in Fort-Royal.


*Monday, February 16.*
I have been reviewing the accounts in preparation for my trip to Fort-Royal. There are a number of mysteries. Father was blustery at first, refusing to respond to my questions, accusing me of ignorance. Gently, I persisted, pointing out discrepancies. At last he broke down. Much of the money had gone to cover gambling debts—but not all. Some covered mistakes he had made managing the plantation. It was the blunders he was ashamed to admit, not the gambling losses—the "debts of honour" he insists are a result of courage, not weakness. "It takes strength to play deep," he said, "to risk one's fortune on the turn of a card." (I refrained from pointing out that it had not been *his* fortune he'd put at risk.)

In spite of his disclosures, there was a sizeable portion left unexplained. "There must be more, Father."

He confessed: four years ago he'd had an amourette with a sewing-woman in Rivière Salée. The woman had given birth. He was beholden to look after her.

I didn't know what to say. "Did she give you a son?" I asked finally. He'd always wanted a son.

"*Another* daughter."

I had a half-sister.*

"She's almost three, cute."

"Does Mother know?"

Father nodded. "Your mother is a saint," he said.


*Tuesday, March 17—Fort-Royal.*

Hortense, Mimi and I arrived in Fort-Royal shortly before noon, splattered with mud. Hortense and I changed before joining my aunt and uncle for the midday meal. After, my aunt excused herself, "for my beauty nap," she said. Then Hortense and her cousins were dispatched with their nannies on an outing to the shore, giving me an opportunity to talk privately with my uncle.

I took a sheet of paper from my basket. "There are two individuals I would like to consult while I am here. Perhaps you could tell me how they might be reached."

Uncle Tascher studied the names, twisting the point of his enormous moustache. "Monsieur de Couvray? It is likely that I will see him this very evening, at the Masonic meeting. If you like, I could set up a meeting."

"Excellent." The palms of my hands were damp. "And the other . . . ?" I asked.

"Monsieur William Browder?" Uncle Tascher looked up. "An English name—I recall seeing it somewhere. Oh, yes—*Captain* Browder. He's enlisted in the navy, I believe, as a translator if I'm not mistaken. I can't imagine what benefit consulting him would be."

"His family used to be our neighbours," I said, my voice tight. "There's a field that has always been shared for grazing, a common— until now, that is. The current tenants have claimed it entirely for their own use."

"But surely this is a matter for the courts."

"A costly procedure, although perhaps a necessary one. In any case, I will require documents, information—"

* *Marie-Josephine Benaguette, "Fifine," born March 17, 1786, to Marie-Louise Benaguette. Eventually Rose's mother took the girl into her own home and in 1806 Rose, as Empress, provided her with a dowry of sixty thousand livres.*

A butler with silver hoops in his ears came to the door, nodded to Uncle Tascher, and disappeared.

"If you'll excuse me," Uncle Tascher said, rising. "My presence is required at Government House." He handed the paper back to me. "My secretary, Monsieur Dufriche, will be able to tell you how Captain Browder may be reached."

I retired to my room. The chambermaid, a girl with dirty hands and an unpleasant odour, helped me take off my dress. My petticoats were damp from the heat. I asked the girl to return in an hour and stretched out under the canopy of gauze netting. A gold cross hung from the bedcurtains.

Forgive me, I prayed.

# *In which I confront the past*

*March 18, 1789.*

I was seated at the writing desk in Uncle's study when Captain Browder was announced, earlier than expected. "Tell him to come in." I smoothed the lace ruffles over the bodice of my silk chemise. Suddenly it seemed too formal.

I opened a book, a volume of Greek history, in order to give the appearance of industry. I cannot begin to transcribe the tumult of my thoughts. I feared I would love him; feared he would disappoint me. Neither thought gave my heart ease.

The leather of my chair creaked as I turned. William stood in the doorway, a shabby black-plumed hat in his hand. His unpowdered black hair was secured at the back with a ribbon. His frock coat, ill-fitting, was patched at one elbow. I remembered my mother's words: béké-goyave.

"Captain Browder," I said. I extended my hand.

William crossed the room, bowed. "Madame la vicomtesse." He smelled of horses.

I withdrew my hand, more for fear he would notice the dampness of my palm than from any sense of propriety. "How good to see you. Please, sit down," I began, the worn phrases affording comfort. "Would you care for a brandy?" I asked.

"No, thank you." He sat down on the stool by the door to the garden. The stool was too short for him. He turned his hat in his hands, studying me.

I looked away. I had forgotten how unnaturally blue his eyes were. "I was grieved to learn of your mother's death," I said. Hanged, it was rumoured, by her own—

"She got what she wanted," he said.

I was disarmed by the bitterness in his voice.

"To be free of it all." He flung his hat onto a low table next to him.

*Freedom.* William's God. His was a life of the sea, a life of freedom, no doubt. Freedom from comfort, freedom from love?

"Did you find happiness, Rose?" he demanded.

"Yes. . . ." I paused, shrugged. "No. My husband and I have separated," I said.

"I'm not surprised."

My cheeks burned. It seemed the entire island was aware of Alexandre's misconduct, Alexandre's accusations.

"Did you love him?" he asked boldly. Too boldly, I thought.

"I was willing to love him," I answered finally.

"That's not the same, is it."

"Your dimples are still there, I see," I said, changing the subject. I felt I had made a mistake.

"So my daughters tease me."

"And your wife?"

He smiled. For a moment I saw the William I knew. "She puts up with me," he said.

"Is that so very difficult?"

"I have yearnings, she says."

"Yes." I studied his face. He still had that boyish look.

"Do you ever think of that fortune you were told?" he asked.

"It comes to me in dreams sometimes." *You will be unhappily married.*

"Good dreams?"

"Bad dreams." Terrible dreams.

"I have a confession to make," he said, after a moment of hesitation. "I wasn't going to come today. But then I changed my mind. I decided I wanted to prove something."

He was interrupted by the sound of a child's voice, footsteps approaching. Mimi and Hortense appeared at the door. William stood.

"Hortense would like . . . to go down to the pier, to watch the boats," Mimi stuttered, her face revealing her surprise.

"That would be fine. Captain Browder, this is my daughter, Hortense.

And you remember Mimi? Madame Mimi we call her now." For Mimi was clearly in a family way.

"Of course I remember." He bowed.

"Grand-maman says that it is not proper to bow to slaves." Hortense pushed her straw hat back off her forehead.

"Hortense! It's not proper for a child to lecture an adult." At six, Hortense had an overly rigid sense of right and wrong and seemed intent on informing everyone on how they should behave.

"Perhaps Captain Browder is what we call 'A New Thinker,'" Mimi explained to my daughter. "Men like that do things differently."

"Oooooh." Hortense regarded William with apprehension.

William nodded. "I might even stand on my head."

Hortense studied him for a long moment and then let out a little laugh.

"Forgive us for interrupting—I can see you are busy." Mimi backed toward the door, pulling Hortense along with her.

"Busy doing *what?*" I heard Hortense demand in the other room.

"I must apologize." I tidied the papers on the desk. "My daughter was rude." I had seen a quill earlier, but now I could not find it—it was not in its holder. I was surprised to note that my hands were trembling slightly.

"I should be going. I shouldn't be here." William was standing by the window, looking out at the garden.

"I did want to talk to you about that field."

William withdrew a document from the pocket of his waistcoat. "This will give you what you need to know." It was a letter of agreement regarding use of the common.

"Do you wish me to return it?" I stood.

"I have no need for it."

"You were saying something, before we were interrupted."

"I don't recall."

I paused. "That you came here today to prove something."

"It wasn't important."

"That wasn't my impression."

He cleared his throat, looked at me. "I came here today with the intention of proving that I no longer loved you."

In the silence, I heard a crow call out four times. I thought of all the nights I'd dreamt of him, the conversations I'd had with him in my mind. The questions I'd wanted to ask, the stories I'd wanted to tell. But the man who stood before me was not William. "I think you should go, Captain Browder," I said.

Captain Browder took his hat. "I was mistaken," he said, turning at the door. "I still love you. Good day, Madame."

*Later.*

Monsieur de Couvray was shown into Uncle's study shortly after four. When he recovered from the discomfort of having to discuss matters of business with a woman, we set to work going over the La Pagerie accounts, reviewing the assets, the land. The low sugar yield indicates exhaustion of the soil, as I suspected; certain fields must be allowed to go to flower and to be replanted from seed.

His other suggestions were less palatable, and I suspect will be so to Mother and Father as well. He observed that there were a number of children in our slave population, our "thinking property" was the term he used. "It is more economical to buy slaves than to breed them," he said.

"It is not intentionally done."

"Perhaps measures should be taken to . . . to inhibit production." He wiped his palms on his buckskin breeches. "Overall, looking at these figures, it is clear that the cost of keep is high in proportion to the work accomplished."

I knew this to be true. Several of the slaves were now either infirm or elderly, I explained.

"If a slave has ceased to be productive," he said, "it is wise to encourage him . . . to *go on*." He puffed on his pipe; the fire had gone out.

"Go?" I was confused. "Go *where*?"

He circled his fingers impatiently. "You know. . . ."

"You don't mean . . . killed?" Surely I'd misunderstood.

"No! Goodness. I wouldn't use *that* word. After all, the methods are humane, and if they are suffering—"

"Monsieur, I do believe my mother and father would be loath to employ such a practice, and I, for one, loathe to suggest it." We talked a short time longer, for the sake of form. I showed him to the door.

*Saturday, March 21.*
I was packing to return to Trois-Islets when Mimi brought me a letter. "Did this come to the house?" I asked, alarmed. I took a seat by the window.

Mimi shook her head no, her dangling earrings making a tinkling sound. "In the market. He asked me to give it to you."

I broke the wax seal.

*Madame Beauharnais:*
*I have discovered information regarding your family's use of the common. It is urgent that you be apprised of it.*
*At your convenience.*

*Your servant, Captain Browder*

I put the letter on the side-table.

"He asked if it would be possible to arrange a meeting," Mimi whispered.

I looked down at my lap. My hands looked like the hands of an old woman.

"Something about a green flash." She looked at me with a puzzled expression.

I held my breath. "Tell him no," I said.

*April 2—Trois-Ilets.*
We've been back in Trois-Ilets for over a week. A feeling of disquiet continues to haunt me. As a youth one dreams of love; by the time one wakes, it is too late.

I've been going for walks in the morning, after chores, in search of solace. In the cool of the forest, my spirit is soothed but not healed. Often I head down the river, toward the sea, but this morning I followed the trace toward Morne Croc-Souris. Before long I had come upon it—

the clearing by the side of the river, the wattle-and-daub shack collapsed, a frangipani bush flowering where the door had been.

*You will be unhappily married.*

Not far from the rubble I saw a crude wooden cross stuck in a mound of dirt covered over with stones. A grave.

*You will be widowed.*

A wind through the forest shook the leaves, a bird called out warning. I approached the pile of stones. The ground was littered with crumpled pieces of paper, feathers, a chunk of bone.

*You will be Queen.*

I felt a cool wind come through me. I was possessed by a light sensation, a feeling of floating on water.

*You will make a beautiful queen*, a boy had once told me.

# In which two worlds claim my heart

*January 4, 1789—Paris*
*Chère Maman,*
    *It has been cold for three weeks. I saw a dead man, frozen. We go walking on the river. When are you coming home?*

                            *A thousand kisses, your son Eugène*


*April 3, 1789—Paris*
*Dear Rose,*
    *A quick note—I have been elected to the Estates General, a representative for the Blois nobility. A spirit of optimism has permeated our land. It's electrifying!*

                    *Your husband, Deputy Alexandre Beauharnais*
*Note—The drawing of Hortense was well executed. Your technique is improving, although the shading would have been more effective in a charcoal, I thought.*
    *And another—I enclose a pamphlet by Sieyès,* What Is the Third Estate? *I recommend you study it.*


*April 15, 1789—Paris*
*Darling!*
    *I've moved back to Paris—it's so thrilling here now! It's the "Roman Republic" all over again—the Goddess of Love rules. Everywhere one goes*

*there is great celebrating, dancing around bonfires. To walk down the street is to become intoxicated by profound sentiment, embraced by everyone one meets, rich and poor, young and old alike.*

*My salon will never be the same. Where before we talked of Beauty, we now talk of Equal Representation.*

*Your loving Aunt Fanny*

*Note—How can you stand being away from the opera for so long?*

*August 11.*

I've been reading the journals that came over on the last boat. I was saddened to learn that the Dauphin died—yet no one seemed to even notice, much less care. I grieve for the Queen. A boy so like Eugène.

*Eugène.* I grow ill with a longing to hold him again. . . . I have been in Martinico for one year.

*July 20, 1789—Fontainebleau*
*Dear Rose,*

*Both Alexandre and François have been elected to the Estates General. Now whenever the two brother-deputies visit on feast-days, they have a frightful row. The Marquis refuses to even discuss political concerns any more, claiming to find "all that" distasteful. "All that" will go away soon, he says, and everything will be back the way it should. He burned all the books by Rousseau in the house, even the signed copy of* Discourse on Inequality. *I hate to think what is going to happen when Alexandre discovers it missing.*

*At least we aren't in Paris—there are twenty thousand troops there now. The strumpets are getting rich, no doubt. As well, every beggar and thief in France has come to the city, swarming at the slightest opportunity. Each district—all sixty of them—has drawn up its own army to keep order. I've taken to carrying a pistol in my bag, even here in Fontainebleau.*

*Don't forget your prayers.*

*Your loving Aunt Désirée*

*Note—You've heard about the riot at the Bastille? Fanny promised she would retrieve some of the stones for me. I'll save one for you, if you like.*

*August 10, 1789—Versailles*
*Dear Rose,*

 *What were before disconnected jottings have now become a fluid system of philosophy, an ether that connects the present to the past. I have long understood how the Roman Empire gave way to the feudal system, which in turn gave way to the modern monarchies. Such a study reveals the oppressive nature of our laws. But it is only now that I begin to understand that it is the Roman Republic in all its glory that we seek to rebuild.*

 *Would that my family could understand the profound nature of the task before us. Unfortunately, they are blinded by history and by the traditional greed of our class. In joining with other enlightened nobles (La Rochefoucauld! Lafayette! The Duc d'Orléans!) to renounce our feudal privileges, I was forced to choose between my family, on the one hand, and my country, on the other. Oh, what a night of profound heroism! What sublime sacrifice! May the night of August 4 burn in my heart for ever.*

 *The sacrifice of my father's regard, of my brother's fraternal embrace is a loss I must bear. The Revolution demands that each citizen make a personal offering for the good of the Nation. I submit with tears of virtue in my eyes, knowing that my pain will be rewarded.*

   *With a noble heart, your husband, Deputy Alexandre Beauharnais*
      *"an honorable and virtuous Republican"*
*Note—I urge you to study the pamphlets I have forwarded, open your heart to the truths you will find therein. One—*A Few Thoughts on the Nature of Reason & Revolution*—I wrote myself. I have worded it simply so that a woman might understand, for I am not of that group that believes women incapable of abstract reasoning.*


*Sunday*
*Chère Maman,*

 *I have my own sword now. My tutor says I might need it. When are you coming home?*

         *A thousand kisses, Eugène*

*December 9.*

A créole man was found dead in a clearing in the woods near Fort-Royal, together with the head of a butchered pig. Blood had been spilled over his hands. Three days before a slave had died on his plantation, imprisoned in a sweltering hut in the sun without food and water.

I hear drumming in the slave village. The moon casts a ghostly light. I see a fire up on the hill, hear shouting and singing. I know the song:

*Never, never, I'll not forget the ranks of Africa.*

*Never, never, I'll not forget their children.*

I despair.


*October 10, 1789—Fontainebleau*
*Dear Rose,*

*The Marquis and I have not been well. Our nerves suffer from the distressing reports in the journals.*

*I am ashamed of my sex. Women—thousands of them, it has been reported—forced our King and Queen to move into that horrid palace in Paris, and now everyone of quality is talking of leaving France. Even the King's brothers have fled, even Madame de Polignac, the royal governess, abandoning her charges. (How could she do that?)*

*But that isn't all of it. Monsieur Ogé, that mulatto from Saint-Domingue, went before the Assembly to demand equal rights for mulattoes—and succeeded! One delegate even suggested that the slaves be freed!\* Everyone, it seems, has lost their reason. If the slaves were allowed to go free, we'd be penniless!*

*Pray for us. . . .*

*Your loving Aunt Désirée*
*Note—Fanny's son Claude and his wife have had a baby girl. \*\* Send your condolences.*


\* *This delegate was hanged when he returned to Saint-Domingue.*
\*\* *Stephanie Beauharnais was later to be adopted by Napoleon and wed to the Grand Duke of Baden, which made her a Grand Duchess of the Court of Würtemberg.*

*January 23, 1790.*

Morin, Mimi's lover and the father of the child she is carrying, was killed in a riot in Fort-Royal. There is nothing I can say to comfort her, for it was men of my race who murdered him.

I stood at the door to her whitewashed hut watching her crumple into the arms of the slave women, listened to their collective moans—and I, who am like a sister to her, was forced to turn away, tears running down my cheeks.

Drums in the mountains. As a child, the steady beat lulled me into sleep. But tonight I do not feel comfort in such sounds. Tonight I hear anger, and a terrible, terrible grief.


*November 5, 1789—Lake Maggiore*
*Darling!*

*Michel de Cubières and I are in a delightful alpine spa. (Remember Michel? The poet with the big lips?) Every evening we play faro in a casino in the village, where a shocking amount of money changes hands. But what is life if one is not prepared to cast all to the winds? One must be brave to be so foolish.*

*The Austrians have been threatening to set up a "cordon sanitaire" across the mountains to keep "dangerous ideas" from coming over from France. Were it not for my mindless chatter and Michel staying quiet—for once!—I doubt very much that they would have let us into their backward little paradise. Fortunately, they neglected to look in the basket that contained the political pamphlets Michel intends to distribute on the streets of Rome.*

*Take care of yourself, darling. I hear your husband has become a Hero of the Revolution. How dashing!*

*Your devoted Aunt Fanny*
*Note—Claude's wife had a girl. He's not taking it well, which disappoints me. I thought we were beyond all that.*


*February 1.*

Mimi lost her child. I went to see her in the infirmary, but she was in a fever and did not comprehend that it was me. I sat beside her for a time, cooling her with strips of linen soaked in rum. She was talking in a dream: *Never, never, I'll not forget . . . Never, never . . .*

Oh, my dear Mimi, how my heart goes out to her. I pray, I pray.

*November 11, 1789—Paris*
*Dear Rose,*

*I have been elected one of three secretaries to the Assembly. I am both honoured and challenged. Fate, surely, is the author of a scheme of such heroic dimensions.*

*I am enclosing a copy of the* Declaration of the Rights of Man, *suitable for framing. I consider involvement in its creation one of the achievements of my life.* \*

*Your husband, Deputy Alexandre Beauharnais*

*Sunday—Fontainebleau*
*Chère Maman,*

*Papa's name is in the news-sheets. I've not seen him for two weeks. Are you ever coming back?*

*A thousand kisses, your son Eugène*

*February 3.*
Mimi has emerged from her fever, wrapped in sorrow like a ghost. The slave women hover around her protectively whenever I approach. "Go away! You curse her!" I do not persist.

*December 7, 1790—Chambéry*
*Darling,*

*The Italians were positively* wild *about my poem "To Frederick the Great*

---

\* *France took the American Bill of Rights one step further. Where Americans proclaimed men free and equal in* their *country, the French proclaimed men free and equal* everywhere.

on the Death of Voltaire." That and one of my novels (Abailard the Pretender, *wouldn't you know—the most naughty of all my works*) is being translated into Italian and will be published there soon. I'm a writer of the world now!

How is my goddaughter Hortense? I am enclosing a leather-bound copy of Erasmus's Manners for Children *for her. It is, at the least, egalitarian. Encourage her to copy the lovely script—the first step toward becoming a writer.*

As you perhaps already know, Marie and François have separated, for reasons of philosophy. Philosophy! At least when Claude (God rest his soul*) and I parted, we did so for reasons of sentiment.

*Your loving Aunt Fanny*

February 23.

Mimi has been put on the field-gang, Mother informed me this afternoon.

"How could you do that! Mimi belongs with *me*, with Hortense!"

Mother put down her needlework. "Apologize for your temper. Mimi asked to be put in the fields."

"But *why?*" I could not comprehend. Field-work was a killing labour.

"I can only presume it is because she has turned against us, because of our race. Were it not for your sensibilities, Rose, I would have sold her, or at least had her whipped. Hate is a dangerous thing in a slave."

I left the room in tears.

December 17, 1790—Fontainebleau
Dear Rose,

*The Marquis and I have suffered a collapse of nerves due to the distressing news about François and Marie. The Marquis is terribly upset, going on about the morals of the young, the stain upon the family name, the lack of commitment to values. I hold my tongue, but in my heart I grieve: for is this*

* Claude de Beauharnais, the Marquis's brother and Fanny's ex-husband, died December 25, 1784.

*not the fruit of our own sins? I have been going to mass twice daily and to my confessor weekly. I urge you to do the same.*

*Your loving Aunt Désirée*

*Note—I am enclosing a bill for one livre, the new paper money we are required to use now, but it's not worth one sou—hold on to your gold.*


Wednesday, March 3.

The island press has been restricted for fear that any further mention of "liberty" would be dangerous. Even the journals we receive from Paris must be hidden away.

"Your husband's letters should be burned," Mother said. She does not approve of Alexandre's views. "As well as Madame Fanny's."

"Along with her novel, perhaps?"

"Indeed," Mother sputtered, crossing herself.

I smiled, for I have seen her glancing into it when she thought no one was looking.


*December 30, 1789—Fontainebleau*

*Dear Rose,*

*Thank you for the lovely Christmas gifts—the Marquis loved his bamboo cane and already the bottle of La Pagerie rum has been consumed. I adore the silver bangles, but especially the set of enamel buttons painted with island scenes—they brought on a feeling of reverie in me. And a crate of coffee beans! What indulgence!*

*Eugène loved all the presents you sent (really, Rose, you must try to refrain from such excess), but the item that pleased him the most—to our own discomfort, I confess—was the foghorn made of shell.*

*Your uncle reports that you have been diligent in your efforts to organize the finances and the management of the properties. You must be having some success, for already we have received a banknote. This money is very badly needed. You can't imagine how expensive everything has become. It is impossible to live on even twelve thousand livres a year now. Nom de Dieu!*

*How is my brother's health? How is your sister Manette? I have sent my gardener on a pilgrimage to Chartres to seek cures. He is devout; I have hope of some success.*

*It has been a gloomy holiday season. No one entertains any more—everyone stays home.*

*Remember—don't neglect your prayers. . . .*

*Your loving Aunt Désirée*


*Christmas Day*
*Chère Maman,*
*Thank you for the foghorn. I have decided to become a sailor. That way I can come see you and my sister Hortense.*

*Eugène*


*May 21.*

As I write at this little table in my room, listening to the heavy dripping of the rain, I wonder if it's possible I ever left this island. France seems like a dream to me, more distant than my childhood.

I sleep with Eugène's miniature under my pillow. Tonight I could not find it. Fear takes my heart—will I *ever* see him again?

## *In which we flee under cannon fire*

*June 3, 1790.*
A mulatto uprising in Saint-Pierre. In his sermon this morning, Father Droppet questioned the existence of a soul in the Negro. After church, talk of weapons. I sleep with a pistol on my side-table.

*July 30.*
Today Mother said, "You must go, Rose—take your daughter, return to France." Her eyes were dark, I could not see her thoughts. "This is no place to raise a child." She pushed a cloth bag across the table at me.

It was a bag of coins—the coins she counted so religiously every day. "I cannot." I pushed the bag away. How could I abandon her with violence threatening, with Father and Manette so ill?

"The English are going to attack. If you don't go now, you will never see your son again. . . ."

Tears came to my eyes. "But—"

"I will not mourn *you!*" And then, her voice low, almost a whisper, "I will not bury *all* my daughters!"

*Later.*
With a heavy heart I have written Uncle Tascher, asking if it is possible to obtain passage to France. . . .

*That evening.*

Uncle Tascher sent back a prompt reply. It is difficult to get passage to France at this time, he said, but not impossible. The openings come quickly, without notice. I must be in Fort-Royal with my movables packed if I am serious about leaving. He advises me to come immediately, for there are rumours of a blockade. "In these turbulent times," he wrote philosophically, sadly I thought, "nothing is as it seems, nothing is as it should be."

*August 1, noon.*

Mother was on the verandah when I went to her this morning, darning socks that had been darned many times before. "You are leaving," she said. She looked out over the garden of flowers I'd tended, the blooms drenched by the rain.

I nodded, turned away. I have become weary of tears.

*August 6.*

We've been packing. All day Hortense has been fighting with Da Gertrude over a rag doll she wants to take with her, but Da Gertrude insists it will bring bad luck. "It was out all night in the light of the moon!" she said with great fear.

*August 7.*

This evening, after dinner, I brushed and braided Manette's hair, the dark plaits falling over her shoulders. I read to her from *Paul et Virginie* until she fell asleep. I sat for a time with the book in my lap, the flame from the candle flickering from the breeze from the open window, looking out at the moon rising behind the tangled branches of the mango tree. Manette and I climbed that same tree when we were children. How does one say goodbye?

*Tuesday, August 10.*

I awoke shortly before dawn. As if by some miracle, it had stopped raining. Quietly I slipped down the stairs and out of the sucrerie, down to the bathing pond. I put my chemise and my head handkerchief on the wet rocks and slipped into the clear water, gasping until I became accustomed to the cold. A frog scuttled into the grass, but other than that there was not a sound but for the tree ferns rustling in the breeze. The scent of the orange tree filled the air.

When the turtledoves began to coo, I emerged, heart heavy. It was time. I dressed and made my final rounds, stopping to talk with the house-slaves. To each I gave a livre. I left three louis with the slave-master to divide among the field-hands. I knew Mother would not approve so I asked him not to tell.

I told Da Gertrude to give Mimi my emerald. "Heal her," I said. Open her heart. Da Gertrude began to cry. I wrapped my arms around her. "Go!" she said, pushing me away.

I went to Father's room.

"So," he said.

I sat down on the straight-back chair next to the bed. It was wobbly, for one of its legs kept coming loose and had been secured, not too successfully, with hemp. A foul odour filled the room, a smell I had become accustomed to, "the smell of death," Mother called it. But I had become too immersed in the mechanical routine of Father's care to think of such things.

I took his hand, for I felt comfortless entertaining such thoughts. His skin felt dry, thin—like the delicate texture of a snake's discarded skin. "Is there anything I can get you?" I asked, for my devotion had taken this form: service.

"You've done enough." His eyes were grey. "Enough for a dying man."

I began to protest, uphold some vain lie—but I knew it would be disrespectful to deny him this, the reality of his passing. I nodded. "I will miss you, Father."

"Princess." He squeezed my hand.

The memory of my childhood dreams came back to me then, the enchantment of my father's stories, told to a dream-struck girl in a hammock under a mango tree, fanning herself lazily with a palm-tree leaf. I kissed his cheek. "My King." I swooped into the courtly curtsy he'd taught me as a girl, regally kicking an imaginary train aside as I turned to go.

He was laughing silently as I left. For a moment I saw that spark again. I did not say goodbye.

At the very last I went to Manette, who was asleep. She looked graven, old, her bedclothes tangled. I did not have the courage to waken her. I kissed her forehead and left. I will never see her again.

It was still very early, only eight in the morning, when Sylvester drove the cart around to the front of the sucrerie. I helped Hortense scramble onto the seat. I turned to Mother. "You will come, to France . . . ?" I could not say "after" . . . after Father dies, after Manette.

She clasped my hands, hard. I climbed into the wagon. Sylvester cracked his whip, the horses pulled forward. As we neared the stone wall, I looked back. Mother was no longer there. I watched the house recede, searching for her face in the windows.

*August 13—Fort-Royal.*
Aunt Tascher is frantic, the house in chaos—there are open packing cases in every room. She and the children are moving to the country, she explained. "It's not safe here!" We left our sea trunk in the carriage house—we will be leaving soon too, I hope.

Hortense and I are sharing a room on the third floor. It is hot—but private. I am sitting at a desk in an alcove overlooking the harbour. Through the rain I can dimly make out where the four warships and several merchant ships are moored. Uncle will be home late. He has much trouble now with government matters and the general restiveness in the population. Tonight he will be able to tell us the situation with respect to our departure for France.

*September 3—Government House.*
There have been riots in town. At a fête yesterday, Governor de Vioménil refused to put on a tricolour cockade, claiming that he would prefer to

die a thousand deaths—which resulted in such violence that he was forced to retract his statement and put on the ribbon, "this pledge of peace, union and concord!" he proclaimed. All this to the sound of musket fire over his head.

A Te Deum was sung and all appeared to be at peace again, but even so, Uncle Tascher has insisted that Hortense and I move into Government House. It is safer for us here, he said. We do not go out any more.

*Monday, September 6.*
There has been an uprising. Uncle Tascher imprisoned the revolutionaries, but then the guards released them and opened fire on the town.

I was at Government House when it happened. Governor de Vioménil ran from room to room, yelling at everyone. Madame de Vioménil fell to her knees, praying loudly. I took Hortense up to our room and read to her from *Fables of La Fontaine,* trying to ignore the sounds of musket fire. All the while I was trembling. Then the parlourmaid came running up the stairs with the news that Uncle Tascher had gone to talk to the rebels in the Fort.

Hortense and I ventured back downstairs to the front parlour where everyone had gathered. The messenger who finally arrived from the Fort was a thin man wearing a dirty wig. "Baron Tascher has been taken hostage," he announced theatrically. The rebels had imprisoned my uncle and were threatening to kill him and every person in the town.

I was helped to a chair. "What did he say about Uncle?" Hortense demanded tearfully. "What does 'hostage' mean?"

The governor was frantic. Aides on all sides were trying to offer him advice. His wife ran after him, yelling, "You can't go!"

He stomped into his study and slammed the door. "He is intent on killing himself!" his wife wept. The musket fire began again, shattering what little confidence we had managed.

Soon after the governor left. His plan was to take refuge at Gros Morne, a village on the way to Trinité, and from there gather support to attack. His wife locked herself in her bedchamber and refused to come out.

I lay in my bed in our little room with Hortense in my arms, trying to calm her, listening to the sound of musket and cannon fire, praying for

Uncle Tascher. Not long after Hortense had finally fallen asleep, I was startled by a knocking on the door. "Who is it?" The night candle threw ghostly shadows.

The door opened—it was the chambermaid.

"Is there news?" I whispered, fearing for Uncle Tascher's life.

"A letter from Commander du Braye." She handed me a sealed folded paper. "I was told it was urgent." There was a sudden retort from a cannon, followed by grapeshot.

"Commander du Braye?" A friend of my uncle, Durand du Braye was the commander of the *Sensible*, one of the warships in the harbour. "What time is it?" I asked.

"Five? Six?" she answered sleepily. She set her lantern on the side-table.

Anxiously, I broke the seal. I had difficulty reading the handwriting for there were big blotches of ink on the page. They were going to set to sea, I finally made out. I must join the ship at once. Commander du Braye cautioned me not to tell anyone, *especially* not the servants. One of his crew would be sent to meet me at Shell Point, south of the village.

I looked up at the chambermaid. She had such a sweet expression— how was it possible that she could be my enemy? "That's strange. He regrets to inform me he must stay in the harbour until given permission to leave. Why would he wake me for this?" I asked, colouring.

The girl shrugged, successfully puzzled.

When she closed the door behind her I got out of bed. How was I to get a child to the shore without being noticed? I put on a petticoat and two dresses, one over the other, as best I could. I had some gold coins in a little cloth bag. I tucked this into my bodice. I would not be able to take much. I wrapped my rosary and a night-dress in a handkerchief along with some of Hortense's clothes and the doll she is so attached to.

It was time to wake Hortense. I almost had her dressed before she began to stir, slumping over onto the bed with every move. "We're going on a boat," I whispered to her. "We must be quick." I pulled her to her feet. "Can you walk?" She was too heavy to carry far.

A loud crack from a musket startled her awake. She nodded. I took her hand and opened the door. We slipped down the stairs. In the foyer a footman was snoring into his chest. I put my finger to my lips, indicating to Hortense that she must be very quiet. I heard a shout out on the street.

I stooped down and kissed her, stroking wisps of curls away from her eyes. "We must be brave," I told her, pulling her hood over her head.

She trusted me completely; it broke my heart, her faith. I led her across the room and slowly opened the big oak door. I was relieved that the footman continued to slumber, our footsteps nothing compared to the turmoil outside.

It was as I closed the door behind us that the reality of battle struck me. A smell of sulphur filled the air. Cracks of grapeshot broke the morning silence. I pulled Hortense forward. There was no time for hesitation. We had only to cross the Savane to get to the shore. It had stopped raining. The ground was soggy under our feet. I skirted the mud puddles. I was beginning to think we might make it safely when cannon fire broke out, followed by a shower of mud at our feet.

*Death*, so very close.

It is said that at such moments, time stops. I think I will never forget looking at Hortense then. I saw her as a baby, and as an old woman too. Then the spell broke and I moved, slowly, as if coming out of a dream, the dawn beautiful and clear before us. Suddenly I saw a bright green ribbon of light across the horizon. "Look!" But as quickly as that it was gone.

At Shell Point there was a man waiting in a rowboat. I lowered Hortense into his big hands. There were shots all around as we made our way over the dark water. When we reached the ship, the man climbed the rope ladder up to the deck, Hortense under one arm.

Cannons fired as the sails were unfurled, but by then we were out of reach and I was below deck, Hortense pressed to my fluttering heart.

I felt the sails catch wind, the ship surge forward. The sound of cannon grew faint. From somewhere up above I could hear a man singing, drunken and off-key: *Ah, ça ira, ça ira, ça ira. . . .*

# IV

*Citoyenne*

*In which I am reunited with my son*

*Friday, October 29, 1790—Toulon.*
We've arrived. We're on land again. I am writing this at a table by a crackling fire. The table does not tip, the ink does not spill . . . for that matter, my hand does not tremble, my stomach does not turn.

Mal de mer for seven weeks! Even now, if I close my eyes, I see a mountain of water towering darkly over me. Whosoever is an atheist has never been to sea.

Our trials are far from over, however. Our meagre clothing—suitable for hot summer days in Martinico, not chilly fall evenings in France—is stained and torn. Nor have we a sou for bread or bed. Fortunately I was able to borrow a sum from Commander du Braye and that together with some money kindly loaned to us by Captain du Roure-Brison* will enable us to make the long journey to Paris.

At least we're alive, I remind myself. Two times the ship took fire— two times good luck they say, luck we were in need of, for it was a stormy crossing. In the Strait of Gibraltar we ran aground. Had not everyone on board—including Hortense, who insisted on "helping"—pulled *mightily* on a rope to pry us loose, we would surely have perished. I have rope burns still.

I will never set foot on a sailing ship again.

* *Captain Scipion du Roure-Brison was on the crew of the* Sensible, *the boat that returned Rose and Hortense to France. He is thought by some historians (lack of evidence notwithstanding) to have been Rose's lover.*

*October 30.*

"Voilà, Madame," the clerk at the post station said with a rough southern accent, handing me the tickets for two places on the mail-coach to Beaucaire. He was wearing leather over his lace cuffs, to protect them.

"Beaucaire? But we wish to go to Paris—"

"That's as far as I can get you." He threw up his hands. "From there . . . who knows! Everything has changed! Everything is being 'improved'—the measures, routes, the *procedures*. I don't even know what district I'm in! But the road is good," he added, perceiving my confusion, "if the bandits don't get you, that is."

"Bandits!" Hortense gasped, grasping my hand.

After purchasing the coach tickets I was able to locate a seamstress shop which would make capes for us quickly (and reasonably). On ship Commander du Braye had been kind enough to loan us some woollens. I can't say that I was unhappy to return them—they were itchy and smelled of fish. He urged me to accept the loan of a pistol, however—"You travel without the protection of a man, Madame."

I declined, at first. Then he told me a story I wish I had not heard and I accepted his offer.

"Make one deep inside pocket," I instructed the seamstress. For the pistol.

*Sunday, October 31, All Saints' Day Eve—Aix.*

After early-morning mass—prayers for surviving the voyage by sea, prayers that we will survive the long land voyage that lies ahead—Commander du Braye escorted us to the post station. I was thankful for our newly made capes, for they disguised our stained and tattered robes.

I very nearly wept saying farewell. Commander du Braye pushed a basket into my hands: a bottle of wine, a roast chicken, some pickled plums, six hard eggs and a two-pound loaf of bread. "Baked here in Toulon," he assured me, for the ship's flour had long become rancid. I accepted his offer reluctantly—we owe him enough as it is.

We were fortunate to get a seat with our backs to the horses. Even so, there were jolts. Shortly before the second post station the route became quite rough, with postillions at the foot of many a hill to help us over.

Several times I feared we would tip. At one pass through the mountains, after the second station, we were asked to walk. One of the passengers—a young man who had been partaking of a flask—refused, letting off his pistol for sport, which caused the horses to bolt and almost overturned the coach with the young man still in it. Once the horses had been recovered, the young man and the driver got into a fearful row—the driver threatening the soldier with his whip. Suddenly the soldier burst into tears and threw his arms around the driver's neck, apologized profusely for abusing a fellow citizen and offered him his flask.

"Why are they hugging now?" Hortense whispered as we, the shaken passengers, climbed back into the coach.

It was late afternoon when we were finally let down at the post station in Aix. We will resume our voyage at dawn. This inn is dirty, and the meal of half-raw little thrushes was not to our liking. Hortense carefully inspected the buns for insects, as has become her custom.


*Monday, November 1, All Saints' Day—Beaucaire.*
Between Aix and Beaucaire we overturned. Only small injuries, but I'm exhausted. Fortunately, our bedsheets here are clean and there appear to be no fleas. We share a room with a clock mender and his wife. I fear there might be improprieties.


*Friday, November 5—Montéliman.*
We have been on a river barge for three days. It is pulled by a team of placid oxen—Joseph, Jos and Jean, Hortense has named them. It is a common flat boat, a large raft-like vessel. In the centre is a shelter under which all the luggage, cargo and passengers are sheltered. Below deck is a stable of sorts for the oxen (we smell it).

It seemed an entirely tranquil, if slow, method of travel and I was congratulating myself on my wisdom when we came to Pont-Saint-Esprit, where the river runs under the arches of a bridge with great force. We accepted the driver's invitation to disembark and walk along the banks with the hoggee—a peasant boy of twelve—until the bridge had been safely navigated. I was apprehensive for the sake of the animals as well as our driver, but the beasts swam calmly under the arches, the driver sitting between the horns of the lead ox.

But that, I am content to say, has been our only excitement. Hortense is in good spirits—a better traveller than her mother, I confess, who is overcome by mal de mer at the slightest movement. She loves the barge, for she may run about and yell to the hoggee, who endures her attentions with patience. Now and again I try to induce her to sit, for the sake of my fellow passengers, holding her on my lap and entertaining her with stories of her big brother Eugène, whom we both grow increasingly anxious to see.

"And Father," Hortense demands, wiggling impatiently again. "Tell me stories of my *father!*"

*Alexandre* . . . I sigh. Where do I begin?

*Thursday, November 11—Lyons.*
We've been able to secure a seat (only one—Hortense will have to sit on my lap) on a mail-coach headed toward Paris—a fairly smooth road, I am told. We should be in Fontainebleau in five days, weather permitting. And then Paris! And then *Eugène*.

*Friday, November 12—Mâcon.*
I'm writing this in bed, by the light of a dirty tallow candle. Hortense is limp at my side, wheezing sweetly. The floor of this inn is covered with fleas, the bed-linens dank with the sweat of others. Lice keep me awake, scratching like a monkey. Endure, endure, I tell myself, shivering with the cold, reluctant to part with five sous for coal.

*November 15—Pont-sur-Yonne.*
At supper tonight there was talk of highwaymen just south of Fontainebleau. In the woods there, four coaches have been taken. A few of us have decided to take another route, through Provins. From there,

we are told, we can take a post-coach to Paris. I have posted a letter to Aunt Désirée informing her of the change in our plans.

*One Station Past Provins.*
Two men on our coach, one a farmer, the other a surgeon, talk between them of politics. They pass a news-sheet back and forth. Now and then a woman, a dealer in candles and cotton bonnets, joins in their conversation and an animated discussion ensues. They talk of the National Assembly.

I listen and remain silent, but I cannot control Hortense. She blurted out that her father was a delegate, a representative of the nobles.

"Does the child speak truly?" the woman asked. For we do not look the part.

I nodded in Hortense's defence.

"There are no more nobles," the surgeon said. He is a young man with no teeth and a hairy wart on his chin. Later, as we passed what appeared to be the burnt-out ruins of a fine old estate, he pointed to it. "The home of a noble. Perhaps it was your home?" He laughed nastily.

At the pewter basin in the post station, I whispered to Hortense that she was not to speak to that man, when his companion, the farmer, came up to us. "Tu t'appelles Madame Beauharnais, n'est-ce pas?" He asked if my husband's name was François.

I was reluctant to answer.

"Alexandre then?" he persisted.

I must have revealed the answer in my eyes, for the burly man threw himself upon me. He turned to the others, crying out: "Madame Beauharnais! La femme de député Alexandre Beauharnais!"

His friends the surgeon and the dealer in bonnets came over and the three of them displayed considerable pleasure at this news. The surgeon apologized for his rude conduct and offered me his cider. I accepted, but with confusion. It is apparently a good thing to be the wife of Deputy Alexandre Beauharnais, but I am too embarrassed to ask why.

*November 17—Mormant.*
Tomorrow—Paris! I can't sleep.

*Thursday, November 18—Paris.*

Fanny's hôtel on Rue de Tournon was badly in need of repair. A window on the second floor had been boarded over. I looked for some sign of life. The once-elegant neighbourhood was deathly quiet. A dilapidated carriage passed pulled by a mismatched pair of nags. The carriage emblems had been painted over. Tattered ribbons hung from the leather traces.

Hortense tugged on my hand, pulled me to the big wood doors, yanked on the bell rope. Soon we heard someone fumbling with the latch and one of the big doors swung open. Before us was a woman, dressed exquisitely in a green silk ball gown festooned with mauve and blue ribbons. Even her hair was done up in the old style, elaborately piled and powdered, decorated with flowers. But the set of her coiffure was slightly off: a wig out of kilter, I thought. Behind her, in the courtyard, was a broken-down carriage with one wheel off.

"May I help you?" she asked. She spoke with an accent—a German accent, I thought.

"Is Comtesse Fanny de Beauharnais in?" I asked, embarrassed by our clothing, fallen to rags.

"Whom may I tell her is calling?" She had a musical voice.

"Her niece, Madame Rose de Beauharnais."

"And Hortense!" my girl said boldly.

Suddenly, from across the courtyard, there appeared a plump woman with wild white hair, her face covered over with rouge. Fanny!

"*Ortensia!* My baby!" Fanny stooped down to look into Hortense's face. Hortense offered her godmother her hand. Fanny gave it a loud kiss, leaving a bright smear of rouge on Hortense's skin.

Fanny embraced me in the Italian manner, with great vigour. She smelled strongly of attar of roses. "It *can't* be you," she said, leading the way into the house. I detected a hint of wine on her breath. "Forgive me, darling, but I've just returned from my Italian tour with Michel." Her voice reverberated through the half-empty rooms.

From the stairway I heard a hiss. I looked up. A girl of about eight or nine stood at the landing, dressed in a white cotton gown. "Émilie?" I recognized the pixie face, the big black eyes: Fanny's granddaughter, Marie's only surviving child. She'd grown tall in the two and a half years since I'd seen her, her limbs long. She gestured to Hortense.

"Remember your cousin Émilie?" I said. Hortense hesitated only a moment and then ran up the stairs.

I followed Fanny through a swinging door into the kitchen. There, seated at a painted table, were a man and a woman. The man's hair was short and unpowdered and he was wearing a peasant's smock.

"Rose!" A woman in man's clothing stood to greet me, her loose curls caught back informally in a linen bonnet. I was astonished to see that it was Marie, Émilie's mother—timid, proper, shy Marie. But something had changed, for the woman I saw before me was quite bold, and certainly not *proper*.

"Why—it's Alexandre's wife!" the man exclaimed. He had big lips and his voice was booming—surprising in a man of his short height. Michel de Cubières, the poet. I had met him at one of Fanny's receptions years ago. He poured a glass of red wine from the bottle in the middle of the table. There were three empty wine bottles lined up on the counter.

Fanny handed me the glass. "Oh, Rose, you have missed the most glorious fêtes."

"The most glorious *Revolution!*" Michel exclaimed, hitting the bare tabletop with his fist.

"Am I not going to be introduced?" the aristocratic woman asked from the door.

"Princess Amalia, Madame Beauharnais; Rose, Princess Amalia." Marie broke off a piece of a breadstick on a platter. "Come, Rose, eat. We're enjoying the servants' day off."

They all laughed, as if this were a joke.

"But Princess Amalia is my servant now," Fanny protested.

*Princess* Amalia? The woman in the wig made a full court bow. I felt I had walked onto a stage in the middle of a comedy and did not know the lines.

"I've come *up* in the world," Fanny said in a stage whisper. "Princess Amalia de Hohenzollern-Sigmaringen is now my kitchen help."

"And *we're* helping clean out the wine cellar," Marie said, her eyes shining.

Michel de Cubières raised his glass. "To housecleaning!"

Fanny pulled out a chair for me to sit on. I backed away. "I must go," I said, stuttering, "to the Collège d'Harcourt. I am anxious to see Eugène."

"Collège d'Harcourt?" Princess Amalia asked.

"But Rose, darling," Fanny stuttered, "you . . ."

"Is . . . is there a problem?" Suddenly I was fearful.

Michel burst into laughter. "I suggest one of you ladies give Madame Beauharnais a looking glass."

How delirious to be clean. How shocking to be full. I've become too accustomed to hunger. After a meal of slipcoat cheese and skerret, and a change into clean linens (provided by Marie) and a walking dress (provided by Fanny), I felt renewed.

Renewed, but far from rested, I might add, for every move I made (even into the water-closet) I was followed by Marie, who felt called upon to provide a minute-by-minute account of every political event of the last six hundred days, as well as Fanny, who kept interrupting her daughter to give me a minute-by-minute account of her recent Italian tour. Finally, I was forced to interrupt. "I must go," I said.

It was not yet three in the afternoon. There was time.

The Collège d'Harcourt is a large institution. Aristocratic, militaristic: there was a sentry at the gate. Everyone was in uniform.

I wandered into the centre court, looking into each boy's face. I feared I would not recognize Eugène, feared he would not know me. He was nine now. He'd been only six when I last saw him.

I knocked on the door to the office. I was introduced to the headmaster, Monsieur de Saint-Hilaire, a portly man in a vivid red frock suit. I explained who I was and my business there. Monsieur de Saint-Hilaire bowed and offered a chair, but I refused. "I haven't seen my son for two and a half years, Monsieur."

After mentioning the tuition, long overdue apparently, Monsieur de Saint-Hilaire ordered a thin boy with boils on his face to escort me to the study hall. I followed the boy through several corridors to a room occupied by only three students. In the far corner was Eugène, glumly hunched over a chalkboard. He seemed older than I had pictured him.

I gave my guide a sou and he ran off. It was then that Eugène looked up, his curly hair falling onto his forehead. He glanced at me and went back to his work with a resigned expression. I was filled with confusion, for no maternal feeling came to aid me.

I stepped back out into the corridor, out of view, and leaned against the wall. I felt short of breath and suddenly unsure. Nothing had prepared me for this—this indifference on my part, this lack of love. I felt tears again, but this time they were tears of dismay.

I resolved to trust whatever Providence offered. I went to the door again. I called out to Eugène this time, softly. He looked up, stood and came to the door with a questioning look. I detected a moment of recognition in his face—but he was insecure, unsure of his young memories. I extended my hand to him. "It *is* me," I whispered, leading him into the hall, out of view of the other students who were watching us. "Maman."

He did not know what to say. I stooped so that I could better see his face. "Did you get the cricket cage I sent you—for your birthday?"

Eugène looked down at the stone floor and pushed the toe of his boot into a crack. I put one hand on his shoulder. The memory of him came to me forcefully then, through the fragile feel of one bony shoulder. "Oh, my boy," I whispered. I took him in my arms and he clung to me, as if he would never let me go.

Little by little the pieces fall into place, the parts make up the whole. Myself, my boy, my girl.

Arriving back at Fanny's, we three sat in the big empty salon on the big empty sofa, a tiny touching cluster down at one end, telling little stories. Shyly. Getting to know one another again.

At nightfall I shook the big featherbed out over them and sang to them, one childhood song after another. I kissed them once and then again—and then again and again. How can there ever be enough?

It is late now as I write. The night is clear; the street lanterns sparkle like diamonds in the dark. From somewhere I hear the sweet sound of a Provençal flute mingled with a violin and a cello. The light from the fire touches the faces of my sleeping children.

A church bell rings, Paris sleeps. But before I blow out the candle, I vow to remember this, this night, to remember that whatever life holds, it is really only this that matters, this fullness of heart.

## *In which I discover my husband*
## *a changed man*

*Monday, November 22, 1790.*
Fanny had tickets to the National Assembly and insisted that I go.
"Watching the Assembly has replaced theatre," she said. She was wearing
a bold ensemble entirely of red, white and blue. "My revolutionary toilette." Apparently the Revolution is the style now in fashionable circles.
"Charming, is it not?" She made a clumsy pirouette. Even her gloves
matched. "And beside, my dear Rose, it is time you saw your husband."

It was a beautiful morning, cold but bright. We hired a fiacre to take us
to the river and across to the Tuileries. The Assembly meets in the former
Palace riding school next to the terrace of the Feuillants's convent. Everywhere there were deputies in black. The gardens were crowded with vendors selling pamphlets and news-sheets, lemonade sellers shouting,
"Freshly made!" People of all classes pressed to gain entrance.

Inside there were public galleries elevated above the Assembly chamber. Fanny chose a bench that was cleaner than others and spread out a
cloth for us to sit on. I noticed a number of elegant women dressed as for
an afternoon stroll in the Bois de Boulogne. Intermixed were men and
women—mostly women—of the serving class, even market women in
one section.

I scanned the faces of the deputies below.

"He isn't here yet," Fanny said, in answer to my thoughts.

A deputy stood and with an air of authority went to the front of the chamber. A woman in back of us cursed. I must have flinched, for Fanny leaned over and whispered, "You should have been here *last* year—she'd have been armed with a pike." She pointed to a man on the far side of the hall. "See Robespierre? He's the one in the powdered wig."

"The tiny aristocrat?" The man I saw was wearing a pale green frock coat and a white lace cravat. He was sitting very quietly with his hands folded in his lap, watching everyone.

Fanny scoffed, snapping her fan shut. "He should have been a priest."

Suddenly there was a tumultuous cheer. I leaned forward to discern what had occasioned the commotion. Fanny pointed to a man who had just entered.

"The peasant?" I asked. He was a thin man dressed in a coarse linen tunic and wearing wood clogs.

"That's Deputy Luzerne. They're cheering because he came *dressed* as a peasant. There's François! In the fourth row. He's wearing one of those dreadful pigtail wigs and a king's hat. Can you see him?"

I placed François by the white plume of his round beaver hat.

But where was Alexandre?

Fanny nudged me in the ribs, nodded toward the far entrance. A man was standing in one of the doors, his long hair curled about his shoulders. He was dressed in a black coat and nankeen pantaloons. It was Alexandre.

"Stop watching me," I protested.

"You still fancy him. Confess."

"You're making up romances." If Fanny wanted to see love in my expression, nothing would prevent her from doing so.

Fortunately, Fanny's attention was distracted by a flurry of shouting from the floor. Two men had stood and were yelling with considerable vigour at another deputy. Finally, order was restored—but with difficulty.

Fanny explained: "Some deputies, your husband among them, are proposing that the clergy be elected officials, government employees. The subject gets them wonderfully heated, don't you think?"

"The clergy—*elected*? But the Pope would never consent to such a proposal," I said, shocked at the notion.

"Who's asking the Pope?" Fanny hissed.

Speakers for and against alternated. Alexandre was the sixth to go to the podium. He expressed himself most persuasively. France was facing financial ruin, he began. The poor were starving, yet the clergy continued to enjoy an exorbitant lifestyle at the people's expense, free from taxation, free from any allegiance to the state. The nobles had given up their special privileges. So in turn must the clergy. . . .

Then Alexandre's brother François spoke, in opposition. He was not as eloquent as Alexandre; his voice did not carry and he was hard to understand. Nevertheless, I found, to my confusion, that I could see his point as well. He argued that in principle such concepts made sense, but in practice the solution proposed was unthinkable. One could not expect men of God to forsake allegiance to the Church.

From there the discussion became extreme, with both sides becoming vociferous. The woman sitting in back of us began cursing again. At last the debate was brought to a close, but without resolution.

"It's that tithe system that gets the Church into so much trouble," Fanny ranted as we were exiting. "If the clergy would only exert a little self-control—but no, they have to live like kings. And at whose expense, I ask you? And all those gloomy parades! Why do they have to clog up the streets *every* Sunday? Aren't feast-days enough?"

"I'd hate to be at the family gathering when this comes up," I said, thinking of Aunt Désirée, who was so devout, and the Marquis, who demanded loyalty, whatever the cause.

We followed the crowd into a large central hall. Alexandre was standing with a group of deputies. He looked up and returned to his discussion.

"He doesn't recognize you." Before I could stop her, Fanny was pushing her way into his group.

Alexandre turned to me with a quizzical look. He broke away and in two steps was in front of me. "Madame Beauharnais," he said, "what a surprise. I learned just this morning you were back." He pushed his fair hair out of his eyes. "I was beginning to fear you would never return. Hortense is with you?"

"She is anxious to see you," I said. I adjusted my gauze fichu; Marie's dress was too small for me. "I thought you gave an excellent speech."

Alexandre glanced toward the hallway where two men, deputies, were trying to get his attention. He looked at me with an apologetic shrug. "I'm sorry, but I must go. You're at Fanny's?"

"For one more week. I've had difficulty obtaining seats on the post coach to Fontainebleau. I'd like to take Eugène with me, for the holidays, if, that is—"

We were interrupted by a plump little man in a white dimity waist-coat.

"Deputy Dunnkirk—you're *just* the man I need to see," Alexandre said. "I'd like you to meet my wife, Madame Beauharnais."

"Your *wife!*" The man gripped me in the comradely embrace that seemed to have become customary in France.

"Deputy Dunnkirk is a *banker*—be kind to him," Alexandre winked.

"The ladies are all *so* kind to me," the little man said sadly.

Alexandre took my hand. "Tonight? You'll be in?" He disappeared into the crowd.

"I didn't know Deputy Beauharnais was married." Deputy Dunnkirk sneezed into an enormous linen handkerchief.

"There you are, darling!" Fanny pressed her thickly painted face between us. "I didn't know you knew Emmery."

"Deputy Dunnkirk, forgive me if I appear abstracted," I said. "I have only been in Paris for a few days, and it is really all so . . ."

"Indeed. We are all of us in a state of confusion. I very much doubt that we will ever recover."

Fanny laughed too loudly. "Dear, dear Emmery. Why do I never see you?"

"You were in Rome, with that wild man. On a tour of propaganda, I am told, preaching to the unenlightened masses. . . ."

"I'm beginning my evenings again, this coming Monday," Fanny said. "I will simply *die* of grief if I don't see you there."

I looked at her. "Monday!" That was only in four days.

"But you don't even have a cook," I exclaimed, as we waited outside for our fiacre.

"*Mon Dieu!* I'd forgotten!" Fanny said, fanning herself furiously in spite of the cold.

*That evening.*

I spent most of the afternoon preparing for Alexandre's visit. I bathed, found a suitable dress, this one a loan from Princess Amalia, one of her *less* formal creations—a teal silk with ivory ribbons and lace, quite the confection. Hortense tried on all of Émilie's big-girl dresses and finally settled on a horrid pink one. It is far too big for her but she will not be persuaded otherwise, especially after Eugène told her she looked "lovely" in it.

Alexandre arrived after supper. Proudly, Eugène performed civilités—showing his father to a seat in the front parlour, ordering refreshments. Hortense refused to leave my side, clinging to me—her eyes never leaving the face of this stranger, her father. She would not allow him near her.

"She will get over it," I assured him, after the children had been taken to bed. I sounded more confident than I felt, for in truth I find Hortense difficult to predict. "You will be pleased to discover that she is quite bright," I told him, "and possesses a number of remarkable abilities."

"I wish I could say the same for our son." Alexandre stood in front of the fire, warming his hands.

"Perhaps Eugène takes after me in the matter of school." I stared into the flames, the heat warming my face.

"He certainly has your nature." He cleared his throat. "Kind, generous . . ." He studied me for a moment. "Charming. That colour quite suits you, Rose."

I flushed.

"Do you ever think of me?" he asked.

"I often think of you."

"Do you think of me *kindly?*"

How honest was I willing to be? "You are an easy man to care for, Alexandre."

"You make it sound facile."

"Is that a fault?"

"I wish you to know that I am a changed man; I feel I have risen from some magnetic slumber. I am intent on putting the foolishness of youth behind me."

We talked for some time of the changes in his life—of his health, the lingering effects of the fever he had suffered in Martinico, which had made a military life untenable. A political career was his only alternative. "Fortuitously," he said, for politics had become his passion. "I should like to tell you more," he said, pulling out a timepiece, "but I promised the Duc d'Orléans I would help prepare a petition. Oh—I almost forgot. I have something for you." He reached into his waistcoat pocket, pulling out an envelope.

"It's from *Mother?*" I recognized the writing.

"Apparently it was delivered to our old hôtel on Rue Neuve-Saint-Charles."

I broke the seal, scanned the contents. Uncle Tascher was safe. Father, Manette, were alive.

"It is bad news?" Alexandre asked, alarmed by my tears.

"No, yes."

"Good news?"

I laughed, handing him the letter to read. "I'm to protect myself against you," I explained.

"Me?"

"Unless, of course, I succeed in reforming you."


*September 23, this year of our Lord, 1790—Trois-Ilets*
*Dear Rose,*

*I trust that my prayers have been answered and that you and Hortense have completed your journey safely. Your father and sister continue to weaken, in spite of my prayers.*

*Your uncle Tascher was released shortly after your departure and in time the rebels were subdued. The disturbance, however, continues. I have had to take measures to ensure discipline with the slaves.*

*The government in France is godless. I have reason to believe that your children's father may be of their party. It is the duty of a mother to help that which is of God overcome that which can only be the work of the Devil. For the sake of your children, Rose, pray for Alexandre's salvation.*

*There is increased talk of war. It may be some time before I am able to write to you again. The English continue to blockade the port. It was only through smugglers and the will of God that I have been able to get this letter to you, should you receive it.*

*Your mother, Madame Claire de Tascher de la Pagerie*

*Wednesday, November 24.*

Everyone has been recruited to help Fanny prepare for her reception. Princess Amalia's brother Frédéric—*Prince* de Salm-Kyrburg—and I were asked to write out the "at home" cards. He's a charming man, quite short, with no chin at all. He was happy to do it, he confided. He and his sister have just built a mansion on Rue de Lille—Hôtel de Salm it is called.* In his drôle German accent he complained that it smelled of plaster, that his sister was forever engaging him in discussions about wall-covering, and that he welcomed any excuse to get out. "Who wants to stay at home all day with servants who snicker at you behind your back?" he said.

"At least you *have* servants," Fanny interrupted. She was covered with flour and seemed a little jolly. She'd been in the kitchen all morning with Jacques, her man-of-all-work, training him to cook, a vocation for which he showed enthusiasm if not promise. I suspected she'd been sipping the cooking wine.

"You mean *masters*," Frédéric said, indulging his passion for paradox.

*November 27.*

Fanny's evening started out well, in spite of many disasters: the goose overcooked, the cake fell in upon itself and a drape in the front parlour caught fire.

Quite a few people came, and the mix was invigorating. Royalists socialized with radicals, artists with bankers. A number of the guests were deputies from the National Assembly. As Alexandre's wife, I am held in high esteem. One deputy even assumed I would be in a position of influence and asked if I would speak to Alexandre on a certain matter.

I was struck with how things have changed. Where before people

---

* *Now the Palace of the Legion of Honour.*

paraded finery, now they boast of economy. Where before our distractions were bouts-rimes and charades, now people amuse themselves with talk of politics . . . and, of course, what is now called "economics": national product, inflation, public debt. (It seems that everyone is writing a plan of finance to save France.)

There were a few poets present, fortunately, several of whom were persuaded to recite from their latest creation—which of course they just happened to have with them. Fanny even got me to play her harp, which I did quite badly, I confess—I haven't practised for some time.

Even so, Deputy Emmery Dunnkirk, the banker Alexandre introduced me to at the Assembly, was effusive in his praise (between explosive sneezes). We talked for some time. He believes he might be able to make contact with Mother, in spite of the English blockade—in any case, he will try. He has clients who have dealings with the Islands, so he is not unfamiliar with the difficulties.

It wasn't until after supper that Alexandre arrived. He joined me in the front parlour. "I was impressed by your article in the *Moniteur* today," I told him. It was a long dissertation on the need for better hospitals.

Alexandre was about to say something when we were joined by a man with an enormous moustache, a deputy from Poitou. "Deputy Beauharnais, you devil, you never told me you had such a lovely wife!"

"Rose—I must say, you've made quite an impression on all my comrades," Alexandre said. "Everywhere I go—"

"Alexandre, I didn't know you had arrived!" Alexandre's cousin Marie interrupted. She was wearing red and blue cockades all over her bodice, the badges of a revolutionary.

"Deputy Beauharnais, how charming to see you!" Princess Amalia joined in. Her hair had been arranged in the old style, stacked high and heavily powdered. Silk ribbons and feathers were stuck into it everywhere.

"Are there hairdressers who still know how to dress hair like that?" the deputy from Poitou asked.

"Hélas! There's a flour shortage and *she's* pouring the stuff onto her hair," Marie said.

Prince Frédéric, who overheard, was about to say something in his sister's defence when we were joined by Deputy Dunnkirk and another deputy, a Monsieur Lyautey, and the discussion turned to the new land tax.

Alexandre and Frédéric excused themselves—they were late for a meeting of a debating society,* "formed under the auspices of the virtues," Alexandre said, putting on his hat. "I will see you and the children in Fontainebleau? Over the holidays?"

"My pleasure."

He took my hand and kissed it with a tender show of feeling. "The *pleasure* will be mine."

---

* *"The Friends of the Constitution"—formerly the Breton Club, and soon to become known as the radical and powerful Jacobin Club. In the interests of clarity, all references have been changed to the "Jacobin Club."*

# In which I suffer a great loss

*Wednesday, December 1, 1790.*
Fontainebleau is a ghost town. The palace gardens have grown wild, the long grass rampant. Gypsies are camped there.

Nevertheless, it was a joyful reunion; the Marquis stuttered, Aunt Désirée wept. They exclaimed how Hortense had grown, pampering her with a multitude of kisses.

The Marquis is frail, as one expects of a man of seventy-six. Indeed, it is a blessing he is with us still. I was relieved to find Aunt Désirée strong in both body and spirit. Their house showed signs of neglect—it is clear that they are getting by on very little.

It did not take Aunt Désirée long to bring up the subject of Alexandre. She has cut out all the articles about him in the news-sheets and pasted them into a big book which she proudly displayed, turning the pages reverently.

She did not say how she felt about his views. I wonder if she thinks of such things. Yet how can she not? Alexandre supported forsaking feudal rights—this alone has cost the Marquis a great deal. And now Alexandre supports the Church being made a government institution. Does Aunt Désirée not understand what this could mean?

"Look at this one," she said. "His name is mentioned five times."

"It's wonderful," I said, turning the pages.


*The next day.*
Aunt Désirée and I had a talk this morning—about finances. It was

impossible to put off. We had to decide what to do about Adélaïde d'Antigny, Alexandre's six-year-old illegitimate daughter we are both of us supporting. It is hard enough to support ourselves. Nevertheless, I could not accept cutting off the girl's care entirely. Aunt Désirée urged me to be firmer with Alexandre. I was making it too easy for him. "If you were to demand more, perhaps he would see the benefit of a reconciliation."

"Perhaps I do not wish a reconciliation." I turned my attention to my needlework.

"Yet you care for him."

"As do any number of women." Alexandre's "successes" were legendary.

Aunt Désirée cleared her throat. There was a moment of silence. "Surely you do not prefer to remain single."

"I believe I have no other option."

Aunt Désirée put down her lacework. "Rose—there is something you should know," she began, as if she were about to reveal a confidence. "A wise woman does not allow her husband's 'amusements' to disturb her, a wise woman closes her eyes. In allowing her husband his freedom, she dominates him!"

I confess I did not know how to respond. I knew my Aunt Désirée to be a woman well versed in the art of getting her way, but I had never suspected that she supported her actions with *philosophy*.

Aunt Désirée, sensing that she had captured my attention, went on. "Alexandre has a taste for tumultuous sensations, he is easily carried away—but surely such excessive sensibility is only proof of a good heart. A family that has suffered the stain of separation can never be repaired. The dishonour will endure for generations to come. I tell you this most painful fact out of the wisdom of my own experience. Rose, you owe it to your children to do everything in your power to bring about a reconciliation between yourself and your husband—the man to whom you were united by *God*."

Now, past dark, I sit in the quiet of my room. The memory of Aunt Désirée's lecture brings a smile to my heart, but the intent of her words brings dismay. I would give my life for my children—I would not hesitate to die for them—but would I live with Alexandre for them?

The lantern throws a flickering light on the walls.

In the light I see security, but in the shadows I see grief . . . in the shadows I see defeat.

*December 13, 1790—Paris*
*Dear Rose,*

*I note that today is the eleventh anniversary of the day on which we were wed. I am writing to commemorate that union, which has brought forth two beautiful children into the world.*

*I intend to come to Fontainebleau for the holidays. No doubt my Royalist brother plans to come as well. It is almost impossible for us to communicate now without becoming heated, but for the sake of family harmony I will attempt to put thoughts of Truth aside.*

*Your husband, Alexandre Beauharnais*

*Note—Make sure Eugène perseveres daily in his studies. Do not allow any exceptions, for in this way his natural inclination toward laziness takes root.*

*Christmas Day.*
Alexandre arrived laden with gifts, including a jewellery case for Hortense and enamelled boot buckles for me. Hortense ended in a frenzy of emotion, weeping her heart out in her room. It was just too much, this sudden regard from this stranger, her father.

I understand her confusion.

*Sunday, December 26.*
What a terrible evening. Aunt Désirée is in the parlour with the Marquis, giving him ether, trying to calm him.

It began after supper, over coffee. The Marquis asked François how things were going in the Assembly. I believe it affronted Alexandre that his father had not asked *him*. In any case, Alexandre interrupted to point out the causes *he* has furthered. It was at this point that François suggested that Alexandre inform their father of his views on the clergy.

"Well, Alexandre," the Marquis asked, "*do* you believe priests should forsake the Church?"

"It is possible to read on his countenance all his projects, Father," François said. "Alexandre not only supported that motion, he was one of the deputies who advocated it."

"Why *should* the clergy be exempt?" Alexandre countered. "It is equality we believe in, yet it is inequality we further—"

"Pretty words," François interrupted, "but they dangerously evade the issue. Honour is not unknown to men of religion. What will you do when the priests refuse? Put them to the lantern?"

Aunt Désirée excused herself from the table. I found her in the parlour, arranging and rearranging the religious relics on the mantelpiece. From the dining parlour I heard Alexandre exclaim, "And that reality is starvation!"

"Is it true?" Aunt Désirée looked paler than I had ever seen her. "Does Alexandre believe that the priests should *renounce* the Pope?" She sank into the chair by the grate. She shivered; the embers did not heat the room. I heard voices from the dining parlour again: François and Alexandre. And then, the Marquis: "I will not have it, Alexandre *de* Beauharnais!" pronouncing the "de" with great spite.*

There was the sound of china breaking. Alexandre strode forcefully down the hall. He banged the front door shut behind him, shaking the walls. As the sound of his horse's hoofs grew faint, Aunt Désirée gave way to tears.


*Friday, December 31.*
Alexandre returned on the last day of the year. He'd ridden a bay gelding all the way from Paris.

---

*\* After the nobility lost their feudal rights (a decree Alexandre supported), it was no longer appropriate to indicate heritage in a name: hence Alexandre de (of) Beauharnais became, simply, Alexandre Beauharnais, a man without lineage. Some individuals got around this by incorporating the "de" into their last name—"de Moulins" becoming "Demoulins," for example.*

"I didn't want to start the New Year unluckily," he told me, taking first Hortense and then Eugène into his arms.

"Did you bring me something?" Hortense asked.

"Of course," Alexandre said. "For the New Year."

Eagerly the children tore open their gifts: a riding whip for Eugène and a blue velvet bag for Hortense.

"And for your mother." He handed me a parcel. Inside was an embroidered muff.

"It's lovely." I kissed his cheek. Eugène and Hortense ran out of the room, giggling.

Alexandre poured himself a brandy. "Has my father forgiven me yet?"

"He's so forgetful now. He likely can't remember what happened."

"I brought him a copy of Hume's *History of England.*"

"You're giving him a book written by a *Protestant?*"

Alexandre slapped his forehead. "I didn't think."

"How long can you stay?"

He made a face. "I've a meeting in the morning, in Paris."

"On a Sunday? On New Year's Day?"

He sighed. "Making history is so time-consuming." He confessed he was uneasy about a speech he planned to give at the Jacobin Club the following week, on the subject of public education. He feared no one would attend. When Robespierre spoke, tickets had to be purchased in advance, but for an unknown such as himself—

There was a commotion in the foyer. Suddenly Aunt Désirée rushed into the room, her hat still on. "Alexandre!" She looked pale. "Have you heard?"

"Heard what?"

"You don't know?" She rummaged around in her handbasket, her hand pressed to her chest.

"Aunt Désirée?" Was she all right?

She pulled a news-sheet out of her basket. "Two thousand créoles have been *murdered* in Saint-Domingue! By slaves!"

"Murdered?" *Two thousand?* I put my hand to my mouth. Mon Dieu.

Alexandre took the journal from her. Cap-François had been

destroyed, the road to the city lined with the bodies of slaves—ten thousand killed, he read.

*Ten* thousand? Had I heard correctly?

"We're ruined!" Aunt Désirée rummaged through the writing desk. "I thought there were some salts in here."

"Behind the quills," I said.

"Our properties are at some distance from Cap-François," Alexandre called out as she headed up the stairs to the Marquis's rooms.

I stood by the fireplace, staring into the flames.

"This is unfortunate," Alexandre said. He was standing at the window, clasping and unclasping the pommel of his sword.

"Yes."

"Perhaps you should be sitting down," he said.

"I will be all right."

"I insist." He cleared his throat. "I bring . . . other news."

I felt apprehensive. I sat down.

"You understand that it is difficult to get mail in or out of Martinico. The British have set up a blockade."

Martinico? I nodded. "Deputy Dunnkirk has been trying to contact my family."

"That's why I came." Alexandre took the chair beside mine. "Emmery asked me to tell you that in spite of the civil war there, he has been able to get through."

"There's a *war* in Martinico?"

"You didn't know?"

My heart began to flutter. "You've had news, Alexandre?"

"Yes."

I felt a tingling sensation in my fingers. "Is it my sister?"

"No."

"Tell me!"

"Your father . . . He—"

I pressed my hands together.

"I'm sorry, Rose. Your father exchanged worlds last November." He put his hand on my shoulder.

I could not catch my breath. *Father.* Tears came to my eyes.

Alexandre took a handkerchief out of his waistcoat pocket and handed it to me. "No doubt you were expecting this. Your father has been ill for a very long time."

"No!"

*January 1, 1791.*
The New Year. It is quiet. No fêtes, no grand balls, no receptions. Instead of perfumed water, stagnant pools fill the fountains.

I wake with a sense of loss. I think of Father, a man so given to dreams.

What did his life mean, in the end?

My mother hated him.

Harsh words, but reality must be respected. And the reality of my father's life was: he suffered, he achieved nothing.

# *In which Alexandre is a hero*

*June 21, 1791—Fontainebleau.*

On my way to the perfumer this morning a placard on a tavern wall caught my attention. In bold letters was the name Beauharnais. Alexandre has been elected President of the National Assembly.*

Immediately I returned to the house. Coming in the door I called out to Aunt Désirée. I summoned the children, who were in the garden. "I have news of your father!"

Aunt Désirée came to the landing. "Is the Marquis in his room?" I asked.

"It's about Father!" Eugène called out. He had tracked mud onto the carpet.

"Is Alexandre all right?" Aunt Désirée asked.

"It's good news."

Aunt Désirée ushered us all into the Marquis's apartment. There, I told them the news. I had to repeat it three times.

"My son? Alexandre? *President* of the National Assembly?" the Marquis exclaimed in disbelief. "But that's not possible!"

I assured him it was so. Other than the King, there was no one more powerful, more important in all the land.

---

* *Although Alexandre's term of office would be for only two weeks—the position of president rotated—this was a prestigious honour.*

*Wednesday, June 22.*

I've been anxious, sleepless without news. *Something* has happened, for the gates to Paris have been closed; no mail, no journals, no couriers have been allowed in or out. It was whispered the King and Queen had fled the country—an unthinkable thought.

It was only this morning, at the procession in town for the feast of the Holy Sacrament, that Aunt Désirée and I were able to obtain a copy of the *Moniteur.* There our fears were confirmed: on the night of the twentieth, in disguise, the King and Queen and their two children escaped by means of the subterranean passages of the palace kitchens. It is thought that the royal berline headed for Varennes.

Quickly we returned to the house, for there was danger of the mob becoming heated. In the Marquis's bedchamber, Aunt Désirée read the journal reports out loud. It was with considerable pride that we learned that Alexandre was being credited with holding the country together— "with a firm and steady hand."

Aunt Désirée read, "President Deputy Alexandre Beauharnais has organized the effort to capture the King—"

"*Capture* the King!" The Marquis was taken with a nervous seizure.

"Not to capture, but to *free* him!" Aunt Désirée rushed for the ether.

The King has not *fled*, he's been "abducted"; he's not to be *captured*, he's to be "freed." If only reality could be changed so easily.


*June 23.*

This afternoon after supper—a lovely repast in honour of my twenty-eighth birthday—we were alarmed by sounds outside on the street. Aunt Désirée's chambermaid went to the window. "There's a crowd in front of the house."

"In front of *this* house?" the Marquis asked.

The children ran to the window. I jumped to my feet, nearly knocking a vase onto the floor. "Get back!" I commanded.

"They're crying out 'Dauphin'!" Eugène said, confused.

"*Mon Dieu,*" Aunt Désirée whispered. "They mean Eugène."

"Because of Alexandre?"

"But the Dauphin is not *here*," Hortense protested. "Is he not in Paris?"

I could not answer, my terror was so acute. The mob was calling my son Dauphin—the future *King*.

*June 27, 1791—Paris*
*Dear Rose,*

*Thank you for writing such a very kind congratulation. And please, forgive me for neglecting your birthday. I am in a delirium. I've not had any sleep for four days. The events of this last week have been overwhelming, for both myself, as well as for the Nation.*

*In moments of despair I recall Rousseau's words—that the best part of Virtue is to accept the yoke of necessity. And so it is with those of us who were born to the nobility, born to bear arms. How enlivening to be relieved of this slavery, to choose, instead, to risk life in honour of that which is True and Just. The sacrifices that we make for the Revolution will be a great benefit to mankind. With the love of Virtue spurring us on, how can we be defeated?*

*Your husband, Alexandre Beauharnais*

*June 30.*

François has taken on the role of the King's defender in the Assembly. "He's going to get us all hanged!" the Marquis sputtered.

Yesterday it was Alexandre's *condemnation* of the King that enraged him.

The brothers fight it out over the King's head on a national stage. Beauharnais *for*, Beauharnais *against* . . . If it isn't one son, it's the other.

*July 6, 1791—Paris*
*Dear Rose,*

*I have been ill, having exhausted my system during the crisis. Thank you for enrolling Eugène in the Collège d'Harcourt for the fall. I had entirely* forgotten. I agree that Hortense would benefit from more formal instruction at this time, as well. You will see to this? Not too costly, however.

*Your husband, Alexandre Beauharnais*

July 18, 1791—Rue de Tournon, Paris
Darling!

It's late, almost midnight, but I feel compelled to write. Alexandre gave a wonderful speech at the Jacobin Club tonight—so uplifting! We were all of us there to applaud him: Marie, Michel de Cubières, Frédéric. Even Princess Amalia came to hear him, in spite of her Royalist leanings. After we all went to the Café Covazza in the Palais-Royal. There Alexandre informed me that you intend to move to Paris, in order that your children might be educated.

Although transported with joy at the thought of seeing you and your wee darlings more often, I thought it would only be fair to warn you what Paris is like right now. It seems we are forever swinging from one extreme to the other, beginning with the sublime and ending in the tragic. Observe:

The week began with the grand fête and procession moving Voltaire's remains to the Pantheon—another of the brilliantly theatrical events orchestrated by the painter David. (Have you met him? He came to my salon once.) Of course I had to go—you know how I feel about our Apostle of Tolerance. The service began in the Masonic Lodge of the Nine Sisters, then wended its way through a number of triumphal arches to the site of the old Bastille. There the coffin rested overnight.

By the time Michel Cubières and I got back Monday morning the roses, myrtles and laurels had been stripped. Representatives of the sections and clubs had turned out in togas and red wool caps (like those awful itchy ones we have to wear at Masonic meetings). The coffin was loaded onto a chariot and pulled to the Pantheon by a team of white horses. I melted with tears.

Thursday, another fête at the Bastille, this time for the Fête de la Fédération. We didn't go (how unpatriotic) but that night the sky was fairly blooming with fire-rockets.

And yesterday, as if we must be punished for enjoying ourselves excessively, there was the tragic riot on the Champ-de-Mars. It began as a peaceful *assembly*—Marie was there with one of her women's groups to sign a petition in favour of a Republic. It got out of hand when two men, spies (or so it is thought), were discovered hiding under the central platform, and were promptly lynched. So Lafayette called out the National Guard, someone in the crowd yelled "Fire!" and now more than fifty are dead.

Thank God Marie was not harmed! Over the course of the day I virtually emptied my bottle of laudanum. It did not help in the least that it was washing week here and the two women I'd hired to help kept disappearing to go off to some fête or demonstration or riot. And now, all these dreary funerals.

If, despite my warnings, you persevere in this matter of your children's education, and move to our entertaining city, I recommend you contact Madame Hosten, a créole widow with three children (only one home still, I believe). I've been told that she has just purchased a hôtel on Rue Saint-Dominique (not too far from Hôtel de Salm), and is looking for someone to help share the expenses. It's in a good district—there, at least, the neighbourhood ruffians aren't out cutting off cats' ears. You will find her a genial woman and will most assuredly not regret my sending you to her.

Your loving Aunt Fanny

July 26, 1791— Rue Saint-Dominique, Paris.
Dear Madame Beauharnais,

Your welcome letter was received yesterday. I take the liberty, through your aunt Madame Fanny Beauharnais, of addressing you a few lines relative to the inducements of my new abode.

The house is large, divided into two apartments, with rooms for domestics on the third floor. My daughter (age twelve) and I occupy the ground floor. The upstairs suite is small but sunny. There is a walled-in garden. The Church of Saint Thomas Aquinas is immediately behind us.

It will give me much pleasure to see you at our residence next Monday evening in order that you might view the accommodations. Hoping to have the pleasure of welcoming yourself and your family as neighbours, I am,

Yours, very truly, Madame Hosten

*Tuesday, August 2—Fontainebleau.*
As arranged, I called on Madame Hosten on Rue Saint-Dominique, in
order to view the apartment. A maid in a day-gown of worked muslin
answered the door and was about to speak when a huge and somewhat
imposing woman appeared behind her. She was wearing a fencing mask
and carrying a sabre in her hand. "Who is it?" she asked, removing the
mask. Her voice was gentle, in contrast to her stance.

"Madame Beauharnais." I put forward my card, somewhat nervously,
I confess. "I believe I am expected."

"What island are *you* from?" the woman exclaimed, recognizing my
accent. She put down her sabre. "No—let me guess. Martinico?"

*She* was Madame Hosten—and she's from Sainte-Lucie. Her family
even knows Father! After showing me the rooms—they are perfect, quite
sunny—she invited me into her downstairs parlour for ginger sweets and
a glass (or two) of pétépié. We talked for hours.

Her name is Aimée. Although big (huge!), she is graceful in manner,
dainty even. She has an acid wit, quite drôle. She is thirty—only two years
older than I am—widowed, yet managing quite well on her own with
three children, two boys aged fifteen and sixteen (serving an apprenticeship in the military), and a girl of twelve, Lucie, still at home. I've feel I've
found a friend.

*September 1—Paris.*
I'm exhausted, we've moved. I've hired a chambermaid, Agathe Rible, a
meek creature who stutters. I assure her she has nothing to fear, but she
only quakes all the more. Already her trembling has resulted in three
glasses shattered.

*September 14.*
In the Assembly today the King pledged an oath of allegiance to the constitution. Firecrackers have been exploding all afternoon. The Revolution
is over!

Alexandre joined us on Rue Saint-Dominique to celebrate. I took his cloak and hat at the door. "Congratulations," I said, embracing him. He looked flushed and his breath smelled of brandy. No doubt there had been many toasts proposed at the Jacobin Club.

Eugène came sliding down the stair-rail and jumped into his father's arms. "You won!"

Alexandre laughed. "We all won."

Hortense came leaping down the stairs after her brother, three steps at a time. "Won what?"

"A constitution," Eugène told her officiously.

"You must feel proud of what you've accomplished," I said, upstairs in our new parlour. It had been an exhausting effort, I knew, to craft a constitution—one that gave France the best of two worlds, a Republic with a monarch. "And relieved."

"It remains to be seen if the King can actually work with it." Alexandre tapped tobacco into his pipe, lit it. "Sharing power will be trying to him, I expect. He was raised to rule his subjects, not to be beholden to them."

"If he were wise, he would use this opportunity to unite France," I said.

"Wisdom is not inherent in kingship, regrettably. And now, no doubt, all the Royalist countries will be sending in their troops to save him from this horrifying development. . . ."

"You believe there will be war?"

"Undoubtedly."

"Austria?"

He nodded. "*And* Prussia, *and*—"

There was a sudden clattering on the stairs. Hortense and Eugène burst into the room. They'd caught a frog in the garden. Alexandre and I helped to make a "home" for the little thing out of a travelling basket. Then, after a meal of mutton and cream fritters, we took the children to the show of paintings at the annual Salon. As we entered the second gallery, there it was: Alexandre's portrait, paired with that of Deputy Robespierre. Eugène and Hortense were of course most pleased, although they fail to comprehend the prestige that attends such an honour. We admired the likeness, which is excellent.

On the way home, we walked along the river, exclaiming as each fire-rocket exploded. Lovers strolled languidly by. The memory of being introduced to Alexandre came back to me then—Alexandre so young, so worldly, so dashing in his white uniform, myself a nervous girl from the Islands, so anxious to please, so willing to offer my heart.

A fire-rocket burst directly overhead. I startled, clutched Alexandre's arm. We laughed. The children, their cheeks pink, went running on ahead. A pleasing portrait, I thought: a man, his wife, two children, out for an evening stroll.

*February, 1792.*

It's as Alexandre predicted: we've become a country under siege. Austrian and Prussian troops assemble at our borders, preparing to march on Paris, preparing to rescue us from democracy. Preparing to rescue our King.

*March 15.*

I've been overcome with the vapours. Daily I am bled. Hortense and Eugène hover, bringing me drinks of tea and rum. Night falls. Alone, I pull myself to my feet, fall to my knees in front of the holy-water stoup. I have not had news from home for over a year. In the silence, fears grow, bloom, take shape.

I resist the cards, resist the temptation to look. But control was never my friend. I dig for them in the writing desk, in the upper corner of the top drawer, next to the bottle of ink. Pretending calm, I lay out the first card.

The Falling Tower: the stones falling, the men tossed and turned as if by some force beyond their control.

I did not need to see the rest: the Wheel of Fortune, Death, the Star turned upside-down.

Manette is dead.

I put the cards away.

Manette—dear little one—I see you in the stars, I see you skipping over the boulders in the river. *Wait for me!* you cry out—to me, your big sister. *Wait for me!*

*April 20.*

Paris has become an armed camp. The Church of Saint Thomas Aquinas is being used to assemble munitions: on the pews guns, muskets, swords, bayonets, even cannon balls are stacked. One sees men with pikes everywhere. Boys too young to fight stand in lines to sign up. Eugène watches them with envy. I pull him away.


*April 21.*

I woke with a feeling of foreboding, so when Alexandre arrived unexpectedly this morning, I felt threatened by vapours. "You're in uniform." I heard footsteps in the street, a woman calling out, distant drumbeats. The fear I'd felt on waking was with me still. "Married men do not have to serve, Alexandre. I don't understand."

"The Republic is in need of officers."* Alexandre put his hands on my shoulders. "Rose, please—don't ask me to go into battle without your blessing."

It was a solemn moment, broken by the discovery of something wiggling inside Alexandre's greatcoat. I cried out. Alexandre drew an animal out of his pocket—a horrid-looking pug, no bigger than a rodent. It had a fawn-coloured body and a black head. "It's a King Charles," he said. It squirmed out of his hands onto the rug. It was sniffing at my feet, making snorting noises, as if it couldn't breathe. "A dog like this is worth ten louis," Alexandre said proudly.

I called for Agathe, my timid chambermaid, but she wouldn't go near it—it looked too much like a rat. "It's only a puppy," I chided her, picking up the little thing up and heading for the children's room, motioning for Alexandre to follow.

"Is it a dog?" Eugène asked, examining its corkscrew tail.

"Does it bite?" Hortense this time, holding out her hand to it. She squealed when it licked her. It growled. "Is it hungry?"

"Can we keep it?" Eugène asked.

* *Before the Revolution, all of the officers had been aristocrats. When the Revolution came, most fled. There were few men left in France who had been trained to lead an army, fewer still with any experience.*

Alexandre looked at me: Would I?

I held out my hand to the little thing. It licked and nipped me, its teeth harmless but sharp. Its nose was flat, pushed into its face. It was a repulsive creature—yet it charmed me. "Fortuné. That's what we will call him."

I do not need to say more. We—Alexandre, the children and I—passed the morning together most enjoyably. When we bid him farewell it was with regret. I gave him a stone I'd had since childhood, a talisman.

"I will keep it with me always." He hesitated at the door as we were parting. "May I kiss you, Rose?"

"Say yes, Maman!" Eugène exclaimed.

I embraced my husband.

"May God be with you!" Hortense cried out as Alexandre passed through the gate. She burst into tears.

"Come now," I chided, drying her cheeks, "a soldier's daughter must not weep." Nor a soldier's wife.

## In which we are at war

April 23, 1792.

There is a curfew in Paris now. By ten the city is dark, silent but for the sound of the guards' boots on the cobblestones and cats fighting in the alleyways. From somewhere, I hear a church bell ring out one note, a lovely, melancholy sound—and so rare now. Most church bells have been melted down for munitions.

April 25, 1792—Valenciennes
Dear Rose,

*I have been assigned to General Biron's staff. Only a fraction of the available troops have been assembled here for fear of risking the safety of the fortified towns. The result is that the war plans are to be executed with very small numbers. On learning this, I had a will made up. I am forwarding it on to you, sealed. It is not to be opened until such time as . . .*

Your husband, Alexandre Beauharnais

May 2, 1792—Valenciennes
Dear Rose,

*Forgive me for alarming you. And thank you for your prayers. If I'm to die of anything, it will likely be frustration. How am I to make soldiers of these farmboys? When they get hungry, bored or have a little fright they take up their muskets and head home.*

*Give the children my love. I keep your talisman with me always.*
*Your husband, Alexandre Beauharnais*


*May 4.*
Alexandre has been in battle against the Austrians. His behaviour was praised in the *Moniteur*. Proudly, I showed the article to the children. We have attached a large map to the wall of the dining area where we trace his progress. As well, we are making a book of clippings from the journals, which is already thick, for the *Moniteur* publishes Alexandre's patriotic articles daily.


*May 17.*
Alexandre sends letters which he instructs me to burn. The revolutionary armies are small, he confides—ill-equipped and untrained. Suspicion rules. The troops do not trust their officers, the officers do not trust their troops. One general was forced to call off a bayonet charge because his troops voted against it, another was murdered by his own men. *By his own men.* Grand Dieu.


*Tuesday, June 19.*
This evening I heard a commotion. I looked out: the streets were jammed with horses, carts filled with possessions. What had happened? I ran downstairs to Aimée's suite.

"Oh, the King has everyone upset," she sighed, stretching out on the chaise with remarkable calm. She was in her white fencing clothes, her sabre on the floor.

Her chambermaid appeared at the door, carrying a portmanteau. "I'll be needing my pay."

Aimée gave me a disgusted look. "They're all in a panic, every last one of them." Reluctantly she went to her writing desk.

"Others have left?" I asked.

The chambermaid cursed. "The Austrians march toward Paris and our own King is going to open the gates wide to let the butchers in! Well—I won't be here!"

Aimée offered the woman paper money but she insisted on coin.

"There goes another one," Aimée sighed when the door slammed shut. "Let's get out the brandy."


*June 21.*

My chambermaid woke me this morning with excitement in her voice. "There was trouble last night." Agathe handed me a bowl of hot chocolate. "The palace was invaded!"

*"Invaded?"*

"The people ran in, took over." She wasn't stuttering.

"Agathe, explain, please—"

Slowly I got the story. Yesterday's feast-day festivities had turned to violence in the night. A mob of men and women had invaded the palace, demanding that the King bring in troops to protect Paris from the Austrians.

"Is the Queen safe?" I asked. "The children?"

Agathe looked at me suspiciously. I realized my mistake. One should never show sympathy for the royal family, especially not for the Queen.


*June 28.*

Agathe insists that the Queen is plotting to burn down the Assembly while all the deputies are in it, that muskets and gunpowder are stored in the basements of all the nunneries. And now Hortense will no longer eat bread. "I might die," she said, for Agathe told her the priests plan to murder everyone by poisoning the holy bread.

"Mademoiselle Agathe told you that?"

Hortense looked at me with a horrified expression. "Maman—it is *Citoyenne* Agathe now, not Mademoiselle."

My daughter, the revolutionary. Now she refuses to speak during meals. It's the patriotic way.

*Monday, July 2.*

Aimée and I went to the Comédie-Italienne to see *Unforeseen Events* with Madame Dugazon playing the soubrette. Princess Amalia had offered us the use of her loge.

"The Queen is expected to be there," Aimée said.

"I didn't think the Queen went out to the theatre any more," I said. She'd let all her loges go months ago, something people held against her.

"There's been pressure on her to make an appearance."

Our loge was directly across from the one the royal family was to use. There was applause when Her Majesty entered, accompanied by her children—the Dauphin, a sweet-faced boy of about seven, and Madame Royale, almost a young woman now. The King's sister Madame Elizabeth and another woman, the children's governess, I guessed, were also with her.

Throughout the performance I watched the Queen's face. It was hard to believe she was only in her thirties, she looked so very aged. The Dauphin, a charming child dressed in the regimentals of the nation, sat on her lap. Now and again the Queen kissed the top of his head. He kept gazing up at her face—he seemed perplexed by her tears.

In the third act, the soubrette and the valet sang a duet. In it Madame Dugazon exclaimed: "Ah! Comme j'aime ma maîtresse!" looking directly at the Queen. Three men in pantaloons jumped up on the stage and threatened the singer.

The Queen's guard hurried the Queen and her entourage out of the theatre. It was, of course, impossible to continue the performance after that.


*Thursday, July 19.*

The Austrians have cut off supplies to Paris—we are entirely without. We whisper—not of gossip, but of grain: where it might be found. (Those who know stay silent.) Every day there are riots for food.

Santerre, Commander of the National Guards, has proposed that all dogs and cats be disposed of, arguing that the food they eat would be better directed toward people.

"What about pain bénit?" Agathe argued. Every Sunday, thousands of loaves of bread are blessed by the priests and left uneaten. "And what about hair loaded with flour powder? What about that!"

My timid maid is timid no longer.


*July 22, Sunday.*
The warning cannon on the Pont-Neuf has been firing every hour. An hour ago a man on horseback, an official caller, yelled out in the street, "La patrie en danger! La patrie en danger!"

The Austrians are coming. . . .

The streets are clogged with carriages. Everyone is trying to get out of Paris, but it is impossible—the gates have been closed! Nobody is allowed in; no one allowed out. We are trapped.


*August 8.*
I have not slept for a week. It's so hot Agathe claims she saw the river boiling. Each day I try to get passes to get out of Paris, but have been unable. The gates are *still* closed!


*August 10.*
Last night masses of people were in the streets. The children were sent home from school this morning. Then, at around nine this evening, just as Frédéric, the Princess, Aimée and I prepared to sit to supper together, the tocsins began to ring.

Frédéric was intent on going to see what was happening. Aimée, Princess Amalia and I tried to dissuade him, but he insisted. Aimée offered him her sabre.

"No—it would look too aristocratic," Frédéric said, taking a meat cleaver instead.

It was almost two in the morning when he returned. The tocsins were still ringing. There was talk of a demonstration at the Palace at daybreak.

"*Another* demonstration?" I asked.

"Who is calling it?" the princess asked.

"The Commune." Frédéric's cheeks were pink. Vats of wine had been set in the street in front of the section house.

"For what purpose?" I feared the Commune.*

"To arrest the King."

*Arrest* the King?

I took a seat. I could not comprehend. Arrest the King? But the King *was* the law.

The tocsins began ringing again at dawn. I went to the window, pulled back the drapes. A group of men, ruffians, were in the street, two carrying pikes. One was wearing the blue tunic of a dockman of Marseille. He saw me at the window and screamed, "Death to the aristocrats!"

I backed away from view. From far away I could hear the faint sound of a musket being fired, followed by grapeshot.

Somewhere, a battle had begun.

*Later that evening.*
The Commune has taken over. Hundreds have been killed, hundreds more arrested.

"We've *got* to get out," I whispered to Aimée. "Get the children out." But how? Who could we trust?

"I've heard that there's a place by the Allée des Invalides, near the Boulevard, where the wall is low. Maybe we could get over there."

"Climb over?" We would have to run through fields in the dark. Eugène and Lucie might be able to, but Hortense . . . ?

No matter how we think it through, it's too dangerous. So we're staying, preparing for the worst.

---

* *The Commune was the municipal government of the city of Paris. Conflicts arose because the city government, which tended to be radical (urban-based), felt that the conservative (rural-based) national government was not doing enough to protect Paris. The Commune, therefore, felt justified in taking control.*

## *In which I take desperate measures*

*Monday, August 13, 1792.*

I was on the balcony when a coach and four pulled into the courtyard. A footman helped lift an elderly woman down. I could not make out her face under the hood of her cape.

A short time later, Agathe brought me a calling card scented with lavender. It was the Comtesse de Montmorin, whose elegant fêtes at the castle in Fontainebleau had so charmed me, whose dear clumsy husband, Comte Luce de Montmorin, the governor of the castle, I'd found so endearing. Why would she be calling on *me?* I wondered, untying my morning cap and reaching for a wig.

The Comtesse's trembling hand clasped mine. "Comte de Montmorin has been arrested—by the Commune!"

"Your husband?"

"They've confused him with Monsieur Armand de Montmorin, the Minister of Foreign Affairs!"

Bungling, forgetful, sweet old Comte Luce de Montmorin—how could anyone have mistaken him for a diplomat? "Which prison?" I asked, shaken.

"The Abbaye."

The *Abbaye*—it was but a short distance from our home; Eugène, Hortense and I had walked by it the day before. All the windows had been boarded over.

"Nobody knows anything! I am desperate—to whom can I turn?"

*Friday, August 17.*
Finally, a response from the Tribunal Jury that has been set up to review the arrests of August tenth. I've been granted an audience this coming Monday with Citoyen Botot, one of the seven directors. I've notes scattered all over the dining-room table, formulating arguments, pleas. My bed is covered with gowns pulled from the cupboard in an effort to select a suitable ensemble. What does one wear when begging a life?

*August 18.*
This morning, as I entered the kitchen, I thought I saw Agathe hastily shove something under the counter. Later, I went to look. It was a pamphlet, official in its presentation, written by an unwhiskered patriot. It claimed that a plot had been uncovered to assassinate the good citizens of Paris during the night of September second to come. According to the pamphlet, this treacherous scheme is to be carried out by aristocrats and priests with the help of those in the prisons, whom the aristocrats and priests intend to set free.

A fabrication, surely. Yet who would promote such a lie? Who would promote such *fear?*

*Monday, August 20, late afternoon, 3:30 P.M.*
Citoyen Botot is a tall, baby-faced older gentleman with a smug, well-fed look. I felt I had met him before.

"I used to sell dental water on Rue des Noyers," he said. He spoke with a hint of a lisp.

L'eau de Botot—of course. "I consulted you years ago," I said.

"Did my remedy help?"

"Yes," I lied.

"My uncle invented it," he said proudly.

He was sympathetic about Comte Luce de Montmorin's mistaken identity but informed me there was little he could accomplish alone. He suggested I attend a reception being held at the home of Deputy Paul Barras in four days. Several members of the Tribunal Jury would be there, he said.

"But I have not even been introduced to Deputy Barras," I said.

"It will be my honour to do so," Citoyen Botot assured me.


*Tuesday, August 21.*

Agathe came back from market today flushed with excitement. She'd seen a man's head cut off—by guillotine.* "The crowd booed!" she said, her pallid complexion pink. "It was over too quickly."


*August 23.*

The children came running into the parlour this afternoon much in a fright. They had heard that our troops to the East had fallen to the Austrians.

"Is it Father?" Eugène asked.

I assured him no, his father was safe.

"But what about us!" Hortense cried.

"It's not the *Austrians* to fear," Agathe hissed. "It's the priests and aristocrats in the prisons who will hold the knife to your heart as you sleep."

Hortense began to wail. It took some effort to calm her.

"Dismiss Agathe," Aimée insisted later that night. We were sitting in our little garden sipping claret, watching the moon and the stars come out.

"It's too dangerous. I dare not." Many, now, are betrayed to the authorities by their domestics.


*Friday, August 24.*

Tonight, the reception at Deputy Barras's. Princess Amalia has offered to loan me one of her beautiful gowns. I have taken a herbal remedy in attempt to calm the fluxations of my stomach. I must go, whatever my condition.

---

* *Decapitation, formerly the privilege of the aristocratic class, was made available to all social classes by means of the guillotine. It was created by Dr. Guillotin, who died of grief over the abuse to which his humanitarian invention had been put.*

*Evening.*

Citoyen Botot and I were shown into an elegantly furnished entryway hung with Gobelin tapestries. An older man of about forty approached us, trailing a sword. He walked with the studied grace of a ballet instructor. He embraced Citoyen Botot, caressed his cheek. "And who is this lovely lady you've brought for me, François?" With a theatrical flourish, Deputy Barras kissed my hand.

"Ah—the famous Deputy Barras." I dropped a deep curtsy.

"I hate to think what I might be famous *for*." He smiled, removing his gold-rimmed lorgnon from his right eye. A diamond on his middle finger caught the light. He was wearing skin-tight yellow silk breeches, high black riding boots and lace everywhere—*very* Ancien Régime. Hardly the revolutionary I had expected, from all I had heard.

"Are there so very many possibilities?" I asked. He smelled strongly of spirit of ambergris.

"Innumerable." By the light of the torches his face was angular, sculpted, with high cheekbones. A sensitive-looking man with sorrowful, puppy-dog eyes. "My dear Botot," he said, taking my arm, "would you be offended if perhaps *I* introduced this lady to my guests?"

As we entered the parlour, I paused to admire a painting by Greuze.

"Later I will show you my collection," Deputy Barras said. "I have an eye for beauty—"

"A weakness, some call it," Botot whispered.

Deputy Barras smiled, a boyish lopsided grin that was rather endearing. "Speaking of beauty, I see you are wearing one of Citoyenne Deperret's creations," he said, noting the intricate lace-and-ribbon design on the shoulder of my gown. "A brilliant designer, but temperamental, I've been told."

"She *is* brilliant," I said. I dared not reveal I had borrowed the ensemble.

Throughout the evening Deputy Barras was quite attentive. (I suspect him of being more interested in the show of seduction than seduction itself.) After the third toast to the Republic I was sufficiently emboldened to express my concerns regarding Comte de Montmorin's arrest. I was encouraged by Deputy Barras's response—

more than the dismissive "We'll see," in any case. He made a point of introducing me to four members of the Tribunal Jury who were present. By the deference they paid Deputy Barras, I could see that it would be wise to cultivate his friendship . . . and no hardship, certainly. He amuses me.

*Tuesday, August 28.*
Tonight it begins. No carriages, no horses on the streets after nine. A crier on horseback proclaimed that the searches would begin at midnight.

What do we have to hide? Aimée burned a quantity of love letters. She read the more private passages out loud before throwing them into the fire. "I wish I had love letters to burn," I said. Alexandre's letters are more like sermons, extolling the virtues of the Republic.

"Leave his out where the authorities can see them," Aimée said.

Agathe watched us furtively and suddenly I wondered: Is my chambermaid a spy?

*August 29.*
It was after one in the morning when the search party came, a group of twelve men pounding on the door. The leader was a Citoyen Wimpfen, a vendor of skins I remembered seeing at our section office. They went through our rooms, insisting that we wake the children so that they could search their beds, stabbing the fur coverlets with their daggers.

Aimée offered them old wine in a decanter and cold river pike. "You'll need this for the hard night's work ahead, citoyens," she told them, pouring out generous glasses which flushed them finely. She is good at this. As for myself, I was afraid they would perceive my trembling.

*August 29, 1792*
*Citoyenne Beauharnais:*
   *Regarding the arrest and imprisonment of Citoyen Montmorin, you have been granted a hearing before the jury in one week, on the fourth day of September, at three in the afternoon.*

*Citoyen Botot*
*Director, Tribunal Jury*

*Thursday, August 30.*
Thousands more have been arrested—clerics, priests, aristocrats. "We're next," Aimée said, strapping on her fencing mask.

*August 28, 1792—Valenciennes*
*Dear Rose,*
   *I have been promoted to maréchal de camp at Strasbourg. I depart tomorrow. I do not know how long it will take to get there as I will be inspecting the garrison towns en route. Do not worry, I have an excellent horse.*
   *Give my love to the children.*

*Your husband, Alexandre Beauharnais*

*September 2.*
Austrian troops are a two-day march from Paris. Panic has taken the city. In a back room, on a small oak table, Aimée and I assemble weapons: a meat cleaver, Aimée's fencing sabre, Commander du Braye's pistol. I touch the cold metal, imagine the worst. Could I? Would I?

*Monday, September 3, evening.*
Eugène's birthday, his eleventh. The sounds of the tocsins filled the air, the slow passing of the hours marked by cannon.

   I pulled the drapes and forbade the children to look out. Calmly I proceeded, pinning up ribbons in celebration of birth, reciting prayers to ward off death. Daggers ever at the ready, I went about the day: children fed, linens mended, bedclothes aired. In little ways one conquers fear.

But now, the children asleep, I wait by the window and watch, listen and wait, the pistol on the table before me. In the dark, fear rules. What would I do if attacked? Would I have the courage to take a life? How are such things done?

*September 4.*
It was two, perhaps three in the morning, when I heard faint laughter and went to the window. The stars and the moon hovered over the city. Tranquillity, I thought, but then, in the dark I saw flickers of light moving. The city was vibrant with flambeaux.

Two boys appeared in the street below, laughing with drunken pleasure.

I looked closer.

They pulled, they pulled, they staggered and fell, they laughed and pulled again.

What was it they pulled?

It was then that I saw. It was the body of a man they were dragging, his long legs white, naked under a black habit—a priest.

I retched and turned, I gasped for air.

As soon as the sky lightened, I changed into my street clothes, pinned on my cockade. I set out for the Rue de Lille. Frédéric was a member of the National Guard. He would know.

It was Princess Amalia who received me, in spite of the early hour. She, too, had not slept. She led me into the garden where she invited me to sit under a blooming acacia. There, in a setting of peace and beauty, she told me what had transpired in the night. The men and women in the prisons had been slaughtered.

I felt faint. "The Comte de Montmorin? He is in the Abbaye—"

Princess Amalia took my hand.

*Mon Dieu.* I had had an appointment to go before the jury that very afternoon. And now it was too late.

It was then that the Princess told me that she and Frédéric were planning to escape France.

"But how? The gates, the guards . . ."

"Frédéric has been able, at great cost, to get passes to Saint-Martin. From there we believe we can get to England."

England. The enemy. But who was the enemy now? The enemy was everywhere.

"You'll . . . you'll lose everything." Their estate, the Hôtel de Salm, everything they owned would be taken by the state, everything but the clothes on their backs.

"Everything but our lives."

"Take us with you." The words leapt from me without thinking. "Me and the children." It was a terrible and fearful thing to do, a terrible and fearful thing to ask someone to do, but I was obsessed with one thought only: to get Hortense and Eugène out of France, to safety.

"Oh, Rose, we couldn't. It's impossible. You would need a passport."

"The children, then." Tears came to my eyes. "You could pretend they were your own."

She reached for me, alarmed. "Rose?"

I began to tremble.

Princess Amalia looked up at the sky. She took a breath. "Yes."

Aimée and Lucie were in the foyer when I entered. I looked away.

"Is something amiss?" Aimée put down her market basket.

"I'm not feeling well," I said. Princess Amalia and Frédéric were leaving at dawn. I'd promised not to tell. In any case, I did not want to. I feared complications, logic—truth. I feared guilt, for thinking only of my own. I hurried up the stairs.

Eugène greeted me with a hug. Hortense ran in with a drawing she had just made. They seemed so very young. A terrible feeling began to rise up in me.

"Maman?" Eugène asked.

I gathered strength. "I have news. I've arranged for a holiday for you both, with Frédéric and Princess Amalia." I had to see this through, and calmly, I knew. Otherwise I would alarm them.

Eugène appeared pleased. I was relieved.

"But I want to go to school," Hortense said.

"There are no more schools. Remember? The schools have all been closed."*

"You're not coming?" Hortense's voice had that high quavering pitch.

I took her in my arms. "I will join you soon," I lied. I kissed the top of her head. Don't cry, I told myself. Don't cry!

It is midnight now. The light from the lamp burns low. I curl strands of the children's hair around my fingers, press them into a locket. Eugène's curls around my finger easily; Hortense's is fine and straight, it defies confinement.

They are sleeping. Eugène is sprawled across his bed, all long legs and arms. He sleeps soundly, without movement. I do not fear for him.

It is Hortense who still needs me, Hortense who will suffer. She is curled in a tense ball, her face frozen into a frown even in sleep. I thank God that Eugène will be with her. He has heart enough for us all.


*September 5.*

It was dawn when we set out, Eugène and I taking turns carrying the canvas haversack. I tried to maintain a festive attitude. The coach and four were in the prince and princess's courtyard, waiting. The driver was not in livery and the family crests had been painted over for fear of drawing attention.

Poor Frédéric was flustered. He couldn't get his sword to tie properly. Eugène helped him. Then the children and I sat down, out of the way, while the princess supervised the packing. So much had been stuffed into a trunk that the valet was unable to close the lid. Princess Amalia was obliged to take a number of robes out.

At last they were ready. I helped the children into the coach. I kissed them and closed the door. The driver cracked his whip, the horses pulled

* Two weeks earlier (August 18, 1792), all religious institutions had been closed by the state. This included most of the schools, which had been run by the Church.

forward. Hortense waved. Eugène pressed his lips to the glass, to make a funny face.

That was the last.

Quickly I headed home. Nearing the Church of Saint Thomas Aquinas, I heard a child singing, a melancholy soprano much like Hortense's sweet voice. I stopped.

I would light a candle, I thought, say a prayer . . . a prayer for safe journey, for my children, but within the dark chapel my intention was thwarted. Labourers were dismantling church ornaments. In a corner a table had been set up and a line of young men had formed: army recruits. At the pews at the front a cleric and several old women were sorting army uniforms.

I stood in the archway, confused.

Two of the labourers moved by me, carrying a heavy statue of the Madonna between them. "Pardon," one said. They loaded the statue onto a handcart and began to pull it away. The labourer in the blue tunic waved to me, as if in a procession.

I recalled Hortense waving. *Goodbye. Goodbye, Maman.*

For how long?

*For ever?*

A feeling of panic came over me. I fell to my knees. The cleric and one of the old women came to my aid. The cleric supported me as best he could to a pew, urging me to rest. "I must go." I pulled away.

I do not remember making my way to Rue Saint-Dominique. I do not remember climbing the stairs. All I remember is standing at the door to the children's room. Scattered all over the floor were Eugène's toy soldiers. One of Hortense's dolls was slumped in a corner.

"Oui?" Agathe was bent over Eugène's bed, as if to straighten it. There was a hollow in the pillow, where Eugène's head had been.

"No!"

Agathe looked at me in confusion.

"Please." Softly this time; I had alarmed her. "Don't." I reached for the door handle to steady myself.

"I'm not to make up the bed?"

"Not just now." My voice was quavering.

Agathe regarded me with suspicion. "I see." She backed away.

I closed the door behind us, turned the key, took a breath. I would have them with me still, their familiar disorder, their rumpled bedclothes—their scent, the imprint of their bodies on the pillows . . . evidence, of their existence.

## *In which I become a good Republican*

*September 8, 1792.*
Aimée is horrified by what I've done.

"I *had* to!"

"You could have at least talked it over with me."

The truth was, I had been afraid to tell her, afraid she'd try to talk me out of it. Afraid she'd say: What about Lucie? What about *my* daughter?

"I promised not to tell!"

"Rose, don't you see? This puts you in such peril!" she ranted, close to tears. "And what about Alexandre? I hate to think what's going to happen to *him* when the authorities find out!"

Alexandre—*mon Dieu.*

*Sunday, September 16.*
Rain, and more rain. I spent the morning in bed, listening to the crackling of the fire, the steady dripping of the rain on the roof, alone with my sad thoughts, a devouring ennui.

At around eleven I must have fallen asleep, for I was dreaming of home, of the salty water of the bay, the tangle of the mangroves. . . . I awoke with a start. Outside, on the street, I heard a child's voice, a girl's bubbling giggle. How cruel, I thought, for a child so like Hortense to call at my window.

I heard the impatient prance of a horse's hoofs on the cobblestones, the front door open, a boy's voice. Was it possible? I went to the landing, clinging to the railing for support. There, in the entryway looking up at me, were Hortense and Eugène.

"Maman!" They clattered up the stairs and into my arms. I clasped them hard, disbelieving. They were confused—and perhaps a little uneasy—by the intensity of my welcome, my tears.

"Father wrote a letter for us to come back," Hortense explained. She seemed pleased by this.

*"Alexandre?"*

Princess Amalia came in the front hallway. Frédéric was behind her, looking harassed. He was wearing his National Guard uniform, now tight on him. I motioned to them to be cautious, for Agathe had come to the landing with a basket of linens.

"Would you like Agathe to make you a hot chocolate?" I asked the children. They followed her happily down into the kitchen. I opened the double sash doors to the parlour. Princess Amalia and Frédéric followed me in, Frédéric checking to make sure there was no one behind the curtains. I closed the doors behind me. "What *happened!*" I whispered.

"We received an estafet close to Saint-Paul," Princess Amalia said in a hushed voice, taking off her feathered hat. Her heavily powdered hair was dressed in an elaborate pouf. "From Alexandre. He demanded that the children be returned to Paris at once." She took a document out of her basket and handed it to me. "It arrived two days before we were to depart for England."

"Alexandre sent you this?" I sank onto the sofa. "How did he find out?"

"*You* didn't inform him?" Princess Amalia glanced at her brother. "We thought . . ."

"Is it possible the government knows?" I asked.

"They have spies everywhere," Frédéric said bitterly.

I didn't know what to think. I was overwhelmed with joy to see Hortense and Eugène again, yet alarmed by the perilous situation into which they had been returned. "But *you* could have gone on to England," I told them.

"Someone had to accompany the children," Princess Amalia explained.

"There was no one we could trust," Frédéric said.

It wasn't until they had left that the enormity of Alexandre's action struck me. The lives of our children, of dear Frédéric and Princess Amalia, have been put at risk. I've penned Alexandre a letter of rage and regret. I watch as it burns in the fire.


*September 21, 1792—Strasbourg*
*Rose,*

*How can you say that I do not understand the situation in Paris! I understand it clearly: the Parisians were overcome with an irrational panic. The Austrians would never have attacked! But even so, to send the children to England? Can you imagine what that would have meant to my career? As a former aristocrat, daily I am required to submit proof of my loyalty.*

*Your much enraged and offended husband, Alexandre*


*Friday, September 21.*
Aimée is intent on my safety. "You're to become a good citoyenne, a model Republican." She's put a red cap and a worsted linen cockade by the door—not even a silk cockade will do—"for *whenever* you go out."

I groaned.

She took the liberty of suggesting that I find a less attractive cape to wear in the streets. "Any show of wealth is dangerous," she said. "Even clean *linens.*" She gave me a cape she'd found in a used clothing shop. It is worn and patched, an unbecoming dirty yellow. "Perfect. You look horrible."


*Saturday, September 22.*
The new Republic dawned wet and dreary. The streets are crowded with people milling about in the rain, sharing wine, singing, celebrating the new Era of Liberty. Dressed in Roman tunics, ragged old army uniforms, mouldy court gowns, they link arms and roam from one neighbourhood to the next.

Aimée has cluttered the front parlour with revolutionary newspapers and magazines. "For our salon," she explained.

"*Our* salon?"

"Every Tuesday evening, revolutionaries welcome," she said, scratching out a guest list. "They're a rowdy bunch—it might even be amusing."


*September 26.*

Our "salon" was a success. There were seventeen guests. Fanny arrived first (looking fashionably rustic). She came with Michel de Cubières (looking fat), her daughter Marie (looking thin) and a Citoyen Lestaing (looking wealthy), a mulatto widower from Saint-Domingue who appeared to be on more than friendly terms with Marie. (Everyone pretended not to be shocked.)

Marie informed me that she has filed for a divorce from François under the new law. "It's easy!" She was wearing a worker-woman cap with an enormous tricolour cockade stuck to the front. "When are you going to divorce Alexandre?"

"I hadn't thought of it," I said. In spite of everything, I still felt Alexandre *was* my husband—the father of my children.

A number of deputies had been invited, including Deputy Barras, who arrived in the company of Citoyen Botot and Deputy Tallien, all of them in spirits.

Deputy Barras kissed my hand. "Citoyenne Beauharnais," he said, his big eyes mournful. "I regretted learning of your friend's—"

Citoyen Botot looked equally stricken. "The timing—" he lisped. He shrugged.

"I have been meaning to write to you both," I said, "to thank you for your help."

"Should aging libertines be trusted in the company of a lady?" a young man in a red frock coat interrupted. Inordinately tall with a bristly head, he moved like a cat.

"Did your mother give you permission to go out tonight, Tallien?" Deputy Barras asked, setting up a table for cards. Citoyen Botot laughed.

"Deputy Tallien is *Secretary* of the Commune?" I asked Aimée later, when I had a chance. "But he's so young." Although gentle in appearance, his manner is one of a gay blade: sarcastic, irreverent, a bit of a wit.

"Hardly five and twenty, the son of a valet. But comely, is he not? And educated, apparently. His father's master made the mistake of educating him. I'm told he quotes Plutarch as well as any noble. In fact, it's said the master *is* his father. Do you not see something aristocratic in his profile? In his nose? A gentle, good-hearted man, by the *looks* of him, but ruthless, they say—one of the Commissaires. Did you hear about that nineteen-year-old woman from Saint-Denis? Disguised as a delegate, she was apprehended in the Assembly carrying sulphuric acid—intended for his face."

"He's a Septembrist?" I thought of Luce de Montmorin, his violent death. How could we have invited a *Septembrist* to our home?

"But influential—he'd be the one to ask about passes out of the city for Princess Amalia and Frédéric." Aimée squeezed my arm. "It's said he fancies aristocratic women."

After innumerable toasts to the Republic, I invited Citoyen Tallien to join me in a game of écarté. He has a weakness for gambling, I perceived. I pleased him greatly by losing. After two games (at a cost of seventeen livres) I summoned the courage to put forward my request on behalf of my friends.

"And allow your friend Frédéric to join the army of the enemy?" Tallien responded.

I had to smile.

"Forgive me if I fail to see the humour," Tallien said.

I explained: "This is perhaps the first time my friend has been regarded as an asset on the battlefield." Dear Frédéric had a reputation for being a coward. He had even had the dishonour to be dismissed from the volunteer National Guard.

Levity or no, Tallien said he doubted that passports could be obtained.

"But there *must* be a way." Were it not for me, Frédéric and Princess Amalia would be in England now, they would be safe.


*September 30, 1792—Strasbourg*
*Rose,*

*How can you accuse me of valuing my own safety over that of my children! I would die for them! And as for Amalia and Frédéric, they are better off in Paris.*

*Alexandre*

*October 2.*

This afternoon I went to Deputy Tallien's office, to ask him once again about passports for Frédéric and Princess Amalia. I was kept waiting for some time. He was working on the layout of *L'Ami des citoyens,* the revolutionary news-sheet he publishes, he explained, when finally he consented to speak to me. He had a deadline to meet, he said.

"Some other time?" I inquired, making the bold step of inviting him to supper.

"Perfect," Aimée said when I told her, offering to keep Eugène and Hortense in her apartment for the night.


*That evening.*

Deputy Tallien is gone; my virtue intact. Tarnished, perhaps, but unsullied.

We spent the evening together, sharing two bottles of wine, which Deputy Tallien clearly enjoys. We played piquet and talked—of the Republic, the constitution, the future. Under a gentle demeanour is a young man who longs to make a difference. He is fervent in his belief in the Revolution, dedicated to a vision of a better world.

"The moderate deputies maintain that the radicals aren't heeding the past," he said, "yet the moderates ignore the present. They refuse to see the poverty that surrounds us."

"It is difficult to understand how one could *not* see it."

We talked of our families, our hopes and aspirations. "You are— twenty-four? Twenty-five?" I asked. "Do you not seek a wife?"

"I seek the wife of a brigadier-general," he said sweetly.

"You know what I mean." I smiled.

"I believe I am incapable of the emotion they call love."

I looked at him, surprised. "That must be a sad feeling."

"It is a secure feeling." He stood to go. "You've not asked about the passes for your friends." He pulled a paper out of his vest pocket. "I've arranged for two to be issued."

The light from a candle reflected in his eyes. "You are kind to have done this," I said.

"Not many call me *kind.*"

"I have another request to make," I said, made bold by wine. "Regarding a girl named Anne-Julie de Béthisy, in the Port-Libre prison. She's only nineteen."* A weeping Marquise de Moulins had contacted me three days earlier about about her niece, imprisoned when the girl's family returned from Germany.

Tallien smiled. "One gets the impression your list may be long. . . ." He leaned toward me.

I stooped suddenly to take up his sword, handed it to him. "I believe it time you fell in love," I said.

He sighed, put a hand to his heart. "Everyone seeks my downfall."

I laughed. He left content; I am relieved.


*Thursday, October 4.*
Frédéric and Princess Amalia departed this morning, quietly, before I could bid them farewell.


*October 9.*
This evening I received a note from Frédéric: "Alas, we're back."

I hurried to the Hôtel de Salm. Frédéric came to the door. He'd been weeping. "It's hopeless. We'll perish!"

Princess Amalia entered. She told me what had happened. They'd set out for Amiens, but at a post station near Clermont their papers had been questioned. No amount of persuasion—"Or gold," Frédéric interjected—could persuade the station-master not to turn them over to the authorities. Fortunately, the precinct commander was more lenient and let them go, provided they returned immediately to Paris.

"And so here we are, in the gayest prison in all of Europe," Frédéric concluded, waving an embroidered handkerchief through the air. "At least *here* we may go to the opera."

* *Anne-Julie de Béthisy was the cousin of the Abbesse de Penthémont. Rose had been introduced to the girl's aunt, Marquise de Moulins (or Demoulins), in Fontainebleau.*

*Friday, October 12.*

A military coach pulled into our courtyard this morning.

"Lieutenant Soufflet," Agathe informed me. "He has a message from your husband."

"From Alexandre?"

"Oui, oui." Lieutenant Soufflet remembered to remove his hat. He seemed a boy—no more than fourteen or fifteen. "Oui," yet again. He felt around in his pockets and handed me a letter.

I recognized Alexandre's hand. *I can no longer trust you. I do not have to remind you of the law.*

"I am to take General Beauharnais's son back to Strasbourg with me." Lieutenant Soufflet spoke these words resolutely, as if he had been practising.

"Eugène is to go to Strasbourg? With you?"

"Oui."

"Now?"

"Oui, oui."

"Surely there has been a mistake!"

I read the note again. *The law.* As the father, Alexandre could command his children back to the dangers of Paris, entrust his son on a long and perilous journey in the care of a boy, expose him to the dangers of a garrison town. I put the note in my pocket. I understood: I had no choice.

Lieutenant Soufflet and I left to fetch Eugène at the joiner's workshop in the Faubourg Saint-Antoine, where he has been serving as an apprentice, as required by the Commune. The fragrant smell of wood dust filled the room. Eugène, busy at a table at the back, did not look up.

I explained to Citoyen Quinette the purpose of my call. He called Eugène over and told him he was dismissed. Eugène looked alarmed. He enjoyed his apprenticeship more than he had ever enjoyed school.

"I will explain," I said.

The large, official coach and the handsome team of horses impressed Eugène, as did the uniform Citoyen Soufflet was wearing, his jaunty hat and long, shiny sword. Eugène brushed the sawdust off his clothes and climbed onto the leather seat.

We returned to Rue Saint-Dominique. It took less than one half-hour to prepare. Proudly, Eugène strapped on his sword. Hortense pushed a drawing into his haversack. I checked over the basket of foodstuffs. "No eggs?" Agathe went to see if there were any hard-cooked.

Lieutenant Soufflet was growing uneasy. It was time. It was raining so we said our farewells at the door. I feared tears, but was instead startled—and, I admit, saddened—by Eugène's enthusiasm. He was going to join his father at the front. What could be closer to a boy's heart?

## In which we grieve for our King

*November 5, 1792.*
Eugène sends brief, mournful letters. Life in Strasbourg is not as he imagined. Instead of being "on the front"—in tents and around campfires, which is how he imagined it—he is enrolled in Collège Nationale, a revolutionary boarding school which he loathes even more than the aristocratic ones.

Hortense struggles over a sash she is making for him. She misses him greatly. We all do.

*November 16.*
I have spent most of this week interviewing applicants for a governess for Hortense. This afternoon I asked my mantua-maker if she might be interested. Her name is Marie de Lannoy, of the ancient Lannoy family of Flanders (she insists)—a homely, vain woman with claims to being an aristocrat. She chatters incessantly, but she can read and I'm desperate. As a former seamstress for the Queen, she will also be able to teach Hortense a trade, fulfilling the legal requirement. She starts next week.

*Monday, November 19.*
"*Mademoiselle* Lannoy, s'il vous plaît." She is stout, with a pockmarked face, buck teeth and bad breath. She has insisted on a bedchamber on the second floor, objecting to the one on the third. Already the cook is cursing,

for she sent her mutton chops back three times. No "tu" or "toi" for this lady, not even to the children, much less to Fortuné, who tried to bite her.

Agathe, our stuttering revolutionary, is the only brave soul among us. She alone refuses to be cowed, boldly addressing her as "*Citoyenne* Lannoy" and taking the liberty of bestowing upon her a vigorous fraternal embrace—much to Mademoiselle Lannoy's obvious discomfort. I confess I was amused.

*November 22.*
Mademoiselle Lannoy will not speak to Agathe. "I will have nothing to do with a Jacobin," she told me firmly.

"Must I remind you," I told her, "my husband is a Jacobin as well as a Brigadier-General in the revolutionary army. We are a *Republican* family."

I have insisted that she take Hortense to all the revolutionary festivals and allow her to play with the bookseller's children. I sound more patriotic than I am, I confess, but Lannoy's arrogance brings out the revolutionary spirit even in me.

*November 18, 1792—Strasbourg*
*Dear Rose,*
*Thank you for your "olive branch"—nor do I want to quarrel. It is important in a time such as ours that all factions be eliminated. We must stand united against the Enemy, against the oppressors of Freedom.*
*Eugène seems to have adjusted and is showing more of a Republican spirit.*
*Your husband, Alexandre Beauharnais*

*Monday, November 26.*
We've become a house of spies. Agathe spies on Lannoy, Lannoy on Agathe. Hortense spies on them both.

Last week Hortense informed me that Agathe sneaks out after petit déjeuner each day—and I've discovered that it is so. Agathe does go out, and furtively so, around ten in the morning. An hour later she is back, her cheeks flushed, her chores undone.

Now I have discovered where it is that she goes. It's the guillotine that draws her, across the river in the Place Louis Quinze—Place de la Révolution now—where daily crowds gather, the vendors selling lemonade, the children playing prisoner's base, the old ladies gossiping as the heads fall.


*November 29.*

This morning I went to my dressmaker on Rue Saint-Honoré. It was with a sinking heart that I saw a cart approaching, three men and a woman on their way to the guillotine, one of the men a youth, really, quite young and weeping, another man doing his best to console him. Five boys were following behind the cart, dancing the farandole.

Shaken, I crossed the street and traced my way back to the palace gardens. There I sought an empty bench under a chestnut tree and sat for a moment, my heart gripped by sorrow. Not far from me, under a chestnut tree, a toy-seller was setting out a tray of tiny guillotines, the kind Hortense and Eugène had often pressed me to buy and I had unpatriotically refused.

I could hear the sounds of the crowd gathering in the Place de la Révolution. Now and then a group would break into song and others would join in and the song would grow in strength and joy. It was a bright and shining morning, and if one could erase the image of the knife, one could not imagine a more innocent festivity.

A cheer sounded and then the cry, "Long live the Republic!"

A head fallen.

What have we become?


*November 22, 1792—Strasbourg*
*Dear Rose,*

*Victory has crowned our arms! I was confident my commanding general, the great Custine, would conquer Mainz—but Frankfurt as well! This victory proves the virtue of our cause. Our Republic will carry the banner of*

*Freedom to all the nations of the world, throw off the oppressive yoke of tyranny! This news has made my job of training the new recruits easier. With glory in their hearts they tackle their work with enthusiasm.*

*Eugène has been ill with a fever, but is now recovering.*

*Your husband, Alexandre Beauharnais*

*December 8, 1792—Strasbourg*
*Dear Rose,*

*Celebration has turned to shame. General Custine's troops were forced to fall back on Mainz, where they are trapped for the winter. Many of my men have deserted. There are rumours that Custine will be arrested, as a result. Don't believe what you read in the journals.*

*Your husband, Alexandre Beauharnais*

*December 23.*

It was with some difficulty that Hortense and I made our way to Fontainebleau for "Christmas." (We dare not call it that now—it is not Christmas we are celebrating, but *Unity,* the official designation.) Most of the horses have been requisitioned for the armies, so the wait for a seat on the post-coach was considerable. I thought to hire a hackney but the drivers were charging four times the normal rate, well beyond our means. So when Frédéric and Princess Amalia offered us the use of their coach and four, I accepted.

And so it was that Hortense (with Fortuné), Lannoy and I set off in such fine style. Although Frédéric and Princess Amalia had long ago taken the precaution of painting over the aristocratic emblems, there was no disguising the fine wood inlay around the windows. Was this the reason the officials at Porte-Saint-Martin would not allow us to pass through? Or was it Lannoy's haughty demeanour? Or Fortuné's incessant growling? Whatever the cause, the guard was reluctant to believe that our papers were authentic. We had to turn back and try another gate. The detour had added two hours to our journey. By the time we arrived in Fontainebleau we were dangerously chilled.

Aunt Désirée burst into tears upon greeting us—it has been many months since we last saw her and the time has been fraught with worry. The Marquis's beard, which used to be grey, has turned a shocking white.

"Don't call him Marquis," Aunt Désirée cautioned fretfully. "It's *citoyen* now."

I suppressed a smile.


*Wednesday, December 26.*
The King's trial has begun. "It's an insult!" Lannoy exclaimed. "The *King* can do no wrong!" She is convinced that the compromising papers found in the iron chest were put there intentionally by Jacobins.*

"Pray hold your tongue, Lannoy!" I whispered, urging her to use caution in her expression. It has been made a crime punishable by death to show support for royalty. "A governess needs her head."

"Fig," she exclaimed. "Fig, I say."

She has certain endearing ways, but one has to look for them.


*Later.*
This evening I was visited by a market woman, a poissarde. The scent of attar of roses gave me pause. In the parlour, she let down her hood. It was Fanny. "Why are you in disguise?" I asked, alarmed.

"I've come to warn you," she hissed, motioning me to be silent. "François has fled. He tried to free the King."

"Mon Dieu." I lowered myself onto a chair. "*Free* the King? From the Temple?" I mouthed these words.

Fanny nodded, taking a pencil and paper out of her basket. *He was part of a group,* she wrote. *A conspiracy.*

I was so stunned by this news I could hardly comprehend. Alexandre's older brother, cautious, quiet, honourable François, had taken the

---

* *On November 2, secret correspondence between the King and the Austrians was discovered in a locked iron chest hidden behind a wooden wall panel in the Tuileries Palace.*

ultimate gamble, the one flamboyant, desperate act of a hero. He had risked his life to free the King.

Fanny pushed another scrap of paper into my hand. *He's gone over to Germany—to join the émigré army at Coblentz!*

I threw the notes into the fire. Would François and Alexandre bear arms against one another then? Would they carry their quarrel unto death?

I heard a door close in the hall. Agathe. I motioned to Fanny to be cautious.

Fanny held out her hand. In it was a gem, a diamond. The lights danced against her skin. "I will take only metal coin, Citoyenne," she said loudly, feigning a knowledge of a market accent I did not know she possessed. (Were I not in such a state of alarm, I might have found it amusing.)

"Is it genuine?" I asked, loud enough to be heard. "What are you asking for it?"

"Not half its value."

"You talked to François?" I whispered when I could be sure that we were alone again.

Fanny nodded. "He came to say goodbye to Émilie. He gave me a letter to give to his father. I am going to try to get out to Fontainebleau tonight. The Marquis must be warned."

Of course. We would all be under suspicion now. "But *how?*" The barriers had been closed all week.

Fanny glanced toward the hall. "I know a sewing-woman who lives by a break in the wall," she whispered, "once used by smugglers."

I heard soft footsteps in the hall again. "And so, my good woman, how much *do* you want for this?"

Fanny scribbled something on a piece of paper: *I'm going into hiding.*

The harsh reality of our lives came true to me then. It was possible—I could not admit to the fact that it was even *likely*—that I might never see Fanny again. The tears I'd been fighting overwhelmed me.

Fanny put the diamond in my hand, pinched my cheek and was gone.

*January 15, 1793—Strasbourg*

*Dear Rose,*

*I am shocked and appalled to learn of my brother's defection. The enemies of the Revolution are too cowardly to face the problems of our day; they look, instead, to the past, to the Age of Chivalry, the Crusades, fancying emigration a modern Crusade. They claim the King is in danger of being guillotined. Absurd! The rage of Europe would be heaped upon us! How foolish do they imagine us to be? They insist that in taking up arms against their own countrymen, they act honourably. They delude themselves!*

*François has put the entire family in danger, cast the stain of the traitor over us all. I fear he might try to contact my father. If a letter is received, it must be turned over unopened to the officials at the section office. Make sure he and Désirée understand the importance of this.*

*My brother's inheritance, all his property and possessions, will be confiscated now, of course, leaving Marie and their daughter Émilie penniless. It goes without saying that Émilie's prospects for a good marriage have been for ever dashed.*

*I can't believe it has come to this. . . . I close in despair,*

*Your husband, Alexandre Beauharnais*

*Tuesday, January 15, 1793.*

The King has been found guilty—of *treason*. Lannoy is profoundly indisposed. We've been giving her hysteric water to revive her.

"Will they kill him?" Hortense asks. "Will they take his head?"

I assure her no. However much the French love liberty, we hold our good King Louis dear.

*January 17.*

I was at my perfumer's shop on the Rue Neuve des Petits Champs when I heard some commotion on the street. A caller on horseback cried out: "The King must die! The King must die!"

I turned to the shopkeeper. She burst into tears and ran from the shop. I walked out the door into the brilliant winter sun. Others, too, lined the street. We looked to one another in shocked silence. Our *King* must die?

*January 21.*
The drums began at dawn. I closed the drapes, but I could not keep out the sound.

Lannoy stayed in her room, praying. Agathe took her a dish of tea.

We heard the drums roll three times. Even Hortense grew silent. I held her in my arms.

The King is dead. We have killed our King.

## In which my husband's star rises and falls

*May 28, 1793.*

Deputy Tallien called this evening, his bristly hair uncovered in spite of a gentle spring rain.

"What is it?" The wife of a soldier always fears news.

"Your husband is going to be promoted," he said.

"Promoted?" It was only two months ago Alexandre had been made General.

"Commander-in-Chief of the Army of the Rhine."

"*Commander*-in-Chief?"

"It's to be announced in the Assembly tomorrow."* Tallien leaned his sword against the wall.

"Can nothing be done to stop it?"

"This is quite an honour, Citoyenne."

I held my tongue. Now, almost three in the morning, I cannot sleep. Alexandre—Commander-in-Chief? I should rejoice, yet fear is the emotion that fills me. A quill is Alexandre's weapon—not a sword. I see myself in a widow's habit, I see my children in black.

---

*\* In fact, Tallien uses the term "Convention." During the Revolution, the name of the elected body was changed several times: on June 17, 1789, the* Estates General *became the* National Assembly, *which in turn became the* Constituent Assembly *in the fall of that same year. With the adoption of the new constitution, on October 1, 1791, the elected body became the* National Legislative Assembly, *which on September 22, 1792, became the* National Convention. *In the interests of making the text less confusing for the reader, the word "Assembly" has been used throughout.*

*May 29.*

I saw Tallien in an archway, his bright tricolour plume setting him off from all the deputies in tall black hats. He told a clerk to show me to a private loge, which, to judge by the luxury of its fittings, must have once belonged to the royal family. It was more like an apartment, with a water-closet and even a fireplace. There were three women there, one in scarlet satin with a daring décolletage. They introduced themselves as guests of Deputy Barras, "en mission to the south, *alas*," the woman in scarlet said.

We fell to watching the proceedings. When Alexandre was proclaimed Commander, Tallien jumped to his feet and applauded. The approval was far from unanimous, however. "Let us be perfectly clear, citoyens," yelled a deputy from the back of the hall. "It is the *Vicomte* Alexandre *de* Beauharnais who has been proclaimed . . . an *aristocrat*." Menacing hisses followed this declaration.

"Congratulations, *Vicomtesse*," the woman with silver paint on her eyelids said.

"*Citoyenne*, s'il te plaît," I said, and quickly rose to go.


*June 3, 1793—Strasbourg*
*Dear Rose,*

*I have been acclaimed, but feel far from secure. The war waged on the battlefield is simple in comparison to that waged in the Assembly. It would be helpful if you made contact with the members of the Committee of Public Safety—Deputy Barère I know is one. We were colleagues together in the Estates General. He could prove useful, but be cautious: In the early years, he had suggested a throne of diamonds for the King, yet at the King's trial he insisted the Tree of Liberty be refreshed by royal blood. No one can be trusted.*

*Your husband, Alexandre Beauharnais*


*Tuesday, June 11.*

I'm exhausted. Every morning I write letters—letters of appeal, letters of guarantee. Every afternoon I sit in on the Assembly sessions, meet with members of the various committees. In the evening I go to the salons the men of influence frequent. I smile, I nod, I inquire.

In this way the wife of Commander-in-Chief Beauharnais has succeeded in getting the sequester lifted on the home of Citoyenne Montlosier and her three children, a stay of execution for Citoyen Dolivier, the release of Deputy Hervilly and the award of a position in the postal service to Citoyen Basire, whose daughter begs coins on the Pont-Neuf. In this way the wife of Commander-in-Chief Beauharnais fights a war of her own.


*June 10.*
The Austrians are gathering strength. Alexandre's letters are disturbing. He is concerned about what might happen if he must lead his men into battle. "My troops are ill-equipped, ill-clothed and ill-fed. I am doing everything I can to train them, increase their morale, but I fear for them. We stand thirty thousand against three hundred thousand, and prayer is no longer the fashion."


*Sunday, June 16, 3:15 P.M.*
Aimée is jubilant. She has succeeded in negotiating a marriage contract for Lucie, now fourteen, to Jean-Henri de Croisoeuil, thirty-four.

"Monsieur de Croisoeuil? Isn't he a Royalist, a counter-revolutionary?"

"But disgustingly *wealthy.*"


*June 15, 1793—Fontainebleau*
*Dear Rose,*

*As you insisted, I have hung a copy of the Declaration of the Rights of Man in a prominent place in our parlour—fortunately, the Marquis cannot see well enough to notice—and just this morning I made a donation to the municipality in exchange for an affidavit declaring my patriotism. But I draw the line at attending the Temple of Reason!*

*I have been trying to persuade the Marquis to send a donation to the Jacobin Club here, along with the patriotic speech which you so thought-*

*fully provided, but he refuses. On this matter you will have to speak to him yourself.*

*I am having great difficulty getting our certificates and papers in order. (Perhaps you have my baptismal records? They would be in the bottom drawer of your escritoire.) Already I have suffered some harassment on this account. At every turn one is required to present papers and passports and if there is the slightest inconsistency . . . !*

*When are you coming to see us here in Fontainebleau? We miss Hortense. I know how busy you are with all your good works, but do try. We are frantic. . . .*

*Your godmother, Aunt Désirée*

*June 21—Fontainebleau.*

Aunt Désirée is uncharacteristically undone. She has been walling up valuables in a corner of the cellar, late at night when the servants are asleep. Both she and the Marquis showed visible relief to see me, and great joy to see Hortense again.

My passport permitted me to stay for one week. This gave me time to talk with Aunt Désirée, determine what should be done. She fears they are under surveillance due to François becoming a major-general in the army of the émigrés. Were it not for the fragile condition of the Marquis's health, they would go into hiding.

"What are we to do?" Aunt Désirée demanded, showing me the extreme unction kit she kept hidden in a crockery pot in the scullery: a hollowed crucifix which held two candles, a few cotton swabs and a vial of blessed oil—in case the Marquis were to die. "Camp in some third-storey garret?" She carefully put the crucifix back. "It would kill him!"

So they keep quiet, pay their help well (better than they can afford), and do nothing to draw attention to themselves.

I was anxious to get them to register loyalty to the Republic, as a protection against arrest. If they didn't, it would certainly not count in their favour. At first the Marquis refused. He could *never* vow allegiance to a government he could not support. "A noble stands by his words." It took considerable persuasion to get him to relent.

The journey to the section house was perilous. Aunt Désirée and I had dressed the Marquis as best we could, taking care that he not look too dignified. With some effort I got him to sport a bonnet rouge. I rehearsed them both on what they were to say and reminded them to use the familiar form. ("To someone I don't even know?" the Marquis demanded. "How rude.") When the clerk at the section office addressed him in the familiar and refused to take off his cap in respect, I trembled. Fortunately the Marquis was too confused to quarrel and Aunt Désirée too nervous. They made their oaths with the appearance of sincerity, and as we came back out into the hot summer sun I congratulated them both.

"For what?" the Marquis scowled, pulling the bonnet rouge from his head.

Quickly, I took the hat from him; I feared he might throw it to the ground. I hung it on a branch of the liberty tree outside the section house—a common act of patriotism. "How generous of you to give up your hat for the Tree of Liberty, Citoyen," I said loudly, for the benefit of some young men passing by.

Slowly we made our way home; as for myself, I am giddy with relief.


*June 25—Paris.*
Deputy Tallien came to our salon tonight. It was in the early hours, after a shocking amount of money had been exchanged at faro, that he told me, in confidence: "Your husband's star continues to rise. He is now being considered for the position of Minister of War."

"For *all* of France?"

"You are not pleased?"

"They will murder him. *That* should please me?"

Deputy Tallien made a careless grin. "They will murder us all," he shrugged, playing his last card.


*Thursday, June 27.*
In the Assembly today Alexandre was nominated for Minister of War. A number of deputies jumped to their feet in protest, including Robespierre. Deputy Barère went to the tribune in front of the President's box.

He read out several of Alexandre's patriotic statements to the papers, accounts of his zeal. Then another deputy came forward. He argued that Commander-in-Chief Alexandre Beauharnais was too valuable to be made Minister of War. He should stay with the Army of the Rhine and continue on to glorious victories. Another deputy countered that if Commander-in-Chief Alexandre Beauharnais could achieve so much at the head of one army, think of what glory would be France's were he placed at the head of *eleven*, as Minister of War.

Eleven . . . *mon Dieu.*

When several deputies protested—yelling that it was an *aristocrat* who was being considered for one of the most powerful positions in the Republic—Deputy Barère jumped up, cried out, "He is my friend! He is my friend!"

The nomination was accepted.

I am ill; I have taken to bed. All our armies were losing. To be Minister of War at this time means certain death. I have sent an estafet to Alexandre, begging him to decline.


*Tuesday, July 30.*

Our Tuesday night salon was somewhat strained. The sudden surrender of our men at Mainz to the Germans, the failure of Alexandre's troops to rescue them, the dishonour to the Republic, threw a feeling of gravity over the evening.

"I have something to show you," Deputy Tallien whispered to me, guiding me into the music room. "A billet your husband sent the Committee. I think you should see it."

He handed me the letter—one page, only half of it filled. In brief blunt words Alexandre expressed rage at the surrender of our troops at Mainz, blaming the commanders there, calling for their execution, demanding that their decapitated heads be sent to the enemy. Indignantly, he insisted that the government accept his resignation, his offer to break his sword.

I handed the letter back. I felt uneasy with Alexandre's blame of the disaster on others, his call for vengeance. "Apparently he is ill," I said.

"How convenient." Deputy Tallien folded the letter, slipped it into his vest pocket. "The enemy attacks, one million Frenchmen prepare for battle and your husband wishes to resign his command." His tone was sarcastic. "This does not reflect well on him, Citoyenne. Indeed, you should be aware that the word 'traitor' has been spoken."

"Rather Commander-in-Chief Beauharnais should have led untrained troops against a professional army ten times the size? Rather he should have led his men to *slaughter?*"

"One leads, willing or not," Deputy Tallien answered. "It takes courage to face one's own death, but even more so the death of others. We are learning this lesson well."

Our conversation was interrupted by a woman and two men, one of whom was in uniform. "Why should dancing no longer be permitted on the streets?" the woman complained, running her fingers lightly across the harp strings.

"It's the other outlawed pleasures* that concern me," the man in uniform said. His companion laughed.

"Deputy Tallien, darling—" The woman took his hand, began a little dance around him. "Why no dancing, pray?"

"Robespierre doesn't care for pleasure, I've heard," the man in uniform said.

"Robespierre doesn't care for women," the other man said.

"Shall I tell Deputy Robespierre you said that?" Tallien's eyes were on the woman, her revealing décolletage.

I stared into the empty fireplace, oblivious to their gaiety. What would become of Alexandre now?


*Saturday, August 10.*
We were awoken at dawn by artillery fire announcing the Festival of Unity.

One must attend these events lest one's patriotism be questioned, so late in the afternoon Aimée, the children and I set out, dressed in Republican

* *The revolutionary government frowned on prostitution as a remnant of the corrupt Ancien Régime.*

garb. We hired a fiacre to take us to the site of the Bastille. At Port-Saint-Paul we were slowed by a procession of men, women and children trudging along in the heat carrying posies of wheat. We decided to get out and follow behind. At the intersection of Rue Saint-Antoine and Rue des Tournelles there was a giant level (signifying equality?), under which everyone was expected to walk. It reminded me of the type of thing one sees at Freemason meetings, and equally mysterious.

On the rubble of the former prison a giant statue of a woman had been erected—Mother Nature. She had a curiously mocking expression, squeezing her bosom with her hands, water gushing out. It was all Aimée and I could do to maintain a suitably reverent attitude. The children, of course, began giggling. I wasn't entirely unhappy when Aimée's daughter Lucie became ill and we had to return home. Later Aimée confessed the reason for her daughter's malady: the girl is with child, and not by Jean-Henri, her fiancé, but by the stationer's son.

"What will you do if the engagement is called off?" I asked.

"Kill her," Aimée said, lunging, her sword-arm extended.


*August 13.*
Jean-Henri has at last consented to marry Lucie, despite his young bride's dishonour. "No doubt the fear of proscription was the motivating factor," Aimée observed wryly. "Vive la Révolution!"


*August 18.*
Lucie is married, at last. The union was blessed to the sound of the crowd in the Place de la Révolution—the mob cheering the execution of General Custine, Alexandre's former commanding officer. He had lost a battle—so off with his head. In spite of the heat, I closed all the windows.

Daily Alexandre sends letters to the Assembly demanding that they accept his resignation. Daily they refuse.

*August 21.*

The Assembly has *finally* accepted Alexandre's resignation—but he is to stay at a distance of thirty leagues from the frontiers, twenty leagues from Paris, a criminal.

I was in the public galleries when the announcement was made. Immediately Deputy Tallien got up and left. I caught up with him in the gardens—with some effort, for his legs are long and he walks with impatience.

"There are other concerns!" he said. He stopped, mercifully. I caught my breath. "Your husband's resignation, the restrictions on his movements, are no longer the issue," he said. "What *is* a concern is his *head*."

"You are cruel!" I was angry at his flippancy.

"Far from it, Citoyenne," he said. "Have I not kept from you the accusations that have been brought against your husband? Have I not held my tongue?"

"Do you think I do not know!" The Army Commissars of Strasbourg had accused Alexandre of spending his time with whores when he should have been preparing for battle. I knew that. I knew more. I knew he'd played court to the daughter of an Army Commissar, Citoyen Rivage—Rivage the Rich he was commonly called. Rivage the Revenger, I would call him now.

"There are more serious charges," Deputy Tallien said. "Some are saying that your husband, an aristocrat in collusion with his brother François, *intentionally* let Mainz fall, *intentionally* betrayed the Republic."

"Who would speak such slander?"

"Deputy Robespierre, for one." Deputy Tallien looked behind him. I followed his gaze. Two men, deputies, stood at the fountain, watching us.

Deputy Tallien spoke in a hushed tone. "Citoyenne Beauharnais, if I may, as a friend—it would behoove you to become invisible. The radicals are going to succeed in pushing through their Law of Suspects, giving the Committee of General Security the power to imprison without *trial*, without *reason* even!"

"Are you not on this committee?"

"No longer—the more radical members have taken control. I caution you not to draw attention to yourself. If you were wise, you would retire from your charitable activities, from your efforts to save all the good people of Paris. *Leave* this city."

I believe I turned pale, for he clasped my arm. "You *must* listen to me! I won't be here to help you. I'm leaving in the morning."

"Leaving?" I confess I was dismayed. I'd become dependent on his help, his protection.

"For Bordeaux. En mission."

"Congratulations." I didn't know how to respond. "Bordeaux is lovely."

"Any place other than Paris is uncivilized, in my opinion."

"Will you be long?"

"Long enough to tame the population, convert the provincials, bring them to heel." He made a comical gesture.

I smiled. He was a boy in so many ways.

He pulled out his timepiece. "I'm expected at a meeting in Rue Saint-Honoré. We're having a guillotine made. The contractor, a German, assured us that it would be ready, but now, of course, he is full of excuses."

A *guillotine*. I reached for my friend's hand. I knew him to be well meaning, a patriot, yet he was so very young, too young for the power he wielded, the intoxicating power over life and death. "Beware, my friend. Don't—"

He stooped to whisper in my ear: "It is *you* who should beware."


*September 1, 1793—Hôtel Croisoeuil, Croissy*
*Dearest Rose,*

*Lucie's pregnancy is not going well. She has been confined to bed. I have moved to Hôtel Croisoeuil in order to care for her and manage the household. I thought this would be a temporary measure, but now I begin to see that it could go on for some time. As a result, I have been forced to consider what should be done with my château here, and it occurred to me: Why don't you move into it? Croissy is safe . . . and I miss you!*

*Love and a thousand kisses, your dearest friend, Aimée*
*Note—My fencing instructor has finally "cut me" (as we say in the Islands). I feinted but did not parry. Touché!*

*September 24.*

Agathe woke me in the night. She'd heard knocking.

"Is it a search party?" I asked, frightened.

"It's at the back door."

I drew the dagger from under my mattress. I put on my dressing gown. Agathe had disappeared. I lit a candle and went to the door. "Who goes there!"

There was no answer. I heard a noise. "Speak, I pray you!"

"Rose?"

I held my breath.

"Rose—is that you? *Please*, open the door!"

The voice was familiar. I opened the door a crack, the knife at my side. There, by the light of the moon, was my husband.

"Alexandre!" I opened the door. He was drenched from the rain. "It is forbidden for you to be in Paris! Why are you here? You are in danger of arrest. Is Eugène with you?"

Alexandre paced. "I had no idea it was like this in Paris now! There are guards everywhere! How am I going to get out?" He'd lost weight. His face looked gaunt and there was a feverish look in his eyes.

"Alexandre—where is Eugène?" I grabbed his arm.

He looked at me. "Eugène?"

Had he been drinking? I could not smell alcohol.

"At school," he said. He strode into the drawing room. He pulled the drapes to one side, peered out.

"You . . . you *left* him, in *Strasbourg?*" I demanded, following him. "But Alexandre, he's only twelve! He can't—"

There were shouts outside on the street. Then a knocking at the front door. "I must get out of here!" Alexandre exclaimed. He leapt toward the kitchen.

"Alexandre . . . !" But before I could stop him, he was gone. "Take care!" I cried as the kitchen door slammed shut.

## *In which I try to escape Paris*

*September 26, 1793.*
We are in Croissy, at last, in this lovely château on the banks of the Seine.
The sky is streaked the most amazing shade of pink. We will be safe here.

*October 4.*
He is here, at last. We sit together, Hortense and I, and look upon him in
amazement. He is taller than I remember, all legs—and so beautiful to
look at, this boy of mine, my son.

He made his way from Strasbourg, in the company of an aide. He carries a sword and knows how to use it. He sits a horse boldly and knows
how to tame it.

He regards me shyly—his mother, a *woman*. He becomes fretful when
I weep.

*October 10.*
Every morning at eleven Aimée comes for a bowl of tea. Often, Abbé
Maynaud de Pancemont from the "church" across the road joins us. He is
a tall man, lanky, his thin ankles sticking out from under a patched white
cape draped in the Roman style.

"It's an Italian *riding* habit," he assured me. For priests are not permitted to wear robes. He enjoys a bit of rum and is fond of romantic poetry.
He has an engaging smile, a big toothy grin. This morning the three of

us played whist and made chit-chat on a matter of great importance in our village: my gardener's courtship of my neighbour's valet's daughter.

There is an air of unrestrained joy about Abbé Maynaud de Pancemont, so it was with disbelief that I learned he'd been in Carmes prison during the September massacres. He was one of the few to survive, his long legs enabling him to leap the wall to safety, to escape the carnage, the murdered bodies of his colleagues stacked ten deep.

We are all of us in hiding here.


*October 17.*
The Queen has been guillotined, accused of crimes beyond imagining.*
Last night she appeared to me in a dream, handing me her head.

"No!" I screamed.

I sat up in the dark, my heart pounding. The night candle had burned down and the moon threw ghostly shapes against the walls. I thought I was in Martinico. I thought I could hear drums, chanting.

I heard a noise outside my door, saw a light moving. I began to tremble.

"Madame?" It was Lannoy, a candle in her hand, her white face framed by her ruffled nightcap. "I heard a scream." She set the pewter candle-holder down.

"Oh, Lannoy," I wept. "Our Queen!"


*October 25, 2:00 P.M.*
Yet another new dictate from the "Nouveau Régime"—we do not have weeks any more, but décades of ten days.** What day is it? What month?

---

* *The Queen was publicly accused, among other things, of taking her eight-year-old son into bed with her and teaching him how to masturbate, to which she responded, with tearful dignity, "I appeal to all mothers here—is such a crime possible?" She was convicted of aiding and abetting foreign powers and conspiring to provoke civil war within France.*
** *To further separate France from the Church, the Gregorian calendar was replaced by a "Republican" calendar, dating from September 22 of the previous year (1792), the date upon which the Republic had been proclaimed.*

I do not know. Is it vendémiaire, the month of vintage? Or brumaire, the month of fog?

This change has made everyone cross. This new, more "natural" order, this romantic calendar of fog, frost, wind and snow, of meadows, flowers, heat and fruit, is nothing but more work. Where have our feast-day Sundays gone? Where our days of rest?*

"It's a plot to befuddle us," Abbé Maynaud said, and perhaps he is right, for befuddled we certainly are. The measures have been changed, the names of our coins, our streets, our deities and now even our days. "They're even revising the next life," he complained, for he has been required to put a sign on the graveyard that reads: Death is eternal sleep.


*October 26.*
A great sadness has fallen over the village. Two weeks ago a flower vendor here went to Paris to testify on behalf of her brother and has not been seen since. Rumours were she'd been arrested for coming to his aid and now it is said that she was guillotined. There is a black mourning wreath on several doors in town, this in spite of the law threatening death to any who grieve a victim of the guillotine.

One hears stories of this sort often now. In most instances I feel it wise to question the veracity of the account, but sometimes, one wonders . . . what if they are *true?*


*Friday, November 1, All Saints' Day.*
As I made my way past the church this morning—on my way to Hôtel Croisoeuil to call on Aimée—Abbé Maynaud beckoned for me to enter. Inside, candles were lit. Although the hour was early five women were on their knees. "In honour of 'Reason'," he whispered, winking. It is All Saints' Day, but we dare not say so.

*\* Previous to the Revolution the French had over thirty feast-days a year in addition to Sundays and Mondays. Under the new revolutionary calendar, there was one day off every ten days plus five or six "jours complémentaires" tacked on at the end of the year—a considerably heavier workload.*

I lit candles for Catherine, Manette and Father—and another for the soul of our Queen. I tremble writing these words.

*November 2.*

Eugène brought me a note today, passed on to him by the postmaster. The wax seal was clumsily made, but it had not been broken. The script was studied, careful, composed—a child's hand. It was from young Émilie, in Paris, informing me that her mother had been taken to prison.

"What is it?" Eugène asked.

I was hesitant to tell him.

"Your aunt Marie has been arrested. She's in Sainte-Pélagie. . . ."

"In *prison?*" He was horrified.

"She is innocent," I quickly assured him. "She has done nothing wrong." How was I to explain? Marie's crime: to have been married to an émigré. That, apparently, was enough to condemn her. Her divorce, her revolutionary activities, her work in support of the Republic were of no importance, apparently. "I must go to her."

"To *Paris?*" Eugène asked. I could see fear in his eyes.

This evening I showed the note to Aimée. "Your son is right," she said. "It's too dangerous in Paris now. You must not draw attention to yourself."

"But how can I *not* go?"

My valise is packed. I leave in the morning. Quietly.

*Sunday, November 3—Paris.*

It rained the entire way to Paris. At one point, where the road was badly rutted, I feared the post-coach might go into the ditch. Near Melun we passed a convoy of grain, escorted by the National Guard. Peasants followed it, on foot, wolves circling prey.

At Fanny's hôtel on Rue de Tournon, I was received by Citoyen Lestaing. Marie's "friend" had apparently moved in.

"And to what do I owe the pleasure of this call?" he asked. He is a slight man, with haunted eyes. He was wearing a white satin dressing gown embroidered with a Roman motif.

"Émilie sent me a note—about her mother." I accepted the offer of a bowl of veal broth. "How is Marie?"

"I send the chambermaid to the prison each day with clean linens. She reports Marie is well."

"You've not seen her?"

I heard footsteps behind me. I turned. There, in the hallway, with one hand on the bannister, was twelve-year-old Émilie.

"I got your note, Émilie," I said.

"You should not have bothered your aunt," Citoyen Lestaing said.

I went to Émilie, took her hand in mine. It was cold. "Have you seen your mother?"

"Émilie!" I looked up into the face of a Negro woman of enormous proportions standing on the landing. The nanny. Émilie ran quickly up the stairs.

"The child is excitable," Citoyen Lestaing said. "It would disturb her to visit a prison."

I turned to him, my heart jumping in my chest. "I appreciate your concern, Citoyen, but I am going to see Marie," I told him, "and I will be taking Émilie with me."

It was shortly after two when Émilie and I set out. When we reached the iron gates to Sainte-Pélagie prison, I took her hand. "You don't have to come in with me."

Émilie clasped the parcel she'd brought to her chest. She had that same pixie look I remembered from when she was a baby. "I want to," she said.

"You are a brave girl."

The gaoler was a big man with a red face. He directed us to the guardhouse where we waited in the company of two men. They were kindly and smoked outside, on the steps. Émilie and I sat side by side on a truckle-bed with a rough woollen blanket pulled over it. Soon the gaoler returned, out of breath from climbing the steps. Marie was behind him.

She looked dishevelled, her dress soiled, the tricolour cockade on her bodice frayed. She attempted to tidy her hair.

"I am here to help," I said, sensing her shame.

"Citoyen Lestaing did not come?"

"He was concerned it would distress you," I lied.

Émilie pressed her parcel into her mother's hands. It contained clean linens and a silver fork, knife and spoon. There was also a porcelain cup, a small box of sewing implements, a novel by Richardson.

The gaoler examined the contents. He saw the knife and took it from her. He opened the small box and removed the scissors. "It is time," he said.

Émilie embraced her mother.

"You must not be a burden!" Marie said.

"We're working to get you out," I told her. I kissed her dirty cheeks. She took off her cockade, shoved it angrily into my hand.

Now, it is late. I am filled with concern. Deputy Tallien is in Bordeaux. Deputy Barras is in the south, I am told, Citoyen Botot with him. To whom can I turn?


*November 5.*

"You are suggesting that *I* make an appeal to the Committee?" Émilie flushed. I doubted momentarily the wisdom of my proposal.

"It is more likely that the Committee will be persuaded by a petition delivered by the prisoner's daughter," I said.

Émilie and I spent the morning preparing. We wrote out the petition, rehearsed. "Imagine that you are in a play," I coached her, for as shy as Émilie is, she blossoms on stage. "Imagine that the members of the Committee are in the audience."

She made a dramatic, pleading gesture.

"That's it!"

Shortly before three I accompanied Émilie to the Tuileries. We were told that the office of the Committee was in the southern section. My heart was pounding as we walked down the wide marble corridors. I thought of the Queen, of her footsteps on the very stones I touched. I thought of her children, orphans now, growing up in a dank prison, alone.

We sat in the anteroom with all the other petitioners, Émilie folding and unfolding her notes. At last her name was called. I gave her a little push. She went through the double doors.

When the doors opened a short time later, it was a sad, diminished Émilie I saw. "I've failed!" she wept. "What if I've failed!"

*November 10.*
Executed this week: Olympe de Gouges, Duc d'Orléans, Citoyenne Roland. Tomorrow, Citoyen Bailly, the astronomer.

*How* can this go on? Even cows cannot be induced into Paris, the smell of blood is so strong.

*Later.*
I leave for Croissy in the morning—without Émilie. I could not persuade her to leave Paris, the city of her mother's imprisonment.

*Monday, January 13, 1794—Croissy.*
Abbé Maynaud looked solemn this morning.

"Is something wrong?"

He handed me a letter. The seal was broken.

"It was broken when I received it," he said.

It was from the Committee. "You read it?" I asked.

"It's not good news."

I scanned the letter. Émilie's appeal had been turned down. No reason was given. I turned the paper over in my hand. So few words, but they meant so much—that a woman, a mother, would stay imprisoned, endanger her health, her heart, perhaps go to the guillotine, lose her head as a drunken mob cheered.

Abbé Maynaud guided me toward a chair. "A glass of brandy?"

"No!" I pulled away. "I must pack my valise," I said.

*January 14.*
I applied this morning for a pass. "So you want to go to Paris again." The postmaster used a tiny model of a guillotine to cut a length of string. He laughed.

I glanced uneasily toward the door. Two men stood watching me.

*Friday, January 17—Paris.*

I am exhausted. It is early evening, a rooster is crowing. I've taken claret to calm my nerves. I will write in the morning. For now, I can't. . . .


*January 18.*

What happened:

As I entered the grand hall, I encountered a most disturbing sight—a long line of men, women, children even. From the bedding and baskets of food, I gathered that some had been there for a long time. I went to the head of the line. "I wish to speak to Deputy Vadier," I told the guard. Vadier's signature had been on Marie's arrest warrant. He and Alexandre had worked together in the Assembly, I recalled.

"So do all these others," the guard smirked.

I handed him a letter I had written. "Would it be possible to have this delivered to Deputy Vadier then?"

The guard opened the big double doors. He gave my envelope to a man in blue velvet sitting at a desk. The man looked up at me briefly.

I smiled: *Please?*

He looked away. No doubt he received such looks all day.

There was nothing to do but wait. Now and then the big oak doors would open and the man in blue velvet would call out a name and one of our numbers would enter. This kept our hopes up for being summoned ourselves.

A few members of the Committee would come and go. Robespierre was one of these. He was wearing a striped satin waistcoat. A woman threw herself to her knees in front of him. She was pulled away by the guards.

Toward noon I began to despair. I saw a man approach—a man I recognized. Deputy Barère! I ran after him, called out his name. He turned.

"Citoyenne Beauharnais." There was something in his face that warned me.

"I've been here all morning, hoping to speak to Deputy Vadier."

"We are exceedingly busy." He ran his hand through his thinning hair, which he had combed to disguise a bald spot.

"If I could just talk to him. . . ."

He shook his head, gave me a look of alarm: *Don't insist.* "I'm afraid that's not possible." The big oak doors closed behind him.

It was nearing five in the afternoon when my name was called. I went to the head of the line. The guard handed me an envelope. I broke open the seal. Inside was a note: *Green salon, north side.* Signed *B.*

It took some time to locate the green salon. When I gave the guard my name he opened the door: I was expected.

Deputy Barère was seated at an elegant writing table. The room was full of ormolu clocks and vases, Gobelin tapestries, several gold and silver tea equipages, a brass statue of the Virgin Mary and three immense candle snuffers. Deputy Barère waited until the door had closed before offering me a seat. "I have put myself in jeopardy meeting with you."

I was feeling short of breath. I heard a cheer outside. "Long live the Republic!" Crowds at the scaffold. I rushed into my speech: "I am seeking release of my sister-in-law, Citoyenne Marie-Françoise Beauharnais, an ardent Republican. She has been imprisoned in Sainte-Pélagie, due to her ex-husband's defection. Yet she divorced him long ago and is not of his party in any way—"

"Citoyenne Beauharnais!" Deputy Barère silenced me with a wave of his hand. "I cannot help your sister-in-law. I have family of my own in prison—I cannot help them! I have consented to meet you only out of a past regard for your husband. You must warn him—he is in danger of arrest." This last he whispered. "And as for you and your children . . ."

The *children* . . . grand Dieu!

"Please understand that you must be *exceedingly* cautious. I can't emphasize this enough—"

"But Citoyen Beauharnais is in Blois," I stuttered. "I can't even write to him to warn him. I have reason to believe that the mail is under surveillance."

"Quite likely." Deputy Barère stood, sighed. "These are . . . *difficult* times. I can say no more." And he was gone.

Lannoy was alarmed by my condition. She brought me a claret. Against persistent admonitions, I insisted on rising. I knew what I had to do. I had to appeal once more to Deputy Vadier, write a letter, for Alexandre's sake, as well as for Marie's. I had to rise and write this letter upon which so much depended, and I had to do so quickly before courage gave way, before fear took possession of me.

It took one hour to compose the draft. Lannoy brought me cup after cup of broth for strength. In spite of the flaws and imperfections, I copied out the final version. As I sprinkled it with sand I silently recited a chant Mimi had once taught me so many many years ago, a prayer to the mystères. I sealed the envelope and sent Lannoy to deliver it. If I waited for a courier, I knew I would tear it to shreds.

*March 4, 1794—Croissy.*
A long walk today, along the river. As I turned back to the château I saw Eugène running toward me, his long legs pumping up and down, up and down.

*What had happened?*
He was crying when he reached me.
Alexandre has been arrested.

*In which I go to the aid of my husband*

*March 6, 1794—Paris.*
I approached the Luxembourg Palace—a prison now—with trepidation, but was soon reassured. Inside, men and women in aristocratic dress mingled freely. Everywhere there were tête-à-têtes, gatherings, the sound of laughter and games. Some of the rooms were elaborately furnished. I saw a woman in a striped polonaise attended by a valet in livery.

I was told to wait in an elegant antechamber. I was offered tea—*real* tea, so rare now. Shortly, Alexandre arrived. I was moved to see him. He was bronzed from country life, his fair hair blonder than usual.

We embraced and exchanged news much as if we were sitting at home in the parlour, not in a prison. He confessed that he was suffering from indigestion, but not from the food, which he said was excellent. He'd met an old friend, an officer with the Esterhazy Hussars, and they'd stayed up most of the night drinking wine and playing billiards.

"All the best people of Paris are here," Alexandre said, as if proud to be included. He gave me a list of books he would like and requested money—a considerable sum, for the privilege of being so comfortably detained cost dear. "I will be out soon, no doubt, but until that happy day, I intend to put this time to good use."

"I wish I had your faith," I said.

After a midday meal, which I ate halfheartedly, I decided to call on Princess Amalia and Frédéric. I was in need of the Princess's sweet temper, Frédéric's drôle wit.

Approaching Hôtel de Salm, I was puzzled by the National Guard standing at their gate. I was allowed to enter the courtyard, only to be turned away at the door by a footman. Princess Amalia was indisposed, he said.

"And Prince Frédéric?"

The valet looked confused. He told me to wait in the anteroom and disappeared into one of the palatial rooms. He returned shortly after. "The Princess will receive you," he said.

He led me to a bedchamber on the second floor where I found Princess Amalia, her eyes red, her wig on the carpet: Frédéric has been arrested, she herself was under house arrest. Hence the guard at her gate.

We collapsed onto the sofa together. I felt numb. All my fears had come to pass. Were it not for me, Frédéric and Princess Amalia would be in England, safe from harm. "Where are they holding him?" I asked.

"I don't even know!" she wept.


*March 9.*

The children and Lannoy will arrive by coach at three. I gathered up my meat-rationing cards, enabling Agathe to purchase a hare. We'll have a meal and then walk over to the Luxembourg to visit their father—a prisoner.


*March 14.*

Alexandre has been transferred to the convent of the Carmelites. My heart sank when I heard. Slovenly, haunted—the Carmes was said to be one of the worst prisons in Paris. I thought of the massacres that had happened there, the stories Abbé Maynaud had told me.

So it was with trepidation that I went today. The gate creaked as the guard opened it. Even from the courtyard, I could smell the stench. I followed the guard through an archway and up some stone steps to a small room. There I was told to wait. Along one wall were dark stains—blood stains, I realized, from where the murderers had leaned their sabres.

Alexandre was ushered in. He looked shaken, uneasy. He wasn't wearing a cravat. I told him I'd still not succeeded in finding out the reason for his arrest. For the first time, he showed impatience. "But there must be a reason! They can't just hold me!"

I left even more determined to find answers.

*Saturday, March 15.*
Deputy Tallien is back in Paris, thank God. I sent him a message: it was urgent that I see him. He returned a note within an hour. I was to come to his office—in disguise. I was to give my name as a Citoyenne Gossec, a perfumer, witness to a shipment of grain that had been destroyed outside the city walls.

The need for disguise puzzled me. I borrowed a dress from Lannoy. By putting a small pillow into a corset I was able to give the appearance of a woman with child. That together with a veiled hat made me sufficiently mysterious.

I arrived at Tallien's office at precisely two. I was let into the anteroom. When Deputy Tallien came to the door, he looked at me without recognition. I smiled and then he realized who I was.

Once within the privacy of his office—which had been elaborately refurnished since I had last been there—we were able to embrace.

"No, I am *not* with child," I smiled, in answer to his questioning look. "Why the necessity of disguise?" I asked, accepting my friend's offer of a glass of Clos-Vougeot.

"I am watched."

*"You?"* He did not look well. "You've returned to Paris unexpectedly."

"Been *recalled* is more accurate."

"Was there a problem?" I thought of the things I'd heard, of the terrible things my friend was rumoured to have been responsible for: a *massacre* in Bordeaux, hundreds of aristocrats executed. Was it possible? I could not believe it.

"You should know that your wish has been granted." He placed his hand over his heart.

"*My* wish?"

"I now know what it is to love."

I could not but smile at such a solemn confession. "That grieves you?" I asked. His expression was one of profound misery.

"The possessor of my affection has an untamed heart—for which I love her all the more, I confess. But I will die as a result—if not of a broken heart, then by the loss of my head on the scaffold." He sat solemnly with his hands before him, his long fingers clasped.

"Pray do not keep me in suspense, my friend."

"The captor of my heart wrote a letter to Citoyen Jullien, Robespierre's nancy-boy sent to spy on me in Bordeaux. In it she gave *him* her undying love, and complained of me, 'the tyrant'! She even tried to persuade him to escape to America with her!"

"She sent this letter to Jullien? How did you come to know of it?"

"The saga, my friend, gets worse." He downed his wine and poured himself another glass. "Jullien forwarded this missive to the Committee of Public Safety. Now it is a public scandal and I'm cast in the role of a fool." He looked forlorn.

"Perhaps it is a plot by Jullien and Robespierre to discredit you. Have you considered that possibility?"

Deputy Tallien shook his head. "I examined the letter. It is in her hand. There can be no mistake. She, the angel who has claimed my heart, she alone is the author of my defeat. Jullien has accused me before the members of the Committee of being her bondslave; I cannot deny it!"

"Where is she now? This angel of yours . . ."

"I've just learned that she is back in Paris. I cannot tell you how it torments me to know that she is near." He stood and began pacing, waving his glass of wine around wildly. "You know her, no doubt. Her name is Thérèse . . . Thérèse Cabarrus."

I was stunned. Thérèse Cabarrus? I had met her at a salon years ago. Even as a girl she had been known for her extraordinary beauty—and her height: "Amazon" she'd been called. She was the daughter of the Treasurer to the King of Spain. Her family was both powerful and wealthy. Thérèse had been one of the few women admitted to Club 89, an exclusive group whose members included Mirabeau, Lafayette, Sieyès, Condorcet. . . . Of course the gossips contended that her contribution was not *philosophical* in nature and had even published a pamphlet to that effect.

Suddenly I understood my friend's lament. Young Deputy Tallien, the humble son of a lowly valet, had given his heart to the wealthiest, most beautiful, most *spirited* woman in all of Europe.

"What a terrible affliction you have wished upon your friend!" he cried. "It is not the guillotine I fear, but the loss of her love!"

I sighed. There was little likelihood that my friend could be attentive to any of *my* requests for help—not in his agitated condition. "Perhaps I can be of assistance," I offered.

And *then* I would see about Alexandre, Frédéric, Marie. . . .


*March 16.*
Thérèse Cabarrus was at her toilette when I entered. It was nine in the morning. She was drinking champagne before an open window that looked out on the Seine. A young woman (I would guess her age at twenty), and strikingly tall, she was wearing a revealing dressing gown with no attempt at modesty. "May I help you?" she asked, turning to greet me. She spoke with a slight Spanish accent. Her voice was deep, soothing, without the ostentation so common to her rank.

I glanced around her bedchamber—everywhere, in and among numerous flowering plants, there were paintings, sculptures, works of art. In the corner was a harpsichord. By the window an unfinished painting on an easel. The abundant trimmings were elegant—yet the effect of the arrangement was unique, bizarre, stimulating to the imagination.

"I am here on behalf of a mutual acquaintance," I began, accepting the offer of a chair.

The chambermaid slipped the dressing gown from Thérèse's shoulders and began massaging her neck. "And who might that be?" Thérèse asked. Her eyes were huge, black—not without wisdom.

"A man who loves you very much."

Thérèse looked at me with a playful expression. "Ah—but there are so many."

I smiled. I believed her. I believed it entirely possible for all the men of Paris to lust after such a creature.

"You find me vain?"

"I find you disarmingly honest," I said.

"Does this disturb you?"

"I appreciate honesty."

She looked at me for a long moment. "We shall be friends," she said.

We finished the bottle of champagne. I informed her that Deputy Jullien had forwarded her letter on to the Committee of Public Safety.

"Grand Dieu!" She put her hands to her heart. "My intention was to discredit Deputy Jullien, for I had discovered that he was spying on Tallien and reporting back to Robespierre. I had intended to tempt him into foolishness."

"You are aware of the danger this puts Deputy Tallien in?"

"Will he ever forgive me?"

"He will forgive you *anything*."


*March 20.*

Deputy Tallien leaps about. He cannot believe his good fortune, cannot believe that a woman as rich and as beautiful and as aristocratic as Thérèse could love *him*. He is beside himself with fretfulness, overcome with sentiments of tenderness, writing sonnets and sighing all day long. It is difficult to keep him focussed on my petitions, but I persist. Daily I visit Alexandre. Daily I visit Frédéric, Marie. The situation worsens.


*April 3.*

I've become ill. Every day brings news of arrests, deaths. I've exhausted myself begging audiences, writing appeals. Deputy Tallien warns me to be more circumspect in my endeavours. "You will be arrested if you persist," he cautioned. "You'd best think of yourself. Your children need a mother."

"My children need a father," I said, fighting back tears.


*April 19.*

Tonight, at dusk, three men came to the door. Fortuné growled. I recognized one of the men from the section office. The other two were unknown to me. I was alarmed lest they enter and find evidence of the Easter drawings I had made the children.

They handed me a paper. "What does this mean?" I asked. It was a search warrant.

Uninvited, the men proceeded into the front parlour.

"The drawings are in the fire," Lannoy whispered.

The men were not gentle with our possessions. They began in the basement and worked up to the attic, where they were excited to discover a locked desk, which they forced open. It was with disappointment that they discovered only patriotic letters from Alexandre (which I had intentionally placed there). They left dejected, having found nothing incriminating.

It is dark now. The flame from the candle sputters. I cannot sleep. I know they will return—for *me*.


*Later.*
It was four in the morning when the banging on the door began. This time they had a warrant for my arrest.

"And for what reason!" Lannoy protested.

"They need no reason," I whispered. To resist would only make it more difficult. I asked Agathe to gather together a few things.

I went to the children's room. I intended to wake them, bid farewell. I thought of their tears. I could not disturb them, sleeping so. I kissed them each, pulled their bedclothes over them, silently said a prayer.

Agathe and Lannoy both began to weep. "Take care of them," I said, as the men led me out the door.

## *In which my husband and I are reconciled*

I was thankful it was night. I would not have wanted witnesses.

My captors were ordinary men, doing a job. One, Citoyen Delmer, the more outspoken of the three, had a wife sick, and was anxious to get home. I was the last call and he was glad it was done. He didn't like taking mothers from their children. "It's good you didn't wake them. It's better that way."

They took me to the convent of the English Ursulines. The turnkey, who smelled of liquor, said there wasn't a chair to sit on, much less a bed.

"Where are we to take her?" Citoyen Delmer saw more work ahead.

The turnkey scowled. Delmer suggested the truckle-bed in the guardroom.

"That's *my* bed," the turnkey said, but he agreed finally.

The next day I asked to be transferred to the Carmes.

"You *want* to go to the Carmes?" The gaoler was a small man with pockmarks on his face.

"My husband is there."

"It's crowded and none too pleasant."

Nonetheless, he complied. At noon, after ham, eggs and dirty water, which made me nauseous, I was loaded into a covered cart along with three others. One was a boy of about fifteen. The other two, a man and wife, were puppeteers, arrested for making a puppet of Charlotte Corday.*

There was straw in the cart, some of it soiled. The cart had been used to bring in prisoners from Versailles the night before, our guard explained.

---

* *The young woman who murdered Deputy Marat.*

As we made our way through the streets people looked in at us and cursed. A boy threw a rotten egg. I turned my head in shame.

At the Carmes we were required to wait as the turnkey, a heavy man named Roblâtre, grumbled over the documents. "Every day they change how it goes," he cursed. "And if I don't get it right . . . !" He rolled his eyes. It was evident from his flushed visage that he was overly fond of the juice of the grape.

We were led down a narrow stone corridor. The smell from the open latrines made me choke. Roblâtre opened a door to a narrow room. The floor was lined with straw pallets, all in a row. Clothing was hung everywhere. The smell of mould was strong.

I was assigned a pallet facing one of the barred windows. To one side a young woman reclined, her golden hair fanned out over her pillow like a halo. "Citoyenne Madame Custine," she introduced herself. "You may call me Delphine."

"Custine? The General—"

"The great General Custine was my husband's father." She had a high, musical voice and spoke in a studied manner, like an actress, with exaggerated feminine flourishes.

"My husband served under General Custine. Alexandre Beauharnais. He is here."

"Oh—Citoyen General Beauharnais! You are his *wife?*"

"You know him?"

"He is my husband's bosom friend." She lay back down on the bed and sighed, her hand over her heart. "General Beauharnais has been drawing my portrait."

A bell was rung in the corridor. I followed Delphine and the others down a labyrinth of stairs into the rectory. There, under the vaulted ceilings, under the scratched-out images of Christ and the Virgin, crude plank tables had been set.

I sought a place on a bench. Bent cutlery was stacked in piles. I sat down facing a stained-glass window. To my left were the wood steps to the altar.

"That's where they read out the names every night," a woman behind me said. The voice sounded like that of Aimée.

I turned. It *was* Aimée. I burst into tears. She squeezed in beside me.

She handed me a teacup. "Here—drink this," she hissed. It was whisky. "I bribed the turnkey." Her cheeks were flushed. I suspected she'd had a bit.

A scrawny woman with dirty fingernails handed me a metal plate of boiled haricots and sardines.

"Ugh, this again." Aimée made a face at the food. "One meal a day and it's garbage."

"What names?" I asked.

"Of the condemned—who goes, who stays, who lives, who dies. It's the nightly entertainment—quite dramatic, I must say."

The lard on the beans was rancid. I put down my fork. The helper woman threw a basket of coarse black bread onto the table. Aimée tore off an end and tucked it down her bodice.

I felt dazed. "When did *you* . . . ?"

"Yesterday morning—but already it seems like a year. They took us all. Jean-Henri—he's over in the men's quarters. Even Lucie, poor child. She's asleep right now, upstairs."

*Lucie?* After losing her first, the girl had quickly become pregnant again—by her husband this time, fortunately.

"She's sick, too ill to eat—if you call this *eating*. I think it was the eggs we ate yesterday—laid under the Ancien Régime."

"We were all arrested at the same time. Curious."

"Do you know why?" she asked.

I shook my head. "Have you seen Alexandre?" Before Aimée could answer the helper woman was taking our plates and our tables and chairs were being moved. The sound in the chapel was deafening. The big double doors opened and a group of men entered. They were unshaven, in dirty shirts and breeches. One wore a kerchief around his head.

"And now the excitement begins," Aimée sighed with mock reverence. "Alexandre will likely be outside. I beat him in a fencing match last night."

"*You* beat Alexandre?" I followed her through a wide corridor that opened onto a walled garden. It was a hot, humid night. The smell of mint was strong. Next to an oak tree I saw Alexandre standing with another man. He looked up as we approached.

"And so it is that fate unites us." Alexandre kissed my hand. "I was told you were here. I can't say that I'm *happy* to see you."

I was introduced to Boyce Custine, a young man with glowing pink cheeks and an eager look. "Welcome," he said, bowing gallantly, "to what we Bucks and Bloods once termed a frolic. C'est bizarre, cela."

"I met your wife," I told him. "We share sleeping quarters."

"Perhaps we could trade places," he said mournfully.

"He's an eager lad, but his wife is reluctant," Alexandre explained. "I've been trying to persuade her to rendezvous with her beloved in the Lovers' Suite."

"The *Lovers'* Suite?"

"A private chamber reserved for married couples," Aimée said, "the rights to which are much coveted, as you can imagine." She had stripped a lilac branch of its leaves and was using it as a makeshift sabre.

"*Except* by the beautiful Delphine," Alexandre said.

"Alas!" Boyce Custine exclaimed theatrically, and we laughed.

We were allowed to mingle in the garden until ten. It seemed strange considering the setting. I was introduced to a variety of people of different political persuasions—from the aristocratic Duchesse Jeanne-Victoire d'Aiguillon to the radical Jacobin, General Santerre.

"*The* General Santerre?" I whispered to Aimée. The tavernkeeper who had proposed killing all the dogs and cats of Paris? The monster who had led the invasion on the Tuileries, who had silenced the King on the scaffold, ordered the drums to roll when the King began to speak?

"All the ladies call him 'Consoler,'" Aimée said. She put her arm through his. Apparently the burly tavernkeeper had become the favourite.

"General Santerre," I said, "I am surprised, I confess, to see a man of your political persuasion *here*."

The Consoler grinned sheepishly, adjusting his red cap. "The way I see it, this way, when they really need me, they'll know *exactly* where to find me."

"Frankly, if you're *not* in here, you're suspect," Alexandre said.


*April 23.*

For two mornings now, Lannoy has brought the children and Alexandre and I have been permitted a short visit. But this morning, Roblâtre would not permit us to see them.

"Tomorrow?" I asked.

Roblâtre shook his head. "There's a new rule." It was morning, yet already he was drunk.

"You mean we may not see them at *all?*" Alexandre demanded.

Roblâtre shrugged. "No longer."

Alexandre struck the chair, sending it flying.


*[Undated]*

I've become ill. Everyone has. We think it was the soup and bouilli last night. Duchesse Jeanne-Victoire d'Aiguillon said it was made from diseased horses' flesh and would not eat it. Others say worse.*


*Later.*

I am weak, confined to my pallet. This afternoon Alexandre brought me the parcel of clean linens Lannoy had delivered. In a petticoat I discovered my fortune-telling cards and a letter written by Eugène. Overcome with joy, I began to weep. Alexandre held me to his heart.


*April 25.*

Now the children are not able to *write* even—our parcels are searched.

"How are we to know how they are, Alexandre?" I wept. There are rumours that the children of prisoners will be taken by the state, placed in the care of "good" Republicans. "They might be ill, they might be dying! We wouldn't even *know!*"


*April 26.*

This morning, as is our custom, Alexandre and I went to the office to collect our parcel of clean linens. The turnkey checked off the items against a list of the contents. He was about to throw the list into the fire when Alexandre

---

* *Some prisoners believed they were fed human flesh.*

asked to see it. The turnkey looked at him suspiciously, but handed it to him nevertheless. Immediately I perceived it was in Eugène's hand.

"Thank you, Citoyen." Alexandre handed the list back to the turnkey, his hand trembling only slightly.

*April 27.*
Every morning now there is a list with our parcel of linens. On one day it is in Eugène's hand, on another in Hortense's. I can sleep now.

*April 28.*
This morning, as I returned from breakfast (pickled herrings—again*), I heard yelping. Suddenly, at my feet, there was a runt of a dog.

*Fortuné!*

I picked him up. He must have slipped past the guards.

"What is it? Is it a dog?" my companion asked uneasily.

Fortuné had a big black ribbon around his neck; it had become entangled in his collar. With some difficulty I got him to hold still so that I could straighten it. Then I felt something. There, concealed under his collar, was a folded piece of paper.

Quickly, I slipped the paper out, hid it in the folds of my skirt. "What an ugly dog. It looks like a rat—don't you think?" I put Fortuné down, pushed him toward the gate, my heart pounding. "Go! Go home!"

It wasn't until Alexandre and I met in the private room that I had the courage to read it. It was a letter from Eugène. They are well—they send their love. I collapsed in tears.

*[Undated]*
Alexandre and I have reconciled.

---

* *Pickled herrings were given to the prisoners in great quantities, provided to the French government by the Dutch in lieu of payment on a debt.*

*In which my worst fear is realized*

*April 30, 1794.*
Citoyen Boyce Custine's name has been called. Delphine fainted when she heard, falling onto the stone floor. We carried her to her pallet. There I cooled her brow. Then she opened her eyes and started screaming. The others became angry. A show of grief upsets everyone, and is considered selfish.

I went to the rectory in search of Alexandre. "Delphine is beside herself," I told him. "She is upsetting the others. I thought I might take her into the private room."

When I got back Aimée had her arms around Delphine, restraining her. "She was pounding on the wall," Aimée said.

"Come." Together Aimée and I were able to control her. Once in the private room Delphine began to calm. I rocked her like a baby. All the while my tears flowed.

*May 3.*
Today, at last, Delphine ate some "bread"—a barley concoction that makes our throats ache. She accepted it without complaint. It has been three days.

*May 4.*
Delphine sat up this morning. "I will require black," she said. She composed a note to her woman-in-waiting. By afternoon she had a new

wardrobe, striking black robes, quite becoming against her fine blonde hair and light blue eyes.

"You look like a princess," I told her.

"I prefer goddess." She rolled her hair in the reflection of the water bucket.

I take it her time of grief is over.


*May 9.*

Delphine has been composing verses which she reads to me each night. "But will *Alexandre* like it?" she asks anxiously when I assure her of its worth.


*Later.*

This afternoon, as I entered the garden, Delphine and Alexandre quickly moved. It was the briefest of movements, no more than a rustle, but Delphine's ready smile told me there was more, told me everything.


*[Undated]*

Delphine cannot suppress her joy. She glows. She sighs. In the night she moans, moves with desire. I know of whom she dreams.


*May 11, a hot afternoon.*

Alexandre's eyes follow Delphine's every move, and I, the aged, lonely wife, must sit idly by and watch this passion unfold, this grand love.

Jealousy possesses me. Jealousy, anger and loneliness—a lethal mix.


*May 12.*

It is unbearably hot. We lounge about the corridors in the most shocking state of undress. The men rarely shave, for water is dear. The women let their hair down, forget modesty. In every dark corner there is a couple seeking the last consolation.

I sit by the slits of windows, taking in air. From a shadow, under a stained bed cover, I see movement. I hear a woman moan, hear a man whisper endearments.

I lean my head against the damp stone wall. Besoin d'être aimé.

I shall die unloved. I shall die alone.


*May 13.*

Today, two newcomers: Madame Elliott, an English gentlewoman (the Duc d'Orléans's mistress and a spy for the English, Aimée insists), and General Lazare Hoche—the hero of the revolution. I could understand why Madame Elliott had been arrested, but General *Hoche* . . . ? A former stableboy, he had demonstrated brilliance on the battlefield. All the Jacobins sang his praise.

"But if you don't *win* the battles . . ." General Hoche made the gesture we have come to know too well: the quick movement of the fingers across the throat.

He is an exceedingly comely young man—thin, tall and with thick black hair and well-defined features; all the women are in a faint over him. It doesn't help that to get to his quarters he must pass through our dormitory. Tonight, as I was reading a journal out loud to the others, Aimée made a swooning gesture as he went by. I cautioned her, glanced up. General Hoche was standing on the stone landing, looking down at me. The sabre scar between his eyes gave him a quizzical look.


*May 14.*

This evening, coming through our sleeping quarters, Lazare Hoche glanced toward me. He made a small movement with his head.

I looked over at Madame Elliott. "Going calling?" she asked, in English. She smiled and demurely looked away.

I summoned the courage to stand. My cheeks were burning. Quickly I slipped up the stone stairs.

At the top there was a narrow passageway leading to another door, heavily bolted. Lazare Hoche pushed it open.

His chamber was small and very deep. At the top of a great wall there was a small window. "My dungeon," he said, lighting a candle. He pulled a covering-sheet over the straw pallet. On a board was a bottle of whisky.

"You have a private room," I said.

"Generals are allowed certain privileges—even in prison."

"Even in death?" Why had I said that?

He took a battered metal camp cup out of a wood crate and filled it from the bottle. He offered me the cup. "May I call you Rose?" he asked.

I took a sip and coughed. The liquor burned my throat. "I am older than you." It was a stupid thing to say. But suddenly I felt so unsure. How old *was* he? Twenty-four, twenty-five? For all he had seen of the world, he seemed but a boy. And I? I felt as old as the earth.

He finished the cup and set it down on the board. "I would like you to stay."

I did not answer. He approached me as one approaches a horse that might shy—firmly, but calmly, with confidence. His skin was rough; his touch gentle.


*[Undated]*

Every night some of our numbers are called. We fall into each other's arms, embraces given, taken, as if they were the last. They are the last.

I play out the cards. They say: This is Heaven, this is Hell. It is as one.


*May 16.*

I've become a night animal. I sleep through the days. Not eating, my body bone, I cleave to my lover, disappear into the stars I see fleetingly through the narrow metal grate.

Lazare. *Hold me!*

For I am dying.

*May 17.*

This night I went to his room. The door was open, the bedclothes in a bundle on the floor.

Citoyen Virolle came to the door. "You could come to *me*."

"Where is Lazare?"

"Among the chosen," Citoyen Virolle said, slurring. He was drunk.

"*Lazare's* name was called?" I retched onto the stones.


*May 19.*

Delphine has complained to the turnkey. My weeping keeps her awake. Duchesse Jeanne-Victoire d'Aiguillon has suggested I move into her cell. There is a vacancy now that her cellmate was called, a hammock of leather-strip webbing.

"A hammock?"

"So the rats won't get you," Jeanne-Victoire said.


*June 23.*

I am thirty-one today. I put on my best gown, in spite of my resolve to save it.* In the garden Alexandre presented me with a drawing he had made of the children, an excellent likeness.

He told me to meet him in the private chamber. "It is not what you think," he added.

"The children—are they . . . ?" Alarmed.

"I dare not speak."

We stood in the private chamber facing one another, our backs against the stone walls. "There is a spy among us," he said. "I have reason to believe I will be called." He told me he would be sacrificed for his country, that he had come to accept his fate. He said he was prepared to die.

---

* *It was common for the women in the prisons to put aside their most elegant ensemble to wear on the day of their execution.*

He asked me to dedicate my life to clearing his name. He had only one wish, and that was to see the children one last time. "Delphine can arrange it."

"Oh?" I have become weary of Delphine.

"One of the rooms upstairs overlooks the garden next door. There's a little house there—a gardener's house. Were the children to be taken there, and were we to stand in the window . . ."

"But what if they were discovered? What if we were seen? It's too dangerous, Alexandre! Surely—"

"It has already been arranged."

I fell silent. It was hot in the little room.

"I thought you'd be pleased." He was irritated.

"Do I have a choice?"

"Tomorrow, at two in the afternoon."

*June 24.*

Alexandre and I waited by the window looking out on the garden. After a short time, we noticed movement on the second floor of the little house. Hortense and Eugène stepped into view.

We stared at one another without moving: parent to child, child to parent.

They looked so *very* beautiful.

Hortense cried out, held out her arms. I heard a guard shout, "Who goes there!" The children were pulled back into the shadows.

It was over as quickly as that.

*July 9.*

Tonight eighteen names were called. So many! We are as sleepwalkers, numb. In the garden, Alexandre accused Citoyen Virolle of being an informer. The little man did not say a word. An hour later his body was found in the rectory. He had been strangled.

*July 17.*
Tonight it was announced: fifty names will be called.
    *Fifty!*
    Is it possible? Fifty of our number—*to die?*
    We begin to comprehend.
    We will *all* of us die.


*July 18.*
Two young men, brothers from Normandie, were the first names called. Hands joined, they leapt down the stone stairwell to their death.
    Two more names were added to the list.


*July 21.*
Names:
    Maurice Gigost,
    Louise Dusault,
    Armand-Thomas Paré,
    Alexandre Beauharnais.
    The sky darkens and the heavens break open with a violent crack. A stray cat trembles, seeks protection under a bench.
    A feeling of dreaminess has come over me. I lie in my hammock, swinging, humming a song from my youth. I can smell the sea.


*July 23.*
Alexandre has been taken to the Conciergerie to stand trial. On Delphine's finger, his talisman—the stone I had given him. This does not matter.


*July 24.*
I have fallen ill. After supper, Jeanne-Victoire came with food, a little wine. There was no news, she said.

"But there must be," I insisted. "What happened at Alexandre's trial? What happened at the Conciergerie?"

"His trial has been postponed." She turned to the window.

*[Undated]*

The ace of spades. Death. I slip it under my pillow.

Turn and turn again, the flower turns to blood. Lovers touch and there is life. A name is called and there is death.

They say I cry. They say I weep.

There is no escape.

*[Undated]*

I rise from my hammock, trembling with fever heat. I go to the window, lean on the grate, press the cold metal bars to my forehead. I search the streets for a sign. "*Someone* knows," I whisper.

I wander into the halls. "Tell me."

Aimée turns her eyes away. "Sleep," she says, guiding me back to my hammock. She spoons bitter wine between my lips, smooths my forehead with a damp grey rag. I hear coughing, voices, far away: "She is resting, now," Jeanne-Victoire says.

Resting, now.

*[Undated]*

In the dark I rise. Fever gives me the vision of a cat. I float through empty halls on cat paws, feel the damp cold of the stones, the air on my skin. All around me spirits hover, caressing.

"I have to know," I say. "Tell me."

They guide me to a paper hidden under a stone. They give me the strength to see. It is there, in the list of the dead, his name: *Alexandre*.

# In which Death calls, and I listen

*[Undated]*

Aimée slips a pair of rusty scissors into my hand. The metal is hot, hot.

I know what has to be done. I set to work, hacking at my hair, clearing a path for the knife. Clean, clean, I sing, watching the pile grow.

*[Undated]*

Aimée comes to me. "Are you dead too?" I ask.

"You are ill," she says. "You have a fever, fever thoughts."

"I hear angels singing."

She puts her head on my bosom.

"Your tears, my friend, anoint me," I say.

"Rose, your name was called," she whispers. "The doctor told them you are too weak to go."

"Did he tell them I was dead?"

She nods, coughs. "He told them soon."

"It's better this way." Better than the mob.

"The angels sing one way or another."

I reach under my pillow, push the wad of hair into her hand.

"For the children?"

I nod. I dare not speak their names. Not with Death so close. Not with Death listening.

"The card too?"

*The ace of spades.* "No!" I grab it back.

Her hand is cold on my arm. "Rose—don't listen to the angels. . . ."

I feel the air turn, the walls begin to crumble. A witch is at my side, her long fingers grasp my wrist. I cry out, pull away. It is the soothsayer, her old black face, her old white hair. I know her, know her . . .

*Remember what I said!* she says.

*[Undated]*

The angels do not sing. The earth pulls me, the stench of the chamberpots, rotting food. I float in, out. Voices come, voices go. Hot hands, cold hands. Cold hands. Cold hands.

*Remember what I said!* she says.

*July 26 (I believe).*

I sat up this morning. Jeanne-Victoire gave me her day's wine. My lips are blistered, my face a mask. "Is it the pox?" I asked, feeling my cheeks. Even so, fear was not with me.

"No, an ague," she said. "We thought you would die."

"I did. Several times."

"Your name was called."

"Aimée told me."

*I told you!* the soothsayer hisses.

I bat my hands about my ears. *Go away! Go away, old woman!*

*July 27.*

I am better today. "Don't get up," Aimée warns, "or they will call your name."

The prison seems almost empty, so many have been called. Even our turnkey has gone to the scaffold, Aimée says. He was too kind to us. Poor drunk Roblâtre.

Now we have Aubert, a Septembrist. He strangles stray kittens with his bare hands, for sport. Each night after supper, he locks us in. No matter.

Outside, I hear drums, great cannonading, hurried footsteps on the cobblestones.

"Something is happening," Jeanne-Victoire says.

*Something is happening,* the soothsayer whispers in my ear.

*I thought you were gone, old woman!*


*July 28.*

At sunrise the turnkey came for my hammock. I stood by the window and watched him take it down.

"But what will Citoyenne Beauharnais sleep on?" Jeanne-Victoire demanded.

"I guess she'll not be needing it any more." He laughed.

Jeanne-Victoire turned pale. As soon as he left she burst into tears.

"Do not cry," I told her.

But she only wept harder. "Forgive me. I am so weak," she said.

*Remember what I said!*

I remembered: I would be unhappily married. I would be widowed.

*There is more!*

"Look, you do not even tremble." Jeanne-Victoire took my hand.

*Say it!*

I took a breath. "I will not die."

Jeanne-Victoire put her arm about my shoulder to comfort me.

*Say it—all of it!*

"I will be Queen," I said. The words came from some other place in me.

"Hush, Rose—there is no queen now," Jeanne-Victoire said sweetly, as if to a child. But the look on her face was uneasy. She thought me mad.

"And you will be my lady-in-waiting," I said.

"You are in a fever still."

She pulled me to the window for air. Weakly, I leaned against the bars. I heard musket shot, cantering horses. In the street a woman was jumping up and down. She picked up her skirt and then a stone, her skirt and then the stone.

"She is trying to tell us something," Jeanne-Victoire said.

The sky was red. Already the heat shimmered over the stones. The woman picked up her skirt, pointed to it.

*"Robe."*

*"Pierre,"* Jeanne-Victoire said, for the stone. "Robespierre. She's saying 'Robespierre.'"

The woman drew her hand across her throat and began to dance wildly.

Jeanne-Victoire turned to me. "Robespierre is dead." She looked uneasy—frightened. "You are saved!"

*Remember what I said!* the old woman said.

# V

## La Merveilleuse

# *In which I walk among the living & the dead*

*July 28, 1794, evening.*
Mirth without bounds. It bubbles forth from the cracks in the stones. With a crackle and a boom, our cell lights up like the day—more firecrackers follow, one upon the other.

The light from my candle throws shadows against the walls. The spirits of this place, this time, are freed. They dance in the shimmering heat. I tie my bundle of cut hair into a knot and toss it between my hands. So close it came. My head.

Grief speaks the refrain. For those who missed the lucky stroke by one single passing of the sun and moon. Grief . . . for Lazare, the old puppeteers, the others, too numerous to list. Grief . . . for Alexandre.

And fear, too, for the bars still close behind us, the guillotine still stands.

*Wednesday, August 6.*
Today two men came through the gates. Deputies. We, the faint, the tattered, gathered like cattle, watching silently. Outside, on the cobblestones, the mob—drunken, gay, dressed in musty ball gowns, tattered silks splattered with mud.

We were herded into the chapel. One of the deputies mounted the pulpit, a sheet of paper in his hand.

Aimée put her arm around me. "Are you all right?"

I laughed; others turned to stare. I laughed without cause. I was one of *those*.

The deputy cleared his throat. "We have come in the name of liberty."

A man cried out. Has not all that has passed and is passing still been done in the name of liberty? We knew liberty—liberty meant *death*.

The deputy continued. "What I have here is a list—"

We trembled. We knew lists. The movements of this ritual were well known to us.

"—a preliminary account, we must assure you, of those whom the new members of the Committee of Public Safety deem innocently accused. The following citizens are free to leave. . . ."

"Do you understand?" Aimée whispered.

"I am not a child," I told her. They thought me mad.

"Citoyenne Rose Beauharnais."

I looked around, frightened. My name had been called.

Aimée clasped my hands. I looked into her weeping eyes. Faces turned to me, friends encircled me. My knees gave way.

I woke on top of a plank table. Someone was stroking my forehead with a damp cloth. I heard a cough, then the words, "She can hear me."

I opened my eyes.

Aimée's eyes reassured me. I looked around at the others.

"Don't you understand, Rose?" Aimée said. "You may go home. You are *free*."

I listened to her words with fear in my heart. *Free?* What did that mean? "Will you come with me?" I asked.

"Soon," she assured me, smoothing rouge over my cheeks. She handed me a basket—my linens, my comb, a handkerchief enclosing my bundle of hair, my tattered cards. "Quick, before they have a change of heart," she hissed.

"I can't leave you here."

"Don't cry! Your children need you."

*My children.*

My friends all crowded around me, helping me to the gate. The mob out on the street was cheering. Four men in the uniform of the National Guard were trying to hold them back. Would they set upon me, tear me limb from limb?

Trembling, clasping my basket, I was pushed out onto the street. The big metal gate closed shut behind me. I looked back. The faces of my friends were wet with tears.

"Where would you be going, Citoyenne?" a woman called out from behind me. Her breath smelled of liquor. She was wearing a court hat, a purple creation covered over with dirty silk flowers and tattered ribbons.

"To the river?" I could not recall.

Rue Saint-Dominique was wider than I remembered, an empty thoroughfare. On the big wood doors a paper had been posted. Sealed, by order of the law; enter on penalty of death. *Death.* I turned away, panic filling me. Where were my children? Where were Hortense and Eugène?

I stumbled down Rue du Belle Chasse. The dogs in the lumberyard growled at me. At Port-de-la-Grenoüillere, I held my hand to my eyes. Light glittered off the river. Across, on the other side, a crowd was gathering in Place de la Révolution, around the guillotine. Still?

I turned toward Princess Amalia's, toward the Hôtel de Salm. Daily the children had gone there to visit, I knew.

The gates to the courtyard were bolted. I shook the bell rope. The chambermaid came running. She peered through the metal bars.

"Citoyenne Beauharnais," I said. I did not say: the *widow* Beauharnais.

A short man appeared between the portico columns. His yellow satin waistcoat glittered with gems. "What is it!" A peasant, by his accent. He was holding a thick horse whip.

"I wish to speak to Citoyenne Amalia Hohenzollern." A feeling of weakness came over me. I grasped the metal bars for support.

"The princess? She and her kind have run across the Rhine, along with all the other vermin."

Princess Amalia . . . in *Germany?* "Her brother, Citoyen Frédéric, is he—"
The maid made a quick motion of one finger across her throat.
Frédéric—*guillotined?* Mon Dieu.

The man commanded the woman to get back to her chores. I grabbed her sleeve through the bars. "Where are my children!" I demanded. "Where are Hortense and Eugène?"

"Their great-aunt came—"
The man cracked his whip.

"Citoyenne Renaudin?"

"No—the short one," she hissed, running.

*Fanny?* Was it possible?

It was Jacques, Fanny's man-of-all-work, who opened the big wooden doors to the courtyard. He suffered a moment of confusion before he realized who I was. I took his leathery hands in mine. My heart was beating wildly. "My children—are they here?"

I followed him into the house. Fortuné came scurrying into the foyer. I scooped him up in my arms; he was a mass of wiggling, his little tongue licking my cheek.

Lannoy appeared at the upstairs landing, Agathe not far behind. "Who is it, Jacques?" Lannoy asked. She regarded me with haughty disapproval.

"Citoyenne Rose!"

"Madame?" Lannoy looked down at me with an expression of disbelief.

I heard a familiar voice behind me. I turned. It was an old woman, her face heavily made-up.

*Fanny.* I put one arm around her shoulders, touched her cheek with my lips, her dry, papery skin. "Thank God you survived," I said, fighting back tears. How long had it been, the nightmare we had endured? Was it possible it was over?

"Mon Dieu, child, you're so thin." She stood back to look at me.

"I've been ill. The children—"

"They're here." Fanny put her fingers around my wrist. "There's hardly anything to you. And your hair . . . !" She smiled, in spite of herself.

"Aunt Désirée? The Marquis? Are they . . . ?"

*Let them be alive,* I prayed.

Then: *Be merciful, let them pass. Please do not ask them to endure the pain of Alexandre's death. . . .*

"They are back in their house now—in Fontainebleau. Before they were in hiding. Charlotte put them up in her basement."

"The cook?" I tried to imagine Aunt Désirée and the Marquis in Charlotte's brusque care. "Do they . . . have they been told?" I held on to the bannister to steady myself. Did *Fanny* even know?

"About Alexandre?" Fanny whispered.

I nodded. Yes.

I heard a girl singing, the sound of a harpsichord. "Hortense?" I went to the door of the music room. Hortense was sitting at the instrument, her back to me. Eugène and Émilie were seated close by. Eugène turned to look at me. His expression said, "Who is this woman?"

Hortense stopped playing. She turned and stared.

I stopped, confused. "Do you not know me?" I let Fortuné down. He stayed by my feet, whimpering to be taken up again. "Fortuné knows who I am."

"Maman?" Eugène's voice cracked.

"It is not," Hortense said.

"They do not believe it is me," I told Fanny. I managed a smile.

"Mon Dieu, it's no wonder—you look like a stray cat!" She ordered the children to approach.

Eugène came up to me bravely, permitting an embrace, followed by Émilie, who burst into tears. Hortense refused, standing behind Eugène. She watched me, her big blue eyes not revealing any emotion. Her father's eyes.

Fanny chided her goddaughter. "Your prayers have been answered and look how you behave."

"I understand," I said. "I'm—"

A sick feeling swept through me, violently this time. I doubled over. Fanny called out to Jacques, who helped me to a bench. "Would you take a dish of broth?" Fanny asked.

I shook my head. I felt too ill. "I need to wash," I said. I took a breath, sat up. The pain had passed. The children—alarmed, no doubt—were standing in a silent clump by the harpsichord, watching. "I'm all right," I told them.

"Fill the copper tub," Fanny told Jacques. "Make it hot."

"There is little wood," he protested.

"Do what you can."

Lannoy helped me up to Fanny's bedchamber. Then she helped me undress, making little clucking noises of dismay. Tears filled her eyes.

"I couldn't wash," I told her, embarrassed by my filth, my bones. "There was no water."

She helped me into the big laundry tub, which Fanny had made fragrant and healing with herbs. After, Fanny brought me a shift, pretty with lace.

I protested. "I am infested."

Fanny shrugged. "So are we all." She led me to a stool.

Slowly, she combed the nits out of my hair, talking—of hiding in an attic in Valenciennes, of returning to Paris to try to get her daughter Marie out of prison (without success), of her own imprisonment in Port-Royal, of Michel de Cubières's heroic rescue.

I listened without hearing. In front of me was a looking glass, framed in ormolu. The woman I saw was a stranger to me. Her gaunt face was lined, aged, without colour. Her teeth were black, her eyes sunken—furtive, fearful eyes.

It was no wonder the children did not know me. This woman was not their mother.

Who, then, was she?

I did not want to know.

As I write this, now, it is almost five in the afternoon. I'm sitting at the writing desk in Fanny's guest room. I've slept, performed a modest toilette, put on one of Fanny's gowns—it hangs loosely from my shoulders.

Outside, on the Rue de Tournon, I hear a bell—a ragpicker's wagon. The sound brings back memories, memories which seem more real to me than this room I inhabit, memories of the Carmes, of the prisoners—my dearest friends—who at this very moment are lying on their straw pallets listening for the sound of the guard's footsteps, listening for the peal of his bell announcing supper.

Strangely, I long to be with them. Here, outside the prison walls, I do not know my place. I am of this world, but not of this world. I am like a zombie, risen from the dead.

*Later that day.*

I rise, dress, eat—go through the simple routines of my day. It is not real; I am performing a part in a play. Yet it is through these simple acts—tying a sash, fastening a button, reading out a sentence in a reader—that Hortense and Eugène begin to know me again. How I long to take them in my arms, *touch* them, but even now I must refrain. I must not alarm them.

*August 8.*

I am stronger today, ready for realities. "Tell me," I told Fanny.

"It is too soon," she said.

"Nothing can wound me." Indeed, I feel I am already dead. I do not tell her this.

She went to her desk and pulled out a blue silk kerchief, folded. There was something inside.

I opened it—hair, long and wavy, chestnut in colour.

"Alexandre's," she said.

I looked up at her.

"I asked the gaoler for it."

"You . . . you were *there*?" I felt a prickly feeling in my hands. "You *saw*?" Did I want to ask? Did I want to know?

"I did not think Alexandre should die alone."

I pressed my face to my knees, fighting back tears. How I revered this woman, her feisty, quirky, stubborn strength.

"Rose! Are you ill?"

I sat up, took a breath. "Forgive me, I was overcome."

"You would have done the same," she said.

Was it true? "He knew you were there, I am sure."

"There's more." Fanny handed me a pamphlet.

I turned it over in my hands. Alexandre's name was on it. "What is it?" I asked. "Alexandre wrote this?" I noticed my name. "It's written to *me*?" I scanned the text:

*I am the victim. . . .*

*The brotherly fondness I have for you . . .*

*Cherish my memory. . . .*

The words shifted and moved before my eyes. "Where did you get this?" I turned the printed sheet over in my hand. One sou, it said, in the lower right-hand corner. "Did you *pay* for it?"

"I got it by the Luxembourg gates. A young man in a toga was selling them. He had a basketful." She paused. "Apparently it's Alexandre's last statement—to you."

*Goodbye, dear friend. . . .*

*Console yourself for the sake of our children. . . .*

I was having difficulty breathing. I stood and went to the window. How like Alexandre to arrange to have his last words *published*, I thought.

"Rose, he was thinking of the family honour, of the children."

"I understand," I said. Two women were helping a drunken man walk down the street. "He'd fallen in love with Madame Custine—General Custine's daughter-in-law."

"Delphine Custine? That silly blonde thing?" Fanny scoffed. "That couldn't have been pleasant for you."

I lowered myself onto the little upholstered stool in front of the fireplace. "I can't recall," I said.


*6:00 P.M.*

Eugène was withdrawn this afternoon—he remained silent throughout supper. "It's nothing!" he insisted.

I followed him to his room. "Something is weighing on you." I sat down next to his table of military figurines.

He shrugged, repositioning four cannon, kneeling to assess the angles.

"Eugène, please, talk to me. It's something to do with your father, isn't it?" No response. "Did anything happen at the workshop this morning? Did Citoyen Quinette say something?" Citoyen Quinette is an excellent cabinetmaker, but known for his temper.

Eugène shook his head.

"Who then? The other lads who work there?"

He would not look at me.

"Did they say something to you?"

I reached to touch his shoulder. Abruptly, he twisted away. "They call me the son of a traitor!" He hid his face in his hands.

"Do you believe them, Eugène?"

"He lost Mainz! He never attacked—instead, he ran!"

"Is that what they say?"

He nodded, tears bursting from him. He wiped them away, embarrassed by his weakness.

"And what do you tell *them?*"

"What *can* I say!"

I studied my son's face. His father—a man he revered, a man who had stood for all that was noble and good—had been put in prison, tried, found guilty, condemned to death. "I will tell you, then," I said, taking a breath. "In war, as in love, it is always complex. You are old enough to begin to understand." I told him of the condition of his father's troops— farmboys without training, without food. I told him of the enemy—professionals outnumbering his father's troops ten to one. I told him of Alexandre's reluctance to lead his men to slaughter.

"To many, to be a hero, one must bask in the blood of others. To many, your father should have led his men to death, risked their lives for the sake of glory. But to me, it proved your father's courage—his courage to risk condemnation, arrest, death even, in order to stand by what he knew to be right. Is *this* not heroic?"

Eugène looked at me with a steady expression.

"You are the son of a good man, Eugène, a man who loved you very much, a man who loved his *country*. A man who lived—and died—for what he believed in. A *hero*. You must never forget that. Your father's memory will be cleared—I promised him that—but it must begin in *your* own heart."

And in my own.


*August 9.*

I don the clothes of the widow Beauharnais. The dull black suits my soul, reflects the death I feel within. Even my children cannot wake me from this slumber. Stiff white gauze tickles my throat. A veil of taffeta covers my boyish curls. I am a ghost. I am a survivor.

I set out for the Faubourg Saint-Antoine. "Place du Trône renversé," I tell the driver.

He puts me down at a corner. I instruct him to wait. I walk the edges. This is where my husband died.

It is a cloudy, hot day. Everywhere children are playing. Did they skip around the guillotine? Did they sing?

I dodge horses, carriages—make my way to the centre. There, despite the curses of the carters, the threat of their whips, I stand. Is *this* the spot?

I am only a moment, waiting. Only a moment, long enough to know that he is not there.

I return to the carriage, instruct my driver once again. This time we head out to the country, outside the city walls. I have been told the way; in any case, my driver seems to know.

He regards my dark robes, my short-cropped hair. "I go often, myself," he tells me. He is wearing a tall hat with yellow tassels. "My son is there. My wife went once, but no more." He needs to talk.

At last, we stop. It is only a farmer's field. It has been dug, mounded, turned. But for that, one would not guess its use.

"The King and Queen are here," the driver tells me. He is proud of this. "It is said they share a pit with Robespierre." He takes down the step. I accept the offer of his rough hand. He wants to be helpful. He has been too much alone in this place.

There are others in the field, four diggers, a pile of lime, a cart nearby. Bodies. Heads.

"Still?" Still more to bury?

"The mountain meets the earth." The driver laughs at his joke. He nods toward an old woman in a spotted muslin dress, sitting in the dirt. "She's always here," he says. He twirls a finger at his temple, meaning: crazy.

Unlike the rest of us, I think with irony.

I scan the broken earth, the weeds. So this is where Alexandre lies. And the others—Lazare? Frédéric? The dear old puppeteers? It comforts me to think of them all together.

I head out across the field. I do not have a plan. At the centre I pick up three stones. One for Hortense, one for Eugène, one for myself. I feel the smooth surfaces. Tokens.

Is that all there is? Is it true, what the Jacobins say—that death is eternal sleep, no more, no less.

The soothsayer said: *You will be unhappily married. You will be widowed.*

I watch as two birds fly through the air—a pair. I wait for some sense of meaning. But there are no answers, only this . . . this awful emptiness.

*In which ghosts come to life*

The dawn was breaking when I set out, accompanied by Jacques. The beggars on the Rue de Vaugirard were still asleep. In front of the Luxembourg a grocer was whipping a donkey in an effort to make the old creature move. We made our way around the quarrelsome pair.

It was a short walk to the Carmes, I knew, but one which bridged two worlds. There are degrees of courage, and I was unsure if I had the will to enter those prison gates again. I was thankful Jacques was with me.

A guard I didn't recognize opened the gate. Jacques knocked on the heavy plank door to the turnkey's office. I heard someone coughing inside. Within, by the light of one tallow candle, the turnkey was hunched over a journal, scowling. A very pregnant Lucie was slumped sleepily on a chair, bursting her seams. Aimée was sitting in the far corner. I was struck by the animal look in her eyes.

She burst into a crazy laugh, which in turn gave way to a rattling cough that stole her very breath. "Am I so very frightful?" she gasped, when she could breathe again.

Jacques took her basket, her meagre possessions. "Ready?"

"What about Jean-Henri?" I asked.

"Croisoeuil?" The turnkey leafed through his papers. "No." Lucie shrugged.

Out on the street an old man came up to us. "Welcome." He handed Lucie a flower.

"How does he know?" She watched the man hobble away.

I took Aimée's hand. I could feel the bones. "We are staying at my Aunt Fanny's on Rue de Tournon," I told her. "It's a short walk from here. Are you strong enough?"

"We're not going to Rue Saint-Dominique?"

"It's been sealed."

"I can't go home?" I saw something crumble within her.

"Come," I said.


*Evening.*

"Are you sure you're all right?" I asked Aimée as I helped her to bed. She seemed strange to me yet.

"I pretend," she said.

I sat down on the bed beside her. It seemed a curious thing to say.

"You're pretending, too. Only you've convinced yourself," she said.

Tears came to my eyes. She was right. I did pretend. I did not speak of the horror I have known. "It's different out here, Aimée. *We're* different."

"The craziness, you mean."

"More than that." I pulled the covering sheet over her, kissed her forehead. "Sleep." I closed the drapes, blew out the candle on the mantle.

"You didn't say what it was, Rose," she said, in the dark.

I stood for a moment. What *was* it? "Shame," I said. In the dark, one word. Shame that we broke down, grovelled, *begged*. Shame for crying out, weeping, beating our heads against the stones. Shame for losing hope, faith, for being willing to forsake everything, *anything*, in barter for life. Shame for knowing fear, its sickening grip.

The shame of the survivor.

"Yes," Aimée whispered. "That too."


*August 11.*

This morning I met with Citoyen Dunnkirk, my banker, attempting to put my finances in order. The news is not good. Martinico has threatened to go over to the English rather than submit to the revolutionary government in France. Citoyen Dunnkirk has reason to believe that Mother has opened her home to the English forces, offered support to the enemy.

"To the *English?*" I thought of Father, of a life spent in battle against "les Goddams." Had Mother offered English officers my father's bed? I was thankful he was dead.

"I assure you that this information will be held in strict confidence. I am aware of the dishonour this could cause you, the suspicion—"

"She is well?" I interrupted. "The plantation—is it . . . ?"

"I don't know if you are aware that your father left a substantial debt—one hundred thousand livres." Citoyen Dunnkirk sneezed into an ugly green kerchief.

"Why was I not—"

"We just found out ourselves. Your mother—a resourceful woman, by all accounts—made an arrangement with her creditors whereby the debt would be paid off over a period of time. Fortunately, the crop was good this year, in spite of the civic turmoil. So good, in fact, she was able to pay off the debt and is reported to have hosted a celebration party for everyone in the village."

"*Mother?*" Surely he was talking about another woman.

"Quite sure, Citoyenne. In fact, we are given to believe that your mother is comfortable, perhaps even well-off. She should have no difficulty providing you with the interest on your holdings—if she can get it to you, that is. Due to the war, *any* correspondence will prove difficult, of course."

"I can't write to her?"

"You could *try*," he shrugged. "Is she aware of your . . . situation?"

"She knows nothing." Nothing of prison, nothing of Alexandre's death.

We reviewed my accounts. I have a sizeable (and growing) debt to Citoyen Dunnkirk, who so kindly advanced funds for the care of the children while Alexandre and I were in prison. "I will repay you," I assured him—but *how?* "I have gems hidden in my rooms on Rue Saint-Dominique. I can sell them, when . . ."

*When* . . . When the seals were removed. When would *that* be?

"It will take time," Citoyen Dunnkirk warned, sneezing again. "The wheels of bureaucracy have always moved slowly—and now . . ." He threw up his hands.

"What about La Ferté?" I asked. Alexandre had invested all of his inheritance in his country estate.

"Your husband's properties have been sequestered. Items of any value have been sold by the government at auction."

"Sold?" There was a painting of Alexandre as a child—I had wanted it for Hortense and Eugène. "And when might *that* sequester be lifted?"

Citoyen Dunnkirk looked at me uncomfortably. "I hate to be the one to tell you this, Citoyenne, but the law gives the government full possession of the property of the condemned. Even if the sequester were to be lifted today, the estate would not accrue to you *or* your children."

Slowly I grasped the situation. According to law, Alexandre died a criminal. The children have been robbed of their inheritance. They face their future with nothing but the clothes on their backs and a blackened name.

I returned to Rue de Tournon shortly before noon. There were a number of people gathered on the street. A woman with a hurdy-gurdy was standing in front of the door to Fanny's hôtel.

"Something is happening," I told Fanny, putting my handbasket down in the foyer. Crowds frightened me.

"They're releasing prisoners at the Luxembourg today." Fanny was holding a stack of books in one arm. "And making a spectacle of it—speeches, a parade apparently."

"Where are the children?" I asked.

"Up at the corner."

I sighed. Watching prisoners being released had become a form of entertainment. "Lucie as well?"

"She consented to go, in spite of the fact that the dress I provided was not judged suitably flattering."

"Neither prison nor pregnancy have dampened that child's vanity," I said. "And Aimée?"

Fanny nodded toward the double doors leading out onto the balcony. "She only just got up. Were you able to get coach tickets to Fontainebleau?"

"I'll try again in the morning." Two times already I'd tried to get a pass.

I stepped outside onto the balcony. Aimée was leaning out over the edge, her hair hanging down loose and long. I thought to say something to her, to caution her against immodesty, but held my tongue. What did it matter, any more?

I put my arm around her shoulders, kissed her forehead. She'd slept for over twenty hours, the sleep of the dead, but even so, she looked exhausted.

"Good," she said, answering a question I had not voiced. She put her hand to her mouth to still a cough.

I looked out over the throng. A woman with a child at her breast was wearing a dress made from a flag. Four young men dressed in togas were making their way slowly down the street carrying a banner proclaiming "la nation." Everyone cheered as they passed.

"This seems like a dream to me," I said. Now and again a wind carried a faint scent of honeysuckle.

Aimée laughed. That awful prison laugh, Fanny called it.

A carriage pulled by a team of old bays turned onto Rue de Tournon. Two open carriages followed. A tall, young man bedecked with red, white and blue ribbons was standing in the last one. The woman in the flag dress began yelling joyously, holding up her baby as if for a blessing.

"Isn't that Tallien?" I asked. Tallien's signature had been on my release form. A stunning young woman sat beside him, scantily dressed in a white toga, a sash with the words "la liberté" draped across one shoulder. Her curly black hair was cut short, like a boy's. "And Thérèse Cabarrus!"

For days the children had been telling me the story: how a beautiful young woman had sent Deputy Tallien a note from prison, hidden along with a dagger in a cabbage, how for love of *her* he had brandished her little dagger in the Assembly, challenged the tyrant Robespierre, ended the Terror.

"Your friends—the new King and Queen," Fanny said, joining us. "That could be useful."

I picked a blossom from a potted rosebush and attempted to toss it into the carriage. I missed and tried again, calling out this time. Thérèse glanced up. She tried to say something to Tallien, but it was too noisy on the street, the crowd too demanding.

Shortly after there was a pounding at the gate. Jacques returned with a message. "A boy," he said. "He said to tell you that the lady with Deputy Tallien invites you to see her."

"Thérèse? Did he give an address?"

"Nine Rue Georges, Chaussée d'Antin. Tomorrow afternoon at three."

"You will see about Marie?" Fanny demanded, grasping my arm.

*August 12.*

A thin boy, only a little older than Eugène, answered the door.* I followed him into a room full of potted flowering bushes. "She will be with you," the boy stuttered, and disappeared.

I heard a woman singing—her voice was lyrical, slightly melancholy; it had a haunting quality. Thérèse Cabarrus stepped into the room. She was dressed in a loose white tunic drapped in the Roman style. Her short, jet-black curls framed her face, her tresses shorn, short and boyish, like my own . . . but for the same reason? I wondered. It did not seem possible. The grey pallor that marked the victims of the Terror, the shadow that enveloped our souls seemed not to have touched her. Was it possible she had even been in prison?

"You do not bear scars," I said, after exchanging civilités. It was bad form to refer to the horrors of the past, but I felt somehow compelled.

She slipped a foot out of a white silk slipper. "See these?" She touched three spots on her toes. "From *rats*."

I put my hand to my throat. I had seen what rats could do.

"May I confide in you?" Her touch on my hand was light, caressing. "When I was taken to La Petite-Force, I was held in a room by eight guards. I was told to remove my clothes." She recounted her tale without emotion. "I knew the danger I was in. The turnkey, a little man with a repulsive face, claimed authority. He ordered the men away. But then he demanded his due."

I looked at her—her clear white skin, her young flushed cheeks. She looked a child, an infinitely vulnerable but voluptuous urchin.

"I used to believe in love," she went on, "but no longer. Perhaps *that* is my scar." She examined my eyes with surprise. "You weep? For *me?*"

"Yet love makes great deeds possible," I said. "I am told you refused on

---

*This is Guéry, the fourteen-year-old son of one of Thérèse's business acquaintances, released the day before from the Luxembourg prison.*

threat of death to sign a statement that would have compromised Deputy Tallien."

"I am cast in the role of a heroine. I enjoy the part, I confess. The lines, the costume, the applause have a certain charm—don't you think?" She smiled, fanning herself. "Forgive me for indulging in theatrics. It is a weakness of mine. But I promise I will always be honest with you. It was not love that inspired my loyalty. It was simply that death ceased to frighten." She closed her fan with a snap. "And *that*, my friend, is *true* freedom."

I heard the sound of a man's voice in the entryway, footsteps. Tallien entered. Close behind him was Deputy Barras, his long sword trailing.

"Rose!" Tallien exclaimed with a boyish grin. He embraced me.

"How good to see you," I said, unexpectedly moved.

"You recall Deputy Barras?" Tallien asked.

"Of course," I said. "The two of you came to my salon on Rue Saint-Dominique, several years ago."

"Citoyenne Beauharnais, what a *pleasure*," Deputy Barras said, taking my hand and kissing it tenderly, in the old style. He smelled of spirit of ambergris. "Has it really been so very long?" he asked, his eyes mournful and tender. He'd gained weight since last I saw him—his leather hunting breeches were tight on him. Even so, he defined elegance.

"Young Guéry showed you in?" Thérèse asked.

Deputy Barras embraced her fondly. "He looks too thin," he told her. "Send him over to my place; I'll fatten him up."

"I'm not letting him anywhere near *you*."

"Unfair!" Deputy Barras lowered himself into a plush pink armchair.

Tallien stood in front of the fireplace. "My condolences, Rose. I was grieved to learn about your husband. . . ."

I nodded yes.

"How unfortunate. Only a few more days and . . . If only . . ."

*If only . . .*

"We are all of us in mourning," I said. All of us in shock. "Everyone lost someone dear." I accepted the glass of cherry brandy the maid offered. I raised my glass to propose a toast. "I would like to express my gratitude. First, to you, Tallien, my dear friend. It was *your* name on my release form."

"I'm sorry I couldn't get you out sooner," he said.

"And, second, to the three of you. I am under the impression that together you saved us from Robespierre, le tyran."

"We 'blood-drinkers'—as he was so fond of calling us—finally got a bit of his." Deputy Barras downed his glass of brandy.

"Tallien and Barras deserve the credit," Thérèse said.

"Didn't you send Tallien a note and a dagger hidden inside a cabbage?" I smiled. "That's what my children tell me."

"I love that story," Thérèse said.

"In truth, we'd been plotting for some time," Tallien said.

"The tip-off was when Robespierre began taking riding lessons," Deputy Barras said, tapping tobacco into his pipe. "When a *politician* begins to ride, prepare for battle—an elementary lesson taught to all students at any military college."

"So Thérèse didn't send a note to Tallien?" I asked.

"You mean the one that refers to our friend's 'notorious cowardice'?" Deputy Barras laughed. Tallien gave him a menacing look.

"I did send a note," Thérèse said. "The gaoler's wife smuggled it out for me. I fabricated the story of the cabbage in order to protect her. It makes a good fable, don't you think?"

"I especially like the part about the little dagger," Deputy Barras said, his big, sorrowful eyes drôle.

"I'm amazed people believe it," Tallien said. "How could one possibly keep a dagger in prison?"

"Ah, but the French love a good story," Deputy Barras said.

"Not that there aren't good stories to be told," Thérèse said.

I put my hands to my ears: I'm listening!

Then all stories began: how they had plotted; how Tallien had brandished a dagger (his own) in the Assembly, confronted Robespierre ("I still can't believe you did that," I told him. "I can't believe it either," he said); how Deputy Barras had boldly taken charge of the military, been the one to arrest Robespierre; how in the middle of the night Deputy Barras had stormed the Temple, seen the Boy—the King's son—alone in his cell.

"You *saw* him?" I asked, interrupting.

The *Boy*. I almost said: *King*. "How old is he now? Ten?" He was only a little younger than Hortense, I recalled, who was eleven now. I remembered seeing him at the theatre, sitting on his mother's lap. I remembered his sweet distress over his mother's tears. How horrible it must be for him, so small a child, an orphan now, alone in a prison cell.

"The Little Capet is small," Deputy Barras said, "too small to be King. *Fortunately.* But ill. He'd been badly tended."

Thérèse tapped my hand with her fan. "I should caution you, Rose: every time the subject of the Boy comes up Deputy Barras begins to weep."

Deputy Barras laughed. "It's so unbearably sad! When I saw him he was dressed in grey rags, lying in this tiny cradle—he refused to sleep in his own big bed for some reason. His face was all puffed up, his hands swollen. Frankly, I've been terrified he might die, so I've ordered him examined, put under care. No sign of rickets, the doctor assures me." He shrugged. "But I'm not sure how old he is, frankly. As for Madame Royale, his sister, she's"—he cupped his hands, indicating breasts—"healthier, although not in the head. She has difficulty speaking. I've been told our dear-departed Robespierre paid her a visit. No doubt she owes her life to his . . . *interest*, you might say. If we're not careful, we'll be having a litter of would-be kings and queens to worry about. Can you imagine a Capet-Robespierre combination? *Terrifying*. But the boy . . . ? Yes, well, nine, eight perhaps? A sweet child. I wish . . ." He sighed.

"Poor Paul," Tallien said, handing him a handkerchief. "Who would have thought that becoming a public parent of the state meant becoming a *parent*."

Deputy Barras wiped his eyes, sighed wryly. "It's a job. The crown jewels, the crown prince and princess"—he rolled his eyes —"the *crown*."

"Don't say that!" Thérèse said.

A footman came to the door with a note on a silver tray.

"Speaking of jobs—" Deputy Barras shoved in his lorgnon and squinted at the note, holding it at arm's length. He handed it to Tallien. "You read it," he said. "You have young eyes."

"They've changed the meeting to this afternoon," Tallien said. "At four."

"The Committee?"

Tallien nodded.

Deputy Barras groaned, pulled out his timepiece. "We'd better get over there." He stood, stretched, his hand on the small of his back. "I'm getting too old for this." He put on his velvet toque hat, adjusting the tricolour plume. "If we leave that group alone for even a minute, there will be another take-over—only our heads will be the ones to roll this time."

"Hold on a moment." Thérèse was rummaging through stacks of loose papers on a writing desk.

"I'll get the horses ready," Deputy Barras said, standing. "Au revoir, Citoyenne." He bowed and kissed my hand.

"My pleasure," I said.

"Here it is." Thérèse handed Tallien a scrap of paper.

"*Another* list?" He groaned.

"The ones with the stars are the most urgent."

He slipped the note into the pocket of his striped redingote. "I'll see."

I stood, withdrawing a list of my own from my velvet bag. Tallien smiled ruefully when he saw it. "I'm surrounded by angels of mercy."

"It's about my cousin," I said. I pointed out Marie's name. "Citoyenne Marie Beauharnais—remember? We'd been working to get her out, before I was imprisoned. But she's still—"

Tallien put up his hands: stop!

"And Jean-Henri Croisoeuil, my friend Aimée's son-in-law," I went on, regardless. "He's in the Carmes, and—"

"I will do what I can," he said, taking my list. "I *promise*. But it's difficult. Robespierre may be dead, but his followers live. They're a tenacious lot."

"If anyone can do it, *you* can," Thérèse said.

Tallien put his hands to his chest, mocking the pose of a hero.

"You jest," I said, "but were it not for your courageous act, we would not be alive today." Tallien smiled uneasily. He was more comfortable in the role of a rogue. "I owe you my life," I said, kissing his cheek. "I will *never* forget it."

*7:00 P.M.*
Thanks to Tallien I was finally able to obtain seats on a post-coach to Fontainebleau. We leave in the morning.

*Thursday, August 14.*
The children and I have been to Fontainebleau and back. I'm exhausted.

It was unsettling to see Aunt Désirée and the Marquis. Aunt Désirée is over fifty now, true, but she looks even older. And the Marquis, at eighty, is an invalid. His mind has begun to wander, his memory weak. Mercifully. Several times he called Eugène by Alexandre's name.

They are back in their own house now. The place had been ransacked, their belongings ruined—but this is trivial in Aunt Désirée's eyes. Her grief for Alexandre is without bounds. I fear for the effect the violence of her feelings will have on her heart. The loss of all of their worldly goods would be enough in itself, but none of it means anything to her. Her one consuming grief, and it is incessant, is the fact of Alexandre's death.

Aunt Désirée was not Alexandre's mother, but she loved him far more than his own mother did, more than I ever did. It is for her I weep.

*That evening.*
So many are being released, one would think the prisons were empty now. Yet even so, Marie remains. "You must be patient," Tallien told me.

"Patient!" Fanny cried out when I told her.

I understood. I was in prison for four months and it very nearly killed me. Marie has been in for over nine months. How much longer can she hold on?

*Friday, August 15.*
Lucie's husband Jean-Henri has finally been released. He, Aimée and Lucie will be returning to Croissy in a few days. I'm hosting a small gathering on their behalf—a reunion of sorts, in spite of Aimée's ill health. General Santerre and my former cellmate Jeanne-Victoire d'Aiguillon will be coming, as well as a number of others recently released from the Carmes.

Lannoy has threatened to quit if "that beast Santerre" sets foot in her house. I reminded her, gently, that this is not her house, that we are guests of my aunt.

Fanny has been trying to console me about my hair. "You look like a Greek shepherd. Even your créole accent is fashionable now."

I nodded, not hearing, examining myself in the looking glass, my cropped hair: "coiffure à la victime," it is called.

"Short curls suit you," Fanny went on. "They make you look young."

*Young?*

Never. Never again.


*Evening.*

The gathering began with discomfort. We were strangers to one another, ill at ease in this world. But with time (and wine) we discovered we could be ourselves again, speaking a language few others could understand, the language of prisoners.

Toward midnight General Santerre introduced a bawdy game of charades that had us howling with laughter. We fell upon one another weeping. It was at this moment that Jacques entered. He whispered something in Fanny's ear.

Fanny glanced at me, made a gesture I did not understand. I cocked my head to one side: pardon?

Everyone in the room grew still. "Mon Dieu," Aimée whispered, looking toward the door. I saw the colour drain from her face.

"Rose?"

It was a man's voice—a familiar voice. My heart jumped. I turned. Lazare Hoche stood before us.

*In which I must bid farewell to those I love*

Lazare smiled. "I am *not* a ghost," he said. "I wish everyone would stop treating me like one."

I stood, approached. In a moment I would faint, I knew.

"Don't, Rose." His voice had that tenderness—that same tenderness I remembered.

"Lazarro?" Speaking helped. I put my hands to my face. "It's just . . . we . . . I thought . . ." Tears flooded my eyes.

He leaned his sword against the wall, took off his hat. "Are you not going to embrace me?" Teasing.

I pressed my cheek against the scratchy wool of his jacket.

Aimée and the others crowded around us. Lazare bowed, a mock gallant. "You ask: Is he dead? Alive?" He laughed.

He was as handsome, as vital as I remembered him. I leaned against the wall. A feeling of light-headedness had come over me.

"I take it this is the *famous* General Hoche." Fanny gave him a beguiling look, a look she reserved for handsome young men, and slipped one arm through his. We followed their slow progression into the salon. "You were said to be dead, General. No doubt you have a story to tell. Perhaps you could entertain us with an account of your resurrection. We have come to love miracles."

Lazare helped Fanny to the sofa by the fireplace, then lowered himself onto a leather armchair close by. I sat with Lucie and Aimée on the sofa opposite. A whirlwind of emotions filled me. I held myself in check, fearful lest my strong feelings became too evident. Lazare. *Alive.*

He seemed a crude man in Fanny's elegant salon, his humble origins evident. And young. Younger than I remembered. A tall man, thin. That had not changed. But pale, I thought. What had happened to him?

General Santerre stood in front of the fireplace, his hands clasped in front of him, a bemused expression on his face.

"You knew about this?" Aimée asked.

General Santerre and Lazare exchanged looks. Lazare accepted a glass of port from Jacques. Then he related his story. He had been kept in a dungeon so deep he'd been forgotten. On the fourth day of August the bars to his cell had been opened. He thought his time had come. He emerged into the light, surprised that there were no guards, no guns, no tumbrils waiting. "The turnkey had his feet on a table. He was singing a rude camp song. I thought of escape, but before I could make a move he gestured: Out! As if shushing a stray cat away. Then yesterday, midday, I ran into our friend, General Santerre, in a cabaret in Les Halles. He told me of this gathering and we devised this little surprise."

Lazare caught my eye and dared to wink. I looked away, my heart beating foolishly. We had been lovers, true—but in that other world, that world of shadow and desperate need. Out here, the rules were different; everything changed. Out here, Lazare was a former stable groom; I a former vicomtesse. Out here, Lazare was a handsome young man, married, a general with a brilliant future . . . and I? Who was I but an impoverished widow, a mother of two, no longer young, no longer pretty.

As the guests departed, I stood back, unsure of what to say. Fanny had long since retired, and Aimée, no fool, disappeared without a word, leaving Lazare and me alone together.

He leaned against the door, looking at me, saying nothing.

"You must not stare so," I said.

"I was grieved to learn of your husband's death."

"He was one of the unlucky ones."

"He was a good man, a good general."

"Did you really think so?"

"You do not know that?"

"A wife sees her husband in a different way."

"And how do you see me?"

"You are as forthright as ever." I smiled.

He put on his hat, took his sword. "If I were to call . . . ?"

I looked toward the stairs. "My children, it is still very . . . I don't know."

"Could we meet? At the Café Lutte in the Palais-Égalité, perhaps?"

"Palais-Royal, you mean?"

He nodded, slipping on his cape. "If you wish to see me, I will be there tomorrow, at one."


*Saturday, August 16.*

Fanny warned me that the Palais-Royal had changed—but even so, I was unprepared for what I saw. Booths and tables were set up in the court-yard, selling everything that could be imagined: confiscated church relics, silver tea services, candlesticks, snuffers, used clothing of every descrip-tion, much of it clearly from the closets of aristocrats now dead, banished or merely impoverished.

And the noise! It was early in the afternoon, but even so, the dance halls and gambling rooms were packed. Young women in transparent gauze gowns hung about the fountains, posing to attract the attention of the young men, themselves dressed outrageously in tight silk.

It was with some relief that I slipped into the quiet of the Café Lutte. A violinist played in one corner. A waiter moved silently over the thick car-pets. Even the most scarred among us looked fresh in the soft candlelight.

Lazare stood as I was shown to his table. "You came," he said. It was with some pleasure, I confess, that I noted relief in his voice.

"You thought I might not?" I asked, allowing him to slip my cape from my shoulders.

He kissed the back of my neck.

I turned to face him. I had prepared a number of things to say: that I was only recently a widow; that it was too soon, my children required all my attention; that it was too complex, not right; that I was ill still, not yet strong; that he was himself married; that what had been begun in a prison, under the threat of death, might not be the same now, here, in this other world. . . .

Yet words escaped me. I lost all will. I found myself accepting his attentions with gratitude. We spent a very short time together in the café. Then I went with him to his rooms.


*August 17.*

I've never known a man like him. Honest, open, boisterous . . . He does not disguise the fact that he was raised in a stable. No, he is proud of it! Crude, bold, gentle—he takes life by storm.

He is a big man: big in heart, big in body, big in soul. He has the power to chase the shadows away, banish ghosts.

He has no patience for etiquette, intellectual games, social protocol. "I am a Republican!" he says proudly. He is a believer, in spite of all he's suffered.

His heart knows no limit. Nor his courage. He is said to be a genius. Young. Fearless. Bright.

"You *know* General Hoche?" Eugène asked, incredulous.

"He is a friend," I told him. Proudly.


*August 19.*

"It's tomorrow you leave, is it not?" I asked Lazare, trying not to show my disquiet. I had known for some time that he would be going to Thionville, to see his young wife. I also knew that he loved her . . . knew the first time he told me of her, knew by the way he spoke her name—*Adélaïde*—that I had no business in his life. Yet I could not turn him away; my need was too great. "When? In the morning?"

We were in his bed, the bedclothes crumpled, sweaty. I stretched out over the pillows, a film of sweat cooling against the oppressive summer heat, the pungent sweet smell of love heavy in the air.

"I wrote her this morning." He stroked my arm, my neck, touched my damp hair. "I told her I wouldn't be coming—that I've been delayed."

"Why?" I dared to ask.

A hint of a smile played around his lips. "You want to know?"

I nodded. I needed to know.

"You want me to answer truthfully?"

"We have agreed to be truthful with one another."

"The truth is I couldn't bear the thought of leaving you."

I buried my face in the pillows, hiding my tears.

He began to make love to me again, but I stilled him. There were things I wanted to tell him, things I could not say. How I woke every night, drenched in sweat, gripped by fear; how at times a faint feeling came over me, a feeling of sickening helplessness; how at dusk I sometimes saw the faces of the dead, pressing at a window; how I felt a lingering shame, still—as if, somehow, I had deserved to be imprisoned; as if, somehow, it had been *my* failing, *my* weakness, *my* fault. But the worst, the most haunting pain, was the cold that had entered my heart. I feared I could no longer love. Not even *him*.

But how could I tell him such things? "Does your wife love you?" I asked instead.

"Is that what you were thinking—of Adélaïde?"

*Adélaïde.* A hard name to speak without tenderness.

"No," I said. "But I hope she does love you—for if she doesn't . . ."

*If . . . if . . .*

"She loves me." Lazare turned onto his back. He rubbed his chin with his hand. He turned toward me. "I don't come to you lightly, Rose—I come because . . . What we've seen, felt, been through—it has scarred us, somehow, set us apart. I—" He stopped. He could not find the words.

"You don't have to explain," I said. "I understand." I pressed my face to his chest. Yes. The shame of the survivor.


*Thursday, August 21.*

Lazare has been reinstated as Chief of the Army at Cherbourg. He leaves in two weeks.

Two weeks. . . .

*August 23.*
Eugène will be thirteen soon—he is coming of age so quickly.

"He should start his military training," Lazare said.

"He should be in *school*." Even I was appalled by his spelling. Yet it was all I could do to pay for his boots.

"I could take him."

Lazare's words registered slowly. "*Take* him?" I asked.

"He could work on my staff—as an apprentice."

"He'd be working, for *you*?" I began to understand. "You'd look after him, keep an eye on him?"

"I like your son, Rose—he's an honest boy, forthright. I wouldn't suggest it if I didn't think he'd do a good job."

"Very well," I said, fighting back tears.

*Saturday, August 30, 3:30 P.M.*
The days go by too quickly. Already, Lazare is preparing to leave. And now Eugène, too, is packing.

*August 31.*
This afternoon, I said to Lazare, "I will see you tomorrow?" There were only a few more days.

He cleared his throat. "Adélaïde is coming. She's bringing my horse. My sword and pistols. I will be needing them."

Suddenly I felt frail. "*Tomorrow?*"

He reached to take me in his arms.

*September 1.*
Eugène will be leaving in the morning—the day before his birthday.

Hortense and I made a birthday cake for him. Without any eggs and very little sugar it was a miracle we could even eat it. We surrounded it with flowers from the garden. "At least these are free," I said.

He has polished his boots three times. My son, thirteen—a soldier.

*Later.*

No word from Lazare. I sent him a note: "Am I not to see you before you leave?"

He arrived two hours later.

"You love her," I said.

He took my hand. His eyes spoke of profound confusion.


*Tuesday, September 2.*

They are gone, Eugène, Lazare.

Eugène did not look back.

How could I say: *Take care.*

How could I say: *Protect my heart.*

## *In which friends comfort & distress me*

*Saturday, September 6, 1794.*

Thérèse and Tallien persuaded me to go out last night, to a concert at the Feydeau. "A cure for melancholy," Thérèse said.

The *Feydeau*—it was easy to be persuaded. Most people had to wait in line three days to get tickets.

Thérèse loaned me a hat with long silver plumes, a matching silver wig and a necklace shaped like a snake.

"Are you going to go out looking like *that?*" Lannoy demanded when she saw me preparing to leave.

"You should see what Thérèse is wearing," I said, amused by her disapproving look.

"It's what Madame Cabarrus *doesn't* wear that attracts notice."

At the theatre there was a terrible crush. The Feydeau is known for its excellent orchestra and the best soloists in Paris, but that isn't the main attraction. "It's the audience," Thérèse said—and she was right. All the fine ladies of Paris arrive as if onto a stage, looking rather like courtesans. No corsets at the Feydeau!

I felt like a star, the crowd lined up three deep to watch the parade, with applause for the most dramatic, the most outrageous. Thérèse, who would look spectacular in a nun's habit, was the obvious favourite.

"You should have been an actress," I told her. The press of the crowd frightened me.

"I *am* an actress," she said.

Inside, it was like a private reception, everyone going from loge to loge, so unlike former times when it was considered improper for a woman to even move from her chair. Fortunée Hamelin was there, an ugly seventeen-year-old créole well known for her ribald wit—"and a body that makes men weep," Tallien moaned. And sweet-faced Madame de Châteaurenaud ("Minerva")—looking like a cream puff in white gauze. And even sweet little Madame de Crény was there, wearing an amusing headpiece with a giant feather sticking straight up. I last saw her when we were both living at the abbey de Penthémont—a saltpetre factory now.

It was an amazing scene—all the aging aristocrats, the former elegant men and women of taste, together with their now-grown children, who, having come of age in the Terror, have cast aside all restraint and dress outrageously. "It reminds me of Carnival in Martinico." I looked out over the audience. We were sitting in Thérèse's luxurious loge, sipping excellent champagne.

"Isn't that Citoyen Loménie's son?" she asked, indicating a youth in a checked coat and an enormous green cravat. "Is that a blond wig he's wearing?" The "Gilded Youths," they were called—our outrageously dressed young men.

"It's the half of thirty-four crowd gone to seed," someone said.

Thérèse turned, spilling her champagne. "Citoyen Fouché! You are forever creeping up behind me."

I attempted to disguise my surprise. Fouché: "the mass murderer of Lyons," the deputy who had signed the most death warrants. Yet the man who stood before me was a slight, ill-kempt, and pockmarked human being with gaps between his teeth and unruly red hair. I'd been told he went mad with grief when his daughter died. How could such a man be a monster?

"Half of thirty-four?" I asked. "I've heard that expression before. What does it signify?"

Thérèse explained: "Half of thirty-four is seventeen. The Boy in the Temple is Louis XVI's heir, seventeenth in line . . ."

"I understand—seventeenth in line for the throne." *The Boy*. Le Petit Roi. "The Little Fellow" was what Hortense called him—an orphan of ten sleeping alone in the Temple prison with rats. And now, according to some, *King*.

Thérèse filled our glasses. "Are not the words 'Révolution Française' an anagram for 'La France veut son Roi'?"*

I looked at her. For a brief, treacherous moment I doubted my friend's Republican conviction.

"Royalists!" Citoyen Fouché cursed. He took a box of snuff out from his waistcoat pocket. "They are stupid, greedy, entirely without morals—and *all* here tonight." With his eyes half closed, he inhaled the fine powder.

"You jest," I said.

Citoyen Fouché brushed the snuff off his waistcoat, smiling slowly. The smile of a man who did not jest.

"Citoyen Fouché knows *everything*," Thérèse said. "He makes himself useful in this way." She leaned toward him, her low décolletage revealing. "It is rumoured you have eyes and ears in every salon, Citoyen."

Citoyen Fouché snapped shut his snuffbox lid, making a sound not unlike a pistol being cocked. "Is there something you wish to tell me, Our Good Lady of Liberty?"

Thérèse tapped Citoyen Fouché's hand with her fan. "You could profit at the gaming tables, you dissemble so well."

The musicians began to warm their instruments. A group of people in the lower levels clapped, then laughed.

Citoyen Fouché turned to go. "Good evening, Citoyennes. I see the concert is about to begin."

"A curious man," I said, after he left.

Thérèse fanned herself languidly. "Did you notice that Iva Théot is here tonight?"

Iva Théot is an older woman, a former duchesse, prominent in society. "Is that significant?" I asked.

"Iva Théot reports to Citoyen Fouché." Thérèse finished off her glass.

"Iva?" Bumbling, matronly Iva Théot—a *spy* for Fouché?

Thérèse laughed. "Rose—you are so easy to shock."

"Conspiring, ladies?" It was Deputy Barras, arm in arm with Tallien.

"Oh, it's the mischief-makers." Thérèse made a face behind her fan.

* *France wants her King.*

• 320 •

"You both look . . . *bright*, shall I say? Deputy Barras—have you been leading my darling astray?"

"Just a little contraband coffee, my dear—six cups."

"Coffee!" Thérèse groaned. "And you didn't bring me any."

Deputy Barras greeted me gallantly, then stooped to kiss Thérèse's hand. "You look exquisite tonight, Thérèse, my child. Good enough to eat. Caution lest you excite an old man's interest."

"Doesn't she?" Tallien put his long fingers around Thérèse's neck.

"What's that unpleasant odour?" Deputy Barras sniffed the air.

"Citoyen Fouché was just here," Thérèse said, and they laughed.

"Have you ever met his wife?" Tallien asked. "The ugliest, the most stupid woman . . ."

"Yet he's devoted to her," Thérèse said. "I find it touching."

"Citoyenne Beauharnais, you *elegant* creature," Deputy Barras said, filling my glass with champagne, "what do we hear from our beautiful man in Cherbourg?"

"General Lazare Hoche is already spoken for, Paul," Thérèse said.

"Alas." Deputy Barras lowered himself gracefully into the chair next to mine. He turned to me with a plaintive expression. "Such is the thanks one gets for saving the man's life."

"*You* saved General Hoche's life?" I was confused. "I thought it was Deputy Carnot who arranged for his release."

Deputy Barras made a theatrical groan. "Carnot! When General Hoche was in the dungeon I was approached by the executioner with a list of the condemned. *I* was the one who scratched out our dear Lazare's name—but you need not tell *him* that. One wouldn't want him to feel beholden to me, *would we?*"

"Hush," Thérèse whispered as the soloist began.

After the concert we went to Garchy's on Rue Richelieu (I had an apricot ice with almond biscuits—*delicious*) where the gaiety continued into the small hours. Deputy Barras entertained us with stories that had us aching with laughter. In company he is the spark that makes a gathering memorable, the master of comedy, of wit. It is hard to believe the rumours one hears. "A man who knows how to play his cards," Thérèse told me in the powder room, referring not to the sport of the gaming tables—a passion both Deputies Barras and Tallien share—but to his unerring instinct for strengthening his political hand.

From Garchy's the men persuaded us to go to a gaming house in the Palais Égalité (I won two livres—in coin—playing faro), and from there, after Tallien lost more than was wise, to the Café Covazza, and *then* to Madame de Châteaurenaud's (*Minerva's*, that is), where we played "magnetism" games, debated reform and gossiped about love.

At dawn we all headed over to a little café on Rue Saint-Honoré where we encountered a number of people who had been at the theatre: wild Fortunée Hamelin and two of her party (*not* her disapproving husband, I noted), tiny Madame de Crény with a tall man named Denon, as well as Citoyen Fouché, oddly enough, sitting alone at a table at the back, an untouched bowl of broth in front of him.

"Do you not enjoy your broth warm, Citoyen?" I asked, stopping to exchange pleasantries.

He shrugged. "Have a seat, Citoyenne Beauharnais?" In spite of the hour, he was sober. Unlike myself.

I took the chair he offered. He asked the waiter to bring a glass, which he filled from the bottle of Hungary water on the table. "Have you been working, perhaps?" I asked. "You do not have the air of a carefree man."

"Yes, I believe I have been working."

"You are not sure?"

"The line between work and play is never entirely clear."

"It is the nature of your work that is not clear."

He looked at me with a steady expression. "You are a woman who appears to speak truthfully—yet in this instance I feel I can be confident that you are fully informed as to the nature of my work. I can only conclude that you are one of those women who gives the impression of candour all the while concealing your hand."

I cocked my head to one side. "I generally win at the gaming tables, too." I smiled.

"Not many regard an ability to dissemble an attribute. Yet it is one of the truly indispensable talents."

"I did not know you to be a philosopher."

"There are many things you do not know about me."

"There are things I know that would surprise you."

"Such as . . . ?"

"Oh—that you feign not to care, yet your heart is tender," I ventured, "and that this distresses you." I observed his look. He appeared amused rather than upset. Perhaps foolishly, I went on. "That you put on an undisturbed air—yet your imagination is easily heated, so you guard against it."

He sat back in his chair and looked at me. "I understand you are in need of money."

I felt heat in my cheeks.

"Forgive me, I have offended you," he said. "You must understand that such matters do not mean anything to me. You are a woman without the protection of a husband—this is not a *fault*, although some would have it so. Your family is distant and in all likelihood impoverished. You have two children to provide for. Furthermore, you play in the company of the rich and reckless. This costs—of course—costs a great deal, but it also pays, does it not? Contacts, properly cultivated, are an invaluable asset. No doubt the balance is to the good. Over *time*, of course." He sat back.

I glanced toward the table at the front. Deputy Barras was observing us.

"Furthermore," Citoyen Fouché went on, "I am aware of the contributions you give to your relatives, as well as to a number of friends. Not to mention neighbours, street beggars, common ruffians. Indeed, your hand is too frequently open. I would advise you to be more cautious."

"You do know everything." I was embarrassed. Was nothing private?

He did not smile. "I will take that as a compliment—but alas, much eludes me. I am in need of assistance in this respect. If you are ever in need, do come to me—I would be most grateful for the services you could provide, services that would be of benefit to the Republic, I should add. I know you to be a sincere patriot." He glanced toward my table, where Tallien was speechifying rather loudly now, Thérèse laughing. "Unlike *some*."

I rose to go, uneasy. "We are all of us patriots, Citoyen Fouché."

"You are leaving me." He refilled his glass with water. "I confess my imagination *has* been heated. You seem to understand a great deal."

"My friends claim I am naive."

"They are mistaken—you see through the masquerade to the true spirit of a man. I have been disarmed. Like a gallant knight in days of old, I am for ever at your service."

I smiled. "I believe you mean it." I gave him a kiss on the cheek and returned to my friends, who teased me at length about my new conquest. I endured, enjoying their good humour—yet I confess that this one brief interchange has disturbed my repose. Citoyen Fouché's words linger still.

*September 10.*

Last night, just after midnight on Rue des Quatre Fils, Tallien was attacked by a ruffian with a pistol. He fell, wounded. When the assassin hit him on the chest with the butt end of his pistol, Tallien let out a cry that woke the neighbours. He was taken to his mother's home, close by.

When I saw him in his mother's humble apartment, I was shaken. He was resting on a bed in the tiny salon, behind a canopy of patched curtains. A bullet had gone through his left shoulder. He'd been bled, but even so, he continued to suffer pain.

"Remember when I said that in a revolution, men must not look behind them?" he asked. "I was wrong."

"It was a Jacobin who tried to kill him," Thérèse told me as we helped Tallien's mother clear the tea cups. Six days earlier Tallien had been expelled from the Jacobin Club for being too liberal in his views.

"You don't think Carrier had anything to do with it, do you?" I asked. Deputy Carrier was President of the Jacobin Club. He was the one who had had Tallien expelled.

"Carrier wouldn't do his own dirty work." Thérèse put a soup bowl down on the wood table. "He would hire some thug to do it for him."

*Dirty work.* It was rumoured that during the Terror, Carrier had ordered over ten thousand executed in Nantes—drowned in the Loire River. *Ten thousand.*

I heard voices. "It's the National Guard!" Tallien's mother cried out, hastily drying her hands on her stained muslin apron. "There's a crowd out on the street!" Her cheeks were pink.

"I'll talk to them," Thérèse said.

There were a number of visitors throughout the morning. The police came twice. Several journalists begged entrance, which Tallien refused, making an exception for a friend who writes for the *Moniteur*. At the end of the day Deputy Barras arrived, laden with spirits and a port pudding he insisted he'd made himself. His eyes filled with tears when he saw his friend's injury. He was accompanied by two fashionably unkempt Gilded Youths, not too much older than Eugène, I thought.

"Bonjour, Monsieur," one of the young men greeted Tallien. He lisped as he talked, as was the fashion, so that it sounded: *Bonzou, monsez*. His breeches were stretched and thin ribbons fell in long curls from the knees.

"We'll kill the assassin for you," the other said. His coat-tails were ragged and the pockets of his vest had been stuffed to make him look deformed. "Just tell us who."

I was chilled by his words. I knew him to be the son of the Duc d'Annonay. He must have been twelve or so when his father was murdered, hacked to death in front of the family home. How could such a thing not scar a child?

"Baptized in blood," Thérèse whispered, after they had left. We were in the kitchen, helping Tallien's mother prepare a tincture for wounds.

"It makes me sad," I said. An entire generation, orphaned by the Revolution, hardened by violence, schooled on the streets. What was to become of them now?

"Did you notice how they talk? Barras says they babble nonsense rhymes while beating Jacobins to death. It's a bit strange, don't you think?"

*Revenge*. Would the violence never stop? "If only there were a way of putting the past behind us," I said.

"Try telling that to Tallien," she said.

By evening Tallien was feeling well enough to begin formulating a plan of attack against the Jacobin Club—against Carrier. "I'm going to demand that hearings be conducted into the atrocities at Nantes," he said, "hearings into Carrier's crimes there. *Thousands* murdered in cold blood. It shouldn't take much to convict him, put him away." This idea gave him strength.

Thérèse and I exchanged looks. "Is this wise?" she asked.

"Shouldn't our goal be to unite all parties?" I suggested, gently, I hoped. "Factions have been our ruin."

"Justice must be done," Tallien said.

"But what if the Assembly becomes enthusiastic about this notion of hearings?" Thérèse asked. "If they decide to look into what happened at Lyons, it will be Citoyen Fouché they put on the stand. If they look into Marseille, it will be our friend Barras."

And if they look into Bordeaux, it will be *Tallien* himself, I thought. Thérèse didn't say that.

"Who among us is innocent?" she went on.

"You." Tallien slid his hand up under her petticoats.

"Innocent!" She laughed.

Quietly, I left, without bidding adieu.

*September 9, 1794—Cherbourg*
*Dear Rose,*

*Forgive my messy scrawl. I did not have a writing master when I was young. The grooms at the stable were my masters and I wouldn't want to tell you what they taught me.*

*Your son is a fine lad—he will make a good soldier.*

*I know I did not handle things very well when I left. Can you forgive me? I do love you.*

*Your soldier, Lazare*

*Saturday, September 12.*

Tallien has recovered—enough to make an appearance at the Odéon Theatre. "My public demands it!" he said, adjusting his sling of red silk.

"*Our* public." Thérèse was dressed in a simple white shift, quite revealing. A string of diamonds threw flecks of dancing light over her breasts.

"*Your* public." Tallien regarded her with devotion.

The theatre was packed, the applause deafening as Thérèse and Tallien entered. People got up on their chairs to see them, cheering and screaming. I felt awed, proud—and frightened.

## *In which I am witness to a wedding*

*September 22, 1794.*

Day One, Year Three of the Republic. I am writing this on a writing desk in a small but elegant suite of rooms on Rue de l'Université. I'm leasing them at a reasonable rate from Madame de Crény ("The Little Woman" Hortense calls her). Hortense and I moved in this morning. It didn't take long—we have so little.

Lannoy has agreed to stay with me in spite of the fact that I am unable to pay her. As well, Agathe will work for board, as will an old man I hired today, Citoyen Gontier, who insists he is strong enough to carry water buckets. So we're settled . . . for the *moment*, in any case. Dear little Madame de Crény is willing to wait three months for the rent. If only, by some miracle, I could get through to Mother. . . .


*September 27.*

Lannoy's brother-in-law has made a fortune buying estates for very little and then selling them at an inflated value. On Lannoy's suggestion, I've appealed to him for a loan—for fifteen *thousand* livres. It seems like a great deal, but how long will it last? I remember when that much money would have kept an aristocrat in pheasant and champagne for three years. Today it won't keep us in fowl and bitter wine for three months.

*Saturday, October 4, evening.*

At Fanny's this evening. She's ill, having succumbed to the vapours brought on by her grief over Marie, I believe—so little success has she had in her constant efforts to get her daughter out of prison. "Can't you do *something?*" she pleaded, breaking down.

What more *can* I do? I've already made several attempts to help Marie, all without success.

"What about that criminal friend of yours?" Fanny persisted. "I bet he could do something."

"Criminal friend?" I grinned. "*Which* one?"


*October 6.*

Deputy Barras pared his fingernails with a penknife as he listened to my appeal. Tall, baby-faced Citoyen Botot, now his secretary, sat by the window taking notes.

After I finished reading my petition, Deputy Barras looked up at me and said, "You sang beautifully at Madame Tallien's last night. You have an unusual voice. Innocent, yet suggestive." He was wearing a double-breasted coat of striped pink silk. His hair was powdered and gathered at the back into a black silk bag.

"You flatter me. . . ." I felt ill at ease. I had conversed with Deputy Barras on a number of occasions—at the theatre, salons, in my own home—but always in the company of friends. He coquetted with me (as is his way with women), yet even so, I feared I was making an imposition asking a favour. I was relieved he'd so warmly agreed to hear my appeal.

"And you are surprisingly accomplished at billiards," he said. "You won three games off Tallien, I noticed."

"Our friend Tallien excels at many things," I said, "but billiards is not one of them. I do not believe it just to surmise that I have any ability at the game."

"Yet you won against Citoyen Rosin as well. You know him, I gather?"

I nodded. I'd met Citoyen Rosin some time ago, at a Freemason meeting. A créole banker of extraordinary means, he'd managed to get his wealth out of Saint-Domingue before it collapsed.

"And his Swiss banker-friend Perré—the man with the burn on his face?"

I nodded. Although disfigured, Perré was particularly charming, I found.

Deputy Barras adjusted his gold-rimmed lorgnon, examined the document before him. "With respect to your cousin . . . Françoise-Marie, Citoyenne Beauharnais—" He shrugged.

"Can nothing be done?"

He made an exasperated gesture. "You must understand: governments come and governments go, but the bureaucracy stays the same. No matter who is in charge there are papers, review boards, committees, procedures. It's an obsession in this country." He cleared his throat, squinted at the paper again. "I see here that her husband, François Beauharnais, *Marquis*, is an émigré, an officer in the Prince of Condé's army. Wounded in the Vendée," he added absently, reading.

François—*wounded?* In the Vendée? I longed for details, but I dared not ask, dared not reveal my concern. "Perhaps you recall meeting her," I said, "at my salon on Rue Saint-Dominique."

Deputy Barras put his fingers to his chin, a posture that displayed to advantage the fine point lace of his shirtsleeve ruffle. "But as the wife of an émigré, and one who has taken up arms against us—"

"Marie divorced her husband some time ago," I protested. I glanced over at Citoyen Botot, intent on his notes.

"Many aristocratic wives divorce their émigré husbands in order to save their fortunes," Deputy Barras said, "*and* their empty heads. It means little, I'm afraid."

"My cousin is a Republican, she belonged to a number of the revolutionary clubs. She and her husband separated for this reason," I persisted.

Deputy Barras sighed. "I will do what I can," he said. He nodded to Botot, who rose and left the room.

"How can I thank you?" I asked. I clutched my silk bag. I had come prepared to pay, but I could not offer much.

"As a matter of fact, there is something you *could* do for me," Deputy Barras said, removing his lorgnon. "I'm involved in a number of fairly large . . . undertakings, I suppose you'd call them. I have need of bankers with a flair for *risk*, shall I say? Citoyens Rosin and Perré have been recommended, but of course, without an introduction, a recommendation . . ."

"I'd be delighted to arrange something," I said, rising. "An evening at my home?"

He took my hand with exaggerated delicacy. "Will I have the pleasure of your company at my salon tonight?" he asked.

I answered him with a bow, honoured.

"On condition you join me in a game of billiards," he said.

"Perhaps we should place a wager on it," I said.

"I take it you intend to win."

"Always."

"You wicked lady."

"Quite," I said, smiling.

As I left I paused to have a word with Citoyen Botot. "Is there any hope?" I whispered.

Startled, Citoyen Botot looked up from the piles of papers covering his desk. "Citoyenne Marie Beauharnais will be released tomorrow—at eleven in the morning," he said, lisping only slightly.


*October 29.*

I encountered Citoyen Fouché at Deputy Barras's salon. "What brings you into these circles?" I asked. He was wearing a mismatched, stained, and ill-fitting ensemble, in spite of the elegance of the gathering. The ribbons on his knee-breeches had come untied.

"I could ask the same of you, Citoyenne Beauharnais," he said. "Although a woman who so willingly listens is always welcome among men of power."

"You are drôle, Citoyen. You evade my question."

"Are you trustworthy?"

"You who know everything about me, ask if I am trustworthy?"

"Last night two deputies were roused from their beds to go to the Temple. Perhaps you know this already."

I shook my head. *"Why?"* The Temple was the prison in which the King's orphan children were being held—Madame Royale and the Boy were there.

Citoyen Fouché looked over his shoulder. "There is a rumour that the

Boy—'King' according to the treacherous among us—is no longer there."

"*Was* he there?"

"There was, indeed, a boy there. But was he the King's son? *That* is not certain."

"But if the Boy is not in the Temple—where is he?" A child of nine, the trump card of nations. So much depending on so small a head.

Citoyen Fouché shrugged. "You tell me. The Royalists want him alive. The Jacobins want him dead. And whoever holds the Boy, holds power over them both."

I saw Deputy Barras coming toward us. I motioned to Citoyen Fouché to be silent.

"So I ask myself," Citoyen Fouché went on, ignoring my caution, "who might want that much power? Who might that be?"

*Tuesday, November 11.*

Mobs in the streets. Deputy Carrier, President of the Jacobin Club, the executioner of thousands, has been arrested for "excessiveness" in the line of duty. The Gilded Youths are howling for his head. Restrained from tearing him limb from limb, they set upon the Jacobin Club.

Then Thérèse arrived to close it down.

*Thérèse.* She took the key to the club herself, fearless of the brawling men, of the violence in their hearts. Thérèse, slipping the key to the Jacobin Club into her bodice, closed the door on history.

"Were you not frightened?" I asked her, astonished. I was reading aloud a report in a news-sheet: "Such a woman as that would be capable of shutting the gates of Hell," a journalist had written.

"I will tell you my secret, Rose," She put her hands to her belly. "God walks with me. I am with child." She burst into tears.

*November 14, late afternoon.*

Thérèse and I stood at the fortuneteller's door for a time, yelling through the delivery slot. There was a chill wind.

"I do not tell fortunes any more!" Citoyenne Lenormand insisted. She refused to open the door. During the Terror she'd been imprisoned for foretelling the death of Robespierre. Ever since she's been reclusive. She would not allow us in.

"But it's me, Thérèse Cabarrus de Fontenoy—I am the one who got you released!" Thérèse cried out.

Finally, the doors opened. Citoyenne Lenormand was a small woman, younger than I imagined, with small dark eyes, quite deep-sunk, under a dirty lace cap.

"I have seen you before," she said to Thérèse. She paused. "Dressed as Liberty . . . when the Luxembourg prisoners were set free."

"You have a good memory." Thérèse untangled her hat strings.

"You have an unforgettable face," the soothsayer said. After civilités, Lenormand instructed Thérèse to sprinkle water over a looking glass placed on a table laid with three covers. "You are about to make an important decision," she said, examining the glass. "It is destined that the union be made. You know of whom I speak?"

Thérèse nodded. Her look was resigned.

"Your path is not an easy one. To your credit, much good will come of this alliance—but you will be the one to pay the price."

Thérèse made a face. "I know."

"You are gifted with vision."

"Cursed."

"Yes," Citoyenne Lenormand said. "It *is* a curse." She turned to me: "I believe I have foretold for you before."

"When I was in the Carmes, a few of us contrived to send you information, from which you deduced our futures."

"Yes. And you *are* a widow now."

I nodded.

"I also predicted that you would remarry, I recall, and that your second husband would be an extraordinary man, known throughout the world."

"That part hasn't come true." I smiled.

"You make light, yet your heart is heavy. Ask me what you wish to know."

"Tell her more about this extraordinary man," Thérèse suggested, grinning at me mischievously.

Citoyenne Lenormand laid out some cards. After a long silence she said, "He will be younger than you. Brilliant, yes. A military man—a general, likely."

Thérèse winked. "I wonder who *that* might be?"

On the way back to Rue de l'Université, Thérèse lectured me. "General Hoche is a rising star—he will do great things." We were in her new red carriage. A gang of children, street urchins, were chasing after us.

"It is true," I said. A miracle worker, people were saying; a genius of war, a genius of peace.

"What I am saying is that he is your rising star—your *extraordinary man*."

I groaned.

"Give me your hand, Rose," she demanded.

"Tallita—you are a Gypsy," I complained. "Confess. A Gypsy queen."

Thérèse smiled, then grew serious. She traced the lines in my palm. "Citoyenne Lenormand is right. You *will* marry a general."

"General Hoche is already married." I pulled my hand away.

"Soldiers get married and divorce once a year, to suit their newest fancy."

"It is not as simple as that. Lazare cares for his wife—I believe he loves her."

"You would be more beneficial to him. You could help him advance in his career."

"Lazare doesn't need my help."

Thérèse made a noise from her throat—an expression of impatience. "May I be frank with you, Rose?"

"Are you ever *not* frank with me?" I smiled.

"You are not getting younger. Your children are charming, true, a credit to you in every way—but in need of an education. Sooner than you think, your daughter will be in need of a dowry, your son a position. This will, cost a great deal. It is *them* you must think of."

"You talk as if there were good prospects everywhere."

"What of Marquis de Caulaincourt? At the Thélusson Ball I saw him following you everywhere, drooling on your shoulder."

"He's been married for two decades, he has eight children, he's almost sixty—"

"He's rich and he dotes on you." Thérèse pulled the fur blanket over her knees.

"Yes, Maman," I said. Thérèse made a playful face. "But what about you?" I asked, changing the subject. "Did you find out what you wanted?"

Thérèse sighed. "I have known since the moment I met Tallien that I was destined to marry him, destined to help others through him—" She paused, looked out the window. We were coming to the river. The spires of Notre-Dame—the "Temple of Reason" now—stood bold and beautiful against the sky. "Destined to soften the rule of his fist," she said softly.

"Tallita!" I was shocked by her words.

"Forgive me. I know you care for him."

"And you *don't?*" Did she not call Tallien her "Lion Amoureux"?

"There are things about him I find distasteful."

I smiled. "You were raised to be a princess," I said. And certainly, Tallien was no prince.

"I was raised to be a courtesan, but we need not get into that. No—I must confess that I entertain the affections of our friend for a number of reasons, but love is not one of them. Not even passion, which is often mistaken for love. Rather, I feel a bond of obligation toward him. He saved my life and the lives of many of my family and friends. And he has suffered as a result." She paused. "I shouldn't be telling you these things." She let down the glass, in spite of the cold, put it back up again.

"You'll not marry him then?"

Thérèse sat back, her eyes brimming with tears. "No," she said. "I will marry him."

"I don't—"

"Have you ever had the feeling you were part of a larger plan?" she asked, interrupting.

I wondered about that. The fact that I was a widow now, that this had been foretold—did that mean that my marriage to Alexandre had been part of a larger plan? Was Alexandre's untimely death *meant* to be?

The coach pulled into the courtyard of my hôtel on Rue de l'Université. "Do you believe this to be so with Tallien?" I asked. I found the idea of destiny both comforting and terrifying.

"When Tallien and I were together in Bordeaux, each night, as I went to bed with him, I liked to think of the lives I had persuaded him to spare that day. In this way I discovered the purpose of my existence."

I did not know what to say. Thérèse was so young, such a carefree soul—and yet, there was this, always *this,* this terrible responsibility she had taken on. Not a day went by that she wasn't pleading for a life. It was a commitment we shared—our religion, some said. "Ladies of mercy," Tallien called us.

"Thérèse—you are an angel," I said, taking up my basket.

The footman opened the door, let down the metal step.

Thérèse touched my shoulder. I turned to look at her. "Will you be godmother?" she asked.

"*Me?*"

She nodded, her cheeks glistening.

"I would be honoured," I said.


*November 10, 1794—Cherbourg*
*Rose,*

*We are in the process of moving to new headquarters in Rennes. I will be coming to Paris to arrange for supplies. The only consolation in this wretched business is that I will once again hold you in my arms.*

*Your soldier, Lazare*


*Sunday, November 16.*
Lazare!


*Monday.*
Lazare brings news of Eugène. Carefully I put forward questions. I do not want to nag. "You're not working him too hard? He's not in any danger? Is

he eating? Are you watching over him?" I have been sleepless with concern. Rennes is in the heart of the Vendée region. I'd heard stories of a civil war there—peasants and aristocrats united against the Republicans. I'd been happier when Eugène was in Cherbourg, facing the English. I didn't want him fighting Frenchmen. It wouldn't be right.

Lazare laughed, lacing up his breeches. "Of course I'm working him hard. Of course he's in danger. It's the army!"

"He's only a boy!"

"Do you not see that *I* feel pride in him? A father's tender care?"

This silenced me. A *father's* tender care?

Lazare held out his hands in a gesture of helplessness. "I have come to love your son, Rose," he confessed, "to regard him as my own."

*November 19.*

Lazare spends his days in meetings with the Committee of Public Safety; nights he spends with me. I take the time I am allowed greedily, my hunger overwhelming.

*November 20.*

Lazare is gone. He was here for only three days—three whirlwind days of passion and tears. Will I ever grow accustomed to such parting?

*November 19, 1794—Rennes*
*Chère Maman,*

*We got to Rennes—on foot! My boots are worn through. (I've enclosed a tracing of my foot and the measure of my leg, for a new pair.) Everyone has lice. But at least I haven't got scabies. We put up in the woods. Yesterday the artilleryman was murdered in town. We are regarded as the enemy!*

*A thousand kisses, your son Eugène*

*November 20.*

An associate of Citoyen Dunnkirk is sailing for America. There is hope of getting through to Mother, so I have spent the day writing and rewriting a letter, writing and rewriting what I must tell her, what she must, in any case, know: that I am a widow, that Hortense and Eugène are without a father, that we are all of us without any means of support.

I am so deeply in debt I know not where to turn. What *are* my choices?


*November 28, 1794—Rennes*
*Rose,*

*My troops are bored—they long for battle. They fail to see glory in an olive branch. Swords are more heroic, I grant you.*

*The peasants only want to pray to their saints. Should we murder them for this? The politicians in Paris insist they go to a Temple of Reason instead. What can these halfway minds be thinking? Faith cannot be legislated.*

*As a result, Royalist sentiment here is strong—a shocking number have hopes of seeing the Boy on the throne of France. This thought disgusts me! What have we fought for, suffered for—if not for Liberty? If the Boy were put on the throne, I'll be sent back to work in a stable.*

*Your soldier, Lazare*


*December 12.*

I went with Thérèse to see her country house this afternoon—La Chaumière she calls it. It is a long drive, outside the city walls. Nevertheless, she is intent on living there. She loves its humble aspect. "No one can understand what I see in it."

It wasn't easy. I was myself surprised. It even has a thatched roof.

"It's bigger than it looks," she assured me.

"The setting is lovely." At the far end of Allée des Veuves, not far from the river, set in the midst of forest, fields, it has a wild, free feeling. I closed my eyes, inhaled the fresh, cold air. Yes, I thought—I *could* understand.

"The first time I came here a hen laid an egg on the doorstep. A sign, no doubt. . . ."

"But of *what*?" I asked, laughing. For Thérèse sees signs everywhere.

*December 16.*

Three Jacobin leaders were guillotined this morning, their heads displayed above a cheering crowd.

"It's starting again," Lannoy said, watching out the window anxiously.

"They say this will put an *end* to it," I said. I could hear someone playing "Ça Ira" on a trumpet.

Lannoy threw me a piercing glance. "Your friends—the 'blood-drinkers'—are they so very different?"

*Saturday, December 20.*

I encountered Citoyen Fouché on Rue Saint-Honoré this afternoon. He asked if I'd heard anything more about the Boy.

"Nothing." Aside from Hortense's constant chatter.

"No whispers at Barras's?"

I shook my head. "Why?"

"Yesterday, three deputies examined the child. Deputy Luzerne is convinced that he is a fraud, that the real Boy has been kidnapped . . . perhaps even killed."

*Killed.* The Boy—*murdered?* "Why do you tell me these things?" Tears came to my eyes.

Citoyen Fouché tipped his hat. "To caution you, Citoyenne. Not everything is as it seems."

*December 26.*

Tonight, Thérèse and Tallien were wed. A small gathering of friends.

"To happiness," I said, embracing Thérèse. At four months, her belly was just beginning to show.

"To Madame Tallien." Tallien raised his glass in toast. "To our Lady of Mercy."

I recalled Thérèse's words: *I am destined to help others through him, destined to soften the rule of his fist.*

The rule of his fist. Was it a bruise her heavy make-up hid?

*In which I learn the true value of friendship*

*Friday, January 2, 1795.*
Daily I cross the river to the Assembly, seeking to have the sequester removed on our belongings, seeking to clear Alexandre's name, seeking restitution, compensation . . . *seeking*.

All along the quay they are there, the thin children, bewildered men, desperate women with babies at their breasts—excrement soiling their clothes, vermin crawling in their hair. I am moved by the defiant look in their eyes. How is it that an entire city can succumb to such misery? How many souls crying out to Heaven, how many prayers? After all that we have suffered, how can we be asked to suffer still? Take my bread, I pray, spare that child. And that. And that. The little hands reaching out, the sunken eyes: this is torture beyond measure.

Defeated, I returned home. Agathe, Lannoy, Gontier were at their work, Hortense at her studies. On the kitchen counter was the one small loaf of bread we were all of us allowed—two ounces per day per person. I slipped it into my basket and returned to the bridge, to the sickly woman with a baby at her breast, four young grabbing at her skirt. I put the loaf in her lap. The children turned to their mother—was it permitted? She tore into the crust like an animal. I averted my eyes.

Later, at home, I heard Agathe cry out: "The bread! It is gone!" She had waited in line for two hours to get it, endured the cold. The small loaf had been there, earlier, she *knew* that, on that very counter, she insisted. Her voice trembled with emotion.

"It can't have disappeared," Lannoy said. Perhaps the bread had been eaten; perhaps Agathe herself was the guilty party, she implied.

"I took it," I told them, stepping into the fray.

Lannoy turned to me with a bewildered expression. "Madame?"

"I gave it to a woman on the Pont-Royal. She had four children. She needed it more than we."

Agathe burst into tears.

*That evening.*

By day I pick my way through evidence of the most appalling poverty. By night I coquette with the newly rich in exclusive salons. Deputy Dumont, a former fowl-fattener, is now fattening himself on confiscated church property. Deputy Nerval, a leather-seller, recently purchased one of the mansions of the Marquise de Neufchâteau—fully furnished, including the horses and carriages—on profits made supplying wormy pork to the Army of the East. Who would know people are starving?

*January 6.*

Lannoy returned from the milliner's with an ashen face. She went directly to her room. "What happened?" I asked Gontier, who had accompanied her. He goes with her everywhere now, a knife concealed in his coat.

He shuffled his feet and stared at the floor. It required patience to get Gontier to speak. I waited. "A woman jumped in the river," he mumbled finally.

"Mademoiselle Lannoy saw this?" Every day people threw themselves into the Seine. Tallien claimed that there were so many now, at Saint-Cloud the job of pulling the bodies out had become overwhelming.

"She had a child strapped to her." Gontier stopped, shifted his weight from one foot to the other. "A big girl . . . like ours."

*Like ours.* Hortense, he meant. A girl as big as that, fighting for her life.

*Thursday, January 8, 7:00 P.M.*

At La Chaumière there is an atmosphere of creative confusion. A work crew toils under Thérèse's direction. She maintains her energy in spite of her pregnancy. She is exacting, she knows what she wants—but invariably it is something unusual. The workmen simply cannot comprehend. Often it takes several attempts before they get it right.

We stay late into the night, going over fabric samples, walking through the rooms. She wishes to create a theatrical, artistic, witty atmosphere: *almost* overdone (this is challenging). It fires my imagination. Now and again we come up with an idea that sets us both dancing.

After, we stand at the doors to the garden, listening to the wolves howl, the wind whistling through the trees, talking of love and life. Another world, so far from the misery that is Paris now—but for the hungry wolves circling, watching and waiting.

*January 2, 1795—Rennes*
*Chère Maman,*
   *I will be needing a new uniform soon. New gaiters, too; mine have entirely worn at the heel.*

                                                            *Your son, Eugène*

*January 8, 1795—Rennes*
*Rose,*
   *Forgive me for not writing more often. I am not a man of letters, as you know. Also, it has been quite the job here; our provisions are terribly inadequate. We do what we can, what we must—and that on very little.*
   *I am pleased with Eugène's progress—he is a fine boy.*

                                                        *Your soldier, Lazare*

*Monday, January 12.*

Under Thérèse's guidance I've realized an excellent profit speculating in saltpetre. Aunt Désirée was horrified. "It is unbecoming for a woman to involve herself in commerce," she scolded. *Until* I told her how much profit I had made (five thousand livres!), and then her own interest was sparked. I intend to reinvest the money in a purchase of lace from Britanny, which I can resell in Paris, yielding an additional twenty per cent.

Citoyenne Rose Beauharnais—*profiteer*. At least now I can send Eugène money for a new uniform.


*January 15, 1795—Hôtel de Caulaincourt, Paris*
*Dear Madame Beauharnais,*

*I am writing to inform you that thanks to your recommendation, General Hoche has kindly awarded my eldest son, Armand, a position as lieutenant in the Army of the Coast. Also, thanks to your efforts, my second son, Auguste, is now gainfully employed as a clerk. I am indebted to you.*

*At your suggestion I have made an appointment to speak to Deputy Coligny about the three years' pay due to me as a retired general. I will keep you informed as to the outcome. Thank you for approaching him on my behalf.*

*I would say more, but even in amoral times such as ours it is deemed unseemly for a man of my advanced age and marital status to write words of "appreciation" to a lovely widow. Perhaps I will see you chez Talliens?*

*I remain, most gratefully and as always,*

*Your dearest and most foolish friend, Marquis de Caulaincourt*
*"a slave to the devil of middle-aged passion"*

*Thursday, January 15.*
Marquis de Caulaincourt has insisted on awarding me ten per cent for my efforts.

"I did it for friendship," I protested.

"I will pay you in coin," he said.

*Gold.* "If you must."

*January 16.*

Tallien has been advising me on how best to draw up a petition requesting that the seals be removed from my belongings on Rue Saint-Dominique. This afternoon I made my presentation to the Committee of Public Safety. Tallien spoke in support: "Certainly it is certain," he began, repeating his words, as was his custom, "my fellow deputies-in-arms are beginning to comprehend that together we must cleanse the wounds of the past, right the wrongs in order for the Tree of Liberty to have fertile ground in which to root."

I repressed a disloyal smile. "Lukewarm-water Tap" is what my friend has been nicknamed in the Assembly, he does go on so.


*Wednesday, January 21.*

Festivities throughout the city, in celebration of the day the King died, two years ago. This in spite of the cold.

I would have stayed in, with Lannoy, who not so secretly mourns the King, but for a ceremony at the Palais-Égalité where Tallien was to be honoured. So I went with Thérèse, who was bundled in an enormous fox cape.

The speeches droned on, followed by singing. The Gilded Youths, resplendent in their crazy finery, dragging heavy clubs, demanded that the band play "Death to the Jacobins."

"There may be trouble," Deputy Barras said.

I suggested we go back to my apartment, which was not far. I was shivering from the cold. Also, I was concerned for Thérèse—at five months she continues to be delicate.

It was cold in my parlour; the fire had died down. We could see our breath. I was about to pull the bell for Gontier to stoke it, when Tallien insisted. "After all, this used to be my father's job," he said.

"Well," Deputy Barras said, lowering himself onto a stool by the fire. He rubbed his hands together. "Two years ago today."

Both Deputy Barras and Tallien had voted for the death of the King. I didn't like to think of that.

The fire caught. "This last year has been blazes." Tallien glanced in my direction. "Pardon my language, Citoyenne Beauharnais—I forget you are a lady." He stood, brushed his hands.

"And what about me?" Thérèse asked, stretching out on my daybed, which I had recently moved into the parlour due to the cold.

Tallien leaned over her, whispered something in her ear. She laughed.

"Perhaps we should request a demonstration." Deputy Barras accepted my offer of a brandy. I filled his glass from a bottle Marquis de Caulaincourt had given me.

"Really, Deputy Barras—you are *so* perverted," Thérèse said.

"Imagine, and in Thérèse's condition . . ." I feigned to be shocked.

"I'm *trying* to imagine, that's my problem." Deputy Barras made a funny face.

Smiling, I threw a fur coverlet over Thérèse.

"Our good, innocent Rose," she said. "Are we embarrassing you?"

"How innocent can she be, I ask you, with a bed in her parlour?" Deputy Barras asked.

"My mother keeps a bed in her parlour," Tallien said. "All the peasants do."

"And sleep there?" Deputy Barras asked. His green-and-black-striped coat had big square buttons with hunting scenes painted on them.

"No, it's only for love-making," Tallien said. (In fact, he used a cruder term.) "When company comes for tea."

"Citoyenne Beauharnais, if I may be so rude as to inquire—why *is* there a bed in your parlour?" Deputy Barras downed his glass.

"It's the only warm room." I took a seat by the fire.

"The other rooms are *colder?*"

We all laughed, but in truth I was beginning to regret having invited them. Seen through their eyes, my small, albeit elegant rooms looked quite humble. Rose, *their* Rose—the former vicomtesse who sipped their expensive champagne—this woman was a fraud, was she not?

"Do you not have fuel?" Thérèse asked, fingering a cameo Tallien had recently bought her for "only" six thousand livres.

"It's difficult to find in quantity now." I did not say: and frightfully dear.

Tallien groaned. "Why didn't you ask? There is more than enough. You'd think there was no fuel to be had in all of Paris, the way people talk."

"Or *bread,*" Deputy Barras added. "Of which there is little, you have to concede."

• 345 •

"The people are too damned lazy to work, and then they come to *us* to complain," Tallien ranted.

I looked from one to the other. How much was in jest? I wasn't sure.

"My friend has become cynical, I'm afraid," Deputy Barras said, in answer to my questioning look. "It is one of the dangers of public life. People expect their representatives to be as gods, to make the foul weather go away."

I sighed, relieved. We were onto safer ground: the weather. I set up a game of faro. We played, laughed, gossiped and gambled (I won seven livres). They left just before midnight, in good spirits.

"We'll be back next Tuesday," Thérèse announced as they were leaving. "For your *salon*."

"I couldn't," I said, horrified.

"Rose—be realistic: you can't afford *not* to. Imagine . . . *Chez Rose*—the most enjoyable salon in all of Paris."

*Chez Rose?* I smiled. "It sounds like a brothel."

"With a bed in the parlour and everything," Deputy Barras said.

"The better to get the deputies to come," Thérèse said.

And so it is set. Next Tuesday. Every Tuesday.


*January 23.*
Oh, it is cold, but we've been warm. Deputy Barras arranged to have a load of wood delivered. There's a huge pile of it outside. Gontier must stand by it to keep the neighbours from stealing it.

I sent Deputy Barras a note: "How can I thank you?"

He sent a note back: "Recommend me to banker Citoyen Rougemont."


*January 31, afternoon.*
By some miracle, I have succeeded. Like a stage director I have assembled the props, moved furniture, created *ambiance*—that mysterious aura that disguises the stains on the sofa, the hole in the rug, the less-than-exquisite fixtures.

My costume I created out of an outdated brocade, Lannoy and I cutting and reassembling the panels into an elegant Grecian design. It took some cajoling to entice her to take up her needle and thread, to use her refined artistry for such a "shameless" dress. Too much arm, too much leg, but worst of all, no corset!

*Later.*
Chez Rose was a success!

Who came: Tallien and Thérèse, of course. Deputy Barras, in the company of old La Montansier (who lived up to her wild reputation). Tiny Madame de Crény and Denon, her beau. Citoyen Fouché, skulking around. Deputy Fréron, raving and drunk, and in the company of an actress. (It is rumoured they have three children.) Fanny, with *both* her current favourites: Michel de Cubières and Rétif de la Bretonne, who got on well with La Montansier—pas de surprise. Fortunée Hamelin, half-naked as usual, and her grumpy husband, who fancied no one. Marquis de Caulaincourt, who *also* got on well with La Montansier, I noticed. Voluptuous Minerva in gauzy white, with a man she introduced as her *fiancé* (that was a surprise). Two of my "prison family": the elegant Grace Elliott, for a short time, and Duchesse Jeanne-Victoire d'Aiguillon—in the company of Mesdames de Broglie, Valance and Bizet, who smoked opium in the water-closet, Thérèse claims (I don't believe her). And dear sneezing Citoyen Dunnkirk, who came with fellow-bankers Citoyens Rougemont, Hottinguer and Perré. (I introduced them all to Deputy Barras.) And last, but certainly not least, my dear Consoler, the wild, radical and wicked General Santerre.

An entertaining, *very* mixed group. "A miracle, no bloodshed," Thérèse said, on leaving.

I would have run short of food were it not for Caulaincourt, who supplied pâté de foie gras from Strasbourg, larded pheasant and an enormous carp stuffed with truffles from Périgord. Not to mention a crate of freshly baked beautiful bread and a basket of fruit (in February!) from Citoyen Dunnkirk. Even Deputy Barras arranged for a half-barrel of excellent red wine to be delivered.

"Celebrating, darling?" Thérèse asked, watching Barras's footman carry in the barrel.

"Celebrating what?" Deputy Barras asked. He looked unusually serious in a Quaker-coloured silk coat and an old-fashioned pigtail wig.

"Being elected President of the Assembly."

"Oh, *that.*"

"You've been elected President?" I recalled when Alexandre had been elected President of the Assembly, remembered our excitement, our pride. How young we were then.

Deputy Barras shrugged. "A nuisance, if you ask me. No—if anything, I'm celebrating the profit I made on a sale of a property two days ago. Five hundred thousand. *Net.*" He grinned, his charming crooked smile.

Five hundred thousand! I could not comprehend such a sum. I practically had to sell my soul to get a loan of a mere five hundred.

"That confiscated Church property on Rue Jacques?" Tallien asked, overhearing.

Deputy Barras smiled, crossed himself. "And the good Lord *was* smiling on me," he said.

At around midnight Barras's secretary Botot came by, in the company of another man, Citoyen Laurent. Lisping, Botot asked if he could speak to Barras. I urged them to come in, but they were reluctant. I wondered if something was amiss.

Deputy Barras came to the door. He stepped into the landing to talk to them. When he came back in he looked drawn.

"Has something happened?" I asked.

"Nothing," he said quickly. Too quickly, I thought.

"Did I not hear Laurent's voice?" Thérèse asked, coming into the foyer on Citoyen Fouché's arm.

"He was just here, with Botot. They had a message for Deputy Barras," I said.

"It's rather late for messages," Thérèse said.

"Ah—Laurent and Botot," Citoyen Fouché said, catching my eye. "The Temple Twosome."

The Temple? The *Boy* is in the Temple. . . .

*February 5.*

At *last,* thanks to Tallien and Deputy Barras, my petition has been approved, the seals removed from my belongings on Rue Saint-Dominique.

I went there this morning—alone. That was how I wished it.

It was strange opening the doors. The rooms were dark, the shutters nailed over the windows. I lit a lantern—and was sickened by what I saw: everything had been pulled to the floor. Vandals.

I walked through the musty rooms, stepping through the litter of my life. My broken and soiled possessions brought forth an abundance of memories. Clothing, scarves, paintings, my guitar—things I had loved. Now ruined.

I gathered my courage and went into the parlour. Gently, I pried away the loose stone in the chimney. I blew into the hole, lest some creatures had taken up residence. Overcoming fear, I put in my hand. Papers. They were still there. Thank God.

Slowly, and with a great sense of relief, I drew out my treasures—my journals, letters, Manette's tapestry, my Bible, a container of dirt from Martinico, my childhood rosary, marriage contract, a little cloth bag of gems. And, at the last, Alexandre's will, sealed with wax.

I lowered myself into an armchair. I was enveloped in a cloud of dust. All that remained of my life was in my lap. I sat for a time thus, as still as the mute objects that surrounded me. How little it all meant, in the end.

My eyes fell upon an object in the corner—my needlework frame. The tapestry I had been working on was still in it, a design of roses, half completed. Miraculously, the needle was still in place. I had the most eerie sense of a life abruptly stopped, a curtain drawn in the middle of a play.

The ghosts began to stir. Not even a year had passed since I had been taken in the night, herded onto a wagon and into a cell. Stripped of my dignity, my health, my faith. Stripped of my youth, my life.

*February 6.*

I sat across from Citoyen Dunnkirk, grasping my basket. There was an uneasiness in his expression that cautioned me.

He cleared his throat and sat forward in his worn leather chair. "I'm afraid that your husband's will is not going to be of much use to you," he said, sneezing into a linen handkerchief.

"What do you mean?"

"Well—" He paused. "He has not left anything to you."

I sat for a moment without responding. Surely, I had misunderstood.

"And second," he went on, mistaking my silence for composure, "do you know of a Mademoiselle Marie-Adélaïde de la Ferté?"

"La Ferté is the name of Alexandre's country estate." But Citoyen Dunnkirk knew that.

"This is a child, a girl born June of 1785, near Cherbourg."

"Perhaps you mean Adélaïde d'Antigny." Adélaïde d'Antigny was Alexandre's illegitimate daughter, whom Aunt Désirée and I were doing our best to support, in spite of the hardships. At nine now, she was a beautiful child, quite bright, with Alexandre's features. "But Adélaïde d'Antigny was born in 1784, in Paris."

"This is a different girl, born the following year. Your deceased husband has left her an annual pension of six hundred livres."

Another illegitimate child? *Two* Adélaïdes?

"As well there is six hundred livres a year to be paid to Movin, your husband's servant, two hundred a year to Richard, the groom, and a one-time payment of an additional two hundred to Sauvage, the second groom—"

"And *nothing* for Hortense or Eugène?" I interrupted. "No mention of *my* name?"

"No doubt he assumed that they would be well provided for by your Island holdings."

I felt short of breath.

Citoyen Dunnkirk cleared his throat again and adjusted the lorgnon in his eye. "You understand, Madame Beauharnais, with respect to Marie-Adélaïde de la Ferté, there may be a way to get around it—"

"Honour it," I said sharply. I was already contributing to the support of one bastard child. How many were there? I thought wearily.

## In which I am warned

February 10, 1795.

La Chaumière has become *the* place to go. Thérèse has had to hire a guard to oversee the door; crowds of hopefuls line the courtyard.

At first there were whispered comments on the absurd location, jokes about the peasant life. But there could be no doubt that everyone is charmed, for inside this modest château is a gem of a palace—the door opens onto a theatrical world of marble columns and Greek statues. The originality of the décor, the artistry that is evident, not to mention the abundant fare and inspired entertainment, certainly make an impression.

But at heart, it is Thérèse everyone seeks. We are as moths to a flame. She embraces us as if it were months since we last met—not last night or the night before that. She is, always, astonishingly beautiful, wearing a simple toga or shift that makes no attempt to hide her growing belly, her swelling breasts. She draws us into the parlour, whispering, "Monsieur Monroe is here, the American Ambassador. And Citoyen Ouvrard, the brilliant financier. . . . Let me introduce you."

Within, guests whisper, ever watchful for others. Contacts are made, broken, alliances formed. After the Assembly's night sitting closes, the deputies arrive in their top hats. The heated debates go on until dawn. *This* is the government, it is said.

*February 12.*

"Thank God you're here!" Thérèse grabbed my hand this evening as I came into the foyer. "Deputy Renan drank the water out of his finger bowl, Citoyen Maurois blew his nose on the tablecloth. Already there have been two fistfights—"

"In the Middle Ages, it fell to the Romans to reform the barbarians," Deputy Barras said. He looked particularly elegant in a embroidered blue satin waistcoat. "Today it falls to Thérèse to demonstrate to the new ruling class *proper* etiquette."

Angry voices burst forth from the parlour. Thérèse raised her eyebrows in exasperation. "But I need help taming this mob!"

And so, my role has been defined: peacemaker. It's a job I apparently do well. I select the most heated guest, engage him in quiet conversation, lure him away—into a walk in the garden, perhaps, if the weather is fine, or through the premises to view the art objects. Soon my "victim" is calm, unmindful of his desire to commit murder only moments before.

Around four in the morning the last guest finally left. Thérèse and I collapsed on the sofa, laughing to tears over these ardent revolutionaries, trying so hard to be rich.


*February 13.*

Thérèse and Tallien persuaded me to go with them to the "Bal des Victimes," at Hôtel Thélusson. I went to Thérèse's early to prepare.

"Your hair is already perfect," she said, fastening a red ribbon around my neck, symbolizing the path for the knife.

"This is bizarre," I said. She was wearing flesh-coloured tights under a revealing gauze gown. As tall as she is, and with her huge belly and breasts, she looked spectacular.

"This is the dance." Thérèse began doing a strange wiggling movement, her head shaking back and forth as if it might come loose.

The streets in front of Hôtel Thélusson were crowded with carriages. Beggars crowded around the entry, vying for attention.

"Doesn't it remind you of the days of the Ancien Régime?" Thérèse whispered. "Of the opera balls?"

A street urchin grabbed the hem of my skirt. Tallien threatened the beggar with his fist. The boy fell back against the dirt. I stopped to make sure he was not hurt, gave him a coin.

"Are executioners allowed in?" someone yelled as Tallien entered.

"It is as *liberator* I am greeted now," Tallien said, attempting a jest.


*February 15.*
I fear Thérèse and Tallien are not getting along.

"Is something wrong?" I asked. Her left cheek was heavily made up. There were the beginnings of tears in her eyes. "I don't understand. He loves you so much."

"His love is killing me!" she cried.


*February 15, 1795—Rennes*
*Rose,*

*My efforts to negotiate peace may meet with success. Pray for me—soon it may be even legal to do so. I long for you.*

*Your soldier, Lazare*


*February 18, 11:00 A.M.*
Lazare has succeeded in negotiating peace with the Vendée rebels, succeeded where so many before him have failed. In exchange for freedom of worship, they will lay down their arms.

"But what about the rest of us," Lannoy grumbled. "Don't we get freedom too?"


*February 21.*
There is great excitement in the streets. Freedom of worship has been granted—to all of France.

"You can put out your little Madonna now," I told Hortense.

"Are you sure?" She is a fearful child.

"The time of hiding is over." Thanks to Lazare.

*Tuesday, February 24.*

Thérèse has not been well; her pregnancy is slowing her down. As a result, she has asked my help in organizing a reception in honour of the Turkish Ambassador. It's to be held next week at Barras's château in Chaillot. Thérèse and I have been going out there every afternoon.

Everything about Deputy Barras is old money: the hounds, the horses, the snifters of fine cognac . . . the degenerate morals. (Marquis de Sade is his *cousin,* he claims: "mon cher cousin.") He even suffers now and then from a mysteriously aristocratic nervous condition that requires hot baths. ("The French pox,* do you think?" Thérèse whispered.) Yet he is not without conscience. He seems to take pride in identifying the coming young men. At first I suspected a prurient interest, but I have found it to be otherwise. In the same way he chooses the winning horse at the races, he enjoys predicting who will hold the political trump card in the years to come. This is not without self-interest—nothing Deputy Barras does is without self-interest—for in this way he assures himself support. He is a master of survival.

Yes, an amusing man, mannered, witty, generous—but with a side to him that is so truly shocking. A libertine, he provides Thérèse and me with daily accounts of his conquests. Were it not for his wit, his stories would surely strike one as sordid—but Thérèse and I end up laughing gustily at his portrayals of coy seduction between grown men. Really, it is all *so* bizarre.

*Saturday.*

What a night! The partridge arrived foul, the fruit did not arrive at all, the violinist arrived drunk and the Turkish Ambassador sent word that he would not be able to attend. Perhaps that was a blessing. . . .

*\* Syphillis or gonorrhea (thought at the time to be the same disease).*

*Tuesday, March 3, late evening.*

Thérèse, preparing for confinement, has been urging me to become more involved in Barras's affairs. "You are exactly the type of woman he needs—aristocratic, elegant, with infallible taste and social skills. Your contacts could prove useful to him. There is *no one* better than you. I told him so myself."

"You told him that?"

"He rewards a woman well, Rose—of *that* I can assure you. And the only thing you have to do is listen to his stories of amorous adventure."

I smiled.

"And keep your son away from him, I should add."

I stopped smiling.


*Friday, March 13.*

I'm exhausted, but pleased. The reception at Barras's went well. Most of the evening was spent around the game tables with a separate area set up for conversation and canapés. At midnight I had a meal served, prepared from Barras's estates: rabbit from his hutches, vegetables from his gardens, wine from his vineyards in Provence. After, I persuaded everyone to play l'hombre. "A child's game!" the guests (including bankers Rosin and Perré) complained before reluctantly consenting—then becoming boisterous participants.

Overall, a success. Deputy Barras seemed pleased. "We will leave pretension to the nouveau riche."

It is late now, time to sleep—ideas swirl: I am filled with fantasies of theatricals, concerts, balls, of elegant meals until dawn. Entertaining on an unlimited budget—*this* is a task I enjoy.


*Saturday, March 28, 3:00 A.M.*

It's late. I'm still at Barras's in Chaillot. The roads are too muddy to risk the return into Paris. Deputy Barras just came in to say goodnight. He was wearing the high-crowned beaver felt hat he reserves for serious gambling. Tonight he'd adorned it with pink and lavender ribbons.

"Your confessions?" he asked, noting my journal. "Put in something scandalous about me. For posterity."

"I've put in what an angel of virtue you are." He smelled of spirit of ambergris, a scent he favours.

"Ah—that *v* word," he groaned, sinking into one of the plush velvet chairs and tossing his hat onto the floor. "Let's not be on about *virtue* again. We had quite enough of that from our dear Robespierre, don't you think?" He took a long sip of whatever it was in the glass in his hand. Spirits likely.

"What did you make of Deputy Valen's comment tonight?" I asked.

"About the Boy?" He bent down to pet Toto, his miniature greyhound.

I nodded. At supper, an elegant affair for twelve, Deputy Valen had expressed the view that it would not take much to install the Boy as King back on the throne of France—a shocking statement, under the circumstances.

Deputy Barras dangled the silk tassel of his robe in front of Toto's nose, to tease him. "I think we've had quite enough of kings," he said, smiling at Toto's antics.

"It is rumoured you favour a return of the monarchy," I persisted, my heart pounding.

"Only a fool would admit it." He looked over at me. "Even to a friend." His big eyes were impossible to interpret. "In any case," he yawned, "I prefer to talk of men, not kings." Toto jumped up on his lap.

"Did Citoyen Lumière not stay?"

Deputy Barras sighed, scratching Toto behind the ears. "Alas, no—his wife was expecting him. His *wife!*"

"And now you only have me."

"And lectures on virtue. . . ." He made a comical face.

"How tiresome," I laughed.


*April 1.*

Agathe returned from the market in tears. Riots in the marketplace—she'd seen a child trampled. Then, as I was preparing to leave to go out to La Chaumière, I thought I heard musket shots. Nevertheless, I sent Gontier for a hackney coach. The driver, dressed in mismatched livery, insisted on a fee three times the normal rate, and that in coin.

"Only fools are out tonight," he said when I objected to the fare.

"What has happened?"

"The Assembly has been attacked." He was a young man, but with no teeth.

The Assembly!

At the end of Pont-Royal there were a number of National Guardsmen on horseback. The coachman cracked his whip; our horses galloped down the quay.

At La Chaumière, coaches and horses filled the courtyard. I saw Tallien, still in his deputy robes. "You're safe!" I embraced him.

He told me what had happened: a mob had invaded the Assembly, demanding food. The Gilded Youths were summoned, who proved cowardly (for all their talk). Then the National Guard had been mobilized. Finally, the instigators had been arrested and peace restored.

"Who was behind it?" I asked.

"Four men." Tallien puffed on his pipe. "'The Four' they are called now—the alumni of the Terror." He listed off the names: Billaud-Varenne, Collot d'Herbois, Barère, Vadier.

"Deputy Barère? Your old *friend?*" Barère and Tallien used to come to our gatherings on Rue Saint-Dominique. I remembered Deputy Barère's support of Alexandre in the Assembly, his fear of helping me when Marie had been arrested. And Vadier, certainly . . . Deputy Vadier had signed my arrest warrant. And yet, years back, they'd all been colleagues of Alexandre's, idealists working together for a better world. Now Alexandre was dead and they were on their way to prison . . . or worse, Guiana.

"Yes," Tallien said with a satisfied air. "Strange—is it not—how history turns?"


*April 2.*

This morning Agathe came to me in an agitated state. "There's a curious man at the door. He insists on speaking with you."

"Curious—in what way?" I asked. There had been sounds of violence, shots fired. I felt uneasy. Today was the day The Four were to be deported to Guiana, expelled from the city on carts. Half of Paris wanted them guillotined, the other half wanted them set free.

"He smells, and he's kind of nervous," Agathe said.

I went to the door. I could hardly see the man's eyes for the scarves he had wrapped about his face.

"Citoyenne Beauharnais—it's me." He put down his fur muff and unwound one of the scarves.

"Citoyen Fouché?"

Agathe hovered nearby. "You may go," I told her.

"I have come to bid farewell," he hissed, after Agathe had withdrawn.

"I don't understand." I took his arm, urged him in.

"The Four have been arrested, deported. As you know. What you might not know is that were it not for Deputy Barras, it would have been 'The Five.' I've been spared, but on condition. I'm to disappear, as it were."

"Disappear? *You?*" I invited him to take a seat beside me on a little bench by the door. "But why?"

"Too much snooping around, I guess." He shrugged. "I'm going to be a pig farmer now."

I smiled. It was difficult to imagine him thus. "I like pigs," I said.

"I forget that you're a farmgirl."

"But where will you be? You and your pigs."

"Not far." He handed me a piece of paper. An address was written on it, in a neat hand. He stood to go. "You are aware, no doubt, of the incident at the hospital, at the Hôtel Dieu?"

"The miracle, you mean?" A dying child had been cured overnight. Hortense had been telling me all about it.

"There are no miracles any more, Citoyenne. You know that."

"You sound sad."

"It's a hoax—with children for pawns! The sick child was moved from the hospital to the Temple, to *pose* as the Boy."

"But where *is* the Boy?" *King. . . .*

"That's what I want to know. Your friend, Lazare—"

"General Hoche?"

"General Hoche stands to be hurt by this. The peace treaty he negotiated with the rebels—I understand that part of the agreement was that the Boy would be restored to the throne."

"General Lazare Hoche would *never* agree to such a thing!"

Citoyen Fouché nodded. "But Director *Barras* might," he said. "Promise, and then not deliver."

I felt a strange tingling feeling coming over me. I could close my eyes to any number of things, but could I close my eyes to this? I only wanted peace.

"How convenient," Citoyen Fouché went on, "if the Boy—or rather, the child everyone *thinks* is the Boy—how very convenient if he were to *die*. . . ." Citoyen Fouché bowed and left, wrapping his face in scarves.

## *In which a child is born & a child dies*

*May 17, 1795.*

I was awoken this morning by Fortuné growling.

"Citoyenne Tallien's footman is at the door," Agathe informed me.

"Thérèse! Is it—" I stumbled into my clothes, threw on a wig, a cloak.

The horses were snorting and pawing at the stones. Thérèse's footman helped me into the new barouche. Immediately the horses pulled forward. They were a fast team. I closed my eyes and held on.

When we arrived at La Chaumière the accoucher was already there. I went to Thérèse's bedside, touched her hand. Thérèse squeezed it hard. Already her night-clothes were soaked.

"Where's Tallien?" I asked.

"He went out last night. With Barras."

I did not ask the obvious. Deputies Tallien and Barras shared a weakness for "the gaming tables of liberty," as they put it. "Well—you'll have a nice surprise for him when he returns," I said.

I fetched cloths and a bowl of water. For hours I stroked her brow, caressed her, spoke words of calm. Shortly before noon the baby came. "I saw her in a dream," she said. There were tears in her eyes. "Rouge me?" she asked.

"You look beautiful as you are." I coloured her cheeks as she requested.

After, she fell into an exhausted sleep. I took the baby—Thermidor-Rose she has been named—and held her in my arms. My goddaughter. She cried for only a moment, a little animal squawk, and then quieted. My breasts responded with a familiar tingling sensation. I sat thus in the rocking chair by the window for some time, looking into the face of this precious little soul, so pure and so new.

If I ever remarry, would I have another? *Could* I?

*June 3.*

Dr. Desault, doctor to the Boy, died suddenly three days ago, of brain fever—or so it was reported. The streets have been buzzing with rumours. For once both Agathe and Lannoy agree: the doctor was poisoned.

I tell them such stories are entirely without grounds, but now the doctor's nephew has spoken, claiming that his uncle the doctor *had* been poisoned, and all because he'd discovered that this child was a fraud, not the Dauphin at all.

"There—you see!" Lannoy and Agathe said in unison.

*June 8.*

At La Chaumière I was met by Tallien. He pulled me into the study. "The Committee of General Security has gone to an emergency meeting. The Dauphin died," he whispered.

"The *Boy?*" I sat down. It was only a week ago that the Boy's doctor had died . . . and now the Boy himself? He was only ten years old.

I recalled Citoyen Fouché's words: *How convenient if the Boy were to die.* I felt a sickening sense of helplessness. "When?" I asked.

"At three this afternoon." It was six now. "You're not to tell *anyone.*" He looked around uneasily. "*Especially* Tallita."

*June 9.*

This afternoon there was an enormous reception planned: an orchestra, a seven-course meal for three hundred (every dignitary in Paris invited), a ball after—all to celebrate the passage of a law allowing restitution to victims of the Terror. It was a significant achievement, deserving of festivity. The new law would begin to heal the wounds of the past. Now Alexandre might be declared unjustly accused, unjustly condemned, his possessions and property returned to his family.

But even so I did not want to go; I could not shake the gloom I felt. However, I had promised; so at midday I set out.

I was greeted by Minerva, her cream-puff cheeks pink with excitement. "Isn't it wonderful!" Her gauzy skirt billowed up around her. "We'll be wealthy again."

She was stopped by the lack of gaiety in my expression. "What's the matter, Rose? After all the work you and Thérèse did to get this law passed, I should think you would happier than anyone."

It was true. Thérèse and I had worked hard. "There has been a disturbing development," I told her. News of the Boy's death was to be announced in the Assembly that morning, I knew. Soon everyone would know. "The Boy died yesterday."

"You mean the King's *son?*" Minerva sat down on one of the lawn chairs, fanning herself furiously. "Oh, dear."

I saw Thérèse approaching, Tallien holding her arm. They were followed by a swarm of men and women, like courtiers to a king and queen. Thérèse was weak still, moving very slowly.

"You should be in childbed." Minerva took her other arm.

"I refuse." Thérèse smiled weakly.

A gentleman rushed to get her a chair. Another held a pastel blue sun umbrella over her.

I glanced at Tallien. "How did they take the news?" I asked.

"The deputies? They were quiet." Tallien looked out over the festive grounds. The manicured gardens opened onto a small lake, where colourful boats floated lazily. A string orchestra was being set up on a floating platform.

"Likely it's the shock of it," I said.

"I'm not sure." He brushed a mosquito off his cheek.

"What else could it be?"

"Suspicion."

*June 11.*

Late at night, last night, a child was buried—quietly, *quickly*.

"What do you think it means?" Thérèse demanded, her baby in her arms. We were walking in her garden. The flowers were blooming, it was a glorious afternoon. "Now everyone's saying that the child that died wasn't really the Boy. Yet it would have been so easy to prove. Why didn't they ask Madame Royale? If anyone would be able to give a positive identification of the Boy's body, one would think it would be his sister."

"Perhaps they didn't want to upset her." I never told Thérèse about my conversations with Citoyen Fouché, my growing uneasiness . . . my suspicions.

"Because they're so tenderhearted? Because they *care* so much about the royal family?" Thérèse gave me a scornful look. "Rose—that makes no sense. Even Barras is being evasive. Why do they have to be so secretive? I don't like it."

I put my arm around her. "Tallita, you shouldn't be thinking such distressing thoughts. You should be resting." I led her back toward the house.


*June 13.*

I've been at Deputy Barras's all afternoon, preparing another reception. "Are you evading me?" he asked, finally. I was in the study writing out the invitations.

I put down the quill. How could I respond? It was true—I *had* been evading him. Ever since the death of the Boy I have had a feeling of disquiet.

Deputy Barras put his hand to his forehead in a theatrical pose. "And even to this, this little query, she remains silent. One hates to contemplate the magnitude of her despair."

"This is not a matter for comedy," I said.

He placed a chair beside me and sat down. "Tragedy?"

"I can't talk about it."

"It's all these nasty rumours. Isn't it."

"There are always nasty rumours."

"But these you believe?"

I looked away. I would have given anything not to be in this position, talking to Deputy Barras now, but I had begun and there was nothing to do but continue. "It is said you have consorted with the enemy—with the English."

Deputy Barras looked at me with an amused expression. "Les God-dams?"

"Is it *true?*"

He smirked. "I dare say the espionage force of an entire nation couldn't have gleaned as much."

"How can you joke?" I cautioned myself to be calm. "Do you think this is a game?"

"This *is* a game, Rose—a complex game. Do not presume to understand." He was angry now.

"You admit it?" I sat back, suddenly short of breath.

"The facts are correct, but the intention mistaken. How better to know the enemy than to be in their league? Or, at the least, to have them *think* you are in their league. A dangerous pastime, true, for one risks condemnation from all sides, but risk has long been my friend, and what risk is too great for the good of the Republic?"

"*Did* you murder the Boy? Did you poison the King's son?"

Deputy Barras made a sigh. "There are things you would prefer not to know," he said.

I felt short of breath. "You—"

He put up his hand. "It's not what you think."

"Then?" My mouth was dry.

"The unpleasant truth is that that child's dear uncle, the Comte d'Artois, paid a considerable sum to see that this was done. He rather fancied the throne for himself, should the opportunity present itself."

I was silent a moment. "The Comte d'Artois?"

Deputy Barras nodded.

"Offered to *pay?*" For his own nephew's *death* . . .

"Paid."

"Paid *you?*"

Deputy Barras nodded again, slowly.

"You did then," I said, coldly, starting to rise. "You—"

"Stay," he said, putting his hand on my arm. "I did *not*. The child—a good lad, you might like to know, a boy I came to be fond of, in my fashion—died naturally of a fever some time ago. On that count I am innocent."

"Why not make it known? Why all this secrecy?"

"Spain would never have signed!" He threw up his hands.

"The peace treaty, you mean."

He nodded wearily.

"So the child who just died was *not* the Boy?"

"*That* child was sickly, deaf and dumb, the son of a nail-maker—a decoy you might say, kept alive for the purpose of forging a peace with Spain. He was destined to die in any case. Nature did our work."

There was a moment of silence. Still, I would not look at him.

"Rose, look at me," he said.

I turned to face him. He did not look like a devil. He looked like an aging, ordinary man.

"You don't believe me," he said, his eyes sorrowful.

"I do believe you," I said. But there was reserve in my heart.

"The question is not, *did* I do it?" He stood abruptly, walked to the window. "The question is—" He pulled the drapes shut. "The question is, *would* I have done it?" He stood for a long moment, his back turned to me. "And the truth is . . . *yes*," I heard him say.

I waited for him to move, say something. "Paul?"

He turned to me, his eyes brimming with tears.

"I don't believe you," I said.


*June 16.*

This morning Barras came to call. It was early; I had a scarf wrapped around my head, créole style. He invited me outside. "I have something to show you." In the courtyard were two handsome black horses harnessed to a gleaming dark green carriage.

"What do you think?" He slapped one of the horses on the flank. "Fine specimens. Hungarian." He opened the door to the carriage. The upholstery was a lush red, the colour of royalty.

"Velvet?" Such luxury is rare now. But then, Deputy Barras never had anything but the best. "It's beautiful. When did you get it?" I asked.

"It's yours."

*"Mine?"*

"In compensation for the carriage and horses your husband left behind in Strasbourg."

He noted my shocked expression with satisfaction. "There's a cow as well—a milk cow. I didn't bring her along. Too slow, you know."

"A *cow?*"

Barras leaned back against the carriage, taking care not to soil his coat on the wheels. "I got them to throw her in."

I began to laugh. A *cow*—we could have butter, milk, cheese. We could have too much, more than we needed. We could have excess—to sell or trade. "But where would I keep her?"

"Must you be so practical?"

"I'm serious." A carriage, two horses, a cow . . . I had no groom, no driver, no hay much less a barn.

"You can stable the horses down the road. And the cow can go to Croissy."

"Croissy? But I'm not renewing the lease."

He looked confused. "Why not?"

I rubbed my thumb and index finger together, meaning: *money.* Barras had his estates, his wolfhounds, his English Thoroughbreds. It was hard for him to comprehend.

"Why didn't you tell me? I've made a small fortune as a result of the meeting you arranged with your friends Rosin and Perré."

And so it is agreed. Barras will take over the Croissy lease.

## *In which intrigue is the rule of the day*

*June 20, 1795.*
A note on my door: "The émigré fleet has left the coast of England, headed for France. They are planning to attack at Quiberon Bay."

Unsigned.

I looked through my writing desk. Finally I found it, the scrap of paper, the one Citoyen Fouché had given me with his address on it. The handwriting was the same.

War. The émigrés are on their way.

I sent a mounted courier to Rennes with a message for Lazare. At the end I hastily penned the words: "Send Eugène home. Quickly."

*Quickly.*


*Wednesday, July 1.*
The émigré forces have attacked. Tallien left for Quiberon Bay in the middle of the night.

Where *is* Eugène?


*Thursday, July 16—Fontainebleau.*
I have come to Fontainebleau to escape the tension in Paris, the fear in my heart, my thoughts of Lazare . . . my worry about *Eugène.*

Only to be assaulted by my aunt.

"Soon it will have been one year," she said.

*One year.* I knew what she was going to say. One year since Alexandre died.

"It is time to think of remarrying, Rose."

"I am too old to marry," I said.

She smiled uneasily. There is truth in my jest.


*July 18—Paris.*

As I climbed the stairs to my suite of rooms, Agathe came running to greet me. "What is it?" I asked.

"Nothing, Madame," she said, falling in behind.

She never called me "Madame," so I was suspicious. I entered the parlour. There, sitting on the sofa, was Eugène, dressed smartly in a dark blue uniform with silver-and-red trim. Tears came to my eyes. He looked so like my father.

I embraced him, trying not to cry. He had grown since I last saw him over ten months ago, tall for a fourteen-year-old. "When did you get here?" I asked, sitting down beside him on the sofa.

"Two hours ago." His voice has not yet deepened.

I took his hand. He pulled away. "Is something the matter?" I asked.

"Why did you make me come back! Just when things were starting to happen!"

It was hot in the room. I stood and went to the window, opened it wider. The air outside was heavy, too; it made little difference.

How was I going to answer? Tell him he was too young to kill, too young to die? That I would not allow him to take up arms against French *émigrés?* That I could not bear the risk of losing him?

"I need you here," I said.

"You have your men friends to help you!" Abruptly he stood and stomped out. I heard the front door slam shut behind him.


*July 20.*

Eugène mopes about the apartment, resentful that I have "caged" him, kept him from the excitement of army life, the glory of war. He takes to the streets where he spars with a rough-looking group.

What am I going to do with him?

*Thursday, July 23.*
It was early, not yet nine when I summoned Eugène. "Do you know the significance of this day?"

He shrugged.

"One year ago your father died." This startled him.

"I have something for you." I got down Alexandre's sword from on top of the cupboard, put it on the table in the dining-parlour. "This was your father's sword. He would have wanted you to have it."

Eugène touched it, picked it up, withdrew it from its sheath. On the handle was engraved the Beauharnais family motto, Serve No Further, and under that, a heart. The family crest had been scratched over with the words "la nation."

"It pleases you?" I asked.

A blush of emotion had spread across his cheeks.

I put my hand on his arm. "Wear it with honour, Eugène." Quickly, I left. I did not want him to see my tears.

*July 23, 1795—Quiberon*
*Rose,*
    *Victory! I carry your ribbon close to my heart.*

                                                   *Your soldier, Lazare*
*Note—Tell Eugène that Sébastien Antier was killed in battle. Eugène and Sébastien were close. Tell him Sébastien died honourably.*

*July 27.*
Victory at Quiberon Bay! Immediately I set out for La Chaumière. It was ten in the morning, early, but already the courtyard was jammed with carriages.

"You've heard?" I exclaimed the moment I saw Thérèse. Through the open door I thought I saw Tallien's bristly head. "Tallien is *back?*"

"He arrived late last night."

"For the banquet tonight?" It was the first-year anniversary of the overthrow of Robespierre.

Thérèse nodded. She looked graven.

"Something is wrong?" I asked. "Is it Lazare—"

"No."

"What is it?" I felt a panic rising within me.

"Over seven hundred prisoners were taken," she whispered.

I did not understand. "Is that not good news?"

"There is talk of execution."

"Of the *prisoners?*"

Thérèse nodded.

"They were taken in battle?" I asked.

"They surrendered, they put down their arms."

"Then by law they cannot be executed."

Thérèse snorted. "There is fear in the air! They will be slaughtered!"

"You are thinking of the past." I put my arms around her. She'd risen from childbed too soon.

"We are the past," she said.


*July 28.*

I was awoken in the middle of the night. It was Thérèse, in distress. She'd had an argument with Tallien, been forced to flee. Indeed, there was evidence she'd not escaped soon enough, for her lip was swollen and her cheek bruised.

"I don't understand." I pressed a cold compress to her face. "I know how much he loves you."

She looked as if she would begin to weep again. "It's my fault. I thought I could reform him. I allowed myself the sin of pride."

"Tallita, please! Don't speak in mysteries." I poured us each a large glass of claret. "What started it? What was the fight about?"

"Have you not heard? About *Sieyès?*" She looked at me incredulously.

I shook my head. Deputy Sieyès was in Holland, I thought.

"He claims he's discovered documents that prove that Tallien is in league with Royalists, with the leaders of the émigré fleet that attacked at Quiberon Bay."

*Tallien?* "But that's not possible, Thérèse." That would mean that Tallien was on the side of the enemy—the very men Lazare fought against in battle.

"It's true, Rose. I knew by the look on his face when I confronted him—but the worst of it is . . . the *worst* of it is his fear of being found out. Now he will go to *any* length to prove himself an anti-Royalist, to prove to the Assembly that he is against the émigrés . . . even if it means *massacring* the prisoners he vowed to save!" She broke into sobs. I held her in my arms. The sun was rising when she finally fell asleep.

It was almost midday when we awoke. Thérèse hurriedly began her toilette, covering the bruise on her cheek with rouge.

"Where are you going?" I did not trust her mood.

"To the Assembly," she said, tying her hat strings.

The doorbell rang.

"It's Deputy Tallien," Agathe informed me.

"You stay here," I told Thérèse.

I went to the front door. Tallien blocked the sun. It was hard to see his face against the bright light. "I have come for Thérèse," he said.

"I don't think it wise for you to see her now," I said. He smelled of liquor.

Suddenly Thérèse appeared behind me. She attempted to push her way past, out the door. "Where are you going—" Tallien grabbed her arm.

"To the Assembly." Thérèse shook herself free. She cursed him in the Spanish tongue.

"It's no use!" he cried.

"What do you mean?" She stared at him, her breathing heavy.

"It's over!" A motion had been passed that morning: the prisoners would be executed.

"Who made the motion?" Thérèse demanded.

Tallien did not deny it. "You don't understand!"

"*You* don't understand. Over seven hundred lives have been sacrificed to save *one*—yours. How can you live with that!"

"You would have *me* sacrificed?"

"Yes!" And louder: *"Yes!"* She ran back to my bedchamber.

"Surely something can be done?" I asked, shaken.

Tallien shook his head. He turned his back, hat in hand, a ruined man.

*July 31, 1795—Rennes*

*Rose,*

*You can imagine my disgrace. I promised* these men life—now all are to *perish! Yet they* surrendered, *they put down their arms! Tallien knows this well—at my request, Sombreuil put his sabre in Tallien's hands! My men saw it! We gave Sombreuil our* word *that his men would be treated as prisoners of war.*

*When Tallien left for Paris, he was determined to secure their safety. Now I am told it was Tallien who made the motion in the Assembly to have them executed, that it was Tallien who waved a dagger through the air, calling for their blood! I cannot comprehend!*

*I am too angry to write words of love. Be cautious. . . .*

*Your soldier, Lazare*

*August 2.*

I called on Tallien. I had heard rumours—that he had lost over ten thousand livres in a single game of faro, that he was drinking heavily. In spite of all that had happened, I felt an obligation toward him. He had been a friend to me when I needed a friend most. He had saved my life. Now it was my turn.

"Get out!" he yelled when he saw me. I backed away, sickened. Empty wine bottles littered the bare wood floor.

"I come as a friend!"

He threw a glass against the wall. "I do not need you!"

Quickly I left.

*August 3.*

I found the courage to call on Tallien again. I found him ill. He was sober, however—we talked for some time. "I know my demons," he confessed.

"Yet you do not know your strengths."

"I am a coward. I do not deserve to be alive."

"Was it a coward who confronted Robespierre?"

"I was in fear of my life!"

"And Thérèse's?"

He put his hands to his face and wept. "And now I've lost her!"

"*This* is your demon," I told him, holding up an empty bottle of wine.

I gave him news of his baby daughter, for whom he displays a sincere devotion. We parted with a tender show of feeling.


*Evening.*

A victory reception at Barras's, thirty-seven guests, many bottles of champagne consumed.

"Army champagne," Barras said, doing the honours.

"The army is supplied with champagne?" I asked. Even water was dear.

"Only *victorious* armies, which of course ours are."

Shortly after nine I was astonished to see Thérèse. She was dressed in a *very* revealing gown, her enormous milk-filled breasts exposed. It was a hot, sultry summer evening and looking at her raised the temperature even higher. Every man in the room regarded her with an expression of both disapproval and lust.

"Should you be here?" I whispered. She smelled of tobacco.

I looked to Barras for help, but found he was filling her glass.

"She should go home, Paul. She may do something she will regret."

"She is not a child."

Shortly before midnight I heard Thérèse's musical voice in the game room: "My entire ensemble weighs no more than two six-livre pieces."

I went to the door. The men had gathered around her. Three women were watching from chairs by the fireplace.

"Including the jewels?" Deputy Nabonide asked.

"Yes." Thérèse's face was flushed, her eyes glazed. *"Everything."*

"I'd bet a louis on that." Deputy Verneuil threw the coin onto a table.

"Any others?" Thérèse posed seductively. There was silence but for the sound of coins hitting coins.

Barras, grinning, ordered a servant to bring a scale.

Thérèse took off her earrings, her rings, handed them to Barras. Then she slipped a sleeve over one shoulder.

I left the room. Soon after I heard a cheer, heard Thérèse's cry—of victory I presumed . . . or was it defeat?

Shortly after, Barras, a young man and Thérèse left together.

My heart sank. I do not have the heart for this life.


*August 4.*

This morning I set out to La Chaumière. I intended to arrive early, so that I could talk to Thérèse.

I found her in her boudoir, splashing cologne onto her silk sheath, to make the thin fabric cling to her naked breasts.

"You come with disapproval in your eyes, my friend." Her own eyes were glazed. Laudanum, I thought.

"I come out of concern, for you." I could hear the baby crying in the other room. "I think you should be cautious. Grief is chasing you. Let it catch you. It will hurt less, in the end."

"You envy my hot blood. I recommend for you a diet of truffles and celery soup, to heat you up." She laughed, a laugh without joy.

"Tallita, I love you—but I can't talk to you when you're like this."

Tears came to her eyes. "See what you've done!" She threw herself down onto her bed.

"Why is it you weep?" I sat down beside her, took her hand. It was soft, without any sense of bone.

"Will you forgive me—for Barras?" she asked.

"Do you care for him?"

"He's an odd duck, but he amuses me."

"In all the world, Tallita, you are likely the only woman who *could* seduce our friend."

"One has to be imaginative," she said wearily.

I smiled. "Rest." I kissed her forehead.

"A pox on these men," she said, closing her eyes.

*In which I am introduced to*

*a strange little man*

*August 6, 1795.*

Everywhere there is talk of divining, cartomancers, fortunetellers, sooth-sayers . . . that mystical realm so much the passion now.

"Rose is always told she will be Queen of France," Thérèse announced at Minerva's this afternoon. She was stretched out on the chaise longue wearing an ivory silk robe and a green wig—the effect was bizarre, startling. ("Les merveilleuses," they call us, the amazing ones.)

"Why—that's horrible," Minerva said, adjusting her white gauze petticoats.

"Only once," I protested, "as a girl in Martinico. The other time, in the Carmes, I was simply told that I would marry a man who would astonish the world." I shrugged. "But what does it mean? My fortunes are extraordinary, yet my life is mundane."

At that moment Barras was introduced. With him was a curious-looking man with short legs and a big head. Minerva stood to greet them.

"Who is that man with Deputy Barras?" Fortunée Hamelin asked, watching the two approach. "Another protégé?" She made a face.

"I may have seen him at the Feydeau," tiny Madame de Crény said.

"If you had, you would *surely* remember," Thérèse said.

The man was remarkable, it was true, but for all the wrong reasons. His long, limp hair hung down around his ears in a sorry attempt at fashion. His skin was sallow and his figure so thin his threadbare breeches seemed to hang.

"Whatever can Barras have in mind?" Thérèse whispered.

We were silenced for the purpose of introductions. "Citoyen Buonaparte, la veuve Beauharnais . . ."

"You are a widow," the stranger said. His accent was rough—unpleasant. Italian? I could not be sure.

"The Republican general, Vicomte Alexandre de Beauharnais, was this lady's husband," Barras said.

Citoyen Buonaparte clasped my hand. His eyes were large, grey in colour, striking. His teeth were good. But there was an intensity in his expression that forbade levity. I was relieved when he was introduced to the others in our group, who seemed to respond to him as silently as I. He took a seat and said no more.

"Well!" Minerva exclaimed, "perhaps we should play charades?"

It seemed that nothing would leaven the mood. The presence of the man in the corner had a sobering effect on us all.

"That Barras!" Thérèse exclaimed in the privacy of Minerva's boudoir. "He has taken his projects too far."

"Deputy Barras pressed me to introduce Citoyen Buonaparte into our circle," Minerva told us. "He is new to Paris and in need of social contacts—"

"He is in need of social *manners*," Thérèse said. "What is he—Corsican or something?"

"Napoleone Buonaparte . . . ? Why is the name familiar?" I asked.

"He was the general who saved Toulon," Minerva said. "Remember?"
Toulon?

"Two years ago—when the English invaded?"

I remembered. The festivities, the dancing, the toasts throughout the night. "So *that's* how Barras knows him," I said. "Wasn't Barras in charge at Toulon?"

"It is impossible for me to believe that that man could be a general, much less a hero," Thérèse said, dusting her face with rice powder.

"My dear citoyennes, is it possible you are blinded by this man's poverty, his lack of breeding?" Minerva asked. "Stand as my witnesses: I predict he will have a great future. I see it in the shape of his chin."

Future or not, Thérèse and I did not stay long—we left on excuse that her baby was ill.

"What a miserable evening," Thérèse groaned, settling into her carriage. "I hope Barras knows better than to drag that Corsican with him everywhere. Next thing you know, he'll be insisting I introduce him at La Chaumière."


*August 9.*

It is just as Thérèse feared—Barras is intent on making a project of the Corsican. He and the strange little man showed up at La Chaumière and now Citoyen Buonaparte comes on his own. Thérèse, ever the soft heart, has offered to help him obtain fabric for a new uniform. "If he's going to be coming here, he should at least have proper clothes," she told me.

"Take care, Tallita—I think he is in love with you," I whispered to her.

"It would seem that Citoyen Buonaparte falls in love easily," she said, rolling her eyes. "He's engaged to marry a girl in Marseille, he talks endlessly about a girl in Châtillon, and now Barras informs me he intends to propose to La Montansier."

"The lady Barras rents his town house from?"

"*Lady?* Rose, you are too kind."

La Montansier was proud of the fact that she had started her career as a prostitute. The loges in the theatres she manages are furnished with extra-wide divans. "But she's over sixty—" I protested.

"And with three million livres hidden under her well-used mattress." Thérèse raised her eyebrows. "In Corsica, apparently, they make no pretense of such matters."


*Tuesday, August 11.*

Last night, close to midnight at La Chaumière, Thérèse came to my side. "Meet me in my boudoir," she whispered.

I extracted myself from my group. When we got to the privacy of her room, she fell onto her bed clutching her sides. "Buonaparte . . . !" She burst into laughter again.

"The Corsican?"

"He's made a proposal of marriage!"

"To *you?*" I stared at her. I smiled imagining it: Thérèse was so much taller than the Corsican. "Just now? In the parlour?"

Thérèse nodded, making a great effort to control herself. "I was with Fortunée, Madame de Crény and Minerva. He came up to us and said, 'Citoyenne Tallien, may I speak with you . . . in private?' So I retired with him to the entryway. And it was there he said, 'Now that you are free, I would like you to consider me.' At first I did not understand. He became a bit impatient. 'I am making you an offer of marriage,' he finally burst out. Then he said, 'Together we could have a great future, for Fortune smiles on me.'"

"He said *that?* That Fortune smiles on him? What a curious thing to say."

"Especially for a man who is in such dire need. If Fortune smiles on him, she should rather start paying attention."

"What did you tell him?"

"I told him he should consider *you* instead," Thérèse said, adjusting the pearl ornaments in her hair in the looking glass.

"No!" She was teasing—surely. "Tallita?"

She never did say. But now the Corsican watches *me*.


*August 12.*

It has been hectic at Barras's. He complains he has no time for the gaming tables, the hunt. "Democracy!" he cursed. "It's so time-consuming! All these tedious meetings."

I pushed a guest list toward him. For two days, I had been trying to get his approval.

"Citoyen Buonaparte? Is he not included?" he asked, looking it over. "The ladies have wearied of my Corsican protégé? You do not perceive his brilliance for his long and, I admit, distasteful hair, his smelly boots. I assure you, he is an ambitious man—he will go far."

"I perceive his ambition," I said, "his ambition to woo every woman of standing in Paris. He shows no moderation in his passion . . . for women of wealth, that is."

"Moderation be damned. Moderation belongs to the past. Napoleone is in need of a wife. Perhaps *you* should oblige him."

With that he was gone. I sighed and added the Corsican's name to the list. I will hear more on this matter, I fear.

*August 14.*
Barras came to my salon last night in the company of the Corsican.

"Do Corsicans never laugh?" Thérèse complained. "He is *so* serious."

Toward the end of the evening I found myself sitting beside Citoyen Napoleone (an *impossible* name to pronounce). In an attempt to make conversation, I complimented him on his valour at Toulon. "It is said you are a genius," I told him.

"Yes," he said.

"You have a large family in Marseille? I am told one of your sisters is particularly charming."

"Who told you that?"

"Deputy Fréron," I said.*

Then abruptly he stood and left the room!

"Is he angry?" I asked Barras. Had I said something to offend him?

"He's a little strange sometimes." Barras took my arm, drew me into the entryway. "I'd like you to befriend him. Get to know him," he whispered.

"He is not an easy man to talk to," I protested. "I don't know if I—"

"If anyone can, Rose, you can," Barras said. He took several coins out of his pocket, slipped them into my hand.

"What's this for?" The three gold louis were worth over seventy livres.

"I can count on you?" he asked.

*August 15.*
"Napoleone has become a regular member of your Tuesday night salon, I see."

Barras and I were enjoying a private lunch in his garden.

* *Louis-Marie-Stanislas Fréron had met Buonaparte's thirteen-year-old sister Maria-Paola in Marseille two years before. They wanted to marry, but met resistance from Madame Buonaparte. Although an educated aristocrat, turned violent revolutionary, Fréron was over thirty, inclined to drink and had had three children by an actress.*

"I am getting to know him," I said. "A little." Napoleone Buonaparte was a complex person; one evening, he talked openly, and the next, he did not say a word. "It is difficult to know where one stands with him."

"And how would one *like* to stand?"

"Why do you ask?"

Barras ordered his butler to bring the dessert. "Do you ever discuss politics with him?"

"He supports the Republic," I said, "if that's what you want to know."

"But with *who* running it?"

"I believe him to be more of a leader than a follower—at least in his own mind."

Barras laughed as he filled my glass. "And *that's* why we must keep our eye on him, my dear."

## *In which I find a home*

*August 16, 1795.*
I have fallen in love . . . with a *house*.

Julie Carreau's, to be precise, on the slopes of Mont-Martre. One approaches it by a long walled-in drive opening onto a most charming setting: a small hôtel, a carriage house, a stable with a garden behind. A tiny, perfect world.

It was a hot day, but cool there, the breeze coming up the mountain from the city. "This is like a country home," I told Julie, "yet close to the heart of the city." I was enchanted.

"I will miss it," she said.

"You are moving?"

"It's small. I can't keep enough staff here. And there's only room for one carriage."

I walked down the garden path. There were rosebushes on both sides. "Are you selling it?"

"Leasing."

"I'll take it." I did not ask the price.

*August 17.*
I signed the lease. Ten thousand livres a year—almost half my allowance from Mother, if it ever comes through. I move in five weeks, on the Republican New Year. I've made arrangements to have my cow brought from Croissy. A house, horses, a cow, garden, staff. A modest establishment, yet even so, so much to attend to . . . so much to *pay* for.

*Wednesday, August 19.*

Thanks to Tallien my appeal for compensation on Alexandre's La Ferté property has been granted. We are to get back the books in his library (an extensive collection), the silver that was confiscated, as well as an advance of ten thousand livres (only!) against the value of the property, which the government sold.

"It will take time for the paperwork to go through," Tallien warned. "It's unlikely that you will see anything until spring."

"How can I thank you?"

"You have done enough already, Rose."

I looked at him with a question in my eyes.

"You are perhaps the only person who overlooks my more visible weaknesses in favour of my more hidden strengths. That is thanks enough."


*August 17, 1795—Rennes*
*Dear Rose,*
*The post is being watched. Give letters and parcels addressed to me to Deputy Barras. The government couriers are secure.*
*I love you.*

*Your soldier, Lazare*


*August 27.*

In the post this afternoon I received a hand-lettered bulletin regarding a school for girls in Saint-Germain-en-Laye, next to Collège Irlandais, a school for boys.

I showed the bulletin to Lannoy. "Madame Campan is running it," I said. I had known Madame Campan's brother and his wife in Croissy—the Augiés. Hortense often played with Adèle, their daughter.

"Ah, Madame Campan!" Lannoy whispered reverently. As former lady-in-waiting to our poor departed Queen, Madame Campan was close to being royal herself, in Lannoy's eyes. "That would be the perfect school for Hortense," she said.

And the Collège Irlandais next door for Eugène.

But for the cost. . . .

*Sunday, August 30.*

Today the children and I visited the two schools in Saint-Germain-en-Laye. Eugène succumbed with resignation. His is a Spartan institution, as one expects in a school for boys. He liked the playing fields.

Madame Campan's school is situated in the adjoining Hôtel de Rohan, a beautiful if run-down estate on a rambling country property. Hortense and her friend Adèle Augié ran about in a fever of excitement. I rejoiced seeing them together again; one would never know, hearing them laugh, that Hortense had not so long ago lost her father, Adèle her mother to the violence of the Terror.

Madame Campan greeted me with elegant simplicity in the foyer. "Please, call me Henriette." She is a plain woman with heavy features. She was wearing a simple black dress, severely cut. Mourning, I wondered? For her sister, the Queen, the Boy? I had heard stories of what she'd been through, her own narrow escapes from death.

She invited me into her office. I was surprised to see a framed copy of the Rights of Man on the wall above her desk. Noting my expression, she slyly turned it over to reveal a portrait of the Queen.

"Comtesse de Montmorin has told me of the heroic efforts you made to save her husband," Madame Campan said, taking a seat beside me.

"Would that I could have saved him from death." And others. "I was grieved to learn of your sister-in-law." I remembered Madame Augié as a sweet-tempered, somewhat distracted woman, always trying to keep track of her three active young daughters.

Madame Campan offered me a cup of weak tea in fine china, slightly cracked. "I tell the girls their mother died in her sleep." Her cup began to rattle in its saucer. Quickly she put it down. "I am mother to them all now. An invalid husband, a son, three nieces to look after as well as a school for one hundred girls." She took up her cup again, took a sip. "I don't have time to mourn."

She outlined the school's program: the girls would be given a classical education with special attention to art (Jean-Baptiste Isabey, a portrait painter I admire, will be teaching there) and history. She glanced at the Queen's portrait. Although hers was a well-to-do establishment, she assured me the girls would not be indulged—they would be taught to cook and to clean up after themselves. "And, as well, in spite of the fashion now, *my* girls will be taught good manners and the art of conversation."

I heard a child shriek. I looked out the window to see Hortense wildly chasing both Eugène and Adèle across the lawn. Manners? Bonne chance, I thought, smiling. "Hortense has a cousin, Émilie—the daughter of an émigré," I said. "Her family is ruined, now, of course. She's in need of education; I'd like to provide for her, but—"

Madame Campan agreed to take both Hortense and Émilie, charging only for Hortense. As well she offered the use of second-hand uniforms. "Adèle speaks so often of your daughter, I regard her as one of the family. I must beg your forgiveness for charging at all."


*September 6.*

I had a meeting scheduled with Barras at his house in Chaillot but the afternoon proved to be too hectic. He'd just come in from a hunt and his excited spaniels were running up and down the halls barking at Toto, the miniature greyhound. There were two men waiting in the foyer and a courier with an urgent message to respond to. "Come back at six," he suggested. "It will be quieter." I gave him a letter to forward on to Lazare (none for me again, alas) and left.

In the evening, however, it was not much different: messengers, men waiting. Barras told them all to go away. "If it isn't the Jacobins, it's the Royalists," he cursed. "We put down one, only to be attacked by the other."

"You're anticipating violence?" I'd noticed an increase in the number of National Guardsmen posted near the Assembly. Now, too, one had to apply for a special passport even to go into that neighbourhood.

"I dare say the worst is yet to come."

"Who is behind it?"

"Sometimes I think it's Royalists disguised as Jacobins. At other times, Jacobins disguised as Royalists. It's the damndest thing."

"Why do you smile?"

"The fact is, who cares? The people are exhausted. How many turned out for this last election? One in thirty? But announce the results, and the rocks come flying."

After supper he got around to the subject of Buonaparte.

"I haven't seen him lately," I said. "Not at any of the salons, not even at the theatre."

"I daresay he's been busy. I got him a job in the topographic department, making maps. Strategic stuff—his passion. A curious enthusiasm."

"Yet you respect him."

"I just wish I could trust him. He's impoverished, with a huge family to support. One wonders what he might do for money. And certainly the Royalists have plenty to throw around. If Buonaparte went over to them . . ."

"It's hard to imagine. If anything, he is a bit of a Jacobin."

"Yes—he's got the rhetoric."

"You doubt his sincerity?"

Barras shrugged. "There is nothing more dangerous—or perhaps the word unpredictable is more accurate—than a revolutionary in want of a fortune."


*September 12—Fontainebleau.*
I've been two days in Fontainebleau, without the children—already Eugène and Hortense are involved in school activities—yet I spent the entire time talking about them. Aunt Désirée and the Marquis were charmed by my reports of what Hortense's teachers were saying, how she is doted on by Madame Campan ("La Petite Bonne," she has been named). "She loves school," I told them. "I don't think I'll ever get her to leave." I've become a little jealous, I confess; Hortense speaks reverently of Madame Campan.

We had a good visit, without Aunt Désirée's customary lectures on the sins of idleness, revels and reading romances. But as I was preparing to leave, she came to my door. I knew by her manner that there was something she wanted to say. Finally, with some hesitation, she confessed she was concerned about rumours she'd heard about Madame Tallien. I assured her Thérèse was an angel, a friend in every way.

"And you're not having anything to do with these criminals who are running the government now, I hope."

"Criminals?"

"Deputy Barra . . . Bassar . . . You know who I mean."

Barras, she meant. I kept quiet. I did not have the heart to tell her that it was "this criminal" who was paying for Hortense and Eugène's education.

*September 15, 1795—Hôtel de Croisoeuil, Croissy*
*Dear Citoyenne Madame Beauharnais,*
*My mother has asked me to respond to your letter, as she is not well. She regrets that she will not be able to come see you. She asked me to congratulate you on acquiring the Talma residence, but also to express her sorrow that you will be giving up the château at Croissy. Do you plan to move your cow? We hope to be seeing you soon. Mother is in need of diversion.*
*Citoyenne Madame Lucie Hosten de Croisoeuil*
*Note—Maman asked me to tell you that she recommends Citoyen Callyot, an excellent cook who can make créole dishes. (I recommend him too!)*

*September 18—Croissy.*
A rainy, melancholy weekend at Croissy, sorting and packing. And going twice daily to visit Aimée.

She is much weakened. It is distressing to see her confined to bed, a situation she does not take to happily. "If I want so much as a dish of tea, I have to ask my daughter for it," she complained. "Fortunately Lucie is still under the impression that I have some authority over her, but soon, no doubt . . ."

"I'd like to meet the person who can succeed in dominating you, Aimée."

She cursed lustily. There is life in her yet.

*September 23.*
The New Year, the new constitution proclaimed. Fireworks late into the night. Thérèse and I watched the display from my garden—my garden! I

am exhausted from the move, but happy. I love my new home. I call it
Chantereine.

*September 25.*
I worked all day in the garden. Fortuné sniffed every mound of dirt,
barked at every bug. Lannoy has begun making drapes for the bedroom
(blue nankeen with red-and-yellow crests). The drawing room looks like
a seamstress's studio, the floor covered over with scraps. I am having six
wooden chairs and a small couch covered. I purchased a Renaud harp
(only three strings missing) and a marble bust of Socrates at a second-
hand shop. Little by little, my home begins to come together. The effect
will be simple, but elegant (I hope).

I've hired a cook, Callyot, a Negro from Sainte-Lucie who makes
créole dishes as well as more traditional fare. (He was recommended to
me by Aimée.)

Agathe ran off with a fowler from the Midi but quickly saw the error
of her ways (he stank of chicken) and returned, not with child we hope.

Gontier is staying on, dear old soul. Fortunately—for he's the only
one who can coax milk from Cleopatra, my cow.

Now all I need is a coachman and a gardener. I am hoping we can
manage on that—for a time. Funds are tight, even with Barras's generous
contributions.

*September 26.*
A hot day, but a breeze was cooling. I worked in my garden again. Mosquitoes hovered, dragonflies circled. Now and again I heard popping
noises and a faint ringing sound—a tocsin, perhaps? The ferment of Paris
seems so very far away. . . .

## *In which we are at war again*

*Monday, September 28, 1795.*

It is so peaceful at Chantereine I was shocked to learn that there had been a riot at the Assembly yesterday. Several hundred people were killed.

"Several *hundred?*"

"Even the Jacobins are beginning to think that only a monarchy can save us." Barras's sword clanked against the fireplace. He had just come from the Military School, where he'd been training a group of men—"My private fighting force, my 'Sacred Battalion.'"

"Not the National Guard?"

"Too civilized," he said. "Upstanding citizens, men of property. How many have ever killed a man? In a conflict, how many will bolt? Half, I predict. They're good for a parade, but not much else. No—I need seasoned killers, men with the smell of blood on their hands."

"And where does one find 'seasoned' killers?"

"In the prisons, of course—thugs, murderers, the occasional terrorist." He accepted my offer of another brandy. "I've got fifteen hundred of them already. I've virtually emptied the prisons."

"No—"

"*My* men," he grinned.

I remembered something Thérèse had once said: *Barras prefers his men coarse, his ladies refined.*

"And the more the merrier, thank you," Barras said, as if reading my thoughts. He pulled out his timepiece. He must go. But first there was something he wanted to ask: Would I seek out Citoyen Buonaparte? "There's a rumour he's been in contact with the Royalists. Whose side is he on? I must know. Things are heating up—"

"But he's busy, you said—with this business of maps."

"You women have your ways. . . . Invite him to your home. Surely this is not a mystery to you."

The project struck me as distasteful.

"Consider the fate of the Republic," Barras insisted, "your *children's* future."


*October 4.*

Citoyen Buonaparte was better clothed than I was accustomed to seeing him, dressed in a new blue uniform. Even so, he looked sickly, his skin sallow, his boots huge on his spindly legs.

I invited him into the garden. I asked Agathe to bring us café au lait. "Made with coffee beans from Martinico," I told him, "and milk from my cow."

He accepted, although he was in a hurry, he said. He could not stay for crêpes. He has been toiling day and night—on a plan to liberate Italy from the Austrians, he said.

I smiled. "You say this in all seriousness."

"One need only believe."

"Is it that simple?" He did not answer. He was absorbed in an examination of the sundial. "You do not credit destiny?" I prompted him.

He turned to me abruptly. "One can become accustomed to appeasing destiny rather than controlling it." He had a strange way of putting things—rather in the manner of proverbs.

"I believe I am of the first party, Citoyen Buonaparte." Although I wasn't sure what he meant.

"*Brigadier-General* Buonaparte," he corrected me.

"Forgive me, I thought—"

"Actually . . ." He smiled. He is almost charming when he smiles. "You may call me Emperor."

"Emperor Buonaparte?" I bowed my head, amused.

He stared at me, his eyes grey, cold but inflamed, unsettling. "I mystify you," he said. "That is understandable. But what I don't understand is why you induced me to call. I confess I have developed something of an attachment for you. Nevertheless, I am under the impression that this feeling is not, at this time, reciprocated."

I stooped to pick a rose. A thorn pricked my finger. Tears came to my eyes, an embarrassing weakness.

"Barras has something to do with this," he persisted.

I turned to him, angry for being so bluntly challenged. "It is clear you favour directness, General Buonaparte. Very well then, yes, it was Deputy Barras."

"And how much did he pay you?" He put on his hat.

"Don't go—"

"I do have pride, Citoyenne." And was gone.

I set out for Barras's in a nervous condition. I was expected—to review social plans, financial arrangements. . . . I had an agenda of my own, however. I wasn't going to do his bidding any longer.

Barras burst into laughter when I told him about my exchange with General Buonaparte.

"I regret I do not see the humour," I said.

"Rose—you are so charming in this mood."

I stood up. "You are not taking my position seriously."

He put his hand on my arm. "Sit, relax. You can't leave now. I asked the cook to make meringues."

"I do not care for dessert." Sitting nonetheless.

"Very well, I will eat your share. Your disposition is sweet enough. I, no doubt, could use a little douceur. Ah, there, you see? I knew I could coax a smile. But please, my friend, accept my apologies. I have caused you distress. I regret to tell you that there have been no letters for you from Lazare. Soldiers are so cruel. But tell me about your children—do they like their schools? By the way, that créole banker you introduced me to has proved to be a *most* profitable contact, did I tell you?"

In short, Barras made himself entirely agreeable. I softened and we talked: of his most recent romantic conquest, the tragedy by Corneille opening at the Comédie-Française in two days, his rabbits.

It was as I was finishing my second meringue that a messenger came.

"Do you recall where the convent of Filles de Saint-Thomas is?" Barras asked, squinting to make out the writing.

"Rue Vivienne, I believe. Why?"

"Apparently it's full of armed men." Barras cursed. "Royalists." He looked at his timepiece, sighed. "And I'd hoped to get some sleep tonight."

I left as he was strapping on his sword, ordering a horse tacked, "getting into war gear," as he put it. I gave him a good luck kiss. "Take care," I said.

He stopped for a moment. Then he smiled, that crooked smile that makes him so endearing. "So tell me, Rose—*can* Buonaparte be trusted?"


*October 5, midnight.*

I'm at Thérèse's. I didn't think she should be alone tonight.

Lieutenant Floraux was just here, cantering dramatically into the courtyard, his horse lathered with sweat. "The National Guard has rebelled!" he cried out, still breathless. He took off his helmet. His hair was short, as is the fashion with the young now, in what is called a Brutus crop. "They've turned on the Assembly, on the Deputies, joined the Royalists!"

"The National Guard?" I asked, incredulous. "Joined the *Royalists?* Are you sure?" I urged him to sit down.

"Not all of them." He gulped down the glass of port I offered him. "Three out of four."

How could a defence be mounted without men? "How many Royalists are there?" I wondered if Jeanne-Victoire d'Aiguillon's nephew was among them. Or Régis de Saale, the Marquis de Caulaincourt's friend. Or Madame Campan's young cousin, only seventeen.

"It is thought they are forty thousand strong."

"*Forty* thousand—mon Dieu!"

"Forty thousand what?" Thérèse asked, coming into the room. She'd been helping the nanny put the baby to bed.

"Royalists," I said weakly, taking a chair.

*October 6, dawn.*

We were awakened by the sound of pounding on the gate. Thérèse's foot-man ran to answer it, yelling for the intruder to be silent. This set a horse whinnying.

It was Lieutenant Floraux again. The government had rallied, he told us. He helped himself to a glass of port. "They've named Deputy Barras General."

"But without the National Guard, who does he command?" I asked.

"He's got some men, a tough-looking group, the Sacred Battalion he calls them. 'Battalion of the Terrorists' others would have it."

A battalion of murderers let loose on the streets of Paris. I was thank-ful the children were in Saint-Germain-en-Laye. "And General Buona-parte? Is . . . is he involved?" I asked.

"The little Corsican? He's second-in-command apparently."

"*Second*-in-command?" Thérèse groaned.

"He may surprise you," I said. *One need only believe.*

"We could use a surprise." Lieutenant Floraux downed his glass.


*10:00 P.M.*

At supper, we thought we heard gunfire. . . .

"Can that be *cannon?*" Thérèse asked, walking the baby back and forth across the room.

We heard a second blast, and another.

Thérèse pressed the infant's head to her heart. "Surely not . . ."

"They wouldn't use *cannon*," I said. "Muskets, but not cannon. Not on citizens." My words were silenced by a volley of ominous booms.

## *In which my heart is broken*

*October 7, 1795.*

Blood on the cobblestones. In front of a church, a market woman wailing, "The butchers! The butchers!"

It is as we feared—a slaughter.

"On *citizens!*" Lannoy ranted angrily. "Your friends, your *virtuous* Republicans, fired *cannon* on citizens!"

What had happened? I set out for Minerva's.

"Have you talked to Barras?" she demanded. "What's going on?"

I shook my head. "Anyone we know hurt?" *Killed*, I meant to ask, was afraid to ask.

"Only rumours. Everyone's upset." We joined a group by the doors to the garden.

"It was the Corsican who gave the command to fire the cannon," Deputy Renouvier was saying.

"That's not what I've been told," a man standing next to him said.

"Corsicans are ruthless," Madame de Méchain argued. "Entirely without morals. Everyone knows that."

"And now, have you heard? He has set up strict supervision of all the theatres and cafés—even the meeting places around fountains are under surveillance. The fountains!"

"I was at the theatre," a sweet-faced young man said, his voice high and tremulous. "There were sentries at the doors of all the boxes. If anyone *dared* voice a request for any but the most *correct* Republican tune, there were over a hundred grenadiers there ready to pounce!"

"Is it not critical that the government gain control?" Deputy Renouvier asked.

"Did we not have enough of control under Robespierre?" the sweet-faced young man argued. "The Corsican is a Jacobin I am told."

"A close friend of Robespierre, I heard," Madame de Méchain said.

"Not exactly." Minerva looked to me for support. "He was a friend of Robespierre's brother."

"Ah, *Bonbon's* friend!" the sweet-faced young man said, and everyone laughed.

The group fell silent. I looked toward the door. It was General Buonaparte, looking over the room with a haughty expression. He took off his hat. The tricolour plume fell off. He stooped to retrieve it, his sword knocking against the door.

As he stood, he spotted me.

"Citoyenne Madame Beauharnais," he said, coming directly to my side, "I—"

"Would you care to walk in the garden, General?" I interrupted him. "I feel the need for air."

Outside, I fanned myself, feeling somewhat faint. "I am fine." I sat down on a stone bench. "Thank you." A man and woman passed. The woman, recognizing General Buonaparte, turned her head in disdain.

Buonaparte broke a branch off a bush, began tearing off the leaves. "The French have a strange way of treating their heroes."

"You feel your actions are beyond reproach, General?"

"I am a military man, not a politician. I do what I am told."

"But perhaps too well, and too quickly."

"The Royalists needed a lesson."

I stood, my cheeks burning. "I do not know the customs in Corsica, General, but the French, as a rule, do not fire cannon on their citizens."

I returned to the parlour, trembling.

I was in the game room with Minerva when Barras arrived. "Congratulations on your victory," Minerva told him, putting down her cards.

He was flushed. He threw himself onto the sofa. "As we soldiers say, when the wine is opened, it must be drunk. To *their* butts," he said, raising his glass. "For once." He laughed and took a long drink.

I looked away.

"Damn your tears!" He threw his glass into the fire. It made a sharp, musical sound.

*October 12.*

It was not yet noon when a member of the National Guard came to my door. All arms were to be turned over to the military authority of Paris. Upon penalty of death.

Eugène, home from school for two days, clasped his father's sword.

"You must do as you are told," I told him. I could see defiance in his eyes.

I asked the guard to excuse us. We went into the parlour. Eugène would not relent. I returned to the guard. "How might one obtain an exemption?" I asked. "This sword means a great deal to my son. It belonged to his father, a Republican general who died little over a year ago."

"Only General Buonaparte can grant an exemption."

Every day it seemed, Buonaparte was promoted. Now he was Military Governor of Paris, and controlled everything.

"You will come with me?" Eugène asked.

"Better to go without me," I said, recalling my last angry words with the General.

*October 13.*

At noon I was surprised by a caller. "General Bona-something," Agathe said.

"General Buonaparte?"

She nodded.

I stood abruptly. What would I say? Our last meeting had not been gentle.

But I had no time to prepare. He was already standing in the door. "Post this at your gate." He thrust a piece of paper into my hand.

It was a notice of exemption. "Does this mean my son may keep his father's sword?"

General Buonaparte nodded. He paused. "On the twelfth day of Vendémiaire,* most of the guns were loaded with blanks. I took care that the citizens had areas available to them that afforded the greatest protection."

His declaration was followed by an awkward silence.

"Surely my opinion cannot matter to you, General," I said.

"You are correct. It does not. Nevertheless, I wish you to understand that I am not entirely without conscience."

"Thank you, General." But already, he had departed.

*October 26.*

The election results have been announced. Under the new constitution, five "Directors" will rule. Barras is one.

"They behead the King, put five in his place," Lannoy grumbled. "And your friend Barras, the worst of the lot."

"Hush, Lannoy!"

*Tuesday, November 3.*

The five Directors had a meeting in the Luxembourg Palace this morning. In the afternoon "Director" Barras gave Thérèse and me a tour.

The palace is in frightful repair, its recent use as a prison all too evident. I recalled my visits to Alexandre there. How different my purpose now. There was no furniture—only a few kitchen chairs and one rickety table. And cold, too—Barras sent a footman out for wood.

The five Directors will move in next week, each into his own suite. Already Barras has a work crew covering his walls with silk. His rabbit hutches have been set up in the gardens, his English Thoroughbreds are already in the stable.

"What good a king without a palace?" he asked, surveying his shabby domain.

"What good a palace without ladies of the court?" Thérèse echoed, taking my arm and his.

* A reference to the Republican calendar.

*December 4, 1795—Fontainebleau*
*Dear Rose,*

*Thank you for your letter. How wonderful that the children are doing so well in school. I miss seeing Hortense on the weekends, although I must admit that a Sunday confirmation class with Madame Campan is possibly the only excuse I would have happily accepted.*

*Your new home sounds delightful—small but charming. I am impressed that already you have had vegetables from your garden. Your mother would be proud. I read your account of getting your cow freshened to the Marquis. We both had a laugh over it. If it weren't for the sad state of my own health and having to tend to the Marquis so religiously, I would accept your invitations to come for a visit.*

*No doubt you have heard about Fanny being sued by some woman claiming to be her daughter—what a scandal! I don't know how Fanny manages to be so cheerful, especially now with Marie marrying a mulatto. I don't dare tell the Marquis—the news would kill him.*

*I know how busy you are, dear, but even so, we long to see you. Do remember what I said about keeping good company.*

*Your loving Aunt Désirée*

Wednesday, December 9.

I've been going to the Luxembourg every day, presenting petitions on behalf of friends, and friends of friends—émigrés, for the most part, wishing to return to France.

"You spend too much time on the welfare of others, Rose," Director Barras said to me this morning. "It is time you considered your own well-being."

"Meaning?"

"Meaning you should be thinking of marriage."

"You have someone in mind, *Père* Barras?"

"Buonaparte."

"I am not wealthy enough for him, I'm afraid." Rumour had it General Buonaparte had just proposed to the recently widowed Madame Permon, a woman old enough to be his mother—but quite well-off.

"I've assured him he would be well rewarded."

I looked to the window, took a breath. Perhaps I had not heard correctly.

"I see you are alarmed." Barras leaned back in his red velvet chair—his "throne" he called it. "Very well, I will explain. Buonaparte has requested command of the Army of Italy. He wishes to pursue a plan to push the Austrians out of Italy." Barras made a gesture meaning: insane! "Of course my fellow Directors do not trust him. They find him abrupt, abrasive . . . overly ambitious. They suspect in him a desire to rule—so they are naturally reluctant to grant him an army, even as pathetic an army as that of the Army of Italy.

"But they are fools, I say. Buonaparte *will* try to take over, it is in his nature—unless, of course, he is kept busy. Unless, of course, he is *controlled*—"

"Unless, of course, he is married to a very good friend of yours," I said.

Barras smiled slowly. "I might not have put it *exactly* that way, my dear."

"How exactly *did* you put it?" I felt an alarming emotion rising within me.

"I explained to Buonaparte that the French Republic was reluctant to promote foreigners to positions of power. I suggested that if he were to marry a Frenchwoman—a certain French widow, for example—perhaps then the Directors would trust him more, and—who was to say?—perhaps *then* the Army of Italy might very well be his."

"You told him that!"

"Think about it, Rose. Buonaparte may be a Corsican, and impoverished, I grant you, but he is a man with a future. I am in a position to guarantee it."

I stood to leave. I was offended by his meddling.

"Rose, must you always be so emotional! You know it is time you married. It's not easy at your age."

I headed for the door.

"I offered him an army!" he yelled after me. "I'm *giving* you a dowry, for God's sake!"

*December 10.*

I have been hours at my toilette. Tiny wrinkles have begun to line my face. My teeth, never well-formed, are turning black. I have lost two in the last year. I smile, and it's a fishwife's grin I see.

I threw my brushes down in despair. The herbal remedies have not succeeded in restoring any regularity to the flowers. Now and again, too, I am weakened (and embarrassed) by frightful flooding.

I am aging.

Marry, my friends say. Soon.

*Friday, December 11.*

At Minerva's last night, General Buonaparte declared his feelings for me. This rather publicly, in the midst of a game of fox and goose. I tossed it off as a jest, but left soon after.

*Tuesday, December 22.*

Minerva came to call. After a glass of wine, news (Madame Royale, the King's unfortunate daughter, has been released from the Temple and sent to Vienne) and idle gossip (Citoyen Léon is taking a mercury treatment*), she asked why I had not been to her salon recently. I confessed my discomfort with the attentions of General Buonaparte. I was reluctant to go to her home lest I discover him there.

"Do you not consider General Buonaparte an acceptable suitor?"

"My heart is taken," I said.

"General Hoche, you mean."

I nodded. My feelings for Lazare were no secret.

"Rose, if I may be so bold—there is something I must tell you. It is your *lover* who is taken."

I put down my glass.

"When the émigrés landed in Quiberon Bay, General Hoche saved the life of a Monsieur de Pout-Bellan. I have it on good authority that he has fallen in love with this man's wife."

* *Venereal disease was treated with mercury.*

I stood, went to the window recess. Lazare—in *love* with another woman?

Minerva came up behind me, put her hand on my shoulder. "Surely you knew that Lazare would never marry you, especially not now, not with his wife expecting a child."

A *baby?*

"Due soon, I believe," she said.

I bit my lip, fought back tears. Why hadn't he written?

"You will come to my salon, Rose?" Minerva asked. "Tonight?"


*That evening.*

I've just returned from Minerva's. General Buonaparte requested the honour of my company at the opera tomorrow evening. I gave him my consent.

## *In which I am courted*

*Wednesday, December 23, 1795.*

General Buonaparte called for me at nine. He was nearly an hour late, and a bit dishevelled, his sash ill-fitting. "I was in a meeting." He did not apologize. He stood in the parlour before the fire cracking his knuckles. He took out his timepiece. "The curtain rises in a few minutes." He leapt for the door. I followed after, bewildered and somewhat offended.

His coach is new, a garish yellow with gold trim, very showy, in bad taste. Inside was no different—the seats were covered in gold brocade, the shades tasselled with pink silk.

We took off at a terrific pace, the coach careening over the bumps and around the corners at a frightful speed. I was momentarily overcome by paralysis. Terror had rendered me speechless. I gripped the sides to steady myself. Finally I summoned the strength to cry out, "Stop!"

General Buonaparte signalled his driver and the coach came to a sudden halt. I fell forward onto the facing seat. I began to laugh.

"We are late." He pulled out his timepiece again. "What is it you want?"

I could not speak for the laughter that had gripped me. Tears ran down my cheeks. Buonaparte regarded me with a puzzled expression. "Too fast?"

I burst into laughter again, nodded through my tears.

Hesitantly, he smiled, a bit unsure. He signalled the driver to go forward again, this time at a more civilized pace. By degrees my laughter came under control. I took several deep breaths. An evening with General Buonaparte—it was not as I had imagined.

It was an enjoyable performance, I thought, yet on the way home General Buonaparte expressed discontent. "The French can't sing, their music has no melody. It grates on the ear. *You* sing for me."

"Here?" We were at the intersection of Rue de Richelieu and Rue Neuve des Petits Champs.

"This is the trouble with the French. They think they cannot sing anywhere, at any time." He launched into an aria I was unfamiliar with. A chimney-sweep turned to stare. "Now you," he commanded.

"I am not a singer."

"Yet you have a lovely speaking voice."

He would not be refused. Quietly, I sang a short refrain from Mozart.

He regarded me seriously. "Not bad. What's your name?"

"You know my name."

"Your full name."

"Marie-Josephe-Rose."

"Joseph is your father's name?"

"Was."

"Was he a good man?"

I smiled. Hardly. "A very good man."

"Very well, I shall call you Josephine, after the heroine in *Le Sourd*. Have you seen it?"

"My name is Rose."

"You are mistaken."

*December 26.*

"Why do you insist on calling me Josephine?" Buonaparte and I had just come from Barras's salon and were on our way to the theatre, to a performance of a work by Molière.

"Do you not find it an attractive name?"

"I am told this is your way with a woman. First you ask her to sing, then you give her a new name."

"You have been talking to your friend Thérèse," he said, disgruntled.

"You can keep no secrets from me, Buonaparte."

*December 29.*

"What is it you *do* all the time?" Thérèse demanded. "You were almost an hour yesterday in the garden."

"We just talk." It was true—driving in the Bois de Boulogne, walking along the quay, sitting in my garden, or in his.

"*Just* talk? Whatever about?"

Music, science, religion . . . there was little that did not interest him, little that escaped his notice.

"You know what people are saying, that he is mad for you."

"We are friends."

"No doubt," Thérèse said, smiling capriciously.


*December 30.*

It was approaching noon when Thérèse's red coach pulled into my courtyard. "Maybe you shouldn't come to La Chaumière tonight," she said, letting down the glass.

"But I must—it's arranged. Buonaparte is coming for me at nine."

"Lazare is back. He will be there tonight."

*Lazare?*

"I thought you should be warned."

Buonaparte and I arrived at La Chaumière shortly before ten. I was relieved that Lazare was not yet there. Even so, I could not be at my ease.

It wasn't until midnight that Lazare arrived, in uniform, in the company of several aides. He saw me and turned away. I took Buonaparte's arm and asked if we might go into the garden for a moment.

"But it's freezing."

"Only for a little air."

After a few moments I was able to compose myself. I had to address Lazare, I knew, had to find the courage to address him. Upon returning to the drawing room, Buonaparte was accosted by Madame de Crény and Fortunée Hamelin, demanding that he read their palms, a magical art for which he claimed to have some talent.

Lazare was standing nearby, by the fire, watching. "How good to see you in Paris," I said, congratulating him on his recent promotion. He regarded me with cold dignity—an expression so chilling I was relieved when Buonaparte joined us.

"And you, General Hoche?" Buonaparte demanded. Lazare put forth his hand. Buonaparte examined it and grinned. "General, you will die young—and in your bed," he said.*

"Alexandre the Great died in his bed, did he not?" I took Buonaparte's arm. "I believe Thérèse wants us in the game room," I said, pulling him away. "That was unnecessary," I hissed.

Buonaparte looked at me. "Do you think me blind?"

I pulled my shawl around my shoulders. "Take me home, Buonaparte," I told him. "I feel quite ill."

It seemed a very long ride back to Chantereine. Buonaparte and I sat silently. "How are you feeling?" he asked as we turned onto Rue Mont-Martre.

"I lied about being unwell," I said.

"I was curious to see how far you would take the charade."

"That's not kind."

"I never said I was a kind man." He paused. "You have an attachment for General Hoche."

I arranged the fur coverlet about my knees. I was thankful for the dark. "I knew him in prison."

"And now?"

"And now General Hoche has a family of his own. Would you care to come in?" I asked as we pulled into my courtyard.

"Would you care to have me?"

I thought for a moment. "Yes," I said. I did not speak untruly. I felt overwhelmed by a feeling of sadness, a feeling that I was too much alone in this life. The cold look in Lazare's eyes had disturbed me in a way no words ever could.

Buonaparte stayed for over an hour. I drank several glasses of Chambertin.

* Lazare Hoche would die in his bed on September 17, 1797, at the age of twenty-nine.

Before he left he said, "I would like permission to kiss you." It seemed a harmless request.

His touch was tentative, unsure, and then urgent. I pulled away. He walked around the room at a vigorous pace.

"Buonaparte?" His manner alarmed me.

Apparently he did not hear, for he did not answer. Then he smiled, a curious smile, I thought, as if he held a great secret. He kissed my hand and was gone.

*January 7, 1796.*
"Are you lovers?" Thérèse demanded, pulling a robe on over her head. She was trying on a variety of ensembles. In two weeks there is going to be a feast at the Luxembourg Palace in honour of the third anniversary of the death of the King and Thérèse was planning her toilette. Robes, petticoats and shawls were strewn all about the room.

"Not in the sense you mean." I held up a shawl for her to consider, a luxurious white lace Barras had given her.

"What other sense is there?" She laughed.

"He intrigues me." General Napoleone Buonaparte was like a tropical day—at one moment exuberant, at the next quiet and moody. He did not inspire respect; rather, he commanded it. I never knew what to expect of him.

"Barras is intent on you marrying him," Thérèse said.

"I don't belong to Barras."

"We all belong to *Director* Barras, my dear." She fastened the pearl buttons on her sleeve. "So what would you answer if Buonaparte proposed?"

I sighed, sat down. "*Marry* Buonaparte?"

"I think our friend the Director is right. I think you should consider. How old is Buonaparte—twenty-six? Remember what Lenormand predicted—that you would marry a brilliant military man, someone younger than you?"

"Hortense weeps at even the thought of me getting married again," I said.

"Has she even met Buonaparte? Why not bring her to the fête at the Palace? She is almost thirteen—it's time she started coming out into society."

*Saturday, January 9.*
At first Hortense was thrilled at the news that we were going to a formal dinner, especially when I showed her the dress Lannoy was making for her.

"It's at the Palace," I said, thinking she would be impressed.

"The Luxembourg?"

I nodded. "Director Barras is hosting it."

"We're going to a reception given by Director *Barras?*" She had a scornful expression on her face. "But, Maman, it was men like him who *murdered* father!"

"Where did you hear such a thing!" Ever since Hortense had started school, she'd begun to have "notions." I'd intended to talk to Madame Campan about it, but withheld, sensing that it was possibly Madame Campan who was the cause. "Were it not for the help of Director Barras, we would never have succeeded in getting back your father's properties," I lectured her. "You owe it to be kind to a man who has done so much to help us."

Finally, she relented; she would go. "But I refuse to speak to criminals and rogues. After all, I'm a Royalist."

I slapped her. We both burst into tears.

*January 21, midnight.*
I'm exhausted. The gala dinner celebration at the Luxembourg Palace was a tremendous success, but it was hardly enjoyable for me. Buonaparte was particularly intense, following my every move. He ate quickly, often with his hands. Hortense sat between us, sullenly refusing to speak.

All the way home Hortense was silent. At last, in bedclothes, she cried out, sobbing, "If you marry that horrid little man, I will never speak to you again!"

I took her in my arms. "I won't," I told her. "I promise."

I promise.

## *In which I must decide*

*Friday, January 22, 1796.*
Buonaparte has made a proposal of marriage. I told him I would consider.

"For how long?" He began pacing the room.

"I will give you an answer in two weeks."

"One week."

"Then the answer will be no."

He smiled. "You are stronger than you look, Josephine. I like that in a woman."

"My name is Rose."


*Saturday, January 23.*
Eugène stood at attention when General Buonaparte came to call. As for Hortense, she turned a cold shoulder. Buonaparte tried his best to charm her, but with little success. For most of the evening Hortense stayed in her room, refusing to come down.

"Try not to be hurtful," I suggested to him.

"I was only teasing." He had accused Hortense of being a bigot because she was preparing to be confirmed.

"She's not a child one can tease. She takes everything seriously."

"Then we *shall* get along."

*January 29, 6:00 P.M.*

"But Thérèse, I am not enamored." Thérèse and I were walking along the quay. It was cold but invigorating, the water grey.

"You care for him as a friend," she said. "He cares for you. Is that not more important?"

"You do not credit love?"

Thérèse scoffed. "Tallien loved me—and all I got were bruises."

"He knows he wronged you." I had been waiting for an opportunity to talk to her about Tallien.

"You've seen him?"

I nodded. "He has changed."

She said nothing.

"He worships you, Thérèse," I persisted. "And he is such a loving father."

She turned on me. "Don't you know how it pains me?" she cried, her eyes full of emotion. "A marriage can survive without passion, Rose, but not without respect. Tell him I'm sorry, but I can't—I just *can't.*"


*January 30.*

"She expresses regret." I tried to soften the news. Tallien had looked so hopeful when I arrived. "She cares for you." This was true.

"But—?"

I shook my head.

I stayed for a time. We played piquet, like in the days of our youth, days before the Terror, days that seem so far away. I talked to him of General Buonaparte, of my doubts and confusion.

"He's an ambitious man," Tallien said. "He will rise. Of that there can be no doubt."

"So Barras says."

"He cares for you? And the children?"

"Yes." Indeed, he seemed to like Hortense and Eugène. "I believe he would be a good father to them."

"And, as a general, a help to your son's military career, no doubt."

"True." That was an important factor.

"Yet you are unsure?"

"We are not lovers."

"That's not difficult to resolve."

"It is not always easy for a woman."

"Is fidelity an issue? Perhaps . . ."

I shrugged. It was customary for married men and women to take lovers—but did I want to live like that?

"I advise you to accept," Tallien said. "It is a gamble—but then . . ." He groaned as I displayed my cards. "But then you have always had a talent for winning games of chance."

*January 31, 1796—Hôtel de Croisoeuil, Croissy*
*Dear Citoyenne Madame Beauharnais,*
   *Come quickly—Mother is not well.*
                    *Citoyenne Madame Lucie Hosten de Croisoeuil*

*February 1, 1796—Hôtel de Croisoeuil, Croissy*
*Dear Citoyenne Madame Beauharnais,*
   *Forgive me for alarming you. Mother is stronger today.*
                    *Citoyenne Madame Lucie Hosten de Croisoeuil*

*Tuesday, February 2—Croissy.*
It was just past noon when my coachman put me down in front of Hôtel de Croisoeuil. Lucie came to the foyer with an infant in her arms. "Madame Beauharnais!" She greeted me most sincerely. "Did you get my second note?" she asked. From somewhere I heard a child laugh.

"How is your mother?" I asked after complimenting her on the birth of her second child—another boy. "What does the doctor say?"

We were interrupted by a scream—a child's. Lucie looked up the stairs. "Quiet!" she yelled. She turned back to me with an angelic expression. "We've moved her downstairs," she said, distracted by the now-howling infant in her arms.

It was dark in the music room; the drapes were drawn, the windows closed. The smell was more touch than sense, a thickening of the air. Gently, I pulled the bedcurtains back. Aimée's eyes were open.

"Aimée." I took her hand, sat by her side. I stroked her damp forehead, studied her face. I did not like what I saw.

"You came." Her voice was husky, hoarse.

"Lucie wrote to me."

"She didn't need to."

"Does talking hurt?"

"I'm so tired."

"I'll rub your feet. Would you like that?"

She nodded. "Tell me news. How is everyone?"

"I am considering an offer of marriage."

"Lazare?"

I shook my head no. "General Buonaparte."

"The man in the journals?"

I nodded.

"Isn't he Italian, Rose? Italians are so unclean."

"He's Corsican."

"That's even worse."

"I wish you could meet him." I longed to tell her of the confusion in my heart, but already she was becoming drowsy, her eyelids fluttering, closing. I sat back down beside her, took her hand. You can't leave me like this, Aimée, I thought. I need you.

Lucie came into the room, a chamber-pot in her hand. I stood up. "She sleeps more and more," Lucie said.

"It will heal her."

"Yes." But neither of us believed this to be so. I took up my basket, my hat. At the door, I turned, looked back. Lucie—so young, so fresh—was standing at the foot of her mother's bed with a resigned look on her face.

"Give her my love," I said. Pray for her soul.


*February 3.*
"I've had a proposal of marriage," I told Fanny. I was at her hôtel on Rue de Tournon, arranging for a delivery of wood.

"You would throw away your liberty?" She looked shocked.

"Liberty to do without." Liberty to sleep alone. "Eugène and Hortense need a father."

"Is it that Corsican I met at your salon?"

"You disapprove?"

"He tells a good ghost story. I rather liked him."

"Most people don't."

"Let them hang. I know the aristocratic matrons of Saint-Germain will stick their noses up over a man with a name they can't pronounce, but who cares about *them* any more?"

"What will Aunt Désirée think?"

"You haven't told her?"

"I haven't the courage."

"She wants you to marry."

"But a Corsican?"

Fanny laughed. "She'd get used to it. Compared to Marie marrying a mulatto, it might even look good. Do you love him?"

"No."

"That's a relief."

*February 4.*

General Schérer, Commander of the Army of Italy, has resigned.

"Why?" I asked, alarmed. Any mention of the Army of Italy brought on an attack of nerves in me.

Buonaparte and I were in his horrible coach, in the Bois de Boulogne. I had persuaded him that in order for me to enjoy the ride, it must be taken at less than full speed, and somewhat reluctantly he had ordered his driver to leave off on the whip.

"Director Carnot sent him my plans for the campaign in Italy," Buonaparte said. "It would appear that General Schérer didn't care for them. He said only the idiot who thought them up would be able to make it work."

"So he resigned? Just like that?"

"Moved over, let's say."

"For you?"

"We shall see. . . ."

"What do you mean?"

"I must have an answer. *Soon.*"

*February 6.*

I felt restless this morning. I decided to go for a drive. On an impulse I asked my driver to take me out to the field where Alexandre was buried.

It looked different from before. Here and there, in patches, grass had grown in, now brown from the frost. The wind blew over the hard lumps of earth. The crazy woman was there, again, in spite of the cold.

I headed out into the field, out to the oak tree in the middle. I leaned my head against the gnarled trunk. How old was this tree? I wondered.

I thought of my life, of the decisions before me. I thought of Hortense, of Eugène. I would turn thirty-three this summer. How many offers of marriage would there be?

"The children must have a father," I said out loud. Could Alexandre hear me? "I cannot manage on my own!"

The crazy woman turned her head toward me, grinned.

I went to her. She was crouched in the dirt. I stooped down beside her. I was surprised to see how young she was, younger than myself. Her clothes were in rags, filthy with excrement. She was shivering.

"You will catch your death out here. Do you have a home?" I asked. "Somewhere you can go?"

"Caesar is coming," she said.

"The Roman?"

"He said he would meet me here."

"You should be inside." Her skin was grey from the cold.

"I am waiting."

I slipped my cloak over her shoulders. "He told me you were to go home," I lied.

"*He* told you that?"

I hesitated. "He told me to give you this." I slipped my little bag of coins into her hand.

She fingered the bag. She looked up at me. Her eyes were deep-set, a dark blue—Alexandre's eyes. Shaken, I turned away.

*Sunday, February 7.*
Another sleepless night. The wind blows against the shutters. I have come to my writing desk by the fire, pulling a patchwork counterpane around my knees. Tomorrow I'm to give Buonaparte my answer. I don't know what it will be.

I get out my cards, hidden away since the Carmes. I feel their worn surfaces, feel the sadness in them still. With fear, I lay them out. At the centre, Conflict. To the future, Union. And the controlling card: Fate.

*February 8.*
I have given Buonaparte my answer.

## *In which I have cause to regret*

*February 9, 1796.*
Eugène took the news philosophically. In fact, I think he was pleased. Hortense, however, was inconsolable. I have betrayed her, she said. She stayed in her room, refusing to eat.


*February 18.*
The banns will be published tomorrow morning. "Have you told anyone?" I asked Buonaparte. "Have you told your family?"

Buonaparte's enormous family: his widowed mother Madame Letizia (whom he worships), his older brother Giuseppe (whom he loves), Lucciano (who shows such promise), Luigi (whom he regards as his son), his sisters ("the three Marias") Maria-Anna, Maria-Paola and Maria-Anunziata, the "baby" Girolamo—twelve now. All of them in Buonaparte's care, all of them needy.

"I've only informed Giuseppe," he said. We were sitting by the fire eating preserved cherries in thick fresh cream. "I wrote him two weeks ago."

Two weeks ago? I hadn't given Buonaparte my answer two weeks ago. "And what was his reponse?" I asked.

"He's furious. He said he should have been consulted, since he's the eldest. He insists I honour my commitment to marry his wife's sister."

"The girl you were engaged to last summer?"

"And now Giuseppe has written Mother."

"And?"

"And now *she* demands I break it off."

"Is this not going to be a problem, Buonaparte? Perhaps we should—"

"No!" he said angrily. "I am my own master."


*February 19.*

Buonaparte has been talking to Barras, Barras has been talking to Thérèse, Thérèse has been talking to me. In this way I have learned that Buonaparte's brother Giuseppe has threatened Buonaparte with a lawsuit for not marrying his sister-in-law!*

"Corsicans spend half their life in court," Thérèse said when I told her. "It's their favourite sport. Ever heard of a vendetta?"

"What am I getting into?"

"Don't worry, Rose. You could charm a snake."

"But Corsican in-laws?"

Thérèse made a doubtful face. "Maybe not."


*February 20.*

I've been to see Citoyen Calmelet, my family advisor, regarding my baptism certificate, which is required for the marriage licence. "I think you are doing the right thing," he told me.

"Not many say so." General Aubert-Dubayet, the Minister of War, had had the audacity to tell me I'd be making a fool of myself if I married Buonaparte. Even Grace Elliott had asked how I could consider marrying a man with such a terrible name.

Citoyen Calmelet nodded. "General Buonaparte is not one to stand on ceremony. This offends some people. But he shows promise and he seems to care for you sincerely. One can see it in his eyes."

"Will you come to the ceremony, be one of my witnesses?"

"I'd be honoured. When is it?"

Seventeen days.

---

* *Bernadine Eugénie Désirée Clary would later marry Bernadotte, who became crown prince of Sweden—making Désirée Crown Princess. Ironically, their son, Oscar I of Sweden, would marry one of Rose's granddaughters.*

*Monday, February 22.*

It was almost noon when I heard the sound of a horse trotting up the laneway. I looked out to see Lazare dismounting from a splendid grey. He handed the reins and his riding crop to my coachman.

Quickly I went to my mirror, rubbed some colour into my cheeks.

Agathe came into my wardrobe. "General Hoche is here to see you."

"Yes, I saw him." I removed my apron. I had intended to work in the garden and the simple muslin gown I was wearing was not flattering.

"Shall I tell him that you will receive him?"

I thought for a moment. Should I? No. "Tell him I am indisposed."

A few moments later I heard a commotion in the hall. I looked up. Lazare was standing in the door. "I want my letters back," he said.

I scoffed. "What letters! I've not had a single letter from you since *August*." I pulled my shawl around my shoulders. "Since you *rescued* Madame de Pout-Bellan's husband."

"Madame de Pout-Bellan? What does she have to do with this?"

"It is said that you love her."

Lazare waved his hand in a gesture of impatience. "Madame de Pout-Bellan? There is nothing . . . ! Nothing, at least, to compare with the way you and Vanakre—"

"Vanakre? Your *footman?*"

"You need not take that aristocratic tone. Vanakre is my aide-de-camp now."

"That's not the point. You thought I'd had an amourette with *Vanakre?*"

"I have *proof!*"

"It would amuse me to see such proof, General Hoche."

Lazare began to pace. "And now you with this"—he cursed, banged his fist on the side-table—"this little *police* general! How could you!"

"Do not speak of General Buonaparte in that way."

"Did you know that only last year he was transferred to an infantry brigade under *my* orders, but he refused, *pretending* to be sick. Did you know the Committee had him demoted for insubordination? And that he offered his services to the Turks! He's an opportunist! He can't be trusted. He only wants the promotion Barras has offered him."

"It has nothing to do with Barras!" I put my hands to my ears.

Lazare grabbed my hands, pulled them away. "Buonaparte's reward for marrying you is the Army of Italy. It is *that* he wants—not *you*."

"Whosoever is appointed to command the Army of Italy will be appointed on the basis of merit." I was trembling. "*All* the directors must approve it—as you well know. In point of fact, it would appear to be Director Carnot who is promoting General Buonaparte."

"Tell me you love him," Lazare demanded.

"I have given him my word."

He stared at me for a long moment. "That's it?"

I turned to the window, took a breath. "I understand congratulations are in order. You are a father, I am told."

"I am. A girl." There was pride in his voice.

I turned to him. "I was never unfaithful to you," I said.

He took my hand. "You're trembling. Do I frighten you?"

"Don't make me cry, Lazare." I pulled my hand away. His touch was gentle. He had always been so very gentle. "Please go."

At the door he turned. "It is true that I have fallen in love with another woman," he said. "My wife."

"You always did love her."

He bowed and was gone. Shortly after I heard the sound of his horse's hoofs cantering up the drive.

I sat for a time by the window, looking out at the grey winter day. Agathe asked if there was anything I wanted.

"Nothing," I said.


*Later.*

I was digging in the garden when a message was delivered. It was a note from Citoyen Dunnkirk: "Come see me."

Was it Mother? Immediately I called for my coach, arriving at Emmery's office shortly before five.

"I am glad you could come so promptly. There is something I think you should know. Your fiancé has been to see me." It was cold. He was sniffling, as usual.

"General Buonaparte?"

"Yes. This morning."

"But *why?*"

"He was inquiring into your financial affairs."

"I have no secrets! He didn't need to ask you."

Citoyen Dunnkirk shrugged.

"What did you tell him?"

"The truth." He blew his nose on a dirty blue kerchief.

"And . . . ?" I didn't know who I was angrier with: Buonaparte or Citoyen Dunnkirk.

"He thought you were wealthier than you are."

I sat for a moment in silence.

"I know it is not my place, Citoyenne, but . . . are you sure this is the man you should marry?"

"I must go." I stood, in fear of my emotions.


*That evening.*

"It's off!" I yelled the moment Buonaparte entered. I had not intended to explode in this way, but the words escaped before I could control myself.

Buonaparte looked behind him. Was I addressing someone other than himself? "Josephine . . . ?"

"And I will *not* be Josephine! I am *Rose*." I paced the room.

Buonaparte threw his hat onto a chair. "Perhaps you could tell me what this is all about," he said, "*Josephine*."

I struck out at him. He caught my wrist, hard. "I warn you never to strike me," he said.

Lannoy came running to the door. Gontier was behind her. "Madame?"

"Leave us alone," Buonaparte commanded. He was not as calm as he pretended.

I nodded to them both. "It's all right."

After they left there was a moment of silence. Outside, a horse whinnied.

"Now, if you would be so kind as to explain?" Buonaparte jabbed at the embers with an iron.

I sat down, clasped my hands in my lap. "I have decided to call off our engagement."

"That much I have gathered. Would it inconvenience you to provide a reason?"

"You have been to see my banker."

"I have."

"You could have come to *me*."

He did not respond.

"You have no affection for me, Buonaparte. In marrying me, you seek only promotion." I would not look at him. "Nothing you can say can persuade me otherwise. Do not try to defend yourself."

"And *you*—are you so . . . ?" He stood. "So free of self-interest? Can you claim that it is only for *affection* for me that you have consented to marry?"

"So much the more reason to abandon this ill-fated union."

He left abruptly. There were tears in his eyes. I do not feel relief.

## *In which we begin again, & yet again*

*February 23, 1796.*
I was still in bed when Agathe informed me that General Buonaparte had arrived.

"I heard the horse," I said. Agathe brought me my white muslin gown. I tied a red scarf about my head and put rouge on my cheeks.

I wasn't looking forward to this meeting. "Stay near," I told Agathe, slipping a shawl around my shoulders, "in case I need you." I shivered from the cold.

Buonaparte was waiting in the drawing room. He was standing by the window examining the bust of Voltaire. He turned to face me when I entered. I could see from his eyes that he had not slept.

"Good afternoon," I said.

"Is it?" He was wearing a dark embroidered coat with a high stand-up collar.

I took a seat to the left of the fire, gesturing for him to take the seat to the right. His boots, which he is in the habit of polishing with some obnoxious substance, threw off a strong odour. I asked Agathe to bring us coffee and toast. "And rum."

Buonaparte and I sat in uncomfortable silence until Agathe returned. She placed the urn and goblets on a serving table and left. "Coffee?" I asked. He refused. I poured myself coffee from the urn, added rum, cream, two heaping spoonfuls of sugar. My spoon made a scraping noise on the bottom of my cup.

"The time has come for truth," he said. He stood. I braced myself for recriminations, justifications. "You have accused me of self-interest in proposing marriage to you. I will answer your charges." He clasped his hands behind his back and then across his chest, and then back behind his back again. "In the beginning, yes, I was attracted by the advantages marriage to you would offer. I saw that you were a woman of influence, a woman who was at ease with men of power and wealth, a woman who bridged both the old world and the new. These qualities would be an asset to me, I knew. And of course there was the plum of the Army of Italy. The Army of Italy! I would have married the most lowly of the market prostitutes to gain command of the Army of Italy."

"You need not insult me, Buonaparte."

"*Insult* you!" He fell to his knees before me. "I intend to honour you as no other woman has been honoured!"

"Rise!" I said, alarmed and embarrassed.

"You *must* hear me!" He took the seat beside mine, grabbed my hand. "Don't you see? I have fallen in *love* with you!"

"Yet you went to see my banker!"

"I will not deny it. It was the act of a coward." He stood back up again. "I was seeking reasons, cause and effect, premise and proof. I was seeking escape."

"From *what*?"

"You. From the emotion that has engulfed me."

I sat back in exasperation. "I dislike riddles," I said.

"You don't understand! When I am with you, it is as if a curtain has been opened, and all that has gone before has been merely an overture. Is this not frightening? I have held a dead man in my arms. I have walked to the mouth of a cannon set to fire. I have faced my mother's fury. Yet *nothing* is as frightening to me as the tenderness that comes over me when I look into your eyes."

Abruptly I stood, went to the window. Fortuné was by the garden wall, by the rosebushes there, digging at something.

"Will you not marry me?" There was desperation in his voice.

I came back to my seat by the fire. "You know I do not love you," I said.

"Yes. I know that."

"You know I am . . . older than you, that I have loved another." Love another still. I did not say that.

"I do."

"Yet even so, you wish to marry me?"

"I wish to worship you."

"Must you be so drôle, Buonaparte?"

"You think I jest."

"Surely, you must." I smiled.

"Forgive me?"

I took his hand. I had never noticed how fine his fingers were, how smooth his skin.

"Join me for a promenade?" he asked.

I stood. We were almost the same height. I felt he was a brother, a companion—"my spirit friend," Mimi would have said. "I will not give up Chantereine," I said, opening the doors onto the garden.

"My hôtel on Rue des Capucines is more prestigious," he said.

"This is my first real home. It is everything to me."

He looked about. "After I liberate Italy, I will require a larger establishment."

"And when might that be, General Buonaparte?" Teasing.

He looked at me with an amused expression. "Shortly after we are married, Josephine."


*Wednesday, February 24.*

"I announced our betrothal to the Directors," Buonaparte told me this evening.

"And what was the response?"

"Positive." He seemed pleased, strutting around. "*Very* positive." He slapped his hands together.


*March 2.*

Buonaparte's footman unloaded a crate of papers into my entryway, Buonaparte coming in after him. "Behold," he said with a dramatic flourish. "The Commander of the Army of Italy."

"It's official now? Were you not expecting it?"

"One can never be entirely sure of such things." He rummaged through the crate of papers.

"And now?"

Buonaparte flipped through the pages of a report.

"And now?" I touched his arm.

He looked at me with a distracted expression.

"And now?"

"And *now* the work begins."


*March 8.*

Buonaparte called for me at noon. I was ready. Together we went to my lawyer's office on the Rue Saint-Honoré. Buonaparte waited in the entryway while my lawyer went over the marriage contract.

"Are you familiar with this contract?" Raguideau asked when I sat down. His dusty office was cluttered with papers and legal forms. The windows looking out onto the Rue Saint-Honoré were covered with grime.

"I am."

"Nevertheless, I am required by law to go over it with you." He is a small man, yet he has an exceptionally deep voice. "Your finances will be kept separate. You will each contribute equally to the costs of maintaining a household. Even the cost of getting married will be shared between you." He spelled out the terms: "Your husband assumes no responsibility for your debts. Other than paying you a nominal sum of fifteen hundred livres a year, you will receive nothing from this union."

He put the papers down on the desk, took off his thick spectacles. "Citoyenne Beauharnais, I must be frank. This man brings you nothing but a cloak and sword. I'm afraid I cannot, in good conscience, advise you to sign this contract."

I felt heat in my cheeks, in spite of the chill. "I have come to sign this contract, Citoyen Raguideau, not to question it."

"Please understand, it would be a *disaster* for you to marry this man."

"So be it." I took up the quill.

Buonaparte was waiting in the hall. He seemed amused. "Only a cloak and sword?"

"You overheard? Are you not offended?" I was angry. Was nothing predictable with him?

"We shall see what a cloak and sword can do!"


*Later.*

The parish bells had just struck four. I was standing by the window, looking out at the garden, when I was startled by a noise. Behind me was Lannoy with a worn leather valise in one hand.

"Are you going somewhere, Lannoy?" I asked. I did not recall that a leave had been arranged.

A vigorous tip of her head almost dislodged her hat, a modest straw creation overpowered by a white-and-blue-striped bow. "I cannot serve that Jacobin!"

"You are leaving me? *Now?*"

"Farewell!" she wailed, throwing herself into my arms.


*March 9.*

Barras and Tallien arrived shortly after seven. Tallien had on his black coat and top hat. He was carrying an umbrella instead of a sword. "His funeral ensemble," Barras said, who was dressed more traditionally in velvet and lace.

I smiled uneasily.

The three of us headed off in Barras's coach. Agathe and Gontier had attached little bouquets of flowers tied with white ribbons to the horses' bridles.

It was exactly eight when we entered the township office, a once-elegant white and gold drawing room decorated with frolicking cupids, now headquarters of the second arrondissement and covered with dust. A fire was dying in the marble fireplace. It was dark: a single candle flickered in a bronze sconce. The large gilt mirrors reflected only shadows.

My adviser Jérôme Calmelet was already there, seated in one of the hard leather chairs. The registrar, Citoyen Leclerq, was going through papers at the desk. A thin lad with a wooden leg sat slumped beside him.

But no sign of Buonaparte. "No doubt he's been held up," Barras said, removing his cape.

We waited. After almost an hour, the registrar stood, yawned, put on his cloak. "I leave you in charge, Antoine," he told the young lad. Citoyen Antoine manoeuvred his wooden leg under the big desk and regarded us with an attempt at authority.

"No doubt he thought he was to be here at nine." Tallien shifted in the uncomfortable chair.

"It is past nine now." My little bouquet of flowers had begun to wilt. "I insist that we leave." I stood. I was angry. I was more than angry; I was humiliated.

"Wait," Barras commanded.

It was past ten when we heard footsteps on the stairs. "He's here," Barras said.

Buonaparte burst into the room followed by a youth in uniform. He went directly up to young Antoine and shook him. "Wake up!"

The lad sat up, blinked.

Buonaparte grabbed my hand, pulled me to my feet. "Marry us," he commanded the lad, pushing a gold band onto my ring finger.

It was over in a few minutes.


We rode back to Chantereine in silence, Buonaparte and I.

"I have decided to change my name. Bonaparte. Napoleon Bonaparte. It's more French. Do you like it?"

I said nothing.

"Is something wrong?"

"If Barras hadn't insisted, I would have left. I don't know why I stayed!"

"So, divorce me in the morning."

"Perhaps I will!"

We didn't exchange another word all the way to Chantereine. I headed immediately up the stairs. I threw the flowers off my bed, embarrassed by the fuss Agathe and Gontier had made. Fortuné growled when Buonaparte entered the room.

"Your footman put your bags in there this afternoon." I nodded toward the wardrobe.

"What about the dog?" Buonaparte asked, returning in his night-clothes. He was wearing a cotton nightcap with a silly-looking tassel on it.

"The dog stays." Fortuné was in his usual place at the foot of the bed.

"I will not sleep with a *dog*."

"Very well, then, you will sleep on the settee." I blew out the lantern.

Buonaparte stumbled toward the bed in the dark. I heard Fortuné growl. Then I heard Buonaparte curse loudly in the Italian tongue.

I sat up, my heart pounding. Fortuné was snarling. "What happened!"

"That dog should be shot!" Buonaparte held up his hand. In the moonlight I could see something dark on it.

"*Mon Dieu!* Is that blood? Did he bite your hand?"

"My leg."

Agathe came running into the room, holding a lantern. Buonaparte's leg was covered with blood. Buonaparte pressed a bedsheet to it to stop the bleeding.

Fortuné was cowering under a chair, baring his fangs.

"A basin of hot water and some bandages," I told Agathe, grabbing Fortuné by the scruff of the neck and shutting the snarling little thing in the wardrobe.

Gontier came to the door, his ruffled nightcap falling into his eyes. "Go for a surgeon," I told him.

"No surgeon will be necessary," Buonaparte said.

"Don't attempt to be a hero over this, Buonaparte," I said. "There is nothing to be gained by it."

"Do you think heroism is something that can be put on, like a cloak!" He turned to Gontier. "I am master of this house now, and I am telling you, do *not* go for the surgeon. I've spent too much time on the battle-field attending to my own wounds to be coddled like a tailor by some ignorant youth." He took one of the bandages Agathe had brought and dipped it into the steaming water. "If your girl could bring some salt?"

"Her name is Agathe. Ask her yourself."

Buonaparte glared at me. "Are we to spend the rest of our lives quar-relling?"

"I believe so." I nodded to Agathe. "If you could fetch the salt? And the cognac," I added.

Buonaparte cleaned and dressed his wound, securing it with two stitches of strong silk which he put in himself, gritting his teeth against the pain. I persuaded him to lie with his leg propped up on a pillow.

"You may go now," I told Agathe and Gontier, who were standing at the foot of the bed, trampling the flowers. "Take Fortuné with you."

"I'm to be woken at six," Buonaparte instructed Agathe.

"That's only a few hours from now," I said.

"I have taken too much time already."

Agathe and Gontier withdrew, taking away the lanterns and a still-snarling Fortuné.

By the light of a single candle I poured two snifters of cognac. I handed one to Buonaparte. He put his hand up in refusal. "I must keep my wits about me," he said.

I sat down on the bed, took a sip of the cognac, sighed. I had wanted a father for my children, security—now it seemed so much more complex.

"You doubt the wisdom of what you've done," he said.

What I've done. Yes. "Must you forever be telling me my thoughts?" I was being churlish, I knew. "I'm sorry," I said. "It has not been a romantic evening." Suddenly I felt tears pressing. Is one allowed to go back, begin again? Can mistakes be undone?

Buonaparte pulled at a pillow.

"Allow me," I said. I put down my glass and adjusted the pillow behind him. He put his hand on my wrist. "There is something I haven't told you."

"Please, no." It was too late for confessions. I pulled my hand away.

"A fortuneteller told me that a widow would be my angel, my lucky star."

I thought of the fortune I'd been foretold. *You will be Queen.*

"You scoff," he said.

"I'm no angel," I said. I lay down beside him.

"You think the woman I love does not exist. You don't believe in Josephine."

His grey eyes were so intense. I looked away.

"Do you believe in *me?*" he asked.

I regarded his profile by the light of the candle. He had a haunted look. What was it that fired him, drove him? It would never give him peace, I knew.

"Are you cold?" He pulled the covering sheet over me.

"Yes," I said. I stilled his hand against my breast.

He seemed unsure what he should do. I felt unsure, myself. Should I blow out the candle? Take off my gown? I felt my age, his youth.

"I have read that if the tip of a woman's breast is touched in a certain way, that she will go mad with pleasure," he said. He sounded like a schoolboy, reciting a lesson. "I amuse you?" he asked, observing my smile.

"You have a scientific mind," I said.

He cupped my breast in his hand, examined it. "Your breast is a perfect example of its kind—round, firm."

"Buonaparte!" A warmth had come into my heart.

I leaned over him. His breath on my face was sweet.

"Truly, you—" He stopped, unable to speak.

I touched a tear that was running down his cheek. It tasted of the sea. "Yes," I said. "I do believe in you."


*Dawn.*

The sun has tinted the sky the most delicate shade of pink. It reminds me of the mornings of my youth. I listen for the animals stirring, the cock, the cow.

Buonaparte, his leg wrapped in a bandage, is asleep. I listen to the sound of his breathing.

I am married. Again.

My husband is not the man I dreamt of as a girl, not my *grand amour*—and certainly not the king the fortuneteller had foretold. Only Buonaparte—strange little Napoleone. Now Napoleon.

And I? Who am *I?*

He calls me Josephine. He says I'm an angel, a saint, his good-luck star. I know I'm no angel, but in truth I have begun to like this Josephine he sees. She is intelligent; she amuses; she is pleasing. She is grace and charm and heart. Unlike Rose: scared, haunted and needy. Unlike Rose with her sad life.

I slip off my wedding ring, a simple gold band. Inside, I see an inscription. I hold it to the light: To Destiny.

# *Chronology*

| 1786 | September 3 | Eugène, five, is now in his father's custody. |
|------|------------|-----------------------------------------------|
| 1788 | July 2 | Rose sails for Martinique. |
|      | August 11 | Rose arrives in Martinique. |
| 1790 | September 6 | Rose sets sail for France under cannon fire. |
|      | October 29 | Rose lands at Toulon. |
|      | November 7 | Rose's father dies. |
| 1791 | June 20 | King and family flee Paris. |
|      | June 21 | Alexandre President of Assembly. |
|      | June 25 | King and Queen are returned to Paris. |
|      | July 31 | Alexandre President of Assembly for a second term. |
|      | September 14 | King pledges oath of allegiance to the new constitution. |
|      | November 4 | Rose's sister Manette dies. |
| 1792 | April 20 | France declares war on Austria. Alexandre joins army. |
|      | April 25 | First use of the guillotine. |
|      | August | Alexandre appointed Chief-of-Staff of the Army of the Rhine. |
|      | August 10–13 | Insurrection. King and Queen are put in prison. |
|      | August 28–30 | Night house searches begin—thousands are arrested. |
|      | September 2 | French troops at Verdun fall to the enemy. Panic in Paris. |
|      | September 2–6 | September massacres. Over 1,000 in the prisons murdered. |
|      |  | Rose sends children away with Frédéric and Amalia. Alexandre commands children return to Paris. |
|      | September 20 | Divorce is made legally possible. |
|      | September 22 | The Republic is proclaimed. |
|      | December 26 | Trial of the King begins. |
| 1793 | January 15 | King declared guilty. |
|      | January 21 | King decapitated. |
|      | May 29 | Alexandre made Commander-in-Chief of Army of the Rhine. |
|      | August 21 | Alexandre's resignation is accepted. |
|      | September 17 | Law of Suspects passed. |
|      | September 26 | Rose moves to Croissy. |

| | | |
|---|---|---|
| | October 16 | The Queen is beheaded. |
| | October 29 | Fanny's daughter Marie is arrested. |
| 1794 | March 2 | Alexandre arrested in Blois. |
| | April 20 | Rose is arrested in Paris. |
| | July 23 | Alexandre is beheaded. |
| | July 28 | Robespierre is beheaded. |
| | August 6 | Rose is released from prison. |
| | September 2 | Hoche leaves Paris for new command. Takes Eugène. |
| | September 9 | Attempted assassination of Tallien. |
| | October 7 | Marie is released from prison. |
| | December 26 | Thérèse (21), pregnant, and Tallien (27) are married. |
| 1795 | February 21 | Religious worship allowed in private dwellings. |
| | May 17 | Thérèse gives birth to Thermidor-Rose. |
| | June 8 | The Dauphin (10) dies in prison. |
| | June 23–27 | Émigré forces land at Quiberon Bay. |
| | July 16–21 | Battle of Quiberon Bay. Hoche leads French troops to victory. |
| | August 17 | Rose signs lease on house on Rue Chantereine. |
| | September 28 | Rose invites Buonaparte to call on her. |
| | October 4–6 | Right-wing insurrection defeated by troops under Barras and Buonaparte. |
| | October 26 | Barras and four others elected Directors of France. Buonaparte takes over Barras's position of General-in-Chief of Army of the Interior. |
| 1796 | January 21 | Gala dinner at Luxembourg Palace. |
| | February 19 | Banns for Rose and Buonaparte's wedding issued. |
| | March 2 | Buonaparte is made Commander-in-Chief of Army of Italy. |
| | March 8 | Marriage contract signed. |
| | March 9 | Rose (32) and Napoleon (26) are married in a civil ceremony. |

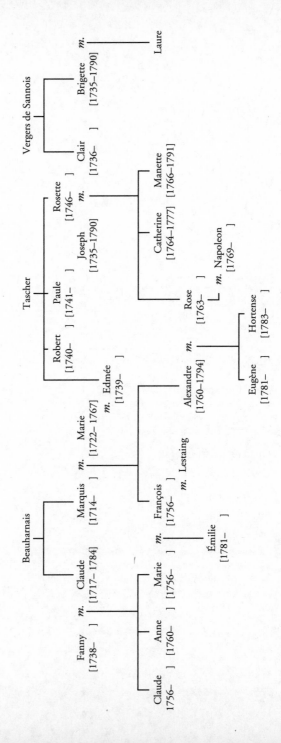

*Genealogy*

# Selected Bibliography

————. *Dictionnaire de biographie française.* Sous la direction de M. Prevost et Roman d'Amat. Librairie Letouzey et Ané, 1954.

————. *Dictionnaire Napoléon.* Sous la direction de Jean Tulard. Fayard, 1987.

Castelot, André. *Josephine, A Biography.* Trans. New York: Harper & Row, 1967.

Catinat, Docteur Maurice. "Une lettre inédite de la future impératrice Joséphine." *Bulletin, 1991.* Rueil-Malmaison: Société des Amis de Malmaison, 1991.

Chevallier, Bernard, and Christophe Pincemaille. *L'impératrice Joséphine.* Paris: Presses de la Renaissance, 1988.

Cole, Hubert. *Joséphine.* London: Heinemann, 1962.

Cronin, Vincent. *Napoleon.* London: Collins, 1971.

Epton, Nina C. *Josephine: The Empress and Her Children.* London: Weidenfeld & Nicolson, 1975.

Jones, Colin. *The Longman Companion to the French Revolution.* London and New York: Longman, 1988.

Knapton, Ernest John. *Empress Josephine.* Cambridge: Harvard University Press, 1963.

Le Normand, Mlle. M. A. *The Historical and Secret Memoirs of the Empress Josephine.* Vol. I & II. Trans. London: H. S. Nichols, 1895.

Minnigerode, Meade. *The Magnificent Comedy; Some aspects of public and private life in Paris, from the fall of Robespierre to the coming of Bonaparte July, 1794–November, 1799.* Murray Hill, New York: Farrar & Rinehart, 1931.

Rose-Rosette, Robert. *Les jeunes années de l'impératrice Joséphine.* Martinique: Publié avec le concours de la Fondation Napoléon, 1992.

Turgeon, F. K. "Fanny de Beauharnais. Biographical Notes and a Bibliography." *Modern Philology,* Aug. 1932.

Wagener, Françoise. *La reine Hortense (1783–1837).* Éditions Jean-Claude Lattès, 1992.

Whitham, J. Mills. *Men and Women of the French Revolution.* New York: The Viking Press, 1933.

# Acknowledgements

For help both general and specific: Eleanor Alwyn, Nathalie Bedard, Gale Bildfell, Elena Diana (Amaritha), Dr. John Goodman, Paul Kropp, Jackie Levitin, Corine Paul, Charis Wahl, John Williamson, and the Golden Girls Plus Bob, especially, Robert Zentner. For editorial suggestions, my main readers: Peggy Bridgland, Judy Holland, Marnie MacKay (ever-patient librarian), Fran Murphy, and especially, Sharon Zentner. For nourishment and wisdom: Janet Calcaterra, Thea Caplan, Pat Jeffries, Kathlyn Lampi, Jenifer McVaugh, Joanne Zomers. For significant teachings at important crossroads: Margaret Atwood, Matt Cohen, Janette Turner Hospital, and especially, Jane Urquhart. For help in the historical labyrinth: William R. Beall, Bernard Chevallier, Dr. Robert Rose-Rosette, and especially, Dr. Maurice Catinat and Dr. Margaret Chrisawn. For fuelling the passion: fellow Napoleonic enthusiasts Tony Kenny, Dr. John McErlean, Derwin Mak, Helen Smith and Robert Snibbe of the Napoleonic Society of America, and especially, deceased Society member David Goudy. For being there from the beginning, Jan Whitford. For being such great editors, great publishers: Iris Tupholme, Maya Mavjee and the rest of the gang at HarperCollins. For being even more pernickety than I am, Bernice Eisenstein. For enthusiasm and understanding: Carrie and Chet Gulland, and especially, Richard Gulland—without whose unquestioning and steadfast support this book never could have been written.

# BOOK TWO

## *Tales of Passion*
## *Tales of Woe*

What is history but a fable agreed upon? — *Napoleon*

Tales of Passion, Tales of Woe
*is a work of fiction based on (and inspired by)*
*the extraordinary life of an extraordinary woman.*

*For my father,*
*who loves stories,*
*and my mother,*
*who loves books.*

In a dark time, the eye begins to see.
                                        —*Theodore Roethke*

*Tales of Passion*
*Tales of Woe*

## Prologue: Marie Antoinette (spirit)

He calls her Josephine.

I approach her with caution. I do not want to startle her, only observe her, writing at her escritoire. It is an old piece of furniture, made in the Islands—a crude design but of sentimental value. She remembers her father sitting at it, cursing over the bills, as she often does herself.

She pauses, looks up, her hand suspended over the page of her journal.

She's not what one would call a beauty, yet he worships her with a passion that verges on madness! Big hazel eyes, I grant you, and yes, long curling lashes, a slender, graceful form, artful dress, etc., etc.— but are these qualities that bewitch? Perhaps it is the caress of her musical voice that has cast a spell. (I know about spells.) No, it's her maddening gentleness that drives him to despair. He wants to consume her, possess her, enchain her! And she . . . well, I see that puzzled look in her eyes.

She glances over her shoulder. There is no one, I assure her. She listens, and hears: the steady ticking of the pendulum clock, the crackling of the fire in the bedchamber. She dips the raven's tail quill in the ink.

I only want to help! History was cruel where I was concerned. They made me into a monster, took my husband, my children, my head.

Beware! I want to warn her. Small deceits, one upon another, destroy faith. You will not miss it until it's gone. Betrayed, one becomes the betrayer. The Devil lights the path. Say what you will, there is no return.

She puts down the quill. A tear? Such thoughts oppress, no doubt. Loyalty defines her; she lives to please.

Such is the luxury of commoners—a conceit, if you will.

She pulls her shawl about her shoulders; I've chilled her, I know. It can't be helped. She knows not the future. I do.

# I

*Our Lady of Victories*

How many lands, how many frontiers separate us!
—*Napoleon, in a letter to Josephine.*

## *In which my new life begins*

*March 10, 1796—Paris, early morning, grey skies.*
I am writing this in my jasmine-scented dressing room, where I might not be discovered by Bonaparte, my husband of one day.

Husband. The word feels foreign on my tongue, as foreign as the maps spread over the dining room table, the sword propped in the corner of my drawing room. As foreign as the man himself.

My face in the glass looks harsh, etched by shadow, reflecting the dark thoughts in my heart.

How unlike me to be melancholy. I'm tempted to black out the words I've just written, tempted to write, instead: I've married, I am happy, all is well. But I've promised myself one thing—to be honest on these pages. However much I am required to dissemble, to flatter and cajole, here I may speak my heart truly. And my heart, in truth, is troubled. I fear I've made a mistake.


*[Undated]*
Josephine Rose Beauharnais Bonaparte
Josephine Rose Bonaparte
Josephine Tascher Beauharnais Bonaparte
Josephine Beauharnais Bonaparte
Josephine Bonaparte
Citoyenne Jospehine Bonaparte
Madame Josephine Bonaparte

Josephine
Josephine
Josephine


*2:30 P.M.*

We've just returned from Saint-Germain. Bonaparte is in a meeting in the study, and I'm back in my dressing room, seeking solace. It seems that everything is going wrong. Where to begin?

This morning, as I was dusting my face with rice powder, preparing to leave, I saw Bonaparte standing in the door. "The coach is ready." He had a riding crop in his hands and was twisting it, bending it. He was anxious, I knew, about going out to Saint-Germain to see my children at their schools. Certainly, I was uneasy myself. I wasn't sure how Hortense and Eugène were going to take the news.

"You're not wearing your new jacket?" I asked, putting on a pair of dangling sapphire earrings. I'd changed into a long-sleeved violet gown over a dotted gauze skirt. It was a new ensemble and I was pleased with the effect, but I couldn't decide which shoes to wear—my lace-up boots or my silk slippers, which went so nicely. It had stopped raining but was damp out. The boots would be more practical. "The boots," I told my scullery maid, who pushed one roughly onto my foot. I made a mental note to begin looking for a lady's maid as soon as Bonaparte left for the south.

As soon as Bonaparte left for the south, and life returned to normal.

Today, tonight and then tomorrow, I thought—twenty-eight hours. Twenty-eight hours of frenetic activity, soldiers coming and going, couriers cantering into the courtyard. Twenty-eight hours of chaos. Every surface of my little house is covered with maps, journals, reports, scraps of paper with lists on them of provisions, names, numbers, schedules. Books are stacked on the dining room table, on the escritoire, by my bed. Twenty-eight more hours of his fumbling caresses and embraces. Bonaparte works and reads with intense concentration—oblivious to me, to the servants—and then falls upon me with a ravenous need. Twenty-eight more hours of dazed bewilderment. Who is this man I have married? Will life ever be "normal" again?

"What's wrong with this jacket?" he demanded.

"It needs mending," I said, smoothing the shoulder. The worn grey wool was pulling at the seams and the edges of the cuffs were frayed. I would have it mended, if I could ever get him out of it. If I could ever get him out of it, I might burn it, I thought, kissing his smooth cheek. "And you look so handsome in the new one." The knee-length tails helped detract from his thin legs and gave the impression of height.

He kissed me and grinned. "I'm not changing," he said, tweaking my ear.


It was a slow journey to Saint-Germain—the rain had made the roads muddy—so it was early afternoon by the time our carriage pulled into the courtyard of Hortense's school. I spotted her on the playing field and waved. As soon as she saw us, she dropped the ball and spun on her heels, covering her face with her hands. Was she crying? I touched Bonaparte's arm to distract him, but it was too late—he'd already seen my daughter's reaction. He gazed across the playing field with a sad expression in his grey eyes.

"Something's wrong," I said. I feared what the problem might be.

"I'll wait for you inside." Bonaparte pulled down on the rim of his new general's hat. The felt was rigid yet and it sat high on his big head.

I squeezed his hand, as lovers do. "I won't be long," I promised.


The ground was soft under my feet. I could feel the damp soaking into my thin-soled boots. A spring breeze carried the scent of ploughed fields. I picked my way around the wet spots, reminding myself that Hortense was young. Reminding myself that it was normal for a girl of twelve (almost thirteen) to have a delicate sensibility, especially considering . . .

Especially considering what she's had to endure. It has been almost two years since the Terror, yet even now my daughter sometimes wakes screaming in the night. Even now she cannot pass the place where her father died without bursting into tears.*

* *Joephine's first husband, Alexandre Beauharnais, the father of her two children— Hortense (twelve) and Eugène (fourteen)—was beheaded on July 23, 1794, at the height of the Terror, the violent phase of the French Revolution in which thousands of aristocrats were guillotined.*

My niece Émilie ran to embrace me. "Is Hortense hurt?" I asked. "What's wrong?" My daughter looked so alone, hunched over by the goal post, her back to us.

"She's crying, Auntie," Émilie said, shivering, her hands pushed into the pockets of her plain woollen smock. "It's the hysterics!"

Hysterics? I'd been warned that girls of fourteen were subject to frightful convulsions, but Hortense was not yet of that age. I lifted the hem of my gown and headed toward my weeping daughter.

"Hortense?" I called out, approaching. I could see her shoulders shaking. "Darling—" I reached out and touched her shoulder. Even through my gloves I could feel her bones—the bones of a girl still, not yet the bones of a woman. I considered turning her, but I knew her stubborn strength. Instead, I walked around to face her.

I was startled by the haunted look in her eyes. Pink blotches covered her freckled cheeks, making her eyes seem abnormally blue—her father's eyes. Her father's critical eyes, following me still. I took her cold, bare hand and pressed it to my heart. "What is it, darling?" Thinking how she'd grown in the last year, thinking that she was tall for her age, and that soon she would be as tall as I am, taller perhaps.

"I'm afraid, Maman." A sob welled up in her.

A gust of wind rustled the leaves. My straw hat flew off my head and dangled down my back by a ribbon. It was not the answer I'd expected. "Of what?"

"That you'll marry him!"

Him: Bonaparte. I tried to speak, but could not. The words stuck in my throat. How could I tell her that the deed had been done, the vows spoken, the contract signed: Bonaparte and I were man and wife. How could I tell her that this man was now her father—for better or for worse, for ever and ever. "Hortense, General Bonaparte is a kind man," I said, reprimanding her gently. "He cares for you sincerely."

"I don't care! I don't care for *him*." Then she hung her head, seeing the stricken look in my eyes. "I'm sorry, Maman!" She took a big breath and exhaled, blowing her cheeks out like a balloon.

I folded her in my arms. "I have to go back. Are you going to be all right?" I felt her nod against my chest. I stroked her soft golden curls. She would need time. We all would. "I'd like you and Eugène to come to Fontainebleau with me next weekend, to see Aunt Désirée and the Marquis," I said, swaying like a mother with an infant in her arms again, lulling her baby to sleep. I felt a thickening in my throat as I recalled the feel of her at birth, her tiny skull, her piercing cry. It *is* going to be all right, I wanted to tell her. (I want to believe it myself.) "Can you come next weekend?" Bonaparte would be gone by then.

The weathered door to the school creaked on its hinges, startling a maid who was perched on a stepladder washing the crystal candelabra. I heard Bonaparte's voice, his lecturing tone. I knocked on the door to the head-mistress's study.

Madame Campan was seated behind her enormous pedestal desk covered with books and stacks of paper. The small room was furnished in the style of the Ancien Régime, ornate, musty and dark. A vase of silk lilies had been placed under the portrait of Queen Marie Antoinette. Two years ago Madame Campan would have lost her life for showing sympathy for the Queen.*

The prim headmistress motioned me in without taking her eyes off her guest. Bonaparte was perched on the edge of a puce Louis XV armchair, holding a teacup and expounding on the uselessness of girls learning Latin. His saucer was swamped—with coffee, I guessed, to judge by the aroma.

When he paused to take a breath, Madame Campan stood to greet me, smoothing the skirt of her gown. Dressed in black, she could have been taken for a maid but for the intricate beaded trim of the head scarf she wore, as if in perpetual mourning. "Forgive me for interrupting," I said, taking the chair beside Bonaparte. He searched my eyes for a clue. This was an awkward situation for him, I knew, a difficult situation for us both. Things were not going according to plan.

"General Bonaparte and I have been discussing education in a Republican

---

* *Madame Campan had been lady-in-waiting to Queen Marie Antoinette, who had been beheaded two-and-a-half years earlier during the Terror, when the monarchy had been abolished and a democratic Republic installed in its place.*

society," Madame Campan said, pulling her head scarf forward. "It isn't often one meets a man who has given this matter thought."

I removed my gloves, tugging on each fingertip. My new gold betrothal ring caught the light. I put my hand over it and said, "General Bonaparte is a philosopher at heart, Madame Campan. He gives all matters thought." I offered Bonaparte a conciliatory little smile.

Bonaparte emptied his teacup and put the cup and saucer on the side table between us. I reached out to keep the table from tipping. "It's late," he told me, pulling out his pocket-watch. "Aren't you going to tell her?"

"Yes," I said, flushing, seeing him through a stranger's eyes: a short, thin man with a sallow complexion, lank hair, shabby attire. A coarse-spoken man with poor manners. An intense, humourless man with fiery eyes—a Corsican, a Revolutionary, an opportunist. My husband. "We have an announcement to make," I told Madame Campan.

Only my closest friends knew that we'd married. I wasn't looking forward to informing my family—nor my acquaintances, for that matter, many of whom would be condescending, I feared, in spite of Bonaparte's recent promotion to General-in-Chief of the Army of Italy. The genteel world would silently judge that I had married beneath me. It would be said that as a widow with two children to educate and place in the world, as an aristocrat without fortune, and indeed, as a woman over the age of thirty, I was desperate. "I—that is, General Bonaparte and I—have married." I took my husband's hand; it was as damp as my own.

Madame Campan sat back abruptly, as if pushed. "Why . . . that's marvellous," she said, with the appearance of sincerity. "What a surprise. But that's marvellous," she repeated. "When?"

"Twenty after ten last night," Bonaparte said, drumming his nails on the arm of his chair. "Twenty-two minutes after, to be exact."

"Well." Madame Campan made a small, dry cough into her fist. "Your children have been very good at keeping this secret, Madame . . . Bonaparte, is it now?" I nodded, grieved to hear my new name spoken, grieved to be giving up the lovely and distinguished name of Beauharnais. "No doubt Hortense and Eugène are . . . ?" She held out her hands, palms up.

I felt my cheeks becoming heated. "That seems to be the problem. General Bonaparte and I came out to Saint-Germain today with the intention of telling my children, but . . ." I tried to swallow.

Madame Campan leaned forward over her desk, her hands tightly clasped. "Hortense does not know?"

"We were going to tell her just now, but she was upset, so I didn't think it wise."

"She was crying," Bonaparte said, shifting his weight.

"How curious," Madame Campan said. "She was so cheerful this morning at breakfast. Do you know why?"

How could I explain without offending Bonaparte? "Perhaps she didn't like seeing me on a man's arm," I said, stretching the truth only a little. "She's so attached to the memory of her father, as you know."

"Oh dear, yes, I see. Your daughter is . . . sensitive." She spoke the word with deliberate care, pressing her hands to her chin in an attitude of prayer. "She feels everything so strongly! Which is why she is gifted in the theatrical arts, I believe, and in the arts in general. She is, as I have often told you, my favourite student." She paused. "May I make a suggestion?"

"Please do! I confess I'm at a loss."

"Perhaps if I told her? Sometimes it's better that way. I could talk to both Hortense and Eugène together."

I glanced at Bonaparte. It was a coward's solution, I knew, but a solution nonetheless. "Good," Bonaparte said, standing.

After, Bonaparte and I stood silently on the bottom stone step of the school, waiting for my coach. "I guess, under the circumstances, we should consider whether or not to visit Eugène now," I said finally, looking out over the fields to Eugène's school next door. On the one hand, I hated not to see him; on the other, I owed four months' tuition. "He's not expecting us," I said, as my carriage creaked to a stop in front of us.

"Back to Paris," Bonaparte told my coachman, opening the carriage door himself. "I approve of Campan's approach," he said, climbing in after me. "She's educated, but she's not a bluestocking. And she's not proud either. I thought she was lady-in-waiting to the Queen."

The carriage pulled through the school gates. I nodded apologetically to the beggarwoman sitting in the dirt with her infant at her breast;

usually I had something for her. "She was," I said, tightening my hat strings. Madame Campan had practically been raised at court. "She was in the Tuileries Palace with the royal family when it was ransacked. A man from Marseille grabbed her and was going to kill her, but someone yelled that they didn't kill women and that saved her."

"She was lucky. I approve that the girls learn to make soup and have to tidy their rooms themselves. I'll enrol my younger sisters."

Bonaparte has four brothers and three sisters—my family now. "Your sisters who are living in Marseille with your mother?" In town now, we were passing the castle, a ruin, like so many.

"I'm going to move them all to Paris."

"That would be lovely," I said, smiling in spite of a pain in my side.

"How much does Campan charge?"

"For the year? Three thousand francs."

"That's ridiculous," he said, opening a book he'd been reading on the way down, the life of Alexandre the Great.

"Eugène's school is even more." And I was paying for my niece Émilie's tuition as well—or trying to. It had been a long time since I'd had any income from home.* My coachman cracked his whip. I let my head fall back against the tufted upholstered seat and closed my eyes, the memory of Hortense's tears coming back to me.

"Not feeling well?"

"I'm fine," I lied.

Now, in the quiet of my little dressing room, I give way to despair. What *am* I going to do? Not long ago I'd promised my daughter that I wouldn't marry Bonaparte. Now she will think I've betrayed her. She is too young to understand what is truly best for her, too young to understand the complexities of love, and of need. Too young to understand that promises made with love may also with love be broken.

* *Josephine's mother, a widow, lived on the family sugar plantation in the Caribbean island of Martinique ("Martinico"), where Josephine had been born and raised. A small percentage of the plantation's earnings constituted Josephine's main source of income—when she received it, that is, which was rarely. Formerly under French rule, the island was now controlled by England.*

*Late evening, I'm not sure how late. Still raining.*

More meetings, visitors. Bonaparte is downstairs still with two of his aides. The smell of cigar smoke fills the air. I'm bathed and dressed for bed, awaiting my husband. This is our last night together before he leaves.

After a fast evening meal (he eats so quickly!), Bonaparte read out loud the letter he'd written to the Directors announcing our marriage. Satisfied, he folded the paper, shoved it into an envelope, dripped wax on it and thumped it with his seal. Then he put the envelope to one side and rummaged through the drawer where the papers were kept, pulling out a sheet of rag bond. He stood and motioned for me to take the seat at the escritoire. "I need a letter to my mother from you."

Of course! I put my lacework aside. He would be seeing his mother in Marseille, informing her of our union—his mother who, according to Corsican custom, should have been asked for permission first. His mother, who would have refused permission had she been asked. His mother, who was opposed to her son's marrying a widow with two children, a woman without a dowry, a woman six years older than her son.

Bonaparte paced, dictating what he thought the letter should say: that she was now my honoured mother, that I was looking forward to meeting her, that I would visit her on my way to Italy to join my husband, that—

There was a sudden rush of pouring rain. I held the raven's tail quill suspended. I was to go to Italy? "But Bonaparte—"

"In six weeks, after I run the Austrians out."

I smiled. Was he joking? I was saved from my dilemma by the sound of a man calling out from the garden, "Open the damned door!"

"Was that Director Barras?" I asked Bonaparte, going to the door to the garden. "It is you!" I kissed my friend's wet cheeks.

"And good evening to you, General Bonaparte, Commander-in-Chief of the Army of Italy," Barras proclaimed in a mock official voice, balancing his gold-tipped walking stick against the wall. "My heartfelt congratulations on your recent appointment." Bonaparte looked sullen, even as the Director shook his hand.*

---

* *The executive authority of the Republic was vested in a council of five directors—"five Majesties." Director Paul Barras was considered the most powerful of the five, and hence the most politically powerful man in the French Republic.*

"Thanks to *you*, Père Barras," I said, draping his military greatcoat over a chair by the fire to dry. Less than a year ago Bonaparte had been unemployed. Barras had been instrumental in getting him a series of promotions, but this last, to General-in-Chief, had taken considerable persuasion on Barras's part. The Directors had been reluctant to grant the command of an army to a Corsican.

"Not bad, not bad," Barras said, turning Bonaparte like a mannequin, examining his new uniform. "A little big at the shoulders perhaps?" His own jacket seemed a little tight on him, I noticed; the tails split open at the back. "But why these frayed epaulettes?"

"What were you doing out in the garden, Paul?" I asked, changing the subject. I'd brought up the matter of the epaulettes earlier, but without success. (Bonaparte is so stubborn!)

"I knocked and no one answered. How you can manage on such a small staff, Rose, is beyond me," Barras said, running his hand through his thinning hair. (Dyed black?)

"I'm looking for a lady's maid, in fact." On learning that I was going to marry a Revolutionary, my former maid had quit. "If you hear of one—"

"Her name is Josephine now," Bonaparte said.

"You're changing your Christian name as well?" Barras frowned, considering. "*Josephine*—yes, I like that, Rose, it rather suits you. As does your gown, I must say. Don't you look lovely. I do know of a maid though. My aunt was telling me of a girl. But only one? You need at least three more. Enough of this Republican simplicity. Republican romanticism, I call it. And speaking of romance, how *are* my lovebirds this miserable evening?"

"Just fine," I said with more enthusiasm than I felt.

"The Directory can only provide me with eight thousand francs," Bonaparte said.

Barras flung back his tails and sat down. (Was he wearing a corset? Barras, at forty, was becoming vain.) "I know, it's not enough, but at least it's not the counterfeit stuff England is flooding us with in an effort to ruin our economy." Raising his hands to heaven. "As if our economy weren't already ruined."

Bonaparte wasn't humoured. "How am I supposed to feed and equip an army on only eight thousand?" He drummed the chessboard with his fingers, sending two pieces tumbling to the floor.

"Prayer?" Barras caught my eye and smiled, his beguiling lopsided grin. "After all, it's legal now—well, almost."

"Barras, you do amuse," I said, offering him a glass of the Clos-Vougeot burgundy I knew he favoured.

"No, thank you—I just came by to drop off the list you asked for, General," he said, handing a folded-up sheet of paper to Bonaparte.

"But these are only the names of the generals," Bonaparte said, scanning the list. "I asked for the names of all the officers in the Army of Italy."

"Even the captains?" Barras stood, reaching for his walking stick.

"Even their aides."

"You're leaving tomorrow evening? I'll get my secretary to bring it over to you in the morning." He punched Bonaparte's shoulder in a soldierly fashion. "Best of luck liberating the Italians from the Austrians, General, as you so nobly put it. Don't neglect to liberate their paintings and sculptures while you're at it, as well as all that gold in the Church coffers. That's where you'll find the money to feed your soldiers." He threw his walking stick into the air and caught it, looking to see whether I had noticed.

Have to go—I hear Bonaparte's footsteps on the stairs.


*March 11, morning, a light rain.*
Sleepy this morning, but smiling. Bonaparte approaches conjugal relations with the fervour of a religious convert and the curiosity of a scientist. He's intent on trying every position described in a book he found at a stall by the river. There are over a hundred, he claims, and we're only on position nine.

Indeed, I'm learning never to predict how things might be with him. He can be imperious and insensitive one minute, tender and devoted the next. Last night we talked and talked . . .

"Like foam on the wave," he told me, caressing my breast.

"I like that," I said, watching the watery undulations that the firelight was making on the wall, thinking of the sea.

"The poetry or this . . . ?"

"That was poetry? *And* that." His hands are soft, his touch surprisingly gentle.

"It's a line from *Carthon* by Ossian. *Her breasts were like foam on the wave, and her eyes like stars of light.*"

It took me a moment to realize who he meant. Bonaparte pronounced the Scottish bard's name like "ocean."

"Alexandre the Great chose Homer as his poet, Julius Caesar chose Virgil—and I have chosen Ossian."

"Bonaparte, you disturb me when you talk like that."

"Why? Don't you like that progression: Alexandre, Caesar . . . *Napoleon*?"

"I'm serious. Can't you be a normal man?"

"Aren't I a 'normal' man?" He pressed against me.

"Well, in that respect, yes." In that respect, absolutely. Except that Bonaparte was insatiable.

"Can I tell you something?"

"Of course!" I was enjoying the quiet intimacy of our talk, this late-night pillow confession.

"Sometimes I think I'm the reincarnation of Alexandre the Great." He glanced at me. "Now you'll think me mad."

"I notice you read about Alexandre the Great a lot," I said, not knowing exactly how to respond to such a statement. It was true—there were things about Bonaparte that seemed strange to me.

"You don't believe in that sort of thing?"

"Sometimes: But not always. When I was a girl, a fortune-teller predicted I would be unhappily married and then widowed."

"So you see? The prediction came true."

"Yes." My first marriage had certainly been an unhappy one. "But she also predicted that I would become Queen."

He propped himself up on one elbow. "That's interesting."

"More than a queen, she said." But not for very long. "So *you* see, predictions are often just foolishness."

"Let's be foolish now."

"*Again?*" I smiled, wrapping my legs around him.

"You have no idea, do you, how beautiful you are. You are the most beautiful woman in Paris."

"Bonaparte, don't be silly."

"I'm serious! Everything about you enchants me. Don't laugh. Sometimes, watching you, I think I'm in the presence of an angel come down to earth."

I stroked his fine, thin hair, looked into his great grey eyes. I felt confused by the intensity of his feeling. I have never been so loved before. My first husband scorned me; Bonaparte worships me. It makes me want to weep. The truth, the terrible truth, is that I feel lonely in my husband's arms. If I am an angel, then why does my heart not open?


Throughout the night, I heard the clock chime one, two, three o'clock. At four bells, Bonaparte wasn't there. I listened for the sound of his footsteps, watched for a flicker of candlelight, but the house was dark, silent. I tried to go back to sleep, but could not, night thoughts haunting me. Night doubts, night fears. Finally I put on my dressing gown, my slippers, and with a candle walked the rooms. From the half-storey landing I saw a light below. I slipped down the stairs and went to the open door of the study. Bonaparte was there, leaning over the octagonal table, holding a lantern above a map. I watched him like a thief. What did he see, looking over that map? He looked so intent. What were his thoughts, his dreams?

"Bonaparte?" I called out, finally.

He looked up, startled. "Josephine," he whispered wondrously, as if he had found me.


*Early afternoon.*

What commotion! I have only a minute. Tonight Bonaparte leaves for the south, to take command of the Army of Italy. The entire household is engaged in frantic activity. My scullery maid is taking in his breeches (he balked at the expense of a tailor). I asked my manservant to put a proper polish on his riding boots and the cook to prepare a basket of travelling provisions—hardtack, hard-cooked eggs, pickled pork brawn, beets. I sent my coachman to the wine merchant for a case of Chambertin—an undrinkable wine, in my estimation, but the one Bonaparte insists on (it's cheap)—and to a parfumerie for the almond meal and rose soap he likes to use on his face. I must remember to boil elecampane root in springwater for his rash. And what else? What have I forgotten? Oh, the—

*A half-hour later—if that!*

Bonaparte burst into the upstairs drawing room and took a seat. I knew what his little smile meant. I told my scullery maid, "Agathe, perhaps I could have a word with my husband—alone."

Bonaparte's rumpled linen shirt was off even before we got to my bedchamber. "Junot and Murat will be here in fifteen minutes."

"That doesn't give much time."

"I can be quick," he said, as if this were an accomplishment.

I turned my back to him so that he could unfasten the buttons on my gown. He ran his cold hands over my breasts, pressed against me. I turned to him and kissed him. He is a small man, but vigorous. And quick, as he said.

"I'd like you to wash," he said, disentangling his pantaloons.

"I was going to." I was taken aback by his soldier bluntness.

Naked (small body, big head), he climbed into the bed and pulled the bed sheet up over him, looking at me expectantly. I went into my dressing room and re-emerged in a gauze nightgown trimmed with violet ribbons. "Take it off," he told me.

I did so reluctantly (Bonaparte is six years my junior) and lay down beside him. "Position ten?" I asked, teasing.

"Twenty-three." He ran his hand over my breast, my belly. "I've jumped ahead."

I smiled. Was he joking? (It is so hard to know with him.)

Then he sat up, said, "Close your eyes. You just lie there." I did as instructed. I felt him crawl down to the end of the bed, felt his hands part my legs, felt the warmth of his breath, his . . .

Mon *Dieu*. I swallowed, took a sharp breath.

Bonaparte was curiously unrushed. A voluptuous warmth came over me. I curled my fingers through his hair as waves of pleasure rose in my blood.

After, I lay for a moment, catching my breath, drying my cheeks on the covering sheet. Bonaparte was sitting on his haunches, regarding me with an awed expression. Then he grinned. "Well, that's the best one so far," he said, swinging his feet onto the floor.

"Come back here," I said, grabbing his hand.


*9:00 P.M.*

A kiss and he is gone.

I hear the crackling of the fire, my scullery maid singing tunelessly in the bath chamber, the heavy tread of my old manservant's wooden shoes on the narrow stairs, carrying up buckets of hot water for my bath. My pug dog Fortuné sniffs in all the corners, looking for "the intruder." I listen to the busy clicking of his little nails on the parquet floor.

The sounds of normal life, I realize. But for the battered tin snuffbox forgotten on the window ledge, the dog-eared volume of Ossian's *Carthon* on the mantel, one would not know that Bonaparte had ever been here. This man, who has come into my life like a whirlwind, has just as suddenly gone, leaving me breathless, dazed . . . and confused, I confess.

## *In which I break the news to my family & friends*

*March 17, 1796—Paris. A bright spring day.*

I've a new maid. She curtsied at the door, lifting the hem of her linen shift. Her long chestnut locks were pulled into a tight braid that hung down her back. She is young, not yet of an age to pin up her hair. "Louise Compoint, Madame," she said, taking in the furnishings. "But I am called Lisette."

I slipped a finger through Fortuné's collar and asked her to come forward. Her mother had been a maid-of-the-wardrobe, she informed me, her father unknown. She'd been "adopted" by the aristocratic family her mother worked for and educated in a convent. Now her mother was dead and the aristocrats had fled during the Revolution. "I can wick lanterns, Madame, as well as dress hair. I understand clear starch and my needlework is good. My mother taught me well."

"This is a small household," I told her. "My lady's maid must serve also as a parlour maid and even as a kitchen maid, should the need arise."

"Yes, Madame. I've churned butter and blackleaded grates. I can also let blood. My mistress was often ailing," she explained, in answer to my startled look.

She is only seventeen, but I liked her forthright spirit. She had a natural grace. "We are a Republican family, Lisette. I will treat you with respect; I expect the same in kind. I permit no followers, and if any man makes advances, I expect you to inform me. You are allowed a half-day off a week to do as you please. Your room is in the basement. It is small, but it has a window and it will be your own."

"Yes, Madame!" Her teeth are excellent.

*March 20, just past noon—still in Paris.*
It was early, not yet ten in the morning, when I heard the children in the foyer. I stood and prepared to face them, clasping my hands to hide my betrothal ring. Nothing has changed, I was going to tell them; marrying Bonaparte did not mean I loved them less.

". . . and then my horse *jumped* the cart." Eugène lumbered into the drawing room with the grace of a heifer. Hortense followed, frowning, pulling at her hat strings.

My daughter greeted me with reserve, stiffening as I embraced her. "My hat, Maman," she said, pulling off her crêpe bonnet, leaving on the white lace cap underneath. I knew by her manner, her averted eyes, that she was angry with me.

"I jumped the grey mare." Eugène smelled of soap and perspiration. I pushed a curl out of his eyes. At fourteen, he would soon disdain his mother's touch, I knew.

"But what's this about jumping carts?" I reproached him.

My new maid came to the door. She looked comely in my cast-off gown of peach chintz. "You rang, Madame Bonaparte?"

*Bonaparte.* Hortense and Eugène exchanged glances. I motioned to Lisette to come forward in order to introduce her. She curtsied to them both. A flush coloured my son's cheeks. Hortense dipped her head, but it was clear her thoughts were elsewhere, her eyes darting about the room—looking for evidence, I realized, of Bonaparte.

"Thank you, Lisette. If you could bring us some hot chocolate? And the comfits." Hortense has a weakness for sweets.

"Maman, it was safe. The mare can jump five feet easily," Eugène said, falling into the down armchair, his legs sprawling.

Hortense lowered herself onto the chair with the horsehair seat, her shoulders back, her posture faultless (for once). I took a seat by the harp. "I understand that Madame Campan has talked to you both about my marriage to General Bonaparte," I said—too bluntly, I thought. Not the way I'd rehearsed this speech in my mind!

"Four days ago," Hortense answered, enunciating precisely.

"Yes, she told us. We know all about it," Eugène said, squirming.

"I want you to know that General Bonaparte cares deeply about both of you." I felt I'd handled things poorly, that I'd let them down. I wanted to reassure them.

"Maman?"

I sat forward eagerly. "Yes, Eugène?"

"Can I go to the Luxembourg Palace this morning, before we leave for Fontainebleau? Director Barras told me I could ride his horses any time I wanted."

I sat back, stupefied. Horses? Was that all my son could think of? How confusing this situation was! "No, Eugène," I said, making an effort to sound calm. "I have another plan. Today is Palm Sunday. I was thinking we would go to mass together."

Hortense looked surprised. (And pleased, I observed with relief.)

"Church?" Eugène groaned, sliding down into the depths of his chair.

"We'll walk," I insisted, standing.

I was surprised by the number of people standing in front of Église Saint-Pierre, enjoying the spring sun before going inside. Not only was it a Décadi* *and* a Sunday (a rare concurrence), but Palm Sunday as well. For once everyone could enjoy a feast-day together—Catholics and Atheists, Royalists and Republicans alike. I put my arms around my children as we climbed the steps. If there could be peace in the nation, then surely there could be peace in my little family.

---

*A new calendar had been established during the Revolution. The ten-day week ended in Décadi, the official day of rest. The names of the months were changed as well: Vendémiaire (the month of vintage), Brumaire (the month of fog), Frimaire (the month of frost) and so forth. Nevertheless, many continued to observe the old calendar, causing considerable confusion.*

*Fontainebleau.*

We weren't able to leave for Fontainebleau until shortly after two, so it was quite late by the time we pulled into the courtyard of the Beauharnais home in Fontainebleau. "I expected you earlier, Rose," Aunt Désirée said, patting at her powdered hair, which was dressed in fat sausage rolls. Her immaculate house smelled of beeswax and turpentine.

"We got off to a late start," I explained, keeping an eye on the children to make sure they took off their muddy boots before walking on the carpet. "We went to church." I knew that this explanation would please.

"Is Grandpapa awake?" Hortense asked.

"Go! Go, my pets! He's been waiting for you both." The children raced up the stairs, pushing and pulling at each other. I did not attempt to quiet them; I was relieved to hear them laughing.

"I've been most anxious for your arrival, Rose," my aunt said, gesturing to me to take a seat. "I have excellent news." She perched on the edge of the green brocade sofa, nervously jiggling an enormous ring of iron keys.

"Oh?" A sick feeling passed through me. I'd come with news myself, and I feared my aunt would not consider it in the least bit excellent.

"My husband died!" she said, crossing herself.

"Monsieur Renaudin?" I had no reason to regret the man's passing. He and my aunt had separated before I'd even been born. Stories of the evil Monsieur Renaudin had excited my imagination as a child—stories of the man who had tried to poison my aunt, and who had (it was later discovered) been imprisoned for trying to poison his own father.

"And so the Marquis has asked for my hand in marriage." Aunt Désirée made this announcement with a girlish flutter of her eyelids.

"That's wonderful!" I said, repressing a smile. The Marquis was over eighty years old—my aunt, a quarter century younger—and I doubted that marriage was much on his mind. "And I take it you've consented?" My religious, proper and socially sensitive aunt had suffered, I knew, from living with the Marquis all these years without the Church's blessing.

"But Father Renard insists we wait a year—out of respect. I'm terrified the Marquis will die before he makes an honest woman of me," she said, picking up the loose sofa pillows one by one, as if looking for something.

She found a coin under one of the pillows and, frowning, put it back. (A test of her servants, I realized.) "So I told Father Renard I'd donate a new candelabra to the church and he finally agreed to six months. I know where I can get a used one for a fraction of what I'd pay in Paris. A good washing down with vinegar will make it like new." The cushions back in place, she pulled a tangle of crumpled handkerchiefs from the depths of her bosom and set to work smoothing them out one at a time on her lap. "And so, Rose, tell me: how are you?"

"Fine! I have news as well." The words came out louder than I'd intended, and far bolder than I felt.

"Has your cow calved, dear?" She put a pastel green handkerchief aside and stuffed the remaining ones back into the crevice of her ample bosom.

"No," I said, taken aback. "At least, not yet. No, I've . . ." My heart was pounding against my ribs! "I've married, Aunt Désirée," I said finally.

Aunt Désirée was holding the green handkerchief to the light, examining it for stains. "Did you say *married*, Rose?" she asked, turning toward me.

I nodded, disquieted by her calm manner.

"Why . . . that's wonderful," she said, crossing herself, "but to whom?"

"To a military man by the name of Napoleon Bonaparte. He's—"

"What type of name is that?" my aunt demanded, frowning suspiciously.

"It's a Corsican name, Aunt Désirée, and—"

"You married a *Corsican*?" She reached for a brass bell and rang it vigorously. "But Rose, Corsicans are . . . they're barbarians, they live like Gypsies. They steal, murder, *lie*—they have no morals whatsoever! And they don't speak a proper language, you can't understand a thing they say."

Fortunately, a parlour maid in a frilled cap appeared just then at the door. "Salts!" my aunt commanded.

"We're out of salts, Madame," the maid stuttered, wiping her palms on her white bibbed apron. "But we do have hysteric water, Madame."*
Aunt Désirée snorted with impatience.

* Hysteric water: a mixture that was said to cure uterine disorders—"an excellent water to prevent fits, or to be taken in faintings." It was made of a mixture of roots of zedoary (similar to ginger), lovage and peony, parsnip seeds, mistletoe, myrrh, castor oil and dried millipedes steeped in mugwort tea and brandy.

"Aunt Désirée, he's not like that at all," I said, as soon as the maid disappeared. "His family is old nobility, and he was educated at the best military schools in France. He's very fond of me, and *especially* fond of the children," I added with feeling.

"Monied nobility, Rose?" With a squinty-eyed look.

"He has a good position as a commanding general," I said, avoiding her question. Not only did Bonaparte have no money, but our marriage contract stipulated that we contribute equally to all our household expenses. "He will be able to help Eugène in his military career." This was my trump card. I was depending on it.

"They made a Corsican a general?" Aunt Désirée demanded, attempting to fan herself with the limp green handkerchief. "A general of *what*?"

"Monsieur Bonaparte is General-in-Chief of the Army of Italy," I said, using "monsieur" in a shameless attempt to appease.

"I've never heard of an Army of Italy. Is it French even?"

"Yes, of course!" I exclaimed—although everything I'd learned about the Army of Italy had led me to believe that it could hardly be called an army at all, more a ragtag collection of drifters and petty criminals, hungry and without uniforms, much less muskets. "He left to take command two days after the ceremony." The wedding seemed like a dream to me now, like something that might not have happened.

"A church ceremony, Rose?" she asked, pulling and twisting the green handkerchief, worrying it.

"No," I admitted. Bonaparte was anti-Church, but I wasn't going to tell her that.

I heard a sniff. Oh dear! Was she weeping? Dismayed, I reached out to comfort her, but she turned on me like a hawk. "Rose, how could you?" she wept, dabbing her cheeks. "How could you have married a man with such a horrible name!"

I'm writing this now in Aunt Désirée's guest room in Fontainebleau. I talked to her at length, trying to calm her. I finally persuaded her to take a glass of hysteric water and lie down. (I had a glass as well.) I regret the way I've handled things, but at the same time, in coming to Bonaparte's defence, in trying to persuade my aunt of the wisdom of what I've done, I began to convince myself. Bonaparte had the words "To Destiny" engraved on the inside of my betrothal ring, for he believes in fate, believes that we are fated. Are we? I wonder. I can only hope that somehow, someday, fate will prove that I have done the right thing. For my family's sake, I dearly hope so.

*March 21—Paris. Almost noon.*
I received my first letter from Bonaparte this morning. So soon! It took me a long time to make out the words, and there are still parts I can't read. Bonaparte's handwriting is as impassioned as his words, which are ardent and tender.

The letter was addressed to Citoyenne Bonaparte in care of Citoyenne Beauharnais, as if Citoyenne Bonaparte were a guest in my house, someone separate from me—which is how I feel yet.

*March 25, sunny, a beautiful day.*
A good (and productive) visit with Thérèse, followed by an amusing few hours with my delightfully eccentric friends.

Thérèse arrived early in her elegant little barouche which she drove *herself* (practising, she explained, to enter the races that would be starting up again in the Bois de Boulogne). "And so how is Madame Bonaparte this fine afternoon?" was the first thing she said. The exotic scent of neroli oil filled my antechamber. She bent her knees to make it easier for Lisette to take her fur-lined cape.

"You're wearing a wig?" I asked, regarding my friend with astonishment. Under a jaunty hat adorned with a heron feather was a mass of blonde ringlets.

"Only twenty francs." She turned her head from side to side to make the curls bounce. "So I bought twenty-seven—and all of them blonde." She pulled both her hat and her wig off, and dug her nails into her scalp. Her own black hair was tightly braided and coiled. "You haven't answered my question," she said, holding up a finger.

"Madame *Bonaparte* is just fine, thank you. I already got a letter from my husband, in fact," I told her. "But there are parts I can't make out." I pulled the letter out of a desk cubby and showed it to her, pointing out the indecipherable passage.

"Mon Dieu, I see what you mean. What a mess," she said, squinting. "I think it's 'perpetual.' 'You are the *perpetual* object of my thoughts.' He signs himself B.P.?"

"For Buona Parte . . . I think."

"Oh la la," she said, reading on. "He's *madly* in love with you."

"That's just the way Corsicans are," I said (flushing), taking the letter back.

"No doubt," Thérèse said with a teasing look. "And your children?" she asked, helping herself to an aniseed-zested licorice comfit. "What do they think of their new papa?"

I made a face. "Hortense burst into tears."

"Because you married?"

"Just because she saw me *with* Bonaparte!"

"If you like, I could have a word with your daughter."

"Madame Campan already did," I quickly assured her. My oh-so-proper daughter disapproved of my friend Thérèse, separated from her husband. *And* Barras. *And* any number of others, for that matter, including her own godmother!*

"Speaking of your daughter, I had a brilliant idea. What about Director Reubell's eldest son?"

I looked at her blankly.

"As a husband—for Hortense."

"But she's not yet even thirteen, Thérèse. And since when have you become a matchmaker?"

"Since I suggested you to the Corsican. Seriously," she said, "the Reubells may be a merchant family, but they're wealthy. And, of course, Reubell being a Director . . . that counts for something, I suppose? They'd likely be willing. Hortense has a noble bloodline, after all."

---

* Fanny Beauharnais, a bohemian poet, is related to Josephine through her first husband. She is Émilie's grandmother and Hortense's godmother. She is being sued at this time by a young woman claiming to be her illegitmate daughter.

"Director Reubell is a radical Jacobin," I said, checking to see whether we had everything we needed: quills, ink, a folio of paper, the files. "An aristocratic genealogy wouldn't make any difference to him one way or—"

Thérèse laughed. "You're joking?"

"Well, in any case she's going to need a dowry."

"How much do you have?"

"Five."

"Five thousand? That's *all*?"

Five thousand in debts was more like it.

"But what about the Island property?"

I shrugged. "With Martinico in British hands, I don't stand to inherit a sou."

Thérèse pinched her cheeks together, considering. "Mind you, anyone can make a million these days. Why don't you get into military supplies? If the Revolutionaries can do it, anybody can." She looked at me. "You find that amusing?"

"Making the small deal now and then is one thing; supplying the military is on another scale altogether."

"The concept is the same—all you need is nerve. I noticed that you beat those two bankers at billiards the other night—the wealthiest men in the French Republic and you humbled them. *That's* nerve, if you ask me."

I smiled. *Well.*

"And look at your Masonic connections, your government connections, your financial connections."

"Those are *social* connections."

"I think you're underrating yourself. You're in an ideal position to make a small fortune, if not a large one. And face it, a fortune is not such a terrible thing. The Revolutionaries are raking it in as fast as they can. They figure it's time for a feast after such a long famine, and you have to admit, they've got a point. Barras says anyone who doesn't get into military supplies is a fool. It's fast money, it's big money, and there's virtually no gamble involved."

"So long as one has the contacts and the money to invest."

"Really, Rose—Josephine! Sorry!—I doubt very much that that would be a problem. After all, you have dear Père Barras, don't you? King of the Profiteers."

I raised my eyebrows. King of the Rotten was what most people called him. "Very well, Mama Tallita, I'll consider." I opened the file marked "Active" and looked at the clock. "We have only one hour."

A review of our projects proved discouraging. We have yet to succeed in getting Citoyen Mérode erased, even though he was put on the List* due to his cousin's emigration. We *have* succeeded, at last, in getting Citoyenne Daco and her son released from prison, but Citoyens Mercier and Pacout remain. Citoyen Pinson, sadly, died. We'll see what we can do to help his widow and five children. In addition to our charities, eleven men and women have approached us for help getting their names taken off the List, getting jobs, getting released from jail. In light of the growing number of requests we decided to meet every week, before the ladies gather to play cards.

"Speaking of whom," I said, hearing a carriage pull into the courtyard.

"Ah, it's the Glories." Glories? "You haven't heard that? That's what Barras calls us," Thérèse explained. "Because we dress for the glory of the Lord."

Glories indeed!** Before I could tell Lisette to please show them in, they'd entered, filling the dining room with their exotic scents, their fluttering fans and bobbing plumes, their silken ruffles swirling with all the erotic sensuality of a harem.

---

* *The List was a listing of émigrés and relations of émigrés forbidden from entering France. Having left the country because of the Revolution, émigrés and even their families were considered enemies of the Republic. Those listed lost all civil rights, had their property confiscated and risked execution if discovered on French soil. The names numbered over a hundred thousand. To be "erased" meant to have your name taken off the List.*

** *In addition to Josephine and Thérèse, the group included Fortunée Hamelin, Madame de Châteaurenaud (called Minerva), and Madame de Crény. Fortunée Hamelin (nineteen) is a créole like Josephine. She is famous for her wit, her daring (un)dress and her dancing. Minerva (thirty-six) is a voluptuous woman known for a mild, sweet manner and an interest in the occult. Madame de Crény (thirty-five), met Josephine when Josephine's first husband, Alexandre, forced her to live in a convent. Thérèse Tallien (twenty-three) is one of the famous beauties of the day. A wonderful teller of stories, she describes herself as a comedian.*

"Ah, it appears we've interrupted a charity meeting," tiny Madame de Crény said, the ends of an enormous red and yellow striped bow flopping down into her eyes like rabbit ears.

"We were just finishing," I said, gathering up the papers.

"Is it true you married the Corsican?" Minerva asked, trying to keep her pug dog from sniffing at my pug dog, who was growling menacingly.

I gave Thérèse an accusing look. "I didn't tell them," she protested. "I'm innocent."

"Hardly!" Fortunée Hamelin was half-naked in spite of the chill spring day; her gown of India gauze shot with silver revealed more than it concealed. (She boasted that her entire ensemble could fit into her embroidered pocket of Irish linen.)

"You must not blame Thérèse," Madame de Crény said, following me into the drawing room where the game table had been set up. "Director Barras is the guilty party."

"As usual." Fortunée propped her mule-heeled slippers on a footstool, displaying to advantage what are generally considered well-turned ankles. (She was wearing drawers!*)

"He has no willpower, the poor dear," Minerva lisped softly.

"And to think he's running this country."

"He *is* running this country." Madame de Crény perched on a chair, swinging her feet.

"Do you think he is dyeing his hair?"

"It must be that opera singer I've seen at his receptions."

"More likely it's her younger brother." (Laughter.)

"*And* he's wearing a corset."

"Just when we ladies have taken ours off."

"*That's* liberation."

"So, Rose, where exactly *is* this husband of yours?" Minerva asked, peering into the study.

"Her husband who loves her *madly.*"

"Thérèse!"

"How romantic."

* Drawers—or pantaloons—were considered men's wear, worn only by women of ill-repute.

"How inconvenient."

"He's in Nice, taking command of the Army of Italy," I explained with pride.

"So are we in an interesting condition yet?"

"It's a little early, don't you think? He left two days after we were married."

"It only takes me one minute," Thérèse groaned.

"And look at me, twelve babies," Minerva boasted. "My husband only has to smile at me and I'm in an interesting condition."

"We've noticed."

"*I've* noticed that most of the women of Paris are in an interesting condition these days."

"It's the style—even virgins are stuffing their gowns with pillows."

"Did you hear? Even Madame Lebon is in an interesting condition."

"No."

"Yes. *Finally.* After five years of marriage, she went to a German doctor. He told her that barrenness is cured by the presence of immoderate heat in a woman accompanied by turgescence."

"Pardon?"

"I think what it means is that a woman must . . . you know, *spasm.*"

"In order to have a child?"

"Apparently, this is a common German belief."

"I've never 'spasmed' with my husband, and believe me, I've had quite a few children by him."

"What's a spasm?"

"The doctor told Madame Lebon that if she were . . ." Fortunée rubbed her fingers together. "Then that proved a spasm had occurred."

"Hardly!"

"What is this, Rose? It is a wig?" Minerva picked up the mass of ringlets.

"Rose is now Josephine," Thérèse said, slipping on the golden curls.

"You're changing your first name?"

"Bonaparte wants me to."

"I thought his name was *Buon*aparte."

"He's changing it." Everything was changing!

"Oh, a wig could be handy. No one would recognize you," Fortunée said.

"I bought twenty-seven of them. Only twenty francs each, so I should be able to make a nice profit on them."

"Real hair. Nice! But why so cheap?"

"Well . . ." Thérèse grimaced. "That's the thing."

"Oh no," Minerva whispered.

"The . . . guillotine?" Madame de Crény squeaked.

"Hair is hair, isn't it?" Fortunée Hamelin said with a shrug. "I'll take three."

Lisette entered the room with a tray of clattering glasses and an open bottle of champagne. She placed it on the side table and stood, smoothing the folds of her ruffled tulle apron.

"Speculation? Loo?" We settled on Speculation, Fortunée insisting on an ante of fifty francs to begin with, "to get the blood racing."

"Oh, I feel lucky today!" Madame de Crény said, wiggling her silver-painted fingernails before shuffling the cards.

Thérèse raised her glass, her ringlets bouncing. "To Josephine Bonaparte."

*In which the past continues to haunt me*

*Mid-afternoon, March 28, 1796.*
Good news: thanks to Barras, the sequester has finally been lifted on Alexandre's property.*

*March 31.*
The Department of Confiscated Goods SW 24 is located in a former convent on Rue de Grenelle, not far from the Invalides. I presented my letter of authorization to the man at the gate, and then again inside to a man sitting at a desk playing solitaire. He held my document to the eight lit candles in a silver candelabra, squinting at the seals and stamps before pulling a ring of keys from a desk drawer (lying next to a pistol) and barking at a man with a matted beard snoring on a sofa: "Gaspard, you dolt!" Taking up a tin lantern, the yawning Gaspard gestured for me to follow him up a set of narrow, dark stairs and through a series of rooms, each one filled from floor to ceiling with crates labelled Comte this, Marquise that—the boxed remnants of lives lost, lives taken.

In the last of the rooms, Gaspard unlatched unpainted wooden shutters over a small window, illuminating a harpsichord, several (lovely) harps, statues, large oil portraits of men on horseback, women with their children . . . I turned away from their staring eyes. It was only by chance that I had survived.

---

* *Josephine's first husband had been convicted (falsely) of conspiring to get out of prison. He was executed, and his property confiscated.*

"316, 317, 318 . . . 322." Gaspard indicated a line of rough-hewn wooden crates on the floor, each labelled Vicomte A. de Beauharnais.

"Is this all there is?" I asked. Seven crates.

*April 1.*
I am overcome with the vapours. I asked Lisette to go for Dr. Cucé, to bleed me, but she offered to do it herself, from my foot. I owed the doctor money, and so I took the chance. Lisette made the cut quickly and with confidence; the bright blood flowed into the chipped porcelain bowl. I feel faint, but pure.

*Late afternoon.*
Stronger now. What happened:

I had risen early in order to help clear a spot in the study for the crates to go. But shortly after eleven, Lisette announced a caller: Louis Bonaparte.

"A young man, heavy-lidded eyes. Italian, I think." Lisette has become forthright in her descriptions.

I was puzzled. I'd never heard of a Louis Bonaparte.

I ran my hand over my hair. I'd dressed in a gown of washed-out blue gauze, the flounce in need of mending—appropriate for a day of going through the musty crates, which I expected to be delivered at any time. "Tell him I'll be a moment," I said, pulling on a pair of silk stockings. I slipped a blue velvet pelisse on over my chemise and rouged my cheeks. An embroidered muslin veil thrown over my shaggy hair gave me a fashionably Roman look. *Bien.*

The young man stood to greet me, slipping a green leather book into the inside pocket of his tailcoat. It was Luigi, Bonaparte's young brother, the brother he regarded as a son! "Napoleon told me to change my name to Louis," he explained. He looked to be Eugène's age, although I understand him to be a year or two older. "I beg you to forgive my calling at such an early hour, Citoyenne Bonaparte," he said respectfully and with a melancholy air. He'd been at a spa in Châtillon and was now on his way to Nice, he explained, to join his brother's staff, as aide-de-camp.

I welcomed him warmly and asked if he would care for a coffee, tea or small beer. He confessed to a longing for my Island coffee, which his brother had told him about. "Alas, the last of my Martinico beans are gone—but my cook, who is himself from the Islands, has discovered an excellent substitute bean from the southern Americas." I rang for Lisette, requesting coffee, chocolate liqueur and a basket of the biscuits my cook had made this morning.

We talked of the spa he had been at, his coming voyage, the danger of ruffians on the roads, the performance of Voltaire's *Brutus* he'd seen at the Théâtre de la Republique the night before. We agreed that the great actor Talma was "diverting beyond moderation" (his words). I told him Talma was an acquaintance of mine, and that he had even once lived in this very house, which astonished him—perhaps because it is so modest an abode. In short, a pleasant conversation.

It was just as Lisette appeared with the coffee that I heard Fortuné barking out on the verandah. "I'm having some things delivered," I explained, standing. "No, please, *stay*, finish your coffee."

Louis downed his coffee and stood, taking a biscuit. "I must be going in any case," he said, accompanying me to the front steps. Two carters were unloading one of the crates—a heavy one, I gathered, from their strained expressions.

"You've made a purchase of a National Property?" Louis asked, observing the seals.

"In a manner of speaking," I said, not wishing to explain that these crates contained my first husband's effects.


The crates practically filled the tiny study. My manservant shifted a few so I could squeeze between them. Then he got a crowbar and began prying off the tops.

The first crate contained household items: china, linens, musty bed curtains. There were surprisingly few personal possessions: an inkstand, an oak box with mother-of-pearl inlay, a blue glass jar of metal military buttons. Some clothing: a pair of riding boots that Eugène might be able to use. Four riding crops, one with a gold handle. But no pistols or swords—stolen, no doubt. And no silver, either. A leather portfolio contained financial records, letters of correspondence. I put these aside for Aunt Désirée and the Marquis. (I did not wish to read them.) And, as I feared, a velvet bag of small linens, garters, a mother-of-pearl hair ornament: Alexandre's "trophies." I threw these away, but then perversely retrieved the hair ornament, which I fancied.

And then there were the books: four large crates. Water had damaged one of them: the pages of the texts were swollen and dusty with mildew. I instructed my manservant to burn these in the garden.

In the remaining crates were a number of valuable texts:
-a complete set of Diderot's encyclopedia, the pages uncut
-the complete works of Voltaire
-a lovely edition of Cicero's *Treatise on Laws* with an embossed morocco cover and hand-stitched spine
-a folio Bible, much thumbed (surprisingly)
-Rousseau's *Discourse on the Origin of Inequality among Men*

There were a number of books about Freemasonry, the natural world, art and architecture. At the bottom of the last crate were a few novels (including, in plain wrapper, *The Life of Frétillon the Wriggler*). And at the last, a sheaf of music and an oak box of artist's supplies. These would be for Hortense.

But other than that, little of value. My children's inheritance.


*Dear Rose,*

*I will be coming to Paris to purchase fabric for my wedding dress on the 4th of April. Will you be in? Perhaps I could pick up the correspondence you mentioned. I was heartbroken to learn that all that lovely silver was missing. Ruffians! It was in the Beauharnais family for six generations.*

*Your loving Aunt Désirée*


*April 4, late afternoon.*
Aunt Désirée hadn't even taken her gloves off before she began to lecture. "Your scullery maid should have disappeared when I came into

the room," she said, running her fingers over my shelves to see if they'd been properly dusted. "She should avert her eyes. And your lady's maid is wearing silk. It makes a rustling sound that is suggestive to men. There will be trouble, I guarantee it. Servants should wear only linen of a dull colour, and certainly no powder. My priest gave me an excellent book on service. I'm reading it out loud to my servants after our evening prayers. You do say a prayer with them all at the end of the day?"

"Things have changed, Aunt Désirée," I said weakly.

She gave me a scathing look. "Rose, my dear child, I had hoped that by now you would have realized that this foolishness about equality has nothing whatsoever to do with servants. It is God's will that they serve us."

She stayed for one hour. I've collapsed, exhausted. At least she didn't get onto the subject of my Corsican husband, "the barbarian."


*Nice, 10 Germinal*

*I haven't spent a day without loving you; not a night has gone by without my taking you in my arms. I haven't even taken a cup of tea without cursing the glory and ambition that separate me from the soul of my life. As I attend to business, at the head of the troops, while touring the camps, you alone are in my heart.*

*And yet you address me formally! How could you write such a letter? And from the 23rd to the 26th, four days passed. What were you doing that you could not write your husband? My spirit is sad; my heart is enslaved; my imagination frightens me.*

*Forgive me! My spirit is occupied with vast projects, yet my heart is tormented by fears. —B.P.*


*April 9.*
"I can't tell you what I suffer the moment I take up a quill," I confessed to the Glories. "My first husband detested my letters, and now Bonaparte." It seemed to be my fate—my curse.

"He's angry because you addressed him formally, as *vous*?"

"But that's how a wife is *supposed* to address her husband." The crown of Madame de Crény's hat was garlanded with tulips secured by a wide bow of black and white striped satin.

"Unless you're the baker's wife."

"How egalitarian do we have to become?"

"He's ardent, I suppose," I said with a disheartened sigh.

Fortunée Hamelin scoffed. "That usually means quick."


*April 10.*
I'm nineteen days late.


*April 11.*
I'm exhausted and have a pain in my side that the motion of a carriage seems to inflame. Troubling conversations at both schools about the children. Too fatigued to explain. For now, fifteen drops of laudanum* and to bed.


*April 12, 1:00 P.M., still in my flannels.*
I feel rested, restored (although that pain persists). What happened—

When we let Hortense down at her school, I was told Madame Campan wished a word with me. I asked Eugène to wait and went inside.

"My purpose in summoning you, Madame Bonaparte," Madame Campan informed me, "is to discuss the possible establishment of the flux. Now that your daughter has turned thirteen, things will begin to move quickly. It is best to think ahead."

It took me a moment to understand what she was referring to. "In my family, we called it the flowers," I said, feeling a bit silly.

"Many do." The headmistress's leather chair creaked as she leaned back. "Or the ordinaries. Our dear departed Queen called it the *general*. The general has come, she would say, or the general is late, or early,

---

* *Laudanum: a solution containing opium, used widely in the eighteenth century for pain, particularly for "women's complaints."*

depending on his whim." Her voice betrayed a quaver. The stoic head-mistress would invariably weaken recalling her years as lady-in-waiting to Queen Marie Antoinette. She cleared her throat. "What I wish to ask you is this: would you like me to send a courier when the time comes? I flat-ter myself on the importance of my role in the hearts and minds—the souls!—of my charges, but when the general calls to escort a girl into the realm of womanhood, it is her mother who should be at her side."

"Of . . . of course," I stuttered.

Madame Campan smiled and leaned forward. "No doubt you have given thought to the matter of corsets."

I nodded, but this time the schoolmistress frowned. "I must advise you to refrain from corsetting your daughter. Such a practice might dam-age her organs. Your daughter is approaching the age of womb disease—one can't be too careful. Madame Bonaparte, you look concerned. Have I alarmed you?"

At Eugène's school the pattern was repeated: my presence was requested by Citoyen Muestro, the headmaster. Eugène groaned, which gave me fair warning that the news would not be good—and it wasn't. Eugène was failing all his subjects, I was informed—all but horsemanship. And furthermore, he'd participated in a prank on the cook, causing a "ghost" to rise up in the henhouse, very nearly giving the man apoplexy. I left the schoolmaster's office shaken, his threat ringing in my ears: "If your son does not begin to apply himself, we will have to ask you to withdraw him from this institution."

Eugène thrust out his chin. "I don't care! I hate school," he said, putting away the scrapbook he was working on.

"You're only fourteen, Eugène. You have to go to school." I made a place for myself on his narrow bed. "You will never get to be an officer if you don't get an education."

"What about General Hoche? He's General-in-Chief and he never went to school."

*Hoche?* It startled me to hear my son speak Lazare's name. Startled me and weakened me. Eugène had only been twelve when his father had died. Throughout that terrible first year he'd been sullen, moody, angry. It had been angels, surely, who had sent us Lazare Hoche, a man with a heart so generous that he could heal even the most shattered soul—my own, Eugène's. He'd taken Eugène into his care, into the army as his aide and apprentice, cared for him like a son. But General Lazare Hoche has a wife and a child of his own—and Eugène now has a father.

*April 13.*
I've been all this morning looking through a book Madame Campan has loaned me, *A Treatise on All the Diseases Incident to Women.* It was written by a physician to King Louis XV. Madame Campan told me Queen Marie Antoinette herself consulted it. There is a great deal in it on all manner of complaints. For example, on the subject of the flowers (the morbid flux, the author calls it):

*The menstruous Purgation is a Flux of Blood issuing monthly from the Uterus. Galen, in his* Book of Bleeding, *attributes the Origin of the Menses to a Plethora. Does not, says he, Nature herself cause an Evacuation in all Women, by throwing forth every Month the superfluous Blood? I imagine that the Female Sex, inasmuch as they heap up a great quantity of Humours by living continually at Home, and not being used to hard Labour or exposed to the Sun, should receive a Discharge of this Fulness, as a Remedy given by Nature.*

*1. The first Fact of this morbid Flux is that it has a stated Time wherein it appears, and this ordinarily from the Age of thirteen to sixteen Years.*

*2. It is known by Experience that the Menses generally cease betwixt forty-five and fifty Years of Age.*

So, it is indeed possible that Hortense, having turned thirteen, might soon begin her periodical sickness. The author cautions against exposing girls of this age to spicy foods or to music in an immoral key. If only I knew which musical keys were immoral!

*April 15.*
A persistent pain in my side and a feverish feeling. And still no sign of the flowers.


*April 17.*
The pendulum clock had just struck two when I heard a horse cantering down the laneway. I went to the front steps. It was Eugène, dismounting a grey gelding covered in lather. He threw the reins around the stone lion statue and bounded up the steps two at a time. "You're riding alone?" I asked, embracing him. The road between Paris and Saint-Germain was isolated, known to be dangerous. "Aren't you supposed to be in school?" His eyes were red-rimmed. Why? "Has something happened?"

"Maman, it's about General Hoche," he said, catching his breath. He pulled a torn sheet out of his vest pocket, a page from *Les Nouvelles*. The newsprint shook in his hand. I squinted to make out the small type: *General Lazare Hoche has been killed in the Vendée.*

"Eugène, it can't be true." Barras would have notified me immediately. But my son was not convinced. "If you like, I'll go to the palace," I assured him. "Director Barras will know for sure."


It was cold in the Luxembourg Palace in spite of the enormous fires burning, the carpets, the hangings, the drapes of crimson damask. And strangely quiet but for the rhythmic swish of the porters' brooms, cleaning up after the daily mêlée of petitioners. I followed the footman through the cavernous reception rooms, my thoughts on that scrap of newsprint folded into the palm of my glove.

Four workmen regilding the wainscotting in the Grande Galérie fell silent as I went by. Only five months before the once-elegant palace had been fit only for vermin and bats. Slowly Barras was having it entirely restored. Slowly it was beginning to look like a palace again—and every bit as intimidating. I glanced in a looking glass, adjusting the tilt of my hat. I was calling on the most powerful man in the French Republic, I reminded myself. It was hard to believe. My dear, eccentric friend, Paul

Barras, was now ruler of the land. "Père Barras," Thérèse and I called him, because of his big-hearted generosity.

"Is Director Barras taking callers?" the footman asked Barras's elderly doorkeeper, who motioned me in with a flourish.

"Entrez!" I heard something shriek from within.

"Bruno, was that a parrot?"

The doorkeeper grinned, his three front teeth missing. I stepped into the room. It took a moment for my eyes to adjust. Barras preferred rooms dark, draped in velvet—a gaming-room ambience.

"Pretty lady!"

"Well said!" Barras was stretched out in his favourite chair, a multicoloured bird perched on his white-gloved hand. "Meet Igor, a gift of the Sultan of Turkey—along with a tiger. But I sent the tiger over to the Jardin des Plantes and kept this clever fellow. It's a little frightening how quickly he learns."

"Ha, ha, ha." The parrot imitated Barras's soft chuckle perfectly.

"Look—Toto's gone into hiding," Barras said with a grin. Only the nose of the miniature greyhound could be seen peeking out from under his desk.

"I had a parrot in Martinico." A vile creature. Cautiously, with one eye on the bird, I kissed my friend's cheek. Barras was wearing a Florentine purple taffeta jacket I'd not seen before. It was pulled in at the waist; he looked as if he might burst. Yes, a corset was likely, I thought. And it was true, I decided: he *had* died his hair black.

Barras eased himself up and nudged the bird onto the perch of a cage set in the window alcove, disentangling a claw from his lace cuffs.

"Damn the Royalists," the bird shrieked.

Barras threw a gold-fringed velvet cover over the cage. "Brandy?" he offered, pouring himself a tumbler. I declined, taking the chair he indicated with a wave of his glass. He sat down across from me, crossing his legs at the ankle. Toto made a mad dash across the room and bounded onto his master's lap. "And to what do I owe the pleasure of this call?" he asked, stroking the dog's head. "I rather expected you at my salon this evening. You'll return tonight? The Sultan will be here and I wish to give the impression of a harem." A roguish grin.

I pulled the article from inside my glove, unfolded it and handed it to him. "Eugène saw a report in *Les Nouvelles* that concerned him." My voice was not as calm as I had hoped.

Barras patted the pockets of his waistcoat, withdrew a gold-rimmed lorgnon and pushed it into his eye socket. "Lazare . . . killed?" He let out a laugh.

I felt a tingling sensation in my chest. "So, it's not true?" I said, sitting forward. Eugène would be anxiously awaiting my return.

"Certainly not. Wishful thinking on the part of some Royalist, no doubt. You can't believe journalists. Haven't I taught you anything? Lazare is unkillable—you know that."

He put Toto down and accompanied me to the door, leaning on my shoulder. "But one question, my dear, before you go." Smiling his charmingly crooked grin. "Why such a fret over Lazare Hoche?" Tweaking my chin. "Madame *Bonaparte.*"

## In which I learn the Facts of Life

*April 20, 1796.*
I've been to see a doctor about the cessation of my monthly illness.
"You've recently married, Madame?" he asked.

"My husband is in Italy now."

"He left—?"

"Twenty-one Ventôse."

Then he asked a number of questions. Are my breasts knotty? (No!) Have I experienced a feeling of fearfulness? Anxiety? (Yes, yes.) Do I suffer from toothache? (All my adult life.) Do I desire to eat loathsome and unwholesome foods such as carrots, raw turnips, roast pig? (I confessed I loved carrots.) Do I fear dying? Do I have forebodings and gloom? Am I overtaken by a fear of undefined evil? Do I suffer from heartburn?

"Excellent, you will carry to term," he said, apparently satisfied with my answers.

"Do you mean, Dr. Cucé, that I am with child?"

"I confirm it."

"But Dr. Cucé—"

"No need to be fearful, Madame," he said, polishing his spectacles with the corner of his jacket. "Although it is not advisable for a woman to procreate after the age of thirty, you need not be concerned about consequences of a fatal nature. You have, as you informed me, already produced two children by your first husband, a procedure that has effectively opened up the channels."

"Dr. Cucé, it's just that I do not feel that I am . . ." My breasts are in no way tender and my belly is not distended. "And what of the pain I am suffering? What of the fever?"

"The pain is . . . ?" He poked his manicured finger in my side.

"Sometimes quite bad," I said, "and at other times only an ache." At that moment, a steady, throbbing, painful ache.

"A minor inflammation of the stomach." He wrote out a recipe for a purging diet-drink and an herbal tea to soak my feet in.

Twenty livres—on account.

Thérèse kissed me on both cheeks and on my forehead, as if bestowing a blessing. "That's wonderful news! Bonaparte is so efficient."

"I just wished I believed it. I'm not in the least bit tender, and this pain is so . . ." Worrisome.

"Did you take the hartshorn, nutmeg and cinnamon powder I sent you? Did you boil it in springwater, as I told you?"

I nodded. "And then I tried a remedy my Aunt Désirée sent me, along with her special prayer. And then another my scullery maid swore on the head of Brutus would curb a morbid condition."

"And nothing helped?"

I shook my head. Something was wrong.

*April 21.*
An amusing caller this afternoon—he helped chase away the vapours.

"Captain Charles." He introduced himself with a theatrical bow. He is young, in his early twenties I would guess, with an alert pixie look. A pretty man, exceptionally well made and with good features, excellent teeth. His thick black hair was pulled back into a braid. His sky blue hussar uniform brought out the extraordinary colour of his eyes—a light aquamarine blue. (Who *is* it he reminds me of?) "I've just arrived from Marseille," he explained, "where I was entrusted with a letter for you." As if by magic, he pulled a document from behind the marble bust of Socrates.

I smiled behind my fan.* A trickster!

The letter was in a woman's hand, the script ill-formed, like that of a child. "It's from General Bonaparte's mother?" *My son has told me of his happy marriage, and henceforth you have my esteem and approval.* "How kind of her to write," I said, suspecting, however, that Bonaparte had dictated her letter as well.

"Yes, the General's mother is so very kind," he echoed, but with a curious long-suffering look that made me wonder if he meant the opposite.

I heard the businesslike clicking of my pug dog's nails on the parquet floor. Fortuné entered the room with the air of a master. "What a charming little dog!" Captain Charles stooped down, holding out his hand.

*Charming?* Most people consider my surly pug ugly. "I beg you to be cautious, Captain. My dog has been known to bite."

Fortuné approached the captain's hand and sniffed it. The captain picked Fortuné up and, with a playful growling sound, rubbed his face in Fortuné's fur. "He's never allowed a stranger to touch him," I said, astonished as much by Fortuné's response as by the captain's.

*April 27.*

"My protégé has done it!" Barras slid off his horse. I came to the garden gate, wiping my hands on my apron. He stepped over the little fence and folded me in his arms, twirling me. "I told them he could do it, but this—this is a miracle." He was in his directorial robes still; one end of the scarlet cape caught on a rosebush.

"Paul, wait." I disentangled him from the thorn. My scullery maid stood frozen in the process of hanging a carpet over the stone wall, her head craned over her shoulder.

"It's unbelievable. Even I never expected . . . !" He was short of breath from such a show of youthful vigour, and dangerously flushed.

"Now, Père Barras," I said, motioning him toward the garden bench, "perhaps I could persuade you to take a seat? And then—at your leisure! I wouldn't want to rush you!—if you could tell me, what is this miracle?" I

---

* *Josephine had bad teeth and was in the habit of smiling with her lips closed or behind a fan.*

removed my apron and used it to brush off the stone bench. "And which protégé?" For Barras had many.

He paced back and forth on the narrow path, kicking up stones. "Your husband. Who else?"

"Bonaparte?" I sat back, tilting my straw hat so that it blocked out the sun in my eyes.

Barras clapped his hands. "He's had a victory!"

I smiled, incredulous. *Already?*

"Yes—at Montenotte." He waved his hands in the air as if deranged. "And with that starved, pathetic little Army of Italy that the Directors were so reluctant to grant him." Pacing again, flinging his cape over his shoulder. "Haven't I always said I have an eye for talent? I told them he could do it. And now they'll have to admit that I was right. *Ha!*"


*April 29.*

Another victory! This one at Millesimo. I've pinned a map to the wall in the study and have tagged it with flagged pins, just as Bonaparte did when planning his campaign.


*April 30.*

And yet another at Dego! "I can't take all this celebrating!" Barras groaned, holding his aching head.


*17 Floréal, Luxembourg Palace*
*My friend,*

*Please forgive this letter—I'm tied up in meetings with the Directors all day. I wanted you to be the first to know: your husband has had four more victories, and in only four days! Twenty-one Austrian flags captured! I'm ordering a fire-rocket show over the river—hang the expense. At this rate, Bonaparte will be opening the Pope's treasure chest soon.*

*I advise you not to grant any interviews to journalists, who will be pressing, I warn you. All information must come from the Directory.*

*Are you unwell? Thérèse mentioned that you've been in bed with a fever. This news will cure, I'm sure. Gather your strength—there will be ceremonies on end.*

*Père Barras*

*Note—I'm negotiating to buy Grosbois. Imagine, the previous residents were the royal family. With luck and a little persuasion (of the gold variety), the royal estate will be mine for a song. It would take millions to make it habitable again, however.*

*May 4.*
Fever, pain again, quite sharp this morning. Dr. Cucé coming soon.

*3:00 P.M.*
Dr. Cucé actually bowed before me. "Madame Bonaparte!" he exclaimed, pronouncing it "Bonne à Pare Té." "All of Paris is delirious! Four more victories and in only four days. My wife was beside herself when I informed her that my honoured patient is Our Lady of Victories. And when she learned that I would be coming to attend to your health today, she practically fainted dead away. If I may be so bold, might you have a small token, something the Hero of Italy has touched? A handkerchief would be excellent, but better—perhaps one of General Bonne à Part Té's hairs? I'd happily waive my fee. No! I insist, don't get up. I'll look myself. In this drawer? This brush?" I nodded, too fatigued to protest and chagrined that the brush had not been cleaned. "Ah, oui!" the doctor exclaimed, extracting a long, dark hair and holding it to the light. He turned to me, his eyes gleaming. "For my wife, of course. You know how women are?"

*May 5.*
Confined to bed still. Thérèse was just here with herbals and good cheer. She showed me an account in the journal *Ami des Lois*. Apparently, someone had sent in verses written in my honour—unsigned, however.

"But I think I know who wrote them," she said. "Wide-Awake."

Captain Charles? (Thérèse has dubbed the amusing trickster Wide-Awake because he's always so bright.) "Don't be silly, Thérèse," I said, pulling the coverlet under my chin. "He's a decade my junior." And in any case, I suspected that the pretty captain might be the type of man who only coquetted with women—nothing more.

"Young men adore you. Look at Bonaparte—he's six years younger than you. And what about Lazare? How many years younger is he?"

"Five," I said, blushing.


*[Undated]*
Slowly, I begin to get better. I detest being sick.


*May 6.*
It was late morning—I'd just had a bath—when I was informed that there were two men downstairs wishing to see me. I considered telling them I wasn't receiving, for I'm not yet fully recovered. "I think one might be your husband's brother," Lisette told me.

Bonaparte's older brother Giuseppe tipped his bicorne hat and bowed from the waist. "I'm called Joseph now," he informed me, displaying the tips of his even teeth. "Charmed to meet you at last." He is both taller and older than Bonaparte, a soft-spoken man with an indolent look. He was expensively if curiously turned out in a yellow tailcoat and matching knee breeches, a little cut-and-thrust sabre covered with gems dangling from his hip. Colonel Junot, one of Bonaparte's aides, stood beside him, cracking his knuckles.

"What a surprise!" I greeted my brother-in-law. "I can't tell you the pleasure this gives me," I said again, aware that I was exclaiming too much. Should I address Bonaparte's brother by his Christian name? Should I offer my condolences on his wife's being delivered of a stillborn? What were the customs in Corsica?

Joseph pulled my hand to his lips and kissed it theatrically with his eyes closed, as if overwhelmed with feeling. I waited for him to finish. "My brother desires me to tell you of his overwhelming love," he said.

"Bonaparte has often told me of his love for *you*," I answered, wondering how I might dry his spittle from my hand. I motioned to Lisette to serve cordials, swiping my hand against my skirt and through the air as I did so, as if I were an exuberant sort of woman. "When did you arrive in Paris? I long for news of Bonaparte. Four victories in four days—it is impossible to imagine!"

"General Bonaparte rode five horses to death," Colonel Junot said, cracking his knuckles again.

Mon Dieu, I thought. "Your journey, how was it?" I asked, my voice thin.

"We came the long way, by sea," Joseph said. "But you will be happy to know, kind sister, that the return shouldn't take longer than one week now that the passage over the Alps has been secured by treaty. Comfortable lodgings have been prepared for you."

Lodgings? I closed my fan. I didn't understand.

"You are to join my brother in Italy, kind sister."

I pulled my train to one side and sat down on the chair next to the harp. "Forgive me, but I'm not sure if I am able to—" Would it be improper to inform him of my interesting condition?

"You do not understand, kind sister," Joseph said softly, the muscles in his jaw twitching. "My brother, the General, he—"

"The General must not be disobeyed," Junot said, twisting his fingers but failing, this time, to crack them.

They left soon after. I've ordered my coach-man to harness the horses—I must talk to Barras.

*5:00 P.M., or shortly after.*
Barras frowned. "But that's impossible. The Directors must first give their consent."

"They seem to be unaware of this."

"The fact is, the Directors wouldn't permit you to go, we wouldn't grant you a passport. It's simply not safe yet. And besides—" He propped his chin in the palm of one hand, regarding me with his puppy-dog eyes.

"I doubt that it would be in our best interest, frankly. You'd distract the Liberator of Italy from his military duties." He made a lecherous grin.

"So the Directors wouldn't allow me to go to Italy?"

He shook his head, the feather in his cap bobbing.

I left shortly after, but not until I'd promised Barras I would attend the first weekend gathering at his new country château. "It will be wonderfully restful," he promised me.


*May 19—Grosbois!*

I am sitting in a chair that was likely sat in by Louis XIV, the Sun King. I am writing at a desk where treaties have been drafted, staying in a château where the great men of history have slept.

I am, frankly, stunned by the magnitude of Grosbois, now Barras's country estate. *This* is a castle.

"What it is, is a headache," Barras said, pointing out all the repairs that are needed to the roof, the foundation, the windows. For it has fallen, to be sure, into neglect. It took two manservants eight full days just to capture and kill the vermin, he told us. (*All* the vermin.)

We are a small party: Thérèse and Tallien (recently reconciled but already bickering, alas), Julie and Talma* (also together again), a Deputy Dolivier (who is also a banker), Fortunée Hamelin (thankfully, her pompous husband stayed at home), Ouvrard and his wife, Lucile Beaucarnot, a singer with the Opéra (Barras's current favourite) and her comely young brother. They are all out walking now, in search of views. I did not feel robust, so I declined.

In any case, it was an excuse to enjoy a short but delicious sleep under silk sheets—under the purple,** Aunt Désirée would say. Soon I'll ring for Lisette and begin dressing for dinner. The water in the basin has been scented with rose petals; a crystal bottle of the finest claret has been placed on the table in front of a flower-filled fireplace. I can smell bread baking.

* *Julie Careau and the great actor François Talma had lived in Josephine's house when previously married.*

** *Under the purple: royal life.*

Three cooks are at work preparing what will no doubt be yet another of Barras's sumptuous feasts. (The menu is before me now.) Barras has arranged for a string ensemble to play as we dine. And then after, sated no doubt, we will retire to a golden salon where Talma will read, I will play the harp while Lucile Beaucarnot sings and—eventually, inevitably!— Thérèse will have us aching with laughter over her hilarious imitations. "And *then* the game room," Barras warned us with a wicked grin, flinging his scarlet cape over his shoulder. He is clearly happy in this role, the grand master, orchestrating our pleasures. I am only too willing to oblige.

*Late (I'm not sure of the time).*
We gathered for dinner at five in full dress. (My new cream-coloured muslin gown embroidered with gold thread was perfect for the occasion.) "May I have the honour?" Barras offered me his arm. We led the small procession into the ancient dining room.

"A fresco by Abraham Bosse?" Thérèse inquired. The walls were painted with a medieval scene.

Barras shrugged. "I just live here."

"How old *is* this place?" Ouvrard said, examining the massive fireplace that dominated one end of the room. He is a tall man, young (in his mid-twenties), exceptionally well-made. The wealthiest man in the French Republic, it is said.

"It has been a royal domain since the thirteenth century. Le Monsieur was the last resident," Barras said. Le Monsieur, the Pretender, the brother of King Louis XVI—and, according to Royalists, King. "We walk in the footsteps of history."

"*You* walk," I corrected him.

We were seated, we ate, each attended by a silent valet. We drank, we got noisy: I took in the news. The deficit was a concern: two hundred and fifty million. The government was going to sell a number of National Properties in an effort to raise money.* The Directors were considering

* *With the Revolution, the government had seized Church property, as well as the estates of émigrés and arrested aristocrats. From time to time, in order to raise money, the Republic put these properties up for sale—usually at a very good price.*

# ⋘ *Dinner Menu* ⋙

1 soup
1 appetizer
6 main dishes
2 roast dishes
6 side-dishes
1 salad
24 dessert dishes

## *Soup*
Monk small onion soup

## *Appetizer*
Sturgeon broiled on a spit

## *Main dishes*
Confidence man sautéed turbot fillets
Eel tartare
Cucumbers stuffed with marrow
Chicken-breast in a puff pastry shell with Béchamel sauce
John Dory fish in a caper sauce
Partridge fillets in rings

## *Roast dishes*
Local gudgeon
Carp in a court-bouillion

## *Side-dishes*
Snow eggs
White beetroot sautéed with ham
Madeira wine jelly
Orange blossom cream fritters
Marie Antoinette lentils in a cream of concentrated veal broth
Artichoke hearts in a shallot vinaigrette

## *Salad*
Shredded celery in a herb-mustard mayonnaise

Twenty-four desserts

introducing new taxes: a patents tax, a stamp duty, land tax. There was talk of a tax on doors and windows, which led to a heated debate.

"The peasants will be forced to live in the dark," Thérèse objected.

"The English do it," Ouvrard observed. "They've done it for years."

"And look at the state of their peasantry."

"The English are taxed for living," Tallien said. "For breathing."

"But they don't have a deficit," Deputy Dolivier said.

"And they don't have every Royalist country in Europe waging war on them for daring to embrace democratic ideals. The fact is," Barras said, assuming his Director's tone, "it costs us a great deal to keep our men in arms. Over half our revenues go to the Ministry of War. A standing army of five hundred thousand requires . . . How much would you guess a day, simply in sacks of wheat? Over six hundred," he said, not waiting for us to guess.

"Six hundred and fifty," Ouvrard corrected. "Seven hundred head of cattle, seventy thousand sacks of oats—a *day*. The horses alone require two million bales a day."

"Spoken as an army supplier," I said.

"Yes, and proud of it," Ouvrard said earnestly. "Although I'm afraid that the title would not be considered worthy in most gatherings."

"Everyone's quick to accuse army suppliers of corruption," Barras said, "but the fact is that the French Republic would have collapsed long ago without them." He made a signal with his hand; the twelve valets moved in unison, filling our glasses with Madeira, taking away the dishes. Then he pulled a deck of cards from out of the side table, threw a sack of coins on the table. "Shall we have a quick game before dessert? How about five hundred to start?" He leaned toward me. "I'll advance you," he whispered, tossing out a second sack. "That's for Madame Bonaparte, lads, but be careful." He winked at his guests, "She plays to win."

(I did: fifteen hundred.)


*May 21—back home in Paris.*
Indisposed again—fever, terrible pain. It was a mistake to go to Grosbois.

I hardly have the strength to hold this quill! I've been examined by three doctors—Thérèse's, Barras's and my own Dr. Cucé. They stood about my bed scratching their heads. Last night the pain was so violent, I feared I would not see the dawn.

*May 24.*
The flowers came on suddenly and frightfully. And with such pain! I feared I was going to die. I felt light, as if I could float. I felt myself flying. Lisette covered me with a bed sheet. "I'm sorry about the mess," I said, closing my eyes.

*Later.*
"Madame Bonaparte, you are healing, the morbid condition of the uterus has improved, but I regret to inform you that you are not . . ."
Not with child, alas. "Was I before, Dr. Cucé?"
He scratched his chin. "A mole, perhaps?"
A mole?

*[Undated]*
From Madame Campan's book:
*A Mole is a Mass generated in the Uterus, which may be mistaken for an Infant in the Womb. Physicians affirm that all Moles are real Conceptions which cannot happen unless there has been some Intercourse between the two Sexes. Nor do they believe that a Woman can become pregnant through Imagination. Hence as often as we meet Moles, we may assure that there has been Co-habitation with Man.*

*May 28.*
I started a letter to Bonaparte, to tell him, but couldn't.

*Every day death leaps around me: is life worth so much fuss? Farewell, Josephine. Stay in Paris, do not write; at least respect my solitude. A thousand knives stab my heart; do not plunge them in deeper. —B.P.*

*23 Prairial*
*Josephine, where will you be when you get this letter? If in Paris, my misery is certain! I have nothing left but to die. —B.P.*

*Late afternoon, around 4:00.*
Thérèse saw the distress in my eyes. "What is it?"

I confessed to her my fears. I told her how disturbing Bonaparte's letters were. "I don't know what to think. He says things that frighten me. It's as if he's in a fever. I'll get a letter telling me to be careful, to take care of my health, not to come to Italy—and then a few days later I get a letter saying that he's going to kill himself because I haven't arrived!"

"Do you think he might be a little . . . ?" She made a twirling motion at her temple.

Tears spilled down my cheeks. "No, of course not." Although, in fact, that was my deepest fear. "It's just that he becomes so upset, I fear he might . . ."

"Step in front of a cannon?"

I nodded, staring down at my hands. They were the hands of an older woman—not my hands, surely. "He wants me with him."

"So go."

"Thérèse! A battlefield is no place for a woman. And what about Hortense and Eugène?"

"Your Aunt Désirée will look after them."

"But my health—"

"Is improving."

I sat back. "You really think I should?" I felt as if I'd been condemned.

She took my hand. "Remember how it was during the Terror, how we were fighting for something bigger than we were?"

I nodded impatiently. What did that have to do with it?

"It's not over yet," she said. "I know, we like to *think* it is. We dance, we play cards, we go to the theatre. I admit it! I'm the first one at a fête and the last one to leave. And why not? We're the survivors. Death tapped us on the shoulder and we escaped. Life is short, so why not enjoy it? But we're fooling ourselves. The Republic is faltering. Everything our loved ones died for is at stake. Our beloved Republic is falling and yet we dance on, trying to ignore it."

"But Thérèse, what does this have to do with whether or not I should go to Italy? Saving the Republic has nothing to do with me," I said, a feeling of anger rising up in me.

"Would you concede that it might have something to do with your husband?"

Yes, I did believe it possible, that much depended on Bonaparte— *why*, I could not say. In my most secret heart, I believed he could save us—and worse, that we needed to be saved.


*Noon, 27 Prairial*
*My life is a perpetual nightmare. A deathly premonition stops me from breathing. I no longer live. I have lost more than life, more than happiness, more than repose. I am almost without hope. If your illness is dangerous, I warn you, I will leave immediately for Paris. —B.P.*

## *In which I finally depart*

*June 19, 1796, early, not yet noon.*
Barras was resistant at first. "It's victory nerves, that's all," he insisted.

"Paul, this is serious. It's more than nerves." I dared not tell him the full extent of my fears, that Bonaparte might be mad.

"Look, it's simply unreasonable of him to expect you to join him."

"Please, listen to me!" Barras looked at me, startled. I'd never raised my voice to him. "If . . . if I don't go to Italy," I said, more calmly this time, "Bonaparte will come here." This was the one argument that was likely to persuade him, I knew.

"To Paris? He would leave his troops in the middle of a campaign?"

Yes, I nodded. He would. He *will.*

"That would get him court-martialled."

I nodded. Ruined! Shot!

"That's strange. He didn't mention any of this in his last letter to me." He looked over the stacks of paper covering his desk. "Here it is," he said, holding a letter up and squinting at it. "Just the usual business—his conditions for the armistice agreement with the Pope."

"Bonaparte is dealing with the Pope?"

Barras smirked. "Getting a little high and mighty, one could say?"

"It's the Republic he represents that is high and mighty."

"That's the problem—that's what's getting the Directors so upset. Bonaparte doesn't represent the Republic, and yet he's acting as if he does. Ah, here's the part." Barras cleared his throat and read out loud. "'I hate women. I am in despair. My wife does not come—she must have a lover who is holding her in Paris.'" Barras looked at me, amused. "So who is this lover?"

"The only man who has been admitted to my bedchamber of late is my doctor, I'm afraid. Fevers are not conducive to romance."

"I must say, you do look frail. Are you even well enough to travel?"


*Early evening—Fontainebleau.*

"Oh!" Aunt Désirée cried out when she saw us. "I wasn't expecting you. Hortense, look at you, a little lady in that bonnet. And you, Eugène, such a handsome lad. You're growing like a cabbage."

Hortense jabbed her brother in the ribs. Eugene grabbed her wrist and tried to pin her arm behind her back.

"Children!" I stooped to give my aunt a kiss, glaring at Eugène. "Why don't you two go out to the stable to make sure the horses are taken care of."

"My groom will look after your horses," Aunt Désirée said, tightening the sash of her squirrel-lined dressing gown.

"The children need to be outside," I whispered as they raced for the door. "It's a long ride from Saint-Germain." The walls shook as the front door slammed shut. "And besides, there is something I need to talk to you about, Aunt Désirée—privately." I settled into the armchair next to the sofa.

My aunt gave me a baleful look over the top of her thick spectacles. "I warn you, Rose, I'm out of salts."

"Still?" I paused. "I have to go to Milan."

"To Italy? But isn't that where the fighting is?"

"I know, Aunt Désirée, it's just that—"

"How would you get there? The roads are so perilous. Even between Fontainebleau and Paris, one risks getting robbed. And what about your health? Just look at how pale you are."

"I'm needed there, Aunt Désirée, my husband—"

"A woman belongs with her *children*. And what about our wedding? The Marquis and I can't get married without you." Sniffing.

I was dismayed. My aunt never used to cry, and now it seemed she was crying all the time. "I have a suggestion to make. Perhaps the priest could marry you and the Marquis before I leave."

"When will that be?"

"Possibly next week," I said, my voice faint.

"Next week!" my aunt shrieked. "Father Renard was reluctant to marry us next month even."

"Perhaps I could explain the problem to him." Pay him a goodly sum. Or promise to.

"But Rose, my gown isn't finished. It isn't even begun."

I heard the children's voices in the foyer. I put my finger to my lips, *shush!*

"The children don't know?"

"What don't we know?" Hortense asked, pulling off her hat.

Eugène grinned at his sister. "A mystery," he hissed.

"You're going to have to tell them sometime," Aunt Désirée said angrily, taking up an embroidery hoop and jabbing a needle into the tautly pulled fabric.

Not now! But it seemed I had no choice. "I'm going to be making a trip," I told them reluctantly.

"Oh?" Hortense looked apprehensive.

"To Milan," I said, with an apologetic dip of my head.

"Where's Milan?" Hortense asked Eugène.

"To the war?" Eugène spoke the word with reverence.

"You're leaving us, Maman?" Hortense's straw hat fell to the floor and rolled for several feet before falling over with a soft *poof*. She backed out the door.

"Hortense!"


I was breathless when I got to the park. "Hortense!" I stopped, catching my breath, one hand pressed against the pain in my side. It was growing dark, the shadows disappearing.

I heard a sob from behind a stone wall. Hortense looked so small sitting in the dirt. I gathered her in my arms. "Sweetheart." I stroked her hair. She was shaking. "Oh, my big girl," I whispered, swallowing hard.

I heard the creaking of wagon wheels, the lazy clip-clop of a horse's hooves on the cobblestones on the other side of the wall. Hortense took a jagged breath. Then, between sobs, it all came out. I would not see her in the year-end play. All the other parents would come, but who would be there to see her? And, at year end, when all the girls went home, where would she go?

"But I'll come back," I promised her.

"I don't believe you!" she sobbed.

*June 20—back home (exhausted). A balmy summer day.*

Aunt Désirée and the dear old Marquis are married at last. ("Kiss me," she yelled, making the sign of the cross over him, "I'm your wife!") Now I must attend to the passports, the financing, a wardrobe. I'll try to see my doctor today, and the apothecary. I'll leave instructions with my manservant to look after the beggar families that come to our gate. I should talk to my lawyer to make sure that my will is in order. I must talk to Joseph Bonaparte soon too—today, if possible. He and Junot will be travelling with us. I must find someone to take my horses; they should be exercised daily. I can't decide what to do about my cow.

Oh—the post-woman just arrived with the mail. Please, let there not be another awful letter from Bonaparte!

*May 4, 1796, La Pagerie, Martinico*
*Madame Bonaparte,*

*Your mother has asked me to write on her behalf. She can no longer hold a quill for the Rheumatism has greatly inflamed her joints.*

*Your mother wishes you well in your marriage. She prays that your husband is a Christian man and that he is of the King's party.*

*However, she declines your offer to come live in France with you. She has used the money you sent to purchase the slave Mimi's freedom, as you specified. We will send her to you as soon as we receive money for passage.*

*I regret to say that there was no income from the plantation last year.*

*Your mother has asked me to pray for you and your children.*

*In the service of the Eternal Lord, Father Droppet*

I've read Father Droppet's letter many times over. It has been a very long time since I've had news of home, and this small token only makes me miserable. I'll send word not to send Mimi until I've returned from Italy. What a blessing it would be to have her with me once again! I'm so relieved she is willing to come.

*June 21.*
"So is it true, darling?" Madame de Crény asked, playing a card. "Are you really going to Italy?"

"Over the Alps," Thérèse informed the Glories, rolling her eyes. (She'd been upset initially—she didn't think I'd actually do it.)

"The Alps? Mon Dieu."

"It's faster than going around," I explained.

"I didn't think it was even possible."

"Bonaparte opened up the route."

"Route de Josephine they're calling it," Thérèse said.

"My husband said he'd move mountains for me, but your husband has actually done it." Minerva looked pleased with her jest.

"Just the thought of those towering precipices makes me sick."

"Not to mention the banditti."

"Did you hear about—"

"Don't tell her!"

"Tell me what?"

"Nothing, darling. *Nothing!* You'll be fine."

*Evening.*
"Bonaparte's brother Joseph can't leave for six days," I informed Barras.

"Did he tell you why?" he smirked, rummaging around in his papers. "He's taking a mercury cure."

I raised my eyebrows. Mercury is used to cure syphilis.

"Having a bit too much fun in town—research for the romantic novel he claims to be writing, no doubt. But can *you* manage it in six days? You'll need to put together a wardrobe—hoops and the rest of it. The Italians are quite provincial."

"Hoops? You can't be serious."

"Servile, tradition-bound, ignorant, superstitious. Dig out your old corsets. *And* a bustle."

I groaned. I'd had my bustles made into pillows long ago.

"And don't forget, Madame Bonaparte, *ma belle merveilleuse*,"* he lectured, pointing a letter opener at me, "always put your handkerchief in your wineglass—only juice for the ladies." I made a face. "And no playing billiards with the men, either, no talking with them about finance and politics." He opened a drawer, riffled through it and then sat back with a puzzled expression. "What am I looking for?"

"Something to do with Italy?"

"Ah, yes!" He took out a file. "I'm to get passports for you, Joseph Bonaparte, Colonel Junot and . . . who else? Oh, that aide-de-camp, the funny little fellow Thérèse calls Wide-Awake. The financial agent—you know who I mean. All the ladies are mad about him."

"Captain Charles?" I was hoping the captain would be able to join us. "He's a financial agent?"

"Oh dear, you didn't know? I wonder if it's supposed to be confidential. I can't remember who told me. He's affiliated with the Bodin Company, apparently. It's hard to imagine—he's so young . . . and so very, very *drôle*."

Drôle, indeed! "At least Fortuné won't bite him. Even my dog finds him amusing."

"You're taking the dog? Mon Dieu, but this is short notice. Why is it I'm always rushing around doing something for Bonaparte? Ah, *here's* what I was looking for. It's a letter from the most beautiful man in the French Republic, our very own General Lazare Hoche. He requests permission to come to Paris." Barras held the letter up with a gloating expression. "Pity you won't be in town."

"You'll see to the passports?" I said, standing.

* *Merveilleuse: an extravagantly (and wildly) dressed woman of the period, typically of the newly rich class of profiteers, bankers and financiers.*

"You're flushed! Forgive me?" He kissed my cheeks. "Ah, but you forgive anything, all my little sins."

"I wouldn't be so sure," I said, tying my hat strings. Remembering to smile.


*June 23.*

"Madame, it's . . . it's . . . !" My maid was actually tongue-tied. "It's the famous General Hoche. Himself!"

"Here? That's impossible," I said, throwing off the down coverlet. It was almost noon, but Dr. Cucé had insisted I get constant rest in preparation for the journey. "General Hoche is in the south. He won't be in Paris until the end of the month."

"I'll go tell him he's not here." The excitement had made Lisette giddy.

"Perhaps there has been a mistake." *Surely* there had been a mistake. "Is this gentleman in his late twenties, tall, with a scar?"

"Broad shoulders, dark eyes," she said, her hands clutched to her heart.

"Lisette, please!" I laughed. "Is my morning gown pressed? Can you find my lace shawl—the one with the silk fringe? Oh, mon Dieu, my hair."


"Rose," Lazare said, turning to face me, taking off his hat. He was bronzed from the sun, his scar white in contrast, snaking down from his forehead onto his right cheek.

"General Hoche." I extended my hand. Lazare. *Lazarro*. He seemed taller than I remembered him. Hercules, Barras called him. "What a pleasant surprise." Joy flooded my heart. "I congratulate you on your recent victories."\* A man of peace, people are hailing him.

"There is no glory but that of the Republic for which I fight."

---

\* *General Lazare Hoche had taken on the difficult task of quelling the uprisings (fuelled by émigrés and England) against the Revolution in the south of France.*

"Of course." I smiled. Lazare believed in the Revolution as if it were a religion—and with good cause. Under the Ancien Régime, he had been nothing more than a dog keeper. Under the Republic, he'd risen to become one of the greatest generals in the land—*the* greatest general, Barras claimed.

I pushed forward a chair. "Care for a cognac?" There was a pitcher of orange juice from breakfast. "Or a pétépié?"

"A pétépié would suit the hour," he said, with a knowing smile.

I poured out a tall glass of juice and added a good measure of rum and absinthe. "You haven't forgotten the pleasures of Martinico," I said, handing him the glass. My hand was trembling slightly; I feared I might spill a drop, feared he might notice.

"Indeed, they haunt me." His fingers touched mine.

The clock on the mantelpiece chimed the hour, echoed a moment later by the clock in my bedchamber. "You have come early to Paris," I said, my voice quavering slightly.

"Just as you, I gather, are departing." He nodded at the open shipping trunk by the door to my bedchamber.

"Yes, I'm leaving for Milan in three days."

"*You're* going to northern Italy?" He sat back. "Is that not risky?"

"I have confidence in my husband, General Hoche."

"As you should," he said, meeting my eyes.

Oh, Lazare, my precious Lazarro. Memories flooded my heart—memories of the fever heat of passion, of love. I stood, went to the window to the left of the fireplace, pushed it open. I still loved him, I realized. Loved him and respected him, for the honour he lived by, his Republican zeal, his passionate commitment to *la liberté*.

"Today is the day of your birth," I heard him say.

"And yours is tomorrow, if I remember correctly." I remembered perfectly.

Lazare came up behind me. I felt the warmth of his hand on my bare shoulder. "My doctor will be calling shortly," I said, turning, my heart pounding violently.

"Are you not well?" he asked with that familiar tenderness that made me weak.

"I'm getting better," I whispered, swallowing. Could he not hear my heart?

"Do you think General Bonaparte would mind if I gave his wife a birthday kiss?" he asked, with a bold and teasing look.

"Yes, General Hoche," I said, looking up at him. I touched the tip of my finger to the cleft of his chin. "I do believe he would mind."

Lazare leaned toward me. I felt his tongue, his heart—my own.


*Later, almost ten in the evening.*

Tonight, after a bowl of broth, I went out to the garden and sat on the bench under the lime tree, my arms wrapped around my knees like a child. The moon bathed the landscape in an eerie light. Lazare's visit had filled me with melancholy. I thought of my mother, so very far away. Was she looking up at the same moon? Did she even think of me? I wondered what had become of them all, my family, the slaves I'd grown up with— my nanny, Da Gertrude and my maid, Mimi. Dear old Sylvester was probably dead. I thought of the graves of my father, my two sisters. I thought of the mound of dirt by the river—the grave of the voodoo priestess. I remembered her terrible words: You will be widowed. You will be Queen.

Overwhelmed by memory, by feelings of longing and loss, I took the Saint Michael medal that Lazare had given me on parting out of my pocket. Saint Michael the Archangel, sword in hand. Saint Michael the warrior saint, standing victorious over the forces of evil.

"I want you to have it," he told me. It had been his mother's, he said. His mother who had died giving birth to him. His peasant mother who could neither read nor write. He told me it would give me courage.

"Truly?" Yes, he said, the courage to do the right thing. I puzzled over some words on the back: *la liberté ou la mort.* "I had it etched on," he explained, somewhat shyly. I told him I would treasure the medal always.

Later, turning from the door, he said, "We never really said goodbye."

"Is this goodbye then?" I asked him.

He never answered, I realize now.

*June 26.*

Lisette woke me gently, touching my shoulder. "There are two big coaches out in the courtyard, Madame."

I went to the window, pulled back the curtain. One of the men on horseback was Bonaparte's courier, Moustache—so named for his enormous appendage. He dismounted and said something to Captain Charles and Junot. Bonaparte's brother Joseph was standing to one side, writing something down in a little book.

A horse whinnied. At the gate a number of mounted guards appeared—nine? ten? "We have an escort?"

"It's a parade!" Lisette said.


*Evening (9:00?)—at Aunt Désirée's in Fontainebleau.*

"Finally!" Aunt Désirée exclaimed when I arrived. She peered out the window. "Where are all the others?"

"They're staying at the inn in town." I felt gritty from the dusty trip down from Paris.

"A man has been waiting over an hour for you to get here. I've been trying to entertain him, but between the lace man coming and then the water carriers . . ." Aunt Désirée led the way into her dark drawing room, the heavy brocade drapes pulled against the afternoon sun. "He doesn't even play trictrac, only piquet, and he says 'tyrant' when he should say 'king.' A gentleman, by his dress, but with plain manners." She made a face. "He blinks."

"Is his name Hamelin?" I asked, pulling off my gloves.

"You *do* know him."

"I'm afraid so." I had hoped Fortunée Hamelin's husband would journey to Italy on his own.

"He's been most impatient for your arrival. I think he might be a Freemason from the way he stands with his feet stuck out at an angle."

"Citoyen Hamelin is the husband of a friend of mine, and yes, a member of Loge Olympique. He's begged leave to come to Italy with us on business." The making-money business. The recovering-from-the-devastation-of-the-Revolution business. The recovering-from-a-weakness-for-horse-racing business, I had reason to suspect.

"I see," Aunt Désirée said with unconcealed contempt, as if the very word business were beneath her. "He has consumed five small beers," she hissed in a créole patois, opening the door to the music room.

"Madame Bonaparte!" Citoyen Hamelin jumped to his feet, blinking rapidly. He was wearing a cutaway tailcoat that stuck out at the back like the wings of a beetle. He took my gloved hand and kissed it, leaving a faint smear of pink rouge. "I was, I confess, beginning to give way to doubt and deliberation. The road is heavy, and one knows the dangers one can encounter, the brigands, the *chauffe-pieds!*"*

"Citoyen Hamelin, you understand, there is no room in our carriages—"

"I will lease a post chaise."

I lowered myself into a chair. "What a good idea," I said weakly.


After Citoyen Hamelin had *finally* departed, I followed my aunt up the narrow stairs to see the dear old Marquis.

At the first-floor landing Aunt Désirée said, "Wait here," in her hushed, sickroom voice. The air was thick with the smell of mothballs. Through the half-closed door I heard her say, "Wake up, Marquis! Rose wants to have a word with you. She's going away, to Italy. No, not me, *Rose*." Then the door opened wide. Sunken into the feather bed was the withered Marquis, a full-bottomed court wig stuck crookedly on his head. "Be quick," my aunt hissed, stepping aside. "He might fall asleep."

Holding onto a bedpost, I leaned over to kiss the dear old man on the forehead. His wig smelled of pomade. "You are looking well, Marquis," I said, marvelling at the dry furrows of his skin.

"Louder," Aunt Désirée said. "He didn't hear you." She was going through the books on the shelves, blowing dust off the spines.

"I am going away, Marquis," I said, loudly this time. "To Italy."

He frowned. "Are the boys downstairs?"

---

* *Chauffe-pieds: literally "hot feet," the term given to the criminals who would extort what they wished by burning the feet of their victims.*

I glanced at Aunt Désirée: oh no. *The boys*—his two sons, Alexandre and François. Alexandre had been dead for almost two years, and François was as much as dead. An émigré, he would be arrested and executed were he even to set foot in the French Republic.

"Forgive me, Rose," the Marquis said tremulously, suddenly clear. "At my age . . ." I took his hand, skin and bones, bones and skin. His new betrothal ring was loose on his finger; it had to be large in order to slip over his big knuckle. He swallowed, his Adam's apple bobbing up and down like a mechanical lever. "I pray for Alexandre every day," he said, his voice raspy. "I prayed for him when he was alive, but it didn't help much. And as for François . . ." He covered his eyes, cursed.

I stroked his hand, my throat tight. Aunt Désirée gave me a warning look.

"So, you remarried," he said finally, recovering himself. "Eugène told me your husband is going after the Austrians."

"Yes." We'd had this conversation several times before.

"Tell him . . ." The old man fought for breath. "Tell him we must get back Mayence."*

*June 27, close to 11:00 A.M., I think—still in Fontainebleau.*
At eight this morning everyone descended on Aunt Désirée's modest town house. I stood on the front steps holding onto a wiggling Fortuné. The small courtyard was a chaos of men, carriages and horses, preparing for departure. Everywhere there was yelling and confusion. Junot was yelling at a postillion who was trying to untangle some harness. Hamelin—"the blinker" I think of him—was yelling at a footman who was trying to cram an enormous sea-trunk into his small post chaise. And everywhere, servants were rushing to and fro, yelling at each other. Only Bonaparte's brother Joseph was silent, standing by the gate writing something in a book.

---

* *The Marquis's son Alexandre, Josephine's first husband, had been arrested for "allowing" the Austrians to invade Mayence (Mainz, in German), on the west bank of the Rhine River. The French traditionally believed that the Rhine River was their natural boundary.*

"I can hold the dog if you wish, Madame Bonaparte," I heard a voice behind me say.

It was funny Captain Charles in his red-tassled boots. He looked shining, his brass buttons gleaming. Gladly I handed Fortuné over. The captain stroked Fortuné's ears and then even kissed the top of my dog's head! "Could I have the honour of showing Madame Bonaparte to her carriage?" He shifted the dog under one arm and offered me the other.

"But what about—?" I looked back over my shoulder. Was everything taken care of?

"I insist, Madame. We must look after you." He opened our carriage door, pulling at the step until it came clattering down. Then, with a twirl of his white gloved hand, he motioned me in.

"We?" My travelling kit was already on the seat: my medications, my Tarot cards, the novel *Clarissa* by an English author, my writing journal (which I'm writing in now).

"The saints and I."

I smiled. He was so sweet. "Who provided the cushions?" There hadn't been cushions on the way down from Paris.

"I did. I recommend that you sit on the side facing away from the horses." Captain Charles jiggled the door to get it to shut. I touched my hand on the windowsill. "Oh, I wouldn't put my hand *there*," he said. I looked at my white glove—it was streaked with grime.

Captain Charles slipped off his gloves. "They will fit you, Madame. I have very small hands. See?" He held up his hand—it was the size of a child's.

I slipped on his glove. It did fit. "You are a gentle and kind man, Captain Charles." I took several deep breaths, laid my head back against the hard, cracked leather. Be strong, I told myself. It wouldn't do to faint. Not now, not at the start of such a long and perilous journey.

# II

## *La Regina*

Ogni talento matta.
(Every talented man is a madman.)
—*Italian proverb*

## *In which I join the Liberator of Italy*

*June 29, 1796—Briare.*

Only two days travelling and already we are miserable. Citoyen
Hamelin is distraught over fleas in his coach. Colonel Junot is made
cross by the slow pace. My brother-in-law Joseph is not in good health
(due to the effects of his mercury cure), and is disinclined to suffer
silently. Thank God, Captain Charles is of our party—he alone is
cheerful.

*July 5—Roanne.*

Today we followed the river road along the Loire to Roanne, a bustling
town of merchants and carters. Passing through the market I heard foreign tongues. Roguish men with long black hair and rusty swords
observed our entourage with hungry interest.

It was dusk by the time we pulled into the courtyard of this humble
inn, the best in the vicinity. The innkeeper ran out to meet us, waving a
leg of chicken in one hand. His beard glistened with grease. He threw the
bone to a dog and started gesticulating wildly to Joseph about a courier
who had been murdered.

"It happened not far from here, to the south," Joseph explained as we
climbed the stone steps to the inn. "The courier was carrying promissory
notes intended for my brother."

"How awful!" I wondered if it was the same courier who had so often
brought me Bonaparte's letters.

"Yes, it was a goodly sum," Joseph said, opening the door to the inn for me.

Inside, the air was sweet with the smell of quince roasting on cinders. I sat down on a bench by the stairs. I had a fever, I feared, and that pain again. "I'll wait here for Lisette," I told my brother-in-law, who wished to examine the accommodations. He put his journal and writing kit on the bench and went upstairs. The journal slipped onto the floor, and as I picked it up I couldn't help but notice an entry that said, "10:15 A.M. J and CC play string game."

Citoyen Hamelin clattered in. Quickly I put Joseph's journal back on top of his writing kit. *Josephine and Captain Charles play string game,* he had written. Cat's cradle, he meant—but why note it down? It was child's play. "Do you realize that the murderer stayed in this very inn?" Hamelin demanded, blinking rapidly. "In the very room I have been assigned?"

Then Lisette entered, followed by Colonel Junot, his nose pink at the tip. She was wearing her travelling gown without the lace insert, I noticed. The innkeeper's wife ran to take her basket.

"*Queen* Lisette, is it now?" Captain Charles said.

She glared at him. "If it gets any hotter, I will die," she said, fluttering her fan.

"It will be even hotter in Milan," Colonel Junot said, cracking his knuckles. "But there are ways to cool off. Vigorous exercise is recommended, the type that works up a sweat."

"How unladylike," Lisette said, glancing up to meet Junot's gaze.


"Is Colonel Junot married?" Lisette asked me later, admiring my necklace before putting it away in its case.

"Colonel Junot has yet to find a woman with a sufficiently large dowry," I said, and then added, "He has a mind to coquet with you, I've noticed."

"You think he fancies me?"

I detected a hopeful tone in her voice. "Colonel Junot is the type of man who will always fancy an attractive young woman." I turned from the looking glass to face her. "Lisette, I hope you understand that it would be unpardonable for you to allow the attentions of an officer."

"I do not encourage Colonel Junot, Madame," she said, helping me into my walking gown.

"You don't neglect to wear your lace insert?"

She flushed. "It needs mending, Madame."

"My sweet Lisette," I said, "you are so young and so very pretty. You must learn to be careful. That's all I'm saying."

*Shortly after 4:00 P.M.*

We've just returned from a refreshing stroll. Feeling weak yet, I leaned on Captain Charles's arm as we walked along the river, the other members of our party going on ahead. We talked like old friends: of fashion (the charming high-crowned leghorn hats that women are wearing now, how they look best with hair loose and flowing); of his birthday (he's twenty-three today, so young); my children (how I miss them already); of novels (he recommended *The Sorrows of Young Werther* by the German writer Goethe). Then we talked of more serious, financial concerns—the shocking depreciation of our currency, the soaring inflation.

"I understand you are a financial agent," I dared to say.

"That is not the sort of thing a soldier would wisely admit to, Madame." The captain brushed a black curl out of his eyes—his blue, blue eyes. "Especially to the wife of his commanding general."

"I assure you, Captain, I will not mention it to anyone." Bonaparte, specifically.

"Then yes, I confess I am an agent—for the Bodin Company, an investment firm based in Lyons. The brothers Bodin—there are two—are from Romans originally. We grew up together."

"I once did business with a speculator in Lyons. I recall he mentioned the name Bodin." I'd made an exceptional profit on a shipment of salt-petre, and then again on an order of lace. "That surprises you?" I asked, perceiving his astonishment.

"Well, it's just that—"

"Women are perfectly capable of doing business, Captain," I chided him.

"Yes, Madame, but you would hardly seem to . . ." He flushed.

I would hardly seem to *need* money, he'd started to say. "I won't bore you with stories of how my children and I went without bread during the Terror, Captain."

"It wouldn't be boring in the least."

"It's really a rather familiar tale by now. Like so many, we lost everything. My husband lost his life; his property was confiscated. I had two children to support, feed and educate. One does what one must in such circumstances." It sounded noble, but the truth was that I enjoyed making deals. Learning to do business had given me an exhilarating feeling of independence.

"And now, Our Lady of Victories, you have everything."

"Everything including debts." As wife of the Liberator of Italy, my expenses had more than doubled. As wife of the Liberator of Italy, I'd been appealed to for any number of charities—charities that it was not in my nature to turn down.

"Perhaps, Madame, I could be of help in that respect." He paused. "I'm sorry, have I offended you?"

"No, not in the least," I stammered, my cheeks blazing, for I'd suddenly realized who the captain reminded me of: William, a boy I had loved in my youth.


*Late now, almost midnight, an evening of tales and tricks.*

The talk at table this evening was much concerned with the murderer, whom the innkeeper, his wife, three daughters, two sons, the innkeeper's sister and her two sons were only too happy to describe in great detail. With each account the villain became more and more sinister. So it didn't help when, just after ten, we were suddenly apprehended by a man in a mask, who jumped into the room with a violent shout.

Junot leapt to his feet, his hand on the pommel of his sword. We gasped, Lisette screamed, but Junot seemed unable to pull his sabre from its scabbard. He cursed crudely, so preoccupied with his dilemma that he failed to notice our laughter—for the man in the mask was none other than Captain Charles.

Junot stood at his place, his blond hair sticking out like a haystack. "What did you do to my sword, Captain?" he demanded, cracking his knuckles.

Captain Charles made what sounded like a frightened duck call and sat down beside me. "How tragic to be murdered on one's birthday," he whispered, cowering as the giant Junot approached. (We saved him!)

*July 10 (Sunday)—Lanslebourg.*
The ascent to the Pass was perilous. We followed a narrow road through thick fir woods, the glaciers glittering above us.

I exchanged a concerned look with Joseph. "Are we actually going to go over?"

"It will be my first time too." He had been writing all morning—notes for his novel, he claimed. "How does this sound? 'The pretty young woman cast a glance upon the handsome soldier, trembling as if she had seen the vault of heaven open.'"

"I like that," I lied.

"I'm not sure about the word handsome," Joseph said. "Virile might be better."

Captain Charles put down the book he was reading (Voltaire's *Lettres philosophiques).* "Are we staying in Lanslebourg?"

"That's where our mules and porters will be," Joseph said.

"We are crossing the mountains on mules?" I asked, alarmed.

"Perhaps you would prefer to be dragged over on a litter. My heroine is going to do it that way, packed in straw."

"Your heroine is going to cross the Alps?"

"The poor girl." Joseph looked up at a towering precipice. "She is exceedingly frightened."

Entering the tiny village of Lanslebourg, I felt we had come upon a new species of human. Everyone seemed deformed in appearance, enormous wens protruding from their necks. The growths are called goiters, I am told, caused by the water.

*July 11, dawn.*

We depart in a half hour. We've been given bear-fur blankets to wrap ourselves in, beaver-skin masks to go over our heads, taffeta eye-shades to protect our eyes from the blinding glare.

The mountains tower above us like giants. A trembling has come over me that has little to do with fever. I've put my miniatures of Hortense and Eugène in the little velvet jewel bag sewn to my petticoat, for heart. Lazare's Saint Michael medal I've tucked into my bodice, for courage.


*Benedictine Abbazia di Novalesa.*

We're over. We were carried in chairs across perilous cliffs by ancient little men. It was even more terrifying than I thought it would be.


*July 12—Turin.*

We were late departing this morning due to a problem with the way our carriage had been reassembled. (It had been carried over the Pass in pieces, on the backs of mules shod with spiked shoes.) Consequently Junot forbade any stops, so by the time we rolled into the tiny but stately city of Turin, I was rather desperate for relief. My heart sank when I saw a regiment of French cavaliers led by a young man in the uniform of an aide-de-camp.

"August!" Junot jumped out of our carriage while it was yet in motion. "What's all this about?"

"The General sent me to escort Madame Bonaparte to Milan." The aide glanced at me, tipped his hat. "But first the King of Sardinia has requested an audience."

Junot cracked his knuckles, grinning. "The King of the Dormice is learning to bow, is he? To us Republicans? That's a good one. Well, I wonder if I should be kind enough to grant his Highness the honour?"

"Perhaps I didn't make myself clear," the young aide stuttered. "His Highness has requested an audience with the General's *wife*."

Lisette has mended the train on my ivory silk gown and unstitched my pearls, which we'd sewn into the hem of a petticoat for security. I've bathed, my hair has been dressed, I've been rouged and powdered. "There," Lisette said, adjusting a pearl-studded ornament in my hair. "You look beautiful." I studied my face in the looking glass, pulling at a curl so that it fell forward. Lisette had plucked my brows into a graceful arc. Yes, by candlelight the King of Sardinia might find me pleasing.

If I didn't melt first, I thought, wiping the perspiration from my brow. Already my gown was damp. I opened the double-sash doors onto the balcony overlooking the piazza. I could see the treetops of the ramparts beyond, and beyond that, in the blue horizon, the icy peaks of Mont Cenis, glittering like an enormous diamond in the sun.

Church bells rang for afternoon vespers. I'd forgotten how lovely bells sound. I watched as a veiled woman in black made her way to church, her eyes fixed on the ground. What will they think of me, these women? Me, the Parisian merveilleuse in her revealing Parisian gown, enjoying her Parisian pleasures . . . her Parisian freedom, I was beginning to understand.

Fortuné yelped at a rapping on the door. "Oh, it's you," Lisette said.

"Please, Mademoiselle," Captain Charles said, "refrain from such an unseemly expression of unrestrained joy." He scooped up Fortuné and rubbed his face in the dog's fur. Then, releasing the delighted dog, he informed me that we would not be going to the palace for another hour.

"An hour!" I'd been waiting forever, it seemed. Waiting to be taken to the palace, waiting to be presented to the king of this realm. Waiting for the laudanum I took for pain to take effect. "Forgive me, Captain Charles. I'm nervous, I confess." I'd never met a king before.

"Why should *you* be nervous?" The captain brushed off a footstool, flipped up his tails and sat down. "I should think it would be the King who has reason to be uneasy. After all, your husband rather badly trounced him."

What was it I feared? That I might do something foolish. That I might become faint, with pain and with fever. That I might embarrass Bonaparte, the Republic. "It's just that I never expected . . ."

"La Gloire?"

La Gloire, indeed! Fame was the last thing I'd expected from marriage to Bonaparte. Strange, intense little Napoleon, the ill-mannered Corsican—a hero now, the Liberator of Italy. The man to whom kings bowed.

Lisette held out a glass of orange water. "I put a little ether in it, Madame. You look pale."

*Late, I'm not sure of the time.*
I survived. It was horrible. (The King fell asleep on his throne!) Barras was right—I should have brought a hoop.

*July 13—Milan.*
Approaching Milan I could hear cheering—it sounded like a lot of people. Bonaparte's brother Joseph stuck his head out the window, holding onto his tricorne hat. A band struck up the *Marseillaise. Amour sacrée de la patrie*, I hummed along, a lump rising in my throat. I wanted to look out, but I didn't think it would be ladylike to be seen hanging out a carriage window. "We should wake Colonel Junot," I said, waving to a gang of urchin boys who were racing beside us.

"What?" Junot sputtered, running his fingers through his hair. "We're in Milan? Already?"

"Is my plume straight?" Joseph asked, adjusting the tilt of his hat. "How do I look?"

"Fine," I said, popping an aniseed comfit into my mouth to sweeten my breath. In fact, all of us looked as if we'd been travelling in rough circumstances for two weeks: rumpled, worn and irritable. It had been a gruelling trip.

The crowd was chanting *Evviva la Francia! Evviva la libertà!* I caught sight of an immense Roman arch festooned with bright banners. "Nervous?" Captain Charles whispered. I answered by widening my eyes. Yes!

There *was* a crowd—men in powdered wigs and old-fashioned court-style jackets, women (the few I could see) in wide-hooped gowns, their heads covered with black scarves. Behind the aristocrats were the peasants in rags, quite a number, a sea of faces. A column of gendarmes stood at attention, the sun glittering off their muskets. I thought of my children, Aunt Désirée. They would have thrilled to see such a crowd.

I recognized Bonaparte's young brother Louis on horseback with the aides. But where was Bonaparte? My stomach felt queasy. I must not be sick, I told myself. Not now.

We came to an abrupt halt. "We're here," Joseph said, with his annoying giggle.

"Finally," Junot said, cracking his knuckles.

A footman in lilac livery opened the carriage door. A breeze blew dust in. I did my best to ignore it—to blink and to smile—for there, standing before me, was my husband, Napoleon Bonaparte.

His face was bronzed by the sun. Backed by the cheering crowd, his soldiers at attention all around him, he had a regal air. "Welcome," he said without smiling. "What took you so long?" he barked at Junot, stepping back so that the footman could let down the step.

*Evviva la libertà!* a man yelled. Fortuné, in his travelling basket, whimpered to be let out.

"Your wife has not been well," Joseph told his brother contritely, his hands pressed between his knees. "We had to make stops."

Bonaparte looked at me, his big grey eyes sombre. The footman was having trouble getting the step down. I felt I was in a dream. The man standing before me seemed a stranger—this man, my husband, the Liberator of Italy.

"May I help?" Captain Charles asked the footman, for the step mechanism had jammed again. "I have had to wrestle that latch many times over the last weeks," he rushed on, aware of his presumption, "and consequently have come to have an intimate knowledge of its perverse ways."

Bonaparte stared at the captain. "You must be Charles, the aide-de-camp."

"General Bonaparte, sir!" The captain saluted.

*Evviva la Francia!* a child cried out.

"Be quick then, Captain—I wish to embrace my wife."

The footman stood back. Captain Charles pressed down on the left side of the step and it gave way with a clatter. Bonaparte took my hand. "Careful!" he said—as if, I realized (heart heavy), I were a woman with child. I stepped down onto the dusty road. He put his hand under my chin. "I have been starved for you."

I smiled, speechless, overcome by the dust, the bright sun, the crowd. Overcome by the intensity of Bonaparte's eyes. "Bonaparte, I—"

He placed his right hand at the nape of my neck, his thumb pressing against my skull. Then he kissed me—without modesty, without restraint, as if, man and woman, husband and wife, we were the only two people on earth. For a moment I resisted, the roar of the crowd in my ears. And then I gave way to him.


My hat slipped off. I grabbed for it, then I stood back, pressing Bonaparte's hand to my heart. Distantly I heard people cheering. He stared at me, his eyes glistening. "We came as quickly as we could," I assured him, but my voice was drowned out by a trumpet blare. "I'm feeling a bit faint." Everything looked bleached. The crowd seemed to shimmer in the heat. I took hold of his arm. The other carriages in our caravan pulled into view: Hamelin's wreck of a hired fiacre, the servants' carriage, the baggage wagon.

A man in yellow-striped rags ran through the line of soldiers. "*Evviva Napoleone!*" he cried out as they pulled him away. "*Evviva la libertà!*"

Bonaparte led me to a carriage harnessed to four grey horses, their brass bells jingling. The ornate berlin was festooned with red, white and blue ribbons; it looked like a feast-day cake. "To cover the Austrian royal insignias," Bonaparte said, lifting a bow to reveal a royal emblem underneath.

"Aren't the others coming with us?" I asked as he handed me in. The upholstery was a pale cream-coloured brocade. I sat down uneasily. My periodic sickness had become unpredictable. I could never be sure what to expect—or when. "What about your brother?" And Junot, for that matter?

"This reception is in *your* honour," Bonaparte said, settling himself beside me and taking my hand. He was thinking of kissing me again, I knew. I opened my fan and fluttered it, leaning my head against the tufted upholstery. The heat was oppressive.

"Perhaps a little air," Bonaparte said, letting down the glass. A bouquet came flying through. He put the glass back up. The crowd was chanting *Evviva la Francia! Evviva Napoleone!* Their fervour frightened me—frightened and amazed me.

I heard the postillion cry out something in Italian. Our carriage swung gently as the team of horses pulled it forward. I put my hand to my side, against the pain.

Crowds cheered as we wound our way through narrow, rutted streets, along waterways and canals thick with barges. The air was filled with the pungent smell of potatoes, chestnuts, aubergines cooking, fish frying. "This is a beautiful city," Bonaparte said, stroking my hand. "You will love it here."

"Yes," I said, although I felt disappointed, in truth. Milan was smaller than I'd expected, and it seemed curiously vacant in spite of the crowds. The few women I saw on the street were dressed entirely in black. The shops had no windows; even the residences were shuttered.

Bonaparte pointed to a sign in the shape of a cardinal's red hat: "A hatter." A pair of scissors signified a tailor; a snake, a chemist; a bleeding foot, leeches. "But the water is unclean," he went on as we crossed over a stinking canal. "We have much to do installing a new sanitation system." A man in a banditti hat, defecating by the side of the road, raised his hand in salute. "And educating the inhabitants," he added.

At one intersection we were obliged to wait for the passage of a cart loaded with an enormous barrel of water. Chained prisoners followed behind, swinging long leather tubes out of which water came, dampening the dust.

We came upon a great square where five goats were grazing. "This must be the famous cathedral," I said, astonished by its grandeur. The church looked even bigger than Notre Dame and far more ornate.

"Three murderers live in there and I can't do a thing about it."*
Masons stopped their work on one of the turrets to cheer as we passed. I
smiled at them and waved. (Like a queen, I thought.) "The façade has
been under construction for five centuries," Bonaparte said. "I intend to
finish it." His statements surprised me. This wasn't a soldier speaking—
this was a ruler.

We pulled through a broad portico into the courtyard of a villa of glittering pink granite. In the centre was a fountain, spurting brown water.
The footman opened our carriage door, his lilac jacket stained from running ahead of our carriage. I stepped down, lifting my skirt up out of the
dust. An enormous number of servants dressed in black bowed at our
approach.

I hung on Bonaparte's arm as he strode up the steps and through two
majestic colonnades into a vast marble hall. I glanced back over my
shoulder. We were being followed by a crowd of noisy, clattering "help."
Everywhere I looked there were men in uniform, standing at attention.
"This is your home," Bonaparte said proudly, sweeping his arm aloft.


Lisette blew dust from her hands. "Our trunks will be brought up soon,
Madame—or so they say." She rolled her eyes. The rigours of travel had
brought out a feisty humour in my maid.

A clock chimed nine bells. Nine? "Do you know the time?" I guessed
it to be around three in the afternoon.

"I think it *is* nine, Madame, but the day begins a half hour after sun-
set, I am told, so the time is always changing, depending on the time of
year." She blew out her cheeks in exasperation.

I smiled. She reminded me of Hortense, and a wave of longing came
over me. "I'll be needing a bath," I told her. I had taken laudanum and
was feeling more at ease, enveloped in a rosy glow.

"I don't think they know about baths here," she said, crinkling her
nose.

---

* *Churches were official sanctuaries. Any criminal who took refuge in a church could
not be arrested.*

Lisette reappeared some time later. "I give up, Madame! I tried French, I tried Latin, I even tried Greek. I told them water, they fetched a mirror— a cracked one. I told them a bath, they brought me a melon rolling around stupidly on a tray."

"We need Bonaparte."

"The General is in a meeting with his officers, Madame," Lisette said, reappearing. "He said he would only be a moment."

But it was over an hour before Bonaparte appeared. A frowning child in a blue smock followed behind him, carrying a vase of flowers.

"I want a bath," I told him, accepting the girl's solemn offering.

Bonaparte raised his eyebrows in expectation.

"But we can't make ourselves understood!" I gave the girl a coin and she ran away giggling.

A copper tub in the shape of a coffin was carried into a little room outside my bedchamber. An endless stream of maids with steaming jugs ran in and out. At last the tub was full. I told them thanks (*grazie*—the only word I know), and indicated that they could go, but they just stood there. "Could you ask them to leave, Bonaparte?" He barked something in Italian and the maids scurried away like a flock of birds, murmuring *prego, prego, prego*.

Lisette helped me off with my gown. I slipped into the soapy water. The ceiling of the little room was painted with cherubs. Lisette's fingers were strong. She massaged my scalp, my neck. My headache dimmed. She helped me into my best nightdress—a cool diaphanous blue silk. I was going to have to tell him.

Bonaparte threw back the bed sheet. I blew out one of the candles and stretched out beside him on the musty feather bed. The laudanum and the bath had brought on a feeling of tenderness in me.

He kissed my cheek innocently, as one kisses a child. I could feel the heat coming off him. "There's something I have to tell you, Bonaparte." I took his hand and pressed it to my cheek. "I'm not with child. Not any more—at least that's what my doctor said." I could not bring myself to tell him that the doctor thought it might only have been a mole. There were things men preferred not to know.

Bonaparte sat up, his arms encircling his knees. "When did this happen?" he asked, staring into the shadows.

"About a month ago." I put my hand on his back. I could feel him rocking slightly. "I was going to write, but then I thought it best to tell you in person."

"This happens," he said, turning back to me with tears in his eyes.

"Oh Bonaparte!" I took him in my arms, my heart aching. If only I could give him what he wanted, what he needed. If only I could return his love.


*Bastille Day, some time after 10:00 P.M. (maybe later).*
We've just returned from a dismal Bastille Day ball. I now understand the meaning of the expression "bored to tears." Bored to *death*.

As we entered the vast, dark ballroom, Bonaparte was hailed. Then we were escorted to a podium where he was hailed yet again. "What do we do now?" I asked him, trying to make myself comfortable on the lumpy chair. Women in the corners whispered behind their fans, regarding me with disapproval. My gown was much more revealing than what the other women were wearing. I regretted not bringing a shawl.

Bonaparte drummed his fingers. "We're the guests of honour. We're required to sit."

All night? I felt like a prisoner of the podium.

We were hours, it seemed, listening to lofty addresses as every noble in Milan was introduced. (One man bowed so low he practically touched his nose to the floor.) My cheeks ached from smiling.

After the introductions Bonaparte was called away for an emergency meeting concerning some military matter. I sat on display, looking out over the dance floor. Thin red, white and blue ribbons had been strung from the rafters. They gave a dismal impression. The air reeked of pomade, garlic and perspiration. A haze of rice powder from the thickly powdered wigs filled the air like a fog. The only laughter came from a cluster of valets standing by an empty marble fireplace. It was a joyless occasion, and I feared it did not bode well for the months to come.

"Is the *bellissima regina*\* permitted to dance with a commoner?" Captain Charles hissed from one side of the podium. He was wearing a charming Chinese ensemble of green silk trimmed with gold, and green slippers to match. "The musicians, although lacking in what a Parisian would call finesse, are, at the least, vigorous." He removed a plume from his velvet toque to fan himself with.

I smiled behind my fan. "First of all, Captain Wide-Awake, let us be clear: I am not a queen."

"You just happen to be seated on a throne?"

"Which is where I'm required to stay, alas."

"How . . . thrilling." With a comical expression.

"Don't make me laugh," I said, laughing.

"Why not?"

"I'm not allowed to enjoy myself. This is a serious position." I sat up straight.

"So, you won't even join us for a cotillion? I thought all Parisian women had a passion for dance."

"In Paris there is only one true passion, Captain," I said, "and that, I fear to say, is the pursuit of wealth."

The captain held up his green-gloved hands and made an expression of mock surprise. "Cynicism in a woman surprises me."

"Forgive me, Captain, I was trying to be clever—a mistake on my part, for I am not a clever woman."

"Yet I believe it fair to say there is truth in your observation. I personally have a passion for the pursuit of wealth, as you put it—or rather, a passion for beautiful things, the one necessitating the other."

"I suffer that weakness myself," I said, smiling ruefully.

"I prefer to think of it as a virtuous flaw, for is not the worship of beautiful things a religion of sorts?"

"You jest and speak of holiness at the same time, Captain. You are a daring man."

\* *Bellissima regina: Italian for "beautiful queen."*

"It is all one, I believe: the holy, the beautiful and the bold—with respect to men, in any case. I cannot speak for women, who, in my observation, regard daring with alarm, and certainly not reverence."

"We all enjoy daring, Captain, men and women alike. Men are driven to be daring on horseback, for example, or on the fields of war. Women, on the other hand, are dealt few wild cards. The few we get we tend to play somewhat innocently, at the dressmaker's, or at the hatter's."

"Or perhaps at . . . ?" He tilted his head in the direction of the gaming room.

"I enjoy games of chance, Captain Charles, but one wouldn't call my approach daring by any means. I am by nature cautious."

"Yet you are said to win."

"I greatly dislike losing," I confessed.

"In that case, I have a wild card to suggest for you," he said. "*Speculation*. It is, after all, the most thrilling of the games of chance, but"—he paused, regarding me seriously—"in the right hands, entails little risk. Just the thing for a woman who is, by nature, cautious."

A portly man dressed in an old-fashioned long velvet coat was heading in my direction. "Excuse me, Captain, but I believe I am about to be accosted."

"Do you require my protection, Madame? I could be your *cavaliere servente*."

"And pray, Captain Charles, what might that be?" I was relieved to see that the man in the long velvet coat had been detained by another.

"The cavaliere servente is one of the few charming customs of this country. When a woman's husband is absent, she requires the attention of a substitute: her cavaliere, who waits upon her hand and foot, who fulfills her every need."

"Her *every* need?" I gave the captain a teasing look. He was the type of man one could coquet with safely.

"Well, excepting, of course, the marital obligations, to which only the husband has a right. It is due to the rigour of this understanding that jealousy rarely arises between a husband and his wife's cavaliere servente."

"Interesting." Both men were advancing toward me now. "Speaking of husbands, Captain Charles, might you know where General Bonaparte is?"

"I believe he is conferring with his officers in the antechamber, Madame."

"Would you do me a favour, Captain?" He jackknifed from the waist. "Would you tell him to come here?"

The captain looked aghast. "Moi?"

"Yes, please."

"You want *me* to tell General Bonaparte what to do?" He mimed a nervous Nellie.

"Yes, my cavaliere servente, I would like you to inform my husband that his wife needs him—*now*."


"I'm afraid I'm not very good at this," I told Bonaparte later, in the privacy of our room. There was a cooling breeze coming from the canal, carrying with it the pungent scent of sewage. "What were all your meetings about?" I asked, closing the shutters.

"The Austrians are advancing again." He took his sword out of its sheath and ran his finger along the edge, examining it. "I think I'll take your horse with me when I go."

"You are leaving, Bonaparte?" *Already?*

"In a few days."

My heart sank. Could I manage in Milan without him? "But why are you taking my horse?"

"You will be coming to join me."

"On campaign? But Bonaparte, won't that be—?"

"You don't think I can live without you, do you?" he grinned, tugging my ear.


*July 16, early morning.*

It seems Bonaparte and I are always parting. The soldiers whistled as we embraced. "For luck," he said, kissing me. He slipped a ribbon from my hair and put it in the pocket next to his heart. "I'll send for you," he said, swinging onto his horse. Then he galloped out the gate, his men scrambling to catch up with him.

## *In which I learn about war*

*Shortly after 5:00 P.M.—still very hot.*

A small afternoon gathering this afternoon. It was impossible! The men stood around the fireplace at one end of the cavernous salon to talk about horses and tell battle stories, while the women sat in the window alcove at the other end of the room discussing fashion, children and dogs. I was relieved when Captain Charles joined in, but shortly a footman came to inform the captain that his horse was ready.

"But you just got here," I said, dismayed. He was the only bright spark in the conversation, frankly.

"General Leclerc expects me in Verona tonight, Madame."

I excused myself from my difficult guests and accompanied the captain to the entryway. "I thought you were my cavaliere servente," I teased him, "and yet already you are abandoning me."

He bowed, a graceful melting movement that a girl might make. "Will you forgive me?" He took my hand and kissed it, his breath warm. "No doubt you will require proof of my attachment. Perhaps there are other ways I could be of service?"

Oh, but he was a naughty boy, I thought, and oh but I was finding it an amusing charade. "What might my cavaliere suggest?"

He took a coin from out of his pocket; before my eyes it became a handful! "My talent, if one could call it that, is an instinct for increase. I guarantee a return of thirty percent." He took his cloak from the maid, his hat, and gave her the coins.

"That's a bold promise, Captain." Was he serious?

"I am said to be bold," he replied, examining his hat in the looking glass, creasing the brim.

Bold, indeed. I adjusted his plume so that it stood straight up. "There," I said, feeling now rather hennish.

"In addition to all the other requirements, I might add," he said, buckling his sword sheath.

"Such as?" I asked, stepping outside where a groom was waiting, holding his horse.

"Discretion." Captain Charles took a fistful of mane and leapt gracefully into the saddle. "Ten thousand, Madame, for starters?" His horse tossed its head, pawing at the cobblestones.

I put up two fingers, twenty. Double or nothing: my game.


*July 23.*

Hidden under an enormous black shawl (like all the women here), I went to church this morning to light a candle for Alexandre. Two years ago today he died.

If I've learned one thing, it is that life is precious and fleeting. I weep to be separated from my children. And I dislike being separated from Bonaparte as well. I prayed to Saint Michael that he would be victorious. Already I want to go home.


*July 17, Saint-Germain*
*Chère Maman,*

*Yesterday General Hoche sent me a letter. Since he makes mention of you, I copy part of it here:*

*"It is with the greatest pleasure that I grant your request for a leave of absence for your friends. Perhaps they will help you forget the losses you have suffered. I will not leave Paris without seeing my dear Eugène. It would have been preferable if his mother had not taken him away from me; I would have made every effort to fulfill my duty toward an unlucky friend."*

*And now, just this afternoon, General Hoche fulfilled his promise and came to see me. Everyone at school was excited, even the teachers! I showed*

*him my scrapbook, which he liked. Then we fenced. He taught me some*
*excellent new moves. He agreed it was time I had a horse of my own.*

*I am improving in my studies. The headmaster does not scowl at me quite*
*so much. I've been riding every day. I saw Hortense twice this week—she is*
*busy with her projects.*

*Your loving son, Eugène*

*H.Q., Castiglione, 4 Thermidor*
*My brothers Louis and Joseph have arrived and assure me your health is*
*restored. It is terribly hot; my soul is burning for you. —B.P.*

*July 24.*
Suddenly there is such a flurry of activity. I'm to meet Bonaparte in Brescia. From there we will go to Verona together.

In the midst of all the packing and preparations, the hapless Citoyen Hamelin ("the blinker") came to call. "Please forgive me, Citoyen, for being distracted," I told him, "but I'm preparing to join my husband in Brescia." I was trying to decide whether I should take my pug dog with me. And what about my medications? Did I have sufficient laudanum? How long would we be gone? "We're leaving tonight and we only found out last—"

Hamelin blinked several times before exclaiming, "Brescia! Madame, the road to Brescia is infested with ruffians. I shall come with you. I will be honoured to risk my life in order that the wife of the General should enjoy a safe voyage." Immediately he headed for the door. "Forgive me, but I must rush off! I must have my muskets cleaned, obtain grease for the carriage wheels. There is nothing more tempting to a rogue than a broken-down vehicle. No, no, Madame—I *insist*."

*Evening—Brescia.*
Bonaparte met us on the road. I joined him in his carriage. "You are well? You look well," he said, regarding me hungrily. "Close the curtains."

The dawn was breaking as our carriages pulled into the courtyard of a villa on the outskirts of Verona.

"Is this where the Pretender lived?" I asked Bonaparte, yawning. I felt exhausted. We'd travelled from Brescia at night, but the road had been jolting and what sleep I'd managed to get had been fitful, disturbed by Bonaparte's ardent caresses.

"It's not as grand as I expected it to be," Bonaparte said, jumping out before our carriage had come to a full stop.

We sat out on the verandah overlooking rolling hills dotted with mulberry trees, drinking coffee and eating fresh figs from a tree in the garden. The air smelled sweetly of cut grass. Bonaparte became animated as he told us stories about the Pretender. "He led a simple life. The people here knew him as Comte de Lille. No one realized he was King Louis XVI's brother. Only his servants knew he was the Pretender to the throne of France."

"How do you know all this, Bonaparte?" I had had three cups of strong coffee and was beginning to feel alert.

"I have spies following him. He's in the north now, in Germany —my men never let him out of their sight. His daily rituals are very regular. He is dressed by eight each morning, a simple ensemble decorated with an insignia, a short sword. Then he sees his chancellor. And then he sits in his study and writes. At midday he stops for a meal—he keeps a frugal table. Then he shuts himself up in his closet and paces back and forth in a state of agitation for a little under one hour. This pattern is repeated every day."

"To think that he sat in this very chair," Citoyen Hamelin said, blinking. He wiggled the arm. "It needs fixing."

"It must be a lonely life," I said, gazing out over the mountains. I thought I saw movement in a dark crevice. Did they have mountain goats in this country? I wondered. I stood and went to the stone balustrade. "What's that moving on the mountain?"

But Bonaparte was occupied telling Hamelin about the last report he had had on the Pretender, the book the Pretender had been reading. "And it's still in the library," he said, "with a marker on page 231. He was on page 204 several months ago, so he can't be a very fast reader."

"Perhaps he did not read from it every day," Hamelin said, blinking. "Perhaps he only read a few days a week. If so, then one could say that he—"

I turned to Bonaparte. "Austrian soldiers wear white uniforms, do they not?"

He came to my side. "I don't see anything."

"Over to the left—see that line of white dots?"

Bonaparte pulled a collapsed glass from out of his pocket, shook it to open it and held it to his eye. "You must leave immediately," he said, letting the glass drop.

We were hours on the road, Lisette, Hamelin and I in the carriage, four dragoons following on horseback. At the fort in Peschiera a portly general with whiskers like sausages rushed out to meet us. "You can't stay here—the Austrians are closing in."

Hamelin and Lisette regarded me with alarm. "My husband instructed us to stay here," I told the general. The air smelled strongly of fish.

"But Madame, what if . . . ?" Hamelin exclaimed.

"Madame Bonaparte," General Guillaume stuttered, "I beg you to consider. If anything were to happen to you, I—"

"I appreciate your concern, General, but we will not move unless ordered to do so by my husband," I repeated, with a firmness that astonished even me. Bonaparte was the only rock I had to hold on to.

I am writing this now in a small stone cell in the basement of the fortress. At least it is cool. An hour ago we had a meal of lake trout washed down with watered Montferrat. We ate in silence. "Leave the horses hitched," I instructed the groom. Lisette and I will share a room. Our valises packed, we will sleep in our clothes. If we sleep.

A numbing fear has enveloped me. That, and anger I confess. How could Bonaparte have put us into this position! Put *me*. For the sake of his lust, he has endangered my life.

*July 31, Sunday—Parma.*

I was woken at dawn by a clatter of horses in the courtyard, the sound of metal clanking against stones.

I touched Lisette's arm. "I think someone has arrived," I whispered. She moaned and turned back into her pillow. "We might have to leave soon. Best to rise," I said, releasing the pedal of the chipped washbasin and splashing my face.

I tied a red scarf around my head créole-style and creamed my cheeks with rouge, blind without a glass. I heard a voice. "It's Junot, I think."

Lisette opened her eyes. "Colonel Junot?"


"It doesn't look good," I overheard Junot saying to General Guillaume as I came down the stone steps into the courtyard. "The Austrians outnumber us three to one."

"Colonel Junot, what has happened?" I asked anxiously.

"We had quite a battle last night." His breath smelled of liquor. "General Bonaparte has set up a command post at Castelnuovo. I'm to take you there, but we must leave immediately."

Hamelin, blinking against the morning sun, appeared at the entrance to the fort, followed by a servant lugging his heavy valise. And then Lisette appeared, carrying a wicker basket.

Junot jumped to the door of our carriage. "Allow me," he said, gesturing us in.

"I'm so sleepy!" Lisette yawned, climbing in after Hamelin. "Did you sleep, Madame?" she asked, smiling with her eyes at Junot.

"A little." I was anxious to join Bonaparte, but anxious as well about leaving the protection of the fort. Nowhere seemed safe.

Junot headed out the open gate on horseback, the dragoons falling in behind. A young dragoon with a pink face jumped onto his horse and trotted to catch up with them. He smiled and tipped his hat at me as he raced by.

"The young men always like *you*, Madame," Lisette teased, handing me a warm roll lined with a sausage.

"Did I miss something?" Hamelin asked, looking up from his book of Italian phrases.

"I remind them of their mothers," I told my maid. The freshly baked bread lifted my spirits, restored faith. We'd not had time to eat.

"Would you be offended if I told you that you remind me of my mother?" she asked.

"Not at all. In fact, you remind me of my daughter." We exchanged an affectionate look.

Our carriage lurched forward. I waved to General Guillaume as we pulled through the gate. He turned away, his hand over his heart. He was frightened for us, I realized, a cold feeling of fear coming over me.

It was cooler along the shores of Lake Garda, the vast water calm, the blue hills in the distance misty. I was relieved not to hear sniper fire.

Lisette and I were playing cat's cradle when we were startled by the ominous boom of a cannon. The carriage halted abruptly; I put out a hand to keep from falling forward. I saw a flash of light, heard musket fire, cannon again. But it was the sound of a horse's scream that chilled me—that, and the violent jolting of our carriage. I realized we might tip. I heard Junot yelling, "Get down, get down, dismount, you idiot!"

"What's happened?" Hamelin hiccupped, pulling down on his hat.

The door to the carriage was thrown open. "Jump!" Junot grabbed Hamelin and yanked him out. A crack of gunfire sent him scrambling.

Lisette leapt into Junot's arms. He let her down and pushed her toward the ditch. I gathered my skirts. I felt strangely calm; even so, I tasted tears. A sudden jolt threw me off balance. I heard a thunderous boom. "Get out!" Junot yelled.

I jumped, scrambling after Hamelin and Lisette, my petticoat tearing. I rolled down an embankment, coming to rest in marshy reeds. I crawled through the mud to the others. Lisette looked deathly pale. I put my arm around her. She was trembling. Or was I?

"My hiccups are gone," Hamelin said, blinking.

I heard the sound of a man crying out. "It must be one of the soldiers." I climbed back up to the top of the embankment.

"Madame, don't! Be careful," Lisette hissed. "Come back!"

I peered through the tall grass. Junot was crouched beside a fallen horse, a big chestnut. It was thrashing, bleeding from a wound in its neck. The other horses were rearing and kicking, trying to free themselves of the entangled harness. It was all the postillion could do to hold onto them while a dragoon cut the traces. And then I saw the young dragoon . . .

I ducked down, my breath shaky. My hand was covered in mud. I wiped it on the grass slowly, as if in a dream, then slid back down the embankment, trembling.

"What's going on?" Hamelin asked, holding a limp Lisette in his arms. Had she fainted? I tried to answer, but I could not, for I had seen the young dragoon, fallen from his horse, his foot caught in the stirrup, his face . . .

"What's wrong with Lisette?" I said finally, gasping.

Hamelin shook her. "I can't get her to wake up."

"Do you have a flask?"

"Oh!" He felt in his pocket, pulled out a leather-covered bottle and handed it to me. "Whisky. There's a little left."

I opened it and held it under Lisette's nose. Her eyelids flickered. I poured some of the liquor over my fingers, wiped it on her forehead, her lips, her nostrils. She moaned. "Sit her up more." I feared she might retch.

Hamelin slumped her forward. Lisette shook her head, looked up at me. "I feel sick, Madame!"

"Have a sip," I said, handing her the flask. "But just a little," I cautioned her, watching her tip back her head. We had to be ready to run.

I heard Junot yell, the crack of a whip, the carriage clattering, horses. We were showered with loose stones. Then Junot came tumbling down the embankment. He cursed when he hit the mud. He crawled over to us, his face frightful with mud and blood. Lisette handed him her handkerchief out of her bodice. "Are you all right?" he asked, pressing her kerchief to his lips.

"It's uncomfortable here," Hamelin said, slapping at a mosquito. They were everywhere now. "This pestilent air—"

"Colonel Junot, we heard the carriage."

"I whipped it on." He cracked his knuckles.

"We're stranded?" Hamelin exclaimed.

"The Austrians will assume you're in it and stop firing. But we've got to get into the woods without their seeing us." Junot started crawling along the ditch. "Can you follow?" I nodded. "Stay down," he hissed.

Once in a more secluded area, not far, we were able to get up out of the mud. Lisette's teeth were chattering, in spite of the heat. "Do you know where we are?" I asked Junot. I put my arm around Lisette, to steady her, steady myself.

"Near Desenzano," Junot said, slapping at a mosquito.

I remembered Desenzano, a village of narrow little streets opening onto the lake. Bonaparte and I had passed through it two nights before on the way to Verona.

I sensed the beat of a horse's hooves. Cocking his musket, Junot went to the edge of the woods. "A carter," he said, returning. "He's stopped to look at the dead horse."

A creaking wagon pulled by a fat red horse came into view. Loaded on the back were crates of chickens. The carter was wearing a black scarf around his head, like a peasant woman. He pulled to a stop when he saw us, said something in Italian. "Can you understand him?" I asked Junot.

"Just get in," Junot said, aiming his musket at the peasant. We climbed onto the wagon, sitting down uneasily on top of the chicken crates. "Go!" Junot said to the driver, climbing up beside him, but the carter just sat there.

"Do you have your little book?" I asked Hamelin.

Hamelin felt around in his pockets, put on his spectacles, ruffled through the pages of his book of Italian phrases. "Nohn sahp-pee-AH-mon DOH-veh chee troh-vee-AH-moh," he said (or something like that).

"What did you say?" Junot demanded.

"We are lost," Hamelin said, blinking. "I think that's what I said."

"We're not lost!" Junot grabbed the peasant's whip and cracked it, flicking the horse's rump. The mare bolted forward, setting the chickens to squawking.

We smelled Desenzano before we saw it. The mare balked, tossing her big head, refusing to go forward. "It's the smell," I said. I put a handkerchief to my nose, my eyes watering.

"There was a battle here last night," Junot said, cracking the whip again. But the mare wasn't budging. Then the driver yelled something at the horse and it pulled forward at last, swishing its plaited tail.

"He said *stupido*, didn't he? I think he told the horse it was stupid." Hamelin leafed through his book of phrases.

"*Stufato*, I thought he said." A feeling of faintness had come over me.

"Stewed meat?" Hamelin read.

Junot glanced back at me. "Cover her eyes."

I tried not to look as we went through the town, but I could not keep out the smell of gunpowder, burned flesh, faint whiffs of a sweet odour. The soft bump of the wagon over a body. The whimpering sounds, like those of a child. "I heard someone call out. Can't we stop?" Then I made the mistake of opening my eyes. Everywhere there were bloated bodies. The cobblestones were awash with blood, drying in the morning sun. Two peasant women were pulling a coat off a dead soldier, a boy with a grey pallor to his skin, vacant eyes. The pickers looked up at us and one of them grinned, toothless as a baby. I pressed Lisette to me, my trembling fingers entangled in her sweat-damp hair.

As we approached Castelnuovo there were herds of cavalry horses tethered, loaded munitions wagons, tents pitched, soldiers everywhere. The smoke of numerous campfires gave the landscape an ethereal look. Tears came to my eyes at the sight of the flag of the French Republic hanging from the thatched roof of a peasant's hut—the temporary headquarters of the Army of Italy.

"What took you so long?" Bonaparte demanded, emerging. "Your escort arrived back well over an hour ago."

"It was rough going," Junot said, saluting, red in the face. He glanced at Lisette. She was staring out over the maize fields.

"It was a good thing I was there," Hamelin said as Bonaparte lifted me down from the wagon.

I fought back tears. "I think I should sit down." And then the sobs came, overwhelming me.

"Get ether," Bonaparte commanded an orderly. He grasped me by the shoulder. "Fight it, don't give in to it." But I had been fighting it for too long. "The Austrians are going to pay dearly for this," I heard him say under his breath.

I drank the ether water the aide brought, coughed. It tasted brackish. That smell was with me still. "Give some to Lisette." She was sitting in the wagon, watching us with a dazed look. Even the chickens in the crates were silent.

"The driver wants a reward," Junot told Bonaparte, cracking his knuckles. "At least, I think he does. Maybe you should talk to him."

"Give him whatever he wants," Bonaparte said, squeezing my hand.

"Are our trunks here? Can we change?" Lisette asked, standing.

Junot put out his hand to help her down. "Careful, she might fall," I told him, my voice tremulous.

"You should eat—it will give you strength." Bonaparte led me into the little cottage with a thatched roof.

Inside, it was dark. The floor was just dirt. The hut was hot, airless, smelling of goats. A table in front of an empty fireplace was covered with reports, illuminated by a tin lantern. An enormous map was nailed to the rough plank wall. Bonaparte led me to a straw pallet. He said something in Italian to a peasant boy with a dirty face. "And salami?" Bonaparte asked, looking back at me. I shook my head, no. I didn't think I could eat.

"The coach will be ready in thirty minutes, General," Junot said, looking in.

"The harness is mended?"

Junot nodded, cracking his knuckles.

"We're leaving you, Bonaparte?" I began to tremble.


Nearing Toscane, we were met by a courier mounted on a black horse slick with lather. "Turn back!" he yelled. "The Austrians are on ahead. They've taken Brescia!"

Mon Dieu, I thought, *Brescia*? Brescia was so close to Milan.

"What are we going to do now?" Hamelin asked, taking out his travel book. "We can't go north, east or west."

"South," Bonaparte said, pacing.

"I want to stay with you!"

He regarded me with an expression I couldn't identify. This man, my husband, wasn't the man I had known in Paris. Here, in the rough-and-tumble atmosphere of the camp, surrounded by men who regarded him with devoted loyalty, he seemed transformed. Confident, expansive, there was a certain nobility to his movements. Like his men I believed in him, felt an aura of security when I was in his presence. "*Please*, Bonaparte."

He knelt down beside me, taking my hands in his. His touch calmed me. "You must understand—the Austrians are closing in. We're anticipating quite a battle. You will be safe in the south."

His eyes told me I must, that it was for the best. I sniffed and nodded. He kissed me with great tenderness. "You were brave this morning," he said with a smile.

"Oh, Bonaparte!" I pressed his fingers to my lips. There was strength in him. I could understand why his men followed him with such absolute devotion—he ennobled them, just as he ennobled me.

He stood and addressed his courier, who was standing in the door, twisting the ends of his massive moustache. "Cross the Po river at Cremona," he told him, tracing the route on the map with a paper knife. "It's less risky there." He scratched something on a paper. "My Uncle Fesch is in Parma. He will give you shelter for the night. Then take him with you south. Tell him that's an order. Head down into Lucques—they are a peaceful people. I'll send word when it's safe to return."

"A kiss?" I said, standing.

"For luck," he smiled, taking me in his arms.

It is past midnight now. We are in Parma, in the home of Bonaparte's Uncle Fesch, a jolly sort of man with a ruddy complexion. A maid just came for my tray, the pastries untouched. "I cannot eat," I told her slowly, in simple French. *Scusatemi*. "I am ill," I added, not untruthfully.

And terrified, still.

And haunted: by the image of a boy's face, his thin body on the dusty road, the smell of Desenzano, the cries of the wounded left to die.

Tears, tears. I begin to tremble. *Mon Dieu.* I am the daughter of a soldier, the widow of a soldier, the wife of a soldier. But until today, I never knew what war was.

# In which I am surrounded by Bonapartes

*October 2, 1796—Milan, a sweltering hot afternoon.*
It has been some time, I see, since I've written here. So much has happened, and yet so much remains the same. Bonaparte is victorious, against all odds. Yet the enemy is a many-headed Hydra. How many armies can the Austrians raise? Every time Bonaparte vanquishes one, yet another rises up in its place. I fear there will never be peace.

Oh, it is the vapours again, surely. I am overcome with malaise. I feel another attack coming on, a strange shimmering at the edges. Migraine, the doctor told me the last time it happened, a paroxysmal pain in the temple. Pain, certainly, for even laudanum could not touch it. The last time I had an attack, I stayed in a darkened room for three days, daring not move or even speak. This land will be my grave, I fear.

*November 23.*
Victory! (Relief.) Once again the Austrians have retreated behind the walls of Mantua.

*December 9.*
Bonaparte is back, his health weakened by a plunge into a swamp. (I pray it is not mal-aria.*) The quiet domestic life we are finally enjoying now

---

* *Mal-aria: malaria, translated in Italian as "bad air," which people believed to be the cause of the disease.*

will help, I hope. How little time we have had together! He's having his portrait painted, we're planning a ball—and, I should add, attending nightly to what Bonaparte refers to as "our project." Maybe now, with time together, we'll succeed.

*December 24, Christmas Eve.*
"Madame?" Lisette curtsied when she realized Bonaparte was sitting in the alcove by the window. "Your sister, General, she is—"

"Maria-Paola? My sister is here?" Bonaparte jumped up. "Already?"

Lisette glanced at me. Oh la la, her eyes said.

"Uff. The boat was disgusting!" Bonaparte's sixteen-year-old sister is a striking girl with curly black hair and sapphire blue eyes—even more beautiful than I'd expected from all I'd heard. "I threw up on the deck, over the side, in the dining hall, in my bunk." She'd plucked her eyebrows into a thin line, like the servant girls. "You're mussing my hair," she protested in bad French, when Bonaparte embraced her. She has a shrill voice. "*This* is where you live? Magnifico!"

Bonaparte turned toward me, his arm around his little sister. "Paganetta," he said proudly.

I nodded, smiling stupidly. *Pagan*etta, indeed. She is only sixteen, yet so womanly. And a spirited girl, it was easy to see, well aware of her charms—*la beauté du diable*.* "Welcome, Maria-Paola, to—"

"I'm not Maria-Paola any more, I'm Pauline."

"Welcome, Pauline, to—"

She swept by me without listening. "Remember, Napoleone, you promised! I get my own suite."

*December 27.*
A constant stream of maids and footmen has been running up and down the hall doing Pauline's bidding. The bed sheets are not sufficiently soft,

* *La beauté du diable: beauty of the devil, or bloom of youth, the sexual appeal of a girl.*

• 552 •

the mirror not sufficiently ornate, the china sugar dish does not match the silver tea equipage and the tapestries hanging on her walls are frayed. I watch this flurry of activity with irritation. I have a reception to prepare for and nothing is getting done.

*December 29.*
I caught Pauline in my wardrobe, hiding in my ball gowns. "I'm playing!" she insisted. (Playing? She's sixteen!) In the reflection of the looking glass I saw her stick her tongue out at me.

"I'd prefer if you didn't 'play' in my suite, Pauline," I said, smiling with all the sweetness I could muster.

*January 7, 1797.*
At the opera last night four young men arrived at our box insisting that they had been invited. Pauline, it turned out, had looked at each of them through the large end of her opera glass (which in this country means, *Come see me*).

Bonaparte only laughed when I told him. "You find that amusing?" I demanded. Frankly, I feel like killing his little sister.

*30 Ventôse, Luxembourg Palace*
*Chère amie,*

 *Terrible news—Thérèse sued Tallien for divorce yesterday. She and the baby and the nanny and three house servants are with me now. Apparently Tallien threatened her with a pistol. I told her I'd do what I could to keep it out of the journals.*

 *And speaking of journals, according to the* République *I'm unable even to write this letter because I've been put in prison for making false bank notes. Ha!*

 *I'm apprehensive regarding the upcoming election. The Royalist faction is gaining strength. Our Minister of Police claims one hundred deputies have made oaths of allegiance to the Pretender. One deputy even had the* *gall to stroll in the Tuileries gardens in red-heeled boots.\**

*Director Letourneur assures us that we need not fear, that all will be under control because he will be patrolling the streets of Paris on horseback. (The dolt!) And as for Director La Réveillière, he is taken up with matters pertaining to a cult he has founded. I advised him that every good religion needed a martyr, and that to make his a success he should get himself hanged. He failed to see the humour.*

*Père Barras*

---

*May 9—Milan.*

We're back in Milan after a difficult three months of travel. In January Bonaparte defeated yet another Austrian army—the *fifth*—and then turned his attention south, to Rome, forcing the Papal states to succumb. Then, with the south secure, he chased the Austrians into the north, until finally, two weeks ago, they agreed to a preliminary peace.

And so, at last, the Austrians are defeated and Bonaparte is victorious. His wife, however, is not. I wage a losing battle with his spirited sister Pauline. This morning I discovered her in the pantry with a footman. "I think you should consider getting your sister married," I told Bonaparte. *Fast.* "General Leclerc is in love with her," I suggested. Victor Leclerc was an absolute fool for the girl. "Everyone calls him the blond Bonaparte because he imitates you." Short, serious, with thin lips and big eyes, Victor Leclerc even looked like Bonaparte, but for his fair colouring.

"His father is a merchant." Bonaparte stood and went to the window, his hands clasped behind his back. "Wealthy, though."

Pauline yawned. "Perhaps you would like to sit down." Bonaparte glanced at me, suddenly unsure. Matters to do with his family flummoxed him completely.

"Perhaps I should go," I said, standing.

"Stay!"

---

\* *Before the Revolution, aristocrats wore boots with high red heels.*

"What's this all about?" Pauline demanded.

"You must have a husband," Bonaparte said.

"I'm already betrothed." Pauline glared. (At me!) "You *might* recall."

"Deputy Fréron is a middle-aged drunk with three illegitimate children by an actress—a bad one."

"He was going to leave her!"

"She claims he married her!"

"Bonaparte?" I touched his hand. He and his sister would only end up brawling at each other. And if anyone was a match for Bonaparte, it was Pauline.

Bonaparte sat down, scowling. "What about General Leclerc?"

Pauline looked from me to her brother and back again. "Little Victor?"

"Marriage would bring many benefits, Pauline," I said. "General Leclerc comes from a wealthy family."

"Flour merchants!"

"He was educated in Paris," I persevered. "The family has a country seat—the château of Montgobert." For all I knew it was a pile of stones.

"What about a trousseau?" she demanded.

"Whatever you like."

"The gowns must be by Signora Tandello."

Bonaparte coughed. Signora Tandello was the most expensive dressmaker in Milan. Yes, I nodded, of course, *anything*.

"How much of a dowry would I get?"

"Joseph and I will have to talk about that," Bonaparte said.

"No doubt a great deal," I added.

Pauline pursed her lips. "Bien."


*May 15, La Chaumière*
*Darling,*

*It is just as well you are in the Land of Antiquity, for the situation in Paris has become worrisome. The election was a disaster. The Royalists have taken control of the legislative councils! Even General Pichegru, who everyone knows is in the pay of the Pretender, was elected President of the Five*

Hundred. I was at a dinner last night where the guests talked quite openly of putting the Pretender on the throne. The Royalists' agents—of whom there are rumoured to be a number in Paris—are throwing gold around quite freely.

My home life is worrisome as well—a disaster, some might say. I was mad to have reconciled with Tallien. I love him with a passion, you know I do, but I simply can't live with his drinking, his wenching and fits of jealous rage. And now it's too late, alas. Every woman in Paris is in an interesting condition, it seems, myself now included.

*Your loving and dearest*
*(and yes, somewhat miserable) friend, Thérèse*
Note—*I heard that your friend Aimée\* died. My sympathy, darling.*


*May 22—Mombello.\*\**

It's a lovely spring evening. Fireflies dance outside the open windows. I am writing this by moonlight. How late is it? I'm not sure. Thérèse's letter disturbed me terribly. I am filled with sorrow, grief. How many lives have been sacrificed for this Revolution of ours, our precious *liberté*? I think of Aimée, all my loved ones who have died. I think of Alexandre. *La liberté ou la mort.* Will their sacrifice be for naught? Will the Royalists be victorious, put a king back on the throne, abolish all that so many have died for?

I kept Lazare's Saint Michael medal close to my heart today—Saint Michael with his sword, Saint Michael fighting tirelessly against the forces of evil. I think of Bonaparte facing the enemy, over and over again. I think, with admiration and pride, of his astonishing victories. But to what end, I can't help but wonder, is he chasing the Royalists out of Italy, establishing a democracy here? What would it matter if Paris were to fall to the enemy?

---

*\* Aimée Hosten, a créole friend of Josephine's with whom she was imprisoned.*

*\*\* A country villa north of Milan that Josephine and Bonaparte leased for the hot summer months.*

*May 30.*

It took a moment for Lieutenant Lavalette to catch his breath. He is not a young man. He took off his hat and straightened his wig, which failed to cover his bald spot. "I arrived in Genoa in the early afternoon, General," he began, standing at attention. "After refreshing myself at my inn, I made straight away for the Assembly and as—"

"Get to the point." Bonaparte drummed his fingers.

"I was informed that your mother was on a vessel in the harbour, General."

"And where is she now?"

"In Genoa, General, I—"

"You left her there? Lieutenant, Genoa is on the verge of an uprising!"

"She insisted," Lavalette stammered. "She said, 'My son is here, I have nothing to fear.'" (Bonaparte smiled.) "I ordered a detachment of cavalry to escort her, General. They will be arriving tomorrow."

*"They?"*

"Your mother and a man—she didn't give his name. And a boy—her son, I think she said. Your brother, General?"

"Girolamo?"

"And two daughters."

"Mon Dieu, Bonaparte," I said, standing abruptly. "That's almost your entire family!"


*June 1.*

We set out to meet them on the road, Bonaparte and I and the two "youngsters"—Pauline and Louis. South of Milan, a carriage came into view escorted by soldiers on horseback. Bonaparte let down the glass. "It's them."

"Put up the glass," Pauline protested.

"Don't screech." Louis covered his ears. He is two years older than Pauline and the two constantly bicker.

"Oh, I feel a fright," I said to Bonaparte. I was fatigued from the heat and parched with thirst.

Bonaparte ran his fingers through his hair. "Maria-Anna has changed her name to Elisa and Maria-Anunziata is now Caroline. But Girolamo's only thirteen. I can still call him Fifi."

"How should I address your mother?" I felt a sick headache coming on. Why had I not thought to take laudanum?

"As Signora Letizia." Bonaparte clasped and unclasped his hands, then wiped his palms on his thighs. "She gave birth to thirteen children; eight survived."

"Remarkable." I didn't know what else to say.

"She is famous for her tiny hands and feet," Pauline said.

"She's from Corsica's Sartène district, well known for bandits and blood vendettas." Bonaparte adjusted his sash. "As a child, I thought my mother was a warrior."

One of our horses whinnied. Bonaparte pounded on the ceiling. I fell forward as the carriage came to a sudden halt. Bonaparte pushed the door open and jumped to the ground.

"Aspetta un momento," Pauline yelled, tying her hat strings. "Napoleone, aspetta!"

The footman let down the step and helped Pauline out of the carriage. I heard shrieks: my Corsican family. I pulled my shawl modestly around my shoulders.

"Madame?" Louis held out a white-gloved hand. "May I offer my protection? The Bonapartes are known to be rowdy."

"How is it you are so gentle, Louis? Are you sure you are a Bonaparte?" I was relieved to see him smile. No more risky remarks, I told myself.

We approached the noisy group. A boy was tumbling in the dust, laughing. Girolamo, no doubt. Bonaparte punched him on the shoulder and the boy punched him back, feigning to box.

"I wonder who that fat man is," Louis said.

An older man with a pudding face was standing by the coach, his mouth hanging open as he watched the Liberator of Italy clasp his young brother in a headlock, the boy cursing like a sailor. "You don't know him?"

A plump girl of about fourteen—Bonaparte's youngest sister Caroline, I expected—was making excited hops in front of Pauline. Regarding everyone with a look of disapproval was a thin, mannish woman with heavy features: Elisa. And at the centre of the commotion was Signora Letizia, a tiny woman clothed in a black linen gown set off rather incongruously by yellow fluted neck-ruches. "You are killing yourself, Napoleone." At least, that is what I thought she said, for her heavy Corsican accent made her difficult to understand.

"Ah, there you are." Bonaparte released his hold on young Girolamo, who went tumbling. He took my arm and turned to face his mother. "Maman, allow me to present my wife, Josephine."

I made a respectful curtsy. "At last I meet my honoured mother," I said, kissing her on both cheeks. She was smaller than I'd expected, but a great deal more frightening.

She frowned, looking me over, and said something to Bonaparte in Italian. Then she turned to her eldest daughter. "Get your husband."

"Now?" Elisa let out a hiccup.

Bonaparte looked from Elisa to the man standing by the coach. "Elisa got married? But I didn't give permission!"

"You are not the head of this family," Signora Letizia informed her son.

"Félix!" Elisa yelled. "Get over here."

"I'm going to get married too!" Pauline displayed her ring.

Bonaparte's mother fixed a baleful look on me, as if I were to blame. A whirlwind of dust stung my eyes. I squeezed Bonaparte's arm. "It's too hot in the sun."


"He's an idiot," Bonaparte fumed in the privacy of our room. "How can Elisa stand him?"

"I don't believe she cares for him in the least." Elisa, it would appear, cared for no one.

"She's not going to get a sou."

No dowry? I could just imagine the maelstrom such a pronouncement would provoke. With the Bonapartes, I was beginning to understand, even the smallest slight was cause for battle. "Do you think your mother will allow Pauline to marry General Leclerc if you don't grant Elisa a dowry?"

Bonaparte scowled.

I covered his hand with my own. "I believe you are right, Bonaparte. I believe your mother is a warrior."


*June 3.*

Bonaparte's Uncle Fesch, his brother Joseph and Joseph's timid wife Julie have arrived, so now all the Bonapartes are here—all but Bonaparte's brother Lucciano, that is, who I'm told refused to come to Italy because of me. (Or rather, I should say *Lucien,* for apparently he has changed his name as well.)

"His wife miscarried," Lisette told me, "and he claims it's your fault." Lisette has become an invaluable informant.

"How could I have had anything to do with it?"

"It's because you prevented Pauline from marrying Deputy Fréron."

"I wasn't the one to forbid it! And in any case, what would that have to do with Lucien's wife's miscarriage?"

"Lucien Bonaparte and Deputy Fréron are friends."

"They are?"

"And that's why General Bonaparte got his brother Lucien assigned to the Army of the North—to get him away from Deputy Fréron. Or rather, you got the General to do it."

"Bonaparte will do something just because I ask him to?" I smiled at the thought.

"And so Lucien Bonaparte and his wife had to move north and then she miscarried—"

"I was so sorry to hear that."

"And so the mishap was your fault."

I frowned, puzzled.

"Because of you, they had to move. When they moved, it happened." Lisette shrugged. "Bonaparte logic."


*June 4 (Pentecost Sunday).*

Our first big family dinner. I am chagrined to discover that the preferred subjects of conversation among the Bonapartes at table are infertility and money.

"Why is there no bambino, Napoleone?" Signora Letizia tapped her knife for emphasis. She had taken the position of honour at the head of the table.

Bonaparte ignored his mother's pointed stare. He was sitting with his arms crossed, glowering. His brother Joseph, as the eldest, had claimed the chair to the right of their mother and it bothered my husband, I knew. (The Bonapartes take any indication of rank very seriously.)

"As the French Ambassador to Rome, I will be making sixty thousand francs a year," Joseph told Uncle Fesch. "As General-in-Chief of the Army of Italy, Napoleone is paid only forty thousand." He picked up a fork, examined it with interest and passed it to his wife, who likewise examined it, turning it over to read the inscription.

"*Magnifico!*" Elisa's husband Félix said, wiping the perspiration from his brow.

"Joseph, you can get some very good deals on sculptures in Rome," Uncle Fesch said, leaning back in his chair.

"Lei e troppo vecchia, Napoleone," Signora Letizia told Bonaparte.

I coughed on a chunk of chipolata sausage in the rice. *Troppo vecchia:* too old. I am too old, she'd told him—too old to have children.

"O primavera, gioventù dell'anno. O gioventù, primavera della vita!"* Pauline sang off-tune.

"Maybe she's barren," Elisa said. (Hiccup.)

"Plombières is an excellent health spa for that problem," Joseph's wife hissed across the table at me. "It's expensive, however." The daughter of a silk merchant, Julie Bonaparte had a straightforward view of the world: profit, loss, supply, demand. Mark-up. And now and again: quality goods.

"What does barren mean?" Girolamo had pressed the bread into dough and formed a moustache with it.

"I'll explain when you're older, Girolamo," Elisa told him.

"I'm thirteen. And I'm changing my name to Jérôme."

"Liar. You're only twelve." Caroline grabbed a chunk of his dough moustache and threw it across the table.

"Maman had thirteen babies, five died," Pauline said.

* *Oh spring, youth of the year! Oh youth, springtime of life!*

"*Magnifico!*" Félix said solemnly.

"Salute. To Maman!"

"Cin-cin!" (Hiccup.)

"Cin-cin, cin-cin." Uncle Fesch raised his glass, oblivious to the chunk of bread dough in his wine.

"Salute." I raised my glass to my new family.

*[Undated]*

Joseph, Elisa, Lucien (not here), Louis, Pauline, Caroline, Jérôme.

Joseph, Elisa, Lucien, Louis, Pauline, Caroline, Jérôme.

I'm getting it.

*June 8.*

"Forty thousand francs," Bonaparte announced to Elisa. "Each."

Bonaparte and Joseph had just returned from a meeting with a notary in Milan to arrange dowries for Elisa and Pauline.

"I'm getting forty thousand?" For a moment I thought Elisa might even smile.

"Well, actually, for you, thirty-five plus three Corsican properties—Vecchia and the two vineyards." Bonaparte shrugged. "It amounts to the same thing."

"Vecchia is damp." Elisa made a face. "What did Pauline get?"

"Forty thousand—in gold." Pauline stuck out her tongue.

*5:15 P.M.*

"Napoleone!"

Bonaparte looked up. "Was that my mother?"

"Napoleone!"

It sounded as if Signora Letizia was outside the door to our suite. "She wishes to speak to you, I believe."

Bonaparte went to the door. "Your footman is asleep," I heard his mother say. "Is l'anziana inside?"

*L'anziana:* the old woman. A surge of anger went through me. This morning, Lisette had heard my mother-in-law refer to me as *la puttana*, Italian for whore! I'd been doing everything in my power to gain my mother-in-law's favour, but nothing seemed to please her. Indeed, even my acts of kindness were viewed as an affront. I made her look like a peasant, she'd told Bonaparte. When I won at reversi, I made her look stupid. (I'd intentionally only won one game out of four.) I was too trusting of my servants—I should sleep with the silver at the foot of my bed. I shouldn't be giving the beggars so much. I laughed too much—I should be silent, like Joseph's wife Julie. And didn't I realize I was too old to wear flowers in my hair? In short, she was determined to detest me.

Bonaparte stepped outside. I could hear his mother talking to him in Italian. Then he burst back into our room, his mother close behind. "*Zitto! Basta!*" Bonaparte stomped his feet.

Signora Letizia crossed her hands over her chest. "Then I refuse consent. Pauline will not marry."

Bonaparte sat down on a chair, his legs stretched out in front of him. He hit the arm of the chair with his fist. "You're telling *me*—the man who waged war on the Pope and won!—you're telling me to arrange a Catholic ceremony for my sisters?"

"Please, Signora Letizia, do sit down." I pulled out a chair for her. She stood ramrod stiff. I searched for a possible compromise. "Could a religious service be performed without anyone knowing?" I asked Bonaparte.

Bonaparte snorted. "Banns would have to be read . . ." He made a circling motion with his hand to mean, and on and on.

Signora Letizia moved toward the door.

"Un momento, Signora Letizia. Per piacere." I turned to Bonaparte. "A dispensation could be granted from having banns read, surely." For a price. "And the ceremony could be performed here, in the little chapel." We could air it out, get rid of the bats. "No one need know. And the civic ceremony could come after."

Silence.

"The civil ceremony must come first," Bonaparte said finally.

"Would that satisfy you, Signora Letizia?" I asked, as gently as I could.

Her lower lip stuck out in a pout. "Elisa too."

"Elisa's already married!"

"Not by the Church."

I touched Bonaparte's arm. What did it matter, one ceremony or two? "They could be at the same time." I didn't dare suggest that our own marriage might also be blessed.

He grunted. I looked over at Signora Letizia. She tipped her head slightly. Did that mean yes? I wasn't sure. "Very well then," I said with more confidence than I felt. I opened the door for Signora Letizia. "We will work out the details this afternoon," I whispered to her. She stomped woodenly out of the room.

I closed the door behind me, but was startled by an explosion of laughter.

"Well done!" Bonaparte embraced me.


*June 14.*

"There's a strange little man to see you." In honour of the festivities Lisette had put on her best gown—a muslin chemise banded by violet shirring that she'd done herself.

"The priest from the village?"

"I . . . I think *not.*"

A little man entered the room, his boots in his hand. His socks were dirty and full of holes. He bowed before me. "Signora Bonaparte?"

"Father Brioschi?" It *was* the priest. But his clothes! "Lisette, ask him if he brought his vestments."

"Habetisne vestimenta?" she asked him in Latin.

"Si." But he just stood there.

"I'll get someone who speaks Italian," Lisette said, heading out the door.

I nudged a wooden chair toward Father Brioschi. "Peccato," he said. *What a shame?* I wondered what he meant. I was saved from the discomfort of this "dialogue" by Lisette returning with Caroline Bonaparte, her plump young body squeezed into a pink taffeta gown covered with a froth of ruffles.

"Caroline, this is Father Brioschi. Could you—?"

"*This* is the priest?"

"Could you ask him whether he has brought his robes?"

"Ha portato i suoi abiti?" The little man said something in Italian and shrugged. "He didn't bring anything," Caroline said.

"Perhaps your uncle has something he could borrow." Uncle Fesch travelled with an elaborate wardrobe, much of it gleaned from the coffers of vanquished Italian nobility and clergy.

Shortly, Lisette returned, staggering under the weight of a jewel-encrusted white wool cape. I displayed it for the humble priest. "Per voi."

He ran his fingers over the glittering surface, whispering something reverent in Italian. "He said it's as lumpy as a diseased sow," Caroline said.


The oratory smelled mouldy in spite of all the flower bouquets. Pauline emerged in a gown so revealing that Father Brioschi was rendered speechless. Victor Leclerc looked on blissfully, his hat cocked sideways, wearing a grey overcoat very much like that of Bonaparte. He could not take his eyes off the wonder of this beauty, his bride. (His bride could not take her eyes off her own reflection in the polished brass.) Then a frowning Elisa and a trembling Félix joined them at the altar—thankfully, no hiccups—and Father Brioschi was finally able to squawk out the lines.

So, now that the ceremonies are over, it's time to prepare for a feast, a reception and a ball. Already, the Bonapartes are bickering over the seating arrangements at table tonight. Already, I'm exhausted.


*[Undated]*

"Is something going on?" Lisette asked, biting off a thread. "Signora Letizia changed her gown."

"Likely it has to do with the viewing today."

"The viewing?" Lisette licked the thread to knot it.

"During the Ancien Régime, the public thronged to Versailles every weekend to watch King Louis XV eat an egg. So, the Bonapartes thought that the public should be allowed to watch Bonaparte eat."

She looked astonished. I put up my hands as if to say, Don't ask me, I have nothing to do with it!

*June 19.*
"They're gone, Madame!" Lisette poured me a glass of champagne.
. "Pour a glass for yourself, Lisette," I offered. I was in a celebratory mood. Jérôme had been sent back to school in Paris. Joseph, his wife Julie and young Caroline Bonaparte had departed for Rome. Louis had been sent to Brescia with dispatches. And now, just this morning, Signora Letizia, Elisa and her hapless husband had left for Corsica.

Leaving only Pauline.

I heard a door slam, a shrill voice.

I clinked my glass against Lisette's and smiled ruefully. *Only* Pauline?

## *In which I receive shocking news*

*June 21, 1797—Mombello.*

"Is this all the mail there is from Paris?" I put down the small stack.

"That's what Moustache said," Lisette said, staring out the window.

"Nothing from my daughter?" Nothing from Eugène, either.

"Just what's there." She burst out laughing. "The footman is drunk! You should see him."

I went through the stack for the third time, more slowly: a letter from my banker; two letters from Barras; three from Aunt Désirée; two from Thérèse; a number from people whose names I did not recognize, the usual requests for favours. And bills, of course. Quite a few.

I tore open a notice from Madame Campan. It was only an announcement about an upcoming recital—a recital I would miss. Attached was a little note: "I thought you would like to know that 'the general' called on your daughter. All is well. She has become a beautiful young woman. She was brilliant in the part of Cassandra in *Agamemnon*."

Lisette was laughing again at the scene outside the window. "Madame, come here—quickly." She turned, puzzled by my silence. "Madame, what is it? Is it bad news?"

"Oh—no." I smoothed out Madame Campan's note. The perspiration from my hand had caused the ink to smear.

Lisette stood up. "Would you like me to get you some orange water?"

I shook my head. How could I explain? I handed her the note. I felt foolish, so suddenly overcome. Somehow, I hadn't realized—had not been prepared.

"That's nice." Lisette turned the note over in her hands, mystified. *A beautiful young woman.* "Yes," I said, blinking back tears.

*June 22.*

"Madame Bonaparte is in the garden," I heard our footman say. I saw a white plume bobbing above the boxwood hedge, heard a young man's voice. A *familiar* voice! I picked up my skirts, hurried down the narrow path, my heart racing.

We very nearly collided. Eugène lifted me in his arms, twirling me clumsily. "I can't believe it, it's actually you," I cried out, my eyes stinging.

He wiggled his hands behind his ears. "Yes, Maman, it's me—truly. Just in time for your birthday."

I took his hands in mine, blinking and sniffing. He remembered! "You didn't write. I wasn't expecting you for another month." It was such a joy to see him.

Sheepishly, he pulled his hands away. "I know, I'm neglecting to wear my riding gloves, I'm neglecting to clip my nails." Imitating my voice, grinning.

"I wasn't thinking that," I protested, laughing. "When did you grow so tall?" Yet still, that boyish face: dimples, freckles across his nose. "How was your journey?"

But before he could answer, he was startled by my new dog sniffing at his boots. "What's this?" he exclaimed, jumping back.

"His name is Pugdog." The tiny black creature sat down by the side of the path, panting like an old dog, his lame leg sticking out to one side.

"What does Fortuné have to say about that?" Eugène bent down to stroke Pugdog's head.

I made a sad face. "Fortuné was killed, Eugène."

"Fortuné!"

"Not long ago. He challenged the cook's mastiff and . . ." My eyes welled up remembering.

"*Fortuné* took on a mastiff?" He scoffed at the thought.

"Come," I said, pulling on his arm, "Bonaparte's in the stable."

My son stopped abruptly on the path. "General Bonaparte?" he stammered.

"He'll be so pleased that you've arrived." I tugged at him again, but he was too big to budge. And then I understood. The stepfather he hardly knew was now a hero, hailed Liberator of Italy. The stepfather he hardly knew was now his commanding general.

*June 23.*

Immediately, Eugène's training has begun. "A superior war is won without fighting," I overheard Bonaparte instructing him this evening, after our meal. "One can use the forces of nature to good effect, but knowledge is the key. Battles are won here." Bonaparte tapped his forehead. "Not here." He put his hand on the pommel of his sword. "Am I understood?"

"Yes, General!" Eugène said eagerly.

Bonaparte caught my eye and grinned.

*June 29, 8:00 P.M. or so. Stiff!*

Eugène, Junot and Captain Charles spurred their horses, raced ahead. Lisette did her best to keep up (she's bold on a horse). I was content to follow at a more leisurely pace, taking a path that edged a pond, relishing the solitude, the vistas. It was a glorious summer day.

Before long I realized I was lost. I was beginning to worry when I saw a man on horseback on the horizon: Captain Charles. I kicked my horse into a gallop. "I was lost!" Laughing, I pulled to a halt beside him, doubling my reins to hold my horse back. The burst of freedom had excited him.

Captain Charles struck a heroic pose. "I returned to rescue a damsel in distress."

"So this is East Wind," I said, looking at the captain's mount. There'd been talk about the horse Captain Charles had recently bought, outrageous speculation about how much he'd paid for her. (The one-hundred-louis ride, Pauline called the mare.) Well built, a glistening black, she radiated both power and beauty.

"Like her?" He stroked his horse's neck. The silver ornaments on her headband sparkled in the light.

The horse was magnificent, without a doubt. And the captain cut an exceptionally handsome figure, I thought, noting the unusual stitching around the cuff of his riding jacket, the square bone buttons. "My father once had the good fortune to own such a horse," I said. "A gambling win. Lady Luck, he called her."

"Mine was luck of a different sort."

Our horses were walking side by side now, in pace. "Oh?"

"I did rather well on a business contract." He swiped a fly off East Wind's ear.

"Through the Bodin brothers?"

"Yes, and as a result they've invited me to join their company. They have profited from buying and selling National Properties, but now they wish to expand into the area of military supplies, specializing in horses."

"For the Army of Italy?"

"I guess it is foolish of me to reveal such a thing." Or simply very trusting, I thought. "May I tell you something in confidence, Madame? As soon as peace is signed, I intend to resign the army. Not every man is meant to be a soldier."

Certainly, it was hard to imagine the captain with a sabre in his hand—hard to imagine him using it. "Military suppliers do very well." Military suppliers became outrageously wealthy overnight.

"With the right connections, yes, but without—" He made a clucking sound that caused his mare to spurt forward. "So far the Bodins have been unsuccessful in their efforts to get a government contract."

"They've applied to the Minister of War?"

"Yes, but without the consent of a certain director, it's useless." He glanced at me.

"Director Barras, by any chance?"

"I understand you are on intimate terms with him."

"Director Barras and I are friends."

"That puts you in a powerful position."

I laughed. "Not really."

"Madame, may I ask you something?" We headed down a steep incline. I leaned to keep my sidesaddle from slipping.

"Certainly," I said. No doubt he wanted me to recommend the Bodin Company to Barras. I am so often appealed to for favours, I've come to recognize the clues.

"Might you consider joining our company? I hope I haven't offended you by suggesting such a thing, Madame."

I pressed my calf against my horse's side, to move her over. "On the contrary." Indeed, it was a most interesting proposition.

"With the right contacts, one could make millions."

*Millions.* My horse pricked her ears. I heard the pounding of hooves. Lisette (in the lead!), followed by Junot and Eugène, appeared at the edge of the woods. They raced toward us at a gallop, yelling and laughing.

"It appears we've been discovered, Captain," I said.

"And now there will be rumours." Captain Charles spurred East Wind. She bucked into a gallop. My horse pulled at the bit, eager to follow. I grabbed her mane and gave her her head, my heart pounding, the wind in my face.


*July 3.*
The Austrian delegates will arrive in one week—representatives of the most ancient royal court of Europe. I'm in a panic! If only I'd had my tooth attended to earlier.


*July 4, late afternoon. (Hot!)*
Dr. Rossi, the dental surgeon, is a little man with bushy red whiskers that he constantly pulls on. He told me a new tooth would successfully root—for a price, nine hundred francs, and this without a guarantee. I explained to him the urgency of my situation; I'm to return in the morning.


*July 5.*
I'm ill! It was *ghastly.*

*Evening, almost midnight (can't sleep from pain).*
What happened:

There was a peasant girl in Dr. Rossi's antechamber when I arrived. She grinned, displaying yellow teeth. Dr. Rossi's maid showed me to a small room, in the middle of which was a leather chair. I was asked to sit and (apologetically) asked to remove my hat, which I did. The doctor entered after a moment, pulling on his whiskers. He peered into my mouth and probed at my bad tooth with a pointed metal object. He seemed pleased by the pain this caused me: "Excellent, excellent."

After his maid gave me morphine for nerves, he excused himself, explaining that he would only be a moment. I heard cries—the peasant girl?—and then he rushed into the room with a bloody tooth pinched in a vise-like tool, two assistants dashing in after him. Involuntarily I shrank back, but the assistants laid hold of me, and the doctor yanked my tooth out and pushed the new tooth into its place. Then one of the assistants held my jaw closed while the other wound my head with a strong strip of linen so that I might not open my mouth.

And so here I am, mute and dazed, bandaged and sedated, with a peasant girl's tooth in my mouth. I dare not get sick.


*July 7.*
My tooth came out—an infection had set in. I'm taking generous doses of laudanum. God meant me to have bad teeth, and to receive the Austrian diplomats thus. Or so I tell myself.


*July 9.*
The Austrian delegates will be here tomorrow. I've been all day in the hands of beauticians: I've been waxed, massaged, pounded and polished. Lisette painted my nails as Eugène quizzed me on the name and title of each diplomat (Cobenzl, Gallo, Merfeld, Ficquelmont), their children, parents, aunts and uncles even, the year each was born, the town. "You know all this, Maman," Eugène said, throwing down the lists.

*July 10, 4:00 P.M. or so.*

They'll be arriving in an hour. "You've never looked more beautiful," Bonaparte told me reverently, taking in the details of my gown, a muslin draped in the style of the ancient Romans. A filigree laurel of gold held back my loose curls.

"It's not too modern?" I studied the effect in the looking glass.

"That's the point. The old world meets the new. Old world *bows* to the new."

New world, indeed. I smiled, for Bonaparte refused to lace his boots with silk ribbons. I knew aristocrats. I feared they would laugh at his laces and round hat.

"Uff! They'll be wearing plebeian shoelaces soon enough," Bonaparte said, giving me a careful kiss before disappearing back into his study to his maps and documents, texts and correspondence—the work that keeps him up all day and all night, day after day. Winning battles had only been a step; the important work was establishing democracy in Italy.

"Kings never worked so hard," I said to Lisette, turning to view myself from the side. I'd become slender in Italy, due to ill health. I was pleased with the effect—it made me look younger.

Captain Charles and Eugène appeared at the door wearing tablecloths for capes and lampshades for hats. "Vee must 'av peace!" they barked in unison, imitating an Austrian accent.

"Don't make me laugh," I pleaded. "I'll ruin my make-up!"


*11:20 P.M.*

It went well! I am pleased. Bonaparte, however, is *not*. I'm having a bath prepared to calm him.

On the whole I found the diplomats to be pleasant—especially the Comte de Cobenzl, the head of the delegation, who speaks elegant French. "I look forward to many pleasant evenings," I told him as they left, adding, daringly, "Citoyens." The Comte de Cobenzl, who heard me distinctly, smiled and embraced me fraternally.

He is an ugly but genial older man with the aristocratic talent of putting everyone at ease. We talked of Corneille's *Le Cid* (parts of which I was surprised to discover Bonaparte had committed to memory); Goethe's new epic *Hermann und Dorothea;* the corresponding theories of electricity and animal magnetism; Mozart's opera *The Marriage of Figaro.* Bonaparte praised his beloved Ossian, which surprised and impressed the Austrians, I could see—they hadn't expected a Republican general to read poetry.

"The charming bastards," Bonaparte cursed as soon as the door closed behind them. "They have no intention whatsoever of negotiating a peace agreement."

*July 14.*
This evening as I was preparing for bed, Bonaparte burst into my dressing room. "They're balking," he said, pacing in front of the wardrobe with his hands behind his back. "They refuse to come to an agreement." He sat down on a little stool. "And why should they? As long as the Royalists are gaining strength in Paris—" He clenched his fists.

*July 16.*
The trouble began before the midday meal. Lisette and I were meeting with two of the cooks, discussing the menu for a reception in honour of the Austrian delegates.

"Solo—" I turned to Lisette. "What is the word for chicken?"

"Pollo."

"Solo pollo." Only chicken. The words rolled off my tongue like a song, as if I were in an opera. A comic opera. Opéra bouffe.

The cooks could not comprehend. No pasta? No salami?

"Lisette, explain to them that that is what the General wishes—" I was interrupted by the sound of someone shouting. It was Bonaparte, yelling in Italian. He only spoke Italian when he was angry. Or amorous.

The two cooks began to laugh.

"What did he say?" I asked Lisette. Bonaparte had been quite explosive of late. The peace talks had not been progressing. The Austrians were not taking him seriously. They were biding their time in the belief that soon the Royalists would be back in power in France.

"He said asswipe, Madame." Lisette flushed.

*Asswipe?* It was unlike Bonaparte to be crude. "Are you sure?" Lisette has been studying Italian, but how would she know a word like that?

"And blazes. And devil."

"The General is savage as . . ." The head chef held up a meat axe, grinned. "Meat. Axe." Enunciating slowly, proudly, in French.

There was another angry outburst. "That haughty, demanding prick!" Napoleon shouted, in French this time. My cheeks burned.

The cook with the wen on his neck snorted. That word he knew.

I stood. "No, you stay," I told Lisette.


Bonaparte was standing with his back to the door. His grey wool waistcoat was stained with perspiration. The scene was one of disorder, the carpet strewn with journals from Paris. I recognized one—the *Mémorial*, a Royalist publication. Berthier, Bonaparte's chief of staff, was sitting at the desk in the corner, staring at the General, a quill in one hand. They seemed frozen in an antique tableau, shadow silhouettes against the light. The very air felt dangerous, like gunpowder, as if it might explode. "The lives of good men have been sacrificed," Bonaparte yelled, breaking the spell. "And for what? Without a peace agreement, what have we accomplished? Nothing!"

"Un momento," I whispered to the hall porter, positioning myself beside the door out of sight, standing purposefully, as if spying on one's husband was the normal thing to do.

"The enemy isn't here, the enemy is in Paris! The Royalists have taken over. The traitors should be arrested, banished! All of them! *Veni, vidi, fugi,* my ass.* The journals should be repressed! They're in the pay of England, of Austria, of every damned Royalist nation in Europe—why should they be tolerated? And the Church fomenting trouble again. *Basta!*

*Veni, vidi, fugi—*Latin for "I came, I saw, I fled"*—was attributed to Napoleon in a Royalist journal in Paris. It plays on the famous line by Caesar,* Veni, vidi, vici, *meaning, "I came, I saw, I conquered."*

Berthier, take this down. Address this to the Emperor. Yes, of course, the Emperor of Austria. Tell him this. Tell him if a peace agreement is not signed by the first of September— No, don't put that. Put . . . what is it? Yes. Put fifteen Fructidor. Let him figure it out. If the peace negotiations are not concluded by fifteen Fructidor, we go to war. You heard me: war!"

I stepped into the doorway. Bonaparte turned to me, his eyes bulging. He looked feverish, emanating a manic energy.

"Has something happened?" I crossed the room and took his hand. He is shortsighted; it is a mistake to address him from a distance. "What's all the shouting about?"

"Shouting?"

"We could hear you in the kitchen."

Bonaparte glanced at his chief of staff, puzzled. "We weren't shouting."


*La Chaumière*
*Darling!*
*A quick note: I've heard rumours that Lazare is being considered for Minister of War. Your husband is to take orders from your former lover? Nom de Dieu!*

*Your most loving, etc., Thérèse*


*July 18, past midnight (can't sleep).*
"May I ask you something?" Bonaparte's hand on my shoulder was cold.

"Of course." I kissed his hand, as if to warm it—warm him.

"How . . . close were you with General Hoche?"

"We were friends."

He snorted. "You were lovers. Everyone knew that."

I pulled the covering sheet up over me. "In prison, yes." A partial truth.

"General Hoche is said to appeal to women. He's a chevalier of the bedchamber, it is said."

"Bonaparte, please, don't be like this." I pressed myself into his arms, pushing through the thicket of elbows and hands he put up as obstacles, pressing against him, knowing his need.

*August 1.*

"What does *res non verba* mean?" Eugène asked, looking up from reading the *Moniteur.*

*Res non verba* was Lazare's motto. I looked over my son's shoulder. The article quoted a speech Lazare had made to his troops. "It means, the thing, not the word—that what you do is more important than what you say," I told Eugène, disconcerted by my son's inability to translate a simple Latin phrase. I heard the sound of spurs jingling outside the door. Hastily, I folded the journal. "Eugène, don't speak of General Hoche around Bonaparte," I said under my breath, standing to greet my husband.

*July 22, Luxembourg Palace, Paris*
*Chère amie,*

*It is almost midnight as I write this. I am in a state, I confess. Forgive my hasty pen. Regrettably, things did not work out with respect to Lazare. It is too complex a matter to explain here. Nobly, he retreated. Whatever you might hear, he did this of his own accord.*

*Director Reubell has gone mad with fear. His delirium recalled to my mind an ancient Oriental proverb: that one should not confuse the sound of the beating of one's heart with the hooves of approaching horses. It is the beating of my own heart that causes me pain. I begin to see that my life has been spent not as a conquering knight, but as a rather pathetic courtier, sitting, ever hopeful, in the antechamber to the boudoir of the Goddess of Love. In all my groping encounters, was it not simply Love I sought? (I recall a little lecture from you, my friend, to this effect.) And yet, having at last been blessed, I submitted not to the light, but to the darkness within.*

*I hear the hooves of approaching horses. By the time you receive this, it will all be over. It is said that the guilty are victorious. If so, I need not fear.*

*Père Barras*

*July 23, Fontainebleau*
*Dear Rose,*

*Imagine General Hoche behaving in such a shameful way! He had nine thousand soldiers quartered at La Ferte-Alais and he as much as admitted that he was going to take over by force. And to think that our Eugène served on his staff.*

*Your godmother, Aunt Désirée*
*Note—I saw Marie-Adélaïde d'Antigny this morning when I stopped by with the money for her education and keep.\* She has just turned eleven, a pretty little thing. I almost wept to see her—she looks just like Alexandre! Please don't forget to send money.*


*July 27, La Chaumière*
*Darling,*

*Lazare was forced to leave Paris under a cloud of suspicion, accused of being a traitor. I am sick with apprehension. Barras refuses to talk about it. If you can shed any light on this mystery, please let me know.*

*Your loving and very dearest friend, Thérèse*


*Wetzlar*
*Rose,*

*Forgive me for writing. I have a courier I can trust—otherwise, I would not compromise you in this fashion.*

*You will have accounts of my disgrace in the journals. I beg you to believe me when I say I did not behave dishonourably. Although clear in conscience, I carry the burden of shame. It is not a mantle I wear willingly. Assure your son that I honoured my vows to the Republic.*

*Should anything happen to me, please, I beg you, help my wife and child.*

*I love you still.*

*Burn this letter.*

*Your soldier, always, Lazare*


\* *Josephine's husband Alexandre had at least three known illegitimate children, one of whom was Marie-Adélaïde d'Antigny. Josephine and Désirée jointly contributed to her support.*

*[Undated]*
Oh, Lazare, Lazarro . . .


*August 4.*
Something happened in Paris—but what? Today, when Bonaparte was meeting with the Austrian delegates, I went through the journals in his office. Apparently, Lazare was named Minister of War, and then there was an outcry due to his youth and he resigned. And then his troops were discovered close to Paris, within a forbidden zone. (From what I can make out, the constitution forbids troops within twelve leagues of the building in which the Legislative Councils meet.) And then he was publicly accused of being a traitor to the Republic.

I cannot make sense of this. There is no greater patriot than Lazare, no man more honourable. It sickens me to think of him publicly reviled, branded with the one word he most deeply loathed: *traitor.*


*September 8—Passariano.* *
We've arrived in Passariano, at last. We are staying in the palace of the last doge of Venice. The courtyard is the size of a military field and the palace itself is huge, ostentatious, ornate. I wander from golden room to golden room, watched by the servants. A fraud, they judge us, Republican imposters.

We won't be here long, I hope.


*September 10.*
Mail from Paris. Trouble again. I'm even more confused than before.


*18 Fructidor, Luxembourg Palace, Paris*
*Chère amie,*
*It is over; I am alive. So, it would seem, is the Republic.*

* *Headquarters had been moved to Passariano north-east of Venice in order to facilitate the peace talks.*

*At dawn I ordered the alarm gun fired. Over sixty Royalist deputies have been arrested. Soon they will all be deported. So be it, the Republic has been saved.*

*Again.*

*Again and again.*

*Directors Carnot and Barthélemy escaped—to Switzerland, it is suspected.\**

*My secretary, Botot, is on his way to Italy with instructions for Bonaparte. Please keep me informed.*

*You are right to suggest that we communicate in cipher. Next time.*

*Père Barras, Director—still*

*Note—Please disregard my last letter. I was, as they say, "in the cups." I vaguely recall writing something about horses.*

*September 9, Fontainebleau*

*Dear Rose,*

*Our government has arrested itself—and just when I was preparing for our move to Saint-Germain. I had to tell the carters to return the following week—at my expense, alas. But there was no way we could travel safely with the roads so agitated. Soldiers were everywhere, cart wheels rumbling over the cobblestones, dragging cannon. Almost two hundred of our elected—yes, elected!—representatives have been taken away in iron cages like wild beasts. Even that lovely General Pichegru, President of the Five Hundred.\*\* Even two Directors! And just because they would not keep Décadi? The King was more just.*

*Your godmother Aunt Désirée*

[Undated]

"Excellent, the Royalists have been kicked out," Bonaparte said, throwing down the *Moniteur.* "*Now* Austria will negotiate."

*\* Director Barras is reported to have thrown a writing desk into a mirror in his rage at discovering that Director Carnot had managed to escape so narrowly that his bed was still warm.*

*\*\* General Pichegru was a Royalist agent.*

*September 20.*

A surprising announcement from Bonaparte. Shortly after two he came into my suite of rooms, sat down across from me. "You've been saying you'd like to see Venice," he said.

I looked up from my embroidery. "We're going to Venice?" I was astonished he would even consider it. Ever since the Venetians had risen up against French soldiers, massacring them in their hospital beds, Bonaparte had conceived a burning hatred for them. An effeminate, treacherous race! he would rant. A city of scoundrels!

He drummed his fingers on the arm of the chair. "No, *you're* going."

And then he explained: the Venetian government, anxious about their fate in the negotiations, had invited him to visit Venice in order to prove their loyalty to the French Republic. He scoffed. "Stinking liars. Of course I won't go, but refusing outright would complicate things. So I'm sending you in my stead."

"But Bonaparte . . ." I paused, trying to take in what he was saying. "This is a job for a diplomat. I can't—"

"I'll tell my secretary to make all the arrangements," he said, standing. "You'll require a gown, something suitably impressive." He hesitated for a moment. "Three hundred francs? Four hundred should do it. Don't worry, the Army of Italy will pay."


"What has happened?" Lisette exclaimed, finding me in the wardrobe, gowns and shawls everywhere. It looked like a field of war.

"I've just learned I'm to go to Venice—"

"That's wonderful!"

"—on a *diplomatic* mission." I groaned. She looked at me with a blank expression. "And the problem is, I'm going to have to dress the part—but in a traditional style."

"So, you'll get gowns made?"

I sighed. Five hundred francs for each gown, three hundred for a cape, one hundred and fifty for hoops, six hundred . . .

Bonaparte insists that I will look sufficiently elegant in a four-hundred-franc gown. As if one gown would suffice! I'm to be fêted day and night for three days in only one ensemble? "My mother wears one gown for weeks at a time," Bonaparte pointed out. Wisely, I held my tongue.

*Venice!*

Coming to Venice has been like falling into a deliciously sensual dream. Everything conspires to make one feel that one is not on this earth, but in some watery magical realm.

My welcome has been overwhelming. A "parade"—in boats!—down the Grand Canal, the citizens hanging from the windows waving banners, showering me with flowers. I'm overwhelmed. And a bit ill, I confess, from so much rich food.

*September 24.*

I have returned to Passariano, to the land of Reality. At my suggestion, the President of the Venetian Republic returned with me in order to press the case for Venice. I regret it now, for Bonaparte was cold, unwelcoming. At dinner, I raised a glass in toast to Venice, spoke warmly of the Venetians, the Revolutionary zeal I saw in the citizens of this newly formed Republic. There was no warmth in Bonaparte's response.

"Murderer," he cursed as the Venetian President's carriage pulled away this morning.

I feel sad and defeated. A diplomat I am not. My heart is too easily engaged.

*September 29.*

I've been busy with official duties. Following my "diplomatic" mission to Venice, I've been called upon to write to the office of the Emperor of Austria, petitioning for the release of French prisoners. (I find these new duties hard to believe myself.) Now, if only I could do something to push the negotiations along. They're proceeding so slowly, and not at all helped, I suspect, by Bonaparte's ill humour. He's not an easy man to live with, and he becomes even more difficult when things are not going his way. "Je le veux!" is his favourite expression. I will it!

*September 30.*
Barras's secretary arrived covered with dust. "I'm too old to travel," Botot said, using his hat plume to brush himself off. "I had no idea the roads would be so rough."

"Did you have trouble from bandits?"

"My valet sent them scurrying." A smug smile.

"Bonaparte is in Udine this afternoon at the headquarters of the Austrian delegation," I told him. The meetings alternate. One day Bonaparte goes to Udine, the next day the Austrians come to Passariano. "He has been looking forward to your arrival." A lie. Bonaparte is convinced that Barras's secretary was being sent to spy on him.

Lisette came skipping down the wide stone steps, her skirts billowing out behind her. "A visitor from Paris! Is there news? Mail?" She came to an abrupt stop in front of us, flushed.

I smiled at her youthful exuberance. "First we must offer our guest refreshment, Lisette—and *then* we'll attack him for news."

News: Lazare Hoche is dead.

I excused myself and set out across the courtyard, alone. Eugène was in the riding arena, I knew, taking a lesson. Inside the stables it was dark, cool, smelling of dung. Two horses in box stalls watched me, munching. The stable boy jumped out of a pile of hay. "Signora!"

"Mi dispiace." I'm sorry. "Non importa." It doesn't matter.

I heard someone yelling from inside the arena. I pushed open the heavy door. Eugène was riding a black horse around the circumference, his face glistening, his horse foaming with sweat. The instructor was standing in the centre, yelling, "Keep your leg on him. Thumbs up. Outside rein!"

I took a seat in the stands. Eugène had turned his horse into the centre of the arena and was talking with his instructor. Then he looked up, saw me and grinned. The instructor turned, bowed deeply. "We are finished, Madame la Générale!"

"I am content to watch, Citoyen." I dreaded breaking the news to Eugène.

Eugène flung himself down beside me. "Did you see that turn on the forehand?" His face was flushed, his hair damp with sweat.

"Quite precise." I stood. "Let's walk in the garden."

He pulled at my arm. "Maman, what is it?"

I scanned the arena. It was empty now. "It's not good news," I said, sitting back down. "Your sister is fine, Aunt Désirée, the Marquis," I assured him, seeing the apprehension in his eyes. "It's about General Hoche, Eugène." I clasped my hands. "He is . . . He passed away." My chin began to quiver in spite of my resolve.

Eugène stared at me, not comprehending. "Dead, you mean? In battle?" With a hint of a stammer.

"No, in his bed. Of an infection in his lungs." I found a handkerchief. "Consumption." My voice was unsteady yet. I took a careful breath. It was inappropriate for *me* to weep.

Eugène leaned forward on his knees, blinking, hitting his riding crop on the bench in front of him. "He died in his *bed*?" He threw down his crop and stood, his face blotched.

"Eugène, I wanted you to—"

His footsteps down the wooden stairs echoed through the arena. I started to rise, to follow him, chase after him, but I stopped myself. He wanted to be alone.

It is late, dark but for a single candle, which is gradually lighting up the room. I am at a marble-topped table in the sitting room, wrapped in a patchwork counterpane. I can hear the hall porter snoring outside our bedchamber door, hear someone singing drunkenly in the courtyard.

The sound of frogs croaking is like a pulse throbbing, a night pulse. I cannot keep my thoughts from wandering, reaching for Lazare. I cannot believe what I have been told: that he is dead, that he died in his bed, robbed of a soldier's heroic death in battle.

My eyes well up, overflowing. When may I grieve? Where? I dare not. All this evening Bonaparte watched me, taking in my red-rimmed eyes, my sad smile.

A woman's truths, how secret they must be. Hidden, buried, only to emerge in the night.

I remember the rough surface of the cold stone walls as I climbed the stairs to Lazare's dank prison cell. I remember the taste of whisky on his tongue, the sputtering sound of a dirty taper burning, the silken texture of his skin. I remember, with wonder—and gratitude—the heat of his love . . . and my own, kindled from ashes.

I found the Saint Michael medal Lazare gave me, stashed away at the bottom of my box of gems. *La liberté ou la mort*, he'd had etched on the back. *Ou la mort.*

*Should anything happen to me,* he had written.

He died of galloping consumption, Botot explained again at dinner, his eyes fixed on his crystal glass of wine. At Wetzlar. He was buried there.

*Should anything happen . . .*

Something catches in my throat. It is bitter, foul, it makes me gag. It is a sudden thought: was Lazare murdered?


*October 1.*

A long talk with Botot this evening. This is what I understand:

The Royalists had changed tactics. Rather than attacking the Republic by force, they decided to try to topple it from within, and to that end succeeded in getting a number of Royalists elected to the Legislative Councils. The goal, of course, was to overthrow the Republic and reinstate a monarchy.

Barras, together with Directors Reubell and La Réveillière, decided to take action. Forming a majority in the Council of the five Directors, they decided to replace Royalist ministers with loyal Republicans (Lazare as Minister of War was one). Fearing that these changes would provoke a Royalist uprising, Barras persuaded Lazare to bring his troops close to Paris.

But here the story fades. Somehow the plan failed, the troops were discovered and Lazare ended up having to leave Paris under a cloud of suspicion, branded a traitor, an enemy of the Republic.

And then, a few weeks later, Barras made a second attempt to oust the Royalists and this time he succeeded. And then Lazare died.

There is more to this, I fear.


*October 3.*

Lisette set a tray down beside my bed. I could hear Eugène's voice in the stairwell, calling for his valet to bring down his riding jacket. I was glad he was going riding; he'd been morose, quiet. "Madame, remember when General Hoche called on you in Paris?" she asked, handing me a mug of frothy hot chocolate. "Just before we left for Italy. It was on your birthday, he brought you roses."

"I don't remember roses," I said, blowing on the steaming chocolate before taking a cautious sip. "Why?" Knowing even as I asked that I was going to regret the question.

"It's awful, Madame. It makes me want to cry. Everyone's saying he was murdered!"


*October 1, La Chaumière*
*Darling,*

*I have just returned from the funeral for Lazare and am overcome with sorrow. The entire nation grieves, stunned by the loss of the Republic's golden boy. He died accused by his enemies, but the people have judged him a saint—a saint of the Revolution. It was a lovely procession of shepherds wearing cypress crowns, their staffs wrapped in black ribbon.*

*Lazare's young wife was there. She looked quite faint, tragic. I suspect she's with child. Lazare's father supported her as best he could, but then he himself was overcome by heart-wrenching sobs, a dreadful keening wail. I weep now even to think of it.*

*I am haunted by the memory of an evening at my salon. Bonaparte was reading everyone's palm, and he looked at Lazare's and predicted that he would die at a young age in his bed. Do you remember that night?*

*The rumours are vicious, of course. Everyone is convinced Lazare was poisoned—and by Barras, of course. (They blame him of every crime!) It's terrible, especially considering how Barras himself is so overcome with grief. He spends entire days in a darkened room, refusing to speak.*

*Tender caresses from Thermidor. And love from the Glories, of course. Will you ever return? Things are so sad here.*

*Your loving and very dearest friend, Thérèse*
*Note—I heard you've hired Vautier to renovate your house. A brilliant choice!*

October 13.
The Austrian delegates dined here tonight. Bonaparte in a surly temper.

[Undated]
Damp today. I've ordered the fires lit. I'm in a melancholy mood. How does one set the stage for peace? I arrange cut flowers, ask the housekeeper to have the silver tea service polished and set out on the buffet, check the liqueur decanters, review the day's menu with the head chef. But despite my best efforts, the fires, the flowers, the succulent food, a gloomy chill pervades. There will be no peace today, I know.

October 15.
"The head of the Austrian delegation wishes to speak with you, Madame." Lisette opened her eyes wide.

"Comte de Cobenzl? Show him in, please!" One did not keep a man of such importance waiting.

As the Comte de Cobenzl entered, my impulse was to bow, but I refrained. As I am the wife of General Bonaparte, the victor, the Comte

Louis de Cobenzl should, in theory, bow to me. We solved the impasse by bowing at precisely the same moment, and with an equal degree of respect.

"I will not be long, Madame Bonaparte," he said, refusing my offer of a chair. "I requested a private audience with you because I am gravely concerned about the future of the negotiations. General Bonaparte has been treating us . . . *rudely*, to be frank. At the least request from us, his temper gives way to violence. No doubt you are aware that he destroyed my prized china tea set."

The day before, in a fit of temper, Bonaparte had thrown Cobenzl's tea set to the ground—the tea set the Comte was so proud of, the one that had been given to him personally by Catherine the Great—exclaiming, as he did so, "I'll break your monarchy like this china!"

"Comte de Cobenzl, please believe me," I said, "I was dismayed when I—"

The Comte put up his hand. "There is much more at stake than a tea service, Madame. If the General continues in this fashion, I'm afraid Austria will have to withdraw from the negotiations."

"Comte de Cobenzl—" Words escaped me. If the Austrian negotiators withdrew, there would be war again.

"My question to you is this: Would you speak to the General?"

Speak to Bonaparte? Was such a thing possible?

"We await the result." The Comte de Cobenzl bowed, I bowed lower, he bowed lower still.


*October 16.*

"You are not to interfere!" Bonaparte showered spittle in his fury.

"I am not interfering!"

Bonaparte had returned from Udine early, fuming; the negotiations had been broken off. War would be resumed in twenty-four hours, he'd threatened. "How can you say that? Yesterday you met with the Comte de Cobenzl privately. You call that not interfering?"

"Have you been spying on me, Bonaparte?"

"This palace is riddled with spies. We are all of us spied upon. Even the spies are spied upon."

I turned to face my husband. "The Comte de Cobenzl came to me of his own accord. He was seeking . . . advice." Was a direct approach wise? So much was at stake. "He feels you have been rude, Bonaparte, that you do not wish to make the peace."

Bonaparte laughed. "He's fortunate to be alive and he complains about niceties. How . . . how *aristocratic*. Cobenzl acts as if he were at a salon, an afternoon tea. And then he demands Mantua. *Mantua!* Mantua is the key. If I were to let the Austrians have Mantua back, they would control Italy again in a very short time. And he wants me to be *civil* in the face of such a demand?"

"Bonaparte . . ." I took his hands in mine. It always surprises me how soft his skin is, how fine his bones. I looked into his eyes. How did one persuade such a man? "There is something I must say."

"I do not hinder you."

"If you treated Cobenzl civilly, perhaps he would be more likely to accede to your wishes."

He looked incredulous. "You are suggesting that I be *nice*?"

"Bonaparte, really, you are so charming when you smile. Who could refuse you?"


*October 17.*
Bonaparte's carriage pulled into the courtyard quite late, almost midnight. I saw him jump down from the carriage, followed by Eugène and Louis. I opened the window. "Peace is signed,"* Eugène called out, holding a flambeau aloft. "Pack for Paris!"

---

* *Historically, the Treaty of Campo-Formio is regarded as both spectacular and shameful. Spectacular because, among other things, the French Republic gained Belgium and the Rhineland (including Mayence), getting back its "natural frontier," and shameful because of the sacrifice of the fledgling Republic of Venice to the Austrians.*

# III

*Profiteer*

The scourge and leprosy of the services! Impudent thievery!
—*Napoleon, on military suppliers*

## *In which problems await me at home*

*December 16, 1797—France!*
"I can understand what people are saying!" Lisette threw her arms in the air and twirled.

I knew her joy. The innkeeper in her crisp white bonnet had a familiar face. Did I not know her? Even the postillion seemed to have mounted his horse in a way that seemed mysteriously *right*.

"Look!" Lisette leapt about the cobblestones. "The sky is French, the mountains are French, the air is French. I bet that horse speaks French." The old nag turned its head. "See?"

*December 17.*
"Where did you learn to load a pistol, Madame?" Lisette looked up from mending the train on one of my gowns.

"In Paris, during the Terror. A friend of mine taught me." A friend now dead, along with so many others. I clicked the chamber shut, slipped on the safety lock. We were travelling with only two mounted escorts; at night, in the inns, I did not feel secure.* I'd sewn my jewels into a little velvet bag, which hung under my gown.

"I love hearing stories about the Revolution, about all the fights and riots. Forgive me, Madame," she said, seeing my stricken expression.

---

* *Napoleon had returned to Paris by way of Rastatt, Germany, where meetings continued regarding the peace accord. Josephine had left Milan at a later date, returning to Paris on her own.*

I handed her the pistol. "Never aim it at a person, even if it's empty."

"I know!"

I smiled. "Have I ever told you that you remind me of my daughter?"

"Many times, Madame."

"Except, of course, that you're a young woman now. Have you given any thought to marriage, Lisette?" She was nineteen. It was time. It was past time, frankly.

"I prefer to serve you, Madame," she said, hiding the pistol at the bottom of her mending basket.

"You may marry and continue to serve me."

"You would permit it, Madame?"* She picked up her mending.

"Do you think I would expect such a sacrifice from you?"

"Other ladies do." She shrugged. "And anyway, who would want to marry me?"

"You're lovely!" But without a dowry, true. "I will be happy to provide you with a dowry."

"Truly?" she asked with an incredulous look.

"On my honour."


*December 19—Lyons.*
There was a letter awaiting me at our inn in Lyons: embossed in gold, it was from Citoyen Louis Bodin of the Bodin Company, inviting me to call.


*December 20, 4:30 P.M., a gloomy day.*
I was, I confess, taken aback by the Bodin estate. I had not expected it to be so imposing. A wide driveway wound through a beautifully manicured park, opening onto enchanting vistas, before coming to the château.

I was guided by a silent footman in a white cravat through a series of elegant rooms to, at the last, a game room, where Louis Bodin (round as a pumpkin and quite pink) was shooting billiards. A sleepy one-eyed

---

* *It was customary to fire servants who married or got pregnant.*

maid with frizzled hair stood in attendance by the high table. In spite of the hour, all the shaded candles in the bronze chandelier had been lit.

"Welcome, Madame Bonaparte." Louis Bodin bowed from the waist. He was welcoming, sincere in manner, yet dignified in spite of his complexion and his youth. Old money, I thought, taking in the antlers over the fireplace, the worn, elegant furnishings, the family portraits, the hound curled by the fire with its chin on its hind paws.

We talked, pleasantries at first, and then of our mutual acquaintance, the irrepressible Captain Charles, our Masonic affiliations, spiritualism (carefully avoiding a discussion of religion), the Treaty of Campo-Formio (avoiding a discussion of politics), his brother Hugo, who ran the company's office in Paris. And then, retiring to a book-lined study where a light collation had been set (Seville oranges, little white boudins, pistachio nuts), we began at last to discuss that which had brought us together: the pursuit of wealth.

Louis Bodin explained that the Bodin Company had profited nicely from the purchase and sale of National Properties, but that due to the increasing scarcity of such "opportunities," the company wished to expand into the more lucrative area of military supplies—specifically, the supply of mounts to the Army of Italy. "We have everything in place to make a success of such a venture," he said. "Everything, that is, but the one essential element—approval by the Directors." He spoke softly, with an enormous orange cat purring on his lap. "As you are no doubt aware, the competition for these contracts is keen. It is perhaps no accident that those who do succeed are the personal acquaintances of one Director in particular." He smiled, displaying brilliantly white false teeth. "Director Barras, of course, with whom, I am given to understand, you have influence."

I considered how I should respond to such a statement. "Director Barras is a friend of mine," I said, a simple statement of fact.

Louis Bodin pushed the cat off his lap and sat forward, his hands on his plump knees. "Madame Bonaparte, would you be . . . That is, would you consider . . . ?" He scratched the end of his nose.

I knew what he wanted to ask. I waited.

He tugged on his shirt cuffs, revealing enormous emerald links.

"Would you consider acting on behalf of the Bodin Company? That is, discussing the merits of our company with Director Barras?" He sat back, his hands on the arms of his chair. "We'd be willing to discuss a partnership arrangement."

"That would depend—"

"On the terms, of course. I understand entirely. For that reason, I took the liberty of preparing a draft contract for you to look over." He retrieved a portfolio from a side table and handed it to me. "Please, at least take it, Madame. You may study it at your leisure."

I held the contract without looking through it. Once back in Paris, I would go over it with my lawyer and then I would decide. I knew that my answer—be it yes or no—would have significant consequences. If no, I would have to find a way to deal with my mounting debt. If yes, I stood to profit—enormously—but not without risk. "Could I presume, Citoyen Bodin, that my involvement would be kept confidential?"

"We fully understand, I can assure you, the sensitive nature of your position."

"Then yes," I said. "I am willing to consider."


*December 28—one stop past Nevers.*
This afternoon, as Lisette and I were airing out the linens, we were startled by four rhythmic raps. "Isn't that Captain Charles's knock?" Lisette asked. "I knew it was you," she said, on opening the door.

For there, drenched and mud-splattered, the plume of his hat broken at the stem and hanging sadly down his back like the tail of some unfortunate creature, was Captain Charles. Pugdog sat up on his cushion, his curled tail wiggling.

"Captain Charles!" I was astonished to see him. "What have you done to yourself?"

"I've been riding like a madman," he said, gallantly doffing his ruined hat, "in the hope of catching up with you."

I motioned to him to take the worn chair by the fireplace. "What an unexpected pleasure."

"I feared you might have reached Paris by now," he said, dusting off his leather breeches before lowering himself into the armchair. He reached down to tug Pugdog's tail, teasing.

"We've had a few breakdowns," I said.

"And ceremonies in every town," Lisette said. "Madame has been making speeches."

I opened my fan. I wanted to talk to the captain about my meeting with Citoyen Bodin—but in private. "Lisette, please bring us some midday collations. And a bottle of that good local wine." After she had left I said, "Captain Charles, we have only a moment. I wish you to know that in Lyons I met with your associate Citoyen Louis Bodin."

"He told me. I understand that you'll be meeting with his brother Hugo in Paris. I must tell you, Madame, we are—"

I put up my hand. "I only told him I would consider." In fact, I was beginning to have reservations. "I hope you understand how important it is that our discussions on this matter never be revealed."

"Of course, I would never—" He stopped abruptly, staring over my shoulder.

I turned. Lisette was standing in the open doorway with a tray in her hand. "Ah, there you are," I said.

*New Year's Day, 1798, 1:00 A.M.*
A day of unexpected twists and turns. I should know better than to try my hand at matchmaking. While Lisette was attending me at toilette this morning, I made a suggestion to her. "I have observed that you and Captain Charles have a companionable relationship, Lisette. Have you considered the possibility of a match?"

"You are serious, Madame?" was her initial response. "Me and Wide-Awake?" She giggled.

"The captain may not be wealthy, Lisette, but someday soon he will be a man of means. Do I have your permission to discuss this with him?"

We dined together, the three of us: Lisette, Captain Charles and I. The cook devised a simple but pleasing repast: a green pea soup (he keeps peas in mutton fat in the cellar over the winter), carp, pickled mush-rooms and small onions, followed by cheeses and sweet chestnuts.

"Captain Charles," Lisette announced after our dishes had been taken away, "perhaps you could take my place at the trictrac board tonight. Madame has given me the night off to go to church." (In fact, *Madame* had told her that she needed to converse privately with the captain, and perhaps Lisette wouldn't mind going out for the evening.)

Captain Charles glanced at Lisette, then at me and then back at Lisette. "*You're* going to church?"

"There are many things about Lisette that are perhaps unknown to you, Captain Charles," I said, dunking a bit of Roquefort in the mulled claret punch (of which we'd all had quite a bit). "Under a gay and buoyant demeanour she hides a serious spiritual nature."

Captain Charles guffawed, and then ducked as Lisette hurled a hard bread roll at him. Was this a good sign? I wasn't sure.

After Lisette departed for church (a bit inebriated, I suspect), the captain and I adjourned to the front drawing room. The room was small, but warm, and it afforded a view of the square. "You may close the door behind you, Captain," I said, ceremoniously lighting three candles.

Captain Charles stood with his hands clasped, like a servant awaiting direction. His ensemble—wide Venetian velvet pantaloons and a silver-embroidered waistcoat—gave him the look of a royal courtier, someone of another time, out of place in our world of egalitarian linen and rough wool. "Please, make yourself comfortable." I poured us each from an opened bottle of still champagne. I handed the one good glass to the captain. "To the New Year."

He sat down on a wooden side chair. I sat on the sofa opposite him. (The down cushions smelled of ducks.) Why this lack of ease? We seemed like strangers to one another. "There are only two more years until the year 1800," I said, offering the captain from a plate of sausage puff pastries and then helping myself to one. "Imagine, a new century."

"Already, the fortune-tellers are making predictions. Have you read them?"

Ah, the predictions—how good of him to bring them up. "I *always* read the predictions, Captain," I said. "And I believe them, I confess."

Captain Charles leaned forward. "The indications are that it will be an excellent year for commercial endeavours."

"Excellent." I opened my ivory fan, then snapped it shut. The subject of marriage is not an easy one to broach. I had hoped that Captain Charles's customary levity would make it easier. I cleared my throat; Captain Charles did likewise. We smiled at this coincidence. "There is something I have been wanting to ask you, Captain," I said finally.

"Concerning the Bodin Company, Madame?"

"No—something to do with matters of the heart. Have you given any thought to taking a wife?"

A laugh escaped him, rather like a snort. I was not sure how to interpret his response. It seemed somehow ironic. Was it possible that my suspicions regarding the captain were true? "I amuse you?" I asked.

"On the contrary, Madame, you enchant me."

He was being silly. "Captain Charles, no jests. I beg you." I put up my hands, palms towards him. "Seriously, as a *friend*, as someone who is concerned with your welfare, I recommend that you marry, raise a family. You are young, but before you know it, your youth will have slipped away. Children give one immeasurable joy."

Captain Charles pushed the toe of his boot against the frayed carpet fringe. "Perhaps you have someone in mind, Madame?"

I nodded, smiling with my eyes. "Guess."

He pursed his lips, a perfect rosette. "Your daughter?"

I laughed, taken aback, I confess. Although I found Captain Charles a charming companion, I did not consider him a suitable match for Hortense. "Forgive me," I said, whisking a crumb off my lap—for his mortified expression made it clear that I had offended him. "It is just that she is so young, Captain, only fourteen. I have yet to consider a husband for her."

"You need not dissemble, mia belissima regina. I know my standing in this world."

I disregarded his statement; clearly, he'd had too much to drink. "I will tell you who I think would make a perfect wife for you," I persevered, tapping my fan against my palm. The bells began to ring, welcoming in the Christian New Year.

"You."

I sat back. "Captain Charles, do be serious!" Many bells were ringing now, a joyful tumult. Where had they come from, these bells?

"The clown, Madame, is always serious." Pulling down on his feathered jockey hat, he made a sloppy bow, kissed me lightly and staggered out the door.

I watched him from the window, weaving on the cobblestones. His hat fell off; he paid it no heed.


*Late afternoon.*

Lisette looked relieved when I told her that Captain Charles had been disinclined to discuss the subject of matrimony. And much to my relief, the captain doesn't remember a thing. My new year's vow: to give up matchmaking.

Tomorrow, Paris!


*January 2—Paris!*

"What took you so long!" Bonaparte crumpled a piece of paper and threw it against the wall. His hair hung down over his ears, giving the impression of a Florida Indian. I was alarmed by his sallow skin, his thin, almost emaciated frame. His health had clearly deteriorated in the six weeks since I'd last seen him. His temper, as well.

His rage had to do with money. The designer I'd hired to make over the house had demanded payment for the renovations—one hundred thousand francs! I sat down, stunned. That was an incomprehensible sum. "One hundred and thirty, in fact," Bonaparte ranted, kicking the flaming logs, making sparks fly. "The house itself is only worth forty, and you don't even own it. The frieze in the dining room isn't even painted by David. It's by one of his students."

There was a frieze in the dining room? "Most of the value is in furnishings, Bonaparte," I said in my defence.

"Most? Even seventy thousand in furniture would be outrageous—I don't care who made it, Jacob Brothers or not! There's no way I'm going to pay for half of this. I'll contribute thirty thousand, but not a sou more."

Leaving *me* with a bill for one hundred thousand? "No doubt there has been a mistake. I'll talk to Vautier." The renovations were the last thing I wanted to deal with, however, after an absence of almost two years. First I had to see Hortense. And then, of course, Aunt Désirée, the dear old Marquis. And then Thérèse—had she had her baby yet? And how was Père Barras? *And* the Glories, of course! Not to mention the business I needed to attend to, my lawyer to see.

"How can there be a mistake? Vautier produced your letters as evidence. You gave him total licence! One never gives total licence."

I removed my gloves, taking in the changes: the Pompeian frescoes, military trophies, chairs upholstered in striped fabric. The renovation was simple, yet elegant. I ran my hand over the surface of the new mahogany desk. The grain seemed to shimmer under my fingertips. I felt I could see deep into the heart of the wood. "Does *none* of it please you, Bonaparte?"

"Come see our beds," he said with a little grin.


Our bedroom had been designed to look like a military tent. "Watch." Bonaparte released a latch and our two beds sprang together with a noisy clatter.

"Clever!" I sat down on one of the stools, covered with chamois leather to resemble a drum. The beds were draped with a canopy of blue and white stripes, the bedposts forged from cannon.

Bonaparte tugged at my arm.

"Not now, Bonaparte," I pleaded, but smiling. "It's not even noon yet, and I need a bath."

"We'll bathe together," he said, pulling at my sleeve, "after."


*Late now, almost 11:00 P.M., a very long day.*

I'd bathed and was changing into an afternoon gown when I heard horses

• *601* •

in the courtyard. A slender young woman in a white riding frock was stepping down from a barouche. A mass of golden curls fell to her shoulders. I put my hands over my mouth. Mon Dieu. Hortense?

"Maman!" Hortense cried out when she saw me, all the airs of une élégante of Paris giving way to that of a girl. Her eyes were an extraordinary blue; how was it possible that that surprised me? She slipped off her cloak, chattering. "Where's Eugène? I saw his horse saddled by the stable. That's Louis Bonaparte's horse? The General's brother is staying here? But why isn't Eugène back yet? I've been telling all my friends he would be returning with you."

My daughter's long fingernails were painted red. And breasts—she had breasts! "Eugène is in Rome," I stuttered. "He'll be—"

"What took you so long? Where were you? Every day there have been notices in the journals that you'd arrived. Maman, what's wrong? Is something wrong?"

"No, nothing," I croaked, taking her in, this lovely young woman.

Aunt Désirée arrived shortly after, barking instructions at two valets who carried the old Marquis into the house by the garden entrance. They deposited him in the down armchair, where he looked about with a dazed expression. I asked my manservant to put on a fire and Lisette to set out the gifts I had brought back from Italy with me.

"Modern," Aunt Désirée said, looking around the drawing room, appraising the changes.

"Grecian is modern?" I stooped to kiss the old Marquis. His beard smelled of brilliantine.

"Bonne à Pare Té!" he said with vigour.

Hortense laughed. Aunt Désirée motioned to her to sit straight, keep her knees together, fold her hands in her lap, and not to laugh so loudly— all in one silent gesture known to all women and girls. Hortense made a prim face, but nevertheless did as instructed. Aunt Désirée gave me a triumphant look. "Hortense, that shawl looks lovely—did your mother bring it back from Italy for you? Where is our famous General, Rose? I bought a flower vase for three francs just because it had his image on it."

"Bonaparte is at the Luxembourg Palace right now, at a meeting with the Directors." I motioned to Louis Bonaparte to join us. "But I'd like to introduce you to Louis, Bonaparte's brother." Hoping that the presence of at least one Bonaparte might appease.

Aunt Désirée gave Louis what I knew to be the appraising look of a woman on the watch for a husband for her niece. "Charmed! How many brothers does General Bonaparte have? And sisters, of course."

"There are a great many of us, and soon to be more," Louis said, tugging at a budding moustache. He glanced at Hortense, a flush colouring his cheeks. My daughter lowered her eyes. "My oldest brother Joseph is in Rome with my sister Caroline—"

"And Eugène," I interjected, arranging gifts on the table—a Roman vase, a glass bowl from Venice, a length of embroidered silk brocade from Genoa as well as a number of pretty trinkets.

"My sister Pauline is in Milan," Louis went on. "She's married and in an interesting condition. And my other married sister who lives in Corsica is also in an interesting condition. And my brother Lucien is in the north, and *his* wife is in an interesting condition, as well. And then there is Jérôme, who is going to school here in Paris."

"Jérôme is only thirteen," I said, chagrined by the parade of fertile Bonaparte women—of which, it was clear, I was not one.

"How nice for Hortense and Eugène to have so many new brothers and sisters," Aunt Désirée exclaimed with too much enthusiasm, perhaps in an effort to display her Christian acceptance of so many Corsican relatives. "I mean aunts and uncles. And *so* many cousins to come," she added, acknowledging the fecundity of the Bonaparte clan.

Louis backed toward the door. He had an English lesson to attend, he explained, and therefore had to take his leave.

"It was a pleasure to meet you," Hortense told him in careful English.

"Thank you, miss. Goodbye," Louis answered in kind, tipping his hat in the English manner.

"What a charming boy," Aunt Désirée said as soon as he was out the door, turning the Roman vase in her hands. I explained to her that it was not "modern" but actually quite ancient. And then we talked of this and of that—the extraordinary welcome Paris had given Bonaparte on his return, Hortense's awards at school, how well Eugène was doing as an aide-de-camp—and then, of course, the gossip:

"Of course, you've heard the news regarding General Hoche." Aunt Désirée had the look of a cat depositing a dead mouse at the foot of its owner. "Regarding his *murder*."

I closed my fan. I opened my fan.

Aunt Désirée leaned forward. "You know what I heard? That it was your friend Director Barras who did it."

"Aunt Désirée," I interupted. I didn't want Hortense to hear false rumours.

"My theory," Aunt Désirée went on, disregarding me, "is that Director Barras, who is known to be greedy, was after the million francs General Hoche embezzled."

"Aunt Désirée, I don't think—"

"It was eight hundred thousand."

I looked at the Marquis in astonishment. He had slumped down so far into his armchair that he was practically doubled over, a dreamy expression in his half-closed eyes. "Did the Marquis speak just now?" I asked.

"He doesn't know what he's talking about," Aunt Désirée said. "It was well over one million."


They stayed for a light repast and then had to leave in order not to unduly tire the Marquis. Hortense is staying with them in town because, as Aunt Désirée informed me, it would be improper for an unmarried young lady to stay in the same house as an unmarried young man, even if that young man is actually her uncle. Tearfully I bade them all adieu and ordered my horses harnessed: I was anxious to see my lawyer about the Bodin Company contract. And then, after that, Thérèse, and after *that*, Barras.


"Thérèse is still in childbed," Tallien (civil, but not sober) informed me.

The baby had been born thirteen days earlier, on the solstice. "A girl," he shrugged. "She died at birth."

"I'm so sorry, Lambert!" I put down the parcel of infant gowns I'd brought from Italy and embraced him. How many times in the past had I done so, thinking him young, thinking he was not so much vulnerable as impressionable, in need of guidance. But now he had the weary fragility of age. Something in him had broken, had not mended. "How is Thérèse taking it?"

"I wouldn't know."

Thérèse was enthroned on the chaise longue in her bedroom. I leaned over to kiss her cheek.

"Did Tallien tell you I've locked him out? Did he tell you why? Of course not. He refused to call a priest! My baby died unbaptized. And then, a few days after, he expects 'service.' I've had it with these men of the people."

Her hand was icy cold. I pressed it between mine to warm it. I felt utterly miserable. I loved her with all my heart, but I loved Tallien too. I'd known him as an idealistic youth.

The maid appeared with a bottle of port, crystal stem glasses. Thérèse wiped her cheeks, embarrassed to be caught crying. "My midwife's orders," she said brightly, clinking the rim of my glass with her own. "I can't tell you how relieved I am to see you. We're all still in shock over Lazare's death. You should have seen his funeral. The streets were thronged—I've never seen anything like it. And now my midwife tells me his widow miscarried, the poor thing. She's only nineteen. A bit touched, though, they say." Thérèse downed her glass. "You're going to Talleyrand's ball tonight?"

"I'm so sorry you won't be there."

"I wasn't invited. It appears that I'm no longer wanted at any gathering that includes virtuous women," she said with obvious irony. "Did you hear what happened at the ball given by Pulchérie de Valence? As soon as I arrived, all the women left."

"I don't understand!" During the Terror Thérèse had saved the lives of many of these so-called virtuous women, often at the risk of her own life.

"I was apparently too public about threatening Tallien with a divorce. Women are supposed to suffer in silence, remember? And then I made the mistake of offering shelter to a young man who had rescued me from bandits one night. He was injured, but a woman of virtue would have sent him away regardless. And *then* there was a horrific scandal over a portrait of me that was hung in the annual Salon. The arbiters of good taste demanded that it be removed."

I smiled. "Were you clothed in this portrait?"

"I've never looked more chaste! No, they didn't approve that the painter portrayed me in my prison cell. Anything to do with the Terror is not to be mentioned in polite society, I gather. I'm not sure I care, frankly."

But she did. I could hear it in her voice.

The door was pushed open by a child in ruffled muslin. "Maman?" It was baby Thermidor—walking, and talking!

"Sweetie, do you remember Josephine, your godmother?"

"Yes," the two-year-old said doubtfully, her chubby fingers stuffed into her mouth.

I held out my arms. Would she come to me? She ran across the room and onto my lap. I felt her tiny fingers pat my neck, tap, tap. I glanced at Thérèse. *She's so beautiful,* I mouthed. But thinking, I confess, how the little girl's future would be ruined if Thérèse and Tallien were to divorce.


After my visit with Thérèse I instructed my coachman to take me to the Luxembourg Palace. The drive seemed to take forever, the streets were in such poor repair. And everywhere, signs of misery. Children in rags ran alongside my carriage, crying for alms. I threw them what coins I had. A boy in a moth-eaten English travelling cap, his ribs showing, beat the others away with a stick. I looked away, sickened, as I pulled through the palace gates and into the privileged realm.


"Damn the Royalists," Barras's parrot squawked as I was shown into the salon. Barras was sitting in an armchair by a roaring fire, petting his miniature greyhound. "Don't get up," I told him, stooping to kiss him.

"No, no, a gentleman must always rise for a lady," he said, lowering Toto onto a tasselled cushion, patting the dog's head apologetically and then pulling himself up out of the chair. "Grand Dieu, my friend, but you do look lovely," he said, his Provençal accent laconic, caressing. "As always."

"Oh, I've made a mess of you," I said, brushing powder from his velvet smoking jacket. He smelled pleasantly of cigars and spirit of ambergris.

"Sit, sit," he insisted.

There was a web of worry lines around his eyes. He seemed to have aged in the year and a half since I'd seen him last—or was it simply that I'd not noticed before? "How *are* you?" I asked, accepting the chair he indicated. He seemed weary, I thought. World-weary. Battle-weary, more likely.

"Oh . . ." He made a dismissive gesture, then let his hand drop. "The usual. I'm getting a new roof put on Grosbois, my modest country abode—now *that's* a job." He cleared his throat. "And now all this fuss over Talleyrand's ball. Too Ancien Régime, according to my fellow Directors, who have only reluctantly consented to go, but in plain dress. We're going to look as out of place as Quakers at a brawl."

The name Lazare Hoche hovered between us, impossible to ignore. "I noticed funeral wreaths at Saint-Roch," I said finally. "My coachman told me there'd been a service just recently in honour of Lazare."

"The official service was three months ago, but people just won't stop! Every time I turn around, I run into some damn procession carrying an effigy of him." He looked away, struggling, I suspected, for control.

I studied my hands, turning my betrothal ring round and round. "You know, ironically, the last time Bonaparte saw him, he predicted that Lazare would die at a young age in his bed. We were at Thérèse and Tallien's that night, before we were married, and Bonaparte was reading everyone's palm. I never told you this story?"

Barras shook his head, his hand over his mouth.

"It comforts me, I confess," I said, my voice quavering dangerously, "to think that maybe it was meant to be." If Death wants you, he will find you: every soldier's creed.

"*Merde.*" Barras buried his face in his hands.

*January 3.*

Oh, what a day, what a night. It began with my cook, who was frantic—Bonaparte would only eat hard-boiled eggs, he claimed. Callyot leaned toward me confidentially. "Because they cannot be tampered with, Madame."

Then the designer arrived; it was impossible to put him off. "I trust the work is pleasing?" Vautier said, handing me a scrap of paper on which the terrifying figure 130,000 francs had been written in a tiny script.

Oh, extraordinarily pleasing. Brilliant. But perhaps somewhat more . . . *costly* than I had anticipated. (By tenfold!)

"As you wrote, nothing but the best for the Liberator of Italy." He bowed.

I'd written him that? "I will have my banker contact you." Thinking, how was I going to come up with the money?

Lisette appeared at the door, one hand on the ivory knob. "The dressmaker, Madame."

I dispatched the designer with extravagant praise and equally extravagant promises. He politely gave way to my frenzied dressmaker. Every woman in Paris required a new gown for the ball, her staff of thirty-two seamstresses had been working day and night, she exclaimed, instructing her footman to display our creations. The gown for Hortense was exquisite, I thought, but the gown for me—a simple yellow tunic of a Grecian design—had an under-chemise made of muslin. "But English muslin is expressly forbidden," I said, dismayed. It had even been printed on the invitations.

Her eyes bulged; I feared she would be taken with apoplexy. "But Madame," she said, lowering her voice to a whisper, "Madame de Chevalley's underskirts are of muslin, as well as those of Madame de la Pinel."

"Neither Madame Chevalley nor Madame de la Pinel is the wife of General Bonaparte," I reminded her gently. As well—although I declined to tell her this—the design lacked elegance. (She'd ruffled the hem!) I repeated my request for simplicity.

"Madame Bonaparte—if I may be so bold—are you sure you want such a plain tunic? I have three girls in my employ devoted entirely to the application of sequins."

No ornaments, I insisted. And no muslin petticoat.

On account, Madame Bonaparte?

Yes, of course—on account.

And then the jeweller, who insisted on being shown in with his case of (I confess) irresistible wares. I selected a lovely strand of gold interlocking leaves. What else would look right with a Grecian tunic? "On account, Madame?"

And so, on it went. Lisette has just arrived with a jug of warm mulled wine. The carriages have been called for nine, she informs me.

"So early!"

It is time for my bath . . .

And perhaps just a bit of laudanum.


Bonaparte sat on a stool beside my toilette table, watching as Lisette made up my hair. He was pleased, he said, with the simplicity of my gown. "We must appear to live within my means."

I refrained from laughing. Even the bachelor generals weren't able to live on a general's salary of forty thousand francs a year, and as for my "simple" tunic—

"How's this?" Louis appeared in the doorway, pulling at the sleeves of a nankeen coat. He'd been ill earlier in the day and still looked pale. (Ever since Italy his health has been uncertain.)

"Ugly!" Jérôme called out from behind his older brother, jealous because he was too young to go to the ball.

Bonaparte jumped to his feet. "Who made that jacket for you?" The collar was of black velvet, the insignia of a Royalist.

"How about your blue one?" I suggested.

"Don't move, Madame!" Lisette sprayed lacquer over my hair. "You look lovely," she said, handing me the looking glass.

I looked hideous! The curls were stuck to my head with a substance that made me look as if I had just been drenched by rain.

Bonaparte pulled out his timepiece. "We're late."

We set out in a light snow, Bonaparte, Louis, Hortense and I. The jingling of the brass bells on the horses' harness made a festive sound. At the Rue de Grenelle we came to a stop. Equipages were backed up all the way to the Seine. Hortense made a peek-hole in the steamed-up glass. Where had all the carriages come from? For years only shabby hacks had been seen on the streets of Paris, and now suddenly the roadway was crowded with elegant landaus, phaetons, barouches and curricles.

It was half-past nine by the time we pulled into the courtyard of the Hôtel Gallifet. A bivouac scene had been created at the entrance—a campfire surrounded by men in uniform, tents. "The fields of Italy," Louis explained to Hortense, offering her his arm. "But for the snow, of course," he added and my daughter laughed.

As we headed up the steps, the double doors were flung open. Four hall porters jumped to take our cloaks. A butler with an operatic voice announced us. The musicians stopped playing and everyone turned to stare. Then a cheer went up and horns blazed out a welcome.

I was overwhelmed by the scene I saw before me. A profusion of candles in enormous hanging chandeliers revealed a crowd of men and women in glittering finery. A man with a shiny forehead was making his way toward us with the help of an ebony cane. He was slithering rather than walking, dragging a club foot, I realized. It was Talleyrand, the famous (infamous) Minister of Foreign Affairs.

He bowed deeply to Bonaparte and then to me, extending two fingers of his right hand as if in benediction. (He had been a bishop, I recalled.) "We have awaited your arrival, Madame la Générale." Only his eyes showed any sign of life. They filled with a fawning reverence whenever they happened to alight upon my husband. My husband, who was ignoring us, however, looking out over the crowd with a hawkish expression, his hands clasped behind his back.

"I am astonished by the beauty of the décor," I told Minister Talleyrand, introducing Hortense, who curtsied, and then Louis, who bowed.

"Delighted," Talleyrand said, his voice a drone.

The playwright Arnault appeared, greeting us shyly. Bonaparte clasped his arm. "Take me about the room, Arnault. We shall engage in discussion; that way no one will accost me." Louis offered to escort Hortense to the ballroom.

Which left me quite suddenly alone with our host. "For this entire evening," he informed me, "I will be your *cavaliere servente*. Is that not how it is done in Italy?" He smiled, an expression that made him look frightful. I heard the musicians warming up. "Come," he said, "you must see my quarrelsome dancers. In a misguided spirit of equality they insisted that if they were to perform for us, they should have the honour of eating with us."

The crowd parted for us as we approached. I moved slightly to one side in order to make room for each swing of his big foot. "And who was the victor in this debate?"

"I am always the victor, Madame."

The orchestra struck up a chord. "Ah. They are about to perform a new dance from Germany. The waltz, I believe they call it." One corner of the Minister's thin lips curled. "It requires that the male and female grasp one another, and so of course the priests are endeavouring to have it condemned."

The ballroom was crowded with musicians, dancers, men standing behind women who were seated, watching. The waltz was a swirling of couples holding each other's arms. I saw Hortense in an alcove with Louis, showing him how it was done.

"Ah, there's Bonaparte." I spotted him in a far corner.

"In my humble estimation, all five Directors together are not worth the General's little finger. Twenty victories are becoming in so young a man. General Bonaparte *is* the Republic." The Minister's toneless drone was at odds with the impassioned nature of his words.

Yes, I nodded, feigning to listen. Bonaparte was heading toward us, arm-in-arm with Arnault. A cluster of men and women were following behind him—like a king's entourage, I thought, a dazed feeling coming over me.

*In which I become involved in intrigues*

*January 4, 1798.*

"Where to, Madame?" my coachman asked, tipping his sheepskin cap. Feeling poorly, I suspected. The drivers and postillions had hob-nobbed and glass-jingled last night, while their masters were enjoying the ball.

"One hundred Rue Honoré," I told Antoine, reading the card on which was printed the Paris address of the Bodin Company. I'd told Bonaparte I was going to call on Thérèse—which was true, in part. After I called in at one hundred Rue Honoré.

A butler in tails opened the oak door. I was shown into a salon so large it required two fireplaces. In a window alcove was a desk covered with files and a counting device.

I heard the even thump, thump, thump of a wooden leg. "Madame Bonaparte?" Hugo Bodin was younger than his brother, but every bit as round, and his complexion even pinker. He pulled on the bell rope. "Captain Charles," he instructed the butler, pushing forward a shield-back chair for me. "I have been anticipating your call, Madame. We are honoured. The fervour of the people for your husband is *electric*, to use a modern word." He lowered himself onto a crimson sofa, his stump stick-ing out to one side like the oar of a boat. "That was quite a fête last night in his honour, I am told. Even we plebeians who were not invited were all 'in a twitter,' as the English say."

"It was an extraordinary display." A ball in the style of the Ancien Régime: a full orchestra, dancers, a feast. "And quite cleverly done. The

Minister of Foreign Affairs transformed his residence to look like the backstage of the opera."

"I was told that that dance the clergy wish to have banned was performed. Wallace? No, valse."

From somewhere in the building, I heard a dog bark. "The captain said to tell you that he will be a moment," the butler announced.

As if on cue the captain appeared, buttoning the top button of a corded white vest figured in gold. "Madame Bonaparte! I hope this means . . . ?"

"I'm not sure," I told them both. "My lawyer and I have gone over the contract carefully, and considering the amount of the investment, I'm afraid that the—"

Hugo held up his hands. "Before you say anything, Madame, you should know that we'd be willing to up your share to twelve per cent."

They'd doubled it. "I appreciate your offer, Citoyen Bodin, but I'm afraid I'd require at least fifteen."

"Done," Hugo said.

Done? I looked from one man to the other. Then I smiled at the captain and said, "Captain Charles, it would appear that we are now business associates."

"Hooray!" Hugo exclaimed in a burst of undignified enthusiasm. We toasted our partnership with thimble-glasses of Chartreuse.

After, in the privacy of my carriage, I laughed at my audacity. Fifteen per cent: a small fortune. A fortune I urgently needed.


Thérèse was thrilled. "You're actually going to do it? You're going to be a partner in a military supply company? That's so daring! You're the only woman I know who has done that."

"But you're the one who told me I should."

"I just can't believe it. You'll be making *millions*."

"Borrowing millions is more like it."

*January 6.*

"It's a large sum," I warned Barras. The leather chair creaked as I shifted my weight. "Four hundred thousand." I was conscious of blinking—once, twice, three times.

Barras sat back, examining his fingernails. Then he grinned. "Welcome to the world of high finance."

High finance, high debt: high profit.


*January 8.*

"There's a Negress outside demanding to see you," Lisette informed me this afternoon. "I told her to go around to the back entrance, but she just stood there."

I fumbled with the window latch and looked out. A Negro woman was standing in the courtyard—a tall, older woman, shivering in a worn wool cloak over a long calico gown. "Mimi?" She looked up, squinting against the sun. "Mimi!"


I did not know how to greet her. It had been over seven years. We'd parted in a difficult time, in a world torn by Revolution, a world divided. It seemed a lifetime ago. "I thought I would never see you again," I said, my eyes filling. She'd been like a sister to me in my youth—a sister, a mother, a friend. It was Mimi who'd taught me to dance, read the cards, make charms, Mimi who had nursed me through childhood fevers, helped birth my babies, Mimi who had been their nanny.

"Yeyette," she said, calling me by my baby name, her warm Island accent music to my ears, "still always weeping." And then she smiled, that big-toothed, big-hearted grin.

We've been talking for hours. I'm *starved* for news of home. "And how is Maman?" was one of my first questions.

Mimi pushed out her big lower lip, the inside pink as an oyster shell. "She can't walk or use her hands."

"How awful!" My mother is a proud woman, independent. She had run the family sugar plantation without any help from my hapless father. After his death she'd worked hard to pay off his debts.

"She says you've married a Jacobin, the Devil himself."

I smiled. I was not surprised. My mother believes in God and the King. "I miss her!"

Mimi touched my hand. "She told me to look after you for her."

My throat tightened. Oh, *Maman.*

*January 9.*
I was reviewing procedures with Mimi when Hortense stuck her head into the room. She started, surprised by the presence of a dark-skinned woman.

"Hortense, do you remember Mimi?"

"My nanny, you mean?" Hortense asked, putting down her portfolio.

"Oh, my Lord." Mimi slapped her hands over her cheeks.

*[Undated]*
News of an uprising in Rome. Lieutenant Duphot, Eugène's friend who was to be married, was killed the night before his wedding. How awful! No word yet from Eugène. I can't sleep.

*January 22.*
It was past midnight when I was awakened by a tap on the door, the sound of the door creaking open. "Madame?" Lisette's candle threw ghostly shadows onto the walls.

I slipped out of bed, my heart aflutter. Bonaparte, asleep, did not stir. "What is it?" My teeth chattering, I pulled on a robe.

"Your son, Madame."

I put my hand over my mouth, fearing the worst.

"He's downstairs!"

"Maman!" Eugène pulled off a boot and lumbered to his feet.

"You're back!" I wept. "I've been frantic with worry."

He held his lantern high, letting out an appreciative whistle. "Is this the right house, Maman? The street name isn't even the same.* And a porter at the gate! He almost didn't let me in."

We talked late into the night, whispering by the fire. So many adventures!

*Twenty-four days of storm at sea . . .*

"I was so sick, I thought I was going to die."

"I get like that too."

*Murderers waking him in the night in Naples . . .*

"Murderers?"

"With these tiny rusty daggers." Laughing about it now.

*The gift of a jewelled sword from the Municipality of Corfu, which he proudly unsheathed for me . . .*

"Are those real rubies? It must be worth a fortune."

"I was thinking of selling it and buying a horse, but Uncle Joseph says I can't—that it was really intended as a gift to the General, and that therefore it belongs to the Bonaparte family."

"He said that?"

*And then, at the last, what happened in Rome, the uprising . . .*

"Is it true—was Lieutenant Duphot . . . ?"

"The night before his wedding, Maman! We were giving a dinner for him when the trouble started. He grabbed his sword and went charging out into the mob. I *tried* to stop him. He fancied himself a hero, and now—" Eugène stopped, a stricken look in his eyes.

*February 9.*

I had planned to meet with Hugo Bodin and Captain Charles today, but it proved to be too difficult. Bonaparte insists on knowing every move I make.

---

* *Rue de la Chantereine had been changed to Rue de la Victoire in honour of Napoleon's victories.*

*February 10.*

Bonaparte departed this morning with Eugène and Louis for an inspection tour of the coast. I stood waving until the carriage was out of sight. Bonaparte will be gone for three weeks—time enough.

*[Undated]*

Barras has agreed to one per cent, but the Minister of War will expect more, he warned me. "And what about General Berthier?" Bonaparte's former chief of staff was now Commander-in-Chief of the Army of Italy.

"Him, too," he said.

Everyone expects a piece of the pie. *Bien.* So long as there is a piece for me.

*February 18.*

I was preparing to go to the Luxembourg Palace to meet with Barras when Bonaparte's carriage pulled up the narrow laneway, the horses steaming in the chilly air. He leapt out while the carriage was still moving.

"You're back early," I said, embracing him—but thinking, I confess, that I had a meeting to get to, and now . . .

"I saw what I needed to see."

"It was not a good trip?" He smelled of the sea.

"The Directors are dreaming. We're in no position to attack England."

His new secretary, Fauvelet Bourrienne, stumbled as he climbed down out of the coach. Then young Louis Bonaparte emerged, yawning and blinking, followed by Eugène, his hair sticking up like a haystack.

"Welcome home!" I said, kissing my son's cheek (stubble?), but worrying about how I would get word to Barras. The Bodin Company business would have to wait.

*February 23.*

Every afternoon Citoyen Talleyrand, the poker-faced Minister of Foreign Affairs, calls and he and Bonaparte disappear into the study. Then I disappear as well—to go to the riding school, I tell my husband. Or to the dressmaker's. Or to visit Thérèse.

All lies. It is "to work" I go—to the Bodin Company office on Rue Honoré. There, over a table covered with parchment and counting machines, we—Captain Charles, Hugo Bodin and I—work out the final details of the proposal: the suppliers, transportation, delivery schedules, but most important, the finances.

I confess that I enjoy this vocation, in spite of my sex. I feel a certain thrill, as if I were visiting a lover. But it is money I court, money that woos me, and the intoxicating power to earn a very great deal.


*February 24.*
I put down the draft of the proposal. Captain Charles's eyes seemed huge in the lantern light, black ink spots. "It's clear, well documented. I think it's ready."

He stood behind me, leafed through to the third page. He smelled of water of roses. "What about this?" He pointed at a paragraph.

"It's fine." His hand was only inches from my breast. He gathered up the papers with exaggerated, busy movements and put them in his blotting book.

I pulled on my gloves, my heart skittering like a leaf in a tempest.


*Late afternoon, around 4:00.*
At last, the Bodin Company proposal is finished. Captain Charles copied it out two times in his neat and tiny script. I'm to deliver it to Barras in the morning. "Wait," the captain called out as I was leaving. He did a handspring and landed on his feet in front of me.

"Yes?" I asked, amused.

He wiggled his fingers over the envelope as if casting a spell.


*February 25.*
"Voilà, the Bodin Company proposal," I told Barras, presenting the portfolio.

Barras pointed his gold-braided hat at the stack of papers on a side table. "Put it there, along with all the others." With a weary, long-suffering look.

I put it on top of the pile and smiled my persuasive best. "The first to be considered, Père Barras?"

Now all we can do is wait. Everything depends on the approval of Schérer, the Minister of War.

*Late afternoon (just before 5:00), still raining.*
"Does the Minister of War ever attend your salon, Fortunée?" I asked, dealing out the cards.

"Citoyen Schérer? Every week."

"Oh, there she goes bragging again," Thérèse said.

"I thought you knew him, Josephine."

"I've conversed with him at Barras's, and I know his wife, but he has yet to come to my salon."

"The Minister of the Interior came to my salon last week. *And* four deputies," Madame de Crény said, swinging her feet.

"Deputies will go to anything."

"I've been trying for months to get the Minister of Foreign Affairs to come to mine and at last I succeeded."

"So I heard."

"You mean you actually lured Talleyrand away from Josephine's salon?"

"All the important men go to *her* salon."

All but Schérer, the Minister of War, I thought—the one man who mattered.

"Invite Geneviève Payan," Fortunée Hamelin told me later, as she was leaving.

The opera singer? "I'm in your debt," I said, embracing her.

*February 26.*
At noon Lisette brought me the calling cards that had been dropped off

over the course of the morning. I sorted through the names, placing them in three piles—those to whom I would send a card, those who required a call, those I would invite to return.

The last card gave me pause. Bordered in black, it was of common design. *La veuve Hoche*. Lazare's widow.

*After 10:00 P.M. (a guess).*
It was dark, the narrow streets muddy. "Are you sure, Madame?" My coachman let down the step, gave me his hand. The house was small, without a courtyard. I nodded. "I won't be long."

"Citoyenne Beauharnais," the widow Hoche said, addressing me by the name of my first husband, by the name Lazare would have called me. Her dark eyes, hidden under the fluted ruffle of a plain linen cap, had a frightened look. She dropped a dutiful curtsy, much as a schoolgirl might greet a teacher, lifting the hem of her stained white apron at each corner. She seemed a wounded bird, a foundling, her shoulders painfully thin. I could not imagine her in Lazare's arms, could not imagine that *this* was the woman he'd loved, the wife he'd betrayed. I had imagined Lazare's wife as a well-made farmgirl, blushing and buxom, with apple cheeks and a hearty laugh. Not this ethereal creature with thin fingers more suited to lace work than to pulling on a cow's teat.

"My profound condolences," I said.

She pushed a wisp of hair back under her cap, blinking. I followed her upstairs to a small sitting room at the end of a dark and narrow passage. A portrait of Lazare hung over a coal fireplace—it made him appear stern. I was surprised to see a crucifix on the wall next to it. I accepted the offer of a chair, clearly the best chair in the room, the place of honour. His young widow took the seat opposite, her hands clasped in her lap. I heard a child's laugh, then little footsteps, hard leather shoes on a bare wooden floor. "Your daughter?" I asked.

The door creaked on its hinges. "This lady was a friend of your father's." Adélaïde Hoche's voice quavered.

The child poked one finger in her ear, and then pointed to the portrait. She was not yet three, I estimated, but a big girl for her age. "She has her father's eyes," I said. And his mouth.

An old woman appeared, scooped up the child. The door closed with a slam that shook the thin walls. I wondered if she was the aunt who had raised Lazare, the peddler of vegetables who went without vegetables in order to save every sou, so determined was she that Lazare would learn to read and write.

We sat for a moment in silence, Adélaïde Hoche sitting on her hands, staring at the floor. From somewhere I could hear a cat meowing plaintively. I was about to make a comment on the indifferent weather when she blurted out, "He said you would help me if I ever needed it."

"General Hoche?" *Should anything happen to me, please, I beg you, help my wife and child.*

"He said I could trust you."

I nodded, yes!

In the other room the child began to cry; the widow tilted her head, assessing the degree of distress. The crying stopped, turned to chatter. "It has to do with Père Hoche . . ." The knuckles of her clasped hands were white.

"General Hoche's father?"

"He's gone back to Thionville to look after things, so I took the chance to talk to you. I'm glad you came. He's coming back tomorrow." She stared at a blue crockery urn on the mantel. "He's in a bad way," she said finally, her chin trembling.

I looked away. I feared she might begin to weep and then we would both be crying, I knew. "It must be terribly hard. Is there anything I can do?"

She paused before saying, "If you could just get the report. Père Hoche tried, but they won't let him see it."

"I don't understand." The autopsy report?

"Père Hoche has become—" She twisted her fingers together. "Maybe if he could just see the report on how his son died, maybe it would help."

"But is there any doubt? Were you not with your husband?"

"He died in my arms," she said with pride.

A sob burst from me. "Forgive me," I said, wiping my cheeks. I'd vowed I would not let it happen.

"I do forgive you," she said with a look of ancient wisdom.

"I understand why he loved you so very much," I said, my eyes brimming.

Immediately after I called on Barras. I was relieved to find him alone. "I've just been to see the widow Hoche," I told him, attempting a casual tone.

He pulled out his lorgnon, looked at me with surprise. "*You* went to see her?"

"She initiated it. She is concerned about her father-in-law."

"Hoche's father? He broke down at the funeral, did you know? It was terrible."

Yes, I'd heard. "The widow feels that Père Hoche has become obsessed, I guess one would say, with his son's death, with trying to find out how he died."

"He knows perfectly well how Lazare died—of consumption. The autopsy made it perfectly clear. It was in all the journals. I don't understand what the problem is."

"Perhaps if he could just see the report."

"That's classified information."

"Paul, you know the rumours," I said softly. "If the autopsy report states that Lazare died of consumption, then why not make it public? It would help—"

"I'll tell you why!" he said, his hands gripping the arms of his chair. "Because there is nothing to hide. I've *had* it with these ignorant, suspicious . . ." He sputtered, seeking yet another invective.

*February 27.*

The door to chez Hoche was ajar. I pulled the bell rope, waited. I heard the child chattering. A tall white-haired man in a heavy wool coat and ribbed stockings came to the door. Lazare's father, Père Hoche—it was easy to see from his bushy eyebrows, the set of his jutting jaw, his proud stance. The child peeked out from between his legs. I introduced myself, handing him my card. "Citoyenne Bonaparte."

"The wife of General Bonaparte?" Père Hoche asked with respect in his voice.

"I knew your son, in the Carmes prison."

"Yes, he told me." With an appraising look.

I flushed. "My profound condolences, Citoyen Hoche."

"Hoche is *my* name," the child said from between her grandpapa's legs.

"Yes, I believe we have been introduced." I smiled.

Squealing, she ran back into the depths of the house.

The old man waved me into the house. "You're here to see Adélaïde?"

"She is expecting me, I believe."

"She told me she was expecting somebody, but she didn't tell me it was the wife of that rascal Bonaparte," he said, lighting a candle enclosed in oiled paper.

I followed his slow progression up the narrow stairs to the dark sitting room. "Sit. I'll tell her you're here." I waited in the spare little room, feeling Lazare's eyes staring down at me. A silk flower had been placed under the portrait, next to the blue urn. I heard a door, footsteps. Adélaïde Hoche appeared, dressed entirely in black, a widow's veil draped around her shoulders. "Père Hoche, please join us. I believe it regards Lazare," she said over her shoulder. She touched the urn on the mantelpiece, crossed herself and sat down.

The old man appeared in the door, filling it. "Oh?"

I glanced from one to the other uneasily. "I'm sorry, but I'm afraid I wasn't able to obtain the report. I was told that the law prevents making it public and—"

"The autopsy report?" Père Hoche asked, stepping into the room.

"But Director Barras assured me himself that the results are clear—your son died of consumption."

Père Hoche slammed his fist against the wall. "Don't you dare speak the name Barras in this house!"

I started, my heart pounding.

"Père Hoche, please," the young widow hissed, but her father-in-law ignored her.

"Yes, my son had consumption, but that wasn't what killed him. You don't get convulsions from consumption. Lazare was *poisoned*."

With the appearance of calm the widow stood, straightened Lazare's portrait. "It is not a good likeness," she said.

## In which I am accused

*February 28, 1798.*
Bonaparte is in a meeting with Talleyrand again. They closet themselves in the study every afternoon. It has become a bit mysterious, for now Bonaparte has forbidden anyone from entering that room. "Even the servants, Bonaparte?" I asked, perplexed. For the study was in shambles.

"Even *you*," he said, tweaking my ear.


*[Undated]*
Books stacked by Bonaparte's bedside—Ossian, Plutarch, the Koran.


*[Undated]*
I felt like a thief in my own house. I lit a candle, looked about. Bonaparte's study was in that familiar state of disarray, that look of volcanic activity. Every surface was covered with papers, journals, scrolls. I picked up a plate with chicken bones on it, to clear it, then put it back exactly where I found it. I held the candle down over the map that was spread out over the carpet—*Egypt*.


*March 1.*
Minister Schérer has yet to even read the Bodin Company proposal. "Why is he taking so long?" I asked Barras. We were standing in an

alcove of his palatial salon, ostensibly to admire a painting that had recently been hung there.

"Because he spends every minute of every day dealing with your husband's proposals, that's why."

I glanced toward the people gathered at the far end of the salon. Joseph was hunched over talking to Bonaparte—lecturing him, I gathered, from the expression on Bonaparte's face. In spite of his retiring nature Joseph took his position as head of the Bonaparte clan seriously. According to Corsican custom his younger siblings were all under his care. Indeed, whatever glory accrued to Bonaparte, Joseph took credit for it; whatever profit, he managed. We're Corsican, Bonaparte would tell me, as if that explained everything.

"Does your husband never sleep?" Barras went on. "We receive at least one memo from him a day, and this in addition to all the meetings he keeps calling."

"Regarding Egypt?" I asked, my eyes on his, watching to see what his reaction would be.

Barras made a sputtering sound. "It's insane, this plan of his," he hissed, grasping my elbow.

"People said the Italian campaign was insane," I said, rising to my husband's defence. But noting—Barras did not deny an Egyptian plan.

He waved his arms through the air in the Provençal manner. "Maybe he's right, who knows? Maybe this *is* the only way to get at England, to cut her off from Asia, her source of wealth."

England: the enemy. For as long as I could remember, it had been thus. We would have peace, were it not for England. We would have prosperity, were it not for England. Almost every man I had ever loved—my hapless father, my dissipated first husband, my honourable Lazare and now even my brilliant and driven second husband—had been consumed by one thought and one thought only: defeating England. "I take it you're not in support," I said.

Barras ran his fingers through his thinning hair. "Officially, yes, of course I'm in support. But privately—and I've told Bonaparte this myself—I have serious reservations. His proposal is based on three assumptions, three *false* assumptions, in my view. First, that it is possible to conquer Egypt, which is doubtful. Second, that he would then be able to establish a connection with India, which is unlikely. And third, that India would then join forces with us to conquer England, which is ludicrous.

"But you know what's *really* mad? My fellow Directors might just go along with it. Personally, I think they'd agree to anything if it meant getting your husband out of the country. His popularity is making them uneasy. Have you seen the Bonaparte dolls the vendors are selling down on the quays?"

"India?" I asked, confused. What did India have to do with it?

Barras regarded me for a long moment. "You didn't know anything about this, did you? You were just guessing."


*[Undated]*
"You might as well tell me about Egypt," I told Bonaparte, putting down my glass of watered wine.

He turned to me with an enigmatic smile.


*March 2.*
Captain Charles did three handsprings in the Bodin Company courtyard. "It's been approved!" he whooped.

At last—the Bodin Company is now the official supplier of horses to the Army of Italy.

"We did it," Hugo Bodin called out from the top step. He clasped his pudgy fists together and raised them in victory.

Captain Charles twirled me. I felt light in his hands. He danced me off my feet, singing, "We're going to be rich, we're going to be rich, we're going to be *stinking* rich!"


*March 5.*
Bonaparte slammed the door behind him. "The Directors gave their consent." He threw his hat at an armchair; it missed and sent a lantern toppling.

"To what?" I asked, righting the lantern, checking to see whether any oil had spilled.

"The invasion of Portugal." *Portugal?* He grinned like a schoolboy. "At least, that's the official story."


*March 10.*

It was our anniversary yesterday—our second. We'd planned a quiet evening, but at four in the afternoon, Bonaparte informed me that Admiral Bruyes and two aides would be joining us for dinner. "I thought we were dining alone, Bonaparte. It's our anniversary."

"It is?"

"We discussed this yesterday."

"Do you have any idea what I do in a week?" he exploded, storming out of our bedchamber.

Later, much later, he returned, repentant. He'd been drinking, which was unusual. "I want to make a baby," he said, fumbling with the bed spring. Our beds flew together with a crash—a sound that could be heard throughout the house, I knew. A sound that set the servants tittering, no doubt.

"I am beginning to despair of ever having another child," I confessed. It had been some time since I'd had the monthly sickness.

"Sterility in a woman is decided in the first three years of married life." He sat down, pulling at his boots. "For a woman over the age of twenty-five, the interval is lengthened."

"You've been studying?" Bonaparte believed anything could be achieved by knowledge—and by will, *his* will.

He planted his hand purposely on my breast. "The womb and the breasts are in sympathy. To excite the womb, one need merely excite the breast."

"Then I should have been with child long ago," I said with a smile.

He tugged at my nightdress, pulling it up over my head. "Queen Anne of Austria brought Louis XIV into the world after twenty-two years of sterility."

Twenty-one years of fidelity was how I understood it. But did not say.

*[Undated]*

From Madame Campan's book, chapter twenty-six, "Of Sterility": *Sterility is a Want of Conception in a Woman of requisite Age who duly suffers the Approaches of Man.*

I don't know what to think. I'm of "requisite age" and I certainly "duly suffer" (!) the approach of a man. I don't understand why I'm not pregnant. For that matter, I don't understand why I no longer have the flowers, in spite of the bitter rue tea Mimi has persuaded me to try.*

*March 13.*

I am . . . yes, *shattered* is the word—betrayed. Bitterness fills my heart. Disbelief. Lisette is gone. Her tears failed to move me.

What happened:

After my morning toilette I took a quick repast in the upstairs drawing room. Lisette, claiming vapours, had gone to her room in the basement. Bonaparte was in the study with Fauvelet, Junot and several other of his aides. Or so I thought.

It was as I was finishing a cup of coffee that Bonaparte came upstairs, asking after Junot. "I thought he was with you," I said.

"I haven't seen him all morning." Perplexed. "Perhaps he went riding."

"Perhaps," I said, standing, suddenly uneasy.

The steep stairs that led down to the servants' quarters in the basement were dark. At the landing I paused. I thought I heard a man's voice. Perhaps it was the cook, or my manservant. But I didn't think so.

At the bottom I stopped, suddenly unsure. The air was colder than above, but stale and smelling of flat-irons. I could simply open the door to Lisette's room—was that not how it was done in plays? Instead, I knocked.

"Tell her I'll be up in a moment," I heard Lisette call out with an irritated tone. The door was thin; I could hear quite clearly.

I knocked again, harder this time, more insistent.

* *Tea made of rue, an evergreen shrub, was commonly used by women wishing to abort.*

"Tell her to hold her horses!" A man's voice: Junot!

"I'll hold *your* horses," I heard Lisette say, giggling, and then, "That woman's going to drive me mad."

*That woman.* I turned the metal latch. The door swung open with a complaining creak. There, nude on a narrow trundle bed under the high dirty window, were Lisette and Junot, Lisette straddling. Both of them turned their faces toward me in a curiously co-ordinated motion.

"Bonaparte is looking for you, Colonel Junot," I said, backing out of the room and closing the door behind me. I went back up the stairs, pushing against both walls for support, my legs unsteady beneath me.

Mimi was in my bedchamber, gathering soiled linen. "I'm fine," I reassured her. "But I'd like to be alone." Her look of tender concern would make me weep, I feared. I heard heavy footsteps downstairs, heard a door open, slam shut, the low rumble of men's voices. I sat down on one of the hard stools by the bed. I'd never seen a man with a woman before, not like that, *en flagrante.* A man with a girl.

I was sipping a second glass of hysteric water when I heard the floorboards creak outside my door and then three light raps. I did not answer.

Three raps again. The latch turned, the door swung open. "Forgive me, Madame," Lisette said, her hands clasped in front of her, her head bowed.

I didn't know what to say. I did not have it in me to forgive her. It was not the deed so much as those words she had spoken: *that woman.* Was that all I was to her? I had come to believe that we shared an affection, one for the other. We'd been through so much together. But clearly, I'd been mistaken. "Gather your things, Lisette."

"Madame, please—!" She pressed her hands to her face.

Was she crying? I doubted it. She reached out to touch my hand as I passed by her, heading out the door. I was not mistaken. Her eyes were clear.

"It was just once, Madame. I promise . . ."

I closed the door behind me, short of breath.

"You'll be sorry," I heard her cry.

"You dismissed your maid?" Bonaparte asked, pulling on his jacket, preparing to go to the Luxembourg Palace for a meeting with the Directors. "But why?"

Junot, leaning against the mantel, observed me, his cold blue eyes unflinching.

"It was a personal matter," I told my husband evenly, avoiding Junot's gaze. There was no point telling Bonaparte. Junot was one of his oldest friends.

"You allowed her too many familiarities. It spoils a maid."

"Yes," I said.

"Next time, you'll know better."

I heard Junot's knuckles crack.

*March 14, midday.*

"Everyone knew," Mimi told me.

"Why didn't you tell me?"

"That's not my way."

"Will you be my lady's maid?"

"An upstairs maid?" Mimi paused, considering.

I touched her hand. "Please, Mimi—I need someone I know I can trust." I felt like a ship without a rudder. I no longer believed in my own judgement.

She made a doubtful face. "I'd have to learn manners."

"But you'll do it?"

She grinned. "I promised your mother I'd look after you, didn't I?"

*March 16.*

Bonaparte's older brother Joseph has taken to dropping in every day for the midday meal. Today he asked for a private consultation with Bonaparte, so I excused myself. They were sequestered for some time. Then Bonaparte's secretary appeared. "The General and his brother wish to speak with you, Madame," Fauvelet Bourrienne informed me, his look uneasy.

Bonaparte had his feet up on his desk and was tapping the desktop with a riding crop. "Leave, Fauvelet," he told his secretary. "And close the door!"

Joseph was slouched in the chair by the fire examining his fingernails. He looked up at me and smiled. It was then that I knew I was in trouble.

"Joseph has just informed me that you have had dealings with a military supply company." Bonaparte glanced over at his brother, who nodded. "The Bodin Company, to be specific, which was recently awarded a contract to provide horses to the Army of Italy."

I glanced from Bonaparte to Joseph and back again. "What are you talking about?" I demanded, my heart pounding.

"Perhaps this will refresh your memory." Joseph withdrew a sheet of paper from his waistcoat pocket and read, "Twenty-one Rue Honoré." He smiled.

Hugo Bodin lived at one hundred Rue Honoré, not twenty-one. "I've never been there."

"Curious," Joseph said, still smiling. "You were seen entering at twenty to eleven on fifteen Ventôse and did not emerge until three that afternoon. You were seen there again on the twenty-second, and then again on the twenty-third."

"Am I being followed?"

"Confess, Josephine!" Bonaparte exploded. "Is that not where you go every day—when you tell me that you go to the riding school to watch your son?"

It was a violent exchange. (I'm trembling still.) "Go ahead, divorce me, if that's what you want!" I ended up screaming. All the while Joseph Bonaparte smiled.


*March 17, late morning, exhausted.*
A sleepless night. Joseph knew everything—the details about the contracts, the finances! How did he find out? Somebody must be informing him. I suspect it might be Jubié, the banker Hugo Bodin has been dealing with. I've dispatched a letter to Captain Charles to warn him, warn Hugo Bodin.

I feel trapped, enraged. What right has Joseph to interfere in my dealings? What right has he to spy on me? For that matter, what right has

Bonaparte to treat me with such contempt! They self-righteously accuse me of crimes of which they themselves are guilty. I'm not married to Bonaparte, I'm married to a Corsican clan—and I despise them.

*11:30 P.M. (can't sleep).*

Bonaparte sat down on his bed. I was on my own, stretched out stiffly in my dressing gown. "You know I am right in this matter," he said coldly, as if from on high.

I did not answer.

"Answer me!" His hands fists.

"You are always *right,* Bonaparte," I said, turning my betrothal ring on my finger. I could have it melted down, I was thinking, made into earrings.

"Admit it—you've been dabbling in military supplies."

*Dabbling.* The word irked me. Did men "dabble"? The fact was, I'd "dabbled" long before we were married, long before we'd met. And I happened to be good at it. The profits paid my rent, enabled me to send my children to school—enabled me to survive. "Yes, Bonaparte, I *dabble.* As do your brothers, as does your Uncle Fesch." As he himself had in Italy. As did virtually all the officers in the army. As did all the *bon ton* of Paris, for that matter.

"It is unseemly for women to mingle in business."

He was talking like an old-fashioned country friar. "Things have changed. Many women—"

"Not my wife!"

"We have an agreement, Bonaparte: you pay for your expenses and I pay for mine." I clenched my hands, digging my nails into my palms. "I'm the one who must pay for Hortense's schooling. I'm the one who must raise a considerable sum for her dowry, who must provide uniforms for my son. How do you expect me to do this, I ask you? I'd be on the street, frankly, if it weren't for my so-called dabbling." (Well, perhaps I was exaggerating a little.)

He stomped out of the room. He is sleeping in the study tonight. *Bien.* He can stay there, for all I care.

*March 18.*

Mimi helped me on with my wool cloak. "Not your fur?" she asked, giving my shoulder a motherly squeeze. "It's cold out."

"I'll be fine." To Mimi, it was always cold. "Should Bonaparte ask, tell him I've gone to the stay-maker's."

She looked at me for a long moment. "But the stay-maker is coming here tomorrow."

"I mean the milliner's," I said, my cheeks heated. I'd never lied to Mimi before. I was becoming a person who did not trust—a person who was not trustworthy. At the door I looked back. "Forgive me?"

In a reckless clatter my coachman drove the horses out the gate. Approaching Monceau Park, I pulled my black shawl from my basket, draped it over my head. My coachman helped me down, cautioning me against the mud. Fortunately, it was no longer raining. An army of beggars cried out, holding out their hands. I gave them a bag of crusts. Where was Captain Charles? I wondered, opening my parasol in spite of the clouds. I'd sent him word to meet me at ten. I felt uneasy entering Monceau Park unescorted. I was relieved, finally, to see a man approaching on a black horse, trotting smartly down the central path. He waved a white plumed hat. I headed for a bench by some Roman columns.

"I meant to get here before you," Captain Charles said, dismounting East Wind with a graceful leap, "but I got tied up making arrangements for Milan." He looped the reins over a branch. Then he pitched two empty wine bottles into the bushes. "Here," he said, taking a silk tasselled scarf out of his saddlebag and spreading it over the stone bench.

I sat down at the far edge in order to give him room—more than he needed. I pulled my cloak tight. It was a damp and miserable day; now I regretted not wearing my fur.

"I talked to Hugo," he said, sitting forward, looking out over the pond. His full lips grazed the edge of his blue neck scarf, tied so that it completely covered his chin. He cleared his throat. "You were right. It was the banker Jubié. It turns out he knows your husband's brother."

"So." I crossed my arms across my chest. I didn't like it when I felt this way—so distant. "And Jubié told Joseph I was involved in the company?" Captain Charles nodded. "But how did *he* come to know? Hugo vowed to keep it confidential."

Captain Charles threw a pebble into the pond. "Hugo said he had to tell him. Otherwise he wouldn't have advanced us the money."

Of course, of course, I thought angrily. I watched the rings of water opening. I wanted to throw something into the pond too, but I felt too old for such games, and that thought made me sad.

"Jubié and your brother-in-law went out on the town, apparently." Captain Charles grinned. "To three taverns, a gambling establishment and a brothel."

I shrugged. I'd heard stories of Joseph's debauchery before, usually from his tearful wife.

"Are you going to quit the company?" he asked.

"No." I couldn't—even if I wanted to. I'd borrowed a small fortune in order to join. If I pulled out now, I'd be ruined. "I'd sooner get a divorce," I lied.

"That would please your brother-in-law. Apparently he told Jubié that he would not rest until he'd succeeded in getting his brother to divorce you," the captain said, tapping a stick against the toe of his boot.

"Oh?" That helped explain why Joseph had been spying on me, his mean little smile. Yet even so, it surprised me. I knew Joseph didn't care for me, but I didn't think he'd go so far as to try to get Bonaparte to divorce me.

"He told the banker that you married his brother for his money."

I laughed, I confess. When we'd married, Bonaparte had had no money. "That's amusing. What *else* did he say?"

"That you have Bonaparte under your spell." I smiled. Well . . . . "And that you're a witch." He made an apologetic shrug.

*A witch?* What had I ever done to Joseph to deserve such a hateful slur?

"I'm sorry, Madame Bonaparte, but I thought you should know. It helps, I think, knowing who you can trust—"

"And who you can't," I said, kicking a pebble. It skittered across the path and into the water. I watched the rings opening, one upon the other. How far did it go, the deceit?

After, I went to Thérèse's. I was in a state. "Look," I told her, pacing, "I can't quit the Bodin Company even if I wanted to." I owed almost half a million francs to Barras alone. The only way to get out was to stay in long enough to pay off my debts.

"May I make a suggestion?" Thérèse said, trying to calm me. "Talk to Bonaparte. Tell him he's been a cheap tightwad—impossible to live with!—that he's put you in an untenable position, that you didn't intend to compromise him by doing what *everybody* in Paris is doing, including all the members of his avaricious family, and then tell him you intend to withdraw. So, maybe extricating yourself will take a little longer than you let on, and maybe he's better off not knowing. From the apoplectic fits he throws over the purchase of a hat, I can guarantee you that he doesn't want to know the extent of your debts. Frankly, all he really wants to hear is that you love him. So why don't you just tell him?" She laughed at my cross expression. "Well, you do, you know. Why don't you just admit it?"

*[Undated]*
"Yeyette?" Mimi set a tray down on the table beside the bed. "I got the cook to make some plantain bread for you." She handed me a piece.

"Oh Mimi, I'm so miserable," I confessed. I'd slept alone for three nights, tossing and turning.

"The General is unhappy, as well."

"Oh?" I bit into the heavenly smelling loaf, my childhood welling up around me in my mind.

"I've never in my life seen a more miserable man."

"Good!" I said, but blinking back tears.

"I think it's time we talked," she said, handing me a flannel to dry my face.

And so we did. I told her how confused I was about Bonaparte, how angry he made me, how exasperating he was. And then I told her how brilliant I believed him to be, how his mind was volcanic, always thinking—and how it frightened me sometimes, knowing the thoughts in his mind, knowing his dreams. I told her how different we were, how hard it was to live with him. And then I told her how alike we were, how we'd both grown up on islands, far from France, how we knew what it was like to be an outsider. And then I told her how he loved me more than anyone had ever loved me, and how he needed me, how I was his good luck star, and how sometimes I felt we were fated.

"Do you think he is your spirit friend?"

"I fear so," I cried, weeping anew.

*March 19, Feast of Saint Joseph.*

I was combing my hair at my dressing table when I heard footsteps in the bedchamber. "Bonaparte?" I called out, standing.

He stuck his head in my dressing room, his hat still on. "There you are."

"I'm . . ." Sorry, I started to say.

Solemnly, he held out a brass-plated chain. "It's your name day today."

The nineteenth of March, of course—feast of Saint Joseph. I was surprised he remembered, surprised he even knew. "How kind of you." I slipped it on. "It's lovely," I lied.

"Josephine, I . . ."

I looked into his great grey eyes, his melancholy eyes so full of dreams. "I know, Bonaparte."

"The Sultan of Turkey has over a hundred wives," Bonaparte told me, "beauties awaiting their turn, devoted to pleasing, to the art of pleasing." He stroked my breast, my hip. "Like my wife." For I please this man, my husband.

"I want to go with you," I told him.

"To Egypt?" he whispered.

"Wherever you go."

*In which I must stay behind*

*March 20, 1798.*

The Black Land—it haunts my thoughts. I have been reading about it, hiding the text under my mattress. We will arrive in June, after the simoon, a suffocating wind that blows across the desert. The temperature will be hot. "I'm a créole," I reassure Bonaparte. "I will be able to take the heat."

There is no rain in Egypt. Every year the Nile River overflows and inundates the land with a slimy substance. But for this, nothing would grow.

A land without water! Even the names of the oases sound dry on my tongue: *Khârgeh, Dâkhel, Farâfra, Sîwa, Bahrîyeh.*

Diseases flourish in that land—plague, cholera, ophthalmia, dysentery . . . even boils so deadly that they can kill a man.

A land of crystalline rock, covered by shifting sand.

A land without trees. It is impossible to imagine such a place. I am curious to see a papyrus plant, from which the paper used throughout the ancient world was made. The lotus is a water lily that grows on the Nile.

Oxen, horses, asses, sheep, goats—familiar creatures. But camels! And cats without tails. (Fortunately, crocodiles are seldom seen.) The pelican, the beloved bird of my youth, abides in the north.

The cities are inhabited by white vultures, which are worshipped—as are certain beasts, reptiles and even vegetables. The sun god is Ra, a hawk-headed man, the moon god is Thoth. Seth is the power of evil, a spirit with a gentle, seductive name.

"Egypt is the first nation known to man," Bonaparte told me with awe in his voice. He works by candlelight on the floor of our bedchamber, studying the maps, tracing the footsteps of Alexandre the Great, Julius Caesar. He dreams of desert sands.

*April 2.*
Meetings here all day preparing for "the expedition"—the *mysterious* expedition. Eugène emerged from the smoke-filled study, laughing with the men. "We're going to Portugal," he told me confidentially.
"Oh?" It is all I can do not to tell him the true destination.

*April 3.*
The widow Hoche called on me today, her worry about Père Hoche over-coming her timidity. Her father-in-law was suffering, rage and grief were burning him up. "Is there nothing you can do?"

*April 4.*
"There's a strange man to see you," Mimi said, crinkling her nose.
It was my old friend Fouché,* looking like a beggar. "How kind of you to come so soon." For I had sent for him only this morning. I offered him a glass of orange water—Fouché did not partake of spirits, I knew. His hooded eyes, his disordered clothes, his stale odour, all brought on a feeling of affection in me. He was an eccentric, this slovenly man, this ardent Revolutionary with bad breath. This man who was devoted to his ugly red-haired wife and all their ugly red-haired children. This man who was making a fortune (I'd heard) as a partner in Company Ouen, a military supply company. This man, the extraordinary spy. "There is a document I need to obtain," I ventured. "Might you be available?"

* *Joseph Fouché was a radical Revolutionary with a reputation for violence (even atrocities) and a penchant for conspiracy.*

He opened his snuffbox. "For a price," he said, sniffing a pinch. I flushed. "You mistake me, Citoyenne. It is information I trade in. I give you what you want, you repay me in kind."

He made it sound so innocent, a simple exchange. But I knew what he meant, in truth. In exchange for whatever answers he might deliver, I would become a spy on his behalf. "I would never compromise a friend," I said.

"That would hardly be necessary. You are no doubt aware that you have a number of enemies who could provide you with numerous opportunities to fulfill such an obligation."

"Perhaps you could begin by telling me who they might be?" I smiled behind my fan.

"It does not take a clairvoyant to see that the Bonapartes wish you dead, but given the inconvenience of being caught with blood on their collective hands, would settle for ruin, no doubt. And in their midst, of late, a rather lovely young woman has been seen—a girl who was, at one time, your lady's maid." He took a small, careful sip of his glass of orange water. "It is a wisdom well understood by our ci-devant nobility that one should never reveal oneself to a man or woman who is in one's pay. Servants thus taken into confidence come to know a great deal, putting them in a position to profit from the sale of such. And profit, even a Revolutionary will tell you, is an irresistible force of Nature. Perhaps it is this young woman who concerns you."

Lisette had been seen with the Bonapartes? I went to the window, my cheeks burning. "No, it is not Citoyenne Compoint."

"Perhaps it has to do with your present state of "—he paused—"embarrassment."

My debts, he meant. "It has nothing to do with that." Appalled, I confess, by how much Fouché knew.

"Then no doubt it regards the somewhat suspect practices of your business associates, the brothers Bodin."

Suspect practices? "The name Bodin is unfamiliar to me, Citoyen Fouché," I told him with splendid calm.

Fouché unbuttoned his jacket, revealing a dapper silver-trimmed waistcoat underneath. "Citoyenne, you are an effective liar, a quality I have always admired in you. Tell me, then—what is it you wish to know?"

"General Hoche's widow has solicited my help." Fouché sat back, surprised. It pleased me, I confess, to startle a man such as Fouché, a professional in the matter of knowing. "Her father-in-law, Père Hoche, the late General Hoche's father, is subject to morbid dreams, rages that have weakened his constitution. He has become obsessed with finding out how his son died."

"Case closed, Citoyenne. It is common knowledge General Hoche died of consumption."

"Specifically, the elder Hoche has tried, without success, to obtain a copy of the autopsy report—"

"Which, being a military matter, is confidential, of course."

I nodded. "So I was told. The fact that no one is permitted to see it has inflamed Père Hoche's imagination further."

"But no doubt Director Barras could obtain a copy for you."

"I'm afraid not." I paused, unsure whether I should tell Fouché how emotional Barras had become at the very mention of it. "The problem is, Père Hoche is convinced his son was poisoned."

"Père Hoche and the rest of Paris." Fouché made a dismissive gesture. "Does he have cause? Or is he feeding off rumours like the rest of us?"

"He claims his son suffered convulsions in his dying moments." I swallowed, a wave of tears rising dangerously within me. "Apparently, convulsions are not symptomatic of consumption."

Fouché bit the inside of one cheek, considering.

"I'm of the view that the father's grief is driving him mad. If he could just see the autopsy report, it might put his imaginings to rest. But after talking to Director Barras, I have come to the conclusion that obtaining a copy of the report will not be easy. Indeed, that it might require a certain degree of, well—"

"Sleuthing?"

I smiled apologetically. "Not to mention discretion. For I'm sure you can understand, Citoyen Fouché, how important it is that my own involvement in this matter be kept strictly confidential."

"Secrecy is my passion, Citoyenne."

*April 6.*

At Barras's salon last night Fouché sidled up to me. "The autopsy report appears to be missing from the Ministry of War's files," he whispered, widening his eyes.

I motioned to him to be silent. Talleyrand had just entered the room.

"I have a contact at the School of Medicine," he went on. "He should be able to give me the name of the surgeon who performed the autopsy."

"How good to see you this evening, Citoyen Talleyrand," I said, giving the Minister of Foreign Affairs my hand.

*April 7.*

"I located the surgeon who performed the autopsy, but he demands one hundred francs," Fouché informed me tonight in the corridor at the Luxembourg Palace. "Are you willing?"

"To pay one hundred francs? Just for a copy of the report?"

Fouché shrugged. "I was surprised he didn't ask for more."

*April 8, Easter Sunday.*

"You got it?" I asked Fouché, my voice thick. I did not care for this, did not care for any of it, neither the seeking nor the finding. I wanted it to be over. Were it not for my promise to help the widow Hoche, I would wash my hands of this business completely.

Fouché arched his thin red eyebrows, his hand on his coat pocket. "I did. But it will not appease the father," he warned, unfolding the single yellowed sheet. "According to the autopsy report, the cause of General Hoche's death is"—he paused for effect—"unknown."

It was not at all what I had expected. Barras himself had told me that the autopsy had determined that Lazare had died of consumption. "So General Hoche did not die of consumption?" I scanned the document and then folded it. I did not want to read it.

"Possibly—because if he had died of consumption, it seems to me that the surgeon would have clearly stated so. But if one were to die of poisoning—let us say, just for the purpose of inquiry—the effects being subtle and therefore mysterious, then the cause of death would, most likely, be reported as—"

"Unknown!" Père Hoche shook the report in the air, as if at the gods. "My son was poisoned. There's nothing unknown about that. And I'll tell you who did it—Director Barras."

I glanced at the widow, dismayed. She was standing by the fireplace, her hand on the blue urn on the mantel. I wanted to speak out in Barras's defence, but I knew that it would only enrage the old man further.

"And I'll tell you why," he ranted on. "Director Barras murdered my son because Lazare had integrity. Speak that word around Director Barras and see if he even knows it. Integrity, honesty, bravery—they're all foreign words to that traitor."

"Can't sleep?" Mimi asked, discovering me in the downstairs drawing room, curled up on the sofa, staring into the embers.

"What time is it?" I asked.

"Two," she said.

I sighed. Would I ever sleep? "I have worries, Mimi."

"I know."

I smiled. Mimi knew everything.

"Want to talk?"

"Not yet," I told her, standing.

"Always remember, we're looking over you," she said, "your mother and I."

I turned at the landing. "Thank you."

*April 9.*
Bonaparte and I have just returned from an evening at Barras's salon. I'm in turmoil over a conversation with Fouché. He informed me that the man who had performed the autopsy had come to his home offering

more information—in exchange for more money, of course. "I took it upon myself to pay on your behalf."

"Oh," I said weakly. I thought the matter was finished. He'd obtained the report. The business was done.

"It seems that after the autopsy, General Hoche's doctor asked that the heart be put aside."

Lazare's heart? Why? I sat down, sickened. I could not bear to think of Lazare's body in this way, as a collection of so many parts.

"Furthermore," Fouché said, sitting down beside me and hunching forward, his elbows on his knees, "there were specks in the lining of the stomach—sufficient to cause suspicion, but insufficient to prove anything."

"Suspicion of what?" I heard a clock chime, followed by another, and then another.

"Of poisoning." He turned to me and smiled. "May I make a suggestion, Citoyenne? Over the years I have learned that success depends on one thing and one thing only—the courage to ask the true question. And with respect, the true question may not be how General Hoche died, but rather who, in fact, killed him."

"Citoyen Fouché, I would like this investigation dropped."

He looked puzzled. "But Citoyenne—"

"I insist!"


*April 10.*

Bonaparte is frantic. There is so much to do, and everything made difficult by the necessity of raising the funds for the expedition—an expedition whose actual destination must remain unknown (to prevent the English from finding out). To that end we have been entertaining every evening—last night the banker Perrégaus; tonight Collot, the munitioner. Those evenings we do not entertain, Bonaparte and I attend Barras's salon at the Luxembourg Palace, where the talk is invariably of what everyone is now calling "Bonaparte's crusade."

*April 11.*

Every evening we receive members of the Académie: engineers, chemists, zoologists, cartographers, antiquarians. Bonaparte is determined to take over one hundred savants with him. He must be persuasive, for the destination remains secret.*

*April 12.*

"*Basta!*" Bonaparte threw his hat onto the carpet, pulled off his boots. "You know the song and dance about Louis being too ill to join the expedition?" He made a sputtering noise. "I just found out the true reason."

"Louis is going to Barèges, for a cure." Ever since we'd returned from Italy, Bonaparte's younger brother had often been unwell. "Isn't he?"

"That's just an excuse." Bonaparte hit a table with his fist. I steadied the clock just before it toppled. "No, it's because he's in love, of all things."

I took Pugdog onto my lap, stroked his silky fur. "Why that's—"

Bonaparte glared. "With Émilie."

"*My* Émilie?" I was astonished.

"The daughter of an émigré," he said, his cheek twitching. "And her parents divorced. And her mother remarried to a mulatto!" He pulled the servant rope. Mimi appeared, tying her apron strings. "Get Louis."

"What do you intend to tell him, Bonaparte?"

"To begin packing for Egypt." Bonaparte glowered into the embers. "And that he's never to see her again. And that she is betrothed."

"But Bonaparte—"

"And that she's to be married in a matter of weeks."

"Married?" I'd seen Émilie a few days ago, and she'd said nothing of the matter. "To whom?"

"That's for you to determine." He strode to the door. "Louis!" I heard him stomping up the stairs.

---

* *Ultimately 167 scholars were persuaded to go, forming a Commission of Arts and Science that would, in turn, be called the Institute of Egypt. Out of this campaign, a twenty-four volume Déscription de l'Égypte was published, upon which the science of Egyptology is founded.*

*April 13.*
Both Bonaparte's brothers Lucien and Joseph have been elected to the
Council of Five Hundred. (Lucien is only twenty-three!) At this rate, the
Republic will be ruled by Bonapartes. *Bien*—so long as they don't rule me.


*April 18.*
Eugène waved a paper in the air, Lavalette hovering behind him. "We're
leaving in four days!"

Four days? "Why so soon?" Bonaparte and I wouldn't be leaving for at
least a month—or so he'd told me.

"At four in the morning," Eugène said, puzzling over the paper. "Lieutenant Lavalette, Louis and I. We're to go in civilian clothes. We're not
allowed to tell anyone that we're aides, and if asked where we're headed,
we're to say we're going to Brest." He looked at Lavalette. "*Brest?*"

"That's likely to keep the English confused," I said.

"If they're only half as confused as we are, they'll be confused,"
Lavalette said.



I heard footsteps on the stairs, light hurried steps punctuated by clicking
spurs—Bonaparte.

"One word before you go, Bonaparte." I stood in the door to stop
him.

"I'm late. What is it?" he demanded, buttoning up his grey uniform
jacket. No matter how many fashionable new jackets I had the tailor
make for him, Bonaparte invariably chose to wear his plain grey one with
the frayed epaulettes.

"Lavalette might be the man we're—"

He squinted at me, confused.

"For Émilie." I nodded toward the front door. "He's in the courtyard."

"Lieutenant Lavalette? You want me to talk to him? *Now?*"

"He's to leave in four days!"

Lavalette stood in the dining room door, his green felt hat in his hand.

"The General has spoken to you?" I asked, standing to greet him.

"Madame Bonaparte, I am . . . I must confess, she is an angel, everything I could ever . . . but"—he ran his hand over his balding head—"but she is a girl, and I'm already twenty-nine."

"Twenty-nine is not so very old, Lieutenant." I'd thought he was older, in fact.

"The General said that the wedding must be held in one week."

One week! Was Émilie to be introduced at the altar? "In that case we should go out to the school tomorrow." Lavalette, Bonaparte, Eugène and I would go. "I will introduce you, and you will make your proposal."

"T-t-tomorrow?"


*April 19.*

Bonaparte had a report to dispatch to the Directory, so it was noon by the time we arrived at the school. Caroline (who has only recently been enrolled) and Hortense came bounding out to join us, Émilie following. "It's such a lovely day, I thought a picnic might be nice," I said, embracing each in turn. Émilie looked charming in her broad-brimmed bonnet: a good omen, I thought.

"I already ate," Caroline said.

I glanced at Lavalette. He was standing with his hands clasped in front of him, gripping a bouquet of wilted violets. "Lieutenant Lavalette, do you know everyone here?" I introduced the girls, but they were more interested in Eugène's new uniform. "Perhaps Eugène will carry the basket," I suggested, taking Bonaparte's arm. I knew a spot under some oak trees.

We proceeded down the wide gravel path. Now and again Caroline cast a glance at Lavalette, at the curious bouquet of wilted flowers he was clutching. She whispered something to Hortense, who burst into giggles. I caught Lavalette's eye. "I know a girl who happens to love violets," I said, nudging Émilie. Wordlessly, Lavalette pushed the bouquet at her. Suddenly the girls fell silent.

We came to the spot I had in mind. Caroline, Émilie and Hortense rushed to help me unpack the basket. Eugène busied himself folding the napkins in cocked-hat fashion. We spread the hemp picnic cloth, laid out the food: flat bread, a mild cheese, roasted hare.

We ate quickly, in silence. Bonaparte threw his bones into the woods. I asked Eugène to entertain us with his imitations. Then the time came to pack the basket. I took Bonaparte's arm. "I'd like to see the pond before we go."

Eugène grabbed Caroline and Hortense by the hand and began running down the path. Émilie made a few steps to follow them. "No!" Eugène called back to her. "You stay."

"Oh, I can't bear it," I told Bonaparte, walking briskly to keep up with him. I glanced over my shoulder. I saw Lavalette bend down and kiss Émilie on top of her head. "I think we can go back now," I said.


*[Undated]*

Louis looked surprised that Émilie is to be married, but other than that he showed no emotion. He was not happy, however, about having to go on the expedition. His health concerns me.


*April 22, Sunday.*

Eugène has been packing. Slipping something into his leather valise (a song Hortense had written for him), I saw his scrapbooks on the shelf. The house was silent: safe. I took down the one about Hoche, opened the glue-stiff pages. It was all there: Lazare's glory, his final disgrace.

What followed were the eulogies: the profound outpouring of a nation's grief over the death of a true Republican, a passionate defender of la liberté. In the words spoken following his death, I could read a lament not so much for Lazare, but for the freedom he had fought for, died for: *la liberté ou la mort.*

Had Lazare been poisoned? Had he died defending la liberté? I closed the scrapbook, put it back on the shelf exactly as I had found it.

*May 4.*

It was on the way home from the theatre that Bonaparte informed me, "We leave tonight."

I put my hand on his wrist. "You don't really mean tonight . . . do you?"

He held his watch fob to the light of the moon. "As soon as we get home. We'll pick up Louis and Eugène in Lyons."

"But . . ." We weren't packed. "But what about Hortense? I can't just leave without—"

*May 9—Toulon.*

It was early when we pulled into the port of Toulon, in spite of a mishap on the road.

"Look," Bonaparte's secretary Fauvelet exclaimed.

Looking out over the harbour I saw the French fleet at anchor, a forest of masts. "Is that *La Pomone?*" I asked. Seventeen years before I'd come to France on *La Pomone*. "How many ships are there?" I'd never seen so many.

"Three hundred and ten," Louis said.

"The greatest fleet in history since the Crusades," Eugène said in an awed whisper.

*10:30 A.M.*

In the market the talk is only of the fleet, where it may be heading. "There is even a booth for placing bets," Eugène said.

"I bet a sou there on Portugal," Mimi said, looking up from her mending.

"Oh?"

"And then there was a rush of bets on Portugal. Everyone thought I knew."

"Which is the favoured destination?" Bonaparte asked, looking up from the volume of poetry he was reading, his beloved Ossian. (*"A tale of the times of old! The deeds of days of other years!"*)

"The Crimea," Mimi said.

Eugène and Louis snickered, imagining that they knew the true destination.

*May 12.*

Bonaparte has been in a flurry of activity, organizing provisions, going over the lists, the ships, the artillery. Going over the maps. Now, he is ready, and impatient. He waits on the wind.

*Evening.*

A wind has risen, but not in the right direction. Bonaparte watches the sky. Hourly, from the widow's walk, he scans the horizon with a spyglass, searching for signs of the enemy.

*May 14.*

This morning, bringing my cup of hot chocolate himself, Bonaparte informed me I would not be going.

A breeze billowed the curtains, filling the room with the rancid smell of the harbour. "Going where?" I asked, confused, pulling the covering sheet over me. I was naked, my sleeping gown tangled somewhere in the sheets. Since reaching Toulon Bonaparte had become even more ardent than usual. Being back in active command had brought out a vigorous energy in him.

He sat down on the bed. I moved over to make room for him. He put his hand on my shoulder, as if to console me, and it was then that I knew what he was going to say. "Bonaparte, no. *Please* don't leave me behind." I felt tears pressing. Stupid tears.

"It's too dangerous—the English are out there. They'll likely attack."

It was silent in the room but for the ticking of a clock. "You never told me that."

He took my hand, kissed it. "When we get to Egypt, I'll send a ship back for you. *La Pomone,* if you like."

I pressed my head against his shoulder. "It frightens me to be separated from you, Bonaparte."

"What is there to be afraid of?"

*His family,* I thought.

*May 15.*

I sit idle as everyone scurries about, preparing for the "crusade." They are filled with excitement, and I, with a feeling of sadness . . . and dread.

*May 18.*

The flags are blowing to the east. Eugène came running up the stairs to my suite. "We're leaving at dawn," he cried out breathlessly, his cheeks rosy.

*May 19.*

All night I could not sleep. At the first hint of light, the first crow of a cock, I slipped out of bed, went to the window. The masts in the harbour were bobbing in the breeze. The weather vane pointed east.

"Where's Fauvelet?" Bonaparte jumped out of bed, fully alert. I helped him into his uniform. He had been shaved the night before, in anticipation of the morning. A knock, three knocks. "There he is."

"General, they're—"

Bonaparte bolted out the door, buttoning his long linen trousers.

I sat down at my toilette table and regarded myself in the glass. The morning light was cruel, the worry lines clear.

Another knock. Fauvelet again, apologetic. "Twenty minutes, Madame."

Twenty! Mimi performed a small miracle, transforming me from an anxious woman who had had no sleep into the elegant wife of General Bonaparte.

Eugène burst in and struck a heroic pose. "Ready?"

There was a call from the first floor. "Coming!" He leapt down the stairs, his hat flying off behind him.

As we came out into the morning sun, a great cry went up. People were waving flags, dressed in a colourful assortment of feast-day clothes. A cluster of people surrounded a man with a board hanging from his shoulders that proclaimed, "Final bets here." The locations were listed along with the odds. I dared not look for fear my expression might give the true destination away. *Portugal,* I kept telling myself. They are sailing to Portugal. The crowd cheered, began singing "Chant du départ."

The moment I'd been dreading came. I took Eugène's hands, examined his face, his soft eyes, the freckles across his nose, thinking: I will always remember him thus, *if*. . .

"How does one tell a soldier to be careful?" I asked, choking up.

"Maman." Squirming, uncomfortable in front of Louis and all his shipmates.

I kissed him quickly, before he could escape. "I'll be joining you." *Soon.*

Bonaparte met me on the railing. I held my handkerchief to my nose. Everyone was watching us, I knew.

"Stay in Toulon until it's clear that we have made it," he said.

"There's a chance you might turn back?"

He stroked a lock of hair out of my eyes. "If we're forced to."

By the English. "Oh, Bonaparte, I hate this." I pressed my cheek against the rough wool of his jacket—that same frayed jacket he'd worn in Italy.

"If you need anything, ask Joseph," he said, his voice thick. "I've told him to give you forty thousand a year."

"But I will be joining you in a few months." Why this talk of a year?

"You'll go to Plombières for the treatment?"

I nodded. The treatment for infertile women.

"When it's safe, I'll send *La Pomone* for you." He kissed me lightly on the cheek. "And then we'll get on with our project."

"General Bonaparte?"

"One moment, Fauvelet." A gust of wind blew hair in my eyes. I held onto my hat. Bonaparte put his hand on my shoulder. "If I should—"

"No, Bonaparte!" The angels watched over him; I had to believe that.

He stopped, his eyes glistening. I pressed my face into his neck. *Please:* "Take care."


I was escorted to a balcony of the Marine Intendancy building, where a number of women were sitting, officers' wives. They shifted so that I might have the best chair. The paymaster came out, carrying a tray of spyglasses. "Oh," we all exclaimed in unison. And then laughed.

I took a spyglass, searched the decks of *L'Orient.* "I see your husband," I told Madame Marmont, a young bride of only sixteen. But no Eugène, no Bonaparte. "By the helm." I showed her how to adjust the glass, so that the focus might be clear.

She put her glass down, blinded by tears. "It's hopeless."

Gunshot! The crowd on the shore began singing *La Marseillaise,* and we all began to sing along. I pressed my glass to my eyes. Finally I spotted Bonaparte in a cluster of men at the helm. I recognized him by his hat. My heart surged with pride to see him. I searched the faces for Louis and Eugène.

"I put my money on Sicily," one of the women said.

"I'm sure it's Africa," Madame Marmont said. "Else why would they take so much water?"

"Even I don't know," I lied.

As the ships weighed anchor, the cannons in the fort were fired and a military band on the shore broke into a brassy hymn. The warships and the fort exchanged salutes. The smell of gunpowder filled the air.

"They're raising the sails!" The wind pulled *L'Orient* forward. A cheer went up on the shore.

"Oh," I cried out. For the huge ship had listed sharply.

"Something's wrong." Madame Marmont jumped to her feet.

"It's dragging bottom!"

"It will right itself," I assured them—Madame *Bonaparte* assured them. But inwardly I was trembling.

"It's righting now."

*Yes.* The huge ship bobbed on the water like a toy. The crowd cheered. Wind filled its gigantic sails, pulled it forward. A lone trumpeter blasted out a note. I waved my soggy handkerchief, but I could no longer see through my tears.

# IV

## *Lobbyist*

"... women are politics."
—*Talleyrand*

## *In which I very nearly die*

*June 14, 1798—Plombières-les-Bains.*
A harrowing voyage, but I'm here at last in the charming mountain spa of Plombières-les-Bains—slate grey houses crammed into a narrow valley as if they had tumbled into a crevice and were too weary to rise. A beautiful setting, cliffs rising to the sky, thick forests all around, the air bracing and clean. But such a small village! (I walked its length in seventeen minutes.) And so much more isolated than I'd expected.

*June 15.*
I met this morning with Dr. Martinet, the water doctor. He is a short man with a trim build and a businesslike air. He wore thick spectacles and a white canvas coat. His hair, which is thinning, was unpowdered, braided at the back into one very long tail, looped and caught up with a white cord. All along one wall of his study were framed testimonials.

"Letters from happy patients," he said with a sweep of his hand. He had moist lips (as if he had been licking them), and moist eyes too, I noticed, as one might expect in a water doctor. "I like to begin by pointing out that our program enjoys a high rate of success." He closed his eyes when he talked. "It is important that the patient begin with this knowledge, for faith—or rather the obedience that faith makes possible—is essential to its successful completion." He opened his eyes.

I sat forward on my chair. The possibility that there might in fact be a cure encouraged me. I had come with prayers in my heart, but little hope, I confess. "I intend to be a model patient, Dr. Martinet."

He leaned back in his cracked leather chair, his hands gripping a board onto which papers had been clipped. "The program is not for those lacking in courage. It requires some degree of both physical and mental strength to successfully complete. But"—he held up an index finger— "nature rewards those who endure. Now, Madame Bonaparte, if you will begin by telling me your history." He peered at me over his spectacles. His eyebrows are thick, bushy (in contrast to his thinning hair), giving him a somewhat diabolical look.

This is what I told him:

I first conceived at the age of sixteen, after only a few months of marriage, but miscarried. My son, Eugène, was then conceived and brought to term. Less than two years later I conceived a daughter. It was a difficult pregnancy and she was born several weeks early.

"But otherwise normal?"

"I had difficulty producing milk." I cleared my throat. "And then—" Did he need to know that Alexandre and I had separated? "Years later my husband died . . . and two years after his death I married General Bonaparte. That was just over two years ago."

"And you have conceived by this union, but miscarried?"

"My doctor thought it might have been a mole."

"Interesting! And then did the flux resume?"

"For a time it was sporadic."

"And the last one was . . . ?"

I wasn't sure exactly. I'd been in Milan. "Over a year ago." Although possibly a year and a half.

"Did you take anything to re-establish the flow?"

I pushed forward the list of herbals (linden blossom, wormwood, coltsfoot) that a doctor in Milan had prescribed, the tea of aloe, gentian root and jalappa. "I also consulted a midwife, who gave me uterus powder." I declined to tell him about the Gypsy I'd gone to in Italy—the one with a well-picked savin bush in her vegetable garden—and the rue tea Mimi had persuaded me to try.*

"But no results?"

"The powder made me ill."

"And your relationship with the General is . . . ?" He licked his upper lip.

I nodded, flushed.

Dr. Martinet tapped his pencil on the desk. "Madame Bonaparte, during the Terror you were held, were you not?"

Imprisoned, he meant. "Yes, I was in the Carmes for four months."

The doctor leaned forward, resting his elbows on the desk. "I must tell you, I have had a significant number of patients who were likewise 'held' during the Terror—women who likewise seem to be suffering from an inexplicable infertility."

I felt a tightening in my chest. "It's true that the flux became unpredictable during that time."

"The effect of shock on the female constitution is proven to be disruptive. If nourishment is lacking, the air oppressive, exercise restricted—any one of these factors is known to affect a woman's capacity to be that which Nature intended her to be, a mother."

"Are you saying that the cessation of my periodic sickness may have been caused by my being in prison?"

"I am suggesting that it may be a very strong possibility. According to my observations, a number of women who have been detained in this way have suffered a cessation of the flow and have plunged, regardless of age, into a condition curiously resembling that of a woman long past the age of reproduction. They have difficulty sleeping, experience an overwhelming anxiety, melancholia—insanity in some cases. And, needless to say, all of them are barren."

"Dr. Martinet, do you mean *menopause?*"

---

* All of these were popular abortive measures. Uterus powder is likely ergot, a black, hard fungus that grows on stalks of rye, an abortive widely used for "bringing on the flowers." Powder made from the leaves of a savin bush, which was often to be seen in the garden of a village midwife, was commonly used. Tea made from rue was considered just as powerful and more reliable than savin, however.

From a book Dr. Martinet loaned me:

*First, one grows stout at the back of the neck, where two prominences form at the lowest cervical vertebrae.*

*The breasts become flat and hard, less spongy.*

*The legs and arms dry up, resembling those of a man.*

*The abdomen enlarges to the extent that the woman may appear to be pregnant.*

*A beard often manifests itself.*


I am at the desk in my sparely furnished room overlooking the main street of Plombières. It is warm. I've opened the double doors wide onto the balcony. I can hear the sounds of horses, carriages, people talking, walking. Somewhere, someone is playing a violin beautifully.

I am shaken, I confess, by my conversation with Dr. Martinet. It had never occurred to me that I might be past the age of fertility. I think of old women, stooped and withered, whiskered and dour, and despair overwhelms me.


*June 16.*

This afternoon I experienced the showers—"the torture chamber" the women here call it. Now I know why.

In an outer chamber I was asked by an attendant to remove my clothes—all of them. In this state of Eve I went into a small steam-filled room occupied by another woman standing in front of a drawn curtain of white canvas.

I was alarmed to hear a man say, "Madame Bonaparte." The voice was coming from behind the curtain. "This is Dr. Martinet speaking. Do not be alarmed; your privacy will be respected. Are you ready?"

The steam was already so thick I felt I might suffocate for want of air. The attendant, a thin woman with a massive nose, was fiddling with a hose and a series of valves. In front of her was a pit, into which she aimed a powerful flow of steaming water. "Get on the mark," she said, holding the pulsating hose to one side. I stood on a faded green circle in the middle of the pit. "Turn around."

"My assistant will aim the flow of the water on the base of the neck." Dr. Martinet's voice seemed ghostly, detached. "She will proceed slowly down the spine. The sensation may be uncomfortable, but be assured that in spite of the stinging sensation, you are not, in fact, being burned. Support bars are provided in case you require support."

I clasped hold of the bars.

"The nape of the neck is the centre of your being, the centre of vitality. The nurse will begin the descent."

The stream of boiling water began to burn its way slowly down my spine. *Uncomfortable!* I would kill him, I vowed, but not quickly. Quickly would be too kind.

At the end of this torture I was so weak that the attendant had to help me into the accompanying room, where I was laid out on a bed and left to sweat in great quantities. A cure, I am told. If I survive.

*2 Prairial, Luxembourg Palace*
*My friend,*

*Paris is seething yet again. Last year we were attacked from the right; this year it's from the left. As feared, the elections resulted in a number of radical Revolutionaries taking seats in the legislature, all of them united in one cause: to bring down the Directors. The committee we set up to review the election results disqualified one in four. You can imagine the reaction.*

*Tallien, unfortunately, was one of those disqualified, and there is nothing I can do to reverse the decision. Thérèse has appealed to me to get him a position with Bonaparte in Egypt. Frankly, I think she just wants him out of the country.*

*Père Barras*

*June 4, Paris*
*Honoured sister,*

*As manager of the Bonaparte Family Trust,* *I have been instructed by my*

---

* *The Trust would be made up almost in its entirety of the estimated eight million francs Bonaparte is thought to have brought back from Italy.*

younger brother to provide you with three thousand francs on the first of each month. I have forwarded a bank note to Citoyen Emmery, your banker. I advise you to manage it responsibly.

In answer to your query, the cost of a cure at Plombières is not the responsibility of the Bonaparte Family Trust. A wife's lack of fecundity is a problem to be borne by the wife. The estate of the husband's family should not be encumbered.

*Familial regards, Joseph Bonaparte*

Rue de Thrévenot, Paris
Dear Rose,

Émilie is now married; I dissolved in tears. You were missed—our little party seemed sadly lacking without you. The bride looked lovely in the dress you had made for her, although mute, which I attributed to a virginal apprehension. But later, on discovering the bride and Hortense in the powder room in tears, I learned that there is more to the story. The bride had apparently confessed to your daughter that she loved another.

I lectured the girls on duty, and spilled milk, and how fate had intended Émilie to marry Lieutenant Lavalette since that is how it turned out—then I left to look after my guests. Eventually the girls appeared, Émilie red-faced and mournful. The groom—a dear man, if a bit of a simpleton—was fortunately oblivious to his young wife's sorrow.

I warned you about allowing the girls to read romantic novels. Now you see the result.

Remember your prayers,
Your godmother, Aunt Désirée

Note—I read in the Publiciste that the fleet is headed for Spain. And I thought they were going to Africa! I'm relieved, I confess. At least in Spain Eugène can go to church.

And another—Madame Campan asked me to remind you about Hortense's and Émilie's tuition.*

* It wasn't unusual for a young married woman to go to a boarding school when her husband was away.

*Chère Maman,*

*I have a terrible confession to make. Émilie is unhappy and it is all my fault. It began in the early spring. Louis Bonaparte had taken to visiting our school, and I told Émilie it was because he fancied her. But the truth, the terrible truth, was that I feared he fancied me and I didn't want anyone to guess! And so then she fell in love with him! And because of that, poor Louis had to go on the crusade and poor Émilie is miserably married. Oh, my dear Maman, I want to die for shame.*

*Your daughter, Hortense*

*[Undated]*

I don't know what to make of Hortense's letter. It dismays me to think that Émilie is unhappy, but at the same time I confess I'm charmed by the admission that Louis may fancy my daughter—my daughter who is so terrified of boys! How am I ever to marry her?

*Corsica*

*Honoured sister,*

*This letter is to inform you that my husband is available to take over the command of the fort in Marseille. Please inform Director Barras that General Bonaparte's brother-in-law is the only suitable candidate for the post. We will move to Marseille in July.*

*Elisa Bonaparte Bacchiocchi*

*[Undated]*

After posting my letters, I took a long walk up the mountain to a little chapel perched at the top of a steep hill, a charming stone structure overlooking the valley. I had to pry open the door. It was musty and damp inside. The silence was heavy, comforting. I sat for a time thus, alone with my thoughts. On impulse, I knelt.

So many prayers tumbled out of my heart! I prayed for the safety of the fleet, for Bonaparte and the boys. I prayed that Émilie would come to love her husband and that my daughter's heart would calm. I prayed for the health of Aunt Désirée and the old Marquis, and for the success of my treatment here. I prayed that the Bodin Company would prosper and that I would soon be able to pay off my debts and provide for my children's future. But above all, I prayed for patience in dealing with Bonaparte's family.

*June 18.*
A day at the baths—huge, steaming pools dotted with heads, women in bright scarves. The cavernous chamber echoed the sounds of laughter, whispered gossip. Shoulders immersed, toes emerging, a knee, two. Floating languorously, a woman laughs, another blows bubbles. A dream world, this.

*[Undated]*
I've had an accident.* Hortense is with me now, thank God. Great pain, despair.

*June 23, Rue de Thrévenot, Paris*
*Dear Rose,*
    *To think that you almost died! I am enclosing an ounce of licorice and*

---

* On June 20, Josephine and three acquaintances were on her balcony when it collapsed. Josephine's injuries were critical. She was immediately wrapped in the skin of a newly slaughtered lamb. For a time it was not known whether she would live, and Hortense was sent for. Josephine's treatment, which was published in a medical journal, consisted of a punishing regime of enemas and douches.
    Dr. Martinet's initial report stated: "Citoyenne Bonaparte was the most seriously injured of the group. She was given a drink of infusion of arnica to stop the bleeding and an enema, which she evacuated, urinating as well. She was immediately put in a warm bath, after which leeches were applied to the most severely bruised parts of her body, as well as to her haemorrhoids, which were swollen. Warm topical remedies and emollients were put on her bruises (apples cooked in water had a good effect). This was followed by compresses soaked in camphor."

coriander seeds your girl could make up into an excellent purge. Scrape the licorice and slice it thin, bruise the seeds and put these both in a pint of water and boil it a little. Strain this water into an ounce of senna and let it sit for six hours. Strain from the senna and drink it while fasting.

Remember your prayers, now more than ever.

Your godmother, Aunt Désirée

Note—My neighbour informed me that the fleet is headed to Spain. She read it in the Messager des Relations Extérieures. But an article in the Postillon de Calais said your husband intended to seize the island of Malta. Isn't that in the other direction?

June 23, La Chaumière

Darling,

The Glories wept to hear of your terrible fall. It's shocking to think that such a thing could happen at a health spa. Barras informs me that the doctor insists you will recover. I'm sending a parcel of remedies. I was comforted to learn that Hortense is with you.

Your loving friend, Thérèse

June 24, Luxembourg Palace

Chère amie,

Dr. Martinet assures me you are out of danger. You must be his only patient; the memos he sends would take hours to prepare, not to mention the reports he has been publishing in a medical journal in which he describes in fulsome detail each and every enema he administers. (Are you aware of this?)

I wrote to General Brune* as you requested. I will let you know as soon as I hear. The last thing you need to worry about right now is the fate of the Bodin Company. Don't worry, my dear, "Papa will fix it."

Père Barras

* The command of the Army of Italy passed from Napoleon to General Berthier, Napoleon's former chief of staff, and then to General Brune. Berthier had favoured the Bodin Company (it is possible he was in on the financial rewards), but General Brune did not and was threatening to cancel the contract.

*July 8.*

It has been eighteen days now. My arms, although still horribly bruised and painful to move, are out of the bandages. At least I am able to feed myself again, and to write, although my script is feeble, like that of an old woman. I am both comforted and plagued by a constant stream of well-wishers.

I can remember very little of the actual fall. The first thing I recall is lying on the street with men standing over me, everything dreamlike. And then the sharp pain of being turned—I'm told I cried out horribly—and then the sickening comfort of something warm and moist on my skin, the woollish smell of blood (for a quick-witted servant had slaughtered a lamb and wrapped me in its still-warm hide). Then the treatments began—the enemas and douches, the baths, the leeches, the bleeding and the infusions. I am determined to get better if only to end the "cure"!

Hortense is doting and sweet (but bored, I fear). "I love you," I told her this morning, as she wheeled me around in my invalid chair. "Whatever happens to me, I don't want to be a burden to you."

She stooped down under my sunshade and kissed me on the cheek. "You *will* walk again, Maman."

This tenderness between us almost makes my suffering worthwhile.


*July 10.*

Again, terrible pain—just when I thought I was getting better. I am overcome with a feeling of hopelessness. It has been twenty days and I still can't stand.


*9 Messidor, Luxembourg Palace*
*Chère amie,*

*I want you to be the first to know. Bonaparte has dodged Nelson's ships and taken Malta—a stroke of incredible good fortune.*

*Père Barras*

*July 16.*
I walked for three minutes. Shooting pain.


*22 Messidor, Luxembourg Palace*
*Chère amie,*

*No doubt you are recovering, judging from the constant stream of petition-ers you have been sending my way. Regarding your requests, please note that I have:*

*1. Found employment for the nephew of the former Abbess of the Convent of Panthémont.*

*2. Seen to it that Bonaparte's doctor's wife, Citoyenne Yvan, was sent her bonus. (She asked me to tell you that Pugdog is content and has even grown plump.)*

*3. Named Citoyen Félix Bacchiocchi, the General's esteemed (sic) brother-in-law, commander of Fort Saint-Nicolas in Marseille. I pray to God that the citizens of that town are never in need of his protection.*

*4. Succeeded (finally—it wasn't easy) in getting the names of three of the five citizens you requested erased from the List.*

*5. And last, but certainly not least, regarding that spirited dancer who was run out of Milan for her so-called convictions (for coquetting with French sol-diers is more to the point), I've succeeded in finding a placement for her with the Opéra-Comique. (She has offered to "repay" me. If only all acts of mercy were so rewarding.)*

*But my question to you, my friend, is this—how do all these strange and rather pathetic characters find their way to you? Do take care, chérie. Your last letter rather alarmed me.*

*Père Barras*


*July 17, Paris*
*Honoured sister:*

*I am aware that forty thousand per annum translates into three thousand three hundred and thirty-three francs a month. One must, however, take the cost of administration into account.*

*I am returning to Dr. Martinet the bills submitted for your treatment since your fall. I have informed him that all expenses incurred in the course of a cure of infertility, however unexpected and unusual, are your responsibility. The Bonaparte Family Trust cannot be held accountable.*

*Familial regards, Joseph Bonaparte*


*July 18, La Chaumière*
*Darling,*

*You would have loved to see the parade here yesterday: eighty wagons loaded with the finest art of Italy were carted with great éclat to the Louvre. Over each enormous case there was a banner proclaiming the contents— Raphael, Titian, Domenichino, Guerchino. It was enough to make even the most uncultured among us swoon. But the triumph, of course, were the four horses of Saint Mark from Venice.*

*Naturally, the Directors neglected to give your husband the credit for bringing all this wonderful loot to Paris. Oh, forgive me, I forget myself—for "liberating works of genius." In Paris, at least, the statue of Apollo may be viewed without his silly fig leaf. If that isn't liberation, what is?*

*Your loving friend, Thérèse*


*August 4, Luxembourg Palace*
*Chère amie,*

*Victories in Egypt! One at El-Ramanyeh, another at Chebreis and then, the coup de grâce, a decisive victory over the Mamelouks near Cairo. "The Battle of the Pyramids" we have named it.*

*I know as heartening as this news is that you will be disappointed over the lack of letters from that land. Unfortunately, the English are high-jacking whatever ships Bonaparte sends in our direction. It has a certain charm, this relationship. We capture their ships, read their mail; they capture our ships, read ours. If only their letters were more interesting.*

*Regarding more mundane matters, you will be amused to know that General Brune came all the way back to Paris from Milan just to complain about the chicanery of certain of our government officials there, including the "shameless plundering" of your charming sister-in-law Pauline Bonaparte* and her accomplice in greed, her husband General Victor Leclerc.

However, before General Brune returned to Milan (stomped back, I should say), I managed to have "a word" with him about the Bodin Company contract. The merest hint of a payback put him in an agreeable disposition. Ah, but these virtuous Republicans are the easiest to bribe.

Père Barras

Note—Forgive me, my dear, but I simply cannot and will not promote Citoyen Lahorie. As a director of this Republic, I must, from time to time, act responsibly. I understand that he was a friend of your first husband and that therefore you wish to help the man, but frankly, he's an idiot.*

August 9.
I walked for ten minutes. I am determined to join Bonaparte in Egypt.

* Lahorie blamed Josephine for Barras's rejection. Consequently, in 1812, he joined a conspiracy to overthrow Napoleon and was shot for treason.

# *In which victories are followed by defeat*

*September 16, 1798—Paris.*

I arrived home to devastating news. Buried in a massive stack of calling cards, parcels, letters of congratulation and the usual demands from bill collectors, there was a note from Barras: *Come see me as soon as you arrive. Urgent.*

I put my hat back on. "What is it, Maman?" Hortense has become sensitive to my moods.

"Director Barras wishes to see me." No doubt it had to do with news from the East regarding Bonaparte. Or perhaps Eugène! I didn't like the word *urgent.*

It took some time to get to the palace—the streets were congested, and everywhere there were signs of festivity, preparations for the Republican Year VII celebrations. On Rue Honoré, an enormous banner depicting Bonaparte with palm trees and pyramids in the background had been hung from the bell tower of a church.

"Madame Bonaparte!" Barras's elderly valet bounded to his feet. "Director Barras has been most anxious for your arrival." Bruno pulled the big oak doors open.

Barras was playing the violin when I entered. He stopped abruptly when he saw me, his gold-rimmed lorgnon falling, swinging on a pink cord, his eyes tender and sad. "I'm so relieved to see you. You've survived the journey? You look thin." His voice sweet, bell-like.

I embraced him, inhaling his familiar scent, spirit of ambergris. How was I? Fine, fine, I lied. In fact, the journey had been painful, but I didn't want to list my aches and pains. "I received your note." Gingerly, I took a seat, for my hip was inflamed after two days in a jolting carriage. "I confess I'm anxious."

"Of course! Of course!" Barras took the chair near mine, shifted uncomfortably. "We've had . . . news," he said, clearing his throat, his Adam's apple bobbing.

"Paul, please tell me—are they all right?" Nothing could be worse than what I imagined.

"Bonaparte, you mean?" Crossing his legs at the ankle.

"Yes—and the boys." Eugène, Louis.

"Of course, yes. They're fine, I assure you, but there has been . . . How should I put it? There's been a bit of a setback. But I assure you, yes, Bonaparte and the boys are safe," he repeated, raising his left hand as if making a vow, "as are most of the men."

*Most?* I tilted my head to one side, my dangling earrings tinkling.

"But the fleet is . . . sunk," he said in a whisper.

*Sunk?* I listened in a daze as Barras explained. After Admiral Brueys anchored the fleet at Aboukir, the English swooped down and destroyed all but four of our ships. The commander of the *Timoléon* set his ship on fire rather than surrender. He died, standing on the deck. Admiral Brueys was cut in two standing at the helm of *L'Orient.* The explosion of the gunpowder in the hold could be heard in Alexandria, twenty-five miles away. The battle went on for three days, the bloodiest ever fought at sea. And yet the English did not lose a single ship.

I put my fist to my lips, overwhelmed by the enormity of the loss. The greatest fleet in history since the Crusades—*gone?* Over three thousand men killed or wounded. All the supplies—including the gold needed to buy provisions—lost.

Barras refilled his glass, spilling spirits onto the carpet. "And, of course, the unfortunate thing is that now the troops are . . ." He cleared his throat again. "Stranded."

My heart began to pound. "But surely we'll rescue them," I said, twisting my handkerchief.

"I can't see how! The English are now in control of the sea. It's doubtful that we'll even be able to get a mail boat through."

A feeling of panic came over me. I had to get home, before I was overcome.

"You understand, we're keeping this confidential," he went on.

"But Paul, an entire fleet, how can you—?"

"The exhibition opens tomorrow! We've planned the most spectacular New Year fête imaginable, to celebrate Bonaparte's victories. And now *this*. The people laugh at us as it is. I'm already accused of every vice, of committing every crime, every petty thievery. To hear people talk, I'm a very busy man. Have you heard the latest epigram? 'If only the Republic could be disem*barras*sed.' Charming, don't you think? And what about that poster of a lance, a lettuce leaf and a rat? It's everywhere; you'll see it. I finally figured it out: *the seventh year will kill them.* * And, you know, I'm starting to think maybe they're—"

"Paul, please, tell me. What does this mean?"

Barras's glass missed the fireplace and shattered against the wall. Toto jumped up, cowering. "What it means is that the *goddamned* English have downed the entire French fleet." He sank back into his chair, his hands over his eyes. "Grand Dieu, I'm going mad."

*September 17.*

Hortense was hopping up and down with excitement. "There are ribbons and bouquets on all the posts."

"And colourful silk banners fluttering in the breeze," Émilie (Madame *Lavalette* now) said.

"That's wonderful," I said, trying to put some enthusiasm in my voice.

Hortense became concerned. "We *are* going to the exhibition, Maman—aren't we?"

It was easier than I thought it would be, accepting congratulations on behalf of my husband's victories, smiling, bowing, nodding—not letting on. I watched as if from a distance the people dancing, singing, staggering in the glow of their country's glory, in the illusion of victory. The

---

* Lancette (lance), laitue (lettuce), rat: *a play on the words* l'an sept les tuera.

realization of defeat would come soon enough. Perhaps it is always thus. Perhaps all victories are false, defeat the inevitable reality.

Or perhaps, more truly, I too did not want to think about what I knew to be true, that the greatest of victories had been followed by the greatest of defeats.

I felt a gentle touch on my shoulder. Barras, looking ill—from last night's tippling, no doubt. "How are you managing?" he asked, his soft voice very nearly drowned out by all the commotion. He was wearing the ceremonial robe of a director, an enormous crimson cashmere cape and a velvet toque with a tricolour plume.

"Not too bad," I said, keeping an eye on Hortense, Caroline, Émilie and Jérôme, who were over by a lemonade vendor. An enclave of Bonapartes sat in a roped-off cluster directly in front of the stage. "It's not as hard as I thought it would be." During the day, that is. During the night it was another matter. "Do *they* know?" I tilted my head in the direction of the Bonapartes—Joseph and his wife Julie, Lucien (back from Corsica), Pauline and Victor Leclerc (recently arrived from Milan). All of them were curiously sullen in the midst of so much festivity.

"Certainly not. That hot-headed Lucien would leak it to the *Moniteur* in a minute, along with accusations that it is the fault of the Directors—my fault, to be specific. Did you know that he's been made Secretary of the Five Hundred?"

"But he was only elected a deputy three months ago."

"He's become quite popular on the strength of his rather vocal opposition to the Directors—on the strength of his opposition to *me*, I should say. And as for that smiling jackal of a man, that mild-mannered—" He raised one bushy eyebrow. "I wouldn't walk a dark alley with Joseph Bonaparte, let's put it that way."

"But why do they all look so glum?"

Barras snorted. "They don't like their seats, they should be up on the stage, the posters should have their faces on them, there should be more posters, the posters aren't big enough." He threw up his hands. "In short, it's not enough. It's never enough for a Bonaparte, apparently. Your husband excepted, of course."

"Of course," I echoed—not paying attention, I confess. An attractive young woman had stooped to exchange a word with Joseph. There was something familiar about her.

"Ready, Director Barras?" It was Director Neufchâteau, the newest member of the council of five Directors, and as Minister of the Interior the mastermind behind the exhibition. I wanted an opportunity to thank him personally for responding to my request that funding to the Vosges municipalities be increased. As well, I had a number of other requests to make. But most important, Bonaparte was going to be in need of allies—especially now.

I gave Director Neufchâteau my hand. "A brilliant display, Director, quite inspiring. I congratulate you." The woman talking to Joseph stood, turned—Lisette! She headed toward a door, the gems in her headdress glittering in the torchlight. Fouché had warned me she'd been consorting with the Bonapartes. Why had she been talking with Joseph? I wondered with apprehension, recalling her words: *You will be sorry!*

The military band began to warm up. I felt a stir in the crowd, craning heads. "Ah, there she is," Barras said, speaking in the Provençal dialect, "our lovely Amazon." I looked toward the entry. It was Thérèse, in shimmering silver and mauve, towering above the crowd. She was followed at a distance by her footman and nanny, carrying Thermidor in petticoats. Thérèse caught my eye, made a look of surprise, waved wildly.

Director Neufchâteau put his gloved hand on Barras's shoulder. "We're being summoned, Director," he said. The two men headed toward the stage.

"I didn't even know you were back," Thérèse exclaimed, folding me in her arms.

I took her hand, feeling suddenly, unaccountably, choked up. It was so good to see her.

Thérèse held me at arm's length. "And how *are* you?"

"I'm going to be all right." I think. "I'm walking, that's the important thing."

"And what do you make of all this?" Thérèse asked before I could tell her about Lisette. "Everyone's gone crazy over your husband. Maybe it's true, what he says—maybe you *are* his Lady of Luck."

I turned away. It was impossible to lie to Thérèse. Fortunately, the nanny appeared with Thermidor, her thumb in her mouth, her big eyes transfixed. "This little one is sleepy," Thérèse said.

"I'm not little," Thermidor said, taking her thumb out of her mouth. "I'm—"

"Three! I know." I took her in my arms. "My, you *are* a big girl now." She smelled of soap. I pressed her silken cheek to mine.

"You will make a wonderful grandmother," Thérèse said.

She hadn't said, *a wonderful mother*.

*September 19.*

A sleepless night. One year ago Lazare died, yet even still he is often in my thoughts. I am no Lady of Luck. Every man I have ever loved has fallen. I am ill at the thought that harm might come to Bonaparte and to Eugène. I have mourned too many loved ones. I plead with my guardian angels: fly, fly! Go to them. Keep them from harm.

*September 21.*

Ah, my dear Glories . . .

"Darling, we're so *relieved* to see you. What have you done with your hair?"

"I love that gown. Turn, turn, let me see."

"Oh, *that's* different, I like the way the sash comes up over the shoulders."

"All of Paris has been singing your husband's praise."

"The French Caesar, my cook calls him."

"Everyone."

"Hail, Caesar!" Fortunée Hamelin was wearing a blue wig. She'd dyed one of Thérèse's blonde ones. "My, but this champagne is excellent," she said, shrugging her shoulders to lower her bodice. "Better get your girl to bring up a few more bottles, *Josephine*. There, you see? I remembered."

"Is it true? Citoyenne Marmont told me that you're going to Egypt with her, that the General is sending *La Pomone* back from Malta just to fetch you."

"That's so romantic. I'd love to have a ship sent for me."

"But are you well enough to travel, darling? I noticed you walking with a bit of a limp."

"We read *all* about your treatment in that medical journal—how ghastly."

"It's a wonder you survived the cure."

"All those enemas—mon Dieu." The bright silk flowers piled high onto the crown of Madame de Crény's ruffled bonnet made her seem even shorter than she was.

"That's one thing I simply can't abide."

"Enemas? Some women actually like them." Minerva giggled.

"And some *men* like giving them."

"Parbleu!" Fortunée Hamelin guffawed.

"It's true. Madame Mercier constantly complains that her husband wants to physic her too much."

"Why, that scamp."

"*Not* that I want to change the subject, *Josephine*, but the big house down the road, the one at the corner of Rue du Mont Blanc—is that the one your sister-in-law and her husband bought?"

"The Leclercs?" I nodded, playing a card. On their return from Milan, Pauline and Victor had purchased (with cash, it was rumoured) the property three houses down. Every time I passed, I saw Pauline's face at a window. My personal spy, I was coming to think of her.

"I think it's nice to have family close by," Madame de Crény said.

Thérèse caught my eye. "Not always," I confessed.

"Oh?" They looked at me expectantly.

"You know you can always trust a Glory," Minerva said, sensing my hesitation.

And then I broke down, told all: how Joseph had vowed to break up my marriage; how Bonaparte's mother called me "the old woman" (and worse!); how Pauline spied on me; how I'd finally come to understand that to Corsicans a wife was nothing, that it was the husband's family that truly mattered, and that my husband's love for me and my children had provoked a profoundly jealous hatred in them.

"Mon Dieu, I've heard about vendettas, but . . . I had no idea," Madame de Crény exclaimed, swinging her feet.

"I'm rather surprised by the fuss over your business dealings. I thought your husband's uncle was an army supplier."

Fesch? I nodded. As well as Joseph. *And* Lucien.

"And not Pauline and Victor Leclerc?"

I rolled my eyes, well, yes . . . them too.

"Is it true they were *recalled* from Milan?"

"For filling their pockets, I heard."

"I heard they bought an estate in Italy."

"*And* are looking to buy a property up near Senlis."

"I thought it was the other brother who was looking for a property near Senlis. What's his name? Lucien. The young one with the thick spectacles."

"But didn't he just buy that big town house on Grand-Rue Vert?"

"On a deputy's salary?"

Fortunée Hamelin whistled. "I *love* this champagne."

"Did you hear about Fortunée's adventure, Josephine?"

"She walked down the Champs-Élysées—*naked* to her waist."

"They dared me." Fortunée Hamelin looked smug.

"She practically started a riot."

"I still don't understand why," Fortunée said. "It's not as if people haven't seen a woman before."

"You should have read all the articles in the journals."

"Speaking of journals." Minerva put down her cards. "Did any of you read that article in *La Révélateur*? Something about the Directors having known for a week about the defeat of our fleet?"

"*What* defeat?"

"That's what I wanted to know."

They turned to me. Tears filled my eyes. Please, no, I didn't want to be the one to tell them.


*November 4.*
Rumours that Alexandria has been burned, that Bonaparte is in retreat.

*November 16.*
Rumours that Bonaparte's army is faltering, that he's surrounded.


*December 12.*
My manservant returned from the market in tears. "General Bonaparte has been killed in Cairo!"

Immediately, I set out for the palace to see Barras. I had resolved not to read the journals, much less to believe them, but this account was impossible to ignore—I *had* to know.

The journey to the palace was a slow one. There were signs of disturbance, more so as I neared the market. Several times my carriage was recognized. One man doffed his hat as if for a funeral procession. I sat back, out of view.

What if Bonaparte *had* been killed?

I burst into tears the moment I saw Barras—in spite of the presence of his guests—for I saw the answer in his eyes. My knees gave way.


As if from a distance I could hear Barras giving out orders for cold cloths and salts. He felt my pulse, pulled back my eyelids. "Please," I said, struggling to sit up. I felt bile in my throat. A circle of faces was looking down on me, men's faces.

"Help me get her onto the bed in the next room," I heard Barras say. He pulled me up. My feet were comically disobedient, my legs like those of a rag doll. Inexplicably, I began to giggle.

"She'll be all right in a moment," Barras said. "She's stronger than she looks."

I was laid out on the bed, my ties loosened, a comforter pulled over me.

I closed my eyes, turned my head. "Tell me," I said. "Tell me what you know."


His name meant "Desert Lion," he'd told his men.

"I didn't know that," I said. Bonaparte had dreamt of riding an elephant, of wearing a turban. "Go on."

*Soldiers!* he'd called out. *From these pyramids, forty centuries of history look down upon you!*

"That's beautiful. He had a way of putting things."

He'd entered Cairo with the Koran in one hand, Thomas Paine's *The Rights of Man* in the other. Triumphant.

"He had a great sense of theatre," I said, closing my eyes, imagining his feeling of exultation at such a moment, what it must have been like for him, his soul infused with the spirit of destiny, walking in the footsteps of Alexandre the Great, of Caesar.

He believed himself chosen. I opened my eyes. "Barras, he can't be dead."

*[Undated]*
Every day, rumours—Bonaparte lives, Bonaparte has perished. I grieve, I rejoice, I grieve again. I begin each day with a prayer, and a conviction that Bonaparte will survive, that he will endure, that he will overcome—but by nightfall, doubt and fear have come into my heart like evil demons.

I have been reading through the letters Bonaparte sent me when we first were married. I read his burning words of love and I want to weep. I have not loved him as I should, have not given him my heart. There are so many things I want to tell him—and now I fear it may be too late.

*[Undated]*
People watch me for clues. "She's not smiling. He must be dead," I over-heard a market woman say.

*December 23.*
I've not been out for two weeks, unable to face the looks of mourning, of exultation. Everywhere I go, I feel eyes.

*January 1, 1799, New Year's Day.*

The bottle of ink in my escritoire was empty. I went upstairs. There were writing supplies in the guest room.

It took an effort to push open the door. I stood for a moment, waited for something to shape itself in the dark. It was light out still, yet with the drapes drawn, no light penetrated. I pulled back the curtains, opened the windows.

What was to become of him? I thought. And what of my son?

A breeze swept into the room, fluttering papers to the floor. The clock under the glass bell struck. Bonaparte had wanted the room made into a second study—but there had been no time, in the end, to even discuss such matters. A desk, I recalled, shelves, and a desk in the corner for his secretary.

Yes, I thought, it will be done. I will get to work now, call in the architects, the furnishers, the drapers—prepare for his return. For he *will* return.

## In which I have enemies everywhere

*January 3, 1799.*

"It's the damned ague again," Barras said from under a mountain of comforters. "A family tradition." His face, surrounded by cambric, looked like an old woman's.

I dislodged Toto from the little chair beside Barras's massive bed, took a seat. It alarmed me to see Barras so weakened.

"It comes, it goes. Don't look so worried." He took a sip of the quinine water his chambermaid brought for him, then spat it out. "You could at least put some brandy in it." She slammed the door behind her.

"My father swore by rum," I said. The room smelled unpleasantly of parrot.

"And *he's* dead." Barras thumped the side of the mattress. Toto jumped up beside him, sniffed around before curling up beside his master.

"So tell me, is there news?" I always felt anxious when summoned.

"I just want you to be assured that all these rumours of Bonaparte's defeat are false. We've had a report that he has assembled an army of one hundred thousand and is going to head into Syria."

"That's wonderful news!" I said, wondering where Syria was. I would look it up on my map when I got home.

"In England they shot cannon from the Tower of London, thinking that he'd been killed. There's even a play running in London called *Death of Bonaparte*, I'm told. Now they're going to have to shoot cannon to announce his resurrection." He laughed. "But there was something in this morning's *London Morning Chronicle* I thought I should show you."

"The English paper?"

He nodded, fishing around in a stack of journals on his bedside table. "My secretary's working on a translation right now. Where are my spectacles? Damn, I can't find anything any more."

"It concerns Bonaparte?" I found his spectacles on the side table and handed them to him. Whenever there was news, I assumed it would be bad.

"I wish I could read English." Barras squinted at the journal, holding it at arm's length. "I wish I could *see*."

"The name Beauharnais is in there," I said, looking over his shoulder. Something about Eugène?

"Ah, there's Botot."

"You're not going to like it," Barras's secretary warned us, a paper in his hand. He read out loud, *"The publication of the letters confidential to be written—"*

*"To be written?* Or *written?"*

"Written. Excuse me. Yes . . . *of the letters confidential* written *by Bonaparte and his men to friends and family in France (letters by our navy intercepted) does a little honour to the morality of our cabinet. Such scandal cannot serve to make good our national to ennoble—"*

"Wait a minute, slow down, Botot. That doesn't make any sense."

"Maybe it's my translation."*

"Go on." I sat forward on my chair. Something about publishing letters?

*"One of these letters confiscated is from Bonaparte to his brother, a song on his wife's debauchery—"*

My *debauchery?*

Botot shrugged. *"Another, from young Beauharnais—"*

Eugène? "One of the letters is from my son?"

---

* The article in the London Morning Chronicle *read: "It is not very creditable ... that the private letters ... which were intercepted, should be published. It derogates from the character of a nation to descend to such gossiping. One of these letters is from Bonaparte to his brother, complaining of the profligacy of his wife; another from young Beauharnais, expressing his hopes that his dear Mama is not so wicked as she is represented! Such are the precious secrets which, to breed mischief in private families, is to be published in French and English."*

"*. . . the hope expresses that his chère maman is less evil than she was represented.*"

"I don't understand." Evil? The air in the room was close, the fire blazing.

"The English intend to *publish* these letters?" Barras demanded, his teeth chattering. "But that's unethical. There are international agreements that apply."

"Damn the Royalists," the parrot suddenly squawked.


*28 Nivôse, Luxembourg Palace*
*Chère amie,*

*We've finally obtained copies of the two letters referred to in the* London Morning Chronicle. *I don't think it wise to send them to you by courier. I will be in this afternoon, if you would care to come by.*

*Père Barras*


*January 17, late afternoon.*

"You'll be comforted to know I intend to have them banned," Barras said, searching through the stacks on his desk.

"Are they that bad?"

"Ah, here's one." He handed it to me. "It's a copy of the letter Bonaparte wrote his brother Joseph. But where's that other one, the one from your son?"

I glanced at the words, *I am undergoing acute domestic distress, for the veil is now entirely rent.*

"The one from Eugène will explain."


*Chère Maman,*

*I have so many things to tell you that I do not know where to begin. For five days Bonaparte has looked very sad, ever since a conversation he had with Junot. From what little I could overhear, it had to do with Captain Charles—that he returned from Italy in your carriage, that he gave you your little dog, even that he is with you now.*

*You know, Maman, that I do not believe a word of it. I am convinced that all this gossip has been made up by your enemies. I love you no less, no less long to embrace you.*

*A million kisses, Eugène*

"This letter is going to be published in England?" I asked.

"*And* the one from Bonaparte to Joseph, apparently. The bastards—the English are totally immoral. We have an unwritten agreement with them to respect private correspondence. Of course, we'll see what we can do to prevent them from making the letters public. My dear, are you all right?"

I tried to swallow. "I think so." I felt so exposed, my life on display. I felt mortified—but angry, as well. What had I done to be ashamed of? Yes, Captain Charles gave me Pugdog; yes, he accompanied me on the return from Italy; and *yes*, he is a friend and I enjoy his company—and why not? "Paul, you understand, don't you, the captain is just a friend."

"Of course! Is our pretty captain even interested in women? But don't worry about rumours, darling, no one will know." He twirled his thumbs, frowning. "I just can't understand why Junot would go out of his way to upset Bonaparte."

"I think I know why," I whispered, remembering Lisette's words: You will be sorry.

*January 24.*

The dressmaker arrived at eleven, her three assistants carrying enormous bolts of fabric samples, boxes of laces and ribbons, books of drawings. I selected a particularly lovely creation. "I do not recommend that one," Henriette said. "Your sister-in-law, Madame Leclerc, has one very like it."

"Pauline Leclerc is one of your clients?"

"And such a curious little thing. Every time we have a fitting—quite often, for she requires a new gown every week—she wants only news of you, Madame."

"She asks you questions about *me?*"

"Indeed, Madame. All about you."


*January 25, afternoon.*

My milliner arrived at three. I showed her the sketch of the gown I had chosen, the fabric samples. "Lola, we've known each other a long time."

"A *very* long time, Madame."

"If I asked you a question, would you tell me the truth?"

"Madame, if I didn't know you better, I would think you had offended me," she said, her eyes bulging out.

"You must forgive me, I am not myself." I wasn't sure how I was going to ask. But I had to know. "Have you made hats for Madame Leclerc?"

"Oh yes, Madame, she has kept my girls quite busy—a new hat each week, sometimes two," she said, a straw form in her hand.

"Does she ever . . . *inquire* of me? I am just curious, that's all."

"She does like to talk, that one." Lola wrapped a length of gauze around the crown of the straw form, fashioning a turban in the manner of the East.

"She *says* things about me?" I asked, looking into the glass, adjusting the plume. The hat didn't suit me.

"Of course, I don't believe a word of it." Lola pulled the hat off me. "If I didn't have my girls to look out for, I would have told her long ago that I wouldn't be making any more hats for her. She's fussy and she's never on time, always keeping me and the girls waiting. And her with *three* lovers."

"Oh?" It was common knowledge that Pauline was having affairs with Generals Moreau, Macdonald and Beurnonville now that her husband had been posted to Lyons.

"And a valet she gets to lift her out of her bath and carry her to her bed. It's not a sin because he's Negro and not really human, *she* says, but still, one can't help but wonder. Really, Madame, she is making a bad name for the General, may God bless him in his trial. And as for you, what she told my girl Doré was that she has seduced all your lovers, one by one, and asked each one who was better, you or she, and what were your—" She flushed, tongue-tied.

"Go on, Lola. I'm finding this amusing."

"Your *tricks* is how she puts it." Lola grinned. Her two front teeth were missing. "You know, Madame—female ways with a man, special things you might do when he's in a heat, things that make him mad for you. I have a few myself. Drives my Lugger crazy—" I liked to think of Lola driving her crippled husband mad with pleasure. "But *then* she says that your lovers say she's just as good, that the only difference is experience. Which I don't believe for even a moment, Madame."

I wasn't sure exactly what Lola didn't believe. "Please inform your girls, Lola, that I have no lovers."

Lola looked at me with an expression of incredulity. "But Madame, even *I* have lovers."

*[Undated]*
I've received three Bodin Company bank notes, but I sent them all directly to Barras to pay off that debt. Others will have to wait. Joseph Bonaparte has cut me off entirely.

*February 1.*
The Seine flooded. Poor Thérèse—her lovely home is waist-high in mud. Barras has taken her in—Thérèse, the little girl, the nanny and eleven servants. I suspect he'll find accommodations for them quickly.

*February 6.*
The Glories met at Thérèse's (beautiful) new house on Rue de Babylone—a "gift" from Barras. After admiring the décor, after debating whether to play commerce, casino or loo, after exchanging news of our children and grandchildren, lovers and spouses, we settled down to what has, of late, become our main topic of conversation—gossip about the Bonaparte clan.

"I finally met the hiccupper," Madame de Crény announced.

"Elisa Bonaparte?"

"She introduced herself to me as a *femme savante*."

"She's here in Paris?" I asked, playing a card. "I thought she and her husband were in Marseille." Sadly, their child had recently died, I knew.

"She left her husband in Marseille and is now living in Paris with her brother Lucien."

"I hear she's started a salon."

"I went. The entire time she reclined on a sofa fanning herself." Thérèse flicked her scarf in an imitation of a woman putting on airs. "Pauline Leclerc was there, as well—*alone*, I might add."

"Serves her right. I heard her three lovers discovered each other—"

"—and all agreed to abandon her!"

But the big news was that Joseph had just purchased Mortefontaine, one of the most regal estates in the country.

"I hear he's pouring millions into it—a lake, an orangery, a theatre."

"Where does the money come from?"

"His wife's dowry?"

I shrugged, pulling in my winnings (eleven francs). Julie's dowry of 100,000 francs was substantial, true, but it was not enough to buy and renovate an estate like Mortefontaine. It just didn't add up.

"*Every* gentleman requires a country seat, Joseph told me."

"And every gentlewoman, I should think," Minerva said, nudging me.

"Poor Josephine. She's the only Bonaparte without a country estate."

I rolled my eyes. *Poor* Josephine indeed.

"I thought you and Bonaparte make an offer on a country château?"

I nodded. "We did, for a place on the Saint-Germain road." Malmaison—a property I'd fallen madly in love with. "But the offer was refused. And then Bonaparte left for Egypt." I'd asked a land agent to look into the purchase again, but I'd yet to hear back.

"Now's the time to buy."

"Prices aren't going to go much lower."


*February 8—at Aunt Désirée and the Marquis's small but lovely new house in Saint-Germain.*

The Marquis is eighty-five today. "I could go at any time," he told me, making an attempt to snap his fingers. Aunt Désirée had dressed him up in his blue velvet smoking jacket.

I smiled. "I think you will live to one hundred."

"I am content to die now but for one thing."

I tucked the comforter around his legs and moved his invalid chair closer to the fire. I knew what it was, this "one thing." He stilled my hand. "Before I die, I must see François," he said, his little rheumy eyes filling. François, his émigré son.

"Marquis, I've tried, but I—" *Can't*, I started to say, but the words, "I'll keep trying" came out instead.

*11 Ventôse—Croissy.*
*Chère Madame Bonaparte,*

*This morning, I spent four hours at Malmaison. If you were as wealthy as is commonly believed, I would tell you only of the charm of the estate—but you require an income property and I am happy to report that Malmaison is just that.*

*The owner suggested 300,000 francs for the grounds (which she claims General Bonaparte offered her last summer) and an additional 25,000 for the furniture. Add to that 15,000 for the agricultural equipment and about 15,000 in taxes would mean that you would have to pay approximately 360,000 francs. If property had not gone down in value, Malmaison would normally sell for 500,000 francs.*

*The land has been in the care of a steward for the last thirty years. He told me that there are 387 arpents of grain, vines, woods and open meadows. The park, which is excellent, consists of 75 arpents, with 312 arpents additional for renting. Letting these out for only 30 francs brings in over 9,000 francs, which added to the 3,000 income from the park brings the total to 12,000. This should reassure you. This year alone they made 120 barrels of wine selling at 50 francs each. The twenty-five farm people who live on the grounds are entirely self-sufficient.*

*The property, which has the advantage of being both practical and pleasant, is one of the nicest I've yet seen.*

*Citoyen Chanorier*

*March 3.*
I've instructed Chanorier to make an offer of 325,000 francs for Malmaison—an excellent value, if I get it.


*March 4.*
Offer accepted! Now all I have to do is come up with the money.


*March 7, Paris*
*Honoured sister,*
    *With respect to the purchase of a country property, I refuse to advance any funds from the Bonaparte Family Trust without direct instruction from my brother. Therefore, if you are to proceed, you will have to do so entirely under your own name.*
*Familial regards, Joseph Bonaparte*


*March 9.*
Citoyen l'Huillier, the estate steward, has agreed to loan fifteen thousand in exchange for a guarantee on his job.


*March 10.*
Twenty-two thousand from Ouvrard (thanks to Thérèse, with whom Ouvrard has been "keeping company") but it's still not enough.


*March 16.*
I just found out that Louis Bonaparte (ill apparently) returned to Paris five days ago with Signora Letizia. Why have they not contacted me? Louis will have news of Bonaparte, of Eugène—I am desperate to talk to him.

*March 17, late morning.*
I've invited all the Bonapartes to a dinner party in Signora Letizia's honour this coming Décadi. My coachman left a few moments ago to deliver invitations. I'm praying this will work.


*Shortly after 4:00.*
"If one had disturbing news about a friend's husband, do you think one should tell the friend?" Minerva fanned herself so vigorously the feathers in her hat fluttered.

"It would depend on the nature of the news, I would think," Madame de Crény said, playing a card.

"Friendship requires honesty, however painful," Thérèse said.

"Do you have *news* regarding a friend's husband?" I asked Minerva, picking up my cards.

"Oh, no."

We played in uncomfortable silence. When the clocks chimed four, I put down my cards. "Minerva, please . . ."

"It's false. Just a rumour."

"Told to you by . . . ?"

She winced. "Your sister-in-law, Pauline Leclerc."

"Oh?" I slapped down a card. "You might as well tell me. I'm bound to hear it eventually, and I'd rather hear it from friends."

"It's just the usual sort of rumour, you know, that the General has taken a mistress, that kind of thing."

The General: my *husband.* I looked around the table. There was more to it, I knew. "And?"

"And the thing is . . ." Madame de Crény stammered.

"He's apparently told her he will *marry* her . . ."

". . . if she gets pregnant."

I threw down my cards.


*March 19.*
The Bonapartes send their regrets—each and every one.

*March 24, Easter.*

I've been three days abed. "Melancholy," the doctor said, insisting that I be bled twice a day from the foot.

*April 9.*

This afternoon, shortly after the midday meal, Mimi announced a caller. "Captain Charles?" Returned from Milan!

But before I could even put down my embroidery hoop, he'd come into the room, twirling like a dancer. "Buon giorno, Signora." He curtsied, holding out his wide Venetian trousers as if he were wearing a skirt.

"If you could bring us some port, Mimi," I said, laughing, "and something to eat. Are you hungry, Captain?" I removed my embroidery basket from a chair.

"As a bear. You have a new maid?"

"Lisette is no longer with me, Captain."

"Oh!" He gave me a sly smile. "Might it have something to do with Colonel Junot?"

"That was part of it," I said, flushing angrily. Had everyone known but me?

"Ah, there's my monster!" Pugdog appeared at the door. "Have we been good?" the captain asked, stroking the dog's head. "Been keeping the lurchers away?"

"He's been sick, in fact." I motioned to Mimi to put the collations on the table beside me.

"Well, my good fellow," Captain Charles said, addressing the dog as if it were a man, "you are in the hands of the kindest woman in all of Europe. Many a man would envy you."

"I regret to say that an international incident has occurred on Pugdog's account."

"Oh?" he said, pulling away as the eager dog tried to lick his chin.

I explained to him what had happened, the letters that had been intercepted by the British. I told him what Eugène had said in his letter, some of the things Junot had told Bonaparte.

"But how did Junot know I gave you Pugdog?"

"Lisette must have told him, of course."

"Ah, so she told Junot, who in turn told your husband."

"Insinuating to him that you and I are . . ." I flushed.

"I confess I find it flattering to be accused of cuckolding the great General Bonaparte." He grinned. "I could go down in history for this."

How young he was, how ignorant in the ways of the world! "I wish I shared your buoyant humour, Captain, but I fear my husband will demand a divorce."

"Over the gift of a dog?" he sputtered.

"Please understand, Bonaparte is an exceedingly jealous man. His emotions are volcanic. The least suspicion grows in his imagination until it rules his reason."

"So, I guess an evening at the Opéra-Comique with your cavaliere servente is out of the question?"

"I go nowhere. I am a prisoner of suspicion. Pauline Leclerc is now my neighbour and she reports to her brothers every move I make. No doubt they will soon be informed of your call. Frankly, if I don't get out of Paris, I'll go mad. I've been looking into purchasing a country property on the Saint-Germain road, but despair of even raising the down payment."

"This may help." Captain Charles withdrew a fat packet from his inside pocket. He twirled it in the air and caught it, presenting it to me formally. "We did rather well on the last delivery."

I felt its substantial weight. *Fifty* thousand livres, he said.


*April 21.*
I've signed. Malmaison is mine.

## *In which I retreat*

*April 23, 1799—Malmaison!*
It is late afternoon. I'm writing these words at my little desk in the boudoir of my country château. A spirit of rebelliousness has come over me. I've not dressed my hair, not painted my face, I'm wearing old "rags"—a cosy déshabillé. A feeling of peace fills me as I look out over the hills, my four hundred acres of woodland and fields dotted with grazing sheep, cows, a few horses. A bull with a ring through its nose is lowing plaintively next to the cowshed. This morning I'll ride the bay mare over every dell and glen, and in the afternoon the gardener and I will lay out an herb garden.

And this evening? This evening I'll listen to the night silence. This evening, I'll sleep content.

This is my home. I will grow old here, die here.


*April 24, morning.*
I have just had a report from my steward. With his face turning red as a turkey-cock and his battered straw hat clutched in his hands, he informed me that the chickens haven't been laying, the clover in the far field is overgrown with hemlock and the winnowing machine is in need of a part (forty francs). Such "problems" are a balm to my battered spirit.


*April 27.*
More and more I retreat from the civilized world. I rise with the sun,

spend my day in the company of the servants, the peasants, the animals. In the early morning I work in the kitchen garden, planting, pulling up weeds, thinning. I think of Paris, of the ferment that is always there, the glitter and wit, with something akin to revulsion.

*[Undated]*

Twice I have set out to go to Paris; twice I have turned back. I have become a country savage.

*May 20.*

Frustrated by my absence, the Glories have descended!

"Ah, darling, now you have everything: a harp, a coach and a château. What more is there?"

"My harp lacks three strings, my coach needs a new shaft and as for my château . . . !" I laughed.

"Don't despair, you can have it repaired," Minerva said to comfort me.

"I confess I love it just as it is," I said, checking under the table to make sure that Pugdog was getting along with my guests' pets. We were five women, four pugs—a zoo.

"The grounds *are* lovely."

"It's perfect," Thérèse said, embracing me. She looked a little plump, I thought. "You might as well know. I'm going to have a baby," she announced sheepishly to the group.

"Oh!"

"Oh?" And Tallien, her husband, in Egypt. And Ouvrard, her lover, married.

"Don't look at me like that!"

We played cards and talked all afternoon, catching up on the news: the assassination of the French envoys in Germany; the depressing military losses in Italy; how one of the Directors had accused Fesch, Lucien and Joseph Bonaparte of pilfering public funds. But most important, the wonderful news that an attempt was going to be made for an Egyptian rescue.

*May 24.*
The rescue attempt failed. Our ships were unable to get through the English blockade. I've been all day in bed.


*June 16.*
A courier came cantering into the courtyard this morning. A letter from Bonaparte? I thought hopefully, recalling the early days of the Italian campaign. But no, of course not. The envelope contained a current issue of the journal *La Feuille du Jour*. Attached to it was a note, unsigned, but in Captain Charles's tidy script—*page 4, top left. I must see you.* On page four there was an article reporting the delivery of unsound horses to the Army of Italy—by the Bodin Company. Apparently, the soldiers had been forced to cross the Alps on lame and feeble mounts, cursing the name Bodin.


Captain Charles's basement rooms at one hundred Rue Honoré are dark. The porter squinted to make out the printing on my card. "Madame Tascher?"

I nodded, giving him my cloak. I was asked to wait in a small drawing room. (I remember wondering whether I heard barking.) I made myself comfortable, taking in the tasteful simplicity of the furnishings—the paintings on the walls, the bouquets of flowers, a side table covered with books (Montesquieu's *Persian Letters* open, face down), a bronze sculpture of a horse—the pleasing clutter of a room much lived in.

"He's receiving," the porter informed me, then led me down a dark passage. We stopped before an antique oak door with a brass knob. I heard a dog barking again. The porter rapped three times.

"Come on in, Claude," I heard a voice call out—Captain Charles.

The porter swung the door open. There, in the centre of a mass of dogs was Captain Charles wearing an artist's frock coat of coarse linen. In his arms was a beagle with one ear missing. "Madame—"

"*Tascher.*"

Gently he lowered the beagle onto the floor and stepped over a long-haired mutt, wiping his hands on his frock coat. His braids had been tied back with a scarlet and black striped ribbon. "You've discovered my secret life," he said shyly, glancing down at his flock.

"Where did they all come from?" How many were there? Eight? Ten?

"I claim them from the streets," he said, removing his coat and ushering me out the door. Underneath he was wearing a scarlet wool cutaway coat with white satin lapels. He closed the door behind him, muffling the yelping.

"And then what do you do with them?" I asked, following him back into the drawing room.

"And then I can't bear to part with them!" he said, pushing forward an upholstered chair. "You've come about the article in *La Feuille du Jour*?"

"It alarmed me."

"The horses that the Bodin Company bought were sound, I assure you. But the horses that were shipped were apparently slaughterhouse animals. The problem appears to be with the dealer."

"Louis and Hugo Bodin are both in Lyons?"

The captain nodded. "I just received a letter from them. There is talk of an inquiry."

This could be the end of us, I thought—the end of *me*. "There's only one person who can help us."


"Grand Dieu," Barras exclaimed when he saw me. "I was beginning to think we'd never see you in Paris again. You're just in time for the celebration." He did a little dance and then winced, his hand on the small of his back. "At last, that braggart Director Treilhard's out—his election as director has been disqualified."

"Ha, ha." The parrot, chuckling like Barras.

"Oh?" Trying to remember who Director Treilhard was. I'd been living in another world. "Why?"

"He's four days too young to be eligible."

"Only four days?"

"Four, four hundred, what does it matter? The law is the law," intoned Barras in a mock deep voice. "The irony is that it was your brother-in-law Lucien Bonaparte who discovered the discrepancy and demanded justice. He himself is four hundred days short of being eligible to be a deputy, and he started screaming about Treilhard's four days. All this at one in the morning. It's a good thing I have a sense of humour."

"Barras, please, have you read that article about the Bodin Company in the—"

"*La Feuille du Jour?* Ah yes, the latest little scandal. The Legislative Councils are outraged, calling for an investigation, of course." He held his hands up, as if under arrest. "And they're just dying to pin it on me. This place is as explosive as a powder keg."

Barras's secretary Botot appeared at the door. "Another deputation to see you, Director."

"That's the third group already today." Barras took me by the elbow, ushering me out.

"Paul, what's going on?"

He kissed me on both cheeks. "Just another coup d'état, a little milk-and-water revolution." He waved gaily, disappearing from view, his words echoing in the vast chamber—*coup d'état, coup d'état, coup d'état.*

"So he can't do anything?" Captain Charles asked, keeping his eyes on the six balls he was juggling.

"I never had a chance to ask him. Things are . . . tense. The last thing he'll want to align himself with right now is the Bodin Company. Maybe later."

"Later will be too late," the captain said, letting the balls drop.

*June 21.*
With a sinking heart, I have written to Barras, begging him to defend the interests of the Bodin Company.

*June 29.*
I was working in the herb garden with Mimi when a hired fiacre pulled through the gates. I squinted to see who it might be. "I think it's that

funny man," Mimi said, for her eyesight is better than mine.

Captain Charles? I untied my apron.

"And a mess of dogs, sounds like," she said.


"We've been turned out," the captain explained as his porter picked the dog hairs off his red shooting jacket. The beagle and a spotted dog pressed their damp, black noses out the carriage window, sniffing. From the variety of barks, I suspected he had brought them all.

"Because of the investigation?" Government payments to the Bodin Company had been withheld until the investigation was complete.

He nodded. "I put all the office files in safe keeping, but as for the dogs—I know it is a lot to ask, but . . . ?"

I started to turn him away, thinking of what might be said, fearing the consequences. But then I thought: how can I let down a friend in such desperate need? Were it not for Captain Charles, I wouldn't even own Malmaison. And who would ever know he was there? I lived in such isolation. "There's a suite of rooms empty in the farmhouse," I told him, wondering as I said the words if I were doing the right thing. "My daughter comes only on the weekends. I'll tell the servants you are my accountant." In fact, I could use his help.

"It won't be for long," he assured me, opening the carriage door and standing back as all the barking, bounding dogs leapt out.


*July 7—Paris.*
Although the Bodin Company contract is still under review, at least we will not be charged. "That's the best I can do," Barras told me. He seemed distant, harassed. I dared not ask him for yet another loan, as I'd intended.


*July 10.*
What a night. Now all is topsy-turvy. Where do I begin? I suppose it was inevitable that the captain and I would become . . . well, perhaps I am being misleading.

It began with inviting the captain to join me in sampling the first bottle of our Malmaison wine. It was, after all, an occasion. We'd learned that the investigation had been dropped. The Bodin Company was going to survive. And besides, the pheasants that a neighbour had been kind enough to give me had been splendidly prepared by my cook and required a "full-bodied" (the captain's words) red.

The first bottle revealed that the wine was, indeed, ready. The captain and I settled into the game room, where, after I noisily beat him at backgammon* (three times!), we propped our stockinged feet up on the big leather hassock and talked: of his family and their need; of his ambition (to own a stud farm, raise horses). I asked him once again why he had never married.

"The woman I love is spoken for," he confessed.

"You won't tell me who she is?" I asked, wondering, I confess, if he was telling the truth. Wondering if the rumours about the captain were true. I took my wineglass in my hand, holding it by the stem. I looked at the captain, held his eye as I raised my glass, emptied it. It is an old-fashioned ritual, this "taking a glass"; I doubted whether he was even familiar with it, young as he is. But gamely he followed suit, holding my eye, downing his glass. I leaned over and filled his glass again. I was conscious of the revealing cut of my gown.

"I'll give you a hint," he said, standing abruptly and propping his hands on the arms of my chair. I could smell the sweet scent of pistachio on his breath. Before I could protest, his lips were upon mine, his tongue soft, seeking. I pulled away. "Why did you do that!" (Shocked, I confess, by his ardour. I'd always considered the captain to be "safe.")

Captain Charles fell back on his haunches. "*Why* is not the question a lady usually asks when she is kissed," he said, rising to his feet, pulling at his coat to try to disguise the rather obvious fact that he was in the manly state. I looked away, a flush heating my cheeks. Perhaps I should take a lover, I thought, thinking of my husband in the arms of another. But was that lover funny little Captain Charles?

* *Backgammon dice were initially tumbled in a noisy iron container and for that reason (some claim) the game was considered ideal by men wishing an opportunity to converse privately with a married woman without arousing suspicion. During the noisy game for two, they would not be overheard.*

The night was foggy. I felt my way cautiously, holding onto Captain Charles's arm for support. We were both of us giggling like schoolchildren, stumbling in the dark, starting at the slightest sound. A snort and low rumble made me jump. "It's just my manservant snoring," he whispered, leading me up the narrow path to the old farmhouse. Inside, two dogs began to bark. "Quiet," Captain Charles hissed through the open window.

I put my hand on his shoulder to keep from swaying. Then he hiccupped and I fell against the wall, trying not to laugh. I remember thinking, I'm in a state, I'm going to regret this.

Captain Charles opened the creaky door to his bedchamber. The room smelled of dog. He lit a lantern and stumbled about the room making it tidy, throwing a woven cloth over the bed. "There." Then he kissed me, pulling me against him. "Please don't change your mind," he whispered, sensing that I might. He pulled at my bodice strings, his fingertips on my breast, his lips, his tongue. I moaned, my hands in his hair. We fell onto the bed. Kiss him, I thought—before you think better of it.

He stood and untied his pantaloons, pulling down his breeches, his drawers. Demurely, I looked away. He stepped towards the bed, and I believe he must have lost his balance, for he began to hop about the room, his ankles tangled in his breeches, the light of the single lantern gleaming off his exposed buttocks, his rather large and bouncing manhood.

And then, I could not help it—I began to laugh. And then the dogs began to bark. Captain Charles pulled up his breeches and ran downstairs to silence them. When he returned I was sitting cross-legged on his bed, drying my cheeks, laughing still but contained, my sides aching. He sat down beside me, confused and shy. "My valet's still snoring," he said.

"Oh, Captain Charles!" I put one hand on his shoulder. I felt him begin to laugh himself. And then we were both of us convulsed.

He kissed me tenderly and helped me to my feet. The moment of danger had passed.

*July 11.*

The captain came to my door this morning with a bouquet of wild flowers. I looked at him for what seemed like a very long time, but was probably little more than a heartbeat or two. I kissed his smooth cheek. "I'm sorry, Captain Charles, I don't know what to say," I said, accepting his kind offering.

*July 13.*

I was awakened by a courier cantering up the drive. Bonaparte had been injured in Egypt, I was solemnly informed, in an attack at Saint-Jean d'Acre.

"A general's wife becomes accustomed to false reports," I reassured the servants, but ordered the carriage harnessed none the less.

"I'm coming with you," Mimi said, running back into the house for her hat.

I stood waiting as my coachman hitched the second horse, a grey gelding. It laid back its ears at the bay, swishing its tail.

"Josephine?" It was Captain Charles, standing by the gate. "I heard the bad news."

A stinging sensation came into my eyes. "No doubt it's just another false report. I'm going into Paris to Luxembourg Palace. Director Barras will know." I jumped at the sudden sound of muskets going off. Bastille Day tomorrow—of course.

Mimi came running, blue hat ribbons aflutter. The carriage leaned as my coachman climbed onto the driver's seat.

Director Barras wasn't receiving, his aide informed me. "His doctor has forbidden any visitors."

"But surely he'll receive me."

"No exceptions." He is a young man, new at the job, fearful of misstep.

"Perhaps you could help me then," I said, the tremor in my voice betraying me.

"It's true. They've been injured," I told Mimi. I felt numb. The enormity of the news was just sinking in. "Both Bonaparte and Eugène."

"Badly?"

"I fear so!" With a shaky breath, I told her what I'd learned. During an attack on Saint-Jean d'Acre, a shell had exploded in the midst of headquarters. A fragment struck Eugène in the head. Bonaparte, himself wounded, risked his life to come to Eugène's aid. A sergeant had thrown himself upon Bonaparte to protect him, but was hit and died.

Mimi put her arm around me. I began to cry.


The horses bent their heads against the wind, heading back to Malmaison. My heart reached for Egypt, for a hot desert land. Fear inflamed my imagination.

Captain Charles was in the game room, sitting by the fire reading a volume of Voltaire's tragedies, his slippers on the leather hassock. He put down the book when he saw me. I took off my hat, my gloves. In a few hours Hortense would arrive. She would be buoyant, excited about the Bastille Day ceremonies tomorrow in our little village of Rueil. And then I would have to tell her—that her beloved brother had a head injury, had not woken. "I'm going to have to ask you to leave," I told Captain Charles.

"I know, your daughter will be arriving soon. I was just going back to the farmhouse in any case." His tone tender. "The news is not . . . ?"

"No. I mean, it's not that."

"What happened?" he asked. "Was General Bonaparte injured?" Captain Charles spoke my husband's name with reverence. "Yes. They don't know how badly. And Eugène, as well. He was struck unconscious from a head injury, so there's a chance that he might be . . ." I thought of the village idiot.

I felt Captain Charles's hand on my shoulder. "I'm so sorry."

I pulled away, out of his reach.

"You don't want me to comfort you?"

I shook my head. He looked like a boy to me, not so very much older than my son. My relationship with the captain was not sinful, but it was not innocent, either. The gods were punishing me, surely! "Captain Charles, I'm . . . I must ask you to leave Malmaison."

"Now?" He looked confused.

"Yes please." How could I pray for my husband and son, with the captain by my side? "I'm sorry!" I fled the room before I could do more harm.

*July 14, Bastille Day.*
Fire rockets, trumpets, a steady drumbeat. I fastened the latch on the leaded window, drew the brocade curtains, muffling the sounds of festivity. I am keeping Hortense with me for a few days.

*July 15, early evening.*
Twice today Hortense and I walked the dusty road to Rueil to light candles in the village church. We have each of us set up a prie-dieu in our bedrooms. Mimi walks in the moonlight, chanting to the voodoo mystères. We have all returned to the gods of our youth.

*July 22—Malmaison.*
Good news—Bonaparte has recovered. But no news yet about Eugène—I'm sick with apprehension.

*Close to midnight—Paris.*
"Director Barras is expecting me," I lied to the aide.

The young man looked at the clock on the mantel. "I guess," he said, still unsure.

I followed him up the grand spiral staircase and through a series of elegant chambers to the last, the smallest and most intimate—the bedchamber of Director Barras. There I found Barras in an alarming condition—pale, too weak to stand. "I'm sorry for keeping you out the other day," he said, waving his hand through the air, then letting it fall onto the bed sheet. "If my enemies were to find out how weak I am—" He made a pistol of his index finger and thumb and aimed it at his temple. "I'm not even letting Talleyrand in. You know he's resigned? Everything's falling to pieces. But at least I was able to get Fouché named Minister of Police. He should be back in Paris in a few weeks. The sooner the better. You wouldn't believe the plots that are brewing. I should be flattered, I guess. Everyone wants to depose me. Even your charming brothers-in-law are circulating the story that I sent Bonaparte into the desert just to get rid of him, that the entire fiasco is my fault."

He was babbling incoherently. I put the palm of my hand on his forehead. "You have a fever. Have you seen your doctor? Have you been bled?"

"Yes, yes, but not bled—not today, in any case. I haven't any blood left." He smiled weakly, his eyes fever bright. "That was good news about Bonaparte. You must be relieved."

"Yes! But I've heard nothing yet about Eugène—"

"My aide didn't tell you? Merde. It's so frustrating. I told him to let you know. These young people are incompetent."

"Tell me what, Paul?" My heart was pounding.

"That your son has fully recovered!"

I put my hand to my chest, put down my head and gave thanks to my son's guardian angels.


*July 23—still in Paris.*
Thérèse told me Captain Charles is staying in old Madame Montaniser's suite in the Palace Égalité. I've sent him a message, asking him to meet me in Monceau Park tomorrow at eleven. I dare not invite him here, not with Pauline Bonaparte watching every move I make.


*July 24.*
The captain was at Monceau Park when I arrived, sitting on the shady bench by the Roman columns. He smiled at my blonde ringlets, for I was wearing one of Thérèse's wigs.

"Would you care to sit, Madame Bonaparte?" he asked, as if we were in a parlour. He'd spread a cloth over the bench.

"Thank you for meeting me," I said, closing my sun parasol. I balanced it against the bench. "I want to apologize." I swallowed. I didn't want to give the wrong impression. He looked so sadly hopeful. "I'm sorry, Captain Charles. I behaved poorly."

"I have an apology to make as well, a confession of sorts." He glanced at me, his eyes the colour of sea-water shallows. "I courted you for what you could give me, for the advantages that you offered, the connections."

I looked away, out over the pond. Two ducks were swimming in the middle. On the far side a girl was pushing a baby in a pram. The captain's words hurt. I had used him—I knew that—but even so they hurt.

"And then I came to love you," he said.

Tears filled my eyes. It all seemed so pathetic, somehow, these little dramas of the heart. I thought of Bonaparte, of Eugène, their struggle for life on far desert sands. "Captain Charles, you are a dear man." I did love him, but as a friend.

We parted with tenderness. The captain agreed to take Pugdog back. I dare not have any reminders of my follies when Bonaparte returns, as I pray he will—*soon*.


*July 27—Malmaison, a glorious summer day.*
Émilie and Hortense are coming for the weekend. I've been all morning in the kitchen with Callyot, helping him with the baking—mille-feuilles, cherry comfits and a delectable apple flan. I miss Pugdog. I keep expecting to see him at my feet, eagerly waiting for a scrap. I am thankful he is in the captain's care.


*July 28.*
Émilie swooned at the dinner table, slumping over into Hortense's arms. A cup fell onto the floor. "I'm sorry," she moaned, her teeth chattering.

Mimi and I carried the shivering girl upstairs, laid her out on the bed.

The chill changed abruptly to a flush of heat, and she begged me to open the windows, which I had just closed.

I told Mimi to run for the doctor in town.

Hortense came to the door. "Is Émilie all right?"

"I don't want you near this room, Hortense." She'd been inoculated as a child, but I wasn't taking any chances.

"Maman!"

"I mean it." I stroked a damp strand of Émilie's hair out of her eyes. I had had a mild case of the pox as a child; it had slightly scarred me, but now I was protected.

*6:00 P.M., waiting for supper.*
The doctor clothed himself completely in a gown, gloves and mask. Émilie took fright when she saw him. I watched his face for some indication. He cleared his throat, stood back, his hands clasped behind his back. "I will return in four days, when the poison has emerged." He paused, his hand on the door handle. "Pity," he said.

*August 1.*
As if by magic, as if by evil, spots have appeared on Émilie's face and neck, exactly as the doctor predicted.

"Give me a looking glass," Émilie demanded. I could not refuse her. "They're little," she said, touching them. "And pointed." Almost with tenderness.

The worst is yet to come.

*August 4.*
I have removed the looking glasses from Émilie's room, but nothing can remove the nauseating smell that thickens the air, the scent of the poison that seeks to kill her.

*[Undated]*

"It's just me, Émilie." I put down the tray of medications. Her eyes had been sealed shut by fever blisters. Her face was unrecognizable now, a monster face.

"Papa?" she cried out.

Tears came to my eyes. She was dreaming of her father François de Beauharnais—her émigré father who had fled France during the Revolution, who could never return. The father she'd not seen since she was a girl of twelve. I sat down on the bed beside her. "No, Émilie, it's me, Auntie Rose."

"Papa!"

Did it matter who she thought I was? "I'm going to put a medication on your face." I dipped a scrap of clean flannel into the glass jar. "It might sting a little," I warned her.

She flinched, then stilled. "I've been waiting for you," she whispered.


*21 Thermidor, Luxembourg Palace*
*Chère amie,*

*Very well, very well. I'll see what I can do about getting François de Beauharnais's name erased. I wouldn't be too hopeful, however. There is a murderous mood in the Councils these days.*

*Speaking of which, opposition against your husband is growing. I'd advise you to give up the life of retirement. I can't fight this battle alone.*

*Père Barras*


*August 29.*

Émilie emerged from sickbed this morning. She lifted her veil and one by one we embraced her, trying our best to conceal the distress in our eyes. Her face is a mass of scars. Thank God she is married already.

## In which I am forgiven (& forgive)

*September 4, 1799.*
Émilie's trials have awakened me from self-pity. If that frail girl can win against Death, surely I can find the strength to take on the Bonaparte clan. I'm moving back to Paris, preparing for battle.

*September 10.*
Today, calls on the Minister of War, Director Gohier (who is now President of the Council of Directors), Barras—trying to revive interest in an Egyptian rescue. It's shocking how indifferent everyone has become to Bonaparte's fate, to the fate of our stranded men.

*September 11.*
I am overcome with frustration. I've been all this week making calls, trying in vain, I fear. Opposition has strengthened against Bonaparte. They, the smug men in power, busy themselves with details, oblivious to the obvious fact that the Republic is falling.

Bonaparte will return (I tell myself, I tell myself), that I cannot doubt. I am resolved not to give up. As a woman, my voice is weak. As a woman, my strength lies in persuading men to act. I will sleep, and then tomorrow I will rise, begin again, make my way back to the offices and homes of the deputies and Ministers and Directors, and with my woman's heart—persistent and nagging, persuasive and flattering, cajoling and flirtatious—I will harry the men who would do my husband ill. Using all the weapons in my arsenal, I will win them to his side.

*September 22, the first day of the Republican Year VIII.*
I've been exhausting myself on Bonaparte's behalf, but today was the hardest. Today I swallowed my pride and called on Joseph Bonaparte. "Madame," he greeted me, bowing neatly from the waist. A smile flickered at the corners of his thin lips. "Forgive me for keeping you waiting. I was with my dancing master," he said, pushing a door open to a tiny room that was more of an antechamber than a drawing room. "My porter informs me that you wish to speak to me about Napoleon," he said, pronouncing his brother's name in the French manner. He checked his timepiece and sat, his hands perched on the knees of his white leather breeches, smiling his unctuous little grin. "I can't be long, I regret to say."

"I won't incommode you, Joseph. As you are aware, the Ministry of War has become indifferent to Bonaparte's plight. Another rescue must be attempted." I laced my fingers together. "If we united, we might have an impact. For your brother's sake . . ."

Joseph shrugged. "It's useless. I've done all that I can."

*October 5.*
*Glorious* news. Bonaparte has had a victory over the Turks at Aboukir. Maybe now men will listen, maybe now they will work for his return.

*October 13—dusk.*
The windows of the palace glimmered with the light of a thousand candles, illuminating the faces of the beggars camped by the Palace gate. "Citoyenne Bonaparte," they called out to me in chorus, and then began singing "Chant du départ," which they knew I would reward with a shower of coins.

Director Gohier's valet announced me with dignity. I stood only for a moment, aware of the heads turning, the stares. There were about twenty or thirty present, a select group. Barras, his scarlet cloak draped dramatically over one shoulder, was on the window seat, conversing with a woman (an opera singer) who regarded him with a bored, voluptuous look. Talleyrand, distinct in black, was standing by the fireplace, leaning on his ebony cane. He looked up, grimaced, his broad forehead glistening. Seated nearby, the assistant to the Minister of War was talking with the Minister of the Interior. Good, I thought, assessing the crowd. Many of the key people I needed to talk to were here.

Director Gohier's wife greeted me with arms outstretched. "I love your hat," she whispered. "A Lola creation? I knew it. I adore those gigantic silk flowers." I enjoyed the Director's wife, but in befriending her I was not blind to the importance of her husband in my cause. The powerful Director Gohier had been vehement in his opposition to Bonaparte. By degrees, I had succeeded in softening him.

After civilities, I joined the group at the hazard table. The dice felt loose and smooth in my hands. I'd won over two hundred francs when I heard Barras say, "Well, look who's here."

I looked toward the big double doors. There, standing without introduction, was the Minister of Police, my friend and spy, Citoyen Fouché. He came straight up to me.

"Citoyen Fouché, how good to see you." But there was something alarming in his expression.

"May I speak to you in private, Citoyenne?" But even before we'd reached the antechamber, he handed me a scrap of paper.

I turned it over in my hand. "What is this? I don't understand."

"Your son sent it. It came by semaphore."*

"Eugène?"

Director Gohier was sitting at the silent whist table, oblivious to all but his cards. "President Director." I leaned to whisper into his ear. "There's something you should know. Bonaparte is back; he's in the south."

Gohier put his cards face down. "If you'll excuse me a moment,

* A message relayed from one vantage point to another by means of flags.

Citoyens, Citoyenne," he said, addressing his guests. He signalled to Barras as he hurried me out of the room.

"With respect, Director Barras, from a legal perspective General Bonaparte has deserted his army." Director Gohier crossed his arms, as if bracing himself against some invisible force. "I ask you, in all honesty, how can we *not* arrest him?"

"Arrest Bonaparte and the nation will rise up against us, I guarantee it," Barras said.

I stood. "Directors Gohier, Barras—please, if you will excuse me. I must go." Both men looked at me as if they'd forgotten I was present. "I'm going to try to meet Bonaparte on the road, before he gets to Paris." Before his brothers get to him.

"Now?" Director Gohier asked, astonished.

"But the roads aren't safe," Gohier's wife exclaimed. "And it's so frightfully cold."

"And the fog," Barras objected.

I felt dazed, a strange combination of both joy and fear. It was true, the fog was thick—too thick to travel, especially at night. "I'll leave at dawn."

"In that little coach of yours?" Director Gohier pulled the bell rope. His valet appeared, scratching his ear. "Tell Philip to ready the government travelling coach." He put up his hand. "I *insist*. It can be made into a sleeping compartment." He grinned at Barras. "Handy that way."

My manservant met me at the door holding up a lantern, which threw a ghostly light. "General Bonaparte is back," the coachman called out to him before I could say anything.

Gontier looked at me, not comprehending. A gust of chill wind blew dead leaves into the foyer. "The General's back from Egypt?" he asked, pulling the door shut against the cold.

I nodded, shivering. "He's in the south. Eugène sent a message, by semaphore."

Hortense appeared in her nightclothes, a red woollen shawl draped over her shoulders. "What's going on?" Yawning and then sneezing.

"General Bonaparte is back," Gontier exclaimed.

"And Eugène is with him," I cried out, my self-control giving way.

Hortense put down her candle. *"Eugène* is back?"

"They landed in the south, two days ago. They're on their way to Paris. I'm going to meet them." I would need linens, provisions, blankets, I thought.

"I'm coming too," Hortense said, her teeth chattering. It was freezing, even in the foyer.

I paused, considered. "But you have a cold, sweetheart."

"I'm better now!"

"I won't be stopping," I cautioned her. "I'll even be sleeping in the coach."

"I don't care."

Her golden curls framed her big blue eyes—her irresistible blue eyes. Bonaparte was fond of Hortense; it might help to have her with me. And I was in need of help. "You'll wear your fur bonnet?"

"Anything!" Even that.


It was still dark when the enormous government travelling coach came rumbling down the narrow little laneway, harnessed to four strong carriage horses. It did not take long to ready it: a charcoal heater, down pillows, fur coverlets, bedpans, medications (laudanum for my nerves and back pain, spirits of hartshorn and Gascoigne's powder for Hortense's cold). We took an enormous basket of provisions: bread, eggs cooked hard, comfits and bonbons for Hortense, wine and brandy for us both.

The sun was just rising when finally we started out, the big coach scraping twice against the garden wall. I waved to the porter, yawning in the door of his shack. The morning felt hopeful.

We careened toward the south. I had thought that we would sleep, but we could not. Hortense was effervescent with excitement. Her beloved brother was alive, he was safe, he was coming home. And myself? I was going to meet my husband.

*October 15 (I think)—Auxerre.*

We have stopped briefly in a posting-station in Auxerre. We have requested a private room while a wheel is being repaired. The response of the people to the news of Bonaparte's return has been overwhelming. All along the route arches of triumph are being built in his honour. Men, women and children line the road in hopes of seeing him pass. Last night the lights from all the torches made a magical effect. "The road to heaven," Hortense said, awed.

Such outpouring of enthusiasm is akin to madness, surely. Whenever we stop, we are mobbed, people crying out, "Is it true? Is the Saviour coming?"

Savage,* I thought I heard the first time. Is the *savage* coming. "Pardon?"

"The Saviour!" a cobbler exclaimed. "*Our* saviour."

*October 16—Châlon-sur-Saône, dawn.*

We've missed him. At Lyons, he took the Bourbon route, west through Nevers, his brothers in close pursuit.

"Ah, they'll get there first," Hortense said, as if this were a game.

"Back to Paris," I told the coachman, my anxiety rising. "Fast."

*October 19—Paris, late morning.*

It was after midnight when our coach pulled up at my gate, the horses steaming. There was a light in the porter's shack, illuminating the sleeping forms of the beggars. The coachman jumped down and pounded on the door. "Chandler, wake up, open the gate."

I nudged Hortense. We were exhausted from five days of travel, eating and sleeping in the coach. Violently jolting over the rough roads had inflamed my back, my hip. The night before I'd been unable to sleep at all. A dreamlike daze possessed me, a curious tingling in my skin. Approaching the dark streets of Paris—the smell of garbage, even in the cold fall air; the mud hardened into ruts; the taste of smoke; the shadows of beggars and ruffians huddled around fires in the alleyways—I felt a sense of doom come over me.

*Sauveur *means saviour;* sauvage *means savage.*

"Are we here?" Hortense asked, sneezing and blowing her nose. "It's so cold. What time is it?"

"We're here." I gathered up my basket, sorting through the travel clutter. I put my hand to my hair; I'd braided it, fastened it with a tortoiseshell comb, but some strands had worked loose. Why didn't the porter open the gate? I took off my gloves so that I could do up the laces of my boots.

The coachman came to the carriage door, holding a torch. "There's a problem," he said, his breath making mist. A freezing blast of air came in the open door.

I pulled the musty fur coverlet around my shoulders. "Is the General not here?" And Eugène!

The coachman nodded. "But the porter—" He stopped.

"What is it, Antoine?" One of our horses whinnied. The porter was standing in the door of his shack, looking out. The shadows from a lantern gave his face a diabolic look.

"He can't open the gate," the coachman said finally.

"Can't open it?" Hortense giggled, tying her hat ribbons.

"What do you mean, he *can't*?"

"General's orders, Citoyenne."

"Bonaparte's ordered the gate locked?" Perhaps it was a security measure.

"The porter said to tell you that your belongings are in his shack, all trunked up."

Hortense looked at me, puzzled.

"I—I don't understand," I said. Trunked up?

"The General, he . . ." The coachman looked up at the night sky, shifting his weight from foot to foot. "He moved your belongings out."

And then I understood—Bonaparte had dared to move me out of my own house, dared to lock my own gate against me, dared to instruct *my* porter to forbid me entrance!

I was furious. I started to get out.

"So we're walking?" Hortense asked, fastening the top button of her cape. "From here?"

It was dark in the verandah antechamber. Hortense pulled the bell rope. I leaned against one of the posts, panting from the effort to keep up with my daughter. "Here comes somebody." Hortense jumped up and down so that she could see in through the little window in the door. "Oh, it's Mimi." Then she shrieked and burst into giggles. "Maman, I see Eugène! I see Eugène!"

"You see him?"

"Oh, he's dark as an Arab!" she hissed, spinning, her hands on her cheeks in mock horror.

The door swung open. "At last—you're back." Mimi rolled her eyes as if to say, You would not believe what's been going on here. "It's your mother and sister," she said over her shoulder.

Eugène was standing in front of the dining room fireplace with a wool blanket draped around his shoulders. He put down the candle, held his arms open wide, the blanket falling.

Hortense threw herself into her brother's arms, bursting into sobs. He held her shyly, blinking. He looked like a young man—thin, tall . . . and so dark.

"Maman," he said, his voice breaking. His voice told me so much— that he loved me, that I was in serious trouble, that he had tried.

He stooped to embrace me. He smelled of cigar smoke, the smell of a man, not a boy. The smell of a soldier, I thought, not without regret. I put my hand on his cheek, surprised by the stubble of beard. He was smiling, yet there was something amiss, a tremor around his eyes, a slight convulsive twitch.

"I can't tell you—" I took a sharp breath. "I love you so much! We . . ." But I could not speak for a choking feeling welled up in me.

"We thought you had died!" Hortense sobbed, all the nights of cold-sweat dreams breaking loose in her. She took a shuddering breath and laughed at herself, and then at the three of us, for we were all weeping.

Sniffing, my breath coming in little gasps, I pulled away. There was so much I wanted to ask him—about Egypt, his injury, how they'd managed to return*—but now was not the time. "Bonaparte—is he . . . ?"

* On August 22, four ships slipped out of Alexandria harbour. By staying close to the coast, they luckily managed to evade the British for six weeks.

"He's in the study," Eugène said.

"Upstairs?" In the room I had had made over for him. I took up a candle.

"Maman, you know . . . ?"

"I know."


As I turned the narrow stairs onto the half-storey landing, a cry escaped me. In the dark at the top of the stairs, a black man had leapt to his feet in front of the door to the study. The light of my candle caught the curved edge of a scimitar, the whites of his eyes, his teeth. "You gave me a fright," I said, catching my breath. He was young, more than a boy, but not quite a man.

He said something to me in a foreign tongue. "I don't understand," I said, stuttering a little. "I am Madame Bonaparte. I must speak to my husband. Is the General in there?" I spoke slowly and simply, so that he might understand. But I kept my distance.

"Bonaparte!" He clasped the pommel of his scimitar.

The name Bonaparte he understood. "Me," I said, pointing at my chest, "me *wife* of Bonaparte." I paused, for effect, then said, "Go!" with a sweep of my free hand.

With relief I saw that he understood and, sweetly obedient, slipped past me down the stairs. I went to the study door, knocked. There was no answer, although I heard movement within. "Bonaparte?" I turned the handle, pushed. "It's me, Josephine!" The door was locked. "Please, open the door." I knocked again, called out. I pressed my ear to the wood. I shook at the handle, turned it, rattled it. "Bonaparte!" Louder this time. "I know you're in there. Please!"

Silence.

It was cold in the corridor. My thoughts were in disorder, slowed by exhaustion, anticipation. And now, I was stumped. I hit the door with my palm. "Bonaparte, let me in! I can explain. It's not what you think." I pressed my forehead against the door. "I love you," I said, but too softly for him to hear. Then I banged on the door, violently, more violently than I'd intended. "I love you," I cried out, weeping now. You *bastard*.

After a long and terrible time, my children came to my aid. Hortense looked distraught. Eugène was standing behind her with a look of pained concern, his cheek twitching. I felt humiliated; how much did they know? I pulled my shawl around my shoulders. Why was it so cold? What season were we in?

Hortense stooped down beside me, caressed a lock of hair out of my eyes, as if I were her child and she my mother. By the light of the single guttering candle she had an ethereal look. "Oh, Maman, please don't cry," she said, handing me a handkerchief.

Her tenderness made me weep all the harder. "He won't open the door."

"We know," Eugène said.

Of course. The house was small. "There must be a key somewhere," I said. Or an *axe*.

"Maman." Eugène looked uncomfortable. "You can't just—"

"There is no key," Mimi hissed up from the ground floor. "I looked. He must have it."

*He*—General Bonaparte. My husband. Hortense and Eugène's step-father. Barricaded on the other side of a small oak door. "This must be what a siege is like," I said. A shadow of pain crossed my son's face.

"Eugène, maybe you could say something to the General," Hortense said in a conspiratorial tone.

"There is something you should know, Hortense." I glanced at Eugène. "Bonaparte believes I have been—"

"It's all right, Maman." Hortense gave me a knowing look, an expression curiously woman-to-woman.

"Just keep trying, Maman," Eugène whispered.

Tears filled my eyes. What had I done to deserve such children? I felt I had somehow tarnished them.

Eugène helped me to my feet. I pressed my forehead against the door. Bonaparte, *please!* Listen to me!


How much can a man take? Now I know: a very great deal. Bonaparte, in any case.

Yet when he finally lifted the latch, it was a shockingly frail man I saw before me. He'd wound grey flannel strips around his head in the manner of a turban. His skin, like Eugène's, was bronzed by the sun. Although his face was in shadow, it was clear that he, too, had been weeping.

We three, my children and I, froze in surprise. After hours of crying, pleading, praying—*cursing*—we'd come to accept the fact of that locked door.


I don't recall the children leaving, only the silence, the sudden awareness that Bonaparte and I were alone. I'd been talking to myself for days, imagining this moment, imagining what I would say. But now, words seemed foreign. "It's cold out here in the corridor," I said finally, starting to shiver.

I followed him into the study and sat down in the leather chair by the fire. The room smelled of cinnamon and ginger. A snuffbox decorated with an Egyptian motif lay open on a side table. A single lantern burned on the desk, which was already covered with papers and reports, books and maps.

Bonaparte pulled the door shut, not so much for privacy, but for warmth, I suspected. "Well? Are you not going to speak?" he said, holding his hands out over the fire. He'd put several waistcoats on over a linen shirt, and over that a heavy woollen smoking jacket. The layers of clothing made him look thin. He grabbed a chair and sat down, leaning on one arm with the air of an indulgent monarch. "You've been *wailing* to be let in, and now that I've opened the door to you, you have nothing to say."

I sat watching him, fighting the anger that was growing in me. "It is you who say nothing."

"I am speaking."

"Without truth, Bonaparte—without heart."

"*You* have the nerve to talk to *me* of heart?"

My self-control gave way. "You claim to love me, yet you are prepared to divorce me based on the gossip of soldiers! It is you who should explain, Bonaparte."

"You *dare* to imply that you are innocent, that you have not—" He hit the arm of his chair with his fist, hard.

I took a breath, held it, held it longer, held it as long as I could stand. "And what about your mistress, Bonaparte—your 'Cleopatra,' as the soldiers called her. You told her you would marry her if she were to bear your child." Blinking, my eyes stinging, trying not to sniff.

"How do you know this?"

"Your brothers and sisters went out of their way to make sure I found out."

He sat back. It was not the answer he'd expected.

"They're so intent on destroying me, they don't care what it might do to you in the process." Caution, I told myself. One wrong word, and forgiveness would be impossible. "They tell you I do not love you."

The light of the lantern shimmered in his eyes. I had found his vulnerable spot, I realized sadly. "I do love you," I said, knowing the truth of those words. I do love this man, this intense, haunted, driven soul. Why, I cannot explain. "And I long for you," I said—meeting his gaze, holding it. Bonaparte is not easily fooled.

It was almost four in the morning when I blew out the candles. We'd crossed the desert and returned, wounded but walking. We had made our confessions (yes), both of sin and of pain. We'd confessed to weakness, to the power of grief. We'd confessed to the desperation of loneliness. I told him I'd not managed well, that weakened by constant attack, I'd fallen.

"Were you unfaithful?" he asked bluntly.

I paused. The time had come to be truthful—but what was the truth? "Not in the sense that you mean." I touched his hand; it was so cold. "Not carnally." Not quite. "But almost." I took a breath. "And you?"

"She got on my nerves."

It felt good to laugh . . . and cry. He told me of the despair he'd felt in that country, convinced that I'd betrayed him, convinced that the Angel of Luck was no longer with him. "Without you . . ."

He made love to me, and then again. "I am with you now," I said.

# V

## *Conspirator*

We are sowing today in tears and blood.
Liberty will be our harvest.
—*Napoleon, to Josephine*

## *In which Eugène is healed*

*October 20, 1799.*

I woke with a start. Fauvelet, Bonaparte's secretary, was shaking him, try-ing to rouse him. I stuck my hand out from under the fur coverlet. An enormous fire was raging in the fireplace, yet even so, I could see my breath. "Greetings, Fauvelet." Groggily. "What time is it?" A sliver of light showed through the drawn curtains. "Is something wrong?"

"No, Madame, the General is always hard to wake—as you know," he added. By the dim light Fauvelet's face looked dark, like Eugène's, like Bonaparte's. "It is seven. I allowed the General to sleep in this morning, but now his brother Deputy Lucien is here to see him." A shy smile. "We have been missing you, Madame," he whispered.

Lucien Bonaparte? I put my hand on my husband's shoulder. He was like a man dead. Everything he did, he did with profound intensity, I thought—work, love, even sleep.

He stirred, then rolled over and embraced me, his eyes closed shut. He smelled like a baby, sweaty and sweet. "Fauvelet, have I introduced you to my lovely wife?" Talking into my nightcap.

Fauvelet pulled back the drapes and morning light filled the room. I was taken aback by how sallow Bonaparte's skin was—his face, although darkened by the sun, had a sickly hue. "Your brother is here to see you," I said, kissing my husband, stilling his roving hands. "Lucien."

Bonaparte rolled over onto his back. "I know, I sent for him," he said, stretching and yawning and talking all at once.

*Sent* for him—when? I started to get up, but Bonaparte put his hand on my shoulder. "Bonaparte!" I did not want to be in the room when Lucien was shown in.

"Remember what I said last night—about the transition to the offensive?"

I fell back against the pillows. *The transition from the defensive to the offensive is a delicate operation, one of the most delicate in war.* "This isn't war."

"No?" Bonaparte smiled. I followed his gaze. Lucien was standing in the door looking rumpled and aged, stooped over like a man of eighty, not like the young man of twenty-four that he is.* His gangling arms hung down out of his coat sleeves. He is a talented young man, fiery and ambitious. I would admire him but for one glaring flaw: he wishes me dead.

"Good morning, Lucien," I said, pulling the comforter under my chin. I wanted to grin—*gloat.* "How nice to see you." Overdoing it, I knew.

He peered at me through his thick spectacles, disbelieving. Then he remembered to bow, lower than was called for, an exaggerated show of subservience—a degree of subservience that signified treachery, to my mind. "I'm leaving, Napoleone," he announced, pronouncing Bonaparte's name in the Italian way. He looked like a disgruntled spider, all long legs and arms. His brother, to whom he clearly felt himself superior, had had the gall to disregard his advice and forgive his wife.

"No, you're not." Bonaparte swung his feet onto the floor. Then, with a mischievous smile, he turned and whacked my bottom. I buried myself under the comforter. If I looked at Lucien, I would burst out laughing, I feared.

At the door, suddenly, carrying a clattering tray, appeared the black-skinned youth I'd encountered the night before. Dressed exotically in bright silks and fur, he looked like a vision out of a storybook. A jewel-encrusted scimitar dangled from a thick silken cord at his waist.

---

* *The young considered it fashionable to look old as well as rumpled: shirts were slept in to give the right effect, servants given new clothes to "break in."*

"Roustam!" my husband said, knotting the sash of his winter robe. The youth bowed, put the tray down on the table beside the bed. "This . . . is . . . my . . . wife," Bonaparte said slowly, pointing at me. "He's a Mameluke, but a good boy," he told me. "A great favourite with the ladies, however. I have to keep an eye on him."

"Good morning, Roustam," I said, reaching for a mug of steaming chocolate.

"And . . . this . . . is . . . my . . . brother . . . but . . . he . . . is . . . furious," Bonaparte said, tugging on Lucien's ear.

The black youth bowed and slipped backward through the door, his scarlet silk slippers making a sliding sound on the parquet floor.

"It's so cold in this country." Bonaparte threw on one of my cashmere shawls, stomping his feet. He took a tiny cup of coffee, gulped it down. A roll disappeared as quickly, crumbs covering the front of his robe. He poked at the fire with the iron, chewing, then threw on two more logs. "There," he said, standing back to watch the flames. He pulled one of the little drum stools over beside the fire and sat down.

"The General fancies himself at camp," I said to the glowering Lucien, attempting to leaven the mood.

Lucien crossed his arms. "Noi dobbiamo parlare, Napoleone." We must talk.

"So talk."

"Privatamente."

"My wife is to be included in all discussions."

"You are a fool!" This with the voice of a man addressing an inferior. "Your wife has played you false. She defames our good name."

I was relieved to hear Bonaparte laugh. "Our good name, you say? And our charming sister Pauline with three lovers? And Elisa throwing herself at the feet of poets one month after the death of her child? And Joseph in a mercury treatment again? And *you,* Lucien, making a fool of yourself over Madame Recamier while your wife languishes in childbed?"

I regarded Bonaparte with astonishment. He had only been back in Paris a short while and yet had managed to discover everything.

"I did not come with the intention of debating family matters," Lucien said, his eyes half-closed.

"Correct. You came because I summoned you."

"Bonaparte, I can—" I put my cup down on the side table.

Bonaparte glared at me as if to say, Don't move. "And sit down, for God's sake," he barked at his brother.

With haughty obedience, Lucien lowered himself onto one of the little stools, his ankles and wrists showing long and bony.

"General? The journals have arrived." I was relieved to see Fauvelet at the door. "But I could come back at another time."

"Now, Fauvelet." Bonaparte motioned to his secretary to take the remaining stool. I sat back against the pillows, resigned. There would be no escape.

Fauvelet ruffled through the stack of journals perched on his knees. "Ah, here's one you should know about. Director Moulins claims you broke quarantine when you landed, that you're bringing the plague to the Republic." His voice was nervous, high.

"Bah! We were forty-seven days at sea, for God's sake, and not one man ill. Is that not sufficient proof?" (I listened to this rebuttal with some relief, I confess.) "And?"

"This one regards Citoyen Bernadotte." Fauvelet cleared his throat.

"Ah, yes, my charming new relative."*

"He sent a letter to the Directors suggesting that you be court-martialled."

"That sounds like something a relation would do." Bonaparte smiled, but I couldn't tell whether he was amused or not. "Like something a *coward* would do."

"He's going around calling you 'The Deserter,'" Lucien informed Bonaparte with unseemly relish. "For abandoning your post."

"*Basta!* I left this country at peace and I return to find it at war. I left it crowned with victories, and I return to find it defeated, impoverished and in great misery. And who, I would ask the good Bernadotte—our once-upon-a-very-short-time Minister of War—who is to blame? That's

---

* Bernadotte had married Eugenie-Désirée Clary, Joseph's wife's sister (and Napoleon's former fiancée). Bernadotte will be crowned King of Sweden, and their son will marry one of Eugène's daughters.

my question to him." Bonaparte hit the mantel with his fist. "Anything else?"

Fauvelet and I exchanged glances. Bonaparte was back.

*October 22, early evening.*

Each day, more soldiers return, bronzed and bearing gifts. Paris is aglow with celebration, abuzz with stories. Wives and daughters parade scarves of exotic silks, fathers and sons proudly wear bejewelled scimitars. Our meals have suddenly become hot with spice. We've been invaded by the East—seduced.

*October 23.*

It's only four in the afternoon and already my little house is bursting with soldiers. "My Egyptians," Bonaparte calls them. Hortense, home from school, powders her nose and studies her reflection in the looking glass before descending the stairs.

Loud and boisterous, the soldiers celebrate their return "to civilization," consuming with great gusto, as if they had been starved. (They were.)

Fearless Murat, swarthy, jewelled and plumed, struts from room to room displaying his battle scars to every servant, the wounds still fresh, barely healed, two holes, one in each cheek. "But not my tongue," he says, sticking it out for examination. The pistol shot went in one cheek beside his ear and exited the other, "without even breaking a tooth," he told me, pulling his thick lips with his fingers.

"You were lucky," I said, stepping back.

"And Junot?" I asked Fauvelet, trying to sound offhand. "Did he not return with Bonaparte?" A number had yet to return, including Tallien (much to Thérèse's relief).*

"Andoche Junot, I regret to say, had to be left behind in the desert"—

* *In Egypt Tallien became blinded in one eye, possibly due to untreated syphilis. On his return he is captured by the English. He does not arrive back in France until 1801, only to discover that his wife Thérèse is living openly with Ouvrard. They divorce and he ends his days in poverty.*

a sly smile—"with *Othello*," he whispered, "the child he had by an Abyssinian slave."

With liquor the men begin to talk—uneasily at first—of the killing heat, the flies, the dysentery. Stories of an ocean of sand, and of thirst. Stories of soldiers blinded by fever. Stories of the Black Plague.

It is the whispered stories that I listen for, and hear—stories of a sea of white turbans, barbaric tortures, French soldiers left in the desert to die of thirst, murdering one another for a cup of water.

"How horrifying!"

"It was different there, Maman," Eugène said, his cheek quivering.

*Close to midnight, a cold evening.*

"So, the domestic spat is resolved? All is well?" Barras greeted me with a bone-crushing embrace. "You'll not join me for a cup of chocolate? My cook has made the most glorious Brussels biscuits. I must say, Eugène looks like a strapping young man. But a bit uneasy? I don't know how to put it, but I see it sometimes in young soldiers." He made a face. "Has he said anything to you? The conventional wisdom is that it's best not to dwell on their experiences, but I'm not so sure. Sometimes it helps to talk. Call me an old woman! But tell me, how is my protégé? I hardly ever see Bonaparte."

"He's working on a paper for the Institut National."

"Ah, yes, something about a stone, I've been told.* How charming. The military man returneth and taketh up the mantle of an academic hermit. A wise posture. One I myself would have recommended, had I been consulted."

"It's not a posture." Although Bonaparte had indeed decided that he should remain out of the public eye to weaken rumours of ambition. And to consider his next move. *At the beginning of a campaign, to advance or not to advance must be carefully considered.* "Won't you come see us?" I asked. Something in Barras's voice suggested that he'd been offended. As well, I was concerned. The Directors had been treating Bonaparte with a

---

* *The stone slab found near the city of Rosetta provided the key to scholars on how to translate Egyptian hieroglyphics. The Rosetta Stone is now in the British Museum.*

conspicuous lack of respect. Jealousy, I suspected. And perhaps fear.

"Is that an invitation from you, or from the General?"

"From us both, of course."

"Of course," Barras said, lowering himself into a chair, his hand on the small of his back. Toto leapt onto his lap. "Have you heard what Director Sieyès said, when he learned that Bonaparte was back?"

"Sieyès was dining with Lucien Bonaparte, was he not?"

"Yes, those two are cosy, I've noticed. When Sieyès was given the news of Bonaparte's return, he is said to have exclaimed, 'The Republic is saved.' Curious, don't you think? I've been wondering about that, wondering what exactly he meant."

"*Sieyès* said that? Are you sure?" Director Sieyès is said to detest Bonaparte—and the feeling is mutual, certainly. I leaned forward in my chair, my eye on the door. "Do you think there is any truth to the rumour that Director Sieyès is plotting?"

"A conspiracy? Every man of politics in Paris is plotting something." Barras carefully lifted Toto back down onto the carpet and tugged the dog's tail playfully. "Rousseau warned that if one were foolish enough to found a Republic, one must be careful not to fill it with malcontents. Malcontents! The French Republic is a nation of malcontents. I've been telling you for years—we're doomed."

*October 24.*

"Bonaparte, there is something I have to ask you." I'd been reading to him from *Carthon*, his favourite poem by Ossian. *Who comes from the land of strangers, with his thousands around him? His face is settled from war.* "It's about Eugène."

Bonaparte looked at me, his eyes glazed, as if in a reverie.

"What happened in Egypt? I mean, what happened to Eugène. I've asked him, but he won't talk." It was more than that. At any inquiry, my openhearted son closed down, his voice became guarded, he looked away, his cheek muscle quivering.

"He fought in battles, he killed men, he was injured." Bonaparte shrugged. "He returned victorious. What more is there?"

*Afternoon.*

I discovered Mimi in the larder, sitting in the dark on the stone-flagged floor. "Are you all right?" I asked, alarmed.

"I overheard the soldiers talking. I found out what happened to Eugène."

I slid down on the floor beside her. "Oh?" Pheasants ripe with maggots were hanging above the slate shelves.

She examined the palm of her left hand, tracing the lines with her fingers. "I don't want to tell you."

I put my hand on her arm. Her skin was smooth and cool. "Please?"

She took a breath: Eugène and another aide, the two youngest, had captured a town of Turks.

"An entire town?"

The men had surrendered, pleading for their lives. Proudly, my son and his companion returned with their prisoners. But Bonaparte could not feed his own men, much less all these Turks. So the prisoners—thousands of them—were driven into the sea to drown. The next day Eugène's partner shot himself.

"Oh no," I whispered.

"There is more," Mimi cautioned me. Eugène was commanded to cross the desert. "He was to deliver a parcel to the Pasha—a warning." I leaned my head back against the wall, closed my eyes. Mimi's voice in the dark closet was low, musical. "A sack of heads."

Sickened, I imagined the shimmering heat, the stench. I imagined the flies, the ghosts. "But that can't be!" Bonaparte would not do such a barbaric thing—and he certainly wouldn't have commanded a boy to do it for him.


Bonaparte was tied up in meetings. I lay down, trying to decide what to do. Finally I got up and went out to the stable, where I found Eugène helping the coachman with a harness. He looked at me expectantly.

"May I talk with you for a moment?" I led us to the bench under the lime tree in the garden. "I've learned what happened with your prisoners—and the warning you had to deliver, to the Pasha." He turned away, biting his cheeks. "I wish you had told me!"

"I couldn't, Maman."

"Why?"

"You wouldn't have understood! You would have wanted to talk to the General about it." He looked at me directly, as if to challenge me. "You would have held it against him."

"Oh, Eugène . . ." But what could I say? He was right.

"Maman, please, *promise* me," he said, blinking back tears. "The General did what he had to do; we all did. You must not say a thing to him about it."

"Maybe Eugène would heal if his head spirits were soothed," Mimi suggested to me later.

Head spirits? And then I remembered. According to voodoo beliefs, head spirits imparted ancient wisdom—without them, one was at the mercy of life, a boat without a rudder.

"A ritual headwashing—to cleanse him, appease the spirits."

"Yes," I said. *Anything.*

"No," Eugène said, his cheek muscle twitching.

"But what would be the harm? It's no different from getting your hair washed."

"It's stupid, that's why."

"Perhaps, but . . . I'll buy you that horse you've been wanting."

"The black thoroughbred?" His mouth fell open. "*Really?* But it's four thousand francs."

I shrugged. *Somehow.* "Tonight?" A deal.

Gathering the ingredients proved easier than I expected. The stall in the market Mimi knew about had everything we needed.

At two in the afternoon I corralled Eugène. "Quiet," I commanded whenever he protested. Mimi mixed the ingredients, chanting, the words coming back to her slowly. She worked her strong fingers into his scalp. I poured buckets upon buckets of clear water over my son's head, murmuring, *I baptize thee, I baptize thee, I baptize thee.*

"That's it?" Eugène asked, rubbing his hair dry.

*October 25.*
One full day, and still no twitch.

*3:00 P.M., a quiet moment.*
Hortense, although polite toward Bonaparte, continues to regard him as a stranger. "I am fine, General Bonaparte," she'll say, or, "Good morning, General Bonaparte." Will he ever be Papa to her?

Eugène also calls Bonaparte "General," but with warmth in his voice. They shared a tent in Egypt, and it is easy to see that they've become close. He's started a new scrapbook, I've noticed, this one on Bonaparte's battles—his victories. Already it is thick. It sits on the shelf next to his childhood books, his scrapbooks on his father and Lazare. "You need room," I told him. "Perhaps you should store these ones in the basement."

He ran his fingers over the old scrapbooks, considering. "No, Maman, there is room for them all," he said, putting them back on the shelf.

This pleased me, I confess.

*Early evening.*
"The Directors had the *nerve* to put me on half-pay," Bonaparte exploded, coming in the door. I was in the drawing room with Hortense, trying to make conversation with Fouché and Bonaparte's brothers, Joseph and Lucien. "They treat me like a civil servant."

I suggested to Hortense that she go.

"Did you talk to Director Sieyès?" Lucien demanded.

I took up my embroidery hoop, my needle. Why would Bonaparte want to talk to Sieyès? And why would Lucien want him to?

"Uff. How anyone can stand the man is beyond me," Bonaparte said, scratching. He'd broken out in boils and was irritated to distraction by a rash.

Joseph noisily sipped his tea. "He would be useful, however."

"Essential," Lucien echoed.

Bonaparte scowled. In Egypt he'd been a king. In Paris he was merely a civil servant, a penitent begging favours at the feet of the five Directors—a cabal of old fools, he called them. "Although he is right about the constitution. It *is* unwieldy," Bonaparte went on, talking to himself, thinking out loud. "Five directors is too many. A three-man executive would be more efficient, one person in charge, the other two advising." Bonaparte paced back and forth in front of the fireplace, his hands behind his back. "And the constant change-over is only creating chaos. We've been reduced to a parliamentary comedy. There is such a thing as overdoing it—holding elections every year has exhausted the population. But the trick will be to change the constitution within the law."

"To do that," Fouché said evenly, "you must have the support of both the Revolutionaries and the Royalists." He'd powdered his hair in an unsuccessful attempt to disguise its ugly red colour.

The three Bonaparte brothers turned to Fouché, as if surprised to discover that he was in the room.

"And do I have that support, Citoyen Fouché, Minister of Police?" Bonaparte asked.

Fouché took out a battered tin snuffbox, tapped it, then pried it open with his thumbnail, which was long, pointed and yellowed. "Yes, General, I believe that you do," he said slowly, taking a sniff of snuff without offering any. "Or, to be more precise—I believe that you will."

*October 26.*

Bonaparte and I set out at seven this evening to see Diderot's *Le Père de famille*. I was looking forward to an evening of entertainment.

Now it is only one hour later and we are already back home, frustrated and dejected—and a little overwhelmed, for as soon as the people recognized Bonaparte they started to cheer and scream, drowning out the voices of the actors. We had to leave in order that the performance could go on. We are prisoners of their adulation.

## *In which I must make a choice*

*October 27, 1799.*

Lieutenant Lavalette gazed around our drawing room. He looked lost, somehow, one of the world's innocents. He clasped my hand, his fat cheeks flushed pink from the cold. "Please tell me, how is Émilie? How is my wife? I did not know! Oh, but I would not have been able to live had I lost her."

"You've not seen her yet? You've not been out to Saint-Germain?"

"I understand you and the General will be going out tomorrow morning."

"And Hortense, and Eugène. Do you wish . . . ? Would you like to come with us?"

"Oh, yes," he exclaimed, clearly terrified to go by himself.

*October 28.*

We set out for Saint-Germain early, Bonaparte, Lavalette, Hortense and I in the carriage, Eugène riding beside us on Pegasus, his splendid new horse. The road was a bit heavy in spots, so it was noon by the time we pulled into the school courtyard.

"General Bonaparte, we are honoured." Madame Campan, wrapped in a black cape, dipped her head. We were ushered into her office—all but Hortense, that is, who went running to find Émilie (to warn her). A bell sounded; the ceiling shook with the sound of stampeding girls. "I'm to fetch your wife, Lieutenant Lavalette?" Madame Campan asked.

"Madame Campan, if you don't mind, I'd like to tell Émilie myself," I said, moving toward the door.

It had been over a year since I'd been in the upper storey of the school. The air was heavy with the smell of pomade and starch. Two girls in the green hats of second-year students were gliding down the hall, arms linked, giggling as they slid on the waxed parquet.

"Hortense is in that room," the girl with golden ringlets said, pointing across the hall.

The door creaked open. "She refuses to go downstairs," Hortense whispered, stepping aside. Émilie was huddled on a narrow bed in the corner, her scars inflamed.

I sat down at the foot of the bed. "Are you afraid, Émilie?" Her husband certainly was.

"No!"

"What is it then?"

"I don't want to be married." (I thought, If you only knew, poor girl, how lucky you are.) And then, her voice low, "To him."

Lieutenant Lavalette's eyes filled with tears when he saw his wife's scarred face. I'd prepared him as best I could, but even so, the sight could only have been a shock, she is so terribly disfigured.

"Ah, so it is true. You've been poxed," Bonaparte said.

Émilie stood in the doorway, her reddened eyes fixed on the toes of her lace-up boots. "Yes, General Bonaparte. Sir." She glanced at Eugène, nodded a furtive, shy greeting. Eugène went up to her, pressed his cousin to his heart. I was touched by my son's tenderness. He'd so comforted Émilie when she was a child of four, and he not much older. "Your husband saved my life," he told her. "More than once."

Lavalette flushed modestly, clutching his hat.

And now perhaps this gentle man might save the heart of this girl, I thought—if only she would let him.

*October 29, early morning.*

"You paid 325,000 for it?" Bonaparte regarded the château of Malmaison, its crumbling façade, the roof in need of repair, the cracked glass on a second-storey window.

"But Bonaparte—" I started to remind him that he himself had offered 300,000, but thought better of it. "It's less than one hour from Paris and the grounds are superb. Plus, the winery alone brings in an income of eight thousand francs annually." Well, seven. "The agent felt it was an exceptional value."

"The chicken coop has more prestige."

But by the end of the day, after riding the property on horseback, looking over the sheep herd and talking with the estate-steward about the sugar content of this year's grape harvest, even Bonaparte had begun to succumb to the charm of the place. At nightfall we sat by the roaring fire playing backgammon, while Hortense played a new composition she had written on the piano and Eugène mended fishing gear.

At nine Bonaparte and I retired, taking candles up to our drafty little bedroom ourselves. We slid between the frigid bed sheets, our teeth chattering, our feet seeking the hot brick wrapped in flannel. Then, in our little cocoon of warmth, we talked and loved, talked and loved.


*Evening—Paris.*

We're back in the city. This afternoon I've meetings with tradesmen. Bonaparte wishes work done on Malmaison—renovations, furnishings, gardens! He loves it there.


*October 30.*

"What are you thinking?" I nudged Bonaparte with my toe. He was sitting on the edge of the bed, motionless as a statue.

"That I should talk to Director Gohier," he said finally, as if waking from a trance.

"Concerning . . . ?"

Fauvelet came to the door, a stack of journals under his arm. "The General's bath awaits," he said grandly.

Bonaparte stood, took the tiny cup of Turkish coffee his secretary handed him, downed it in one swallow. "Concerning getting elected director."

*3:00 P.M.*

"*Basta.*" Bonaparte pulled at his boots, kicking one free. It went flying across the foyer and hit the door.

"Director Gohier wasn't helpful?" I followed him, retrieving his boots. They were filthy, in need of a polish.

Bonaparte threw himself down on a chair and glared into the fire. He was wearing the pair of leather breeches that the actor Talma had lent him, so that he would have something presentable to wear to meetings with the Directors. They should have been returned. I tugged at his toe to get his attention.

"I told him I wanted to be a director."

"And what was his response?" Both in Italy and in Egypt Bonaparte had proved his genius for administration. If he were one of the five Directors, perhaps the Republic would—

"He laughed at me! 'You're too young, the constitution doesn't allow it, it wouldn't be legal.'" Bonaparte's voice was mocking. "Legal! The constitution is strangling this country and they refuse to do anything about it. They pray at the altar of the law, as if it were the word of God, this thing, this constitution they serve. They forget that it is the other way around—*we* made the laws, *we* created the constitution and *we* can change it." Pacing, his hands behind his back. "And if they won't, I will!"

*October 31.*

A hectic but exciting day at Malmaison, planning gardens, supervising improvements. Hortense's new horse was delivered, a lovely bay cob mare. It raced around the paddock, whinnying to Pegasus. "Thank you for the horse, General Bonaparte," Hortense said, addressing her stepfather as if he were a guest—an honoured guest, but a guest none the less.

In the late afternoon the four of us—Bonaparte, Eugène, Hortense and I—surveyed the grounds on horseback, talking with the workers. Then Eugène and Bonaparte raced their horses back to the château.

"You know, Hortense, it would please Bonaparte if you called him Papa," I said to her, our horses walking lazily.

"Yes, Maman," she said, her eyes welling up with tears.


*[Undated]*

This evening I noticed Bonaparte standing in front of the pianoforte, studying a sheet of music—*Partant pour la Syrie*, a marching song Hortense wrote when she was sick with worry about her brother in Egypt.

"That's one of Hortense's compositions," I said.

"It's good," he said thoughtfully, flicking one corner with his fingernail.


*November 1—back in Paris.*

"Do you know what Minister Fouché told me?" Fortunée Hamelin asked, stooping to tie the leather thong of her Roman-style sandal. "He suspects someone fairly high up in the government may be in league with the Royalists." She sat up, demurely tucking a breast back into her bodice.

"How high up?" Madame de Crény asked, playing a card.

"A director."

"Can't get any higher than that."

"*That's* interesting. I heard that one of the directors was sending copies of all the minutes and correspondence to England."

"What an awful thought!"

"And so, of course, everyone suspects Barras."

"Ah, poor Père Barras, everybody's favourite bad boy."

"My linen maid is convinced the Royalists gave Director Barras five million."

"I heard two million."

"Rumours!"

"But that's not the worst of it."

"Oh?"

"The worst of it, is they're saying that General Hoche found out, and so Barras had him—"

No! *Don't* say it.

"—poisoned."

And now, alone in my dressing room, I prepare for bed. I've bathed, powdered, done up my hair in a pretty lace nightcap. Waiting for Bonaparte, who is in meetings still. It is a peaceful picture I see in the glass, a woman writing in her journal. The candlelight throws a soft halo of light. Yet within me there is no peace, for I am disturbed by some of the things that the Glories said this afternoon. Gossip, I know, but even so, an evil seed of doubt has been planted in my heart. I think I know Barras—but do I? I thought I knew Lisette.

*November 2, late.*

Thérèse looked like a goddess of fertility, comfortably enthroned in Ouvrard's opulent box at the Opéra-Comique. At six months, her belly prominent, her bosom abundant, she was a vision of voluptuous femininity.

"I feel I haven't seen you for a decade," I said, kissing her. "Sorry I'm late." The three hammer strokes had sounded as I'd entered the lobby, but then there had been greetings to exchange with Fortunée Hamelin and Madame de Crény.

On stage two actors were engaged in a heated debate, two ladies under a "tree" looking on, bemused, fluttering enormous feather fans. "You haven't missed anything." Thérèse took my hand and didn't let it go.

The two men began chasing the two women around a bush. The people in the pit stood up and started yelling, waving their arms. "Is Ouvrard not here?" I asked.

"He detests opéra bouffe." Thérèse leaned forward into the glare of the gaslights. "Oh, there he is—with Talleyrand. Ah, and look—" She nodded to the left. "Our newly elected President of the Five Hundred." She stuck her nose in the air, a mocking gesture.

Lucien Bonaparte? I ducked back out of view. "I told Bonaparte I was at the riding school. He doesn't approve of the Opéra-Comique. He thinks I should only go to the Théâtre de la République." But the truth was, I didn't want him to know I was meeting Thérèse.

"He's getting to be such a snob." But smiling. "How *is* our darling boy?"

Thérèse considered Bonaparte a friend, but a history of favours and affection did not hold much credit in his eyes, I'd discovered—especially now, with her illicit pregnancy so visible. "Busy."

"I hear you've started your evenings again. From what I gather, all of Paris comes to your salon." She poured a glass of champagne, handed it to me. "Don't worry, darling, I won't embarrass you. I've been a social outcast for so long it doesn't even bother me."

A big man in the pit stood up and shook his fist at the stage. Others were pulling at him, trying to get him to sit down.

"Well! I knew the loveliest ladies would be in Ouvrard's box." Barras, his legendary hat askew, appeared with Toto tucked under one arm, wrapped in a red cashmere scarf. "So the General let you out tonight, Madame Bonaparte?"

"You brought Toto to the theatre?" I put out my hands.

"He's not feeling well. The two of us actually."

"He's cold," I said, tightening the scarf around the quivering creature. The miniature greyhound resembled a rat more than a dog.

"You'll join us, darling?" Thérèse asked.

"Is the General among us?" Barras looked behind the curtain. A stone on his little finger caught the light—an enormous ruby. "Or is he still in hiding?"

Barras had been drinking, I suspected. There was something dangerous in his manner. "I couldn't induce Bonaparte to venture out," I said. The public's enthusiasm for my husband made appearances difficult. But I couldn't say that to Barras.

"A wise move. We've had reports that his army want to kill him—for deserting them in that godforsaken land." He smirked. "For leaving them to die."

Thérèse threw me a look of caution.

"Forgive me, ladies! We are enjoying an evening of light opera, are we not? Certainly not tragedy, of which the much-applauded General does not approve." In fact, Bonaparte enjoyed tragedy, loved classical theatre, but I didn't think it wise to correct him. "Of course not," he ranted on. "The General understands Parisians. They want only victory, glory, a glittery show. But caution, Citoyennes—for they weary quickly. Indeed, one must ask, does such a fickle people even deserve democracy? Perhaps there is something to be said for the stability of a monarchy. The French are a feminine people—they *long* to be dominated." He smiled. "What a shocking thing to say! How fortunate to be among friends."


*November 3.*

Shortly after eleven I heard the sound of a horse galloping down the lane. Only Bonaparte galloped into the courtyard—he knew no other pace. Then I heard the front door slam.

"How did it go?" I'd been waiting for him to return.

"How did *what* go?" Tossing his hat onto a table.

"Your meeting with Barras," I said, taking up his hat, wiping the rain from the brim.

Bonaparte threw himself into a chair by the fire. "Well, you were right about one thing—Barras agrees that a change is in order." He jumped back to his feet. "Indeed, he even told me the Republic is in need of someone to take the helm, a man with vision, a military man who enjoys the confidence of the people."

Yes, I nodded, almost fearfully. It was obvious to everyone who that man was.

"He even informed me that he has the man picked out." Bonaparte paused for effect. "General Hedouville."

Hedouville? Who was Hedouville?

Bonaparte hit the wall with this fist. "Exactly! Hedouville is a nobody. Barras insults me by making such a suggestion. Wasting—my—time." He enunciated each word with spite.

I took a breath, not moving. "No doubt there has been a misunderstanding."

Bonaparte stomped out of the room, knocking an ancient Egyptian vase to the floor as he went by.


*November 4.*

"I've decided to go with Director Sieyès," Bonaparte informed me at breakfast.

"But—" Sieyès and Bonaparte detested each other!

"The romance of the Revolution is finished; it's time to begin its history." He downed his scalding coffee in one gulp and wiped his mouth with the back of his hand. "Can I count on you?"

"I don't understand." Count on me for what?

"To help out, talk to people, be persuasive. You're good at that. But you'll have to keep quiet about the plan. No talking to your Glories."

"There's a plan?"

"Director Sieyès has had one worked out for some time, as it turns out."

Ah, I thought, so the rumours are true—Director Sieyès has been plotting something.

"First, the five Directors resign. Second, Directors Sieyès and Ducos and I form a new executive council. Third, we craft a workable constitution. Sieyès assumes it will be the one he has been working on, of course." He scoffed. "But everything within the law."

It sounded so logical—so easy. "And Barras will agree to resign?"

Bonaparte poured himself a second cup of coffee, scooped in four heaping spoons of sugar. "He'll have no choice."

I paused before asking, "What do you mean?"

"I mean he'll be powerless, we'll be stronger."

Suddenly I understood what Bonaparte was saying. He was going to overthrow Barras—by force, if need be. "But Bonaparte, Barras has helped you so much. If it weren't for him . . ." I started to say, If it weren't for Barras, we wouldn't be married. If it weren't for Barras, Bonaparte would be nobody. But these were not words one could say to a man like Bonaparte. "Why can't Barras be included? You said yourself he believes something needs to be done."

"He'd want to be in charge. The people are not going to support a new effort if they see him at the helm. They'll think it's just another money grab on his part, just another way to milk the Treasury for his personal gain."

"There's no evidence to support those rumours! All we really know for *certain* is that Barras has been your most loyal supporter."

"That's not a factor any longer. There are more important issues."

"This is heartless." I threw down my embroidery.

"You'd likely not say that if you knew that your so-called friend is conspiring with the Royalists."

"That's a terrible thing to say!"

"Correction—it's a terrible thing to do."

I stared out the window, unseeing. War times are not moral times, Barras had once told me. But there were things I preferred not to know.

"The Royalists have long been seeking someone inside the French Republic to help put a king back on the throne—someone high up, someone powerful and someone who could be swayed by their gold. Your friend—"

"Our friend, *your* friend, Bonaparte. This is just conjecture. You don't have proof."

"Look at Grosbois, look at the way Barras throws money around. Do you think one can live like that on a director's salary, on gambling wins?"

I swallowed with difficulty. "Just because Barras is wealthy doesn't mean he's in league with the Royalists. Barras voted for the death of the King. He believes in the Republic."

"Barras believes in himself! Open your eyes, Josephine—he has been bought. This is no longer a personal matter. Too much is at stake. Do you think I make these decisions lightly?" He paused before saying, almost sadly, "There *is* evidence. Fouché has being going through General Hoche's papers."

I felt a strange sense of detachment, as if this were a story I had already heard. Barras was in league with the Royalists. If this were true, as I feared it must be, then what of the rest? What of all the other rumours—that Lazare had found out, that Barras had had him poisoned?

I felt weakened, sick at heart. I thought of the man I knew—big-hearted, generous Père Barras, a dedicated Republican, an ardent anti-Royalist. I thought of the tears I'd seen in his eyes when he spoke of Lazare. *This* was the Barras I knew in my heart. The other Barras seemed a fiction, a character in a play. "Are you sure, Bonaparte?"

Bonaparte put his arm around me. He saw that I was shaken, heard the dismay in my voice. "Josephine, my angel, we must be brave. We can't afford to fool ourselves. The Republic—and all that it stands for—will either survive, or it will perish."

"I know, Bonaparte, but—"

"Please, listen to me." He held my face in his hands. His skin felt soft and cool, soothing against my hot cheeks. "If you're with me, you can't be with Barras. It's as simple as that."

"You would ask me to betray a friend?"

"I am asking you to help save the Republic," Bonaparte told me gently, wiping my cheek with his thumb.

I laid my head on his shoulder. "What do you want me to do?" If I could not trust my heart, what could I trust?

"Just be your charming self. Don't let on. Barras must suspect nothing."

I nodded slowly. Very well then. "Can you promise me one thing?"

He kissed me lightly.

"Barras must be spared."

"I told you, this will be bloodless."

"There are other ways to ruin a man."

## *In which we have "a day" (or two)*

*November 4, 1799, evening, around 9:00 P.M.*

Barras greeted us with open arms. "I've opened a bottle of excellent Clos-Vougeot. Did I tell you about the string quartet I've hired for later? I'm determined to conquer that German dance—what is it called? *Valse?* Un. Deux. Trois. Un. Deux. Trois. You see, it is not in the least bit complex, just a triangle, but somehow, by this means, one must move about the room. There's a trick to it. Un. Deux. Trois. Un. Deux. Trois. Ta la! You see, I've got it." He danced ahead of us into a salon where a small table had been laid with three covers, the fine crystal and golden flatware glittering in the candlelight. Gold-plated serving dishes had been placed on a side table. The air was sweet with the smell of juniper. "General? You will have a glass?" Barras pulled hard on the cork, sniffed it.

"I have my own, thank you," Bonaparte said, signalling to Roustam to step forward.

Barras looked with astonishment at the bottle of wine Roustam was uncorking. "A health measure," I rushed to explain.

"You have not been well, General? You must talk to my doctor. He'll be joining us later. He is oh-so-very wicked with the enemas." A peal of laughter. "Pardi! But I am full of animal spirits tonight. I must be getting sick. It is always the first sign."

The footman pulled out a seat for me. He started to pull one out for Bonaparte, but Roustam stepped in. A maid removed three golden lids: thrushes in a juniper dressing, rice with saffron, fat white asparagus with purple tips.

Two maids rolled in a trolley. Barras lifted a silver cover. "Ah, a most excellent tunny, esteemed for its beneficial effects on a troubled digestion, you'll be happy to know, General. You'll not be offended if I do the honours?" He scooped asparagus onto my plate. "We are, after all, like family here. I've been in the kitchen all morning, coaching my new chef on how a court bouillon is to be properly rendered—how it must be coaxed into being," he said, dipping and licking his index finger. "Grand Dieu, I believe he has a knack for it. General? May I have the honour of . . . No?"

Roustam had placed a hard-boiled egg on Bonaparte's plate. It rolled around the brim. Bonaparte cracked it against the edge of the table.

My hand jerked, nearly toppling my glass. What could I say? "Barras, have you seen that play that just opened at that little theatre on Rue du Bac? *Les Femmes Politiques,* I think it is."

"The play Thérèse is so upset about?* No, I've been too damn busy with Grosbois renovations. This new roof—what a mess. I haven't been out at all. Fortunately, watching Director Sieyès taking horseback riding lessons from my window here is entertainment enough. Every morning he manages to fall off. It's getting so a crowd turns out just to watch. I'm starting to think we could charge for admission. The last time I was so amused was watching Robespierre learn to ride."

"Sieyès is a little old to be taking up horseback riding, isn't he?" I could feel the heat in my cheeks. I knew that Director Sieyès was intent on riding beside Bonaparte—when the time came.

"What is it they teach in military school, General: when a politician begins to ride, prepare for battle?"

Bonaparte wiped the egg from his lips with his lap cloth and handed his plate and glass to Roustam. "No. When a politician betrays the people"— Bonaparte pushed back his chair—"that's when the battle begins."

*[Undated]*
"Just so you know, we're saying Director Barras is aware of the plan, that he's with us." Bonaparte tapped a stack of correspondence with his silver-tipped riding whip.

* *Thérèse believed that the play was about her.*

I nodded yes. Yet another deceit.

I have become a person I do not care for.

*November 5.*

President Director Gohier arrived punctually at four, as is his custom, carrying a bouquet of roses. "For the loveliest lady in Paris," he said, giving me a rather wet kiss.

Shortly after, Minister of Police Fouché arrived, skulking into the room in a dishevelled state, smelling of garlic and fish. I was on the settee by the fire, sitting with Director Gohier, enjoying a conversation about theatre. I moved over to make room for Fouché.

"What's the news, Citoyen Minister of Police?" Director Gohier asked.

"There is no news," Fouché said, feigning weariness.

"But surely there is something," Gohier said.

"Only rumours," Fouché said, catching my eye.

"About?"

"Just the usual about a conspiracy."

"Conspiracy," I exclaimed, shocked that he would so boldly speak the truth.

Fortunately, my shock gave the impression of ignorance, for Director Gohier, spilling his tea, echoed, "Conspiracy?"

"Yes, conspiracy," Fouché repeated without a trace of emotion. "But trust me, Citoyen Director, I know what's going on. If there were truth to the rumour, heads would be rolling by now, don't you think?" He laughed.

"Citoyen Fouché, how can you laugh about such a thing?" I pressed my hands to my heart.

Director Gohier put his arm about my shoulder. "Don't worry, my dear," he said to reassure me. "The Minister of Police knows what he is talking about."

All the while Bonaparte was leaning against the fireplace mantel watching—watching and smiling.

*November 6, just after 1:00 P.M.*

Bonaparte has just left for the banquet in honour of the Republic's military victories. I could tell by his embrace, his damp hand, that he was uneasy—as well as by the basket of provisions Roustam was carrying: a bottle of Malmaison wine, three hard-boiled eggs.

*9:20 P.M.*

Bonaparte didn't return home until almost eight. I took his wet hat. "Where have you been?" I demanded, keeping my voice low so that our guests would not overhear. I'd been in knots worrying.

He glanced over my shoulder into the drawing room, which was crowded with savants, politicians, military men, all talking politics, tense and conspiratorial. "I went to Lucien's after the banquet to make the final arrangements."

The *final* arrangements? "How was the banquet?"

"A dismal affair." I helped him off with his greatcoat. One of the boils on his neck was inflamed again. "The place was freezing," he said.

The playwright Arnault came up behind me. "General," he said under his breath, "Talleyrand sent me to find out what time tomorrow we—"

"Day *after* tomorrow," Bonaparte told him.

"But General, a day's delay, is that not . . . ?"

*Dangerous,* he started to say.

Our guests fell silent as Bonaparte entered the drawing room. Throughout the evening they watched to see who he invited back into his study—for whom the door was closed and for whom it was kept open. All the while I entertained gaily as if nothing was going on, as if I knew nothing.

Which may be the case, in fact. I calm and I charm, I amuse and I placate, but increasingly I have the sense that a great deal more is at stake than I realize, that the game has changed and I do not know the rules.

*November 7, morning.*

I woke to the sound of Bonaparte's tuneless singing. I remembered that it was Septidi, the second Septidi in Brumaire, and that the Glories would be gathering at Thérèse's for a coffee party. I decided to send word I wouldn't be able to come. Ill, I would be.

Ill I am, in fact—in spirit, in soul. I can't face Thérèse right now, can't bring myself to lie to her, to say, No, nothing's going on, there is no plan, no conspiracy to overthrow Père Barras.

Bonaparte just stuck his head in the room and told me to send Hortense and Caroline back to school in Saint-Germain—*today*. I protested that they had been looking forward to a ball that was going to be held tomorrow. Couldn't they stay one day longer? His answer worries me: "I don't want them anywhere near Paris," he said.

There is more to this than what I've been told, I fear.

*Darling,*

*The Glories were sad to hear that you're not well. Perhaps you are suffering from the same ague Barras seems to be afflicted with right now—of all times, the poor dear, what with his cousin from Avignon visiting with all five of her girls. The palace is swarming with little Barrases—it's like a girls' school there!*

*Get well. Soon it will be the turn of the century. Imagine! We are all of us already planning our gowns.*

*Your loving and dearest friend, Thérèse*

*Note—Good news. Barras promised to get that odious play closed down.*

*November 8.*
Bonaparte returned from the palace shortly before noon. "You saw Barras? How is he?" I asked anxiously.

"He doesn't suspect a thing. I told him I'd like to see him tonight, at eleven, so that we might talk privately."

"And will you?"

"Of course not."

Lie, detract, deflect. So this is what it is like to be a conspirator, I thought—to put on the face of a friend, to plan that friend's undoing. I can only pray that it will be over soon, and that after I will become, once again, a person who speaks truly.

I heard a curse, the sound of a horse prancing. I opened the sash windows, leaned out. The coachman, Antoine, had an enormous black horse by the reins and was trying with difficulty to control it. "Whose horse is that?" It wasn't Pegasus, Eugène's new mount. This horse was bigger—and fiery.

Bonaparte joined me at the window. "Admiral Bruix has lent me his stallion for tomorrow."

*"You're* going to ride that horse?"

Bonaparte looked at me, amused. "You don't believe I can?"


*[Undated]*

Bonaparte is happy, industrious, cheerful even: writing dispatches, speeches, preparing for what's to come—preparing for a victory. "How does this sound?" he asked, reading out loud: *"Nothing in history resembles the end of the eighteenth century, and nothing at the end of the eighteenth century resembles the present moment."*

"Perfect," I said, frightened.


*7:20 P.M.*

"This jacket suits you," I told Eugène, picking a hair off his lapel. It is a becoming dark green, cut away in the front, tails in the back, and a high turned-over collar.

"It's too new, too pressed," he complained.

"You're going out?"

"I'm going to the Recamier ball at Bagatelle—I told you last week. Don't you remember?"

I groaned. Everything was happening so fast, it was impossible to keep track. Every evening there had been meetings late into the night.

"Why aren't the girls here? I thought they were all excited about it.

And oh, about tomorrow," he said, heading out the door, "I think I'll invite that juggler I told you about—the one I met at the Palais Égalité. And maybe his friend the mime artist."

Mon Dieu—his breakfast party. I'd forgotten. "Eugène, I'm sorry, but I'm afraid I'm going to have to ask you to cancel it," I called after him.

"Maman!" He gave an exasperated groan.

"It's just that we have so many coming as it is."

"So I gather! What's going on?"

*November 9.*

I woke to the smell of smoke. I pushed back the bed curtain, alarmed. The fire in the fireplace illuminated Mimi's face, her white morning gown. "Oh, it's you," I said, whispering so as not to waken Bonaparte. "What time is it?"

"Just past six." She pushed open the heavy drapes.

"Six!" I swung my feet onto the cold floor. Thinking: day one, day two, and then it will be over. That is the plan. Thinking: today is day one. Today it begins.

Mimi draped a cashmere shawl over my nightclothes. "There's frost on the ground," she said, giving my shoulder a squeeze. "And men in the courtyard."

"Already?" I pushed my feet into a pair of fur slippers and shuffled to the alcove window.

"I invited them in, but they said they preferred to stay outside." She rolled her eyes. "Soldiers."

"What time is it? Is Fauvelet here yet?" Bonaparte asked, abruptly opening his eyes. "Where's Roustam? Roustam!"

Roustam, wearing a thick turban of wool for warmth, looked in at the door. "Master?" He bowed, putting down the tray of shaving implements on the dressing table, the crockery bowl of steaming hot water.

"Get Gontier up here, and the groom," Bonaparte commanded Mimi. He sat down in the hard leather chair, pulling a fur throw from the bed and draping it over his knees. He tilted back his head, exposing his throat. "And Antoine!" he ordered, causing Roustam's brush of thick lather to catch his ear.

I went downstairs to the kitchen to see how the cook was managing. Breakfast invitations had been sent out to over one hundred military officers. Did we even have china for that many?

Callyot, unfortunately, was about to have an apoplectic fit. The yeast dough for the bread had not risen due to the unseasonable frost. We contrived to cover the pans with a comforter, lining them up near the ovens. Then Eugène came tumbling down the narrow stairs, groggy from not enough sleep, and starving, he said. "Why is everyone in uniform? What's going on?"

"I suggest you get in uniform as well," I said, handing him a roll which he consumed in one gulp. "And best saddle your horse."

It was still dark when Talleyrand arrived. "I didn't think you rose before noon," I said, serving him the beer soup I knew he favoured.

"I haven't been to bed yet."

"You won't have a coffee?" The smell of beans roasting filled the house.

"My brain does not require nourishment," he said without expression.

"You are so calm, Citoyen." Unlike the rest of us!

"Perhaps you forget, Madame, I am always the victor."

Immediately he was joined by Bonaparte and the two moved slowly toward the door, Talleyrand's big boot making a scraping noise on the parquet floor. "Be respectful," I overheard Bonaparte telling him, "but make sure he understands that he has no choice."

"Is Talleyrand going to see Director Barras?" I asked Fauvelet, my voice low so that the men in the drawing room would not overhear. "To persuade him to resign?"

"With the help of two million francs," Fauvelet said, biting the nail of his thumb.

Two *million?* I mouthed the words, made frog eyes. "That *is* persuasive."

"Yes, if Talleyrand doesn't pocket it for himself."*

I went the rounds of the drawing room, making light conversation, but it wasn't easy: everyone was tense, sipping champagne, all the while watching the door to the study. I heard the sound of trumpets.

Two messengers of state stooped as they came through the door, careful not to crush the plumes on their hats. "An official message for General Bonaparte," one announced, sniffing from the cold. "From the Council of the Ancients."** Pox scars, enflamed by the chill air, gave him a feverish look.

Everyone in the drawing room parted as I led the two men through to the study. "Get Eugène," Bonaparte's secretary told me. "The General wants him."

Eugène leapt to his feet when I summoned him. Flustered, he disappeared into Bonaparte's study, then reappeared shortly after smelling of cigar smoke. "I have to go," he told me, strapping on his father's sword.

"You'll be needing this," I said, handing him his hat. "What's going on?" Not that a mere mother had any right to know.

"I have to make an announcement—to the Council of the Ancients! I'm to tell them the General is coming." He made a nervous face, chewing at his nails in mock terror.

I smiled at his charming antics. He is eighteen now, but often acts like a boy. "You'll be fine," I assured him. Although, in fact, when it came to theatre Eugène had always been one to forget his lines.

The courtyard was crowded with men in uniform, all waiting—for what, they didn't know. They watched with interest as Eugène mounted his horse. He tipped his hat—proud, I knew, to be riding such a fine creature in the uniform of an aide-de-camp—and cantered down the

---

* *It's not known whether Barras ever received this money; it is possible Talleyrand did in fact keep it.*

** *Napoleon was expecting a decree from the Council of the Ancients giving him control of the troops in Paris. This was the first step in the plan.*

laneway. I went back into the house where I discovered Bonaparte in the dining room, talking to Fauvelet. He gave me a quick kiss. "It's time."

The men in the courtyard cheered when Bonaparte emerged. *The king of mighty deeds,* I thought, recalling a line from Ossian. He addressed them from the top step as if he were on campaign. Suddenly—magically!—the sun came out and there was a clashing of swords and a jubilant tossing of hats. *The sunbeam pours its bright stream before him, a thousand spears glitter around.*

Antoine, the coachman, emerged from the stable with the black stallion, the horse rearing in spite of the stud chain over its nose. Someone held the stirrup as Bonaparte mounted. The stallion shied, very nearly unhorsing Bonaparte. He yelled to his men, pulling back on the reins. The horse reared, then bolted down the narrow lane, shaking its head and bucking, the men in pursuit.

Suddenly it seemed so quiet. I turned, surprised to discover Fauvelet behind me. "You're not going with him?" Except for the servants, the house was empty now. Empty for the first time in what seemed like months.

"Madame," he said, observing the distress in my eyes, "be assured that the plan is a good one—"

"I know, Fauvelet." Today the Directors would resign. Tomorrow a temporary committee would be formed to craft a workable constitution. All within the law—a bloodless coup. "I guess I'm not very good at this, at being a conspirator."

"Madame, I beg to differ. I believe you are very good at it."

A day in history does not have any special weather; there is nothing unusual about the way it unfolds. The cow must be milked, linens freshened, bread baked. But for the skipping of my heart, my silent prayers, but for my anxious watching at the window, listening for the sound of horses in the laneway—a day like any other.

It was shortly after noon when Bonaparte's courier Moustache came trotting into the courtyard with the news that General Moreau had agreed to take command of the troops guarding the Luxembourg Palace.

Fauvelet jumped up. "That's the key!" He confessed that he had, in truth, been a little bit worried—more worried than he'd let on, in any case.

"But why must the palace be kept under guard?" I asked.

"Directors Gohier and Moulins are being kept prisoner there," Moustache said.

Prisoner! "What about Director Barras?"

"He's gone to his country estate, under escort."

Under guard, he meant. Mon Dieu.

A night of betrayal, a night of prayer. Mimi helped me into bed, gave me hysteric water and laudanum, piled me high with comforters. Yet even so, warmth eluded me. I waited, clutching Lazare's Saint Michael's medal, startling at the slightest movement, the shadows. Full of fear, remorse. Waiting for my husband, my son. Waiting. And praying. *La liberté ou la mort.*

It was very nearly midnight when I heard the sound of horses in the courtyard. I met Bonaparte and Eugène at the door. "Thank God, you're safe!" I cried out, embracing them both. I was so relieved to see them. My son yawned, indifferent to danger, and stumbled up the stairs to bed.

"You were worried? Why?" Bonaparte asked, unbuckling his sword. "Everything's going smoothly, according to plan."

"I'm . . . frightened." *Terrified.* "I'm worried that Barras might try something, send some of his ruffians to—* Is there enough of a guard outside, do you think?" We seemed so exposed.

"There's no need. Roustam will sleep outside our door," Bonaparte said, but he nevertheless pulled out a brace of pistols, cocking them to see

* In his memoirs—published one hundred years later—Barras confessed that he had in fact arranged for assassins to kill Bonaparte, but had called them off at the last minute.

if they were loaded. He came around to my side of the bed and put one on the table beside me. "Just in case," he said, tugging my ear.

Bonaparte, accustomed to battle and battle nerves, made feverish love and then immediately fell asleep. I lay beside him for what seemed like hours, my heart's blood pounding: *la liberté ou la mort, ou la mort, ou la mort.*

*November 10.*
Day two. I woke with a start, pulled the bell rope. What time was it? I could hear commotion out in the courtyard. Bonaparte wasn't in bed—why hadn't he wakened me?

"They're almost ready to leave," Mimi said, rushing in with a lantern. She went to the window, pulled back the curtain. "The General is in the courtyard now."

By the light of the flambeau, I could see Bonaparte adjusting his saddle. "Quick, tell him I must see him."

"Now?"

I grabbed her elbow. "Insist on it."

Bonaparte ran up the stairs, his spurs jingling. I pulled him to me, kissed him. "For luck," I said, my eyes filling. He pressed his forehead against mine, his eyes closed as if in prayer. Everything depended on this day.

*Just after 6:00 P.M.*
Still no word. It's so quiet I can hear the candles dripping.

*8:15 P.M.*
A crowd has gathered at the gate. I sent my manservant to inquire. He returned with a hangdog look. "They think there's been an attempt on the General's life, Madame."

"An attempt?" I repeated, imagining the words *wound, injure, cripple, maim*. Imagining the word *killed*.


Shortly after the clocks struck ten—in unison, a rare and almost mystical occurrence—a carriage pulled into the courtyard. I recognized the white horses, the Leclercs' ornate carriage. Pauline fell into her valet's arms and was carried to the house, followed by a woman in black, Signora Letizia! I rushed to the door, opened it myself. Pauline was sobbing hysterically. "What happened?" I cried out, panic rising in me.

"It's just a mother fit," Signora Letizia said, stomping into the house.

I asked Mimi to fetch hysteric water and whisky.

"Brandy," Pauline said between gasps for air.

Signora Letizia took a chair by the roaring fire. "We went to the theatre," she said, looking about the room with obvious disapproval. She thinks my taste too expensive, I've been told, but at the same time lacking sufficient display. "We were in act two—"

"What does it matter which act?" Pauline cried out, pulling at her handkerchief. "The comedian Eleviou stopped the performance—" She was interrupted by Mimi's entrance into the room with a tray of glasses and bottles containing hysteric water, laudanum, salts and brandy. Pauline pushed the hysteric water aside and poured herself a brandy, dousing it liberally with laudanum and downing it in one choking gulp. "He stopped the performance to announce that the traitors of the Republic—"

"She made a scene." Signora Letizia imitated the sound of loud weeping.

"—had tried to assassinate my brother."

I gripped the arms of my chair. Assassinated? "Bonaparte has been . . . ?" A sob rose in my throat.

"No. At the gate a lady told me my son was *king*," Signora Letizia said.

I stood up, went to the window, pulled back the drape. A chill came off the glass. King?

"The General has saved the Republic!" Bonaparte's courier Moustache smelled of liquor. "The spirit of the Republic has saved the General!"

"What did he say?" Signora Letizia demanded. "The spirit saves who?"

"He said Bonaparte has had a victory," I said slowly, so that my mother-in-law would understand.

"Ah, victory," she said, flashing her even teeth.

*Almost midnight.*

A cold pouring rain. Signora Letizia and Pauline left about a half-hour ago, thank God. I am alone again, alone with my thoughts, my prayers— keeping vigil. I think of the men on horseback in the rain, of Bonaparte and Eugène. I think of Barras out at Grosbois, alone like myself. I see him walking the cold and empty halls—drunk, likely, weaving and raging. Betrayed.

Fouché just came and went, bringing the news that victory had not been as easy as they had hoped. In the end, force had been required.

Force? "But everything was to be done within the law."

"It's law now," he smirked.

*Almost 2:00 in the morning, still raining.*

Eugène is home—at last!—soaking wet, but exhilarated by battle, a battle won. "Deputies were running all over the place, holding up their togas like ladies. Their red capes are everywhere—on the bushes, in the trees."

"And Bonaparte?"

He laughed. "That black stallion very nearly threw him. He looked a fright. His face was covered with blood—"

"Blood!"

"—from scratching that boil," he assured me.

*Dawn.*

Bonaparte and Fauvelet didn't return until four in the morning. I was sitting up in the dark when they came into the bedchamber, Fauvelet carrying a lantern, teasing Bonaparte about "talking foolishness."

I threw my arms around my husband. "What foolishness?" Examining his face in the dim lantern light, I could see traces of something dark. As Eugène had said, it looked as if Bonaparte had scratched his boil. I would treat it with plantain water in the morning, I thought. I made a mental note to talk to my cook.

Bonaparte threw his jacket over a chair. "I guess I got *a bit* carried away," he confessed.

"Tell me!"

Fauvelet let out a little giggle. "The General announced to the Five Hundred that he was the God of War and the God of Fortune," he said, setting the lantern down on a drum stool.

I looked at Bonaparte, amused. "Both?"

"I didn't say I *was* God," Bonaparte protested, putting out a foot so that Fauvelet could pull off his boot. "It just sounded as if I did."

"So tell me, what happened? How did it go?" I crawled back into the bed and pulled the comforters up to my chin, like a child eager to hear a bedtime story. And so I was told:

*How Lucien had been the hero of the day—*

"Lucien?"

Bonaparte shrugged as if to say, Who would have guessed?

*How Lucien had publicly threatened to stab Bonaparte if he were ever a traitor to Liberty—*

"He told them he'd stab you?"

"With his dagger drawn," Fauvelet exclaimed, demonstrating.

*How Lucien had thrown down his toga and jumped on it—*

"At the Tribunal?" Incredulous.

"Like this." Fauvelet jumped up and down.

"But he put it back on." Bonaparte was drinking cognac—something I'd never seen him do.

*How fearless Murat had led the charge—*

"There was a charge?" Alarmed.

"They were rising up against me!" Bonaparte pulled a flannel night-shirt over his head.

*And how, confronted by a pressing crowd, Bonaparte had started to faint.*

"Really?" How awful.

Fauvelet rolled his eyes as if to say, Yes, *really.*

"I hate that feeling," Bonaparte said.

*And how it had been Lucien who had chased after the fleeing deputies in the dark, and had gathered together a sufficient number to pass a decree establishing a new government.*

"So there are no longer directors?"

"Gone," Fauvelet said, yawning. "Instead, there are three consuls who have full executive—"

"Three *provisional* consuls," Bonaparte corrected him.

"Yes. General Bonaparte, together with Sieyès and Ducos, who—"

"Good night, Fauvelet." Bonaparte cut him short, slipping under the covers and burrowing close to me for warmth. I wrapped my arms and legs around him, kissed him. "And oh, don't forget—" Bonaparte lifted his head just as his secretary was about to shut the door. "Tomorrow we sleep in the palace."

# VI

## *Angel of Mercy*

The Age of Fable is over;
the Reign of History has begun.
—*Josephine, to Thérèse Tallien*

## *In which I must live in a haunted palace*

*November 11, 1799.*

Hortense and Caroline arrived shortly before the evening meal. "Maman, it was so exciting!" Hortense exclaimed.

"I want to tell it." Caroline pressed her hands to her heart. "Joachim sent four grenadiers of the guard—"

"Commander Murat, you mean?"

"Yes . . . Joachim Murat sent four grenadiers to our school to tell me that the Republic had been saved by my brother." She fell back onto the sofa, as if in a swoon.

"Well, they weren't sent just to tell you," Hortense said.

"They were!"

"They came out to the school in the middle of the night?"

"Yes, and pounded on the door with the pommels of their swords!" Hortense said.

"No—with their muskets."

"Madame Campan must have been terrified." Those of us who had survived the Terror knew only too well the horror of that sound—the pounding on a door in the dead of night.

"We all were," Caroline exclaimed. "It was so romantic!"

The children are thrilled that we will be moving into the Luxembourg Palace.

"I wonder if it's haunted," Hortense said.

"Of course it's haunted," Bonaparte told her.

We crowded into our little carriage: Bonaparte and I, Caroline, Hortense, Eugène and Fauvelet. "Will we get a bigger carriage?" I asked. Ours was too small for us and inclined to break down—something that worried me on the isolated road to Malmaison. There were rumoured to be bandits in the quarry.

Bonaparte scowled. "The coaches at the palace seem to have disappeared. *And* the horses." He glanced at Fauvelet. "Make a note to check the crown jewels."

"But we'll have our very own riding arena," Eugène said.

"Is there a piano?" Hortense asked.

"I'm afraid all we have acquired are debts," Bonaparte said, drumming his fingers. And a broken country to mend. And a hungry people to feed.


The Gohiers' suite was very much unchanged. Their bed linens were rumpled, a mug of cold chocolate sat on the windowsill. I felt like an interloper, a thief.

"It will do," Bonaparte said, looking around. "We'll live in this suite, I'll work in the one below."

The salon was darker than I remembered, sombre and pretentious. Every few years a new director had moved in. The result was a nightmare hodgepodge of styles, all of them pompous. I did not want to live here, but I'd entered a realm in which personal choice was no longer relevant. "Could we redecorate?"

"We won't be here long," Bonaparte said.

"No?" I asked, hopeful. Hortense, Caroline and Eugène were racing up and down the marble staircase, yelling to make echoes. I wondered if my children remembered coming to see their father here, during the Terror, when the palace had been used as a prison.

Bonaparte circled the room, his hands clasped behind his back. "As soon as a new constitution is ratified, we'll move into the Tuileries."

The *Tuileries?* My heart sank. The Palace of Kings. The palace of beggars was more accurate. That dank, depressing structure had stood empty for almost a decade, home to vagrants and rats, no doubt—home to restless spirits.

"What about Barras's suite?" I asked. "Have you looked at it?"

"Haven't had a chance."

"Maybe I will," I said, suddenly anxious.


*4:00 P.M.*

Bruno leapt to open the door to Barras's former suite for me. "You're still here?" I said, shocked to see him.

"Madame, I was born here," he said with dignity.

I understood. He'd served first the King, then the Revolutionaries, then Director Barras, and now Bonaparte. It didn't really matter whom. It was the building he was loyal to, the palace itself. "I'm glad to see you, Bruno. I'm going to need your help."

He opened the wood shutters to let some light in and busied himself building a fire. I sat down in the chair by the window. A red velvet throw had been draped over one side of it, giving off a strong scent of spirit of ambergris. I'd never seen this room so bright, I realized. Barras liked it dark. The afternoon sun sparkled in the tiny crystal beads of the huge candelabra. I bent down to smooth a corner of the carpet. The parrot cage was still there, I noticed, the wire door open. There was a china cup half-filled with cold coffee on the table, beside a stack of journals. A violin case was open on the floor, Barras's violin laid on the upholstered bench. The music stand had been knocked over. I stood, righted it, put the music sheet back on the stand. Everything seemed familiar, yet strange. I thought I knew Barras so well, but now I wasn't sure. Was he a Royalist? Was he a murderer? I could not say for sure that he *wasn't*. All the rules had been broken. Now, anything seemed possible.

My reflection in the gilded bronze mirror startled me. I saw an elegant woman in a classical gown of fine muslin, her short curls veiled. She pulls her red cashmere shawl around her, for warmth. This was the home of her friend, but he no longer lives here. Her own home sits empty and she lives in the rooms of a stranger.

The fire roared, catching. "There," Bruno said, pleased, jumping back to admire the blaze.

"Is Barras's study open?" I asked.

"The office or the cabinet? I have the keys to all the rooms, Madame."

"The cabinet." Where Barras worked each morning, where he attended to his private correspondence.

I followed Bruno through two rooms to a small door off Barras's bed-chamber. It resembled the door of a confessional. Bruno knocked before inserting the key. "Habit," he explained with a sheepish grin. He opened the door, lit a lantern and bounded back into position against the wain-scotting, his eyes fixed on the ceiling.

Entering Barras's cabinet was like entering a cave: dark and remote from the world. I inhaled the scent of old wood. The furnishings were of plain design—which surprised me, for Barras loved opulence. I took in the shelves of books, the hourglass, the compass next to the marble quill holder on the desk, the globe, the oil portrait of a woman—his mother, I suspected, from the set of her eyes. I straightened it. The safe door hung open, the contents emptied. I ran my finger over the desktop. I wanted to look through the drawers, but I felt uneasy with Bruno watching. "Thank you, Bruno," I said, emerging. "No, don't lock it," I added. I would come back.


*After midnight.*

I don't know what I was looking for. I don't know what I expected to find. I knew Barras would be clever enough to empty the drawers and files of anything incriminating. And I was right, so I knew that the three letters I found had been left there intentionally—for Bonaparte's eyes. I recognized Lazare's loopy script right away. The letters were addressed to me. Three letters of love.

Now it is the dead of night. Bonaparte is fast asleep. I've read the letters, burned them. (Oh, my heart!) Lazare had written them to me at the end of 1795, when Bonaparte had been courting me—and Barras had been urging me to consider marrying him. I loved Lazare against all reason, and so was blind to Bonaparte. But then Lazare had stopped writing—or so I had thought. Assuming that I'd been forgotten, I gave in to Bonaparte's attentions.

And now, with a feeling of helpless anger and dismay, I understand. Barras had intentionally withheld Lazare's letters from me in the hope that I would marry Bonaparte. Bien. I can live with that, for I have come to believe that fate, however convoluted, however indirect, had intended for me to meet and marry Bonaparte.

But what I find truly shattering is the realization of why he'd held onto them. There is only one explanation: as long as Barras had those letters, he had the power to ruin me.


*November 21.*
Our first evening entertaining at "home": a long sober game of whist with the Consuls: Bonaparte, Sieyès (dry, taciturn, wrinkled beyond his years) and Ducos (nervously watching Sieyès and Bonaparte, imitating each by turn). After the game, the men took out their snuffboxes and discussed constitutional law. Yawning behind my fan I excused myself and went to the window, "for air."

It was a beautiful night, clear but cold. It smelled as if it might snow.

"A constitution should be short and obscure," I heard Bonaparte say.

"Yes, short," Ducos echoed, clearing his throat.

I heard a duck call outside. On the street side of the metal gates stood a man and three women—Fortunée Hamelin, Minerva and Madame de Crény! The man did a handspring: Captain Charles! I waved, threw them a kiss. Come out, come out, they gestured. I shook my head: I can't, sorry. (Oh, *so* sorry!) They began to sing an aria from *Don Giovanni*.

"The rabble are noisy tonight," Sieyès observed.

I closed the window, the drapes.


*November 22.*
"I'm sorry, Madame Bonaparte, Madame Tallien is not receiving."

"Still? Please, I must see her."

Thérèse's butler closed the door.

*[Undated]*
Every morning Bonaparte begins work at eight, whistling tunelessly. He reappears every few hours, kisses me, exchanges pleasantries, an amusing story, has a quick collation, a coffee or a sip of watered wine (usually a coffee), advises me on my toilette and disappears again, singing.

He is full of optimism. "My government will be a government of spirit and of youth." He says this in the face of the hordes of beggars on the streets, the robber bands everywhere, the nation's staggering debt. No detail is overlooked. This morning he ordered bulls imported from Switzerland to give strength to French herds, trees to be planted along all our roads. The Ministers are exhausted trying to keep up with him, for he requires daily reports.

And nightly, when a normal man would be entirely depleted by the events of the day, he attacks with the same zeal "our project." I'm not married to a man, I'm married to a whirlwind!

*November 29.*
"I'm sorry, Madame Bonaparte, Madame Tallien is not receiving."

Not receiving *me*.

*[Undated]*
Bonaparte is going mad working out a new constitution with Sieyès, who is both slow and illogical. For a price (a high one) Sieyès has at last agreed to step aside. Now, I pray, things will begin to move.

*December 24, Christmas Eve.*
There is great celebrating in the streets. The new constitution has been announced. "The Revolution is over!" people cry out, tears streaming.

Over? I want to believe this. I want to believe these words.

*December 25, Christmas Day.*
A lovely family gathering here this morning: Aunt Désirée, Hortense and Eugène. (It was too chilly for the Marquis to travel.) The children and I enjoyed taking Aunt Désirée on a tour. Aunt Désirée admired the black "Eagle" cooking range with a coal grate in the kitchen, and the elaborate network of bells and cords for summoning servants. The children insisted on showing her the secret passages. (I kept thinking I could hear Barras laughing.) Aunt Désirée left me with careful instructions on the use of Goddard's powder to polish silver and the proper way to clean walls lined with brocade (brush down and then rub with tissue followed by a soft silk duster).

Now, a quiet moment before preparing for the Bonapartes tonight. Bonaparte is busy drafting a letter to the King of England, proposing peace. Peace! A spirit of optimism has come over us all.

*December 31.*
Today is the last day of the eighteenth century. It seems that everyone in Paris (except me) is festive, gay, *drunk*—openly celebrating, for mercifully Bonaparte has allowed the Christian holidays to be observed. Wisely, rather, for it would have been impossible to ignore this significant turning.

*January 1, 1800!*
This is the first day of a new century. Just imagine! Everything I do, every move I make, has a careful yet excited feeling of beginning anew. This morning Bonaparte and I lingered long in our big feather bed, laughing and whispering, teasing and coquetting, working on "our project" (as he so solemnly puts it). I had a hint of the flowers two weeks ago. I am filled with hope.

*Later.*
One hundred and fifty-seven hackney cabs lined up outside the Palais Egalité to buy sugared almonds and marrons glacés. "Just like in the days

of the Ancien Régime," Eugène said, chewing a sugared almond, his chin dusted with powdered sugar. "I guess it wasn't all bad," he added, licking his lips.

*[Undated]*
I have been reading to Bonaparte every evening before he drops off to sleep.* This is a quiet time for us, a precious moment. He makes love to me, and then we talk, of our astonishing life, the challenges we each face, the exciting possibilities that lie ahead. And then I read to him, usually from his beloved Ossian. This evening the worn leather volume was not in its usual spot beside the bed. "I've burned it," he said, more in sorrow than in anger.

"Why?" I was shocked. Bonaparte took that book with him everywhere.

"It was a fake," he said. "I found out they're looking into it in Scotland."

"They weren't the words of Ossian?" I found that impossible to believe.

"No, someone made them up, and then claimed that Ossian had written them. Fooled us all." Embittered. "It just shows, doesn't it, that nothing can be trusted."

"But Bonaparte, the beauty in the words—nothing can take that away. Certain things one can trust absolutely." I put my hand against his cheek.

*January 2.*
It's official now. "We're moving to the Tuileries," Bonaparte has informed me.

The palace of the Bourbon kings.
The palace of our dead King.
And Queen.

---

* *Josephine was said to have a low, musical voice. When she read to Napoleon, the servants would hover outside the door to listen.*

*January 3.*

Mimi stood on the dirty cobblestones, looking up at the façade of the Tuileries Palace. Obscene messages, revolutionary emblems and slogans had been painted all over the walls. There were dark stains on the cobblestones—bloodstains, I feared. "What a mess," Mimi said, frowning.

The doors were stuck; it had been a long time since they'd been opened. Two men together (the architect and a journalist) were unable to loosen the seal. Then Bonaparte threw himself against it and the doors fell open. We laughed to see him fly.

"How easy for *you* to enter this Palace of Kings, Consul," the journalist said. "One would think you were expected."

"Palace of the *Government*, we're calling it now," Bonaparte corrected him.

"Yes, Consul!" He took out a paper, lead pencil.

I peered into the vast depths. The windows were high, dirty, some boarded over. It was cold, too, colder than outside. And musty. It smelled of old air.

"The hard part will not be moving in," Bonaparte said, brushing off his shoulders. "The hard part will be staying. Antoine, get the torches," he ordered our coachman. "I've a country to run."

"And the shawls!" I called after him.

"I'll get them," Mimi said, sprinting down the steps two at a time.


We were like a medieval procession in that place, some ancient doomsday rite. Antoine, torch held high, bravely took the lead, hitting a stick against the walls to scare off rats.

"Oh," Mimi said, clasping my hand.

"This must have been the King's suite," Bonaparte said, studying a plan. He looked up, around, paced off the room. "This will be my office. I'll receive in that room there." The room with the throne.

We descended to a lower level, darker, mustier and colder: the Queen's rooms.

"This place is gloomy, Consul General," the journalist said, his deep voice echoing in the empty rooms.

"Gloomy like all grandeur," Bonaparte said.

"The Committee of General Security met in this room," the architect said, examining the fireplace façade. "I recognize the detail on the chimney face. The Queen could not bear monotony—everything had to be ornate."

"Yes," the journalist said, his voice a whisper. We were in that forbidden realm: the realm of the past.

"Then that room over there, the reception area, must have been where Robespierre—" I put my hand to my eyes and pressed until I saw stars, but the image remained: of the tyrant, wounded, stretched out on top of a table with Blount, his faithful Great Dane, whimpering, licking his hand. Had Robespierre not died that day, I would not be . . .

It was then that I saw her, the figure of a woman in white, standing by the wardrobe.


They laid me out on the cold floor, my shawl under my head. Mimi fanned me, stirring up dust. I coughed, struggled to sit up. All of them were standing over me with worried expressions. "I'm fine," I assured them.

"She'll be fine," Bonaparte said, tugging at my hand.

"I'll get her, General," Mimi said, her hand supporting my head.

I leaned on Mimi for support. She was steady, not trembling. "Oh Mimi, wasn't she a fright!" I whispered. The men were examining the windows. I put my hand to my chest. A shakiness had come over me, and a chill; it seemed to come from within me, from inside my very bones.

Mimi frowned. "Who?"

"That woman by the wardrobe." Breathing in, out, in, out.

She had been mannish, her jaw firmly set, her hair cropped short, ill-covered by a ruffled cap. She'd been wearing a white gown with long sleeves, plain. "You must have seen her. She was standing by the wardrobe door. How could you not have seen her?" She was so clear.

"Oh-oh," Mimi said, screwing up her face.

Then I remembered where I'd seen that face, the jaw clenched against adversity. At Citoyen David's studio—his rough pen portrait of Queen Marie Antoinette, on her way to the scaffold.

*January 7.*

Too busy to write: working day and night getting the Tuileries Palace in condition to live in. It is ten o'clock in the morning and already I have selected fabric for all the drapes, met with my frantic cook about what the Tuileries kitchen will need (everything had been stolen: there's not even a stockpot) and met with Madame Campan about protocol and staff. (Madame Campan's experience as lady-in-waiting to the Queen makes her invaluable to me now. It's so overwhelming: my cook alone will require three assistant chefs in the kitchen. No wonder he's having fits.)

Tomorrow I'll attend to my wardrobe.

I'm hearing Barras's chuckle from somewhere in this palace. We are all of us going mad.


*January 17.*

Bonaparte came into my drawing room at noon. He sat down, staring into the fire. "Murat just asked for Caroline's hand."

"Oh?" Relieved, I confess. A week before I'd discovered Murat and Caroline sprawled on a sofa.

"Murat's the thirteenth child of an innkeeper; I don't want to mingle my blood with his. I was thinking more of General Moreau."

"But Bonaparte—"

"Perhaps it would be wisest to wait. In a short time it's possible I could marry her into royalty." He smiled. "Now that's a thought."

"Murat is brave," I persisted. A swearing swashbuckler so much the fashion now. A swashbuckler in peacock plumes. "He served you well at the Battle of Aboukir, and at Saint-Cloud."

"Brave isn't enough. He's not intelligent, he's uneducated and he's of lowly birth—"

"He suits Caroline perfectly."


*Waiting to be called to supper.*

An amusing exchange. "Are you sure this is what you want?" Bonaparte demanded of his young sister.

Caroline sat primly on the sofa, muslin ruffles everywhere. "I love him."

"That's easy to say now, but as your brother I must warn you, when he's naked, a big brute of a man like that, and in a state of desire, you're not going to find him so very—"

She burst into a peal of delighted giggles.

*January 18.*

It's done, the contract has been signed in the presence of every Bonaparte in Paris: Signora Letizia, the five brothers, two sisters, Uncle Fesch. And, as well, a tiny trio of Beauharnais: myself, Hortense and Eugène.

The house-poor brothers were scarcely able to scrape together a dowry of thirty thousand francs, ten thousand less than Elisa and Pauline each received when they were married, so at the last moment Bonaparte added a lovely pearl necklace. I frowned when I saw it. It looked familiar. It was familiar: it was my own.

*January 20.*

The iridescent pearls, loose on a black satin cloth, reflected the candlelight. "I've never seen pearls so . . ." So *pure.*

"Indeed, Madame, these are that rarest of gems, the round saltwater pink pearl." Monsieur Lamarck spoke in a reverent hush. "It is *impossible* to find pearls of this size and perfection: look at these ugly baroque pearls, Madame, to compare: covered with blisters. They resemble potatoes. Or look at this set of freshwater pearls, shaped like little wine barrels. But *these* pearls—" He handed me a magnifying glass, pulled a lantern closer. "These pearls have lustre." He murmured the word "lustre" confidentially, as if he were imparting dangerous information. "And *iridescence.* Observe: rainbows. *Captured* within. Indeed, Madame, it is an exceptionally thick layer of nacre that makes them so"—he rolled his eyes erotically—"*hypnotic.* Some claim that the nacre has healing powers—but that is strictly conjecture and as you know, Madame, we deal *only* in fact. Observe, Madame, a fact: they are imperfect. A *perfect* pearl is an imperfect pearl. Did you know, the Queen of Spain wears green pearls?" Whispering now. "Her jeweller should be hanged. But these pearls, Madame, these pearls are without question the finest in the world. Even a queen could wear them with confidence. Oh, forgive me." Withdrawing an enormous handkerchief from his gold-embroidered waistcoat pocket. "Excuse me, Madame." Sniffing. "I got carried away. Now, where was I—yes, the price. The price is five hundred thousand francs."

I swallowed, my mouth suddenly dry.

"Y-y-yes?" Monsieur Lamarck slipped off his spectacles, cleaned them with a corner of his handkerchief, put them back on. "Did I hear you correctly, Madame? Was it *yes* that you said?"


What has come over me, what have I done? I am made breathless by my daring, shaken by my foolishness—giddy by my gall! Such money! The price of a vast estate contained in a necklace. I look upon them entranced; it's as if they have cast a spell over me. I am transformed, bewitched! How am I to pay? I'll find a way, for I cannot be parted from them. I put on these gems, and I *am* a queen. Grand Dieu.

# In which I must sleep in
# Marie Antoinette's bed

*January 21, 1800.*

This evening Bonaparte handed me a thick file.

"What is this?" But I knew: it was the List—the names of the French aristocrats who were forbidden from returning to the Republic. For years Thérèse and I had lobbied to get names removed. Each small success had been a battle won.

"I'd like you to determine who should be taken off," Bonaparte said, opening his battered tin snuffbox.

I stared at him, not comprehending. "You want me to decide?" To name who was innocent, who guilty—rule whose life would be ruined, whose life saved?

"If you prefer, I could get Duroc to do it."

Duroc, the most heartless of Bonaparte's aides. "No, I'll do it!"

Now, alone in my boudoir, I look through the thick file, the names of so many thousands of men and women, and I am overwhelmed. Can I do this? I pray for strength.

*February 5.*

"Don't blame your hall porter," I told Thérèse. "I pushed my way past him. May I come in?" I stepped boldly into the room. "I heard you had your baby, a girl."

Thérèse regarded me without a smile. Swaddled at her side was the infant, only a few days old. I stood for a moment in uncomfortable silence, remembering Thérèse as I'd first met her, her eyes so dark, so seeking. Eyes of wisdom, of innocence. And now, tired eyes. "I need your help going over the List. I've been asked to name the émigrés who should be allowed to return."

"Back to the Republic?"

I nodded. "But it's a big job, too big for me." One of Thérèse's canaries broke into song.

"Come in then," she said finally. "And take off your coat," she added in an exasperated tone, as if it was too difficult to maintain, this chill, an unnatural thing.

I put down the basket of comfits and toys I'd brought and leaned over the bed. "She's beautiful. She looks just like Thermidor when she was born. What's her name?"

"Clémence."

*Mercy. Forgiveness.* "Yes."

Thérèse touched my hand. "How are you doing, Rose?" Addressing me by my former name. My old self. Not my new self.

"Surviving." I shrugged.

"You and I, we'd hoped for more," she said, gesturing to a chair beside the bed.

Before long we were sharing confessions. I spilled out my heart to her, telling her how dismal it was to live in the palace, about all the boring fêtes, the tedious ceremonies, the Queen's ghost. "Forgive me," I said when the clock chimed three. "I promised myself I wouldn't stay long." It was unfair of me to unburden myself to this woman in childbed. I pulled my shawl around my shoulders and stood—but there was more, we both knew, a name not yet spoken. "How is he doing?" I asked finally.

"You care?" Yet her tone was curiously gentle.

Yes, I nodded. I cared. In spite of everything.

"He's drinking too much, gambling recklessly, his health is not good— but then all that's to be expected, I think, under the circumstances."

I felt the weight of her accusation. "You don't understand."

"Then enlighten me, please." Her huge eyes swimming.

"I had reason. That's all I can say."

She stared at me for a long moment. "I know Barras was taking Royalist money, but that was no reason to betray him. He was playing all sides. That's his way—he makes no secret of it. He was taking their money and using it against them." The baby made a chirping noise.

"Is that what he told you?"

"You don't believe it?" Thérèse asked, putting the infant to breast.

I felt a familiar tingling in my own breasts. "It's more complex than that, Thérèse." More deadly.

"He didn't poison Lazare, if that's what you're thinking. He broke down one night, told me everything."

"Oh?" Wine talking, no doubt—wine and tears, a potent mix. Wine and tears and rage. I knew Barras so well. But not well enough, as it turned out. I sat back down on the little upholstered chair by her toilette table. "But Lazare *was* poisoned?"

She nodded. "By a Royalist agent."

I propped my elbow on the table and rested my chin in the palm of my hand. Trying to take this in. "The Royalist agent Barras was taking money from?" My words hung in the silence.

She paused before saying, "One of them."

I glanced at my friend in the looking glass. Then I turned to face her. "But why?"

"Do you really want to know?"

I nodded, but fearful.

"Lazare found out what Barras was doing. So then he knew too much. The agent was worried he might talk."

So. A Royalist agent poisoned Lazare to silence him, to protect his dirty secret that Director Barras, the most powerful man in the French Republic, was in his pay.

"Barras went mad when he found out," Thérèse said, switching the baby to her other breast. "He wanted to strangle the man."

When did this happen? I wondered, thinking back. I was stunned by the realization that Thérèse had known and had kept it from me. "You knew all along." We had all been deceiving each other—a thought that did not comfort me in the least.

"We're all guilty," she said with a sweet-sad smile.

Except Lazare, I thought.

"*And so you see,*" Thérèse sang to her baby, quoting a line from *Candide*, "*the new world is no better than the old.*"

<br>

*8:30 P.M.*

Adélaïde Hoche sat upright in her chair like a schoolgirl, her hands folded neatly in her lap. Her eyes look frightened. Père Hoche stood behind her.

"I just want you both to know I found out what happened. At least, what likely happened," I said.

Père Hoche leaned forward, one hand on the back of Adélaïde's wooden chair, the other hand on his cane, a thick oak cudgel. One could kill with such a stick, I thought.

I began: "Director Barras had been taking money from the Royalists." Père Hoche cursed. "It's hard to know for sure what his intention was," I persisted. He'd been taking money from the Pretender faction as well as from the Orléanists, I explained. He'd been dealing with all parties, as was his way, but holding his cards close, playing his own game. Then, when he learned that evidence had been found exposing the Pretender agents, he decided to jump ship. To cover himself, he attacked the Pretender group—but the plan failed (at least the first time) and Lazare took the blame.

"They called my son a traitor."

"He had to go along with it, Père Hoche," I told him, as gently as I could. Lazare would have preferred musketfire to such a slur, I knew. Traitors were scum in his eyes. The scar on his face was testimony to the passion of his creed: as a youth of sixteen, he'd challenged a grenadier in his barracks who was spying for bribes. They'd duelled on Mont-Martre on a cold winter's day. The spy had scarred him, a badge Lazare had worn proudly. "If Director Barras had been accused, the Republic would have fallen. The agents knew that, so they tried to expose Barras. The agent for the Pretender must have shown your son proof that Director Barras had accepted their bribe money."

I could imagine the depth of Lazare's disillusionment, his disgust. "The Royalists were trying to get your son to turn against the Director, but it didn't work," I went on. "He knew what was at stake. Then the agent must have panicked, because General Hoche, their worst enemy, knew too much—knew everything."

"And so the agent poisoned him," Adélaïde said, her voice clear and strong. She was standing with one hand on the mantel—on the blue urn.

The urn. Mon Dieu, I thought, suddenly remembering what Fouché had said, about Lazare's heart. "Yes," I said, sickened, my throat tight. I heard the child laughing. I glanced up at Lazare's portrait, for strength. "Director Barras had nothing to do with it." The truth was not so simple, however. The truth was that Lazare, the brave innocent, had fallen victim to one of Barras's greedy intrigues.

*February 6.*
The final vote on the new constitution has been tallied. Bonaparte is now First Consul. Three million voted in favour—and less than two thousand voted against.* It's a miracle.

*[Undated]*
I knew by Fauvelet's flustered look that he had something to say to me, something I wasn't going to like. "It's about your debts, Madame. The First Consul wishes to have them settled."

"And so Bonaparte sent you?" Coward!

Fauvelet nodded. "I'm to ask you the total sum." He scratched his chin. "He will pay them. He only asks that you withdraw from all speculative endeavours now and in the future, Madame."

I paced around him as he talked. In truth, there was no other way. My debts were beyond my ability to settle. It wasn't all hats! (Although

* *The actual vote was 3,009,445 in favour, 1,562 against. Sieyès and Ducos stepped down to be replaced by Cambacérès as Second Consul and Lebrun as Third.*

I did owe for thirty-eight—how did that happen?) The big bills were substantial: Bodin Company debts, a National Property I'd invested in and Malmaison alone accounted for over one million. And the pearls, mon Dieu.

It is done: I've withdrawn from the Bodin Company. Bonaparte settled my debts. There were tears.

*February 7.*
"Damn, Washington died," Bonaparte said, throwing down a dispatch.
  "The American?"
  "Of all times. Now I'll have to show mourning." He looked over a calendar. "How many days left?"
  How many days until we moved to the Tuileries Palace, he meant. "Eleven," I said, examining the calendar. Just thinking about the move induced a panic in me. There was so much to do, so much that had to be accomplished in so little time. The walls were not yet plastered. And the floors—the workers were *supposed* to have begun work on them three days ago.
  "Perfect, ten days of mourning: and *then* the move."

*February 14.*
A good meeting with Thérèse. We're making progress going over the List. It's so much easier with the two of us.

*February 16.*
"You sent for me, Citoyenne?" Émilie's husband Lavalette stood before me at attention, as if for a military review.
  I begged him to be seated. "I have a favour to ask of you, Lieutenant Lavalette. However, I am hesitant, as it entails a certain degree of personal danger. I need someone to go into Austria—"

Lavalette registered surprise.

"—in order to locate a certain individual, an emigré whose name has finally been removed from the List. I need you to help that individual cross the border back into France." No easy task.

"May I ask who?"

"Certainly, but you must vow not to tell a soul, not even your wife." I paused, smiled. "François Beauharnais." Émilie's father, the Marquis's son.

*February 17—Tuileries Palace.*

I am writing this at my escritoire in what will soon be my new drawing room—the yellow room, I call it. I feel uneasy, at odds with the taste of the Queen, who occupied these rooms before me. Every surface—the walls, the ceiling, even the floor—is covered with ornament.

Will I ever be happy here? Was she? I wonder. (I doubt it.)

I'm exhausted, I remind myself. Even now, there are trunks to be unpacked, put away. But the dining and reception rooms are finally presentable, the heavy brocade drapes hung only an hour ago. Day after tomorrow . . .

*February 18.*

Everything should be ready for tomorrow's move—the grand parade, the reception, the dinner. Ready in *theory*, anyway. In reality, every time I go to look over the work, something is amiss. The workers were only this afternoon laying the carpets. And now, my cook is ill with an ague.

*February 19.*

Eugène's uniform has been mended and Hortense has finally determined the right shade of ribbon (a lovely blue-green) to go with her gown. Bonaparte just rushed in and we went through the order of events one last time. "Make sure Hortense is watching just after the cavalry," he whispered to me. But he wouldn't say why.

*Shortly after 5:00—a quiet moment.*

"I hate all this." Bonaparte tore at his sash.

"Be still."

"You look majestic, General," Fauvelet said, helping Bonaparte on with his jacket.

"I've never seen you looking so . . . pressed," I said with a smile. Bonaparte was most comfortable in old, worn clothes.

"Is that supposed to be a compliment?" He did not smile. "Fauvelet, you're lucky. You don't have to make a fool of yourself in public, as I do."

"Madame Bonaparte?" One of the movers gestured toward a mountain of trunks. "Do these *all* go?"

I nodded. Moving, on top of everything else. Any minute, I would collapse. "As you have said yourself, Bonaparte, the people need to see you, they need a spectacle."

"So you do listen to me."

"Bonaparte, I'm always listening." Tweaking *his* ear.

Hortense, Émilie and Caroline came gliding into the room, twirled for inspection. I fixed Hortense's hair ribbon. Caroline's dress was tight on her, but there was nothing to be done. (Is she in an interesting condition? I wondered. Already?) "You should see Joachim's new plume for his hat," Caroline said. "It cost three hundred francs."

"What's that terrible racket?" I looked toward the door.

Eugène appeared, straddling a chair, rocking and jumping it into the room as if it were a horse. The girls and I burst into laughter. He jumped off, tamed his "steed," saluted. "Well?" Grinning. Showing off his new uniform, the uniform of the Consular Guards.

"Oh," said Hortense, breathlessly, "all the girls will be throwing their bouquets at you."

"So long as they don't throw them at my husband." Caroline crimped the bow in her hair, so that it would stand better. "See how it droops?"

Our coachman appeared at the door wearing tails. "Your coach is ready, Madame."

I looked at the clock on the mantelpiece. We were on time—miraculously. I glanced in the glass: I felt I had too much make-up on, like an actress preparing to go on stage. And then I realized that I was an actress, and this was a stage.

"Come, darling. It's time!" Caroline said to Hortense and Émilie, putting on an exaggerated air of grandeur as she swept into the corridor.

I caught Bonaparte's eye, smiled—children!—but he was preoccupied. The valet was helping him on with his boots. "I'll see you later then—after the revue?" And before the dinner, I thought, which reminded me: had the silver been packed? Worrying: should I take my new pug dogs with me now?

Bonaparte stood, pulling at the bootstrap. "I can't get my foot in." The boot went flying.

I touched his shoulder. He turned, as if startled. Addressing soldiers, Bonaparte was at ease; addressing civilians terrified him. Every Royalist country in Europe would be praying for a stumble. "It's going to be splendid," I said, giving him a kiss.


The parade *was* splendid. Eugène looked wonderful (as did his new horse Pegasus), and of course the crowds went wild for Bonaparte. It was a moving moment when the tattered flags of the Army of Italy went by. Bonaparte removed his hat and bowed his head; the crowd suddenly became hushed, reverent. This little man with such big dreams has filled all our hearts with hope. If there are angels (and there must be, surely), they are with him now.

Indeed, even my daughter is falling under his spell. As soon as the cavalry went by she, Émilie and Caroline excused themselves to go to the powder room. I remembered Bonaparte's instruction just in time. "Wait, Hortense." The military band was marching out into the courtyard, the brass instruments bright in the sun. "Just one moment, *please*."

"Why?" Caroline demanded as Hortense slipped back into her chair overlooking the palace courtyard. The members of the band were in position and an orderly was running across the courtyard with a stool for the conductor to stand on.

"I don't really know." The conductor mounted the stool and lifted his baton. The musicians raised their instruments and the opening

Partant pour la Syrie

No 1.

Piano.

chords were struck. The piece sounded familiar, yet I could not place it.

Hortense sat forward, her hands on her knees.

"Can we go now?" Caroline asked, standing by the door. Hortense raised her index finger.

"Hortense, isn't that your song, the marching song you wrote?" I asked. "*Partant pour la Syrie?*"

"Hush," she cried out. "I want to hear it!"


*Evening.*

"What did you think?" Bonaparte asked, bursting into my dressing room. "I thought it went rather well."

"It was brilliant," I said. He hadn't noticed Hortense sitting by the door.

"Why is it so dark in here? Where are the children? What did your daughter think?"

I looked at Hortense in the looking glass, smiled. Bonaparte followed my gaze. "Oh!" he said, taken aback.

Hortense stood, her hands clasped in front of her. "I was so honoured."

Bonaparte smiled and tugged her ear. (Gently, for once!) "You were surprised? Good. The musicians want to know if you would write another for them."

Hortense nodded, tongue-tied, a flush covering her pale cheeks. "Caroline is expecting me!" she cried and bolted out the door.

"Is she pleased, do you think?" Bonaparte asked, puzzled.

"She's overcome." I pressed his hand to my cheek. "That was a very nice thing for you to do."

"It's a good piece," he said, shrugging, sitting down so that the valet could pull off his riding boots. "Why do you have the drapes drawn?"

"People look in." I'd had a fright earlier when I saw a man's face pressed against the iron grill. "But it's dark in here even when the drapes are pulled back." The rooms are set below ground level; the windows are high on the wall. Sitting, one cannot look out. "Your new breeches are on top of the trunk with your sash."

In moments he reappeared, his valet following him like a shadow.

"Excellent," I said, although the fit wasn't perfect. There hadn't been time.

Mimi came to the door, lovely in a new muslin gown. "Third Consul Lebrun and his wife are—"

"Already?" I looked at the clock. It was only five! We weren't expecting guests to arrive until six.

"Good," Bonaparte said, pulling on his dress shoes. "I need to talk to him about the deficit."

"I'll only be a moment." I stood in front of the large looking glass as Mimi fastened my pearls. The Queen had studied her image in this very glass, I thought.


After dinner with the Consuls (boring!), I went on ahead to the bedroom, to prepare for my husband. I dismissed Mimi. Alone, I bathed, changed into a simple flannel gown. I was weary of lace and pageantry. Wrapped in a comforter, I sat by the fire thinking of the woman who had once sat thus, in this room, by this fireplace, also waiting for her husband to join her. Her husband: King Louis XVI. I recalled the day he was guillotined, the slow, steady roll of the drums. And then I recalled the day of the Queen's death less than a year later, a ghost of a woman already, widowed, her children taken from her. She was thirty-eight when she died, only a few years older than I am now.

Queen Marie-Antoinette. How curious it is for me to be living here, writing at her escritoire. How curious, and how very unreal.


Bonaparte arrived as the clocks chimed midnight. "I'll ring for the valet," he said.

"No, don't." I helped him out of his coat.

In his nightshirt, his head wrapped in one of my madras scarves, he regarded the room thoughtfully. "Well." He took in the bronze-trimmed mahogany bed, a monument of (ugly) ornate ormolu.

"I still can't believe we live here." I did not say, I can't accept that this horrible place is now my home.

Bonaparte went to the grandiose bed, pulled out the little step. "Come, little créole." Smiling, he bowed at the waist, arms wide, like a courtier. "Step into the bed of kings."


"Bonaparte, don't you feel as if you're in a dream?" The centre of the enormous bed was like a valley; we kept rolling into it. (I'll have a new mattress made.)

Bonaparte grunted, on the verge of sleep, and pulled me closer, his arms around my waist. "Yes," he said a moment later, "a dream of my creation."

I lacked the courage to ask him what that dream entailed. "I keep thinking of all the things that happened in this room, the kings and the queens who have slept in this bed." The kings and the queens who have lost their lives.

"And I keep thinking how lovely you are, how I'm luckier than any of those kings." His hands were roving again.

"Bonaparte, I'm serious. It frightens me, being here, living here. I don't belong."

"You're questioning God when you make such a statement." He propped himself up on his elbow.

I rolled over onto my back, looked into his sad-serious eyes. "What do you mean?" There was no limit to Bonaparte's energy, to his dreams, to what he aimed to achieve. Was it faith that gave him courage?

"Remember the fortune you were told, that you would be Queen?"

Tears came to my eyes. "I don't want to be a queen, Bonaparte."

"But I'll need you beside me," he said, joking gently.

I put my hand on his cheek. "I love you."


I lay beside my husband for what seemed like hours, listening to the sounds of the night. I could hear the prostitutes laughing in the gardens, whisperings outside our windows. I lay listening to my heart, and to the strange, silent dark of the cold marble corridors.

The bells had just rung out one note when I felt it again, that chill. Bonaparte, often so deep in sleep I fear him dead, murmured and turned, pulling the comforters around him, as if he too could feel it. I sat up, watchful. I saw a light approaching.

"Mimi?" I hissed. My heart began to pound. Only bad news came thus, in the night. I pulled the comforter around me. Why was it suddenly so very cold? And then I saw her again: that plain white gown, that plain white cap. The Queen—in prison clothes. A cry escaped me, I reached out for Bonaparte. The moment I touched him, she began to recede, fade. And then the room was dark again, and silent, but for the pounding of my heart.

# *In which I am called Angel of Mercy*

*February 22, 1800.*

"Twenty-seven already this morning," Mimi told me, her eyes wide.

Twenty-seven petitioners? Yesterday there had been twelve, and nineteen the day before. Proud, starving aristocrats, trembling beggars. Weeping women, tongue-tied men, stuttering children: all desperate, all needing help.

"Madame Bonaparte." The girl bowed. The elderly woman accompanying her was dressed in the uncomfortable style of the Ancien Régime. With the help of a walking stick she struggled to stand.

"Oh, please, do sit," I insisted. Her bustle had slipped sideways, giving her a deformed look.

"M-M-Madame B-B-Bonne . . ." the old woman stuttered, but she could get no further.

*"Bon à Parté,* Grandmaman." The girl threw me an embarrassed look.

"Mademoiselle de Malesherbes, is it not?" The girl had come to me weeks earlier. I guessed her to be twelve years in age, thirteen perhaps.

"You remember!" She flushed.

What I remembered was the charm of her devotion to her grandmother, whose name had been put on the List during the Revolution and who was destined to die in Germany, alone, far from her family, her loved ones.

I took the elderly woman's hand. "Then you must be Countess de Malesherbes."

"In Germany they call you the Angel of Mercy," the old woman said, her voice clear now. She had a vise-like grip on my hand. "I want you to come to my funeral."

I smiled. "I trust it will not be soon."

"It will be a splendid fête. My daughters have promised."

"We have come to say thank you," the girl said.

"And God bless!"

Over twenty petitioners later, I was growing fatigued. No wonder thrones are cushioned. "Only one more," the hall porter informed me. "Mademoiselle Compoint."

I tilted my head to one side. "Pardon?"

He squinted at the card. "Mademoiselle Louise Compoint."

Lisette?

"I could tell her to return tomorrow, Madame."

I drummed the arm of my chair—as Bonaparte so often does, I realized. Soon I would have all his nervous mannerisms—his twitches, his tics. Soon I might even have his short temper. If only I had his judgement, I thought. Should I refuse to receive Lisette? "Send her in," I said finally, putting back my shoulders.

She looked older than I expected. There were frown creases between her eyes that her heavy make-up could not hide. She looked like a grisette,* I thought, with an unexpected feeling of sympathy . . . and guilt. I knew what happened to maids who were let go without a reference, knew what choices they had.

"Madame," she said, standing nervously before me as she had stood only four years before. "I have come to beg your forgiveness." She dropped her head, a subservient gesture as superficial as her words.

"Forgiveness is a great deal to ask." I didn't like the feeling that had come over me, the realization that I had power and she had none. "Tell me why you have come," I said finally.

* Grisette: a lady of easy virtue.

"I wish to marry, Madame—but I am in need of a dowry."

Ah, of course: she had come for money. Once upon a time, in a more trusting time, I had promised her a dowry. "You are betrothed?" I asked, both angry and repentant. None of us was innocent, if the truth were to be told.

"Almost, Madame. If I had a dowry, an English jockey would marry me, he said."

"Would you be moving to England then?"

"Yes, Madame."

"Very well then."*


*Evening.*

Fouché slumped into the chair by the fire. "Discouraged, Citoyen?" I asked. The Minister of Police had just had a meeting with Bonaparte.

"I confess to defeat. It appears I've been unsuccessful in my attempt to dissuade the First Consul from going ahead with his plan to resurrect the odious custom of the masked ball." He made a wry face. "The Laundresses Guild won out, I regret to say."**

"You will get no support from me on that score, I'm afraid." It had been over seven years since the last masked ball. All of Paris was in a state of excited anticipation, the shops displaying costumes, fanciful creations. It was impossible to buy bright silk. Everyone, it seemed, wanted to go as an Egyptian god, a Mameluke, a Turk or a harem dancer. I myself was going as a butterfly. And Bonaparte—whom I had finally persuaded to attend—as Caesar.

"That surprises me not in the least," Fouché said, tapping his snuff-box. Made of black and gold enamel, it matched his jacket exactly—a fashionable detail curiously out of place in a slovenly man. "But then, the safety of the good citizens of Paris is not your responsibility."

He offered me a pinch of snuff. I refused. "Am I being reprimanded, Citoyen Minister of Police?"

* *The marriage ended poorly and Lisette died in misery.*

** *The Launderesses Guild, one of the most powerful in Paris, had been lobbying for the return of the Mardi Gras because of all the laundry work the festivities generated.*

• 792 •

Fouché snapped closed his pretty little box and slipped it into his pocket. "Put masks on the good citizens of Paris and give them, for one night, the freedom to act without consequences?" He shrugged. "Nous verrons."

*Sunday.*

"You haven't told Émilie? She doesn't know?" Aunt Désirée was dusting her china figurines for the third time in ten minutes.

"Do you think I should have?" I asked, looking out the window into the courtyard. Why were they late? It was quarter-past three. Lavalette and his *very* special charge—Émilie's father and *my* former brother-in-law, Vicomte François de Beauharnais—were supposed to have been here fifteen minutes earlier, one full hour before Émilie herself was due to arrive. The anticipation was unendurable.

"When I told the Marquis that his son was coming, the shock almost killed him. Imagine if François had walked in without any warning? Émilie is frail, she might . . ." Aunt Désirée blinked, sniffed. "Oh dear, François is not even here and already I'm weeping!"

I helped her to the sofa and rang for her maid to bring hysteric water. "*And* the salts," Aunt Désirée exclaimed, fanning herself. "I sent the scullery maid to the apothecary this morning just to make sure we had them on hand. Oh!" she shrieked when the doorbell sounded. "It's them." With a terrified expression.

"Sit down, sit down," I said soothingly, but practically pushing her back onto the sofa. "You stay here."

"Is my hair all right?"

"You've never looked lovelier," I assured her, hurrying into the foyer where I found Lavalette helping a middle-aged man off with his jacket. It was François, looking heavier, true, and curiously old-fashioned in his powdered periwig, but distinguished, gentle François nonetheless. Without ceremony I rushed to him and took his hands in mine, blinking back tears; he looked so very much like Alexandre.

"Rose?" He folded me in his arms. It had been . . . how long? Seven years since he'd fled? In those terrible seven years his brother had been guillotined; the King and Queen had been beheaded; we'd endured a Reign of Terror and established not one but three Republics (trying to get it right). And I had remarried, a man who had saved the nation, and the Palace of Kings was now my home. "You haven't changed a bit," he said, drying his eyes.


"Fou-Fou?" Aunt Désirée exclaimed the moment François entered the drawing room, calling him by his baby name. François stooped to give the woman who had been a mother to him a tender kiss. "You look so old!" she exclaimed, crossing herself. And then she started to bawl. "I'm going to be fine, don't worry, don't worry!" she cried out, honking into an enormous kerchief.

François helped her to her feet and took her in his arms, his chin resting on the top of her coiffured hair, blinking and blinking, shyly patting her heaving back.

"That's enough!" Aunt Désirée said, standing back, sniffling. "So. There. I've wept and now I'm finished. Let's go see your father, lest he die before you even get up the stairs. Did you know that we're married now? You may call me Maman."

"Maman," François echoed obediently, smiling with tender affection.

I caught Lavalette's eye. "Émilie will be here at four," I whispered to him, glancing at the clock. Only fifteen more minutes.

"I'll wait for her down here," he said, taking off his silly round hat and running his hand across his balding head. "Does she know?"

I rolled my eyes, shook my head and ran up the stairs.

François was standing on the landing outside his father's door, his hand on the crystal knob. "Désirée—*Maman*—told me to wait out here," he said, his voice nervous.

"Go, go," I said, taking hold of his elbow, urging him in.


The room smelled of aromatic vinegar and roses.

"Father?" François said, with a hint of disbelief in his voice. The shrunken man in the feather bed was not the stern patriarch he'd known.

"Let's wait downstairs," I whispered to my aunt.

The Marquis held out his trembling hand. François pressed his father's fingers to his lips. His face was glistening with tears and his lower lip was quivering uncontrollably.

I tugged at my aunt's sleeve. "Let's leave them alone together," I repeated. Frankly, I didn't know how much more my heart could take. But just as I said that, I heard light footsteps on the stairs—Émilie?

She appeared in the door, her veil covering her face.

"François, there's someone here to see you," Aunt Désirée said.

Émilie began backing out of the room, but her husband was behind her—she couldn't. "Don't be frightened, sweetheart," I said, reaching for her hand.

"Émilie?" Her father's voice was thick with emotion.

"Don't be silly," Aunt Désirée said. "This is your father."

With aristocratic gentility, François bowed. Émilie slowly raised her veil.

"Very well, that's enough tears for today!" Aunt Désirée said, opening the window and taking a deep breath of cold air. "Whew!" she exclaimed, fanning herself. "Whew."


*[Undated]*

A blissful day at Malmaison. Rollicking games of Prisoner's Base with the children on the lawn, Bonaparte laughing. We debated (noisily!) who would play what parts in the play we've decided to put on (Corneille's *Mélite*). And then, chess in the evening in front of the fire, Bonaparte cheating (or trying to), the children teasing, in an uproar! "You can't do that, Papa," Hortense blurted out, objecting.

*Papa.* Bonaparte smiled, caught my eye. He looked as if he'd just been blessed.


*February 25.*

"Why are you laughing?" Bonaparte stood before us in a badly draped white toga, a haphazard crown of gold leaves circling his brow.

I tried to control the laughter that was welling up in me, but it kept overflowing, sending first Hortense and then Eugène into a fit. Bonaparte looked so serious.

"That's it. I'm not going," he said, pulling off the crown. Four golden leaves fluttered to the floor.

"Bonaparte, no!" We all jumped up in protest. "It's perfect," I assured him, and then Hortense and Eugène joined in. "With your Roman features, your profile, it gives you a heroic look."

He regarded us without expression. "Then what, may I ask, do you find so amusing?"

"*We* know you are Bonaparte," Hortense said, sweetly taking his arm.

"Nobody else will," Eugène joined in.

"You'll be in disguise," I assured him.


Of course Bonaparte was recognized immediately. The ballroom was thronged, yet the crowd parted reverently when he approached. (Fortunately, no laughs.)

I clasped his hand—it was clammy. Crowds made him uneasy, I knew. Perhaps he was right, perhaps this had been a mistake, I thought. I looked over my shoulder. Roustam, dressed as himself, was not far behind.

"Is that Émilie?" I asked Hortense, nodding toward a young woman in a medieval gown, a veil covering her face. She was standing with her husband Lavalette (a knight) and another man I could not place at first. Her father François, I realized suddenly, dressed as a Revolutionary in long pants, short jacket and bonnet rouge.

"And isn't that Aunt Désirée?" Eugène asked.

"I don't believe it," I said. Aunt Désirée, dressed incongruously as a Gypsy, was seated beside the dear old Marquis, who was wearing his old (*very* old) Commander-of-the-Navy hat.

"There's Caroline, with Murat," Hortense said.

"Ah!" The Viking and the belly dancer—staring into each other's eyes. (Who would have thought that a rough soldier like Murat would fall so deeply in love, and with a girl like Caroline—his *wife*?)

A man in a black hood appeared before us: Fouché, dressed as Death. "I'll stay close by," he assured us.

"How comforting," I said.

Suddenly there was a flurry of excitement by the door, raucous cheers, rude hoots. Four women had made a rather dramatic entrance dressed as wood nymphs, their brief tunics (transparent over flesh-coloured shifts, so they looked naked) ending at their knees.

"Maman!" Hortense hissed. "It's Citoyenne Tallien—with her legs showing." She looked away, horrified.

My Glories! Followed by Fortunée's blinking husband Hamelin (dressed as a Venetian gondoliere) and a pretty little man dressed as a jester—Captain Charles? An old woman dressed as a harlot clung to his arm: Madame Montaniser. Rich old Madame Montaniser.

Bonaparte turned to Fouché. "Those women are half-naked. It's unacceptable."

"I'll take care of it," Fouché said.

The contredanse was about to begin. "No, wait." I grabbed Fouché's sleeve. "I'll talk to them."


Thérèse embraced me with open arms. "I have to tell you something." I pulled her into an alcove. How was I going to put it? "There's a bit of a problem." I took a breath. "Bonaparte is concerned about . . . dress." *Un*dress. "So." I swallowed. "So it might be best if you left, you and the others."

"But we just got here." She had to raise her voice to be heard.

I grimaced. "I'm afraid you will be asked to go—by the police—unless you leave." A tall man appeared at the edge of the dance floor, his hand on the small of his back. He was wearing a mask—the face of Lazare Hoche. I put my hand to my heart.

"We haven't done anything wrong," Thérèse said.

The man in the mask turned to face me and then disappeared into the crowd.

"It has to do with . . . changes," I said, my heart pounding violently against my ribs. Was it who I feared it might be? "Setting new standards." And personal sacrifice. I felt my eyes filling. I swallowed, took a careful breath. I didn't want my make-up to smear. "Thérèse, please, don't you see?" The musicians began to play. "The Age of Fable is over, and the Reign of—" I blinked back tears. The Reign of History, I'd started to say.

"Look," she said, taking my hand, "I do understand. I know it can't be easy." She kissed my cheeks. "I'll tell the—"

But she was interrupted by Fortunée Hamelin, her forehead glistening, her bare breasts heaving. "Isn't this wonderful? Parbleu, what a fête. Thérèse, Ouvrard wants you. We need one more to make a set. *Love* your costume, Josephine." Fortunée grabbed Thérèse's hand, swirled her off into the sea of revellers.

I stood for a moment, my back against a pillar, watching the revelry. I felt dizzy from the press of the crowd, the unsettling costumes, the masked eyes without warmth.

"Madame Bonaparte, do not disappear on me again."

"Oh, it's you, Fouché." He always approached so silently.

"There is something you should be aware of." He was, perhaps, the only sober person in the room—except for my husband. "Paul Barras is here. I recommend caution."

I nodded. I knew.

"He's wearing a mask that resembles the face of General Lazare Hoche."

Fouché led me back to the head table. "Ah, there you are." Bonaparte was irked: young Jérôme, already drunk, had challenged one of Pauline's lovers to a duel. He took my hand. His sad, serious expression was a welcome contrast, somehow, to the crazed gaiety all around me. "Why are you trembling?" he asked. I heard a woman laughing loudly. I looked back over my shoulder. Captain Charles was juggling balls for old Madame Montaniser. "Did you talk to Thérèse?" Bonaparte pressed my fingers to his lips.

I nodded, blinking back tears. We had only each other, I realized. But it was enough. Indeed, it was a very great deal.

"What did you tell her?"

"I told her things had changed." Things *had* changed.

"Consul General," Fouché interrupted, "I've just been informed that the musicians intend to play Chant au départ. I think you should—" But he'd no sooner said the words than the opening chords were struck. Suddenly, everyone was cheering: *Vive Bonaparte! Peace with Bonaparte!*

"I think you would be safer on the platform, Consul General."

Bonaparte clasped my hand and tilted his head toward the platform.

"Me?"

"I want you beside me."

Fouché pushed his way through to the steps, Bonaparte and I following in his wake. When we emerged onto the platform, a cheer went up. *Vive Bonaparte!*

Over the heads of the crowd, I saw a scuffle at the back by the big double doors. Four gendarmes were escorting out the man in the Hoche mask: Père Barras. My throat tightened.

The noise was getting louder and wilder. Some had started to sing the *Marseillaise*. The ballroom walls seemed to shake with a roar of cheers: *Vive Bonaparte! Vive la République! The Revolution is over!*

I saw Joseph and Lucien Bonaparte, dressed as pirates, standing by a pillar. I bowed to them. (Gloating: Yes! I confess it.) Then I felt a tugging at my hem. It was Mademoiselle Malesherbes, my sweet young petitioner, dressed as a violet. Her grandmother, Countess de Malesherbes (with a jester's hat on), was slumped into an invalid's chair beside her. "Consulesse Bon à Parté." The girl had to yell in order to be heard. "My grandmother wants me to tell you: *Long live the Angel of Mercy.*"

I smiled and made a little wave at the countess, who clapped, grinning toothlessly.

"The Revolution is over!" a man yelled nearby, his tears ghoulishly streaking his black and white harlequin make-up.

I saw François Beauharnais in the crowd, standing by a statue of Venus, one arm clasped around his daughter's shoulders. Lieutenant Lavalette was standing behind them, hovering. He bent down to say something to his wife. Émilie lifted her veil and smiled.

It was then that I noticed Thérèse at the back of the ballroom, following Fortunée Hamelin, Minerva and Madame de Crény out the big double doors. My Glories! Thérèse threw me a kiss, waved goodbye. "Ahr-ree-veh-dayr-chee!" I heard Fortunée's husband Hamelin yell as the doors closed behind them.

*The Age of Fable is over . . .*

Then, strangely, I could see the cheering faces, but I couldn't hear the shouts. And it was then that I saw her again, in the shadow behind the two pillars: that face, set jaw, the ruffled white cap.

I touched Bonaparte's arm and I could hear again. The roaring in my ears mingled with the cheers. *The Revolution is over! over! over!*

"Long live the Angel of Mercy!" The girl tipped back her grand-mother's chair, spun it around, the old woman cackling.

"Bow," Bonaparte whispered, squeezing my hand.

I bowed and a great cheer went up. I glanced at Bonaparte. Was that for *me*?

"They love you," he said.

*Us,* I realized.

He held up my hand. We bowed to the cheering crowd.

*The Age of Fable is over . . . the Reign of History has begun.*

# *Chronology*

| | | |
|---|---|---|
| July 18-22 | Barras persuades Lazare Hoche to bring troops close to Paris. When discovered, Hoche is accused and leaves Paris under a cloud of suspicion. | |
| summer | Eugène joins Napoleon's staff in Italy. | |
| September 4 | "Journée du 18 Fructidor," led by Barras. Fifty-three deputies, suspected Royalists, are arrested. | |
| September 19 | Hoche dies at Wetzlar, Germany. | |
| October 17 | Napoleon and the Austrians sign the Treaty of Campo-Formio. Eugène takes news of the treaty to Venice, Corfu and Rome. | |
| November 16 | Napoleon leaves Milan for Paris by way of Rastadt, where the treaty will be ratified. | |
| December 20 | Thérèse and Tallien's baby dies at birth. | |
| 1798 | January 2 | Josephine returns to Paris. |
| | January 3 | Talleyrand gives a ball in Napoleon's honour. |
| | January 22 | Eugène arrives back in Paris. |
| | March 5 | The Directors approve Napoleon's plan to invade Egypt. |
| | March 16 | Napoleon and Joseph accuse Josephine of being involved in the Bodin Company. |
| | May 4 | Josephine and Napoleon leave for Toulon, where the fleet will depart for Egypt. |
| | May 18 | Émilie marries Lavelette. |
| | May 19 | The fleet sets sail from Toulon without Josephine. |
| | June 14 | Josephine arrives in the mountain spa of Plombières, where she undertakes a treatment for infertility. |
| | June 20 | Josephine falls from a balcony and is seriously injured. |
| | July 21 | Napoleon is victorious at the Battle of the Pyramids. |
| | July 24 | Napoleon enters Cairo in triumph. |
| | July 27 | Eugène writes from Egypt that Napoleon had been told suspicious details concerning Captain Charles and Josephine. Napoleon writes similarly to Joseph. Both letters are intercepted by the British. |
| | August 1 | The French fleet is destroyed by the British in the Battle of the Nile at Abukir. |

| | | |
|---|---|---|
| | September 16 | Josephine arrives back in Paris. |
| | November 24 | The contents of Eugène's and Napoleon's letters are alluded to in the *London Morning Chronicle*. |
| | December | Rumours of Napoleon's death. |
| 1799 | March 19 | Both Napoleon and Eugène are wounded during the siege of St. John d'Acre, Eugène seriously. |
| | April 21 | Josephine buys Malmaison. |
| | June | The Bodin Company comes under investigation. |
| | October 9 | Napoleon sails into Fréjus harbour on the French Riviera. |
| | October 13 | Josephine and Hortense leave at dawn to meet Napoleon on the road. (They miss.) |
| | October 16 | Napoleon and Eugène arrive in Paris. |
| | October 18 | Josephine and Hortense arrive back in Paris. Bonaparte has locked Josephine out. Reconciliation. |
| | November 9-10 | "Coup d'État du 18 Brumaire." Napoleon becomes First Consul. |
| | November 12 | Napoleon and Josephine move to the Luxembourg Palace. |
| 1800 | February 1 | Thérèse gives birth to a girl, fathered by Ouvrard. |
| | February 18 | Results of the vote on the new constitution announced: 3,011,007 in favour, 1,526 opposed. |
| | February 19 | With ceremony, Napoleon and Josephine move into the Tuileries Palace. |

# *Characters*

*Adélaïde Hoche:* Lazare Hoche's young wife

*Agathe:* Josephine's scullery maid

*Alexandre Beauharnais:* Josephine's first husband; guillotined during the Terror

*Antoine:* the coachman

*Barras, Paul:* a director; Josephine's friend and mentor

*Botot, François:* Barras's secretary

*Bruno:* Barras's hall porter

*Callyot:* Josephine's cook

*Caroline (Maria-Anunziata) Bonaparte:* Napoleon's youngest sister

*Charles, Captain Hippolyte ("Wide-Awake"):* Josephine's intimate friend and business partner

*Crény, Madame de:* one of the Glories

*Désirée Renaudin:* Josephine's godmother and aunt; she lives with the Marquis

*Elisa (Maria-Anna) Bonaparte:* the oldest of Napoleon's sisters; married to Félix Bacchiochi

*Émilie Beauharnais:* Josephine's niece

*Eugène Beauharnais:* Josephine's son

*Fauvelet Bourrienne:* Napoleon's secretary

*Fesch:* Bonaparte's uncle (by marriage)

*Fortuné:* Josephine's first pug dog

*Fortunée Hamelin:* one of the Glories

*Fouché, Joseph:* Josephine's friend, talented in undercover work

*Gontier:* Josephine's manservant

*Hortense Beauharnais:* Josephine's daughter

*Hugo and Louis Bodin:* Josephine's business partners

*Igor:* Barras's parrot

*Jérôme (Girolamo, Fifi) Bonaparte:* Napoleon's brother, his youngest sibling

*Joseph (Giuseppe) Bonaparte:* Napoleon's older brother, married to Julie Clary

*Julie Clary:* Joseph's quiet wife

*Junot Andoche:* one of Napoleon's aides

*Lazare (Lazarro) Hoche:* Josephine's former lover

*Lavalette:* one of Bonaparte's aides-de-camp

*Letizia Bonaparte:* Napoleon's mother

*Lisette (Louise) Compoint:* Josephine's lady's maid

*Louis (Luigi) Bonaparte:* Napoleon's younger brother whom he raised like a son

*Lucien (Lucciano) Bonaparte:* Napoleon's fiery younger brother

*Marquis de Beauharnais:* the father of Alexandre, Josephine's first husband, and François, Émilie's father

*Mimi:* Josephine's childhood maid, a mulatto from Martinique

*Minerva (Madame de Châteaurenaud):* one of the Glories

*Moustache:* Napoleon's courier

*Napoleon (Napoleone, in Italian) Bonaparte:* Josephine's husband.

*Ouvrard:* a financial genius

*Pauline (Maria-Paola, Paganetta) Bonaparte:* Napoleon's beautiful and spirited younger sister

*Pegasus:* Eugène's horse

*Père Hoche:* Lazare Hoche's father

*Pugdog:* Josephine's second pug dog

*Talleyrand, Charles–Maurice:* a former bishop, sometimes Minister of Foreign Affairs, always influential

*Tallien, Lambert:* Thérèse's husband

*Thérèse (Tallita, "Amazon") Tallien:* Josephine's closest friend, one of the Glories

*Toto:* Barras's minature greyhound

*Genealogies*

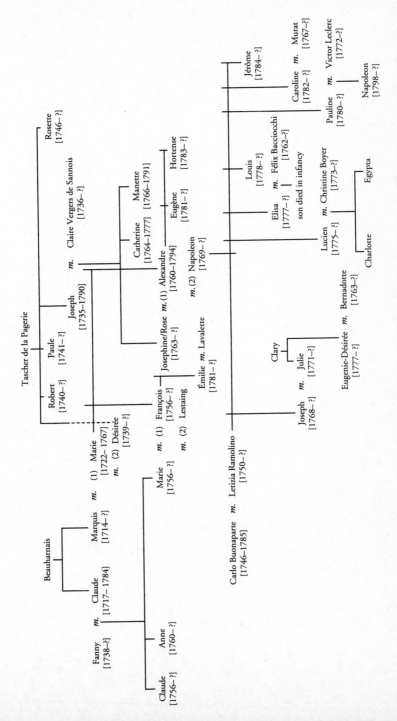

# Selected Bibliography

In addition to several hundred reference and general texts, I largely depended on the following books in writing *Tales of Passion, Tales of Woe*. I've starred the titles I recommend to readers who wish to read more about Josephine and the Napoleonic era.

Allinson, Alfred. *The Days of the Directoire*. New York: John Lane, The Bodley Company, 1910.

Aulard, A. *Paris pendant la Réaction Thermidorienne*. Vol. 3–5. Paris: Maison Quantin, 1902.

———. *Paris sous le Consulat*. Vol. 1. Paris: Maison Quantin, 1903.

Barras, Paul. *Memoirs of Barras, Member of the Directorate*. Vol. 1–4. Edited, with a general introduction, prefaces and appendices by George Duruy. Translated by Charles E. Roche. London: Harper & Brothers, 1895.

Bernard, J. F. *Talleyrand, A Biography*. New York: G.P. Putnam's Sons, 1973.

Bonaparte, Napoleon. *Letters and documents of Napoleon*. Vol. 1, *The Rise to Power*. Selected and translated by John Eldred Howard. London: The Cresset Press, 1961.

Bonnechose, Emile de. *Lazare Hoche.* Translated by Emile Pernet. Toronto: Willing & Williamson, 1881.

Bourrienne, Louis Antoine Fauvelet de. *Memoirs of Napoleon Bonaparte.* Vol. 1– 4. Edited by R.W. Phipps. New York: Charles Scribner's Sons, 1892.

*Bruce, Evangeline. *Napoleon and Josephine: The Improbable Marriage.* New York: Scribner, 1995.

*Catinat, Maurice, Bernard Chevallier and Christophe Pincemaille, editors. *Impératrice Joséphine: Correspondance, 1782-1814.* Paris: Histoire Payot, 1996.

Cerf, Léon, ed. *Letters of Napoleon to Josephine.* New York: Brentano's, 1931.

*Chevallier, Bernard, and Christophe Pincemaille. *L'impératrice Joséphine.* Presses de la Renaissance. 37 rue du Four, Paris 75006. 1988.

Cole, Hubert. *Fouché: The Unprincipled Patriot.* London: Eyre & Spottiswoode, 1971.

*———. *Joséphine.* London: Heinemann, 1962.

———. *The Betrayers: Joachim and Caroline Murat.* London: Eyre Methuen, 1972.

*Cronin, Vincent. *Napoleon.* London: Collins, 1971.

Dupre, Huntley. *Lazare Carnot: Republican Patriot.* Philadelphia: Porcupine Press, 1975.

Goodspeed, D. J. *Bayonets at St Cloud; the Story of the 18th Brumaire.* Toronto: Macmillan, 1965.

*Hortense, Queen. *The Memoirs of Queen Hortense*. Published by arrangement with Prince Napoleon. Edited by Jean Hanoteau. Translated by Arthur K. Griggs. Vol. 1 and 2. New York: Cosmopolitan Book Corporation, 1927.

Hubert, Gérard. *Malmaison*. Translated by C. de Chabannes. Paris: Editions de la Réunion des musées nationaux, 1989.

*Knapton, Ernest John. *Empress Josephine*. Cambridge, MA: Harvard University Press, 1963.

Markham, Felix. *Napoleon*. New York: New American Library, 1963.

Mossiker, Frances. *Napoleon and Josephine: The Biography of a Marriage*. New York: Simon and Schuster, 1964.

*Oman, Carola. *Napoleon's Viceroy: Eugène de Beauharnais*. New York: Funk and Wagnalls, 1966.

Saint-Amand, Imbert de. *Citizeness Bonaparte*. New York: Charles Scribner's Sons, 1899.

Sorel, Albert. *Bonaparte et Hoche en 1797*. Paris: Librairie Plon, 1896.

Tourtier-Bonazzi, Chantal de, ed. *Napoléon Lettres d'Amour à Joséphine*. Paris: Fayard, 1981.

Woronoff, Denis. *The Thermidorean Regime and the Directory, 1794-1799*. Translated by Julian Jackson. Cambridge: Cambridge University Press, 1984.

*Notes*

This novel spans the most controversial years of Josephine's life. If she has what one would call a bad reputation, it arises largely out of her actions during these four and a half years—or rather, her actions as described by a number of historians. When I began my work on Josephine, I assumed that these scandalous stories about her were true. Through years of research and consultation, however, I came to change my view. I am well aware of the accepted version of Josephine's life, well aware that this novel presents a view of her that is unique in the literature. It is my hope that a study of Josephine will someday be undertaken reexamining primary sources, and that the rumours surrounding her will then be reassessed.

The following have been excerpted from authentic documents: the letters from Napoleon throughout; Director Barras's dinner menu on page 501; the Hoche letter that Eugène quotes on page 539; Dr. Martinet's medical report on page 664; the article from *London Morning Chronicle* on page 682; the letter Eugène writes Josephine on page 683; Citoyen Chanorier's letter regarding Malmaison on page 688; the musical score written by Hortense on page 785; the various passages quoted from Jean Astruc's *A Treatise on All the Diseases Incident to Women* and other medical books. Note, as well, that the prediction that Josephine would become Queen of France is referred to as early as 1797, well before she is crowned in 1804.

Some readers may have noticed that the Hoche child was a boy in the early printings of *The Many Lives & Secret Sorrows of Josephine B.*, and a girl in *Tales of Passion, Tales of Woe*. In researching this novel I discovered my error.

Regarding currency: It is difficult to determine the value of a franc at this period in French history. Before the Revolution, estimates place the value of the franc (then called a "livre") somewhere between $1.25 and $4.50 U.S. In the period after the Terror, the economy was unstable and inflation soared. In 1795, for example, the year before Napoleon and Josephine married, a loaf of bread could cost as much as 1,400 francs, and a barrel of potatoes, 17,000.

## Acknowledgements

At times the creation of this novel resembled a team effort. Although solitary in my work, I could feel the collective goodwill of a number of people. First and foremost I'd like to credit my editor and publisher, Iris Tupholme, for the hours of creative think-sessions, her ebullient good humour, sound advice and inspired suggestions. Thanks also to Karen Hanson at Harper-Collins Canada for her careful scrutiny, Valerie Applebee, who volunteered to be part of the editorial team, Becky Vogan for her sensitive final polish, and Maya Mavjee, for her editorial feedback in the early stages. Warm thanks to Carol Shields, who was closely involved in the first draft, for her encouragement and wisdom. Both Peggy Bridgland and Fiona Foster were perceptive and supportive editors.

A number of readers gave invaluable feedback at various stages: Janet Calcaterra, Thea Caplan, Dorothy Goodman, Marnie MacKay, Jenifer McVaugh, Carmen Mullins, Sharon and Bob Zentner. Two book clubs took the time to read a draft of this novel and meet to discuss it. I'd like to thank the members of the Scarborough Book Club IV in Calgary, Alberta, and the Chapters 110 Bloor St. Book Club in Toronto, Ontario, for their insights.

A number of men and women helped me in my travel research. Prof. Egmont Lee provided the information I needed to locate Mombello north of Milan. Maurice Moncet was kind enough to open up Grosbois (now a museum) after closing hours and give me a private tour. As well, I'd like to credit the many individuals whose names I do not know who went out of their way to help: the caretaker who showed me around

Mombello (now a school); the housekeeper who showed me Josephine's rooms in the Serbelloni Palace (now government offices) in Milan; the men and women at Plombière-les-Bains who enthusiastically subjected me to a variety of water treatments.

I'd like also to thank Marc Sebanc for his help with Latin translations, Simone Lee and her mother, Prof. Valeria Lee, for help with Italian, and Translingua at the University of Ottawa (especially Christine Hug) for help with French.

A very special thanks to my two historical consultants, Dr. Margaret Chrishawn and Dr. Maurice Catinat, who gave generously of their time and knowledge. And thanks as well to Tony Kenny for passing on his extensive Napoleonic library to me: it is a daily blessing.

Story ideas come from far and near. In my community, specifically, I'd like to thank Christina Anderman for her ghost story and Fran Murphy for her parrot tales. Jim and Tish Smith put aside a stack of old medical books for me that inspired me to delve further. Chaz Este showed up at my door with a beautiful book on eighteenth-century interiors that he was willing to lend "indefinitely."

I'd also like to thank my readers, especially Lady Corry, who kept asking, "When is it coming out?" For emotional support, thanks to WWW (Wilno Women Writers), my Humber group, and to Internet writing cronies. But most of all I give a heartfelt thanks to my family: my son Chet, my daughter Carrie, and especially, my husband Richard. I could not have written this book without their support, both tangible and emotional.

# BOOK THREE

## The Last
## Great Dance
## on Earth

History is a story, as told by the victor.
—*Napoleon*

The Last Great Dance on Earth
*is a work of fiction based on (and inspired by)*
*the extraordinary life of Josephine Bonaparte.*

*For Chet and Carrie,*
*prince and princess*

I will not stand before you as time passes;
I will stand before you eternally.

—*Oscar Bearinger, "Masks and Shadows"*

*The Last
Great Dance
on Earth*

# I

## *La Bonaparte*

I was not born for such grandeur.
—*Josephine, in a letter to her daughter Hortense*

# *In which peace seems an impossible dream*

*March 2, 1800—Tuileries Palace, Paris.*
"Josephine . . . Come see the moon."

I woke with a start. A man was nudging my shoulder, his face illuminated by candlelight. "Bonaparte, it's *you*," I said, clasping his hand. I'd been dreaming of home, of my beautiful Martinico, dreaming of the sea. But I was not on a tropical island. I was in the dank, opulent palace, in the bed of Marie Antoinette and King Louis XVI—the bed of the dead. I pressed Bonaparte's fingers against my cheek. "What time is it?"

"Almost three. Come outside with me."

"Now?" I asked, but threw back the covers.

"It's a little chilly," he said, draping a cape over my shoulders.


A full moon hung over the river, bathing the gardens in a radiant light. "It reminds me of something you once wrote to me," I said, taking Bonaparte's hand. "That we are born, we live and we die—in the midst of the marvelous."

"I don't remember writing that," he said, heading toward the steps that lead down to the flower beds.

The fertile scent of spring was heavy in the air. Bonaparte brushed off a stone bench for us to sit on. I leaned my head on his shoulder, overcome with a feeling of longing. It is the season of renewal, yet I remain barren—in spite of love, in spite of prayers.

"I think best in the open air," Bonaparte said. "My thoughts are more expansive." By moonlight, in profile, he looked like a Roman statue. "See those shacks down by the laundry boats? Every citizen should have a proper home—and clean water. I'm thinking of a canal system to bring it in. And more hospitals—there should never be more than one patient to a bed. And bridges across the river would be beautiful as well as practical. Imagine it! I intend to make Paris the most beautiful city of all time."

"You will do it," I said, with confidence. What could stop him? Already so much has changed. Before Bonaparte, everything was chaos, and now prosperity prevails and France is made whole again—*I* am made whole again. Not long ago I was a widow, a survivor of the Terror, a frightened mother of two children. Now I look upon my life with wonder, for everywhere there is abundance—of wealth, certainly, and even glory, but mainly of heart. As Madame Bonaparte—indeed, as *Josephine*—I have felt my spirit blossom. This intense little man I married has inspired me to believe once again in heroes, in destiny, but above all in the miracle of love.

It was at this moment that I found the courage to voice the question I have long been afraid to ask: "Bonaparte, what if . . . ?" What if we can't have a child?

An owl's plaintive call pierced the night silence. "We must not give up hope," Bonaparte said gently. "Destiny has blessed us in so many ways."

Blessed me, certainly—blessed Hortense and Eugène, my fatherless children. "*You* have blessed us," I told him truly.

*Je le veux*, Bonaparte so often says. I will it!

If only he could will a child into being.


*March 6.*
Tonight, after a performance at the Opéra, Bonaparte was thrown a bouquet by a girl in a revealing gown, her plaited straw bonnet tied with blue ribbons. "I'll hold that," I offered.

Later I discovered a note tucked in it, inviting the First Consul to a rendezvous. I threw it into the fire. Daily, it seems, Bonaparte receives an invitation from some young maiden eager to sacrifice her virtue to "the saviour of France."

*March 7.*

I knew from the way Bonaparte pitched his battered tricorne hat across the room that the news was not good. "They refused my offer of an armistice," he said with a tone of defeat. His hat missed the chair and fell onto the carpet, startling the three pugs sleeping on a cushion by the fire.

"Again?"

"Refused to even consider it." Bonaparte threw himself into the down-stuffed armchair; two feathers floated free. "Refused to even *discuss* it." His cheek twitched. "*Pacem nolo quia infida*," he said, mocking an English accent.

"The English said that?" I rescued Bonaparte's hat from the pugs.

"No peace with . . . the infidel?" Hortense translated slowly, looking up from a charcoal sketch she was working on. She pushed a flaxen curl out of her eyes, leaving a smudge of black above her brow.

"And *we're* the infidel?" I asked (indignant).

Bonaparte got up and began to pace, his hands clenched behind his back. "The British flog their own soldiers and accuse *us* of brutality. They violate international agreements and accuse *us* of lawlessness. They pay every Royalist nation in Europe to wage war against us and accuse *us* of starting conflicts! If they don't want war, why don't they try to end it?"

"Papa, you must not give up," Hortense said with feeling. Peace is something my daughter has never known, I realized sadly. When has France not been at war with England?

"I will never give up," Bonaparte said with quiet intensity, that spirit his soldiers call *le feu sacré*: the will to be victorious—or die.

*March 9—Malmaison, our fourth-year anniversary.*

We stayed all morning in bed. Bonaparte's hopeful enthusiasm for conceiving a child makes me sad. Every time we have marital congress (often!) he names the baby—a boy, of course. This morning it was Géry—Napoleon Géry Bonaparte. Last week it was Baudouin, Gilles, Jean. Tonight, who will it be? Jacques? Benoît? Donatien?

I go along with this game, yet I know I'll not conceive. I had a hint of a show several months ago, but no longer, in spite of the tincture of senna I take to keep my body open, the endless restoratives and expulsives I consume—birthwort boiled in beer, syrup of savin, powdered aloe and iron—all bitter to the taste and bitter to the soul.

2:45 P.M.—*a lovely spring afternoon.*
"I have the perfect cure," Madame Frangeau said, pulling her cap so that the lappets would hang properly. "It has never failed."

I observed the midwife with astonishment. She was as eccentrically dressed as I'd been told to expect, her shirred gown covered with the fringes and tassels that had been the fashion before the Revolution. "Ergot?" I guessed. The mould was said to be infallible (except in my case).

"No, not ergot, not jalapa, not even scammony. Come with me."

I followed her out of her modest abode and over the cobblestones to the door of a house on a narrow street. "Madame Frangeau," I protested, "I don't think I should—"

"Madame Bonaparte, I am the midwife," she informed me with authority, pounding on the door.

And indeed, she did have authority, for all the household jumped at her command. I followed her into a bedchamber where she told a woman in bed, "Don't stir! I have need only of your infant." She instructed me to sit in the nursery, to slip my gown off my shoulders, whereupon, having cleansed me, she put the swaddled infant to my breast. "I will return in a half hour," she said, and abandoned me.

I was shaken by the beauty of this week-old baby at my breast—its milky sweet smell, the silken down of its skull—but also by the humiliation I felt being tended in this way.

Dutifully, the exuberant and confident midwife returned, dispatching me with salves and herbs and instructions to "congress" at *least* once a day. "You must drown in your husband's vital fluid."

It is my tears I am drowning in! On return I broke down, exhausted by all the "cures" I've tried, frustrated by my body's stubborn refusal to respond.

*Evening, not yet 9:00 P.M.*

Bonaparte pulled the cord of a little silk sachet, trying to unknot it. "Zut!" he said, slicing it with a meat knife. He shook the contents out over the dinner table. An enormous diamond glittered among the dirty china, the chicken bones, the half-empty plates of peas, plum pudding and cod-liver canapés. "A bauble for our anniversary," he said, flicking it toward me, as if it were a plaything.

"How many carats is that?" Hortense asked, her eyes wide.

"One hundred and forty," Bonaparte said. "King Louis XV wore it in his coronation crown. The police finally found it in a pawnshop."

"So *this* is the Regent diamond," I said, holding the translucent gem between my fingers, losing myself in its light.

*March 10.*

Time is a woman's enemy, it is said. This morning I sat before my toilette mirror, examining my face. I am thirty-six, six years older than my husband. On impulse I sent for "my" diamond. The embroidered blue velvet case was placed reverently before me. Gently, I edged the gem out of its nest.

"Hold it at your ear," Hortense whispered, as if we were in some sacred place.

I sat back, examining the effect in the glass.

"Pour l'amour du ciel," the maid said, crossing herself.

By diamond light, I seemed transformed: younger. I glanced uneasily over my shoulder, imagining the spirit of Queen Marie Antoinette looking on. She knew the irresistible lure of a brilliant—and now, alas, so do I.

*March 29, 1:15 P.M.—Tuileries Palace.*

I am writing this by the light of three candles. It is afternoon, yet dark in this room, the curtains drawn against the curious eyes of the men and women in the public gardens outside.

Hortense is to join me soon. We're going to Citoyen Despréaux's annual—

*Much later, after midnight, everyone asleep (but me).*
—Citoyen Despréaux's annual dance recital, that is.

I was interrupted earlier by Bonaparte, who showed up unexpectedly—as he does so often—humming "la Marseillaise" (badly). "I have an idea for Hortense," he said, sitting down in his chair beside my toilette table. He picked up a crystal pot of pomade and examined the etched design, the details. "General Moreau," he said, sniffing the pomade, rubbing some on his fingertips, then putting it back down and picking up a silver hair ornament. (Bonaparte is never still!)

"Ah," I said, considering. General Moreau *is* a possibility—a popular general, dapper, always in powder, with the manners of a gentleman. "But too old for Hortense, perhaps?" General Moreau is close to forty, a few years older than I am, and a good ten years older than Bonaparte.

"Did I hear my name?" Hortense asked, appearing in the door.

"Your mother was telling me what a charming young lady you've become," Bonaparte said with a fond look at his stepdaughter.

"Indeed! That gown looks lovely on you." The cut flattered Hortense's lithe figure. The silver threads shimmered in the candlelight.

"That isn't English muslin, is it?" Bonaparte asked, frowning.

"Of course not, Papa." Hortense made a neat pirouette.

"Bravo!" we cheered.

"But I'm having trouble with the minuet," she said. "In the first figure, when passing, I'm to do a temps de courante *and* a demi-jeté."

"Instead of a pas de menuet?"

"Only on the first pass, Maman. Otherwise, it looks affected—or so the dance master says. And *this* pas de menuet has two demi-coupés and two pas marchés en pointe."

"Bah," Bonaparte said.

"Why don't you show us," I suggested.

"Papa, I need you to be my partner," she said, tugging on Bonaparte's hand.

"I'll play one of Handel's minuets." I took a seat at the harpsichord.

Reluctantly, Bonaparte stood. He placed his feet in a ninety-degree turnout and stuck out his hand. "Well?" he said to me over his shoulder.

"First Consul?" Bonaparte's secretary interrupted from the door. "Citoyen Cadoudal is here to see you." Fauvelet Bourrienne's chin quivered in an attempt not to smile at the sight of Bonaparte attempting a plié. "I suggest we not keep him waiting—he's an ox of a man, and spitting everywhere."

"Cadoudal, the *Royalist* agent?" I asked, confused—and not a little alarmed. Cadoudal is the leader of the rebel faction—the faction intent on putting a Bourbon king back on the throne. The faction intent on deposing Bonaparte.

"He's early," Bonaparte said, putting on his three-cornered hat and heading out the door—relieved, no doubt, to escape the minuet.


Bonaparte's young sister Caroline was standing outside the recital hall when Hortense and I arrived. She was dressed in a short-sleeved ball gown more suited to an evening fête; only a thin froth of organdy ruffles served for a sleeve. "Joachim will be here in five minutes," she said, chewing on a thumbnail. "I made him practise cabrioles for a half-hour this morning."

"Why cabrioles?" Hortense asked. "I thought you were to demonstrate a gavotte."

"Le Maudit! We are?" Caroline took a snuffbox out of a gaudy bead reticule.

The dance master opened the door. "Ah, Madame Bonaparte— mother of my *best* pupil! How kind of you to honour us with your presence." Citoyen Despréaux patted his brow with a neatly folded lavender handkerchief.

"My husband will be here any moment," Caroline informed him, taking a pinch of snuff. "General Murat," she added, in answer to the dance master's puzzled expression.

"Of course!" Citoyen Despréaux exclaimed, casting a concerned look at Caroline's exposed arms. "You are to perform the gavotte. Mademoiselle Hortense, if you would be so kind? I'd like to consult with you regarding the layout of the room." With a studied balletic motion, Citoyen Despréaux gestured my daughter in.

"I'll see you after, sweetheart," I told Hortense, blowing her a kiss. "Is your mother inside?" I asked Caroline, lingering. She seemed forlorn, all alone.

"She's not coming," Caroline said, snapping the snuffbox shut. "She's visiting Pauline today." This with a hint of chagrin. Of Bonaparte's three sisters, beautiful (and spoiled) Pauline is clearly the favourite. Elisa, although plain, is lauded as "literary" . . . and young Caroline? Poor Caroline is illiterate and, although not plain, with her common extremities, thick neck, muscular build and what Bonaparte calls a "warrior spirit," she is certainly not what one would ever call *engaging*.

"Ah, there's your husband," I said. It was all I could do not to smile watching Joachim Murat swagger toward us, a big, muscular soldier dressed entirely in bright pink: a pink velvet coat with tails, pink satin knee breeches, even a flat pink hat embellished with pink-and-black striped feathers.

Caroline opened the timepiece that was dangling from a heavy chain around her neck. "He's three-and-a-half minutes late."

Citoyen Despréaux positioned himself before the twenty or so assembled guests—the family and friends of his students. "Bonjour! We will open our recital with the most regal of dances, the traditional minuet, a dance whose very simplicity reveals *all*: the education, the grace and—dare I say it?—the *class* of the performer. But first, the walk: the cornerstone of good breeding." He motioned to his students, who circled self-consciously.

"Observe how perfectly *this* young lady moves," he said, indicating Hortense. "The very essence of unaffected fluidity! Now, perhaps if I could have a young man to—Ah, Citoyen Eugène, fantastique."

I turned to see my son at the door, a black felt hat on his head, his unruly curls escaping. Grinning sheepishly, he approached the dance master. "But I'm in boots," I heard him whisper to Citoyen Despréaux. "I didn't expect to—"

"I only wish you to demonstrate a bow, my good fellow."

Dutifully, Eugène raised his right arm to shoulder height, clasped his hat by the brim and, slipping his left foot forward, bowed deeply.

"Voilà, the *perfect* bow," Citoyen Despréaux said, touching his lavender handkerchief to the outside corner of each eye. "Merci, Citoyen Eugène, you may be seated."

"It's a good thing he didn't call attention to my walk," Eugène whispered, taking the seat beside me. I smiled—his *lumbering* walk, Bonaparte and I call it.

Overall, the recital went well—Hortense performed brilliantly. Eugène and I were so proud! Even Caroline and Joachim managed, although Joachim made too many circles and ended up at the wrong end of the room—a common error, certainly, but one Citoyen Despréaux unfortunately felt called upon to note.

After, Caroline, Joachim, Hortense and Eugène went out for ices. I pleaded fatigue and returned to the Tuileries Palace, only to find Bonaparte in a temper, pacing back and forth in front of a blazing fire. The Minister of Foreign Affairs was sitting in front of the fire screen, watching him with a bored expression.

"Madame Bonaparte," Talleyrand said with a catlike purr. "It is always a pleasure to see you, but especially this evening. The First Consul is in need of your calming influence."

"Do not mock me, Talleyrand," Bonaparte barked. "It's not *your* life on the line."

I put my hands on Bonaparte's shoulders (to calm, yes) as I kissed each cheek. "The meeting with Citoyen Cadoudal did not go well?"

"He would strangle me with his own hands given half the chance."

"I don't know why this comes as a surprise to you, First Consul," Talleyrand said. "Citoyen Cadoudal wants a Bourbon king back on the throne and you're rather inconveniently in the way."

"The French people are standing in the way—not *me*. Two hundred years of Bourbon rule was two hundred years too many." Bonaparte threw himself into the chair closest to the fire, his chin buried in his hand.

"The Bourbons, of course, argue that two hundred years of rule confers permanence," Talleyrand said, lacing his long fingers together with a fluid motion. "They created that red-velvet-upholstered symbol of power in the throne room; they consider it *theirs*. And so long as it remains empty, I venture they will do everything in their power to get it back."

"And England will do everything in *its* power to help them."

"Correct."

"You both make it sound so hopeless," I said, taking up my basket of needlework. "Is peace an impossibility?"

"'Impossible' is not a French word," Bonaparte said.

"There is peace, and there is lasting peace," Talleyrand observed philosophically. "History has proven that the only lasting peace is a blood knot, the mingling of enemy blood—and not on the battlefield, First Consul, but in the boudoir. Peace through marriage: a time-honoured tradition."

"What are you getting at, Minister Talleyrand?" Bonaparte demanded. "You know I don't have a son or daughter to marry off to some lout."

"You have a stepson, the comely and honourable Eugène Beauharnais—"

"A boy yet, only eighteen."

"—*and* a stepdaughter, the virtuous and accomplished Mademoiselle Hortense." Talleyrand tipped his head in my direction. "Who, being female and nearing her seventeenth birthday, is at an ideal age to marry."

"I'm beginning to think you are serious, Minister Talleyrand," Bonaparte said. "Marry Hortense to an Englishman? The English would never condescend to join one of their blue-blooded ilk to anyone even remotely related to me. Have you not read the English journals?" He grabbed a paper from a pile on the floor and tossed it to the Minister of Foreign Affairs. "Top right. It will tell you who I am in the eyes of 'Les Goddamns.'"

"Ah, yes. 'An indefinable being,'" Talleyrand read out loud in English, a hint of a smile playing about his mouth, "'half-African, half-European, a Mediterranean mulatto.'"

"Basta!" Bonaparte grabbed the news-sheet and threw it into the fire, watching as it burst into flames.

"I wasn't thinking of mating your daughter to the English, frankly," the Minister of Foreign Affairs said evenly. "I was thinking of Georges Cadoudal."

"Oh, Minister Talleyrand, I trust you jest," I said faintly, my embroidery thread knotting.

## In which we have reason to fear

*April 9, 1800, 2:20 P.M.—in the downstairs drawing room at Malmaison,
a lovely afternoon.*

We made the four-hour journey out to Malmaison seeking country
quiet—only to find everything in a state of chaos. The hothouse is almost
but not quite roofed, the drapes almost but not quite hung, the fireplace
mantel in Bonaparte's cabinet almost but not quite completed. And now,
as if all that isn't enough, the first cook is upset because the second cook
put away a jelly-bag wet, and the second cook is upset because the first
cook expects him to empty the hog pails. (It's a sign of what my life has
become that I have *two* angry cooks to contend with—and this at our
country château.) Then my flower gardener—not the kitchen gardener or
the groundskeeper—tremulously informed me that three cartloads of lilac
bushes had been delivered: could he leave them in the front courtyard?
Put them behind the farmhouse, I told him. "We're expecting guests."

As soon as he left, Hortense and Caroline came into the room with
their fête gowns on, which they paraded for me to admire.

"How much did Hortense's gown cost?" Caroline wanted to know,
swishing the gold fringe at the hem to reveal a spangled satin petticoat
underneath. "Mine was four hundred and twenty-three francs."

"I believe Hortense's gown was less," I lied, to satisfy Caroline. Hortense's simple gown of fine ivory cotton was draped to imitate a toga.

"Your gown is beautiful, Caroline," Hortense said, in an attempt to
appease.

*You* are beautiful, I wanted to tell my daughter. Slender, graceful, her head crowned in golden curls, Hortense reminds me of an angel.

"Madame Frangeau says I have the look of a boy-producing woman." Caroline positioned herself in front of the full-length mirror and pushed up her bosom.

"Madame Frangeau, the midwife?" Hortense asked, her voice filled with awe. Caroline is only one year older than she, but Caroline is married and knows the secrets of women—secrets that mystify (and frighten) my daughter.

"But just to be sure, I drink plenty of red wine." Caroline leaned close to the mirror to examine her face—that flawless rosebud complexion that gives her a girlish countenance quite at odds with her masculine neck and shoulders.

"But isn't it the man who is supposed to drink wine?" Hortense asked. "Before . . ." She flushed.

"I'm not convinced one can determine the sex of a child." Four years of trying to conceive had made me a reluctant expert on the subject.

"Madame Frangeau says you can," Caroline said. "She knows all sorts of tricks. She says it's a wife's duty to produce a child, that a woman who fails to do so has been cursed. Maybe you should talk to her about your problem, Aunt Josephine."

My *problem*. "I already have," I said, chagrined, leaving the room to get my basket of embroidery threads.

"Maybe it's not my mother's fault," I overheard Hortense say on my return. I paused at the door. "After all, she had me and Eugène."

"There's one way to find out," Caroline said. "If Napoleon got another woman pregnant, then it would be clear that—" (The gall of that girl!)

"Caroline!" my loyal daughter objected.

"I didn't say Napoleon should do it, just that that's how one could make a determination. And speaking of making a determination, now that you're going to be seventeen, don't you think it's time you married?"

My cue to enter. "I happen to know a few young men who would love to be considered by Hortense—Citoyen Mun for one."

Caroline made duck-lips. "He's a gabbler and a boor."

"There are other qualities to consider," I suggested, but thinking, I confess, that *gabbler* and *boor* well described Caroline's own husband, Joachim Murat.

"I am going to marry for *love*," Hortense said, clasping her hands to her heart.

"There are many forms of love," I said cautiously. Hortense's romantic notions concern me. "An arranged marriage will often blossom into sincere devotion, while a romantic union withers with age."

"My husband loves me," Caroline said. "He does anything I tell him."

I heard footsteps approaching, a rustle of silk. Mimi appeared in the door, her hands on her wide hips. "Yeyette," she said, addressing me by my childhood name,* "the architects said to tell you the hothouse will be finished next week." She rolled her eyes up, as if to the heavens. "But it won't be finished for two months, I'll wager you."

"And we *know* that Mimi can tell the future," Hortense said, smiling at her former nanny.

"But can she say when someone's going to die?" Caroline demanded. "In Corsica, there are women who go out at night and kill an animal, but before the animal dies, they look into the animal's eyes and see someone's face and then that person dies. It's true! Any Corsican will tell you."

"No doubt, but that's not the type of thing Mimi does," I said, with an apologetic look at Mimi.

"So what *does* she do? My mother had a Negress who could predict the weather with sticks." Caroline took the last three macaroons on the plate.

"Mimi predicts the future from cards," I said.

"Then get her to tell us our futures," Caroline persisted. "I want to find out if Joachim and I will make a *you know* before he leaves on campaign in two days. Hortense could find out if she's ever going to marry, and—who knows, Aunt Josephine—maybe *you* could find out if you're ever going to be able to—"

"Do you have your cards with you?" I asked Mimi, interrupting.

"First, the birthday girl," Mimi said with a good-natured grin, pulling the worn pack out of her apron pocket.

"Oh no," Hortense said, as if faced with her doom.

---

* *Josephine's childhood name was Rose and her nickname Yeyette. Mimi had been a slave on Josephine's family's sugar plantation in Martinique ("Martinico"). She and Josephine grew up together and had a sisterly relationship. It is possible that they were, in fact, half-sisters; Josephine's father may have been Mimi's father. Josephine had purchased Mimi's freedom a few years previously.*

We watched in silence as Mimi laid out the cards in rows, seven cards wide. The Death card with its ghoulish skeleton turned up in the fifth row—but that can mean many things, I thought: *transformation, change*. The Lovers card was in the row above it. "I see a husband, and I see love," I said. But not necessarily together.

Mimi nodded slowly, pulling at her lower lip. "You will have four babies."

Hortense beamed.

"By two men," Mimi added, frowning.

"Aha!" Caroline opened her snuffbox and inhaled a pinch.

"Two marriages?" I asked. How did Mimi see that?

But Mimi had already pulled in the cards and handed me the deck to shuffle. "How about I do yours now, Yeyette?"

"Why am I *always* last?" Caroline brushed snuff off her bodice.

"Patience, Madame Caroline, we'll get to you," Mimi said, taking the cards back and laying them out. "Oh-oh—there she is again."

"You jest." But there it was: the Empress card, the Empress with her weary, unhappy eyes.

"My mother is often told she will be queen," Hortense explained to Caroline. "Even when she was a girl in Martinico she was told that—by a voodoo priestess."

"Oh, let's not talk of it!" The memory of that afternoon disturbs me still.

Caroline shrugged. "She lives in the Palace of Kings. That's almost like being a queen."

I heard a horse approaching at a gallop. "Palace of the *Government*, we call it now," I reminded Caroline, going to the window. "It's Bonaparte," I said, relieved to see his little white Arabian racing through the gate.

"I was accosted by hooligans," Bonaparte exclaimed, sliding off his horse.

Mon Dieu, no! "Near the quarry?" His hat was askew and there was dust on his uniform—but then, Bonaparte always looks a shambles. "Did you outrace them?" I asked, brushing off his frayed jacket. Bonaparte's horse is small, but fast.

He laughed and tweaked my ear. "Bandits wouldn't dare lay a hand on me. Don't you know that? Where is everyone?"

Everyone: the Bonapartes, he meant—his Corsican clan. Mother Signora Letizia, jolly Uncle Fesch and all his brothers and sisters: Joseph "the Elder" and his wife Julie, Elisa "the intellectual" and her husband Félix, Pauline "the beauty" and her husband Victor—and Caroline and Joachim, of course. Is that everyone? Oh, how could I forget young Jérôme—"the scamp"? (Bonaparte has decided to send the rambunctious fifteen-year-old to sea soon because of his extravagant debts, inclination to duel and absolute disregard for any form of study.)

Lucien "the fireball" is at his country estate and Louis "the poet" is in Brest, so that makes eleven Bonapartes. Hortense, Eugène and I bring the total to fifteen. I'll have a word with my quarrelling cooks.

*April 10—a balmy spring morning at Malmaison, cows lowing, lambs bleating.*

My daughter is seventeen today! "Now you are a woman," I told her. Her eyes filled with apprehension. I pulled back the bed-curtains to reveal a mountain of parcels, an entire wardrobe in the latest fashion—a wardrobe such as a woman wears.

My chatterbox girl was momentarily speechless. Then oh, what pleasure, opening one parcel after another, exclaiming over the laces and trimmings, the flounces and frills on all the gowns. There were quite a number: three for morning wear, two for afternoon (but suitable for receiving), two silk gowns for evening, a walking gown, a ball gown and even a lovely riding habit—accompanied, of course, by a parasol and numerous bonnets, gloves and slippers.

"This is like a trousseau, Maman," Hortense said, overwhelmed. "One would think I was getting married."

"As you will *soon*, no doubt." At this her expression darkened.

It was a beautiful afternoon for a birthday fête—we dined off tables set up on the lawn. We had just finished sherbet and syrup when who should canter up the driveway but Bonaparte's young brother Louis, holding a bouquet of hyacinths aloft like a torch.

"Louis is back from Brest already?" Bonaparte asked, squinting.

Louis dismounted his lathered horse and presented the flowers to Hortense. "Love is nature's cloth, embroidered by imagination," he said, bowing like an old-fashioned knight.

"Have you been reading romantic novels, Louis?" Hortense gave him a mocking look.

"Voltaire," he said, flushing. He looked comely in a bottle-green riding jacket, his wavy chestnut hair cut to shoulder length in the style now popular with the young.

"Who is Voltaire?" Jérôme "the scamp" asked, throwing a bread roll at one of the pugs, hitting it hard on the head.

"Maybe if you listened to your tutors once in a while you'd learn," Elisa said, between hiccups.

"The flowers are lovely, Louis," I exclaimed, to soften my daughter's teasing—and divert the argumentative Bonapartes.

"You made excellent time," Bonaparte said, embracing his brother.

"Louis is a good rider," my ever-cheerful Eugène said.

"When he's not falling off," Caroline said, helping herself to the last of the cream.

"Magnifico!" Elisa's husband Félix exclaimed. (Why?)

"A fearless rider," Bonaparte said. "I owe my life to him."

"Blood is everything," Signora Letizia said, taking out her knitting.

"Salúte!" pink-cheeked Uncle Fesch said in Italian, emptying his wine glass before a servant refilled it.

"Louis has a fast horse," Joachim Murat said, twirling a pink silk tassel. "He paid a lot of money for it—several thousand francs."

"I *love* a horse with a big chest," Pauline said, pulling down her sleeves to better display her perfect white shoulders, "and *strong* flanks."

"I have dispatches for you, Napoleon," Louis said, pleased to have met with his older brother's approval. "As you thought, English warships are blockading Brest. Our ships can't get out to sea."

"Maudits anglais," Bonaparte swore under his breath.

"Maudits anglais," Pauline's husband Victor echoed.

"You've arrived just in time," I said, inviting Louis to take a seat between me and Hortense. "We're having a ball tonight."

"At which even Papa will dance," Hortense said.

"Napoleon?" Louis asked with a sceptical look.

"I can dance perfectly well." Bonaparte looked disconcerted when we all burst into laughter.

"Other than *country* dances?" Hortense teased.

"Bah! What's wrong with country dances? They're jolly—and at least one gets a little exercise," Bonaparte said, and with that he pulled Hortense to her feet and spun her about the lawn, humming loudly (but tunelessly), while two pugs scurried after. I turned to see the servants hiding behind the bushes, doubled over laughing.


*April 11, early evening (beautiful weather).*

Proudly, we bid our soldiers adieu this morning—Eugène, Louis and Joachim, each sitting on his horse so proudly, riding off to join their regiments. (Joachim has embellished his uniform with pink gewgaws—even his horse's saddle blanket is pink. Bizarre.)

It is sad to see so many empty chairs around the table. Bonaparte mopes. He wishes he were riding out with the men. He will be joining them soon enough, I know.


*April 12—back in Paris (alas).*

Caroline has been miserable, stomping from one room to the next. I have been trying to console her, assuming that she was melancholy because her husband was gone, but it turned out she is furious because he hasn't been assigned an army of his own.

"Maybe she's a little sensitive right now because she's . . . *you know*," Hortense whispered to me from the harpsichord bench.

"Is she?"

"She must be. She told me they . . . *you know*, all night long." Hortense struck a chord, flushing furiously.

*April 28—Malmaison.*
I am writing this at the breakfast table to the sound of Caroline retching.


*Noyon*
*Chère Maman,*
   *We were days in the rain from Corbeil. Soon I expect we'll be setting out over the Alps to Italy.* *

   *The renovations at Malmaison that you described amaze me: arcades and moving mirrors? I like the idea of one big room on the ground floor instead of three little ones—better for a ball.*

   *I'm surprised Hortense has rejected Citoyen Mun—I thought he was an excellent choice. I'll think of some other possibilities.*

   *A million kisses,*

                              *Your loving son, Eugène (Captain Beauharnais)*


*April 30.*
At a salon last night, Caroline's singing was received with audible snickers. "Someone should tell her not to perform with such zest," a woman whispered to me. "People will think her impure."

   The comment angered me, and I rose to Caroline's defence—Bonaparte "zest," after all, has saved the nation—but, in truth, someone does need to have a word with the girl. She tries so hard to be noticed, but her dramatic grimaces, her quivering lips and panting sighs are only viewed as laughable.


*May 1—Malmaison, blowing rain.*
When I suggested to Caroline that her "wonderful" singing would be better appreciated if she were to perform quietly, without embellishments, she turned on me!

   "I don't need *your* help," she said with such spite that I was left speechless.

---

* *"Italy" in 1800 comprised various independent states, including several northern territories claimed by Austria.*

"Sometimes I don't know what to make of Caroline," I told Mimi later.

"She's dangerous, Yeyette," Mimi said. "I saw it in her cards."

I had to laugh. When I think of Caroline, I imagine a plump powder-puff of a girl. Jealous, yes, and temperamental, certainly—but *dangerous*?

*[Undated]*

Mimi slipped me a folded note with my morning cup of hot chocolate. "Just as I thought," she said.

*I workd in the Dineing Room all week. Shee say to her Husband they wood have Everything but for the Old Woman & her 2 Children. Shee say the 1st Consul must get rid of Her. Shee say Shee will find a way.*

"I don't understand," I said, perplexed. The note was crudely written on the brown paper used to wrap fish in. "Who is this 'shee'?"

"Madame Caroline." Mimi looked smug. "I told you she's not to be trusted."

I reread the note. Was I "the old woman"? "Who wrote this?"

"One of Madame Caroline's footmen."

"You've got a *spy* in Caroline's household?"

"Old Gontier's nephew. He can be trusted."

"Mimi, that's not a good idea! Please—don't do it again."

"So I have to pay him myself?"

"How much?" I said with a laugh. (Fifty francs—mon Dieu.)

*11:20 P.M.*

I keep rereading the spy note, puzzling over it. Can I believe it? Can I afford not to?

*May 3.*

I am writing this in the downstairs drawing room at Malmaison, at my lovely new escritoire—mahogany, with Egyptian touches in gold, *very* elegant. It is after three o'clock. Soon I'll go down to the kitchen to see how the dinner preparations are coming along. Quite well, I suspect, from the fragrant scent of roast chicken (Bonaparte's favourite) that fills the air. I just sent two of the domestics to ride out to meet Bonaparte on the road. I worry about his safety, frankly. "But whatever you do, don't let on that I sent you to meet him," I warned them.

*May 4—still at Malmaison (we return to Paris in the morning).*
Old Gontier, my man-of-all-work, informed me around one this afternoon that the stonemasons had left, that the mantel was finally finished.

At last, I thought. The stone dust has been driving us mad.

"But Agathe says to come see," Gontier said. "There's something she wants to show you."

The mantel looked excellent, although the scullery maid had quite a job to do cleaning up the dust. "You wanted me to see something, Agathe?"

She got up off her knees, wiping her hands on her stained apron. "This." She pointed to a snuffbox on the desk.

I recognized the intricate mother-of-pearl inlay in a Roman motif. "It's Bonaparte's."

"But the First Consul's is chipped on one corner."

She was right. All Bonaparte's possessions are scarred in some way. "Perhaps someone left it here," I suggested, feeling its weight. But why an exact replica? "Agathe, could you ask the groom to send for Fouché?" I said, carefully putting the box back down.

"The Minister of Police?"

Yes, I nodded. My old friend—the man who knows everything.

"Poison," Fouché said, prying the snuffbox open with his long yellow thumbnail. "When inhaled, it will cause the victim to expire within one revolution of the minute hand."

Poison! I sat down, opened my fan. If it hadn't been for Agathe's apprehension, her sharp eye . . . ! "Are you sure, Fouché?" Had murderers been in our midst—in our *home*? The masons, perhaps? I'd offered them refreshment, inquired after their well-being.

"Someone went to some trouble making a replica." Fouché traced the inlay with his finger. "The First Consul must be notified immediately."

"He's here now," I said, hearing a horse. Only Bonaparte comes through the gate at a gallop—he knows no other pace.

"*Poison* in my snuffbox?" Bonaparte scoffed.

"It's not really yours, Bonaparte," I told him. "It just looks like yours."

"It's an excellent reproduction. Who made it?"

"One of the stonemasons, likely," Fouché said.

"But *why*?"

"Certainly, there are any number of possibilities, First Consul. Revolutionaries long for a return to anarchy and the Royalists for a return to monarchy. Extremists of every persuasion want you dead. It is, one might say, the price of your popularity."

"It looks like snuff." Bonaparte started to take a pinch. I grabbed his hand. "I'm not *that* easy to kill off," he said, laughing.

"Bonaparte, at the very least you shouldn't ride alone," I told him. "You should have someone with you." And guards at all times, and . . .

"Bah!" Bonaparte said, glowering.

"First Consul, with respect, I suggest you consider it," Fouché said. "A minimum of precaution would put your wife at ease. For some reason, she prefers you alive."

"I refuse to be coddled like some feckless ninny!"

"Don't worry," Fouché told me later, on leaving. "We'll protect him. We'll just have to make sure he doesn't know it."

## In which I try (but fail) to accept

*May 5, 1800, 11:45 P.M.—Tuileries Palace.*
Bonaparte and I had just returned from the Opéra when his sister and brother were announced.

"Joseph has something urgent to discuss with you before you go," Caroline said. Bonaparte's older brother Joseph stood behind her, dressed entirely in pale yellow brocade.

"Before I go where?" Bonaparte demanded.

"To Italy," Caroline answered, offering her snuffbox to her brothers before taking a pinch herself. (She claims it calms her sickness of the stomach, which has been violent throughout her first month.)

"How did you find out I'm leaving? No one is supposed to know."

"What we want to know is what happens if you get killed," Caroline said, refusing my offer of a chair. Joseph sat down instead, his hands pressed between his knees.

"If I die—or rather, *when* I die—I'll be put in a coffin," Bonaparte said evenly, reaching for a paper knife and slicing open an envelope.

"It's not a jesting matter, Napoleon! Who would run this country?" Caroline paced with her hands behind her back (as Bonaparte so often does), her masculine movements at odds with her ensemble: a gauze creation wildly embellished with bows and wired flowers.

"According to the Constitution, the Second Consul," Bonaparte said, looking up from the letter.

"Cambacérès?" Joseph's voice was tinged with disgust.

"*That* would set an interesting example for the nation," Caroline said scornfully. "Imagine—the French Republic led by a man who claims that a country is governed by good dinner parties, whose passions run to food, expensive wine and young men."

"Second Consul Cambacérès is a highly capable individual." Bonaparte crumpled the letter and hurled it into the roaring fire.

Oh-oh, I thought. I rang for the butler: a collation. *Anything.*

"Your successor must be within the clan," Caroline said, squaring her shoulders.

"And I am the eldest," Joseph said, scratching the end of his nose.

Bonaparte looked at his brother and laughed. "*You* want my job, Joseph? You don't know what's involved. You'd have to rise before eleven. You might actually have to work a day or two."

"It is our right!" Caroline said, her cherub cheeks pink, her eyes blazing.

"*My* right," Joseph said.

"The French Republic is not a family fiefdom!" Bonaparte exploded.

By the time the butler arrived with a tray of wine and sweetmeats, they had departed in a temper. Mon Dieu.

*6:30 in the morning (cold).*
Bonaparte left before dawn. "I'll be back in a month, I promise," he said, pulling a greatcoat on over his consul's uniform.

"Please, Bonaparte, take me with you." My trunk was packed!

"I need you in Paris, Josephine. No matter what you hear, you must act as if all is well."

"Even if I hear what?" I asked warily.

"Even if you hear that I've been defeated, or that I've been killed. Even if you hear that your son has been—"

*No!* I put my fingers over his mouth.

"The public will be watching. They will assume that you know. *Always* tell people I am victorious."

"But what if the rumours are true?"

"I'm not going to be defeated. I have you, don't I? My guardian angel," he said, kissing me tenderly—his good-luck kiss, he calls it.

*Le 21 Floréal,\* Geneva*

*I love you very much. My Josephine is very dear to me. A thousand kindnesses to the little cousin. Advise her to be wise, do you hear? N.*


*May 14—Malmaison.*

Hortense squinted to make out Bonaparte's messy scrawl. "I think that says 'little cousin,' Maman." She frowned. "What little cousin?"

"Are you sure that's what it says?" I asked, taking the letter back—flushing, I confess. Bonaparte has a habit of referring to a very private part of me by code name. "It must mean something else," I said, turning so that she might not see my smile.


*May 24, 1800, Aosta*
*Chère Maman,*

*A quick note just to let you know that we are over the Alps. The passage took five days. It was icy—we literally slid into Italy! So large an army has not crossed the Saint-Bernard Pass since the days of Charlemagne. It made me realize how much can be accomplished by a leader who has perseverance and knows his own mind. You know of whom I speak.*

*Your devoted son, Eugène*
*Note—Citoyen Henri Robiquet is a good possibility.*


*May 30—Paris.*

"My brother has requested that I give you thirty thousand francs out of his account, Madame," Joseph said with a hint of a bow. "I thought it wise to take care of the matter before I made my departure." Belatedly, he removed his hat and stuck it under his arm.

"You're leaving, Joseph?"

"I'm departing for Italy this afternoon."

---

\* *May 10. A new calendar had been established during the Revolution. The months were named after the natural world. (Floréal, for example, meant month of flowers.) The weeks were ten days long and ended with "Décadi," the day of rest. Confusion resulted because people continued to use the traditional calendar.*

"You'll be seeing Bonaparte? If only I had known—I could have accompanied you."

"It was an abrupt decision."

"Is there a problem?" I asked, suddenly fearful.

"My brother Napoleon may die."

I felt for the back of a chair to steady myself. "Whatever do you mean?"

"And Lucien has claimed the right to succession."

"Lucien *Bonaparte*? What right?" I asked, confused. Anyway, wasn't Lucien in mourning for his wife?

"Exactly! Lucien may be Minister of the Interior, but I am thirty-two and Lucien has only just turned twenty-five. I am the eldest. It is *my* right, not his. This must be settled immediately, before Napoleon is killed in battle."

"Oh," I said weakly. "Of course."


*June 14, Saint-Germain-en-Laye*
*Chère Madame Bonaparte,*
*I know how busy you are these days with official and unofficial duties, but perhaps you could spare a moment of your time for your poor aunt and her ailing husband? The Marquis has taken a turn. If you are unable to call, at least pray for him.*

*Your godmother, Aunt Désirée*


*June 17—Saint-Germain.*
Aunt Désirée met me at the door, her face white with rice powder. "Thank God you're here! The Marquis is dying—from strawberries, of all things."

"Aunt Désirée, please don't alarm me. Are you serious?" I don't know why the possibility of the old Marquis's demise surprised me. We'd celebrated his eighty-seventh birthday not long ago. It was a miracle he was alive, but because he had lived so long, I'd come to think he would always be with us.

"Oh yes, I assure you, he is at the heavenly gates. My goodness, but it's a hectic business. The doctor has been here three times today already, and each time costs eleven livres—I mean francs. What *do* we call money now? I wish they'd stop changing the names of things. Perhaps you could have a word with your husband about it."

"It is francs now." The air was as thick as that in a hothouse. There were fresh-cut flowers on every surface. "Did you get my letter about Eugène being safely over the Alps?"

"And that's another thing," Aunt Désirée said, her hand on the stair railing. "If we're at war with England, why are we fighting Austria? And if we're fighting Austria, why are we fighting in Italy?"

"It's hard to explain," I said, following Aunt Désirée's ample posterior up the stairs. How did we get onto politics? And what about the Marquis! "The flowers are beautiful," I observed, changing the subject.

"The mayor of Saint-Germain sends us a fresh bouquet every day," Aunt Désirée said, her taffeta skirts swishing with a voluptuous languor I found disconcerting, under the circumstances. "Monsieur Pierre, we call him. He and the Marquis played piquet together every evening—until the Marquis ate all those strawberries and started dying, that is," she said, coming to a stop in front of the Marquis's bedchamber, catching her breath. "Monsieur Pierre won every game, and so that's why he sends flowers."

"Oh," I said, trying to figure out the logic.

"The doctor applied leeches to the Marquis's stomach and then a laxative blister, which very nearly carried him off right then and there," Aunt Désirée hissed, so that a maid dusting the wainscotting should not hear. "Frankly, the doctor is a simpleton! He objects to the turpentine enemas I give the Marquis, when it's perfectly obvious that I've been keeping my husband alive all these years with them."

*Turpentine?*

"Mixed with snail water," she assured me, her hand on the crystal doorknob, "which I make with sweet wine from the Canary Islands—but where am I supposed to buy Canary wine now? If I'd known there was going to be war with England again, I'd have bought a supply. Maybe next time your husband decides to make war, he can let me know ahead of time."

Aunt Désirée had so many misconceptions, I didn't know where to begin. "Bonaparte tried to get England to agree to a peace, but—"

"The solution is plain to see, my dear. If we gave the Pretender his rightful throne back, England would leave us alone."

Put a Bourbon king back on the throne? Had we gone through the Revolution for nothing? "Aunt Désirée, it's not—"

"I don't care what people say," Aunt Désirée said with conviction. "Too much freedom is not a good thing. What's wrong with feudalism? It's impossible to get good help these days, for one thing. Marquis de Beauharnais," she yelled, throwing open the door. "It's Rose to see you. You remember: *Yeyette*. Or Josephine, as she's calling herself now."

The Marquis, sunk deep into the centre of a thick feather bed, turned his head slowly. "You know—Madame *Bonaparte*," Aunt Désirée yelled in his ear.

"Bon à Part Té!" the dear man croaked.


*June 18—still in Saint-Germain.*
I'm taking a quiet moment to reflect (strengthen). The Marquis went quietly—"Like a lamp without oil," Aunt Désirée said—in the arms of his wife and his son François. Even dear old Aunt Fanny managed to arrive "in time," dressed for the occasion in a sequined ball gown of tattered ruffles.

The Marquis's last words were whispered to me: "Marry Hortense to a man with good teeth." I told Aunt Désirée that he said, "I married a good woman."

I'm surprised, frankly, to feel so overcome. The Marquis had a good long life, and he didn't suffer. May God be with him, may he rest in peace.


*June 21—back in Paris.*
A mounted courier sent by the Minister of Police brought me back to Paris in a state of alarm. "You look pale," Fouché observed, on greeting me.

"I'm anxious, I confess." Paris seemed deserted. "Why are the streets so empty?" And why had he sent for me?

"Everyone has headed south in the expectation of hearing news from

Italy," he said, tugging at his stained cuffs. My friend was expensively attired, but even so the effect managed to be shoddy.

"What news?"

"The city is rife with rumours. In every café in the Faubourg Saint-Antoine idlers are claiming that your husband's army has been defeated in Italy. The opposition is openly making plans to snatch the Republic from the grasp of 'the Corsican'—as they call the First Consul."

"Bonaparte has been defeated?" How was that possible?

"As well, there are rumours—false, no doubt—of the First Consul's death."

I put my hand to my heart. *Rumours*, he'd said. "Is nothing known? Have there been any reports?"

"There *has* been a setback, apparently."

"Fouché, *please*, be honest with me," I said, my voice tremulous. "Is it possible that the stories are true?"

"It would be misleading to deny it." Fouché cleared his throat. "You should know that there is also talk of your son—of his death," he added quietly.

I clasped the arms of my chair. I would not be able to endure such a loss!

"It's only gossip," Fouché assured me, handing me a crumpled cambric handkerchief. "You must not dwell on it. All eyes will be on you tonight."

The reception for the foreign ambassadors! "Minister Fouché, I can't possibly go. I've already sent a message to the Minister of Foreign Affairs explaining that there has been a death in my family, that I am unable to do the honours. And now, what with this news . . ."

"But you *must* be there. The factions are poised, ready to attack. At the least hint that the First Consul has fallen, the nation will be plunged into civil war." At this Fouché's eyes widened. "Which is why we are counting on *you* to play the part of Victory."

*Nearly 2:00 in the morning.*

I recalled Hortense's acting lessons as I spoke my lines, presenting the backs of my hands, elevating them on the word "victory," my eyes sweeping the room as my arms gradually ascended to the highest point. "The First Consul is not only alive, but victorious!"

Following a measured applause, I turned away (trembling). Had they believed me?

"I think so," Fouché said, without moving his lips.

It was into this strained atmosphere that a messenger was announced shortly after midnight. My heart jumped when I saw that it was Moustache, Bonaparte's courier. Grinning under the impressive facial appendage which had earned him his nickname, the mud-splattered rider laid two tattered Austrian flags at my feet. Bonaparte *had* been victorious!

*June 22, Sunday.*
Salvoes of artillery announced the victory at noon. Giddy with delirium, the servants danced down the halls. "The Funds have gone up seven points," Mimi announced, calculating an excellent profit.

*Milan*
*Chère Maman,*

*Before the Austrians knew it, we were upon them! I led a charge and captured an Austrian officer—che buona fortuna! Papa has promoted me to head of my squadron.*

*We had a good skirmish in spite of the difficulties. The plains of Marengo were not very good for cavalry—too many streams and ditches. Pegasus was cut on the flank but will heal—luckily, for many horses were lost. I was fortunate to get away with only two sabre cuts on my saddle cloth.*

*The citizens of this country have hailed us as heroes—you should see the celebrating!*

*Papa said to tell you he will write soon.*

*A million kisses,*

*Your proud son, Eugène*
*Note—It's true what they say, Maman: Italian women are very pretty.*

*June 24.*

"I'm told that the people of Milan have gone mad with gratitude, that the women literally throw themselves at the feet of our soldiers," the artist Isabey said, studying his cards.

"Italian women are *so* hot-blooded," the actor Talma said.

"All women have a weakness for a conqueror," the writer Madame de Souza said, artfully using her cards as a fan.

"Oh?" I said, pulling in my winnings. Bonaparte has not been writing.

*July 2, or rather July 3, after 3:00 in the morning (can't sleep).*
Bonaparte returned quietly, before midnight. Within an hour, crowds had gathered in the gardens, men, women and children waving flambeaux: an eerie, ghostly sight.

"We rejoice in you," I said, wrapping my arms around my husband, holding him. Holding him.

*July 4.*
Bonaparte is home; he is victorious, all is well. Why, then, do I feel so melancholy—so alone?

*July 5—Malmaison for the day.*
"How *are* you, darling?" my dear friend Thérèse asked, straightening her wig of infantine blond—her disguise.* I must have sighed heavily, for she spread her bejewelled fingers and exclaimed, "Mon Dieu, that bad?"

"Can't I hide anything from you, Mama Tallita?" Thérèse and I have been through much together. One might even say she saved my life. Certainly, she enriches it with her wit and wisdom—and abundant heart.

"You know better than to even try," she said, tapping my knuckles with her painted fan.

---

* *Thérèse was separated from her husband (Tallien) and living openly with a married man (Ouvrard), by whom she had a number of children. Publicly, she was perceived as a "fallen woman," and Napoleon did not want Josephine to associate with her. Nevertheless, the two friends continued to meet secretly at Malmaison.*

I confessed the reason for my depression of spirits: my suspicion that Bonaparte was having an amourette with another woman. "Since his return from Italy, he has been curt with me, impatient without reason." Thérèse winced. "You've heard something?" I asked.

"It's just a rumour—something about that Italian singer from Milan."

"La Grassini." Of course! Young and voluptuous, La Grassini is renowned for her passionate nature, her angelic voice. Two years ago I arranged for her to sing for us in Italy. I remember Bonaparte's enthusiasm, remember the buxom Italian singer's caressing eyes. Bonaparte had been oblivious to her all-too-obvious invitation—then.

*July 6, 4:15 P.M.—Paris.*

"Is it true that the prima donna of La Scala has come to Paris?"

"La Grassini?" Fouché withdrew a battered tin snuffbox from his vest pocket. "She arrived in a carriage drawn by eight black horses, rather hard to miss. All the people of Paris saw her."

"And what else have all the people of Paris seen?"

He gazed at me with his heavy-lidded eyes. "Perhaps you should first tell me what you yourself see."

"It is natural to become watchful, when suspicions are aroused." I paused, turning my wedding ring. It had become oblong, rather than round; it fit my finger perfectly. Too perfectly, perhaps. I could no longer remove it. "Do you know what I would dislike? I would hate to be the last person to know if my husband were . . ." I felt my cheeks becoming heated.

"Exercising the right of kings?"

I nodded. More and more, I was learning about the "right of kings." I counted silently to three and then looked up at him. "No doubt you would know."

"It is my business to know." Fouché spit into a spittoon. "As you suspect," he said, wiping his mouth on his sleeve, "your husband has fallen for La Grassini's charms."

"A soldier's wife understands these things," I managed to say. "It will blow over, like a squall."

"You are wise, Madame, the perfect wife."

*[Undated]*
The perfect wife is angry! The perfect wife spent a fortune this afternoon, ordering five hats, six pairs of gloves, four pairs of slippers and two pairs of boots, not to mention a number of small linens in fine cambric, embroidered and laced and beribboned. Not to mention a new gown by Leroy, the most celebrated designer in Paris.


*July 7, 3:45 P.M.—hot!*
"A Bastille Day ensemble? A gown for the wife of the victor?" Leroy's eyes glazed over, as if a vision had come to him, a vision of mystical dimensions. "Mais oui! I see antique ivory gauze, *swirls* of cascading silk with appliquéd gold laurel leaves, a *plush* golden velvet shawl, embroidered in gold and edged with ermine. Laced slippers, long gold gloves with pearl buttons—of course!—a bandeau of laurel leaves made of pearls . . ."

"Perfect." *Wife of the victor.*

"But Madame Josephine," Leroy said, tugging on the knot of his starched azure neckcloth, "the First Consul is frugal, and . . ."

The *frugal* First Consul is spending twenty thousand francs a month on a mistress, I happen to know. "You were saying, Citoyen?"

"Well, it's only fair to warn you that ermine is . . . Well, right now I'm afraid it is perhaps a little *dear*, perhaps too . . . ?"

"Spare no expense."


*July 9—Tuileries.*
Madame de Souza announced at whist this afternoon that after the age of thirty a woman cannot expect to have first place in her husband's heart, that she should be content to be second.

"That would be worse than death itself," I said heatedly (losing the round).


*July 10—Malmaison (bright moon, dark thoughts).*
"I hate to tell you this, darling, but she's right," Thérèse said, giving me a vial of Compound Spirit of Lavender—a remedy for women feeling a

great sinking. "If it's not La Grassini, it's bound to be some other trollop. Husbands are like that. It's one of the things a wife must accept. Has he been doing his duty by you?"

I nodded. If anything, Bonaparte's attentions have been more ardent than before.

"Then what do you have to complain of? Just because he has a mistress doesn't mean he doesn't love you."

Love? Bonaparte had not loved me—he'd *worshipped* me. "You don't understand!" How could I possibly explain what it was like to be loved by a man such as Bonaparte, to be his muse, his angel, the object of his all-consuming passion? Am I to lie beside him now while he dreams of La Grassini, smell her musky scent on him, hear the joy in his voice as he sings, knowing that it is love for another that inspires him? "Accept it, Thérèse? Never!"

"Do you want your husband's enduring love?"

"Of course," I said angrily.

"Then repeat after me: I *accept*—with love, grace and magnanimity." She laughed. "And no gritting of teeth."

*[Undated]*
Three hats, two gowns, seven pairs of slippers, five pairs of silk stockings, two shawls, a necklace of rubies and pearls.

*July 14, Bastille Day, almost midnight.*
It was almost time to leave for the Bastille Day fête when Eugène arrived from Milan. "You made it!" I threw my arms around my son. He smelled of horses—horses and campfire smoke.

"Oh là là, Maman!"

"Is something wrong?" I asked, alarmed by his outburst.

"No, not at all. It's *you*. You look . . . beautiful!"

Eugène and his chasseurs escorted Bonaparte and me to the Invalides. A deafening cheer went up as we pulled through the gates of the Champs-de-Mars, the enormous field a sea of faces.

Inside, the Invalides was packed, the air oppressive. I was moved to tears as Eugène solemnly presented the captured enemy flags. Then Mademoiselle Grassini sang, filling the vault with (I had to admit) heavenly sounds. It pleased me to note that she has developed a double chin and was wearing too much Spanish Red.*

* *Spanish Red: red dye in a horsehair pad, used as a blusher.*

## In which we are very nearly killed

*July 22, 1800—Paris.*
At the Théâtre Français tonight, the police apprehended a man aiming at Bonaparte with a peashooter.

Bonaparte laughed when Fouché informed him. "You're serious—a peashooter? They're going to have to do better than that."


*August 7.*
I can't sleep. This morning ruffians were caught lurking in the quarry on the high road to Malmaison. Their intention was to attack Bonaparte as we returned to Paris.


*August 9—very hot.*
Fouché sidled up to me at tonight's salon. "No, don't tell me," I said, my heart jumping in my chest. "I can't take it!"

"Calm yourself. I merely wish to inform you that La Grassini is discontented with your husband."

"Oh, thank God! I thought perhaps there had been another attempt on Bonaparte's life." In every shadow I saw a man with a knife. The slightest noise confirmed my fears. "What did you say about La Grassini?"

"She complained of the First Consul at the salon of the Minister of Foreign Affairs last night."

"*You* were at Talleyrand's?" Talleyrand and Fouché are arch-enemies.

"My spies keep me informed. La Grassini confided to those assembled at the whist table that the First Consul's lovemaking was . . . *unsatisfying* was how she put it." He pronounced the word "unsatisfying" with unseemly relish.

"I take no comfort whatsoever in her indiscretion." How dare she!

*October 10—Paris, very late.*

On returning from the Opéra tonight, Bonaparte and I found Fouché waiting for us in the Yellow Salon, tapping his foot. The Minister of Police was not happy. The commotion we'd heard during the performance had been his men apprehending assassins armed with daggers and pistols—men intent on murdering Bonaparte!

I scooped up my train and sat down on the edge of a stool. "Assassins?" But what shocked me even more was that Bonaparte had known about the plot for weeks, but had not informed Fouché, thinking that he would lure the conspirators out into the open himself. "Bonaparte, you knew those men would be at the Opéra?" I was stunned—and *angry*. How could he be so cavalier? Not only had he put himself at risk, he'd put *me* at risk as well.

"Your husband not only knew the assassins would be there tonight," Fouché said, "he arranged to provide them with the money they needed in order to carry out their scheme. Have you any idea, First Consul, how close you came to getting murdered?"

I trembled for Fouché. Bonaparte does not take a scolding well, however justified.

"The plan worked, Minister Fouché." Bonaparte paced under the crystal chandelier. "I'm fed up with Revolutionaries intent on my demise—and so I took action. If this little episode proved anything, it proved that there is a great deal going on in this city that you are entirely unaware of. You don't know anything!"

"Respectfully, First Consul, I know a very great deal," Fouché said, his lips thin. "I know, for example, that a man in a greatcoat regularly emerges from the palace, gets into a hired fiacre and goes to 762 Rue Caumartin, an abode which he has leased for the use of a well-applauded

Italian singer. A short time after, the man in the greatcoat reappears and returns to the palace. Within an hour of his departure, a tall young man, a violinist, is seen to enter the home of the energetic Grassini, who—"

"Get out!" Bonaparte kicked a burning log.

I followed Fouché into the antechamber. "How could you do that to him!"

"Devotion wears many masks. The First Consul endangers himself by such conduct."

"You humiliate him in the name of duty?" I turned on my heel, trembling with emotion.

I found Bonaparte in the bedchamber, sitting on our big bed, unlacing his boots himself. "We can pretend I was not witness to that scene," I said, sitting down at my embroidery frame by the fire.

"Just as you have pretended not to know, Josephine?"

I picked up my embroidery needle, checked the colour of the thread, a shimmering light blue, the colour of a summer sky. My hand was shaking. "Yes." I put down the needle. "*Please*, Bonaparte, get up and pace the way you usually do. I don't like it when you are so still."

"I'm surprised you aren't angry."

"I've been angry. Now I'm angry at *her*." La Signorina Grassini had not only seduced my husband—worse, she had made a cuckold of him.

"I've been a fool."

I put aside my frame and went to him. "Don't be angry at Fouché," I said, taking his hands in mine—his soft, feminine hands of which he is so proud. "He spoke out of devotion for you."

"Do you know how much I love you, Josephine?" The firelight danced in his grey eyes.

Later, in Bonaparte's arms, I took advantage of his gratitude to persuade him to take at least a few precautions against attack. And no more trying to ferret out assassins on his own! Reluctantly, he consented. "You love me too much," he complained.

"We all do!"

*October 18—Tuileries Palace, Paris.*

Early this morning, Fouché was shown into our bedchamber. I sat up, alarmed. It was dark still. "This must be urgent, Citoyen Minister of Police," Bonaparte said, instantly alert.

"A bomb stuffed with nails and grapeshot exploded behind the Salpêtrière convent a few hours ago. The culprits got away, but I have reason to think they had you in mind, First Consul. I thought you would want to know."

"Mon Dieu, Bonaparte—a *bomb*?" Would there never be an end to it?


*Christmas Eve—Paris.*

The worst has happened. At least we are alive, I remind myself.

It is three in the morning now as I write this. I'm in the little sitting room next to our bedchamber. The embers cast a dying light. I've given up trying to sleep. Perhaps if I write it out, the memory of this evening will stop haunting me.

Caroline, eight months along now, joined Hortense, Bonaparte and me for dinner. We were looking forward to going to the opening of Haydn's *La Création*—all of us but Bonaparte, that is, who announced that he'd changed his mind, he had work to do. (Even on Christmas Eve.)

"Please come," I begged him, knowing how disappointed the public would be not to see him, how unhappy they would be to see only *me*. "You've been working so hard lately." Day and night, his energy was boundless. "It's going to be splendid." (Oh, recalling those words! If anything had happened to him, if he had been killed!) "It would please me," I said finally, knowing he would not refuse.


The coaches were lined up in the courtyard in readiness. A footman jumped to open the door of the first carriage for Bonaparte and his aides. "The ladies will follow with Colonel Rapp," Bonaparte instructed César, his coachman, who grinned broadly, clearly in his cups. César cracked his whip and the horses charged out the gate.

"We do not need to follow *quite* so quickly," I instructed our driver as Hortense and Caroline were handed in. I was about to follow them when

Colonel Rapp suggested that my shawl, which is embroidered with an Egyptian motif, would look lovely arranged in the Egyptian manner, tied at the waist. I paused to change it. We owe our lives to this delay!

This next part is painful to recount. As our carriage turned the corner onto Rue Nicaise, we were thrown into the air by an explosion. Colonel Rapp yelled at us to cover our heads. I remember the sound of timbers cracking, the strong smell of gunpowder.

"It's a plot to murder Bonaparte!" I cried out. (I'm ashamed to admit that I lost my head.) There was rubble all over the street, and what seemed to be a very great number of people, some writhing, some lying still—*bodies*, I realized with a shock. And then, slowly, a chorus of cries filled the air.

Suddenly our coach was flying pell-mell. "Stop!" I heard myself scream. The horses had bolted, taken the bit. "Turn back, they've killed him!" The memory of it makes me tremble even now.

Our carriage finally pulled to a stop in the Tuileries courtyard. "You will excuse me, ladies?" Colonel Rapp said, struggling with the carriage door mechanism. He hit it with his fist and jumped out.

It seems a dream to me now—much of it in fog, yet other scenes sharp, the memory painful. "There has been an explosion on the Rue Nicaise," I heard the coachman say. "Grand Dieu, things were flying!"

I recall someone asking if the First Consul had been injured.

"I don't think so," our driver answered. "He went on ahead."

"Are you all right?" I asked the girls, my voice shaky. Hortense appeared calm, though pale. "Caroline?" What a terrible thing to happen to a young woman in her delicate condition!

"Where's a footman?" Caroline said, looking out the shattered window. "Why doesn't someone come to hand us down?"

Hortense pulled a handkerchief out of her reticule. "Imagine what would have happened if we had left a few seconds earlier!"

If I hadn't stopped to rearrange my shawl, if I hadn't . . .

"It was just a house on fire," Caroline said.

A footman came running. Limping after him was a cavalier with a gash under his chin, leading his horse by the reins. "The First Consul was not injured!" the cavalier said, his voice quavering.

"Thank God," Hortense whispered.

"Are you sure?" I demanded. "Did you *see* him?"

"He is at the Opéra, Madame Bonaparte—you are to join him there. Another carriage is being prepared for you."

I was to go to the Opéra? I wasn't sure I could even walk! "Of course," I said, pulling my shawl around me, as if this was what one did after a violent explosion: one proceeded to the Opéra. A prick of pain reminded me that there was glass everywhere. "What happened? Do you know?" I asked as he handed me down. I felt tremulous, but I could stand.

"Apparently a barrel of gunpowder exploded."

"A barrel?" The explosion had lifted our carriage into the air! "Were many people hurt?" *Killed.*

"I suggest you take a different route," the soldier said over his shoulder, giving Caroline a hand.

People were crowding into the courtyard. I saw Mimi making her way through to us, wiping her hands on her apron.

"There's been an explosion!" Hortense cried out to her.

"Bonaparte's all right. I'm to join him at the Opéra."

"*You're* going, Yeyette?" Mimi asked, frowning.

"I'm fine." I needed to see Bonaparte; I needed to know he was safe.

"I'm coming with you, Maman," Hortense said, her blue eyes swimming.

"What's happened to your hand?" There was blood on her left thumb.

"It's just a little cut, from the glass."

"It has stopped bleeding," Mimi said, examining the wound. She withdrew a patch of plaster from her pocket and secured it to Hortense's hand with a handkerchief. "Stay close to your mother," I heard her whisper as a carriage pulled up beside us.

"What about me?"

"Caroline, you really must—"

"I'll look after Madame Caroline," Mimi assured me, her hand firmly on Caroline's shoulder.

"Best send for the midwife, just to be sure," I called out as we pulled away. "Madame . . . " My mind was in a fog.

"Madame Frangeau," Hortense called back as our carriage pulled into the roadway, the soldier escort riding alongside, his horse wild-eyed.

Bonaparte was sitting in the theatre box drinking an amber liquor. "Josephine," he said, standing and removing his hat. And then, with a little bow, "Is something the matter?"

Did he not know? Talleyrand caught my eye, made a gesture with his hand behind Bonaparte's back: Be quiet, stay calm, the First Consul knows, the audience is watching.

"You're just in time," Bonaparte said, turning toward the stage. Madame Barbier-Walbonne's voice filled the hall—the oratorio had begun.

I wrapped my shawl around me, as if by bundling myself tightly, I might stop the trembling. Hortense put her bandaged hand on my shoulder, to calm. I stroked her fingertips. How close death had come.


Once we were back in the privacy of our suite at the Tuileries, Bona-parte's calm gave way to fury. "Every time I turn around, someone's trying to kill me," he raged at Talleyrand. "Têtes des mules! It's all these bomb-making Revolutionaries, longing for the days of anarchy and violence, the same fanatics who were responsible for the explosion at the Salpêtrière convent, no doubt."

"*And* the Opéra plot," Talleyrand observed, propping his gold-tipped walking stick against the arm of the chair. "And likely the snuffbox plot, too, for all we know."

"This is intolerable." Bonaparte threw a log on the flaming fire, send-ing sparks flying.

"Did the Minister of Police ever convict any of these Revolutionaries?" Talleyrand asked. "His friends and colleagues, one might note."

"And what is that supposed to mean?" Bonaparte demanded, his fists on his hips.

"It means that Fouché should be arrested and shot, in my opinion."

Shot! Talleyrand's words shocked me.

"There has been enough bloodshed tonight, Minister Talleyrand," I was relieved to hear Bonaparte say, passing off Talleyrand's remark as a joke.

Shortly after Talleyrand left, Fouché himself was announced. "Where have you been?" Bonaparte demanded.

"At the site of the explosion, First Consul," Fouché said, touching the brim of his battered hat. "Seven killed and over twenty injured."

Mon Dieu!

"I suggest you give your drunken coachman a reward, First Consul," Fouché continued, tugging at his stained linen cuffs. "Had he not been so reckless, you would be dead. The keg of gunpowder appears to have been set intentionally."

"Damned Revolutionaries!"

"They would like to murder you, certainly, but they are not guilty of this act."

"Surely you're not going to claim that it was the work of the Royalists," Bonaparte scoffed. "Royalists may intrigue, but they do not stoop to violence."

"I say it, and what's more, I will prove it."


*January 2, 1801—Malmaison.*
"I'm so relieved you're all right, darling!" Thérèse exclaimed, removing a leather mask,* a cloak, a hat *and* a wig. "I very nearly died when I read the news-sheets." She embraced me vigorously, enveloping me in a cloud of neroli oil. "How terrifying it must have been!"

"I'm at the end of my strength," I confessed. Fouché insists that Bonaparte's Mameluke bodyguard follow him everywhere. Roustam even sleeps outside our bedchamber door at night. "As well, Fouché has posted two guards *inside* our bedroom," I told her. Every few hours they wake Bonaparte, who assigns a new password. Accustomed to sleeping on the battlefield, Bonaparte falls quickly back to sleep. I, however, lie awake all night, fears swirling, trying to ignore the presence of the guards.

Thérèse tapped a flower-shaped beauty patch stuck to her chin. "Make sure you have your doctor bleed you, but not much, just a bit. Cooling laxatives are called for—an infusion of senna with salts. It will be over soon, won't it? I heard that the police have discovered the owner of that cart."

A cart with a barrel of gunpowder in it: the "infernal machine" everyone

---

* *It was not uncommon for a woman to wear a leather mask to protect her skin from the weather.*

is calling it. "They know who he is, but they can't find him, Thérèse!" One Petit François—a man with a scar over his left eye. "So long as he walks free, I cannot feel safe, no matter how many guards watch over us."

*January 6—Tuileries Palace.*
Given that human temperament is composed of four humours—blood, bile, phlegm and melancholy—I'd say that the members of Bonaparte's family have an excess of bile.

Oh, how uncharitable of me! But truly, sometimes they are too much even for Bonaparte. "I turn into a wet hen around them," he told me last night after Kings' Day with the clan—or rather Cake Day, as we're to call it now.

After sharing the latest news (the scar-faced man has yet to be found), plans for the season, and the usual discussion regarding status, money and bowels, we got onto that other clan favourite: my fertility—or lack thereof.

It began innocently enough, with Caroline announcing that her midwife had told her that her baby-soon-to-be-born is a boy.

"Because of all that red wine you've been drinking," Pauline said, resplendent in a revealing gown of white satin.

"It's the man who is supposed to drink the wine," Bonaparte said.

"That's what *I* thought." Hortense blushed.

"What would you know about such things?" Caroline said. Swathed in ruffles and sequins, her big belly prominent, she looked like a carnival balloon.

"What does it matter whether your child is a boy or not?" Elisa asked Caroline. "It won't be a Bonaparte. It will only be a Murat."

"At least that's better than a Bacchiochi," Caroline retorted.

"Magnifico!" Elisa's husband Félix exclaimed. (Why?)

"Blood is everything," Signora Letizia said, frowning at her knitting.

"Speaking of Bonaparte offspring, I have an announcement to make." Joseph pressed his hands between his knees. "*My* wife is expecting a child."

"Our prayers have been answered," Uncle Fesch sang cheerily, swirling wine in his goblet and then holding it to the light.

"Cin-cin! Cin-cin!" Everyone raised a glass.

"That's wonderful news, Julie." I caught Bonaparte's eye. If Julie and Joseph could conceive a child after years of trying, then perhaps we could, too.

"I credit the waters of Plombières," Julie told me.

"Not *my* waters?" Joseph looked pleased with his bad jest.

"Aunt Josephine already went to Plombières—in 1796," Caroline said. "It didn't help her."

"That's likely because of her age," Elisa said, holding her breath to prevent a paroxysm of hiccuping.

"Spa waters can be dangerously exciting," Uncle Fesch observed, his cheeks heated by the fumes of the wine.

"Pauline has been unable to have a child since our son was born almost three years ago," Victor Leclerc said, adjusting the set of his tricorne hat—an exact replica of Bonaparte's.

"And we've tried *everything*," Pauline said, languorously fanning herself with a peacock feather. "The doctors say I'm a mystery."

"Mystery, dear sister? Erotomaniacs are often unable to procreate." Caroline shot her sister a gloating look.

"Erotomaniacs?" Hortense looked confused.

"I'll explain later," I mouthed to her.

"*Or* it could be due to an abnormal state of the blood," Caroline observed. (Addressing me!) "Certain diseases—which I will not mention in front of Mother—are believed to inhibit conception."

"How long before dinner, Josephine?" Bonaparte asked, pacing again.

"I had thirteen children," Signora Letizia said, twirling yarn around her stiff index finger.* "Five of them died."

"A wife has a Christian obligation to produce children," Uncle Fesch said.

"Sons," Joseph said, giving his wife a tight smile.


*January 22.*
Caroline has had her baby—a boy, just as the midwife predicted. I've

---

* *Due to an injury, Signora Letizia could not bend her index finger.*

sent over one of our cooks. Caroline's cook has resigned in protest because Signora Letizia insists on keeping a live frog in the kitchen in case the baby shows symptoms of thrush. I pray that this does not happen, for if it does, the infant will be induced to suck on the live frog's head.


*[Undated]*
Can't sleep. Still no sign of the scar-faced man.


*January 31—Paris.*
At last! This morning, the police discovered the scar-faced man asleep in a bed in a garret. He confessed, revealing the name of the man who had paid him to explode the bomb—the name of the man who had paid him to *murder* Bonaparte. "Georges Cadoudal," Fouché said with a slow (smug) smile. "Safely in England, regrettably."

The Royalist agent! "So you were right, Fouché—it *was* a Royalist plot," I said.

"It is proverbial," Fouché said, offering Bonaparte a pinch of snuff before taking one himself. "The Seine flows and Royalists intrigue. It is the nature of things."

"Intrigue and murder are not the same, Minister Fouché." Bonaparte paced in front of the fireplace with his hands clasped behind his back. "The devil!" he cursed, halting abruptly. "England's behind this."

## In which my daughter is impossible to please

*July 5, 1801—a hot Sunday morning at Malmaison.*
It's confirmed: Hortense, her cousin Émilie and Bonaparte's mother are
coming with me to Plombières. Colonel Rapp, who is to accompany us,
has just informed me that we are to be escorted by a detachment of
cavalry and three aides. The last time I went to the spa, I had only Mimi
for company. My life has become so complex—now we require a carriage
just for our trunks of ball gowns.

*July 8 (I think)—Toul, very hot.*
We have stopped for a few moments at an inn while the horses are
changed and the wheels cooled—tempers cooled. The girls are lively,
Signora Letizia disapproving, Colonel Rapp ill. I endure.

*July 10—Plombières-les-Bains.*
We've arrived, at last—the trip was harrowing.*

* *Hortense and her cousin Émilie composed the following letter about the journey: "Never has
there been a more agonizing journey to Plombières. Bonaparte mère showed courage.
Madame Josephine trembled in fear. Mademoiselle Hortense and Madame Lavalette argued
over a bottle of eau de Cologne. Colonel Rapp made us stop frequently in order to ease his bile.
He slept while we forgot our troubles in the wine of Champagne.*

*"The second day was easier, but the good Colonel Rapp was suffering still. We encouraged
him to have a good meal, but our hopes crumbled when, arriving in Toul, we found only a
miserable auberge which offered nothing but a little spinach in lamp oil and red asparagus*

"Madame Bonaparte," the spa doctor said, regarding me with rheumy eyes, "I, more than anyone, understand the delicate nature of this subject. When the reproductive powers are defective, few women have the courage to speak to a physician. It is evidence of your sincere wish to give your husband the fruit of your love that you have returned to Plombières. The condition can be rectified, but first you must tell me *everything*."

"Everything?" Flushing, I recounted the efforts Bonaparte and I had made to produce a child—the periods of abstinence followed by periods of coital activity, the techniques Bonaparte had undertaken in order to expel slowly, the herbs I'd taken to increase my "receptivity."

"And yet nothing." Dr. Martinet studied the thick file of papers. "From what your doctor in Paris indicates, there hasn't been a show since . . ."

"For over a year," I admitted. And that merely a hint.

"On your previous visit, we ruled out malformation of the canal. As well, the feminine characteristics are clearly in evidence." He pushed his spectacles onto the bridge of his nose. "It's therefore likely that a morbid condition of the blood is to blame."

I felt my cheeks becoming heated. Did he think I might have some shameful disease?

"A chronic decline! When the blood has become bankrupt, there often follows a failure of the reproductive function, leading to derangement." His spectacles magnified his eyes. "It is generally believed that an enfeebled uterus is the cause, but I am of the opinion that that organ is entirely dependent."

"Oh?" I said, confused.

"The causes of a uterine decline are indolence, nutritional perversion or the taking of drastic medicines."

---

simmered in sour milk. (*We would have loved to see the gourmets of our household seated at this disgusting meal!*) *We left Toul in order to eat at Nancy because we'd been starved for two days.*

"*We were joyfully welcomed when we arrived in Plombières. The illuminated village, the booming cannon, all the pretty women standing in the windows helped us not to feel sorry about being away from Malmaison.*

"*This is the exact story of our trip, certified to be true.*"

Did he suspect me of indolence? "I eat well," I said, wondering what constituted nutritional perversion and whether Mimi's rabbit-bone remedy might be considered a drastic medicine. Three knife-tips of bone shaved off the ankle of a rabbit shot on one of the first three Fridays in March were believed to stimulate the uterus. (But had failed to stimulate mine, alas.)

"Of course you do, Madame Bonaparte! In *your* case, acute suppression of the menses was caused by a violent disturbance, suffered due to imprisonment during the Terror. Such derangement of the blood calls for *baths*: foot baths, sitz baths, even vapour baths are proven to be beneficial."

"I take baths daily, Dr. Martinet." A practice Mimi considered ruinous.

"And you've been ingesting the uterine tonic I prescribed?"

"The viburnum? Dutifully." I sat forward on the hard oak chair. "Dr. Martinet, may I ask you something?" I ventured hesitantly, clutching my fan. "I'm thirty-seven years old, as you know—far from young, admittedly, but not yet what one could call . . ." I paused, not knowing what word to use. "You once suggested it possible that I was in the turn of life."* And if so, could I please turn back?


*July 17.*
When not taking the waters and all manner of remedies, I'm entirely occupied with delicate and time-consuming discussions sounding out the parents of prospective husbands for my lovely but persnickety daughter. There are a few excellent possibilities. I am hopeful.


*Sunday afternoon, July 26.*
"I don't like him." Hortense crossed her arms over her chest.

"But Hortense," I said, trying not to let my exasperation show, "Eugène even recommends him. Citoyen Robiquet is a gentleman, intelligent and well-educated. He has such good manners." I felt like a fair vendor, hawking my wares. "Don't you like the way he enters a room?

---

* *Josephine began menopause in her early thirties, likely due to the trauma of her imprisonment during the Terror.*

The way he ties his neckcloth? *Very* elegant. And so charming! And from a very good family." *Wealthy.* "What do you not like about him?"

My daughter refused to say, her expression glaring defiance. Later, I learned the reason for her stubborn refusal: she'd discovered the young man rolling on the floor with one of my pugs. "Undignified," she pronounced, refusing to be swayed.

*[Undated]*
"Too short."

*[Undated]*
"Too tall."

*[Undated]*
"Too—"

"No! Don't tell me!" I clasped my hands together—hard. I felt like strangling my daughter. The objection to one young man had been that he could not dance; the problem with another was that he had eruptions on his cheek. (Only two.) And yet another wore a silly hat. (High fashion in England.) All honest young men of good family! "Let me guess." I paced in front of the fireplace, as Bonaparte does when he is angry. "He's too educated, not educated enough. Too wealthy, not wealthy enough. Too aristocratic, too common, too . . ."

Hortense's chin puckered. "My thoughts exactly!" she exploded angrily, and stomped out of the room.

I give up!

*July 29, 1801, Saint-Jean-de-Maurienne*
*Chère Maman,*
*Hortense has rejected all those suitors—even Citoyen Robiquet? I'll try to think of some other possibilities. She's not easy to please!*
*I was elated to learn that England has finally agreed to negotiate. You see?*

*Papa's tactic is working: force Austria to sign a peace treaty, and then England will have to follow.*

*A million kisses,*

*Your loving son, Eugène*

*Note—I've sent Uncle Joseph a note of congratulations on the birth of his daughter, although a letter of condolence might have been more in keeping, knowing how much he had hoped for a son.*


*August 1, very hot—Plombières.*

We're packing, getting ready to head back home. Hortense slumps about with a long face. Marry she *must*.


*August 8—Malmaison.*

Bonaparte greeted me with a lusty embrace. I feel like a field in spring— plowed and well-fertilized.


*August 17—Malmaison.*

Family gathering here tonight. Caroline brought Achille, who is seven months old already. She is feeling ill, she announced, suffering nausea and vomitings every morning. (Yes, she is with child again.)

Bonaparte held little Achille for almost one hour. My throat tightened watching him. What a good father he would be, doting and proud.

Faith, the water doctor told me. I must have faith.


*August 25, 10:15 P.M.*

Bonaparte was in a playful humour tonight as we gathered in the drawing room before dinner. Hortense (looking lovely in her new spotted silk gown trimmed with lilac ribbons) was sitting on the settee, working at her frame. "Well," Bonaparte said, reaching over to tug her ear, "I've just been to your room and read all your love letters." He often teases Hortense in this way, but this time, instead of smiling and shrugging, she made an awkward excuse and hurriedly left the room.

Bonaparte and I looked at each other: what was *that* about? When she returned for dinner, Bonaparte asked if she had secrets. "No, Papa!" she said, then chattered non-stop about her acting lessons, how much she was learning from the great actor Talma, about the ball she and Caroline had gone to the night before, so charming a fête she "almost suffocated" (the highest praise). "Both Citoyen Dupaty and Citoyen Trénis danced a quadrille with Madame Récamier," she chatted on (and on). *Everyone* said (she said), and *she* agreed, that Citoyen Trénis is a much better dancer than Citoyen Dupaty, that even Citoyen Laffitte is a better dancer than Citoyen Dupaty, and Citoyen Laffitte does not know how to make the grand bow with the hat. Citoyen Trénis's jetés have verve, she said, and although they perhaps lack in grace, his spirit is lively and vigorous, and as for . . .

After exactly fourteen minutes (as usual), Bonaparte threw down his napkin. "You'll excuse me?"

Hortense and I were left in silence. "Now," I said with a smile, passing her some bonbons on a platter, "about running off to your room so mysteriously—is there anything my daughter might want to tell her mother?"

And then, with obvious relief, Hortense confessed that Bonaparte's aide, Christophe Duroc, had slipped a letter into *Lives of the Saints*, a book she had been reading.

"*Duroc* wrote you a letter?" I asked, concerned. I don't care for Christophe Duroc (phlegm), and not just because he is known as "the procurer." He is handsome, in a fashion, and fanatically loyal to Bonaparte, but his manner is cold—I can't imagine him loving a woman. And in any case, it is improper for a young man to write a girl a letter; many a reputation has been ruined for less.

"I did not open it, Maman," Hortense hastened to assure me—but confessing that she *had* tried to read it without breaking the seal. "I only wished to see how a man proposed."

*Proposed!* "Hortense, a gentleman who respects a young woman wouldn't propose without discussing it with her parents first," I said carefully. And a gentleman who respected a girl wouldn't write to her unless they were already engaged.

*September 2—Paris.*
It has been almost one month since I returned from Plombières, and still no change. *Faith.*


*September 3.*
Bonaparte's young brother Louis has taken to joining us in the drawing room evenings, reading aloud from Young's *Night Thoughts* while Hortense sketches and I sit at my tapestry frame. (Bonaparte, of course, is usually in his cabinet immersed in work.) Now and then Louis will look up and gaze at Hortense as she applies charcoal to a self-portrait.

I wonder—


*September 5, late afternoon.*
Is it possible that Louis is in love with Hortense? He, Bonaparte and I were enjoying a pleasant conversation yesterday evening on the subject of German literature when Hortense came into the room. Abruptly Louis stopped talking. No persuasion on our part could induce the crimson-flushed young man to continue. "The silent one," Hortense teased, oblivious to the powerful effect she has on him.


*Shortly after 2:00 A.M.—can't sleep.*
Why haven't I considered Louis before? He is twenty-four (a good age), serious in his demeanour, not unattractive, intelligent. Educated, literary. Since his fall from a horse in Italy, his health has been a concern—he uses his right hand with increasing difficulty—but it is not a congenital problem and will no doubt improve with treatment. He's a bit moody, sometimes, but gentle (he dotes on his mongrel water spaniel). Generous features, a nice height. Excellent teeth.


*September 8.*
I've been to see Madame Campan for advice on staff. As a former lady-in-waiting to Queen Marie Antoinette, she is invaluable, but as Hortense's

former schoolmistress, she is even more so. I told her all I've been going through trying to find a suitable husband for Hortense, all the excellent young men who have been introduced to my daughter, how she has rejected them all. I told Madame Campan my concerns: that Hortense has formed an ideal in her mind that no man can live up to, that the novels she reads have given her romantic notions, that she is intent on a love marriage, a practice that is becoming more and more common, true, but so often ends in misery.

Madame Campan looked alarmed. "A *love* marriage is out of the question," she said firmly, smoothing her black gown, which was modest in design, without frippery or devices. "Young people are swayed by emotion—they are unable to choose wisely. Your daughter is intelligent. I am confident she will come to the conclusion that the French system is superior to any other. Who do you have in mind?"

I told her that although I'd not yet discussed it with Bonaparte, I was coming to the conclusion that his brother Louis might be ideal.

Madame Campan sat back with a satisfied look. "I was going to suggest that you consider Louis. Even if he were a repulsive candidate, I would recommend him, for the benefits to you, your husband—indeed, the nation—are abundantly clear to all concerned."

*Abundantly clear.* "Certainly, but—"

"But fortunately, he is not a repulsive candidate. Louis is a reflective individual. He is kind and has simple tastes, as does Hortense. They share a poetic sensibility. And his feelings for your daughter?"

"Frankly, I'm beginning to suspect Louis may be in love with her."

"They would have handsome children."

Oh yes! And what a joy it would be for Bonaparte and for me. Their children would unite us, console us if we are never able to . . .


*September 8—Paris.*
"Josephine?" Bonaparte nudged my shoulder. "Are you awake? I've been thinking: what about Louis? As a possible . . . *you know*, for Hortense."

"What a good idea!" I said, wrapping my arms around him. "Why didn't I think of it?"

*September 10.*

"Bonaparte, we must do something about Hortense and Louis."

"Do what?" Bonaparte asked, closing the book he was reading, a history of the Emperor Charlemagne, holding his place with his finger.

"You know—what you talked about."

"That's a woman's job," he said, opening up the book again. (Breaking its spine.)

"But someone needs to talk to Louis, and really, it should be you."

"What do I know of such matters?"

"More than you think," I said with a smile.


*[Undated]*

"So I talked to my brother." Bonaparte sat down beside my toilette table, examined my gown (approvingly), the embroidered lawn, the décolleté. "Louis *is* in love with—"

"Bonaparte!" I hissed, rolling my eyes in the direction of my hairdresser.

Citoyen Duplan laughed, fluffing out my side curls. He'd persuaded me to try a rhubarb and white wine tint, which gave my chestnut hair a hint of gold. "Madame Josephine, you know me better than that."

"I know you too well."

Then Bonaparte's secretary appeared at the door. (It's always like this now: bustle and turmoil.) "First Consul, Minister Talleyrand wishes to have a word with you."

I took my husband's hand. "And?" What about *Louis*?

"And he agreed," Bonaparte said with a shrug, standing up.

"That's all?"

"I'm not in the room!" Duplan said, digging in his case of combs. "I'm invisible."

"He was going to anyway, he said." Bonaparte lowered his voice. "Now someone needs to talk to you-know-who, see if you-know-who would be . . . you know: *receptive*."

"Nowhere to be seen!" Duplan exclaimed, throwing up his hands, turning his back.

"I don't think I should be the one to discuss it with her." It would put too much pressure on her. "Best to have someone outside the family, I think."

"Fauvelet could do it," Bonaparte said.

"Certainly," Fauvelet said. "Do what, First Consul?" I heard him say as he followed Bonaparte out.

"Citoyen Duplan, I'm serious, don't you dare say a word," I told my hairdresser immediately after the door had closed. "Not even a whisper." *Especially* not a whisper.


*4:30 or so.*

This afternoon, when Bonaparte's secretary came to model the new jacket I'd designed for him (it's excellent—even Bonaparte has requested one), I told Fauvelet our thoughts. "Louis is gentle and affectionate and he cares for Hortense sincerely. Were they to marry . . ." I outlined the benefits to all concerned. "I agree with Bonaparte that you are the ideal person to approach Hortense on this delicate matter." Well—perhaps not ideal, but . . .

"I know, Madame Josephine, the First Consul discussed this with me, but I don't think I could—"

"You and Hortense play in theatricals together. You have a companionable relationship. *Please.* Would you mind? Could you just find out what her feelings might be?"


*September 13.*

"She wept, Madame."

Wept! "Why? What did she say?"

Fauvelet shrugged his thin shoulders. "She didn't."

"Well—what did you tell her?"

"That she owed it to her country."

Mon Dieu.

"And that the First Consul and you had decided."

"Didn't you point out Louis's good qualities?"

Fauvelet looked at me quizzically. "Louis has good qualities?"

"Didn't you point out how gentle and sensitive and intelligent he is?

Didn't you tell her that Louis loves her?" As I had instructed him to say!

"I started to, Madame, but I don't know if she heard me." He pursed his lips. "She was crying awfully hard. Don't worry!" He held up his hands, as if surrendering to an enemy. "She *assured* me she would never do anything to displease you."

Hortense has asked for eight days to consider. Now, alone at my escritoire, I am full of remorse. How difficult this is. Are we doing the right thing?


*September 15—Malmaison.*
I observe my daughter's sad look and have to turn away. "She must decide herself," Bonaparte told me, taking me in his arms.


*September 16.*
Madame Campan is with Hortense now. I can hear the low murmur of their voices, the muffled sound of Hortense weeping. I can't bear it.


*Later.*
I walked Madame Campan to her carriage. "She will be fine," she said. "You must be patient."

"What is Hortense's objection?" Why is my daughter so miserable? We are not asking her to marry a repugnant old man. Certainly *that* sort of thing happens all the time. "Does she dislike Louis? Bonaparte and I were under the impression that she cares for him."

Madame Campan leaned toward me. "I think she expects to feel *rapture*," she said. I frowned. "Exactly!" she exclaimed. "Of course she cares for Louis. He's just not her *ideal*. Hortense has always been very . . . theatrical, one could say, but in the best sense! Sensitive, certainly. Romantic, I'm afraid. She'll come round—you'll see."


*September 17.*
Bonaparte has issued an ultimatum to England: unless a peace treaty is

concluded, negotiations will be broken off. "And as for your daughter . . ."
he said, pressing for resolution.

Four more days.


*September 21, early afternoon—Tuileries Palace.*
Fauvelet poked his head in the door. "Madame Josephine?"

I looked up from my fancy-work.

"She has agreed. She said she would not stand in the way of your happiness."

I scrambled for my handkerchief, my chin quivering.

## *In which my daughter finally marries*

*September 22, 1801, almost 10:00 P.M.—a rainy day in Paris.*
Louis looked terrified. "You wish to speak to me, Napoleon?"

"Yes, sit," Bonaparte said, throwing a crumpled paper into the roaring fire. "Hortense has agreed to consider an offer of marriage, were one submitted to her." I cringed. Bonaparte can be so blunt! "I recommend her. She is a sweet and virtuous girl."

Just then Hortense came into the room with a bound music book in her hand. Seeing Louis, she turned and fled.

"A bit timid, perhaps," Bonaparte said, bemused.


*[Undated]*
Now all that remains is for Louis to make his declaration to Hortense. The two are painful to watch, always at opposite ends of a room, always silent. Bonaparte and I wait . . . and wait and *wait*. How long can this go on?


*October 3, 1801, Saint-Jean-de-Maurienne*
*Chère Maman,*

*A quick note (the courier is leaving soon). The news that England has finally agreed to sign a peace treaty is glorious!*

*Victor wrote that he has been put in charge of the fleet sailing to Saint-*

*Domingue.\* What a splendid command! This is his opportunity to prove his worth. Pauline must be pleased.*

*Hortense hasn't written for some time. Too busy entertaining suitors?*

*A thousand kisses, I am well,*

*Your loving son, Eugène*


*October 14.*

"Perhaps you should have a word with Louis," I suggested to Bonaparte. "Encourage him to . . . *you know.*" Propose! Simply getting the young man to *speak* to my daughter was going to be a problem.

"What do I know of these things?"

"Would you prefer that I take care of it?" Our big ball was coming up: the perfect setting.


*October 21, 6:00 A.M.—Malmaison.*

Oh, it's early in the morning, but I'm too fraught to linger in bed. My heart is aswirl with feelings of joy, doubt—but most of all, relief.

Bonaparte and I opened the ball last night with a minuet. (He only missed two steps.) "What are you going to say to Louis?" he hissed, for we had decided that the time had come.

Presentation of the right hand: "What do you think I should say?"

Presentation of the left hand: "Tell him to get on with it!"


I induced the shy suitor to sit beside me. "Louis, do you think it would be improper for a woman to request a dance with a man?" A cotillion had been announced and couples were proceeding onto the floor.

"I believe it is the man who must always ask," he said solemnly.

"Pity," I said, with what I hoped would be a giveaway smile. Unfortunately, he didn't understand. "Would you find it shocking, then, were I

---

\* *The preliminary peace treaty with England opened up the Atlantic Ocean, which had been previously controlled by England's fleet. Saint-Domingue (Haiti now) had been in French hands for some time, but France had been unable to sail there. Troops were required in order to quell an insurrection.*

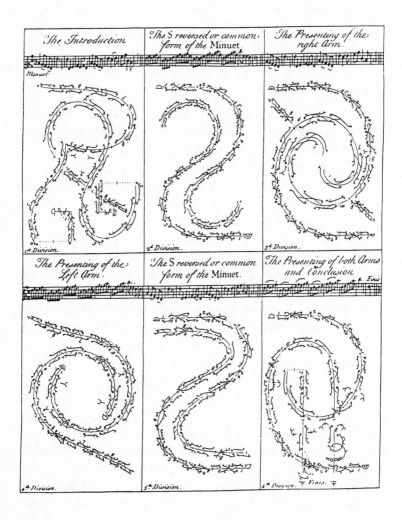

to inform you that if you were to ask the honour of my hand in the dance, I would be happy to accept?"

He looked at me in all seriousness, a small frown between his eyes. (*Nice* eyes. Madame Campan is right: their children would be handsome.) "You'd like to dance, Aunt Josephine?"

"I'd be delighted." He led me out onto the dance floor. Hortense was sitting with Caroline near the musicians; I wiggled my fingers at them.

"Your daughter is usually one of the first on the floor."

"She is passionate about dance."

"She dances well," he said as the music began.

"As do you, Louis." Although, in truth, his movements lacked confidence. Perhaps with time Hortense could . . .

"I aim only not to make a fool of myself," he said as we proceeded down.

"You underestimate your abilities." This was true. Louis has exceptional qualities. Turning my head (the old women sitting at the edges of the dance floor knew how to read lips), I said, "Louis, Bonaparte and I have been thinking about you and Hortense. Have you given any thought to *when* you might make a proposal? Tonight might—"

"No! I mean, yes." Louis missed a step, and try as he might, could not correct it.

"I'm breathless," I lied. "I believe I should sit down." It was a faux pas to leave the floor in the middle of a piece, but at least we were at the bottom of the dance.

He escorted me to my chair. "Won't you join me for a moment?" I asked with authority, offering the empty seat next to mine. Dutifully he sat down beside me, his eyes darting about with the look of a captured animal. Men! I thought, so valiant on the battlefield, so timid in the parlour. "As I was saying—" I would have to be firm. "Bonaparte is anxious to settle the matter. He feels you should declare yourself to Hortense—*tonight*. There she is now," I said, pointing with my fan.

Louis looked stricken. "But now she's with Caroline *and* Émilie."

A dance would be too challenging for Louis under the circumstances, I realized. "You could invite her for a stroll in the garden." I touched his elbow, urging him to stand. One step, and he would be committed. But that step! "Go," I hissed.

*[Undated]*

The clan received the news in chilly silence. Slowly, Signora Letizia got to her feet and held up her glass of verjuice, her stiff index finger pointing at Hortense as if in accusation. "Now you will be one of us," she said, and sat down.

After, in the drawing room, as Hortense sang one of her new compositions and I accompanied her on the harp, I sensed an undercurrent of hisses, sharp glances, covert hand movements—a flurry, it seemed, of secretive murmurs.

*October 29, 1801, Saint-Jean-de-Maurienne*
*Chère Maman,*

*What a surprise! I'm delighted. Louis is perfect for Hortense; they suit each other in so many ways. Has a date been set? Just think—I may be an uncle next year!*

*Your loving son, Eugène*

*Note—I'm thinking of growing a goatee.*

*November 17, 1801, Saint-Jean-de-Maurienne*
*Chère Maman,*

*Very well, no goatee!*

*I've finally decided on my wedding gift: two horses, one a roan mare and the other a bay stallion, both sired by Pegasus. What do you think? Would you mind keeping them at Malmaison until Hortense and Louis have their own establishment?*

*Your loving son, Eugène*

*December 18, 1801, Saint-Jean-de-Maurienne*
*Chère Maman,*

*You should know that the details of the wedding gown you are having made for Hortense are lost on your son. What do I know of silk and fine lace? But would it be possible to have Hortense's portrait painted wearing the gown? That, at the least, might console me for not being at the ceremony in person.*

*I've been getting my regiment ready to join you and Papa in Lyons next month. I regret that I can't be in Paris for the big event—too much to do!*

*Your loving son, Eugène*
*Note—Hortense wrote that Pauline is unhappy about having to go to Saint-Domingue with Victor. I've heard it said that Papa wanted to get Pauline out of Paris, away from a number of admirers. (You can see how bored I am: I've stooped to gossip. Forgive me!)*

*December 25—Christmas Day.*
Christmas dinner with the clan. "I'm so happy that Hortense and Louis are getting married, Aunt Josephine," Caroline told me, piling her plate high with pudding and tarts. "Just think, Hortense and I will be sisters, as well as bosom friends—and Napoleon will be Hortense's brother," Caroline said, catching Louis's eye. "That must please him; Napoleon is so *very* fond of Hortense. Everyone is talking about what a *close* family we are."

*December 26, early morning.*
Something in Caroline's expression last night made me uneasy. Against my better judgement, I've asked Mimi to contact her spy. "I was going to anyway," she told me with a grin.

*[Undated]*
Mimi slipped me a note this morning. "From Gontier's nephew?" I recognized the crude script.

"It isn't very nice," she warned me.

I tucked the note into my sleeve.

*This Evinng Mme Carolin told her Brother Louis he must not marry the Old Woman's daughter. Shee told Him Peopl say the 1st Consul is Lover of Mlle Hortens. Louis said that is a Lie, that it is not True, that He will marry Her. Mme Carolin broke 5 dishes Shee so angry.*

I'm enraged! My hand is trembling as I write this.

*December 29.*

And so, in spite of opposition, rumours and suspicion, plans proceed for the marriage of a Beauharnais, the daughter of "the Old Woman," to a Bonaparte. The contract will be signed on January first—in only three days; the ceremony to be held the day after. The wedding gown is almost finished. Leroy has outdone himself.

*December 30.*

Hortense was ill all night. Overcome with hysterics, she raged and wept. She could not possibly marry Louis, she finally confessed. "I have given my heart to another!" she said, falling against the pillows.

I folded and unfolded my hands, folded them again. What was my daughter telling me?

"I love Christophe Duroc," she wailed.

*11:20 A.M.*

"She's very upset. I don't think she can go through with it."

Bonaparte threw down his book in exasperation. "What do you mean? She has to! Everything is set."

"She's in love with one of your aides—with Duroc."

"Christophe?" Bonaparte snorted with amusement.

*Very late—past midnight (can't sleep).*

This evening before retiring, Bonaparte informed me that he'd offered Hortense to Christophe Duroc. "You did *what?*" It took me a moment to even respond.

"As we discussed," he said, pacing in his nightshirt. "I told Fauvelet to tell Christophe that I'd give him half a million and the command of the Eighth Military Division at Toulon on condition that the wedding take place in two days and they leave for Toulon immediately."

*Toulon?* "Fauvelet spoke to him this evening?" I gasped.

"Yes, he informed Christophe of the offer before Christophe left for the Opéra. He gave Fauvelet his refusal on his return."

"Christophe Duroc *refused* her?"

"He wants to live in Paris, he said. He doesn't want to live in Toulon."

My poor daughter! Christophe Duroc entertains no affection for her whatsoever, for he responded to the offer quite crudely, telling Fauvelet that he couldn't be bothered, that he was on his way to a whorehouse.

The air in Hortense's bedchamber was close. "Hortense?" I parted the embroidered bed-curtains. Hortense was sitting against the pillows, the counterpane pulled up to her chin. "How are you feeling?"

"I am fine, Maman," she said, her voice measured. "Thank you for inquiring."

She is young, I reminded myself, subject to moods. I sat down beside her. "There's something I have to tell you." There was no other way, or time. "I know you entertain a hope of marrying Christophe Duroc. I discussed the matter with Bonaparte, and he offered, but . . . Duroc refused," I said, as gently as I could.

"You're just saying that! You don't want me to marry him," she sobbed, throwing pillows. "Where are you going?" she demanded when she saw that I was leaving.

"I'm going to summon Fauvelet," I said, trying to remain calm. "He will tell you himself what Christophe Duroc said."

"Don't go!" she wept, her shoulders heaving.

I took her in my arms. She was so hot! "I'm sending for a doctor."

*December 31, New Year's Eve.*

With considerable difficulty I managed to get Bonaparte to postpone the wedding. "Two days," I said. "Dr. Corvisart feels she will be well enough by then." Dr. Corvisart is the only doctor Bonaparte trusts.

"You don't understand!" Bonaparte exploded. (Everyone is being so temperamental! There is too much going on at once.) "Several hundred Italian delegates are expecting me in Lyons to inaugurate their new republic. All the arrangements are going to have to be changed. Do you have any idea what this entails?"

"She just can't do it, Bonaparte!"

"A two-day delay?" Louis looked suspicious. "It will make a poor impression," he said, drawing his head into his shoulders. "May I inquire why?" He didn't feel that a wedding date should be changed under any circumstances, he said.

"She's really quite ill. Believe me, Louis, it will make an even poorer impression if you go ahead with it: She can barely sit up, she's so weak."


*January 2, 1802, early morning.*

Hortense has recovered—well enough, in any case. And so we will proceed with the signing of the contract, the civil ceremony, the religious ceremony—dragging my reluctant daughter into the holy state of matrimony.

"All girls feel that way," Madame Campan assured me. "Hortense is more expressive than most."

More stubborn than most!


*Sunday, January 3.*

The contract has been signed, so at least *that* ordeal is behind us—and an ordeal it was. Bonaparte's mother scowled the entire time; Caroline and Joseph smiled falsely. In spite of my resolve, I wept, which distressed the groom. Only Hortense seemed unperturbed (aloof).

After the signing, Bonaparte presented Hortense with the stunning diamond necklace set we'd had made for her. "Thank you," she said, but without any emotion. She is *determined* that nothing please her.


*January 4, just after 8:00 A.M.*

I woke with the dawn and have already accomplished a great deal: reviewed the menus, arranged with Leroy to make one last alteration to Hortense's gorgeous wedding gown (it's a surprise for her), sent a letter asking Cardinal Caprara to officiate at the religious ceremony to be held at the little house on Rue de la Victoire after the civil ceremony.

Frankly, I'm in such fits over this wedding that I keep forgetting Bonaparte and I will be leaving for Lyons in a few days and will be away for a month. I'll see whether Hortense and Louis would like to stay at Malmaison, look after all the animals.

Hortense and Louis. Hortense and Louis. Hortense and Louis.

Louis and Hortense.

Madame Louis Bonaparte.

Madame Louis.

Madame.


*11:45 P.M. A long day.*

Shortly before nine I knocked on the door to Hortense's room. She emerged in a plain crêpe gown, carrying a small orange-blossom bouquet. "You're not dressed? It's time to go upstairs. Everyone is waiting."

"I *am* dressed," my daughter informed me.

I looked at Mimi in confusion. "What happened to the wedding gown?" The exquisite gown of white satin. "Was it not delivered?" And what about the diamonds Bonaparte had given her? Hortense was wearing a single strand of inferior pearls.

Mimi rolled her eyes as if to say: I give up. "The bride prefers to be simply attired."

I pressed my lips together, trying as best I could to hide my frustration. It would do no good whatsoever to argue, I knew. "You look lovely," I lied.


It was a grim affair, in truth. We stood solemnly as the mayor joined Louis and my daughter in marriage. The family and the Second and Third Consuls watched the proceedings without any indication of joy. Bonaparte was impatient to have it over with quickly. (He had work to do!) I feigned happiness, but it was difficult: Hortense looked so miserable. Louis regarded her anxiously—my heart went out to him.

After, the cheerless party proceeded to the little house on Rue de la Victoire, where Cardinal Caprara had been waiting in his canonicals for hours. (He'd misunderstood the time.) After champagne, which I hoped would make the gathering at least a little bit gay (it didn't), Cardinal Caprara joined Hortense and Louis in the eyes of God. And so the knot is truly tied, for better or for worse.

Bonaparte wished the two well, and then he and the two Consuls immediately departed—they had much to do to prepare for the trip to Lyons, they said. While waiting for dinner to be announced, Caroline mentioned to the Cardinal that she and Joachim had only had a civil marriage and that someday soon they intended to be married by the Church.

Cardinal Caprara examined his timepiece, a heavy gold instrument dangling on a thick chain. "I could marry you now, if you like. It would only take a half hour or so," he assured me, for the table had been set.

I glanced at Hortense and Louis, sitting glum-faced on the sofa. "You wouldn't object?" It was, after all, their happy day. (Hardly.)

"Of course not," Hortense said dutifully, but then added, "that is, if my *husband* does not object."

"No, I do not object," Louis said, his voice so quiet that it was hard to hear.

"Anyone else wish to marry?" the jolly Cardinal said after he'd rushed Caroline (six months along and already enormous) and Joachim through the ceremony.

"Pity the First Consul isn't here, Maman," Hortense said, and then wisely bit her tongue, for it isn't generally known that Bonaparte and I have never been joined by the Church. At the time, it was not possible*—and now it is awkward.

Then, as dinner was announced, Cardinal Caprara took his leave: "I'm afraid I am expected elsewhere."

"Before you go, Cardinal Caprara, would you mind? If you could . . ." I looked around to make sure no one could hear. "If you could bless their bed." It is an old custom, and who can say? Perhaps it will help. Certainly Hortense and Louis are in need of a blessing.

---

* *Catholicism had been outlawed during the Revolution.*

## *In which we are all of us blessed*

*January 31, 1802—Paris, home again, 7:30 P.M. approximately.*
We're back, at last. The trip to Lyons was . . . well, surprising. The adulation! But also all the pomp, the tiring ceremonials. It helped that Eugène joined us there, so proud with his regiment.

Speaking of whom—he has just arrived. He's anxious to go see his sister—as am I!

*9:45 P.M.*
Eugène lifted Hortense off her feet in a big bear hug. "Madame Louis! You haven't changed a bit."

"I'm the happiest woman in the world," she said (catching my eye), chatting on about Louis's problematic health, the art class they are taking together, a pug dog's litter, a lame horse, old Gontier's trouble with his back. Then Louis joined us and Hortense fell silent as he talked of this and that, clasping her hand in his, never taking his eyes off her.

I'm *so* relieved.

*February 18—Malmaison.*
Louis looked so proud. I knew right away what he was going to say! "The midwife informs us that although it is too early to know for *sure*, my wife is likely with child."

"That's wonderful!" I exclaimed, embracing Hortense—restraining myself from crushing her, so great was my joy.

Eugène heartily shook Louis's hand. (His weak hand: I cringed.) "I guess this means I'm going to be an uncle." He struck a dignified pose that made us laugh.

"How do you feel?" I asked Hortense anxiously. I feel so protective of her!

"Sick!" Hortense moaned.

"Good, then it will be a boy." Bonaparte tweaked Hortense's ear. "Joseph has a girl. Lucien has girls. It's about time we had a boy Bonaparte."

My daughter is going to have a *baby*—I'm delirious!


*February 23, a chilly afternoon.*
Louis's plan to go to a spa for a health cure is an excellent idea (clearly, he needs it) except for one thing: he expects Hortense to accompany him. I'm ill with concern! Barèges is so far. It would take over a week to get there, and the roads are terribly primitive. I've persuaded Dr. Corvisart to have a word with Hortense about the dangers of such an expedition for a young woman in her condition.


*February 28, Sunday and a Décadi—Malmaison.*
Hortense has dark circles under her eyes. Louis has been waking her in the middle of the night. "He weeps, Maman! He says if I loved him, I would follow him anywhere."

"You explained to him what the doctor said?"

Hortense nodded. "And so I told him I'd go with him, but that if I miscarried, it would be *his* responsibility."

"Hortense, you can't risk that!" I said, my hands clasping her shoulders.


*March 1—Tuileries Palace.*
"He wept as the carriage pulled away, Maman," Hortense said, collapsing into my arms. "He says he can't live without me!"

Oh, the early years of marriage are so passionate, I thought—so *stormy*.

"Bonaparte said things like that when we were first married," I told her, to soothe. "Corsican men are extreme in love—or maybe just Bonaparte men," I added with a smile. Extreme in everything, I might have said: love, hate, ambition, pride. "Louis's health concerns him, I know. The waters will help. And once the baby comes, things will settle down. You're lucky to be married to a man who loves you so much. And something tells me he'll be a devoted parent."

Hortense smiled through her tears. "He has already filled a closet with toys."


*March 27, 11:30 A.M.*
It's official now—England has actually *signed* a peace treaty. "Your island is French again," Bonaparte told me with a kiss, as if presenting me with a gift: my beloved Martinico.

"Ah, just think of the cashmere shawls we'll be able to buy now," Caroline said, eating macaroons by the handful. (She's enormous—only one more month.)

"And gowns of English muslin." Hortense gave me a private wink— we've been wearing English muslin all along, only telling Bonaparte that the fabric is French leno.

"And English plants for an English garden," I mused. I've already written letters to England, to botanists there.


*March 30.*
I've sent a parcel to Martinico, sent Mother portraits of Bonaparte, me and the children along with a gold box beautifully decorated with diamonds. Inside, I've tucked some gold medals and coins in honour of Bonaparte's victories.

Now that the seas are safe to travel, I'm hoping Mother can be persuaded to move to France. I've also suggested that Uncle Robert send my goddaughter, fifteen now. Young Stéphanie would benefit from a year at Madame Campan's school before marrying.

*April 6—Paris.*

Peace was signed with England less than twelve days ago and already Paris is swarming with Lord Such-and-Suches and Lady So-and-Sos, going about town with their quaint umbrellas and their noses stuck in the air. This in spite of the fact that they are incredibly *impressed*, blinking their eyes, disbelieving, taking in the glory of our new Republic—taking in our fine clothes, our glittering entertainments, our vitality, our *pride*. Expecting squalor and disarray, they are stunned to find a well-managed, thriving country, shocked by our fine new hospitals (especially the one just opened for children—the first of its kind), our schools, our roads. Everywhere one looks there is construction: a new quay, bridges, monuments. "I wish to make France the envy of all nations," Bonaparte told me not long ago—and I believe he has already succeeded.

*April 8.*

Wonders upon wonders: now there will be peace with the Church. "We'll celebrate Easter Sunday in the Cathedral of Notre-Dame," Bonaparte told me.

Celebrate in regal style: all the servants to be in livery.

"Easter Sunday?" Leroy exclaimed. The distraught dress designer placed the back of his wrist to his brow and closed his eyes. Only ten days.

*April 18—Easter Sunday in Paris.*

The church bells of Paris are ringing again. What a glorious sound! Bonaparte opened the casement windows and stood at the sill in his nightshirt, as if breathing in the deep resounding peal of Emmanuel, the big bell of Notre-Dame—silent for how long? Ten years?

Our morning reverie was shattered by a salvo of guns that made the windows (and my heart) tremble. "I have everything I could wish for," Bonaparte said solemnly. Peace with England. Peace with the Church. "If only . . ."

If only we could have a child.

*April 26.*
Very busy. Caroline has had her baby—a little girl, named after Signora Letizia. A difficult labour.


*June 4—Paris.*
To the Opéra tonight to see *Hecuba*. The applause for Bonaparte was tumultuous. When Priam said to Achilles, "You fulfill the hopes of the nation," I thought the walls would tumble, the cheering was so great. The audience demanded that the line be repeated, and repeated yet again.

It does not seem to matter how often it happens—the fervour of the people continues to overwhelm me. Overwhelm me and frighten me, for where will it lead?


*June 10—Malmaison, a beautiful summer day.*
Thérèse lifted her veil of white muslin held in place by a crown of roses. "My divorce from Tallien is now official, so I'm dressing as a virgin," she announced. "What's wrong?" she demanded, looking at me closely.

I hesitated—but to whom could I speak truly? "The people are so grateful, they will give Bonaparte anything he should ask for."

"The world! And even then, it would not be as much as he has given us." She laughed at my expression. (Thérèse isn't given to adulation.) "Don't look so surprised. I can see as well as anyone that your husband has accomplished the impossible—and to think what a fool he seemed when we first met him. Remember how we laughed at his toothpick legs in those big smelly boots? Ah, now I've got you smiling. So tell me, what do you fear he will ask for?"

"People are saying that he should be named First Consul for Life—"

"Of course. *Everyone* is voting in favour."

"—with the right to name a successor."

"I didn't know about that part."

"What's the difference between that and a king? Sometimes I worry that in striving to become legitimate in the eyes of the world, we are becoming what we fought so hard to change."

"It's not really the same. It's being voted on, after all—it's up to the people to decide what they want. And even if Bonaparte were voted king, he would be a citizen-king."

"I know, I know," I argued, "but already some people are telling him that the right to name his heir isn't enough—that the office should be hereditary." His *family*, in particular—insisting that the office should fall to one of them.

"Ah, now I understand. You and Bonaparte have no children."

"And I'm beginning to think we never will."

"Have you tried—?"

"Everything!" I've given up animal foods, liquors of a spirituous nature. I've endeavoured to keep my body open by ingesting tincture of senna, Epsom salts and other laxatives. (Oh, the results.) I've even had leeches applied to my temples. "I'm going to Plombières soon for yet another cure, but I confess, I . . ."

Thérèse placed her hand over mine. "Darling, you must have faith."


*July 2—Plombières.*
The water doctor is hopeful. "The waters are making you ill. That is a good sign."


*July 7—Plombières, hot.*
A miracle—I've had a hint of a show! "Return to Paris immediately," the water doctor ordered, prescribing tonics and potions. "Constant relations, and no moving about after. Keep your hips propped up on a pillow for at least two hours."

I'm packing.


*July 14, Bastille Day—Paris.*
I've prepared for bed like a bride. A pagan spirit is in the air: tonight twelve girls, dowered by the city, were married to soldiers at the Bastille Day banquet. Bonaparte looked splendid in his Lyons coat of crimson satin laced with gold. "Like a king," his family told him with satisfied smiles. A king requiring an heir.

*July 29.*
The results of the vote have been published. Over five million citizens voted in favour, less than ten thousand against.


*August 2—Malmaison.*
Today it is official. Bonaparte is now First Consul for *Life*.

"What will this mean?" I asked him as we walked along a path banked by blooming roses.

He picked a yellow blossom, held it to his nose, his eyes closed, as if lost in sensation. "Things are going to change," he said, opening his eyes.

First: we must double our staff. "But Bonaparte—"

Second: Malmaison is too small. We must move to the palace of Saint-Cloud. "But Bonaparte—"

And third: he is to be addressed as Napoleon. "But Bonaparte—"


*August 6.*
This afternoon Madame Campan and I toured the palace of Saint-Cloud, making long (*long*) lists of what is needed, *who* is needed: ladies-in-waiting, torch boys, pages, footmen . . . My head is reeling. I'm writing this in bed.


*August 8—Tuileries.*
"It's a supernatural materialization," Fouché reported. "The Church has found a saint for your husband: Saint Napoleon." From now on, August 15 will be known as Saint Napoleon's day.

"So who is this Saint Napoleon, anyway?" Hortense demanded, looking up from copying out scripts of the one-act comedy she is directing—as well as acting in, in spite of being seven months along. (At least it gets her mind off her long-absent husband, still in treatment at the spa.)

"Some lazy reprobate, no doubt," Eugène said with a boyish grin, ducking Bonaparte's attempt to tug his ear.

*August 11—Malmaison.*

Hortense is frantic. "Maman, what am I going to do? My costume is too small for me *already* and Fauvelet *still* doesn't know his lines."

"Don't worry!" In her condition, it isn't good to get distraught. Calm is required. "We'll get Leroy to make alterations to your costume, and Eugène can coach Fauvelet every night. It's going to be wonderful."

"How do you know?"

"The best actor in Europe happened to tell me."

"*Talma* told you that?" Beaming—for there could be no greater praise.


*Fort de France, Martinico*

*Chère Yeyette, my beloved niece,*

*You must understand—your goddaughter Stéphanie is still a girl. I appreciate the advantages of having her educated in France, and I am certainly not concerned knowing that you and your illustrious husband would make sure that she was well looked after, but her mother and I cannot bring ourselves to send her across that perilous body of water, no matter how peaceful the seas might be at this time.*

*I regret to tell you, as well, that there isn't any hope of persuading your mother to sail to France, in spite of the gracious invitation the First Consul has extended. She remains firmly of the Royalist persuasion.*

*Your most humble etc. uncle, Robert Tascher*


*August 12, late afternoon—Paris.*

Bonaparte threw an English journal into the fire and sat glaring at it as it burst into flames. "Riff-raff!" His expression alarmed me, but also provoked my curiosity. "You don't want to know about this, Josephine," he warned me, sensing my thoughts.

"But now, of course, you must tell me."

He jumped to his feet and began to pace, his hands behind his back. "The English journals are circulating the rumour that Hortense has already given birth."

I shrugged. "They're simply mistaken."

He stopped short, his hands fists. "And that therefore Hortense was with child at the time she married." He paused before he added, "And that I am the father of her child."

I watched an ash fragment float up the chimney. "That's what was in that news-sheet?"

"And they call this peace!" Bonaparte kicked the burning logs.

"We must make sure Hortense never learns of this."

"Nor Louis," Bonaparte said quietly, under his breath.


*August 15, Saint Napoleon's day (!)—Malmaison.*

What a birthday fête! Has there ever been one like it? Saint Napoleon, indeed. (Saint Napoleon, who is only thirty-three today—so young!)

The reception at the palace this morning went smoothly. It was followed by a glorious concert (three hundred musicians playing Cherubini, Méhul, Rameau—heavenly). Then, after a Te Deum at Notre-Dame, we caravanned in flower-festooned carriages out the long road to Malmaison for a garden fête. The weather, for all my fretting, turned out to be perfect: a clear blue sky, not a cloud.

"Our prayers have been answered." Uncle Fesch, who was made a bishop today, raised yet another toast.

"The sun always shines on Papa," Hortense said, ebullient in her gaiety, for her one-act comedy had gone off splendidly, well-clapped. ("Fantastique! Formidable!" Talma was heard to exclaim over the cheers.)

Even Bonaparte enjoyed himself. He insisted Hortense lead a dance with Eugène, in spite of her condition. "Do it for Saint Napoleon," he said with his irresistibly charming smile.


*August 16.*

Hortense is so upset! There's an article in today's *Journal de Paris* about her dancing at Bonaparte's birthday fête last night. "Why did they have to say I was seven months with child?" she demanded.

"May I see it?" Bonaparte's secretary handed me the news-sheet.

"And look, Maman, someone even wrote a stupid poem about me.

'On seeing Madame Louis Bonaparte, seven months pregnant, dance on August 15.'"

"Do you know who wrote this, Fauvelet?" No author was credited, but I had a suspicion.

"Certainly not, Madame Josephine," Fauvelet Bourrienne exclaimed, moving his hand in the epic style of delivery, as if the upper arm—the "oratorical weapon," Talma called it—were completely detached from the body.

"Someone with no literary talent whatsoever," Hortense ranted.

"None whatsoever," Fauvelet echoed, but colouring.

I pressed my lips together to keep from smiling. *So.*

Hortense burst into tears. "Why did they have to say anything at all? I didn't even want to dance. I wouldn't have if Papa hadn't *insisted.*"

Fauvelet looked stricken.

*Don't worry, it's all right,* I mouthed, putting my arm around Hortense and leading her out the sash doors into the rose garden. Clearly Bonaparte had wanted Hortense to dance for a reason. No doubt he had asked Fauvelet to write the poem about her and publish it in the paper—thus proving to the English scandalmongers that Hortense had not yet given birth, quelling the evil rumours. "You're such a lovely dancer, Hortense. That's why people write about you. Don't fret, *please* don't fret."

*September 14—Malmaison.*
"I've come to bid you farewell," Fouché said, standing in the foyer at Malmaison.

"You're going away?" I asked, distracted, for I'd just come from Saint-Cloud, where workmen are trying to finish the renovations before Bonaparte and I move in four days from now. I've been trying to figure out what type of bed-curtains would suit our bed there. Its unique boat-shape makes it a challenge. A velvet in a terre d'Égypte hue would be perfect, I've decided, but it requires something more: perhaps a gold fringe to make the embroidery stand out.

"It appears I've been let go."

Slowly Fouché's words penetrated my harried thoughts. I leaned against a crate. *Let go,* did he say?

"Well—demoted."

"You're no longer Minister of Police?"

"*Senator* Fouché." He spoke the title with contempt. "A perfectly useless position."

"I can't believe that!" Fouché is the best Minister of Police imaginable. How can Bonaparte manage without him? If there is trouble, Fouché knows of it. If there are assassins plotting, Fouché finds them. "Bonaparte did this?" Fouché is the only one of Bonaparte's ministers who has the courage to speak truthfully to him. He has often angered Bonaparte—true!—but Bonaparte owes his life to him.

"Apparently my services are no longer needed."

"I don't understand." But I suspected the reason. Fouché argued against Bonaparte's being made First Consul for Life, and this enraged Bonaparte's family. Too, Fouché is my ally.

"Another clan victory," Fouché said with a smirk.


*Early morning.*

Last night I tried to talk to Bonaparte about Fouché, but it proved difficult. "I was advised," was all he would say. I dared not broach the subject of his family's influence, their greedy nature—their hatred of *me*. Bonaparte is master of Europe—but when it comes to his family, he weakens dangerously. *Blood is everything*, his mother often says. *Blood is our only strength.* Blood is your only weakness, I want to tell him—but do not dare.


*September 18—Saint-Cloud.*

Exhausted! We moved in the rain. The rooms at Saint-Cloud are spacious, but cold. As soon as it clears, Bonaparte and I are going for a ride in the park.


*Sunday, September 19.*

The midwife estimates that Hortense's baby could come as early as the first of October, several weeks before previously thought. She told Hortense that it is easy to miscalculate with a boy.

"She thinks it's a boy? That's wonderful!" A girl grandchild I would love—with all my heart—but a boy would solve so much.

"But Maman, that would be three days *short* of nine months since we married," she said, looking up from a drawing she was working on, a copy of an infant by Greuze. "What would Louis think?" Louis, who was expected home from the spa any day soon.

And what would the English scandalmongers write, I thought—but did not say.


*September 21—Saint-Cloud, sunny and bright.*
Louis returned from the spa yesterday, but alas, all is *not* well. His health, unfortunately, is not improved, to judge by his extreme disability. (His right hand is so crippled he can't use it.) His spirits are tormented, as well, for he threatens to drown himself if the baby is born early!

"But Louis knows that you are virtuous," I told my daughter, looking for a way to make peace between them.

"Of course he knows, Maman, but all he cares about is how it would *look*, what people would think."

"He loves you—you know that." If Louis heard the rumours circulating in England, it would inflame him, no doubt. That he had not said anything to Hortense was to his credit. "Periods of separation are difficult."

We talked as we walked along the rutted cart paths edging the fields. I eased my daughter's fiery spirit—or tried to—by urging her to be gentle with herself, as well as with her husband. "Louis has been away for seven months—a very long time. There's often a period of turmoil on the return." I know this all too well. "It's best not to allow yourself to become heated, especially in your condition." I put my arm around my poor lumbering daughter. It will certainly not help matters if this child *does* come early.


*October 7—Saint-Cloud.*
It is now nine months plus three days since Hortense and Louis married. "I'm saved," Hortense said, her hands clasped as if in prayer.

Hortense has always been given to drama, to melodrama—but in truth, we are all relieved.

*October 10.*
Late this morning a horse cantered up the drive and into the courtyard. I headed out to the terrace to see who it might be, but even as I opened the door, Eugène came bounding up the steps, yelling at me to hurry.

"Is it Hortense?" I cried out, made fearful by his state of alarm.

"It's happening, Maman—I was with her when it started! Louis says to come *quickly.*"

I didn't think the drive from Saint-Cloud into the heart of Paris could be made in under two hours: now I know that it can. We left Saint-Cloud at 10:05, and at exactly 11:48 Eugène and I were at the door of Hortense and Louis's town house, pulling impatiently on the bell rope.

"Yoo-hoo!" We turned to see a woman dressed in an old-fashioned red gown covered by an apron festooned with ribbons. She was balancing what looked to be a birthing stool on top of her head with one hand and holding a leather portmanteau with the other. "I can't unlatch the gate."

"Madame Frangeau!"

"The midwife?" Eugène hurried to let her in.

I greeted the good woman, but just then the front door opened. "Madame Frangeau?" Louis said, his afflicted right hand clawed over his heart. (Awful.) "At last."

"Louis, how is Hortense?" And then, from within the house, I heard a cry. Oh no!

Louis held up the index finger of his good hand to silence me, examining a pocket watch that he clutched with the other, counting off the seconds. "Good," he said, dropping the watch into his pocket.

"Dr. Jean-Louis Baudelocque will be here after he finishes his meal, Citoyen," the midwife informed Louis, untying a kerchief.

"*After?*" Louis asked anxiously.

"Truth is, he just gets in the way," she hissed in my direction, stepping aside as the hall porter carried the stool and portmanteau up the stairs.

Louis hurried after the porter, talking over his shoulder to Madame Frangeau. "My wife's pains are coming often now. I think she's near."

"Someone should let Bonaparte know what's happening," I suggested to Eugène, who was standing in the courtyard looking bewildered.

"I will!" he said, relieved to have a task.

"He's working at the palace today," I called out, but my son was already on his way out the gate.


The lying-in room smelled strongly of cloves. Madame Frangeau was closing the windows, barking instructions to the two maids.

"Maman!" Hortense gasped when she saw me. Louis was seated beside her, stroking her hand.

"How are you, darling?" My sweet, my treasure, my heart! She looked like a girl in the big bed, a girl with golden locks, her big blue eyes peeking out from under the lace frill of her nightcap. A frail slip of a girl with an enormous belly.

"She's splendid," Madame Frangeau said. "Now, Madame Josephine, if you could sit yourself here, out of the way, while I take your daughter's measures."

Obediently I sat down on the opposite side of the bed. Hortense writhed as a wave of pain came over her. "Dear God," she cried out.

I swallowed, took a breath as the midwife cheered her on. "That's the way! The louder the better. Let the neighbours know. Let all of Paris know!"

Dr. Jean-Louis Baudelocque didn't arrive until shortly before three. The child—the most perfect I've ever seen—was born shortly before nine. Although it was not a long labour—eight hours in all?—it was not an easy one. My daughter suffered!

I will never forget that beautiful sound—the baby's first lusty wail. "It's a boy," Louis whispered, as if in disbelief at his good fortune.

A *boy*. I felt light-headed, blessed.

"A boy!" I heard a maid yell in the hall.

"A boy!" I heard someone call outside in the courtyard—the coachman likely. Somewhere in the house a bell was rung. Oh, the excitement!

I wanted to run out into the street, ring the bells of Notre-Dame.

"Good work, Madame Louis. You've given your husband a healthy baby boy," Madame Frangeau said, holding the red and screaming infant up for Hortense to see. (*Careful!* I wanted to cry out.) "Wash him up, measure and swaddle him," she told the nursemaid. "He's perfectly well-made," she added, as if speaking of an object, "not a flaw that I can see." Louis followed the nursemaid out of the room in a daze.

Dr. Baudelocque tapped my daughter's knee through the covering sheet. "One more push, Madame Louis, and the business will be done."

"We don't want the womb climbing back up!" the midwife said, as if it were a thing alive.

Hortense winced, but did not cry out. I stroked her damp forehead with a cloth dipped in rosewater. It is early yet, I know, the danger not yet past. Heaven's gates stay open nine days for a woman in childbed.

Louis reappeared with a proud look in his eyes. He knelt beside the bed and kissed Hortense's hand. I was moved to tears—his simple action was so noble.

"He is well, *our son*?" my daughter asked.

"Six pounds, two ounces, and eighteen inches long," he said, his eyes glistening.

"That's an excellent weight," I said.

"He looks small to me," Louis said excitedly, "but the nursemaid told me he's big—and very well made."

The nursemaid appeared with the baby in her arms, tightly swaddled and peaceful now. "Oh, Hortense, he's an angel," I said, a lump rising in my throat. Napoleon-Charles he will be named—so it has already been decreed. Little Napoleon.

"Our Dauphin," the nursemaid said, putting him into Hortense's arms.

"Hold your tongue," I heard Louis hiss at the nurse.

"Bonjour, little Napoleon," Hortense whispered, gazing into the eyes of her son, her cheeks wet with tears.

*In which I have suspicions*

*October 13, 1802—Saint-Cloud, a chilly day.*
Hortense is being treated like royalty for having produced the first male Bonaparte grandchild. Even Signora Letizia conferred begrudging congratulations on the mother of "her son's son." And now Eugène has been made Colonel of the Guards (quite an honour—he's only twenty-one), although the title "Uncle" excites him more, in truth.

Unfortunately, such Beauharnais glory has excited clan jealousy—further aggravated by today's birth notice in *Le Moniteur*. Hortense's name is printed in small capitals. "They don't do that for any of *us*," Caroline said, clutching baby Letizia in petticoats, little Achille sitting beside her sucking his thumb. "Don't we count?" She is with child again, but it does not seem to calm her. If anything, becoming a mother has turned Caroline into a lioness.

"Make sure you contact *Le Moniteur*," I suggested to Bonaparte's secretary later. "All family members must be treated *exactly* the same."


*October 14—in Paris for a few days with Hortense.*
Madame Frangeau (*General* Frangeau, Eugène calls her) has ordered Hortense to be wrapped in a feather comforter and the fires in her room kept blazing, "to sweat the poisons out," she said.

"Of course," I agreed, but tactfully suggested that the maids put branches of apple on the fire, for the air in the lying-in chamber has become heavy.

"I'm *drowning* in my bodily fluids," Hortense complained. She maintains her good humour in spite of Madame Frangeau's insistence that she lie flat for one full week, not moving even to allow the bed to be made, or to change her underclothes.

"It would be certain death," Madame Frangeau informed us.

"Only a few more days," I comforted my daughter, gazing upon the precious face of the newborn in my arms (falling in love). "It's wise to be cautious."


*October 15—still in Paris.*
Nine days. Madame Frangeau has allowed Hortense to sit up—but she's not to get out of bed for another five. "If I hear that your feet have so much as *touched* the floor, there will be hell to pay."


*October 20—Saint-Cloud.*
"I've come to bid you farewell, Madame Josephine." Bonaparte's secretary stood forlornly before me.

"Farewell, Fauvelet?" I asked, pulling off my gloves, my thoughts on Hortense and the baby. Little Napoleon is sleeping better now that his wet-nurse has agreed to abstain from fruit and vegetables.

"I've . . . I've been let go."

"Pardon?"

He repeated what he'd said, but even then I could not comprehend. Let go? Fauvelet Bourrienne was not only an excellent secretary, he was Bonaparte's oldest friend. "But why?"

He waggled his fingers. "Oh, I made some investments, and . . ." He shrugged, shoving his hands deep into the pockets of his redingote. "*Indiscretions*, the First Consul said."

"But Fauvelet, everybody plays the Funds."

Fauvelet flushed. "I guess I took advantage of my position."

"I still don't understand." Doesn't everyone "take advantage"? What about the investments that Bonaparte's brothers and sisters have made—even his mother? What about those made by Minister Talleyrand, for that matter, who regularly profits from knowledge of international developments, who considers such "income" his due? "Did Bonaparte's family have anything to do with this?" I demanded. Fauvelet is my ally—something the clan holds against him.

He hunched his shoulders. "Well . . ."

*November 15—still at Saint-Cloud (chilly).*
Little Napoleon was christened this morning. Bonaparte and I, as godparents, held him proudly. He was an angel—not even a whimper. ("Everyone knows that if a baby doesn't cry at his christening he will die," Caroline said later. That girl!)

We returned to Louis and Hortense's house where Louis, entirely on his own and much to my daughter's surprise, had arranged a fête in her honour. Hortense's closest friends were there—her cousin Émilie, the three Auguié sisters and Caroline.

Soon after, Hortense's former schoolmistress, Madame Campan, arrived and then all the other members of the Bonaparte clan. Lucien came with his two girls. Elisa appeared in a bizarre ensemble she'd designed herself, a composite of Egyptian, Roman and Greek styles that she expects every woman in Paris to adopt. "Joseph sends regrets," she announced (but later disclosed that he felt it disrespectful of Louis to celebrate the birth of a son so soon after he himself had suffered such a grievous disappointment in the birth of yet another daughter—a second). And last, jolly Uncle "Bishop" Fesch arrived with Bonaparte's mother. Signora Letizia stood in the centre of the room refusing all offers until Bonaparte led her to the chair of honour on the right of the hearth.

It was as Caroline was trying to get little Achille to show everyone how he can wave that Aunt Désirée—dressed in a youthful Grecian style!—made a dramatic entrance with dear old fusty Aunt Fanny, who appeared shrunken but vigorous as ever, her thick face paint smudged. With the bravado of an author who has just received a literary award, she read aloud a rather drawn-out verse she'd written in honour of her goddaughter's son, "the new Apollo." I was becoming concerned about the length of Aunt Fanny's recitation (Bonaparte was starting to twitch), when Eugène arrived in his new uniform as Colonel of the Consul Guards, and all the girls made a fuss, causing him to blush.

Once all the guests had arrived, and everyone was comfortably settled, and the children were quieted with bribes of comfits, we talked of the excitement in Paris over the coming debut at the Théâtre-Français of Talma's protégée, an actress of only fifteen. Then we exchanged news of Jérôme and Pauline, both in the Islands. Of young Jérôme, not much could be said—only that he had written for more money (as usual)—but Pauline is reported to like Saint-Domingue after all, "in spite of the snakes and savages."

After a collation Louis solemnly presented Hortense with a stunning set of rubies. She was overwhelmed, I believe, for there were tears in her eyes as she thanked him quite sweetly. Then the true jewel of my daughter's crown, her beautiful baby, was brought in by the nursemaid for everyone to admire. He belched quite splendidly, which made us all cheer. The children squealed and jumped up and down to see his pink little face, as Louis and Hortense and the doting godparents—Bonaparte and I—looked on proudly.

I can't remember a gathering when my family and the Bonaparte clan have been so united—if one can call it that. I suspect Aunt Fanny with her careless ways (she sat on the arm of a chair) and Aunt Désirée with her girlish pretensions (flowers in her hair at sixty!) horrified Signora Letizia. Oh, that evil eye! Yet all in all, and in spite of the jealousies, it was a lovely family fête, thanks largely to the children. I induced them to sit quietly near me so that they could stay with the adults. Little Napoleon lay in my arms the entire time.

"Ah, portrait of a mother," Caroline said, holding out her thumb and squinting at me as an artist might. "Pity—"

*Fort de France, Martinico*
*Chère Yeyette, my beloved niece,*
    *We promise, we'll consider your offer and talk it over with Stéphanie. She's a spirited girl. You'll be pleased with your goddaughter, should you ever have an opportunity to meet her.*
    *The house you purchased for your mother in town is magnificent. Now all we have to do is prise her out of her ramshackle abode in Trois-Ilets.*
                  *Your well-meaning uncle, Robert Tascher*

A meeting with Madame Campan this afternoon, regarding the staff required for Saint-Cloud, their duties and functions. "One lady-in-waiting isn't enough," she said, looking over my notes.

I confessed I didn't know what exactly a lady-in-waiting *did*.

"Ladies-in-waiting do just that: wait."

"But for what?"

"For whatever you fancy. To join you for a game of chance, or a walk in the garden. To hold your fan should you care to dance. To call for a servant to bring refreshment, should you suffer a sudden and unexpected thirst. To read to you as you work at your frame. To amuse your guests with intelligent and pleasing conversation. To reflect well upon you, by virtue of their reputation and breeding. In short, to make your life pleasing. I suggest you begin with four."

"Won't that be too many?"

"At the speed at which your husband's destiny is unfolding, Madame Bonaparte, I predict that you will soon require five times that number."

Just then my dame d'annonce opened one of the double doors and exclaimed, "Citoyen Talma!" so loudly that I let out a little shriek. "Madame Campan, perhaps you could help with the training of the staff," I suggested under my breath as the great actor entered with an air of regal authority—made somewhat difficult by the sheepskin cap he was wearing and a silly little muff he had hanging from a cord around his neck.

Slipping off his hat and tucking it under his right arm, Talma looked slowly about the room, his eyes lingering on the bronze chandeliers, the yellow velvet chairs, *us*. With a fluid motion, he placed his right gloved hand behind his back (without letting the hat slip), the other extended, palm up, and bowed deeply. "Ladies," he said, his voice resonant. "My pleasure." Then, with a nervous, almost tragic intensity, he slipped off his gloves and ran his fingers through his unpowdered hair. "How was that?"

"Excellent!" I said, clapping. "Madame Campan, what do you think? Was that not a perfect entry?"

"Commanding," Madame Campan agreed. "But the gloves stay on."

I persuaded Talma to join us for a glass of Chablis. We shared the news we'd each gleaned in various salons, reviews of the various spectacles we'd attended, the excitement about his young protégée, Mademoiselle Georges. The volatile actor confessed that he was fraught with concern that she would fail him. "She's a child, and yet she is to play Clytemnestra! What does she know about maternal feelings? Grand Dieu! I will never survive this debut."

Shortly after Talma was summoned by Bonaparte, Madame Campan took her leave as well. I saw her out through the labyrinth of corridors to her carriage. On return, passing Bonaparte's cabinet, I heard sounds of violence: a terrifying shriek. The guards came running, their hands on the pommels of their swords, and threw open the cabinet door to reveal two startled men: Bonaparte standing about three feet from Talma, who was holding a plumed quill aloft like a dagger.

"What is it?" Bonaparte demanded, turning.

I looked at Talma and then back at my husband. "It sounded as if someone was being murdered!"

Talma burst into laughter. "I told you that you should consider a career on the stage, First Consul."

Sheepishly, Bonaparte showed me the papers in his hand: a play script. "I was helping Talma rehearse a murder scene," he said.


*November 20—Saint-Cloud.*
I've been interviewing applicants for the various staff positions all week. It's exhausting—and I've several more to interview tomorrow.

A wonderful respite today when Hortense came with the baby. Bonaparte and I turned into silly beings, cooing and talking nonsense, making faces and peering into the face of this perplexed little one— notre petit chou.

"You see?" Bonaparte said when the baby made a face. "He knows me."

I *love* being a grandmother.


*November 21, still raining.*
"Madame Rémusat?" I hadn't seen Claire Rémusat for over a decade— she'd been a girl then. Clari, we'd called her. Although she was a young woman now, I recognized her sharp little nose and lively eyes.

"Madame Bonaparte," she said, dropping her head. Her graceful move showed respect, but displayed good breeding, as well.

Short and a little plump, there was something childlike about her; she seemed younger than her twenty-two years, perhaps due to her archaic pleated cap.

I led her to the chair by the fire. "Do you mind if I call you Claire?" During the Terror, she and Hortense had played with dolls together, but that wasn't the only thing they had in common. Tragically, both girls had lost a father to the guillotine. (Oh, those terrible days . . . )

"I would be honoured, Madame Bonaparte," she said, straightening the neck ruffle of her old-fashioned gown, "but most people still call me Clari." She placed her hands in her lap, one hand over another (to cover a stain on her glove).

"Hortense tells me that you are married and have two children."

"Two boys," she said, her melancholy eyes brightening. "One five years and quick, the other two years, but an infant in his growth and mind." She swallowed before adding, with heartfelt emotion, "Madame Bonaparte, you are well-known for your generous heart, for your willingness to help the unfortunate. The Angel of Mercy, people call you, because you further the cause of every petition that is made to you—you never turn anyone away. We lost everything during the Revolution. We have not a sou. I beseech you, please help us."

"I am the one in need of help," I assured her. The daughter of an impoverished aristocratic family, Clari no doubt found it humbling to beg employment. "I am in need of someone to accompany me—a lady-in-waiting. The salary is only twelve thousand francs, but you would share the position with several others, so you would still have time for your family."

"You are so kind!"

"And your husband?" I asked. "The First Consul might be able to employ him, as well."

"I will be forever indebted," she said, clasping my hands, her composure giving way.

*November 23, late morning.*
Bonaparte has approved my selection of ladies-in-waiting (except for the Duchess d'Aiguillon,* alas). Madame Lucay, Madame de Copons del Llor, and Madame Lauriston will report in shifts, beginning in a few weeks. Clari Rémusat will begin immediately. Her husband will be one of Bonaparte's chamberlains, as well—which solves their monetary embarrassment.

*November 27.*
Clari Rémusat, her husband and children moved into a suite at Saint-Cloud yesterday. She is quick-witted and cultured, and seems eager to be of assistance—certainly, I can use help.

*November 29—Saint-Cloud, chilly.*
"I picked up your parcel in town, Madame," Clari announced from the door, pushing back the hood of her cloak.

"I'm so glad you're here," I said, making smiling wide-eyes at Clari's two boys, their cheeks red from the wind. "I'd like your advice." I'd been studying a book of Greek statues that my architects had loaned me, and I was trying to get my shawl to fall in the manner of one statue in particular.

"We got held up on the Rue Saint-Honoré," Clari said, handing her youngest child into her nursemaid's arms. "You should see the lineup at the Théâtre-Français! Even at noon there was a long queue."

"A lady got hurt and the police were there," her eldest boy Charles said, one hand clutching the skirt of his mother's gown.

"Oh dear!" I told the boy, putting my hands to my cheeks—or pretending to. I was *not* to touch my face. Citoyen Isabey, Hortense's art instructor, had attended to my make-up and regarded my face as a work of art.

"It's true." The child nodded. He is an exceptionally sombre five-year-old, mature for his years.

"Apparently, there was a bit of a press when Mademoiselle Georges

---

* *The Duchess d'Aiguillon had shared a prison cell with Josephine during the Terror. She was not permitted to hold a position at court because she had been divorced.*

arrived," Clari said. "The Venus of Paris, people are calling the girl. Is it true she's only fifteen?"

It was after six by the time Bonaparte and I arrived at the theatre. "Not a seat empty," the theatre manager told us, escorting us to our box. "And now, may the performance begin," he announced, bowing deeply as the audience cheered.

Over the balustrade I looked to see what faces I recognized, nodding to acknowledge Minister Talleyrand, and the Second and Third Consuls, Cambacérès and Lebrun. In the third tier, way at the back, I thought I recognized Fouché, sitting alone. "*Everyone* is here," I whispered to Bonaparte. Caroline and Joachim (in pink), Elisa and Félix. "*And* Joseph," I said—but not with Julie. "Ah, it's your mother." I made a little wave to them all, but they didn't wave back.

By the end of the first act, the audience was becoming restless, in spite of Talma's riveting performance as Achilles. Everyone had come to see Mademoiselle Georges play Clytemnestra, and she was not to appear until the second act. So when the curtain opened, the claque cheered loudly.

At last the moment arrived: Clytemnestra stepped onto the stage. She *is* beautiful—tall!—but from our close vantage point, I could see that the poor girl was trembling. "Mon Dieu, Bonaparte, she can't speak," I whispered. Fortunately, the appreciative murmur of the crowd seemed to give the young actress courage and she began to recite her lines—somewhat mechanically, however, and without that fire that one senses in the great artists of the theatre.

It was during the third act that the trouble began. My heart jumped at the first hiss. It seemed to come from the benches toward the front. Then increasingly the critics became more and more vocal until, during the fourth and final act, there was a very long hiss during one of Mademoiselle Georges's speeches. Then the pit erupted: shouting, raising canes and umbrellas. Blows were exchanged!

Poor Mademoiselle Georges stuttered out a few lines. She looked as if she might faint. "Courage, Georges!" I heard someone yell out, and at this the young actress's voice became strong—angry even—and the audience fell silent. At the final curtain, the audience burst into cheers.

*December 1, early evening—Saint-Cloud.*

Talma struck a pose, his eyes raised in prayer, his shoulders thrown back, signifying pride. "Even Geoffroy, that idiot of a critic, was impressed with my protégée's masterful performance," he said, crossing both hands on his chest, casting his eyes down slowly and bowing his noble head.

"Bravo!" Clari clapped with delight. The famous theatre critic had recently lashed out against Talma, calling him a "Quaker of dramatic art." Talma's new school of acting, in Geoffroy's view, should be banished for tampering with the incantatory alexandrine.

"That's wonderful," I exclaimed, feeling that perhaps it was Talma who should be commended for a masterful performance. Although certainly beautiful, Mademoiselle Georges tends to speak her lines in a monotonous drawl, and that, to my mind, hinders perfect elocution. Still, she is only fifteen. "We should send her a note of congratulation, Bonaparte."

"I've already seen to it," Bonaparte said, staring out onto the terrace, lost in thought.


*December 16—cold!*

Troubling news from the Islands. Things are not going well in Saint-Domingue—apparently there has been a revolt. "Damn Victor Leclerc!" Bonaparte ranted. "I gave him my best men, our most seasoned soldiers, and even then he can't manage so much as a skirmish."


*December 22—still at Saint-Cloud.*

I confess I'm growing weary of Mademoiselle Georges—weary of the cult of enthusiasm that attends her every move. Or is it simply that I am growing old, and am jealous of her youth?

Bonaparte and I arrived late at the theatre. Mademoiselle Georges was centre stage, drawling a monologue. (There I go again!) The audience applauded our appearance, demanding that the actors start over—which they did.

All in all, it was a passable performance, I thought—at least on the part of the young actress. There was one curious moment when Mademoiselle

Georges said the line, "If I have charmed Cinna, I shall charm other men as well," and the audience craned to look at Bonaparte.

"It appears they think you've been charmed," I said, touching my husband's hand (watching his eyes).


*December 23.*

Terrible news—Victor Leclerc is *dead*. He died in Saint-Domingue of yellow fever. We are stunned to hear it. Bonaparte's beautiful sister Pauline is now a widow.

Bonaparte's new secretary brought the bulletin just after Bonaparte and I had finished our midday meal. "It regards your sister's husband, First Consul," Méneval said.

Bonaparte scanned the bulletin, then folded it, creasing it methodically. "My poor sister," he said, standing.

Victor Leclerc, dead at thirty-six. (He was older than I thought.) "The blond Bonaparte" we called him because of his habit of adopting Bonaparte's movements, even Bonaparte's expressions—which was why he irritated Bonaparte so much, I think.

We aren't sure how to proceed, frankly. Victor's family must be notified, of course. Who is to do it? My heart goes out to his mother and father, flour merchants, so very proud of their son.


*[Undated]*

The news is even worse than we originally thought. A vast percentage of the men sent to Saint-Domingue have died of yellow fever. The numbers are stupefying: of the twenty-eight thousand who sailed, fewer than ten thousand remain. *Mon Dieu.* How is that possible?

Bonaparte is overcome. This evening I placed his coffee at his elbow, touched his hand so that he knew it was there, returned to my frame. All the while he sat motionless, his hand over his mouth.


*February 12, 1803.*

Pauline is back, her husband in a lead coffin, her beautiful black hair shorn, entombed with Victor's body. She is enfeebled, both physically and emotionally. "They all died," she said weakly, kissing Bonaparte's hands. "Every last one of them."


*February 19, early—not yet 9:00 A.M. (and cold).*
England is refusing to honour the terms of the peace treaty. Bonaparte is not sleeping well, if at all.

"Stay, Bonaparte," I said, reaching for him in the middle of the night.

"I'll sleep when I'm dead," he said, pulling away.

I feel old in his presence—unappealing, without grace. I feel like a beggar, scrambling.


*February 28—Paris.*
"Mimi?" I found her in the wardrobe. I'd debated all morning about taking this step, was debating even as I spoke.

"I wish I could find that new lace veil, the silk one," she said, going through an open trunk. "I know I saw it here not long ago."

"Maybe it's at Malmaison. Or at Saint-Cloud." I never know where anything is anymore. I sat down on the little velvet stool in front of the chimney. "I was wondering, have you heard any rumours?"

Mimi closed the lid of the trunk. "About?"

I shrugged. "Oh, about Bonaparte and a woman."

"There are always rumours."

"For example?"

She blew out her cheeks. "Flowers are being sent upstairs of late."

"To the room above Bonaparte's cabinet?"

She screwed up her face.

"You could find out for me. You could ask Roustam, or Bonaparte's valet—or even Hugo, the cabinet guard." Even the new secretary would know, I realized with chagrin. "*Please*, Mimi."

I may be played false, but I'll be damned if I am going to be played for a fool.

*March 2, 2:30 P.M.*

"There's a young woman who comes most every afternoon around four, and . . ." Mimi put up her hands. "And that's *all* I know."


*March 3.*

"It's that actress everyone is talking about."

Mademoiselle Georges. I knew it! "The girl," I said.

"She's not a girl anymore."


*March 12—gloomy Tuileries.*

"Your powder was smudged tonight," Bonaparte said as I slipped under the covering sheet.

Of course it was—I'd been crying! Our weekly dinner for over one hundred in the Gallery of Diana had been unusually trying. Conversation kept coming around to theatre, to the "brilliance" of Mademoiselle Georges. Glances in my direction made it clear that everyone knows. "I'm miserable, Bonaparte."

Bonaparte took a candle and disappeared into the wardrobe. He looked ghostly re-emerging, the light from the candle throwing shadows over his face. "I couldn't find a handkerchief," he said, handing me a madras head scarf. "Now—what's this all about?"

I could tell from his tone that he knew the answer. "It concerns your amourette . . . with Mademoiselle Georges."

He sat down on the end of the bed, his nightcap askew.

"There's no use in denying it!" At the last theatrical we'd attended, Mademoiselle Georges had the audacity to wear *my* lace veil on stage.

Bonaparte crossed his arms. "Why should my amusements matter to you? I'm not going to fall in love."

"But Bonaparte, it's not right—"

"It is *my* right!"


*[Undated]*

Clari discovered me in my dressing room in tears. The gentle touch of her hand on mine unleashed my torrent of woes. She, so sweetly comforting and wise beyond her years, advised me to be patient. "This is but a temporary affair, Madame. It will pass, time will cure."

I know, I know, I nodded—but I was raging within. Plump, aging La Grassini was one thing—this beautiful young actress is another matter altogether.

"Just ignore it, that's my advice. It's your gentle acceptance that the First Consul loves. He will return to you, in time."

Gentle acceptance? I imagine Bonaparte in the arms of that girl and I weep tears of despair! I imagine her young, supple body—so responsive and fertile—and I feel withered within. I am not a young woman, and in truth, I fear I am older than my years, for my passion is no longer of the flesh. Passion of heart I have—oh yes—and spirit in abundance. But no amount of salves, lotions and face paint can disguise the dryness of my skin, my thinning hair—my waning lust.

Oh, I know this emotion all too well, this humiliating jealousy, this *fear*. My first husband was a coxcomb, true—and he never did love me. Bonaparte does: I know that! And it is *this* that frightens me—the possible loss of his love.

## In which Bonaparte is deceived

*March 14, 1803—Saint-Germain-en-Laye.*

In spite of the wind and driving rain, I set out for Saint-Germain early this morning. The hastily penned note from Aunt Désirée's new husband*—sent by courier, no less—worried me: "Come quickly, your aunt is gravely ill."

Therefore I was relieved (but also, I confess, not a little surprised) to find Aunt Désirée, her husband Monsieur Pierre *and* Aunt Fanny enjoying brandy and crumpets.

"What are *you* doing here?" Aunt Désirée demanded, trying to rise from the chaise longue.

"Gentle b-b-beloved," Monsieur Pierre stuttered (for this is what he calls her!), "you have been ailing, and I thought—"

"You thought I was dying?" Aunt Désirée said in accusation.

The poor man turned crimson.

"Stop stuttering and pour my niece a brandy, Monsieur Pierre," Aunt Fanny said. "She's been out in all that fresh air. Grand Dieu, if anyone's apt to die today, it's going to be her, and then we'll all be the worse for it. She brings the First Consul good luck—everyone says so. God knows where we'd be without *her*."

"So all the more reason for the First Consul to stay *home*," Aunt Désirée said with an all-too-knowing look.

---

* *Not long after the Marquis's death, Désirée married the mayor of Saint-Germain-en-Laye, Pierre Danès de Montardat.*

"And not to be going out all the time to the *theatricals*," Aunt Fanny said, emptying her glass of brandy and holding it out for more.

"I'm fine, thank you," I told Monsieur Pierre, declining a glass. "You have not been well?" I asked Aunt Désirée—intentionally changing the subject. It was humiliating to discover that Bonaparte's amourette with Mademoiselle Georges was talked about even in Saint-Germain.

"Your Aunt Désirée has endocarditis," Monsieur Pierre said.

"Which rhymes with nothing," Aunt Fanny said, frowning.

"It's something to do with the heart," Aunt Désirée explained, fluttering her hands over her bosom, "with the irritation of blood passing through it. At least that's what the doctor said, but what does *he* know? I'm the picture of health, as you can see."

However, not long after Aunt Fanny departed and Monsieur Pierre excused himself to go to his club, Aunt Désirée did, in fact, become quite ill—an attack coming on suddenly and severely. I helped her to her chamber where she collapsed into her musty feather bed.

"I'm sending for a doctor," I insisted.

"No, wait," she said, gesturing me back to her bedside.

"Aunt Désirée—rest. You must not talk!"

"This is important! I speak from your mother's grave."

*Mother's* grave? But Mother isn't dead!

"Just listen! To keep a husband, a wife must be cheerful and understanding, but above all, *blind*."

I promised to heed her advice on the condition that she rest and allow me to send for the doctor. He's with her now.


*5:20 P.M.*

Mon Dieu, we've lost her. The doctor left with assurances that Aunt Désirée was not in danger. I was preparing the tincture he'd prescribed when she began to turn blue, struggling for breath.

"Aunt Désirée!" I cried out, overcome with alarm. She was slipping away, and there was no one to help, no one I could turn to. I ran to the door and yelled for the servants. Someone!

"Above all, be blind!" she gasped.

I was trying to calm her when she suddenly stopped breathing and died in my arms.

I persuaded a very distraught Monsieur Pierre to retire as I helped the maids lay Aunt Désirée out. I moved without tears, my heart curiously still. Gently, I closed her eyes, arranged her limbs, helped wash and dress her. We debated: should she wear stays? "She wouldn't want to be without them," I finally decided. Even in death. Even in the hereafter.

After all was done, I dismissed the servants, and sat by her side as the candles melted down. Oh, Aunt Désirée, how can *you* leave me?

*March 19, Saint Joseph's Day—Tuileries.*
I returned from Aunt Désirée's funeral in a melancholic state of mind, so it seemed only fitting to find Bonaparte sitting in a darkened room, the drapes closed against the bright spring sun. He got up, but did not pace. "I've been in meetings with the Minister of the Marine," he said, leaning against the fireplace mantel.

Decrès? "And . . . ?"

"You know how he has become so much slimmer of late? I suspected that there was a petticoat in the picture, but never in a thousand years would I have guessed whom the old dog was courting." He snorted. "My sister Pauline, the bereft widow."

I was not surprised to hear that Pauline is receiving callers. Mourning is boring, she had said when last we saw her. But *Decrès*? "I guess it's time to look for a husband for her, Bonaparte," I told him, picking a long black hair off his collar. *Above all, be blind*, I heard a familiar voice say.

*Fort de France, Martinico*
*Chère Yeyette, my beloved niece,*
    *This morning Stéphanie sailed on* Le Dard *for Brest, France. She is only fifteen, so you can understand a father's concern. Have you arranged a chaperone for her? Were it not for the prospect of a proper education and a good marriage, my wife and I would have kept her near.*

*Your mother objected that the chicken coop attached to the magnificent house you bought for her in Fort de France was not sufficiently large. I ordered a larger one built, but chicken coop or no chicken coop, your mother refuses to be moved from her ramshackle country abode.*

*God bless you.*

*Your fond but aging uncle, Robert Tascher*

*April 8, Good Friday.*
I've just hired Mademoiselle Avrillion, an impoverished aristocrat of impeccable credentials: quiet, serious, virtuous. She'll help with the wardrobe for now, and when my goddaughter Stéphanie arrives from Martinico, she'll be the girl's chaperone.

*When* young Stéphanie arrives!

*April 28.*
Bonaparte is in a temper of frustration. England is flagrantly breaking the terms of the peace treaty. "Peace hasn't proved profitable for them," he said. "The perfidious British are doing everything they can to provoke war again."

*May 17.*
I've never been so upset. I don't know what to do, where to begin.

England has seized French ships near Brest. Bonaparte made sure I was sitting down before he told me, very gently and with assurances that all would eventually be well, that the ship *Le Dard* was one of those captured, and that my goddaughter had been taken captive.

I listened, I heard, but I didn't understand what he was saying. "Stéphanie has been kidnapped, you mean? By the British?"

There were tears in Bonaparte's eyes as he nodded, *yes.*

*May 22.*
The British are holding Stéphanie at Portsmouth and refuse to return her!

"Bonaparte, how can they do this? She's only a child!"

"Maudits anglais," Bonaparte cursed, pacing.

*May 25—back at Saint-Cloud.*
England has opened fire. Its navy captured one of our ships, killed ten men, wounded as many more.

No word on Stéphanie. I can't sleep.

*June 10.*
Bonaparte has received an offer from England to return Stéphanie, but along with a demand for trade concessions he felt he couldn't responsibly accept! I wept and begged and finally he agreed. We're both weak with emotion.

*June 14, 11:15 A.M.—Saint-Cloud.*
At last: Stéphanie will be returned. We are *so* relieved. "But she won't be here for a month at least," Bonaparte told me.

My breathing was coming in sharp gasps. "It's all right," he said, holding me close. "It's going to be all right."

*June 19.*
"I have to tour the north coast," Bonaparte informed me this morning. Of course, I nodded. War preparations. A fleet of flat-bottomed boats was being built, I knew—ships that could battle England's fleet, ships that could invade. "I want you to accompany me. Spare no expense. I must make a strong impression."

"Very well, Bonaparte," I told him, only too happy to oblige. "But are you prepared to pay?" Bonaparte wants me to be luxuriously attired in a new gown every evening, but he balks at paying the bills. "In advance," I persisted, suggesting an allowance not only for myself but also for Clari, the lady-in-waiting who will accompany me.

"Madame, how does one begin to dispense such a sum?" Clari asked me later in all seriousness, for Bonaparte has given her thirty thousand francs.

"Don't worry, Clari. It's really quite easy," I said, beginning a list of what I will need to take—but thinking, I confess, of what I will be leaving behind: a certain Mademoiselle Georges.


*June 23.*
We are ready, trunks packed, jewels in a velvet-lined strongbox. I've prepared for this trip as if for battle: my munitions are my gowns, my ointments, my salves.

I am forty today—an old woman, many would say, at an age when a woman has no claim on her husband's passions. I think with affection of Aunt Désirée, the seductive swish of her taffeta skirts. "Too old? Nonsense!"

"Every battle should have a definite object," Bonaparte says, and for me the object of this battle is his heart. In the north I will have Bonaparte to myself.


*June 25, I think—Amiens (overcast).*
The route to Amiens was decorated with a profusion of garlands, the streets and squares thronged with people cheering Bonaparte's arrival. In the heart of the city our carriage was forced to a halt. We heard the coachman protesting—for the people were unhitching our horses. Bonaparte looked uneasy. Crowds make him nervous, I know. Who is to say what might happen? And then a thunderous cheer went up and our carriage began to roll forward again—slowly, for we were being pulled by the people, so great was their adulation. Even Bonaparte's eyes were glistening.


*June 26—a Sunday.*
As I write this, I am deafened by the cheers of an enormous crowd at our window, crying out over and over, so fervently that the words become a heartbeat, a prayer: Long live Bonaparte! Long live Bonaparte! Long live Bonaparte!

I watch my husband, standing still as a statue. The cheers are a roar one can almost feel, a wave of rapture. What is he thinking?

"It's frightening, isn't it?" I have to raise my voice to be heard. "Who could ever have imagined *this*?"

"I did," he says, without turning, his tone strangely melancholy.

*[Undated]*

Bonaparte has succeeded in persuading most of the northern countries to close their ports to English goods. "Now if only I could stop the *exports* to England."

Russian hemp, for example, which gets sent to England to make rope for the British fleet. "Without rigging"—Bonaparte made a downward motion with his thumb—"even the invincible sink."

*July 7—Lille.*

Bonaparte threw a scented letter onto my embroidery frame. I recognized Pauline's unschooled hand. "Seems my beautiful sister has fully recovered from her devastating grief." He sat down, frowning as he counted silently on his fingers. "But she'll have to wait. It won't be a year until November."

"What won't be?" I asked, confused, trying to decipher Pauline's misspellings. "She's asking your permission to marry?" *Already?* Not Minister of the Marine Decrès, surely. I read on. "Prince Borghèse?"

Clari looked up from her lacework. Oh là là, her eyes said.

*Oh là là*, indeed! Prince Borghèse is the son of one of the wealthiest and most aristocratic families of Italy. I hate to think of the airs Pauline will put on if she becomes a princess.

*July 14, Bastille Day—Ghent.*

An exhausting day: audiences, visits to a public monument, two factories, a dinner followed by a reception, then the theatre. Bonaparte fell asleep during the after-piece in comic verse. "I'm not made for pleasure," he said wearily, untying his neckcloth.

"Yet some forms of pleasure suit you very well." I smiled archly over my bare shoulder as I turned back the bed covers.

*August 12, 10:30 P.M.—Saint-Cloud again, at last.*
Louis, Hortense and the baby welcomed us home. Little Napoleon, big and healthy at nine months, gurgled at Bonaparte, which pleased him greatly. As we sat in the family drawing room, talking of this and that, the baby fell asleep in Bonaparte's arms—a precious portrait. Oh, how we love this child!

*August 21.*
Stéphanie has arrived! Bonaparte and I have collapsed.

She's . . . oh, how to describe her? She is tall, for one thing, a giant of a girl with the body of a woman and the restless energy of a two-year-old. "I had the best time in England," she exclaimed, smothering us in her embrace. "Getting kidnapped was so much fun!"

"When does she begin boarding school?" Bonaparte asked faintly, exhausted after only an hour of the girl's constant chatter.

In two days, I told him. In the meantime, Mademoiselle Avrillion is charged with containing this cyclone of energy. And as for Madame Campan—she's got a challenge ahead!

*October 24—Saint-Cloud, very late, long past midnight (can't sleep).*
We've survived Pauline's engagement dinner—nearly two hundred covers. There were fourteen of us at the head table: Bonaparte and I, Prince Camillo Borghèse and Pauline, Lucien, Elisa and Félix, Joseph and Julie, Louis and Hortense, Joachim and Caroline, Eugène.

Prince Camillo Borghèse is well made, surprisingly ignorant, shockingly wealthy. Pauline was already flaunting the famous Borghèse diamonds. Lucien and Joseph seemed uneasy—why? Elisa hiccupped through dinner, as usual. Joachim was more fancifully dressed than Caroline, in his pink velvet toque dripping with ostrich feathers. Eugène dutifully attended to the (constant) needs of Signora Letizia—even going so far as to fill her nostrils with snuff.

Much of the conversation was in Italian, for the benefit of Prince Borghèse, who seemed, however, not to understand what was being discussed regardless of the language. Pauline insisted on feeding him chicken morsels herself, the grease dripping onto his gold-embroidered silk vest.

"I can see why Paris is abuzz with gossip about *those* two," I told Eugène later, setting up for a game of billiards. I took the opening shot, a strong one that scattered the balls with a gratifying clatter.

Eugène shrugged, chalking his cue. By the light of the candles, he appeared to be flushed. Was it wine? No, I didn't think so. My son is moderate in his habits (at least around family). "Prince Borghèse is a good match for Pauline," he said, not meeting my eyes.

"Fortunately, they don't seem to mind waiting to marry," I said, studying the table.

"Maman . . ."

"Piffle," I said, missing my shot.

"Maman, there's something I've got to tell you. But you must promise not to tell Papa."

"You know I can't promise that, Eugène."

"Well . . ." He grimaced. "Pauline and Prince Borghèse are already married."

"They're . . . ?" *Married?*

"The first of September, Maman, at Mortefontaine—seven weeks ago. Joseph and Lucien were in on it," he went on nervously. "Julie told her dressmaker, who in turn told Hortense, who of course told—"

Hortense knew! "And she didn't tell *me*? And no one told Bonaparte?" *Mon Dieu.* I could just imagine the explosion. War with England is one thing—but to be played for a fool by his own family is another matter altogether. "Eugène, Bonaparte is going to be furious. He's just announced Pauline's engagement."

"That's why you mustn't tell him, Maman!"

"They're *what?*"

I nodded, my mouth dry. "September first," I said finally, swallowing.

"They've been married for two *months?*"

"But only a church service, not the legal one. I suppose that makes a difference?" Timidly!

"Sacrebleu! I can't believe it," Bonaparte muttered. "Who do they think I am? Some puppet they can play with—pull my strings, then put me away in a box when I get in the way?" He came to an abrupt stop, staring into the fire. "I suppose they all knew."

"I just found out myself," I said, rushing to assure him. "I debated whether or not to tell you. I know how much you have on your mind right now, and . . ." I held out my hands, palms up, a gesture of appeasement. "But in the end, I thought you would prefer to know."

"I'm leaving immediately for Boulogne on an urgent military matter," he said, sitting down at the escritoire, rummaging around for a quill, then scratching something on a scrap of paper. "Inform Pauline that I'm leaving with the express intention of *not* being present at the farce of her so-called wedding. I'll be away for two weeks."

"Bonaparte, it might be best if—"

"And furthermore!" His quill snapped, splattering droplets of ink onto his shirt. He pulled out the drawer of the secretaire with such force that it ended up in his lap, the contents strewn, sand everywhere. Quickly I scooped up a quill from the floor and handed it to him. "And furthermore," he went on, oblivious to the mess, "advise her that it would be in her best interest if she and her idiot husband departed for Rome before I return."

*November 6, Sunday—Mortefontaine.*

"Bonaparte said to send his regrets." I embraced Pauline. She was drenched in a syrupy scent that caught in my throat, made me cough. "He was called away on an urgent military matter." I made a peaceable half-bow to Prince Borghèse (who could have used some scent).

"You don't have to lie, beloved sister." The "bride" broke into a mirthful giggle. "I guess I surprised him!"

"Yes, the First Consul was . . . *surprised*," I said, putting off informing her of Bonaparte's demand that she and her husband leave Paris immediately. Perhaps after the ceremony, I thought. But after the ceremony, Bonaparte's brother Lucien made an announcement that he himself had remarried one week before!

"I'm happy for you, Lucien," I lied, numb with shock.

Now, in the quiet of my room, I feel a sick head pain coming on, imagining Bonaparte's fury—deceived not once, but twice.


*November 10—Saint-Cloud.*
Family dinner tonight. Pauline agreed that she and Prince Borghèse will leave Paris before Bonaparte returns—on condition that she is formally "presented" at Saint-Cloud. Reluctantly I consented.


*November 13, Sunday.*
I should have guessed that *Princess* Pauline would make a theatrical event of the occasion. She and Prince Borghèse arrived at Saint-Cloud in a carriage drawn by six white horses, outriders in livery before and after carrying torches. My dame d'annonce threw open the double doors and announced (or rather, yelled), "Prince and Princess Borghèse."

Pauline entered the salon in a halo of blinding light, for she had adorned herself with virtually all the Borghèse diamonds. Her head, ears, neck and arms were loaded with a gaudy display of the priceless brilliants. Shuffling her feet to give the impression of floating, she approached me with her head bent forward in that strange position she considers regal.

"*Madame*," she said, bowing (slightly) before me, holding her hands rigid in order to avoid an unsightly bend at the wrist. Her eyes swept the crowd. *She* is a princess, and "a *real* one," she informed everyone, I'm told, coquetting with the men and loudly referring to her husband the prince as "that idiot."

They leave for Rome tomorrow.

"So!" Bonaparte yawned. "How did it go with Pauline?"

"As well as could be expected," I said cautiously, pulling the covers up over us. "They left five days ago for Rome." I didn't want to tell him about Lucien, but I knew I had to. "I have bad news, however." Quick, I thought, get it over with! "Lucien has married as well." I braced for an explosion, but there was only silence. "Madame Jouberthou, the widow of a broker." I winced before adding, "They married after the birth of their son." (But *before* they were sure that her husband was, in fact, dead. This I refrained from saying.)

"Lucien has a son?"

"Six months old now."

"I don't understand. He told me he'd consider marrying the Queen of Etruria,"* Bonaparte said, trying to comprehend. "And he was already married when he told me that?" He was silent for what seemed a long time. "Sometimes I wonder if my family even cares about me," he said finally.

"Your family loves you."

He took me in his arms. "I only have you."

We talked until dawn—of his mother, his brothers and sisters, Hortense and Eugène. We shared our enchantment with little Napoleon. Bonaparte said that although we would miss seeing the baby every day, he thought it would be good for Hortense and Louis to live in Compiègne for a time, Louis to take command of the troops stationed there. We talked of the challenges ahead, of preparing to battle England—and then, very late, Bonaparte began to talk of what was truly on his mind.

"What will happen if I die? What will become of France?" It was an outpouring of emotion, as if he had needed to unburden himself. "Who can I talk to? Who can I trust?"

I put his hand to my heart.

---

* *Etruria was an independent principality along the Mediterranean coast. A family alliance would have given Napoleon control over the port of Genoa—strategically important in the war against England.*

*November 24.*

"I'm tired of going out to the theatre every night," Bonaparte said last night. "Let's stay in—just the two of us." This with an amorous look.

Mimi grinned at me as she closed the door behind her. No flowers are being sent up to the little room.

## *In which once again we have reason to fear*

I didn't know whether to be relieved or alarmed to hear Fouché announced late this evening. I knew he would not have called at such an hour without a reason.

"Ah, Senator Fouché, it's good to see you," Bonaparte said, inviting him to join us in our private suite. "A Corsican will always invite a caller to his hearth," he added, attempting to be convivial.

It was chilly in the drawing room. Bonaparte fanned the embers. "And so?" he said, turning to face his former Minister of Police, his arms crossed. "You must have something to report."

"Bonaparte!" I said, pouring our guest a glass of verjuice. "Do we not inquire, first, as to Madame Fouché, all the charming Fouché children?" I smiled at my friend as I handed him the grape drink I knew he preferred. "Everyone is well?"

"As well as can be expected," Fouché said, downing the glass. "Yes, First Consul, I thought you might be interested to know that the Royalist agent Cadoudal is back in Paris—plotting your death yet again."

Cadoudal! The Royalist agent responsible for the Christmas Eve bomb—the "infernal machine"? I looked at Bonaparte, alarmed. "But I thought Cadoudal was in England."

"It appears he has been in town for several months," Fouché said evenly, "working on behalf of the Pretender. Financed by England, no doubt."

"That's impossible!" Bonaparte exploded.

"As you so often point out, First Consul, 'impossible' is not a French word."

"Cadoudal is as big as an ox. I ask you, how could he be in this city without the police being aware of it?"

"I asked myself the same question. How *could* they have missed him? According to my informants, Georges Cadoudal was hoisted by ship cable up a 250-foot cliff close to Dieppe on the fourth of Fructidor—August twenty-first. No doubt your police know the spot: certainly it is well-known to smugglers."

"End of August? Mon Dieu, Bonaparte—that's almost five months ago."

Bonaparte faced Fouché, his hands fists. "If this is a ruse on your part to discredit the police so that you will be reinstated as minister, it won't do any good."

"I didn't expect that you would believe me, First Consul," Fouché said, handing Bonaparte a scrap of paper. "I suggest you ask your police to have a word with this man at the abode indicated. His hours are regular. He's there until 9:50 every morning. He'll tell you what you need to know. In any case, it would be prudent to double or triple the number of guards you have protecting you." In the doorway, he tipped his hat. "At your service, First Consul, as always."

"Sacrebleu! This again," Bonaparte cursed.


*February 5, Sunday—Paris.*

I was preparing to go calling this afternoon when Bonaparte appeared. He sat down in his customary armchair next to my toilette table, fiddling with the crystal stopper of a bottle of lavender water. "Where are you going?" he asked.

"Madame de Souza is receiving this afternoon." I smoothed another dab of ceruse* under my eyes. I had not been sleeping well.

"Madame de Souza, the wife of the Spanish ambassador, and a writer of romances." Bonaparte pushed out his lips, as if considering this information.

---

* Ceruse was a thick paste made with white lead—and consequently corrosive and poisonous. It was used for several centuries as a make-up base, with devastating consequences.

"It's a pre-carnival fête, she said, in lieu of a ball," I explained, leaning into the glass to see how my make-up looked, then leaning back, squinting to get the effect. "Idle chatter, ladies mostly—the type of thing you hate. I made excuses for you."

But he wasn't listening. "I'd like you to take an escort," he said, drumming his fingers.

"But Bonaparte, it's only minutes away, and I'll have the pages with me, as well as two guards." The usual parade. (Oh, for the days when I could go out alone!) "Getting an escort together would take at least thirty minutes and I'm running behind as it is."

"Josephine . . ." He paused, sitting forward, leaning his forearms on his knees. "Fouché was right. Cadoudal *is* in Paris, along with a number of other assassins, as it turns out."

"A *number*?" Bonaparte rarely showed alarm, but something in his manner—the very stillness of his expression—made me wary.

"Twenty-four, to be precise."

"In Paris!" I reached for a handkerchief, pressed it to my mouth, inhaled the calming scent of lavender.

His hand felt hot on my shoulder. "We're hiring more guards and closing the gates to the city at night."

But the assassins were *in* the city, not outside. "Bonaparte, we *need* Fouché."

"Don't worry. Unofficially Fouché will be overseeing everything."

"That's reassuring," I said, sitting back. Maybe, with Fouché watching, we will be safe.


*Shortly after 11:00 P.M.*
The city gates are to be closed from seven each evening to six the next morning. Searches have begun of all carriages and wagons, looking for evidence of Cadoudal, his accomplices.

"Just like *those* days," Clari said, meaning the Terror. Only this time, we're the ones closing the gates, we're the ones searching.

*February 8—late, almost midnight.*

"What is this about?" Signora Letizia jabbed her stiff finger at a copy of *Le Moniteur.*

"What it's about, Maman, is that England has hired a Royalist thug to murder your son," Caroline answered, lingering over the word *murder* for effect.

"Ca-doo-dahl?"

"But don't worry," I said, offering my mother-in-law the seat of honour. "The police have it well in hand." Fouché, in fact—but that I could not say. I dared not even hint that the man the clan had persuaded Bonaparte to demote had been the one to uncover the plot. Had it not been for Fouché, Bonaparte might well be dead.

"Worry? The Funds are up," Elisa said between hiccups.

"Nothing like a little crisis to stimulate the economy," Joseph responded with a satisfied look. "I've a meeting at the Bourse tomorrow morning, Maman. Would you like me to speak with the man who handles your investments?"

"Naturalmente," Signora Letizia said, her knitting needles clattering.

"Perhaps now is as good a time as any to make a family announcement." Joseph smiled uneasily. "I've word from the Islands that Jérôme has married an American girl in Baltimore."

Mon Dieu, I thought, glancing at Bonaparte. Not another one.

"That's impossible," Bonaparte said evenly. "Jérôme's only nineteen. Legally, he can't marry without permission."

"He can in America, apparently," Joseph said.

"Basta!"

First Pauline, then Lucien, and now Jérôme.


*February 10—Tuileries.*

Louis and Hortense arrived from Compiègne last night. "Did you get my letter?" I asked, embracing my daughter. She has put on weight, which pleases me. "You didn't bring the baby?"

"He's asleep in his basket," Louis said, stepping aside to let the maid in with a tray. "What's going on? We had a difficult time getting through the city gates."

"The police have uncovered another plot against Bonaparte." How much could I tell them? "Remember Cadoudal?"

Hortense looked at me, alarmed. "*He's* in Paris?"

"He is believed to be here somewhere."

"But I thought he was in England," Louis said.

"No doubt he's in the *pay* of England," I said.

We heard tuneless singing outside the door, and then a baby's squeal. Bonaparte appeared in the doorway with little Napoleon in his arms. "At least *he* likes my singing," he said with a grin.


*February 14, Shrove Tuesday—Tuileries.*
Still no sign of Cadoudal, but a Royalist in the Abbaye Prison has admitted coming to France with him. The plan, he said, was to kidnap Bonaparte. The essential coup, they called it.

"Kidnap? That's a ruse. The only way to get rid of me is to kill me," Bonaparte ranted.

Frankly, we are all shocked. According to this Royalist's confession, General *Moreau* is implicated, one of the most popular generals in the Republican armies. How can that be?


*4:35 P.M.*
Bonaparte is constantly in meetings with the Special Council. Now and again he emerges with a drawn look.


*February 15, very early.*
Bonaparte didn't sleep at all last night, tossing this way and that until the covering sheet was in a damp knot. With the first light of dawn, he sat up. "I've come to a decision."

I knew from the slump of his shoulders what it would be.

*February 16.*
The news of Moreau's arrest was made public this morning. Everyone is stunned. Even the market was silent, Mimi told me.

*March 8—Malmaison.*
I persuaded Bonaparte that we should move to Malmaison for a few weeks to escape the tension in Paris, but even here, in this beautiful season, fear robs us of repose. Couriers come and go, officials with leather portfolios and sombre expressions. Daily Bonaparte is in meetings, locked up with his advisors. Still no sign of Cadoudal.

*March 9—our eighth-year anniversary.*
Our anniversary dinner was interrupted by a caller: Fouché. "Show him in," Bonaparte said, pushing back his plate of chicken bones.

Fouché appeared in mud-splattered top boots. "Cadoudal has been found."

"Arrested?"

"One of the conspirators alerted us to a plan to move him to another hiding spot. We apprehended his cabriolet on Place St-Étienne-du-Mont, but in the struggle he managed to escape."

"Answer my question, Fouché," Bonaparte said. "*Has* Cadoudal been arrested?"

"His carriage only got as far as Place de l'Odéon, where he was cut off by two policemen. One grabbed the horse, and Cadoudal shot him dead. The second officer was shot in the hip as he attempted to hit Cadoudal with a club. Then Cadoudal jumped from the carriage—"

"Now I know you're deceiving me. Cadoudal jump? He is a big man—he finds just stepping down out of a carriage difficult."

"First Consul, I may be devious, but I never lie. As Cadoudal began to run, the wounded officer—with the help of two brave citizens, I should add—managed to grab him and hit him over the head."

"So he *is* in custody. Has he confessed?"

"Only that he came to Paris with the intention of overthrowing you. His attitude is . . . well, certainly not repentant. When informed that the policeman he'd killed was a husband and father, he suggested we send bachelors on such missions next time."

"The bastard."

"The *wealthy* bastard. His pockets were stuffed with English gold. They have paid him well."

"Give it to the officer's widow."

"We already have."

Immediately after Fouché left, Talleyrand appeared. "We have apprehended Cadoudal, First Consul," he said, bowing deeply, his voice fawning.

"I am already aware of that, Minister Talleyrand. Fouché was just here."

Talleyrand blinked slowly. Only a crease on each side of his mouth gave any indication of the displeasure he must have felt at his rival's getting the rightful credit for the arrest. "I have been studying the documents found in Cadoudal's effects." Talleyrand presented a portfolio of papers, holding it out reverently in white-gloved hands as if offering up a sacrament.

Bonaparte pulled the parchment papers out and quickly riffled through them. "Explain," he said, throwing them down.

"According to these documents, First Consul, Cadoudal and his men were waiting for someone they referred to as 'the prince' to join them before they made their move."

Bonaparte paced. "What prince?"

"Perhaps we should discuss this in your office, First Consul."

"Speak!"

"Two of Cadoudal's servants have been questioned. They each declared that every ten or twelve days a gentleman came to call on Cadoudal—a man of middle height, corpulent and balding. Cadoudal always met him at the door, so apparently he was a person of consequence. When he was in the room, nobody sat down."

"And you think this man is 'the prince.'"

"It is a logical conclusion."

"A Bourbon prince?"

"Likely."

"It doesn't sound like either the Pretender or his brother."

"But the Duke d'Enghien resides one hundred and thirty leagues from Paris, First Consul—just across the Rhine river at Ettenheim."

"Enghien fought against us in Italy," Bonaparte said, frowning.

"The last hope of the house of Bourbon, it is said. It's possible that the plan was for Enghien to come to Paris as soon as you were"—Talleyrand paused for effect—"*dispensed* with. As a Bourbon representative, so to speak, he would have held Paris until the Pretender arrived from England and mounted the throne."

"The Duke d'Enghien is slender, Minister Talleyrand, is he not?" I asked, turning. He is said to be a charming man, and handsome—certainly not corpulent and balding. It is rumoured he has secretly married Princess de Rohan-Rochefort—la belle Charlotte. "In his late twenties, I would guess, and—"

But the men were already on their way out the door. Their voices grew faint until I could hear no longer. "I believe, First Consul, that . . . a lesson to those . . . endless conspiracies . . . the shedding of royal . . ."

*The shedding of royal blood*, I believe I heard Talleyrand say.


Now, recalling that conversation, playing it over in my mind, I am more and more uneasy. Why was Talleyrand pressing Bonaparte to suspect the Duke d'Enghien—a Bourbon prince beloved by Royalists everywhere?

I don't trust Talleyrand, frankly. He reminds me of a snake—he sheds coats too easily. He expresses admiration for, even worship of, Bonaparte—but is he sincere? He is known to take bribes, to extort enormous sums in his international dealings. His "loyalty" is of the kind that is bought for money, I suspect.


*March 18—Paris.*

Before Mass this morning Bonaparte told me, his voice so low I could hardly hear him, "We've arrested the Duke d'Enghien."

At first I didn't understand. "But isn't the Duke d'Enghien in Germany?"

"What does it matter? What is important is the charge: conspiring to commit murder—*my* murder."

On the long ride out to Malmaison, I broke down, confiding to Clari that the Duke d'Enghien had been arrested.

"Arrested for what, Madame?" She burst into tears, confiding that as a girl, she had kept an etching of the Duke d'Enghien in a secret spot under her mattress.

"I believe they intend to have him tried in connection with the conspiracy."

"But *he* can't be guilty!"

"Then he will be found innocent and go free," I reassured her.

Clari's agitation was extreme. It had been a mistake to confide in her, I realized. She is young, not skilled in the art of deception. "You must not let Bonaparte know that I have told you," I cautioned her as our carriage pulled through the Malmaison gates.

"Oh no, Madame, never!"

"So you must try to stop *weeping*," I said with a smile, handing her my handkerchief.

"Yes, Madame," she sobbed.

*March 19, Saint Joseph's Day.*
"Women know nothing about such matters!"

"Bonaparte, I cannot be silent on this." My attempts to seduce my husband into listening had met with failure.

"If I don't act firmly—*now*—I will have to go on and on prosecuting conspirators, exiling this man, condemning that man, without end. Is that what you want?"

"Surely it is not so simple."

"You forget that it is the Bourbons who are the cause of the turmoil in France. *They* are the ones seeking to murder me."

"But what if the Duke d'Enghien is innocent? General Moreau was arrested over a month ago. If the Duke d'Enghien is part of the conspiracy, would he have remained at Ettenheim? Cadoudal's servants reported that the mystery prince was corpulent. The Duke d'Enghien is said to be slender."

"There is evidence!"

"But Bonaparte, even if the Duke d'Enghien is guilty, if you were to convict him"—*execute* him, I feared—"all of Europe would rise up against you." The stain of royal blood is indelible, it is said.

"Do you want me killed?" He clenched his hands. "I must show the Bourbons who they're dealing with. I must give them a taste of the terror they are trying to inflict on me. I must show them I'm not to be trifled with—and I'm not!"

*March 20, 8:00 A.M.*

Gazing out over the gardens, I saw Bonaparte walking the paths between the flower beds, his pace and gestures agitated, as if arguing with himself. How small he seemed, pacing among the roses. "Little Bonaparte" I had once thought of him—before he'd become a giant in our eyes. (Our hearts!) I know how ardently he wishes to do the right thing, and I am beginning to comprehend how hard that can be.

*9:20 P.M.*

Around noon Hortense dropped little Napoleon off for me to look after—never have I more welcomed a child's innocent prattle. "I'll see you tomorrow?" I asked, kissing my daughter goodbye.

She and Louis were joining Caroline and Joachim for dinner, she said. She was running late, the boulevards had been congested—was something going on?

I shook my head. She is newly again with child. If only I could protect her from the realities of the world! I was thankful she left quickly, before she could see Clari's reddened eyes, before she looked too closely at my own.

*March 21.*

I was going to Bonaparte's cabinet this morning to drop off the usual petitions when I heard him yelling: "What do you mean? Didn't he get my letter?"

I paused outside the door, holding my breath. I heard a man say something, then cough. Was it Savary, Bonaparte's aide? "I saw him on the road," the man said. It *was* Savary. "He didn't get your letter until this morning." Another cough. "When it was too late."

*Too late?*

"What do you mean, this morning? I gave that letter to you last night with the instructions that it was to go directly to the Prefect of Police!"

"I gave it to his valet."

"I didn't say to give it to his valet. I ordered you to give it to the man himself! Do you realize what you've done?"

I heard footsteps approaching behind me: one of the guards. "Do you wish to speak with the First Consul, Madame Josephine?" Hugo asked, his deep voice announcing my presence.

Bonaparte came to the door. "Josephine." He looked pale. "You are dismissed," he told Savary coldly, over his shoulder. The aide hurried out the door between us. "Come in," Bonaparte said, "I have something to tell you." I lowered myself onto a wooden armchair. "The Duke d'Enghien has been executed."*

* Napoleon had sent the Prefect of Police a letter saying that he wished to talk to the Duke d'Enghien, but the letter wasn't delivered until after Enghien had been executed. Fouché was later to say that the Duke d'Enghien's execution was "worse than a mistake, it was a blunder."

## *In which a prophecy is fulfilled*

I found Savary in the drawing room. "General Savary, I would appreciate it if you could tell me—" Did I really want to know? "How did it happen?"

"There was a tribunal, and then . . ." Savary wiped the perspiration off his forehead with his sleeve. "And then the Duke was taken to one of the trenches outside the château."

"A moat, you mean?" I had never been to Vincennes.

He nodded. "A dry one."

A canary burst into song. "No last words?"

"Just that he didn't want a blindfold." Savary felt in his jacket pocket, withdrawing a ring, a folded handkerchief and a sheet of paper. "Earlier he asked that his wife get these. Princess de Rohan-Rochefort, he said."

*La belle Charlotte.* The letter was short and tender—*love eternal*—the ring a simple gold band with an insignia on it. "And what's this?" I asked, unfolding the handkerchief.

It is late now. I am at my escritoire. Before me is a ring, a letter, a handkerchief containing a lock of hair: the remnants of a life.

I study these artifacts, half-expecting them to speak, give me an answer. Was the Duke d'Enghien guilty of conspiring to murder my husband? Or was he innocent, and unjustly executed by him?

As I write this, Bonaparte sits in the chair by the fire, watching the flames—as if expecting to see an answer there himself.

*March 23—Paris, windy.*
"I would say that the people of Paris are *unsettled*," Fouché responded, in answer to my question. "They've been flocking out to Vincennes to view the trench, tossing in bouquets. Of course, that damn dog doesn't help."

"What dog?"

"The Duke d'Enghien's dog. It stands over its master's grave, howling day and night."

"Bring it to me."

"I suggest you reconsider. The First Consul would not care to—"

"I know someone who would very much appreciate having that dog."

*March 24.*
Princess de Rohan-Rochefort resides in Worms. I've sent the Duke d'Enghien's last effects to her in the care of Moustache, along with the trembling dog—Mohilow by name—strapped into a wicker travelling basket. Against my better judgement, I included a note of sympathy.

*March 25—Paris.*
Both Bonaparte and I were uneasy setting out for the Opéra tonight. It was our first public appearance in Paris since the Duke d'Enghien's execution. "Are you trembling?" Bonaparte asked, taking my arm. His face was pale as death.

"Just a little chilled," I lied.

Immediately on entering our box, Bonaparte went to the front, showing himself to the audience. On hearing cheers, applause, Bonaparte turned, took my hand. *Relief.*

*March 27—almost midnight.*
Fouché arrived late at the drawing room tonight. "Ironically, the support for the First Consul has, if anything, increased," he said when I told him about our experience at the Opéra. "The Revolutionaries feel that he is finally one of them—now that he has blood on his hands."

"Fouché, please, you know it's not—"

"And as for the Royalists," he droned on, "they are entirely diverted by rumours of a crown."

A *crown*. The thought made me tremble! "I understand that there was a motion in the Senate today inviting Bonaparte to make his glory immortal." What did that mean—*immortal*?

"This latest attempt on the First Consul's life has made people desperate for security," Fouché said, stroking the mottled skin on the back of his hand. "It is generally believed that some form of monarchy would bring peace—and peace, of course, would bring prosperity. If a king is required, a citizen-king crowned by the people might not be such a bad thing. That the First Consul can now be counted on not to be in league with the Bourbons makes him all the more trustworthy."

"Fouché, if I didn't know you better, I'd think that you yourself might be in favour of a monarchy."

"I made the motion."

"*You* made the motion about glory immortal?" I was momentarily speechless. "But you opposed Bonaparte being made First Consul for *Life*."

"Do you wish me back as Minister of Police?"

Oh yes!

"I want my department back. Any fool can see what's required." He smiled, a ghoulish expression on him. "If there is one thing I've learned over the years, it's that flexibility is the key to survival."

*April 5—a gorgeous day.*

Bonaparte leaned against the fireplace mantel, his arms crossed. He cleared his throat.

I put down my cup of coffee. I knew that look. Bonaparte had something to tell me—something I was not going to like.

"Josephine, my advisors are saying that a hereditary system of succession would put an end to the threats against my life."

*Hereditary.* Glory eternal. "Is that what is being proposed?" My voice betrayed my apprehension.

"Yes, that succession be hereditary in the male line, by order of primogeniture. A traditional arrangement. This is the model that is being suggested, in any case."

"And so Joseph would be your successor?" How awful!

"That is Joseph's view, unfortunately. But ideally, the heir would be my son, a child raised to the role."

I looked away, blinking. There was no heir; there would never be an heir! All the mineral waters in all the spas of Europe could not give me what I wanted more than anything in the world: Bonaparte's child.

*Very late—everyone asleep.*

"Bonaparte, there's something we should discuss."

He yawned. "Now?"

"Tomorrow, if you wish. In the morning."

He pushed back his nightcap, turned to me. "You look beautiful in the moonlight."

"You want to talk about it now?"

"I don't want to talk at all," he said, pulling me close.

"So what was it?"

"What was what?" I yawned with contentment.

"What you wanted to discuss."

"Oh . . ." I never wanted to talk about it, frankly!

"Oh *that*," he said, understanding.

I nodded against his shoulder. He was damp with perspiration, smelling sweetly of lemon.

"You should know that I'm insisting on the right to adopt," he said softly, caressing my cheek.

I pulled away. "You'd be able to *adopt* an heir?" Of course my first thought was of Eugène.

"The child would have to be a blood Bonaparte—one of my brothers' sons."

"Little Napoleon?" Smiling.

"Come back here," he said.

*April 7.*

I was surprised this morning to see our courtyard crowded with men in uniform, on horseback. "Bonaparte, why such a large escort?" And everyone in formal livery—even the pages. Perhaps I had misunderstood. "Aren't we just going to see Louis and Hortense?"

"This is an official visit," he said, pulling at the ruffle edge on his sleeve.

Hortense came down the stairs to meet us with little Napoleon in her arms. "You must not run down the stairs like that!" I admonished her (in spite of my resolve not to be overly protective). She is large for three months, already beginning to show.

"What's this about?" Hortense gave us both a quick kiss. "Is there a military review today?"

"Nonan!" little Napoleon cried out to his uncle, squirming to be let down. Bonaparte took the boy from Hortense and tipped him upside down, making him squeal.

"Careful, Bonaparte!"

"Again," the child demanded, giggling.

Hortense, tucking a lock of hair under her cap, looked out into the courtyard. "Look at all the soldiers."

"Perhaps we should have sent word first. You were painting?" I asked. A week ago she'd begun a portrait of Eugène, and was finding it challenging.

Hortense ran her long red-lacquered fingernails over her smock. "Earlier, while my sweet one was having a nap."

"No!" the boy protested, sticking his fingers in his mouth.

"Not now," Hortense reassured him with a kiss.

"Where is Louis?" Bonaparte demanded, letting the nanny take the baby from him.

"Out. He didn't tell me where, just that he wouldn't be long."

"Perhaps we might wait?" I suggested to Bonaparte.

"I'll be in the garden," Bonaparte said darkly.

"Maman, what is this all about?" Hortense led the way into her drawing room, inviting me to sit beside her on the sofa.

Hortense tended not to follow politics. I didn't know how much she knew. "Are you aware that a new constitution is being proposed?"

She nodded. "The Civil Code?"*

"The Civil Code is an important part of it, certainly, but there's more." I paused, unsure how to explain. "As you know, this last conspiracy has raised concerns once again about Bonaparte's safety—and, consequently, concerns about the stability of the nation. Our enemies know that if Bonaparte were to be assassinated, the French Republic would fall." Was she following me? I took her hand. "But if a system of hereditary succession were in place, the nation would endure."

"I thought you were against that, Maman."

"I've come to understand the reasoning. The attempts on Bonaparte's life must stop!"

"But what good is a hereditary system if you and Papa don't have have an heir?" She bit her lip, regretting her words.

"Bonaparte is going to insist on the right to adopt."

"Eugène?"

"To be legitimate, the adopted heir must be a Bonaparte." My daughter looked suddenly wary. I smiled apologetically, a pleading look. "Bonaparte would like to adopt little Napoleon as his successor."

"But he's only eighteen months old, Maman!"

"Nothing would change," I started to assure her, but was diverted by Bonaparte, standing at the door.

"I can't wait any longer," he said, beckoning me and then disappearing.

"Should I mention this to Louis?" Hortense asked, her voice thin.

"Bonaparte should be the one to say something, I think."

"Maman, if Papa suggests it, Louis will be against it on principle."


Bonaparte was seated in the carriage, impatiently tapping his sword against the floor. Soldiers on horseback were lined up behind the carriage in double file, the horses sleepy in the morning sun.

* *The Civil Code (Code Civile des Français, later renamed Code Napoléon): a combination of Roman law, existing French law and the egalitarian principles of the Revolution. It remains the basis for jurisprudence in many countries of the world today.*

"I told her," I said as the footman handed me in. "She's apprehensive, I think, but—" My train caught on the carriage door. Just as I freed it, a man on horseback came through the gate. "It's Louis." He looked alarmed by the sight of so many soldiers in his courtyard.

"Zut," Bonaparte said, annoyed at his brother for being late—late for an appointment Louis knew nothing about. Hortense was right, I thought. It would be a mistake for Bonaparte to approach Louis.

"I'll talk to him," I said, opening the carriage door.


First I had to assure Louis that nothing terrible had happened—that his son had not been murdered nor his wife abducted. "The First Consul and I came today regarding a matter of great importance to the nation," I began, "a matter that would someday bestow a very great honour on you and your son." I paused. The setting was less than ideal. We were standing in the entry, everyone watching. "We don't expect an answer, only that you consider what we are proposing."

"Which is?"

"As you know, Bonaparte must have a successor. The amendment that is being drafted to the Constitution will give him the right to adopt an heir—little Napoleon."

Louis tilted his head toward his hunched-up shoulder, cradled his weak hand. "My *son*?"

Oh dear, I thought. Louis's immediate concern was that he himself would not be the successor. "Such a fine prospect for a son might help console a father for not being named heir himself," I said, giving him an imploring look.


*April 8, Sunday.*

Hortense was just here, very upset. Caroline called on her last night: accosted her is perhaps more accurate. In an angry tone Caroline informed Hortense that she had learned of Bonaparte's proposal to adopt little Napoleon and was prepared to fight it! Little Napoleon would be the crown prince, but *her* children would be "nobodies" (her word), and she would not stand for such an injustice.

"I don't understand," Hortense said tearfully. "I thought she was my friend."

*[Undated]*
Mimi slipped me a note this morning. "It's just as you suspected," she said with a grimace.

*Mme Carolin told Louis He must not let the 1st Consul take his son. Shee told him the Old Woman wants the 1st Consul to dis-inherit all the Clan. Shee told him He wood hav to bow down to His own Son. Shee told Him that Peopl say the 1st Consul is the Father of his Child. Shee told Him that if the 1st Consul wants a Son, He must divorse the Old Woman.*

*April 9.*
Louis has sent an angry letter to Bonaparte. "He demands to know why I want to disinherit him," Bonaparte said. "He can't stand the thought that little Napoleon would be his superior. He says he'd rather die than bow his head to his son."

"He wrote that?" I asked, pretending to be surprised.

"*And* that he'd leave France and take his son with him," Bonaparte said quietly.

Pour l'amour de Dieu!

"*And* that the only solution to the problem of an heir is for me to—" Bonaparte stopped. "Listen," he said, his voice thick, "according to the new constitution, I will have the right to adopt the boy when he turns eighteen. Louis will come around, with time."

Louis, perhaps—but what about Caroline?

*April 23, evening, almost 9:00, I believe.*
Tonight Bonaparte informed me the Legislature has voted in favour of hereditary succession. "It will become law in less than a month. At that point, everything is going to have to change."

"Again?" We'd been in a constant state of change for years, it seemed.

"We're going to have to have a legitimate court, more servants—"

I sighed. We already had far more than I could manage.

"—and ritual." He made a circling motion with one hand. "And costumes."

"Livery, you mean?" We already had "costumes," as he put it.

"You'll see to it?"

"I will, King Bonaparte," I said with a teasing smile (wondering when I should break the news to him how much new liveries would cost).

"No, never king."

"No?" Hopeful!

"The title 'king' reminds people of the Bourbons. My title must be more expansive, more of antiquity. 'Emperor' harks back to the Roman Empire and the reign of Charlemagne. It alarms some people because it's vague and conveys a sense of immensity—but that's what appeals to me. What's wrong with immensity?"

"You're serious." *Emperor?*

He smiled at my puzzled expression. "Emperor Napoleon." This with theatrical flair, his hand in his vest.

*11:20 P.M.*

Yeyette, Rose, Mademoiselle Tascher, Citoyenne Beauharnais, Madame Bonaparte: *Empress.*

Grands Dieux. It's just a courtesy title, I tell myself—it doesn't give me any official standing.

I tell myself. I tell myself.

*April 26, late afternoon.*

A long meeting today with Madame Campan, who has agreed to help organize our household—our "court." (I'm so relieved.) "You must have aristocrats serving you," she said, looking over the list of those who might be invited. "Men and women of the most ancient houses of France."

The nobility of history: Chevreuse, Montmorency, Mortemart. The names alone terrify me. "Madame Campan, with respect, the men and women of those families do not even deign to speak to me. How could they possibly serve me?"

"The nobility are raised to bow, to be bowed to. They understand the power that subservience confers. It's the wife of a soldier who will balk at the notion of lowering her head, for fear of being taken for a maid. What about Countess de la Rochefoucauld?" she said, flicking the paper with her finger. "A Rochefoucauld would impress. Others would then follow."

No doubt. The Rochefoucauld name is one of the oldest—and most revered.

"She's your cousin, is she not?"

"A distant cousin," I said, "through the family of my first husband. She was at Plombières last time I went." Chastulé de la Rochefoucauld does make me laugh. A hunchback with a plain countenance, she nevertheless approaches life with humour and wit.

"It would be a victory to persuade a Rochefoucauld to be your lady of honour. It's one of the most powerful positions at court. She would manage your staff, your appointments, your budget and ledgers. Anyone who wishes to call on you must apply first to her. Such a position might interest her."

"I very much doubt that she would agree, however." Chastulé is fond of me, but blistering in her condemnation of Bonaparte—"that upstart Corsican," she is said to call him.

"I believe she might. The family is said to be seriously embarrassed."


*May 4—sunny!*
For the sum of three hundred thousand francs, *plus* an annual salary of eighty thousand (with guaranteed increases each year), *plus* a position for her husband, Countess Chastulé de la Rochefoucauld has agreed to be my lady of honour.

"Ha!" she exclaimed. "When do I start? Next month? Fine. Whoever said aristocrats had principles? Wave a little gold in front of my eyes and I'm yours, ready to serve in the house of the devil. Not that *you're* the devil." She tugged on my elbow—gestured to me to bend down so that she could kiss my cheek. "Ha! You see, Your Majesty. Everyone bows to a hunchback."

*Your Majesty,* did she say?

### May 6.

Bonaparte insists that once the Empire is officially proclaimed, once we are named Emperor and Empress, everything we do—what we say, how we move, what we wear—must be done according to royal tradition (*legitimacy*).

I've been studying an ancient book that was found in the palace library: *The Code.* Over eight hundred articles outline what is done in any situation an emperor or empress might encounter. Even so, much is left unsaid. Consequently, I've been consulting Madame Campan. She explains how things were done in the days of kings and queens—how people were addressed, what privileges were accorded to whom. We go over the procedures, the rules and forms, considering what to keep, what to reject. Poor Clari's hand is cramped from writing down all that Madame Campan dictates—over two hundred pages already.

### May 17.

Subject to ratification by the people, tomorrow the Republic will be formally entrusted to a hereditary emperor.

"Are you ready?" Bonaparte asked.

"I'm not sure." How did one prepare for such a thing?

Bonaparte told me what to expect: Cambacérès, Arch-Chancellor now, will come from the Senate with a delegation in order to make the official pronouncement. The officials will go first to Bonaparte, make their presentation, and then they will come to me.

Madame Campan and I have been going over the elaborate procedures. How foreign it all seems. "Look upon it as a performance," she told me, sensing my apprehension. "Look upon it as your greatest role."

*May 18.*

I was dressed long before I heard the clatter in the courtyard announcing the arrival of Arch-Chancellor *de* Cambacérès (now) and his large delegation: men from the Senate, the ministers and the councillors escorted by a regiment of cuirassiers. De Cambacérès entered my apartment with great pomp, coming to a halt six paces from me. (Why so far? I thought. Is this what it means—that from now on no one will dare come near me?) Then, dropping a full court bow—as full as he could manage with his large belly, that is—de Cambacérès spoke the one word I never wanted to hear: *Empress.*

# II

## The Good Empress

How unhappy a throne makes one.
—*Josephine, in a letter to Eugène*

## *In which we become a "court"*

*May 18, 1804—Saint-Cloud, thunder and lightning still.*
Empire. Emperor. Empress. It has been little over a day since the Empire was proclaimed, and already we have become like animals, snarling over a bone. It frightens me to see what greed can do to people.

But I jump ahead of myself.

After the proclamation, there was a formal state dinner—an *Imperial* occasion, our first. (Three footmen for each guest, and Bonaparte unhappy because Talleyrand used the aristocratic word "supper" on the invitations instead of the more plebeian "dinner.")

The family, the officials and the officers of the household assembled in the Grand Salon, awaiting Bonaparte—or rather, awaiting the *Emperor*, as we are to call him now. Of the family: Hortense and Louis, Eugène, Elisa and Félix, Caroline and Joachim, Joseph and Julie—a smaller number of Bonapartes than usual because Signora Letizia, Uncle Fesch, Lucien and Pauline are all in Italy, and young Jérôme is still in America.

Duroc—looking bandy-legged in the Imperial skin-tight knee breeches—informed everyone that Joseph and Louis are now to be addressed as Prince, their wives as Princess. Caroline cast furious glances at her husband, who was slouched in the corner in his circus finery, tossing one of the new coins in the air (Emperor Napoleon on one side, the French Republic on the other).

The *Emperor* arrived promptly at six and saluted the new princes and princesses as well as *Madame* Caroline, *Monsieur* Joachim, *Monsieur* Eugène and so forth. Caroline's expression had taken on a hard aspect.

Just then a violent thunderstorm broke outside. A flash of lightning followed by a roll of thunder sent the pugs scurrying.

Duroc announced that we were to proceed to the table, and both Louis and Joseph claimed the honour of following Bonaparte. "I am the eldest," I heard Joseph hiss, urging his wife to step ahead of Hortense. Caroline grabbed her husband's arm and strutted by. I glanced back at Eugène—he was standing by the fireplace with a bored expression, quite content to be at the end of the line.

Bonaparte placed me on his right, inviting "Princess" Hortense to sit on his left. Caroline choked gulping down a glass of water, so great was her distress.

*May 19—Saint-Cloud, beginning to clear.*

Caroline and Joachim arrived early for the family dinner. Caroline, her smile fixed and bright, was dressed in a gown of ruffled green silk, her bosom adorned with a string of paste gems. Battle gear, I thought. (For once she outshone her husband.) It was a more informal occasion than the imperial dinner the night before—but consequently became somewhat raucous. Fortunately, Hortense and Julie were not present.

Caroline was conspicuously silent throughout the meal. Bonaparte—in an effort to be obliging, I am sure—did not complete in his usual fourteen minutes, but lingered, encouraging us to finish each course. After desserts (Caroline helped herself to a generous slice of the almond cheesecake, eight figs and virtually all the Gruyère), I suggested that we retire to the drawing room for coffee. Bonaparte bolted from his chair as if the doors to his prison cell had been opened. I purposely allowed Caroline to proceed ahead of me out of the room.

When everyone was settled, the butler brought in the coffee service on a tray. "I'll have a barley water," Caroline demanded.

"Are you not well?" Bonaparte asked his sister.

"What do you care about my health?" she said with such violence that the butler very nearly upended his tray. And then it came out: why were his own sisters to be condemned to obscurity, while strangers were loaded with honours?

"That's right," Elisa chimed in, setting down her coffee.

"Joseph's wife and Louis's wife are not strangers," Bonaparte observed with admirable calm (his thigh muscle twitching, I noticed).

"Julie and Hortense are not Bonapartes and yet *they* are princesses, while your own flesh-and-blood sisters are nobodies!"

"I distribute honours as I deem right for the nation," Bonaparte said, "not to fulfill *your* personal vanity."

"You think it's baubles I seek? I'm concerned with posterity, my *children's* future," Caroline said bitterly.

"Your children are not in the—"

Not in the line of succession, Bonaparte was going to say, but before he could finish, Caroline broke in. "They are your nephews and nieces— your *blood* relatives. They will be commoners! Is that what you want?"

I got up and closed the windows. It wouldn't do for this quarrel to be reported in the journals.

"One would think I had deprived you of the crown of our father, the late king," Bonaparte said sarcastically.

"You expect me to bow down before Hortense?" Caroline shrieked.

"Or Julie?" Elisa added, scowling.

"You dishonour your own flesh and blood!" And with that, Caroline placed the back of her hand to her brow and sank to the floor, her voluminous silks billowing out all around her.

"Caroline?" Joachim looked down at his wife, puzzled to see her stretched out at his feet.

The pugs, delighted to have someone at their level, started licking her face. When she didn't respond, I realized that she wasn't acting. "Juste ciel, Bonaparte!" I sent the butler for smelling salts. Bonaparte knelt beside Caroline and shook her shoulder, trying to get her to rise. "Hold some spirits under her nose," I suggested, but there was no need, for her eyelids began to flutter.

Bonaparte sat back on his heels, shaken. "Look," he said, addressing his family. "I'll give it some thought."

"And what about my husband?" Caroline demanded, sitting up.

*June 2—Malmaison for the day.*
"*Princess* Caroline? All of Paris is laughing!" Thérèse reported, fluttering

her neroli-scented fan. "She parades through the streets as if she really *were* royalty. But people love *you*—it's said you seem born to the role."

Born to it? Hardly!

*June 12—Saint-Cloud.*
Bonaparte has been in a meeting with the Special Council for three hours. The men come and go. Now and again I hear the word "coronation."

*[Undated]*
There *is* to be a coronation: the date has been set for July 14, Bastille Day. Only one month from now!

*[Undated]*
I'm so relieved. The coronation date has been put forward to November 9 (18 Brumaire*).

*June 16.*
An exhausting day reviewing the proposed staff list with Madame Campan. Here is what my household will look like, so far:

First almoner: Prince Ferdinand, often in his cups, but Bonaparte insists because he's cousin to the Duke d'Enghien. ("Fusion," Bonaparte decrees.)

First equerry: Monsieur d'Harville, the most powerful person in my household. Count Etiquette, I've named him, for that will be his task— to make sure everything is done properly. Not an easy job.

Five chamberlains: the first chamberlain will be General Nansouty, a wonderful cavalry officer, according to Eugène.

Introducer of the ambassadors: Monsieur de Beaumont, with his comical high voice.

---

* *18 Brumaire: date of the coup in 1799 which overthrew the government of France and instituted Napoleon as First Consul.*

Intendant of the household: Monsieur Hainguerlot.

Lady of honour: little Chastulé.

Ladies-in-waiting: I'm going to hold it to twelve, although Madame Campan insists I will need twice that number. Clari will be first lady-in-waiting.

Mistress of the wardrobe: Mademoiselle Avrillion.

Chambermaids (four, at present).

Dames d'annonce: Madame Campan says I'll need at least four more.

Pages: six charming boys, very proud of their uniforms.

Valets de chambre (six).

Ushers (four).

Footmen (eight).

Coachmen (three).

Errand-runner: quick little Benoist.


No wonder I'm having trouble sleeping. It's a terrifying list, and Bonaparte's staff is three times as many. I think with longing of my life of eight years ago—my staff of four.


*June 19.*

The Empire unfolds in lists: the staff announcements will be made tomorrow, the swearing-in ceremony in two weeks, everyone to begin shortly after. Et voilà: *court.*


*July 1—Paris.*

"Court" officially opened this morning—it was not a perfect debut.

My newly sworn-in aristocratic ladies-in-waiting regarded the comings and goings in a daze. They are happy to be back in the familiar milieu of a palace—except for the pace we keep here, which is so . . . well, *wrong.* Bonaparte insists that every step of every royal ritual be performed—but everyone must hurry it up, he hasn't got all day, he has work to do! So we go through the ancient genuflections in double time, as if to the beat of a drum.

Fouché, who joined us for dinner, observed the commotion with a hint of a smile. "I suppose I have this to look forward to," he said, as the cook's maid crashed into the footman coming through the door, a china dish of quails spilling onto the carpet.

"Oh?" I inquired, ordering three bottles of our best champagne brought up from the cellar. Bonaparte had just made the announcement that Fouché was going to be reinstated as Minister of Police—a celebration was called for.

"Fouché is the new owner of Grosbois," Bonaparte explained, tearing off the end of a loaf of bread.

"General Moreau's château?" I was astonished. I know the château of Grosbois well (too well)—"the house of traitors" I've come to think of it as.*

"General Moreau was happy to sell it to me for half a million," Fouché said, dragging his lace cuffs through the soup. Even in extravagant finery he looked slovenly, his smell sour, his buttons mismatched.

"Next I suppose you'll be wanting a title, *Citoyen*," Bonaparte teased, reaching over to tweak Fouché's ear.


*July 2, 4:45 P.M.*

After dictation this morning, Madame Campan and I walked through the rooms of the Apartment of Honour, reviewing the staff, their roles, the procedures. The porter at the door of the antechamber stood disdainfully, halberd in hand. "You must strike it on the floor at Her Majesty's approach," Madame Campan told him. "And the lackeys?" She looked over the crowd of pages and footmen to the men in green coats with red waistcoats and black breeches. They jumped to attention, clattering their swords against the furniture. "As soon as Her Majesty is announced, you must unroll a carpet." Patiently, I waited.

In this manner we made our way through the antechamber to the first drawing room (nodding to the pages, the citizens awaiting an audience,

---

* Before General Moreau—who was exiled to America after being found guilty of involvement in the Cadoudal conspiracy—the ancient château had been owned by Josephine and Napoleon's friend Paul Barras, who had conspired with the Royalists and was overthrown by Napoleon.

the officers not on duty), the second drawing room (everyone jumping up and bowing: the aides-de-camp, officers and their wives, the usher, chamberlain, equerry), until we reached my drawing room—or rather, the room in which I receive the most honoured of my guests.

"*Both* doors are opened for the Emperor and Empress," Madame Campan instructed the ushers, who positioned the chairs and stools appropriately: armchairs for Bonaparte, his mother and me, chairs for the princesses, stools for everyone else. "Your Majesty," Madame Campan hissed, when she saw me about to wearily lower myself onto a stool close at hand. "An *empress* must never . . ."

Must never, must never, must never . . .


*July 4—very hot.*
Who would have imagined that the life of an empress could be so complex? Walking, for instance: simply strolling from one room to another must be done in concert with two pages (becurled and berib-boned): one six steps in front, one behind, carrying my train. "Ready?" I whisper to them, for I must catch their attention before I make a step, lest I move too quickly, lest we end up in a jumble.


*July 5.*
Monsieur Despréaux, the dance master, is beside himself with frustra-tion. Bonaparte expects him to transform us into true-blood aristocrats in a matter of weeks. "Easier said than done," Monsieur Despréaux laments.

Everyone complains. They ache from the drills, the constant exer-cises—all just to learn how to walk, how to enter a room, doff a hat, *bow*.

"And is the Emperor not to . . . ?" Monsieur Despréaux mentioned hesitantly.

Bonaparte scoffed at the notion that *he* should take lessons from the dance master. "I create myself," he said, not untruthfully. However, I've noticed that he is frequently closeted with Talma, of late, and is moving with a bit more grace (not much). Now and again I catch him observing himself in my looking glass, checking his position.

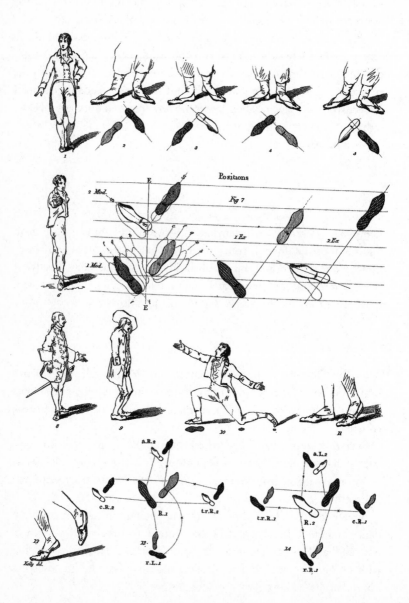

Positions

Fig 7

*July 9.*

Dress rehearsal in three days. Everyone at court is to be presented, execute a proper bow. "We are not ready," Monsieur Despréaux gasped, pressing his neatly folded handkerchief to the corner of each eye.

*July 12, late afternoon.*

Oh, mon Dieu, what an entertainment. Bonaparte sat on his throne, I sat on mine. (They are cushioned, fortunately.) The Princesses—Hortense, Julie, Elisa, Caroline, Pauline—sat on tabourets. Prince Joseph, Prince Louis and the officers stood at attention on either side. Then the procession began: my ladies-in-waiting, the marshals and generals with their wives (some trembling), the officials and ministers—all in court dress. First the ladies came to the throne and curtsied, and then the gentlemen, who bowed. All the while Monsieur Despréaux stood to one side hissing: *Shoulders back, elbow up, chin forward! Relax!*

It was all I could do not to laugh—and all Bonaparte could do to sit still, for it took a *very* long time. After an hour, he signalled to Monsieur Despréaux to hurry things up—he didn't have all day!—and the pace increased so much that the men were racing to the throne, jackknifing into a deep court bow, and then racing backwards, very nearly tripping up the next in line.

*July 17.*

Princess Dolgorouki, who attended the drawing room at the Tuileries two nights ago, is going around Paris saying that "it" undoubtedly is a great power, but certainly *not* a court.

"Not a court? What does it take!" Bonaparte fumed. "Your attendants must all be countesses," he said, and at a stroke of his pen, countesses they all become. They smile disdainfully behind their fans: *parvenu.* (But accept the titles, nonetheless.)

*[Undated]*

"Your Majesty, the Emperor has asked me to" —Dr. Corvisart shuffled uneasily through the stack of papers in his hand— "address the problem of your . . ."

My infertility, he meant. I looked away, downcast in my spirits.

"You've been to Plombières a number of times, Your Majesty," Dr. Corvisart said, squaring the papers and setting them neatly in front of him on the writing-table. "Perhaps a change is in order. I recommend the waters at Aix-la-Chapelle."

"The spa near Brussels?"

"The waters there are said to be good for . . ." He shrugged. "It's worth a try."

A futile try, we both knew. We are all of us pretending.


*July 19.*

Cannon signalled Bonaparte's departure for his northern tour. I'm staying in Paris for a few days before departing for Aix-la-Chapelle—staying behind in the palace, alone.

Well, alone except for a staff of hundreds. I'm at a loss, I confess. The household has become like some large beast, impossible to tame. "That's *my* job, Your Majesty," Monsieur d'Harville (Count Etiquette) assured me, handing me my schedule for the day. My marching orders.


*July 21—Saint-Cloud, early afternoon.*

I've been deceived. Count Etiquette is not my servant, he's my jailer! He is present at each audience, standing behind my chair. With every move I make, his hand is out—to help, which is kind, but according to etiquette, *his* is the hand I must wait patiently for, regardless of the number of helping hands present, for *he* is the highest officer of my household. "It's an honour to serve you, Your Majesty," he reminds me officiously.

This morning, preparing to leave for Aix-la-Chapelle, I remembered that I'd forgotten to ask that my new cashmere shawl be edged. I crossed two halls to find Agathe, whose handiwork I know to be precise. I was shortly informed by Count Etiquette that all orders to servants must be given through him, and him alone—that to do otherwise would, in his words, "compromise the dignity of the throne."

"I may not speak to my own maid?" Agathe has been with me for over a decade!

"It would be contrary to the Code to suggest that your Imperial Majesty may not speak to a person, even to a servant," the count informed me, his voice unctuous, "but I would not be doing my duty if I did not inform Your Majesty that there are formalities to be observed."

Grands Dieux! I can't get used to being "Empress"—I detest it, frankly. If I drop so much as a fan, I may not stoop to pick it up. The most "honoured" lady-in-waiting present must first retrieve it, then hand it to Count Etiquette, who then hands it to me.

I wasn't raised for such a confining role. How I long for the delicious freedom of being a simple citizen, just to stroll along the Champs-Elysées on a sunny afternoon and go to Frascati for an ice. I informed Count Etiquette—with a smile and carefree air that I hoped would temper my words—that although such etiquette was entirely suitable to one born into a world of restraint, it was not always perfectly suitable for me, and that, therefore, on occasion, I would continue to give my orders directly.

I've since repented this burst of "rebellion." I am fortunate that Count Etiquette has accepted this position—and a difficult one it is, tutoring us parvenus on royal procedures. Somehow, I must find the patience to be an empress.

*[Undated]*

We are crawling through Europe, my four ladies-in-waiting, two chamberlains, two chambermaids (one ill), an equerry, master of the horse, private secretary, butler, two ushers and ten footmen in addition to an army of coachmen and kitchen staff . . . *and* a financial controller, who is tearing out his hair at the expense. At each relay we require over seventy horses and twenty postillions. To move this group in concert is a monumental task—and all just to escort *me* to a spa.

I am reminded of an incident in my childhood: when a swarm of bees surrounded us, Mimi courageously reached for the queen bee and carried her to an open field, the swarm following.

I am the queen bee, and this is my swarm.

*July 30—Aix-la-Chapelle, about 8:00 in the evening.*
We've arrived, at last, in Aix-la-Chapelle, a sordid little town—
"wretched," my ladies say (a word I hear often from them), in spite of its
glorious history, its monumental cathedral, its treasure: the body of
Charlemagne, Emperor of the West.

*September 3.*
Bonaparte has arrived and suddenly this sleepy town awakes. Banners are
flying everywhere. Even the nags roped to crude carts sport ribbons.

*September 7.*
After a Te Deum in the Cathedral of Aix, Bonaparte was given the talisman Charlemagne wore on his collar when going into battle. Tonight
Bonaparte returned to the talisman again and again, holding it in his
hand, studying it, turning it. "Charlemagne was crowned by the Pope,"
he said, "and I will be as well."

"You will go to Rome?"

"Pope Pius VII will come to me."

I smiled, but perhaps it had the appearance of a scoff, for Bonaparte
tugged my ear. "You don't believe me?"

*August 19, 1804, Paris*
*Chère Maman,*

*How is the treatment going? What do the doctors say? I enjoyed your
account of turning down the bone from Charlemagne's arm. Everyone thinks
your response clever.\**

*Don't worry so much about me! Louis will be returning from Plombières
next month. Until then I am quite busy organizing the layette. I feel enormous, but the midwife assures me I am just as I should be at seven months.*

*It is terribly hot here in Paris. Little Napoleon, the charm of my days, is*

---

\* *Josephine refused the bone fragment, saying that she had for her own support an arm as
strong as Charlemagne's.*

*talking more and more. His favourite word is "no," however!*

*Your loving daughter, Hortense*

*Note—I have just this moment had news that Pauline's son died of a fever in Rome. How terribly sad—Dermide was such a dear child. Poor Pauline—first Victor and now their son. I don't know how one could survive the death of a child.*


*September 12, 1804, Saint-Leu*
*Chère Maman,*

Louis returned to Paris on the eighth, and immediately we set off to Saint-Leu. Our new country château is beautiful! We wanted to have some time here before returning to Paris for my confinement in one month.

The château requires repairs, but even so, our sojourn here has been restful. Health permitting, Louis and his beloved water spaniel roam the hills and fields as I busy myself in domestic pleasures. I was in the kitchen all this morning, helping put up some delicious fruit preserves. Yesterday we made soap and next week it will be candles. Little Napoleon "helps," of course. He is much happier now that his papa is home.

His poor papa, whose health was not improved by this last spa treatment. Dr. Corvisart is of the belief that Louis suffers from chronic rheumatism, as you suspected. He's been taking spirit vapour-baths every evening along with regular doses of extract of smartweed in addition to the anuric tablets Dr. Corvisart prescribed. These do seem to help temper the pain. He's been told to avoid mutton, goose and pork—all of which he is sorely fond of. It's no wonder his spirits suffer now and again.

Whatever you do, Maman, don't worry: I'm well cared for. I'm enclosing a "drawing" little Napoleon made for you. That big scribble in the lower right corner is me!

*Your loving daughter, Hortense*


*October 7, Sunday—Saint-Cloud.*

I returned to Paris ahead of Bonaparte in order to be with Hortense during her confinement—only to discover that she and Louis are *still* at their country estate. She's due any day now!

*October 9.*

"What took you so long? You should have been here weeks ago," I scolded my daughter (embracing her). "Look at you!" For she is *huge* with child and carrying quite low. "You shouldn't be travelling over rough roads."

"Maman, don't worry! The midwife assured me I have lots of time. The countryside was healing."

Yet she seemed uneasy. "Is that a sentry box in the garden?" I asked, looking out her bedchamber window. The guard was standing directly below. "And the garden walls are new, are they not?" The stone walls had been built up so high that a good part of the kitchen garden was now in shadow. The place had the feeling of a prison.

"For security," Hortense said, weaving a white ribbon through the lace edge of an infant cap.

"Because of a follower?" Since the Empire had been proclaimed, both Hortense and I had been plagued by strange men—harmless simpletons, for the most part.

"No," she assured me (but colouring—why?).

I gave her the bag of bulbs I'd brought from my travels and was explaining how they should be planted when little Napoleon ran into the room and bounded into my arms. "Oh, you are so big!" With a studious expression he pried open two fingers. "I know," I said with a smile, kissing him. Our beautiful Prince—our *heir*. "Tomorrow you will be two." I gave him one of the (many) gifts I'd brought: a small wooden sword from his Uncle Napoleon.

"From Nonan the soldier?" The child clasped the gift to his breast with such earnest sincerity that both Hortense and I laughed.

"Your Majesty?" The governess curtsied. "May I . . . ?" Little Napoleon's cap had come off.

"No!" The boy squirmed as his governess tried to put it back on.

"Your Uncle Napoleon wears one just like it," I told him, which changed his outlook immediately. He settled happily into my lap, clutching his new toy.

Soon Louis arrived with an aide-de-camp, Monsieur Flahaut. "I wondered whose carriage that was," Louis said. He limped coming in and seemed to walk with difficulty. One would take him for a man of fifty instead of the young man of twenty-six that he is.

"How good to see you, Louis—and *you*, Monsieur Flahaut," I added, dipping my head to the aide-de-camp, my friend Madame de Souza's son.

"Your Majesty," Flahaut answered with a graceful bow. A pretty man with elegant manners; it is easy to see why the women fuss over him. (Indeed, it is rumoured Caroline fancies him.)

Louis stooped to kiss Hortense on the cheek. "You are well, my precious love?"

"Oh yes, perfectly well, darling," she said with a bright smile.

What a lovely portrait, I thought: the young, happy mother, the doting father.


*October 11—quite late now (exhausted).*
It was still dark when Mimi woke me, whispering, "Your daughter's footman is here. Her confinement has begun!"

Bonaparte was asleep, dead to the world. I slipped out of bed, following Mimi into the adjoining room. "What time is it?" I asked, wrapping a cashmere scarf about my head.

"Twenty after three," she said, checking a yawn.

"Are the horses harnessed?"

"Slow down, Your Majesty." Mimi smiled, handing me a mug of hot chocolate. "You can't go out like that. What will Count Etiquette say? The baby will take its imperial time and you should, too."

But I felt there was a fire under me; I could not be idle imagining my daughter's discomfort. I quickly slipped on the gown Mimi brought from the wardrobe and left. Empress or not, my daughter was having a baby.


Louis met me at the door, en déshabillé. "Oh," he said, as if surprised to see me. "I thought you were the accoucheur."

I removed my cape and gave it to a butler in livery (thankful that Mimi had persuaded me to dress respectably). "But the midwife is here? How is Hortense?" I asked, trying to get my hat ribbons untied, for in my haste I had knotted them. "Has the Arch-Chancellor been sent for?" Impatiently I pulled the hat off my head, tearing one of the ribbons.

Louis gave me a puzzled look. "De Cambacérès?"

"There must be a witness at Imperial family births, remember? According to the new protocol."* This *had* been discussed, had it not? The amended Constitution decreed that an official witness must be present at the birth of any child in the line of succession.

"Pour l'amour de Dieu," Louis muttered, and headed up the stairs.

The accoucheur didn't arrive until just before noon. Shortly after, Arch-Chancellor de Cambacérès arrived in a carriage drawn by six horses and accompanied by six pages, a footman and a chamberlain. The servants kept the Arch-Chancellor content at the dining table with dishes of bloated herring à la Dublin, mutton kidneys and several glasses of an excellent Madeira. (De Cambacérès related all this to me later in detail.)

The baby was born at half-past two. Another boy! "A good specimen," the midwife pronounced. De Cambacérès saw enough through his silver-rimmed lorgnette to fulfill his duty as a royal witness (but not so much as to upset his stomach). Louis examined the baby thoroughly before he was swaddled by the nursemaid.

"What a blessing: two sons," I told him. "He looks like you."

"Do you think?" Louis said.

My daughter pressed my hand against her cheek. "Isn't he beautiful, Maman?" she said, the colour rising in her cheeks.

"*You're* beautiful," I said. How brave she had been.

* *Queen Marie Antoinette and queens before her had been required to give birth in a room crowded with gawking witnesses.*

## *In which I am offered a crown*

*October 15, 1804—Saint-Cloud.*

"The Pope has finally answered," Bonaparte informed me as I came in the door. "It's not official yet, but he's agreed: he'll come to Paris."*

"To crown you?" I asked absently, putting down my basket. I'd been with Hortense all morning and was sick with concern. The new baby—Petit we're calling him—is thriving, but Hortense herself is still not strong, not eating well, if at all.

"Call the architects, set up a meeting for later this afternoon. I'm free at five. The Pope will stay in the Pavillon de Flore. We'll need to renovate." He paused at the door. "What's the matter? You don't think it will suit?"

"Bonaparte, I'm sorry. I guess I wasn't . . . Did you say the *Pope* is coming? You're serious? You're not jesting?"

"I told you before."

"It's just that . . . How does one do that—receive the Pope?"

Bonaparte let out a little laugh. "What's the problem? *I'm* the Emperor."

*October 16.*

Hortense has milk fever. She's in terrible pain, her breasts hard and

---

* *The Pope was initially reluctant to crown "the murderer of the Duke d'Enghien." He only agreed after promises of concessions to the Church—though these were never fulfilled.*

inflamed. A bread-and-milk poultice has done little to relieve her distress. The doctor will consider bleeding her if she does not improve by the morning.

*[Undated]*

Fifty-six rooms are going to be redecorated to house Pope Pius VII and his entourage.

Fifty-six rooms: imagine! I remember, not long ago, when a new bedstead was too great an expense.

Between tending Hortense and preparing for the coronation, I'm run ragged.

*October 17—Saint-Cloud.*

Busy! This morning I met with fashion designer Leroy and artists Jacques-Louis David and Isabey about the new court dress. I finally succeeded in persuading them that it would be brutal to resume the hoop. French women simply won't tolerate such a medieval construction! What we have decided on is simple but elegant: a dress very much like the gowns worn today, but with the addition of a long mantle and a ruff. Although impractical, a ruff is, no doubt, becoming. Leroy has suggested one with long points, made of tulle embroidered with gold or silver. It attaches at the shoulders and comes up high behind the head, as in the portraits of Catherine de Medici. My ladies are in ecstasies.

*October 19—a beautiful fall evening.*

"I've got it—*finally*." The poet Chénier was euphoric.

"Got what?" I asked.

"The subject for the tragedy the Emperor has asked me to write in commemoration of the coronation."

"Ha! It should be a comedy, the way things have been going around here," Chastulé said.

"All the poets in the Empire have been asked to create a piece to celebrate the coronation, Your Majesty," Clari explained.

"Aren't you going to ask about my subject, Your Majesty?" The poet scratched his head.

"Oh, yes, of course, Monsieur Chénier. Forgive me. What is the subject you've decided on?"

"The Emperor Cyrus!" Talma's voice boomed behind us, making us jump. "Played by guess who?" The actor struck a heroic pose, looking for all the world like a Roman statue in spite of the curious costume he was wearing.

"I was going to tell her," Chénier complained.

"Talma! What on earth are you wearing?" The tight breeches did not flatter his figure. The vain actor usually took pains to disguise his bowed legs.

"You don't know, Your Majesty?" Talma twirled. "*This* is the new court dress."

"Are you serious?" I frowned in disbelief. It was an ensemble in the style of the Renaissance, an embroidered satin doublet with a ruff and *puffed* pantaloons over skin-tight breeches, silk stockings and white high-heeled shoes with rosettes.

"The Emperor approved it this afternoon, but we can't decide what to call it. What do you think? Spanish?" With a twirl. "À la Henri IV?" Another twirl. "The Troubadour? That's what *I* suggested." Three twirls, the short cape flying. "But who am I to say? I was merely" —he threw the velvet cape across his shoulder and strutted across the drawing room— "the *model*."

"Bonaparte is going to wear that?"

Talma threw the black hat festooned with ostrich feathers into the air. "Apparently." He caught it and positioned it back on his head. The plumes bobbed comically. "Or at least something like it. What His Majesty actually said was" —and here he imitated Bonaparte's voice and movements exactly— "'Enough. That's it. Don't bother me anymore about it! I have better things to do than to decide about lace. Do whatever you think. Just get out of here.'" At which the actor flung himself into the air as if propelled by some invisible force and landed on his backside.

"Talma," I gasped. "Are you all right?"

The famous actor stood, brushed himself off, and before our very eyes *transformed*, as if by magic, into a Roman figure once again.

*October 20, 6:00 P.M. or so.*

"Please, darling, just try a little," I coaxed my daughter, trying to tempt her with a crumb of the rhubarb cake she had loved as a child. "Show little Napoleon." I smiled down at my grandson, who studied his mother with a grave expression.

"Make it like a horse," he said, showing me the trick his Uncle Napoleon uses to get food into *him.*

Obligingly, I made it like a horse, and my daughter fainted dead away.

I'm so worried! Afterwards, perplexed and concerned, I dropped in to see Eugène, who was himself frantic. His mare had rejected her foal and he was spending days and nights in the stable trying to save the little thing. On top of all that, he was going crazy with the renovations being done to his house.* I helped with some decisions about wallcoverings and drapes—and then we talked about Hortense. "She *is* getting better, Maman," he assured me, for he calls on her every day.

He will make some young woman a wonderful husband—in time—but for now I get the feeling that he'd rather be with his horses.

*October 25.*

Hortense has been relieved of her milk, which has been causing her such terrible pain.

*10:20 P.M.—Saint-Cloud.*

The coronation was to be held in two weeks—but this evening Bonaparte learned that the Holy Father hasn't even left Rome yet! Consequently the coronation has been put forward to December 2. Frankly, I'm relieved. There is *so* much to do.

*October 26, late, after 2:00 in the morning—can't sleep.*

Tonight, after Bonaparte returned to his cabinet to work, Eugène

---

* *Napoleon had given Eugène the use of Hôtel Villeroy, 78 Rue de Lille. It is now the German embassy.*

suggested a game of billiards. He played well, though with too much force—I won the first game, he won the second, but not without a struggle. By the third we were laughing and talking: of his newest mount, of finding a good (quiet) riding horse for me, of Hortense—who is sitting up and eating—and her beautiful boys. Then we talked of my growing staff, my need to hire yet more ladies-in-waiting (as Madame Campan had long ago predicted).

"Madame Duchâtel would be good," Eugène blurted out.

"Adèle Duchâtel?"

"She asked if I could help her get a position." Flushing.

Aha, I thought—winsome Adèle Duchâtel had caught my son's fancy. Certainly she is a beauty: slender, with an abundance of golden hair, blue eyes, good teeth. On the other hand, she is tall, and her nose is a bit beaky. I find her manners cold, but perhaps she is simply shy. "I think Madame Duchâtel would be a lovely addition to my staff, Eugène, but I'm not sure she's qualified." Adèle Duchâtel is married to an elderly, disagreeable man, a councillor of state. His status doesn't merit a position for his wife at court, regardless of her personal charm.

"*Please*, Maman."

I took up my cue and circled the table, assessing the shots. Thinking: it is time my son started dreaming of something other than horses. Thinking: Adèle Duchâtel has a husband, so marriage wouldn't be a possibility. That is good. The choice of a wife for Eugène will have to be dictated by political concerns—he understands that, understands that it is one of the sacrifices demanded by our position. "I'll see what I can do," I said, sinking two balls.

"Promise you won't tell Hortense or Papa?"

"I promise," I said, ruffling his hair. My boy.


*October 27.*
Madame Duchâtel begins tonight, at our ball. I've sent a note to Eugène.


*Past midnight.*
It was painful to observe Eugène courting Adèle Duchâtel, painful to see

his confusion, for she refused his invitation to the contredanse.

Eugène slouched against the wall all night with a despondent air. "Come to my drawing room tomorrow evening," I suggested.

*October 30.*
Bonaparte lingers in the drawing room each evening of late. Tonight he cautioned Madame Duchâtel against taking a green olive. "An olive in the evening will upset your stomach," he said, and the girl lowered her eyes.

"And we wouldn't want *that*," Caroline said, putting her arm around Adèle's shoulders.

"Perhaps a brandied cherry?" Eugène offered, ever hopeful.

*[Undated]*
Bonaparte is being gallant. I'm suspicious.

*October 31, Décadi—Tuileries.*
This morning a model of the interior of the cathedral of Notre-Dame was set up on a table in the Yellow Salon. Cardboard figures of the people in the procession were lined up in order.

"Where is yours, Maman?" Eugène asked, studying the layout before we joined the clan for dinner. I pointed to the figure that represented me, standing on the mantel. "Why isn't it on the table with the others?" he asked, perplexed.

"Because they haven't decided where to put me yet."

"They?" He tilted his head in the direction of the room where the Bonapartes were assembled.

"*They* argue that I'm not to be part of the ceremony, that I'm to be merely a witness," I whispered, taking his arm as we entered the room, the family all rising to bow.

*November 3—Saint-Cloud.*
I've ruined everything! This evening at around seven, Bonaparte left the

drawing room. A short time later, Madame Duchâtel got up from her embroidery frame and left as well. I waited for her return: five minutes, ten minutes, twenty.

Finally I could stand it no longer. I called Clari over to a window recess and told her that if anyone asked where I was, to say that I had been summoned by the Emperor. "Where are you going?" she asked, her tone apprehensive.

"I've got to find out if something is going on." I slipped away before she could protest.

I proceeded in the direction of Bonaparte's cabinet. I told myself he was working, as he often did in the evening. No doubt Madame Duchâtel was simply indisposed and had retired. There were any number of explanations.

These were the thoughts going through my mind. But what would I say to Bonaparte? I wondered, stopping outside the door to his cabinet. I would ask him if he wished to play a game of chess. No, he would know that I would not venture through the cold, dark corridors to ask such a thing. I decided to tell him that I needed a private moment to talk with him regarding my concerns about Hortense, her health.

The antechamber to Bonaparte's cabinet was dark. The moonlight illuminated the sleeping form of a guard. Stools had been positioned around the perimeter of the room, a room at rest. I tapped lightly on the door to the cabinet. No answer. The guard stirred, but did not wake. Was the door locked? I lifted the iron latch and the door swung open. The room was empty. I slipped up the stairs behind the bookcase, the stairs that led to the private suite of rooms above. Bonaparte had recently had the rooms redecorated.

At the top, I heard voices—Bonaparte's, and that of a young woman: Adèle Duchâtel.

Foolishly, I knocked on the door. (Why? What possessed me?) I heard scurrying about, then the door opened: Bonaparte, shirtless. "What are *you* doing here?" he demanded. Behind him, in the shadows, I could see the frightened girl.

I knew from the tone of his voice that I should not speak, yet heedlessly I cried out, "This is wrong, Bonaparte!"

Enraged, he picked up a stool and brought it down with force against the stone hearth. The girl let out a squeal. "Get out!" he yelled. "Get out of my sight!"

I tumbled down the stairs, letting the pewter candle holder clatter onto the stones. I heard the door slam shut, the bolt slide into place and I was plunged into darkness.

Trembling, I hurried back to the salon. With others present, I would be safe—at least this is what I told myself. In truth, I was not myself. I'd never seen Bonaparte in such a rage, and it frightened me—frightened and angered me.

Four of my ladies were still around the game table by the fire. Clari was at her frame. They all stood when I entered, bowed. "Please, be seated, continue," I told them, taking my place behind my embroidery frame. I took up my needle. I'd been working on the stem of a vine, in cross-stitch. I made a stitch, but it was unruly.

The only sounds in the room were the crackling of the fire, the shuffling of cards and an occasional groan or murmur from the players. Thoughts of Bonaparte's infidelity, his rage kept coming back to me. "Clari," I called out, my voice shaky—and louder than I'd intended. She jerked her head up, regarding me with a look of caution. "I'm . . . retiring for the evening. Please attend me." Good, I thought, standing, at least I'm not trembling.

I looked about my bedchamber as if I'd never seen it before. "Your Majesty?" Clari inquired from the door.

"I . . ." But no sooner had I opened my mouth than tears spilled. "I discovered them," I managed to say. "Bonaparte and Madame Duchâtel." My hands felt like ice, yet my heart was racing. "He's furious! Soon he will come here, and . . ."

"*Please*, Your Majesty, permit me to go! His Majesty would be furious were he to think that you confided in me. It will be best if he finds you alone."

I sat down at my toilette table, fussing without thinking over my baubles. I put a pearl ornament in my hair, then took it out. It was sharp—it might inflict harm.

Shortly after, the door flew open: Bonaparte, in stocking feet. He came into my room, snorting like a bull about to charge. "How dare you spy on me!" he yelled. "I will not put up with it!"

It humiliates me now even to think of it, for I cowered like an animal. I crouched trembling but dry-eyed as he destroyed what he could, throwing bottles and gems against the looking glass (glass shattering everywhere), splintering the leg of my Jacob toilette chair, tearing the lace bed-curtains.

"You're to move out immediately." He sneezed, overwhelmed by the jasmine scent that filled the air. "We'll work out the details of the divorce proceedings next week," he said, holding a handkerchief over his mouth and nose.

And then the door slammed shut.


The floor was strewn with debris. A clock chimed eight bells. Only eight? I stood and, stepping carefully, reached for the servants' bell rope. A chambermaid came to the door. "Please tell Madame Clari that I'd like to speak with her," I told her, my voice surprisingly calm. "I believe she is in the Yellow Salon."

The girl took a long, gaping look at the floor, and stifling a nervous giggle, hurried off down the hall.


Clari found me at my toilette table, looking into my shattered image. "Oh, Your Majesty!" she exclaimed, dismayed by the state of my room. "Are you all right?"

"Yes," I said dreamily. "You are going to Paris tonight?"

"Our coach has been called for nine," she said, stooping to pick up a broken crystal decanter, and then another, putting these on a side table. "Oh là là! Perhaps you'd prefer if I stayed."

"Others can attend to it. I'd like you to go to Paris and call on my son. Tell him . . ." I leaned my chin on my hand.

"Your Majesty?" Clari asked, retrieving a powder puff from under the bed.

"Tell him the Emperor and I have had a . . . disagreement," I said. "Tell him the Emperor has demanded a divorce." And then I broke down.


"Maman?" Eugène called to me from the door of my bedchamber. The light from the lantern he was carrying made him look like an angel—which he is, to me. "Are you awake?" he asked softly, glancing around the room. The glass had been swept up and the bed-curtains and vanity quickly replaced, but even so, he must have sensed that something was different.

"Come in," I said, sitting up, pulling on my bed jacket. "I was just lying here." Cursing. Praying. *Repenting.* "Do you know what happened? Have you talked to Bonaparte?" I wasn't crying any more.

He nodded, putting the lantern down on the little table beside my bed. "He's upset," he said, lowering himself onto a stool.

I wondered how much Bonaparte had told him. "Did he tell you he wants a divorce?" My voice quavered in spite of myself. "Did he tell you I discovered him with a woman?" I wondered if Eugène knew *who* it was I had found Bonaparte with.

My son nodded in a matter-of-fact way. (Good, I thought. He doesn't know it was Adèle Duchâtel.) "I told Papa I would follow you into exile—"

*Exile!* Was I to be banished?

"—even if it meant going back to Martinico with you." He smiled sweetly, so full of love.


*November 4, late morning—just rising.*
"I suppose you've heard?" I asked Mimi as she handed me a dish of morning chocolate. My hands were unsteady; I had to be careful not to spill any.

"Gontier and Agathe told me," Mimi said, slipping a note under my pillow.

*This Evinng Princes Carolin told her Husband that her Plan workd. The Emperor bedded the girl & the jelos Old Woman found Him with Her naked. Now the Emperor will Divors the Old Woman & they will have Everything.*

Mimi gave me an orange-blossom infusion, to calm. "I told you she's a witch," she said.


*November 5.*

"How was the family dinner last night?" I asked Hortense (peeking at the sleeping baby in the bassinet, blowing him a kiss). The weekly clan dinner had been held at the home of Bonaparte's mother. I had not been invited, of course.

"I was too ill to go," Hortense said, sitting forward so that the maid could plump the big feather pillows. "*Fortunately,*" she hissed, as the maid closed the door behind her.

"Oh?" I asked, placing a pretty box of comfits on her bedside table. Although still confined to bed, Hortense seems better. There is spirit in her voice.

"The Bonapartes have been . . . how should I put it?" She reached for a comfit. "Rather openly pleased, one might say, over recent *developments.*"

"I'm not surprised."

"But they're gloating so openly over what they see as their 'victory,' they've managed to annoy Papa. I gather he had a big fight with them last night."

"Bonaparte?" *That* surprised me. "Was Eugène there?"

"No, I wasn't invited," said a voice at the door.

"Eugène!" I jumped up to embrace my son. "What a surprise." He smelled of winter chill.

"Maman and I were just talking . . . about *Papa,*" Hortense said self-consciously.

"Oh?" Eugène said, leaning against the windowsill and crossing his arms.

Hortense widened her eyes at her brother.

I glanced from one to another. Something was up. This "encounter" had been planned. "Oh?" I echoed.

"Maman, Eugène and I have been thinking," Hortense said finally. "About?"

Eugène shrugged sheepishly. "You and Papa."

"Oh." I inhaled sharply. *That.*

"It's just that Papa is a young man, Maman," Hortense said, flushing.

Eugène cleared his throat. "It's natural for a man to . . . you know."

I sat forward, my hands on my knees. "Are you taking *Bonaparte's* side?" They didn't understand!

"We don't think you need to feel jealous, that's all," Eugène said. "Papa loves you."

Hortense nodded, her eyes filling. "And we love him."

*November 6, 7:00 P.M.*

Thérèse was shocked, and not a little reprimanding. "You did what?" she exclaimed, very much flurried. "You walked in on them—*intentionally*? Are you crazy? After all I've told you? And what about your dear departed Aunt Désirée? I thought you promised her to 'be blind'—on her deathbed! I know, I know—it's hard not to notice when it's right under your nose, but where else is an emperor supposed to go? It's not as if he can wander the streets like an ordinary soldier. No wonder he's provoked! Oh, forgive me, I'm sorry. It's cruel to harangue, but trust me, my dear, *dear* friend—you don't want to be divorced. It's hell!"

*November 7.*

I knocked on Bonaparte's cabinet door. It was early; I knew he would be working. "Entrez."

Courage, I told myself, and pushed open the door.

"Josephine!" Bonaparte stood, taken aback. For a moment I thought he looked happy to see me, but then his expression changed, growing severe. "I've a meeting in fifteen minutes with Talleyrand."

"It will only take a moment, but I can return later," I said. "Whenever you wish."

He paused before motioning me in, slouching back down in his chair. "What do you want?"

"I want . . ." What did I want? I wanted Bonaparte at my side—I wanted my husband, my "spirit-friend." I wanted our quiet moments together, our rides in the park, our early morning walks in the garden. I wanted our consoling moments of tenderness. "I want peace between us," I said finally.

"I don't see how that's possible."

"You mistake me, Bonaparte. You believe I am motivated by jealousy. It is more than that. What you call innocent dalliances are damaging your image with the people."

"You spy on me in the interests of policy? Josephine, you are not a good liar."

He was right. I *was* lying—to him, as well as to myself. What *was* the truth? "I will own that my preference is for fidelity, Bonaparte, but I believe I can learn to live without it if I must—so long as I have your love."

"I do love you," he said angrily. "This . . . *business* means nothing to me. It is merely an amusement."

"Yet you become harsh toward me."

"Because you wish to control me—and I will not be controlled!"

"Very well then, I see a solution. I will raise no objection, and you will not be harsh." I opened my hands.

"I may do as I please?"

"With my blessing," I lied.


*This Evinng Princes Carolin told Prince Joseph that the Emperor is a Fool. Shee say the Emperor must divors the Old Woman. Shee & Prince Joseph will talk to Him tomorrow Evinng at 8 hours.*


*November 10, Décadi.*
"Good evening, dear sister." Joseph kissed me on both cheeks. "You look especially lovely tonight. Doesn't she, Caroline?"

"Indeed," Caroline said. "That gown must have cost a million francs."

"Thank you both so much." We were all lying—smiling from the teeth out, as Bonaparte says. "You are so very kind." Like a rabid fox. "I understand you have a meeting with the Emperor at eight," I said, glancing at the clock.

*Shortly before midnight.*

Bonaparte tore off his jacket in angry frustration. "What is it?" I asked, helping him with his vest.

"Do you know why Joseph does not want you crowned? Because it would be against his interests. *His* interests—it has nothing to do with policy, with what might benefit the Empire."

"I don't understand." I'm to be *crowned*? I thought they had met to persuade Bonaparte to divorce me.

"Because if *you* are crowned, then Louis's children will stand above his, Joseph said, because then *Louis's* children will be the grandsons of an empress. Bah," he growled, struggling to get his nightshirt on, his head finally popping through. "Do you know what it takes to make a tyrant out of me?" He threw back the bed-curtain with such violence that one tie tore free. "My family, *that's* what it takes. All they have to do is speak, and I become a monster. Sacrebleu! You're going to be crowned all right, even if it takes two hundred thousand soldiers."

"You're serious?"

"Of course I'm serious. I'm always serious."

I felt breathless with anxiety. Me—*crowned*? "I don't know if that's such a good idea." A crown would elevate my status. I'd have courtiers aplenty—as well as enemies. "Is it even customary?" I'd never heard of a woman being crowned.

"Not in the least."

"But then why?"

"To spite them!"

"Bonaparte, that's not a good reason," I said with a teasing smile.

"You're right. It is a mistake to jest. However, I *am* perfectly serious. I will crown you. You married me when I was nobody. I want you beside me." Taking my hand, pulling me toward the bed.

"Bonaparte—I'm going to have to consider."

"You'd turn down a crown?"

Easily! "I need to think about it." And talk to my children.

*November 11, evening, late.*

"Oh, that's frightening, Maman." Hortense (standing, *walking*) covered her cheeks with her hands.

"I know!" I didn't want a crown; I didn't even want Bonaparte crowned.

"Papa suggested this?" Eugène asked. "What would it mean, exactly? You're already Empress. How would being crowned change that?"

"From what I can make out, I would become more of a symbol of the Empire, so that wherever I went, whatever I did, I would have to be shown the respect due the crown."

Hortense rolled her eyes. "*They* won't like it."

The clan, she meant. "Not in the least."

"Because it will strengthen your position," Eugène observed.

Strengthen my tie to Bonaparte. "Frankly, that's the only argument in favour," I said.

"And a good one, Maman," Hortense said.

*[Undated]*

Yes, no, yes, no.

Yes.

No.

Yes?

Oh, if only I could sleep!

*November 12, 10:20 A.M.*

I went early this morning to Bonaparte's cabinet. He looked up from his big desk, which was covered with plans and drawings and memoranda regarding the coronation. "I've decided to accept your offer," I told him.

"What offer?"

Had he changed his mind? "To be crowned."

"Ah!" He stood and came around to me, pulling me into his arms.

## In which I am crowned

*November 15, 1804—Saint-Cloud.*

"Mon Dieu, Maman, you should see how crowded Paris has become," Eugène said, his cloak thrown back. "The population has doubled, I swear, people everywhere! And now, with all the troops that have been ordered in, it's crazy."

He said that already people are desperate to get tickets to the coronation, that one family has paid three hundred francs for a second-floor window just so they can watch the procession. Tickets are even being sold to see the preparations that are being made inside Notre-Dame. Yesterday, one man got knocked senseless by a stone that came loose from all the hammering. "I've never seen anything like it, Maman. All the masons in Paris are occupied, even the carpenters. How am I to get the work completed on my house?"

"Would you like me to ask Messieurs Percier and Fontaine?" I suggested, but immediately regretted it. Our Imperial architects are overwhelmed with the task of transforming Notre-Dame and renovating both the Tuileries and Fontainebleau palaces in anticipation of the Pope's arrival. "I'll be meeting with them in . . ." I glanced at the clock. That late already? "In ten minutes."

"No, Maman." Eugène put up his hands. "They're too expensive. And besides, I don't want a Roman temple, or even a Greek one. I just want it to be a comfortable house . . . with a *splendid* ballroom," he added with a grin.

"Eugène, does this mean that you're giving a ball? Oh, your sister is going to be so pleased. Surely, you'll need my help. I could—"

"No, Maman, I want to do it myself!" He turned at the door. "One thing, though. Do you mind if I hire your musicians?"

"Of course not." Eugène is an enthusiastic dancer—music-mad, as Hortense says.

He grinned, twirling his hat on his index finger (or trying to). "I happen to know that one of your ladies-in-waiting is very fond of them."

Adèle Duchâtel. I started to say something, to warn my son—but I couldn't bring myself to tell him about Bonaparte and . . .

Bonaparte and Adèle.

"Above all, be blind," dear Aunt Désirée told me on her deathbed. If only it were easy! I promised Bonaparte that I would no longer object to what he calls his "amusements." I appear calm and accepting, but inside I feel a whirlwind of emotion: jealousy, fear—anger—but also, curiously, a feeling of peace, for I do know that Bonaparte loves me. Loves me, and what's more: needs me.

Last night he woke me as he so often does, wanting me to come walk with him in the moonlight. The gardens were dusted with an early frost, giving the landscape an eerie glow. We walked and talked until the chill set in, then we tiptoed back to the warmth of our bed, whispering like naughty schoolchildren.

*November 17.*
Bonaparte was in a Special Council meeting all afternoon. I wondered what such an important gathering might concern—war? peace?—and was rather disconcerted to discover that it had to do with who is to carry my train during the coronation. Joseph has lodged a formal protest on behalf of the female Bonapartes: they flatly refuse.

*November 18, early evening.*
A compromise has been struck. Caroline, Pauline and Elisa have finally consented to carry my train—or rather (as it must now be worded), to "hold up the mantle," which is to be viewed as "an attribute of sovereignty."

"But on condition that the princesses' trains are in turn carried by their chamberlains," I explained to Jacques-Louis David, who is co-ordinating the procession.

"That's ridiculous," he complained. "You're going to look like a centipede!"


*November 19.*

"We'll need the crown jewels for our meeting with the jewellers," Bonaparte told me at breakfast, and suddenly we were all of us in a flurry. We had to get down the Code to see how it was done. To obtain the jewels, the Emperor (Bonaparte) must instruct the Grand Chamberlain (Talleyrand) to give a written order on behalf of the Treasurer-general (Monsieur Estève) to the Master of the Wardrobe (Clari's husband) for those pertaining to the Emperor (Bonaparte), and to the Lady of Honour (Chastulé) for those pertaining to the Empress (me). It has taken us all morning to work this out.


*November 20, early afternoon.*

Bonaparte's mother will not make it to Paris in time for the coronation. She lingered too long visiting her beloved son Lucien in Milan. "Sacrebleu," Bonaparte said, but softly, with a melancholy air.


*November 21.*

Tomorrow we go to Fontainebleau in anticipation of the Holy Father's arrival. I doubt that I'll sleep.


*November 25, Sunday—Fontainebleau.*

Pope Pius VII arrived at noon along with Bonaparte's Uncle Fesch (now a Cardinal), and all the members of a fairly large papal entourage: sixteen cardinals and bishops and well over a hundred clerics (*all* of them excitable—oh, it's noisy here).

Everyone in the château lined up to welcome His Holiness at the door. He stooped coming in, perhaps out of habit, for he is very tall—

he towers over Bonaparte. He was dressed entirely in white, shivering in a long cape draped in the manner of a Roman statue. (I've ordered his fireplaces stoked hot—I'm concerned that the chill might harm his health, which is not robust and considerably weakened by the strenuous winter journey.) Even his shoes—unfortunately thin for this climate—were white, although muddy from alighting to meet Bonaparte at Croix de Saint-Hérem. He's grave, dignified, a simple man, more like a man of fifty than the sixty-two years he is, in fact. Perhaps it is his coal-black hair (does he colour it, I wonder?), so striking against his white robes, his peasant's sheepskin cap, his slender hands and long fingernails. His voice is curious: high and somewhat nasal. He speaks excellent French, but with an Italian accent, pronouncing *u* as *ou*. A man of gentle manners—unlike his entourage of rough and noisy priests (spitting everywhere!). He has a pallid complexion, although this may be due to a cup of sour broth he mentioned taking at a posting house this morning.

After a brief reception, Talleyrand escorted the Pope to his apartment, where he is resting now. How, I do not know, for the palace resounds with the voices of his entourage, yelling boisterously in Italian. "The Holy Father may be gentle and mannerly, but it is evident that his people are not," Clari observed primly, taking up her needlework.


*Late evening.*
After his rest, His Holiness met with Bonaparte for about a half-hour. Then Bonaparte conducted him to the Hall of the Great Officers where we had an informal dinner of only six covers: the Holy Father and his secretary, Bonaparte and me, Eugène (who remembered not to break bread before grace) and Louis (who did not). The Pope ate and drank with enthusiasm. He *loved* the turkey stuffed with truffles and the sauté of lark fillets.

Before he retired, His Holiness presented me with a ring. It is an amethyst encircled with diamonds, simply cut, simply set, exceptionally clear. And blessed by the Pope. "Thank you," I said, looking into his benevolent eyes.

"Daughter," he said.

I must gather the courage to speak, make my confession—soon. Tomorrow?

*November 26.*
The Pope was taken aback when I confessed that Bonaparte and I had not been married by the Church. "I was not aware."

"Forgive me," I said. "I have spoken without the Emperor's knowledge, Your Holiness." Much less his consent!

*Early afternoon.*
Bonaparte entered my dressing room scowling. "There seems to be a problem," he said, taking a chair by the side of my toilette table. "We have to be married by the Church, otherwise the coronation is off; the Pope refuses."

I feigned an expression of consternation.

"Zut." Bonaparte snapped one of my combs in frustration.

*November 27—back in Paris.*
This morning the terrace resounded with the sound of people crying out for the Pope, kneeling to receive his benediction. He brought only a few rosaries and medallions to give out and already they are gone. "I was told that the French are not religious," he said, his voice plaintive. He blesses whatever objects are brought to him: eyeglasses, inkpots, even a pair of scissors. Both Royalists and Revolutionaries come for his blessing, even Jacques-Louis David, an atheist. The Holy Father has captured our spirits, our hearts.

*November 28, 7:30 P.M.*
"And the oil I'm to anoint you with?" the Pope inquired this afternoon, at our daily meeting working out all the (endless) details. "I understand that there is a flask of holy oil that has been used since Clovis was

anointed in 496." The Holy Father is an amateur historian, and proud of his knowledge.

Bonaparte frowned, puzzled.

"It was destroyed, Sire," Bonaparte's secretary spoke up. "During the Revolution."

"We will begin a new tradition," Bonaparte said, commanding his secretary to have a suitable flask made.

I flushed: the ancient flask had been destroyed after my first husband proposed (and I quote, for I remember it well) "that the baubles of tyranny and superstition be burned on the altar of the Fatherland."


*[Undated]*
Chaos! The hundred and forty Spanish horses purchased for the coronation procession have all been delivered at once.


*November 29—Tuileries, not yet noon.*
We had a tour of the work being done on the cathedral this morning. Amazing. Two of the side altars and the choir screen have been removed and tiers of seats installed on either side of the nave. "Painted cardboard will give it a Greco-Egyptian style," Jacques-Louis David explained.

"Not Roman?" I asked.

"That, too," he said, pointing out that the bare stone walls will be entirely covered over with flags, tapestries and velvet hangings.

"What a stage," Talma exclaimed, throwing out his hands, his voice echoing in the huge vault.


*4:45 P.M.*
A terrible rehearsal. We're *still* tripping all over ourselves.

"I'm to carry some bit of bone?" Joachim protested on being assigned the relic of Charlemagne. Eugène, after all, is to carry the coronation ring.

As a result Bonaparte decreed that Joachim will carry my crown, which of course infuriates Caroline.

Is there to be no end to it? Now Jacques-Louis David is beside himself. The master of ceremonies assigned him to a seat in the stands at the coronation and he very nearly had a fit, threatening a duel. He'd been promised a box so that he could set up his impedimenta, work on his drawings undisturbed. I was called upon to settle the matter: yes, he absolutely did require a box directly above and in front of the altar in order to set up his easels and make sketches, and no, a duel would absolutely *not* be permitted.

A duel! I confess I almost laughed at the thought of this ardent Revolutionary settling a rather minor conflict in such an aristocratic manner. We are all going mad.


*November 30—only two more days.*

This morning, first thing, Bonaparte came to me at my toilette, hiding something behind his back. "What are you up to now, Bonaparte?" I asked, for he had that playful look.

"I want you to try something on." He brought a glittering ornament out from behind his back and twirled it in the air as if it were a trinket. He caught it neatly and held it out with one hand, holding it by the gold cross perched on top.

My crown! "Bonaparte, isn't it heavy?"

"Exceedingly. Take it!"

"I've never seen anything quite so beautiful," I said, a lump rising in my throat. Or so frightening.

"Try it on." He reminded me of an eager boy.

The crown sat snug on my head. The jeweller had devised a padded velvet band around the inside, but even so, I felt a head pain threatening. "It's perfect," I said.


*December 1—only one more day.*

It is one-thirty, a cold winter afternoon. I'm in my dressing room, awaiting my entourage. We will have one last rehearsal in preparation for tomorrow. Outside in the courtyard I hear César yelling. Thirty carriages to make ready, a hundred and forty horses to groom. No wonder he is raving.

The fervour, frankly, is unnerving. Two of my ladies are planning to rise at two in the morning just to have their hair dressed. It seems that everyone in Paris is going mad with last-minute preparations. Three orchestras—four hundred and fifty musicians in all—have been rehearsing. Scribes have been busy copying out over seventeen *thousand* pages of music for the choir of four hundred. And every tailor in Paris, it seems, is sleepless from making uniforms for how many soldiers? Eighty thousand, I think Bonaparte said, just to guard the route.

I'm not frantic, but nervous, yes: tomorrow I will be crowned Empress in the Cathedral of Notre-Dame. In all this, I keep forgetting that Bonaparte and I are to be married tonight.


*1:20 A.M.*

At midnight, between salvos of cannon and thunder, Bonaparte and I were married before God by his jolly uncle, Cardinal Fesch, in front of a makeshift altar set up in Bonaparte's cabinet. It was done quickly, without fuss, much like our first, civil, ceremony.

"I am your wife, forever and ever," I told Bonaparte. A truth. He clasped my hands and pressed them to his chest.


*December 2 (or rather December 3).*

It is almost two in the morning. Bonaparte sleeps. It is snowing lightly again. I am wrapped in a fur, sitting at the little escritoire by the fire—embers now. My crown is set carelessly on my toilette table, next to my diamond tiara. I start for a moment, considering the danger, the temptation to thieves, and then remind myself that Roustam is asleep outside our door, recall the great number of guards who watch over us as we rest: Bonaparte and me, man and wife, Emperor and Empress.

It has been a very long day. I was woken by gun salutes at six this morning, followed by a deafening tumult of bells. "Well, Your Majesty?" Mimi said with a grin, handing me a cup of hot chocolate. "This is your big day. Too bad your mother couldn't be here to see it." She laughed. "Your mother in her mended socks."

My mother, who is convinced I've married an ogre. I felt Bonaparte's side of the bed. He'd risen? Already?

"The Emperor is in his cabinet," Mimi said, clearing a spot for a plate of rolls.

"He's working?" I don't know why I was surprised.

"You know what I was thinking of, Yeyette? Remember the fortune the obeah woman told you back home on Martinico? You were only thirteen."

"Fourteen," I said, biting into the hot roll. How could I forget? *You will be Queen.* And then I recalled the words: *But not for very long.* Did the voodoo priestess really say that? I couldn't remember. It all seemed a dream to me: a bad dream.

"I told you she was never wrong. Did you sleep?"

"Thanks to you." Mimi and her box of magic herbs. "Is that *rain*?" It had been snowing when Bonaparte and I had gone to bed.

"It's miserable out," Mimi said, pulling back the drapes. "The streets are a mess."

Reluctantly I swung my feet out from under the warm covers. "That's a shame," I said, thinking of the crowds huddled in the cold. Thinking of the freezing cathedral. Concerned about the Pope, his frail health.

I looked out into the courtyard. Already it was thronged with people, shivering in the slush, the soaked banners and flags hanging from the balconies.


The morning unfolded like a fairy tale. Chastulé brought in my diamonds: the diadem, belt, necklace and earrings. Clari and Mademoiselle Avrillion staggered under the weight of my white satin gown, heavy with gold and silver embroidery. Chastulé assessed me up and down, her hands on her hips. "Ha! We begin with the chemise."

After I was clothed, Isabey was announced with his big wooden box of paints and powders, to "create" (his word) my face. I sat before my looking glass, fingering the ring the Pope had given me, watching as I was slowly transformed: my bosom and face whitened with ceruse ("Venetian—the finest, mixed with egg white, much preferred over powdered pig bone," Isabey said in all seriousness), veins lightly delineated with blue liner, cheeks rouged with Spanish Red, eyebrows defined with black lead.

"A little belladonna?" Isabey suggested, lining my eyes with a hint of kohl.

"The poison?" I asked, alarmed.

"To give a wide-eyed *sensual* look."* He opened his eyes wide, to demonstrate.

"I prefer to see!" And live.

Then Monsieur Duplan, my wonderful hairdresser, began, powdering my hair with gold dust before dressing it. "Oh, that's *beautiful*, Your Majesty," Clari said, watching every new development with great interest.

"Ha, you look not a day older than twenty-five," Chastulé said.

Perhaps if one didn't look too closely, I thought. "You're magicians," I told Isabey and Duplan, who hovered like proud parents.

"But remember, Your Majesty, no laughing—and certainly no weeping," Isabey cautioned. "We don't want you to flake."

And then came time to put on my gown and my jewels. Chastulé stood on a stool to position the diamond diadem. She breathed heavily with the exertion as she fastened the necklace, my earrings and belt. Then she pulled me over to the big looking glass.

I regarded the image. *You will be Queen.* Feeling a little faint, I sat down. It was only half-past seven. I felt I'd been up for days . . . for a lifetime.

"She's in here," I heard a woman's yell from the other room, followed by a hiccup. Elisa? Soon Pauline and Elisa appeared, and behind them Caroline, huffing and complaining about the weight of her train, her tight stays.

"Is it supposed to stand up like this?" Pauline asked, fussing with her ruff.

Following the three princesses were Joachim (in a pink-lined cape), Joseph and Julie, Louis and Hortense . . . and, breaking free of his nursemaid, little Napoleon. I held my arms open and he came bounding into my arms. "Careful," the nursemaid cried out.

I kissed the boy, and stood him up so that I could admire his uniform. "He looks so handsome," I told Hortense (who is healthier now, but still wan, still thin), wiping a smudge of rouge from the boy's

---

* *Belladonna, or deadly nightshade, dilated the pupils, imparting a languorous look of desire.*

cheek. "Sit here, near your grandmaman," I whispered, pulling out the little upholstered armchair I had had made especially for his visits.

He climbed up onto it and sat watching us, sucking two fingers. Bonaparte entered the room in a purple velvet tunic and plumed black velvet toque. "I feel like a stuffed monkey," he said.

I hid my smile behind my hand.

Little Napoleon let out a delighted squeal. "Nonan the monkey?"

We laughed as Bonaparte chased his nephew around the room making monkey noises, his silly cape flying. The Emperor!

And then all my lovely ladies arrived, looking so beautiful in their white silk gowns, their long sleeves embroidered in gold. They paraded for our benefit, protesting as the pugs stepped on their trains.

Bonaparte stood before the glass with his brothers Joseph and Louis. "If only our father could see us now," he said. I knew what he was thinking: if only his mother could be here, too. And *mine*, so far away in Martinico, I thought, tears rising, checking to make sure that my earrings were secure.


It was still raining when we were summoned to our carriages. Bonaparte and I were escorted to the Imperial coach—a glittering conveyance ornamented all over with stars and laurel leaves, Bonaparte's bee emblems. I thought I might be transported to some magical place were I to set foot in it. I recalled the soiled trundle that had taken me to prison in the dead of night—how long ago? A decade?

I looked up at the coach driver, so high up on the box. César tipped his green-and-white feathered hat and grinned, pleased, no doubt, to be looking so fine in gold-embroidered silk stockings, his wide green coat trimmed with gold lace. The eight rather impatient grey horses pawed at the cobblestones, tossing their white head-plumes.

I got in first so that I might be seated on Bonaparte's right, followed by Joseph (who was irked: he'd expected to be awarded the seat of honour next to Bonaparte, I suspect) and Louis (his cloak covering his enfeebled arm). Bonaparte drummed his fingers on his knee, examining the white velvet upholstery embroidered in gold, the golden lightning bolts on the ceiling, the golden N crowned with laurels. Trying (still) to loosen his itchy lace cravat, pulling down on his toque with its eight rows of diamonds, picking at the bees embroidered on his cape. Impatient! Finally, cannon and a salvo of artillery announced our departure. I was relieved to be moving—although *moving* is perhaps not the right word. Crawling would have been faster.

We were hours, it seemed, traversing the short distance from the Tuileries to Notre-Dame. It was so cold! (There was no foot-warmer in the coach—only a bearskin underfoot.) I smiled and nodded to the crowd along Rue Saint-Honoré as the three brothers talked: of the ceremony planned for the fifth of December on the Champ-de-Mars, Chénier's new tragedy opening this coming weekend, the fête the city of Paris was planning, the cost of the renovations that had been made to the Hôtel Brienne in anticipation of Signora Letizia's arrival—whenever *that* might be.

Soldiers were lined three deep along the route. From somewhere I could hear kettledrums and trumpets. Hawkers were selling sausages and rolls. (Suddenly I was so hungry.) All around our carriage the Imperial Guard rode, the bravest of the brave, Bonaparte called them, his "old moustaches"—revolutionaries who had fought beside him in Italy and Egypt, following now in great state to see their "little corporal" (as they called him) crowned Emperor. Eugène was with them, proudly riding Pegasus.

"You look beautiful, Maman," he mouthed and then grinned, that look of bedazzlement that was becoming so familiar. I wondered if he thought of the crowds he'd seen on these streets as a boy, thronging to watch the tumbrel carrying prisoners to the guillotine. I wondered if he remembered—as he regarded his mother in her golden carriage—catching a glimpse of her through the window of her prison. I wondered if he remembered crying for bread, going to sleep hungry. I wondered if he thought of his father.

Yes, I thought then, looking out over the cheering throng, nodding and waving, nodding and waving (just like a queen), I believe my son does think of such things. Perhaps we were all of us recalling those days. Perhaps it was the memory of that terrible time that was at the heart of the wild joy that seemed to fill our beautiful city, in spite of the cold and the damp. *Long live the Emperor!* Long live the man who has saved us, I thought, giving my (impatient) husband an appreciative look. *Long live Napoleon!*

It was eleven by the time we arrived at the west entrance of Notre-Dame. Cannons went off, bells pealed and the crowd cheered. As we stepped out of the carriage, the sun came out. "Ah," Bonaparte said, as if he'd been expecting it.

It was warm, at least, inside the archbishop's palace next to the cathedral, the fires blazing brightly. All the running to and fro made it seem like backstage at a theatre. It took four valets to help Bonaparte into his Imperial robes. "Well?" Bonaparte said, turning to face me. *Emperor!* (Although, in truth, he looked more like the king of diamonds on a deck of cards, dwarfed by his enormous ermine mantle.) His expression was vaguely distressed—perhaps because of the weight. My own mantle was so heavy I could hardly move, even with the reluctant princesses helping to carry it.

Then, at last, we began the procession into the cathedral. Ahead of me were the heralds, the pages, the Master of Ceremony (looking distractedly around to make sure we were all in order), a glowering Joachim with my beautiful crown on a crimson cushion, the chamberlains and equerries, each ten paces apart. "Now?" I asked Count Etiquette. I looked back to make sure that the Princesses (Elisa, Caroline, Pauline, Hortense and Julie) were ready to bear the weight of my long train—and that *their* chamberlains were positioned, in turn, to carry theirs.

On a signal from Count Etiquette, we all began to move—very, *very* slowly. A centipede, indeed! Just before I entered the doors of the cathedral, I glanced behind me, smiled at my daughter. Behind her I could see Bonaparte motioning to Joseph, Louis, de Cambacérès and Lebrun to hurry up, pick up his mantle. And behind *him*, after the marshals, I spotted the face of my cheerful son, waiting so patiently. I searched the crowd for little Napoleon and his governess, finally spotting them near the door of the cathedral. I kissed the air and little Napoleon grinned, opening and closing his hand: bye-bye, Grandmaman. Bye-bye.

I don't believe I will ever forget that moment, entering Notre-Dame. The audience lost its dignity and burst into applause as the four orchestras played a triumphal march. The light streaming in the brightly coloured windows, the enormous tapestries, the painted backdrops, pigeons swooping high above the glittering crowd, the hat plumes bobbing, gems sparkling, all made it appear like a scene out of the *Arabian Nights*.

I'm told it was after one o'clock when we reached the altar. I can believe it, for we proceeded at a snail's pace. Pope Pius VII, who had been waiting in the cold for hours, was seated near the Grand Altar in his simple white robe. *My daughter*, his eyes said as we approached.

As the angelic choir sang Paisiello's *Coronation Mass,* Bonaparte and I climbed the steps to the thrones in front of the altar. I was relieved to have something to sit on. Bonaparte looked calm, as if he were crowned every day.

Then the ceremony began. The Pope, intoning Mass in his high nasal voice, blessed the Imperial emblems: the ring, the sword, the mantle, the sceptre. (Twice I saw Bonaparte stifle a yawn.) Then, after *Veni Creator,* Bonaparte and I knelt on the big velvet cushions and the Holy Father took up the (new) flask of holy oil, anointing first Bonaparte and then me with the triple unction, intoning, *Diffuse, O Lord, by my hands, the treasures of your grace and benediction on your servant.* Bonaparte was listening with a pious expression, but I suspected that he didn't like having the oil on his hands and was wondering what to do about it, whether or not he could wipe it off somehow.

Then the Pope took Bonaparte's crown from its cushion on the altar and Bonaparte, removing his golden wreath, took it from him and, turning to the crowd, placed it on his head himself. (Everyone gasped!) Just then a loose pebble fell from the ceiling and hit his shoulder but he did not flinch. His face shone with a radiance I'd never seen in it before. He looked . . . *heroic*—that is the only word I can think to describe it. I moved toward the altar and knelt before my husband, my hands clasped in prayer.

I'd never experienced such silence; surely it was the silence of heaven. As I knelt there, waiting, my life welled up before me. I thought of my beloved father; how I wished he could see me. Tears spilled onto my gloves as Bonaparte approached. Trying hard not to weep, I studied the embroidered bees on his white satin slippers. I felt him fussing with my hair, felt the weight of the crown—and then felt him lift it off. I raised my eyes, a little concerned: was there a problem? Was my tiara in the way? He was looking down at me with my crown in his hands and the hint of a smile in his eyes, as if to say: Maybe I will, and maybe I won't. As if to say: Don't be so sure. As if to say: This is my gift to you, this is *our* moment. As if to say: I love you with all my heart, and I want the world to know it.

Only Bonaparte would have the audacity to tease at such a moment. I held my breath; it wouldn't do to laugh! And then I felt him place the crown firmly on my head and a murmur went through the crowd, a reverent hush. A calm feeling of courage filled me and I stood, my knees steady. I was there by the grace of God.

But *not*, certainly, by the grace of Bonaparte's sisters, for as I started to climb the steps up toward the altar, I was yanked back and very nearly toppled.* I heard Bonaparte hiss something sharply and I was freed.

The rest of the ceremony went by as if in a dream. The chorus sang, "May the Emperor live forever." The heralds proclaimed in full (and wonderfully sonorous) voice, "The most glorious and most august Napoleon, Emperor of the French people, is anointed, crowned and enthroned!"

"Vive l'Empereur!"

"Vive l'Empereur!"

"Vive l'Empereur!"

The thick stone walls of the ancient cathedral shook as hundreds of cannon were fired outside and the great bell of Notre-Dame began to ring. As we emerged into the bright winter sun, fire-rockets flared. Already the dancing had begun.

* *A member of the assembly wrote: "Nothing could have been more comical than the way the Bonaparte sisters acted. One sulked, another held smelling salts under her nose, and the third let the mantle drop."*

## *In which Bonaparte honours my son*

The Emperor and I dined alone, infused by the glow of glory. (And with relief that it was over.) "Leave it on," Bonaparte said, as Chastulé was about to remove my crown. "It becomes you." Over a simple meal of roast chicken with crayfish butter, hashed apples and a vanilla soufflé (which Bonaparte ate first), we talked, chattering like children. He'd not even noticed the stone that had hit his shoulder, and yes, he'd barked at his unruly sisters. "Imagine if I had fallen over backwards!" I said, both of us laughing now that it was over.

After, we joined everyone in the Yellow Salon: family, officials and household staff. Over the booming of cannon and the hiss and cackle of the fire-rockets outside, we shared story after story. My ladies demonstrated how, on the way to the cathedral, they'd had to pick their way through the slush in their silk slippers, shivering in the icy wind. There had been one uncomfortable moment when the crowd near the market had laughed at the Pope's prelate in his broad-brimmed hat, riding a white mule and carrying a huge cross. Uncle "Cardinal" Fesch, flushed with fine wine, told how his nephew—the Emperor—had poked him in the backside with the Imperial sceptre.

Bonaparte grinned. "It got you moving, didn't it, Uncle?" (Little Napoleon giggled, half-asleep in my arms.)

"And were those *stones* that fell from the vault?" Hortense asked, taking the baby Petit from his nursemaid.

"It was the birds I worried about."

"With reason," Eugène said with a laugh.

"And what happened at the altar, Your Majesty?" Chastulé asked. "It looked as if you were going to fall over. That mantle must be heavy."

"It *was* heavy," I said, glancing at the Bonaparte sisters. "Ask the princesses," I suggested with an innocent air.

"And were you weeping, Your Majesty, when the Emperor put the crown on your head?" Clari asked.

"I couldn't help it," I told Isabey, who looked mortified at the damage to his handiwork. "I tried not to."

And then everyone began to chatter at once:

"Sire, did His Holiness know that you were going to put the crown on yourself?"

"Ah, so it was planned that way."*

"It was glorious, just glorious."

"A day I will never, ever, ever, ever, *ever* forget."

I sat and listened, taking it all in, caressing my sweet little Napoleon, now asleep in my arms. I caught Bonaparte's eye and smiled. Our day. Over at last.

*December 18, late afternoon—Paris.*
Madame Mère (as she is to be called now) has finally arrived back in Paris—none too happy, and certainly not the least bit apologetic about having missed the most important event of her amazing son's life. She regards the magnificence Bonaparte has bestowed upon the family and the nation with something akin to contempt. "So long as it lasts," she said sceptically, ferreting coins away.

She was too ill to come to the last family gathering—sick with chagrin, her daughters reported, over having to buy a length of expensive silk for a gown. She has rationed her cooks to one dishcloth, one apron, one towel a day, and refuses to buy more than three half-pound loaves of bread at a time. "We have to bring bread when we dine there," Caroline complained to Bonaparte.

"You must *spend* the money I give you," Bonaparte later instructed his

---

* *In crowning himself, Napoleon was following a ceremony Charlemagne had ordered when his son was crowned.*

mother. "You must entertain, keep an open house, be generous with your staff. It is the aristocratic way."

*January 6, 1805, morning—Sunday and Kings' Day (cold).*
Fouché, looking uncharacteristically dapper in a fur-lined cloak, sidled up to me at last night's ball in my honour. "Why are you smiling?" I asked. "It makes me uneasy."

"I thought you might be interested in two items in the latest police report." He blinked his eyes slowly. "Concerning members of your family."

"Perhaps." Of course I wanted to know!

"One concerns the Emperor's youngest brother."

"Jérôme?" The scamp.

"He and his bride are apparently on the frigate *La Didon*, returning to France—to the welcoming arms of his brother the Emperor."

"Welcoming?" I rolled my eyes. It was doubtful that Bonaparte would agree even to see Jérôme. "And the second item in the report?"

"Concerns your son."

*Eugène?* In a police report! "It doesn't have anything to do with Adèle Duchâtel, does it?"

"Ah, the devious Madame Duchâtel—that's another matter altogether. No, the report divulged rumours of a possible marriage between your son and Princess Auguste-Amélie of Bavaria—the most beautiful princess in Europe, it is said." Fouché studied my reaction. "The Princess's family is one of the most ancient and distinguished in all of Europe."

*Indeed.* Princess Auguste's family has ruled Bavaria for eight centuries—the blood of Charlemagne flows in her veins. "The rumours are unfounded. Princess Auguste is betrothed to Prince Charles of the House of Baden." Unfortunately!

*January 18.*
Tired, a troubled sleep. Eugène's ball in his newly renovated town house last night was a success, especially with the young. The revelry went on until dawn—or so I'm told, for Bonaparte and I left early, shortly after

Caroline and Hortense's duet. (Caroline braying, trying to compete with Hortense, the crowd crying out for an encore from my daughter—painful.)

"Your fête is a big success," I told Eugène, on taking my leave.

"I suppose," he said, uncharacteristically morose.

I've since learned the reason for my son's dejection. Caroline had cruelly informed him that the woman he courted had been "taken" by his stepfather.

*January 19, Décadi—close to midnight.*
A blizzard howls both outside and in—Bonaparte is in a foul temper.

*January 21.*
Eugène called on me at my morning toilette, his hat damp from melted snow. "Papa has ordered me to leave with my regiment."

Leave? For where?

"For Milan."*

"*Now*, Eugène?" The storm was severe. It was difficult to ride across town, much less over the Alps.

"Within twenty-four hours," Eugène said, handing me the order. "I don't understand, unless . . ."

Unless Bonaparte wanted Eugène out of Paris. "Eugène, may I ask you something?" Something I had no business knowing. "Have you done anything that might have angered Bonaparte?" His evasive look gave the answer. "Something to do with Adèle Duchâtel, perhaps?"

And then Eugène confessed: he'd been upset, he said. He'd called Adèle a coquette (and worse, I suspect). "I told her I'd tell her husband about . . . you know." He tapped the tip of his riding whip against the toe of his boot.

About Adèle and Bonaparte. What was I to say? It was such a complex web. "And so?"

---

* *Napoleon was sending troops to Milan in order to protect Italy from invasion by Austria, which tended to view northern Italy as its domain.*

He hunched his shoulders. "And so she said she would tell the Emperor about *me*."

He seemed so much a boy still, all fluster and freckles, hardly equal to this bedchamber duel with his Emperor stepfather. "And what might there be to tell, Eugène?"

"Maman, she'd have to lie," he said, blushing angrily. "I got nowhere!"

*January 22.*

This morning my obedient, loyal son headed off into the storm at the head of nine hundred chasseurs and grenadiers. I am struggling with my conscience. I promised Eugène I wouldn't say anything to Bonaparte.

*[Undated]*

"Zut," Bonaparte said under his breath, pacing. "So Adèle lied to me about Eugène. That was devious on her part—devious and manipulative. I'm afraid you're going to have to let her go."

"You want *me* to dismiss your mistress, Bonaparte?"

The thought gives me pleasure, I confess.

*February 1.*

Today Bonaparte made an announcement to the Senate, naming Eugène Prince and Vice-Arch-Chancellor.

*February 24—noisy: carnival parade starting outside.*

I should have guessed that this would happen. An enraged (and hiccupping) Elisa descended upon Bonaparte: "Eugène is a prince now, even Joachim is a prince—so why not Félix? What about *my* husband?"

*This* is a problem. Elisa's husband is lazy and inept and alienates everyone with his haughty rudeness. "I must get them out of Paris," Bonaparte said, scratching his head.

*March 19, Saint Joseph's Day.*
Bonaparte has found a solution to his sister's complaints: he is awarding
Elisa and Félix the little kingdom of Piombino in northern Italy.

"How charming," Caroline commented with biting sarcasm. "My
sister is to rule an army of four soldiers."

"Better than ruling only one soldier," Elisa said evenly—meaning
Caroline's husband Joachim.


*March 21—Saint-Cloud.*
I've been busy getting everything ready for the baby's baptism on the
weekend—by the Pope no less. (He has wisely decided to linger in Paris,
waiting for the passage over the Alps to clear.) Bonaparte insists that
Hortense and Louis's second son be baptized exactly as a Dauphin would
have been baptized during the Ancien Régime. Complex! The Holy
Father has confided that he's never performed a baptism before, much
less an Imperial one.


*March 22.*
Caroline has had her baby, another girl. "Bad timing," Bonaparte said
during our evening ride. "She expects the infant to be baptized along
with Hortense and Louis's boy next week."

"But wouldn't that mean two entirely different ceremonies?" Caroline's children are not in the line of succession—the ceremony would not
be the same.

"Exactly. I'll tell her it would take too long," he said.


*[Undated]*
Caroline's in a rage!


*March 24, Sunday, 4:00 P.M.—Saint-Cloud.*
And so it has been done: Hortense and Louis's baby Petit was baptized by
the Pope (with Uncle Fesch prompting): Napoleon-Louis, he has been

named. The five-month-old obliged us by crying the entire time. Bonaparte, the proud godfather, held the squalling child at the font. Madame Mère, as godmother, stood beside Bonaparte, scowling in her expensive new gown. The baby finally quieted, sucking on Bonaparte's finger.

And now, that behind us, we rush to get ready to leave for Milan in one week—one more coronation to get through. Bonaparte is to be crowned King of Italy—unless he can succeed in persuading one of his brothers to take his place, that is (to avoid alarming the Royalist nations).


*March 28.*
Monsieur Rémusat left this morning for Italy—escorted by a sizeable guard. He carried with him the Imperial insignia and Crown jewels. Clari is in tears at the thought of her husband having to endure the "wretched Savoy roads and their ignorant postillions." And the bandits! Bandits just waiting to murder her husband in order to get their hands on his treasure. But most of all she is in a fret over the Mont Cenis pass, "with its steep descents and no wall at all on the outer edge!" In spite of my assurances that I myself have crossed two times over "that fatal" Mont Cenis, she continues to be convinced that her husband will perish. In comforting her, in assuring her that there is no danger, I begin to conquer my own fear. I try to think only of the pleasure of seeing Eugène in Milan, try not to think of the mountains that must be crossed to get to him.


*March 30—snow!*
I'm "in a state of perturbation" (as Clari puts it)—but it's not only me. *Everyone*, it seems, is in a fluster, getting ready to depart in two days. The servants can't figure out who to take orders from, whom to give orders *to*.

And then excitement beyond measure: the new Imperial travelling coach was delivered and everyone went out in the snow-covered courtyard to gawk at the enormous berline. The outside is plain—intentionally, so as not to attract bandits. The only indication that it is an Imperial coach is a small coat of arms on the door.

Inside, the coach is remarkable, for it is divided into two compartments. In the one at the front are two deep seats, separated by an armrest. Opposite is a bank of drawers, equipped with toilet articles and a table service, as well as a desk. In the back compartment is a bed that can be made into a sofa.

I let the children of the household climb inside—they scrambled from one compartment to another. "*My* seat," little Napoleon said, climbing into the leather chair opposite the desk—Bonaparte's chair.

"He'll make a fine emperor someday," I heard a maid say.

"Our Crown Prince."

Our *heir*.


*April 1—Fontainebleau.*
The coach is remarkably comfortable: the big body swings on wide leather straps attached to heavy springs. "Time to try out that bed," Bonaparte said meaningfully as soon as we had passed the Paris gate. He pulled the blinds and took my hand. And so our first Imperial expedition is off to an excellent start, the Emperor (*and* Empress) content.


*April 22—Palazzo Stupinigi, near Turin.*
We crossed the Alps without incident. In fact, the weather was glorious, the vistas stimulating to the imagination, bringing back memories of youth. A decade ago I crossed the Alps into Italy to join my new husband on his first campaign. I remember my fear then, the wonder of a journey into an unknown world. If I had known then what an amazing journey it would, in fact, turn out to be . . .

Eugène, so bronzed from the sun he looks like a peasant, met us at this regal lodge not far from Turin. He and Bonaparte immediately set off on a hunt. I've bathed, changed into an evening toilette. The intoxicating scent of spring is in the air.


*April 24—still at Palazzo Stupinigi.*
We've had word that Bonaparte's young brother Jérôme is in Turin! He's

sailed from America to Portugal and come on horseback into Italy, seeking his Emperor brother's favour—and approval of his marriage. Eugène has just left with the unhappy message that Bonaparte refuses to receive his youngest sibling, refuses to recognize "that girl" as his wife.

"*Forgive* him?" Bonaparte ranted when Eugène and I pleaded for him to reconcile with Jérôme. "He's lucky I haven't court-martialled him for desertion!"

*1:20 A.M.*

On hearing a horse trot into the courtyard, I crept down the stairs in my dressing gown and cap, shielding the candle flame against the warm breeze that billowed the curtains. "Oh, Maman, it really is a little sad," Eugène said, unbuckling his spurs. "He does care for her."

"It's a matter of policy, Eugène." *Policy* has nothing to do with love and individual happiness. Policy has to do with peace and prosperity. Policy has to do with the well-being of a people, of a nation.

Eugène threw down his hat. "That's what I told him. I explained that with power came responsibilities, that the Imperial family must set the example and that an illegal marriage could not be condoned." All this in the mock voice of Bonaparte.

"And he accepted?"

"Not until I told him Papa would find him a buxom princess to marry."

"You didn't!" Both of us laughing.

*A balmy evening, May 6—Alessandria.*

Jérôme and Bonaparte embraced. With promises of a princess and a crown someday soon, Jérôme has agreed to have his "marriage" declared null and void.

The young man set off this morning, waving his hat from the high road. "That scamp," Bonaparte said, shaking his head, his eyes misty.

*May 8—Milan.*
We're in Milan, in the royal palace facing the cathedral. How noisy it is! The thick stone walls shake (I swear) every time the bells ring, which is often. We've a water closet, but the arrangement of the rooms is awkward, our bedchamber uncomfortably small. Bonaparte is already pacing it off, deciding how it's to be renovated.


*May 24, close to 11:00 A.M.*
Yesterday a mounted detachment was sent to Monza to bring back the Iron Crown. It's a simple band of gold (not iron) about three inches high, decorated with a few irregular gems. Rather crude for a crown, I thought, but Bonaparte held it as if it were made of diamonds. "Charlemagne wore this crown," he said reverently, placing it on his head to see if it would fit (it's a little small).

"Is it decided?" I asked, shifting it forward on his head. "You're to be King of Italy?" Certainly that's what the Italians want, but England and the other Royalist nations won't like it, that much is clear. Any indication that France is growing in power and prosperity alarms them.

"I tried to talk one of my brothers into it, but . . ." He made a gesture of futility. His brothers don't want to give up their place in the line of succession for the French crown.

"So you will be King, but you'll appoint someone to rule?" I asked, emboldened by the moment.

"Curious to know who that might be?" he teased, tugging my ear. And then, his countenance suddenly serious, he added, "Joachim was the obvious choice. He speaks the language and has commanded troops here."

"You say he *was* the obvious choice." Not any longer?

"Prince Bully-Boy is none too popular here, it would appear. He's made a number of enemies."


*May 26—a superb day.*
Yet another coronation behind us. Bonaparte shocked everyone by walking in carrying Charlemagne's crown under his arm, like a hat.

Now everyone awaits the big announcement: whom will he name Viceroy?

*June 7.*
"You appointed *Eugène?*"

"I thought this was what you wanted," Bonaparte said, perplexed.

"Oh yes!" I said, but overcome by the realization that my son would no longer be living in Paris, or even in France; overcome knowing, suddenly, how very, very much I was going to miss him.

*[Undated]*
"Maman, I can't sleep for worrying," Eugène confessed. "I'm only twenty-three."

"You have the best of teachers. Bonaparte has so much confidence in you."

"I'm going to miss you and Hortense—and what about her boys? Little Napoleon will forget me."

"We'll just have to find you a wife," I teased. *Soon.*

*July 6—Genoa.*
As feared, England has joined with Austria and Russia to wage war against us—yet another Royalist coalition determined to put an end to the French Republic.*

"I must leave for Paris immediately," Bonaparte said, ordering the travel carriage. I begged to return with him. "There will be no stops," he warned. "I'm going to travel night and day."

Yes, I nodded, ringing for a maid to pack my trunks. Now I am ready; *he* is not.

* *England was involved financially, paying Russia and Austria to send troops against France.*

*July 11—Fontainebleau.*
We arrived at Fontainebleau before anyone expected us. The flustered cooks managed to find some tough mutton for us to eat.

Immediately I fell into bed (my feet swollen) and slept for hours, waking dazed. People can't believe that we travelled from Genoa in eighty-five hours—a *record*—and this with a three-hour delay on Mont Cenis due to a storm. "This comet called Bonaparte," Hortense once said. This comet indeed! Sometimes I feel I'm hanging on for dear life.


*Milan*
*Chère Maman,*
*You will be pleased to know that I'm following up on your suggestion to establish a nursery-garden in order to supply trees to all my kingdom. Fruit trees are unknown here. Any recommendations?*

*I've also been thinking of creating a museum to display the fine works of art hidden away in the cellars of the monasteries and churches. I have so many dreams: of a library, a museum of natural history, a medical museum (don't laugh). I think a school of design might do well here, too.*

*I get daily letters from Papa. I'm learning so much from him.**

* *Napoleon's instructions to Eugène on how to rule Italy included these guidelines: "We live in an age where one cannot underestimate the perversity of the human heart. I cannot empha-sise enough the importance of circumspection and prudence. Italians are naturally more deceit-ful than the French. The way to earn their respect is not to trust anyone. Dissimulation is natural at a certain age; for you, it must be a matter of principle. When you have spoken openly, tell yourself that you have made a mistake, and resolve not to do it again.*

*"There will come a time when you will understand that there is little difference between one nationality and another. The goal of your administration is the well-being of my Italian subjects. You must sacrifice the things you care most about, and embrace customs which you dislike. In Italy, you must forget the glory of being French. You must persuade Italians that you love them. They know that there is no love without respect. Learn their language, social-ize, take part in their festivities. Approve of what they approve of, and love what they love.*

*"Speak as little as possible. You do not have enough training, and your education is insuffi-cient for you to take part freely in discussions. Although Viceroy, you are only twenty-three. People may flatter you, but everyone will realize how little you know. You will earn more respect by virtue of your potential than by what you are today.*

*"Do not imitate me; you must be more reserved.*

*"Rarely preside over Council of State. You do not have enough knowledge to do so with*

*A million kisses. I miss you and Hortense terribly. Kiss my nephews for me, remind them of their lonely uncle.*

*Your Prince Eugène, Viceroy of Italy*
*Note—You'll be happy to know that my efforts to reduce the violence in the city have already had results.*


*July 19—Paris.*
Caroline flashed a smile. "Joachim and I wish to convey sincere congratulations on your son's appointment as Viceroy of Italy," she said, her fingertips pressed together. "Don't we, Joachim?"

"The Emperor is flawless in his wisdom." Joachim doffed his pink hat and bowed, straightening with difficulty.

"What's wrong with your leg?" Bonaparte demanded. "Better get in shape. We'll be riding out soon." Riding out to war again.

"Oh, it's nothing!" Caroline said, answering for her husband—but I've since discovered the cause of Joachim's leg injury. On learning of Eugène's promotion, he broke his sword over his knee in a rage.

*success. When you do preside, do not speak. They will listen to you, but they will soon see that you are not competent. One cannot measure the strength of a prince who remains silent.*

*"Do not be overly friendly to foreigners—there is little to be gained from them. An ambassador will never speak well of you because it is his job to speak poorly. The foreign ambassadors are, in a manner of speaking, official spies. Preferably, surround yourself with young Italian men; the old ones are useless."*

## In which my son falls truly in love

*September 2, 1805, late afternoon—Malmaison.*
It has been some time since I opened these pages. Anger impels me to pick up a quill once again. Anger and fear, I confess. This afternoon Caroline called to announce in a tone of victory that Joachim has been named Bonaparte's second-in-command in the coming campaign. "How surprising that Louis was not chosen, or even Eugène," she said, purring like a cat with her claws out.

"Eugène is quite busy governing Italy." And doing so well!

"It must be difficult without a wife," she said, helping herself to a fistful of aromatic pastilles. "*Speaking* of which, I heard the most astonishing rumour. It's being said that Eugène is going to marry Princess Auguste of Bavaria."

"Princess Auguste is betrothed to Prince Charles," I said evenly.

I was so relieved when she left! Whatever marriage negotiations are undertaken, the last person I would want to know about them is Caroline.


*September 9.*
Austria has invaded Bavaria. "They must be stopped," Bonaparte said, closeting himself with the Minister of War. Soon, I know, he will announce that we're leaving. I've already sent silver, linen and furniture on ahead to Strasbourg.

*September 23, the first day of the Republican New Year.*
We leave in the morning, before dawn. The carriages, *fifty* of them, are lined up. I've been reviewing the lists. Bonaparte has just told me to make sure the telescope and compass have been packed. Which reminds me: dentifrice powder (for me) and wart paste (for Bonaparte).

I must make sure that the cooks prepare dishes we can take with us. Bonaparte doesn't believe in stopping for something as unnecessary as eating, much less answering a call of nature.


*September 26, I think.*
We're in Strasbourg, another flying trip. Keeping up with Bonaparte will be the death of me! We left at four in the morning and travelled without stopping for two days. At each posting house, the wheels had to be cooled with buckets of water. But no, I will *not* complain, lest Bonaparte command I stay behind.

And as to staying behind—the carriage carrying all the kitchen utensils broke down en route. Of the fifty carriages (the dust was terrible), only five were able to keep up.

Already Bonaparte is at work, organizing an attack on the Austrians. "Speed is my weapon."*


*October 1—Strasbourg.*
Bonaparte left this morning. "A kiss—for luck," he said, pulling on his battered hat. It has been five years since he rode to battle. He was anxious, I knew, and eager.

"I will be thinking of you." Praying for him. (This I did not say.) "I put barley water in the berline—in the top right-hand cabinet." That and a number of other remedies that helped "keep the balance," as he put it.

"We won't be long," he called out as the carriage pulled forward. "I promise you."

---

* *The Austrians believed Napoleon and his army were still on the Channel coast. It was an understandable assumption: never in history had so large an army been moved so quickly.*

*12 Vendémiaire, 11:00 P.M., Munich*
*The enemy has been beaten, lost its head, and everyone is telling me that it*
*was the happiest campaign, the shortest and the most brilliant ever made.*
*The weather is terrible. I change clothes twice a day because of the rain. I love*
*and embrace you. N.*


*October 23—Strasbourg.*
Great Patience, Little Patience, Windmill. Every night I lay out the
cards, praying for victory, fearing defeat. Tonight I won all three games:
"They are victorious," I announced to my ladies. A short time later a
breathless courier was announced: Victory! I gave him my pearl ring, so
great was my joy.


*27 Vendémiaire, Elchingen*
*I did what I intended. I destroyed the Austrian army. Now I'm going after*
*the Russians. They are lost. Adieu, a thousand kisses everywhere. N.*


*Yesterday I made thirty-three thousand men put down their arms. I took*
*sixty or seventy thousand prisoners, more than ninety flags and two hundred*
*cannon. Never in the annals of military history has there been such a cata-*
*strophe. I have a bit of a cold. N.*


*October 27—Strasbourg.*
The wife of Bonaparte's chamberlain stood with her hands clasped in
front of her. "I have a message from the Emperor, Your Majesty," she
told me.

She had just come from Munich. I'd been expecting to hear something—something too delicate to entrust to a military courier. Something to do with the spoils of war. Something to do with the hand of a
princess.

"The Emperor asked me to tell you that he has discussed a certain
matter with King Maximilian of Bavaria."

"Indeed?" I said, opening my fan. No doubt King Maximilian was grateful to Bonaparte for liberating his country from the Austrians: but *how* grateful? "And did he say King Maximilian was amenable?"

"Everything has been arranged, Your Majesty," she said with a bow.

I'm to travel to Munich, she said, giving me Bonaparte's detailed instructions itemizing exactly how much I'm to spend on gifts, whose carriage is to precede my own and whose is to follow. I'm to be heralded in every town by the ringing of bells, cannonading, drumming and trumpeting. I'm to accept the homage as my due. I am the wife of the victor.

*November 21, 1805, Paris*
*Chère Maman,*

*Paris has been dispirited without you and the Emperor. Louis is with his regiment on the north coast, in case England invades. I am alone with my angels right now, but not for long. My dear friend Mademoiselle Adèle Auguié has agreed to be my lady's maid—she'll be starting next week. You can imagine how happy this makes me.*

*We read* Le Moniteur *for the names of the injured. Louis will want information pertaining to his aide-de-camp, Monsieur Flahaut. He was wounded at Lambach. Do you know anything?*

*Little Napoleon sends his love. He is sweet with Petit, who has just begun to crawl. They both suffered a bit of an ague that was going around, but are recovering well. My own health is improving with each day. I've been taking your tonics—don't worry.*

*Your loving daughter, Princess Hortense*

*Note—I enclose an account of the disaster in Spain: twenty ships captured!\**
*Fortunately the Emperor's victories in Germany help to console us for the loss. It is said all our luck is with him. It is also said that you are his luck, Maman.*

*December 4—a posting house somewhere en route to Munich.*
Karlsruhe, Stuttgart, Ulm, Augsburg. Everywhere I go, I cast out gifts—

---

\* *On October 21, 1805, the French-Spanish fleet was defeated by England off Cape Trafalgar, on the southwest coast of Spain.*

ebony snuffboxes, enamel miniatures, gems of every size and hue. I feel like a fairy godmother. (And I love it.)

*December 5, Munich—snow, very cold.*
I'm in Munich finally, at the royal palace—called the Residenz. This is a gay country, although curious. The women pile flowers on top of their heads with feathers and bits of chiffon tucked in, using an enormous number of little pins with diamond heads on them. And no face paint, no Spanish Red, and many wearing stays and awkward hoops. Their carriages, much like our old mail coaches, are unusually wide just so that the ladies in their hoops can fit in. (Even then it isn't easy.) Sad-looking nags are harnessed to the carriages with rope. Turning a corner is, of course, difficult.

The Residenz itself is more like a city than a palace. How many court-yards—seven? There are eight galleries and even a museum, I'm told. It's a maze, each apartment suite decorated in a different era: Renaissance, baroque. Mine is luxurious rococo. We have been greeted like royalty.

Well, we *are* royalty, I remind myself. However, walking these ancient halls hung with the portraits of illustrious ancestors dating back centuries makes me feel very much what I am, in fact: *a parvenue.*

Tomorrow the receptions begin. I'm anxious to meet King Maximilian, Princess Auguste's father.

*December 6—Munich.*
"Please, call me Max," King Maximilian said in flawless French. "Everyone else does, even my servants." He laughed gaily.

What a charming man! Tall, handsome, a noble face (in spite of a ruddy complexion), robust for his age, which I take to be about fifty.

He was guarded, however, on the subject of his daughter. "She will agree, I am quite sure."

"She has *not* agreed?"

King Max threw up his hands. "I can't force her."

I've since made inquiries and discovered that Princess Auguste has refused to break her engagement to Prince Charles. She is encouraged in this by her stepmother. As well, the Princess's governess and an aunt are said to be opposed to marriage with Eugène.

All this has me terribly worried. Tomorrow I've been invited to dine with King Max and his family. I've laid out my gifts, sent for a jeweller.

Chastulé will accompany me: the Rochefoucauld name will inspire respect. I've instructed her that she is to entertain our hosts with stories of what a good horseman my handsome Eugène is, how he excels at the hunt, what a fine ruler he is. (I'd prefer to tell them how much Eugène loves children, how gentle and kind-hearted he is, but I'm not sure that they would approve.) Chastulé will praise my son and I will modestly protest. My battle plan.

*December 8.*
Oh, my goodness, she *is* lovely. Tall (I made sure to mention how very tall Eugène is), and *so* beautiful, but in an entirely natural, unstudied way. Seventeen years old with a sylphlike figure—she reminds me of Hortense. A lovely complexion, big dark eyes—*soft* eyes. Shy, gracious—I saw my grandchildren in her lovely arms.

But she is, as well, loyal. She is fond of her pudgy cousin and refuses to break her engagement to him. And headstrong, too, for she resists her father's will.

*[Undated]*
"Ha. It's the three women we must first convince, Your Majesty," Chastulé said.

*The three women*: the stepmother ("Madame Hard-face," Chastulé calls her), the governess ("Madame Fat-face") and the aunt ("Madame Old-face").

"Chastulé, you're cruel," I protested, laughing.

*14 Frimaire, Austerlitz*
*I've concluded a truce. The Battle of Austerlitz is the best I have ever fought. Forty-five flags, more than one hundred and fifty cannon and thirty thousand prisoners—plus twenty thousand killed, a horrible spectacle.*

*Tsar Alexandre is in despair. He showed neither talent nor bravery.**

*Finally peace has returned to the continent. One can only hope that peace will now come to the world.*

*Adieu, my good friend. I very much long to embrace you. N.*

*December 19—Munich.*
Caroline has arrived. We kissed and pretended to be happy to see one another. I'm in dread of her finding out about the delicate negotiations going on right now.

*[Undated]*
Auguste is holding firm. "What do you think it will take?" I asked Chastulé, discouraged.

"To get the Princess to consent?" Chastulé made herself comfortable in one of the enormous armchairs, swinging her feet back and forth like a child. "Well, for one thing, the Three Faces object because there's no crown," she said. "Ha. Yes, a crown *always* helps."

The crown of Italy. "Of course," I said, shrugging, "but—"

"Or if your son were to be named *heir* to the crown. Even King Max objects that Eugène is 'merely' a French gentleman."

"I thought King Max favoured this match."

"He has consented to it, Your Majesty, but that does not mean he favours it."

"But Eugène is a prince, Chastulé. How can King Max say he's 'merely' a gentleman?"

"Prince-*parvenu*, and not even the Emperor's son."

---

* *The Russian Tsar Alexandre wrote to a French general after the battle of Austerlitz: "Tell your master that I am going away. Tell him that he performed miracles yesterday, that the battle has increased my admiration for him, that he is a man predestined by Heaven, that it will take a hundred years for my army to equal his."*

"So if Bonaparte were to formally adopt Eugène as his son and declare him heir to the crown of Italy . . . ?"

"That would help."

I paused, smiling slowly. "If that's what it takes, Chastulé, then perhaps that's what the Princess should demand."

*December 21.*

"Ha. The Three Faces are very long this morning, Your Majesty."

My heart jumped. "The Princess has accepted?"

"Not quite, but she *has* agreed to consider breaking off her engagement to Prince Charles."

"In order to marry Eugène?"

"Not quite. I'm told there are *conditions*." Chastulé grinned.

*December 23—Munich.*

"Is Princess Auguste betrothed?" Caroline asked as we dined tonight.

"Yes," I said, lying with conviction. "To Prince Charles."

*December 31, early—not yet 9:00 A.M.*

Bonaparte arrived just before midnight last night—chilled, weary and *furious* that the wedding contract has not yet been signed. "But she hasn't agreed to it, Bonaparte!"

*4:20 P.M.*

"I'm sending for Eugène," Bonaparte announced.

"She agreed?" *Finally!*

"But on two conditions: one, that I adopt Eugène, and two, that he be made heir to the throne of Italy."

"And so . . . ?"

Bonaparte shrugged. "And so I said yes," he replied with a sheepish smile.

*January 1, 1806, New Year's Day—a Wednesday (not Primidi—hurrah!*
*No more Republican calendar).* *

Caroline has had a nervous fit and taken to her bed. "I wouldn't go to too much trouble, Your Majesty," Chastulé said as I was preparing a basket of healing tinctures and salves to take to her. "It's said Princess Caroline is indisposed because of Prince Eugène's engagement, because now your son's children will take precedence over her little monsters. It's even said she tried to convince the Emperor that he should divorce you and marry Princess Auguste himself."

Mon Dieu, that girl . . .

*January 6, Kings' Day—Monday.*

Now Auguste is ill. The wedding will have to be postponed, we've been told. Bonaparte sent Dr. Corvisart over to "help."

"I could find nothing amiss," the doctor reported back.

"The girl is dissembling," Bonaparte said, smiling at her nerve.

I'm praying that Eugène will get here soon. Until the vows are spoken, I won't be able to sleep.

*January 7, Munich—snowing again.*

Auguste has "miraculously" recovered, but is now claiming a sprained ankle. The wedding will have to be postponed, we were told yet again—until after the Emperor leaves for Paris, her stepmother said.

"They're stalling," Chastulé said. "Once the Emperor is out of Munich, they'll back out."

Bonaparte gave his "assurance" that he'll stay in Munich until the young couple is wed, *whenever* that may be.

Checkmate.

*[Undated]*
Now *I* am ill.

---

* As of this date, the French Empire officially returned to the Gregorian calendar.

*January 10, Friday morning.*

I was woken by my husband. "I have a surprise for you," he said, grinning mischievously. I *screeched*! In the door I saw Eugène. "Grand Dieu, at *last* you've arrived." I clasped his hands, kissed him. "You look as if you've been on a horse for a week." He hadn't shaved and his hair was uncombed. "You've grown a moustache?" It looks horrible on him!

"You don't like it?" he asked, pulling on one point.

"Sweetheart, you are the handsomest prince in all of Europe, but that moustache will have to go. Bonaparte, send someone for the barber. We'll have to get Eugène cleaned up before we introduce him to Princess Auguste," I said, squeezing my son's hand, my heart in a flutter.

Eugène looked at Bonaparte and then back at me.

"What does that look mean?" Slowly it dawned on me. "Bonaparte, you didn't!"

"It was fine, Maman, truly."

"Bonaparte, you took Eugène to meet Princess Auguste—*already*? Without telling me?" I was furious with them both.

"You haven't been well, Josephine. I didn't want to wake you."

"Well, now I'm really sick." All our plans were ruined—and all because of an ugly moustache! "How *could* you? Just look at him. He's a *mess*."

Eugène handed me a handkerchief. "It's all right, Maman," he said, laughing.

"Your son arrived at ten this morning, precisely when he said he would." Bonaparte gave Eugène an approving nod. "I took him directly to King Max—nothing formal, just a family affair, or so I had to assure him."

"I *was* a bit nervous, I admit."

"Actually, I had to pull him along." Bonaparte rocked on his heels in front of the fire.

"And so . . . ? How did it go? What happened!"

"King Max commanded his daughter to enter," Bonaparte explained. "She did, but just stood staring at the floor. I think she was even trembling."

"Auguste didn't expect to be introduced like that, without any warning," Eugène said.

"Go on, Bonaparte," I said slowly. There was something in my son's voice . . . a manly gentleness, a protective caring. *Auguste*, he said.

"That's pretty much it. We parents left the room so that they could be alone together."

"And?" My hands over my mouth like a child.

"She was upset, Maman. She told me she'd only agreed to marry me for the sake of her father."

Oh no! So it hadn't gone well.

"I told her that if she really was against the marriage, I would do everything in my power to prevent it."

"Eugène, you didn't!" I looked at Bonaparte, alarmed. Had my son no idea how important this was?

Bonaparte grinned. "I don't think we need to worry, Josephine. When Eugène and the Princess came out of the room, they were holding hands."

"She's . . . *pleased* with you, Eugène?"

My son smiled shyly. "I think we're in love, Maman."

Bonaparte reached over and tugged a lock of Eugène's hair. "The charmer."


*January 12, a beautiful Sunday.*

This afternoon, in a quiet ceremony, Bonaparte adopted Eugène as his son and designated him heir to the throne of Italy. He embraced Eugène with love in his eyes. The look in Caroline's eyes was of another sort.


*Monday.*

"Caroline is too ill to come," Joachim told Bonaparte, his chin buried in a ruff of artificial pink lace. "She sends her regrets."

Bonaparte looked up from cleaning his fingernails with a coral toothpick. "Ill with bile, I venture."

"Ill with good reason."

I glanced from Joachim to Bonaparte, not a little concerned. Now was not the time for a brouhaha. In two hours the contract was to be signed, followed by the civil wedding ceremony.

Bonaparte frowned, methodically tucking the toothpick into its gold case. "And what might that *good* reason be?"

"These royal fops scorn us." Joachim spat into a spittoon.

"What do I care what they think? You are jealous, face it. Eugène's children will have the blood of Charlemagne in their veins. They are not even born and their future is writ large on the pages of history. And you say this is a bad thing? I see it as a great victory—equal to the victory at Austerlitz."

In fury, Joachim knocked a vase over with his sword on his way out. "You see, Josephine?" Bonaparte said, picking up the book he had been reading. "Our people don't even know how to walk properly."


*January 14.*

At seven this evening in the Royal Chapel, Eugène was married to Princess Auguste-Amélie of Bavaria. The young couple could not take their eyes off each other. We bask in the glow of this miraculous love.

As is the royal custom (we've learned), Bonaparte and I saw the newly-wed couple to the door of their suite. "So," said Bonaparte, clearing his throat. "I guess this is it." He grasped Eugène's hand and gave it a mighty shake.

I embraced my new daughter-in-law. "I can't tell you how happy I am." *Truly.*

Auguste looked up at Eugène and slipped her hand into his. "Well, I guess this is it," Eugène said, repeating Bonaparte's words.

I kissed them both (a blessing) and took Bonaparte's arm, tugging him away. We meandered down the wide marble halls arm in arm, the portraits of centuries looking down upon us.

## In which we are devastated

*January 27, 1806—Paris, at last.*

Tears sprang into my eyes when I saw Hortense. "Are you not eating?" I exclaimed, embracing her. She is so gaunt.

"I am fine, Maman," she assured me. "Now, tell me *everything*."

With pleasure I described how wonderful Auguste is, Eugène's happiness, how much in love they are. "If only I could have been there," Hortense said wistfully. "Louis would not allow me to go."

"No doubt he was concerned about the rough roads, especially in this season." Especially considering her health.

We talked for a time of this and of that—of the boys, Louis's latest (bizarre) treatments,* a song she was composing. I described the curious fashions worn in Munich, the elaborate royal rituals we'd observed there. I told her that the new furniture Messieurs Fontaine and Percier had designed for my suite at the Tuileries was hideous, but that I was pleased with the chambermaid my hairdresser Duplan had recommended. Hortense had been using Duplan herself, she said—did I mind if he dressed her hair on Wednesday?

"Are you and Louis planning to go see Talma play Manlius that night?" I asked.

But before she could answer, we were diverted by the sound of the

---

* *Believing that skin eruptions would draw the "morbid humours" out of Louis's body, Dr. Corvisart was intentionally exposing Louis to scabies by having him wear the unwashed linens of a diseased man. Another treatment involved "bathing" in steaming entrails.*

children outside the open door. Little Napoleon ran into my arms. "I can count, Grandmaman."

"That's wonderful," I said, covering his cheeks with kisses, counting with each one.

The baby staggered toward me and then fell onto the carpet. I held my breath, waiting for a howl. Instead he scampered at a crawl to my feet and, grasping my gown, pulled himself up. I hoisted him onto my lap, little Napoleon close beside me. "Oh, what treasures you have given us," I told my daughter, my heart overflowing.

*Wednesday, January 29.*
We didn't get to the theatre until the end of the first scene. Seeing Bonaparte, the audience cheered with such passion that the actors decided to begin the play again. We stayed to the end. Talma got a standing ovation—even the critic Geoffroy was observed to applaud.

Caroline and Joachim were there with an entourage, including a comely maid in a daring ensemble, Caroline's new reader—whom Caroline took special pains to introduce to Bonaparte, I noticed. I'm watchful.

*March 2, Sunday.*
Bonaparte made a number of announcements to the family tonight: in addition to naming Joseph King of Naples, he will add Lucca to Elisa's domain, and will name Joachim and Caroline Duke and Duchess of Berg.

Caroline looked as if she'd eaten something sour. "Berg isn't even a kingdom," I heard her hiss to Joachim.

"But maybe it comes with the droit de cuissage,"* he said, guffawing.

*March 5.*
Bonaparte has just returned from the Murats' country estate—where he

---

* *Droit de cuissage: the feudal right of a lord to sleep with the bride of a subject on their wedding night.*

went to hunt, he told me cheerfully, taking me into his arms. I pretended to believe his lie. He smelt of a boudoir, not a stable.

*Princes Carolin builtt a litle House for her Readr. This day the Emperor was 2 hours with the Readr in it.*

*[Undated]*
Oh, I *do* find this difficult. How do other women manage to be so accepting of a husband's mistress? I may pretend to "be blind," but I rage within!

*April 10.*
"The Kingdom of Holland has formally requested a sovereign from us," Bonaparte informed me at dinner tonight.

This had been rumoured. Caroline expected that the crown of Holland would go to her husband.

"I'm considering Louis." Bonaparte opened his snuff tin, but closed it without taking a pinch. "Hortense would be Queen, of course."

"Oh?" I said, dissembling my surprise. Louis didn't seem to have the energy to walk, much less to rule a nation. And as for Hortense . . . "Do you think Louis would want such a position?"

"What he *wants* has nothing to do with it. We do what we do because we must, because it is the will of destiny."

I nodded, but thinking, I confess, that we do what we do because it is Bonaparte's will.

*June 1, Sunday—Saint-Cloud, a glorious day.*
At the Bonaparte family dinner tonight, Bonaparte made the announcement that at the request of Holland, Louis will be their King, Hortense their Queen.

Now both Hortense and Caroline are miserable. Caroline wants a crown; Hortense does not.

*June 12, Thursday.*

Bonaparte and I bade farewell to Louis and Hortense this morning (King and Queen!), farewell to little Napoleon and Petit. "Bye-bye, Grandmaman," little Napoleon said solemnly. "Bye-bye, Nonan the Soldier." Giving his beloved uncle a salute.

"Take care of your brother," Bonaparte said, tugging little Napoleon's ear. (Little Napoleon, his heir—Bonaparte is uneasy about letting the child out of France, I know.)

"*And* your mother," I said, eyes stinging. God knows when we will see them again.

*June 15.*

"I wish I didn't have to give this to you," Mimi whispered, slipping a scrap of paper into my hand.

*Princes Carolins Readr is 3 Months With Child—by the Emperor, Shee says.*

*July 14, Bastille Day—Saint-Cloud.*

I've been ill for over a month, in bed with a fever.

*Tuesday, August 19—Rambouillet.*

We're at Rambouillet, a dank and cheerless hunting abode. Caroline arrived with a full suite to attend her, including her reader, clearly with child. Bonaparte has been gay.

As I write this, the court makes merry dancing to fiddlers. Fifteen wolves were bagged today.

*August 26, 1806, Milan*
*Chère Maman,*

*I have the most wonderful news: my lovely Auguste is with child. Don't worry—we are taking the utmost care.*

*The news of the Prussian advance is disturbing. I'm putting the Army of Italy on a war footing in case we are needed.*

*Auguste sends her love.*

*Your loving and happy son, Eugène*

*Note—I'm not in the least bit surprised to learn that Pauline and her prince have separated.*


*[Undated]*

"Auguste will have a girl," Bonaparte predicted.

"Why do you say that?"

"Charlemagne's son Pépin—the one he sent to rule Italy—had daughters. Five daughters and one son. Eugène will have the same."

"Excuse me for being confused, Bonaparte," I said with a smile, "but I thought you were the embodiment of Alexandre the Great." He'd once told me as much!

"Charlemagne's reign is, in fact, closer to mine," he said in all seriousness.

This curious comment sent me into the library for information on the ancient Emperor of the West. The similarities are striking: Charlemagne was not tall, but he was strong, with a thick neck. He dressed simply. He was temperate in his eating and drinking and, like Bonaparte, remedied illness by fasting. Also like Bonaparte, he was in the habit of rising several times during the night to work. Charlemagne crossed the Alps into Italy and he was crowned Emperor by the Pope.

I was amused by the parallels until I read that Charlemagne repudiated his first wife, by whom he had no children, and married a woman of high birth, by whom he did have children.


*September 6, Saturday, 7:10 P.M.—Paris.*

It was a hot afternoon for a military review: Bonaparte sweltered in his black beaver hat and greatcoat. In spite of the marching bands, the stirring spectacle of bayonets glittering, flags waving, the heart-stopping cavalry charge—in spite of all this, the crowds seemed curiously silent. They watched sombrely as the soldiers marched by.

"Funds down," Mimi said.

There is a sense of departure in the air, a sense of something ending. Our men will soon be marching out to war.

*September 24.*
Bonaparte is humming "Malbrough." Tomorrow he leaves on campaign.

*Gera, October 13, 2:00 A.M.*
*I am at Gera today, ma bonne amie. Things are going very well. The Queen of Prussia is at Erfurt. If she wishes to see a battle, she will have that cruel pleasure. I am well. I've gained weight since I saw you. All thine, N.*

*October 16, Weimar*
*Everything has gone as I calculated. Never has an army been so beaten and so completely lost. The fatigue, the bivouacs and the watches have fattened me. Adieu, ma bonne amie. All thine, N.*

*November 2, Berlin*
*We have taken Stettin. Everything is going as well as possible and I'm very satisfied. I miss the pleasure of seeing you, but I hope that it will not be long. Adieu, mon amie. All thine, N.*

*December 3, Posen, 6:00 in the evening*
*You must calm yourself. I wrote you you could come when winter had passed; thus you must wait. The greater one is, the less one can do as one pleases. One depends on events and circumstances. As for myself, I am a slave, and my master is the nature of things. N.*

*New Year's Day, 1807.*
Caroline's reader has given birth to a boy.


*January 16, 1807*
*My dear, your unhappiness pains me. Why the tears? Have you no courage? I will see you soon. Show character and strength of spirit. Adieu, I love you. N.*


*January 18, 1807, Warsaw*
*I'm told that you always cry. Fie! That's terrible! Be worthy of me and have more character. I love you very much, but if you cry all the time, I will think you are without courage. I do not like cowards. An empress must have heart, even down to the small cousins. Speaking of which, I kiss them. They must be low, because you are always sad. Adieu, mon amie, I kiss you. N.*


*Tuesday, February 10—Paris.*
The carnival season is gay; I am not. I'm trying to be the empress that Bonaparte wishes me to be, one with spirit and character. As it is, I'm an empress with a head pain. They've been coming frequently again.


*Mon amie, your letter grieved me—it was too sad. Your heart is excellent, but your powers of reasoning are weak. You experience things wonderfully, but you think poorly. There, enough quarrelling. I want you to be happy with your lot—not grumbling and crying, but cheerful and gay. The nights are long. N.*


*February 9, 3:00 in the morning*
*Mon amie, we had a big battle yesterday. Victory was with me, but I lost many men. The enemy's loss, which was considerably greater, does not console me. I love you. All thine, N.*

*February 14, 1807*
*Mon amie, I'm still at Eylau. This country is strewn with the dead and the wounded. It is not the prettiest part of war. One suffers and the soul is oppressed to see so many victims. However, I did what I wanted and repulsed the enemy. Calm yourself, and be gay. All thine, N.*

*[Undated]*
Publicly we celebrate victory; privately we mourn. Daily couriers arrive with lists of the dead, the wounded, the missing. I'm mortified how close Bonaparte himself came to death, how he exposes himself to danger.

*March 15, 1807, Milan*
*Chère Maman,*
   *Wonderful news! At 6:47 last night, Auguste gave birth to a beautiful baby girl. I hope you and Papa aren't disappointed. I'm going to write to him now, to tell him we'd be delighted if he chose a name for her.*
   *My Auguste was as brave as any soldier, Maman. She is remarkably well, and the baby is sucking strongly. How is it possible for one's heart to be so full?*
   *Thank you for the bulletins you sent on the Eylau victory. It's excellent news, but oh, the losses! I understand that you are upset the Emperor exposed himself to danger. You must have faith, Mama—Papa is blessed by Lady Luck. Did you know that the soldiers are convinced that* you *are his Lady Luck?*
   *A million kisses,*

*Your son, a father! Eugène*

*April 28, La Hague*
*Chère Maman,*
   *Little Napoleon is very sick with measles. I have been up for two nights. Pray for our dear little prince, Maman.*
                    *Your devoted (and worried) daughter, Hortense*

*Chère Maman,*

    *This is just a quickly scribbled note to let you know that our prayers have been answered: little Napoleon has recovered.*

                              *Your devoted (and very much relieved) daughter, Hortense*


*May 5, Tuesday.*

I was awoken before dawn by Mimi. "There's a courier downstairs. He rode all the way from La Hague without stopping." She handed me a cap. "He insists on speaking to you."

The mud-splattered courier had a message from King Louis of Holland, he said. Prince Napoleon's condition had worsened. The child had developed a congestion in the chest and was having difficulty breathing. King Louis wished me to send Dr. Corvisart.

"Order the Master of the Horse to have our travelling carriage harnessed to our fastest horses," I commanded a sleepy chamberlain. "Have the cook put together a basket of provisions. Have the controller provide a purse of coins, both French francs and Dutch florins. Dr. Corvisart will be leaving immediately for Holland."

"Immediately?"

"Immediately!"


*[Undated]*

I feel like a sleepwalker, not of this earth. A light drizzle, the dank smell of the gardens, a pale early morning light envelop me. I know that when I wake from this dream, life will never again be the same. The fabric of our happiness has been forever rent.

Little Napoleon is dead.


*May 6, 1807*

*Aunt Josephine:*

    *I'm leaving tonight for Holland. My brother King Louis will need me. I've instructed Arch-Chancellor de Cambacérès to organize everything for your journey. I suggest you meet your daughter at the Château de Laëken near Brussels.*

*Princess Caroline*

*May 15—Château de Laëken, Brussels.*
Hortense endured my embrace with patience. "Good afternoon, Maman," she said—but without any emotion.

"Oh, darling!" Her manner confused me.

"Hortense," Louis said, "your hat."

"Thank you," she said, slowly reaching out her hand, dreamlike. "He liked the flowers on it. He wouldn't want me to lose it." And then, to Clari, "He is dead, you know."

Petit tugged his father's hand. "Brother?" Louis motioned to the child to be silent.

"It doesn't matter what the boy says," Caroline said, gesturing to the servants to move the trunks out of her way. "She's not listening."

We followed Hortense into the great hall. She stood looking around at the entryway, the walls covered with tapestries. There was a chill about her; she seemed of another world. "*He* was here with me not long ago. I held him on my knees—there." She pointed to an upholstered chair. And then she fell silent and would not speak.

*Early evening, 6:20, I think—awaiting dinner.*
Louis and I sat on a musty sofa in the château library, Dr. Corvisart on a cracked leather armchair opposite us. I gave Louis a look of sympathy. "You are being admirably strong." It was true.

"At heart I weep," Louis said with feeling. And then he recounted how it had happened: little Napoleon had recovered, but then suddenly his face turned blue and he began to have difficulty breathing. They summoned the best doctors in Holland—

"Well-respected medical practitioners, Your Majesty," Dr. Corvisart assured me. "Your grandson had the best treatment available anywhere."

The doctors administered leeches and a course of blistering, but they were unable to check the disease's progress. "At that point I sent for Dr. Corvisart," Louis said, his voice tremulous. In desperation they even tried English Powder, a quack remedy. "It was a miracle," Louis said. "Little Napoleon sat up in bed and asked to play Go Fish."

I smiled through my tears. I had taught him how to play that game.

"And then he relapsed." We waited in silence as Louis struggled to continue. "Hortense leaned over to kiss him. He said, *Bonjour, Maman*, and closed his eyes." Louis looked at me, his cheeks glistening. "And that was it."

I put my trembling hands to my lips in a gesture of prayer. How were we ever going to bear it?

"Hortense fell to the floor in a swoon. Her eyes were open, but she was not responding. She . . ." Louis stopped, overcome.

"Your Majesty, your daughter was in a state of paralysis for over six hours," Dr. Corvisart said.

"In the morning she was able to speak, but"—Louis clasped his hands together to still the trembling—"she has yet to shed a single tear."

"You must understand, Your Majesty, your daughter is not herself," Dr. Corvisart said gently. "One must be patient. It's as if she is in a walking coma."

He recommended a voyage, a stay at a spa—to which Louis readily agreed. "Would you look after Petit?" he asked.

Oh, *yes*.


*[Undated]*

This morning Caroline offered Petit a little cake and, without realizing what I was doing, I grabbed the sweet out of his hand. The confused child bawled.

Caroline stood looking at me steadily. "I'm . . . I'm sorry," I stammered, and gave the cake back to Petit.

"Would you like one, Aunt Josephine?" Caroline asked with a baby-faced smile.

Now, on reflection, I realize that I don't trust Caroline around Petit, don't trust her not to try to harm the child in some way. What an evil thought! Caroline is not the monster: I am.

*Sunday, May 17—Château de Laëken, Brussels.*
This morning after Mass Hortense and I walked in silence down to the pond at the end of the park. "He threw pebbles in the water here," she said.

I burst into sobs. "I'm sorry, it's just that—" But I couldn't explain, couldn't tell her that I grieved not only for little Napoleon, but for my daughter, too.

"I am fortunate," she said with a smile that chilled me, "for I feel nothing. Otherwise I would suffer."


*Thursday, May 21—Château de Laëken, Brussels.*
Tears, *finally*—but oh, how painful.

Hortense and I were on our afternoon walk. I'd stopped to have a word with a neighbour. Hortense wandered off, but shortly after a cry of anguish set me running. I found her seated on a bench, writhing. "Maman, I can't bear it!" she wept, falling into my arms. My heart was breaking for her, for the pain of her despair, yet it was with dismay that I saw that glazed look come over her once again. She pulled herself free and sat up. "Ah, that's better," she said. "I can't feel anything now."

## In which we must be gay

*May 14, 1807, Finckenstein*
*I understand your sorrow over the death of poor little Napoleon. You can imagine what I feel. I wish I were near you. You have had the good fortune never to have lost a child, but it is one of the painful realities of life. Take care of yourself and trust in my feelings for you. N.*


*May 22, 1807, Milan*
*Chère Maman,*

    *Poor, poor Hortense, poor Louis: how they must suffer! Auguste and I clasp our little one close—our beautiful little Josephine she has been named. (At Papa's request, Maman.) If only we could keep her from harm, forever and ever. How hard it is, becoming a parent.*

*Your faithful son, Eugène*


*June 7, 1807, Paris*
*Darling,*

    *I weep for you! There is nothing more devastating than the death of a child—and such a child. If a visit would help console, please allow me the honour.*

*Your loyal friend, Thérèse*

*June 10, afternoon—Malmaison.*

I broke down the moment I saw Thérèse, upsetting sweet Petit. Thérèse cheered him with a gift of a tin shovel set. "So you can play in the mud—although perhaps princes are not allowed?" she added with a worried look.

"May I, Grandmaman?" Petit asked, his big eyes filled with hope.

"Of course," I said, stroking his fine curls. He's been delicate since the tragic loss of his big brother, not eating well and waking often in the night. He misses his mother and father, I know. Daily we send his "letters" (scribbles) to their spa in the Pyrenees, so very far away. Far from the devastating pain of grief, I pray.

"You and Mimi," I added, gesturing to Mimi to take the child. "Grandmaman Josephine allows mud play," I explained to Thérèse, leading the way out the double-sash doors to the garden, "but *Maman* Hortense does not." And then I started to weep again, remembering how little Napoleon had loved to play in the puddles. Thérèse didn't say a word, just took my arm. We walked in the garden thus while I blubbered like a fool. "Forgive me!"

Thérèse led me to a bench by the pond where we sat for a moment in silence, watching the two black swans glide over the surface of the water. In the distance we could see the gazelles grazing in a meadow, the baby gazelle bounding about. "And how is the Emperor taking it?" Thérèse asked.

"He writes me to have courage, but I'm told he weeps." Poor Bonaparte. He rarely broke down, especially in front of his men. "He loved that child so much."

"Little Napoleon was his chosen heir."

"That's just it! But it feels wrong to think about *that*—about the political consequences, the personal consequences."

"Yet how can you not?" Thérèse asked, giving me her handkerchief.

"It's true. Since little Napoleon's death, it seems that everyone is obsessed with one thought: what would happen if Bonaparte were to die? Who would be the heir? Heir! If I hear that word one more time, I will scream. I'm sorry," I said, taking hold. "The concerns are just. If Bonaparte *were* to die without an heir, chaos would reign. There would be civil war, no doubt, over who would take his place."

"Princess Caroline is saying her husband should be the one."

"To rule?" A look gave away my thoughts.

"Joachim would make a good queen," Thérèse said, letting out a throaty laugh.

"And Caroline a good king, for that matter," I said ruefully, drying my cheeks, my eyes.

"That girl *really* wants a crown."

"I don't know why anyone would."

"Oh, my poor sad Empress," Thérèse said, squeezing my hand.

"But Empress for how long, Thérèse?" I told her about Caroline's reader, about the boy she had given birth to—Bonaparte's child. "Now that Bonaparte knows he can father a child, what's to keep him from divorcing me and marrying a woman who can give him a son? Especially *now*—with everyone so desperate for an heir."

Thérèse smiled. "I just happened to have heard something that may be a cure for the vapours."

What she told me astonishes me yet: that Joachim had been heard to brag that Caroline's reader had been bored by the Emperor's attentions, but had been very pleased with *his*. "Joachim may be the child's father?" And not Bonaparte?

"Murat would seem to have it so."

"Does Caroline know he was 'visiting' her reader, do you think?"

"My guess is she not only knew about it, she set it up."

"Why would she do that?"

"Think about it: they wanted the girl to get in a certain way."

Of course: it made perfect diabolical sense. "So Joachim seduced the girl in order to make her pregnant?" In order to fool Bonaparte into thinking *he* could father a child. In order to induce Bonaparte to divorce *me*.

"I'd make sure the Emperor learned of this, if I were you," Thérèse said.

"Of course," I said, overwhelmed with sensation: relief certainly, but indignation, too, for Bonaparte's sake, at having been so ill-used.


*Mon amie, by the time you read this letter, peace will have been signed and Jérôme will be King of Westphalia. I love you and hope to learn that you are happy and gay. N.*

*July 12, Sunday.*

"*Jérôme* is going to be a king?" Caroline could not conceal her rage.

"*Is* a king," I corrected her, going through the papers on my escritoire. I didn't have time for one of Caroline's tantrums, frankly. Bonaparte had written with instructions that the celebrations of the peace were to be lavish, "a show of Oriental splendour." Even Chastulé had taken to her bed, overcome with all that had to be attended to: the celebrations of the peace, Jérôme and Princess Catherine of Württemberg's wedding, to be followed by two months of festivities at Fontainebleau. Every sovereign of Europe would be attending. Where were we going to put them all?

Caroline stomped her foot. "Jérôme has a crown, Napoleon has a crown, Joseph has a crown, Louis has a crown. Even Elisa has a stupid little crown. Everyone has a crown but *me!*"

*Saturday, July 25, morning, very hot.*

"Ah, crowns," Fouché said, "it seems that there can never be enough."

Oh, I am weary, so weary of conflict, of intrigue and doubt. If only Bonaparte would return. Last night I sprinkled my covering sheet with the lemon scent he uses. It has been ten months.

*July 27, Monday.*

At five this morning I was awoken by a commotion in the courtyard. Mimi came rushing in. "It's the *Emperor!*"

Oh, mon Dieu. I jumped out of bed. "Mimi, hurry, fetch my best nightdress," I said, splashing water on my face. "And my new lace bonnet." I sat down at my toilette table. I looked old. There wasn't time (nor enough light) to apply a proper face.

"Is this the one you meant?" Mimi said, panting, for the wardrobe is in the attic and the stairs are steep. She held out a lovely nightdress and cap.

"Oh no. I mean, it's gorgeous—but it's English muslin. Don't worry," I assured her, taking the bonnet and slipping it over my dishevelled hair. "I'll wrap myself in a shawl." I dusted my nose with rice flour. "The one I wore last night—the rose one." A good colour in the morning light.

"I saw it in the antechamber," Mimi said, running out the door and almost immediately returning with it. I dabbed on the lavender water Bonaparte favoured (lightly—not too much), threw the shawl around my shoulders, took one last anxious look in the long glass (not too bad: the effect was rumpled but slightly erotic), slipped into my slippers (a new gold-embroidered pair—perfect) and rushed out the door.

I stood at the entry, taking in the scene: five Imperial carriages thick with dust, grooms and postillions unharnessing the steaming horses, servants struggling under the weight of huge trunks. Jérôme, Joachim, Duroc . . . everyone—but where was Bonaparte? And then I heard a man yell, "I already told you. I do not repeat myself."

Was it Bonaparte? It sounded like him, yet the voice was harsh.

"Ah, there you are," he said, appearing behind the Imperial coach. I saw old Gontier hobbling toward the stable with a miserable look on his face.

"Oh, Bonaparte." I said, embracing him. Tears welled up, in spite of myself. It had been a very difficult ten months without him, and now that it was over, I felt my courage weakening.

"Why are you crying?" he said, standing back.

"I'm so happy to see you." I was confused, in truth. Bonaparte's voice was different, as was his manner. This man was neither husband nor friend nor lover. "*Sire*," I added, with an apologetic smile. It is often difficult after a long separation, I reminded myself. It takes time to get to know one another once again.

"Your Majesty?" Clari's husband, Monsieur Rémusat, was accompanied by four pages. In spite of the hour they were all in full livery. "I am informed that you wish to speak to me." He and the four pages bowed in unison, their plumed hats crushed against their hearts. (Clearly, they'd been rehearsing.)

"Yes, fire that old man. I don't want to see his face again." And with that Bonaparte marched into the château, leaving me on the steps.

Monsieur Rémusat offered me his arm. "Don't worry, Your Majesty," he whispered. "According to the Code, first the Emperor returns, and *then*, a few days later, the husband."

"Of course," I said, smiling at his gentle humour. Strangely, I felt even lonelier than before, now that Bonaparte was back. "But don't fire Gontier," I told him as we followed Bonaparte into the château. "Or rather," I added quickly, seeing the look of consternation on Monsieur Rémusat's face, "assure Monsieur Gontier that he will be reinstated—when the *husband* returns, that is."


*Wednesday.*

Not long ago the Governor of Paris stormed out of Bonaparte's cabinet, and, shortly after, Joachim was announced.

Clari leaned forward over her embroidery hoop. "Do you suppose the Emperor has found out about Governor Junot and . . . ?"

Junot and *Caroline*, she meant.

"I wonder if the Emperor also knows about all those other men his sister has been receiving," Chastulé whispered.

"What other men?"

"You don't know, Your Majesty?" Clari asked. "Princess Caroline lured the Austrian ambassador into her bedchamber, which she'd strewn with rose petals I've been told."

Rose petals! Caroline had come out to Malmaison not long ago asking me for sacks of them—for a tincture she was making, she'd told me. (Some tincture.)

"Ha! As well as Talleyrand—"

"That's impossible," Clari objected, flushing. (I suspect she's sweet on the dour Minister of Foreign Affairs.)

"—*and* the Minister of Police," Chastulé went on.

Fouché? "Now *that's* impossible," I said.

"Everyone's calling Prince Murat Prince Cuckold," Mademoiselle Avrillion joined in, looking up from mending one of my petticoats.

"But it doesn't seem to bother him. I was hoping for a duel, at least," Chastulé said.

"That's because Princess Caroline told him that she does it for *him*," Clari confided.

"That's a good one," Chastulé said. "I'll remember it the next time my husband catches a lover in my bed."

"To seek advantage, she told him."

"Caroline told Joachim that?" I could understand the advantages Fouché, Talleyrand and the Austrian ambassador might have to offer—but Junot? "I don't understand how the Governor of Paris could—"

"He commands the troops in the city, doesn't he?" Mademoiselle Avrillion asked.

"Ha! You never know when a cannon or two might come in handy."


*August 15—Saint Napoleon's Day.*
As I write this, fire-rockets flare, lighting up the night. Paris has given itself over to revelry: tournaments, plays, concerts, illuminations and ballets. Everywhere there is some kind of festivity in celebration of Saint Napoleon's Day—in celebration of Napoleon, Emperor and peacemaker.

Bonaparte and I watched the celebrations from the Tuileries balcony. The crowd cheered to see their hero, Napoleon the Great.

Napoleon the Unapproachable. He takes everything in with a frown. He is not a happy man—and I, certainly, am *not* a happy woman. It's just as well I'm so desperately busy preparing for Jérôme's wedding festivities, the arrival of a royal bride.


*Sunday, August 23—Tuileries.*
This morning Jérôme and (buxom) Princess Catherine were married in the Gallery of Diana in the presence of the entire court (eight hundred now). Jérôme looked dazzling in his suit of white satin embroidered in gold. We are in a frenzy of forced gaiety.


*August 27, 11:20 P.M.—the family drawing room, Saint-Cloud.*
Mimi came to fetch me during the second act of *Cinna*. She signalled me from the door. "I'm wanted about something," I whispered to Bonaparte, and slipped away.

"Hortense is back," Mimi said, her hands crossed over her heart.

"Here? Now!" I followed Mimi out of the theatre and through the orangerie to the château.

Hortense laid her head on my shoulder as if weary, as if she needed a mother's shoulder to rest on. "I'm better, Maman," she said.

"I can see that," I said—and it *was* true. She spoke from her heart.

"Have I interrupted something?" she asked, looking out at the courtyard, crowded with equipages.

"*Cinna* is being performed. I'll send for Bonaparte."

"No, wait, Maman. That's Papa's favourite play. There will be plenty of time."

"Shall I go get Petit?" Mimi suggested with a grin.

"He's up?" Hortense sounded hopeful.

"I'll wake him," Mimi said. "He's been talking about his maman every day."

"His maman who is looking well," I told my daughter.

"It was a good trip," she said, caressing my cheek—as if I were *her* child. "I've been writing songs." She paused, raising her eyes. "For *him*."

*Him.* Little Napoleon. As if his spirit hovered. "Petit has been wonderful. I have so many stories to tell you. He's the sweetest child." But frail and fearful of late, often waking in the night. "Ah, he's up," I said, on hearing the child's sleepy chatter.

Mimi appeared with the boy in her arms. "Oh, Petit!" Hortense said, her voice tremulous. I knew what she was thinking, that he looked so very like little Napoleon. And yet so different.

The child stared at his mother and then hid his face in Mimi's neck.

"Three months is a lifetime to a child," I said, fearing a problem. "Remember how you felt, darling, when I got out of prison? You didn't even recognize me."

"I don't remember," Hortense said, leaning down to catch her boy's eyes. She covered her face with her hands and surprised him with a peek-a-boo. Petit studied his mother sombrely, his thumb in his mouth, a hint of a smile in his eyes. She did another peek-a-boo for him, eliciting a tiny giggle. Then she opened her hands and he dove into her arms. She pressed him against her heart, tears streaming onto his fair curls, cooing, "Oh, my Petit, my sweet Petit." Mimi and I stood sniffing, our hearts full of love and sorrow.

"Ah, there you are." It was Bonaparte, standing in the door.

"Papa! *Sire.*" Hortense made a respectful dip, balancing her child in her arms. She swiped one eye with the back of her free hand.

"*Still* weeping?" he said reproachfully. "You've cried enough over your son. You're not the only woman to have suffered a loss. Other women are braver than you, especially considering that you have a child who needs you. Now that you are back, smile and be gay—and not one tear!" And with that he left.

Hortense lowered herself onto the little bench by the door. "How can Papa reproach me like that?" she asked, her breath coming in sharp gasps.

"Try to understand, Hortense," I said, motioning to Mimi to take Petit. "Bonaparte is just as upset as we are, but he believes we make it worse by weeping." Sorrow unnerved him, made him uncomfortable.

"Doesn't he understand how a mother feels?"

"He believes being stern will help you." I put my arm around her thin shoulders. "He loves you."

It is true. Bonaparte has a great, *great* heart. If only I could find it.

*Sunday morning at Malmaison, lovely—not too hot yet.*

I've just talked with the housekeeper and the head cook about the family dinner tonight: Madame Mère, Julie,* Louis and Hortense, Pauline, Caroline and Joachim, Jérôme and Princess Catherine, Stéphanie and Émilie, Bonaparte and me. Is that everyone? Table for thirteen. And all the children, of course: Petit, Julie's girls (Zenaïde and Charlotte), Caroline's four (Achille, Letizia, Lucien and Louise). Mimi is organizing a picnic for them out under the oak trees.

*10:10 P.M.*

The dinner went fairly well—for a Bonaparte gathering, that is. Joachim was so transparently obsequious toward Bonaparte—offering him his snuffbox, bowing not only in greeting, but with *every* sentence—it annoyed both Louis and Jérôme, who addressed him as "Prince Bully-Boy," much to Joachim's annoyance. Caroline, as well,

---

* *Although Joseph had moved to Naples to reign as king, his wife Julie and their two daughters continued to live in Paris. In Naples Joseph lived openly with the Duchess d'Atri.*

seemed in a temper—this business of crowns, no doubt. But worst of all, Pauline—who was carried in on a tasselled silk litter by four Negroes dressed as Mamelukes—berated Hortense for wearing black: "Your son was only five when he died. You're not supposed to wear mourning."

My god-daughter Stéphanie was a little giddy, but otherwise restrained, thanks to Madame Campan's stern tutelage. Hortense only pretended to eat, I noticed. Then, as the desserts were being brought out, she abruptly excused herself from the table.

I found her in the water closet with a china bowl in her lap, Louis beside her. Her face was flushed, beaded with perspiration. "It's all right, Maman," she said, seeing the concern in my eyes. She looked at Louis. "Should I tell her?"

"Hortense is with child again," Louis said.

Caroline flushed on hearing the news—her heated complexion visible even through a thick layer of ceruse. She gave Joachim "a look," a very slight widening of her kohl-lined eyes. "How wonderful," she said with a bright smile, methodically tapping a beauty patch stuck on her chin. "What a surprise."

At the close of the evening, Louis proposed a toast. He and Hortense would be returning to their kingdom, he said, and so consequently, they must bid everyone adieu.

"Cin-cin! Cin-cin!" Jérôme called out, spilling wine on his new (and doting) wife.

"Blood is everything," Madame Mère said.

"No, Maman: you're supposed to say salúte."

"Salúte."

"Salúte!"

"Santé," I echoed faintly, weak with concern.

*[Undated]*

Alarming news: Hortense is consumptive. "Does that mean she has consumption?" I asked Dr. Corvisart. People die of that disease!

"It's more of a tendency in that direction," he told me. "No doubt she will recover, but I'm concerned that the climate of Holland might be too . . ." He made a grimace. "A damp climate might—"

"Harm her health?"

"Especially in her delicate condition." He cleared his throat. "And I've concern about the child, as well. He is sickly, and one doesn't want to take any risks."

*Dieu nous en garde!*

*September 19.*

Louis has returned to Holland alone—without his wife, without his son. "But he left *furious* at me, Maman," Hortense sobbed.

"Dr. Corvisart explained it to him, didn't he? About the dangers?"

"I don't know. Louis wouldn't even speak to me!"

*Sunday morning.*

Caroline's ball last night was shocking in its splendour: tightrope walkers and acrobats, a miniature village in the garden. As Caroline and Joachim (tipsy) escorted Jérôme's bride to a replica of her summer chalet, a choir dressed in peasant costumes appeared, singing the traditional songs of her country.

It was a triumph, of course. Caroline made sure Bonaparte was aware of all that she had done to further his glory. She also made sure, I later discovered, that a rumour was circulated that Hortense is with child by a man named Monsieur Decazes.

*4:45 P.M.*

"I believe I've discovered the reason for Louis's temper," I told my daughter. "Do you know Monsieur Decazes?"

"He was at the spa, mourning the death of his wife."

"It seems that there is a rumour going around that he is the father of the child you are carrying."

"Monsieur Decazes?" Hortense wrinkled her nose. "That's . . . that's crazy, Maman."

"I agree! I was outraged. But it might help explain why Louis was so angry. Perhaps if you were to—"

"It explains nothing! How could Louis believe something like that about me?"

"Well . . ." I understood what it was like to be consumed by jealousy, knew how it could make a person act.

"All a man has to do is look at me and Louis is convinced of my infidelity. I will never forgive him!"

"But Hortense, don't you think maybe—"

"Never!" she cried, bolting for the door.

I put my arm out to prevent her from running out of the room.

"Let me out!" she demanded.

"I want the truth, Hortense."

"I'll tell you the truth!" she said, her voice tremulous. "But it won't be what you expect. The truth is something you don't want to hear. The truth is that Louis torments me! He *hires* people to spy on me. He has me followed. *Every* outing I make he assumes has a romantic purpose— even to visit a relative's deathbed! He listens at my door at night, he opens my mail. I might as well live in a convent. Do you know how he begins each day? With a search of my closets. Is that how a man is supposed to regard his wife?"

I listened in stunned silence as she sobbed out years of torment. I could not believe what she was saying, yet suddenly it all made sense—the high wall Louis had had built around their house, the sentry posted below Hortense's bedchamber window. "I'm so sorry, Hortense," was all I could say. If only I had known! If only she had told me! But perhaps it was true, what she said: perhaps I hadn't wanted to hear.

"You know what he tells me, Maman, about *you*? He says you're a harlot. He says you're not my mother, that Madame Mère is my mother now—and she detests me! He says any love I show you is a stab against him! He's in a constant rage. I cannot even speak to a man without Louis threatening to run him through. I've *never* been untrue to him, Maman, yet he treats me like a criminal," she sobbed. "Every time I try to please him, he finds something in me to hate, something to doubt. He loves his dog more than he loves me! I can't bear it any longer. Please, *please* don't make me go back to him. I fear it will be the death of me!"

And then she gave way to a convulsive fit of coughing that frightened me terribly. I took her in my arms, rocking her like a baby. Slowly the coughing eased. "Forgive me, Hortense—I've been blind." And worse—wilfully so. "But now I know."

And now, I vow, things will be different.

## *In which I am betrayed*

*September 22, 1807—Fontainebleau.*
At last we are settled at Fontainebleau for a month of hunting and festivities—*all* of us. (Moving a court is not easy.) Settled, but in chaos still, everyone rushing about trying to find trunks, getting lost in the vast corridors, frazzled from lack of sleep. Even the actors and actresses are in hysterics. They are to perform Corneille's *Horace* in less than two hours, "and our props haven't even arrived," Talma exclaimed, the back of his hand to his forehead.


*Thursday, September 24, 4:45 P.M.*
Duroc addressed the assembled court this morning. Here are the rules:

One evening a week the Emperor will receive. On that evening there will be music followed by cards.

On another evening I'm to hold a reception at which cards will be played. (But not for money: Bonaparte insists.)

Two evenings a week there will be a tragedy performed. (No comedies: Bonaparte considers them a waste of time.)

As well, the Princes and the Ministers are required to give dinners, inviting all the members of the court. Duroc, as Grand Marshal, and Chastulé, as lady of honour, are required to do the same, laying covers for twenty-five. A table will be provided for any who have not received an invitation to dine elsewhere.

"I want to dine at *that* table," Hortense whispered.

"And finally," Duroc said, raising his voice, "only the Emperor and Empress will have the liberty of dining alone—*should* they choose to do so."

There was a rustle of fine silks, a tinkling of gold pendants, a murmur—of envy, I realized, over the privilege of privacy. Fortunately the assembly was diverted by Duroc's announcement that for the deer hunt, the gentlemen were required to wear a green coat with gold or silver lace, white cashmere breeches and riding boots without flaps. The shooting costume was to be "a simple green coat without any ornament but white buttons," Duroc said, looking expressly at Joachim, who was known to embellish even his nightcap. "But on those buttons, some characteristic of the species being hunted is to be engraved."

"The prick," Joachim guffawed.

Duroc ignored him, and continued by saying that hunting costumes would be required as well for the ladies and their households, and for this purpose the designer Leroy had been engaged. At this point Monsieur Leroy, flustered but clearly enjoying the acclaim, was called upon to display his creation: a tunic, rather like a short redingote, over a gown of embroidered white satin. I applauded, which signalled to the assembly that they could do likewise.

So on this pretty note court was adjourned. The first hunt is to be held in four days at eight in the morning. Tardiness is forbidden. The Emperor has spoken.


*September 27, Sunday—Fontainebleau.*
"We must be a court!" Bonaparte exploded, hitting the table with the flat of his hands. "A *real* court, with dancing and gaiety. I will it!"

*I will it.* If only it were as easy as that! Bonaparte has everyone terrified. It is impossible to be gay. My ladies are so fearful of being publicly reprimanded that they don't dare speak, much less *enjoy* themselves.

"Zut. I've brought hundreds of people to Fontainebleau to amuse themselves. I've arranged *every* sort of entertainment for them and yet they just sit with long faces."

"Pleasure cannot be summoned by the beat of the drum, Your Majesty," Talleyrand observed in his expressionless manner.

"How long are we here for?" Hortense asked plaintively, later.

Six weeks. Six *long* weeks.

*Wednesday.*

The first "crowns" (as Chastulé calls them) have arrived from Germany—the brothers Prince Mecklenburg and Prince Mecklenburg-Schwerin, charming young men with old-fashioned manners. Prince Mecklenburg-Schwerin, recently widowed (his wife was the Russian Tsar's sister), hovered at the edge of my drawing room last night. Understandably he refrained from joining us at the whist table, but sat to one side, watching how I played my cards with apparent interest. Later, when ices were served, he confided that he has not been well. I offered him condolences but immediately regretted it, for he seemed suddenly close to tears. "Forgive me, Your Majesty. It was a mistake to come to Fontainebleau," he said, touching a lace-edged handkerchief to the corner of each eye. "I only came because I wished to persuade the Emperor to withdraw his troops from my country."

"Have you discussed this with the Emperor?"

"Yes, this afternoon, but . . ." He looked discouraged.

"Give it time," I suggested, tendering an invitation to both him and his brother to join us in our box for the theatrical performance tomorrow evening.

*[Undated]*

"I see you've made a conquest," Bonaparte said. "It's a good thing I'm not a jealous husband."

"Hardly," I said, but with an edge of regret. There was a time when Bonaparte *had* been a jealous husband. "Prince Mecklenburg-Schwerin's wife died not long ago. He talks to me of his grief." I paused, considering how best to proceed. "He's very impressed by you."

"That I doubt. He is disappointed in me. He wants me to withdraw my troops. That's out of the question. These princes seem to think I should come in with my soldiers, liberate their country and then, job done, just leave. They live in another world."

"So there's *no* chance that our troops will be withdrawn . . . someday?" I took his hand in mine.

"I take it the Prince has recruited you to advance his cause," he said, tweaking my ear—hard.


*La Pagerie, Martinico*
*Madame Bonaparte,*
*I regret to inform you that your mother has been taken by the Lord. She changed worlds at 3:47 P.M. on the eighth of July, at La Pagerie. I was the only person in attendance, not counting the slaves. I will notify you if there is anything left of value once the estate debts have been paid.*
*In the service of the Eternal Lord, Father Droppet*


*Fort de France, Martinico*
*Chère Yeyette, my beloved niece,*
*Our profound condolences on the passing of your dear mother. You did what you could to make her last years comfortable.*
*Stéphanie writes that she may be wed soon—and to a prince? Is this possible? Surely she is jesting.*
*God bless you,*

*Your aging uncle, Robert Tascher*
*Note—Father Droppet is going to send you the accounts of the estate, such as they are. Be sure to check his numbers. He is known to be "imaginative."*


*Saturday evening.*
"I understand how you feel," Prince Mecklenburg-Schwerin said. "Grief sets one apart."

"Yes," I said, clutching my handkerchief.

"There will be a period of mourning?"

I shook my head. Bonaparte didn't want the news of my mother's death made public. A period of official mourning would put an end to the festivities. I understood, but a part of me rebelled. Was no one to mourn her? I felt so alone in my grief. "The timing is . . ." I waved my soggy handkerchief through the air.

"Inconvenient?"

"It makes me sad, nonetheless. Hortense and I are the only mourners in all of France."

He slipped a narrow black silk ribbon off his queue and threaded it through a buttonhole on his jacket, tying it in a tidy bow. "There," he said. "I wager you thought I wouldn't know how to tie a bow."

"I admit it crossed my mind," I said with a smile.

"A bit unusual as a mourning ensemble, but I believe the Almighty will understand."


*October 4, Sunday.*
Mimi, Hortense, Chastulé, Clari and even Monsieur Etiquette are now all sporting a little black ribbon. I feel strengthened beyond measure.


*October 5—Fontainebleau, 2:00 P.M.*
Caroline joined the hunt this morning wearing a little black ribbon tied to a buttonhole. "It's the fashion," she informed everyone. "Haven't you noticed?"


*Thursday, October 8, very late, possibly 2:00 A.M.*
Every evening before dinner, Bonaparte and I go for a ride through the woods. He drives and I try not to ask him to slow down. It's a welcome hour, for me, a chance to be alone with Bonaparte (if one doesn't count the mounted escort riding fore and aft).

Often we ride in silence—that comfortable silence of the long-married—but tonight Bonaparte was cheerful (unusual for him these days) and we talked amiably of this and that: of Jérôme's latest mischief, the foreign princes. And then, as if it were inconsequential, he informed me that he was having an amourette with my reader. "Your spies will inform you in any case," he said, glancing at me to gauge my reaction.

"Madame Gazzani?" How could I not have known? "I appreciate how discreet you've been. And Madame Gazzani, as well."

"You're not angry?"

"Bonaparte, there are only two things I wish for. One, your happiness. And two . . ." I paused, feeling the calming lull of the even clip-clop of the horses' hoofs. I'd given up even wishing for a child, I realized sadly.

"And two . . . ?" He turned the horses in the direction of the palace.

"And two, I wish for your love."

He pulled in the reins, bringing the horses to a halt. "Don't you know how much I love you?"

"I do know that, Bonaparte," I said. "That's what makes it so hard."


*Saturday afternoon.*

Carlotta put a vase of roses on my escritoire. "Thank you, Carlotta."

She curtsied. "It is my pleasure to serve you, Your Majesty."

I believed her. "I would like you to join us tonight, Carlotta, in the drawing room." The girl was no doubt bored to tears, relegated to her small attic room.

"But Your Majesty, I'm merely a . . ."

Merely a reader, she started to say. Readers are not granted drawing room privileges; my ladies would no doubt object.

"It would please the Emperor, Carlotta," I said with a knowing smile.


And now—at long last—I believe I have finally begun to understand. Carlotta has become my gift to Bonaparte, like some succulent fruit I place before my husband. In loving her, he must love me. In loving her, he must feel beholden.


*October 25, Sunday.*

This morning, returning from Mass, Fouché (lurking in a window recess) pulled me aside. "I have a matter of grave importance to discuss with you, Your Majesty," he said, clearing his throat. He glanced toward the door, where a guard was stationed.

"Oh," I said, not a little concerned. His manner was uneasy. And when had he ever addressed me as "Your Majesty"?

He pulled a tightly rolled paper out of his inside coat pocket and handed it to me. Sunlight caught the diamond in the ring on his little finger.

Warily I slipped off the silk cord and unrolled the scroll. The script—Fouché's—was tiny, difficult to make out. "I'm afraid I don't have my reading spectacles with me."

"Read it later, Your Majesty. I'd like you to . . . *reflect* on the contents."

"And what is it, may I ask?" Why were we being so polite with each other?

"It's a draft of a letter I suggest you send to the Senate."

"You think *I* should write a letter to the Senate?" *Why?*

"You are no doubt aware of the public fears that as the Emperor ages, he will follow in the traces of Sardanapalus."

I wasn't sure what he was talking about, but I thought it sounded like something concerning Bonaparte's health.

"Even the general public, so deserving of peace and security, is crying out. As devoted as they are to you, Your Majesty, they are even more devoted to the Emperor and the Empire he has created—an Empire which they know will crumble upon his death."

Did Bonaparte have a life-threatening disease? Was there something I did not know? "Fouché, is the Emperor—?"

"The Emperor suffers, Your Majesty," Fouché said, taking out an ivory snuffbox adorned with precious gems, "for he has reached the painful conclusion that a compelling political necessity, however abhorrent to him personally, must be undertaken for reasons of state. Yet, as brave as he is on the battlefield, he lacks the courage to speak to you on this matter."

My hands became cold, and my heart began to skitter. A nervous apprehension filled my veins. This had nothing to do with Bonaparte's health. "And what matter might this be?"

Fouché sniffed a pinch of snuff, then dusted off the tip of his nose. "Why, the matter of a divorce, Your Majesty."

"You're suggesting that I—?"

"I'm suggesting that you write to the Senate, informing them that you are willing to make this sacrifice for the good of the nation. I know how devoted you are to the Emperor, and I believe your love for him is such that you would sacrifice your life, if it meant that *his* would be spared."

I leaned against the wall. This is it, I thought. Bonaparte doesn't have the courage to speak to me, and so he has arranged to have Fouché speak on his behalf. The coward!

"Our soldiers are willing to sacrifice their lives for their country," Fouché said, grasping my elbow. "It is rare for a woman to have an opportunity to prove her devotion, her—"

"I must know one thing," I said abruptly. I felt on the edge of a precipice. I feared I might lose control, but I had to know. "Minister Fouché, did the Emperor *ask* you to speak to me about this?"

"Although I know the Emperor's thoughts on this matter, I had no order from him," Fouché said evenly, examining a timepiece which hung from his breeches on a heavy gold chain. "I regret to say that I must bring an end to this melancholy interview, Your Majesty, for I have an urgent appointment."

And without even so much as a bow, he left. Hortense found me shortly after, standing near the window recess clutching the drapes.


*[Undated]*

I went to Bonaparte's room early this morning, just after seven. I thought it best to talk to him before his work began, so I was surprised to find him dressed in a hunting coat, with his valet helping him on with his Hessian boots. "You're not going on the hunt, Josephine?" He pulled on his left boot and stood to embrace me. "Not feeling well?"

"No, I'm not—not going on the hunt, that is." I'd forgotten entirely. "Bonaparte, I need to talk to you." It was hot in the room; a fire was roaring.

"Fine," Bonaparte said, sitting down and sticking out his right foot.

"Privately," I said, clasping Fouché's letter, which I'd rolled into a tight tube and secured with a yellow ribbon, the colour of betrayal.

Bonaparte stood and stomped his foot. "That's good," he told Constant, dismissing him. He led me to one of the chairs by the fire.

"You're pale. You must be cold." He kicked the burning log, sending embers flying, and then sat down, watching the flames.

"I always imagine that you're thinking of camp when you look at a fire like that," I said, fumbling to untie the ribbon, which had become knotted.

"Josephine, I'm willing to talk, but I can't take all morning. The Austrian ambassador is expecting me. What's the problem?"

"It's . . . complex," I said, finally succeeding in sliding the ribbon off and handing him the rolled-up letter.

"This is for me?" He tried to get it to lie flat on his thigh. "Who wrote it?" Squinting.

"Your Minister of Police."

"Fouché wrote this?" He held the paper close to his face and then back, at arm's length. "My eyes are getting so weak," he complained. "Haven't those spectacles been delivered yet?"

How could Bonaparte be thinking of such details? Our life was falling apart and all he could think about were his new spectacles. "Yes, *Fouché*," I said, making an effort to sound calm. "He gave it to me yesterday, after Mass. He . . . he suggests that I write such a letter to the Senate."

"Basta," Bonaparte exclaimed, reading. He threw the document into the flames.

"You knew nothing about this?"

"Of course not. Fouché has no business in our bed."

I pulled a handkerchief from my bodice. (I'd thought to bring several.) It was difficult to gauge Bonaparte's reaction. Was he pretending to be innocent? "I was so afraid that you might have asked Fouché to do this terrible thing," I said, my voice breaking.

"Josephine, I am quite capable of bringing up such a matter myself. I have no need to get Fouché to talk to you on my behalf." There fell an uncomfortable silence. Bonaparte cleared his throat. "And so, since we *are* speaking of it, I will ask you: What do you think?"

"I think you should dismiss him," I said, knowing perfectly well that that was not what Bonaparte meant.

"Fouché?" Bonaparte scoffed. "His crime, if anything, is an excess of zeal. He acted out of devotion, to me and to the Empire."

*Devotion.* It was the same word Fouché had used. "Devotion to *his* self-interest," I said heatedly. "You are surrounded by flatterers, Bonaparte. They delude you into thinking that by divorcing me and marrying a young and fertile princess, you would be rendering a great service to your country."

"Josephine, you must not—"

"You asked me what I think and I will tell you!" I persisted, twisting my handkerchief into a rope—a rope to hang myself with. "If I believed for even a moment that by our divorcing peace would come and the Empire would prosper—*if* I thought that, I would do it! But I *don't* think that." My brave speech broke down in stupid female whimpers. "I will be honest, Bonaparte, since we must speak of this. I do fear for myself, for I love you. I don't care about my crown, or my rank. All I care about is you."

"Josephine—"

"I *beg* you to listen to me! I believe they are wrong. I fear that they are pushing you down a path that will lead to your downfall, and the downfall of the Empire with you. *They* don't care about your happiness—they only care about their own. They are greedy and fearful and do not understand you as I do."

Bonaparte watched me, his big grey eyes glistening. "I have one more thing to say," I said, "and then I will go. You and I have travelled a very great distance together. Indeed, in many ways I believe that our . . . our *destiny* is so extraordinary that it must be directed by Providence." I paused, afraid of saying what I truly feared might be true—that in some mysterious way, Bonaparte's extraordinary luck was linked to *me,* to our union. "We've talked of this before," I said instead, my heart pounding. He nodded, very slightly, but an acknowledgement nonetheless. "You put me on a throne, Bonaparte. It would not be right for me to step down from it. If you ask me to, I will. I want you to know that. But you will have to be the one to say so."

"I couldn't, Josephine," he said, his voice a whisper. I fell into his arms. The valet found us thus, weeping and embracing.


*November 20—back in Paris.*
"I was tempted to burn this one," Mimi said, handing me a scrap of paper.

*Princes Carolin & her Husband were with Min. Fouchay last Evinng. Min. Fouchay say Everything wood be easyer if the Empress wood die.*


*[Undated]*
It is late, two in the morning; everyone is asleep. Bonaparte is on the way to Italy. I am alone in the palace—alone with my fear. My ring of keys sits on the desktop before me. They sprawl, a long-legged insect—an insect with the insidious power to open locked doors.

One of the keys—a heavy, slightly rusted one—is the key to Bonaparte's cabinet. I could, if I dared, open that door, look into his files. I know where to look, know where Fouché's police reports are kept. I can see that leather portfolio as if it were lying in front of me now: black cowhide, thick and unbending, secured with a grosgrain white ribbon, stained from having been tied and untied by men with snuff on their fingers.

I could go—*now*. Discover exactly what is being said behind my back, know once and for all who my enemies truly are. The secretary is not here, nor is the valet; Roustam is not asleep outside the bedchamber door. They are all with Bonaparte in Italy, with Bonaparte always. But what of the others, the night watchmen, the guards?

No, I will go in the morning, early. I will tell Hugo, the cabinet guard, that I need to get something out of the Emperor's files—something he wished to have sent to him. I will bring Hugo a coffee laced with cognac, to cheer and distract.


Police Report of November 17: *People were astonished not to see the Empress on Tuesday at the performance of* Trajan. *It was said that she was upset. Most spoke of the dissolution of the Imperial marriage. This news is the talk of all classes, and the truth is that there is not one who does not view it as a guarantee of peace.*


Police report of November 19: *At court, in the homes of the princes, in all the salons, people are talking of the dissolution of the marriage. The people who are in the confidence of the Empress share the opinion that the Emperor would not resort to this rupture. They say that the Empress is adored in France; that her popularity is useful to the Emperor as well as to the Empire; that the good fortune of both the one and the other depends on the duration of this union; that the Empress is the Emperor's talisman; that their separation would be the end of their good fortune.*

*The other part of the court—the part which regards the dissolution as necessary to the establishment of the dynasty—try to prepare her for this event, giving her advice that they judge appropriate to the situation.*

*In the Imperial family, there is one opinion only: they are all unanimously in favour of a divorce.*

*December 2—Malmaison.*
I became suddenly ill last night after the fête for the ambassadors. Mimi insisted I empty my stomach, making me take mustard mixed with warm water and tickling the back of my throat with a goose feather. Then she sent for Dr. Corvisart, who pronounced my symptoms "puzzling."

"And if I were being poisoned," I asked him weakly, "what would my symptoms be?"

"Your Majesty, who would do such a thing?" he said gently—but not answering my question.

*[Undated]*
I'm still quite ill . . . and frightened. There are some, I know, who wish me dead.

*January 2, 1808—Tuileries.*
"Josephine?" I heard a man say as I slept. The voice was soft, caressing: Bonaparte's voice. Was I dreaming? I opened my eyes, swollen shut with fever. It *was* Bonaparte, standing at the side of the bed with a New Year's gift in his hand—a box of pink, white and blue sugared almonds. He put the box down and took my hand. "They told me you were ill, but . . ." His eyes filled.

"I had a bad reaction to a purge," I reassured him weakly. So Dr. Corvisart insisted—nothing more. "I'm getting better."

"You *must*," he said, clasping my hand so hard it hurt.

*January 12—Paris.*
Stronger today. I spent an hour this afternoon making the final plans for Stéphanie's wedding next month to Prince d'Aremberg.

*Fort de France, Martinico*
*Chère Yeyette, my beloved niece,*
   *My wife and I are grateful for the part you have played in making the arrangements for Stéphanie's marriage. It is hard to imagine that our little girl will be a princess. Remind her not to let her stockings sag and to cover her mouth when she burps.*
   *God bless you,*

                                        *Your aging uncle, Robert Tascher*

*February 1—Tuileries.*
Preparing to go to Hortense's for Stéphanie's wedding, I was startled by a pounding on the door. It was Bonaparte's valet. "Your Majesty, come quickly—the Emperor is terribly sick. I think it's one of his episodes!"*

   I scooped up my train and rushed up the dark stone staircase after Constant, my heart's blood pounding. "It happened just as the Emperor got out of his bath, Your Majesty," Constant said, trying to hold the light so that I might see better. "He forbids me to summon Dr. Corvisart. He said he had need only of you."

   We stumbled into Bonaparte's suite. The roaring fire and a candle on a table afforded little light. Constant raised his lantern in the direction of the bed where Bonaparte was buried under the covers. His face was grey. "Speak to me, Bonaparte!"

   Wordlessly Bonaparte grasped my arm and, in spite of my finery,

---

* Napoleon had occasional seizures of an epileptic nature.

pulled me into the bed. A tremor seemed to go through him. Was it the falling sickness? "Constant, get the vial." The valet looked confused. "The nitrite of amyl—in the Emperor's travelling case."

"Josephine!" Bonaparte blurted out finally.

Constant reappeared. "Two or three drops on a handkerchief," I told him.

"Oh dear, oh dear," the flustered valet murmured, pulling out a handkerchief, dosing it and handing it to me.

"Breathe," I said, holding the cloth to his nose.

"Josephine, I can't *live* without you," he said finally, gasping.

*Mon Dieu,* I thought. "Bonaparte, we can't go on like this," I heard myself say, holding him to my heart, stroking his fine hair, as if he were an infant I was soothing.


*Saturday, April 2—sad.*
Bonaparte just left for the south—very quickly. (As quickly and as secretly as an entourage of thirty-six carriages can leave, that is.) Officially it's being said that he's making an inspection tour of Bordeaux, but in truth he intends to study the situation in Spain.

"Don't be long," he said, holding me in his arms. I'm to join him in a few days.


*April 6—Saint-Cloud.*
I've just returned from seeing Hortense, bidding her farewell and Godspeed, for I leave in the morning to join Bonaparte in the south. I leave with a worried heart.

I took her a number of pretty items to add to her layette—as well as a copy of Madame de Souza's new novel, *Eugène de Rothelin*\*—and promised to return in time for her confinement in six weeks. As I was folding a tiny flannel waistcoat and putting it on the table next to the

---

\* *Madame de Souza's son, Charles Flahaut, was in love with Hortense. The novel's main character, Eugène de Rothelin, is believed to be based on Flahaut and the character Athénaïs on Hortense.*

cradle, I saw something black at the bottom of a travelling basket of embroidered muslin.

"What is this?" I asked Hortense—for it looked like a shroud.

"Oh nothing," she said uneasily. "Just a length of fabric the dressmaker left here."

She wept when I left. She is a young woman alone now; no husband to plague her, but no husband to care for her, either.

As I was getting into my carriage, I saw Hortense's friend Mademoiselle Adèle Auguié—now her lady's maid—returning with Petit. I called out to them.

"I'm . . ." I am concerned about Hortense, I wanted to tell Adèle. "I regret having to leave at this time."

"Don't worry, Your Majesty. We'll look after your daughter," Adèle said, smiling down at the boy. "Won't we?"

I wanted to ask her about that length of black cloth, but dared not. "I know you will," I said.


*April 10—Palais de Bordeaux.*
Bonaparte welcomed me with open arms. He was relieved to see me, much in need of my help with a demanding (and sensitive) social calendar. I'm exhausted from the journey, but will nonetheless attend a reception tonight.


*April 24, 1808, Paris*
*Your Majesty,*
*You will be relieved to know that Queen Hortense has been delivered of a boy—almost a month early! Both mother and son are safely out of danger.*

*On the twentieth of April, a Wednesday, Princess Caroline invited your daughter and Petit to a fête. In spite of Queen Hortense's delicate health, she decided to attend (travelling lying down in the carriage). It was to be a fête for children, with a number of nursemaids and nannies and parents and even important officials standing about watching Princess Caroline's children swing from the lamps and terrorize the guests. In short, the usual circus; and a circus it was, complete with clowns and tightrope dancers performing above* the children's heads! Every time one of them slipped (which was often), Queen Hortense clutched my hand. We were both terrified that one of the performers would fall onto the children—and, in particular, onto our sweet Petit. (It is my contention that Queen Hortense's alarm precipitated the contractions.)

Arch-Chancellor de Cambacérès was standing beside us and, claiming to feel ill, begged your daughter's permission to leave in order to return to his home and have leeches applied.

Queen Hortense assured him she would not be needing him—that she would not go into confinement that night—but as if Providence were reminding us all who was in charge, within an hour of the Arch-Chancellor's departure, her first pain came. Quickly the contractions became violent, and it was with great difficulty that we managed to get her back home, where the midwife and Arch-Chancellor de Cambacérès soon joined us, the poor Arch-Chancellor with three leeches still stuck to his back. (This story has been the cause of much merriment in Paris!)

The baby was born nearly lifeless and terribly, terribly small. You can imagine our fear! Bathed in wine and wrapped in cotton, he revived, but then we began to have concerns for Queen Hortense, for her pulse had become irregular.

She is delicate yet, Your Majesty, but three days have gone by and the doctor assures us that your daughter is out of danger. Queen Hortense specifically asked me to tell you that you are not to return to Paris. The Emperor has need of you, and believe me, your daughter is well looked after. Petit, especially, is tender in his care of both his mother and new brother.

As you suggested, Dr. Jean-Louis Baudelocque was awarded a gift of ten thousand francs in a gold box adorned with diamonds, and Madame Frangeau a handsome ring.

Please forgive the mess this quill has made.

Your humble servant,

Mademoiselle Adèle Auguié

Note—I've notified King Louis.

And another—Unfortunately, the early arrival of this child has led to all manner of rumours, in spite of the accoucheur's declaration that the baby was a month premature.

*[Undated]*
Bonaparte discovered me weeping over Adèle's letter. "Your daughter has had another son. Is that not cause for celebration?"

"I wasn't beside her!"

He comforted me tenderly. We walked hand in hand through the gardens.

*April 27, Wednesday, I think—Château Marrac (not far from Bayonne).*
How wonderful to be close to the sea again. I can smell it in the air.

By the morning light I see that this room has been decorated in soft violet and yellow silks. Our bed (which we share here), of a beautiful cherrywood, is topped by a crown. The drawing room has been made to look like a tent with the sides looped up—a blue satin tent braided with violet and yellow. A sofa (not very comfortable), armchairs and a footstool are covered in a striped blue silk trimmed with yellow. There's even a bathing chamber with a wooden tub in it—which is being filled for me now.

A tall Basque maid in rope-soled shoes has just brought me a dish of chocolate and marzipan. "A gift from the Emperor," she said—or rather, that's what I *think* she said, for they speak a curious language here. (Euskara?) "He say to say he *love* you," she added in French, enunciating the words proudly.

*May 5.*
The King of Spain has ceded to France. Bonaparte has persuaded Joseph to give up Naples and take the crown of Spain. "Not Joachim?" I asked, relieved but surprised. Caroline had made it clear that the Spanish crown was to go to her husband.

"Bah!" Bonaparte muttered. "Joachim has bungled things here. I'll give him Naples. That should make Caroline happy. She'll have a crown at last."

But not the crown she wanted. Not a *big* crown.

*Friday afternoon.*

There is something in this salty, bracing breeze that enlarges our spirits. The melancholy cries of the gulls sing "home" to us both. How alike Bonaparte and I are, both born and raised on islands, the sea ever before us.

If only we could live like this forever, far from the intrigues of Paris. We talked late last night, whispering in the dark: "When we're old and grey, we'll have a little château by the sea," he said sleepily. "You'll tend the flowers and I'll tend the vegetables."

*[Undated]*

Bonaparte and I arrived back at the château giddy this afternoon. My maids shook their heads in wonderment at my wind-tousled hair, my bare feet. "The Emperor took my shoes and hid them," I explained, and then burst into laughter at their puzzled faces. A maid is preparing a bath for me now, for I've sand in my hair, my ears.

The day was glorious. We set off at a fast pace in one of the new light carriages and soon were within sight of the ocean. "Ah," said Bonaparte, inhaling, taking my hand. The sun sparkled off the water.

As soon as we came to a deserted beach, Bonaparte ordered our driver to stop. "Too wild, do you think?" he asked, examining the rocky cove.

"It's perfect," I said, tying my hat ribbons.

At the sand's edge I kicked off my shoes and tucked up my skirt. I heard Bonaparte call out behind me, and I bolted into a run. He caught me, the foaming wave swirling around our feet. We were laughing and out of breath. He tried to push me into the water, but I twisted away, escaping his reach.

We were how long thus, playing like children? Hours. An eternity.

I wonder what our guards thought, watching their Emperor and Empress running back and forth along the shore, watching as we fell laughing onto the sand, watching as we walked hand in hand—watching as we embraced.

Perhaps they thought we were very much in love.

# In which we return to the camp of the enemy

*August 15, 1808, Bonaparte's thirty-ninth birthday—Saint-Cloud.*
Bonaparte and I were both rumpled and weary as our carriage pulled into Saint-Cloud. We'd slept in the coach the night before, but even so, there was no time to bathe—only time for a change of clothes and a quick repast.

I'm writing this now in the drawing room off the garden, the doors open wide, waiting for Bonaparte to emerge from his cabinet on the other side of the courtyard. In a few minutes we're to receive the Senate, then go to Mass and a Te Deum in honour of "Saint Napoleon."

I'm anxious to see Hortense, Petit, the new baby, but it will have to wait. (Wretched duty!) It's hard to believe that we've been away for over four months—four *wonderful* months.

*Late afternoon.*
"He's a good baby," Hortense said fondly, handing the infant to me.

"Oh, Hortense, he's . . ." In fact, I was alarmed. The baby seems small, with the exception of his head, which is big. "He's beautiful," I said, and with truth. He has the ancient beauty of a new soul.

"His name is Oui-Oui," sweet Petit said, standing beside me, his dimpled hand on my knee. I bent forward to give the boy a noisy kiss. "Tickles," he said, but then added, "Again?"

"*Later* we'll have a rumpus," I said. "But right now, I think you might want to have a look at"—I nodded in the direction of the door and dropped my voice to a stage whisper—"something I brought you." His eyes widened. "Did the coachman bring it in?" I asked Adèle.

"The coachman *and* the butler," she said. "It's heavy!"

"Maman, *what* have you brought?" Hortense asked, stretching out on the chaise longue.

"Yes, Grandmaman, *what* have you brought?" Petit echoed as the sound of great clattering on the parquet floors was heard in the hall. The butler appeared, pulling a model of a warship on wheels (and trying, in spite of it, to appear dignified).

Petit turned to me, a look of wonderment on his face. "Yes, for *you*," I said, rocking the infant, who had started to fuss.

"Say, Thank you, Grandmaman," Hortense called out as Petit ran to the wondrous object.

"Thank you, thank you, thank you, Grandmaman!" the child sang.


*Monday morning, August 22.*
A ball last night. "I'm the one who won Spain," I heard Joachim boast, well in his cups. "I'm the one who should have gotten that crown, not Joseph. He can't even ride a horse. And what do I get as thanks? Naples! But maybe at least Joseph will leave the Duchess d'Atri behind for me." Guffaw, guffaw.

He's gone, at last. He left for Naples this morning. That poor kingdom.


*August 28, Sunday.*
A family gathering at Malmaison: Madame Mère, Pauline, Julie Bonaparte and her girls, Hortense and sweet Petit. The children loved the orangutan, dressed comically in a gown. Its antics had them screaming with laughter. Then Bonaparte pretended to be a bear, much to the delight of the children *and* the pugs.


*September 10, 1808, Milan*
*Chère Maman,*
    *Little Josephine is walking. You should see her—she is so charming! My*

*lovely Auguste is exceptionally well, considering her condition (three more months). Please tell Papa that I have taken his advice to spend more time at home with the family—no more working until midnight.*

*A million kisses,*

*Your loving son, Eugène*

*Note—I am hopeful that Papa will be able to come to an understanding with Tsar Alexandre at the upcoming conference in Erfurt. If he can get Russia to agree to support a blockade against England, England will be forced to negotiate for peace.*

*September 16, Friday.*

It seems that everyone—our best actors and actresses, my cooks, even Dr. Corvisart—is going to Erfurt in Saxony . . . for the peace talks, it is said, but what is whispered is that Bonaparte will be meeting with Tsar Alexandre to discuss marriage to the Tsar's sister.

"Nonsense," Bonaparte told me tonight when I teased him about this rumour. "Talleyrand, explain to my wife that my meetings with the Tsar will be strictly political."

"Your Majesty, the meetings will be strictly political."

"And royal marriages are not political?"

As a result of this "innocent" banter, I could not sleep last night and have been in bed all day. Every hour or so, Bonaparte pops his head through the bed-curtains. "You worry too much," he said, suspecting the cause of my malaise. "You shouldn't listen to the gossips."

*September 22—Saint-Cloud.*

Bonaparte left for Erfurt at five this morning. He embraced me farewell, kissed me with feeling. "I'll be back in a month. Promise you won't worry?"

"I promise," I lied.

*September 26, Monday—Malmaison.*

Thérèse's hat was even more fanciful than usual: an exotic confection of birds and flowers. "What is there to worry about?" she asked, getting right to the point. "Has the Emperor ever made a woman pregnant? No! He's not about to divorce you and marry some young thing only to make a public fool of himself."

"That's the one thing that consoles me," I confessed—and that makes me sadder still.


*October 19.*
Bonaparte arrived back from the peace talks laden with magnificent Russian furs. "Why the disguise?" I asked, for he was dressed as an advocate in a black wool cape.

"I had need of speed. Spain is in trouble."

"You're *returning* to Spain?"

"Joseph has abandoned Madrid, fled without even a struggle! King Pepe Coxo, the Spaniards call him—vice-ridden incompetent. With family like mine, I have no need of enemies."

"Will there be no end to war?"

"Do you think I seek it?" he asked sadly.


*Saturday, October 29—Rambouillet.*
Bonaparte refuses to allow me to accompany him to Spain. "It's too dangerous," he insisted. "The Spaniards are unpredictable."

Murderous, he meant. I pressed my cheek against his heart. If he only knew how much I worried! My attention was drawn to something under his vest. "What's this?" It felt like a soft, small sachet, about an inch in circumference. Bonaparte pulled away. "What is it?" I persisted. His hands were cold.

"Josephine, you wouldn't want me to be . . ."

I closed my eyes. It was poison, I realized, in case of capture.


*November 13—Paris, the awful Tuileries.*
I've moved back into the Tuileries: the dark, dank palace—now garishly renovated, alas. I'm too ill to care, frankly, too upset about the Spanish

campaign, trembling every time I think of that terrible, impossible war. Bonaparte wouldn't even be there had he not been advised that the Spaniards were eager for "liberation." And now, once in, how does one withdraw? Certainly not Bonaparte. *Le feu sacré.* He'd be the last to admit defeat—especially to England.

*December 4, Sunday.*
The most astonishing news—the most *disturbing* news. Talleyrand invited Fouché to his home on Rue de Varenne. They were seen to walk arm in arm through the rooms. "But Fouché and Talleyrand detest one another," I said.

"When enemies unite, there is bound to be trouble," Chastulé said.

*December 22, 1808, Milan*
*Chère Maman,*

*I have succeeded in intercepting a letter that Governor Junot sent to Queen Caroline in Naples. As you suspected, Talleyrand and Fouché are in league to put Joachim on the throne of the French Empire—should the Emperor be killed in battle, they will have it, but the scheme looks suspect in my view. Caroline has even set up a communication system between Paris and Naples so that her husband can quickly be summoned. Junot guaranteed her military "protection"—you know what that means.*

*I've alerted the Emperor, who will no doubt return to Paris immediately. The enemy are not in Spain—they are at home, and in the intimacy of his family circle.*

*My lovely Auguste is well. The midwife says "any day."* *

*Your ever loyal son, Eugène*

*Tuesday—Malmaison.*
"So *that's* what Caroline was up to," Thérèse said. "She's been planning this little coup for some time. I have to say, I admire the little vixen. She

---

* *A daughter, Eugénie, was born the following day, on December 23.*

figured she needed Fouché on her side so she honeyed him. Junot, as Governor of Paris, controls the militia, and so she dragged him into her bed. And—of course—an intimate relationship with the Austrian Ambassador *would* prove to be helpful were she to become Queen of France. What a terrifying thought! You alerted the Emperor?"

"Eugène did."

"Let's pray he gets back soon."


*January 23, 1809—Tuileries.*

Bonaparte is back from Spain, roaring at everyone. Talleyrand has been demoted,* but Fouché, alas, is still Minister of Police. The man who knows everything knows too much, it would appear. "It's safer to keep him near," Bonaparte said.

And what of his sister Caroline? I dared not ask. *Blood is everything.*


*April 12—Saint-Cloud, 10:00 P.M.*

An hour ago, as we were dining, a message came announcing that Austria has invaded Munich—*again.* Between war in the southwest and war in the northeast, Bonaparte is run ragged.


*Saturday, April 15—Strasbourg.*

Nothing in Bonaparte's manner warned me: no loud and tuneless humming of "Malbrough," no rush of last-minute preparations. After a late dinner he returned to his cabinet to work—as usual. I played whist with my ladies until one and then retired. I think it was shortly after three that I was awoken by the sound of a horse's whinny. I sat up, puzzled. Wagon wheels? I went to the window, drew back the drapes: there, in the courtyard below, was Bonaparte's travelling carriage. Servants, grooms and aides were rushing about with flambeaux . . . and there was *Bonaparte*, pulling on his hat. The footman opened the carriage door and let down the step.

---

* *Talleyrand went directly to the Austrians, offering "services" in exchange for one million francs.*

He was leaving—without even a good-luck kiss? I groped through the dark rooms to the entry, knocking over a table. I flew down the steps and into the carriage.

"Josephine?" Bonaparte was startled to see me.

"You can't leave without telling me, Bonaparte!"

"I was afraid you would insist on going, and—"

"Well, you were right."

"But you can't just—"

"Sire, we're ready to set out." Duroc glanced at me, puzzled. What was the Empress doing in the coach in her nightdress and cap?

"That's fine," I said, with an attempt at authority.

"But Josephine, you're not even dressed."

"I'm serious," I growled, which made Bonaparte laugh.

"Order the Empress's trunks sent on to Strasbourg," he told Duroc, draping his greatcoat over my shoulders. "Ah, Josephine, whatever am I going to do with you?" he sighed as we passed through the Paris gates and onto the cobbled avenue.


*Sunday morning—Strasbourg.*
We've only just arrived in Strasbourg and already Bonaparte is leaving to join his army—yet another hurried departure, another tearful leave-taking, another quick good-luck kiss. I've set out the candles, the cards: keeping vigil yet again.


*May 6, noon*
*Mon amie, the cannonball that touched me caused no wound—it barely grazed the Achilles tendon. My health is excellent. Don't be anxious. Things are going very well here. All thine, N.*


*Schönbrunn, May 12, 1809*
*I am master of Vienna. Everything is going perfectly. My health is very good.*
*N.*

*May 27*
*Eugène has joined me with his army. He has achieved the mission I assigned him, almost entirely destroying the enemy army in front of him. I am very well. All thine, N.*


*[Undated]*
News from headquarters: the Emperor is victorious.

Rumours from headquarters: the Emperor is often in the company of a young Polish countess.

Go back home, Bonaparte writes. Don't join me here.

I am packing, returning with regret.


*September 20—Malmaison.*
"It's the Minister of Foreign Affairs, Your Majesty, Monsieur Maret, or rather"—Clari stuck her nose in the air in imitation of a haughty demeanour—"the *Duke* de Bassano."

"Are you sure, Clari?" I thought Hugues Maret was in Germany, with Bonaparte.

But it was, indeed, the Minister of Foreign Affairs—Citoyen Maret, as I think of him. (After all, I've known him since before the Revolution.) "Forgive my surprise, Minister Maret. I thought you were with the Emperor."

"I was, Your Majesty," he said, sticking his nose in the air, just as Clari had demonstrated. "I've a message from him."

"A letter?"

"No, Your Majesty. A verbal communication."

"Would you care to walk in the garden, Minister Maret?"

Two of the pugs got lazily to their feet and sniffed the Minister's boots. He smiled down at them, showing false teeth. "That would be delightful," he said, taking two steps back.

The day was crisp and bright. "And how is the Emperor?" I asked, picking a decayed leaf off a potted auricula. The Emperor my husband; the Emperor in the arms of his Polish mistress. My husband whom I missed very, very much, nonetheless.

"The Emperor is exceptionally well, Your Majesty," Minister Maret said, jumping to open the grille-work gate for me.

I stopped on the path to inhale the scent of a bloom. *Rosa Longifolia, Rosa Pulila, Rosa Orbessanea,* I recited silently in my mind. "You said you had a message for me." I broke off a bloom long past its prime; the petals scattered on the stones. "From the Emperor."

"I do," he said, and fell silent.

"Then perhaps you might tell me what it is?" I suggested gently.

"Your Majesty, perhaps we . . . That is, perhaps you . . ." He waved his arm over a bench.

He wanted me to sit. Wary, I sat down, gathering my shawl around my shoulders.

"Your Majesty, the Emperor has a proposal to make to you, one which he wishes you to know arises out of the deep well of his love for you." Minister Maret licked his thin lips. "It's respecting a woman, Your Majesty, Countess Walewska. I am given to understand that you are aware that she and the Emperor . . . ?"

"Yes, Minister Maret, I am aware."

"The young lady is confirmed to be with child, Your Majesty."

*Rosa Longifolia, Rosa Pulila, Rosa Orbessanea.* "The Emperor's child?"

Minister Maret nodded, not meeting my eyes.

"And there can be no doubt?"

Minister Maret coughed into his fist. "It is early yet, Your Majesty, so it's possible that *things* may not develop, but as to the parentage, there is no doubt whatsoever."

A child—after so many years. *His* child. It must seem a miracle to him. "The Emperor must be very happy," I said, a lump rising in my throat. "But surely this is not why you have come all the way back to Paris, Minister Maret."

"Indeed, Your Majesty, I have come with a highly confidential and delicate proposition. The Emperor wishes to know if you might consider . . . *adopting* this child."

Bonaparte's child? Oh, yes! "I might."

"And more, the Emperor wishes to know if you would be willing to feign a pregnancy—so that the child would appear to be your own."

"You may tell the Emperor that I will do *anything.*"

*[Undated]*

So. A young Polish countess is with child by Bonaparte. I'm told she is shy, gentle, sincere in her love for my husband. I am told she is called his "Polish wife." Oh, my murderous thoughts! She is my undoing—*his* undoing. Is that *gentle*? Is that *sincere*?


*October 1, 1809, Schönbrunn Palace*
*Your Majesty,*

The Emperor, who is in Raab, has charged me with letting you know that Dr. Corvisart regretfully demurred not so much on account of his considerable integrity as a physician, but because of his conviction that the undertaking would be eventually discovered with disastrous results. He has persuaded the Emperor not to pursue this course of action.

Burn this letter.

*Your devoted servant, Hugues Maret,*
*Minister of Foreign Affairs*


*October 14, 1809, Schönbrunn*
*Your Majesty,*

You mistake me. I am in full sympathy with your plea. I understand the importance of this issue, both to the Emperor and yourself, and especially to the Empire. However, as a physician, I appreciate the risks involved. When the eyes of the world are upon one, even the truest action will appear false. I warned the Emperor, and I now caution you against a folly which, however well intended, would lead to the Emperor's disgrace.

The Emperor's health is excellent. The delirious joy we have all felt since the signing of the peace accord has been darkened by the attempt on his life. The Emperor would like to pardon the overzealous student who attempted to pull a knife on him, but the young man foolishly insists on declaring his guilt. That the lad very nearly succeeded has us all somewhat shaken, as you can imagine. I wish to assure you that the Emperor was not hurt in any way. This is not being made public as it would no doubt inflame concerns about the future of the Empire.

*Your most humble servant, Dr. Corvisart*

*October 26, Thursday.*

Moustache came cantering through the gate. "Your Majesty," he yelled to me in the rose garden. "The Emperor is in Fontainebleau!"

"But . . ." Bonaparte wasn't expected back until late tomorrow, at the earliest.

"May I make a suggestion, Your Majesty?" Moustache pulled at one end of his massive appendage. "*Hurry.*"


It was almost six by the time I got to Fontainebleau. I found Bonaparte alone, sitting at a table in the drawing room. "It's about time," he said, looking up briefly, then lowering his eyes.

"Bonaparte, *please* don't be cross."

"Is it too much to ask my wife to be here to greet me after an absence of over six months?"

"Sire," I said, using the formal salutation, "if I may be allowed the impertinence of reminding you, you wrote that you would not be arriving until tomorrow night, at the earliest. My ladies and I were planning to arrive tomorrow morning, in order to be in readiness."

"I suppose it would have *inconvenienced* you to have come a few days early?"

"In all our years together, Bonaparte, this is the first time I've been late to meet you. Just once! We've been apart for half a year, and this is how you welcome me?"

He pressed his hands against his chest, as if he'd been wounded.


*Saturday, October 28—Fontainebleau.*

Once again, we are required to be gay. Three nights a week for theatre, the rest of the week for receptions, one evening at the Emperor's salon, perhaps a ball. When nothing is planned, Chastulé sets up game tables in her drawing room.

Daily Bonaparte hunts, and with a frightening energy, galloping as far as twenty leagues. When not hunting, he is shooting with falcons.

In the evening, at dinner, theatre, receptions and balls, we are careful around each other, our speech and movements studied. Now and again

I see him watching me with a melancholy expression. I know what he is thinking: should he divorce me, or should he not?

*October 29, Sunday—raining.*
Bonaparte's sister Pauline arrived three days ago with a blue-eyed, lascivious lady-in-waiting. Smiling mysteriously, Mademoiselle Christine follows Bonaparte's every move, all the while swinging a huge gold cross on a velvet ribbon, as if trying to entrance him.

*[Undated]*
The light from Pauline's windows is bright: it illuminates the courtyard, the guards standing by the fountain. A door onto the balcony opens and suddenly I hear the sound of violins, merriment. I hear Bonaparte's voice, Mademoiselle Christine's shrill giggle.

*[Undated]*
"I think you should just smile and pretend not to notice, Your Majesty," Clari said.

"I would take a lover," Chastulé said. "The Prince of Mecklenburg-Schwerin will be arriving soon, will he not?"

"That's what *they* would like me to do," I said. What the Bonaparte clan wanted me to do, certainly—in the hope that I would make a fatal error. "I think Bonaparte is intentionally trying to make himself unlovable—"

"Ha! And succeeding."

"—for a reason." My reader adjusted the shawl around my shoulders. I gave Carlotta a sympathetic look. We had both of us been rejected. "I know Bonaparte. He is acting a part. He wants me to look upon . . ." I stopped. I could not speak the word "divorce." "He wants me to look upon a separation as a desirable thing."

"Maman," Hortense interjected, her voice wistful and sad, "perhaps he is right. Perhaps it would be a desirable thing."

I looked down at my needlework, tears blurring the stitches.

*Wednesday, November 8.*
I'm writing this in a golden room. I'm adorned with diamonds, my finest gown, a hat. Damn him!

Oh forgive me, for I am frightened. For my own weak soul, yes, but also for Bonaparte, my exasperating husband, the *Emperor*. This man who is capable of being so heroic—so saintly—but who is also capable of being base and destructive.

Yes, I am frightened, for myself, for Bonaparte, for my children, but also for all the people of this nation who have honoured me with such devotion. I concede: I have lost the battle, and the battle was over Bonaparte's heart.

*You will be Queen,* a voodoo fortune-teller once told me. How clearly I remember those terrible words. *But not for very long.*

I don't care! I don't want to be Queen, Monarch, Empress. I don't want to sit on a throne. The crown has only made me miserable. But I have the misfortune to want very much to sit beside the man on the throne. It is not the Emperor I love, but the *man*. And who else loves *him?* Nobody.


*November 13.*
A fearful slaughter. I'm ill.

For days Bonaparte has been talking about a boar hunt. Today the Emperor got his way: *Je le veux.*

We drove out to where a huge pen had been built in a clearing: the ladies in their hunting finery, their plumes and velvet jackets over gowns of white satin. We climbed up onto a high stand, trembling with nervousness. The men were all standing on a huge platform that had been built in the centre of a pen, loading their guns. Soon we heard fearful sounds, a savage grunting and snorting as over eighty wild boars, stampeded into the pen. Then Bonaparte and the men proceeded to kill them all. The squeals of fear filled the air with a sound I cannot forget. The ladies tittered at first, and then paled.

It has become torture here. Tomorrow, thank God, we return to Paris.

*November 14.*

Paris: city of whispers. I enter a room, and suddenly there is silence, embarrassed smiles. Isabey, making up my face each morning, says nothing about my red-rimmed eyes. "Perhaps a little ceruse?" he suggests, applying the thick white base. I look in the mirror and my face is a mask. "But no crying, Your Majesty," he scolds me tenderly, and tears fill my eyes once again.

*November 15.*

"Monsieur Calumet?" The man who had been my legal advisor years ago had aged. Why was I surprised?

"Madame Bonaparte," he said, rising with difficulty. He hesitated to extend his bare hand. "*Empress,* Your Majesty. Forgive me."

"How are you, kind sir?" I asked, taking a seat. Monsieur Calumet had been witness to my civil marriage to Bonaparte. How things have changed. Now diamonds adorn my headdress and tears my heart.

"Oh," he said, his voice quavering, "your husband has been good to us all. Long live the Emperor!"

This with a burst of emotion that quite took me aback. "I'm afraid I've come about a . . . delicate matter, Monsieur," I began, my hands on my knees, like a schoolgirl. "I wish to consult with you regarding the legitimacy of my marriage—at least in the eyes of the Church. Have you had a chance to consider the document I had sent to you?"

"The Catholic certificate of marriage?" He withdrew it from a drawer and placed it carefully before him. "Your Majesty, forgive me for being the one to tell you, but I'm afraid that there is a problem."

"Oh?" I said, my heart sinking. This was my last hope.

"According to Church law, the requisite witnesses were not present."

"*What* requisite witnesses?"

"The priest of your district, for one. Your Majesty, I do not wish to . . ." He cleared his throat, his hand to his chest.

"Monsieur Calumet, I have come to you because I know I can count on you to tell me the truth. Honesty is rare when one sits on a throne."

He looked away. "Your Majesty, the truth is that this document is worth nothing."

*Nothing?* The word burned! I am your wife forever, I told Bonaparte that night. Is that nothing?

I returned to the palace in a daze. I stood before the fire in my bedchamber for a time, this "worthless" document in my hand. Twice, I started to throw it into the flames . . . and twice I held back. In the end I sent Mimi for the oak strongbox. I've locked it back in there, along with my old journals, along with Bonaparte's fiery letters of love.

It is true: documents are worth nothing. What binds is the heart—the heart's true story. I love Bonaparte and Bonaparte loves me. We *are* man and wife. Come what may, come what will.

*December 1, Friday.*
Bonaparte has spoken.

I wore a wide-brimmed hat to dinner, to hide my eyes. We ate in silence, our attendants standing like statues behind us. Our plates were put on the table, then taken away, the food untouched.

"What time is it?" Bonaparte asked one of the kitchen officers, mechanically hitting his knife against the side of his glass.

"Five to seven, Your Majesty."

Bonaparte stood and headed into the drawing room. I followed, a lap cloth pressed against my mouth. I felt I was moving through deep water, that every step I made required all my concentration. We eat, Bonaparte stands, I follow him. We've been through this ritual for all the days of our life together, but suddenly, it seemed foreign.

The drawing room was stifling hot. The butler entered with the usual tray, standing before me so that I might have the honour of pouring the Emperor's coffee. I reached for the silver jug, but Bonaparte was there before me. Watching me steadily, *defiantly*, he poured his own coffee, spooned in the sugar, and drank. He put the empty cup on the tray and made a dismissive motion, closing the door behind the flustered attendant.

"Josephine," he said, turning to face me, "we must divorce."

He wanted me to see reason. The security of the Empire required this sacrifice. He relied on my devotion to give my consent. "This is a great and noble sacrifice we must make," he said firmly.

"You are wrong, Bonaparte. This would be a mistake! We would live to regret it."

There is no solidity to his dynasty without an heir, he repeated. He'd come to see the absolute necessity of it. The Empire must endure more than a day; it must endure for all eternity.

"Name Eugène heir," I argued. "You've trained him well. He's loyal and devoted to you. He understands your aims, your vision. You *know* the nation would benefit." The Empire would flourish! "You can *trust* him. Under Eugène, your legacy would endure."

"He is not a Bonaparte."

*Blood is everything.* "Then what about your nephews? What about Petit?"

"It's not the same as a son, born to the purple, raised in a palace. I *must* have a child of my own, Josephine. It's cruel of you to deprive me!"

And then I began to weep. "You don't know the pain we will suffer." I felt crazed, beyond reason.

"I will always love you. I will come to visit you—often."

"Don't you understand? It will not be the same!" He was deluding himself. This man who prided himself on his clear vision did not know his own heart.

"I *promise* you," he went on, as if words would heal. "You will keep your title. I will give you five million a year. You may have Malmaison. I'll buy you a country château—anything! I'll make you Queen of Rome. You will have your own domain."

"Bonaparte, no! Whatever you do, *please*—don't send me away." I envisioned myself alone and unloved. I fell on the carpet, giving way to pitiful sobbing.

·

I remember very little of what followed. I was carried down the narrow passage to my room and Dr. Corvisart was summoned. "You've suffered a violent attack of nerves, Your Majesty."

Hortense appeared before me through a laudanum blur. "Eugène and I will follow you," she told me. "Together we'll lead a quiet life. It will be peaceful. We will know true happiness."

I wrapped my arms around her thin shoulders. Mother and daughter, we were both alone in the world. It is perhaps best that she does not know what lies ahead, I thought. I felt like a Cassandra, calling out futile warnings of impending doom. Destiny has been crossed; the downward slide will now begin.

## In which we must part

At eight, as is her custom, my maid of the wardrobe entered my bedchamber with a selection of gowns. "Come in, Mademoiselle Avrillion," I said, parting the bed-curtains. "I have something to tell you, but first, make sure that the door is closed." I fell back against the pillows. I still felt weak, but calmer.

Mademoiselle Avrillion put down her basket and smoothed her skirt, her expression apprehensive. We'd all been expecting the worst, waiting for the sky to fall—knowing that it would, but not knowing when. Not knowing how life would go on after.

But life does go on. I took a breath and began. "The Emperor informed me that he has decided to—" In telling her, I was again overcome. I struggled to finish. "He has decided to pronounce a divorce." Mademoiselle Avrillion clapped her hands over her mouth, let out a cry. "However, everything must appear normal for the time being."

"That's cruel of him, Your Majesty." Her look was defiant—loyal.

"The Emperor suffers," I told her firmly. "He does what he must."


And so, by the bright winter light, my new life begins. I look ravaged, yet I will play the part, assume the costume of the Empress, recall her calm and charitable heart. After the celebration of the peace, Bonaparte will make a public announcement. As for this moment, I'm suffering an indisposition, that's all.

Brave words, but as soon as Mademoiselle Avrillion left, I gave in to despair. How can I do this? I've a reception at Malmaison tomorrow, and the day after is the big celebration, a ball. And then more balls and fêtes, and fêtes and balls, all in a spirit of gaiety. How will I find the courage, the strength?

*Saturday, December 2—Malmaison.*

It is late. I'm writing this at the little mahogany writing table in Bonaparte's bedchamber at Malmaison. I'm in my nightgown, warmed by the bearskin I've pulled off the bed.

The sovereigns have all departed, even Bonaparte, who decided to return to the Tuileries in preparation for the morrow—in spite of the snow and freezing rain. "This is your lucky day," I told him, on leaving. He looked puzzled. "The second of December." The anniversary of the coronation: how could he forget?

"Oh," he said, shrugging, as if luck no longer mattered.

It is a relief to be alone now. The hardest part was receiving the family. Queen Caroline and King Joachim, newly arrived back from Naples, watched me closely. They suspect, I know. And what will they do, I wonder, when they learn that they have won the day, won the battle, won the war? They will proclaim a victory, no doubt. They will have the Emperor to themselves, at last—all his power and all his riches. And all his heart, they will assume—not knowing his heart, not realizing that this sacrifice will harden him.

It is now almost two, I suspect. The fire has burnt down; I begin to feel the winter chill. My portrait by the bed is in shadow—Bonaparte's favourite, though not mine.

Five years ago today Bonaparte crowned me Empress. Oh, it was the most glorious day! I accepted that crown as if it were a betrothal ring, thinking that it would bind me to my husband. And now . . . *now* I see that it is the one thing that has pushed me away from him. Without issue, I have no right to that throne—no right, indeed, to the Emperor's Imperial bed. As Empress, there was only one thing I was required to do: provide the link to the past and to the future, secure the Emperor's place in history. In the womb of an Empress, the future unfolds. She is the past, she is the present, she is the future. And I? I was never an Empress. Only Yeyette, Rose, Josephine—an ordinary woman from Martinico. An ordinary woman who loves her husband.

How much does it matter, in the end, my love for Bonaparte? Not much, truly, when balanced against the needs of a nation. Indeed, it *is* a sacrifice we are making, Bonaparte and I—a noble sacrifice. I only pray that it will not be made in vain, that my fears are unfounded. "Superstitious nonsense," as Bonaparte would say, "womanish imaginings." (Pretending not to be superstitious himself.)

Oh, Bonaparte—how hard it is for me to comprehend the changes that lie before us. I feel you in this room with me now—your light lemon scent lingers. Your spirit is everywhere. A half-empty crystal champagne glass engraved with your monogram is on the table beside a stack of journals, coins, a snuffbox. A small, battered medal catches my eye: Charlemagne's talisman, carelessly tossed in among the pocket clutter. A book you were reading—*History of the Revolutions of the Roman Empire*—is facedown on a chair beside the bed, the spine cracked, the pages dog-eared. Your vest is thrown over the arm of the black leather chair. A crumpled news-sheet litters the carpet.

The clock has just chimed two. I don't want to leave this room, this moment so full of memory, but I've a difficult day tomorrow, I know. I will lock the door when I leave, forbid entry. It will always be here for me.

*Sunday.*

First, a Te Deum at Notre-Dame. I was not to go there in the Emperor's coach, was not to sit beside him, Duroc explained, his manner officious, as if I were a servant he was instructing. Rather, I was to sit with Caroline and Jérôme's wife, Catherine. "The Emperor wishes the people to begin to be prepared," Duroc said. "He wishes it to be conjectured."

*Conjectured.* Of course. Rumours would be circulated, hints given, predictions printed in the popular journals. And perhaps it is for the best. Perhaps in this way I, too, will begin to be "prepared."

"Does anyone in the household know?" I asked.

"Only the Imperial family, Madame."

Madame. Not *Your Majesty*—just *Madame*. Well, so be it, I thought, swallowing hard.


"Madame Bonaparte," Caroline said with a bright (smug) smile. "How lovely you look this afternoon."

"How kind of you to say so," I replied with a bright (false) smile. "*Queen* Caroline." (How trivial it all seemed to me, in truth, catching a glimpse of the tomb of little Napoleon tucked into a corner of that vast cathedral.)

After Mass, the Imperial cortège drove to the Legislature, where Bonaparte was received with thunderous cheers. My heavy heart gladdened to the sound of "Hail to the Peacemaker! Long live the Emperor!" From habit and affection, Bonaparte glanced over his shoulder at me, sharing the moment.

At five the cortège returned to the Tuileries, where we received the foreign ambassadors before proceeding into the Gallery of Diana for the Imperial banquet. (My last, thank God—how I hate them.) King Joseph was seated on my left, Madame Mère on my right. King Louis, newly arrived from Holland, sat next to his mother (with whom he is staying). Bonaparte sat directly across from me, with the King of Saxony on his right. Hortense was on his left. I avoided my daughter's eyes, for fear I might weep.

And then, of course, all the others: the King of Württemberg, King Jérôme and his wife Catherine, a conspicuously gay Princess Pauline, King Joachim in pink silk embroidered with gold stars—and, of course, an exultant Queen Caroline, ordering the servants about as if she were in charge, as if *she* were the hostess.

Bonaparte seemed anxious, motioning to the chamberlain for no purpose, wiping his mouth even when he wasn't eating, creating a growing pile of soiled napkins behind him.*

We ate without speaking, each silently attended by three footmen, the

* *After a napkin was used once, it was thrown behind the diner's chair and a new one was supplied.*

only voices those of the carvers, passing the trays to the footmen. I don't believe I was ever so glad to see Bonaparte rise. Immediately everyone stood, turned, advanced one pace toward the line of butlers, who offered trays. With trembling hands I squeezed lemon into the white bowl, cleansed my mouth and swished the tips of my fingers in the blue bowl. To think I've finally mastered this little ritual, I thought, tossing my napkin into Caroline's pile.

*December 4, Monday—Paris.*
My demise—my loss of a throne, a crown, a husband—begins to be "conjectured." At the military review this morning, a market woman placed flowers at my feet, as if I had died.

The review was followed by a fête given by the city of Paris, with the court of the Hôtel de Ville transformed into an enormous ballroom. I'd been instructed to go alone. My ladies would be there to meet me, I was told, but when I entered, I found the foyer empty, the small drawing room beside the grand staircase where the attendants waited deserted. Where were my ladies, my entourage? The head butler came running down the marble stairs. "Your attendants have been seated," he said, out of breath.

"I'm to enter alone?"

"It is the Emperor's wish."

*I will it.* Bien. Drums sounded my entry into the Grand Salon. I could hear the hushed whispers as I made my way to the dais: an Empress without an Emperor. As I approached the throne, my knees began to give way. Quickly I was handed into the velvet-cushioned throne. I sat back, faced the crowd.

The drums beat again, and Bonaparte entered with Caroline on his arm, Jérôme following behind.

Caroline caught my eye, glowing with the triumph of victory.

*December 5—Paris, shortly before dinner.*
A message from Eugène—he'll be here in a few days.

*Thursday.*

I was at my toilette when Hortense appeared at the door, her cheeks flushed and her eyes glistening. "Eugène is here!"

I pressed my hands to my heart. I hadn't seen my son since he and Auguste had married—almost four years ago now.

"He's with the Emperor," she said, touching her cheek to mine. "Are you sure you're all right?"

"I'm . . . *fine*." I reached for the vial of herbal essence Dr. Corvisart had prescribed, for nerves. I put a drop on my finger and held it to my nose, inhaled slowly. I had not been sleeping, and already this morning I'd had one of my "tropical storms"—a torrent of tears that seemed to come upon me unexpectedly and without warning. I inhaled again and sat back. "I'm all right," I repeated (but with tears welling up). "I've been—"

I was interrupted by the thundering sound of footsteps in the private passage. "Come in," I called out at the sound of Bonaparte's characteristic *rap-rap*. How I've missed that sound!

Bonaparte stumbled into the room, blinking against the light. "Hortense *is* here," he said over his shoulder.

And then close behind him appeared a tall, good-looking young man with broad shoulders and honest, smiling eyes: Eugène! I stood to embrace my beloved son. "Oh, mon Dieu, Eugène, you look so old!" So handsome—so manly.

He swung me playfully in his embrace, crooning, "Oh Maman, Maman, Maman . . ."

"And you've grown sideburns." And a kingdom. And two daughters. "You look wonderful," I said, blinking back tears. "Doesn't he?" I said, turning to Bonaparte—*Papa*. "Doesn't he?" Turning to Hortense.

"Oh Maman, *don't*," Eugène said, his eyes brimming. He pulled me against his chest, patting my back, stilling my sudden sobs.

"Hold her, Eugène." Hortense saw my knees beginning to buckle.

Supported by them both, I regained my strength. "Forgive me. I'm sorry." I glanced up. Bonaparte was staring at the three of us, his cheeks wet with tears.

"Oh, Papa," Hortense whispered, pulling him into the circle of our embrace.

*December 8.*

As we married, so we must divorce: with ceremony.

We begin with specifics: who, what, when, where. The date has been set for a week from today, next Friday. Evening, court attire. Reception in the throne room, the ceremony itself in Bonaparte's cabinet. In the presence of family and a few officials, Bonaparte will make a statement, I will follow, and then the legal document will be signed. Arch-Chancellor de Cambacérès will see to the legalities. His secretary will send out the invitations.

"As you wish," I said, my mouth dry.

*[Undated]*

"Your Majesty, did I understand you correctly? There is to be no lace, no embroidery, no pearls—*nothing?*"

"The gown must be plain, Monsieur Leroy," I said, "like one a nun would wear."

*[Undated]*

Arch-Chancellor de Cambacérès has given me a draft of a divorce statement he thinks would be appropriate. I cannot speak his words. I will write it myself.

*[Undated]*

I tried to write my divorce statement this morning—gave up in tears.

*No longer having any hope of conceiving children, I give my beloved husband proof of my devotion by . . .*

By divorcing him.

Oh, mon Dieu—this is not the right thing to do, Bonaparte!

*December 13, Wednesday evening.*
An exhausting day attending to my charities, my wardrobe.* To bed. Tomorrow there is a formal reception followed by dinner in the Gallery of Diana. I've begged permission not to attend, but I'm told I must. It will be my last appearance as Empress.

*I declare that, no longer having any hope of conceiving children, I am willing to give my husband proof of my devotion by . . .*

*December 14.*
The reception and dinner were difficult. At least it is over. "It always gives me a head pain anyway," I told Chastulé as she took my crown away.

*I declare that, no longer having any hope of conceiving children, which would satisfy the interests of France, I am willing to give the greatest proof of my love and devotion by . . .*

*December 15, Friday.*
Leroy has delivered my gown. "I finally understand, Your Majesty," he said. "You wish to adorn yourself in precious gems. The simplicity of the gown will be what designers call a counterpoint."

"No, Monsieur Leroy, I intend not to wear a single gem." Only my wedding ring, which I will wear to my grave.

He looked at me as if I'd gone mad—and perhaps he is right.

Mademoiselle Avrillion came for me shortly before nine. "Your Majesty, are you ready? The Emperor is expecting you in his cabinet."

* *Josephine doubled her usual contribution to charity and, as well, gave away 72 pieces of lace, 380 gowns, 17 shawls, 146 bonnets and hats, 39 lengths of cloth, and 785 pairs of boots and slippers—virtually every pair she owned.*

"I am ready."

She burst into tears. "You should see them all."

"They've arrived?" Already?

"They're in the throne room, Your Majesty. I've never seen Caroline and Pauline looking so grand. Even Madame Mère is wearing a fuchsia-and-yellow brocade—and rubies! One would think it was carnival. I will be honest, now that we are leaving. I think that they're beastly individuals and I detest them!"

At the landing, I sent Mademoiselle Avrillion away. "I'll be all right," I assured her, proceeding through the antechamber, the waiting room, the drawing room, nodding to the guards, the maids. Hugo, his chin puckered in misery, threw open the door to Bonaparte's cabinet. "The Emperor is expecting you, Your Majesty." Bowing deeply.

Bonaparte was seated on the chaise by the fireplace, his back to the door. "Josephine!" He jumped to his feet. He was wearing a blue velvet suit richly embroidered in gold. He wiped his hands on his breeches and came to me, hands extended, as if I were a guest he'd been expecting. But stopped short. "The family will be shown in soon. I thought you would sit here, by the writing table." He pulled out the antique chair.

Slowly, I sat down. The chair needed to be reupholstered, I noticed—the silk piping was beginning to fray. The fabric was an unusual shade of green kersey. It would be difficult to match. I vaguely recalled that a length of it had been stored in the attic wardrobe. I should let Bonaparte's chamberlain know.

"Josephine, are you all right?" Bonaparte patted my shoulder, very lightly—as if afraid to touch me.

I nodded, swallowing, my eyes stinging. A gold quill stand had been placed on the table before me in readiness, a parchment beside it. I put my own parchment down, smoothing it out so that it lay flat. *I declare that* . . .

Bonaparte took up a matching chair and placed it in front of the fire. "And I will sit here. Everyone else can sit on the stools—but for my mother, of course. I thought perhaps she might sit on the chaise. What do you think?"

"Your mother doesn't care to sit too close to a fire."

"She doesn't?"

Nor too far. "Perhaps if the chaise were placed against the wall," I suggested.

"Good idea," he said, shoving the chaise into place and then tugging at the corner of the carpet to straighten it.

The big pendulum clock began to sound the hour.

*One.*

*Two.*

*Three.*

At the fourth chime the door creaked open. "Your Majesty, it is time," Christophe Duroc informed Bonaparte (without glancing at me). He was wearing the grandest of his Grand Marshal ensembles: an enormous cape with a batwing collar made stiff with bone.

*Five.*

*Six.*

*Seven.* Bonaparte and I looked at each other for what seemed a very long moment.

*Eight.* Let's leave, I felt like crying out. Let's escape to some island, frolic in the surf, grow flowers and vegetables. Let's grow old together, fumbling and fond.

*Nine.*

"Send them in," Bonaparte said, looking away.

I could hear Caroline's voice, and then Pauline's shrill giggle. I pulled out a fresh handkerchief, took a deep breath.

Duroc announced everyone in order of status. First Madame Mère (smiling), then Louis—leaning heavily on two walking sticks, his expression hooded—followed at a distance by Hortense, Jérôme and his wife, Caroline and Joachim (snickering), Julie (Joseph is in Spain), Eugène and, at the last, a giggling Pauline.

Hortense reached for the back of my chair as Eugène strode across the room to stand beside Bonaparte. My son crossed his arms on his chest and stared at the carpet, paler than I'd ever seen him.

I touched my daughter's hand and looked up at her. Her red-rimmed eyes glistening, her face streaked by tears—that sensitive face so full of intelligence, so full of grace. No wonder the Bonaparte sisters loathe her, I thought. Hortense is everything they are not.

Arch-Chancellor de Cambacérès came in, his cape pulled back to better display the medals and ribbons that covered his vest, followed by dignified Count Regnault, the clan lawyer. We lapsed into the uncomfortable fifteen minutes of silence required by the Code, broken only by Hortense's sniffs, one muffled occurrence of flatulence (Joachim, I suspect), Pauline's and Caroline's whispers. I caught Bonaparte's eye. He smiled wanly and looked away. My throat tightened and a wave of tears rose up within me. I took a deep breath, tracing a circle on the head of the gilt-bronze gryphon that ornamented the arm of my chair. *I declare that . . .*

Bonaparte broke the silence. "You have been summoned here," he began, "to witness the declaration the Empress and I are obliged to make." He cleared his throat. "We are divorcing."

Eugène reached out for the mantel. He was trembling, I realized with alarm. Hortense stifled a sob. I caressed her fingers, my eyes fixed on my husband.

He read quickly at first, as if racing to get the ordeal over with. Then he paused. "She has adorned fifteen years of my life. The memory of those years will be forever inscribed on my heart," he read haltingly, finishing with difficulty.

I felt Hortense squeeze my shoulder. It was my turn.

The parchment shook in my hands. "I declare that . . ." I began to read, but at the words, *Everything I have comes from his kindness,* I broke down, and handed the paper to Count Regnault. Leaning one elbow on the table, I listened as he read my words, so true and so heartfelt: *The dissolution of my marriage will make no change in the feelings of my heart. The Emperor will always find in me his truest friend.*

Count Regnault put the paper on the table and pulled out a handkerchief to wipe his eyes.

Bonaparte sat motionless. Through a blur of tears, I saw my son's stricken face. Cambacérès indicated to Bonaparte that the time had come to sign the official document. Bonaparte stood and scratched out his signature—that messy scrawl I knew so well.

"Josephine?" he said then, with a sweet-sad smile, handing me the quill.

*4:30 A.M.*
The night sky is lightening. I don't believe I've slept at all.

It was close to midnight when I gave way to my heart. En déshabille, I fumbled up the connecting passage, lighting my way with a single candle. The guard woke with a start when I rapped on Bonaparte's door. He looked at me, confused, his hand on the pommel of his sword. "It's just me, the Empress Josephine." Fortunately, Bonaparte's valet opened the door.

"Your Majesty," he said, astonished as much by my unexpected call as by my disordered appearance.

"Who is it, Constant?" I heard Bonaparte call out. I stepped into the room. By the light of a lantern on the washstand, I saw that Bonaparte was in bed, under a pile of comforters.

"Bonaparte, I just wanted to—" I began calmly, but my voice suddenly went high, like that of a child in pain. "I don't know if I have the strength to do this," I gasped.

Bonaparte sat up, his nightcap slipping off. I fell sobbing into his arms. "Courage," he said, tender and caressing. I touched his cheek, now wet with tears. "Oh, Josephine, how am I ever going to manage without you?" he whispered, holding me close.

*Saturday, almost 2:00 P.M.*
I will be leaving soon, leaving the palace, never to return, leaving my place beside Bonaparte. Soon another empress—young, royal, fertile—will sit at this desk. I have no illusions. Bonaparte will come to love her; that is her right. She will be the mother of his children.

And I, who will I be? I will be "the other one," growing old alone.

I've sprinkled the room with my light lavender scent. He will never, *ever* forget me.

"Ready, Maman?" Hortense touched my shoulder, a gentle motion that gave me strength.

"What about the pups?" I asked, slipping a veil over my head to hide my tear-streaked cheeks. Two days ago, one of the pugs had given birth to a litter.

"Don't worry, they're in Mademoiselle Avrillion's carriage," Hortense said, taking my hand. "Along with the canaries," she added with a smile.

All the servants were lined up in the entry. As soon as they saw me, saw that the moment had come, a terrible wail rose up, a heart-rending lamentation that echoed off the marble surfaces. I was blinded by tears; Hortense pulled me forward.

"Oh dear," I heard her say, once we were out the door. There was a crowd in the courtyard, standing in the cold winter rain. "It's the good Empress Josephine!" I heard a woman call out. Hortense hurried me into the carriage. As the horses pulled forward at a fast pace, Hortense reached to close the leather curtains. I did not look back.

# III

## The Other One

If he is happy, I will have no regrets.
—*Josephine*

## In which a king is born

*Sunday, December 17, 1809—Malmaison.*
I woke this morning to the sound of Mimi humming a familiar créole song. "*He's* here," she said, poking her head through the bed-curtains.

"Bonaparte?" I sat up, my heart jumping.

"The Emperor awaits you in the garden," an aide I didn't recognize informed me, neither addressing me as Empress nor bowing, merely ducking his head.

"In the rain?" I asked. It was more of a drizzle now, but damp nonetheless. I sent Mimi for boots and an umbrella—not the English one—a cape and a hat.

The aides followed like an unwelcome shadow to the rose garden gate. Bonaparte, pacing at the far end in his familiar grey coat, turned to face me. He touched the brim of his tricorne hat, as if in salute.

The aides lined up like sentries along the fence—close enough to watch, I realized. Bonaparte stepped back as I drew near. I understood: we were not to embrace.

"I didn't expect to see you so soon." I took a shaky breath, another. Tears would upset him, I knew.

"I needed to know how you were doing." He looked grim—his eyes red-rimmed.

I dared not answer, for fear of speaking truly.

"Let's walk, Josephine," he said gently, offering his arm.

*December 17, 8:00 P.M.*

*Mon amie, I found you weaker today than you should be. You must not surrender to such a devastating melancholy. You must find happiness, and above all, you must care for your health, which is so precious to me.*

*Never doubt my constant and tender feelings. You do not understand me if you think I can be happy if you are not at peace.*

*Adieu, sleep well. N.*


*December 21—Malmaison.*

Thérèse burst into tears when she saw me. "I told you never to get divorced!" she said angrily. "I told you it was hell." And then she embraced me, held me tight. "Forgive me!" she cried, enveloping me in a cloud of her familiar neroli oil scent. "You *love* the brute—and he loves you. That makes it even worse."


*Sunday.*

Bonaparte removed his hat, held it over his heart. "I'd like you, Hortense and Eugène to join me for dinner tomorrow. Christmas dinner," he added, as if I did not know.


*Monday, Christmas Day.*

"That was the most miserable meal I've ever experienced," Hortense exclaimed on our return.

I stroked one of the pugs' ears. The dog looked up at me with sorrowful eyes, as if she knew my thoughts. It *had* been miserable. Bonaparte had sat silently throughout the entire meal, now and then wiping his eyes.

One sweet note: the tender welcome of Bonaparte's staff. "The Emperor misses you terribly, Your Majesty," Constant whispered to me. "We all do."

It seems lonelier here now at Malmaison. I see him still, walking in the garden, working at his desk.

Oh, Bonaparte . . . how hard this is!

*January 1, 1810—Malmaison, almost dinnertime.*

What a terrible way to begin the year.

The ordeal began after the noonday meal. The servants of the household were instructed to enter the music room one by one. I was to give them a New Year's gift, and they in turn were to declare themselves: tell me if they would be staying with me or seeking employment elsewhere.

"Chastulé, perhaps you could record what everyone says," I suggested.

"Ha! But who will write down *my* declaration?"

"You wish to declare yourself now?"

"Why wait?"

"Countess d'Arberg, could you? Would you mind?" My tall, elegant lady-in-waiting did her best to squeeze into Chastulé's little chair and desk.

"Don't I get my gift first?" Chastulé demanded. "It's the one on the right, with the scarlet bow." Countess d'Arberg checked the tag and handed it to her. "My husband insists I stay with the court," Chastulé said, pinning the diamond brooch to her bodice. "I have my family to think of, and you won't be needing a lady of honour any more since you won't be entertaining and holding drawing rooms or suppers." She glanced at what Countess d'Arberg had written. "I said *suppers*, not dinners."

"You're leaving me, Chastulé?" I felt her words as a blow.

"I've already written to the Emperor, Madame," she said, edging toward the door.

"Just send in Carlotta, if you would, Countess de la Rochefoucauld," Countess d'Arberg said coolly.

The door slammed shut behind Chastulé. The silence was oppressive. Even the canaries were still. "Would you care to be my lady of honour?" I asked Countess d'Arberg weakly.

"I've coveted the position ever since I joined your household, Your Majesty," she said, efficiently blotting the ledger book and turning the page.

I was surprised. Countess d'Arberg is a Belgian aristocrat of German extraction, allied to the ruling houses of Germany. I had assumed that she would want to stay with the court.

The door creaked open. "Your Majesty, you summoned me?" Carlotta's dark eyes widened seeing Countess d'Arberg seated at Chastulé's little escritoire.

"You were," I said, guarded. Carlotta would leave me, too, no doubt. "Today everyone is to make a declaration, as you know."

Carlotta coloured as she said, "I want to serve you, Your Majesty—that is, if you will have me. Forgive me—have I said something wrong?" she asked, puzzled by my reaction.

"I assure you, Madame Gazzani, you have not," Countess d'Arberg said, giving my reader her gift.

"And this, as well, Carlotta," I said, taking a ring off my finger, pressing it into her hand.

And so, throughout the afternoon, there were many, many tears. A significant number of the servants will be leaving—understandable, I tell myself. A few will retire with a pension. (Agathe is one, alas. She is betrothed to the groundskeeper at Fontainebleau.) Clari would have liked to stay, she assured me, but for health reasons begged to be allowed to retire. I will miss her.

It's a smaller household now, but a good one. Mademoiselle Avrillion will stay, as mistress of the wardrobe. Mimi will stay, of course, and old Gontier. "I'll see you to your grave, Your Majesty," he declared, leaning on a cane, one hand pressed to his heart.


*February 6, almost midnight.*
Eugène pulled on a pug's tail and growled playfully. "Sorry I'm late, Maman."

"And?" I put down my needlework. He had set out late this afternoon for the Austrian Embassy to deliver Bonaparte's formal request for the hand of Archduchess Marie-Louise.* "How did the Austrian ambassador respond?" The offer had been made on condition that an answer be given within a day. The seventeen-year-old Archduchess would not even be consulted.

---

* It was important for Josephine and her children to show public support for the new marriage. Indeed, both Eugène and Hortense (as well as Josephine) were involved in the discussions as to which royal princess should be chosen.

"The contract will be signed tomorrow at noon."

"I suppose this is cause for celebration."

"I suppose," he echoed, embracing me.


*February 14.*

Eugène has left to return to Milan. "I'll be back soon," he promised, "with Auguste." For Bonaparte's wedding, he did not say.


*Saturday noon.*

*Le Moniteur* is full of news about the preparations that are being made for "the wedding of the century," all the fêtes and spectacles that are being planned.

"Your Majesty, perhaps it would be best not to read the news-sheets," Countess d'Arberg said gently, bringing me a cup of tea (and slipping the journal away).


*Monday, February 19—a bit of a drizzle.*

"Uncle doesn't like his dance lessons," Oui-Oui told me this afternoon.

Bonaparte is taking dance lessons?

"Aunt Caroline said he must learn," Petit explained.

"Well, of course," I said, dissembling. How many times had I tried to persuade Bonaparte to learn to dance only to be told no, impossible, don't even mention it! And *now*—now that he will have a young wife— he has decided to learn.

"*And* he has a new shiny suit with a high collar." Petit demonstrated how high with his fingers.

"But it's too tight," Oui-Oui said with a giggle.


*February 20, Tuesday.*

My hairdresser was miserable this morning—and now I am, too. "I'm sorry, Your Majesty, but—"

"Monsieur Duplan, you've been dressing my hair for over a decade."

"Queen Caroline is helping the Emperor set up the new household and insists that—"

Insists that from now on, Duplan—*my* Duplan—is to be hairdresser to one woman and one woman only: the soon-to-be-Empress Marie-Louise. "I understand," I said, but fuming, I confess. It is one thing to lose a husband and a crown, quite another to lose a hairdresser.

*[Undated]*

"Not you, too, Monsieur Leroy." How was I to manage without my dress designer? I'd discovered Leroy! I'd been his patroness. Together we'd created a new fashion.

"Your Majesty, you know I would far prefer to make gowns for you," he said tearfully, his manicured hands pressed to his rouged cheeks. "But—"

*[Undated]*

"Dr. Corvisart, please don't tell me that you won't be able to attend me any more."

"Now, now," Dr. Corvisart said thoughtfully, taking my pulse. He sat down across from me, his thumb on his chin—preparing to tell me I was dying, no doubt. "Your Majesty, your eyesight has become quite weak," he observed. "Do you weep often?"

"No," I said, weeping.

He smiled. "I will be honest. Your nerves have suffered quite seriously *and*, dare I say, your heart."

I pressed my hands to my chest. I *was* dying; I knew it! "What's wrong with my heart?" Dr. Corvisart is a heart specialist—he has written a medical text on the subject.

"I believe it is broken," he said gently, handing me a cambric hand-kerchief. "The waters of Aix-les-Bains are excellent for nerves." Tapping the end of his pencil against his cheek. "June would be a good time to go—not too hot and not too cold," he said, marking it on his calendar.

"But Dr. Corvisart, I've never been to that spa." Aix-les-Bains was southeast, in the mountains bordering Italy.

"Exactly," he said. "No memories."

*Friday night, March 9, quite late.*
Fire-rockets brighten the night sky. Another fête, no doubt, to celebrate the coming wedding—another fête to which I haven't been invited.

Fourteen years ago today, Bonaparte and I married.


*March 12*
*Mon amie, I hope you will be happy with the Château de Navarre. You will see in it another proof of my wish to please. It's not far from the village of Évreux, about thirteen posting houses from Paris—twenty-eight leagues, to be exact. Joachim, who arranged for the purchase, informs me that the château was designed by Mansart, the architect of Versailles, and that it is famed for its gardens. You could go on March 25 and spend the month of April there. Adieu, N.*


*March 12, Monday—Malmaison.*
"Why March 25?" Countess d'Arberg asked, examining the calendar. "Oh," she said, and fell silent.

March 25: two days before Archduchess Marie-Louise is expected to arrive in France.


*March 20.*
Hortense has just left in a flutter. Every king and queen in Europe is coming to the wedding. "Where are all these sovereigns going to stay?" she demanded. Jérôme and Catherine alone had arrived with a suite of over thirty servants. "And all requiring a bed, Maman—impossible!"

I remembered the problems Chastulé and I had had in December, trying to find suitable accommodation for everyone during the peace celebrations. One can't put kings and queens in just any establishment. "Chastulé should be able to help," I suggested.

"You don't know, Maman? Papa sent her packing. He was furious that she refused to stay with you."

Countess d'Arberg caught my eye and smiled.

*March 24.*

Eugène and his lovely Auguste arrived (exhausted). Soon they'll leave to join Bonaparte at Compiègne to join the party that welcomes the young bride to France.

"Aren't you going to the country, Maman?" Eugène asked anxiously. "Didn't Papa buy you a château? Shouldn't you be there now?"

Don't worry, I assured him. "I'm leaving in the morning." I won't be around when *she* comes to Paris.

Don't worry, don't worry, don't worry. The old Empress will be long gone.


*March 29, Thursday—Château de Navarre.*

My château—my "gift" from Bonaparte.

My curse, I fear. The people of Évreux have named it "the saucepan." The ugly cube structure is topped by a bizarre dome, intended at one time to support an enormous statue. One enters into a dark circular hall—the only light from slits two stories up. And all around, opening onto this hall, are strange triangular rooms.

The chair I'm sitting on, like all the furniture here, is ancient and uncomfortable. I had a splintered oak table moved close to the (smoking) fireplace because it is so very cold. None of the windows both opens and closes. Some cannot be opened, but most, unfortunately, cannot be closed, so swollen is the wood from the damp.

Mademoiselle Avrillion is with me now, huddled by the fire. The bedchambers are small, cold, *dismal*. Each day we burn fifteen cartloads of wood and seven sacks of coal, and even so, we shiver.

"The grounds are lovely," Mademoiselle Avrillion said quietly, as if reading my thoughts.

Yes, I agreed: were it not for the bogs and the stagnant pools.


*[Undated]*

Four servants left today, two yesterday . . . and who can blame them?

*[Undated]*
Three cartloads of furniture arrived from Paris this afternoon. The servants descended on them like starving men attacking a banquet table. A distressing melee ensued, the servants fighting over stools and bed frames while the driver cried out for them to stop. (Futile.)


*April 1, April Fish Day—Château de Navarre.*
As I write this, Bonaparte and Marie-Louise are being joined in marriage.

We have made some progress clearing the swamp. Very cold still, bitter. My health suffers.


*April 5, Thursday.*
In spite of my resolve, I have read the accounts of the wedding in the journals. The crowds along the Champs-Élysées were so thick the troops had difficulty restraining them. Eight thousand were in attendance at the ceremony. (Who carried the bride's train? I wonder.) The usual concerts, fire-rockets and fountains gushing with wine. Food was distributed as prizes in a lottery.* (No banquets?) At one signal from the palace, the entire city was illuminated—I would like to have seen *that*.

It's only eight, but I'm going to bed. We've sealed the window cracks with wax, which helps. I wonder if Uncle Fesch remembered to bless their bed.


*April 18—Château de Navarre.*
I could not believe my eyes, for who should be announced this evening as I was playing trictrac with the Bishop of Évreux but my son! I jumped to my feet and threw my arms around him, forgetting all sense of propriety. "Why have you come?" I demanded, suddenly alarmed. Was Hortense all right? Her boys! And what about Bonaparte? Was he . . . ?

Eugène held up his hands. "Everyone's fine. Papa got your letter. He

---

* *The prizes: 4,800 pâtés, 1,200 tongues, 3,000 sausages, 140 turkeys, 360 capons, 360 chickens, and 1,000 legs and 1,000 shoulders of mutton.*

sent me to tell you that he'll give you the money you need for repairs."

"But no letter from him?"

"He said to tell you he would write soon. He wanted me to have a look, see how you're doing." Eugène frowned at the rotting windowsill. "Well," he said, his hands on his hips. "I see the problem."

"It's really much improved." In my joy to see my son, my complaints had vanished. "And the fishing here is excellent, I'm told. Isn't it, Bishop? Oh, forgive me, I've neglected civilities. Prince Eugène, Viceroy of Italy, may I have the honour of introducing you to the Bishop of Évreux. The king of trictrac, we call him."

"A defeated king, alas," the old man said, struggling to rise.

"Please, stay seated," my son insisted, lowering himself onto the (hard) sofa.

"No, no, I only care to get trounced once in an evening," the Bishop said, taking his leave. "Tomorrow evening, Your Majesty, as usual?"

"A charming man," Eugène said, after he'd left.

"He has saved my life here," I said, sitting beside my son and taking his hand. "And how *is* Bonaparte?" How is the *Empress*? I wanted to ask, but dared not. Not yet.

"Papa is well," he said, after a moment's hesitation. "Although—" He grinned. "Although he has had to make a few *adjustments*."

I frowned. Bonaparte did not care for "adjustments."

"She calls him Popo, for one thing."

Emperor Popo?

"She likes her bedroom icy cold."

Bonaparte could not tolerate the cold!

"She becomes *vexed* if rushed."

"Oh-oh."

"And she *refuses* to watch tragedies." Eugène sighed. "Consequently the court is required to sit through a burlesque every single night, while the—"

"Bonaparte as well?" I couldn't imagine him sitting through a comedy.

"—while the Emperor sleeps in his chair."

"And does he . . . ?" I tilted my head, smiled, my finger on my chin—as if posing a light, almost fanciful question. "Does he *love* her, do you think?"

Eugène looked down at the worn carpet. "It's different, Maman."

*Thursday, early afternoon—Château de Navarre.*
A lovely morning with my son. I showed him the new herb bed, my roses and lilacs, the pretty cascades and pools, the charming vistas. "Already you've created a paradise here," he said.

"It's peaceful." Isolated, in truth: but I didn't want him to worry. "And just think: no intrigues."

"No *clan*, you mean," he said, for even the new Empress has been made to suffer. "Even Auguste," he confided.*

*June 10, Sunday—Malmaison.*
I'm back at Malmaison again, at last. It is quiet except for the distant crack and fizz of the fire-rockets. Most of my staff are in Paris at the fêtes in honour of the Emperor and Empress. The servants will return drunken and gay. I plan to be asleep.

*Mon amie, I'd like very much to see you. I need to know that you are happy and well. Never doubt the sincerity of my feelings for you. They shall last until I die. N.*

*June 13.*
Bonaparte arrived this morning precisely at ten. A startled maid directed him to the garden, where I was tending roses. I hurried toward him, then stopped short. (We were being watched.) I *would* not weep!

We sat side by side on a curved stone bench for over an hour—talking

---

* *Eugène's wife Auguste wrote her brother regarding the Bonaparte family: "When one has known them at close quarters one can only despise them. I could never have conceived anything so abominable as their ill-breeding. It is torture to have to go about with such people."*

and talking, as if nothing has changed between us. "I understand Prince Mecklenburg-Schwerin made you a proposal," he said.

"Who told you that?" I'd been touched (and surprised) by the offer, but had not given it more than a moment's thought.

"So it's true? I think you should accept."

"He's young. It wouldn't be fair to him." And in my heart I was still married, still very much in love with my husband.

At my urging, Bonaparte talked to me about Marie-Louise, his difficulties and concerns. (She's not pregnant yet, which worries me.) "And unfortunately she's exceedingly jealous of you," he said. "She was upset to learn that you are back at Malmaison. I had to use the utmost secrecy to come see you today."

"Perhaps if I met her." I want Marie-Louise to regard me as an older sister, as someone she can confide in, learn from. I could help her. I could tell her what pleased the Emperor—and what did not. I could tell her how to tend to his delicate health, how to calm his easily ruffled temper.

"Impossible! She's a child in many ways." Bonaparte stood, paced. "And perhaps she is right, perhaps she has good reason to be jealous. It's likely for the best that you will be going to Aix-les-Bains to take the waters soon."

For the best that I go away—and stay away.


*June 18—Aix-les-Bains.*
I've arrived at the spa, exhausted from days and nights of travel. Already I long for home.


*July 6, 1810*
*Chère Maman,*
   *I've just received shocking news: I don't know what to make of it. In what Papa calls an "act of madness," Louis has abdicated the throne of Holland, disappearing with his beloved dog.\**

---

\* *The water spaniel jumped out the open window of Louis's carriage at a posting house. It fell under the wheels and was crushed to death.*

So I am no longer a queen, Maman. I am not unhappy, I confess. I have no ambition but to lead a quiet life with my boys.

I hope the spa treatment at Aix-les-Bains is proving beneficial for your nerves. Is it true that Madame de Souza and her son Charles are both there? Perhaps I will visit.

Your loving and dutiful daughter, Hortense

Note—I spoke with Madame Clari Rémusat at Talleyrand's salon. She looks remarkably well.

And another—Empress Marie-Louise is suspected to be with child.


September 14, Saint-Cloud
Mon amie, the Empress has been with child for four months. She is well. Do not doubt the interest I take in you, the feelings I have for you. N.


November 11—Malmaison.
I am back at Malmaison, but for only a few weeks. I've had a fever, but I'm better today. Dr. Corvisart has ordered rest. The Château de Navarre won't be ready until the end of next week, in any case.


6:15 P.M.
Countess d'Arberg has just informed me that an Imperial baptism was held yesterday. Bonaparte and Marie-Louise baptized a number of infants—sons and daughters of the grandees of the Empire. Every baby girl brought to the font was named Josephine, unfortunately. This will only inflame Marie-Louise's jealousy of me. I had hoped it would be different. I don't want to go to damp, cold Navarre right now, but I know I must.


December 9, 1810, Milan
Chère Maman,
I'm now the father of a big, healthy son. The labour was difficult, but my lovely Auguste seems to be out of danger. Don't worry—we'll do exactly as the midwife says.

*My girls are thrilled to have a brother. Augustus Karl Eugen Napoleon he will be named—Augustus, for short. Do you like it? Little Josephine asked me to send you this drawing she made of him. You can see that he has a healthy crop of black hair. Eugénie has decided that Augustus is her doll—she will be two on Christmas Eve. It's hard to believe. Where does the time go?*

*I think your decision to go to Navarre until after the birth is wise, Maman.*

*I must be off—I hear the baby crying!*

*Your very proud and happy son, Eugène*


*March 19, 1811—Château de Navarre, Évreux.*

The villagers of Évreux came in carts harnessed to field nags, reciting verses that they'd written in my honour. They presented me with a bust they'd had made of me, decorated with a crown of wilting spring flowers.


*March 20—Château de Navarre.*

I was resting, nursing a head pain, when I heard the bells begin to ring in town. "The child is born!" I heard someone call out. A gun salute was followed by another a minute later, and then another, and then another. The silence after the twenty-first salute seemed an eternity. And then . . . one more. *Twenty-two* guns: a boy!*

Thank God! My sacrifice has not been in vain. The Empire has an heir.

---

* *Twenty-one guns announced the birth of a girl, a hundred and one a boy. In Paris, on hearing the decisive twenty-second shot, the* Gazette de France *reported: "One single cry, one alone rose in Paris and made the walls of that old palace where the hero's son had just been born tremble, and round which the crowd was so thick that there was not room even for a fly. Flags waved in the air, handkerchiefs fluttered—people ran hither and thither, embracing one another, announcing the news with laughter and tears of joy."*

*In which all is for naught*

*March 21, 1811—Château de Navarre.*
Eugène embraced me at the door, sweeping me off my feet. "Our prayers have been answered."

"Bonaparte must be overjoyed!"

"He commanded me to come to you immediately," he said, leaning against the wall so that a servant could pull off his muddy boots. "He's going to write to you tonight, he said. He can't take his eyes off the baby."

"Coffee and breakfast cakes," I told a maid. "And a bottle of champagne," I called out to her. "Come," I said, taking my son's hand, pulling him into the drawing room. "I want to hear *all* about it."

And I did. Grands Dieux—the young Empress had very nearly died. "Oh, the poor girl."

"It was awful, Maman. They had to pull the baby out by the feet. Marie-Louise fainted dead away, mercifully. The accoucheur was in a frightful state. *Imagine.* At one point he told Papa that he was going to have to choose between the life of the child and the life of the Empress. Papa never hesitated—he told the doctor to save Marie-Louise."

"But she's all right?"

"It's early yet, of course. She seems well—fatigued, of course."

"And the baby?" King of Rome.

"A big boy."

Mon Dieu—and feet first.

"They thought he was dead, but he revived. A lusty crier," he said, grinning broadly.

"Bonaparte loves children so much." A child, at last—and a *son*. "And so, no doubt, there is much celebrating in Paris?"

"Except on the part of the *sisters*," Eugène said, imitating their long faces. "All they could think of was that their influence would be lessened, that *their* children would lose rank."

"Why does that not surprise me?" I said as the maid came in with a collation. "A toast," I said, handing my son a glass of champagne. "To the King of Rome. To *peace*."

"To the Emperor!"

"*And* to his wife," I said, raising my glass. I sacrificed my marriage for this baby, but young Marie-Louise had very nearly sacrificed her life.


*March 22, Paris*
*Mon amie, I received your letter. Thank you. My son is big and very well. He has my chest, my mouth and my eyes. I hope that he will accomplish his destiny. N.*


*April 2—Malmaison, at last.*
How beautiful Malmaison is, the air sweet, the flowers blooming. I've been all morning with my gardeners. Yet even so my thoughts pull ever toward Paris, toward *them*.


*May 18, Saturday.*
My daughter appeared like a fairy angel, her cheeks pink under a lime green velvet hat with a high feathered crown. She has gained weight, which is encouraging. I suspect she's in love (at last), for she blushed when I inquired about aide-de-camp Charles Flahaut.

She stayed only an hour, telling me all about the new baby. "He's big and handsome—although he does take after *her*," she said, wrinkling her nose.

"But people say the Empress Marie-Louise is pretty."

"Big jaw, Maman." (We giggled, I confess.)

She told me Marie-Louise is childlike in her attachment to the

Emperor, that she weeps to be separated from him for even a minute, but also does not care to travel. "That makes it difficult," I said, concerned. "An emperor must travel." Especially Bonaparte.

"Especially now," Hortense said, filling me in. Russia is refusing to enforce the blockade against England.

"I don't understand. Tsar Alexandre agreed. He gave Bonaparte his word."

"And now there is even talk of war," she said with a grimace.

With Russia? What a terrible thought! "Does it look serious?"

Hortense started to answer when her boys came running; they wanted to ride the pony, they said. "I'm afraid we must go," Hortense told them, tying her hat-strings. "I have an engagement in town."

I persuaded her to leave the children with me for a few days. We waved until her coach was out of sight and then I rang for cakes while the pony was being tacked up. All the while we chattered, chattered, chattered. Petit and Oui-Oui are so sweetly excited about the new baby in the family—"Little King," they call him.

Petit is mature for a six-year-old, I think, but Oui-Oui is still very much a baby. He seems a bit anxious about being three now. "Uncle says I am grown," he told me solemnly. Their Uncle Napoleon, who insists on their company at his midday meal, who supervises their lessons, who is tending a rose garden at Saint-Cloud.

"Himself?" I asked, incredulous.

"He's going to be a gardener when he grows up," Oui-Oui told me.

"Yes, I think so." Oh Bonaparte! "And what about the Empress? Do you see her often?"

Petit shrugged. "I don't think she likes us. We're wiggly, she says."

"But Grandmaman does!" Oui-Oui sang, diving into my arms.


*[Undated]*
Petit, to Mimi: "Maman spoils me when I'm good, but Grandmaman spoils me all the time."

And this afternoon, in the woods, Oui-Oui threw his cap in the air, exclaiming, "Oh, how I love nature!"

How I love *them*.

Hortense came for the boys this morning. She looked distressed about something, so I lured her into the rose garden to talk. At last she confessed: Caroline, who is supposed to stand as godmother at the baptism, can't leave Naples. She has asked Hortense to take her place.

"That's quite an honour," I said.

"But the ceremony will be held in Notre-Dame, Maman."

Then I understood. Little Napoleon's tomb is there. "You haven't been in since . . . ?"

She shook her head. "I'm so afraid I'll break down!"


*June 9, Sunday.*

Little King was baptized today. The procession schedule was posted in the market: at two o'clock the Imperial coaches would arrive at Notre-Dame.

I'd planned a number of activities to keep my mind occupied, but with the gun salutes and church bells ringing, it was impossible. At noon I told Mimi: "We're going." She looked alarmed. "Incognito," I assured her. I would wear a broad-brimmed hat and a mask. "I *have* to see." Had to see the Empress, the *baby*. "We'll take the landau." It is a plain vehicle, without insignia, used for riding in the park when the weather is good. "If we leave now, we can get there in time."

I hadn't reckoned on the crowds, however. It was well after three by the time the coach driver had fought his way into the heart of the city. I asked Antoine to let us down a few blocks from the route. "We'll walk."

The streets were thronged. It was all the troops could do to hold people back. Festive banners had been hung from the rooftops and everywhere I looked I saw garlands of flowers. "Let's wait here," I told Mimi, ducking into a recess. Stone steps leading up to the door of a boot-maker's shop afforded a view over the heads of the crowd.

And wait we did: four, four-thirty, five. The crowd began to thin, the hungry citizens reluctantly returning home. Mimi and I edged our way closer to the street. By luck, we found a spot that gave us a clear view. At five-thirty, at last, guns sounded and bells rang.

"What do you suppose that means?" a woman standing beside us asked.

"That the Emperor and Empress have just left the palace," I told her.

"It won't be long now," someone behind us said. My heart thrilled to the distant sound of drums, a marching band.

"They're coming!" a man behind us yelled.

I looked at Mimi and grinned. "It's exciting on the street."

"I see it," a child straddling a man's shoulders cried out as the glittering coronation coach pulled into view, drawn by eight white horses, just like out of a fairy tale. "Where's the baby?" the boy demanded.

Bonaparte, in purple velvet and gold, looked out over the crowd. He's thinking of his work, I thought. He's wondering how long this ceremony is going to take. He's gauging the enthusiasm of the people. He's thinking how uncomfortable his jacket is.

"Empress Marie-Louise is prettier than I expected her to be," Mimi said, covering her face with her shawl.

Marie-Louise. Big lower lip, strong jaw, plump. I thought she'd be more attractive. And she seemed bored—disdainful even. "She's younger than I expected." Only a girl. She was dressed—not very elegantly—in white satin, wearing a diadem of brilliants. *My* diadem.

"The other one used to smile," the woman beside us said. "This one never does."

"I see the baby!" the boy cried out behind us. "He's in the next carriage. He's dressed in white with red ribbons."

Everyone craned to see as the second carriage pulled into view. The King of Rome was held by Madame de Montesquiou, his nanny. The fat, complacent baby was sucking his thumb. I blew him a kiss, my blessing.

*Monday, June 10, 4:30 or so—Malmaison.*
Hortense was full of stories about the Imperial baptism. "I'm so relieved that it's over." She'd gone to Notre-Dame the night before and persuaded the guards to let her in. In the empty cathedral she'd fallen to her knees before little Napoleon's tomb and wept. "It was a good thing," she assured me, seeing my stricken look. "The next day I was able to get through the ceremony without a tear."

Now that the baptism is over, she would like to take the waters, she said. Could I look after the boys? (Gladly!) On leaving, she embraced me somewhat stiffly, and with reserve. Something about the way she walks makes me think of a woman with child. No—*surely* she would tell me.

*Lake Maggiore, September 2, 1811*
*Chère Maman,*
*I must stay away longer than I expected. My health is a little frail.*
*I am sending some trinkets for Petit and Oui-Oui. How I miss them! Embrace them for me. Speak to them often of their maman. I hope to be back in October. Will they even remember me after four months?*
*How are your eyes? (No weeping, remember!) Are you applying the salve I sent you?*
*I smiled, I confess, on learning that you are trying to make "economies." Your heart is too good, maman. Your hand is always open.*
*Ah, my tender, gentle maman—the trials of this world do weigh upon me. We are punished for our pleasures; if only we were rewarded for our pain.*
*Your loving and dutiful daughter, Hortense*

*October 11—Malmaison.*
Hortense returned in time for Petit's seventh-year birthday fête. She is thinner, and has an air of melancholy. I suspect, but will not ask; know, but cannot say.

*[Undated]*
Bonaparte came to see me today. He seemed gloomy—it was clear that there is much on his mind. "Tsar Alexandre refuses to enforce the blockade against England," he said, his hands on his knees. "And he promised! He's shipping hemp to England—he *knows* it's used to make rigging for their Navy. A continental blockade is the only way to get England to the peace table."

I watched Bonaparte go out the gate with a heavy heart. There will be war again soon, I fear. I saw it in his eyes. *Le feu sacré.*

*February 11, 1812, Shrove Tuesday—Malmaison.*

Carnival. Tonight there is a costume ball at the Tuileries—a ball to which I have not been invited, of course. Hortense will be performing a quadrille. She was here yesterday, showing me her intricate choreography, the lovely costumes. "Please come, Maman. I want you to see it! Nobody would know. You'd be in costume."

I told her it was too risky, but that was only a partial truth. I cannot bear the thought of seeing Bonaparte attend to his young wife while I stand alone in the shadows.

*February 12, Ash Wednesday.*

"Your daughter's quadrille was *brilliant*," Mademoiselle Avrillion told me. "You should have heard the cheers! Men were standing on their chairs to see her perform. What a talent she has, every move so precise, so light, so . . ." She made a floating motion with her hand. "So *elegant*. And her troupe of dancers—they were absolutely magical. It brought tears to my eyes to see them. Queen Caroline looked as if she was going to have a fit, she was so angry. Oh, everyone clapped for her dance certainly, but only out of politeness. All that dreadful clumping! And the Emperor? He loved your daughter's quadrille, it was easy enough to see, but otherwise . . . ? Three times I saw him yawn and pull out his timepiece. And when he and the Empress stood to take their leave, you know what I heard him hiss at her? 'Try to be graceful.'"

"Oh, the poor girl."

"Your Majesty, she didn't smile, not even once."

*Monday, early afternoon at Malmaison, March 9.*

Bonaparte stood at a distance, in full view of his aides. It had been months since we'd seen one another, but I had been expecting him. It was, after all, our sixteenth wedding anniversary.

"You've gained weight," he said with a smile.

"So have you." Even so, he looked unhealthy. "How are you, Bonaparte?"

"Well enough." He needed to get back in shape, he said, for the coming campaign. He'd been hunting every day in the Bois de

Boulogne, to toughen himself. He'd managed to "disappear" this morning, in order to visit me.

"You can stay a few minutes?" I invited him to join me on the stone bench under the tulip tree. "I want to hear all about your son." He would have his first birthday in two days.

"He's a big, healthy boy—a bit of a temper, though."

Like his father, I thought fondly. "Petit and Oui-Oui tell me so many stories about him. I think it's wonderful, the time you take with the children."

"Marie-Louise thinks it unnatural."

I'd heard that Marie-Louise rarely saw her baby, that weeks went by without her sending for him. "Certainly it's unusual for a man to enjoy the company of children the way you do." To *dote* on them. "I'd love to see your son, Bonaparte."

"I've been thinking about that," he said. "It will have to be arranged carefully, so that Marie-Louise does not find out."


*[Undated]*
Baron de Canisy, first equerry to the Little King, has let me know that Madame de Montesquiou will be taking the child to the park of Bagatelle next Sunday. I am to wait for her in the little château there.


*Sunday, a beautiful spring day, bright and crisp.*
I rode to Bagatelle, as arranged.* As soon as I saw the Imperial carriage approaching, I went to the little room at the back. Soon the matronly figure of Madame de Montesquiou appeared with the baby in her arms. I stood, bowed: the King of Rome.

"What a *surprise* to see you, Your Majesty," Madame de Montesquiou

---

* Madame de Montesquiou has left the following account: "I arranged with Baron de Canisy that I would tell him as I got into the carriage that I left him the choice where we would go. A little time later, I would call out to him that if the baby needed to stop, we would go to Bagatelle. In effect, we arrived there. In entering the courtyard, Baron de Canisy announced, with a show of surprise, that the Empress Josephine was there. I responded that it was too late to turn back—it would be improper."

said in carrying tones. (This was the fiction we'd arranged.) "I'm going to rest with the baby here for a moment," she told her attendants in the other room.

She sat down beside me, gently prying open the baby's grip on her hat ribbon. "You see what a good baby he is? Watch." She bounced him on her knees to make him laugh.

Big forehead, heavy jaw. "He takes after the Empress," I said, catching the baby's eye, making a funny face at him. He gazed at me for a long moment and then jammed his fist into his mouth. Lively eyes—Bonaparte's eyes.

"But his spirit is that of his father," the nanny said with a laugh, struggling to hold onto the baby as he squirmed to climb down. "Quite *wilful*."

I reached into my basket and brought out a wooden doughnut with brightly coloured objects attached to it, dangled it in front of him. He reached for it, missed, and then reached for it again, closing his fingers around the ring.

"Do you think he'd mind?" I asked, patting my knees.

"He's become particular," she said, "but we could try. He doesn't even let his mother hold him." She shifted the baby onto my lap.

He was quiet, absorbed in the toy. In a reverie of emotion, I inhaled his sweet baby scent, and something else, a hint of lemon. "He smells like the Emperor," I said, grinning (eyes stinging).

"He was with his papa just before we came. His papa who said to send you his regards." She looked at me tenderly. "His papa who still misses you very much, Your Majesty," she added quietly.


*April 17, late afternoon.*
Bonaparte leaned forward, his forearms on his knees. We were sitting, as had become our custom, on the curved stone bench in the rose garden, under the tulip tree. "I've sent for Eugène," he told me. "I'm giving him command of the 4th Corps: eighty thousand men. He should be pleased."

"Then it's true, what everyone is saying, that there is going to be war?" Bonaparte's silence gave me the answer. "Who will act as Regent while you are away?"

"I'm not sure who I can trust."

*April 22—Malmaison.*

Eugène has arrived. First he called on Hortense, who lent him a carriage to take to Saint-Cloud. "So you've already been to see Bonaparte?" I asked.

"He was in meetings. He said to come back for dinner." Eugène looked at the clock on the mantel. "Maybe I have time to go fishing."

I laughed. "What you have time for is a talk with your mother. I want to hear all about the children." Josephine, five; Eugénie, three; Augustus, one (already).

"And Auguste is due again in only three months," Eugène said, proudly showing me the chain of miniature portraits he carried with him, one for each child. "I promised her the war would be over by then."

The *war.* "She's going to miss you." And worry.

"I already miss *her*, Maman." He started when the pendulum clock began to strike the hour. "Papa's waiting!"


*9:15 P.M., a balmy evening.*

"Well?" I demanded, meeting Eugène at the door. I'd been anxiously waiting for him to return.

"I got to hold the baby—Little King, as the boys call him. But only for a moment. He was fussing—teething, his nurse said. Twelve teeth at thirteen months bodes well, don't you think?"

"And your meeting with Bonaparte?"

He took off his hat and ran his fingers through his hair. "He asked me to act as Regent while he's on campaign."

"That's wonderful!" I said, pretending to be surprised.

"I refused, Maman."

I put my hand to my chest. Refused?

"It's a great honour, I know, but how could I sit at a desk in Paris while my men were fighting?"

So much more was at stake than a battle or two! Didn't he see that? "What did Bonaparte say?" I asked, disheartened.

"He said he'd have felt the same."

*April 30.*
Every able man in the Empire, it seems, has rushed to join La Grande
Armée.* I am guarded by sixteen disabled soldiers, who sadly must stay
behind. All of my good horses have been drafted.


*May 2, Saturday, late afternoon.*
Bands blaring, bells pealing, Eugène and his men left for Poland this
morning, their muskets decorated with flowers, people hanging out the
windows cheering: our glorious Grande Armée.


*Friday, May 8, storm threatening.*
"I've come to say goodbye," Bonaparte said, his eyes solemn.

"It has been a long time since you left on campaign."

"I had hoped it wouldn't come to this."

Yes, certainly. The marriage to Marie-Louise, the birth of an heir—all
this should have secured a lasting peace.

"At least I leave knowing that if anything should happen to me, the
Empire will endure in my son."

"You will miss him."

We were both of us uncomfortable, both aware that this was the first time
he'd be going into battle without a "good luck" embrace. He looked at me
for a long moment, and then his footman opened the carriage door. I
watched the carriage pull through the gates, not even daring to blow a kiss.

* The Grande Armée (Grand Army) was the largest army of all time. It was made up of
200,000 men from France, 150,000 from Germany, 80,000 from Italy, 60,000 from Poland and
110,000 volunteers from other countries.

## In which we are defeated

*November 18, 1812—Malmaison.*
We've been months without news, rumours only. We wait and we worry. We worry and we pray.


*November 30, Monday.*
A young woman, not more than twenty, accompanied by an elderly maid, came out to Malmaison today. Mademoiselle Aurélie de Beaumont, she introduced herself, turning her straw hat in her white-gloved hands. Her father, Monsieur de Beaumont, was the bosom friend of Monsieur Bataille.

Auguste Bataille? "Monsieur Bataille is one of my son's aides."

She nodded, withdrawing some folded papers from the crown of her hat. "He has been sending my father letters."

"Of the campaign?" My heart jumped. News—*true* news, is rare. The official bulletins sent to Paris cannot be trusted, I know.

"My father suggested that I copy the letters out for you. He thought you might desire to have news of your son, Your Majesty."

"Yes," I said, almost breathless.

"This is one of the originals." Aurélie showed me a scrap of paper. The writing was minuscule, crossed.* "Sometimes I have to use a glass to make it out." She promised to return when the next letter came.

---

* *A letter was said to be "crossed" when the letter-writer filled a sheet of paper, then turned the page sideways and continued writing across the filled-in sheet.*

*Plock. Mon ami, we've been in this Polish town for almost two weeks, await-ing orders from the Emperor. It feels as if we're in the middle of nowhere. A number of us have fallen ill. The Prince Eugène's baggage and horses have finally arrived so he will be able to tour his regiments. Salut et amitiés, Bataille.*

*Thorn. Mon ami, we're expecting the Emperor any day. I've been busy trying to find food for the troops and hay for the horses. We were allotted some corn, three hundred bulls and thirty thousand bushels of oats, but the corn was green and the horses got colic, and many of the soldiers have dysentery from the sour black bread. Salut, Bataille.*

*Soldau. Mon ami, from Thorn we marched to Soldau. The villages are wretched. Prince Eugène sleeps in a tent, in spite of the cold. We have eighty thousand men to feed and only a few sacks of corn. Amitiés pour toujours, Bataille.*

*Late evening.*
Plock, Thorn, Soldau. I've found a map in Bonaparte's cabinet and am tracing the route. They are so very far away.

*Mon ami, we are in Russia now, looking for an army to fight. It's a dull landscape—nothing but trees (a few birches) and sand. It's after ten P.M. but so bright I am writing this without a candle. The sun wakes us at two in the morning. Toujours, Bataille.*

*Vitebsk. Mon ami, how can we go on? By day we boil; by night we freeze. We've over three hundred sick soldiers—our men are dying of sunstroke. Thousands of horses have perished. The Emperor arrived last night. He insists on pressing on to Smolensk. Ten more days, if we survive. Adieu, Bataille.*

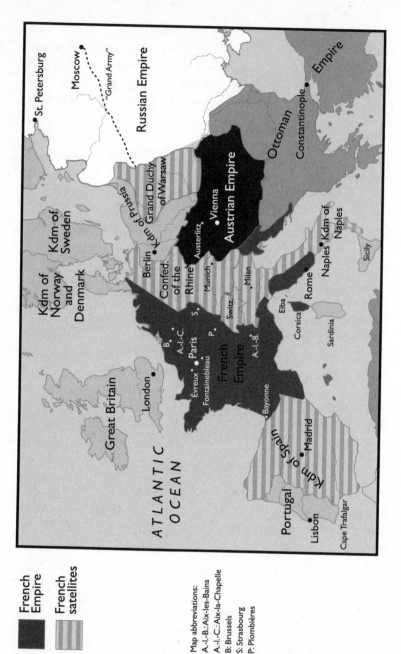

French Empire

French satellites

Map abbreviations:
A.-l.-B.: Aix-les-Bains
A.-l.-C.: Aix-la-Chapelle
B: Brussels
S: Strasbourg
P: Plombières

*December 3—Malmaison.*
I'm ill with concern. Bataille's letters both reassure and dismay. I worked all morning in the hothouse with the gardeners, but my thoughts turn always toward the northeast, toward Russia, that barren land.

*Mon ami, we've made it to Smolensk, a heap of smoking ruins. Moscow is "only" two hundred miles more, the Emperor tells us—but one mile more will kill us. The farther we chase after the enemy, the farther we are from home, the farther from food and shelter. Amitiés, Bataille.*

*Mon ami, the Russian army has come to a stop—at last we will see battle. Some Cossacks were taken prisoner—savages with bandy legs. They gulped down tumblers of brandy as if it were water, holding their empty glasses out for more. Their horses are stumpy and have long tails. They're much impressed by King Murat, his plumes and glitter. They have asked to have him as their "hetman." They're welcome to him! Salut, Bataille.*

*Mon ami, it was bloody. Prince Eugène was rallying his troops when thousands of Cossacks fell on his reserve. He galloped back to face them head-to-head. A victory, yes, but hard won. Adieu, excéllent ami, Bataille.*

*Mon ami, as we crested a hill and caught sight of the city, the soldiers broke into a run crying out, "Moscow! Moscow!" The spires and onion-shaped domes glittered in the sun like a mirage—and a mirage it is, for the Russians, a barbarous race devoid of all honour, have set fire to it, the most magnificent ancient city in all of Europe. As I write this, flames light up the sky. We are sheltered in a small wooden house outside the city. The landscape is dreary: cabbage fields and more cabbage fields. Amitiés, Bataille.*

*December 14—Malmaison, cold, but bright.*

I was honoured this afternoon by a visit from Countess Walewska and her child: "the Polish wife" and her son by Bonaparte. (He looks *just* like Bonaparte—I was so moved.) It has taken numerous entreaties to persuade the young Countess to call on me, but now that she has, she will return, I hope. We are uniquely united by our prayers for a singular man. She turned pale and very nearly swooned after I showed her the letters from Bataille.

*Mon ami, the Tsar has not responded to the Emperor's request for peace. King Murat has persuaded the Emperor that the Russians are in disarray and that the Cossacks are ready to quit. Therefore, we press on. Amitiés, Bataille.*

*Mon ami, King Murat was defeated by the Cossacks so we're on the move again, heading for home, if we can make it. We're a sorry spectacle, soldiers pushing wheelbarrows of looted treasure, a rabble of prostitutes following after. The cannon keep getting stuck in the mud. À toi pour toujours, Bataille.*

*Mon ami, Prince Eugène had a glorious battle, worthy of every honour, but we've suffered heavy casualties, and now a frost has lamed hundreds of our horses overnight. In consequence, the Emperor ordered all the carts emptied into a lake. We watched as priceless works of art sank through the ice. The enormous cross of Ivan the Terrible was the last to disappear, like some dreadful omen of doom. Cossacks harass us. They encircle us, whooping like wild beasts. We march in a freezing fog. We are at the end of the world. Bataille.*

[Undated]

"Your Majesty, would you prefer it if I did not bring you the letters?" Mademoiselle Aurélie asked, clutching her straw hat.

"No! Please, you *must* bring them," I said, giving her two of my rings.

*Mon ami, what was left of the Grande Armée was destroyed on the icy marshes. Those who escaped drowning were set upon by Cossacks. Prince Eugène managed to save what was left of his troops. Luck stays with him, such as it is. Two horses have been shot from under him. Bataille.*

*December 17, Thursday, chilly.*
A stunned despair hangs over Paris. The extent of our losses in Russia—the death of so many of our men—has finally been revealed in *Le Moniteur*. Every heart is filled with the terrible apprehension that a loved one will likely not return. I am sick with fear for Eugène, Bonaparte.

*December 19, Saturday—Malmaison.*
The familiar sight of Bonaparte's courier cantering up the drive stopped my heart. I pushed the window open, leaned out. "Monsieur Moustache! What's happened?"

"The Emperor is at the palace," he yelled up.

"Bonaparte? He's in *Paris*?" How was that possible?

Moustache nodded, catching his breath. "He sent me to tell you. And to let you know that your son is well."

That's the last I remember, for I fainted.

*Sunday.*
Bonaparte looked like a Cossack in his bear coat and hat. His face was dark, burnt from the sun. "I can't stay long." He took my hand, did not let it go. "Come outside."

We sat on the cold stone bench under the tulip tree, its branches bare, the winter garden grey and featureless. I listened to his account with tears in my heart. He'd hastened back to calm the populace, he said. He feared people would panic on learning the extent of the losses. The campaign would have been glorious if the Russian winter had not come early, and had not been so severe. All he needed was to raise another army.

I could not speak. *Another* army? Where will the soldiers come from?

Did he not see that we are a nation of women—a nation of women in mourning? The only men left are either old or crippled.

Four hundred thousand is all it would take, he said.

*February 28, 1813.*

Carnival season opens as the wounded return, yet even so the fêtes and the balls go on—"the balls for wooden legs," people call them now.

Every day, it seems, we learn of some new tragedy. One of Carlotta's brothers has died in Russia. Mademoiselle Avrillion's aunt has lost two sons, and the third son who did return lost his hands due to frost.

*March 6.*

We've been working all week making lint bandages for the wounded. My drawing room looks like a hospital.

*Wednesday, April 14—Malmaison.*

Bonaparte and I sat for two hours this morning under our tulip tree. He told me charming stories about his son, now two and temperamental, and complained of his young wife (she wipes her mouth after he kisses her). Then he began to speak of the war, the coming campaign, his conviction that he will be victorious this time, that a peace will be signed. "But not a dishonourable peace. Not a peace at any price."

I want to believe him—and why should I not? Has he not wrought miracles?

He touched my hand before he left, promising to give Eugène my love. "My prayers are always with you."

"I was happy here," he said, looking out over the gardens.

*April 26, Mansfeld*
*Chère Maman,*
*Forgive my penmanship: I've developed a bit of rheumatism.*

*My army is on the move again, riding out to join the Emperor. I'm confident that this new campaign will be over quickly and that soon there will be peace. Both sides long for it.*

*Take care, lovely Maman, and give my love to my sister and her boys. We sing her songs often—they give us courage.*

*Your loving son, Eugène*

*May 5.*
Bonaparte has had a victory! "Funds up to 76.90," Mimi said.

*Friday, May 7.*
*Another* victory! Cannons have been booming all morning.

*May 12, 1813, Lützen*
*Chère Maman,*

*The big battle has been won. The Emperor is allowing me to return to Milan—to my beautiful Auguste and our children. I'm to raise and train another army.*

*I bade the Emperor Godspeed about an hour ago. He looked worn. We are all weary. I've been at war for a year.*

*Your devoted son, Eugène*

*June 11, a glorious day.*
At last, an armistice has been signed. Dare we believe we shall have peace?

*August 23, Monday, early evening.*
The Emperor of Austria has denounced the armistice, declared war on France. Mon Dieu—Marie-Louise's *father*. How could he turn on us—turn on his own *daughter?*

*October 30—Malmaison.*

Disaster at Leipzig. I wept when I read the words: *The French army has lost.* Reduced to only forty thousand men!

I've locked myself in my room—to pace, pray, weep. Against all better judgement, I've written Bonaparte.*

*November 9.*

Bonaparte is back, at the head of his defeated army. He returned without fanfare, without cannon or marching bands.

*December 2.*

On this, the anniversary of the coronation, on Bonaparte's "lucky" day, I received a distressed letter from Milan—from my lovely Auguste. Her father, jolly King Max of Bavaria, has joined the enemy! Furthermore, he tried to persuade Eugène to do so as well.

Of course Eugène refused. "God gave me an angel as a husband," Auguste wrote. And God gave an angel to him.

*January 3, 1814, Monday.*

Hortense's cheeks were flushed. "Maman, terrible news! An army of over one hundred thousand Cossacks has crossed the Rhine and is headed for Paris. I've never seen the Empress Marie-Louise so upset. Do you know what she told me? That she takes bad luck with her wherever she goes, that everyone who comes near her is made to suffer."

"And what did Bonaparte say?"

"He told her that's superstitious nonsense."

"No—I mean about the Cossacks!"

"He said not to worry—he has a plan."

---

* *Josephine wrote: "Sire, I saw in the bulletin that you suffered a great loss and I wept. Your sorrows are mine, they will always be in my heart. I am writing you because I am not able to resist the need to tell you this, in the same way that I am unable to stop loving you with all my heart."*

*January 14.*

A call has been sounded: soldiers needed.

"I'm going to volunteer," Oui-Oui told me in all seriousness.

"Me, too," Petit echoed.

I explained that there were age requirements.

"Uncle said he wanted us."

"Everyone," Oui-Oui explained gravely. "Even *old* men."

Even old men, indeed: dear old Gontier just informed me that he was going to enlist. "Gontier, you mustn't!" He is over sixty, I am sure.

But nothing I could do or say would dissuade him. I gave him a good pony, one of the few I have left, so many have been drafted.


*Saturday, January 22.*

Bonaparte stood by his carriage as he told me that he was leaving for battle in the morning. In three months he would be either victorious or dead.

*Le feu sacré.* "I didn't come to make you weep," he said, perplexed by my response.

I tried to dissemble my fear. All of Europe has joined forces against him. He has only fifty thousand men. Victory is impossible!

But "impossible" is not a French word, I reminded myself. "May I—" Kiss you, I almost said. "I would like to wish you good luck." Dropping a curtsey.

Bonaparte looked at me for a long moment. "Remember me, Josephine," he said, stepping back, tipping his hat.


*February 4.*

Terrible rumours—it's being said that Bonaparte's troops have been repulsed, forced to retreat onto French soil. I don't know what to believe. I sent Mimi into Paris to find out what she could. She returned with a worried look: prayers are being said at Notre-Dame and the Louvre's collections are being packed.

*February 18, 1814, Milan*
*Chère Maman,*

*I fear this will distress you terribly, but you must know. Caroline and Joachim have joined the enemy and this morning Joachim made an open declaration of war against the Army of Italy—against me. I do not need to tell you the degree of my disgust—nor the depth of my sympathy for the Emperor. Such a "family" he must suffer.*

*Your loyal son, Eugène*


*March 28.*
People are coming into Paris in droves, fleeing in advance of the enemy.

"Bonaparte will save us," I assured Hortense, rolling lint bandages, stacking them up. "He calculates everything so carefully, taking into account every possible outcome. Surprise has always been his strategy. No doubt this is part of his plan."


*[Undated]*
A cobbler from town just came to warn me that he has met wounded soldiers on the road. They've told him the enemy is near. What does that mean: *near?*


*Tuileries. Maman, we've learned that the enemy is approaching from the south. Empress Marie-Louise intends to flee Paris in the morning with the baby. You must go to Navarre—immediately. Take every precaution. Don't worry about me and the boys. I'll get word to you. Hortense.*


*March 29—Mantes, 7:20 P.M.*
Hortense's note came after midnight, in the dead of night. I woke everyone, gave the order that we would be leaving Malmaison in the morning, taking as much as we could with us. We've decided to leave the farm

animals, the orangutan and the birds in the care of the groundskeeper, but to take the pugs and the horses.

Mimi and I stayed up stitching my gems into the lining of a wadded skirt. The remaining jewellery we put into strongboxes, along with the oak box of Bonaparte's letters—my true treasure. It was almost three in the morning when we finished. We would be leaving early, at seven—there was not much time for sleep. I bade Mimi goodnight and got into bed. I lay there for some time, listening to the spring rain, thinking of Empress Marie-Louise all alone in that big ormolu bed in the Tuileries Palace. Was she sleeping? Or, like me, was she tormented with fear and doubt—and *guilt*, surely, at fleeing Paris.

I got out of bed. Taking the night candle, I slipped down the stairs and walked through the château. Would my beloved Malmaison be ravaged by Cossacks, my treasures carried off? I ran my fingers over the harp strings—the light, rippling sound brought back the memory of summer evenings. What a magical place Malmaison has been—what a magical *life* I've had here.

I went into the study—the room Bonaparte had worked in, built an empire in. I spun the globe. Where is he?

I returned to bed with a heavy heart. At dawn I woke sweating. It was grey and raining, a cold spring drizzle that made me shiver. No point lighting a fire, I told Mimi, slipping into my wadded gown.

We didn't reach Mantes until nightfall. It was slow going with all the horses in the pouring rain.

This inn is full of people escaping Paris. I am Madame Mercier, I tell them. Nothing is known; everything whispered. I am dead with exhaustion, but rest eludes me. Where is Hortense as I write this? Where is Bonaparte? What is happening in Paris?

# *In which I entertain the enemy*

*April 1, 1814—Navarre.*

It was the sound of boys' voices in the cavernous entry that brought me to my feet. I very nearly collided with Hortense at the door. "Mon Dieu, it *is* you!" I threw my arms around her, pressed her to my heart. "Forgive me, we've been tormented not knowing."

The servants crowded into the room. Hortense paused before announcing, "We've capitulated."

There was a moment of incomprehension, followed by cries of disbelief.

"Where is the Emperor?" I demanded.

"Maman, I don't know! All I know is that a treaty of surrender has been signed and that the Empress and the baby are in the southwest, at Blois."


*Saturday, April 2.*

"The army wouldn't take me," old Gontier said sheepishly. He returned to Malmaison on my sturdy little pony only to be told that we'd fled to the north. He's been three days travelling to reach us.

He left Paris on Wednesday, he said. In the morning he heard cannon in the direction of Saint-Chaumont. As he headed out, he saw Russian soldiers on the road. "Well-behaved lads wearing caps with green leaves stuck in them." There had been no sign of plunder or violence, he said, which is a great relief to us all. (Though hard to believe.)

*Sunday.*
As Hortense slept, I took the boys to Mass at the cathedral in Évreux. The town was quiet—there was little to indicate that France had fallen. The Imperial sign over the posting house had been taken down, but nothing put up in its place.

"Are you sad, Grandmaman?" Petit asked. He is tall for a boy of nine; his name no longer suits him.

"Very."

"I am, too," Oui-Oui said, snuggling into me for warmth. The weather was bright, but brisk. "I had to leave my rocking horse behind," he told me, his lip quivering.

"I will get you a new one," I promised.

"No, Grandmaman," Petit solemnly informed me. "Maman says we must suffer like everyone, that we are nobodies now."


*April 4, Monday—Château de Navarre.*
At last, a note from my groundskeeper: Russian guards have been assigned to protect Malmaison. He included a copy of *Le Moniteur*, but all that it contained was Tsar Alexandre's proclamation.

Where is Bonaparte? What is happening?


*April 7.*
Shattering news. The Pretender is to take back the throne.


*Later . . .*
Worse news yet. *Talleyrand* is at the head of the new provisional government, in league with the enemy.

Chameleon! Opportunist! That he should prove a traitor does not surprise me in the least. Indeed, I am calmed by the revelation of his true colours. But what dismays me beyond measure is the story that it was *Clari* who helped him, that it was she who opened the gates of Paris to the enemy.

We've received journals from Paris. I'm filled with disgust, a bitter taste. Is there no honour? No loyalty? Bonaparte's marshals—men he favoured and raised to glory—have rushed to publicly proclaim themselves in favour of the Pretender. These men—*soldiers*—swore fidelity and allegiance to Bonaparte, and now they attack him, portray him as an ogre.

Disillusion has weakened my heart. Defeat at the hands of the enemy is nothing compared to this corruption from within. I weep for Bonaparte, for us all.

*April 8.*

Mimi woke me in the night, tugging gently on my toes. "There's someone downstairs who would like to see you, Yeyette—Monsieur de Maussion. The bookkeeper," she reminded me, lighting a lamp. "He has news of the Emperor, he said."

"Of Bonaparte?" I sat up, my heart pounding.

Monsieur de Maussion stood by the dying fire in the drawing room. He was wearing a short green hunting coat. A small travelling pistol hung from his broad belt. "Your Majesty," he said, bowing stiffly from the waist. "I beg forgiveness for disturbing your repose."

"I am told you have news of the Emperor," I said, taking a seat, neglecting civilities in my anxiety. I gestured to him to sit down in the chair opposite, but he stood ramrod-stiff, as if at attention.

"The Emperor is at Fontainebleau," he announced. "He has abdicated and will be sent into exile. I've been—"

"Exile?" I was alarmed, but relieved, as well. At least Bonaparte was not to be executed.

"To Elba, Your Majesty. I've been—"

"Where is Elba?"

"Elba is a small island in the Mediterranean, Your Majesty, separated from the Italian mainland by the Strait of Piombino. I've been—"

"A very *small* island, is it not, Monsieur?"

"Between one and three-and-a-half leagues in width, Your Majesty, six leagues in length. I've been—"

"But that's smaller than the park at Malmaison!"

"I do not recall the dimensions of the park at Malmaison, Your Majesty. I've been—"

"Have you *seen* the Emperor, Monsieur de Maussion? Have you talked to him?"

"I have seen him, Your Majesty, but no, I have not spoken with him. I've been—"

"*Please* tell me: how did he look to you?"

Monsieur de Maussion frowned. "Like the Emperor, Your Majesty."

I pressed my fist against my mouth. If only I could see Bonaparte! I would know in a glance how he was feeling. I would know if he was sleeping, if he was eating, if his stomach—oh, his sensitive stomach!—was upsetting him. I would know by the abruptness of his movements if a falling fit might be threatening. "Yes, of course," I said weakly, remembering myself. "Did he look . . . *well*, did you think?" I asked, using the cuff of my sleeve to dry my eyes. It wasn't fair, I knew, to ask this man to see with the eyes of a wife.

"Yes, Your Majesty. I've been asked by the French Ambassador to Russia, the Duke de Vicenza, to—"

"De Caulaincourt?"

Monsieur de Maussion nodded. "Yes, he asked me to—"

"De Caulaincourt is with the Emperor?" Gentle, aristocratic Armand de Caulaincourt. It would comfort me to know that he was with Bonaparte.

"Yes, Your Majesty. He sent me expressly to tell you to do what you can." This last in a rush of words for fear I would yet again interrupt.

"What does that mean?" *Do what you can.*

"It means that you try to seek favour for yourself and your children at the court of the enemy, Your Majesty."


*April 13.*

A note from Armand de Caulaincourt. He urges me to return to Paris—it's in my best interest, he said. It behooves me to show myself, press my case with the Tsar. It is the Emperor's wish. *Je le veux.*

And then, a note at the bottom, in the secretary's tidy script: *Your Majesty, it is urgent that they be persuaded to be charitable with respect to the Emperor.*

I'm packing.

"Very well," Hortense said, but in a tone that suggested she did not approve.

"You don't think I should go," I said.

"Do what you want, Maman," she said, "but I won't be going with you."

"You'll stay here?" I was relieved, frankly. She and the boys would be safer at Navarre.

"I've decided I must go to Blois, to see the Empress."

"But Hortense, that's risky!" A show of allegiance to the Empress would be held against her. "You must think of your future, and that of your boys."

"It's my duty, Maman," she insisted. "Marie-Louise is young and very much alone. Imagine the torment she must feel! You have raised me to do what is honourable."

"I understand," I said, turning away, both furious and proud.


*April 15, Friday—Malmaison.*

It was disconcerting to see Russian guards at the gates to Malmaison. I tried to explain who I was, but it wasn't until my groundskeeper came hobbling that I was allowed in. "What happened?" I asked, alarmed, for he had bandages on his head and one arm was in a sling.

"Cossacks. I tried to stop them, Your Majesty, but—" He shrugged, a movement that made him wince. "They broke the leg off the table in the entryway, but that was all. It was the orangutan that scared them away."

And so it was with a sense of disbelief that I walked back into my home of priceless treasures to find it all untouched. But for the Russians at my gate, one would not know that the nation had fallen.

*[Undated]*

Oh, the stories: that the theatres in Paris closed for only one day—the day Paris capitulated—that the actors carried on even as cannon boomed. That it was Joseph Bonaparte who gave the order to raise the white flag of surrender and then disappeared, not even handing over command. (Just as he had in Madrid—the coward!) That everyone in Paris is wearing a Bourbon white rosette, that Bourbon banners are everywhere. (Ingrates!) That the Pretender's brother, the Count d'Artois, has arrived, that he wears a powdered wig topped by a silly hat. That his servants wear strange Gothic tunics with enormous crosses hanging from the buttonholes. That Cossacks sleep with their boots on. That shopkeepers are doing a brisk trade. That in the Tuileries Palace they have simply pasted Bourbon fleur-de-lis over the Imperial bees. That Talma played for the Tsar and was forced by the crowd to proclaim, "Long live King Louis XVIII," but left the stage in tears. (Poor man.) That Empress Marie-Louise's father, the Emperor of Austria, paraded down the Champs-Élysées in full daylight, not even trying to hide the fact that he had profited from his daughter's misfortune. That the people were falling over themselves to bow before the new regime, claiming that they'd detested "that monster" Napoleon. That even his family has deserted him.

How devastating all this is.

*Almost midnight (can't sleep).*

Clari looked like a matron in her bonnet, clutching a wicker basket. "I was afraid you would not receive me," she said, fingering the gold cross that hung from a yellow velvet ribbon around her neck.

"It is not in my nature to hold a grudge," I said, feeling vindictive nonetheless. She had betrayed Bonaparte, the nation, *me*. "Speak your business." And go.

"The Tsar Alexandre begs permission to call on you."

"I take it you are his servant, then?"

"I help out where I can." Her sharp nose in the air.

"I understand you helped the enemy enter Paris." Clari and Talleyrand. "Such helpfulness is well rewarded, I expect."

"I did not intend to hurt *you*."

"I think you should go."

"Will you consent to receive the Tsar? It would be to Napoleon's advantage for you to do so."

"How dare you speak his name!" A vase fell to the floor, shattered. "He murdered the Duke d'Enghien!"

"You're a fool. If anyone can be held responsible for the death of the Duke d'Enghien, it is your friend Talleyrand. He's the one who persuaded Bonaparte to arrest the Duke."

"He told me you would say that."

I took two steps toward her, trembling.

"Forgive me, Your Majesty," she whispered, backing out through the door.

*April 16, Saturday.*

Tsar Alexandre arrived attended by only a few guards. "I am honoured," he said, bowing before me. He is attractive, a man of middle years—thirty-five? thirty-six?—imposingly tall, with golden curls, pale blue eyes.

I was surprised (and reassured) by his show of respect. I am the ex-wife of an ex-emperor. He is the victor, ruler of one of the most powerful countries on earth. "Your Majesty," I answered with self-loathing, "the honour is all mine." As I spoke, he stooped close, and I recalled that he was slightly deaf. "The honour is all mine," I repeated, raising my voice, flushing (knowing the servants could hear).

I took him on the usual tour of Malmaison—through the gallery, the music room, the theatre, the rose garden, the hothouse—and even through the dairy (my Swiss cows interested him). I found him easy to talk to, for his French is excellent and his mind of an inquiring nature. (So like Bonaparte in that respect.) He wanted to know about the grafting technique my gardeners had been using with success on evergreen shrubs, how much sun was advisable on tulip beds, what proportion of cow-dung was added to the compost used for the auriculas, how much milk my cows yielded.

We paused in front of the hothouses, talking of theatre: he'd been to see Talma in *Iphigénie en Aulide* at the Théâtre Français and had been tremendously moved. "Although," he said, "there was an incident afterward that was painful to witness, I confess."

"I have heard of it." Poor Talma—I was beginning to fear his mind had turned. He'd physically attacked Geoffroy for having written a critical review.

"The actor remains attached to the Emperor. His feelings are honourable and should be respected."

"We *all* remain attached to the Emperor," I said with more heat than was wise.

"I understand," the Tsar said with feeling.

But it is you who have destroyed him! my heart cried out.

It was then that we were—fortunately perhaps—diverted by the sound of children's voices: Petit and Oui-Oui! They raced down the path, stopping short when they saw the tall and imposing stranger beside me. "Come, come," I said, stooping to embrace them. Why were they at Malmaison? Hortense had taken the boys with her to Blois, to see the Empress Marie-Louise. "I'd like to introduce you to Tsar Alexandre of Russia."

Petit looked concerned. "It's all right," I whispered. "Make your best bow."

The Tsar smiled and bowed in turn.

"Where is your mother?" I asked anxiously.

"She's coming *slowly*. She has to stop to admire *everything*," Oui-Oui said, dramatically rolling his eyes.

"We didn't stay long at Blois," Petit informed us, pulling at a ringlet. (Oh dear, I thought. Now the Tsar will know that Hortense went to see Empress Marie-Louise.)

"We've been in a carriage for *days*," Oui-Oui said, rolling his eyes yet again.

Hortense had stopped beside one of the rose beds. I waved to catch her eye. She smiled—*There* you are!—then frowned, twirling her percale sun umbrella, taking in the figure beside me.

"We're over here, Maman," Petit said.

"With a Cossack," Oui-Oui cried out, throwing up his cap.

"Shush," Petit said, frowning at his younger brother.

Tsar Alexandre laughed. (I was relieved.)

"I'm so happy to see you," I said, embracing my daughter.

"Malmaison looks fine. Nothing was taken?"

"Thanks to the Tsar Alexandre," I said, introducing my daughter.

"Honoured," she said coolly, with only a slight dip of her head.

"Can I offer you both an ice and tea?" Hortense wasn't helping!

"Cossacks drink vodka," Oui-Oui said.

"Pardon?" Hortense said with a reproving look.

"I'd be delighted," the Tsar said. "And yes, if you had vodka . . ."
Pulling the brim of the child's cap down over his eyes.


"He impresses me," I told Hortense after the Tsar had left. "He seems sincere in his desire to put an end to the conflicts."

Hortense shrugged.

"You disapprove of my receiving him, don't you?"

"We discussed this at Navarre, Maman. I understand your reasoning perfectly."

"Then why . . . ?"

"It was disconcerting, I admit, seeing *you* entertaining the enemy."

"Hortense, Tsar Alexandre has the power to help you and your children." As well as the power to ruin them.

"There is nothing we need."

"Now is not the time for idealism! Do you want to be exiled from France, never to return? It might be wise to be civil, at least for the sake of your boys. And, need I remind you, for Eugène's sake, *my* sake—*Bonaparte's* sake. Who do you think must make the decision about Bonaparte's future? The Tsar—that man you treated so rudely."

We both burst into tears. "Oh, forgive me, Maman! I've had such a terrible two days."

And then it all came out: how after Hortense's long and arduous trip to Blois, the Empress Marie-Louise had kept her waiting, how when she'd finally received Hortense, she'd told her that it would be best, perhaps, if Hortense left, because her father, the Emperor of Austria, was coming to get her, and how the one thing that *really* worried her was that her father might force her to follow Bonaparte into exile.

I sat for a moment in stunned silence. "But I thought Marie-Louise was sincerely attached to Bonaparte. I thought you said she couldn't stand to be separated from him even for one day."

"I thought so, too, Maman."

Poor Bonaparte! Everyone is deserting him, even his wife. "And the boy?" The son he loves so much.

Hortense smiled sadly. "He was so happy to see Petit and Oui-Oui. You know what he told them? That he knows he's not a king any more because he doesn't have any pages. Madame de Montesquiou told me he cries for his papa."

I stood and went to the fireplace, holding my hands out over the embers. "I'd go to Bonaparte in a minute if I could."

Hortense came up behind me, held me in her arms. "I know you would, Maman."


*Early evening.*

The sight of the horse cantering up the laneway puzzled me. The rider looked familiar, yet I could not place him. I went to the garden gate, my basket full of cut roses. "Moustache?" But I wasn't sure. "What's happened to your . . . ?" I pointed to my upper lip.

"I cut it off and gave it to the Emperor," he said, handing a letter to me. "I told him he already has my heart; he might as well have my namesake."

How touching, I wanted to say, but could not speak. The letter was from Bonaparte.


*Fontainebleau*

*I wrote you on the eighth of this month (it was Friday), but perhaps you never received my letter. The fighting was still going on so it may have been intercepted.*

*I won't repeat what I said—I complained then about my situation. Today I am better. I've had an enormous weight lifted from me.*

*So many things have not been told. So many have a false opinion! I loaded benefits on thousands of poor wretches. What did they do for me? They betrayed me—yes, all of them. With the exception of good Eugène, so worthy of you and me.*

*Adieu, my dear Josephine. Resign yourself as I have. I will never forget you. N.*

"Thank you," I told Moustache, slipping a diamond ring off my hand. He'd aged during his years as Bonaparte's courier; his face was lined with furrows. "How is he?"

"The Emperor?"

I leaned toward him. "Yes." *Tell me.*

"He's . . . not well, Your Majesty." His voice had a pleading quality.

I nodded. *And?*

He looked away. "I'm told he tried to poison himself."

There was a century of silence, heavy and ponderous and dangerous. "*Tried?*"

"Apparently it was not strong enough."

"Thank you, Moustache," I said weakly, turning away.


Grand Dieu. I *must* get to him.


*Very late, past 2:00 A.M., I think.*

Perhaps I'm going mad. My emotions rage within me. Oh, Bonaparte! I feel so helpless—


*Monday.*

Shortly after dinner I called for my carriage. "Fontainebleau," I told the driver.

"But Your Majesty . . ." It would take hours and the roads were not safe, Antoine said. "And what about an escort?" The men were just sitting down to eat.

"I won't be needing them," I informed him. "I'll be travelling incognito." *Alone.*


The leather mask was curiously reassuring. I was of the world, but not part of it. Lulled by the sway of the coach, I watched the sun set, the moon rise, the outline of the hills become liquid and dark. I sat as if in a trance, without thinking.

Nearing Fontainebleau, we stopped at a posting house to refresh the horses. "Where in Fontainebleau?" Antoine asked.

"The château."

"But . . ." The Emperor was inside the château. It would be heavily under guard.

"I am expected," I said, and even believed it to be true.

As we neared the sentry hut by the main gate, I perceived my foolishness. There were Russian guards everywhere.

I thumped the ceiling of the carriage roof with my fist: stop, please! I had to reconsider. "Your Majesty?" my driver called down.

"Wait a moment, Antoine." A few lights were visible in the château: Bonaparte's suite. A light went out, then flickered.

Out, on, out, on—as if someone were pacing back and forth, back and forth. "Pull over to the side of the roadway," I said, my eyes on that light. On. Out. On. Out. And then on.

I waited, listening to the frogs croaking—so very like Martinico, I thought, but for the wind, which carried no scent of the sea. "Home now," I said, tears streaming.

## In which my heart is with my husband

*April 19, 1814, Tuesday—Malmaison.*
"The French ambassador to Russia wishes to speak to you, Your Majesty."

Armand de Caulaincourt! At last. "Thank you for coming so promptly," I told him, once civilities had been exchanged, once we'd made what has become a ritual acknowledgment that the world has changed, and that we are all rather deceitfully playing new roles.

"I've been intending to call in any case, Your Majesty." His blue eyes looked sad, resigned.

"About the Emperor?"

There was a moment of embarrassed hesitation. Which emperor? "About the Tsar Alexandre," he said apologetically.

"But you've seen Bonaparte? You've been to Fontainebleau?"

"Yes, Your Majesty. I've been with him throughout his . . . this terrible ordeal."

Ah! I thought, as if I had come upon a treasure. "I've been so anxious for news of him, Armand," I said, dropping all formality. "I've been told terrible things." I toyed with my handkerchief, already damp. "I've heard—" How did one ask such a thing? "Is it true, did the Emperor try to . . . ?"

"I'm afraid so, Your Majesty." Armand sat forward. "I don't know if you are aware, but before the last Spanish campaign, the Emperor had taken to wearing a small sachet suspended from a ribbon around his neck."

The sachet!

"It contained a deadly mix of belladonna and white hellebore, in case of capture in battle. He did consume it, but it was old, no longer potent." He smiled ruefully. "You can imagine the Emperor's frustration."

"But it must have made him terribly sick." I felt ill at the thought. Bonaparte is so sensitive. The least thing causes him terrible pain.

"Very." Constant stuck his finger down Bonaparte's throat, to make him retch, he told me. "Then I forced him to drink milk. We thought he was dying," Armand said, his voice thick. "And *he* thought so, too. At the time he asked me to tell you that you'd been very much on his mind."

The sound of a canary singing broke the poignant silence. Oh, Bonaparte! "When will he be leaving for Elba, Armand?"

"Tomorrow."

Oh, mon Dieu, so soon! "I *must* see him." One last time. *Please.*

Armand shook his head, not meeting my eyes. "I'm sorry, but it just isn't possible. The Emperor hopes to be reunited with his wife and child. Anything that might jeopardize that reunion must not—" He stopped. It pained him to have to explain.

"I understand," I lied, thinking with bitterness of Marie-Louise's reluctance. "I would never do anything that might cause the Emperor more pain than he has already had to endure."

A maid entered with a tray of refreshments. I took the opportunity to recover my composure. "You said you wished to speak to me about the Tsar Alexandre," I said, lifting my cup of tea, testing the steadiness of my hand. I took a careful sip. "He paid me a call several days ago. I found him to be respectful and courteous."

"As ambassador to Russia, I've come to know Tsar Alexandre well. Certainly he honours me with his confidence. The last time I saw him, he appeared dejected. He confided to me that your daughter had received him coldly."

"Hortense and I had a talk after he left," I told Armand, chagrined. "These are *difficult* times. Hortense is fierce in her loyalty. However, I believe she now understands the importance of diplomacy."

"He would very much like to call again, Your Majesty, and has asked if this coming Friday might suit you, for supper."

"Of course." One did not refuse such a request.

"You are wise. The Emperor likely would have been executed had it not been for the Tsar's intervention."

Before he left, I gave Armand a small parcel of things to give to Bonaparte, things he would be able to take with him into exile: a miniature of myself (from the first year of our marriage), Hortense's book of songs, some bulbs—including an asphodel lily, so helpful for his sensitive digestion. "And *this*," I said, enclosing the talisman Charlemagne had worn, heading into battle. "Tell him . . ." I turned away. Tell him I'll be waiting.

*April 20, Wednesday.*

In bed all day. I hardly have the strength to walk. I can't bear the thought of Bonaparte's isolation.

I imagine him saying farewell to his men, riding captive in a carriage, surrounded by Russian guards. They will likely take the road to Lyons, but this time there will be no triumphal arches, no cheering crowds. This time it will be different.

I see him so clearly! He sits motionless (for once), watching but unseeing. What are his thoughts?

He will travel incognito, no doubt, but even so people will line the road to watch him pass—their "little corporal," this man they once worshipped as if he were God. Oh, such glory! Will the world ever see the like of it again? It's like a dream now.

And, as in a dream, I see the people standing in silent witness, watching his carriage as it trundles by. They lower their heads, as if for a funeral procession. The veterans with their wooden legs—are they there? Yes, I see them with tears in their eyes.

He did not want it so.

Adieu, Bonaparte. My spirit-friend.

*[Undated]*

I have given away almost half of my wardrobe to the servants. They are overjoyed. Tomorrow I will go through my papers. I've a ringing in my ears that prevents me from sleeping. I've so little strength. Where is he now?

*April 22, Friday.*
Tsar Alexandre came to dinner tonight. He played with the boys—Hortense was gracious and even charming. I watched as if from a distance, thinking of Bonaparte.

*May 3.*
A gloomy day. The Pretender—King Louis XVIII now—has entered Paris. I'm told that the crowd was large, but unenthusiastic. "He's boring," Carlotta reported, as if this were an evil thing. I listen with indifference, my thoughts elsewhere.

*May 8.*
Eugène has arrived from Milan. He held me in his arms, telling me not to worry so, telling me that he'd been to the palace to see the King.
    "Already?"
    "It went better than I thought it would."
    If my children are taken care of, then I can rest, I thought. "I've been sorting through my things. I have something I'd like to give Auguste." Eugène looked at my diamonds in astonishment. "Don't worry, I'm giving quite a few to Hortense, as well. And I've a crate of things I'm putting aside for you."
    He looked at me for a long moment, his eyes filling. "Aren't you going to need them, Maman?"

*[Undated]*
Hortense, Eugène, the Tsar Alexandre: young, ardent, idealistic. How ironic that they have formed a friendship. I sit by the fire and make polite

conversation, but my heart is far, far away, on a small Mediterranean island. *Elba.* He should be there by now. The sea.


*May 12, Thursday.*
"But Maman, you *must* come," Hortense begged. She's invited Tsar Alexandre to her country château at Saint-Leu and now she is anxious. "After all, aren't *you* the one who insisted I entertain him? It won't be the same without you."

"I know," I protested, "but—" The ringing in my ears has become constant, making sleep impossible. I've been having spells of dizziness and malaise. And melancholy—oh, melancholy.

"But you'll come?"

"Of course, darling." I smiled.


*May 14—Saint-Leu.*
I managed the journey to Saint-Leu well enough, but shortly after I arrived yet another of my spells came on. How they frighten me! I'm in the guestroom, recovering. Mademoiselle Avrillion has brought me an infusion of lemon water and orange flowers. The weather is cold and damp—it was foolish of me to have gone for a ride in Hortense's open calèche. I can hear Tsar Alexandre's and Eugène's voices downstairs, Hortense's musical laugh.

I must gather strength for the dinner hour. "Restore the balance," Bonaparte used to say. Oh, Bonaparte!


*May 15—Saint-Leu still.*
The carriage is being prepared for my return to Malmaison. I'm still not well. While I have the energy, I want to record my conversation with the Tsar last night.

Before dinner, I sent word that I wished to see him. He came immediately to my room. "Your Majesty," he said, "I fear we have tired you. Don't stand," he insisted, asking leave to take the chair closest to me.

"Tsar Alexandre, I am—"

"Your Majesty, I implore you—please call me Alex. I command it," he said with a smile.

"Very well, then, *Alex*."

"I have a confession to make." He placed his right hand over his heart. "I love your family." I searched for a dry handkerchief, weakening again.

"Oh, you see, I *have* wearied you."

"Tsar—*Alex*, I mean, I must speak frankly. I am anxious about what is to become of Hortense and Eugène. I won't be able to sleep until their futures are settled."

"I will see to it immediately," he said, kissing my hand.

If only I could believe him. Bonaparte trusted him, and was betrayed.

*May 16, Monday—Malmaison.*
Home again, but still *so* ill. A devastating weakness has come over me, an unbearable sorrow. Dr. Horeau prescribed an emetic, which has not helped.

*May 23.*
Eugène escorted me to my bedchamber after dinner tonight with guests.

"I'm fine," I insisted.

He put his hand on my forehead. "You must rest, Maman."

"I *will* rest, Eugène—once it's determined how you and Hortense are to be looked after."

"Maman, Maman, Maman."

Hortense came to my room shortly after. "Eugène said you aren't well."

"I'm just a little tired."

"I'm calling the doctor."

*Tuesday.*
"Dr. Horeau is right, you should not receive guests," Mimi said. "You should be in bed."

"Did Dr. Horeau tell you to say that?"

Mimi reached her hand out to feel my forehead but I ducked away. I had a fever, I knew, but it was slight. "Send the cook up," I insisted. The Tsar and the Russian Grand Dukes would be coming for dinner. The menu had to be carefully considered. Any day now, they—"the Powers," Mimi calls them—will make a decision about Hortense and Eugène.

*May 26.*

Slight fever, light-headed. I'm writing this in bed, covered with a terrible rash. Hortense wants to summon her doctor, but that would upset Dr. Horeau, I know. "I will do whatever you tell me," I told him. Now I've a disgusting plaster on my throat.

Still no word from "the Powers."

*[Undated]*

Hortense looked puzzled when I told her I needed her to fetch a box hidden behind my hats. "Please—get it down for me," I told her.

"Why don't I get a manservant to help?"

"No," I said, falling back against the damp pillows.

The oak strongbox *was* heavy, to judge by Hortense's pink cheeks, the beads of perspiration along her hairline. She plunked it down on the bedside table. "No, on the bed," I said, struggling to sit. "The key is in the upper left drawer of my escritoire—under the box of calling cards."

The metal felt cold in my hands. I fiddled with the lock and eventually got it to open. And there it all was: my old journals, the Church marriage certificate, Bonaparte's letters tied up in a scarlet ribbon. These I took out, carefully. Mere scraps of paper—yet such passion, such burning love. "I'd like you to put these in a safe spot," I told Hortense. She leaned forward to reach for them. "But not yet," I said, pulling back. I wasn't ready to let them go. "And these," I said, indicating the old journals. "I'd like you to burn them . . . when the time comes." Hortense looked confused. "Can I trust you?" She made a tiny nod, her expression wary. "And one other thing: you must not read them."

"Maman, why are you doing this?"

"Just *promise.*"

She exhaled with exasperation. "Yes, Maman," she said, like a dutiful schoolgirl.

I smiled. "Do you know how much I love you?"

Her eyes filled. "Yes, Maman." A sniff. Two. She pulled a handkerchief out of her bodice. "And I love you!"

I opened my arms and she fell into bed beside me, as if she were a girl again, not the woman she'd become. I held her close until her breathing steadied. The pendulum clock rang four gongs. And then, in the heavy silence that followed, I asked, very quietly, "Hortense, is there anything you want to tell me?"

"No, Maman, why do you ask?" she said, sitting up and wiping her cheeks with the backs of her hands.

"It doesn't matter." *Remember that.*

*[Undated]*

I can't talk, but I can write. My throat! The children are so very dear. I see the distress in their eyes—the *fear*. I love them so much! At least they have each other.

Oh, Bonaparte, if only . . .

*Postscript*

Sire, Emperor (Papa),

I am writing to you now with tears in my heart. Your beloved Josephine passed away suddenly. We still cannot comprehend that she is no longer with us. Our distress is made more bearable knowing that she lived a full life, a life full of love. She loved us. She loved you—profoundly.

She got chilled riding in the Montmorency woods and developed a fatal infection in her throat. However, it would seem to have begun earlier, for after your exile, her constitution steadily weakened. Mademoiselle Avrillion tells us that she was subject to episodes of a devouring melancholy—so very unlike her, as you know.

It didn't help that she insisted on rising, insisted on entertaining. She was anxious about me and Hortense, how our futures would be decided. We have just now learned that we will not be exiled, that we may keep our properties and the titles that go with them. So perhaps she rests in peace.

But at what a cost! On the return from Saint-Leu, her doctor-in-ordinary advised a small dose of ipecacuanha as a corrective. Although suffering, she seemed better, well enough even to breakfast with guests. That night she tried to join us in a game of prison-bars on the lawn, but had to sit down. After the guests left, she attempted to take her customary stroll through the rose gardens, but became so weak she could not walk and had to be helped back to the château. It was at this point that we began to be alarmed. A few days in retirement revived her once again, but on reading in the news-sheets that little Napoleon's body was to be exhumed, she *relapsed.** Even so, she persevered in her efforts to persuade the Austrian and Russian rulers on our behalf.

Had I known how ill she was, I would have stopped her, Sire. (Not that she would have listened. Her doctor tells us he begged her to stay in bed.) When I left that afternoon, she seemed to have worsened. Although her doctor assured us that she had no fever and was not in danger, she was having difficulty speaking. I think this was on the Monday, which would make it the twenty-third of May. The next morning she woke with pain in her throat. Dr. Horeau administered a purgative and tried to persuade her to stay in bed. She refused: the Tsar and the Russian Grand Dukes were expected for dinner. She rallied, but partway into the meal was forced to excuse herself. I saw her to her room.

Wednesday she woke covered with a rash. She'd had a terrible night, Mimi told me: pains in her chest, fluxions of the stomach, a shivering fever. The rash did go away in the evening. Even so Hortense insisted that a plaster be applied to her throat.

On Friday the Tsar sent his own doctor, Sir James Wylie—a Scot, not an Englishman. All three doctors were concerned: the back of Maman's throat was dark crimson. That night her fever raged. A blister was applied between her shoulders, and mustard plasters to her feet.

But it was too late, Sire. We were losing the battle. Saturday morning her fever was high and it was hard to feel her pulse. She breathed with difficulty and was in pain, slipping in and out of delirium. In a futile effort to save her, the doctors applied a plaster to her chest. Hortense brought her boys, but Maman became agitated for fear the air in the room would harm them.

Whitsunday, May 29, the doctors told us there was no hope.† We sent for the curate to administer the last rites. He wasn't home, so Hortense's tutor, Abbé Bertrand, was summoned. At eleven Maman received the last rites. When Hortense and I appeared in the door, she held out her arms to us, but was unable to speak. Oh, the love in her eyes! Hortense swooned and had to be carried to her chamber.

---

* Out of sympathy (and friendship), Tsar Alexandre arranged for the child to be entombed in the chapel of Hortense's château at Saint-Leu.

† An autopsy on Josephine's body revealed an inflamed trachea with a gangrenous spot on the larynx. The lungs were choked with blood.

*At that moment Mimi cried out to me in alarm. I rushed to the bed. Maman slumped against me and I knew she was gone. I held her thus for a time, feeling her spirit like a brilliant light all around me.*

*Mimi told me to go to Hortense—she would put Yeyette to rest, she said, weeping. Hortense was in her room, still insensible. She roused herself, took one look at my eyes and began to weep. "At least you'll have each other," Maman had told me several weeks ago. I hadn't been listening, Sire. She was saying farewell, and I hadn't been listening.*

*Soon after, Hortense and I left for Saint-Leu. We are here now. Hortense is still overcome. It will take time.*

*As you can imagine, the citizens of this nation are overwhelmed with grief at the news that their "Good Empress Josephine" is no longer with them. I was told by old Gontier that the gate could not be opened for the mountain of bouquets piled high there, that the long road from Paris to Malmaison has been thronged with people with tears in their eyes—peasants and aristocrats alike.*

*She was placed in a double casket. Over twenty thousand people came all the way out to Malmaison to pay their last respects. Astonishing. Even the gate here at Saint-Leu is covered with bouquets and letters of sympathy. Really, Papa, it touches us deeply to see such an outpouring of love.*

*"Tell him I am waiting," Maman told Hortense a few days before her death. Fever talk, we thought at the time, but now it all seems so clear. Mimi, who was with her through that last feverish night, says her last words were of you.*

*Did she know how much we loved her? If Maman's death has taught me anything, Sire, it is that one must speak one's heart when one can. I love and honour you as my Emperor and commanding general, but above all as my father. Bon courage, as Corsicans say. May God be with you. I know her spirit will be.*

*Your faithful and devoted son, Eugène*

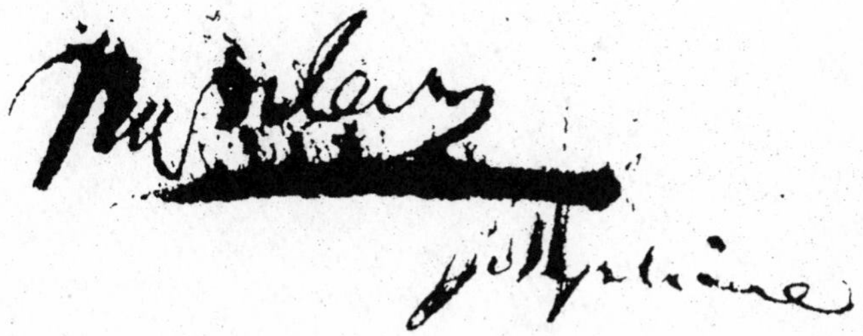

# *Epilogue*

Napoleon escaped from the island of Elba one year later and returned to France, chasing out the Bourbon King Louis XVIII and the Royalists, including Talleyrand and all the others who had betrayed him. (Fouché, who stayed, betrayed Napoleon as well by sending his war plans to England.) This was the period known as the Hundred Days, which ended with Napoleon's defeat by the British and their allies at the Battle of Waterloo. This time Napoleon was banished to St. Helena, a remote island off the southern tip of Africa. He died six years later at the age of fifty-one—of stomach cancer, some say; of poisoning, others claim. His pleas to his mother and Uncle Fesch to send medical help were dismissed by them as a British ploy. They had been convinced by a mystic that Napoleon was perfectly well. On his deathbed Napoleon is reported to have said, with emotion: "I have just seen my good Josephine. She told me we were going to see each other again and that we would never again be separated. She promised me."

All the members of the Bonaparte clan were banished from France.

Madame Mère, who retired to Rome with her half-brother Fesch and daughter Pauline, refused to speak to Caroline after Caroline's betrayal of Napoleon. She died after a fall at the age of eighty-six.

Joseph emigrated to the United States as "Count de Survilliers," making a considerable amount of money on speculative ventures. He died in Florence at the age of seventy-six.

Lucien returned to France to help Napoleon during the Hundred Days. He was refused permission to join Napoleon on St. Helena, and lived out his life in Italy with his wife and eleven children.

Elisa fled to Italy as "Countess de Campignano." She died of a fever near Trieste at forty-three.

Pauline also fled to Italy, where she lived from time to time with her mother in Rome, and even, at the end of her life, with her estranged husband Prince Borghèse. Of all the Bonaparte siblings, Pauline was the most loyal to Napoleon in exile, even managing to visit him on Elba in spite of her delicate health. She died in Florence at the age of forty-five, dressed in a ballgown, with a mirror in her hand.

After abdicating the throne of Holland, Louis settled in Italy, leading a quiet life as a gentleman of letters. He wrote a melancholy novel (*Marie*, about a man who is forced to marry a woman he does not love), poetry and various works relating to Holland and the Empire. He died of apoplexy at the age of sixty-six.

Caroline, deposed Queen of Naples, was considered too dangerous to be allowed to live near any members of her family, and died in isolation in Florence as the "Duchess de Lipona," an anagram for Naples (Napoli). Her husband, Joachim Murat, was executed by a firing squad at the age of forty-eight, clutching portraits of his children. Foolhardy as ever, he had attempted to recover his kingdom of Naples with only thirty men.

Jérôme settled first in Switzerland and then in Italy. He returned to France eventually and lived to see the reign of Napoleon III (Oui-Oui). It is through Jérôme that the Bonaparte name exists today.


The Empress Marie-Louise, object of a deliberate plot on the part of the Austrians to keep her from joining Napoleon, succumbed enthusiastically to the sexual prowess of Count Neipperg, the chamberlain assigned to her for just that purpose. She became indifferent to the fate of her son by Napoleon. The boy—Napoleon II—died of tuberculosis at the age of twenty-two, without issue. ("My life would have been different," he reportedly said, "had Josephine been my mother.") Marie-Louise died in Vienna at the age of fifty-six.

Hortense came to Napoleon's assistance during the Hundred Days, and consequently was exiled after Waterloo. She settled in Switzerland, where she died at the age of fifty-four. Her eldest surviving son, Napoleon-Louis (Petit), died in battle at the age of twenty-seven. Louis-Napoleon (Oui-Oui) was elected to the presidency of France after the Revolution of 1848, becoming Emperor of the French under the name Napoleon III.

Hortense's lover, Charles Flahaut—believed to be Talleyrand's illegitimate son—asked Hortense to marry him, but she refused because Louis was opposed to a divorce, and ultimately Flahaut married another woman. Their illegitimate son, Charles Auguste Demorny, was prominent in the government of Napoleon III, his unacknowledged half-brother.

On condition that Eugène never take up arms again (which prevented him from coming to Napoleon's aid during the Hundred Days), Eugène was offered the title Duke de Leuchtenberg by Tsar Alexandre. Eugène, Auguste and their children settled in Munich, living happily and quietly. He died of apoplexy at the age of forty-three.

Of seven children, six grew to maturity. Each married into royalty:

Josephine married the Crown Prince of Sweden (son of General Bernadotte and Eugénie-Désirée Clary—Joseph and Julie's nephew), becoming Queen of Sweden.

Eugénie married Prince Frederick Hohenzollern-Sigmaringen, a German prince.

Augustus married Queen Maria II of Portugal (but died shortly after).

Amélie married the Emperor of Brazil.

Théodelinde married Guillaume de Württemberg, a German count.

Maximilian married Grand Duchess Maria, daughter of the Tsar of Russia.

Through Eugène, Josephine's progeny live on in most of the royal houses of the world today.

# Chronology

March 9, 1800. Napoleon and Josephine's fourth-year anniversary.

March 29, 1800. Napoleon meets with Royalist agent Cadoudal.

June 18, 1800. The Marquis de Beauharnais dies at Saint-Germain-en-Laye at the age of eighty-six.

October 10, 1800. The Opéra plot: revolutionaries attempt to assassinate Napoleon at the Opéra.

December 24, 1800. Royalist assassination attempt by exploding gunpowder nearly succeeds.

February 9, 1801. Lunéville peace treaty is signed with Austria.

July 7 to August 5, 1801. Josephine goes to the spa at Plombières to be treated for infertility.

January 4, 1802. Hortense and Louis marry.

March 27, 1802. Amiens peace treaty is signed with Britain.

April 18, 1802. Concordat with the Church is celebrated.

June 15 to July 12, 1802. Josephine returns to the spa at Plombières to undergo another treatment for infertility.

August 2, 1802. Napoleon is declared First Consul for Life as the result of a popular vote. (Fouché opposed.)

September 14, 1802. Fouché is demoted.

October 10, 1802. Hortense and Louis's first child is born, Napoleon-Charles.

November 1 or 2, 1802. Pauline Bonaparte's husband, Victor Leclerc, dies of yellow fever in Saint-Domingue (Haiti today).

March 14, 1803. Josephine's Aunt Désirée dies.

May 1803. Josephine's goddaughter, Stéphanie Tascher, fifteen, sails from Martinique on *Le Dard*.

Shortly before May 18, 1803. *Le Dard* is captured by the British.

May 18, 1803. England declares war on France.

August 18, 1803. Stéphanie arrives in France by ship from England, after being held hostage.

February 4, 1804. A Royalist plot to kidnap Napoleon is discovered.

February 19, 1804. General Moreau is arrested.

March 9, 1804. Georges Cadoudal is arrested.

March 15, 1804. Duke d'Enghien is arrested in Germany.

March 21, 1804. Duke d'Enghien is "tried" and executed.

March 27, 1804. Fouché makes a motion in the Senate inviting Napoleon to make his glory "immortal."

April 7, 1804. Napoleon and Josephine ask Louis if they can adopt his son. (Refused.)

May 18, 1804. A new constitution based on the Civil Code is proclaimed. Napoleon is proclaimed hereditary Emperor by a national plebiscite.

June 28, 1804. Cadoudal is executed. General Moreau is banished.

July 10, 1804. Fouché is reinstated as Minister of Police.

July 30–September 11, 1804. Josephine goes to Aix-la-Chapelle to take a treatment for infertility.

October 11, 1804. Hortense and Louis's second son, Napoleon-Louis, is born in Paris.

November 25, 1804. Napoleon receives Pope Pius VII at Fontainebleau.

December 1, 1804. Josephine and Napoleon are married by the Church.

December 2, 1804. Coronation at Notre-Dame. Napoleon and Josephine are crowned Emperor and Empress of the French.

May 26, 1805. Napoleon is crowned King of Italy in Milan.

June 7, 1805. Eugène is named Viceroy of the Kingdom of Italy.

August 1 to August 30, 1805. Josephine goes to Plombières-les-Bains for yet another treatment for infertility.

October 21, 1805. Battle of Trafalgar. The French fleet is defeated.

December 2, 1805. Napoleon scores a decisive victory in the Battle of Austerlitz.

January 14, 1806. Eugène marries Princess Auguste-Amélie of Bavaria in Munich.

June 5, 1806. Louis and Hortense are formally proclaimed King and Queen of Holland.

December 13, 1806. Caroline's reader, Éléonore Denuelle, gives birth to a son, Léon, thought to be fathered by Napoleon (but possibly by Joachim Murat).

May 4, 1807. Louis and Hortense's eldest son, Napoleon-Charles, dies.

July 27, 1807. Napoleon returns after an absence of ten months.

April 21, 1808. Hortense and Louis's third son, Louis-Napoleon, is born prematurely.

December 1808. Eugène intercepts a letter revealing a plot to put Joachim Murat on the throne should Napoleon be killed in battle. Napoleon is alerted.

January 23, 1809. Napoleon returns to Paris from Spain and, shortly afterwards, Talleyrand is demoted.

End of September 1809. Countess Marie Walewska becomes pregnant by Napoleon.

November 30, 1809. Napoleon tells Josephine that they must divorce.

December 15, 1809. Formal divorce ceremony.

December 16, 1809. Josephine moves out of the Tuileries Palace.

March 27, 1810. Napoleon and Austrian Archduchess Marie-Louise meet for the first time at Compiègne.

March 29, 1810. Josephine moves to the Château de Navarre at Évreux.

April 1, 1810. Napoleon and Marie-Louise are married at Saint-Cloud.

May 4, 1810. Napoleon's mistress, Countess Marie Walewska, gives birth to a son in Warsaw.

March 20, 1811. Napoleon and Marie-Louise's son, François-Charles-Joseph-Napoleon II, King of Rome, is born.

September 15 or 16, 1811. Charles Flahaut and Hortense's son is born.

December 17, 1812. *Le Moniteur* prints the XXIX Bulletin, outlining the massive losses of the Grande Armée in Russia.

August 10, 1813. Austria joins the Allies.

August 26–27, 1813. Napoleon defeats the Allies at the Battle of Dresden.

October 16–19, 1813. Battle of Leipzig. Napoleon's army is defeated and reduced to 40,000.

November 22, 1813. Speaking on behalf of the Allies, Auguste's father, King Max of Bavaria, tries (unsuccessfully) to induce Eugène to abandon Napoleon.

February 15, 1814. Joachim Murat makes a declaration of war against Eugène.

March 28, 1814. Empress Marie-Louise and the Bonapartes make a decision to abandon Paris. Josephine gets an urgent message from Hortense: flee.

March 29, 1814. Josephine leaves Malmaison to go to Évreux.

April 1, 1814. Hortense and her two boys arrive at Évreux with the news that Paris has capitulated.

April 6, 1814. Napoleon abdicates.

April 16, 1814. Tsar Alexandre visits Josephine at Malmaison.

May 14, 1814. Tsar Alexandre visits Josephine, Hortense and Eugène at Saint-Leu. Josephine catches a chill.

May 29, 1814. Josephine dies at noon.

February 26, 1815. Napoleon escapes Elba.

March 21, 1815. Napoleon returns to Paris

June 18, 1815. Napoleon is defeated at Waterloo.

June 22, 1815. Napoleon abdicates a second time.

October 15, 1815. Napoleon arrives at Jamestown, St. Helena.

May 5, 1821. Napoleon dies.

# Characters

Agathe: Josephine's scullery maid.

Arberg, Countess d': Josephine's second lady of honour, replacing Chastulé.

Auguié, Adèle: Madame Campan's niece and Hortense's closest friend, as well as her maid.

Avrillion, Mademoiselle: Josephine's mistress of the wardrobe.

Bacchiochi, Elisa Bonaparte (Princess of Piombino, Grand Duchess): Napoleon's eldest sister; married to Félix.

Beauharnais, Eugène (Viceroy of Italy): Josephine's son by her first husband; married Princess Auguste-Amélie of Bavaria and had six children.

Beauharnais, Fanny: Josephine's aunt through her first husband; poet and eccentric.

Beauharnais, Marquis de: the father of Alexandre, Josephine's first husband; married to Josephine's Aunt Désirée.

Bonaparte, Hortense Beauharnais (Queen of Holland): Josephine's daughter by her first husband; married Napoleon's brother Louis and had four sons (little Napoleon, Petit and Oui-Oui by her husband; Charles Auguste Demorny by Charles Flahaut).

Bonaparte, Jérôme (King of Westphalia): Napoleon's youngest sibling; first married Elizabeth Patterson (annulled), then Princess Catherine of Württemberg; one child by his first wife, four by his second.

Bonaparte, Joseph (King of Naples, King of Spain): Napoleon's older brother; married to Julie Clary, by whom he had two daughters.

Bonaparte, Letizia (Signora Letizia, Madame Mère): Napoleon's mother.

Bonaparte, Louis (King of Holland): Napoleon's brother; married Hortense and had three sons.

Bonaparte, Lucien: Napoleon's brother; disowned by him; first married Christine, with whom he had two children; widowed, he married Alexandrine, with whom he had eleven.

Bonaparte, Napoleon (Emperor of the French, King of Italy): first wife, Josephine; second wife, Marie-Louise, by whom he had one son, Napoleon-François-Charles-Joseph.

Borghèse, Pauline Bonaparte (Princess Borghèse): Napoleon's sister, renowned for her beauty; first married to Victor Leclerc, then widowed; subsequently married Prince Camillo Borghèse. Dermide, her son by Leclerc, died at the age of six.

Bourrienne, Fauvelet: Napoleon's first secretary.

Cadoudal, Georges: Royalist agent, convicted of conspiracy.

Cambacérès, Jean-Jacques de: Second Consul, Arch-Chancellor.

Campan, Madame: schoolmistress and former lady-in-waiting to Queen Marie Antoinette.

Caulaincourt, Armand de: French Ambassador to Russia, Minister of Foreign Affairs. Josephine had known his family since before the Revolution and had helped them during the Terror.

Chimay, Thérèse Tallien (Princess de Chimay): Josephine's close friend. Divorced from Tallien (who died indigent, likely suffering from venereal disease) and the mother of a number of illegitimate children by the financier Ouvrard. Ostracized by the court and polite society, she nevertheless married Prince de Chimay. One of her sons by Chimay married a woman whose biological father is believed to have been Napoleon.

Constant: Napoleon's valet.

Corvisart, Dr. Jean: Imperial doctor to Napoleon and Josephine for many years, then doctor to Empress Marie-Louise. He conspired with the Austrians to help keep Marie-Louise and her son from joining Napoleon on Elba by telling her that her health was not strong enough for such a voyage.

Denuelle, Éléonore: Caroline's reader, Napoleon's mistress. Her claim that Napoleon was the father of her son, Léon, was later substantiated.

Désirée, Aunt: see Montardat.

Despréaux, Monsieur: dance master.

Duchâtel, Adèle: Josephine's lady-in-waiting; mistress to Napoleon, courted by Eugène.

Duplan, Monsieur: hairdresser.

Duroc, Christophe: Napoleon's aide and Hortense's first love.

Fesch, Joseph (Archbishop of Lyons, Cardinal): Napoleon's uncle by marriage.

Flahaut, Charles: Hortense's lover and father of her son Charles Auguste Demorny (raised by Flahaut's mother, the romance novelist Madame de Souza, with financial help from Hortense).

Fouché: Minister of Police, at various times; intriguer.

Frangeau, Madame: midwife.

Gazzani, Carlotta: Josephine's reader and Napoleon's mistress (briefly).

Georges, Mademoiselle: actress, Napoleon's mistress.

Gontier: Josephine's elderly manservant.

Grassini: Italian singer, Napoleon's mistress.

Horeau, Dr.: Dr. Corvisart's student; Josephine's physician at the time of her death.

Isabey: portrait artist, art teacher, Josephine's make-up artist.

Junot, Andoche: Napoleon's aide; Governor of Paris; Caroline's lover.

Lavalette, Émilie Beauharnais: Josephine's niece by her first husband; married to Lavalette. After Napoleon's second and final defeat, Émilie disguised herself as a man and took her husband's place in prison (where he'd been condemned to death), allowing him to escape to Bavaria. Tragically, while in prison, she suffered a miscarriage and lost her sanity. Pardoned in 1822, Lavalette returned to his wife in France, but she did not recognize him. However, his attentive care partially restored her memory and their last years together were happy ones.

Leroy, Monsieur: fashion designer.

Méneval: Napoleon's secretary, replacing Fauvelet Bourrienne.

Mimi: Josephine's childhood maid; a mulatto from Martinique, formerly a slave. She married one of Napoleon's cabinet guards and during the Hundred Days gave refuge to Hortense.

Montardat, Désirée: Josephine's godmother and aunt; first married to Monsieur Renaudin, who was suspected of trying to murder her. Her second husband was Marquis de Beauharnais, the father of Josephine's first husband. Shortly after the Marquis's death, she married Pierre Danès de Montardat ("Monsieur Pierre"), the mayor of Saint-Germain-en-Laye.

Moreau: popular general convicted of conspiracy; exiled to America but returned from exile to join the Russian forces. He was killed by a French cannonball at the Battle of Dresden in 1813.

Moustache: Napoleon's courier.

Murat, Caroline Bonaparte (Duchess de Berg, Queen of Naples): Napoleon's youngest sister; married to Joachim Murat, with whom she had four children.

Murat, Joachim (Duke de Berg, King of Naples): Caroline Bonaparte's husband.

Rémusat, Claire ("Clari"): lady-in-waiting to Josephine.

Rochefoucauld, Chastulé, Countess de la: Josephine's distant cousin and lady of honour.

Roustam: Napoleon's Mameluke bodyguard.

Talleyrand: Minister of Foreign Affairs and traitor.

Talma: the most renowned actor of his day.

Tascher, Stéphanie: Josephine's niece and goddaughter.

Thérèse: see Chimay.

Walewska, Countess Marie: Napoleon's Polish mistress, the mother of his son Alexandre.

# Beauharnais Genealogy

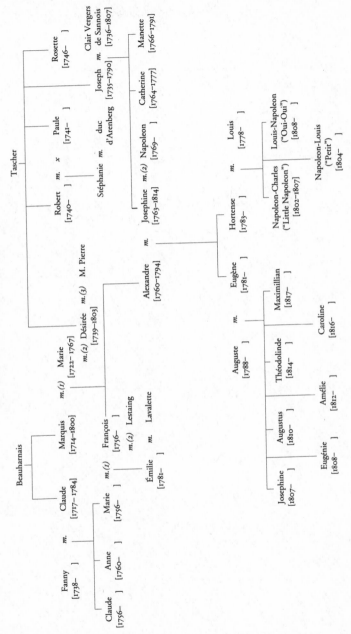

# Bonaparte Genealogy

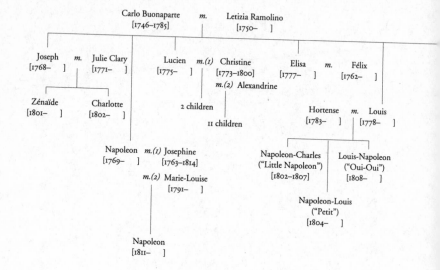

Carlo Buonaparte [1746–1785] *m.* Letizia Ramolino [1750– ]

Joseph [1768– ] *m.* Julie Clary [1771– ]

Lucien [1775– ] *m.(1)* Christine [1773–1800]
*m.(2)* Alexandrine

Elisa [1777– ] *m.* Félix [1762– ]

Zénaïde [1801– ]    Charlotte [1802– ]

2 children

11 children

Hortense [1783– ] *m.* Louis [1778– ]

Napoleon [1769– ] *m.(1)* Josephine [1763–1814]
*m.(2)* Marie-Louise [1791– ]

Napoleon-Charles ("Little Napoleon") [1802–1807]    Louis-Napoleon ("Oui-Oui") [1808– ]

Napoleon-Louis ("Petit") [1804– ]

Napoleon [1811– ]

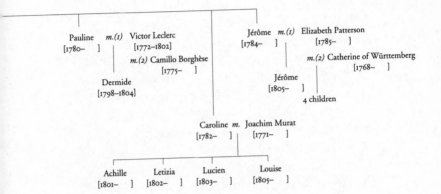

Pauline    *m.(1)*    Victor Leclerc
[1780–  ]         [1772–1802]

           *m.(2)* Camillo Borghèse
                  [1775–  ]

     Dermide
     [1798–1804]

Jérôme    *m.(1)*    Elizabeth Patterson
[1784–  ]         [1785–  ]

           *m.(2)* Catherine of Württemberg
                  [1768–  ]

     Jérôme
     [1805–  ]

        4 children

Caroline    *m.*    Joachim Murat
[1782–  ]         [1771–  ]

Achille      Letizia      Lucien      Louise
[1801–  ]    [1802–  ]    [1803–  ]    [1805–  ]

# Selected Bibliography

Anyone who ventures into the Napoleonic Empire is quickly overwhelmed by the vast number of books that have been published on all aspects of the period. After over a decade of immersion in this moment in history, I still feel I have only scratched the surface. My bibliography now lists almost four hundred titles; I will note only a few.

Researching this novel, I was highly entertained—"diverted" is a suitably eighteenth-century word—by the many memoirs of the period: those of Mademoiselle Avrillion, Fauvelet Bourrienne, Las Cases, Constant, Madame Ducrest, Baron Fain, Fouché, Madame Junot, Méneval, Madame Rémusat, and especially Hortense. In all cases it was necessary to judge the veracity and objectivity of the author (who was, in many cases, a ghost writer), making the search for "truth" rather like trying to find one's way through the hall of mirrors at a fun fair.

For information about Josephine, my mainstays have continued to be: *Impératrice Joséphine, Correspondance, 1782-1814,* compiled and edited by Maurice Catinat, Bernard Chevallier and Christophe Pincemaille (Paris: Histoire Payot, 1996) and *L'impératrice Joséphine* by Bernard Chevallier and Christophe Pincemaille (Paris: Presses de la Renaissance, 1988) as well as Ernest John Knapton's *Empress Josephine* (Cambridge, Massachusetts: Harvard University Press, 1963). An award-winning biography was published as I was in the final stages of this work: Françoise Wagener's *L'Impératrice Joséphine (1763–1814)* (Paris: Flammarion, 1999).

It is difficult to select one particular book about Napoleon: there are so many. Although decidedly pro-Napoleon, Vincent Cronin's *Napoleon*

(London: Collins, 1971) remains one of the best, in my opinion. At the very least it is highly readable and captures the spirit of the time. Frank McLynn's *Napoleon: A Biography* (London: Pimlico, 1998) is a recent and balanced account I consulted frequently.

Other books of note: Joan Bear's *Caroline Murat* (London: Collins, 1972); Jean-Paul Bertaud's *Bonaparte et le duc d'Enghien; le duel des deux Frances* (Paris: Robert Laffont, 1972); Hubert Cole's *The Betrayers: Joachim and Caroline Murat* (London: Eyre Methuen, 1972) and *Fouché: The Unprincipled Patriot* (London: Eyre & Spottiswoode, 1971); Émile Dard's *Napoleon and Talleyrand* (London: Philip Allan & Co., Ltd., 1937); Walter Geer's *Napoleon and His Family: The Story of a Corsican Clan* (London: George Allen & Unwin Ltd., 1928); Carola Oman's *Napoleon's Viceroy: Eugène de Beauharnais* (New York: Funk and Wagnall, 1966); Jean Tulard's *Fouché* (Paris: Fayard, 1998) and *Murat* (Paris: Fayard, 1999).

Three books in particular provided a wealth of wonderful detail: Bernard Chevallier's award-winning *L'art de vivre au temps de Joséphine* (Paris: Flammarion, 1998); Maurice Guerrini's *Napoleon and Paris: Thirty Years of History* (New York: Walker and Company, 1967); Frédéric Masson's *Joséphine, Empress and Queen,* (Paris and London: Goupil & Co., 1899).

I am often asked to recommend a non-fiction book on the subject of Josephine and Napoleon. Evangeline Bruce's *Napoleon and Josephine: The Improbable Marriage* (New York: Scribner, 1995) is excellent—a highly readable and generally accurate account of both personal and political worlds.

In closing, a word of caution: this subject is addictive.

*Note*

With the exception of the letter of March 12, 1810 (to which information has been added), Napoleon's letters throughout are edited versions of those he actually wrote to Josephine. The police reports (pages 1071–1072) are likewise authentic, as are Hortense and Émilie's account of the journey to Plombières (pages 874–875), Napoleon's instructions to Eugène on how to rule Italy (pages 1022–1023), and Josephine's letter to Napoleon (page 1144). The translations are my own, with help from Bernard Turle.

The illustration on page 888 of minuet notation is from *The Art of Dancing* by Kellom Tomlinson, published in 1735. The illustration on page 972 showing how to bow is from *Chironomia; or A Treatise on Rhetorical Delivery* by Gilbert Austin, originally published in 1806. The map on page 1138 is based, with permission, on a map by Hyperhistory Online.

## Acknowledgements

There have been times over the last three years when I felt that the spirits were putting roadblocks in my path, that there was a conspiracy to prevent this book from drawing to a close—a conspiracy in which I was, no doubt, an unconscious accomplice, for this hasn't been an easy book to finish. It ends a decade of daily interaction with Josephine and her family, closes a curtain on a world that has become home to me.

Perhaps the most difficult part of writing this novel was having to simplify a very complex narrative. Many delightful characters and fascinating stories had to be cut: readers familiar with the period will miss Fanny Beauharnais's granddaughter Stéphanie (*another* spirited Stéphanie); the several Tascher boys sent from Martinique to take advantage of the caring protection of their Empress aunt; Talleyrand's marriage to the delightfully clueless Madame Grand; General Bernadotte and his wife (Napoleon's first love, Eugénie-Désirée Clary), who became King and Queen of Sweden; the colourful Spanish royalty, most especially the unforgettable Prince of Peace. Any of these people could easily be the subject of a novel.

But most of all I have felt inadequate to the task of properly portraying Napoleon, his strengths and weaknesses, his vision and blindness, his heroic accomplishments and grievous failings. As well, the political picture—so vast and so complex—had to be simplified. Notably missing is the story of Toussaint's defence of Saint-Domingue (Haiti today) and his tragic death in France, as well as the story of the arrest and imprisonment of the Pope. This novel represents only the tip of the iceberg.

Of those individuals I have chosen to include, my apologies to their descendants if I have misrepresented them in any way. I hope my respect and love for them shows, even in their villainy.

Researching this book in Europe, I owe special thanks to Yves Carlier, the curator of Fontainebleau, who took me on a tour behind the scenes of that amazing château, and the staff of the Archives Municipales in Évreux. And, as always, I owe a special thanks to Bernard Chevallier and Dr. Catinat at Malmaison. Dr. Catinat has happily answered my numerous questions for almost a decade. His knowledge and perception of "notre héroïne" have influenced me greatly.

Special appreciation is due to all those on various Net history forums who took the time to give me specific information, notably: Bruno Nackaerts, Beryl Bernardi, Cori Hauer-Galambos, Yves Martin, and especially Tom Holmberg, who made perceptive and helpful suggestions after reading an early draft. Military historian Dr. Margaret Chrisawn not only answered my frequent questions, but combed the final text for errors (those errors that remain are entirely my responsibility). My debt to her since the inception of this trilogy is immense. Historian Dr. John McErlean kept me posted of new publications and developments; Irène Delage at Le Souvenir Napoléonien helped find obscure references; John Ballantrae provided tarot expertise; hemp activist Robert Anderman provided an interesting perspective regarding the Russian campaign; and Marshall Pynkoski and Jeannette Zingg of Opéra Atelier opened my eyes to the intricate world of eighteenth-century dance.

The members of the Algonquin Book Club (Penney Carson-Mak, Shirley Felker, Bonnie Ference, Catherine Lee, Rhoda Levert, Joanne Paine and Cathleen Sullivan) gave an exceptionally helpful critique of an early draft. My hard-working readers proved invaluable yet again: Peggy Bridgland, Janet Calcaterra, Thea Caplan, Dorothy Goodman, Marnie MacKay, Jenifer McVaugh, Carmen Mullins, Fran Murphy, Robin Paige, Chris Pollock, and especially my parents, Robert and Sharon Zentner. Kristine Puopolo at Scribners made very helpful suggestions. The sensitive work of Fiona Foster, a talented editor, is apparent on every page. A "triple salvo of bravos" to Judy Holland, who read two drafts and each time gave me the benefit of her considerable expertise as an editor, writer and teacher.

Thanks to Jan Whitford, whose early faith has at last been rewarded, and to my "home team" at HarperCollins Canada: Karen Hanson, Roy Nicol, Magda Nusink, Lorissa Sengara, Rebecca Vogan—and especially, especially, *especially* my editor and publisher, Iris Tupholme, who wept reading each draft.

And, as always, I thank my husband Richard, who picked me up when I fell down, brushed me off and gently but firmly turned me back in the direction of the eighteenth century.

# About the author

# About the book

Ideas,
interviews
& features

# Read on

# Author Biography

SANDRA GULLAND was born in Florida in 1944. Her father was an airline pilot, so the family moved often, living in Rio de Janeiro, Brazil, then Florida again before settling in Berkeley, California.

In the fall of 1970 Sandra moved to Canada to teach Grade 2 in an Inuit village in northern Labrador, an experience she describes as "amazing." Later, she worked as a book editor in Toronto, and in 1977 she married Richard Gulland. She gave birth to a daughter and son, and in 1980 the family moved to a log cabin near Killaloe (population 600), in northern Ontario. Sandra started an editorial and writing service and became the principal of a parent-run alternative school. All the while, she grew vegetables (or "tried to grow vegetables," as she puts it), raised chickens and pigs, and developed a lifelong fascination with horses. Meanwhile, and always, she was writing.

Sandra's consuming interest in Josephine Bonaparte was sparked in 1972 when she read a biography of her. Decades of in-depth research followed, which included investigative trips to France, Italy and Martinique, consultations with period scholars and learning French.

*The Many Lives & Secret Sorrows of Josephine B.* was published in 1995. It was followed in 1998 by *Tales of Passion, Tales of Woe* and *The Last Great Dance on Earth* in 2000. The Josephine B. Trilogy is now published in eleven languages. Napoleon said that he "conquered countries but that Josephine conquered hearts," Gulland says. "It's amazing. She continues to do so."

JERRY BAUER

*Sandra Gulland*

Sandra and her husband now live half the year in San Miguel de Allende, Mexico, and half in northern Ontario. She is currently writing a novel set in 17th-century France.

৵

# Animating History: The Challenges of Writing an Historical Novel about Josephine

*From a speech presented by Sandra Gulland to the Napoleonic Society of America in 1993, two years prior to the publication of the first book in the trilogy*

Over fifteen years ago, in the course of my work as an editor for a book publisher, I read a short biography of Josephine's life. I was overcome. As a joke I sometimes say it was as if lightning struck, but it was, in truth, a turning point for me. I was captured (or, should I say, kidnapped) by Josephine—her heart, her intelligence, her grace, her courage.

For me, the desire to learn about Josephine—to understand her—took all the predictable forms: I spent too much money on books; I collected tacky memorabilia; I travelled long distances to go to museum exhibits; I grew teary-eyed on the cobblestones of Paris. Eventually (and inevitably), the desire to learn about her led to the impulse to write about her in order to ▶

> ❝ I was captured by Josephine— her heart, her intelligence, her grace, her courage. ❞

3

discover answers to my questions: What was life like for her? What did being Josephine feel like? So I proceeded, one page at a time. Had I known what I was getting into, I would never have begun. Only a fool would knowingly undertake a work of this nature.

The first challenge, of course, was the research. Obviously, I had to learn about the times—all of the times: from the *ancien régime*, the Revolution, the Terror, the days of Thermidor, the Consulate, the Empire. I had to come to grips not only with the waves upon waves of political upheaval but also, of course, with the finer details of dress and deportment, manners, food and transportation. Not only did I have to research the life of Josephine but also the lives of all of the significant people she knew.

The second challenge was (and continues to be) learning the French language. When I began I thought that there was enough material available in English to keep me in libraries for a lifetime. I was right—there is—but eventually, as my research became more specific, I needed to consult works that were only available in French. I also had to be able to pronounce my characters' names!

The third challenge was trying to figure out what actually happened. Both historians and novelists create stories to link fact A to fact B. Histories conflict; experts differ. As a novelist I can't say: "Exactly why Josephine returned to Martinique is not known." I have to create a reason. I have to make a statement. But harder than sorting out facts has been wading through the interpretations histo-

> Had I known what I was getting into, I would never have begun. Only a fool would knowingly undertake a work of this nature.

4

rians have made about Josephine—their assumptions which, over time, have come to be regarded as fact. If she:

- spent time with a man, it was assumed she was sleeping with him.
- said she was ill, it was assumed she was lying.
- bought works of art, it was said she was a "hoarder" or a "spendthrift" rather than a "collector" or a "patron of the arts."
- wept, it was said she was frivolous, or weak, or manipulative.

During her months in prison, for example, she is portrayed as weeping uncontrollably, demoralizing the other inmates. Historians neglect to quote accounts of her courage in prison. They neglect to mention that the one woman who complained of Josephine was Delphine de Custine, who Josephine nursed through a violent bereavement and who recovered sufficiently to fall into the arms of Josephine's husband, Alexandre. I'm not sure, under the circumstances, that Delphine had a right to be critical of Josephine, and I resent that Delphine's words have been passed on unqualified for hundreds of years.

Another weeping episode often cited occurred when Josephine was leaving Paris to join Napoleon in Italy. It is true—she did weep. The traditional explanation for her tears is that she couldn't bear to leave the gay life of constant parties and theatre in Paris. What is not mentioned is that Josephine, at the early age of thirty-two, was apparently going through menopause brought on by the stress of her prison experience. One can only imagine the emotional confusion—the nightmare— ▶

“ Historians neglect to quote accounts of Josephine's courage in prison. ”

5

of dealing with an early menopause in an age that knew little about menopause at all. Furthermore, she had developed complications of a "feminine nature" and was, in fact, quite ill. In leaving Paris, she was leaving behind one of her dearest friends, who was dying. She was also leaving behind her children at the delicate ages of thirteen and fifteen. When would she see them again? What mother would not be distressed leaving teenagers behind? Her daughter was just about to be confirmed, and Josephine, her mother, would not be there. This was tantamount, at the time, to not being present at a daughter's wedding. Given all of this, I believe it is safe to say that Josephine had very good reasons for weeping.

In general, my feeling is that Josephine has been harshly judged. Few seem willing to question the assumptions made in the past. Few seem willing to see things from her perspective, to walk in her shoes, to give her the benefit of the doubt. And that, precisely, was one of my intentions when I began my novel—to give Josephine a chance to speak, to give her a voice.

Which brings me to the greatest challenge of all: writing the novel. The main problem with writing historical fiction about a person's life is creating drama and tension. A life does not

- unfold in chapters. (You may have noticed this.)
- have "a message," an underlying theme— yet a novel must.
- build slowly but steadily to a climax.
- restrict itself to three main characters.

> One of my intentions when I began my novel was to give Josephine a chance to speak, to give her a voice.

6

With the last draft of *The Many Lives &
Secret Sorrows of Josephine B.*, I was asked to
include a cast of characters. I was shocked
and depressed to count eighty characters
in Josephine's life—and this was before her
life with Napoleon began! Which brings
me to another problem—nearly everyone,
it seemed, was named François or Marie or
both. Imagine a novel swarming with characters named François!

Another more serious problem is resisting
the desire to put something in a novel just
because it is exciting new information. For
example, when I met with Bernard Chevallier
and Dr. Catinat at Malmaison, both of them
were quite excited by the new discovery that
Josephine had been a Freemason. Through
the Freemasons, she had met influential and
wealthy bankers from the Islands. This put
her in a powerful position. Specifically, Josephine was able to introduce Barras to these
contacts. Dr. Catinat is of the opinion that in
the exchange of money and favours between
Josephine and Barras, Barras came out on
top. Furthermore, he believes (and I concur)
that Josephine and Barras were not lovers.

Increasingly, through new research, I get
the sense of Josephine as a rather "modern"
woman: not a promiscuous woman at all, but
rather, a woman who had many male friends;
a woman who networked with men, who was
comfortable in the working world of men; a
woman who had financial dealings with men
in an age when women did not work at all,
much less handle money.

But the problem for me is that I wanted to
put all of this in my novel, but I couldn't. In
the case of Josephine's involvement with ▶

> " I get the
> sense of Josephine
> as a rather "mod-
> ern" woman: a
> woman who had
> financial dealings
> with men in an
> age when women
> did not work at
> all, much less
> handle money. "

the Freemasons, it was next to impossible for me to find specific information on secret societies. Regarding her bank wheeling and dealing, rising and falling interest rates do not make for good reading. The point is: a novel has to work on its own terms. A novel that is merely a dramatized account of historical facts will never come to life. And bringing history to life is what writing historical fiction is all about.

This brings me to the last and most frightening challenge I encountered: What right had I to make a statement about Josephine? The most difficult challenge has been finding the gall, the courage to take on this subject. How would you like to have Napoleon as a character in a novel you were writing? It's frightening!

I have a quote by Beckett pinned up over my desk. It says: "How can I do this?" And the answer is: "How can I not?"

❦

# An Interview with Sandra Gulland

*The dresses worn by women are often described as "gauzy" or "revealing"—especially the one worn by Thérèse in* **The Many Lives & Secret Sorrows of Josephine B.**, *when she wagers on the weight of her ensemble. This seems so risqué for the time—but was it?*
Thérèse reputedly would brag that her gown was so flimsy she could pull it through the

> **❝ What right had I to make a statement about Josephine? The most difficult challenge has been finding the gall, the courage to take on this subject. ❞**

ring on her finger. It was a risqué time, similar to the flapper era of the 1920s. The two periods share a celebratory spirit of people who have survived a very close brush with death. No doubt this influenced the times, added to the "live for the moment" fervour.

*Malmaison sounds absolutely delightful; you've described it and its contents lovingly through Josephine. Have you been to the Musée du château de Malmaison? Did any of your research take you to the other locations mentioned?*

I find it essential to see the places I'm writing about. Researching Josephine's life, I travelled to France, Martinique, northern Italy and Germany, visiting the places in which she stayed. Some were difficult to find, and all were surprising. I've been to the prison where she was held in Paris, attended Mass at her family church in Martinique, had treatments in the mountain spa she frequently went to, seen where she was born, and where she died. By going to the places where she lived, walking where she walked, looking out a window as she surely did, she began to come alive for me.

Josephine's spirit is most clearly evident at Malmaison. It's a beautiful home. As a museum, it has been faithfully restored. I highly recommend a trip there. For each book in the trilogy, I went to Malmaison at least once. In the offices or in the attic, rooms that used to house Josephine's wardrobe, I would meet with historian Dr. Catinat and sometimes with chief curator Bernard Chevallier, two individuals who know more about Josephine than anyone in the world. No matter how many times I visited ▶

> ❝ By going to the places where Josephine lived, walking where she walked, looking out a window as she surely did, she began to come alive for me. ❞

**An Interview with Sandra Gulland** (*continued*)

Malmaison, I never felt I got enough of the place. After each visit, I would walk into Rueil-Malmaison to the church on the village square, where Josephine's and Hortense's tombs lie. If the church was open, I would buy a rose from the flower shop on the square and place it on Josephine's tomb. I'm hoping that more and more roses will mysteriously appear there over time.

*There are so many wonderful details about food and drink in the books: Napoleon's preference for Chambertin (oft-described as "an undrinkable wine"), the rum-and-absinthe cocktail called pétépié, Barras's Brussels biscuits and, of course, his extravagant dinner menu, to name but a few. Are there stories behind these and why you chose to include them? Were there any other "interesting edibles" that you came across in your research that didn't make it into the book?*

As often as possible, I try to use factual details. Napoleon did drink the red wine Chambertin (mixed with water) and I was delighted to find the actual dinner menu for one of Barras's parties. It brought the elegance of the evening to life for me. Napoleon's table manners and tastes were less refined than those of Barras, to be sure. It was said that Napoleon's manners were of the barrack room, and I think his taste in food was as well. He preferred simple food, and ate quickly, with his fingers. Speed seemed to be what he valued most. He liked chicken but hated to wait for one to be cooked. He would have his cooks prepare a fresh one every half

> **I would walk into Rueil-Malmaison where Josephine's and Hortense's tombs lie. If the church was open, I would buy a rose and place it on Josephine's tomb.**

hour so that one was always ready for him. Chicken Marengo, which I didn't mention in the diaries, is a chicken dish Napoleon came to be very fond of, one that was initially cooked for him after a victory when on campaign. From that time on, it was served after each victorious battle.

*There seems to be no other breed of dog than the pug in all of France! Was the breed the height of fashion, or is there another explanation for Josephine and "the Glories's" fascination with them?*
There were many types of dogs favoured by the aristocratic families of that era: Newfoundlanders and mastiffs (as guard dogs), spaniels, hounds for hunting—but ladies preferred small dogs like toy poodles and pugs, dogs that could charmingly be carried about in a travelling basket. Josephine's first pug, Fortuné, was famous for his bad temper; he even bit Napoleon on the leg on their wedding night.

*The artist Jacques-Louis David makes a cameo appearance just prior to Napoleon's coronation. He complains of inappropriate sightlines for his work on what eventually became the grand mural* The Coronation of the Emperor Napoleon I and the Coronation of the Empress Josephine in Notre-Dame Cathedral. *An inconvenience to Josephine, perhaps, but his painting proved a great help to you in preparing the setting, the costumes, and the details, one would imagine.*
The story of David's creation of the magnificent coronation scene could be a book in itself. All of what is related in the novel is ▶

❝ The story of David's creation of the magnificent coronation scene could be a book in itself. ❞

based on fact, but there was much more that I would have liked to include as well. I wrote several additional scenes about the painting, which I ended up cutting. One man was furious because he was portrayed without his wig; the artist proclaimed that he would not sully his paintbrushes to create such a lie— yet there are lies aplenty. Napoleon's mother, who never showed up to his coronation (a humiliation to him), is shown prominently. Maids, not Napoleon's sisters, are shown holding Josephine's train (the sisters insisted on this). In the duplicate of this painting at Versailles, David was somehow persuaded to show Napoleon's vain sister Pauline in a pink gown, making her stand out from all the others. Napoleon said of the painting that one didn't look at it so much as walk into it. It does have that effect.

*You create a believable scene of a "regular family" as the members of the court in the Yellow Salon chatter about the coronation: the ladies having to traipse through mud, Napoleon poking Uncle Fesch in the behind, the stone falling on Napoleon—and, of course, the significant moment when Bonaparte crowns himself emperor. Are all of these details fact?*
There is so much documented detail available on the coronation that writing this scene was really a matter of describing it moment by moment as it had been described by others. The terrible weather is fact, as is Napoleon playfully poking his uncle, the stone falling

**❝** Napoleon said of the painting that one didn't look at it so much as walk into it. It does have that effect. **❞**

during the ceremony, the gasp of the crowd as Napoleon crowned himself. Some of what happened could not have been seen by Josephine at the time, so it had to be related to her (and therefore, to the reader) later, in discussion. In all of the amazing events that unfolded during this era, it was important for me to remember that these were essentially family occasions.

**The Last Great Dance on Earth** *opens with Napoleon presenting Josephine with the Regent diamond. Where is the diamond now?*
When Napoleon went into exile in Elba, his second wife, Marie-Louise, fled, taking the Regent diamond with her. Her father, Emperor Francis I of Austria, later returned it to France where it became part of the crown jewels. In 1887, France sold many of the crown jewels at auction but kept the Regent. When the Germans invaded Paris in 1940, the diamond was hidden behind a stone panel in Chambord, a royal château near Blois in the Loire Valley. The Regent diamond is now displayed in the Galerie d'Apollon of the Louvre in Paris.

> ❝ In all of the amazing events that unfolded during this era, it was important for me to remember that these were essentially family occasions. ❞

# Recommended Reading

*Citizens; A Chronicle of the French Revolution,*
Simon Schama

*Napoleon and Josephine: The Improbable
Marriage,* Evangeline Bruce

**Memoirs and biographies:**
*The Memoirs of Queen Hortense, Hortense,
consort of Louis Bonaparte, King of Holland,
1783–1837*

*The Rose of Martinique,* Andrea Stuart

*More Than a Queen: The Story of Josephine
Bonaparte,* Frances Mossiker

*Napoleon,* Vincent Cronin

*Napoleon's Viceroy: Eugène de Beauharnais,*
Carola Oman

**If the actress Mademoiselle George intrigued
you, read her life story in these books:**
*A Favourite of Napoleon: Memoirs of Made-
moiselle George,* Marguerite Joséphine
Weimer George

*Napoleon and Mademoiselle George,* Edith
Saunders

**For more on Madame Mère, the imposing
matriarch of the Bonaparte clan:**
*Napoleon's Mother,* Alain Decaux

*For further reading on the court fashion designer Louis Leroy, and on Napoleon's influence on fashion:*
*Dressed to Rule: Royal and Court Costume from Louis XIV to Elizabeth II*, Philip Mansel

*For more information on the "Corsican Clan":*
*Napoleon and His Family: The Story of a Corsican Clan*, Walter Geer

# Web Detective

For more information on the author and the books in the series: *www.sandragulland.com*

For a very thorough website devoted to the Napoleonic era, with emphasis on military history and warfare: *www.napoleonguide.com*

Discover Martinique, the island on which Josephine was born and raised: *www.la-martinique.net*

For more on the French Revolution: *http://chnm.gmu.edu/revolution/chap9a.html*

For an interesting lesson on the placement of mouches —the beauty marks placed on faces, often to hide pock marks: *http://collections.ic.gc.ca/louisbourg/weird.html*

For more on Fanny, Josephine's eccentric aunt: *http://poesie.webnet.fr/auteurs/beauharnais.html*

For more on Malmaison (in French only): *www.chateau-malmaison.fr/* ▶

For more information and images of Fountainebleau and the Tuileries Palace:
*www.georgianindex.net/Napoleon/Fontainebleau/Fontainebleau.html*
*www.georgianindex.net/Napoleon/Tuileries/Tuileries.html*

For a history of the Regent Diamond:
*www.georgianindex.net/gems/Regent_diamond.html*
*http://famousdiamonds.tripod.com/regentdiamond.html*

For more on Mademoiselle George, the actress and mistress of Napoleon: *www.cadytech.com/dumas/related/napoleon_by_morlock.php*

To view Jacques-Louis David's painting of the coronation: *www.artchive.com/artchive/D/david/consecration.jpg.html*

To better understand the French Republican calendar: *www.gefrance.com/calrep/calen.htm*

For a list of films about Napoleon:
*www.napoleon.org/en/gallery/cinema/*

For an interview with Sandra Gulland as part of an educational website for the PBS Napoleon series: *www.pbs.org/empires/napoleon/n_josephine/courtship/page_1.html*

❧